SARUM

SARUM

The Novel of England

Edward Rutherfurd

CROWN PUBLISHERS, INC.

New York

This book is dedicated to those who built and to those who are now trying to save Salisbury Spire.

Illustrated maps by Alison Borthwick
Area of Detail map by Jacques Chazaud
Copyright © 1987 by Edward Rutherfurd

Published in the United States in 1987 by Crown Publishers, Inc., 225 Park Avenue South, New York, New York 10003 and represented in Canada by the Canadian MANDA Group.

First Published in Great Britain in 1987 by Century-Hutchinson Ltd.

CROWN is a trademark of Crown Publishers, Inc.

Manufactured in the United States of America

Library of Congress Cataloging-in-Publication Data

Rutherfurd, Edward.
Sarum.
I. Title.
PR6068.U88S27   1987   823′.914   87-6710
ISBN 0-517-56338-X

10 9 8 7 6 5

First American Edition

Contents

OLD SARUM

Journey to Sarum / 3
The Barrow / 40
The Henge / 69
Sorviodunum / 141
Twilight / 235
The Two Rivers / 281
The Castle / 327

NEW SARUM

The Founding / 375
The Death / 501
The Rose / 559
A Journey from Sarum / 582
New World / 598
The Unrest / 661
The Calm / 723
Boney / 775
Empire / 823
The Henge II / 871
The Encampment / 873
The Spire / 891

Preface

The name *Sarum*

THE WORD SARUM is, strictly speaking, an inaccurate rendering of the abbreviation used by medieval scribes when they wished to write the name of the place called Salisbury.

But having misread the scribal hand, men found the name pleasing; and the term Sarum has been used in writing and probably in speech for seven hundred and fifty years, to describe the town, the diocese and the area of Salisbury.

For purposes of clarity, I have chosen throughout this novel to apply the term Sarum to the immediate area around the city. When describing the individual settlements or towns on the site, I have used the names they carried at the time reached in the narrative – Sorviodunum in Roman times, Sarisberie in Norman, and Salisbury thereafter. Old Sarum is the proper name of the original town and is used as such in context.

The novel *Sarum*

Sarum is a novel and to see it as anything else would be a mistake.

All the families of Porteus, Wilson, Shockley, Mason, Godfrey, Moody, Barnikel are fictitious as are, therefore, their individual parts in all events described.

But in following the story of these imaginary families down the centuries I have tried, insofar as is possible, to set them amongst people and events that either did exist, or might have done.

In the prehistoric chapters I have felt free to choose dates and telescope developments somewhat, but under advice from those experts who have so kindly assisted me.

However, the reader may care to note that the date of the separation of the island of Britain from the European mainland is usually set somewhere between 9,000 and 6,000 B.C.

Of the religious, astronomical and building practices at Stonehenge nothing can be said with certainty and I have felt free to make my own selection from the many theories suggested.

There and elsewhere I have also placed in the text, from time to time, items of historical information which may help to orientate the reader who is not intimately familiar with English history. These are not, and make no pretence to being a detailed historical account. They are merely signposts.

Topography and Avonsford

There are so many villages, hillforts, and other natural features around Sarum, that in order to avoid a bewildering confusion of settings, I have found it necessary to make one alteration to the landscape. The village of Avonsford does not exist. It is an amalgam of places and buildings drawn from all over the area and I have sited it – somewhere – in the valley of the river Avon that lies to the north of Salisbury and which I have chosen to call, for purposes of narrative convenience, the Avon valley. It may be of interest that the following features, in particular, which I have sited at Avonsford all exist, or have existed, within a few miles radius of Salisbury: an iron age farm, a Roman villa, fields called Paradise and Purgatory, the miz-maze, earthwork enclosures, dewponds, fulling mills, dovecotes, manor houses as detailed, churches with box pews.

Where other local places have had different names at different periods, I have chosen the most familiar – as in the case of Grovely Wood and Clarendon Forest. Longford appears a little closer to Clarendon than it is.

Salisbury street names have also changed over time; but generally I have chosen not to confuse the reader with this information.

Otherwise places in the text – Salisbury, Christchurch, Wilton, Old Sarum – are as described.

Family names and origins

Of the fictional families in the story – Wilson, Mason and Godfrey are all common names which may be found in almost any English town. The derivations given in the story for the first two are those normally given; the derivation for the Godfreys of Avonsford is invented, but typical of one way in which names were derived from Norman originals.

There was, as it happens, a real Godfrey in Salisbury some centuries ago who became mayor of the town and his family, with its different origin, makes a brief appearance in our story, and is clearly distinguished from the fictional family.

Shockley is a rarer name and the derivation I have given is likely.

As for the derivation of the much rarer name of Barnikel, this belongs to English folklore, but I like to believe it. The name Porteus is found more usually in the north – often Porteous. Its Roman derivation is invented. Names do not, unfortunately go back so far.

But families do. In recent decades, historians and archaeologists seem to have discovered increasing evidence of continuity of occupation in many areas of England. While it is generally true that the Saxon Settlement tended to push the British people westward, there is no reason to suppose that none remained where they were. The idea that there may be people in the Sarum area today whose bloodlines go back to the occupants of the region in Celtic or pre-Celtic times cannot be proved, but is not entirely fanciful.

[vii]

The Dune

I have deliberately chosen to use the modern and familiar term *dune* for the hillfort of Old Sarum. Properly this should be written dūn.

Summary

No place in England, I believe, has a longer visible history of building and occupation than the Sarum region. The wealth of archaeological information, let alone historical record is so overwhelming that even a novelist, wishing to convey anything near the full story of the place would have to write a book three or four times as long as I have done.

Faced with such an embarrassment of riches, the author can only make a personal selection and hope that in doing so, he may have conveyed something of the wonder of the place.

ENGLAND

BATH

SALISBURY
PLAIN

Stonehenge

LONDON

Thames

Wylye

Bourne

Nadder

SALISBURY

Ebble

SOUTHAMPTON

Avon

CHRISTCHURCH

Isle of
Wight

ENGLISH CHANNEL

ENGLISH

AREA OF
DETAIL

0   20   40   60   80   100

Miles

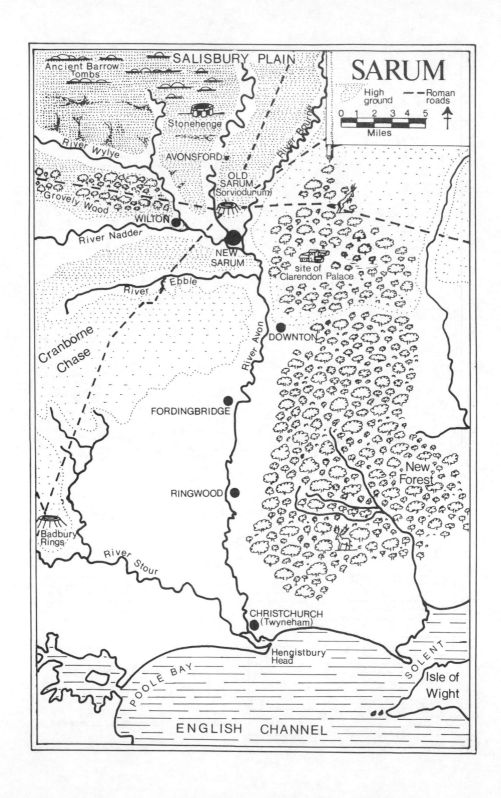

SALISBURY PLAIN

SARUM

High ground — Roman roads

0 1 2 3 4 5
Miles

Ancient Barrow Tombs

Stonehenge

AVONSFORD

River Wylye

River Bourne

OLD SARUM (Sorviodunum)

Grovely Wood

WILTON

River Nadder

NEW SARUM

site of Clarendon Palace

River Ebble

River

DOWNTON

Cranborne Chase

River Avon

FORDINGBRIDGE

RINGWOOD

New Forest

Badbury Rings

River Stour

CHRISTCHURCH (Twyneham)

Hengistbury Head

POOLE BAY

SOLENT

Isle of Wight

ENGLISH CHANNEL

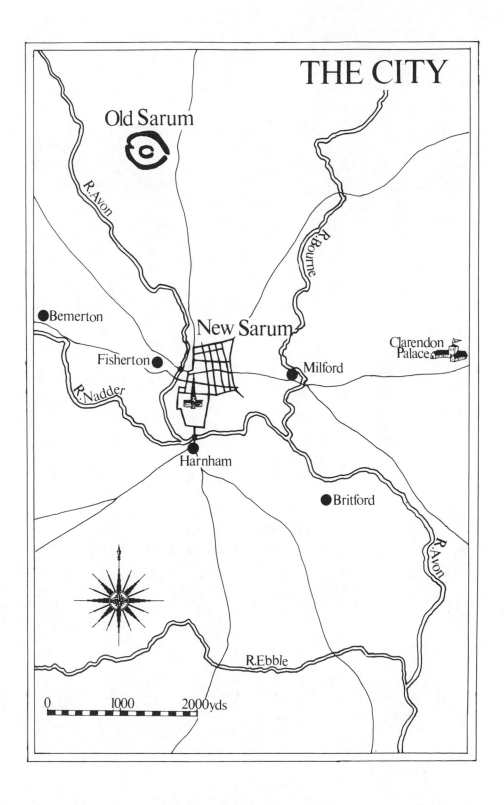

THE CITY

Old Sarum

R. Avon

R. Bourne

Bemerton

New Sarum

Fisherton

Milford

Clarendon Palace

R. Nadder

Harnham

Britford

R. Avon

R. Ebble

0   1000   2000 yds

FAMILY TREES

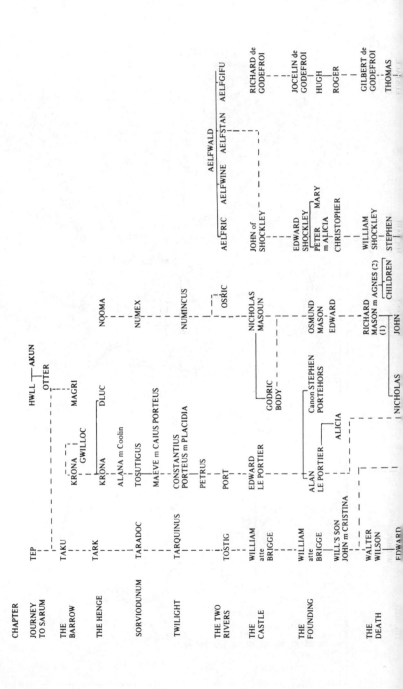

CHAPTER							
JOURNEY TO SARUM	TEP		HWLL ─┬─ AKUN				
			OTTER			NOOMA	
THE BARROW	TAKU		KRONA ─┬─ MAGRI				
			GWILLOC			NUMEX	
THE HENGE	TARK		DLUC				
			KRONA				
			ALANA m Coolin				
SORVIODUNUM	TARADOC		TOSUTIGUS			NUMINCUS	
			MAEVE m CAIUS PORTEUS				
TWILIGHT	TARQUINUS		CONSTANTIUS PORTEUS m PLACIDIA			OSRIC	
			PETRUS				
THE TWO RIVERS	TOSTIG		PORT			NICHOLAS MASOUN	
			EDWARD LE PORTIER		GODRIC BODY		
THE CASTLE	WILLIAM atte BRIGGE					OSMUND MASON	
					Canon STEPHEN PORTEHORS	EDWARD	
THE FOUNDING	WILLIAM atte BRIGGE		ALAN LE PORTIER				
			ALICIA				
	WILL'S SON JOHN m CRISTINA					RICHARD MASON m AGNES (2)	
THE DEATH	WALTER WILSON					(1)	CHILDREN
				NICHOLAS		JOHN	
	EDWARD						

AELFWALD

AELFRIC	AELFWINE	AELFSTAN	AELFGIFU
JOHN of SHOCKLEY			RICHARD de GODEFROI
EDWARD SHOCKLEY	MARY		JOCELIN de GODEFROI
PETER m ALICIA			HUGH
CHRISTOPHER			ROGER
WILLIAM SHOCKLEY			GILBERT de GODEFROI
STEPHEN			THOMAS

EUSTACE GODFREY

OLIVER ISABELLA

PIERS NELLIE GODFREY

JACOB GODFREY

DANIEL GODFREY

Sir KERSEY GODFREY

MICHAEL SHOCKLEY

REGINALD

EDWARD SHOCKLEY m KATHERINE MOODY

WILLIAM SHOCKLEY

OBADIAH MARGARET SAMUEL
EDMUND NATHANIEL

JONATHAN SHOCKLEY
(1)
(2)
MARY m ADAM

RALPH SHOCKLEY m AGNES

BERNARD JANE

FRANCES

PATRICIA SHOCKLEY

STEPHEN SHOCKLEY

ADAM SHOCKLEY

MAGGIE

BENEDICT MASON

PETER MASON m ABIGAIL

WILLIAM MASON

BENJAMIN ELI

DANIEL MASON

DANIEL MASON

JOHN MASON

OSBERT MASON

SUSAN

STEPHEN FIELD

Canon NICODEMUS PORTEUS m FRANCES SHOCKLEY

JOSEPH PORTERS

ALAN PORTERS

JOHN WILSON

WILL WILSON

Captain JACK WILSON m NELLIE GODFREY

FIENNES WILSON

Midshipman ROBERT WILSON

Brigadier ARCHIBALD FOREST–WILSON m Patricia Shockley

JENNIFER m

ROBERT FOREST

THOMAS FOREST

GILES

Sir HENRY FOREST

GEORGE

Sir GEORGE FOREST

JOSHUA becomes LORD FOREST

LORD FOREST

THE ROSE

JOURNEY FROM SARUM

THE NEW WORLD

THE UNREST

THE CALM

BONEY

EMPIRE

THE HENGE II

THE ENCAMPMENT

THE SPIRE

OLD SARUM

Journey to Sarum

FIRST, BEFORE THE beginning of Sarum, came a time when the world was a colder and darker place.

Over a huge area of the northern hemisphere – perhaps a sixth of the whole globe – stretched a mighty covering of ice. It lay over all of northern Asia; it covered Canada, Scandinavia and about two thirds of the future land of Britain. Had it been possible to cross this gigantic continent of ice, the journey would have been some five thousand miles from whichever direction it was approached. The volume of the ice was stupendous; even at its outer edge it was thirty feet high.

In a desolate, dark belt to the south of the ice lay a vast subarctic wasteland of empty tundra, several hundred miles across.

This was the colder, darker world, some twenty thousand years before the birth of Christ.

Since the huge casing of ice contained a considerable portion of the earth's water, the seas were lower than those in later times – some did not exist at all – and so the lands to the south stood higher, their sheer cliffs frowning upon empty chasms that have long since vanished under the waters.

The northern world was a quieter place too. Over the ice, and the tundra, there reigned a silence that seemed to have no end. True, there were terrible winds, huge blizzards that howled across the land of ice; true, in the arctic tundra there were sparse forms of life – a meagre vegetation, small groups of hardy animals – which eked out a bleak existence in the freezing wastes; but to all intents the land was empty: thousands upon thousands of miles of desert; and in the vast glacial cap itself, all forms of life and the seas which might have spawned them were locked up in the great stasis of the ice.

Such was the last Ice Age. Before, there had been many like it; after it, there will be many more. And in the gaps between these ages, men have come and gone upon the northern lands.

Centuries passed; thousands of years passed, and nothing changed, nor seemed likely to. Then, at some time around 10,000 B.C., a change began to occur: at the outer edge of the frozen wastes, the temperature began to rise. It was not enough to be noticed in a decade, hardly in a century, and it did not yet have any effect upon the ice; but it rose nonetheless. Centuries passed. It rose a little more. And then the ice cap began to melt. Still the process was gradual: a stream here, a small river there; blocks of ice a few yards across in one place, half a mile in another, breaking away from the edge of the ice cap, a process hardly noticeable against the thousands of miles of the vast continent of ice that remained. But slowly this melting gathered pace. New land, tundra, emerged from under the ice; new rivers were born; ice floes moved southwards into the seas, which began to rise. A new ferment was in progress upon the surface of the earth. Century after century, the face of the continents changed as new lands began to define themselves and new life began, cautiously, to spread across the earth.

The last Ice Age was in retreat.

For several thousand years this process continued.

About seven thousand five hundred years before the birth of Christ, in the still bleak and uninviting season that was summer in those northern lands, a single hunter undertook a journey that was impossible. His name, as nearly as it can be written, was Hwll.

When she heard the plan, his woman Akun first looked at him in disbelief and then protested.

"No one will go with us," she argued. "How shall we find food without help?"

"I can hunt alone," he replied. "We shall eat."

She shook her head vigorously in disbelief.

"This place that you speak of; it does not exist."

"It does." Hwll knew that it did. His father had told him, and his father's father before that. Though he did not know it, the information was already several centuries old.

"We shall die," Akun said simply.

They were standing on the ridge above their camp: a pitiful little cluster of wigwams made of reindeer skins and supported on long poles, which the five families that comprised their hunting group had set up when the winter snows departed. Across the ridge, as far as the eye could see, stretched the empty expanse of coarse grey-brown grass, dotted with the occasional bush, dwarf birch or clump of rocks, to which ragged lichen and stringy moss had attached themselves. Grey clouds scudded over the brown land, driven by a chill north east wind.

This was the tundra. For when the ice of the last glacial age began to retreat, it laid bare a desolate region that extended uninterrupted across the entire northern Eurasian land mass. From Scotland to China, in these vast, empty spaces similar in climate to Siberia today, small bands of hunters known to archaeologists as Upper Paleolithic, followed by Mesolithic man, had followed the sparse game that roamed the barren wastes. Stocky bison, reindeer, wild horse and the stately elk would appear on the horizon, then disappear again, and the hunters would follow, often for many days, in order to make their kill and survive another season. It was a cold, precarious life that continued for hundreds of generations.

It was in the extreme north west corner of this gigantic tundra region that Hwll and his woman found themselves.

He was typical of these wanderers, who were of no single racial type. He was five foot seven, just above average height, with high cheekbones, coal black eyes, a deeply rutted and weatherbeaten face with skin that seemed to have been worn like the landscape into innumerable valleys, creeks and gullies; he had half his teeth, which were yellow, and a full black beard now flecked with grey. He was twenty-eight: ripe middle age in that region and at that time. The crude jerkin and leggings that he wore were made of reindeer skin and fox fur, held together with toggles made of bone; for the art of stitching clothes together had not yet reached his people. On his feet were soft moccasin boots. He wore no ornaments. Thus naturally camouflaged in the tundra, he resembled a shaggy brown plant of some indeterminate kind, from the top of which hung the thickly tangled mass of his hair. When he stood stock still, his spear raised ready to throw, he could be mistaken at twenty yards for a stunted tree. The broad-set eyes under his deeply scored forehead and bushy brows were cautious and intelligent.

He was a good provider, known amongst the other hunters as a skilful tracker, and for many years the little group had lived and hunted undisturbed in a region approximately fifty miles east to west and forty north to south. They followed game, they fished, and it was the moon goddess who watched over all hunters that they trusted to protect their precarious way of life. In summer they lived in tents; in winter they built semi-subterranean houses, cutting them into the side of a hill and facing them with brushwood: crude shelters, but well designed to conserve precious body heat. He had taken Akun as his woman ten years before and in that time he had fathered five children, two of whom had survived: a boy of five and a girl of eight.

And now he was preparing to embark on an immense trek to an unknown place! Akun shook her head in despair.

The reasons for Hwll's extraordinary plan were simple. For three years now, the hunting had been poor, and that last winter the little group had nearly ceased to exist. In vain he had searched in the snow, day after day, for the tell-tale tracks that might lead him to food. Day after day he had come back disappointed, having found only the trail of a single arctic fox, or the minute scuffling patterns of the lemmings which then inhabited the region. The little band had subsisted on a store of nuts and roots that they had gathered in the preceding months, and even that store had been nearly exhausted. He had watched the women and children grow wasted, and almost despaired. Nor had the weather given them any respite, for it had been bitterly cold, with continuous icy winds from the north. Then at last, he saw a party of reindeer, and the hunters, calling on their last reserves of strength, had managed to separate one from the group and kill it. This single lucky find had saved them from starvation: the flesh of the animal gave them meat and its precious blood gave them the salt which they would otherwise have lacked. Despite this kill, the end of the winter saw one of the women and three of the children dead.

Spring came and, in place of the snow, revealed a cold, marshy wasteland where small flowers and ragged grasses grew. Usually this change of season meant that they would encounter the bison, who cropped over the new shoots on the high ground during the early months of summer. But this year the hunters had found no bison. They met only wild horse, whose meat was tough and which was hard to catch.

"If the bison do not come, then the hunting here is over," Hwll said to himself, and throughout the early summer as the pale sun coaxed the vegetation into flower, and the ground became firmer underfoot, they had travelled in a wide circle, twenty miles in radius, in search of game; but still there was almost nothing. The group was half starving and he was sure they would not survive another winter.

It was then that Hwll made his decision.

"I am travelling south," he told the others, "to the warm lands. If we leave now, we can reach them before the snows." He said this to encourage them, because in fact he did not know how long the journey would take. "I am going to cross the great forest of the east," he said, "and go south to where the lands are rich and men live in caves. Who will come with me?"

It was a brave statement and it was based on the ancient store of oral tradition which was all he knew. The geography that had been handed down to Hwll through scores of generations by word of mouth was fairly simple. Far to the north, it was said – he did not know how far – the land grew colder and even more inhospitable until finally one reached a great wall of ice, as high as five men, that cut across the landscape from east to west. The ice wall had no beginning and no end. Beyond it lay the ice plateau, a shimmering white land that extended northwards for ever: for the land of ice had no end. Far to the west lay a sea, and that, too, had no end. To the south lay tundra, and thick forests, until one reached a sea too wide to cross. On three sides, therefore, the way was cut off. But to the south east there was a more inviting prospect. First one walked south many days until a great ridge of high ground arose, and down this it was possible to travel easily for several more days. Then from this ridge, turning east, one could cross other, lesser ridges, until a gently shelving plain led to a huge forest through which there were tracks that could safely be followed. By crossing the eastern forest it was possible to by-pass the southern sea; at the end of the forest began a great steppe, and when he reached that, he must turn south again and travel for many days until he reached those fabled warm lands where the people lived in caves.

"There it is much warmer," he had been told, "and the hunting is good."

Vague as it was, all this information was correct. For Hwll was standing in what would one day be called the north of England. Far to the north, the ice wall of the last glacial age, some thirty feet deep, had been retreating steadily and was still melting; only centuries before it had covered the place where their camp was now. To the west lay the Atlantic Ocean. With the exception of the island of Ireland, about which he did not know, the water continued until it reached the coast of North America, and would not be crossed for nearly nine thousand years. To the south lay the midlands and the broad lowlands of southern England, and further still the large estuary of the river Rhine had, with other rivers, been slowly carving out the small sea now called the English Channel for several thousand years. To the south east however, lay the great land bridge that joined the peninsula of Britain to the continent of Eurasia. Here, a vast plain stretched unbroken, forest interspersed with steppe, from eastern Britain for two and a half thousand miles to the snow-capped Ural Mountains of central Russia.

Across this land mass the hunters of the northern hemisphere had wandered for tens of thousands of years: moving south when successive Ice Ages came, and north once more each time the ice receded. Because of these migrations, Hwll's ancestors could have been traced to many lands: to the Russian steppe, to the Baltic, to Iberia and the Mediterranean. It was the distant memory of these travels that had been handed down to him and which formed the basis of his world view now. Two centuries before, his ancestors had roamed through the huge eastern forest onto the British peninsula and had followed the game north to the area in which he now found himself. In his ambitious journey to the warm lands of the Mediterranean basin, fifteen hundred miles to the south, he would therefore be retracing their steps. Had he realised how far it was he might never have started; but he did not. All he knew was that the warmer lands existed and that it was time to go in search of them.

The plan was daring. It would also have been sound – had it not been for one fatal flaw of which he could not possibly have been aware, and which would bring it crashing down in ruins.

But when, later that day Hwll asked: "Who will come with me?" there was silence from the rest of the band. They had hunted there for generations and they had always somehow survived. Who knew if the warm lands really existed, or what kind of hostile people might live there if they did? Try as he might, Hwll could not persuade anyone to join him; and it was only several days later, after many furious arguments, that Akun came, sullenly and under protest.

There was a warm sun in the sky on the morning that they left the other four families, who stood watching them sadly until they were out of sight, certain that, whatever privations they themselves faced, Hwll and his family must surely die. For five days they walked south; the going was easy because the ground was firm and dry; in all directions, the brown tundra stretched to the horizon. They had taken with them a small quantity of dried meat, some berries, and a tent which Hwll and Akun carried between them. They travelled at a slow pace to conserve the strength of the two children, but nonetheless, they covered a solid ten miles a day, and Hwll was satisfied. Bleak as it was, the landscape was criss-crossed with little streams, and usually he was able to catch a fish to feed his family. On the third day he even killed a hare, using his slender bow and arrow with its long flint head; and always he kept an eye on the sky where the movement of the occasional eagle or kite might indicate food on the ground below. They spoke little; even the children were silent, sensing that they would need all their resources to survive the journey.

The boy was a sturdy little fellow with large, thoughtful eyes. He did not walk very fast, but he had a look of concentrated determination on his face. Hwll hoped it would be enough to carry him through. The girl, Vata, was a stringy, wiry creature, like a young deer, he thought. She looked the more delicate, but he suspected she was the tougher of the two.

On the fifth day they reached their first objective: the ridge.

It rose magnificently above the tundra – a huge natural causeway several hundred feet high, running for two hundred miles down the east side of Britain before it curved westwards across country for two hundred miles more, and finally turned south again to end its journey in the sea. A little before it reached the sea, this limestone, Jurassic ridge would skirt in the centre of southern Britain, a huge plateau of chalk, from which other long ridges spread out across the land like the tentacles of some giant octopus. Throughout prehistoric times, and even afterwards, these ridges were the great arterial roads along which men travelled – the natural and gigantic highways made for men by the land itself.

The views from the ridge were magnificent and even Akun smiled with wonder as she joined Hwll to look at them. They could see for fifty miles. As they began to make their way along it, they found that there were patches of wood and scrub so that they did not need to descend from the ridge to seek shelter at night. But as the days passed and the little family wandered on alone, it was sometimes difficult not to lose heart. Hwll, however, was set in his purpose. Grim-faced, silent, and determined, he led them down the ridge, and all the time in his mind's eye, he tried to picture the southern lands where the weather was warm and the hunting was good. At such times he would look back at his two children and at Akun, to remind himself that it was for them that he had undertaken this astonishing migration.

Akun: there was a prize! A glow of warmth suffused his body when he looked at her. She had been twelve when they met, one of another group of wanderers who had entered the area where his people hunted. Such meetings were rare and were treated as a cause for celebration – and above all for the exchange of mates: for these simple hunters knew from the experience of centuries that they must keep their own bloodstock strong by seeking other hunters with whom to breed. He was a skilful young tracker without a woman; she was a good-looking girl just past puberty. There was no need even to discuss the matter; the two parties hunted together and, for a small payment of flint arrowheads, she was given to him by her father.

She was twenty-two now, entering middle life, but better looking than most of the tough, weatherbeaten women of her age. Her colouring was lighter than his. She had a rich brown mane of hair, though it was now greased with animal fat and matted from recent rains; her eyes were an unusual hazel colour and her mouth, pursed though it often was against the cold winds, was wide and sensual. She had most of her teeth, and her face had not yet developed the deep wrinkles that one day would make it resemble the cracked clay bed of an empty stream in a time of drought.

It was her body, though, that made the determined face of the hunter break into a tender smile. Smoother than the squat, hirsute bodies of the other women he knew, her skin had a rich, lustrous quality that set the blood racing in his veins. He would still catch his breath with wonder when he thought of the magnificent, swelling curves of her breasts and the rounded, powerful body in the full flower of its womanhood.

There was, in the tundra summer, a glorious, all too short period of less than a month when it was warm; and at this magical time, he and Akun would go down to one of the many streams that ran through the landscape and bathe together in the cold, sparkling waters. Afterwards she would stretch out her magnificent body in the warm sun and then, in an access of joy at the sight of her, and at the continuing strength of his own manhood, Hwll would throw himself upon her. She would laugh, a low, rich laugh that seemed to come from the earth itself, and languidly raise that wide, tantalising, sensuous mouth to his.

She was indeed a wonder! She knew with an infallible instinct where to find the best berries and nuts; she was deft in making nets for fishing. Perhaps, he hoped, they might still have another son: but not in the tundra, he vowed: they would reach the warm lands first.

It was twenty days after they had first set out, that Hwll and his family descended from the ridge and began to walk towards the east. The land now was flat and there was more vegetation. Woods were growing beside the streams; long reeds and grasses waved in the breeze. Hwll noticed these changes with pleasure; but the light wind came from the east and it was still cold.

He had been right about the children. Vata was very thin; her face was pinched and her head hunched forward; but she had kept on doggedly. The boy was starting to worry him. For three days he had been walking with his thumb in his mouth – a bad sign. Twice, the day before, he had stopped, refusing to go on. Both Hwll and Akun knew what they must do: if they gave in once, the boy would break the necessary rhythm of their journey. He must not be allowed to think that they would wait. And so they left him standing there, watching his parents moving slowly away from him until they receded into the distance. It was Vata who finally turned back and dragged him along, and when he caught up at last there were huge tears in his eyes. For the rest of that day he refused even to look at his parents. He did not fall behind again, though.

That night they camped in the shelter of the woods, and Hwll caught two fish in a stream. Akun sat opposite him, a small fire burning between them; the two children huddled close to her.

"How far is it to the forest?" she now asked. During the twenty days that they had travelled, she had said nothing about the journey which she had so opposed. She had spent her energy keeping the children alive and he was grateful for the silence between them, even though he knew that it was also a form of protest. Perhaps her question now meant that she was ready to show her anger, he thought, but her face was expressionless. He was too tired to concern himself anyway.

"Six days journey, I think," he said, and fell asleep.

Five days passed. They came to another ridge and crossed it. There were many streams to get over; some of the land was marshy and the going was more difficult. But he was fascinated by the gradual change in the landscape. Bleak as the plain was, it contained far more vegetation than there had been in the tundra to the north; and though it was still very empty, game was not so sparse. The children barely noticed the change, for now even the boy was too dazed to protest: his thumb was no longer in his mouth; he and Vata moved like automatons, staring straight ahead of themselves as though in a dream while Akun strode beside them at her stately walk. But they kept a steady pace and he did not let them cover more than ten to twelve miles a day, conserving the last reserves of their strength.

"Soon you will see the great forest," he promised them. And each day, to encourage them, he repeated what his father had told him. "It has many kinds of different trees, and plenty of game, and strange birds and animals that you have never seen before. It is a wonderful place." They would listen to him, then stare blankly, straight ahead, and he prayed to the goddess of the moon, who watched over all hunters, that this information was correct.

On the sixth day disaster struck, and when it did so, it came in a form unlike anything the hunter had ever dreamed of.

He woke at dawn, to a clear, chilly day. Akun and the children, wrapped in furs and huddled together beside a clump of bushes, were still sleeping. He stood up, sniffing the air and staring towards the east where a watery sun was rising. At once his instincts told him that something was wrong.

But what? At first he thought it was something in the air, which had a curious, clinging quality. Then he thought the trouble was something else and his brow contracted to a frown. Finally he heard it.

It was the faintest of sounds: so faint that it would never have been picked up by any man other than a skilled tracker like himself, who could discern a single buffalo three miles away by putting his ear to the ground. What he heard now, and what in his sleep had troubled him all night, was a barely perceptible murmur, a rumbling in the earth, somewhere to the east. He put his ear to the ground and remained still for a while. There was no mistaking it: some of the time it was little more than a hiss; but it was accompanied by other grating and cracking sounds, as though large objects were striking against each other. He frowned again. Whatever it was, this sound was not made by any animal: not even a herd of bison or wild horse could generate such a trembling of the earth. Hwll shook his head in puzzlement.

He stood up. "The air," he muttered. There was, undeniably, something strange about the air as well. Then he realised what it was. The faint breeze smelt of salt.

But why should the air smell of salt, when he was close to the great forest? And what was the curious noise ahead?

He woke Akun.

"Something is wrong," he told her. "I must go and see. Wait for me here."

All morning he travelled east at a trot. By late morning he had covered fifteen miles, and the sounds ahead were growing loud. More than once he heard a resounding crack, and the murmur had turned into an ominous rumble. But it was when he came to a patch of rising ground and had reached the top that he froze in horror.

Ahead of him, where the forest should have been, was water.

It was not a stream, not a river, but water without end: a sea! And the sea was on the move, as ice floes stretching out as far as he could see, drifted past, going south. He could hardly believe his eyes.

Along the shoreline, small ice floes buffeted the vegetation, and tiny waves beat on the ground. This was the hissing sound he had heard. Further out, the tops of great trees were still visible here and there, sticking out of the water; and occasionally a small iceberg would crack and splinter the wood as it rubbed against them. So that had been the strange cracking sound that had puzzled him!

Before his very eyes, lay the entrance to the great forest he had been seeking; and here was a new sea, moving inexorably southward, gouging out a mighty channel and sweeping earth, rock and tree before it.

Hwll had seen the rivers swollen with ice floes in the spring, and he surmised correctly that some new and gigantic thaw must have taken place in the north to produce this flow of waters. Whatever the cause, the implication was terrible. The forest he wanted to cross was now under the sea. For all he knew, so were the distant eastern plains and the warm lands to the south. Who could tell? But one thing was certain: there would be no crossing for him and his family. The ambitious plan for the great trek was destroyed; all the efforts they had made on their long journey had been wasted. The land to the east, if it still existed, was now cut off.

With a short gesture of despair he sat down, stared at the scene before him, and tried to put his thoughts in order. There was much to think about. When had this calamity begun, he wondered, and were the waters still rising? For if they continued to rise, they might engulf the land in which he was standing as well, even perhaps the ridge that he had left six days before. It was a thought which terrified him. For then, he considered, perhaps there will be nothing left. Perhaps this was the end of the world.

But Hwll was a practical man. He stayed where he was all afternoon, and as the sun went down he noted carefully the exact level the waters had reached. Having done so, he hunched his furs over his shoulders and waited for the dawn.

All night the hunter considered the huge forces that could unleash such a flood; for he saw that they must be powerful gods indeed. He thought with sadness of the great forest full of game that lay before him under the dark waters. For reasons that he could not have explained it moved him profoundly.

In the morning, he could detect no raising of the water level. But still he did not move. Patiently he settled down for another day and another night, minutely observing the great flood. By the end of that day he had discovered that there was a small tide, and had noted its high and low points. Then, all through the remaining night he sat awake by the shore, sniffing the salt sea air and listening in that vast emptiness to the hiss, crack and moan of the slow decline of an ice age.

[11]

On the second morning, he was satisfied. If the waters were still rising, they were doing so slowly, and unless there was a further deluge of water after this, he had time at least to lead his family to high ground where they might be safe. He rose stiffly and turned to go back to Akun. Already new plans were forming in the hunter's tenacious mind.

What Hwll had witnessed was the creation of the island of Britain. The great forest which he had tried to cross lay off what is now known as Dogger Bank, in the North Sea. During a short period of time – very probably in the space of a few generations – the vast melting floes of the northern ice cap had passed a critical point and had broken through the land barrier across the northern sea, flooding the low-lying plain that joined Britain to Eurasia. Around this time also – the chronology is still uncertain – the land bridge across the Straits of Dover, which had been the south eastern extremity of another of the great chalk ridges of Britain, had also been breached. The land that Hwll's ancestors had crossed was all gone, and for the whole of his short life, he had no longer been living on a peninsula of Eurasia, but on a new island. Because of that arctic flood Britain was born, and for the rest of her history, her people would be separate, protected from the outside world by a savage sea.

When he reached Akun, he explained to her in a few words what had happened.

"So, shall we go back?" she asked.

He shook his head. "No." He had come too far to go back now, and besides, it seemed to him possible that further south there might yet be higher ground that the sea had not been able to swallow up. Perhaps there was still a way over.

"We will go south along the coast," he said. "There may be another way across."

Akun stared at him angrily. He knew that she was near revolt. Vata's eyes were sunken; but the little boy disturbed him more: he was past fatigue; there was a strange apartness about him.

"He is leaving us," Akun said simply.

He knew it was true. The little fellow's spirit had almost gone; if they did not recover it soon, he would die. Hwll had seen such things before.

Akun held both children close. They clung to her silently, hardly knowing what was happening to them, taking comfort from their mother's warmth and the rancid but familiar smell of the pelts she wore. He was sorry for them, but there could be no turning back.

"We go on," he said. He would not give up now.

The journey seemed endless, and at no point did they see anything to the east except the churning waters. But ten days later, one change was evident which gave him cause for new hope. They had left the tundra.

They encountered marshes, and large woods. Trees appeared that they had never seen before: elm, alder, ash and oak, birch and even pine. They investigated each one in turn. The pine in particular they smelt with interest, and felt the sticky gum that oozed from its soft bark. There were huge luxuriant rushes by the water, and lush green grass in enormous tufts. Signs of game appeared; one morning when he was trapping a fish in a stream, the children came to his side and silently led him a hundred paces upstream. There, ahead of him, were two long brown animals with silky fur playing on the riverbank in the sunlight. They had not seen otters before and for the first time in months, the travellers smiled with pleasure. That same night, however, they heard another new sound – the eerie, chilling cry of wolves in the woods – and they huddled close together in fear.

For the curious paradox, which Hwll had no means of understanding, was that the very flood which cut him off from the lands to the south was part of a process which was providing him with exactly the warmth that he sought, there, where he already was. As the ice cap melted in the distant north, and the seas rose, the temperature of Britain had risen too, and would continue to do so for another four thousand years. The tundra region from which Hwll had come was itself a belt that was moving north as the ice retreated; and as the generations passed, three hundred miles to the south it was already becoming appreciably warmer. Hwll was entering these warm lands now, without needing to cross the eastern forest at all. They were the warm southern lands of the new island of Britain.

Despite this fact, Hwll was not yet ready to abandon his quest for the fabled lands to the south; there, he still believed, lay safety.

The following day, he made a mistake. After they had walked all morning he found his way south barred by a large stretch of water, on the other side of which he could see land. Obsessed as he was with the lands to the south, he said:

"It's the southern sea."

But Akun shook her head.

"I think it's a river," she replied. And so it proved to be. For they had come upon the estuary of the river Thames.

They followed the river inland for two days and crossed it easily by making a small raft. Then, once again, Hwll headed his little party south east.

"If there is a way across," he said, "I think it will be here."

If the land joining Dover to France had not already been washed away, he would have been correct, and six days later he reached the high, chalky cliffs of the south eastern tip of the island.

This time they did see what they had been looking for: jutting over the horizon was the clear outline of the tall, grey shoreline of the European mainland. It was there: but it was unattainable. Hwll and Akun stared across the English Channel and said nothing. At their feet, the chalk cliffs descended in a sheer drop for two hundred feet, and at their base the angry waters of the channel buffeted the coast.

"This time I am sure . . ." he began.

Akun nodded. The distant shores were the path to the warm lands of the south; and the churning waters below were the reason why they would never reach them. The cliffs where they were standing had once clearly been part of a great ridge that crossed the sea, but the waters had washed it away as they pressed south and west into the funnel of the Dover Straits.

[13]

"We could cross with a raft," he started hopefully, although he knew that they would not. In that angry sea they would unquestionably be destroyed on any raft that they knew how to build; for they were looking at one of the most treacherous patches of water in Europe.

The quest had failed. He had been defeated. Now it was time for Akun to speak.

"We cannot go south any more," she said bluntly. "And we cannot hunt alone. We must find other hunters now."

It was true. And yet . . . He pursed his lips. Even at this moment of defeat his active mind was busily sketching new plans. They had come down the east coast and he knew for certain that water barred his way in that direction. But was it possible that there might, after all, be a land bridge across further west? Although he had no reason to think so, the persistent fellow refused, even now, to give up all his hopes. And if they found no land bridge in the west perhaps at least they would find another hunting group. Lastly, he was determined to find high ground. If another flood came, who knew how much land it might engulf? He did not want to be caught on the lowlands if the sea came in; he wanted to be able to flee to the mountains.

"We'll try going west then," he announced.

For twenty more days they travelled steadily westwards along the chalk and gravel cliffs, always with the sound of the sea on their left. On the second day the distant coastline opposite dipped low on the horizon and disappeared entirely by nightfall. They never saw it again. Looking inland he could sometimes see hills and ridges running parallel with the shore.

The fundamental facts of the geography of prehistoric Britain that Hwll was discovering were fairly simple, and governed much of Britain's history since. To the north lay ice and mountains; to the south, the sea; and across the rich lands in between, the huge network of ridges divided the country into high ground and lowlands. Southern Britain, into which Hwll was now travelling, consisted of three main entities: water, alluvial land and chalk – rolling ridges of it lightly covered with trees; and in the alluvial land below stretched huge warm forests and marshes.

Several times now Akun asked him to stop for a few days and camp. But he was resolute.

"Not yet," he reminded her. "We must find other hunters before the summer is over." And he pressed on.

At last, however, there were signs which gave them encouragement: signs that other hunters had passed that way not long before. Twice they came upon clearings made in the trees and marks where fires had been lit. Once they discovered a broken bow.

"Soon we will find them," he promised.

At the end of three weeks they came upon a sight which confirmed all Hwll's fears, and determined the course of the last stage of the journey. This was the estuary of a huge river that rolled impressively towards them from the west, so wide and deep that it was clear they must now turn

[14]

inland to follow along its bank. At this point, it ran almost parallel with the coast and as they walked along it, they could still see a line of the cliffs a few miles away to the south.

It was later that day that Hwll saw what he had feared: five or six miles away to the south, the line of cliffs was broken. The sea had breached it, formed a gully, and then poured in, flooding a large part of the low-lying area between the coastline and the river. He looked at it with dread.

"You see," he explained to Akun, "the sea has come through the cliffs. It is breaking in everywhere. The sea has not only cut us off, but I think perhaps it will wear down all the cliffs and swallow up the whole land. That is why we must find high ground."

He was right. In the coming centuries, the sea would break through again and again, flooding the coastal areas and wearing down the chalk cliffs. The whole chalk coastline of southern Britain would disappear under the waves, and miles of land be flooded. The great river Solent, on whose banks they stood, was to disappear completely into the sea, and all that remains of this original chalk coastline of Britain is the single, diamond-shaped chunk standing off the southern coasts that is called the Isle of Wight.

"But first we must camp," she reminded him. "The children cannot go on."

"Soon," he replied, but he could see that she was right. Vata no longer even opened her eyes as she walked. The little boy had fallen three times that morning.

Now Hwll picked him up and put him on his shoulders.

"Soon," he promised once again.

Still with their faces west towards the setting sun, the little family turned inland, and Hwll began to look for a suitable place.

The next day he discovered the lake.

It was a small, low hill about five miles inland that first attracted his attention. It looked like a place from which he could spy out the land and where they could camp at least for the night. When he reached the place, however, he was surprised and delighted to find that hidden below it and in his path lay a shallow lake about half a mile across. At its eastern end, a small outlet carried its waters away towards the sea. Tracking round the lake he found that it was fed from the north and the west by two small rivers. On its northern side was a flat, empty marsh.

The water, sheltered by the hill, was very still; there was a sweet smell of fern, mud and water reed. Over the surface of the lake, a heron rose and seagulls cried. Protected from the wind it was warm. It did not take him long to make a small raft and cross the little stretch of water.

From the top of the hill he looked inland; all the way to the horizon now, he could see low wooded ridges succeeding each other. He turned to Akun and pointed.

"That is the way that we must go."

There were two months of summer left. This was clearly the place to rest and recoup their strength.

[15]

"We shall stay here for ten days," he said. "Then we go inland." And with a sigh of relief, Akun and the two children made their way down the hill to the shallow water's edge.

The lake turned out to be a magical place, and Hwll was delighted to find that it abounded in game. The hill embraced the water like a protective arm, and animals that he had never seen before paraded themselves there: swans, a pair of herons, even a flock of pelicans waded by the water's edge. On the open ground beyond the marsh, the soil was peaty and covered with heather, and a troupe of wild horses galloped across it one morning before vanishing towards the low wooded ridges to the north. In the rivers he found trout and salmon; one day he even crossed the Solent on a raft and reached the rock pools by the sea, returning with crabs and mussels which they cooked over the fire that night.

The children were beginning to recover their strength. Hwll smiled one morning to see Vata being chased by her little brother along the shallow waters by the lake's edge.

"We could stay here for the winter," Akun said. "There is plenty of food." It was true; they could build their winter quarters in the shelter of the hill. But he shook his head.

"We must go on," he said. "We must find high ground."

Nothing would shake his fear of the terrible force of the sea.

"You will kill us," said Akun angrily. But she prepared to move on.

The end of Hwll's remarkable journey was in fact closer than he thought. But it was not to be accomplished alone.

Before leaving the lake, Hwll had decided to reconnoitre the land immediately to the north, and so one morning he began to work his way up the river, towards the first of the low ridges he had seen from the hill. The banks were lightly wooded and the river, which was only thirty feet across, glided by at a gentle pace. River fowl ducked in and out of the rushes; long green river weeds waved their tendrils in the stream and he could see the large brown fish that paused silently just beneath the surface. He had followed the river five miles, when to his great surprise he almost walked over a camp.

It was in a small clearing by the bank. It consisted of two low huts made of mud, brushwood and reeds. The sloping roofs of the huts were covered with turf and they seemed to grow out of the ground like a pair of untidy fungi. Tethered by the riverbank was a dugout.

Startled, he halted. There was no fire, but he thought he could smell smoke, as if one had been put out recently. The camp seemed to be empty. Cautiously, he moved forward towards one of the huts. And then suddenly he became aware of a small man, with narrow-set eyes and a crooked back watching him intently from the cover of the reeds, fifteen yards away. In his hands he held a bow, fitted with an arrow which was pointed straight at Hwll's heart. Neither man moved.

Tep, who was the owner of the camp, had watched Hwll's approach for some time. As a precaution, he had hidden his family in the woods, before taking up his position; and although he could have killed Hwll, he had decided to watch him instead. One never knew, the stranger might be useful in some way.

As Hwll would discover, he was a cautious and cunning hunter; but apart from these two attributes, his character had no redeeming qualities whatever.

He had a face like a rat, with narrow eyes, a long nose, a pointed chin, pointed teeth, unusual, carrot-coloured hair, a shuffling walk and one very distinctive inherited peculiarity: his toes were so long that he could even grip small objects with them. He was mean-minded, vicious without provocation, and untrustworthy. Some time before, he and his family had lived with a group of hunters fifteen miles to the north east of the lake; but after a furious quarrel about the distribution of meat after a hunt – where he had demonstrably tried to cheat the other hunters – they had cast him out. He was a pariah in the region and few of the scattered folk there cared to deal with him. But Hwll knew none of this.

Hwll made a sign to indicate that he had come in peace. Tep did not lower his arrow, but nodded to him to speak.

In the next few minutes the two men discovered that although they spoke different dialects, they could make themselves understood well enough with the aid of sign language and Hwll, anxious to secure aid if he could, told this curious figure about his journey.

"Are you alone?" Tep asked suspiciously.

"I have a woman and two children," Hwll told him.

Slowly Tep lowered his aim.

"Walk in front," he instructed. "I will come and see."

By the end of the day, Tep had inspected the new arrivals and decided that it would be wise to make friends with the stranger from the north. He had a son who would one day need a woman; perhaps Hwll's girl would do.

When he understood that Hwll was looking for high ground, his calculating eyes lit up.

"I know such a place," he assured Hwll. "There are many valleys, full of game, but above them there is high ground," he indicated a great height, "many days journey across."

"Where?" asked Hwll.

Tep looked thoughtful. "It is far away," he said finally, "and the journey is not easy; but I can guide you." He paused. "Hunt with me first," he suggested. "Then I will show you the way."

Although Hwll was not sure he could trust the little man, this was not an offer that any hunter could refuse; and indeed, after the endless days of loneliness, he was not sorry once again to have a companion.

"I must reach the high ground before winter," he said.

"I promise that you shall," Tep replied.

Thus began the curious relationship between the hunter from the tundra and the hunter from the southern woods. Tep had four children. His first woman had died, so he had travelled to the west and stolen another from a band of hunters, when she was little more than a girl. Her name was Ulla and two of the children were hers. She was a round-faced creature with large brown eyes that wore a perpetually frightened look, and a scrawny body. The children all resembled their father, running swiftly through the woods on their long-toed feet and catching small animals with a ferocious dexterity that was frightening.

It was Tep's intention, by whatever means, to keep Hwll and his family with him until he had reached an understanding that, at the least, he should have the little girl for one of his sons. But, disingenuous though it was, his offer had advantages for the newcomers. While Hwll made his camp in the clearing, Tep showed him all the best fishing grounds. One day he also took him some miles west along the seashore and showed the northerner something he had never seen before: an oyster bed. Soon he had taught Hwll and his son how to dive for the oysters and prise them from the bed below with a knife; so adept did the boy become that they called him Otter, like the little animals who built their houses under the water, and the name stuck. That night both families feasted by the side of the lake on trout, mussels and the oysters which were swallowed whole, while the reflection of the stars shimmered on the clear water. Never had the family from the tundra eaten so well, and again Akun demanded:

"Why not stay here?"

But Hwll was anxious to go on and the next day he reminded Tep of his promise to show him the high ground; once more, however, the cunning little man temporised.

"First, let us hunt deer together," he insisted. "When we have killed a deer, then I will show you the high ground."

Hwll was reluctant this time to delay any further, but he finally agreed to this plan.

"But after that, I must find the high ground before winter," he insisted.

"I promise," Tep assured him. "We hunt at the full moon."

There was one other reason why Hwll agreed to delay. Skilful as he was in the tundra, he saw clearly that in these southern woods, Tep was a better hunter than he.

In the open tundra, where game was so scarce, men hunted in groups and followed their prey for days, wearing it down before moving in for the kill. But Tep hunted alone, in woods where game was plentiful and varied. Roe deer, the swift wild horse, hare, grey partridge, swans and geese were all easy prey. More dangerous were the wild boar and brown bear; and fellow hunters were the polecat, the fox, the wolf, badger, stoat and weasel. Blackberries grew on the edge of the clearings, and juniper berries. There were edible fungi and grasses. All these animals and plants, the narrow-faced man with the bent back understood. He knew everything that was edible and where it could be found.

His weapons were more varied too. In the tundra Hwll had carried a single spear and a bow and arrow. The ends were made of flint, carefully chipped to a razor-sharp serrated edge, and bound to the shaft with twine. But Tep's weapons had many different heads, each one for a different animal. They were smoother, usually chisel-ended rather than pointed; his arrow heads fitted neatly into a notch in the shaft, and some of his spearheads had a socket into which the handle could fit snugly. The spear he used to catch fish had barbs so that the fish would not slip off; in particular Hwll admired the delicate, lancet-like arrows Tep used to kill the fox so that its fur remained undamaged.

Nor were these the only differences. Tep's clothes, unlike his, were close-fitting and sewn together with twine made from animal gut. He wore a single jerkin and loincloth in summer, and added long leggings in winter. But he could also dress himself as a fox, or a deer, wearing the animal's head over his face to complete the camouflage. And Ulla made baskets of osier and beautifully carved bowls of wood superior to anything Akun could have attempted.

For though he did not know it, Hwll was one of the last of his kind. All over the northern hemisphere, the Palaeolithic hunters, the wanderers of the tundra, were gradually being displaced as the warm forests crept northwards and more sophisticated Mesolithic forest hunters like Tep took over the land.

Several days now passed as they waited for the full moon, and Hwll was careful to ensure that this time was put to good use. He learned from Tep how to make better weapons and how to set cunning traps in the woods, while Ulla showed Akun how to weave baskets. Something approaching friendship arose between the two families, and Hwll was bound to admit that, so far, meeting them had been to his advantage.

Each night now, as they stood beside the river, or down at the lake, the two men watched the moon, the goddess of all hunters, grow larger and more splendid in the sky. For both men, it was this silver goddess whom they revered above other gods, for the animals altered their behaviour according to her seasons, and was it not by her light that men hunted in the long nights?

The nights passed, then at last the moon became full and they knew the eve of their hunt had arrived; it was time now to prepare themselves and to perform the necessary rituals in honour of the goddess.

On the shore beside the sheltered lake they built a fire. As the moon rose high over the lake in the night sky, its reflection gleamed at them in the waters.

"She comes to drink," said Tep, and as they watched the silver disc shimmering on the lake, it did indeed seem as though she had dived under its waters to drink.

While their children built up the fire, the two men performed a curious but most important ritual. Over his head, Tep held the antlers of a deer killed the year before, and very slowly, he danced round the fire, imitating exactly the deer's delicate walk, its pauses, the quick, nervous turn of the head as it looked about for signs of danger. While Tep so perfectly acted the part of the deer, so that the children gazed at him in wonder, Hwll stalked him round the fire, with infinite care, exactly as he would when the hunt began. With meticulous precision, the men rehearsed every detail of the hunt – how the deer would be found, how stalked, and finally how it would be shot and die, while the women and children watched each move intently. This ritual was not only the hunter's way of instructing the children in the ways of the hunt. It was a rehearsal, a piece of magic performed in the sight of the moon goddess, to ensure that their desires were known to her and that they would be given a kill the next day.

So brilliantly did Tep the hunter act his part, that it seemed as if he had, in truth, become a deer, taking on the animal's soul, and sacrificing himself to the will of the hunter. When they killed the next day, both men understood that the spirit of the chosen deer would already have been promised to and accepted by the moon, and its body to themselves: nothing was left to chance. After this ceremony was done, the little group fell very quiet, knowing that an important and ancient magic had taken place amongst them, while the fire crackled and the moon continued on her silent way across the sky.

The following morning, a few miles up river, Hwll and Tep, accompanied by Tep's older son, a wiry boy of ten, found and killed a magnificent stag. They ferried it back to Tep's camp where the two women carefully skinned it, cut the meat away from the carcass and collected the blood in a leather pouch. They would feast that night, but even so, they would be able to keep back most of the meat, slicing it into strips and drying it in the sun. Meanwhile, shallow trays of seawater that had been left to evaporate now provided salt which they sprinkled over the meat to preserve it. Thanks to their care, the meat would last for weeks.

Before the feast, however, a second and most important ceremony had still to be performed by the men. When the meat had been removed from the carcass, the women handed them the skin. Inside the skin they placed the deer's heart, and then the men filled the remainder with stones and sewed the skin together again. Together Hwll and Tep lifted the deer across the dugout, and as the moon was rising, they paddled down stream towards the lake.

It was already dark when they reached the lake's placid waters, and the moon was high. Silently they pushed out to the middle and there they tipped the weighted carcass overboard. At once it sank to the bottom.

"Now the moon may eat as well as drink," said Hwll reverently, and they turned the dugout and paddled upstream to where their own feast was waiting.

The meat of the deer was for them, but its form and its spirit belonged to the moon goddess who had given them good hunting.

The two families ate well that night. The smell of the succulent roasting meat drifted across the river; and as Hwll looked at his children, now romping on the ground, and at his contented wife, he was tempted to move no further. But later in the night, when he buried himself in the warmth of Akun's still magnificent body he vowed:

"I'll find the high ground – and we shall live well too."

The very next morning Tep approached Hwll solemnly. It was now time for him to redeem his promise and show them the way inland; Hwll wondered what trickery the wily hunter would try.

Tep came straight to the point.

"Your girl. I want her for my boy," he stated. "If you give her, I will show you the way to the high ground."

Hwll considered. Tep had broken his word, but the bargain could be worse. At some stage the girl would have to be given to a man, and Tep's son was a good hunter.

"Take me there," he countered, "and if it is as you say then he may have the girl."

After a suitable pause Tep agreed to this, and the next day both families began to follow the river upstream. Tep led them at a leisurely pace.

It was good land. The fertile alluvial soil had been deposited by retreating waters, during millions of years, over a broad gravel plain. As they went along, Tep excelled himself in catching fish for them: trout, tasty eels, perch, pike and the delicately flavoured grayling. He seemed determined to please his new friends.

Only one thing worried Hwll – they were moving at such a slow pace, covering only five miles a day. It was now late summer. Would they reach the place before winter set in? Repeatedly he questioned the little man.

But whenever he heard this, Tep only grinned and shook his head.

They travelled up river, at a snail's pace, for five days. On the fifth day, they found themselves in a broad, shallow valley between gently sloping ridges. But these shelving hills were hardly high ground and Hwll was amazed therefore when Tep suddenly said to him:

"Climb that slope ahead and you will see it."

A small rise lay just ahead, by a bend in the river; together they walked up it, and as they reached the top, Tep said:

"This is the place where the five rivers meet."

And then Hwll saw it, directly ahead.

It was as though a huge bowl, miles across, had been scooped out of the land to form a broad system of wood and marshland surrounded on east, west and north sides by ridges. Even from where they stood, he could see that these ridges were of considerable size, and rose steeply. In one place he could see a sharp escarpment; in another, a daunting slope. Just right of the centre of this arrangement of ridges, a single wooded hill pushed forward from the edge of the high ground into the bowl, and behind it he could see the entrance to one of several valleys that cut through the uplands.

"There are three valleys," Tep explained. "West, north and north east." He pointed to the entrances of each. "That hill," he indicated the one near the centre, "guards the entrance to the northern valley; that's the smallest of the three. There's a river coming out of each valley, except that the western valley has two rivers. They join near the valley entrance." He made a sweeping motion with his hand. "Down there, all the rivers run together and then they make a big loop around the south west."

Hwll could see the big curve of the flowing waters near the centre of the bowl, before it flowed towards them.

"The fifth river joins from the west, just upstream from here," Tep concluded. "See, it's like this:" and he put his left hand on the ground, palm upwards, with fingers and thumb outstretched. "Like a man's hand. We're here." He indicated his wrist.

The analogy was perfect.

"And the high ground?" Hwll asked eagerly.

"In front of you." Tep indicated the huge ridges. "Once you climb the ridge to the north, it is all high ground. You can walk across it for days."

So it proved, when, two hours later, the two men stood at the top of the northern ridge some hundred and fifty feet above the valley floor. The panorama in every direction was magnificent, but what pleased Hwll was the view to the north. As far as the eye could see, a gigantic plateau of high, lightly wooded ground unfolded itself in ridge after ridge. Only the wind hissed quietly over this vast empty space. His broad face broke into a smile. At last: this was what he wanted. Even if the sea broke down the cliffs and swamped the low ground across which he had been travelling, it would never, he was sure, be able to break down this huge plateau. He was safe.

He turned to look at the rivers in the marshy ground below, where the swans made their stately way upon the water.

"This is where I will stay," he said.

He had found Sarum.

For the great plateau he had reached was Salisbury Plain, the huge, empty tract of high ground where all the natural land roads in southern England meet. From this rolling upland, the long ridges spread out south-west, east and north including, far to the north, the part of the great Jurassic ridge down which he had begun his journey from the tundra. To the east also stretched another ridge he had already encountered: for he had stood upon its last section as he stared across the Straits of Dover, where the sea had cut through it like a knife. These and other ridges, extending hundreds of miles over the island, all ran down to the great central hub of Salisbury Plain.

He looked at it with awe.

"It's like a sea," he murmured. "The land folds like waves."

He would have been astonished to know how close to the truth this statement was. For the geology of Salisbury Plain is not unduly complicated. About sixty-five million years ago, the plain and most of southern Britain lay under water, and when subsequently the sea receded in the so-called Cretaceous period, a massive layer of chalk, sometimes hundreds of feet thick and forming the covering of the ridges, was laid over the older shelf of Jurassic limestone beneath. It is this chalk which forms the soil of the high ground. Recently however – that is to say in roughly the last two million years – the wind and water of a long succession of ice ages interspersed with warm spells produced a very thin, very delicate sediment of earth over the chalk; and it was in this rich and shallow earth that the trees he saw were growing. This was the land of Salisbury Plain.

It was deserted. But Hwll was by no means the first hunter to encounter the place. Hunters had intermittently made the plateau and the valleys below their home for a period of a quarter of a million years, roaming over them, leaving small traces of their passing – arrowheads, the bones of animals – in the shifting soil, and then passing out of sight. They too had recognised the benefits of this little collection of valleys.

"The place is as you said," he remarked dryly to Tep. He knew now that the cunning little hunter had deliberately misled him in the first place by indicating that the place was hard to find. Obviously, he would easily have discovered it himself simply by walking up river. No wonder Tep had taken them north so slowly! But though he had been cheated, he had made a promise, and there was nothing to be gained by quarrelling with the only fellow hunter he had been able to find since he left the tundra.

"When the time comes," he said, meaning the moment when the girl reached puberty, "your son may come for her." And with that, he turned back to the valley below.

The following day, he investigated the area thoroughly, paying particular attention to the hill that protected the entrance to the northern valley. It rose steeply, jutting out from the edge of the high chalk ridge like a sentry post. From the top of the hill there was a magnificent view in every direction; and at the bottom, the ground sloped gently to the river.

"I think this is the place," he said to Akun, and she nodded. So on the south west side of the hill, which faced towards the place where the five rivers met, they built their shelter together. It lay in a small hollow with the hill behind it and a lip of ground in front, so that it had complete protection from the wind but, at the same time, an unsurpassed view. A tangle of stunted trees gave further cover.

To Hwll's surprise, Tep did not return to his own camp down river. The truth was that the little hunter was tired of living as an outcast, and glad to find someone who knew nothing of his bad reputation. So the day after Hwll selected his hill, Tep came to him.

"It is better that I stay here and hunt with you," he said; and although Hwll did not trust him, he had to acknowledge the sense of this arrangement.

Two miles away, where the two western rivers met, Tep and his family set up their curious, ramshackle shelters by the river bank.

In this way, the two families came to occupy Sarum, hunting the high ground and the valleys where game was abundant. Never again did Hwll have to face starvation as he had in the tundra, and although his journey south had been cut off, he had found his warm lands.

So began a new community of hunters at the place where the rivers met. They were not entirely alone, however. Seven miles to the east two other families had a similar camp on a wooden slope above a stream; and beside a marsh ten miles to the west along the river where Tep had built his huts, a friendly group of three families had settled in marsh huts, raised above the water on long poles for protection. To the north, however, as far as Hwll could discover, the plateau was empty.

In Britain at that time, this was still a dense population, for the entire island probably contained less than five thousand souls.

[23]

Sarum proved to be a place of many wonders. The two families could find enough food in the nearby valleys all year round without needing to move their camps. There were abundant roe deer; there were wild horse, elk, and sometimes bison and reindeer on the cooler plateau above. Once or twice, a brown bear with its clumsy gait even appeared; and while there were wolves in the forests too, they usually avoided the humans if they could. On the river there were swans, and at the harbour storks, pelicans and herons, though the last were not good to eat; there were many birds, including the tasty grey partridge and delicate lapwing. There were beavers, foxes, badgers; and sometimes all the families in the area came together to hunt the dangerous wild boar, with his villainous flashing tusks and his delicious meat. On the slopes Akun could find juniper, blackthorn and hawthorn berries; in the rivers Tep caught trout, salmon, pike, perch, grayling and eels. The hunters had a varied diet.

Many animals however were as yet missing from the scene: there were of course no house mice, although field mice could be found in the woods. There were no rats; there were no sheep, no domestic pigs or cattle, no pheasant and, though hares existed, there were no rabbits, nor would there be until the Normans introduced them six and a half thousand years later.

There was timber of many kinds: oak, ash, elder, pine; there was clay; and embedded in the chalk everywhere were deposits of flint useful for making arrowheads. In one place in particular, on the high ground a few miles to the east of the valley, there was a hollow in the ground which led to a small, natural open flint mine; and when he and Tep dug down a few feet, they found wonderful stone that they could easily quarry.

He and Akun did not entirely abandon the way of life they had known in the open tundra. Neither of them cared for the stuffy hut in which Tep lived all the year round. In winter they cut a large square hole well into the hillside and faced its entrance with brushwood and reeds, to keep in the heat; but when spring came, they erected their tent on the warm slopes overlooking the valley, and raised the flaps so that the breeze could ventilate their home with the sweet smell of spring leaves and summer grasses.

The winters were still long and hard, and the east wind could whip up a blizzard on the high ground quite as terrible as any they had known in the north; but when spring came, it was a warm, tumultuous affair unlike the meagre season they had known before: the clear streams from the melting snow coursed down from the high ground into the valleys, and below their hill, the little river would suddenly swell into a roaring spate and the long green riverweeds, which normally drifted listlessly in the current, would be stretched almost horizontal by the weight of waters pressing south and carrying with them a heavy rich sediment of chalk and mud.

But because he had come from the open tundra, it was above all on the bleak, silent high ground that Hwll liked to wander. In summer on a cloudless day, it often felt as though he could reach out and touch the sky; and when winter came and a biting east wind whipped the snow from the tops of the trees, the place reminded him still more of the vast, implacable emptiness of the tundra he had once loved.

It was, however, the midsummer of the year after their arrival that he discovered one of the greatest beauties of the area. He and Akun had wandered alone on to the high ground one sunny afternoon, and some miles north, they had come across a huge clearing. It had been made on a gently sloping hillside some thirty years before by a band of hunters who had camped there for several years and cut down all the surrounding trees. Cowslips grew there, and the delicate horseshoe vetch; but what puzzled Hwll was that the ground seemed to have a strange, blue colour, unlike anything he had ever seen before. What could it be? It was Akun who solved the problem. Laughing, she ran forward into the clearing, clapping her hands. As she did so, the blue field dissolved before his eyes, and upwards of a hundred thousand blue butterflies, startled, rose into the air and almost blinded him with their crazy flutterings of wings. These were the adonis blues and the chalkhill blues that made any empty spaces on the plain their special home. As he watched Akun in this cloud of blue wings, Hwll felt his heart once again leap for joy. Rushing to her, he pulled her to the ground and they made passionate love in the field.

For three years the families lived together in peace, and Hwll's broad, craggy face creased into ever deeper lines of contentment as he watched his family grow. The boy, Otter, grew into a strong, stocky little fellow, bright and capable; he and Tep's children took to hunting along the valleys in a pack and soon Otter had proved himself as adept as any of them in trapping the small animals they hunted. As for Vata, the little girl, she had Akun's magnificent hazel eyes from birth and by the time she was eight she was so strikingly like her mother that it sometimes made Hwll burst out laughing; he delighted in her company and he was only sorry that he had promised her to Tep's boy, who showed every sign of being as hard and untrustworthy as his father. But the promise had been made and it seemed he could do nothing about it. Despite this one regret, his joy seemed almost complete when, early in the second year of their new life he saw that Akun was going to have another child: and that summer she gave birth to a second fine son. It seemed then to the hunter that the goddess of the moon, to whom he sacrificed an animal every year, had blessed him and his family indeed.

As for Tep, he was glad no longer to be an outcast. He and Hwll often hunted together, and sometimes he would disappear down river in his dugout and return a few days later with pelican meat or some other delicacy from the lake, or with the bright plumage of one of the lake birds that Ulla, smiling for once, would weave into one of her baskets. Ulla's own life changed little. Sometimes she would appear with a black eye or some other mark of the beatings Tep gave her from time to time; but she rarely complained about the life of drudgery she led.

It was not until the fourth year of the new settlement, in the summer, that an event took place which nearly destroyed both families.

The preceding winter had been exceptionally long and hard and in the middle of it, Ulla had fallen sick. Though she was still only twenty, the intense cold and her hard life took their toll, and it seemed that she would die. Tep and his children tended her, in their careless way, but soon she had descended into a sickly silence and she showed no sign of recovery. After a few days, it was left to Akun to sit with her in the small hut in which Tep left her alone, to keep a fire alight for her and to feed her the warm broth which was the only food she could swallow. Her already meagre body was wasted; some days she shivered uncontrollably and Akun could only shake her head when Hwll asked about her condition. When, at midwinter, a huge blizzard blew into the valley for three successive days so that Akun could not make even the two mile journey from the hill camp to the hut by the river, she assumed that Ulla had died. But somehow she had not. The frail life force that had given her the passive resistance to survive with Tep and his family now enabled her to survive the cruel cold, and after the blizzard she very slowly began to mend.

It was because of her care for Ulla that a new, if somewhat unwelcome, friendship developed between Tep and Akun. One day in early spring she was surprised when the hunched form of the little hunter arrived at the hill camp bearing a large fish which he solemnly handed to her.

"For you," he explained. "You looked after Ulla."

She accepted this gift of gratitude with a friendly smile and, as custom demanded, offered him a place at the little fire and gave him food in return.

A few days later, he appeared again, this time with another fish and a hare. Akun was not sure she should accept more gifts from him; but since she did not want to offend him, she took them and once again thanked him with a smile.

Since then, Tep had on a number of occasions continued apparently chance meetings with her, either near the hill camp or in the valley below, and since she spent time with Ulla, who depended on her for company, it was impossible to avoid the foxy-faced hunter. She fell gradually into a polite familiarity with him which seemed to please him, and he continued to give her presents of food from time to time. When she once or twice asked Hwll if she should accept them, he only shrugged and said:

"Tep hunts with me; it is better he should be our friend."

And so she did not bring the matter up again.

It was one morning in late summer, when Hwll had gone tracking deer with Otter, that she left her baby at the camp with Vata and went down into the valley. In the woods east of the valley entrance there were berries and she knew that by now they would be ripe. As she made her way to the spot, she had the feeling that she was being followed, but though she stopped a number of times, she was unable to see anyone. The place she selected to pick the berries was a small clearing where blackberry bushes abounded, and she had already filled one of the two pouches she had brought with her when, quite suddenly, she realised that Tep was in the clearing with her. He had crept up on her stealthily and now he stood at her side. She could see that he had bathed in the river that morning so that his normally dirty body and straggly beard were less evil-smelling than usual. His shock of grizzled carrot hair stood up briskly from his head.

Although he had surprised her, she greeted him calmly as usual, but

[26]

there was something in his manner that alarmed her, and as she continued to move along the line of the bush, she found that he was moving beside her. He said nothing. She was not sure what she should do. Then, as she reached out to a high cluster of berries, the sly little fellow slid his hand quickly forward and firmly took her breast.

She froze. Although she was somewhat taller and heavier than the wiry hunter, she feared his strength.

While her body was motionless, her mind was working fast: she realised at once the enormous danger of the situation. For Tep to attempt to steal another hunter's woman was to risk a fight, probably to the death, and unless Tep had already planned to kill Hwll, which was unlikely, she could not believe that he was deliberately provoking such a crisis. So he must think that she would welcome these illicit advances. Immediately her mind ran over their recent meetings. She had smiled at him, accepted his gifts, not just once, but several times; she had made him welcome when he visited their camp and she had fallen into the habit of easy familiarity with him in Ulla's presence. Clearly he had mistaken these tokens of friendship for signs that she would encourage him, and now he had taken the first positive step. She must act fast, before it was too late.

So she turned, keeping her face impassive, and taking his hand gently but firmly by the wrist, she removed it from her breast, shaking her head gravely at the same time. She did not speak because she did not trust herself to find the right words. She hoped this action would be enough.

It was not. Tep had brooded about the full-bodied woman on the hill for many long months, and Ulla's bouts of sickness had increased his hunger and restlessness; cautious and calculating though he was, he had for some time persuaded himself that Akun's friendly attitude was meant to encourage him, and he was in no mood to be denied. At this first sign of rejection his face registered disbelief, then his eyes narrowed to slits. Slowly he reached out with his hand again.

Now Akun made her great mistake. Instead of remaining calm, she panicked. She struck his hand away with a gesture of disgust and then, contemptuously, she spat into his face.

Even as she did so, she realised the terrible error she had made. His face contorted into a spasm of hurt and rage; his eyes hardened into angry lust; and before she knew what had happened, he had ducked under her arm, seized her round the waist and with an ease that was terrifying, thrown her to the ground. Then, with a single, vicious movement, he ripped the shirt of leather off her shoulder and tore it down over her breasts. They were still magnificent, full and heavy; his lips curled into a snarl of lust.

She hit out wildly, no longer thinking of anything but escape. Swinging her fist with all her force at his face, she caught him on the side of the head and sent him sprawling; but only for a moment: before she could get up he had pulled out his long, bone hunting knife and with a cry of rage he threw himself upon her. This time she felt the sinewy strength of his arms as they pinioned her, his hard little face pressed against hers, and the knife held tight against her throat; and she knew that there was nothing she could do.

[27]

If she were to have any hope of getting away from him, Akun knew that she must make him relax; and so, deliberately, she let her body go limp. Then, hiding her anger, she ran her hands down his hunched little form, just as she would have done had it been Hwll; she raised one knee, seeming to invite him. Slowly she felt him loosen his grip on her, but still cautiously. She waited. He raised his face and she forced herself to smile at him. He was deceived. With a sudden grin of satisfaction he pushed her legs apart and thrust at her, and still, as he entered her, she seemed to encourage him. His face creased with a look of triumph; and he released the knife.

Before even his quick wits could anticipate her, she had it in her hand. She slashed upwards at his face with all her force. There was a scream of anguish, as he threw himself back away from her and his hand clapped to his face. She had sliced open his right eye.

Akun did not stop. As he rolled in agony on the ground, she ran through the wood, still holding his knife in one hand and pulling her clothes around her with the other. She did not stop until she reached the camp on the hill; and there, until Hwll returned, she stood on guard with one of Hwll's bows and a quiver of arrows, in case Tep should think of following her.

As events turned out, she need not have done so.

It was late afternoon when Hwll returned. Still trembling with rage and fear she told him what had occurred.

"You must kill him," she said, "or I am sure he will try to kill us both."

Hwll's face darkened with rage, and his first impulse was to do exactly as she suggested. But after a moment he became thoughtful.

It was a simple if unspoken rule of life amongst the hunters in those deserted regions that strife between families must at all costs be avoided. The population was tiny: life was precious; mates must be found each generation. If he killed Tep and started a feud with his family, then Tep's sons, when they were full grown, would seek revenge. In a few years, both families could be destroyed. He shook his head: that was not the way. It was this simple instinct for preservation that had kept the peace in many of the hunting communities in those empty spaces.

"I will consider what must be done," he said. And all that night he sat alone in front of their tent, pondering this difficult problem.

By dawn it was clear to him that there was only one possible solution; early that morning he took both his spear and his bow, and moved softly through the woods towards Tep's camp. He moved cautiously. Tep would expect reprisals; he might be in hiding; he might try to ambush him. He made a circle round the camp by the river before closing in.

As he expected, the huts were deserted, although Tep's dugout was still resting on the riverbank nearby.

Carefully choosing a position where he could not be surprised from behind, he placed his spear beside him and sat down to wait, laying his bow across his legs. He had the feeling that Tep was nearby and probably watching him, but there was no sign of him. The morning passed; the sun reached its high point and slowly began to descend, but still there was no movement except that of the swans drifting by on the river, and no sound but that of the birds and the soft breeze rustling in the trees. Hwll waited, knowing that his patience would be rewarded.

It was mid-afternoon when Tep appeared. He came slowly forward from a clump of trees opposite, moving haltingly, as though he did not trust himself, and as he drew closer Hwll saw the reason for his shaky gait: his right eye was nothing but a mass of pulp around which the blood had hardened; he would never see with it again.

Silently the two men faced each other, both watching cautiously in case the other attacked. Then Hwll spoke.

"You must leave here," he said simply. "Go back to your camp down river."

It was the only solution and both men knew it.

Tep considered.

"My boy, your girl," he ventured.

"No." Hwll shook his head. He did not feel bound to honour his promise to give little Vata to Tep's son any more; and he was not sorry for the excuse to end this rather unsatisfactory arrangement. For some time he had considered a boy from the camp of hunters to the east – a cheerful, lively boy like his own son who had appeared with his father the last time there had been a gathering of men to hunt boar.

Tep said nothing for a moment. He could not argue with Hwll's decision; but it was the second time that he had been cast out of a community and he knew that the prospects for his son now of finding a woman were bleak. There was still something else on his mind however.

"When the bison came over the high ground," he began, "my sons . . ."

Since their arrival at the place where the rivers met, the high point of each year had been the time in late spring when he and Hwll, accompanied usually by hunters from other camps, had trekked across the high ground to find the bison who might appear briefly from the north west at that season. It was a thrilling and dangerous exercise and they often followed the lumbering beasts for days at a time. It was a form of hunting closer to that which Hwll had practised in the tundra but Tep, too, had excelled at it and his son showed promise of doing the same. It was not a form of hunting to be undertaken alone and Tep was anxious that he and his sons should not be excluded from ever joining in again.

Hwll considered the request. He knew how bitter the blow was to the little hunter, but he did not want to restore him to the area.

"You may camp here one month, every other year," he decided finally. "Your sons may hunt if I send for them. But you may not visit our camp, and if you touch Akun again, I and the other hunters will kill you."

Tep had no doubt that Hwll could carry out this threat: he was respected by the other hunting families and, knowing the case, they would support him. He hung his head.

"We shall speak of this no more," Hwll concluded. "You can come for the bison in two years. I will send for you."

In this way the two men parted and Hwll prevented further bloodshed in the valley. Akun was angry that Tep had not been killed, but she had to accept Hwll's wise decision.

So began a new phase in the life of the wanderer and his little family. Hwll and his son now hunted alone in the valleys, except when the other families in the region joined them for the boar and bison hunts; and Tep returned to his life on the river as an outcast. Occasionally Akun would warn Hwll to expect trouble.

"He or his sons will have to steal their women; they may kill for them," she said, but Hwll was not concerned.

"They will not dare attack any of the families in this region," he replied, "for fear of revenge. If they do as you say, they will steal from far away, as Tep stole Ulla before."

In the second year after the incident, Tep reappeared with his family and camped by the river where he had lived before. His two sons, one a youth, the other a boy, were allowed by Hwll to accompany the other hunters when they tracked the bison, and at the kill received their share. Tep remained at his camp and kept out of sight. The family was subdued, conscious of their disgrace, and departed quietly at the appointed time.

It was two years later that the problem of the outcast family was resolved, in an unexpected way.

They had arrived in early spring, somewhat before the other hunters had gathered, and set up their camp as usual. As yet no bison had appeared, but already Hwll was busy tracking over the high ground, looking for signs of them.

One morning he went out, taking with him Otter and Tep's eldest son. He took a route almost due north across the wooded ridges but although he covered the ground swiftly, by midday they had found nothing. Accordingly they cut across to the west a few miles and descended the valley to the river.

"We'll follow it down until we get back to camp," Hwll announced. "Perhaps we'll find something on the way."

The hunter and the two youths made their way carefully down river. The banks were wooded, but occasionally they came upon patches of marsh which they had to skirt, or upon clearings where lush grasses grew and where deer often came to drink and graze. The river was still in its spring spate and moved by swiftly and heavily on their right. For several hours they continued their slow journey, watching for signs; but neither down by the river, nor on the valley ridges above did they see any evidence of the bison.

It was late afternoon, and the sun was already low over the ridge opposite when Hwll pulled up sharply and stared ahead in astonishment.

Then he whispered a single word to himself:

"Auroch."

Of all the animals on the island of Britain at that time, the most dangerous and the most highly prized by the hunters was the auroch. It was every hunter's ambition to kill one but they were so rare that even to catch sight of the animal could be counted as good luck.

Hwll had seen an auroch only once before, when he was a boy in the tundra; now only two hundred paces away stood a single beast grazing quietly by the river bank, in front of a small clump of trees.

The auroch was the prince of beasts: it resembled a black bull, but was about twice the size, standing over six feet high at the shoulder. From nose to tail it was about ten feet long and weighed many tons; although cumbersome, it was almost unstoppable once it began to charge. The aurochs roamed in small groups of usually a dozen or less, and all the other animals feared them – as well they might: for beside one of these mastodons even a full grown bison looked puny.

It was, above all, the horns of the auroch that were such a wonder. Hwll had never forgotten the time when he had seen one killed. The hunting party led by his father had taken half a day to wear it down, hurling spear after spear into the huge form. When finally, weary of the struggle, it had sunk to its knees and a brave young hunter had run forward and cut its throat, he too had rushed forward in the ecstasy of the moment to seize the horns – and found to his amazement that he could not reach across them. Even his father had only just been able to do so and Hwll still trembled when he thought of it.

The auroch did not survive. Although small herds were to be found all over Europe in prehistoric times, it was too large and too fierce to be domesticated by man – and too clumsy to escape the hunters. Over the centuries its numbers shrank until it finally became extinct – or almost. For in the seventeenth century, in an obscure corner of Poland, a single auroch was found in a forest. No one knew how it came to be there, but there is written evidence from the time, given by reliable witnesses, that the huge beast did indeed exist. That was its last appearance. No example of this prehistoric species has ever been seen since.

Motioning the two youths to remain where they were, Hwll began to move cautiously closer. The auroch was alone and had not picked up his scent. Keeping to the trees he crept forward further. Once, for a heart-stopping moment, it raised its head and stared straight towards him, and he froze; but then it lowered its gigantic horns again and continued to graze. It was a cow, not a bull, that had somehow become separated from the rest of the group, and though he watched for some time he could see no sign of its companions.

The fact that it was a cow did not make the auroch less dangerous; at the first attack the animal was capable of charging any hunting party with devastating force. But if one could bring it down – what a prize!

"Give me this auroch," he prayed. "Moon Goddess, I have sacrificed to you many times; give me, once, the mighty auroch."

The sun was sinking fast and the auroch showed no sign that it intended to move. It would probably spend the night by the river and rejoin its group the following day. Taking careful note of the spot, he returned to the others and the three of them slipped away into the woods.

He was tempted to attack the auroch there and then – anything rather than allow such a prize to escape! Excited though he was, however, he knew that it would be foolish to try to kill the huge beast alone; but what should he do? Darkness was about to fall and he was still far to the north of his own camp. The nearest camp where other hunters might be found was over twelve miles away through the woods.

"We need help," he said, "but where?"

All three were silent; then Tep's son spoke.

"I can bring my father. His aim is still good."

Hwll considered the proposition. He was torn: on the one hand he had no wish to hunt with Tep again; on the other he desperately wanted the auroch. With Tep that made four hunters. But Tep had only one eye – could his aim still be good?

"Tell him to meet me at the river before dawn," he said finally. "We'll have the auroch."

It was already after dusk when he came up the hill to the camp, and Akun could tell from his walk that he was excited. When he squatted by the fire, she saw that his eyes were shining. Then, in a few words, and using dramatic gestures, he told her about the auroch.

"Tep is ready," he announced. "He will bring his older son and we shall hunt at dawn."

One man, one cripple and two boys. At once Akun was afraid. Her youngest child was still a baby, and she could not afford to lose her man to an auroch.

"Go to the other camps," she said. "Get a hunting party."

But Hwll shook his head.

"No time. It will be gone by early morning."

"It's madness," she protested.

"The auroch is big, but it's slow," he countered. "We can lame it, then follow until it grows weak. Wear it down." It was the method of hunting used in the tundra and no one understood it better.

But if they made even one mistake, they could just as easily be killed, and Akun looked at him in despair. She knew his obstinate nature, though – it had brought them to Sarum from the tundra; and so she only shook her head.

"My son will say that his father killed the mighty auroch," he said with pride.

The little party was on the move before dawn. Tep and his son each carried a bow and two spears, as did Otter. Hwll brought spears and a heavy axe made of a broad flint head he had obtained from his quarry, fastened to a shaft of oak. The arrows would weaken the beast; but the spears with their long, deadly heads of sharpened flint would pierce the auroch's strong hide and embed themselves deeply. Since the technique of the hunters would be to maim the auroch, it was important that the first spear should strike deep behind the shoulder, slowing the beast down and working its way in towards the heart. After the first assault, the hunters would follow it relentlessly, striking again and again, until the auroch was finally so exhausted that they could move in for the kill. Then Hwll would slit open its throat with his knife. It was an effective method, but it was essential that the first attack be successful: for if they failed to maim the beast, then it would either career away, or it would turn on them and destroy them. All four hunters knew they risked death that morning.

[32]

With suppressed excitement, they made their way along the riverbank, in the early dawn when the birds had just begun the first, tentative sounds of their dawn chorus.

"Let it still be there," Hwll softly prayed, as he searched the darkness.

The first grey light was appearing when they reached the place where the auroch had been the day before. As the earliest tinge of dawn lit the horizon, it was just possible to make out, about half a mile away, a dark shape by a bend in the river. His hand clenched on the handle of his axe.

"It's there," he whispered.

The hunt was conducted in silence. A faint wind was blowing from the south up the river. The four hunters fanned out, keeping up wind in the cover of the trees, or the clumps of reeds in the clearing.

The sun rose over the ridge, breaking through the grey clouds. The auroch continued to graze, and the hunters remained invisible.

The attack was sudden. In perfect unison, all four hunters rose and hurled their spears. They came from three sides, and were all within thirty feet of the auroch when they threw. It had been an expert piece of stalking.

Hwll watched the auroch's head jerk violently as it let out a bellow that echoed down the valley. And at the same instant, he knew that the attack had failed.

His own spear had been well aimed. It had struck behind the shoulder but it had failed to penetrate deeply. Otter's had struck the auroch's throat, but had not done much damage either. Both Tep and his son had missed completely. It was the worst possible combination: the animal was enraged but not badly hurt.

The disaster took place in seconds.

In a fury the auroch wheeled about, stamping its huge hoofs and searching for its attackers. It was Tep that the auroch saw: for he had come across the clearing with only the reeds for cover. The auroch put down its tremendous head, and charged. The cunning little hunter with the long toes had no chance. He faced death calmly, his hard, mean little face staring straight at the huge form rushing towards him. At the last moment, knowing that it was useless, he made a dart to one side, but the auroch's great horns caught him and with a single burst of blood, Hwll saw his small body broken apart. Tossing the body high into the air, the auroch thundered forward towards the trees and a moment later he could hear the great beast stumbling about in the wood, snapping the spears off against the tree trunks. The hunters made no attempt to follow.

Tep was dead: a sad little mess of flesh and blood, scarcely recognisable. Without a word, they carried him back to the camp and that evening they buried him on the high ground, under a small cairn of stones.

The death of Tep left the little community with a new problem, and one that had to be solved quickly. Ulla was still of child-bearing age, and her family, except for her son, who was still a youth, had no protector. But there was no available man in the area. They could not be sent down river again alone.

No words were spoken between Hwll and Akun on the subject but both of them knew what must happen.

Two days after the death of Tep, Akun herself strode down the hill to the camp by the river and brought the family there up to her own camp on the hill. There, forty paces along the slope, they set to work to build a new shelter: it consisted of two parts, one for Ulla and one for her children.

Ulla said nothing. It was hard to know whether she was frightened by the loss of her protector or glad that Tep, who had always bullied her, was gone. In any case, her new status was uncomplicated: she and her children were now under Hwll's protection. Akun inspected the girl carefully while they built her new home. She was a stringy, unsatisfactory creature used to being treated as a workhorse by Tep. But she had survived, if nothing else, and Akun had no doubt that she would have more children.

She explained the matter to Ulla simply and succinctly:

"Hwll will be your man now; we shall both be his women. But I am the senior woman and you will obey me."

Ulla said nothing, but made a token nod of submission. For many years she had learned how to submit.

It was Hwll who was most affected by the change. Akun had been his woman for many years and when he thought of a woman, it was she alone who came into his mind. Now all was to be changed and it gave him a profound sense of unease.

While the two women prepared Ulla's new home, the hunter went off alone. He was gone several days and when he returned, he said nothing about his absence, but moved quietly about the camp with a new look of satisfaction on his face.

During his time away, he had wandered along the valley to the west. Some miles away he had often noticed an unusual slope above the river. There, instead of the usual chalk, the ground exposed a long rib of soft grey rock with a wonderful texture and colour, quite unlike anything else in the area. He had passed it many times and noticed the curious grey light it seemed to return when the sun struck it. The only stone that he had any use for was flint, and so he had passed by the grey stone without giving it much thought. But now, in this crisis in his life, a strange new idea had formed in his mind.

At the rockface he had searched the ground for some time, picking up lumps of stone and discarding them, until finally, with a grunt of satisfaction, he found what he was looking for. It was a lump about the size of his fist, oval in shape and smooth to the touch. The stone was not hard, and settling down on his haunches beside an oak tree, he began to work it with a flint.

That night he stayed by the grey rockface, and the next day he strode up to the high ground he loved. All the time he worked the stone, hardly pausing. Several times he washed it in a stream, and by the end of the second day he had begun to polish it. On the third day, his work was finished, and putting the stone in a pouch, he went back to the camp on the hill.

The figure that he had so painstakingly carved was remarkable. It resembled a short, squat female torso and head. The face was indicated by a ridge for the nose and three little holes for eyes and mouth. It was crude. And yet, taken as a whole it had an extraordinary beauty: for this primitive little sculpture was nothing less than Akun herself; the heavy, full breasts, the rounded, fertile stomach and hips, the big, muscular buttocks – it was the essence of his woman that the hunter had created, and he stroked the little figure lovingly.

What had possessed him to carve in stone? He could not say. Something about the feel of it, the way it caught the light, the wonderful heaviness of it had taken his fancy. Perhaps the challenge of the thing. At all events, he was pleased with it. Akun was fertile, the mother of his children. She was everything that he knew about a woman; and the curious little figure, he felt sure, would bring him good fortune.

The following day, taking the little stone figure with him, Hwll went to the hut where Ulla awaited him, and there he lay with her for seven days before returning to Akun. This practice he repeated, at different phases of the moon, all through that winter and the following spring. And in the autumn, Ulla produced a child: a handsome boy baby which, unlike its half brothers and sisters, did not have long toes.

For seven more years Hwll continued this pattern of life, producing three more children. And always, each time he lay with Ulla, he took with him the little stone figure he had made.

If Hwll was the father of the valley, there was never any doubt about who was the senior woman.

Akun had not come so far, against her will, not to enjoy the advantages that were now due to her. In her high, sheltered camp near the top of the hill she would come out each day onto the little lip of ground that formed a sort of natural walk in front of it, and as she moved along the line of gnarled trees, it was the signal for the girls and younger women in the camp below to run up to her and do her bidding.

She taught them – how to skin game, how best to trim the skins of every different animal, how to cook and preserve their meat. Sometimes she would lead all the women into the woods and direct them in their search for herbs and roots, moving about herself briskly, prodding the ground with a stick.

Only once, as the new family of Hwll grew up, did Ulla attempt to challenge her authority, by rashly giving her own daughter an order contradicting Akun's instructions. She had done it in front of the whole family, including Hwll. For a second, Akun looked at her with contempt, then gave her a blow that sent her flying off the edge of the lip and rolling thirty feet down the slope over gnarled roots and thorny bushes. No one said anything. Bruised and bleeding. Ulla looked up once, with rage in her eye, at the powerful stocky form above her, then reverted at once to her usual submissiveness. She did not cross Akun again and the camp lived in peace.

The future of the valley seemed assured. The little tribe which Hwll and Tep had fathered hunted the area with skill and success.

Because of Hwll's protection, even Tep's sons were able to find brides in the region. He saw his own son now lead the hunt. Soon another generation would take over, and Hwll was content.

Yet he was not content. At first he could not say why. He and Akun, both in their thirties and approaching old age, could look back upon great achievements: he had led his family on their epic journey from the tundra; he had found the warm lands. They had hunted well and raised fine families. Both of them were now treated with honour and respect – surely he had done all that it was possible to do.

But with each passing season, the feeling of unease and disquiet grew stronger within the old hunter: it was a deep sense that his work was not complete, that something of vital importance was still missing from the life of the place where the five rivers met. It distressed him and it would not leave him.

He took to visiting the high ground alone, withdrawing somewhat from the life of the camp, even from Akun herself, whom he loved. He would spend days up there. Sometimes he would make a small sacrifice to the moon goddess who had watched over him so faithfully; at other times he would find a high spot from which there was an uninterrupted view in every direction and he would gaze for long hours over the empty landscape of wooded ridges which reminded him of the bleak spaces of the tundra. It was the huge elemental forces – the open sky, one day azure blue, the next grey, lowering and savage, the ridges that swept endlessly to the horizon like a sea, the whistling breezes and the great silences – it was these things which both frightened him and comforted him as well.

At such times Hwll would remember his father and the many things which he had told him about the world and about the gods who directed the huge forces of nature; he would remember the directions that had been handed down to him and which, despite the fact that they had proved inaccurate, had nonetheless brought him south on his epic journey. He thought of the terrible things he had witnessed on that journey, and the meaning of it all. The contemplation of these things moved him profoundly.

And to the gods he would whisper:

"Show me what it is that I have failed to do, what further act I must perform."

And one day, as the wind hissed over the trees, he heard it give him his answer:

"You must tell it, Hwll. You must tell the story of your journey, and of your ancestors, and of the gods, so that these things will be remembered and not be lost."

He heard it distinctly; there was no mistaking the whispering voice. But still he was troubled.

"How shall I tell these things?" he cried out loud.

Then the voice of the gods – for this was surely what the whisper must be – replied:

"Listen."

It was evening when Hwll came down to the camp; and his family never forgot his look when he approached them: for his wrinkled face was suffused with a radiance they had never seen before, and his eyes had a faraway stare.

Whatever it was that Hwll had heard from the gods, it was not to be told just yet. For only a few days after he came down from the high ground, the long winter began.

It seemed to be endless that year; at times the old hunter wondered: did I come so far, only for this? The cold was bitter, as bad as he had ever known in the tundra. The river was frozen over so hard that it took the men most of the day to break through a hole through which they could fish in the water beneath. In the valley, a great silence had fallen, and for days on end only a few birds appeared to move. Soon they were dying, and the silence grew deeper. On the high ground above, there was no movement and no sound either, except for the steady, persistent hiss of the north east wind, day after day, bringing snow like a wet haze, snow that drifted quietly into piles so deep that when he looked out now, Hwll could not even see the trees.

Thanks to Akun and the women, they had plentiful stores. Fish could still be caught; sometimes there was a little game. Hwll consoled himself with the thought: this will never be like the land we travelled from. When spring comes, there will be game again.

Only one thing grieved him: Akun.

She had known for some time that soon a winter would come which must be her last. At first there were only small signs – a slight stiffness in the joints, a tooth unexpectedly loosening, or cracking on a bone. Twice recently she had lost a tooth, felt it suddenly under her tongue, tasted the blood. On each occasion, she had stuffed grass into the gap and hoped that Hwll had not noticed. She did not want to admit what was taking place.

But this winter, something worse was happening to her.

It was not just her joints: they might ache in the cold, damp winter, but the spring sun had always seemed to make them better. No, this was something of a different nature, something less easy to define: it was an inner coldness, that often made her shiver when she was alone, and which obstinately refused to leave her, even when she huddled close to the fire or slept, wrapped in furs, beside the warm body of old Hwll. Her body was growing gaunt; she looked sadly at the now flaccid and wrinkled shapes that had once been her splendid breasts. Several times, when there was no one to see, and the terrible cold from the snow came insistently into the shelter in the long hours when Hwll had gone out onto the ridge, she found frozen tears on her cheek. The winter seemed endless.

But it was not even this coldness within that told her what was to come. It was when she awoke, one day in the depth of that long winter and realised that she did not care any more. Then, without regret she knew: this winter will be my last.

The spring was very late that year, but when it came, it came with a huge rushing of waters; the sun broke through, warm and strong; the whole valley burst into violent life and the river was, once again, a torrent. Hwll, grey-haired, thinner than before, but still in his old age a useful hunter, led her each day to her accustomed place on the little lip of ground overlooking the valley; but it no longer pleased her. She retired to the shelter each day when he was gone; and even in summer, she could only be persuaded out for a little time.

He said nothing, but he understood, and it grieved him to know that he was soon to lose her.

It was one night that summer, when the whole extended family sat round the fire they had built on the side of the little hill above the valley entrance, and after they had eaten the sweet-smelling meat of the deer, and gorged themselves with the berries that were so abundant, Hwll ordered silence: and then, with words that had been given him by the wind itself, he completed his life's work by passing on to them the great treasure of his knowledge.

That night, and many more times, in words that they could memorise easily, so that the past would be preserved when he had died, he told them all he knew: he told them about the wall of ice and the tundra in the north, about the great seas to the west and south, and about the mountains and forests far away in the east. He told them about the gods and about the great causeway across the sea. And then, he told them the story he had heard in the wind, of how the sea had cut them off.

"In the beginning," he explained, "there were two great gods: the sun, and the moon his wife, who watches over all hunters. And they had two children: the god of the forest, and the god of the sea. And the god of the forest lived in the great forest to the east that was full of game; and the god of the sea lived in the north, near the great wall of ice.

"The sun and moon loved the forest god, and gave him much land. But he was never satisfied and always asked for more. This made the sea god angry, for he was given no land.

"A year passed, and still the forest god asked for land. And the sea god was more angry still.

"The next year, the forest god asked for more land, saying: 'My mother the moon likes men to hunt; give us more land for forest, so that they may do so.'

"Now the water god was angry; and he went to his father the sun and said: 'Father punish my brother who is never satisfied.'

"And so the sun god became a huge white swan, he flew over the ice in the north, again and again, and the ice melted.

"When the ice melted, there arose a sea; and the sea came down from the north in a huge wave and it swept over all the land there and it covered the forest to the east. And the waters remained."

Then, carried away by the memory of the terrible sight he had seen, and moved to the depths by the thought of the vanished forest, the hunter's voice rose to a chant:

"So the forest lay under the sea, and the animals too, the birds and the beasts, they are all there still, under the dark waters.

"You can hear their cries in the waves.

"The path to the east is lost, and we are an island, cut off from the rest of the land.

"The waters are rising still; each year they rise, taking more land.

"They will take the shore, they will take the lake, they will take the valley.

"But the high ground will remain, for the waters cannot reach it.

"Here, my children, we are safe, until the world ends.

"Give sacrifice to the gods. Salah."

His song was ended. The listeners who heard these sobering words, and knowing they came to him from the gods, remained silent for some time.

When Hwll died, three years after Akun, they buried him beside her on the high ground. With him they buried the little stone figure that he had made of her.

And for many generations, at Sarum, it was the time of the hunter.

The Barrow

APPROXIMATELY THREE THOUSAND five hundred years passed, and in the remote northern island of Britain, as far as we can tell, very little happened. To the north, the ice cap retreated to something like its present arctic position, and the sea continued to rise and devour new land, so that the inland lake by the hill became instead a protected harbour, most of the land between the hill and the old chalk cliffs having been washed away. The temperature too had continued to rise, so that in the northern part of the island, the tundra departed, and cool forests took its place. The reindeer, the bison and the elk gradually disappeared from the land.

But in the place where the five rivers met, the descendants of Magri and Taku, and others like them, continued to hunt undisturbed, and if a few adventurous folk succeeded in crossing the Channel to the island from time to time, they too followed the ancient hunting ways of the region during this long period.

But elsewhere, the story was very different; for some time before 5,000 B.C., the greatest revolution that the western world has ever known took place. It started in the Middle East and from there it spread over most of Europe: this revolution was the introduction of farming.

It changed everything. It was the beginning of the modern world. Following game, a single family even in a region like Sarum had needed many miles of land over which to roam in search of food; but for sowing crops and raising livestock, a few dozens of acres was enough and food could be stored. It was the beginning of wealth as it has been known ever since. Whereas up to this point in history, man had been only a figure in the landscape, now he began to dominate the land, controlling it and shaping it to his own purpose.

By four thousand years before the birth of Christ, these epoch-making changes had produced extraordinary results.

In the warm and fertile lands between the great rivers Tigris and Euphrates in present day Iran, an inventive and busy people – the Sumerians – were building the world's first hill towns. They were made of mud and brick and their summits were crowned with temples. Elsewhere in the Middle East, other peoples were developing new and sophisticated crafts: in Egypt they made linen; in Mesopotamia, clever jewellers were combining copper brought down from the mountains with glass, in beautiful and intricate patterns to make the ornamental work called faience. On the coast of Saudi Arabia, divers searched the oyster beds for pearls which they exported, and in the Levant, merchants were putting out to sea in small ships rigged with square leather sails, carrying cargoes of copper, ivory and brightly painted pottery.

Further north, in Europe, there were no towns. But in that huge belt of land stretching from the Danube to the Baltic, farmers were planting crops, raising livestock, and burning the stubble to enrich the soil; and they were building huge wooden barns and houses, sometimes a hundred feet long. Further west, in Brittany on the northern coast of France, the farmers were learning to decorate their stonework and pottery with elaborate patterns of spirals, arcs and circles that seemed to have no end.

The Neolithic Age of farmers and builders in stone was well under way, and the age of the new metal alloy, bronze, would soon begin.

But not in Britain.

For in Britain, cut off by the sea from these developments, it was still the time of the hunter.

One summer morning, about four thousand years before Christ, a party of six small boats entered the shallow harbour by the hill and turned up the slow moving river that led towards Sarum.

The boats were made of brightly painted skins stretched over a wooden framework; they were each about fifteen feet long, broad, with a fairly shallow draught, and they had been paddled across the English Channel at great risk from the coast of Brittany. They had no sails and were really designed for river work, but luckily the weather during their crossing had been unusually calm.

There were twenty fighting men in the boats, together with their women and children; both men and women wielded the paddles and they wore simple sleeveless jerkins made of leather or woven wool which left their arms conveniently bare for this hard work. The boats also contained four dogs, eight lambs, twelve small calves, ten piglets and a quantity of supplies, including the all-important clay pots that contained seeds for sowing. The fleeces of the lambs were coloured a rich golden brown.

There were two figures of particular note in the party. In the stern of the last boat sat a massive man. He did not paddle or take any active part in the proceedings, but sat very still as though conscious that he was a precious object to be taken reverently from place to place. He was middle-aged and of only middle height: his massiveness derived from his gigantic girth and weight. His head was round and bald. He had oiled both body and head so that the latter now caught the sun and shone. His watery eyes were set wide apart and were never still; he wheezed continually. This was the medicine man, and his presence would ensure that the greatest of all the gods, the sun god, looked upon the enterprise with favour.

The other, and still more striking figure was that of the leader of the band, a big thick-set bull of a man with a black beard, a huge nose that jutted out from his face like some rugged promontory, and small, angry eyes. As the boats moved swiftly across the shallow waters he stood in the prow of the foremost, directing operations. At his feet lay an enormous black club. His fierce eyes scanned the banks for signs of any enemy, but he saw that the place was deserted.

He was wrong. On the northern edge of the harbour, concealed behind a bank of reeds, a single hunter had been watching the six boats intently ever since they first appeared in the narrow entrance that led to the sea. He was a small, wiry man; his shock of bristling black hair and his narrow face gave him the look of some small, stoat-like animal; he also had long prehensile toes, a characteristic he shared with a number of hunters in the area. He was sitting in a simple dugout – well suited to those calm waters, but slow and primitive compared with the six long boats that had just glided by. As soon as they had passed, he abandoned it and, using the tracks the hunters knew, loped quickly inland through the woods. In this way, he was able to head off the boats as they made their way upstream; he did not pause, however, but continued on his way.

The leader of the new arrivals was a remarkable figure and, along the coast from which he came, already a legend in his own lifetime. They called him Krona the Warrior.

He had started life as a simple farmer, undistinguished from the other modest smallholders who lived in the region. He would certainly have remained just that – an even-tempered fellow with a healthy young family – had it not been for one of those sudden tragedies which can jolt a man's, or a community's life, into some wholly different course.

In Krona's case, it was the invasion of a marauding tribe which changed everything. They arrived suddenly and without warning in that coastal region early one summer; no one knew exactly where they had come from, nor what impetus had driven them to travel; but they seemed to have arrived from the east. It was a pattern that was to be repeated for thousands of years in the troubled history of Europe. Again and again such invaders – sometimes a party of raiders, sometimes an entire people – would come sweeping into western Europe with terrifying force; they came from Scandinavia, from the Germanic plains, from the distant steppes of central Asia; some stayed and settled, others came, ravaged and departed.

The marauders who came to devastate Krona's region were a comparatively insignificant group, a nameless but brutal tribe of tall and swarthy people who camped in huge leather tents, and whose only interest was in hunting, stealing and destroying. They had made their base about a hundred miles to the north east and each spring they had swept along the coast in war parties, burning the isolated farms and settlements who were ill-equipped to resist these surprise attacks. One day, when Krona had been away on a visit further along the coast, they had swooped down upon his area, and when he returned it was to find his farm burned, his wife and four children all dead, and his livestock taken. When he saw this, he vowed:

"There will be vengeance."

The next year, when the invaders came whooping through the fields, they suddenly encountered an organised force of thirty men drawn from farms all over the region. The farmers were well armed and lying in wait for them, and after a hard struggle, the invaders were driven off. To their amazement, Krona and his men then followed them relentlessly, day after day, in an effort to obliterate them. For Krona now sought only one thing: revenge.

The same pattern was repeated the following year when the invaders returned in greater force; and in succeeding years.

Soon Krona was able to muster fifty or sixty men, and because they were fighting for their own homesteads, they were easily worth twice that number of raiders. They wore blue warpaint, and they would lie in ambush for their enemies and hit them with a devastating fusillade of flint tipped arrows. The insurgents began to dread them. But it was in hand to hand fighting that they were most feared. They wielded short axes of polished stone and they were methodical and merciless.

Krona himself however, only ever carried one weapon: it was a huge oak club, blackened with age. The heavy end was formed by a big knot in the wood; into the thin end he had fitted a vicious spike of flint. It was a terrible weapon, and with it Krona could club a man to death with a single blow, or slit him open with one tearing upward sweep – and it was impossible to tell which kind of blow to expect.

When he was not fighting, he reverted to being a peaceable farmer, and so it was that the saying arose in the region:

"You can argue with Krona; but never argue with his club."

After a dozen years of this warfare, the invaders wisely left the region alone and turned their attention further south and peace returned for the time being.

But there was a sense of unease in the area. There was the fear that the raiders might return. There was also a pressure on the land, for though the soil in Krona's region was poor and easily exhausted, other farmers had been tempted to come there to enjoy his protection and now the place was overcrowded. Finally, the younger farmers who had fought with Krona and enjoyed a taste of action found they were growing restless. They had discovered that they could defeat these savage tribesmen: what else could they do? A spirit of adventure was in the air; and as these young farmers looked about them, a desire arose to find new land: but where?

"The island across the sea is said to be rich," one declared. "No one lives there except some hunters. If we go there, we can take all the land we want."

"If the hunters don't kill you first," another laughed.

"Krona might lead us," suggested a third.

And so it came about. Krona was tired of fighting; he was growing old now, nearly forty and although he had defended them so stoutly, he too found that he was ready to leave the lands where his first family had been murdered and avenged. Despite his age, he had taken a new wife – a high-spirited girl who had given him two boys – and he soon agreed to lead the party to the island in search of a new settlement.

Now, as he took his first look at the island, he was pleased with what he saw.

The harbour was sheltered. As they went up the river, the banks were wooded – he saw no signs of any settlers there before them – but he could see that the land was rich. However, this low-lying and indefensible terrain was not what the cautious leader was looking for, and he urged the boats forward. They pushed up river some ten miles and then camped for the night.

It was on the afternoon of the next day that he reached the place where the five rivers met; and as soon as he saw the bowl of land and the surrounding hills he smiled. At his urging the boats soon reached the entrance to the northern valley and the hill which guarded it. Its natural defensive position was obvious.

"We settle here," Krona declared.

But there remained the question of what to do about any hunters they encountered.

Krona was not only a brave warrior; he was also a shrewd and wise leader of men, and his instructions to his men had been given carefully.

"Do not attack any hunter," he told them. "They know the terrain and they can destroy us. If we are to live here in peace we must win them to our side."

This strategy was to be tested at once; for as the six boats pulled into the bank, Krona saw that along the edge of the trees, which were set back some ten yards from the water at that point, a dozen men had silently stepped forward, their bows and arrows at the ready. They had been warned of the boats' arrival the night before by the long-toed hunter named Taku, who had run all the way from the harbour to prepare his people. They did not move, but watched the newcomers suspiciously.

Slowly, and alone, Krona stepped out on to the bank. He laid his club ceremoniously on the ground as a signal that he had come in peace, and walked towards the hunters. The conversation between them, which had to be carried out in sign language, went as follows:

KRONA: I have come in peace.
HUNTERS: Where from?
KRONA: Across the sea.

This caused a murmur of astonishment.

KRONA: I bring you gifts.

At his signal, Krona's young wife, Liam, now brought forward a magnificent pottery bowl, and a tunic made of woven cloth, that she herself had thickly embroidered with beads and gems. The hunters inspected both, first cautiously and then with wonder. The workmanship of the bowl was remarkable. It was a large, rounded object, which looked almost like a leather bag. Its surface contained tiny grits of flint, giving it a consistency like a biscuit and it had been fired to a rich dark brown colour. They had seen nothing like it before. Quickly it was passed from hand to hand. As for the tunic, it, too, was unlike anything they possessed. The cloth was woven and the whole front was covered with brightly coloured

[44]

beads, drops of amber, and even pearls that had reached Krona by a circuitous route through friendly merchants from the south.

HUNTERS: What do you want?
KRONA: To live in this valley.
HUNTERS: These are our hunting grounds. You cannot hunt here or there will not be enough game.
KRONA: We do not wish to hunt.

The hunters looked at one another. This made no sense at all. How could the strangers live if they did not hunt?

KRONA (*seeing their mystification*): We bring our own animals.

He showed them the animals in the boats. The hunters could still make nothing of this.

KRONA: We want only the valley. All the other hunting grounds are yours. If you give us the valley, we will give you many gifts. But you must leave the valley and not hunt there. That must be our agreement. If you do this, we will live in peace.

To give emphasis to his words, the women now brought from the boats six more of the fine bowls and three more tunics. To the hunters this seemed riches indeed.

Krona waited without moving while they conferred amongst themselves. Taku, who had preceded the boats from the harbour, argued that they should kill the newcomers.

"They are lying," he said. "They will hunt all over our lands. Kill them now and take their gifts." Several of the hunters agreed with him.

"What Taku says may be true," a stout elderly man called Magri replied. "But they are strong and well armed. Let them enter the valley. If they keep their word, it is well. If they have lied, then we can wait and ambush them later, when they are not prepared."

After some further argument, this wise and provisional plan was agreed.

And so that day, in a matter of minutes, Krona bought the valley and the little hill of Sarum; the hunters, pleased with their new riches, departed to their camps along the rivers.

The next morning Krona stalked up the small valley, pointing with his club to the boundaries that were to divide each homestead from the next. He allotted to each man and his family a parcel of land on the well-drained slopes that rose high above the river. There each family would be able to clear the ground, sow crops and raise their stock for generations to come. He inspected the river, and smiled to find it full of fish; his hard, weatherbeaten face creased with pleasure as he saw the swans which had built their nest in the reeds on the riverbank opposite the hill where he had decided to build his own farm.

[45]

And now a most important event took place. Leading the entire band of settlers up the hill, with a speed and agility that were astonishing for a man his size, the medicine man directed them to clear a space at its summit some thirty feet across. Men, women and children all set to: for this was important and sacred work that no able-bodied person who feared the sun god could neglect. This took several hours, but when it was done, not only had they made a fine clearing, but they had also opened up a magnificent view. All around on the northern side they saw the endless folds of the lightly wooded high ground: below, and to the south, the broad rich valley of wood and marshland led into the blue distance, to the sea from which they had come; and a murmur of approval went up.

Calling them to order, the medicine man commanded them to build a large fire in the centre; and while this was being done, he prepared himself for the all-important ceremony that was about to take place by painting his face chalk white with the powder he always carried with him. He also made a small incision in his finger and with the blood from this, he painted circles round his eyes.

When all this work was completed, Krona himself solemnly led forward a lamb, one of the eight on which the future of the community's flocks was to depend. No higher proof of their reverence for the sun god could be given than this present to him of such a precious commodity.

Then, in his high, but carrying voice, the medicine man cried out:

"Oh sun god, look down upon us now. You who shall bring us seedtime and harvest in this new land, you sun who direct the seasons, you who fatten our sheep and cattle and smile upon our crops – our lives and our valley are yours: accept our sacrifice."

Quickly he slit the lamb's throat and laid it on the pyre; then, using the dry sticks which he rubbed into flame, with twigs and dried moss for kindling, he started the fire. As the sacrificial pyre began to burn, and to send its smoke into the cloudy sky over the valley, he moved solemnly from one person to another, carefully cutting a lock of hair from each; when he had obtained hair from everybody present, he threw it all into the flames, thus ensuring that the sun god knew that each of the settlers was equally associated with the sacrifice. As though in answer, the sun suddenly appeared from behind one of the clouds and for a few moments, the bare summit of the little hill was bathed in light.

The settlement had been founded.

The changes that took place in the coming months astonished the hunters, who watched from the ridges nearby. At once the settlers began to clear the slopes of trees by felling and burning, and the women began scraping the earth and planting their precious grain on the thin soil. Beside these little plots, the men used the felled timber to build stout houses, surrounding them with palisades of wattle. On the upper slopes, the children guarded the community's precious flock of brown fleeced sheep, and watched to see that the cattle did not wander onto the growing corn. At night, the animals would be brought down to Krona's farmstead, and though the wolves' echoing cry was often heard from the nearby woods at night, Krona saw that the livestock was carefully guarded and none was lost. Incomprehensible as most of this activity was to them, the hunters were impressed. The settlers obviously meant business. Krona's men meanwhile, under his instructions, made no attempt to meet the hunters. They went about their business and remained strictly in the valley.

The settlers were pleased with their new home, and none more so than Krona himself. He enjoyed his young wife with her proud walk and her flashing eyes. He smiled to see his two little boys following behind her slim lightly-stepping figure as she went down the slope into the valley.

He might be getting old, but Liam was fiercely proud of him; and now, in this new land, he could almost forget the pain of the family he had lost.

In the first months, however, two incidents occurred which established the future relationship between the two communities.

Just before the first snows came, the long-toed hunter Taku followed a handsome deer down the valley. The deer got away; Taku killed one of the precious calves and started to pull it up the slope under cover of the trees. It was a foolish thing to do; he was seen by one of the women and before he had reached the top of the slope he was caught. Three of the settlers, furious at this outrage, dragged the wiry little hunter down the valley to Krona's farm, collecting others on the way so that it was a large group of half the settlers in the valley and their families who clustered in front of the farm on the hill.

As Krona faced the angry little crowd, he considered the situation carefully. The trespass must be punished; and the killing of the all important calf merited death. But against this, he had also to think of the settlers' relationship with the hunters. He stared at Taku thoughtfully, and then he looked at his long toes.

KRONA: You have killed one of our animals. The penalty is death. Do you understand?

Taku said nothing.

KRONA: You should die. But instead, you shall take a message to your people to warn them. We have come in peace, but they must not touch our animals.

He turned to the settlers, and cried:
"His toes are too long!"
Then he signalled to the medicine man, who at once stepped forward, and with a sharp flint knife cut off the last joint of Taku's big toes. The hunter yelped with pain.

KRONA: You will not run into the valley again.

The settlers thought this a great joke, and Taku hobbled away. No hunter ever touched the animals in the valley again.

[47]

The second incident occurred during the winter. It was particularly cold and long, and even the river had frozen solid. At this time, with the first harvest not yet arrived and the livestock still no more than a few precious animals needed for breeding, the farmers nearly starved. Then it was Magri, the stout hunter and his son who came down into the valley from the high ground one day, carrying between them a deer they had killed. They dropped it in front of Krona's house and moved away without a word.

From that time onwards, the settlers and the hunters lived in peace.

There were many things that puzzled the hunters, and many that interested them.

They were fascinated by the long painted boats which the settlers let them inspect. Taku in particular, who despite his punishment, struck up a curious friendship with several of the farmers, was delighted with them.

"They are strong, but so light," he marvelled as he hobbled round them. There was no question that the boats made of skins were larger, more manoeuvrable, in every way superior to his own dugout.

The women were amazed by the woven clothes, and both men and women impressed by the solid timber houses. But for a long time, the entire complex business of sowing crops and raising livestock confused them; and they were deeply puzzled by the way that the farmers took the livestock into their own houses to protect them during the winter months. It was normal and sensible for the farmer and his family to sleep next to animals on which their life depended, but to the hunters this seemed strange indeed.

By the end of the second year however, with the first crops harvested and the stock beginning to increase in number, they had to admit that the settlers had kept their word. They lived in the valley, and they had not needed to encroach upon the hunting grounds outside.

"They eat well," the women said.

"But they live like women," old Magri retorted. He pitted his wits against the animals he hunted; he roamed free over the great ridges under the open sky, where the wind moaned. The static, confined life of the farmer harvesting his crops and keeping his animals in pens had no appeal for him.

"It is not a life for a man," he stated, and the other hunters agreed with him.

Two more years passed, and now the hunters could hardly recognise the valley any more.

On the hill overlooking the river Krona's farm now consisted of a stout wooden building thirty feet long and fifteen deep with a sloping thatch roof and a large doorway to let in light and air. Around it were grouped several small outhouses. Beside the hill, on the slopes, where the soil was light and well-drained, small plots of various shapes had been laid out, their borders marked with stones. He had sown them with wheat, barley and flax, after cross ploughing them with a light ard – a small hoe with a flint head – which he could handle, if necessary, without even the aid of an animal. This process of ploughing fields first one way, and then at right angles, was the most efficient way of breaking up the soil with so light an implement. Near the huts were two pits, six feet deep and four across, lined with plaited straw; in these, and in their pots, they would store the grain. Beside the river, pigs and cattle wandered, and on the high ground above the fields, a few sheep cropped the coarse grass that grew in patches cleared among the scattered trees. All the way up the little northern valley, the pattern was the same, as the trees were destroyed and the land taken up instead by crops and livestock.

The hunters gazed at it all with increasing wonder.

It was a tiny beginning – the clearing of the slopes of a small, obscure valley in the midst of an immense forest that covered most of the island: an almost invisible scratch on the surface of the landscape.

And yet for the landscape of much of Britain, such early clearings were to have profound significance.

For when Krona and his men started to cut down trees on the edge of the high ground, they began a process whose result would be a permanent change in the composition of the soil. Previous ages had created the rich topsoil which covered the chalk downlands of Britain, and the trees which covered the ridges held this topsoil, often only inches thick, in place. When men cut down the trees, this fragile covering was exposed at once to wind and rain, and in many places it would be washed downhill, leaving behind only a harsh chalky soil full of flints. Sometimes trees would grow again in such places before the topsoil was gone; often man or his animals destroyed them once more. If the topsoil were displaced, the chalky soil remaining was good enough for growing corn, or grazing sheep on the turf covering that would form when it was not ploughed; indeed, the process brought much new life to the land – cowslips, buttercups, huge quantities of butterflies, all of which found the fields their natural habitat – but the woods did not grow there again.

Once begun, this destructive process had a momentum of its own. The chalky soil was often exhausted by the corn and the land had to be left fallow. Then the farmers would turn sheep on to it to crop the stubble and manure the ground, while more woodland was cut down for sowing. As generations passed, the sheep increased rapidly in number, and the human population increased too, so that the process of land clearance was accelerated still further. The farmers proceeded with a ruthless destructive efficiency: experiments have shown that with their flint axes, three men could clear six hundred square yards of birchwood in three hours. And as the centuries passed and more settlers came, all over southern England, these neolithic farmers cleared the light forest cover from the chalkland soils which they could so easily till.

The bare, sweeping chalk downs of southern England, familiar today, are not a natural feature of the landscape: they were created by prehistoric man.

There was another feature of the settlement which intrigued the hunters.

For in the third year, when the settlers' precious little herd of cattle was beginning to grow, Krona ordered all the men to come to the hill at the foot of the valley, and there, under his direction, a short distance from the medicine man's sacred circle, they stripped away the remaining trees and shrubs from the hilltop and laid out a rectangle, forty paces long and twenty wide, heaping around it a modest wall of earth. For this was to be the corral, in which the cattle could be protected and watched over at night. When this work was done, and Krona looked at the sturdy earthwork, and the plots of corn on the nearby slopes, his fierce face broke into a smile. Now the valley was starting to look like a proper settlement.

So far, the relationship between the hunters and the settlers had developed as Krona had hoped it would. The two communities lived well apart, but when they met, there was little trouble, and soon the enclosure on Krona's hill became a meeting place and the focus of a sporadic but lively barter trade between them. To the enclosure the hunters would bring furs and flints, and occasionally a fine deer they had killed; and the settlers brought woven cloth and pottery. Before long both sides knew a few necessary words of the other's language.

The incident with Taku was forgotten. Since he could not hunt easily on his maimed feet, he became the most expert of fishermen, and soon he was allowed to take the farmers along the five rivers in the boats he admired so much, showing them the best places to fish.

It was when the settlement was six years old that this precarious harmony was broken and an open warfare broke out that nearly destroyed the settlement. It was the medicine man's fault.

Twice a year, at the start of winter and at the time of harvest, the medicine man would paint his face chalk white and go down the valley to Krona's hill. Waddling and wheezing, he would climb to the top of the little promontory and there, watched by the settlers, he would perform the sacrifice to the sun god. In winter, he asked for a good harvest. And after the harvest, the community gave thanks. On each occasion he would sacrifice an animal, usually a lamb.

The hunters were afraid of the medicine man. They knew that he sacrificed to the sun god but not to the moon goddess – and like most hunters, they had more reverence for the moon. Besides this, there was something about the fat, smooth-headed man with the shifting eyes that made them distrustful of his power. They trusted Krona, but they avoided the medicine man whenever possible.

His power in the valley, however, was considerable. If a child were sick, he would be summoned to cure it. When a new plot had been cleared, he would walk slowly round the bounds with the farmer, muttering an incantation. Whenever an animal was killed, a choice cut would be sent to the medicine man in payment for his services; he lived well and was second in influence only to Krona. And if, unlike Krona, he was not brave, he was cunning and ruthless to make up for it.

In the sixth year, despite a fine spring and a warm early summer, there were heavy rains soon afterwards which continued non-stop for twenty days. The harvest was ruined.

Although the community had enough stores to last them through the winter, the failure of the harvest was a serious blow. Such a disaster could only mean that the sun god was offended with them for some reason and to placate him and ensure a good crop the following year, the medicine man made a special sacrifice of four lambs that winter, repeating this costly gesture again in the spring.

That summer was an anxious time, not only for the farmers, but for the medicine man as well: for his magic was being tested and all eyes were now upon him. The spring and early summer were fine, however, and with a renewed confidence he waddled round the farmhouses, inspecting the extra land that had been sown, and predicted a bumper harvest. But then, at midsummer, the rains came yet again, and for a second time the entire harvest was ruined. This year the settlers faced real hardship.

If this second failure of the harvest brought the threat of hunger to the farmers, it brought an even greater threat to the medicine man. For it was clear to all the settlers that the sun god must be angry and that the sacrifices of the medicine man had not worked.

"The sun god has turned his face away," they acknowledged. "He does not speak to the medicine man; he has refused the sacrifices."

The medicine man had failed and as each day passed, there were signs of the settlers' anger and his declining influence with them that he could not ignore. There were sullen murmurs about him in the homesteads. Women with sick children did not go to him and the men avoided his company. One day, at the cattle enclosure, he even saw a settler woman whose child had stumbled into some poison ivy, accept gratefully a herbal cure from one of the hunters. He had waddled forward to stop this, but the woman had taken the herbs and quickly left without looking at him.

One day a small deputation arrived at the farm on the hill to see Krona.

"The medicine man has brought two years of rains," they complained. "He is displeasing the gods and we should drive him out."

After they had gone, Liam joined her voice to theirs.

"He has failed," she reminded him, "and besides, he is not to be trusted."

The ageing chief knew that his proud young wife resented the influence of the medicine man in the valley, and he understood the feelings of the settlers, but he was unwilling to do such a thing.

"We shall not be hasty," he decreed. "Speak to me of this no more."

But from that day, the medicine man noticed that whenever Krona saw him his weatherbeaten face took on a hard and angry stare that was frightening. Still more disturbing was the suggestion he overheard a young farmer make to some companions, none of whom disagreed with him:

"I think the sun god has no power in this place," he said. "Perhaps it belongs to the moon goddess the hunters worship and we should sacrifice to her instead."

When he heard this, he knew that he had not much time.

It was at this critical moment, when the very future of the settlement in

[51]

the valley seemed in doubt, that an event took place that was to give the medicine man his opportunity.

Early one morning, near the end of summer, a single man walked slowly out of the woods to the east and entered the place where the five rivers met. He was very old – probably older than any other man living in the south of the island; he carried a staff to lean on and walked with a shuffle; and his sudden arrival caused a flurry of excitement amongst the hunters.

They had not seen him for twelve years and his presence amongst them meant that there would be a great feast in his honour, when important matters such as the arrival of the settlers would be discussed, and his advice sought. For no man was more revered, and none wiser, than this old man, who might appear only once or twice in the lifetime of a hunter.

He was the soothsayer.

There were several soothsayers on the island at that time – strange figures who usually lived alone, travelling through the forests from one isolated camp to another; and wherever they went, the hunters welcomed them as honoured guests. They were mysterious, disappearing into the forests sometimes for months at a time; they were wise, for they knew every secret of the forest, every root that cured sickness, and the habits of every animal. The soothsayer who approached was especially revered because he was known to have magical powers, and to be able to predict the movements of game and of the weather.

"He is protected by the forest god," Magri explained to one of the farmers. "And when the moon is full, he converses alone with the moon goddess and she tells him her secrets. We call him the Old Man of the Woods."

He was very old: over sixty at a time when few men lived to be fifty. His knowledge was indeed extraordinary: for with all the ancient lore of the natural world, he also carried in his head a vast store of knowledge concerning the hunters themselves. He knew the family histories of most of the settlements in the south of the island; he was a great teller of tales; he was in truth the keeper of the hunters' culture.

"He will tell many stories," Magri told a farmer, "and then he will make a great sacrifice to the moon goddess, to give us good hunting."

It was when he heard of this visitor that the medicine man knew what he must do.

A few nights later, a remarkable sight could be seen at the place where the five rivers met. On the riverbank, where the river made its lazy sweep to the south west, two large fires were burning. Over one of these, a wild horse was roasting and over the other, a deer. Between the fires, in a large circle, sat no less than fifteen families of hunters who had come from miles around to hear the old man. The blue smoke rose into the late summer night. The hunters ate well; there was a constant murmur and occasional bursts of laughter from the festivities beside the crackling fires. It was many years since there had been such a large gathering, not since long before the settlers had come to their valley, and as they feasted on the meat, the fish and berries that the land had always given them, the hunters could almost forget that anything had changed.

In the place of honour sat the soothsayer. He was a strange figure: none of the hunters had ever seen a human being so old. He had once been a man of average height, but age had shrunk him and now he was tiny. His body was like a little stunted tree, his bones and joints showing through like branches and knots in the wood. His hair was silver white and the long strands from his head and his beard brushed the ground where he sat. His skin was very clear, almost translucent, yet the surface was broken into tiny wrinkles, so many and so small that the eye could hardly pick them out. He sat very still, cross-legged, his long staff laid in front of him, and as he gazed at the faces round him his pale blue eyes seemed almost to look through those they rested upon. Although the hunters offered him every delicacy they knew, he ate little.

They had told the soothsayer about the settlers and he had listened carefully, but had made no comment yet: that would be discussed at the conference the hunters would hold the following day. For the moment, the soothsayer would content himself with reminding his people about their past, as only he could. He sat with his hands folded in his lap until the moment should arrive.

At last, when the feast was over, the hunters fell silent and it was then that the soothsayer began to speak. At first his voice was little more than a whisper, but in the hushed silence it cut through the night like a ray of light; and as he warmed to his theme, his voice, too, rose to a magical, tuneful chant that seemed to come from very far away.

First he related tales of ancient hunting days: how their distant ancestors at Sarum had killed auroch, bison and boar in the region. Then he told stories of the gods. Then he described the land and its geography, and the other people he had seen in his travels round the island. The hunters were spellbound. The scent of woodsmoke and roasted meat hung heavily in the air. He told them about the lineage of their families, who had settled at Sarum, where they had come from and when they had come; their names and deeds lived in his memory and those sitting around him felt the wonder of knowing their own ancient history.

Finally, he came to the oldest story of all, of how the island was formed, of the great wall of ice in the north, how the sun melted it and how the sea covered the great forest of the east. This was the ancient story that Hwll the hunter had composed over three thousand years before, and it had travelled all over the island during that time, with remarkably little alteration. The old man told it wonderfully in his singing voice, just as countless generations of soothsayers before had done; and the hunters were as lost in the story as he was. As the river made its faint sound nearby, and the fires rustled, the old man's chant rang out clearly. The listeners could see it all: the great wall of ice, the frozen tundra, the angry sun god flying over the ice like a swan, and the mighty flood of waters that rushed south and engulfed the forest.

Rhythmically, the old man chanted:

They are all gone, under the sea,
They are all gone, under the waters:
The game and the birds,
The foxes and the deer,
And the oak and the elm.
The way to the east is lost;
And the sea is rising still.

Now the old man's voice sank to a whisper.

But under the dark waters
The forest is still alive.
Stand on the shore and listen –
You can hear the forest creatures;
You can hear their voices crying in the waves.

The attack came suddenly and without warning. As the old man reached the end of his tale, the silence was broken by a shout from outside the circle. The astonished hunters turned and saw that they were completely surrounded by fighting men who stood in the shadows, impassive but fully armed. Before they knew what was happening, they saw the medicine man detach himself from the shadows; with a surprising agility, he stepped quickly over the seated hunters and waddled to the centre of the circle. His face was painted white; around his eyes were circles of blood. He moved with purpose.

Whatever the reason for this intrusion, there was nothing the hunters could do, since none of them was armed. There was a tense silence.

The medicine man had prepared his ground carefully and he had moved with speed and cunning. Keeping his action secret from Krona, who he knew would not support him, he had hurried stealthily that afternoon from one farm to another at the north end of the valley with a simple and persuasive message: so persuasive that by dusk he had collected a force of fourteen young warriors eager to see action and convinced that their medicine man had discovered the cause of the bad harvests. At dusk, and before Krona had discovered what was taking place, the party slipped out of the valley in their boats and made towards the place where the rivers met.

His plan was bold. If it worked, he would at a stroke recover his prestige, and make his position stronger than ever before.

The conversation which now took place between the medicine man and Magri, who as the senior man spoke for the hunters, was to be remembered for generations.

MEDICINE MAN: We come in peace.
MAGRI: What do you want?
MEDICINE MAN: (pointing to the soothsayer) Who is this man?
MAGRI: The soothsayer.
MEDICINE MAN: He is evil. We have come to punish him.
MAGRI: He is a holy man.

MEDICINE MAN:	(*excited*) He is a devil!
	He lives in the forest and tells lies. He has secret meetings with the moon goddess and he tells you not to worship the sun god.
MAGRI:	(*reasonably*) But the moon goddess protects hunters.
MEDICINE MAN:	The sun god is greater. He makes the seasons and gives us good harvests. All other gods are less than him. But now he has turned his face from the valley. Twice he has destroyed our harvests.
MAGRI:	The rain destroyed your crops.
MEDICINE MAN:	(*pointing*) He is the cause! He has taught the hunters evil magic! He tells you not to sacrifice to the sun god. The hunters must not listen to him any more. The sun god says that he must die.

There was a gasp of stupefaction. The soothsayer did not move.

"Evil!" screamed the medicine man, who had been working himself up to a pitch of rage. "Evil."

At this signal, while the circle of hunters was still stunned at what was taking place, two young warriors ran forward, seized the old man and dragged him away into the shadows. The hunters rose in fury, but the medicine man had anticipated them. With a speed that was remarkable for a man his size, he had already leaped out of the circle as the soothsayer was being taken, and the hunters now found themselves faced with twelve warriors with spears raised.

"Those who do not worship the sun god must die," the medicine man cried in exaltation. "Remember." And within moments, the warriors had vanished into the darkness in their boats.

When they reached the valley, the war party headed north, to a spot on the ridge above the medicine man's house and there, watched by the warriors, the medicine man executed the soothsayer, who still had not spoken a word. He burned his head and his heart on a little fire and announced with confidence:

"Next year, there will be a good harvest."

The outrage had been committed, and once done, there could be no turning back. The news of the killing, so quickly accomplished, reached Krona at dawn when a party of the triumphant murderers came to his house with flickering torches to announce the great deed they had performed. When he heard it, the old warrior's face grew dark with anger.

"You fools," he shouted. "Now there will be fighting!" But he could see at once that they were not heeding him, and silently he cursed the medicine man.

Liam knew what should be done:

"You must kill the medicine man" she declared. "I said he could not be trusted, and now he has defied you."

But Krona sadly shook his head. He was too wise to suppose that the situation could be remedied for the present. There was nothing to be done except ensure that each farm was well fortified.

The attacks came the next morning and they continued for three days. A farm was burned down; but it was chiefly the hunters who suffered. Expert stalkers though the hunters were, Krona's men were battle-hardened warriors who built stout palisades which they attacked without success. By the third day, six of the hunters were dead.

The medicine man was delighted by these events. His authority was greater than ever, and though he took no risks himself, he encouraged the warriors to press home their attacks.

It was on the third day of this useless killing that Krona took matters into his own hands. Slowly and deliberately, he walked down the hill at the valley entrance to the river, and when he reached the place by the river bank where the settlers had first landed, and where he knew the hunters could see him, he laid his club on the ground, and quietly sat down to wait.

There could be no mistaking his intention.

In the early afternoon, Magri appeared, and sat down opposite him.

KRONA: The killing must stop.
MAGRI: Why did your men kill the soothsayer?

Krona understood exactly why the medicine man had acted in this way. He was appalled by the folly of the action and would rather have disowned it. But he knew that if he did that, the hunters would think the settlers weak and divided and might press their attack still more strongly: and by the same token, if the settlers thought that he was siding with the hunters, they would no longer listen to him and they would follow the medicine man into who knew what new madness that he might devise. Whatever Krona did, the medicine man had won, and he cursed the fat man's cunning.

KRONA: He came with evil magic. The sun god punished the valley
           because of him.
MAGRI: So you say.
KRONA: The sun god has spoken to our medicine man. He was
           angry with the soothsayer. It was the sun god who ordered
           his killing. You must understand.
MAGRI: So you say.
KRONA: It is so.

Magri was silent for some time. From the first moment that he had seen the settlers, he sensed their superior power; because of it, he had counselled the hunters to give them the valley when Taku and others had wanted to kill them. Had it been a mistake after all? It certainly appeared so: his people had been insulted; now they were being killed. For the first time in countless generations the little community of hunters was threatened with exile or extinction, and it was up to him to find some way of saving them.

MAGRI:	Your medicine man says we must worship the sun. But hunters worship the moon goddess. If we do not worship her, she will desert us and we shall have no hunting.
KRONA:	You can worship both. You can honour the sun also, then we shall be your friends again.
MAGRI:	My people are angry.
KRONA:	If our people make war, the killing will be terrible. Our men are warriors and the hunters will be destroyed. We must make peace and exchange gifts once more.
MAGRI:	How do we know the medicine man will not kill again?
KRONA:	The sun god is satisfied. There will be no more killing.

The next four days were tense. The hunters did not attack again, but it took all Krona's powers of persuasion to hold the younger settlers back. Had he not done so, the hunters would probably have been exterminated; but as it was, an uneasy truce was established.

All through the winter, both the settlers and the hunters went about their business anxiously; any move on either side might have started another crisis. There was no trading at the enclosure, but Krona reflected that this was probably a blessing – it was better that the two sides did not meet.

The following summer there was a bumper harvest. The medicine man had triumphed.

His success was complete; his authority now was greater than ever. He waddled about the valley in a stately manner and took gifts from the farmers – not because he needed them but to remind the people of his special relationship with the gods.

"He speaks to the sun god," they said. The farmers were respectful; and the hunters were cowed.

At the summit of Krona's hill, the medicine man now made his clearing into a small temple. It consisted of ten large tree stumps set in a circle in the middle of the clearing. In the centre of this little circle, which was only fifteen feet across, he would now build his fire and there, with the help of a young man whom he had selected to be his assistant, he made the sacrifices to the sun god. Twice a year not only the settlers attended, but a small party of hunters too would silently appear from the woods, bringing with them a deer to be given to the settlers' god.

"He burns his fires above your house," Liam protested to Krona. "He makes himself chief of the valley." She could not understand his patience.

And when the hunters in the bowl of land to the south, or on the ridges opposite, saw the column of blue smoke rising from the hilltop they knew that the medicine man was powerful indeed.

In the forest, however, far out of his sight, they made their own sacrifices to the moon goddess who protected all hunters, and performed the old dances before the hunt at full moon, as their ancestors had done since time began.

But still Krona watched, and did nothing.

For despite the arrogance of the medicine man, the two communities were slowly returning to a state of peace. At the trading post in the enclosure, the barter trade between hunters and settlers cautiously resumed. And although the passage of a few years could not remove the fear and distrust that the hunters still had of the settlers and their medicine man, on the surface at least all was calm.

The fact that this state continued unbroken was mostly the work of the two old men: Krona and Magri.

Krona was determined to maintain peace. He had come to the island because he knew that the sea wall would protect the new settlement from the kind of marauders who had destroyed his farm and his family when he was a young man, and he had no wish to see the valley become involved in a useless and bloody dispute with the hunters. He hated the course of action that the medicine man had followed; but even if he suffered personal humiliation, he knew he must still be patient.

"This madness must run its course," he muttered; and he did not oppose the medicine man.

Instead, he occupied himself quietly on his farm and in all matters except those concerning the sacrifices of the gods, he remained the most influential voice in the community. He became attached to a particular spot immediately in front of the oblong house and there, on one of the big sacks in which the farmers stored the wool from their sheep, he was often to be seen, with his club resting at his feet as a symbol of authority, gazing over the settlement that he had founded. The farmers still came to him as the arbiter of their disputes and even the medicine man approached the old warrior on his sack with some caution. But on most days, Krona was content to sit there alone, attended only by Liam, his sharp, fierce eyes watching the winding river below and the swans that silently glided upon it.

It was to this place that Magri often came. He too was growing old, and he too knew the value of patience. The two men would sit quietly opposite each other, perhaps only exchanging a few words during the course of several hours, but always treating each other with the respectful politeness which they knew must be maintained if harmony were to be preserved between their two peoples, and by this means many small disputes that arose between the communities, which could have become dangerous, were quietly and peacefully settled.

It was during these conversations that Magri gradually conceived the remarkable idea which was to decide the course of the settlement's history for many generations.

For often the old hunter would question Krona about his life on the other side of the sea. Gradually he learned about the coastal community that Krona had left, about the hundreds of other farming settlements that existed on the mainland, and as he came to realise their full extent he was deeply thoughtful.

"If there are so many farms," he said one day, "then the time will come when other settlers cross the sea to this island. They will arrive, as you did, and they will take more of our valleys."

"Perhaps," Krona replied. "But the sea is dangerous. They may not come."

"They will come. It will be so," Magri answered calmly, and his weatherbeaten old face was sad. "There will be many of them, too strong for us; and they will destroy my people."

For the more he observed the life of the farmers, the greater he understood their power to be. Already the young men were building new farms and clearing more land further up the valley. He saw the small herds of livestock, the flocks of sheep who were steadily taking over the higher ground, and he knew that nothing could stop them.

"You make the land itself obey you," he reflected. "The sun god is very strong."

"If more settlers come," Krona said truthfully, "the hunters will have to make peace with them, and with their gods."

The old hunter turned these matters over in his mind for many months; and finally he came to the remarkable decision which he announced to his people when they were next gathered together for a big hunt.

When they heard Magri's proposal, the hunters were dumbfounded.

"We cannot agree to such a thing," they protested. But he was determined and argued his case again and again, for he was certain that only in this way could he protect his people for the future.

"The sun god makes the settlers strong," he told them. "We cannot resist them. It will be better if we do what I suggest."

This dispute amongst the hunters, of which the settlers in the valley remained ignorant, lasted for two years; and at the end of that time the authority and arguments of the old man gained his idea a grudging acceptance.

It was a surprise to Krona one summer when he saw Magri approaching with a small deputation consisting of the limping figure of Taku and two of the older hunters, together with two girls who walked behind them. He greeted them politely and the men quietly sat on the ground in front of his farm, while the two girls stood silently a short distance away. Krona wondered what this visit could mean.

Magri began slowly.

"For over three years there has been peace between our peoples," he said. "We have brought sacrifices to the medicine man and we have kept our promise not to hunt in the valley."

"And we have not disturbed your hunting grounds," Krona reminded him.

"It is true. But every year," Magri continued, "your people clear more land and one day they will want more land than there is in the valley."

"We have all the land we need," Krona assured him.

"For the moment, perhaps," Magri replied. "And for the moment we have peace. But in time your farmers will want to take more, for each year your cattle and your sheep increase in number and you cut down more trees. It must be so," he insisted. "And already," he warned, "our young men are getting restless. If your people want more land, they will say that it is time to drive them from the valley; they have not forgotten the killings and this time they will be well prepared. Many will die."

"We can stop them," Krona said. "You and I."

Magri shook his head.

"We are growing old," he replied. "In a few years we shall have gone; our advice will be forgotten."

Krona was silent. He knew that what Magri said was probably true, and it was the prospect of the peace being destroyed which he feared most. The old man's words filled him with dismay.

"What is it you propose?" he asked.

"We must make sure that there is peace for many generations," Magri said. "There is only one way," he explained: "the peoples who live where the five rivers meet must become one people."

Krona stared at him. "How?"

"You must become our leader. We place ourselves under your protection. Will you accept?"

This surprising proposal was followed by absolute silence.

"But our peoples have different ways," Krona objected at last.

"We must learn the ways of your people," Magri replied.

"Your gods . . ." Krona began.

"We make sacrifices to the moon goddess who protects hunters," Magri said. "But we see that the sun god is greater. We have seen his power," he acknowledged truthfully. "We worship both, but the sun is the greatest of the gods."

"And do your people agree to this thing?" Krona asked.

"Yes. If you will protect their hunting grounds, they will call you their chief and give you gifts," he replied. For even the more rebellious of the young hunters respected Krona's word and acknowledged the fairness of his rough justice.

Krona considered.

"It is agreed," he said finally. "From today, I will be Krona, the protector of the hunting grounds."

Magri rose and led the two girls forward. Krona now saw that they were just past puberty. Both had dark good looks, small, lithe figures and they stepped lightly over the ground.

"Two of your young men need women," he said. "Take these."

It was true that there were two young farmers without women at that moment. Krona looked at the two girls with admiration, and saw at once the wisdom of the old man's gift.

"They will have to learn your ways," Magri said. "But you will teach them."

"We accept your gift," Krona replied. And as the hunters rose to leave he knew that a new era had begun.

The new arrangements worked well. In the years that followed, it was to Krona's hill that both the farmers and the hunters came for the settlement of disputes, and he dispensed his rough justice impartially. He and Magri also insisted that all the hunters should attend the sacrifices to the sun god and so, twice a year, ten families of hunters led by Magri and Taku would enter the valley and make their way up to the little temple at the top of the hill where Krona and the medicine man would solemnly greet them. Then with the whole community of farmers on one side of the clearing, and the hunters on the other, the medicine man – who was pleased with this new extension of his authority – would make the sacrifices to the greatest of all the gods. After this all-important ceremony, there would be a feast and then, in the enclosure, Krona would call a council of the older men from both communities at which matters of weight could be discussed.

It was at such a meeting, in the third year of Krona's leadership, that an important decision was taken. For some time the flocks of sheep had grown at a healthy rate, providing excellent meat, and wool which the women spun and then wove into the cloth that the hunters had so much admired when they first came. But lately the quality of the wool had been poor and it was clear that a new strain was needed in the settlers' flocks.

"We need sheep with the finest wool, no matter what size," one of the farmers said. "Cross-bred with the big ones we have . . ." he made a sign to indicate the excellence of the result.

"But we can't get them on the island," another said. "We'll have to make the crossing again," he added reluctantly. Few of the settlers were anxious to brave the English Channel a second time in their fragile boats.

Krona, however, was firm.

"We'll get more sheep and cattle," he decided. "Improve the quality of all our livestock. We can get all we need from the farmers on the coast of the mainland. But we must go soon, while the summer weather lasts."

"What can we trade?" the first farmer asked. "Our pottery and our basketwork?"

Krona considered briefly, then shook his head.

"No," he said, "we have something better." And he turned to Magri and Taku. "We need skins, pelts, fur," he said. "The farmers on the mainland will make a good exchange for those."

It was true: these items were greatly prized by the farmers on the north European coast, and the island was rich in all of them.

"Taku shall arrange it," Krona concluded.

In the last few years, the lame hunter had become a remarkable trader, taking the big skin canoes up and down the five rivers and even along the coast in search of goods which he brought back to the settlement. Now it took him only a few days to amass an impressive cargo, enough to fill two of the biggest canoes. There were deer skins, fox furs, badger pelts and even some bison skins which had made their way down the island's network of rivers from the north. These activities of Taku's were the first beginning of what was to become a substantial island trade; and with justifiable pride Taku hobbled from one pile to another, pointing out the high quality of each pelt.

"It is enough," Krona said when he had inspected them. But if he thought that Taku was satisfied, he was mistaken; for now the lame hunter laid before the chief his most important request.

"Let me go with them," he asked, "with my son," and he indicated the eldest of his sons, a young man who appeared to be a carbon copy of his father.

Krona paused. Would he be useful?

"We can paddle," Taku added. Indeed the hunter and all his children had made themselves accomplished boatmen. But still Krona was not sure. He wondered if the settlers manning the boats would accept his presence? To his surprise, however, there was general support for the idea. The former criminal turned ubiquitous trader had become quite a popular figure, arriving unexpectedly at farmsteads, but always with some new item that he had found to please the farmer or his woman.

"Very well," Krona said. "Let him go with his son."

That night Taku addressed his children solemnly.

"We shall cross the sea," he said. "Perhaps we shall not come back. But even if we do not, other voyages will be made, in the future, and men will return. You must do as I have done. Use the boats, and trade: that is the best way for our family."

For when Krona had originally lamed him and severely reduced his ability to hunt, he had unknowingly done Taku a great favour. Necessity had driven the hunter to find another way to subsist, and as the settlement grew, he had seen what the other hunters had failed to understand, that such a community must trade. Since the farmers were few in number and busy clearing the land, he had seen his chance and begun to act as a carrier of furs and game, a middleman on the five rivers. Now he perceived that bigger opportunities would open out with a crossing over the sea and he was determined to be a part of this new activity. He operated by instinct – for he had never seen a developed trading community such as already existed on mainland Europe; but his instincts were good.

The voyage was a success. The farmers got all the livestock they needed; the cattle enclosure had to be enlarged; and Taku had also found some small sheep with the finest wool. But most important of all, he and his son saw the larger settlements and the vigorous trade that was developing on the mainland.

"You were right to make peace with the settlers," Taku confided to Magri. "They are even more powerful than we thought." And to his son he said: "We need bigger boats now. We must trade across the sea."

As the new era of prosperity developed at Sarum, only one nagging problem remained to trouble Krona as he entered the last phase of his old age – for he was nearly fifty now – and that was how to find a leader for the two communities to succeed him.

Liam was not in doubt.

"Name our son," she urged. Their elder boy was thirteen now. In a few years he would be a man. As she gazed at her old husband with pride and tenderness, she was sure she could look after him and keep him alive long enough to see his strong young son become a fitting leader. "They will follow him, even if he is young, because he is your son and you have chosen him," she argued.

But Krona knew it could not be.

"One day my son will be chief," he promised Liam, "but not yet."

It would be a difficult choice. For despite the peace that seemed to have settled over the place, the hunters still lived a life apart, worshipped the moon goddess, and made no attempt to raise livestock or sow corn themselves. He needed to choose a man who could command authority amongst the dominant settlers, but who was sympathetic to the hunters as well.

The solution to this problem presented itself unexpectedly.

When old Magri had brought the two girls to Krona's camp, the chief had decided to give one of them to a promising young farmer named Gwilloc, who was distantly related to him. Gwilloc was a tall man of twenty-two with a long, intelligent face; the other farmers called him the dark man because his hair, his thick beard and his eyes were all jet black; and his dark and swarthy look was made more striking by his tallness. He spoke little, but when he did, his words were listened to with respect. Gwilloc accepted the girl from Krona without complaint and before long there were three children, all of them with striking dark good looks; Krona noticed with interest that these children seemed to be equally at home with both the settlers and the hunters, and he smiled at Magri's wisdom in making the gift of the girls. In a few generations, he could see, the two peoples, despite their different cultures, might merge into one.

But such a blending would take time, and meanwhile, it was young Gwilloc who now presented Krona with a new and unexpected development.

At the time when Taku was preparing for his voyage across the sea, Gwilloc came to Krona and asked permission to stake out a new farm.

"My brother and his family will take over the farm we have been sharing," he explained: "for he has three sons now. It is time for me to start a new one."

This request was reasonable enough. But when Krona asked what place he had in mind the young farmer named a spot outside the valley.

"But our farms are all in the valley," Krona said. "There is good land there."

"The land opposite the valley entrance, to the south west of where the rivers meet, is even better," Gwilloc replied. "And there," he added to the old man's surprise, "my woman will be nearer her own people."

This was a new idea that had not occurred to Krona before.

"We gave our word to the hunters to stay in the valley," he said. "I promised to protect their hunting grounds." Such an extension of their settlement would provoke exactly the kind of bad feeling he was trying to avoid. "You are a fool," he told the young farmer.

"What if I can persuade the hunters to agree that my farm should be here?" Gwilloc asked, undismayed.

Krona shrugged. If that were the case, then he would have no objection.

"They will not agree," he said.

But to his surprise, ten days earlier, Magri and another hunter

[63]

approached him and proposed that Gwilloc's farm should be situated exactly at the spot he had requested.

"But that is on a hunting ground," he said.

Magri nodded.

"But this farm would lie at the entrance to the western valley; and the hunting there is less good than to the east. If there are to be new farms, let them be in the western valley," he replied; the other hunter nodded.

"We promised to stay in the northern valley," Krona persisted. "And we keep our promises. There is plenty of land there."

The second hunter smiled.

"You make promises, but look at the way your farms advance. Sooner or later the hunters know you will want to leave the valley. Better to have Gwilloc, whose woman is one of us, than another of your farmers."

"The children of Gwilloc already begin to hunt with our children," Magri explained. "In time they will respect our hunting grounds the more if they have lived amongst our people. It is better this way."

At this moment Krona saw who it was who should succeed him as chief.

In the five years that followed, Krona lived contentedly. In the third year, during a particularly long and harsh winter, old Magri died and automatically, since he was the next oldest, Taku filled his place as the spokesman for the scattered bands of hunters. The following spring the medicine man became sick and at the time of the harvest, he too died; his place was taken by his assistant: a cool-headed young man who was in much awe of Krona and who was careful to do nothing to upset the hunters.

From the time that he set up his new farm opposite the valley entrance, Krona took care to watch Gwilloc closely and to give him every chance to prove himself as a worthy leader.

Whenever there was a council or discussion of importance, he called him to his side; and frequently he sent him with instructions to act for him in smaller matters. Gwilloc was quick to respond, and since he well understood both communities, his words carried weight. He was a good farmer and the land he had chosen was well-sited. He and his family prospered.

The marks of Krona's favour were immediately understood by the farmers and since Gwilloc's reputation was high, no words were raised against him as he quietly but steadily established himself as the old man's successor.

Each year the old warrior moved about less and he was aware of a stiffening in all his limbs. The great bull neck began to sag, and his powerful form grew thinner: but even near the end, he was still an imposing figure. Whenever the sun was warm, he could still be seen in front of his farm, attended now by several of the younger women to help Liam, and, as ever, watching the swans make their nests on the banks of the river below.

It was in his usual place, on a sunny afternoon in late spring, that Krona quietly and suddenly died. He had reached the considerable age of fifty-four.

The next day a council was held and Gwilloc was immediately chosen as the new chief.

Gwilloc's first act as chief began a process which was to continue for nearly four thousand years, a process which would alter the landscape of Sarum for all time to come.

"We must honour Krona, who founded this settlement and who kept peace in the place where the five rivers meet," he announced. "We must not let his greatness be forgotten."

There was general agreement, but some uncertainty about what to do.

"We should build a pile of stones over his grave," said one farmer. But several of those present felt this was not enough.

Finally Gwilloc supplied the answer.

"We shall build him a house," he said, "where his soul may live at peace for ever."

And so he selected a place on the high ground a few miles north of the valley entrance; it was a deserted spot at the top of a ridge, with a magnificent view over the high ground and the valley below. There, on his orders, the hunters and settlers came, each day, clearing the whole area of trees before they began to build. First they made a small house of wood and placed Krona's body inside it. Beside him they put his club, the sack of wool on which he used to sit, and they killed one of the swans he liked to watch and placed it there as well.

But next, they did something that had never been done before. First they sealed the wooden tomb; then, using deers' antlers as picks, on either side of it they dug two enormous parallel ditches in the chalk, a hundred feet long and ten apart, piling the earth in the centre to create a mound. Day after day they continued. The mound grew. Soon it completely covered Krona's wooden tomb, which lay at its south east end. But still the work went on until the hundred foot mound rose over six feet high along its entire length.

This work took two months of hard labour to complete; when it was done, Gwilloc made them pack the chalk sides and the top of the mound hard. The final result was a long, impressive monument that rose out of the ground like a huge, upturned boat. By day, it struck the eyes with its harsh, white glare; and under the moonlight, it gave off a pale, ghostly glow.

"Now Krona has his house," Gwilloc said. "Here he lives for ever."

Both settlers and hunters looked with wonder and delight at the huge earthwork that they had made; and each knew that, from now on, this clearing on the high ground would be a holy place.

On Gwilloc's instructions, the medicine man then sacrificed a lamb to the sun god, and a deer to the moon goddess of the hunters as well, so that nothing should be left undone as they laid the old chief to rest.

Often in the years that followed, when he had difficult decisions to make, Gwilloc would come alone to the clearing on the high ground and sit silently beside the long white tomb that he had made.

"Tell me, Krona, what I must do," he would ask. At such times, it seemed to him that the old man's spirit spoke to him quietly, giving him good advice; and he would return to the valley, strengthened.

This was not the only manifestation of Krona's abiding presence: for often, when the summer thunder rolled over the ridges the people of Sarum would look at each other and say:

"That's Krona, rumbling in his house."

Years afterwards, when he in turn had chosen one of Krona's sons to succeed him, Gwilloc marked out for himself and his family a similar though more modest tomb half a mile away, so that his spirit also should remain properly housed near the place where the rivers met.

And so began at Sarum the first building of the great earth tombs known as long barrows that are the distinguishing mark of Neolithic Britain and which have lasted for over five thousand years. From this time on, through generation after generation, other tombs would arise out of the ground in the Sarum area as farming communities cleared and settled the land. Sometimes the barrows became the tombs of families or groups, but others continued to be built as memorials to some individual great man. Their use spread further afield over Britain. As millennia passed they took on many forms – some round, some saucer-shaped. But it is on the high rolling downland of Salisbury Plain that to this day one of the greatest concentrations of all can be seen, where several hundred barrows overgrown with grass – brooding presences from the island's ancient days – dot mile after mile of the landscape.

As Magri had predicted, not only did the settlers leave the northern valley in time and spread over many of the old hunting grounds, but other settlers, too, came from across the sea.

For the arrival of Krona was only one of many similar migrations, both to the island of Britain and to the more distant land of Ireland in the west, to which the settlers came in a steady trickle, braving the dangerous northern waters in their tiny craft. They built small wooden farmsteads, sowed corn or raised livestock, or, like those at Sarum, they did both. Their earthwork enclosures were used as meeting places, where cattle could be bartered, or sometimes for defence; they built barrows; they cleared the ridges for their flocks of squat brown sheep. Wherever they settled, they dominated the land. And out of this sporadic settlement grew the great civilisation known as the Neolithic culture of Britain.

It took about two thousand years.

This next two thousand years of Britain's history are reasonably well documented by archaeologists. The barrows, settlements and implements of the farmers have been found in quantities which allow scholars to identify many varieties of culture. One area somewhat to the north of Sarum, has given its name – Windmill Hill – to the culture which produced surface flint quarries and causewayed earthworks. In Yorkshire to the north, the settlers found the lustrous stone called jet, which they used for making necklaces and ornaments. And in Cornwall, Wales and the Lake District, communities of miners developed, who cut into the volcanic rock of those regions and made axes superior to any seen before. Cut off from the rest of Europe, the island continued to develop its own rich and distinctive life.

It may be supposed, though it cannot be proved, that the island's original and sparse population of hunters was absorbed by the gradual infiltration of these Neolithic farming folk. But although the land under agriculture could support much larger communities, the numbers of people were still very small. The population of settlers in the entire island by 2,000 B.C. may have been no more than forty thousand souls – a huge increase from the old hunting community – but still leaving vast tracts of the country completely untouched. And who knows what primitive folk may have continued to roam, undisturbed, in these deserted wastes.

But the Sarum area in the heart of Wessex, with its upland soil which was so easy to till with the light plough, was not only agricultural – it became one of the natural centres of Neolithic Britain. The ridges and trackways along which hunters like Hwll had once travelled now brought traders from far away. From the south, traders from along the coast, or even across the sea, could come to the natural harbour under the shelter of the hill and make their way up stream to the place where the five rivers met. Situated at this junction of ridgeway and waterway, it was natural that Sarum should become a place of importance.

Around 2,500 B.C., a further change occurred in Britain. Wonderful flat-bottomed pottery appeared, as it did elsewhere in Europe, which, on account of its shape, archaeologists have called Beaker, and which may be traced to sources in Iberia, and on the river Rhine. About this time also, the islanders acquired from across the sea first copper and then, soon after, the new alloy of tin and copper known as bronze. With this they began to make weapons, fine jewellery and many small implements. But bronze was soft. Though easy to work with, it did not revolutionise either warfare, or more important, agriculture. Its effect on the island was not profound.

But the glory of the island, and of Sarum in particular, during these long centuries was not made of metal, nor was metal important in its construction. The glory of the island was made of stone.

This was the magnificent collection of circular stone temples that rested on the high ground: the henges. Even today, they are awesome to look upon. Huge stones, each weighing many tons, were set up with a sharp, geometric precision on the bare ridges. Some of them cover several acres. Their engineering is extraordinary: and the power of those who could organise the huge teams of men needed to erect them is impressive. They stand as stately memorials (relegating even the barrows to insignificance) to the science and the ambition of the rulers of those days.

These henges are known nowhere else in northern Europe; but in Britain they are found all over the island, from Cornwall to the northern tip of Scotland. Their development lasted many centuries: they were first made of earth, then of wood and finally of stone. They were always circular, and their entrances usually oriented on an axis that pointed them towards the rising sun at the summer solstice. But that was only the beginning of the science of the henges, and to this day, archaeologists and mathematicians are still studying the religious and astronomical properties of these remarkable temples. The largest concentration of them lies in the area around Sarum. Thirty miles north west lay the huge henge at the village of Avebury. Nearer were several smaller ones including a fine henge made of wood. But the greatest and most impressive henge of all is Stonehenge on the high ground north of Sarum.

It was begun early – soon after 3,000 B.C. At first it consisted of a circular earth wall enclosure, its entrance oriented on the rising sun at summer solstice. Just inside the earth wall, soon afterwards, was set up an inner circle of fifty-six posts, evenly spaced. There were also large stones framing the entrance. Around 2,100 B.C. a stone circle was begun near the centre with bluestone rocks. It was one of the most remarkable feats of Neolithic engineering: for each of the sacred bluestones stood over six feet high, weighed four tons, and had been brought, at a time when the builders had not the benefit of the wheel, a distance of some two hundred and forty miles by sea, land and river from the distant Preseli Mountains of South Wales. The completed circle would have required over sixty of these stones.

But around 2,000 B.C. something very strange occurred. For some reason, the building with the bluestones which was half completed, suddenly stopped. The bluestones were removed from the site. And then, miraculously a new building was begun. It had a stately avenue that led from the entrance between earthwork walls for six hundred yards across the rolling high ground. Its gigantic grey stones dwarfed the previous bluestones. Its design and its magnificence was unlike anything that the island had ever seen before.

The Henge

2,000 B.C.

THERE WERE STILL a few hours before the dawn.

In the centre of the great temple of Stonehenge, the six priests waited expectantly for their orders: it was some time since the High Priest had last spoken.

To an observer who did not understand the secret workings of the henge, the scene would have seemed strange indeed. The priests who stood respectfully at their posts were each dressed in a simple long robe woven from undyed lambs' wool, their feet encased in sturdy leather boots to protect against the cold and their heads, except for a V shaped wedge of hair with its point between the eyes, shaved bare. In their hands each priest held two or three long sticks with pointed tips.

Apart from the priests, there was only one other person in the henge: in the gateway, bound with strong leather ropes and long ago terrified into silence, lay a young criminal who was to be sacrificed to the sun god at dawn.

Dluc, the High Priest did not seem to be aware of any of them. His tall, rangy figure in its long grey robes stood as motionless as a stone. In his right hand he held his ceremonial staff the top of which, carved in bronze and decorated with gold, was in the elegant shape of a swan – the symbol of the sun god. In his left hand was a large ball of twine made of flax. His gaunt, clean-shaven face was impassive: his eyes were fixed on a distant point on the horizon.

He had good reason to be preoccupied. For some time now it had been clear that – unless the gods could be pacified – the ancient territory of Sarum and its sacred grounds were doomed to destruction. But what could he do to avert it? And how much time did he have?

"If Krona should fall sick . . ." he murmured to himself. It was a terrible thought, which he tried to dismiss from his mind – but it would not go away.

Imperceptibly his fingers tightened round his staff.

But there were other duties to perform and much work to be done that night. Breaking his painful reverie, he suddenly pointed the staff at four different spots in the circle and gave a curt order:

"Place the markers."

The priests hurried to the places he had indicated and at each one, drove a stick into the ground. This night, as every night, the astronomer priests of Stonehenge were busy measuring the heavens.

There was a half moon high in the cold autumn sky. It was a night full of stars. The dew on the bare ridges, which swept majestically away on every side, caused them to shimmer in the moonlight.

On every ridge of the sacred region, chalk barrows jutted out of the turf–some long, others round–pale forms which glimmered, even from miles away, like ghostly ships, frozen upon a vast unmoving sea. For the dead watched over the living at Sarum, and were honoured accordingly.

The sacred grounds extended for many miles across this rolling landscape; they contained not only burial mounds, but also small temples of wood and earthwork enclosures – the monuments of centuries during which this high ground had been reserved as an area apart. No place on the island was more hallowed, and pilgrims would come down the chalk ridgeways many days' journey to visit the sacred plateau.

At the centre of these precincts, on a gently rolling slope, stood the magic henge.

It was huge: a circular chalk bank, three hundred and twenty feet across and surrounded by a deep ditch, enclosed the inner sanctum. This was unusual: for normally the ditch of the island henges lay inside their banks, not outside. "But we are different," its priests proudly declared. From the entrance on the north east side, a broad avenue between earth walls cut a straight, ceremonial path for six hundred yards across the landscape. At the point where it joined the sanctum, a pair of huge grey stones formed the gateway through which only the priests and their sacrificial victims ever passed. Within, there were two small mounds used for astronomical observations, an outer circle of fifty-six wooden markers which the present High Priest had carefully restored, and a double inner circle – as yet only half completed – of standing stones. These were the sacred bluestones.

The henge was already eight hundred years old and it was a place of mystic significance. Not only was it the site at which the priests made the ritual sacrifices to the sun god and the moon goddess: it had important astronomical properties central to the ordering of all activities in the huge territory of Sarum and its great chief Krona.

And though there were larger henges, like the huge complex to the north west known as Avebury, where a neighbouring chief reigned over a lesser people, Dluc always reminded his priests: "The proportions of our henge are better; and we are superior astronomers, too."

For the henge was perfect: on Midsummer Day, the summer solstice, the sun rose over the horizon exactly opposite the entrance and sent its first crimson flash straight along the avenue, between the stones at the gateway and into the centre of the circle. At the winter solstice, the sun set in exactly the opposite direction, so that its last rays sent their parting glow over the bluestones and along the great ceremonial way. At the henge, using wooden markers as the sun progressed round the heavens, the priests kept tally of the days and ordered the calendar; they calculated the dates of the solstice and the equinox, they regulated the times for sowing and for harvesting and all the other observances listed in the sacred sayings of the priests. The henge was their gigantic sundial that told the days of the year.

Over the henge, Dluc knew, and over all Sarum, the sun god presided. His brooding presence lay over the high ground and over the valleys. In the morning and in the evening when his powerful rays struck the bare ridges round the place where the five rivers met, and threw huge shadows across the bowl of land, every man knew that the sun was watching him. At midday, his awful light blasted the dry chalk so that it hurt the eyes to look at it. Sun gave day and night, summer and winter, spring and harvest: the sun gave – and the sun took away: the sun was absolute.

As the priests scurried about, Dluc moved slowly from one of the pointed sticks to another, unrolling his ball of twine and pausing occasionally to check a sighting line. At such times, in the quiet of the temple, his intellectual, ascetic nature could break free from the troubles that beset the land. With only the deferential priests and the silent bluestones for company, Dluc made his abstruse measurements and calculations in his lonely effort to solve the greatest of all the mysteries of the heavens.

The interruption came in the form of two swift-footed runners, who carried between them an empty litter. They moved across the sacred ground with remarkable speed, their bare, hardened feet making a hiss as they left their prints in the dew.

When they arrived at the henge, they came quickly to the entrance of the sanctum where they prostrated themselves. One of the young priests pointed them out to the High Priest. Dluc frowned.

"What is the meaning of this interruption?"

"It is Krona, High Priest," they answered without looking up – for it was an offence for a servant to look at the High Priest. "He sends for you."

"Before dawn?" He glared at them. Then a thought struck him. "Is he sick?"

The two men hesitated.

"We do not know," the older of them said, "but he is very angry," he added, and his companion nodded emphatically.

Dluc suppressed a sigh.

"I will come."

Indicating to the priest that they were to sacrifice the young criminal lying near his feet as soon as the sun rose, he stepped into the waiting litter.

They carried him at a smooth, rapid run and the seven miles over the high ground to the place where the five rivers met was soon covered. For this was the heart of Sarum and the residence of the great chief Krona.

Since time out of mind, the family of the chief had ruled at Sarum. Claiming direct descent from the legendary Krona the Warrior whose long barrow on the high ground was still venerated, a list of no less than eighty generations of the family had been ceremoniously recited by the priests when the last chief's reign had been inaugurated. To emphasise the continuity of their rule, each chief took the same name – Krona – on his succession, and the office of High Priest was usually also occupied by some other member of the family. This was the case now, for Dluc was the chief's half brother.

When Dluc arrived, the moon was still high, bathing the place in light. It was a fine sight, calculated to impress. The tops of the horseshoe of ridges overlooking the bowl of land had been scraped bare and along them stretched a line of palisades, manned by Krona's guards. As the visitor approaching along the river looked upward, this was the skyline that greeted him, a bleak reminder that at Sarum the power of the chief was absolute. In the centre of the horseshoe, on the summit of the hill that guarded the valley entrance, stood his house: a large wooden structure daubed white and surrounded by an outer wall which was coloured red. It stared out impassively over the tops of the trees below. Inside the wall was a series of courtyards and store houses, as well as the quarters of Krona himself.

In the valley below the hill was a small trading post through which all the goods that passed along the five rivers or down to the harbour in the south must pass: for trade, like every other activity at Sarum, was regulated by the chief.

As he looked out at this scene, Dluc's gaunt face softened into a half smile. "Sarum the fortunate," he murmured to himself, remembering better times.

The five rivers had always been the centre of Sarum's power; but now the powerful Krona's rule extended over large tracts of land in all directions. To the south, he controlled the river all the way to the harbour; to the north, all the sacred grounds and beyond; to east and west his rule extended for nearly twenty miles. No territory on the island was richer or better placed. The traders from the north brought marvellous axes of polished stone; from the east fine pottery; gold, intricately worked, came from the magician artisans of Ireland; amber, jet, pearls and all manner of wonders came through the harbour from distant lands. The people were rich: the brown sheep grazed for a day's journey along the ridges. Fields of wheat, flax and barley covered the slopes; the valleys were full of cattle and pigs. In the woods, trappers found pelts to sell downriver and Krona hunted his deer and his wild boar.

There were nearly three thousand souls in this territory, which had never been conquered. And for generations, all over the island it had been said:

"No chief is greater than Krona; no family more noble than his, which rules over Sarum the fortunate."

Sarum the fortunate. Was it still blessed? Would the gods still smile upon it? These were the questions that now occupied Dluc's mind as he was carried into the house on the hill.

Three torches on wooden tripods were burning in the little enclosure in front of the chief's quarters. On the wall, on the thatched roof, over the door, hung scores of antlers, horns and boars' heads, the trophies of Krona's many hunting expeditions – for the magnificent hunts and lavish entertainments of the chief had been renowned far across the islands, until recently.

Without hesitation, the tall priest swept in through the doorway.

Inside, the wax tapers were lit. A servant stood trembling by the entrance, and fell to the ground as soon as he saw Dluc appear.

"Where is Krona?" the priest demanded.

"In the inner room."

He strode on.

The inner room was a smaller chamber separated from the main room by a heavy curtain, and it was here that Krona slept. Dluc brushed the curtain aside.

Only a single taper lit the room, and for a moment Dluc had to pause, to accustom his eyes to the shadows.

Near him, kneeling on the floor, her body doubled up and shaking with fear, was a girl whom he recognised as a farmer's daughter he had sent to Krona the month before, the latest in the series of new wives that the great chief had recently taken. She was a plump creature of fifteen with a wide, inviting mouth, soft young breasts and broad hips made for child bearing. He frowned to see her in such an attitude. The chief had seemed pleased with her a few days before.

Then he saw Krona.

In recent months, since the tragedy that now threatened the survival of Sarum, the chief had changed dramatically. His commanding eyes had become sunken, his huge, manly form had grown thinner, and his shoulders had begun to stoop, as though under the weight of a great burden. His full, flowing black beard was now streaked with grey. But despite his troubles, nothing had altered the noble bearing of Sarum's chief.

Krona was standing in the far corner of the room, in front of the large couch covered with furs on which he normally slept. He was half hidden in the shadows. Beside him, on the floor, the priest could make out the form of Ina, his senior wife; she had been with him since he was little more than a boy, and though she was starting to grow old now, he knew that the powerful chief was devoted to her. As his eyes became accustomed to the shadow, the priest saw that something had taken place within Krona's spirit. His shoulders were hunched in anger and misery; his face was haggard. His nose, always aquiline, now seemed to curve down like a great beak; and his sunken eyes had in them a look of wildness that Dluc had never seen before. He was motionless: he looked like a huge, ominous bird of prey.

"I have come," Dluc said softly.

For several moments Krona did not speak. When he did at last, his voice was little more than a hoarse whisper.

"She has taken away my manhood." He pointed at the girl crouching on the floor.

Dluc glanced down at her.

"Take her," the chief went on. "Sacrifice her to the sun god, High Priest, so that I can be a man again."

Dluc considered. The human sacrifices at the temple were regulated by strict customs. Only criminals, or those chosen by the priests on the most

[73]

important festivals were killed. The High Priest did not sacrifice a girl without reason, even if Krona himself wanted it.

The priest shook his head.

"Do you understand?" Krona hissed from his corner, "she has taken my manhood. I can do nothing."

"I have many cures for impotence. A potion will restore you," Dluc replied calmly.

Krona shook his head. His eyes stared at the priest angrily. Then, slowly, he slid down and sat on the couch.

"No potions," he said wearily.

Now Ina moved closer to him. His faithful companion for many years, she had carefully supervised each of the new wives, instructing them how to please him, watched over them and advised them. She touched the chief's leg lightly with her hand and stroked it softly, trying to calm him. Then, slowly and very gently, with her greying hair falling forward over her face, she leaned over his lap and, pulling aside his robe, she took her husband's member in her mouth and caressed it.

Dluc watched, admiring not for the first time, the love of this dutiful woman for the great chief.

He saw her head sway from side to side, saw her look up with a hopeful smile into Krona's haggard face, and then resume her task, gently persuading, before finally touching her husband affectionately on his leg and returning to her position at his feet. She looked up at Dluc with sadness in her eyes and shook her head.

"No potions," the chief repeated. "Give the girl to the gods, or there will be no heirs for the house of Krona."

Dluc sighed. For this was the problem that threatened Sarum with destruction.

It had been news of the arrival of a merchant ship from a distant country that had caused the party to go down river to the harbour, and Dluc had looked forward to the journey, both because the harbour with its low, sheltering hill, its herons and pelicans always gave him pleasure, and also because he liked to question the sailors about the wonders they had seen on their voyage.

The journey had begun well, a large party travelling in ten of the big canoes with their brightly painted skins; Krona sat with his two sons, magnificent in a crimson robe, in the first, as they skimmed down the river which was at its lowest level in the midsummer heat. Everywhere there was a heavy smell of grass, riverweed and mud.

In mid-afternoon they entered the long still stretch of harbour water and at once they saw the merchants' boat, moored by the trading post on the south side of the harbour.

It was a remarkable vessel. The traders who came from along the coast or across the sea from the mainland to the south used curraghs: boats of skin stretched over wooden frames, similar to the river canoes except that they were broader and had deeper draughts. The merchant sailors rowed these boats although sometimes, when the wind was in the right quarter, they would raise a small sail on a pole to aid the oarsmen. But this new vessel was twice the size of any curragh that Dluc had seen before, and not only its frame, but its sides, too, were made of wood, the planks neatly joined one to another and sealed with pitch. In the centre was a thick mast, secured into the spine of the craft below, and rolled on a crossbeam was a large, square leather sail. At the back of this amazing vessel was a huge rudder which both steered the boat and stabilised it so thoroughly that although the sailors had oars, the master mariner could, by using the sail and rudder together, drive the vessel forward, even when the wind was not directly behind it. There were no craftsmen on the island who could build such a vessel.

The mariners in the ship were short, stocky, round-headed men with wide cheekbones, olive skins and dark curly beards that seemed to have been oiled, for they gleamed in the sunlight. They spoke a strange language, but they had brought with them a merchant from the mainland who could interpret for them.

Their cargo was impressive: huge vessels of wine, which the islanders had not tasted before; lengths of linen, encrusted with precious beads and stones; amber, which the islanders knew how to work; huge pearls; and magnificent jewellery.

"What are you looking for?" Krona asked.

"Pelts," they said, "and hunting dogs. We saw hounds from this island across the sea – they are the best in the world."

The chief and his sons were delighted with the merchants' goods. The wine they found thinner and sweeter than the island's native dark beer, but less sweet and potent than the mead which the farmers of Sarum made from the honey they collected in the woods. Many goods were bartered. And finally, for each of his two sons, Krona chose a small bronze dagger, decorated with gold – finer even than the metalwork that came from the craftsmen of Ireland – and encrusted with flashing gems unlike any they had seen before.

For each of these daggers, the merchants demanded six pairs of hounds; and when Dluc protested at such a price, Krona threw back his long head and laughed.

"How else can a great chief honour his sons?" he cried. "I have other hounds."

The memory of that sunny day was still vivid to the priest: Krona stalking impressively amongst the merchants, his head high, his eyes shining, his harsh laugh ringing over the waters of the harbour; and his two sons, the elder sixteen, the younger fourteen, both his children by faithful Ina, walking beside him.

Like their parents, both were tall and well made, with noble features and flashing black eyes. The younger was just starting his first beard. The sons of Krona were wonderful hunters, never trembling before the boar, or even the rare and mighty auroch. Dluc could see them so clearly in their short green cloaks, fastening the splendid daggers into their belts and smiling at their father. His heart had gone out to this handsome pair.

"The sons of Krona will rule after him," the chief said. "Let them be adorned like chiefs."

But while the chief and his sons made their bargains with the merchants, Dluc had asked the sailors other questions.

"Where have you come from?"

"From a great sea, far to the south, that extends from east to west several months' sailing," they told him.

He nodded. He knew of this sea's existence from other merchants. But usually at this time, the sporadic trade between Britain and the Mediterranean was conducted through intermediaries who controlled trade on the great rivers of south-west Europe, and others on the northern coast of France. It was rare indeed for merchants, even in search of new goods to barter, to undertake such a long voyage round the Atlantic coast of Europe to the distant island in the north.

These mariners were of particular interest to the astronomer priest, because he knew that they steered their long course by the stars and he was anxious to elicit all the information from them that he could. He was not disappointed.

The leader of the mariners told him many things. A fat man with a round head that was entirely bald, and small, intelligent eyes surrounded by deep creases, he soon became so voluble that the interpreter could hardly keep up with him.

"Not only is it hotter in our lands," he said, "but the sun rises higher in the sky – so high that it is nearly overhead. And once," he went on, "I made a long journey – many months – far to the south of our lands. And there I saw things stranger still; for there were other constellations of stars over the horizon: stars that I had never seen before." He shook his round head. "How do you explain that?"

Dluc had heard such tales before and he had decided that they must be true. For there must surely be stars, he thought, which are so far away to the south that their angle above the horizon would be too low to allow him to see them clearly. After all, did one not lose sight of distant lands, even across the sea, for the same reason? And similarly, since the sun at its greatest height was still to the south of Sarum, it must be that at some point in that direction, it would indeed pass directly overhead in its daily course over the land.

When he discovered that the merchant had actually come near such a place he became eager.

"How far – how far to the south before the sun is overhead?"

The mariner thought.

"Hard to tell. Perhaps a four months sailing – maybe six months."

Dluc was thoughtful.

"And the sun was overhead?"

"Nearly."

Six months sailing. The distance was very inexact, but it was at least a rough indication of the magnitude of the distance. And as he considered the matter, the normally severe face of the priest relaxed into a smile. For if he knew the distance along the ground from the island to the point where the sun was overhead, and since he knew, with minute accuracy, the angle of the sun at its highest point, it seemed to the priest that he could with his sticks and lines, by the simple method of triangulation, make an estimate of the sun's distance from the earth – an important piece of information that was nowhere recorded in the sacred sayings of the priests.

Many similar speculations entered the mind of this intelligent priest. If the angle of the sun changed – as he saw that it must – then was there a region far to the north, where the sun itself would be so low on the horizon as to be almost invisible? Or was such a point already off the end of the world?

And where was the end of the world? Had the mariner ever seen it?

"No. But I have met a man who has."

"Where was it?"

"He would not tell me."

"He was probably lying," Dluc replied sadly.

Nonetheless, it had seemed to him that day that the gods were smiling on Sarum. Both the powerful chief, his fine sons, and he himself had been satisfied with their day's work; and that night, by the harbour's edge, they feasted with the merchants.

On the morning after the feast, the mariners had decided to leave, since they intended to make their way west along the coast where they could find tin, and then across to Ireland to seek gold before they journeyed south again.

Dluc would never forget that day. It dawned bright and clear; at sunrise he sacrificed a sheep by the water's edge to give the mariners a safe journey; and by mid-morning, when a brisk south easterly breeze had sprung up, bringing with it small banks of clouds that gathered along the horizon, the mariners took their leave.

It was as they pushed away from the jetty and rowed slowly out into the harbour that there was a cry of merriment from the islanders' boats; three of them suddenly left the bank and sped out into the shallow waters to accompany the visitors round the headland. Both Krona's sons were in this party and as they raced past after the larger vessel they waved gaily.

"Farewell," they cried. "We're going south with the merchants!" They paddled furiously to shouts of laughter and encouragement from the bank.

Krona, the priest and their attendants climbed the hill so that they could watch the progress of the boats as they left the harbour and went out to sea.

The sky was now becoming grey and overcast; but there were breaks in the heavy clouds, and through these huge rays of sunshine burst down making shining patches on the dull sea below. As the boats rounded the eastern point of the headland and slipped through the narrow channel into the open sea, the wind was already starting to blow more strongly, catching the tops of the little waves and sending the surf skimming over the surface. Having passed the point and turned towards the west, the boats began to leave the shore behind, and though the water was choppy, they managed well. It was a brave sight: the stout boat of the merchants pushing out firmly into the sea and just behind it, dipping and bobbing, the three brightly painted canoes gaily following. Slowly the boats came level with Krona and his party, all the time drifting further away from the shore.

"They go too far," Krona murmured. The canoes were two miles out, perhaps more. They now seemed very small, sometimes disappearing entirely behind a rolling wave.

Then Dluc saw the storm. At first it seemed to be only a single brown cloud somewhat darker and heavier than the others, rising harmlessly over the eastern horizon; but then – and with astonishing speed – it grew: below the single cloud now he saw others, huge banks of them all along the horizon, not brown, but black and threatening. Within minutes, the storm rose in the east like an enormous, dark bird: first the head, then the great angry wings, swooping over the water.

At the first sign, he had touched Krona's arm and pointed; and as soon as the chief saw the storm he frowned.

"If they don't turn back at once," he began, "they'll be caught."

As Dluc stared into the barrelling thunderous cloud, it seemed to him no longer like a bird, but now like a huge dark flower that was opening towards them. He gazed at it in horror. The canoes however, eagerly pressing west behind the wooden boat, did not appear to see the storm behind them; for the sky above was still bright.

The party on the hill shouted to the boats, but it was futile: they were far out of earshot, and still drifting further from the shore. At last the mariners' wooden boat, with its sail hoisted, began to run before the wind and plough away towards the west; only then did the canoes turn around and start to creep back eastwards towards the point. Now they too could see the storm approaching. Their progress was painfully slow.

"Run for the shore, you fools," the chief muttered.

It was the only sensible course. The beach was sandy, and the waves would have carried them in. But they continued boldly back towards the point, where the cross currents were always treacherous and where now the coming storm was whipping the sea into a froth.

"They are mad!" Krona cried.

When the storm reached them, it seemed that the whole world was plunged into darkness. The sea rose like a wounded animal, and huge waves began to thrash the shore. The wind threw the salt spray up even to the hilltop where it stung the faces of the watchers and forced them to turn away. After a few minutes, Dluc could not even see the canoes. Surely now they must be making for the shore. But in seas like that, could any canoe stay afloat?

As he saw his two sons caught in that terrible storm, even great Krona trembled.

"Save us brother," he cried urgently to the priest. "Speak with the gods."

In a loud voice Dluc cried out the ritual prayers to the sea god. He took gold dust from a little pouch on his belt and hurled it towards the water.

But the prayers, and the gold dust, were thrown back in his face by the wind.

For some reason, the storm struck only the sea. In front of the hill were roaring waters and blinding rain; yet behind it in the harbour, the surface was ruffled only by tiny waves no bigger than a man's hand. It was a strange sight.

The canoes never reached the shore. That terrible day, as the stout merchant ship continued on its way towards the west, Krona lost both his sons. Their bodies were found, many days later, far along the shore. Dluc buried them at Sarum.

For the first time in her history, Sarum was without an heir. Krona had no other brothers: of the entire family at present, only the chief and the High Priest were living, and Dluc as a priest had vowed never to know woman.

The peace that Sarum had known for generations came from the fact that the family were strong and known to be favoured by the gods. No other chief on the island, however jealous he might be of Sarum's wealth, would be likely to attack the guardians of the sacred grounds. But without the family of Krona to rule with a firm hand, it might be a very different story. The territory would dissolve into chaos.

From that day, a cloud of sadness settled over Krona's spirit and over the place where the five rivers met; all over the island it was said:

"The gods have turned their faces from Sarum the fortunate: even sun himself no longer loves the guardians of Stonehenge."

And indeed, when the following month there was an eclipse of the sun, Krona turned to the High Priest and said:

"I think we are doomed."

The physical change in Krona had begun then. His jet black hair began to turn grey, his tall, proud body to stoop; his piercing eyes seemed to be glazed over and he would spend long days alone in his house, occasionally summoning Dluc to ask him:

"Do you believe that the gods have cursed me and our family?"

To this question Dluc had no definite answer.

"It is clear that the gods have punished us," he said, "but we must discover what it is that they want us to do."

"Discover quickly," Krona replied. "If I die and the house of Krona ends . . ."

There was no need to say more. Each day Dluc made sacrifices and prayed to the gods at the temple, so far with no result. But both he and the chief knew only too well the most urgent need: Krona must have new heirs.

It was many years since faithful Ina had given her husband his two fine sons. Dluc had watched the effect upon her of their loss.

Always quiet, always dignified: when her two sons had triumphed in the chase, they had stood tall and proud before their father and she, though she smiled her approval, seldom said a word; but if in some way they had failed, it was to Ina they would come, avoiding Krona if they could, and then, though she suffered with them, she was wise and never showed it. Always she was the same – the quiet centre of the family; and if the chief and she had left behind the early days of their passion, Krona would still turn to her with affection and say: "Come to me now, mother of my sons."

Now they were gone. What was left? The searing pain she had borne, as was her way, in silence. And strangely, though she knew that his love for her was bound up in their sons, the loss of them had awakened in her a renewed passion – not to restore their family, for that she knew she could never do now, but to heal with her love the stricken, wounded man she saw before her.

She had tried. She had failed.

"I shall not give him more children," she told Dluc; and it was she who had then urged the chief:

"You must take new wives, young women who will give you children. Let the priest choose them for you."

And so, early that winter, the process of finding Krona's new wives had begun.

Soon after the autumn equinox, Dluc had made a great sacrifice: fifty-six oxen, fifty-six rams, and fifty-six sheep. When it was done, he had brought to the chief two young girls of good family.

He had lain with each, many times.

Spring had come, then summer; the harvest had been poor, spoilt by heavy rains; neither girl conceived; and the people of Sarum were discouraged.

"The curse is not lifted," they said, "not even by the great sacrifice."

In his heart, the High Priest knew that they were right. He knew it even when he made the sacrifices. The great slaughter had been useless: whatever it was the gods wanted, they were not appeased.

Krona was depressed.

"You are not old yet," Dluc reminded him, although it grieved him to look upon this sad, grey-haired man who had been a magnificent chief in the full pride of his manhood only months before. "We will find others."

It was some time after the summer solstice that he brought this latest girl to Krona. With her ripe, inviting and rather plump young body, even Krona, who had seemed to take little pleasure in the other girls, smiled when he saw her. The priest had chosen her because in the recent bad harvest her father's crops, for some reason, had been excellent, and since the gods had clearly marked her father out for their special favour, he was hopeful that at last he had found a bride who would be pleasing to them.

Now he was looking at her, cowering on the floor, while the chief stared at him with eyes that were wild, and Ina sadly shook her head.

"Very well," he said at last. "It shall be as you wish." He did not believe that sacrificing the girl would do any good, but it was better to try every remedy. He did so at dawn the following day, with a heavy heart; and that same evening, Krona reported to him that he was well again.

"Send me more girls," he urged.

But this time Dluc did not. For it was clear from the signs from the gods – and his own instincts also told him – that the causes of their present troubles were deep-rooted. They would not be overcome by making a sacrifice and sending the chief another girl.

"I do not think our sacrifices are enough," he told the chief. "We must do more."

"What?"

Dluc shook his head.

"I don't know. But we must find out. We shall read the auguries."

This process, by which the priests asked the gods direct questions and received their answers was a lengthy one which Dluc did not like to use: not because he had any doubts that the gods would reply, but because of the extraordinary difficulty of interpreting their answers, against which his precise, mathematical mind secretly rebelled. In this instance however, he could see no other course. For several days the priests roamed the woods, netting birds which they kept in cages, where they were fed with grain into which was mixed all kinds of other material – herbs and grasses, gold dust, tiny pellets of stone and coloured earth – all of which would leave a tiny residue for inspection in their gut.

Early one morning, when over a hundred birds had been collected, fed, and brought in their cages to the henge, Dluc aided by a circle of priests began the delicate task of reading the signs.

Carefully, using a small bronze knife, he slit the bird's breast open and then, with sharp sticks, pulled out its intestines for inspection, cutting here and there to see what signs could be found which would indicate the wishes of the gods.

The questions were simple, and before opening each bird, Dluc called them out:

"Tell us, great sun god, is Krona to have an heir?"

To this, by noting the sex and state of the innards of each of ten birds, an affirmative answer was soon reached, and Dluc gave a sigh of relief.

But to the following questions, the answers were less simple. What must be done to appease the gods? No less than three kinds of intestine were discovered, suggesting three different conditions, each of which caused gasps of astonishment as they were understood; and several times as the priests peered at them Dluc had to call:

"More birds."

Thirty-three were inspected before Dluc said:

"Then we are all agreed?" and his priests, glancing at one another in apprehension, nodded.

But it was the last question: "How are we to know Krona's chosen bride?" that produced the strangest and most enigmatic answer of all, for in each bird, and twenty were opened, small specks of gold dust were found in the very top of the intestine: a very rare phenomenon which was repeated again and again. At last, when the priests had agreed on the message that the entrails conveyed, they were hardly less puzzled than when they had begun.

Dluc gave Krona the news that night.

"You will have an heir," the priest assured him. "But first, the gods demand a new henge, made of stone." This was the meaning of the pellets of stone found in many of the birds. "It is to be greater than any temple built before."

Krona nodded.

"If it is the will of the gods, let the work be done."

"The gods demand that you give your firstborn child to be sacrificed. After that, you will have a son who will succeed you. It will be your pledge that you submit to the power of sun, and he demands it."

It was a terrible message. Krona weakly protested:

"I am growing old. Will there be time?"

"The gods will grant you time," Dluc assured him. "Your son will be a great chief."

The chief sighed. "And who is to be my bride?"

Dluc frowned. This was the part of the message that had puzzled the priests most.

"Her head will be crowned with gold," he replied.

Krona stared at him. "What does that mean?"

"I am not sure," the High Priest confessed. "Perhaps that she is the daughter of a great chief."

"Find her quickly," Krona growled.

There was one other condition laid down by the gods in the auguries, and it was this one that had caused the priests to look at each other with such apprehension: it was the date by which the new henge must be completed:

The henge must be finished by the day when the sun looks into the moon's full face along the avenue.

To the astronomer priests who knew the mysteries of Stonehenge, this cryptic statement could only have one meaning.

For their henge was a wonderful and complex instrument. Not only did the sun's shadow on the markers tell the days of the year; many other wonders took place there.

"At the summer solstice," the older priests explained to the novices, "in certain years, not only does the sun god rise along the avenue, but the moon goddess sets opposite him. And at mid-winter solstice, the positions are reversed; and while sun departs in the south west, moon rises along the avenue." Sun and moon, male and female, summer and winter: all of these perfect oppositions were contained in the great circle.

There were many other subtle coincidences and angles between the solar and lunar paths. "And these do not occur so perfectly at other henges in the far north," the priests declared, "by which we know that our henge is especially favoured by the gods."

In fact this was correct, although their science was not able to discover the true reason. For the relationships between the sun and moon will alter at different latitudes on the globe.

But there were greater secrets than this. Some time after the henge was first built, its astronomers made another discovery: that the moon in its orbit round the earth does not follow a single path, but that it oscillates from side to side in a subtle cycle of its own, which is repeated every nineteen years.

"There at the entrance," the novices were told, "the priests of old set up the markers to record the shifts of the moon goddess back and forth along the horizon. For at each winter solstice, she returns to a slightly different spot when she rises – you would never notice it from one year to the next unless you marked the spot, but it is so. And she swings from side to side, back and forth along the horizon, once every nineteen years. That is what we call the sacred moonswing.

"The observation took one hundred years," the priest would continue, thus reminding the novitiates that this degree of precision and dedication would be expected from them too.

Nor was this all. For though the solar year does not divide neatly into twenty-nine day lunar months, it was Dluc himself who had discovered, by patient calculation, that a coincidence between solar and lunar years could be arranged on a long count of nineteen years – a discovery always ascribed to Meton the Greek, some two millennia later.

"It is one of the greatest secrets in the sacred sayings of the priests," the novices were told – that the moon goddess only shows the same face, on the same day, once in nineteen years."

And this was the significance of the augury. For Dluc and his priests, from their meticulous recordings, knew that soon a rare and notable event was due to take place in the heavens. At the end of the present nineteen-year moonswing, already nearly half completed, not only would the sun at midsummer solstice rise opposite the moon and exactly down the centre of the avenue, but on that precise day it would be full. It was a huge astronomical coincidence, an opposition more perfect than any seen for generations: and it was due to take place at the end of that very moonswing – in ten years' time.

"How can such a huge work be accomplished in so short a time?" a young priest cried.

"By the will of the gods," Dluc replied coldly.

For several days, Dluc pondered the new temple design. Into it he put all his knowledge of the mysteries of the gods, the intricate pattern of their motions in the heavens, the magic numbers the priests derived from the motions of the sun and moon and the succession of the days – all of this and more went into his design, until finally he was satisfied and murmured to himself: "Truly this will be a hymn to the gods, a marvel in stone."

It was. The henge that Dluc designed was far taller than any temple on the island. The bluestones stood six to eight feet high, and were sacred. But the High Priest decided to replace them with the mighty sarsen stones that came from the downland nearly twenty miles away, and which would stand three times as high. At the centre, he would place five huge free-standing arches, each consisting of two uprights with a lintel across the top of them, and arranged in a half circle around the altar, with the open end towards the entrance and the avenue. These were the five trilithons which would stare down upon the sacrifices. Then, in place of the half-completed bluestone circle, a massive ring of thirty huge sarsens would be built, supporting lintels which would be joined together to form a perfect, unbroken circle. It was a sophisticated, daring design, and he pondered it for many days, making careful drawings of the various parts with chalk on pieces of bark.

When he had completed this work, he summoned the priests and declared: "The design is ready. Now we need a builder to supervise the work. Who shall it be?"

After some discussion it was agreed:

"Nooma shall build the new Stonehenge."

Nooma the stonemason was a curious little figure; and a few mornings later the priests gazed in mild contempt as the mason in his leather apron waddled towards the henge, his over-large grizzled head nodding sagely at his own thoughts as he went along.

His ancestors, who were potters, had been tall; but fate had decreed that Nooma, while being blessed with a head that was huge and statuesque, should be given to go with it a body that was short, stocky and bandy-legged. The result was that his solemn round head with its ageless face sat on his shoulders like an enormous and rather absurd egg. His hands were small, with short fingers and thumbs that were little more than stumps. Shy and reserved and still unmarried, he usually spoke little, unless something in his work excited him, when he would start to tremble, break into voluble, unexpected eloquence and wave his little arms about wildly. But most of the time, his quiet eyes were serious and trusting, and this often made people take advantage of him.

If his appearance was absurd, it was misleading. For generations his family had been fine craftsmen – potters and carpenters usually – and he had all their skill. The stubby fingers, that looked ill-suited to delicate work, could produce miracles. Although only twenty-five, he had worked all over the island since he was a boy and was said to be the best stone worker living.

Nooma was excited that the priests had chosen him to build the new henge: not only was this a great honour that made him stick out his chest with pride, but it was also a challenge to his craftsmanship; and he hurried towards the sacred grounds with eager anticipation.

But when he heard the priests' instructions, and when finally he comprehended the enormous scale of their plan, and the short time in which the work was to be completed, his solemn eyes grew larger. Despite the chill autumn day, he felt small beads of perspiration breaking out on his broad forehead.

"Such huge stones? Completed in ten years?" It was a wail of dismay.

The priests took no notice of his protests, and now the little mason began to tremble with fear. How could such a vast temple be completed so quickly. It would need an army of masons! But as he looked into the impassive faces of Dluc's priests, he had no doubt of his fate if he failed him.

"They will give me to the sun god," he thought. "They will sacrifice me at dawn."

When the priests next showed him the drawings that the High Priest had made, and he bent his head to study them, his large oval face fell even further.

"Nothing like this has ever been done before," he muttered as he stared at the great arches. And jabbing his finger at one of the drawings he protested: "How am I to do that?"

For Dluc's designs made clear that each of the massive stone lintels of the ring of sarsens was to be slightly curved so that together they would form a perfect circle. How could such huge stones be transformed – thirty of them – into identical blocks each shaped with such precision?

"You must find a way," they told him.

Nooma shook his head slowly. "I shall certainly be led to the altar stone," he thought sadly.

But there was nothing he could do. The priests could not be refused. Somehow, he must devise a way to build this huge new henge.

"I should need fifty masons to work under me," he said finally. "And as for labourers . . ." He tried to calculate the size of the army of men that would be needed to haul such enormous stones. For each sarsen would weigh up to thirty-five tons – the largest half as much again – and would have to be moved nearly twenty miles across the rolling high ground. "Why," he exclaimed, "it would take five hundred men at least, and teams of oxen too."

But the priests were unmoved by these astounding demands.

"You shall have all the men you need, and the oxen," he was informed.

Nooma thought. The practical problems of organising such a force, of feeding and housing them would occupy much time. He could not do this and supervise the stone-working alone. "I shall need help to organise the men," he said.

"Choose whom you wish."

The little fellow considered.

"I should like Tark the riverman," he said.

It was a good choice. No one on the five rivers was cleverer than Tark, the best known and most highly regarded of all the riverfolk. The riverfolk at Sarum were an extensive tribe, somewhat apart from the farmers, and mostly descended in one way or another from the crafty fishermen and hunters who had first inhabited the place millennia before. It was not uncommon to see mean, hard little faces and long toes which bore a remarkable similarity to those of Tep the hunter, along the riverbanks of any of the five rivers, as these people went about their business as trappers, fishermen and traders. Water rats they were often called by the Sarum people.

Tark was of this tribe, but a nobler specimen than most. Though he, too, had the long toes of the water rat, he was a tall, good-looking man with strong, rugged features, long black hair which he swept back, and a black beard which he kept meticulously trimmed and singed. His eyes, black as jet, could be hard when he was driving a bargain, but could also become gentle and luminous, especially when he sang, which he did in a fine, tuneful bass; and it was partly for this reason that he was well known from the trading post to the port to be popular with the women. Tark was an expert trader, with six boats and men of his own working under him. He was everywhere, even crossing the sea sometimes in search of slaves or special items that he knew would please Krona or the priests. Above all, he was wily in his dealing with the priests, always making himself useful to them, while at the same time seeing to it that each transaction was to his benefit. He liked the little mason, whom he found slightly absurd, admired his craftsmanship and had formed a kind of friendship with him, often letting him have small items from his river-trading which the mason would never have been clever enough to bargain for himself.

Nooma was sure that he would know how to organise the provisioning and quartering of his men, and he was right.

"You have a month to prepare," the priests told the mason. "At the next new moon, work must begin."

In the days that followed, Nooma found that his needs were more than supplied. The priests moved from house to house, picking young men whenever they were needed. Before the work was done, over a third of the adult male population would be engaged on the task at any one time. Under Tark's direction, grain stores were built near the site from which the sarsens would be brought, and the work of felling trees, which would be used as rollers over which the huge stones could be moved, was begun.

By the end of the month, despite the huge size of the task before him, Nooma felt the first dawning of a new confidence. Encouraged by Tark, who was delighted by such an opportunity to make himself useful to the priests, he began to go about his great work with a new optimism and before the end of the month confided to the trader: "Perhaps, after all, it can be done."

While the preparations were in hand, he also set his mind to the technical problems presented by the stones themselves: how were they to be handled, and above all, how were such cumbersome objects to be fitted together in so precise a design?

It was in this that Nooma showed a practical genius which amply justified the choice that the priests had made in putting the work under his hands.

For when he came to report to the priests at the end of the month, the little mason was brimming with suppressed excitement.

As he outlined his plans, jabbing the air with his stubby little fingers, he announced:

"We must cut the stones into their final shape before we move them."

The priests were surprised. It had been assumed that the rough hewn rocks would be brought to the henge before they were shaped. But Nooma shook his head.

"First," he explained, "it is foolish to move the sarsens before they are almost shaped, because they will be heavier. And second, if we cut and dress the stones at the henge, the mess will be enormous: thousands of stone chippings to carry away."

[86]

"Then you mean to shape every stone of the temple a day's journey away, carry the finished stones to the sacred ground and assemble them there?" One of the priests asked in astonishment.

He nodded calmly. "Why not?"

Next he produced his own drawings.

To produce the identically curved lintels he proposed to make a wooden block, along which each stone could be cut, and in order to fix them in place he had devised an ingenious solution.

"See," he explained, "at the top of each upright we can make two tenons – these bumps – and on the underside of each lintel two matching sockets for the tenons to fit into."

He pointed them out to the priests.

"They will be fitted into each other just as we do blocks of wood," he explained. "And then," he continued, "I can make tongue and groove joints at the end of the lintels so that each one slots into the next."

"They will be solid," the priest who had spoken before remarked.

"Solid!" the quiet little fellow suddenly burst out. "Why, each stone will be married to the next like husband to wife. The temple will be indestructible!" He was flushed with excitement.

It was from that moment that the priests knew the new temple of Stonehenge would be a masterpiece; and that night, when they gave Dluc an account of the mason's plans, the High Priest was pleased.

If only the High Priest's problems had been so easily resolved. For the question of Krona and his heir remained and as the months passed, it was only his faith in the sun god that kept him from despair: often it seemed to Dluc that they were labouring in a great darkness. At times it even appeared that the gods themselves were deliberately confusing them. A suitable bride had to be found: but where? The auguries had said that her head would be crowned with gold – but what did it mean? It might only signify that she would be the daughter of a chief, for it was often the custom for such girls to wear a circlet of gold in their hair when they were married; but this explanation did not satisfy him: he was sure that the augury meant something more. And indeed, though messengers were sent to chiefs all over the island, they failed to find any bride who was suitable.

It was then that one of the older priests suggested:

"The land of Ireland is called the golden because of its fine jewellers. Perhaps the girl is to come from there."

And since the searches on the island had been useless, it was decided to send a priest to that distant western land to see if he could find a bride there. But it was a long and dangerous journey and Dluc was uncertain whom to send until a young priest named Omnic, tall and stately and with the fire of courage and dedication in his eyes stood up and cried:

"Send me, High Priest. I shall be safe, for I know that this journey is the will of the sun god."

So Dluc sacrificed two rams, Krona gave him fine gifts, and three days later, in a small curragh, he set out from the harbour with only three men to accompany him.

He was gone for two years.

During this time, while Nooma and his masons cut ten of the great sarsens, Krona's spirit became less sad: the haggard look left his face, he made several visits to see the work progressing, and he even began to hunt again. He resumed his life with Ina. What must she feel, Dluc sometimes wondered, sharing Krona's bed once again, yet knowing it must be for only a short time, until his new bride should arrive? At first he had noticed an air of contentment about her; the lines in her still handsome face had seemed to be smoothed; but as the months passed, and Krona started to look forward to the approach of his new bride with more and more obvious impatience, the priest observed new lines, of irritation, around her mouth and as time wore on, not only her face, but her whole body seemed to take on an air of resignation.

Once, when he had asked her what she thought of the chief's health, she had given him a sad smile: "Krona is well. But let his new bride come soon."

And indeed, Krona's impatience became increasingly clear. When they discussed the future, his eyes were concerned and sometimes he would take the High Priest by the arm and say:

"Sacrifice another ram to the sun god, so that Omnic may return soon with my bride."

Each time Dluc did as he asked, and always he reminded him:

"Do not despair. We are building the new temple. If we obey the gods, they will keep their promise."

But Krona was still fearful.

"Tell the masons to work quickly," he urged. "Time is passing and soon I shall be old."

They were anxious years. To the High Priest they seemed to be long periods of darkness, pierced through occasionally with rays of hope: like the cloudy days interspersed with sunshine that were such a feature of the high ground in the spring and autumn of each year.

At the sarsens' quarry the work continued all year round, only halting when the weather made it impossible to continue.

It was a strange place. It lay on an empty tract of downland, and, properly speaking, it was not a quarry at all. For the huge sarsen boulders from which the henge was to be made were not buried under the ground, but lay on the surface – hundreds of long, low humps of rock, rising only a few feet above the ground – so that from a distance it looked as if the landscape was covered by a flock of motionless, giant grey sheep.

Never had Nooma been busier: his squat form bustled everywhere in a heavy leather apron, his hair full of dust; but he had about him now an air of quiet authority and his word was never questioned as he showed the men how to cut and shape the huge rocks.

Discipline was strict. The men working at the quarry or felling trees on the ridges were kept in camps for months at a time. At the great festivals of the year, the summer and winter solstices and the spring and autumn equinoxes, the priests ordered Tark to bring slave girls to the camp, and the best workers were rewarded with them for two days, after which their work began again. At such times, Tark had always seen to it that Nooma had the pick of them.

The workers on the henge who were not already married were forbidden by the priests to take a wife; but in the second year, as a reward for his services, Nooma was told that he might do so.

This posed the mason with a problem. "I have no time to look for a wife," he muttered as he surveyed the busy scene around him. Yet the thought of it excited him. Accordingly, one spring morning, he walked down to the trading post to consult his friend Tark.

"I need a girl," he said.

Tark grinned. It was known that his own sexual appetites were prodigious. He kept several slave girls besides his wife and he had more than once let Nooma know that, without the knowledge of his priests, he could procure him a slave girl whenever he wanted.

But when Nooma explained that it was a wife he required, the river-trader grew serious. He listened carefully to his friend and then replied: "Come back in three days. I will make enquiries."

He was as good as his word. When Nooma returned, he had already spoken with several families along the five rivers who had suitable daughters, and had found that all of them would be glad to give a girl to the skilful builder of the henge, who was in such favour with the priests.

Carefully he outlined the merits of each.

"But the best is Katesh, daughter of Pendak the potter, who lives along the western river," he said. "Her father is anxious to please the priests: he would part with the girl for five pelts; and for a girl like that, the normal marriage price would be twenty."

"Is she so good-looking?" the mason asked.

"A beauty. I've seen her," the trader assured him. "Black eyes, soft hair, and her body . . ." he made a lewd sign and laughed. "I envy you."

Two days later, when Nooma saw the girl, he had to agree with his friend's description.

She was thirteen, and the first thing he noticed were her large, lustrous black eyes and pale, creamy skin. She was a little taller than the mason. Her black hair fell to her waist; and though she stood quietly when her father brought her forward from the little hut beside his pottery, there was something challenging about the way she held her shapely young body, that stirred the mason to immediate excitement.

While he spoke to her father he was aware that the girl was watching him, and though her eyes carefully never met his, he knew that every point about him had been carefully noted. He wondered whether what she saw had pleased her.

He made his decision on the spot.

"I will take her," he told the potter, who was delighted by the match.

A few days later he and Tark came up the river to the potter's house, the five pelts were paid, and the girl was his. Slowly they paddled back to the place where the five rivers met, while Tark gently hummed a tune to himself, and the mason grinned almost foolishly at his good fortune.

When Nooma had brought her to the small house he had prepared in the northern valley, and she had silently cooked the customary meal of wheat cakes and meat, he rose to his feet the moment the meal was eaten and raised her up in his strong little arms. While he watched with a gasp of delight, she took off the loose woollen robe that all the women wore, and he saw her fresh, sweet-smelling body and her firm young breasts. Only then did she raise her large eyes slowly to his, and he saw their cautious uncertainty, and also an unmistakeable challenge: he guessed that she was wondering if this small man would be able to satisfy her.

The months that followed were a time of new joy and excitement for the little mason, as he explored each night his wife's young body. He would hurry back from the henge now before dusk fell, when he might have lingered before, so that it became a joke with all the masons as they saw his bandy-legged little form hurrying urgently towards his wife.

Fate had not been kind to Katesh. She was a lively, good-looking girl who could, in the normal course of events, have expected a rich choice of husbands from the farmers around. It was her bad luck that her father was so anxious to please the priests. When she heard that the mason had been asking for her she was dismayed.

"I have heard about him," she cried. "They say he is small and ugly with a huge head."

"He is the finest mason on the island," her father told her, "and he is very popular with the priests."

"But what if I do not like him?" she protested.

"You'll be lucky if he'll have you," she was told.

When she first saw Nooma, her worst fears were confirmed. While the little mason saw that she was discreetly eyeing him, he little guessed the unhappy thoughts that were going through her mind.

"He is ugly," she thought, "but I can bear that if I must. He is shorter than me. That's not so terrible. But he is . . ." she did not want to think of it: "he is absurd," she acknowledged. "How shall I love him?"

That night as she thought of the young man – undefined but handsome – that she had always dreamed would be her husband, and as she realised that the rest of her life might be spent with this worthy fellow with his big solemn head, his bandy legs and the funny little hands that she had observed that day, she wept bitter tears.

For two days, she pleaded with her father, but each time he turned his face away as though he could not hear her, and her mother only shook her head sadly.

"You must obey your father," she told the girl. "He will choose the right husband for you."

When the mason came for her and paid her father the absurdly low price that he had asked, she hid in the house and wept until her parents came in to fetch her. Then her mother firmly gave her the advice – it was really an order – that was to see her through the rest of her life:

"Remember Katesh, you are thirteen now – grown up. You must make your husband believe that you love him. And you must always obey him, that is your duty. Make sure you do both these things or you will suffer."

In the coming years, she did her best. But on that sunny day, as the boat carried her towards her new home, and she looked up at the towering ridges and the broad, sweeping spaces of Sarum under the clear blue sky, it seemed to the young girl that the rest of her life was ordained to be a long and terrible sacrifice.

She remembered her mother's words.

Night after night, as the little mason made vigorous love to her, thinking that he impressed her with his strength and passion, she tried to pretend that she, too, was carried away; and since the mason was filled with pride and excitement, it did not occur to him that his young bride might not be delighted with his passionate attention, his endless thrusts and his grunts of pleasure.

Indeed, knowing the excitement she caused her little husband did give Katesh a momentary delight and satisfaction; but she was glad that on most days she was alone, and she did not look forward to the nights when he returned.

Several times the mason took her to see the henge, where already the sacred bluestones were being moved to one side to make way for the new sarsens. Each time she noticed the grins of amusement on the faces of the labourers, and sensed the lewd jokes they were making in whispers as the bandy-legged mason led her proudly along; each time she secretly cursed the gods for giving her a husband whom she could not love.

It was at this time that the mason made a remarkable discovery. In order to make sure that he had fully understood the priests' designs, he had made for himself a little wooden model of the new henge. It was a fine piece of work, every measurement precisely to scale, and when the priests saw it, they nodded their approval: this was exactly the temple they wanted. But although the priests were satisfied, Nooma was not. Something about the model – he could not at first say what it was – displeased him; and for several days he studied it until he thought he understood the cause.

What he did next made Katesh wonder if he had lost his mind, and delighted the children from the neighbouring farms. Each night now, before retiring to bed, by the light of a taper, he would fashion curious little wooden arches, even tiny henges a few inches high, each one with a subtly different shape; then, at sunrise and sunset he would place these little structures on the turf and lie on the ground, watching them intently as the light caught them.

"Look, Nooma is playing his game again," the children would cry. And they would fall on him, ruffle his hair and often knock over the tiny henges and arches until the place looked like a battleground.

"They aren't even straight, your arches," Katesh remarked.

But the little mason good-naturedly shook the children off, set up his models again, and resumed his intense observation.

When, after nearly a month of this strange behaviour, he was finally satisfied, Nooma gathered up the original model of the henge together with several of his curious arches, and took them to the priests.

"The new henge is badly designed," he told them bluntly. "It won't look right." To their surprise he placed his models on the ground and explained "See how the light catches the uprights where they join the lintels. Although they are straight, they appear to get closer together towards the top. The building looks top-heavy." Then he showed them the little arches he had made. "You see – I have tapered the uprights towards the top, and the effect is lighter. The columns seem to be straighter; even though they are not." To strengthen his point, he showed them a drawing. "This is how it should be."

And when the priests looked, it was undeniably so.

What Nooma had observed was the phenomenon, well known to the Greeks, of entasis – the bending of pillars; and to this day it can be seen that the upright sarsens of Stonehenge are tapered towards the top, a sophistication unknown in any other prehistoric building in northern Europe.

It was in the spring of the next year that Katesh told Nooma that she was pregnant. His face lit up with a grin.

"When will the baby come?" he asked eagerly.

"At the start of winter," she said. "Around the feast of Winter Day, I think." She was glad at least to make her little husband happy.

"It will be a boy," he said. "A fine mason."

And swelling with pride, the mason gave a sheep to the priests for sacrifice, to ensure the blessing of the gods on his first child.

In the following months, he went about his work with a light heart; in the evenings he would sit for hours contentedly in his hut and look with pride and admiration at the swelling body of his young wife.

As autumn came and winter approached, and Nooma became daily more excited by the obvious approach of his child, his spirit of optimism was in stark contrast to the prevailing mood at Sarum.

For no word had been heard from Omnic.

As the months passed, Krona asked, with growing insistence:

"Where is my bride?"

Though the High Priest constantly assured him: "The gods will provide her. Be patient," he himself was beginning to be concerned.

"Perhaps Omnic has drowned. We should find another," Krona suggested gloomily. And Dluc had to admit to himself that the chief might be right. The cloud of depression had returned to Sarum and seemed to be settling.

"If there is no sign of your bride by Winter Day," he finally said, "then we will send out other priests. You shall have a wife before midwinter."

In the late autumn, to keep his own spirits up and to encourage the workers on the henge, the High Priest decided himself to visit the sarsen site to inspect Nooma's progress with the stones.

[92]

It was a windswept afternoon when he arrived. Grey shafts of sunlight burst through the fissures in the heavy grey clouds and lit the bare landscape harshly. The cold north-east wind that drove the clouds over the moorland threw the dust from the stonework into the masons' and the priests' eyes.

Nooma, in his heavy leather apron, his grizzled hair powdered with dust, prostrated himself in front of the High Priest and at his command quickly conducted him round the site.

It was extraordinary what he had done. Already three huge sarsens lay ready to be moved, and several others were nearing completion. As the party threaded their way through the knots of men they came upon a huge rock that was about to be worked into shape. It lay along the surface, seven feet across and as long as ten men.

Nooma patted it.

"I can make one of the tallest uprights from this one," he said with confidence, and pointed to where a group of men were busily engaged near the centre of the rock. "This is where we cut it," he explained, and he showed the High Priest a deep V-shaped groove that he had made across the stone. Underneath, at the same place, the men had dug a trench in the ground which they had just filled with brushwood.

The act of cutting through the rock was a remarkable operation, and Dluc remained to watch it. First the men lit the brushwood and then they busily stoked it, pushing fresh wood into the trench with long poles. Soon the heat had become tremendous and the rock grew so hot that no-one could touch it. Nooma urged the men on. After a while, the rock began to glow, but still the mason was not satisfied. Then finally, when the air around the rock seemed to pulsate with the heat, and the men's faces were burning, he gave the order: "Now the water;" and quickly the men ran forward with leather buckets of water which they emptied into the V; there was an explosion of steam.

"More! more!" he called and they slopped the water in, jumping back so as not to be scalded. The process went on for several frantic moments, and then there was a great crack and all the men cheered.

As the steam cleared, it could be seen that a fissure had opened right through the red hot rock at the point where the split had been made. There was no sarsen, however large, that the mason could not reduce in this way.

Then Nooma led the party of priests over the rest of the site. The sarsens were in all stages of preparation and Nooma supervised everything. In particular, he watched over the dressing of the stones, which his masons did by pounding them with hard, round stones, which removed a little of the surface at a time.

"You see," he explained to them, "the men always strike downwards, from the top of the upright towards the bottom. That way, every stone will have a consistent surface."

When the priest inspected a finished sarsen, he could see that it was covered with minute grooves all aligned in the same direction, giving it a single grain so that when the stones were all in position, the light would

[93]

always strike a vertical edge, enhancing the graceful effect of the whole.

Truly, he could see, Nooma was a master of his craft.

It was just as the High Priest was admiring this work that a messenger came running over the downland towards them.

"High Priest," he cried, "you must come at once to Sarum: Krona is sick."

He was more than sick: he seemed to be dying. The High Priest learned that a fever had seized him the very day that he had left for the quarry, but the chief had ignored it. By the time the priests were called, it had grown rapidly worse and soon they had despaired of saving him.

When Dluc entered Krona's house, he was lying on a bed of straw; there was a lull in the fever and he lay very still, shivering only occasionally. His flesh was grey; his eyes were glazed, but fixed on the roof above him, and he did not appear to notice the priest. Dluc had seen men like this before; but none who had lived.

On the floor at his side, like a shadow, sat the stately figure of Ina. She had grown old suddenly, as the island women often did: her body was bent, her hair, which was now white, had grown thin. She was very quiet and he could see that she had been weeping.

Dluc murmured a few words to the chief, but he did not hear them.

"He will die," Ina said. Quietly she leant forward and wiped his brow.

"It is the will of the gods that he should live," the priest replied firmly. Ina said nothing.

Brave words: yet was his faith so strong? Dluc knew that he had spoken them to make himself believe. He knew all the secrets of medicine – and he knew that there were maladies of the spirit which none of them could cure.

Even so, he made potions of verbena, that sweet smelling and most efficacious of all herbs, and with these potions moistened the chief's brow and his lips, while he prayed to the gods. The night passed and there was no change.

For two days his life hung in the balance. They were terrible days for the High Priest. Could it be that the gods had deserted Sarum after all? Was the new temple not as they had ordered? It seemed to him that he no longer knew himself.

The news of Krona's sickness had spread all along the rivers. In every valley, the people of Sarum went about their business silently; what would happen if Krona died? No one knew. During those days, all Sarum seemed to be living with a sense of doom.

Then, in the darkness, came a glorious ray of sunlight.

Omnic returned; and with him he brought a bride.

They came up the river in a large curragh – twice the size of the boat in which he had left – which was painted white. Wise Omnic, remembering the message of the auguries, which all the people knew, had covered the girl's head not only with a coronet of gold, but an intricate golden net that reached down her back, and he had made her stand in the front of the boat so that the people in the settlements along the river would see her clearly as the boat passed. His choice was excellent: the girl was tall, high-breasted and slim. She was not beautiful; she had a long nose, solemn grey eyes and her skin was pitted; but she was the daughter of an Irish chief who had parted with her for a handsome payment, and her mother and grandmother had each borne twelve healthy children.

Omnic had been thorough. He had not only taught her the dialect of the Sarum area on their long journey, but had carefully explained to her every aspect of her new role. The girl had made little comment, but the priest thought she had understood him well enough.

News of their coming reached the hill at Sarum well ahead of their arrival and Dluc was waiting on the riverbank to receive them. When she stepped out of the boat and he conducted her up to Krona's house, his heart rose; not because she was graceful – she was not – but because she, at least, seemed certain of her destiny. Whether guided by her own instincts, or by what Omnic had told her, she took charge of the situation at once. On entering the house she went straight to the bed where Krona lay and, taking no notice of Ina, in her strange accents she spoke firmly to the chief.

"I am Raka, your wife. You must get well, for you are to have children again."

Ever since he had been a child, no time had been more magic to Krona than the ancient feast of Winter Day. Of all the feasts that were celebrated, this was the oldest, and although the priests set the date of the festival by the solar calendar – it fell thirty-nine days after the autumn equinox – it was thought that these rites were older even than the henge itself. Since time immemorial each farmer had performed the rite on the eve of Winter Day in his own house, before he killed the livestock he did not want to shelter during the cold months ahead. The farmers used to say that on Winter Day itself, even the sun god is asleep and that the spirits come out of their graves to walk among the living. The rite of Winter's Eve was especially important, because that was when each farmer asked the gods to make his fields fertile.

In the presence of this strange woman from the western islands, the chief felt his spirits slowly returning. The pallor left his face; his eyes grew clearer, but above all, a small hope, like an inner warmth, deep within his body, began to grow again.

"I had lost faith in the gods," he confided to the High Priest on the third day of his recovery. "It was as though, after my sons . . . Krona had begun to die."

Dluc nodded.

"When Krona dies, Sarum also dies," he said. "But now?"

"I am still weak," the chief confessed. "But I begin to live again."

Indeed, his recovery was remarkable. Raka and Ina were constantly at his side. The girl said little. She seemed to be self-sufficient. But each day she would look into Krona's eyes and tell him; "You will soon be well," in a voice that made it seem like a statement of fact rather than a hope. And from this Krona continued to draw strength and comfort.

[95]

"She knows I shall be well," he told the priest. "She is the one sent by the gods. This time I am sure of it."

On the fifth day Dluc said: "It is time to set a marriage day."

To which Krona replied: "Let it be the eve of Winter Day, in three days' time. No day in the calendar is more lucky."

The ceremony took place as night was falling, in the main room of Krona's house. All the tapers were lit, and twenty of Sarum's most important families crowded into the room.

"Let the couple come forward," Dluc called, and Krona stepped forward with Raka. He looked younger and stronger than he had for many months, and the priest rejoiced to see the great chief he had loved restored to something like his former self. Then, following the time-honoured custom on Winter's Eve, Dluc said loudly:

"Let the corn maiden enter."

Old Ina and her serving woman brought in that strange and wonderful figure which, even then, brought a flush of excitement into Krona's heart: two cubits long, made of braided cornstalks cunningly woven together to form a female figure with huge breasts and legs spread wide apart, the corn maiden was the image of fertility. The women laid her carefully on a bench in the centre of the room. Next Dluc called out:

"Sun, bless this fair maiden and let her be fruitful." And all those present cried: "See she is fruitful!"

As soon as these words had been said, Ina and her women slowly danced around the corn maiden three times, pausing to bow as they completed each circle.

As Dluc performed the next part of the ceremony he thought of Krona. He took a heavy oak club, black with age, and laid it between the maiden's open legs.

"We have ploughed and sown," the men all cried. "See that we reap!"

For the second time, Ina and her women went three times round the corn maiden, and this time they clapped their hands and made provocative signs to indicate to the corn maiden that she must be fruitful.

The ceremony of the corn maiden was complete; she would lie there, the club between her legs, until sunset the following day. Then Dluc led Krona and the girl forward.

"Greatest of all gods, sun," he cried, "giver of life: bless the marriage of this man and woman and let her, too, be fruitful."

All the men and women in the room clapped their hands. Then he placed a circle of gold upon the girl's head.

"Raka," the priest said earnestly, "you are chosen by the gods."

And as Chief Krona looked at the corn maiden, that wonderful, pregnant symbol of the fields that reminded him so vividly of his childhood; as he gazed fondly at his faithful old wife and stared in wonder at the strange girl by his side; as he went through the time honoured ritual of this most magical day of the year – when even the implacable sun god slept – he felt a glow of happiness and excitement in his body that he had not felt for many years. It was like a great warmth. It seemed to him that on this day his spirit had been reborn.

This time both Krona and the High Priest really believed that Sarum had come to an end of her troubles.

A few days later, in the modest hut in the northern valley, a small event took place that gave the mason more joy than the knowledge that at last Krona had found his chosen bride.

His son was born: a splendid little boy with a large round head, huge, serious eyes and stubby little hands with short thumbs; when Nooma held the boy up high and inspected him he grinned with satisfaction.

"You'll be a fine mason one day," he chuckled. "Look at his hands." He handed the baby back to Katesh and stroked her hair affectionately. "Soon we'll have a team of little masons," he said enthusiastically; and she smiled weakly.

At the next full moon, just before the first frosts came, a feast was held at the little hut in the valley. The mason carefully laid out rush mats on the ground outside, while Katesh prepared a meal, the centrepiece of which was the greatest delicacy the valley knew – a whole sucking pig which she turned slowly on a spit over the open fire. There were wheat cakes, ripe berries and – most important after the pig – great flagons of the dark ale of the region and the thick, sweet and highly alcoholic mead, fermented from the honey that had been scooped from the nests of the bees in the surrounding woods.

To this feast he invited his best masons, the family of Katesh, his friend Tark and – without whom the feast would have no meaning – one of the priests: for it was the privilege of the priests to name the child.

Before the sun set, the baby was brought out and shown to the priest.

He was a serious young man. Like all the priests he wore a single heavy robe of undyed brown wool and his head was shaved in the customary way into a single V, with its point between the eyes. For some time he stood silently, gazing severely from the large, solemn head of the baby to the equally solemn face of the little mason. Then suddenly his stern expression creased into a laugh.

"The son is like the father. Let him be called Noo-ma-ti," he said, smiling.

This was a clever pun, for it meant both 'like-Nooma' and 'man-of-stone'. The party shouted with delight at the appropriateness of the name and the feast began.

At the end of the feast, when the sweet and heady mead was drunk and Nooma felt his whole being glow with warmth, it was the turn of Tark the riverman to lead the guests in song. And as he began in his rich, deep voice, the men gladly followed his lead. They sang the old hunting songs of the region, and some others of a more bawdy nature. But while the men rolled about and frequently sang out of tune, Tark was always still, his dark, lean face like a glowing wooden instrument from which there came always a wonderful, melodious tune. At last he said:

"Now, a lullaby for the child."

And very softly, while the men and women listened silently, he began a slow rhythmic song which seemed to curl up into the air and disperse like the woodsmoke rising from the glowing embers of the fire; it was a strange old song about a forest, full of animals and birds, that lay under the sea. It was a haunting song; and all the time that he sang, his dark eyes, which seemed to be focused on the far distance, wandered round the circle of happy faces by the fire.

That night, when the guests had gone, Katesh said: "He is a fine singer, your friend Tark." And the little mason warmly agreed, before he fell contentedly asleep.

Three days later, Nooma began to move the first of the completed sarsens to the henge.

He had chosen this time of the year because it was then that the first frosts had made the ground hard, so that the huge weight of the sarsens would not cause them to get bogged down.

"We can get the sarsens half way to the henge before the snows come," Nooma said. "Perhaps they will go over the snow too."

On his orders, each sarsen was strapped to a framework of timber, and hundreds of trees had been felled and their trunks stacked at points along the route, to be used as rollers over which the frames could be guided. The route was carefully chosen, keeping as much as possible to the higher ground where the going was easy. He began this work with five hundred men and a hundred teams of oxen.

The men worked efficiently, but Nooma had soon found that the oxen were a problem.

"The obstinacy of these beasts," one of the priests said to him, "is greater even than the obstinacy of men." And it was certainly true.

A single pair, or even a team of oxen could be driven easily enough. But to pull one of the huge stones, many pairs of oxen, twenty or thirty were needed, and though their strength was enormous, their movements were spasmodic.

"They are impossible to handle," the mason cried in despair, and he called for more teams of men to replace them.

In the end, the oxen were used only on the uphill slopes, where their extra power was useful in helping the disciplined teams of men who pulled steadily on the leather ropes and sang as they worked.

When the snows came, Nooma tried to build a great sled under one of the sarsens, but the weight of the stone was so great that it sank into the snow and was impossible to budge; and the moving of sarsens had to stop until the early spring.

It was in the spring, soon after the equinox, that the news for which Sarum had waited so long finally came. Raka was pregnant.

She was a strange creature. As the months passed, she still spoke little, complained about nothing, asked for nothing, had no friends and no enemies; she was always at Krona's side; and of the other women in the house, including old Ina, she took no notice at all. She did not insult them; but it was as if they did not exist. There might have been complaints at such conduct: old Ina, though she said nothing, walked about the house in dejection; but now that the girl was with child, no one could speak a word against her. The fate of Sarum rested in her belly.

Was the girl happy, Dluc once or twice asked himself? Who knew? And truth to tell, who cared? She had been brought there for a purpose; there could be no doubt about her destiny; and she was fulfilling her task.

Above all, Krona was happy. Each day, it seemed to the chief that he drew strength from Raka, and each day, as he saw her belly swell, he would exclaim: "The gods sent you to us."

As the spring ended, there was every sign that there would be a brilliant summer that year: a seemingly endless succession of hot, still days followed each other and on the broad slopes above the five rivers, the heavy corn seemed to promise a bumper harvest. Sarum, at last, was at peace with the gods and Krona was full of hope. A month before the summer solstice Nooma began to erect the first of the huge grey trilithon arches of the new Stonehenge.

And during these months, the mason too was contented. After all, his wife had given him a son. The work on the henge was proceeding quickly. Like all the people of Sarum, he was conscious of a lightening of his spirit now that Raka was with child and the gods smiled upon its valleys and ridges once again.

It was true that from before the time that their son was born he had seen that Katesh was sometimes irritable and short-tempered, but he put this down to trivial causes, and their life together continued placidly enough. Indeed, the girl proved herself a good wife: she cooked well and the leather jerkins he wore were now beautifully trimmed with fur. Her care for him was everything it should be: and if sometimes her response to his enthusiastic and energetic lovemaking was lukewarm, the little fellow was still so excited by her splendid young body that he hardly thought anything of it. When he came home to find her sitting cross-legged by the fire in front of the hut with their little son and saw her smile of welcome, he would lift her up and carry her indoors just as he had when they first married.

Often he was away; for it would sometimes be necessary to camp at the sarsen site for a month at a time; and during these periods Katesh was left alone to fill the time caring for their little plot of ground on the hillside, and sitting with the other women who lived in that part of the valley. But many of the men were away for long periods while the great work on the henge continued, and Katesh never complained.

Truly, she was a good wife.

Sometimes, if he had been absent for a while, Nooma would consult his friend Tark the riverman, and ask him:

"What can I give Katesh that will please her on my return?"

Tark would tell him to wait and then, after one of his visits to the harbour, he would return with some fine ornament or a string of gleaming beads that he had traded with the merchants who came from across the sea.

"These are the things women like," he told the mason. When Nooma gave these presents to Katesh, she flushed with pleasure, and the little mason grinned to see that he had made his wife happy.

It was during the late spring, when he was returning to the valley one evening, that Nooma made a small discovery which delighted him. Beside the path that led down from the ridge, he had often noticed a small thorn tree whose roots for some reason had pushed up through the ground so that one had to be careful not to trip over them. That day he carelessly caught his foot in one of these, and almost fell. And it was in turning to look at the root, that he noticed it had pushed up a small piece of stone which must have been lying under the surface. He stopped to look at it. To his surprise, he saw that the little lump of grey stone, which was no bigger than his fist, had already been carved – crudely but unmistakably – into the form of a little woman, squat and full-bodied. Something about the curious little figure pleased him as he cradled it in his stubby hands. He saw and felt how the carver had succeeded in reproducing lovingly the big, firm curves of the squat little woman, how he had captured the very essence of her boundless fertility.

"The man who made this loved his woman," he murmured. And he pushed it into the leather pouch he wore on his belt and took it home with him.

In a corner of his hut he had a pile of such objects – flint arrowheads, spearheads, and stones with curious formations that he had found and which he delighted to study, noting the grain and the secret inner forces of the rock that had caused each strange shape. Onto this pile he placed the little figure that Hwll the hunter had made of his woman Akun, thousands of years before, and there for many years it remained.

It was during the long warm days of summer that Nooma began to erect the first arches of the new Stonehenge.

The raising of the sarsens was a delicate matter. The huge uprights were brought to the edge of the pit that had been dug for them so that a few feet overlapped the edge. Then ropes were attached, and two hundred men would lever and haul the stones, inch by inch, into an upright position – one group pulling the ropes over a high wooden frame while another pushed in props behind the slowly rising stone. Gradually it would slip into the pit – the greatest trilithon was set eight feet deep – and gangs of men would pack in the chalk filling around it.

When it came to raising the lintels – each weighing several tons and needing to be lifted twenty feet into the air – the labourers had at first been uncertain which was the best way to proceed.

Nooma supplied the answer at once.

"It's easy," he explained. "Just build a wooden scaffold under the lintel and raise it." He showed then what he meant, using a pebble and some twigs. "We raise the stone with levers at one end and slip a wooden pole under. The same the other end. Then lay two more poles over them, crossways so that you have a square. Then you lever the stone up again over the crosspoles, exactly as before. And you do this again and again, securing the scaffolding underneath with ropes as you go." His quick fingers arranged the twigs so that the workers saw the stone rise before their eyes. "When the scaffolding is as high as the uprights, we lever the lintel across into place."

It worked very well. Under Nooma's direction, the scaffolding was built and the lintels slowly rose. By the festival of the solstice, two of the tallest trilithon arches at the centre of the henge were in place.

They were awesome: and when the people saw them at the festival, there was a gasp of wonder.

"The new temple will be the greatest ever built," they said; and they were right.

The harvest was the best in living memory; Krona now smiled as the High Priest had not seen him do for years; Raka grew big with child.

"The sun god smiles on us at last," Krona said to the priest, who nodded in agreement.

And summer passed and early autumn came, before the blow fell.

It was a warm, clear night in early autumn; the moon was in the thirteenth year of her cycle, with six years left before the great henge must be completed. Dluc and Krona were quietly conversing together in his house on the hill, and the High Priest was looking forward to his usual visit to the henge later that night, when suddenly a scream from another room brought both men hastily from their conference.

Raka had gone into early labour; and as soon as Dluc looked at her, he knew that something was badly wrong.

The rest of that night remained in his memory as a succession of blurred images: of Krona, distracted, cursing him; of his own, desperate prayers to the gods, and his awful conviction that they were useless; of Ina, as always, silent and strong, holding the poor girl in her arms; of the chief, ashen, leaving the room like a sleep-walker. But above all, it was the blood that he remembered. It seemed to be everywhere, as though a sacrifice had been messily performed. It covered the bed, the floor, even the walls. She had been dead, and so had the child before it left her body; it lay on the floor, a small, bloody, grey bundle of flesh, the death of all their hopes.

Then, while Ina, shaking her head, gathered up the dead child, her women began to keen and moan over Raka's body, scattering herbs as they did so. And he, too, had wept.

He remembered the blood; and he remembered Krona's face, when he went to him afterwards.

The chief was sitting alone in an out-house in which only two candles were lit; but by their light the priest could see his face clearly. It was more terrible than any human face he had seen: for it was not angry, nor in despair: it was blank.

When Dluc came towards him he stared as though he could see through him and, even before he spoke, the priest knew that he was mad.

Another, though quite insignificant series of events had been taking place in the valley below, during that summer.

It was by chance that Katesh had been standing by the riverbank below the hut one brilliant day in early summer when Tark the riverman had also chanced to bring Nooma the mason down the river from the henge to his home.

The water was moving slowly, and the long green waterweeds caused tiny eddies and ripples which caught the sun so that, as she watched with her baby, the surface of the water seemed to dance with light.

Katesh was contented that day. As she closed her eyes and let the warm sun play on her face, and then looked down at the chubby baby gurgling happily beside her, she felt a peacefulness she had not known for many months.

She had followed her mother's advice. She had put all other thoughts out of her mind and tried to make her strange little husband happy; and in a way she had been rewarded.

For she loved her baby; as for her husband, if the other women sometimes smiled at his appearance, they were always quick to say:

"But you are lucky Katesh: your husband is the greatest mason of them all."

She saw the canoe when it was still some distance away. Nooma had his back to her; Tark was paddling.

As she saw the squat little form of her husband, his broad strong back leaning forward as he earnestly made some point to the riverman, and the tall, spare form of Tark, as he quietly listened and guided the canoe down the stream, she could not help noticing how curious the little mason looked beside the riverman. For an instant – no longer she thought than one of the flashes of sunlight upon the surface of the river – it seemed to her that the small form of Nooma was that of a stranger, while that of Tark . . . she could not say what; but she watched the canoe with fascination as his long arms gently lifted and dipped the paddle in the stream.

When they came ashore, the little mason leapt on to the bank with a cry of joy, took his wife in his arms, and then lifted up his baby son and showed him to Tark, saying "Here's a fine young mason," before he led them all up the path to his hut.

It was the first time that she had been near the riverman for some months. She had seen him pass in one of his boats from time to time though, and had seen him giving orders at the trading post. Her husband had often spoken highly of him too, and she had learned from the women that he had another reputation, which did not surprise her. She had been curious about him.

But now she found that his presence disturbed her.

Nooma, in search of something, had dived inside the hut, leaving her alone with him in the sunlight outside. As a good wife should, she offered him wheat cakes and drink and sat modestly on the ground while he ate, looking up at him only when he spoke to her the formal compliments that custom required. Even so, she felt herself blush.

Tark the riverman looked down at the mason's young wife. She was little more than a girl. And he understood at once everything that was passing in her mind. He smiled pleasantly at her, noting once again the points about her that had first made him tell Nooma that she was the best of the girls he had seen. She was indeed, with her dark eyes and creamy skin.

Above all he felt sorry for her.

"I did this poor girl no favour when I told the mason about her," he thought. Had she ever known passion with this squat fellow who was now bustling around in his hut looking for some stone he had picked up that he wanted to show him? He doubted it. He felt sorry for her; but there was nothing he could do now.

Just then, Nooma appeared triumphantly with his stone.

"Look," he exclaimed as he handed Tark the little figure of the ancient hunter's woman; "isn't it fine workmanship?" As Tark turned the little figure over in his long fingers, and felt the firm, voluptuous curves of it, he had to agree that the mason was right.

"The carver loved his woman," Nooma grinned, "as I love mine." As Nooma put his arm round Katesh's waist, Tark found that he was looking into her eyes.

Katesh looked down at once. She had not meant to look at him. And for the rest of the time that Tark was there, she kept her eyes downcast.

What was it about the tall figure that made her afraid she would blush if she looked at him again? Was it the memory of his rich voice and his far-away eyes when he had sung that night after Noo-ma-ti had been named? Was it something she had seen just then, as he paddled down the stream? Was it the fact that he was close to her now, that she knew he guessed the feelings that she had hardly even allowed herself to think?

She thought she was glad when he left.

"Isn't he a fine fellow?" Nooma said enthusiastically, as Tark walked down to his boat.

"He is too tall," she replied.

"Most women like him," Nooma laughed.

"I prefer my husband," she said, and pulled him to her.

Did she, after that day, go more often to the riverbank? She did not think she did.

It was almost a month later that Tark pulled in to the bank one afternoon to exchange a few words with her. His boat was laden with goods that he was taking up from the harbour to the henge and politely she enquired:

"Were you trading with merchants from over the sea?"

He nodded. "They brought things from many lands."

Then he explained to her where each of the items in the boat came from: the rich cloths from the far south, the bronze knives from the north, the richly decorated belts from cunning artisans who lived in the east. She was impressed with this knowledge and the fact that he spoke of these distant places with such familiarity. Her shyness with him grew less.

"Have you been to these places?" she asked.

"Some, but not all," he told her easily. Then, stepping out of the boat and sitting beside it on the riverbank, he gave her some account of the journeys he had made across the sea in the course of his trading, of the merchants he had met and the stories they had told him. No one had ever spoken to Katesh of such things before; she was entranced; and when he left her to continue on his way, she watched him thoughtfully until he disappeared around a bend in the river.

Often, from that day, he would pause to speak a few words to her as he passed; and as time went by, she could not help contrasting the sense of power and ease which exuded from every movement he made, and the roving life he led, with the short, jerky movements of her husband who only bustled, like a beetle, from the sarsen site to the henge and back again. As the summer days passed, she would sit by the river with Noo-ma-ti and watch the elegant swans: and when one of them stretched its great neck and, with a beating of its wings, took off so easily from the water to soar into the air, she thought of the river-trader who so calmly crossed the seas.

It was an early afternoon in mid-summer and Katesh and Noo-ma-ti were by the riverbank. Katesh had eaten some wheat cakes and fed the baby, and now he lay in her lap, his eyes closed. Katesh felt drowsy, and lifting the baby gently she placed him beside her on the ground, then stretched out herself, curling her arm round the child. The smell of the riverweed was good. The water made gentle, rippling sounds, as it flowed past below her feet. Lazily she turned her face towards the sun, which was directly above a clump of trees and closed her eyes.

She woke with a start. The sun was still high, but had moved some way from its previous position. And the baby was gone.

She looked to right and left but there was no sign of Noo-ma-ti. Quickly she inspected the riverbank. How far would the child have gone?

Beginning now to fear the worst she started to run along the bank downstream, her eyes anxiously scanning the water. But she found nothing, and with a pounding heart, and a terrible, ice-cold mind, she thought: the baby is drowned, and I shall not even find him.

Still scanning the water, she returned along the bank. Those long river weeds with their waving green tendrils could so easily drag a baby under the water and then conceal it. The pounding of her heart grew stronger as she approached the empty spot where she had been.

Then she saw him.

The baby was on the bank where he had crawled, only ten yards from the spot where she had fallen asleep. There was a small bush there and the child must have lain concealed behind it when she ran down river in her panic. But now, little Noo-ma-ti was sitting perilously on the edge of the bank, and as she watched, slowly, it seemed deliberately, he leaned forward and fell into the water. There was eddy in the current at that point, and at once, before Katesh could even move herself, it carried the baby which floated quietly, face downwards, out into the stream.

She screamed. But there was nobody there. Then she threw herself into the river.

As she frantically thrashed towards midstream, the river weeds caught her.

They were so soft, yet so insistent. They wrapped themselves around her legs, holding her back, and seemed to wish to embrace her arms. It

[104]

was as though she was in one of those dreams in which, despite her will, her body was forced into slow motion. The baby was already nearly level with her, out of reach and about to glide past. She shouted frantically.

Tark's canoe came round the bend of the river with a speed that was astonishing. He had heard the scream, and his long arms now made fast, powerful strokes with the paddle so that the light boat sped over the water. He saw everything at a glance; and as Katesh saw her baby drift past her, out of reach, the canoe rushed after it. As he came level with the child, Tark scooped it into his boat with a single gesture, and sent his canoe skimming to the bank. Moments later, having pressed the water out of the child and made sure that it was still breathing, he turned his attention to its mother, who was now struggling to get her legs disentangled from the weeds. He dived into the water and swam easily towards her with powerful strokes; in seconds, his strong arms were round her, and Katesh found herself supported and soon lifted out of the water on to the bank.

As his long, dark body came dripping out of the river, she had just time to notice the dark hairs on his arms, and the drops of water that fell from his beard as he smiled before she half ran, half clambered along the bank to her baby.

They went together up the path to the hut, and whilst she was inside wrapping the baby in a woollen shawl, Tark built up a fire in front of the hut and sat cheerfully in front of it to dry himself. He made her sit down opposite and eat. While she shivered from shock, he calmly sat watching her, the steam hissing from his leather jerkin, and when she tried to thank him, the riverman smiled down at her and laughed softly.

"The river is dangerous, Katesh, like a woman. You never know what she will do next. So be careful of her."

He ran his hand through his long black hair and smoothed his beard. His black eyes, she saw, were watching her thoughtfully.

When he had dried himself, he rose to go. Katesh rose too. As she put out her hand to thank him, he took it gently and held it. She looked up into his face.

For the first time in her life she felt a rushing current of excitement pass through her whole body; it was more violent, more urgent than anything she had felt in her life before. She could not help herself; she trembled.

Tark said nothing, but he knew. He moved closer. She felt her lips part on her upturned face, saw his head about to swoop down upon it.

Then, to her surprise, his face looked instead to a point somewhere behind her, and, still holding her hand, he called in a friendly voice:

"Nooma, you come at a good time. Your son has been swimming!" as the little mason approached his hut from the path.

When, soon afterwards, Tark left them, Nooma turned to her and said:

"You may not like Tark, but he has saved our son's life. He is a good man."

Katesh herself was frightened by the effect that Tark now had upon her and she tried to put him out of her mind.

Most of the time she was successful. She stayed away from the riverbank where she might see him, and the trader though he often passed, made no efforts to seek her out.

The summer passed. Two months after the solstice, the priests ordered the harvesting to begin.

The harvesting was completed quickly in the northern valley that year, and in the final days, Katesh went to help the family of a neighbouring farmer to get the last of his corn in. Nooma was away.

The work was hard and she enjoyed it. She and the farmer's wife took turns to sit in the shade with Noo-ma-ti and the children of the farmer who were too young to work with the adults in the field.

By early evening, the last of the fields was cleared, and all the women went to the farmhouse to prepare a meal to celebrate the completion of their work. It was just as the sun was setting and the men were coming towards the fire that a happy shout came from below the farm towards the river, and a few moments later the farmer appeared, his face wreathed in smiles.

"Look who I have found passing us on the river!" he cried. "He shall sing to us tonight." And behind him came Tark.

Before she could stop herself, she looked at him. She had not spoken to him since the incident in the river, and now that she saw him once again, the trembling sensation that had come over her then – and which she had afterwards told herself was caused by nothing more than the shock of the occasion – now came to her again more violently than even before. Fortunately, in the shadows, and with all eyes on the riverman, no one noticed.

As the stars came out and the farmers sat round the fire, once again Tark led the singing. The men called for all kinds of songs: some bawdy, some recounting hunting feats. Once again, it was Tark who finally said softly:

"And now a lullaby."

It was indeed a wonderful song that he loved to sing: lilting, mournful, yet soothing. And the words, Katesh thought, were so strange: for the song was more than a lullaby: it told the story of a forest long ago, full of great trees, and birds and animals; and how one day the gods tired of the noise of the forest and decided to send it to sleep: so they sent a great sea to cover it like a blanket. But although the forest slept under the sea, from time to time, the sounds of the animals living below the waters would be heard in the waves.

Sleep baby sleep:
The waters are over the forest
Sleep, pretty one sleep:
The birds are all under the sea.

What was it about that lilting melody that stirred her so deeply? Feelings, passions she had only half dreamed of, never known how to name, seemed to be spoken of in the haunting words.

"Aie," she murmured, "it is beautiful."

Sleep pretty one, sleep
Dreams of the forest will come to you;
Sleep pretty one, sleep
Hear the voice of the birds in the waves;
Let the birds sing you a lullaby
Sleep, baby, sleep on the waves.

His face was so strong, his body, she knew, so hard. But his faraway eyes and his voice were so gentle. Katesh rocked back and forth to the song and wondered what it meant, this strange and wonderful feeling that stirred her.

Later that night, taking little Noo-ma-ti who was fast asleep, she slipped away from the circle and returned alone to the little hut; after she had put the child in his little cradle, she sat outside in the warm night, and gazed at the stars.

The song haunted her, and so did the riverman.

A little later she thought she heard the soft sound of his paddling in the river below, and she strained her eyes to pick out his canoe in the darkness; but she could not.

Then she saw him. He came softly up the path, making no sound, his tall lean form moving like a great cat.

And as he drew close, she forgot her husband, her child, everything as instinctively she rose to meet him.

His voice came softly through the shadows:

"Did you know I would come?"

Her mouth open, her eyes half closed, with a gasp she felt herself in his strong arms, pressed against him.

"The lullaby was for you," he whispered.

She felt his careful hands begin to take the covering from her shoulders, and his mouth descended on hers. Instinctively, they moved together into the hut.

Nooma the mason had been away at the sarsen site for a month, but at last, on a warm day in the late summer he set out to walk over the high ground to Sarum. He had planned to leave by early afternoon to reach his home by dusk.

But there was much to do that day and it was already late afternoon when the sturdy little mason set out to walk home to his wife. On the way, he rested twice. Once, at dusk, he heard a wolf's cry, but he ignored it.

Night had fallen long before he reached the ridge above the valley and a few stars were visible through the thin clouds. The moon had not yet risen. A light dew had already fallen on the turf. On the high ground above, which only the sheep inhabited, there was the faint, tangy smell of the sheep droppings; but as he began to descend from the ridge, another welcome smell greeted him: the scent of woodsmoke hanging in the air over the hut below. Although the mason was tired from his long walk, his heart began to beat faster as he thought of his wife in the valley below. With a new burst of energy, he went down the path, and as he did so he decided to shout her name: "Katesh," so that it echoed across the valley. Immediately, several dogs from nearby farmsteads began to bark and Nooma grinned.

"Katesh!" he shouted again, "Nooma is back!" Chuckling to himself at the din he had created, he hurried down the path.

From a turn in the path he could see the hut. It lay about three hundred paces away and he could make out its shadow clearly. There was a small fire burning in front of it. Immediately above and below the ground had been cleared, but to the right of the hut were the trees of a little coppice. Further along the valley, a dog was still barking; but otherwise, everything was silent. "Katesh!" he bellowed happily once again.

At that moment he saw it. A figure, he was almost certain, slipped stealthily out of the little hut, moved past the fire, and went quickly across into the shadow of the trees. He stopped, peered into the darkness and blinked. Surely he must have been mistaken. And yet he could have sworn that he had seen a tall and familiar figure there – familiar not only by its shape, but because of that particular, long-toed, loping walk which he knew so well belonged only to Tark the riverman.

His heart was suddenly beating wildly. He bustled down the path and rushed breathlessly in through the doorway of the hut.

Katesh had just taken Tark in her arms when she heard her husband's call, and in an instant the spell of the moment was broken.

"Go," she whispered desperately, "Go!"

What had she done? With a rush of guilt she pulled herself together. How could she so nearly have betrayed her little husband?

As his moonlike face appeared in the doorway she rose to greet him with a smile as he looked about him in angry suspicion.

"Who was here?" he cried, staring at her.

"No one," she lied, praying that he would believe her.

"I thought I saw someone."

She shook her head.

But Nooma turned, and bustled away towards the woods.

Dluc the High Priest had no doubt that Krona had been driven insane by grief. The priest could hardly blame him. Nor, when he remembered the room full of blood had he any power to comfort him. He could only hope that Krona would recover himself. For at present, he was obviously mad.

Even so, on that fatal day, when Raka lay dead, Krona's first words had taken him completely by surprise.

"The moon goddess watches over hunters, doesn't she?"

Dluc stared at him. Every child knew that the sun gave seedtime and harvest and that the moon goddess watched over hunting, as she had always done. For the moment he did not know how to respond.

"You are a priest," he cried. "Answer."

[108]

"She does," Dluc replied.

"And she also watches over the houses of the dead?"

"Of course." The tombs of the ancestors on the high ground were also under her special protection.

He nodded slowly, then indicated the walls of the room.

"This," he said bitterly, "is the house of the dead."

The priest was silent. What could he say?

"You priests," he went on, "you begin your prayers: 'Sun, giver of life.'" Suddenly he pounded his fist into his hand. "But to Krona, the sun gives nothing but death," he screamed.

Dluc tried to interrupt him, but he took no notice. His eyes were blazing with anger and he began to rave.

"Krona is given death: he accepts it! We shall not worship the sun at our henge any more. We'll worship the moon and her alone. Sarum shall no longer be called the Fortunate. It shall be called: the Place of Death!"

The priest began to protest at this blasphemy; but Krona did not hear him.

"We shall sacrifice to the sun god no more," he shouted. "The sun is dead in Sarum. Each month you shall sacrifice to the moon goddess, and to her only. And your new henge – that too shall be to honour her."

After this he fell silent for a time. Dluc, thinking that perhaps his grief had now made him unconscious, rose to leave. But his voice rasped out, cutting through the shadows.

"Where is Omnic?"

"At the house of the priests."

"He brought the girl from Ireland. He said she would give me sons." He paused and Dluc wondered what direction his thoughts would take next. When he continued, his voice was almost a groan. "He lied: and he is a traitor."

"You are mad," Dluc cried.

Again, he ignored him.

"Omnic must die," he said.

This was worse than madness: it was sacrilege.

"He is a priest," Dluc blazed. "His body is sacred." But he could see that Krona's eyes were staring into space and that the chief no longer heard him. He left.

He could not believe that even Krona in his madness would dare to lay hands on one of the priests of Stonehenge; but he took no chances, and that very night he had the faithful priest taken along the river to the west and hidden in the woods a day's journey from Sarum. It was as well that he did: the next day Krona's men came to the henge looking for Omnic and when they found that he had gone they reported back to Krona that he must have been hidden. Krona sent for the High Priest at once.

"You have hidden Omnic," he shouted.

Dluc said nothing. He saw that Krona was little changed from the previous day except that now he looked at him with suspicion and fear, and it made him sad.

"So you desert me too?" he muttered.

"No," Dluc replied. "But I will not desert the gods."

He shook his head.

"They have deserted me. Bring me Omnic."

"No."

He began to curse, but Dluc left him and the next day, he sent the worthy young priest to a temple far away in the mountains of Wales where he would be safe.

There were times during the next five years, when Dluc wondered if Krona would try to kill him too.

For now at Sarum a reign of terror began. The darkness of Krona's spirit descended on the entire territory like a terrible blight. Word of events there had soon travelled all over the island and beyond, and before long, even the visiting merchants would not venture up the river from the harbour.

"Sarum is a place for the dead," they said.

And so it seemed.

A month after the tragedy of Raka, old Ina died, and from then on there was no one who could alter Krona's moods. He was silent and morose; he withdrew his spirit and soon retired completely into his house. For months at a time he would be invisible to all but his closest servants; and yet in his seclusion he was all the more terrible.

Not only did his anger, and his passion for the moon goddess grow obsessive, but he became suspicious. The people of Sarum were terrified.

For his servants were everywhere. The workers in the fields, the traders at the port, the farmers who owed him tribute – and even the priests in the temple – all were watched. His spies were endlessly inquisitive and reported to him each day.

Those were the years when it became common to hear a farmer say to his wife:

"Be careful what you say: Krona is listening."

During this time, Krona forbade any public celebration of the festivals of the sun god: the great feasts at the solstices and equinoxes ceased. Instead, rites were performed each month when the moon was full, followed by dances and feasts. Whenever Dluc protested at this reversal of the natural order Krona would shout at him furiously.

"If you do not honour the moon goddess," he would cry, "then I will stop the building of the henge."

Yet despite these terrors, Dluc remained calm.

"Be patient," he told his priests. "The building of the henge must continue. These terrible times will pass and the will of the gods will be made clear."

He also gave orders that the ceremonies to honour the sun god should continue in secret; and often he prayed to him:

"Give me strength, Sun, in this time of darkness; guide my hand."

But it was the sacrifices which were sickening.

In his quest for an heir, Krona no longer asked for help from the priests, but he developed his own system, which he claimed was dictated by the moon goddess.

Once every three months, his servants would stalk from farm to farm, looking for young girls. When they found one to their liking they would seize her and take her to Krona. At first the farmers were hopeful that this was an honour which might bring riches to their family. They soon learned better. The girls were forced to be at Krona's side day and night, ministering to his every need. Dluc would see them when he had business at the chief's house: wide-eyed, frightened, cooped up like animals with the ageing tyrant; and if ever he was not with them himself, they were watched by his servants. He would keep them like this for three months. At the end of that time, the girl was watched with particular care, and if she still menstruated, then Krona would give her to the temple and order the priests to sacrifice her to the moon goddess. Three months was all the time he gave them to get pregnant, never more.

The first time it happened, Dluc refused to perform such a monstrous rite. Krona grew furious.

"Give her to the moon goddess," he raved. "She accepts my sacrifices though the sun does not!" When the priest still tried to argue, he swore: "Then I will kill her myself." And again he threatened: "If you will not perform my sacrifice, I will stop the work on the henge."

Sometimes, after this, he would be calmer, put out his hand and take Dluc by the arm. "Sarum must have an heir," he would remind him urgently. "Time is passing." And Dluc would shake his head, for he had no solution to offer.

In the end, the High Priest always did as Krona asked. It seemed to him that the girls would be better sacrificed than murdered by Krona: for those sacrificed to the gods were received by them at once after death, and walked with the spirits on the sacred grounds.

Every three months a new girl was sacrificed on the altar, while the henge slowly grew, and Krona's servants would go out to find another victim for his bed. The farmers began to hide their daughters to save them from this fate, but such attempts were useless. Krona's servants were cunning, their spies were everywhere; nothing and no one could escape them. And often they would come to the chosen house at night, dragging the girl from her couch, slashing and hacking at her parents with their terrible stone axes if they dared to protest.

As for Krona, it seemed to Dluc that he became more than ever like a bird of prey. Physically he did not deteriorate. Indeed, apart from the fact that his hair was grey, he looked as fit as he had been in years. But he was, in a way, no longer a man, so hardened had he become by this appalling way of life. He cast off each girl as casually as if she had been one of his cattle to be slaughtered.

When the red harvest moon appeared, no one at Sarum rejoiced any more, as they used to do.

"See," people whispered, "Krona has filled the moon with blood."

None of Krona's girls conceived. The priests sacrificed nineteen of them.

Krona knew, for nothing was hidden from him, that the priests still performed secret rites to the sun god. Many times he summoned the High Priest to him and raged:

"You make the moon goddess angry!" And each time that another girl failed to conceive he shouted: "This is all your fault." Several times he became so angry that Dluc feared for his life, but even in his rage Krona hesitated to strike down the High Priest. And it occurred to Dluc that perhaps even in his madness, the chief was still secretly afraid of the sun god.

The work on the new Stonehenge went on. But with what a change! The men no longer sang hymns as they dragged the sarsens over the chalk ridges: they were silent and sullen; even Nooma's masons had to be watched carefully.

"Sarum is cursed," they said. "What's the use of building a new temple?"

And sometimes the priests had to whip the labourers to make them approach the sacred grounds at all.

Somehow faithful Nooma, his solemn face serene, his little hands always busy, led the masons and kept them all at work. But despite the beauty of the new building, which was already becoming apparent, it was often a long and bitter task, and sometimes when he was alone in the henge at night, the High Priest would cry out into the sky:

"Give me a sign, Sun and Moon – give me some sign, at least, that we are doing your will."

Nearly five years of Krona's madness had passed when Dluc sacrificed the nineteenth of his luckless victims. She was little more than a child – a dark haired, dark eyed, creature with a pretty little red mouth. Her terror when she was dragged from her parent's hut to the house on the hill was heart rending. Dluc had seen her with Krona twice in the three months she was allotted to give him an heir and watched her pathetic attempts to please him, which the chief accepted with a coldness that was terrible. He knew that it was said that a woman who is frightened is more likely to conceive; but in the case of Krona's women, it seemed to make no difference. When Dluc slit her throat, her wild, child's eyes gazed up at him as though to ask: "Why?"

And to that question the High Priest knew that he had no answer.

When Katesh looked back, she could no longer say exactly when her painful love had begun. Was it on that first day when he had paddled the canoe that took her with her husband to her new home in the valley? She remembered that he had quietly hummed as they went along. Had he looked at her?

But no, she was sure it was not then.

Was it one of the times when she had seen his tall, handsome figure hovering over the little mason as they discussed the building of the henge? Or when once she had seen him throw back his powerful head to laugh, and she had noticed the shape of his mouth, turned up to the sun? Was it one of these times?

She did not think so.

Surely then it was the time when he had sung, after the naming of Noo-ma-ti, when his voice had seemed to caress the circle of people round the fire and when, as Nooma's head had fallen sleepily on her shoulder, she had found herself looking straight into his eyes, so clear and understanding.

Yet she did not think it was even then, nor when he had rescued her baby in the river.

No, it was that night after the harvest when, though they had hardly looked at each other all evening, she had known that he would come to her.

And since then – it seemed to her that once the process of her passion had begun, nothing in the world could be more beautiful than her pain.

Nooma had been suspicious, that first night. But he had found no trace of Tark in the woods, nor of his canoe in the river; and finally he had decided that, after all, he must have been mistaken.

In the months that followed, as Sarum plunged into gloom after the death of Raka, she had done all she could to make the mason happy and she had been careful to avoid Tark. Several times she went with Nooma to the henge and admired the work as the sarsens continued to rise.

And indeed it was a remarkable sight. For already, a quarter of the arches were up, and the mason moved briskly about in the dust, directing everything.

"My husband is a great man," she said to him on these occasions, and walked obediently behind him to let the labourers know that the mason was respected by his wife.

The winter passed, and the spring. She looked after her husband and child and even believed for a time that she had forgotten Tark.

The following summer, when Krona had already taken the fourth of his victims, Nooma went to the sarsen site and stayed there for two months.

When Tark came up the path, she thought of hiding; but instead she gathered her courage, stepped forward and greeted him politely. He was respectful.

"I bring a message from Nooma. He will be at the site for another month. There is much work."

She nodded. With Krona's rages and the anxiousness of the priests, Nooma was especially careful to see that no criticisms could be made of his work on the henge.

"I thank you, Tark," she replied correctly. And as custom required, she offered him food and drink.

Sensing her thoughts, Tark sat at a distance from her, and spoke generally of the henge, of events at the harbour, and of the rumours about Krona and his wives.

Cleverly he interested her so that gradually she forgot her reserve. She had been left alone for a long time and she began to ply him with questions: What did the merchants say about Sarum? Were the priests satisfied with the work on the henge?

[113]

For a long time they spoke, and his answers to her questions fascinated her; the shadows were already lengthening when he rose to go.

Two days later he came again. This time she was less reserved.

Two days after that, just after dusk had fallen, she heard the faint sound of his paddle in the river below, and knew that he would come to her.

Even then, after they had kissed passionately and moved inside, she paused. The reproachful figure of the mason rose up before her eyes. If she did this thing, how she would hurt him; and what terrible punishment would the gods visit upon her?

She trembled, turning her face away from Tark, not daring to look at him. But now, having got so far, she realised that she wanted the riverman with a pain that she could hardly endure, and so at last, letting her clothes fall from her, she turned her naked body towards him with a little cry.

"Ease my pain."

The passion of Katesh took place that summer and, when Nooma returned to supervise the hauling of the sarsens, the autumn that followed it.

She came to know every feature of the riverman's body, became obsessed by it.

Sometimes her fear of the gods, and of her husband if he found out, caused her to tremble. But then the memory of her lover's touch, the shape of the back of his neck as he laughed, his soft eyes and gentle voice, obliterated everything else. She longed to have his child, to flee with him over the sea; but all this she knew was impossible: she would only steal a dangerous and forbidden passion during the dark days and nights of Krona's rage at Sarum.

And the danger was very great.

"Krona's spies are everywhere," she would say. "If we are seen and reported to the priests . . ."

"I am careful," Tark assured her. "We shall not be seen."

For under the laws of Sarum, if a husband could prove to the priests that his wife had lain with another man, she was sacrificed to the gods, while the other man was liable to pay the cuckolded husband a heavy fine.

When she thought of this, Katesh shook her head in terror and moaned to herself:

"Why did the gods not give me another husband?"

Tark was so different from the little mason. Sometimes he would lean back, the silky black hairs on his chest catching the light from the taper, stretch all his limbs like a cat, and she would mount him with a little gasp of joy while he slowly smiled; then she would tell him to be still while she rhythmically moved and stretched herself, arching back, upon his taut body. But above all, she loved simply to hold him in her arms, glancing from time to time into his soft, sleepy eyes, and cradling the powerful head that relaxed, when he slept, so that it often seemed to her like that of a child.

[114]

Unlike Nooma, Tark was a skilful lover, who took his time. He was so gentle, she thought, feeling her, teasing her, encouraging her to come again and again.

When the mason came home, she did her best to appear pleased to see him. She submitted to his lovemaking and tried to make him happy, as before.

She was sometimes almost overcome with guilt at what she had done with Tark, and again and again promised herself that it would stop. But each time that Nooma departed, and she saw the riverman, her resolve broke down once more.

It was in early winter that she made the terrible discovery that she might be pregnant.

Nooma had been away for a month. Now the gods would punish her!

"He will discover!" she cried. And she wept bitterly for the pain she would cause the worthy mason who had given her, in his clumsy, well-meaning way, nothing but kindness.

"He will give me to the priests," she wailed. She deserved such a fate, she knew, but it was terrible to think of it.

Then Tark told her what she must do.

The next day, Nooma was surprised when his friend came striding across the ridges to where the gangs of men were hauling the sarsens; and still more surprised when Tark took him to one side.

"Let me supervise the labourers," he said. "The work at the henge is being badly done. Go there at once and supervise it or the priests will begin to complain."

Grateful for the advice, Nooma set off at once and when he got to the henge, although he could see no signs of bad work that would have caused immediate complaint, he noticed a number of small mistakes the masons were making and corrected them at once.

"That Tark is more of a perfectionist than I," he chuckled to himself.

He was glad that he had come back. For when he reached his home, an extraordinary change had come over Katesh.

He was completely unprepared for the reception that awaited him. When he first arrived, she prepared food for him as usual while he sat by the fire in the doorway of the hut and played with his son. But while he ate, he noticed her looking at him in a way that was new; and that night when they lay together, she made love to him with a passion unlike anything that she had ever shown before.

The next night the same thing occurred again. And the next. It seemed that suddenly his wife had fallen violently in love with him; and the little mason, though he was astonished, rubbed his little hands together with joy. Now, when he told her about the wonder of the henge, or his work with the stones, or the problems he had overcome with his masons and labourers, instead of nodding absently, as she had usually done before, her face was full of admiration and she would ask him to tell her more.

"My husband is the greatest mason in the whole island," she would smile. "All Sarum says so."

[115]

And the mason was gratified that his young wife appreciated him.

All that winter, Nooma experienced an excitement and happiness that was even greater than that of the first year of their marriage. Katesh did everything she could to please him; and at nights her moans and cries of passion aroused him to new heights. Then, in the spring, he saw to his joy that at last his hopes had been realised and that Katesh was pregnant again; when he felt her belly with his strong little hands and kissed her, Katesh smiled at him happily, whispering:

"I think we shall have many more."

Early in the summer, Nooma gave a sheep to the priests for his new child.

While all Sarum suffered under Krona's madness and while the girls continued to be sacrificed, Nooma went quietly about his business with a happiness that it seemed nothing could shake.

His greatest delight at that time was to take his son with him to the henge. The boy was such an exact replica of his father that even the priests would smile with amusement as the two bandy-legged figures, one a diminutive version of the other, waddled around the henge to survey the work. Noo-ma-ti had quick little hands and loved to model figures with the clay his father brought him.

"He will be a master craftsman," Nooma told the priests proudly. "Better than me."

He would show the tiny boy the great sarsens he had made, running his hands over them lovingly and explaining the properties of the grey stone.

"You will learn to work stone," he told the boy, "and to love the henge."

For as the years had passed, the henge itself had begun to exercise a fascination upon the mason. Normally he would never have been allowed inside the earth circle, but his building work took him into the most sacred precincts so often that he grew used to the place and the ways of the priests. He came to love the broad encircling bank, the silent sanctum within, and the great avenue that pointed like an arrow at the dawn on the horizon. At the end of the day's work, when dusk fell and the masons and labourers laid down their tools and departed, Nooma would often linger there, quietly tolerated by the silent priests as they went about their nightly tasks. The henge, he realised, had a strange, echoing quality about it when one stood inside and the light receded from the empty sky above. Was it the wide circle of the chalk bank? Was it the sarsens as the temple neared completion? He could not say; but he knew that it affected him.

He was fascinated also by the activities of the priests. Some things they did he understood. Each day at dawn, for instance, a careful note was made of the sun's position as it rose; precise sightings were taken over the fifty-six wooden markers that stood in their circle just inside the perimeter wall. Each day he would watch as the priests noted the small difference in the sun's position from the day before, adding each to their tally; and before long he found that he, too, could reckon the days and months with precision.

But some of their other activities baffled him. As dusk fell, little parties of priests would move about on the high ground around the henge carrying sticks and long strings of flax. With these they would take sightings of the stars, noting the motions of the moon and the planets, quietly pacing about until the first signs of dawn appeared, making ever more complex patterns with their sticks and lines until often the whole ground was covered with these strange constructions, and Nooma would return to Katesh, shaking his head in wonder and saying:

"The ways of the priests are very strange."

As the summer continued and Katesh grew big, Nooma was excited.

"It will be another boy," he said, "another mason. I am sure of it."

Katesh laughed whenever she heard this. "I think it's a girl," she told him.

"Perhaps," he admitted, but immediately brightened: "Then she will look like you," he decided happily.

One day when he held her belly and felt the child kicking inside he remarked:

"I think it is bigger than Noo-ma-ti was. When is it due?"

Katesh shrugged.

"When it arrives. Two months I think."

"I still think it is bigger than the boy," he said.

But soon afterwards, when he was at the henge, he realised that his wife had made a small error. Glancing at the fifty-six calendar posts, he realised that the sun's position had only changed by six months since his return. The child could not be due for three months. He grinned to himself at his wife's carelessness with the dates.

"She will have to wait a little longer than she thinks," he chuckled; but just then one of the workers came to him with a problem and the matter went out of his mind.

It was only at night, during those terrible years, that the spirit of the High Priest found peace.

At night he would go up to the sacred high ground, walking alone past the pale chalk houses of the dead, and enter the great circle of the henge. There, and only there, in the silence under the huge blackness of the night sky he could recover his spirit. And despite all Krona's madness and Sarum's grief, it was during those years some of his best, his most precise observation of the heavenly bodies was accomplished.

The stars were his companions. Each night he looked up and saw the constellations shining down upon the henge: the ram, the deer, the auroch, and the constellation he loved the most of all, the stately swan that filled the northern sky – these were his faithful friends. So too was the milky way that stretched across the panoply of stars like a gleaming chalk path leading down to the horizon. Whatever madness was passing there below, the stars still shone with a pure and constant light, and when he saw them his faith in the immutable gods would return.

He found comfort in the secret mathematics of the heavens. It was he who had restored the fifty-six wooden markers to their honoured place within the circle of the sanctum's walls: for had not the ancient priests, in the course of their endless tabulations, discovered the mystic properties of that sacred number? Was it not true that between three solar years and three lunar years of thirteen lunar months, there was an interval of fifty-six days? And was it not also true that between five solar years and five lunar years, if this time the lunar year was reckoned as twelve lunations, there would be an identical interval of fifty-six days? It was! In these secret ways, he knew, the gods revealed their harmonies to the priests who honoured them and studied their movements with reverence.

It was during this period that he charted the motions of the five moving stars. For countless generations the astronomers had recorded the appearance and disappearance of these wanderers across the heavens and had decided that they must be the sons and daughters of the sun and moon. But they had never been able to discover the exact pattern of their movements and the magic numbers which, they knew, must govern these motions. Night after night his gaunt, angular figure could be seen as he silently placed markers on the ground, joining them with lengths of twine in his efforts to discover these secrets; and often there were so many of these markers spread over the henge that in the morning the junior priests would whisper:

"See, Dluc the spider has been weaving his web again."

He thought that he had established the pattern for two of them, which he added to the sacred sayings of the priests. But the other three continued to baffle him.

Each night, when he had made his observations, he waited for the dawn and then, as the sun god rose over the horizon in all his glory he would cry out:

"Greatest of all gods, Sun, Dluc has not deserted you! This is still your temple."

There was one mystery however, above all others, that Dluc wished to solve; and when Nooma had seen the priests go out, night after night, it was on this, the High Priest's life's work, that they were so busily engaged.

Each month, as he surveyed the results of the labours he had ordered, he would pace about and burst out "Why – why do all our efforts fail? Why do the gods hide from us their greatest secrets?"

"Priests have tried to solve the problem for many generations," the other priests replied.

But to Dluc, this was no comfort.

What the High Priest was so anxious to discover was the pattern that underlay the most significant, and the most dramatic of all the alignments in the heavens: the eclipse of the sun. After all, the astronomers had succeeded in establishing all the sun's movements and some, at least, of the moon's. Why was it so difficult to discover this particular feature of their relative motions?

For despite all his meticulous recordings, Dluc knew neither that the earth was round, nor could he know the basic organisation of the solar system, without which knowledge such a prediction was, mathematically, almost an impossibility. But since he did not know this, and since he was a perfectionist, the High Priest continued, night after night, to send his priests out on their thankless task.

"It shall be my life's work," he muttered. Indeed, the discovery of the secret of this celestial phenomenon, when the moon goddess dared to cover the face of the sun god himself, was dearer to his heart than even the building of the new Stonehenge.

Her size had only made Nooma suppose that the child would be large. He was taken by surprise when Katesh gave birth to a daughter a month early.

She seemed delighted; never before had the little mason seen his wife look so happy. When he came to her, she held the child up for him proudly to inspect.

"It's a girl," she said with a tired laugh. "You shall have another mason next time."

And Nooma eagerly took the baby in his arms.

But then he frowned.

The child was not premature. He could see that at once. And as he looked more carefully, he noticed other things: it had a long, narrow head, unlike his; even at its birth, he could see that its fingers and toes were unusually long, too. Like those of Tark.

He stared at Katesh in silence; but she did not seem to sense anything amiss: her whole mind was full of her happiness with the child. She even smiled at him.

Carefully he handed the baby back to her; then, after a few words with the women who were helping her, he went outside.

It was warm. Slowly and thoughtfully, he made his way up the path to the high ground and there, looking over the sweeping ridges, he considered what he should do.

There was no doubt in his mind – the child was not his. It had been conceived while he was away at the quarry, and he had no doubt either that the father was Tark. Bitterly the mason thought of Katesh's sudden passion for him when he had returned: now he understood the reason for it – she had guessed already that she was pregnant; in silent disgust he paced along the ridge and as he thought about how he had been made a fool of by both his wife and his friend, the little fellow clasped and unclasped his stubby hands in rage.

It was some hours before he came down, having reached no conclusion.

That evening he ate alone; then, as the stars came out, he sat in front of the hut by himself and went over the alternatives again.

By the custom of Sarum, he knew, he could accuse his wife to the priests, and if she was found guilty, then she would be put to death and Tark would have to pay him compensation. That was the punishment for such a crime, and for a time Nooma considered it.

But he had loved Katesh once; he could not give her up to such a fate.

He would not even punish her: everyone knew the fate of cuckolded husbands: instead of being admired as the great mason, he would be laughed at as the bandy-legged little fellow whose wife so easily deceived him. Why should he subject himself to that? He shook his head. No, he would not even say anything; but from now on he would ignore her; his pride was too hurt: his love for her had died.

But as he brooded about what had happened, it was the tall, mocking figure of Tark, his friend, who rose up, again and again before his eyes.

For several hours more, he sat in silence, making his plans, nodding to himself from time to time; and could the people of Sarum have seen the little mason then, they would have been surprised: for his eyes were hard as stone.

At last, when he was satisfied, Nooma slowly rose. Inside, the tapers were still burning as Katesh, rather pale, lay asleep with her baby. He glanced at his wife, but looked away in disgust. Then he glanced at the baby. It, too, was asleep; but now the mason's kindly face softened as he reached out a stubby finger to touch its face.

"You shall not suffer," he murmured. "You have done no wrong."

Then he moved over to where Noo-ma-ti lay and smiled. The boy at least was his; that was one consolation.

A few minutes later however, as he lay on his own bed of straw, the mason's face grew hard again, as he thought of Tark, and now he whispered:

"I will have revenge!"

It was a quiet summer night without a moon. The white circle of Stonehenge on its rolling ground stared up into the black and silver heavens like a single, huge all-seeing eye.

Alone in the henge, Dluc the High Priest concentrated on the stars, wiping from his mind the memory of the nineteenth of Krona's girls that he had sacrificed that morning; trying to forget for a few hours that only a year remained before the henge was due to be completed.

He had chosen to be alone that night, and since there was no moon, no measurements could be made in the prediction of the eclipse. With a sigh, he relaxed his long body and let his eye wander over the glittering sky.

And then he saw it.

It was on the western side of the great constellation of the swan; a small but very bright star that he had never seen before, and as he looked carefully he saw that behind it in a broad V-shape stretched a gleaming cloud of light. This, he knew at once, was one of those strangest of all the heavenly bodies, the wanderers which the people called the stars with hair and which appeared only once or twice in a life time. The astronomers had kept records in the sacred sayings of every one for centuries, and since there was no pattern in their movements, they knew for certain that they were special signs to them from the gods. He gazed at the new star intently and as he did so, he realised its most remarkable feature – the trail of hair behind this messenger from the gods was not silver, as the sayings told them to expect, but golden.

"The head of this star is crowned with gold," he said aloud. As he did so, he realised the huge significance the statement might have. Could it be that, at last, the time of their salvation had come? Surely that must be the meaning of such a portent in the sky; yet after so many disappointments he could hardly bring himself to believe it.

He watched it carefully all night: it was moving slowly and growing larger.

By the following night, all the people of Sarum had seen it. The priests gathered at the henge and together they watched the golden-haired star and made exact note of its movements. It grew brighter still and before dawn it had moved half way into the constellation of the swan. On that second day, even after dawn had broken, it could still be seen in the early morning sky.

It was then that the High Priest showed both his faith and his courage.

In front of all the priests he firmly declared:

"The gods have not deserted Sarum or their faithful priests. This is the sign for which we have waited." And then he added: "Bring me a ram, so that I can sacrifice it at once to the greatest of all gods, sun. And let all Sarum know that the sun is honoured again at the temple today."

Soon after first light, messengers came to the henge from Krona to ask the meaning of the portent in the sky. And with a new confidence the High Priest declared:

"Tell Krona that the head of the star was crowned with gold. The time of our salvation is near: his bride who will give him heirs is coming and he must prepare himself."

"Where is she?" his priests asked him. "Where are we to find her?"

"The star entered the constellation of the swan," he told them, "and the swan is the form that the sun god takes when he flies over the water. I believe we should search for her upon the water."

Since his discovery of Katesh's deception, Nooma the mason had spent little time at his house. Partly this was because the pressure on him to supervise the dressing of the sarsens was so great; and partly it was out of choice.

He said nothing to her; nor did he allow his behaviour to change towards Tark, with whom he continued to work.

There was, however, a subtle change in his manner. Where he had been either quiet or enthusiastic, he now became abrupt, giving his orders curtly to the masons, and sending the labourers to their tasks with little more than a nod. But since he bore such a large responsibility, and since his skill and knowledge were unquestioned, the gradual change seemed normal to those around him who had come, with the passing of the years, to regard the curious-looking little fellow first with respect and even with awe.

From time to time he now took to going down river to the harbour whenever he heard that a merchant ship was coming in – for they usually had slave girls in their cargo. When he saw a girl he liked, he would buy her and take her to the hut he occupied near the sarsen site. It was widely known that he did so, but if news of it reached Katesh, she never mentioned the subject to him.

It was shortly after the comet was seen that he made one of these journeys.

He arrived at mid-afternoon, and as soon as he entered the long, still stretch of protected water, he saw the newly arrived merchant ship, moored by the jetty in the lee of the hill.

It was a stout, wooden vessel, with a double bank of oars that had made its long journey from a port on the Atlantic shore of Europe, skirting the dangerous coasts before it crossed to the island.

The little jetty was already crowded with people. Word had spread rapidly; farmers from all over the territory had hurried down the rivers, and were now jostling for a chance to see the boat and inspect its cargo.

The sailors were an interesting sight: small, dark, swarthy folk with bronzed skins from the south, but it was their leader whom Nooma especially noticed. About his own age, he had a bald round head, and a black beard that grew in hundreds of gleaming, tightly rolled curls, cut close and square. He had soft brown eyes, a snub nose, an engaging smile in which he displayed a fine row of white teeth, and a gentle, coaxing voice that seemed almost to ooze out of his throat: the sailors called him honey tongue. On his fingers he wore a dozen gold rings, which he clinked together constantly.

While the crowd watched in fascination, he brought forth his wares. There were jewelled ornaments which flashed in the sun, huge coils of beads, amphorae of wine, wonderful coloured cloths. Then with a flourish and a loud click of his fingers he made the sailors hold up the strangest pelt that Nooma had ever seen. It was like a huge lynx, but many times larger with a magnificent head, huge teeth and claws so large that Nooma shuddered to see them. Strangest of all was the animal's strange colouring; it was striped black and ochre.

"This creature could rip an ox apart," Nooma murmured to his neighbour, and he wondered what kind of animal this could be and where it came from.

But stranger things than a tiger skin from distant eastern trade routes had filtered through the Mediterranean and up to the northern sea ports before that.

Then came the merchant's special prize. He built up to it splendidly. Using his whole body to emphasise his points, and accompanied by wonderfully enticing sounds of appreciation that seemed to arise from his belly, he let them know in a spoken pantomine that they were about to see something they had never seen before: a special gift from the gods – a human wonder. It was a girl he explained – but not just a girl: she was the most beautiful creature in the world, a princess in her own country, sold tragically into slavery. A virgin too. Of fifteen. This was the usual patter of any competent trader selling a slave, but the olive-skinned merchant did it so well that the crowd grew tense with expectation. When he judged that the dramatic moment had arrived, he once again clicked his fingers, and the sailors led forward a figure covered from head to foot in a heavy cloth. With a flourish he whipped it off: and the crowd gasped.

On the deck of the little ship stood a girl, entirely naked, and unlike anything they had ever seen before. Her eyes, which stared straight over the heads of the crowd, were blue. And her hair, which caught the sun so that it flashed, was golden!

It was the first time that a blonde woman had ever been seen on the island.

So stunned was the crowd that for minutes there was silence, and the shrewd merchant watched with satisfaction.

Nooma stood quite still; but his mouth had fallen open. It seemed to him that this extraordinary vision of loveliness was as far above all other women as the henge was above all temples. He noticed her well-formed body, her pale and delicately coloured skin, her wonderful, hard young breasts. But above all, it was the faraway blue eyes and the magnificent, the abundant golden hair that fascinated him. It seemed to him that she belonged not to the race of men but to the gods themselves. He could hardly believe that this marvellous creature was an ordinary woman at all.

The hair was genuine, the merchant assured them. To prove his point, he plucked several hairs from her head, and one also from her body, and passed them round for inspection. The girl, Nooma noticed, winced, but gave no cry of pain, and her eyes never left the horizon on which they were fixed.

She had been captured the previous year from one of the many and nameless tribes which roamed the vast, uncharted expanses that stretched between the eastern Mediterranean and distant Asia. She had been transported west, and then sold to the captain of a vessel which traded up the great rivers of south west Europe. Finally she had been seen by this clever trader as he was about to leave for the northern island and he had at once appreciated her value to the dark-haired islanders and paid a good price for her.

To Nooma she was a revelation. Suddenly the little fellow experienced emotions, passions, that he had never known before. It seemed to his dazzled eyes that the girl was above even the passage of time itself; he felt the years drop away and the blood race in his veins. He forgot his age, his unfaithful wife, his humble life. Above everything else in the world, he wanted to own this wonder. He must have the girl.

As the merchant began the bidding, the little mason forgot his reserve and began to shout, jumping up and waving his arms.

"Five pelts! Five pelts!" he cried.

The crowd laughed. The bid was ridiculous for such a rarity as this. The price for her would be far beyond anything Nooma the mason could afford and only the richest farmers could think of her. But Nooma was completely oblivious to everything except the girl.

"Twenty pelts," he shouted wildly. Such a sum was a fortune to him.

Still there were more laughs.

Then, abruptly, the auction stopped. It did so at a sign from one of the priests who now stepped forward. Calmly he went up to the merchant, the crowd parting to let him pass, and in a few words let the merchant know that the girl was to be reserved for the temple. The trader bowed his head respectfully and the girl was immediately covered again. The merchant was well-pleased. He knew that the priests would pay a good price.

A sigh went up from the crowd as the girl was quickly removed from their sight. No doubt she was to be reserved for a sacrifice, probably at the dedication of the new henge. As Nooma saw it, he opened his mouth to cry out in protest at such a terrible fate, but he realised that this was futile and remained silent. The power of the priests could not be questioned. Moments later he discovered that there were tears on his cheeks.

When the priests brought the girl to the High Priest and explained where they had found her, he stared at her in wonder. As they uncovered her, the sunlight caught her golden hair so that it flashed. Dluc slowly nodded:

"This," he murmured, "surely this must be the one. For truly, her head is crowned with gold." And he ascertained that the long, soft golden hair was indeed genuine.

"Where are you from?" he asked.

The girl spoke no language that they knew; but by sign language she let them know that she came from far to the east, from a place where there were snow-capped mountains. She was the daughter of a chief killed in battle, she claimed. This was the story most slaves told, hoping to get special consideration, but Dluc considered that in her case it might be true. In any case, he was sure that he knew what he must do.

A few hours later he climbed the hill to Krona's house and announced without hesitation:

"This is the girl foretold by the auguries. The curse over Sarum has been lifted. She will give you heirs."

Krona stared at the girl. He put his long hands through her hair wonderingly, pulled out several strands and inspected them.

"Is this really the one?" he asked.

"I am sure," Dluc replied.

"Perhaps," he murmured. "Perhaps it is so." And staring at her in almost childlike surprise, for the first time in many months, he smiled.

"What is her name?" he asked.

Dluc thought.

"Menona," he said, which meant She Who is Promised.

The next day, Dluc married Krona and the girl.

But before he did so he said firmly to the chief:

"You must sacrifice a ram to the sun and acknowledge that he is the greatest of all the gods."

And Krona bowed his head and said:

"Let it be done at once."

When he heard those words, the High Priest knew that the reign of terror had ended.

During the night that followed, Dluc stood alone in the henge; many times he looked up into the heavens and murmured:

"Never again, Sun, never will I doubt you!"

At dawn he sacrificed the ram.

In an astonishingly short time, the years seemed to fall away from the chief. He came out of his house on the hill; he inspected his many fields; and once again he began to receive merchants. The network of spies was forgotten and just as they used to, the farmers now approached him without fear to receive justice and to get his advice.

The girl was a marvel. Dluc had explained to her in sign language that she had been sent by the gods to this great chief and that she was to provide him with children, and once she understood she nodded calmly. She seemed pleased with her lot, and indeed, Krona's house was an improvement on the merchant ship or the prospect of life as a slave. Dluc soon came to believe for he watched her carefully, that she was indeed the daughter of a chief herself; for her hands were soft, not like those of an ordinary woman, and once in Krona's house, she carried herself with the dignity of a chief's daughter.

What was certain was that the gods had sent her. Although she did not speak the islanders' language, she seemed always to understand Krona's wishes and it was a joy to see the old chief's face light up whenever he saw her.

As for being his companion in bed – when the High Priest enquired if all was well, the old chief grinned at him like a boy.

Dluc believed it was now safe to recall Omnic from his mountain hiding place, and that autumn, at the festival of the equinox, the ceremonies to the sun god were resumed with all their former splendour, and Krona led the people of Sarum as, once again, they worshipped in peace at the sacred henge.

But for Nooma the mason, the summer brought no lightening of spirits but a new fear, that rose like a cloud over the horizon and soon seemed to cover the whole sky.

The work on the henge was falling behind.

It was the fault of the masons shaping the stones. For the last two years Nooma had been fighting a battle to keep their work moving swiftly. First one or two would fall sick and have to be replaced. Then the replacements would need to be trained, or mistakes would be made. With his time now divided between the quarry and the henge, it was difficult for the mason to supervise everything, and at times he knew that his men had become discouraged.

But the result of this was that over a period of five years, not enough sarsens reached the henge.

All that summer he had chivvied the masons, for before the equinox, all the sarsens should be completed and ready for transportation; but as that day approached, he could see that the final shaping of the stones would not be finished.

The great dedication of the henge was due to take place the following summer. If the ground was soft in the spring, and it often was, then it would be too late to try to take any more sarsens to the henge. There was only one thing to do.

"We shall have to transport all the sarsens to the henge now," the mason said. "We can finish shaping them there."

When he reported his difficulties to the priests, he could see that they were angry. The will of the gods and the fate of Sarum was not to be jeopardised by the failure of the little mason to complete his appointed task. When the priests reported to Dluc, the High Priest frowned dangerously.

"If necessary, every man in Sarum shall work on the henge," he ordered. "There must be no delays."

And an order went out that day that the priest would marry no man in Sarum who had passed fifteen summers if he did not work at hauling the stones that year.

By three days after the equinox, nearly a thousand men were assembled at the sarsen site, and helping to supervise them was Tark the riverman.

Tark felt sorry for the little mason. Though he had admittedly stolen his wife, it did not lessen his respect for the craftsman and he did all he could to help him now. He was everywhere, finding provisions, preparing extra tents to house the men as they hauled the sarsens over the ridges, and encouraging the men.

Nooma saw this. But what he saw above all, were the eyes of the priests as he made the final preparations. For now their eyes when they looked at him were hard and cold, and inwardly the mason trembled.

There were ten sarsens to move. Two journeys were needed. One by one the sarsens were strapped to the frames, and on the fifth day after the equinox, the enormous caravan began to make its way across the ridges, raising a steady cloud of dust.

It was four days before Winter Day when the five sarsens reached the henge. Never before had the journey been done so quickly, and the men, already exhausted by the crippling pace that had been set, returned to begin their journey for the second time. More slowly this time, despite the urging of Nooma, Tark and the frequent whippings of the priests, the men dragged their ungainly burdens along.

The disaster, when it struck, came in the form of a snowstorm – a three-day blizzard more violent, and much earlier in the year, than any the mason could remember. For three days it raged without stopping, a searing north-easterly wind driving the snow into enormous drifts. During this time, the men were crowded into hastily erected huts and deerskin tents in which they huddled miserably. The sudden cold was terrible. By the third day, a hundred men had frostbite.

Nooma watched the snow with terror. Before his eyes, first the wooden runners, then the frames, and finally even the huge sarsens themselves began to disappear in the snow. Two of the sarsens were on an incline where the snow was rapidly drifting; on the second day, he and Tark had to go out into the raging blizzard and place stakes around each sarsen to mark the spot where it lay. By the third day, only the top of the stakes could be seen.

On the third day, the blizzard stopped.

When Nooma looked out over the high ground his heart sank. For mile after mile, the snow lay thick. The rifts and gullies had completely disappeared in the snowdrifts. The sky was clearing, but it was cold and there was no sign that the snow would melt. Perhaps it would stay there all winter. And anyway, even if the snow did melt, the ground would be so sodden that it might be late spring before the stones could be moved again. Furiously his mind made the necessary calculations. In that event, could the henge be finished on time? He did not think so.

Later that morning, a party of three priests sent by Dluc approached across the snow.

With scarcely a word to the mason, they inspected the sarsens and stared at the white ridges.

"How will you move them?" they finally asked.

Nooma looked miserably at the ground.

"I do not know."

"Find a way," they told him, and departed across the snow.

The mason hunched his shoulders and thought. He knew now very well what fate awaited him if he failed.

Meanwhile, the men were becoming restive. They were cold; many were ill; one man who had wandered away from the tents in the blizzard had died. They wanted to go home. Nooma did not know what to do. He stamped about in the snow and made one attempt to move a sarsen on a huge sled. He knew it would fail. It did. Tark moved amongst the men, trying to keep their spirits up; but even he did not have much success.

By the afternoon, Nooma wanted to let the men return to their homes; but the priests accompanying them forbade it.

"The High Priest requires you to finish the task," they said. "Stay here until you do."

When three men tried to escape, the priests caught them and flogged them unmercifully, and left them bleeding in the snow. There were no more attempts to leave.

For two more cold and bitter days, Nooma and his thousand men waited, inadequately camped, on the cold, bare ridge; and at the end of that time, Nooma could only see the prospect of a miracle from the gods themselves, or the failure of all his plans and his own execution.

When Dluc had recovered from his first fury at the incompetence of the mason in falling behind with the work, and when he got over his shock at the sudden snowstorm, he knew what he must do.

At the henge, in the thick snow, a space was hurriedly cleared on the altar stone, and Dluc himself sacrificed six rams to the sun god, while the priests knelt in the snow.

"Great sun," he cried, "your servant Dluc has placed his trust in you. We await your will."

And conquering his doubts he told the priests:

"The temple will be built. It is the will of the gods. The sun god will help us."

The sun god heard them.

For on the third day, a warm wind blew up from the south west, bringing with it a heavy rain that fell steadily all day, and began a general thaw. Then, that same night, while the drenched ridges were awash, the wind changed yet again, the sky cleared, and there was a heavy frost. The temperature plummeted, and the following morning when Nooma looked out from the camp, he saw an extraordinary scene.

It was unlike anything he had witnessed before. For mile after mile, as far as the eye could see, over the rolling ridges and under a clear blue sky, there lay a sparkling land of solid ice; as the sun struck the ground, it dazzled him. He stamped on the ground. It was hard as iron. He took a stone out of his pouch and hurled it. The stone bounced and slithered away for a hundred yards.

Nooma smiled.

"I think," he muttered, "that now we can move the sarsens."

He was right. For now he could construct the huge sleds, as he had tried so unsuccessfully to do before; and this time they worked. When the teams of men hauled on the long leather ropes, the mighty stones on their sleds now hissed easily over the unyielding ice on the bare ridges.

There were still problems. On the long downward slopes between the ridges, it was necessary for two or three small teams of men to go in front, to steer the sleds; the bulk of the men on these occasions being placed behind the stones, steadying them and preventing them from rushing forward down the slope. But their foothold on the slippery ice was precarious and the danger was always that the stones would go out of control. Twice this happened – the sleds plunged forward wildly, dragging the teams along behind for painful yards, until the ropes snapped; and then hurtled forward on to the men in front, crushing them. Twenty men were killed in the two incidents, and many more were injured; but the stones crossed the land of ice.

The frost held for over a month and by the midwinter solstice, all the sarsens were at the henge.

But although one danger was past, the cloud over Nooma's life remained; for as he looked at the ten, unfinished stones, at the pits still to be dug, and at the dour faces of the priests, he wondered: "Shall I, even after this, complete the henge in time?"

But Krona was filled with a new confidence. For just as the great blanket of ice formed over the high ground, the gods kept another of their promises and Menona let him know that she was pregnant.

Once again, Dluc sacrificed a sheep to the gods who had kept faith with Sarum. Even Nooma the mason, beset as he was with troubles, smiled with relief when he heard of it.

The period from that cold midwinter to the summer was a busy one at

Sarum; but with each succeeding month, both the priests and the people felt a lightening of their spirits.

Nooma worked feverishly with his masons. The remaining sarsens were hurriedly beaten into shape and each day the labourers carried away dozens of baskets full of chippings and deposited them in pits they had dug some distance from the sacred grounds. Other gangs of labourers were needed to raise the huge sarsens into place as the circle was completed.

Above all however, Nooma found that he had to supervise the masons to make sure that in these last, critical stages, no mistakes were made.

As for Tark, who saw the mason almost every day, he observed no change in Nooma's manner towards him.

Soon after the birth of the little girl, whom they had called Pia, he had visited Katesh.

"Does he know?" he had asked.

She shook her head. "I do not think so."

"Does he show any anger towards you?"

She shrugged. "He is away at the henge so much. He has never spoken to me of it."

Tark considered. "He has given me no sign either," he remarked, marvelling at the simplicity of the mason.

As the months had passed, Nooma had still seen little of his wife, and Tark had seen him several times with slave girls; but he attached no special significance to this. No doubt the mason was seeking variety.

Several times he returned to Katesh, but each time she was reserved towards him.

"What we did must be over now," she told him. "I have forgotten."

He saw that she was lying and saw the effort it cost her. Despite the neglect of the mason, she was now determined to remain faithful to him.

"The gods punish me," she said simply. "I have deserved it."

When Nooma was at home, though he paid only perfunctory attention to his wife, he found to his surprise that he delighted to watch Noo-ma-ti playing with little Pia, and he would often take them both in his arms and carry them round the hut in triumph while they shouted with joy. Although she was not his, he took a special pleasure in the fact that little Pia adored him and would often sit staring at him fascinated, with her large round eyes.

Often now, Dluc came to look at his work, to make sure for himself that the new Stonehenge would be completed on time, and Krona too now emerged from his seclusion to inspect the temple.

As the spring progressed, Menona grew larger.

Though they looked forward to the birth of Krona's child, neither the High Priest nor the chief had forgotten the instructions of the gods set out in the auguries, that his first born was to be given to the gods.

"The auguries must be obeyed in every detail," Dluc reminded his priests.

But Krona showed no alarm at this. "I feel a young man again," he told the priest. "I think I shall have many sons before I die."

Before the winter was over, to the delight of all Sarum, he several times went hunting in the woods again.

Under Nooma's ceaseless care, the last of the huge sarsens were made ready. By the end of spring, all the uprights were in place, with only five lintels remaining to be finished and lifted into place; and it was announced that as soon as the work was completed, a great feast would be held for all the labourers.

The dedication of the temple was to be an impressive and solemn affair. Already, pilgrims from all over the island were approaching the sacred high ground along the chalk ridges. For the dedication of a new temple, not only a huge sacrifice of animals was called for in the sacred sayings of the priests, but an impressive human sacrifice as well.

"The great sacrifice is necessary," Dluc reminded the priests, "to show the gods we honour them. Nineteen shall be sacrificed: one for each year of the sacred moonswing." And the priests were told to consider carefully who they should be.

There was less than a month to go before the summer solstice and for Nooma the mason, the completion of the henge and the realisation of all his plans was now rapidly approaching.

"Less than a month," he told himself, "and all will be accomplished."

The two remaining tasks were simple enough. It was necessary only to scoop out the two sockets on the underside of each lintel, into which the tendon joints on the uprights would fit, and to raise them on the scaffolding. He enjoyed this operation, delighting in its simple efficiency and precision. The construction of the scaffolding was straightforward, and when fastened with ropes it was strong. The only moment requiring delicate handling was when the heavy lintel was carefully levered across from the scaffolding on to the uprights and slotted into position. He took a particular pride in the skill with which this was done, always supervising this operation in person.

One evening in the late spring, after his men had left the henge, Nooma lingered as he often did, to watch the priests begin their nightly vigil under the stars. It was a fine night, although the moon had not yet risen, and the few priests already there took no notice of him. Quietly the diligent mason checked on the work that had been done, even climbing the scaffolding and spending some time on his final check, adjusting a rope here and there, making sure that everything was exactly as he required it.

When he had finished, and he gazed at the silent grey temple around him, so nearly perfect, he spoke a single prayer aloud to the sun god.

"Great sun, let the work of your servant Nooma, who had laboured so hard, be completed perfectly."

And with that he returned home contented.

It was the following morning that Nooma had to meet Tark at the henge to discuss the arrangements for the great feast that was soon to take place. Over a thousand people would be fed on a broad stretch of open ground on the riverbank in the valley about a mile from the henge and there were many matters to organise.

It was just as the two men were deep in conversation at one side of the henge that a call from the masons told Nooma that his men were about to lever a lintel across from the scaffolding into its final position. Still talking to Tark, and paying no very close attention to the workers, Nooma waddled across, with the riverman loping beside him, and took up his normal station on the ground directly underneath the lintel, to supervise the delicate task. Tark, beside him, noticed with admiration the expert way in which the huge stone was slowly moved out to the edge of the scaffolding and across the narrow gap on to the uprights. He was so busy watching that at first he did not hear what the mason was saying.

Then he did, and gazed down at him in amazement. The absurd little fellow's normally solemn face was contorted into a mask of rage and hatred such as he would not have believed possible. Between his teeth he hissed:

"You lie with my wife, riverman! You gave her the child! Do you expect that I will forgive?"

He stared at Nooma in surprise. He did not think the mason had realised. But as he did so, it was now Tark who blanched: for as he looked into the transformed face of the mason, he understood the meaning of his words, and for the first time in many years, the riverman was afraid. Never had he seen anger so absolute, so condensed as now, to his astonishment, he saw in the eyes of his strange little friend.

And at that moment he knew that Nooma was going to kill him.

How it happened that one side of the scaffolding suddenly collapsed that morning, no one could ever explain.

Tark the riverman, who happened to be standing underneath and had just opened his mouth to say something, had hardly even time to look up as the four tons of the stone lintel that was being moved tipped off the edge of the scaffolding, struck the side of the uprights and crashed down upon him, striking his head and crushing the life out of him immediately.

No one had noticed anything amiss with the scaffolding. All eyes, until the moment when it collapsed, had been on the delicately balanced lintel. Two of the workers on it had fallen too. One broke his collarbone, the other a leg. But Nooma, who had been directly under the lintel, by a miracle of luck, managed to throw himself to one side and escaped with only bruises.

Two days later the lintel was successfully raised into place.

The priests made no comment on the accident. Nooma hoped that they had not guessed the truth.

When Nooma described the accident to Katesh, he saw her grow pale; her lips quivered; for a moment she seemed to stagger, reaching out for something to support her. And then she stood silently, looking at the ground.

"It is only by the will of the gods that I was not killed myself," he said.

Katesh did not seem to hear. But Nooma could see that she was holding back her tears; and the little mason secretly rejoiced.

Then suddenly, Katesh looked up, and her large dark eyes looked straight into his. She did not try to hide her secret; she let her little husband see the pain in her eyes. With complete honesty, for the first time in their lives together, their eyes met; and Katesh saw, as she thought she had heard, triumph in his expression. It was at that moment she knew with absolute certainty what the mason had done.

And Nooma, in his triumph, saw in his wife's eyes the naked soul of a woman who has lost her lover, and for a moment, in his way, he felt ashamed. But then the mason saw the expression in his wife's eyes change from one of pain to hatred and contempt. It was only for an instant, before she lowered them; but in those moments the marriage of Nooma and his wife achieved, for the only time, complete honesty, and at the same time ended.

In the following days, Katesh moved about the hut quietly. She fed her husband and did all that a wife should: but as if he was a stranger. They neither spoke unnecessarily, nor approached each other.

Though Nooma had assumed that nothing could now go wrong at the henge, he was mistaken. Three days after the death of Tark, as he was inspecting the last of the lintels to be raised, he suddenly noticed that something was amiss. The socket on the underside was in the wrong place. He stared at it in astonishment. It was too far towards the centre by the span of a man's head. This was a serious matter. Not only would a new hole have to be quickly made, but the lintel was no longer perfect, as every stone on the sacred henge should be. Had there been any time, it should have been replaced. But there were only days until the solstice. It was impossible to do anything.

How had this happened, he demanded angrily? Someone, it seemed, had made a careless scratch mark on the stone and one of the younger masons, seeing this, had assumed that it marked the spot where the hole should go. Before anyone knew what had happened, it had been hollowed out. It was a simple, and foolish mistake. But it was Nooma's fault that it had occurred.

The hole would be just visible from beneath the completed arch. He could not, even if he wanted to, hide it from the priests. Miserably, he had to report the matter.

"I cannot make a new stone in time," he ruefully explained.

The priest inspecting it gave him a cold stare that made him tremble.

"The mistake must be invisible," he said. "And the stone must be put in place."

The mason prepared a plug of clay and filled the hole; and across the plug he placed a disc of grey stone that he made from chippings; and when he had done this, his work was so good that no one but himself could even find the place where the mistake had been made. But the lintel was no longer perfect: the henge contained a tiny flaw; when he thought of this news reaching the High Priest, he shook. Neither the priests, nor the gods, would be able to forgive this.

"They will sacrifice me to the sun," he muttered sadly. "After all, that is how it will end."

However, the lintel was raised into place, and with five days to spare before the all-important solstice, the new Stonehenge was complete.

Half proud, half terrified, at the feast for the labourers held by the river the following night, Nooma drank himself to sleep.

But the next morning, one thought kept coming to his mind: "I have killed a man; I have made an error in the building of the sacred henge. Nothing is hidden from the priests: they will destroy me."

It was nearly dawn. The moon was still high.

As Dluc the High Priest surveyed the new temple that the mason had built, he experienced a profound emotion.

"It is complete," he murmured. For it seemed to him that not only the building itself, not only a cycle of the sun and moon were now completed, but also that the terrible journey along which the people of Sarum had passed had now reached its completion, which the perfect circle of stones symbolised. Sun and moon, day and night, winter and summer, the spring time and the harvest: all these things seemed to him to be contained in the henge: all Sarum's life and all its destiny lay in the stones that recorded the endless procession of the days and the harmony of the heavens.

It was five days before the solstice, and, that day, as he always had in times gone by, Chief Krona was to hunt the boar.

As dawn approached, Dluc called his litter, and gave the runners their orders.

It was the custom that before the hunt, he would perform the ritual asking the moon goddess to bless the huntsmen, and so, soon after dawn, he arrived in the broad clearing which lay at the foot of the escarpment by the entrance to the eastern valley, where the hunters were meeting.

Ah, the beauty of it! When he saw them, he too felt young again. There were fifty hunters, in their thick leather jerkins, carrying bows, heavy quivers of arrows and the short, heavy spears with flint tips that were used for hunting the boar. They were standing in groups, joking together. Krona was in the centre of it all, just as he used to be: tall and impressive, with his flowing beard, all white now, and wearing the jaunty headdress with long green feathers stuck in it that he favoured for hunting. His harsh laugh rang round the clearing, as he jested easily with the huntsmen. Beside him rested the light litter made of pine, and carried by four sure-footed runners, which would carry him over the ground while the other men walked or ran beside him. He wore a short green cloak and in his belt was a magnificent hunting knife made of flint. This was Krona the chief as he truly was: how his brother the priest rejoiced to see him like that once more!

The men were delighted to be hunting with the chief again. Old Muna the chief huntsman, his hair grizzled and his face now very red, with his stocky figure in its crimson and black tunic, was everywhere. On his head he wore the small set of antlers that were his badge of office, and in his hand he held a hunting horn decorated with bronze and gold. He was cheerfully directing the men who handled the hounds – eight couples of the sleek, swift hunting dogs, who could follow a scent all day, and whose excited pants sent steam into the cold morning air. With Muna was his grandson, a wide-eyed boy of ten. It was the boy's first hunt.

"Krona has promised that he will blood this boy himself if we kill today," the old man grinned. Hearing this, the chief turned.

Krona looked at the boy's eager face and remembered how, at his age, his own father, following the ancient custom, had lifted a portion of the dead animal when he was in at his first kill, and wiped the blood across his cheek. He had carefully kept that mark on his face for a month, for it had been the first mark of his manhood. "You'll be blooded," he laughed.

Then Krona called for silence, and the High Priest spoke the simple, ancient words of the hunting ritual:

"Moon goddess, who watches over all hunters, to whom the spirits of all dead animals belong, watch over us and give us good hunting today."

Muna gave a short blast on his horn, Krona stepped into his litter, and the whole party moved off through the woods, up the eastern valley.

That was how afterwards, the High Priest liked to remember Krona – a gallant figure, a great chief, hunting the woods at Sarum.

They brought him back that night.

Although the Sarum huntsmen believed that their method of hunting the boar was the best, it had several disadvantages. If the boar deceived the hunters, he could easily kill one of them; and if the boar was driven according to plan, then the chief was always exposed to the animal's charge. But Krona in particular favoured this Sarum method. The procedure was that when the hounds seemed to have cornered the boar, usually in a thicket, the hunters would fan out in a long line and make a slow encircling movement. Then, when the circle was closed, those behind the boar would advance through the wood, making as much noise as possible and driving the boar out of his hiding place towards the centre where the chief, surrounded by the best hunters would be waiting. Using this method, Krona saw many fine kills take place before him; but those driving the boar took a terrible risk if the boar should turn on them with his flashing tusks, and there was always the risk that one day the boar would break through Krona's hunters and gore the chief himself.

He was still alive when they brought his body into the valley that evening.

The hunt had gone according to plan: the boar had been driven towards the place where Krona waited, had hurled itself across the clearing, where the hunters waited. But then the disaster had taken place. Whether because they were out of practice or whether because the boar was more cunning than most, the ferocious animal had broken straight through the line of hunters and burst upon Krona himself before getting away. There were terrible wounds in the chief's stomach where the beast's tusks had ripped him open, tearing the flesh to shreds. He had lost much blood and he was already a pale grey colour. When Dluc saw him, he thought he would die that night.

The High Priest did what he could for the friend of his youth: for that is how Krona now seemed to him – neither the great chief of Sarum, nor the monster who sacrificed the nineteen girls in those darkest days; but his friend, wounded and in pain. He bound up his wounds; he helped him drink a little of a broth he made with herbs, and with Menona he tended him through the night.

Krona lay dying. He knew it. His wounds were deep and already beginning to fester – they were far beyond any medicine, or even the High Priest's prayers.

And now began the last, and the hardest of all the trials sent to Sarum by the gods.

For neither man had forgotten the promise that had been made when they first began work on the new Stonehenge. Krona's first born child was to be given to the gods for a sacrifice; and in return, the auguries had claimed, he was to be given a second, who would be his heir.

The High Priest pondered: the auguries had been clear – and had they not foretold everything, so far, exactly as it had happened? Yet it was obvious, beyond all doubt, that the chief could never father another child. If he kept his promise to the gods, then the house of Krona would end, the new temple would have been built in vain, and in return for their faith it seemed that the gods would visit upon them and upon Sarum the punishment of death and darkness. But why?

Dluc hesitated. He was not sure what to do or what to say. Finally, when the two men were alone, it was Krona who spoke.

"You cannot sacrifice the child." It was no more than a whisper, but it went straight to the priest's heart. He was silent. He could not look at the chief.

"The child is all we have," Krona said softly. It was true. But still Dluc could not answer. Painfully the chief raised himself on his elbow and stared at him intently. "Promise me," he whispered, "you will not give the child to the gods."

Dluc almost wept. But he was the High Priest, and he knew what must be done. Had he not sworn to Sun himself. "Never again, never will I doubt?"

"The gods must be obeyed," he said.

"Save my child, priest!" the chief cried out in agony, before falling back.

Dluc thought of the nineteen girls that he had sacrificed without mercy; now it seemed that the gods had ordained he too should suffer pain. But what did it all mean? He did not know, but he knew what he must say.

"We cannot question the gods," he replied.

Did he believe that the gods would keep their promise at that moment? Did he, the High Priest, trust them this time?

For a moment he thought Krona would burst out with rage, but then he saw that the chief no longer had the strength. Instead, he did what was harder to bear: he reasoned with him.

Gently, patiently, as a friend, Krona explained to the priest why he must not do this terrible thing. "My firstborn were already given to the gods when my sons were drowned," he said, "you priests have misunderstood the auguries." He assailed him with every argument; he told Dluc that he must not destroy Sarum, reminded him of the chaos that would follow if he died without an heir. His reasoning was perfect. But it was useless.

"The gods must be obeyed," Dluc told him. "We must trust them and they will not desert us." But Krona only shook his head.

The day wore on and neither the High Priest nor Krona would give way. With an incredible strength of will, he held on to life, sometimes reasoning with the priest, at other times abusing him. Once he even threatened his life. But he knew by then that he was powerless; in this matter no one, not even his servants, would dare to question the will of the High Priest.

It was while they continued this grim argument, that Menona went into labour. She had been shocked by the sight of Krona's wounds, and that evening, quite suddenly, she began. She was almost a month early. They took her to a small chamber at the back of the house, where two women skilled in childbirth looked after her.

Now Krona became desperate. As the sun set and the tapers were lit, he pleaded with the priest again and again, crying out in agony so great that Dluc feared it would kill him:

"Priest, I am dying. Save my child!"

Dluc wept. He turned his face away because he could not look at Krona. He trembled. But still he held firm. And at last, in the middle of the night, he heard the cry of the newborn child, and strode out of the room.

It was only then, at the end of his last trial, that Dluc came to understand the beauty, the perfect symmetry of the workings of the gods. For the sight that greeted his eyes was so wonderful that it made him cry out for joy.

In their hands the women held not one, but two children that the golden-haired girl had given to Sarum: a boy and a girl. Although premature, both were healthy. Menona was smiling weakly.

"Give me the first born," the priest severely commanded; and, as he knew they would, they handed him the baby girl. "To the gods, we have promised the first born," he cried. "And now Sarum has an heir."

It was the eve of the solstice.

Before the festival of the dedication could be celebrated, there was for the people of Sarum one terrible day that must be gone through.

The family of Nooma the mason rose at dawn, and, looking at each other apprehensively, sat by their hut in the valley.

For on this day, all Sarum knew, the nineteen sacrificial victims were to be chosen; and the people trembled as little parties of priests solemnly went from farm to farm, from the valleys to the harbour, pointing the ceremonial bronze knife at their victims and leading them away. There was no way of guessing whom the priests would choose. Sometimes it was a malefactor, or someone who had rashly offended them; but it was just as likely to be a blameless labourer, or a rich farmer's daughter. No one of either sex, of any age or from any family was immune. For the priests were too wise to let any man or woman think that he or she could escape the absolute rule of the sun god or his chosen priests.

As Nooma and his family waited in their hut, he was very much afraid. His mind was troubled by several things. There was the imperfect lintel that he should never have allowed to happen. Would the priests forgive that? Surely not. And the murder of Tark. Had the priests guessed? The mason wiped his head and found that there were beads of perspiration there. Of course they knew. It was foolish to think for a moment that there was anything that could be hidden from them.

"I think they will come for me," he finally whispered aloud.

Katesh looked at the little fellow in surprise.

"For the builder of the henge?" She shrugged. "I do not think so."

Nooma said nothing. He did not share her confidence. Would Katesh mind if he were chosen, he suddenly wondered? Probably not. Then, fearfully, he looked at the children. The ways of the priests were inscrutable. What if, to punish him, they chose one of them? There would be children amongst the victims: you could be sure of that. He realised the sorrow he would feel if they took little Pia, who even then was staring up at him with her large, trusting eyes.

And as for Noo-ma-ti . . .

"If they will only take me, and not the boy," he silently prayed.

The day wore on, in silence. The sun began to sink.

"They will not come here at all," Katesh stated. And the mason began to think that, after all, she was correct.

They came. Two priests, one young, one old, walking slowly down the path towards the hut, just as the shadows from the nearby trees were lengthening towards them. When they reached the hut, where the little family now stood trembling before them, the young priest took out a long, thin bronze knife and handed it silently to the older, who pointed it.

As he did so, and the mason saw that it pointed at his little son, he cried out: "No! Take me! I have murdered! I have defiled the temple! I should die!" And he threw himself forward.

But the young priest was shaking his head. And, confused, Nooma turned and saw his mistake: for the knife was not pointing at Noo-ma-ti at all, but at Katesh, who was standing immediately behind the boy, and whose large eyes were now staring at the young priest in disbelief.

"It is the will of the gods," the young priest said.

Then Nooma knew that the priests were all-seeing and that their rule, though cruel, had a terrible justice.

The ceremonies began at dusk.

Already, nearly four thousand people were gathered on the slopes surrounding the henge. In the place of honour, where Krona himself should have been standing, two chosen men stood, one bearing the chief's breastplate, chased with gold, the other holding his ceremonial mace with its zig-zag decoration of amber set in gold.

As the sun sank towards the horizon, the priests arrived: a long procession of them followed by the party in charge of those who were to be sacrificed. They made their way slowly to the entrance of the avenue, where they waited for the sun to set.

The priests, except for Dluc himself, were dressed in white, and the crimson rays of the evening sun caught their robes.

On this greatest of days, the High Priest was dressed in a magnificent robe of red and white, sparkling with precious stones. His long face was painted white. On his head he wore the tall headdress of bronze decorated with a golden disc that flashed in the sunlight, and in his hand everyone could see the long staff, with its shining top shaped in the form of a swan. Taller by far than all those around him, he was an awesome figure.

The sun departed, dusk fell, and the crowd prepared for the silent vigil that would last through this shortest night of the year. Shortly after dark, the full moon slowly rose.

Nooma the mason stared across at the great henge, his life's work. The perfect circle of grey stones stood in the eye of the henge bathed in the pure white light of the moon, and casting huge shadows that slowly altered their shape and revolved as the night passed. Between the stones he could see the innermost sanctum, the semi circle of trilithons, and the terrifying slab of the altar stone. Of all that had happened to him, he wondered, had anything been of significance except this huge, demanding, temple of stone? Truly the power of the priests was terrible he thought, and silently he put one arm round his son and held Pia close – knowing that both children must grow up in the shadow of the henge.

Slowly the night passed.

At the first, just perceptible lightening of the eastern horizon, the priests began a slow, monotonous chant; then they began to move at a stately pace, up the six hundred yards of the avenue towards the circle of stone. In the faint half light Nooma peered to try to see the sacrificial victims, but he could not. He tightened his grip upon the children.

"Your mother is lucky," he told them. "She is to be given as a special gift to the gods." Pia's large eyes gazed at him, uncomprehending; but Noo-ma-ti, who half understood what was passing, began to sob.

For his part, the mason felt no emotion. The rule of the priests and of their henge was too awesome, at such moments, to leave men time for their own emotions. He shifted his weight from foot to foot.

In the east, above the horizon – the sky was beginning to glimmer.

And in the centre of the henge, still and silent as a stone, the gaunt figure of Dluc the High Priest waited by the altar stone.

Just before the procession had started to move up the avenue, they had brought him word that Krona had died. Soon he would lie in a great white tomb on the high ground, his spirit at rest. The High Priest was glad that the chief had found release. It was fitting that Krona should have passed to the next world to walk with the spirits at this moment of renewal.

For as the new henge waited for the sun god to show his face, the High Priest realised that it was only now that he himself had understood the importance of all that had passed since the death of Krona's sons.

For how was it that the sacred sayings of the priests began? What were the opening words – before the long history of Sarum; before the story of the great flood that cut off the path to the east and made the land an island; before the endless catalogue of all the observed motions of the heavenly bodies, that took the novices two years to learn; before the recital and explanation of the mystic numbers: what were the all important words that preceded it all?

Sun rules the skies.
Sun gives; Sun takes away;
Nothing that is
Is so by chance.

That was the meaning of the new henge; that was the meaning of the stones, of the nineteen girls that Krona killed, of the nineteen years of the sacred moonswing and the perfect opposition of sun and moon which he was about to witness. That was why the henge was perfect, fitted together in a perfect circle, indestructible. That was why a new heir had been born out of the suffering of Krona and his people. Had he dared to doubt?

Nothing takes place by chance. The purposes of the gods may be hidden, but they are absolute, perfect in their terrible symmetry and order; and as fixed as the stars. This was what Dluc now understood as even he had never understood before.

And for men on earth, there was only one course: obedience. This was the message of the curse that had fallen upon Sarum, of the death of the chief and his sons. This was the message of the sacrifices.

Men build to honour the gods. And men may try to measure the heavens. But that is all. They may not question: they must obey.

It was almost sunrise. Drops of dew had formed on the High Priest's robes.

Soon the great moment was coming.

As the sky lightened, it could be seen that the full moon had moved to a point a little above the western horizon, and exactly opposite the avenue. In the east now, as the sky above started to turn to a deep, luminous blue, the horizon line began to shimmer with light, first a thin, silvery line, then a crimson and saffron gleam. The chant of the priests grew louder. The crowd grew tense. The horizon began to glow; and now the whole east was turning to magenta, turquoise, azure, and the horizon was throbbing. Opposite, the moon was just above the ridges.

It came, the rim of the sun god, the first flash of his burning rays that struck like an arrow along the avenue to the heart of the henge. At that same instant, the chanting stopped, and the terrible silence that followed was broken only by the faint sound, within the henge, of the first victim being dropped on to the altar stone.

Dluc stared into the face of the sun. Slowly he raised Krona's first-born child, in both his hands, high over his head, showing her to the god and cried:

Greatest of all gods, Sun,
Great Moon,
Your servants obey.

At the new Stonehenge, the sun god came to his kingdom; his huge, golden orb, pulsating with light, rose over the horizon into the turquoise sky. And opposite, for long, silent minutes, the silver orb of the moon hung facing him, in perfect opposition across the perfect circle of the henge, before dipping below the horizon. Sun god and moon goddess had shown their faces to the people.

As the victims were placed on the altar stone in rapid succession, Nooma strained to see them. The seventh was Katesh. He saw her pale body being held by two priests, saw it hit the stone and arch in horror as the bloody knife of the priest rose, flashed in the sun, and fell.

Dluc the High Priest never discovered how to predict an eclipse of the sun.

Sorviodunum

SOME TWO THOUSAND years after the building of the sarsen circle at
Stonehenge, in A.D. 42, the most powerful man in the world had never
heard of Sarum or its temple of stone.

The dominions of the Emperor Claudius, ruler of the mighty Roman
Empire, extended from Persia in the east to Spain in the west; from Africa
in the south to France and parts of Germany in the north. The
Mediterranean Sea was his private lake and few men in the whole course
of human history have ever wielded greater earthly power.

Despite his great empire, and his many talents as a scholar and a ruler,
Claudius was considered something of a joke. He was lame, he stuttered,
and though he came from a family which over centuries had provided
many great generals, he himself had no victories to his name.

This was the situation, in the year 42, that he proposed to change.

It surprised nobody that he chose Britain. After all, everyone in Rome
knew that it was time that the distant island in the north was brought into
the civilised world.

Julius Caesar had led an expedition there a century before; and only
three years ago, the previous emperor, Claudius's nephew Caligula, had
prepared a great invasion of the island, which had never taken place.

He would undertake the conquest himself, he announced, thereby
completing what his illustrious ancestor Julius Caesar began.

Julius Caesar's detailed account of his doings on the island in 55 and 54
B.C. were well known – although there were still a few diehard wits in
Rome who insisted that the island did not in fact exist and that Caesar had
invented the place. It pleased Claudius to link his own name in this way
with that of the greatest commander Rome had ever known.

"But apart from Caesar's writings, almost nothing is known about the
island," his commanders complained.

Nonsense, the scholar emperor had told them, a great deal was known.

This was an overstatement; but it was true that for centuries accounts of
the island had been written, usually by Greek merchants, who had
journeyed to the land of mists across the sea; and only a few years before,
his own kinsman – the old Emperor Tiberius – had commissioned the
great geographer Strabo to prepare a treatise on its trade. Britain, it
seemed, was rich. The merchants of Gaul bought quantities of corn,
hides, cattle and the island's famous hunting dogs from their British
counterparts. The country contained minerals: gold and silver, iron, lead
and tin. The tin Claudius could not at present use: for at this time the

province of Iberia was already producing more tin than Rome could use and to keep the Iberians quiet, the empire had already been forced to make their tin mining a protected industry. But the gold and lead, if they could be found, would be useful.

The reports of the merchants were still more encouraging. "The islanders are always quarrelling amongst themselves," they stated. "They make it a point of honour to fight. And afterwards," they laughed, "we hurry across and the winners sell us many fine slaves."

The Britons bought many Roman luxuries, they explained, and in particular wine from the Mediterranean to supplement the beer and mead they had made for themselves since ancient times. "Some of them have even minted gold coins," they said; and they were able to show examples, struck for a British king in the east, that was a very passable imitation of one of the imperial sesterces.

What were their ports and landing places? Claudius and his advisers wanted to know. On this subject the merchants could give detailed information. It seemed there were many, and particular attention was paid to those nearest the coast of Gaul, at the Dover Straits; but they knew about many others too. There was one in particular which lay half way along the south coast – a great trading emporium with a shallow natural harbour protected from the sea by a low hill. "It is fortified; but the harbour is splendid for landing troops," they reported. "We sell a huge quantity of wine there, and they pay us in their own coin of silver and gold."

But Claudius was not interested. He already knew that his armies would land at the narrow straits opposite Gaul, far from this port. He never discovered that there was a place twenty-five miles north of this wonderful harbour, a magical place where five rivers met.

The emperor was satisfied with what he learned.

"I am sure," he could tell any doubtful senators, "that once Britain is part of the empire, it will pay for itself." That, after all, was what mattered most.

There were other considerations too, which a wise ruler could not ignore.

For the obscure island had become something of a trouble spot. Many of the islanders were Celtic tribesmen like the people of Gaul; and when Caesar had conquered Gaul in the previous century, some of those who had fought most fiercely with him, members of the so-called Belgic tribes – half German and half Celtic – had finally decamped to Britain with their loathsome priesthood – the Druids – whence they frequently sent raiding parties over to the mainland, and this had become a major irritation to the empire.

When Rome conquered Britain, it could not only stop these tiresome raids on Gaul but it could also exterminate, once and for all, these Druids who were such an abomination to the gods.

In its early days at least, the Roman Empire tolerated most religions. But the Druids were an exception, and Claudius had a particular loathing for these Celtic priests because they practised human sacrifice. It was not that any right-thinking Roman objected to the shedding of human blood:

that was done in the public theatres every day. But the Druids' human sacrifices seemed to Claudius, who loved Roman tradition, nothing less than an obscene and disgusting mockery of the proper Roman sacrifices of animals – the ancient and sacred art of the *haruspices*, who divined the future by inspecting the entrails of the animals they killed. Had he not himself spent vast sums on encouraging this noble pursuit, and awarded scholarships to young diviners? These Druids encouraged the raiders on Gaul, and defiled the earth with their filthy abominations. He would know how to deal with them.

He pressed ahead with urgency, pushing the military suppliers to their limits.

"The conquest could be accomplished another year," suggested some harassed officials. But Claudius shook his head.

He had a good reason for his haste. For when Caligula had prepared the expedition that turned into such a fiasco, he had pulled together four of Rome's powerful legions. This army had been disbanded, but two of the legions were still kicking their heels on the banks of the river Rhine. No emperor who valued the purple or his life, ever left two well-armed legions close to home with nothing to do. They had an uncomfortable habit of growing bored, and proclaiming a new emperor. The invasion must proceed at once.

In A.D. 42 therefore, the conquest of Britain was almost inevitable. And if there was any remaining doubt about the matter, the islanders destroyed it themselves.

Every few years, in the course of their frequent quarrels, one of the colourful and big moustachioed island chiefs would send an appeal to Rome for help against his neighbour, offering payment in return. Sometimes they even left the island and came to plead their cause. Claudius had seen one of them in Rome; he had been fascinated and amused by the man's incredible garrulity and obvious disingenuousness. But they were never taken seriously; Rome saw many rulers from every corner of the known world and knew who must be listened to and who could be ignored. But recently a certain British king, Verica, friendly to Rome, had been driven out of his kingdom by a new and unruly chief of the tribe of the Catuvellauni called Caractacus, and Verica had fled to Rome for sanctuary. In an act of consummate foolishness, bold Caractacus sent a message demanding his extradition, and when Claudius had properly ignored it, Caractacus sent a raiding party to the coast of Gaul.

It was an insult. Claudius could hardly believe his luck. To anyone who still doubted the wisdom of the expedition he could now protest, with righteous indignation: "Rome has been insulted!" It always worked.

He selected his generals carefully. For when he chose for himself, instead of letting his wife do it, Claudius was a brilliant picker of men; and he announced that he would go over the sea in person to be present at the victory.

"When the Britons see me," he declared, "they will be struck dumb with fear and amazement." When his courtiers looked surprised, he explained: "I shall ride an elephant."

[143]

In order to understand the events that were now about to take place in the distant island in the north, it is necessary first to go back some way in time.

For around 1300 B.C., a new and extraordinary people entered the story of the western world.

They began their epic voyage through history very quietly: archaeologists have identified them at this early date as a minor community of farmers living in obscurity on the banks of the great river Danube in the heart of south-eastern Europe. Whether these insignificant folk constituted a tribe it is hard to say: they were certainly not a race; and although in later times they would idealise themselves in the figures of the tall, fair-haired, and blue-eyed warriors of legend, it would probably be more accurate to say that, in common with most of the peoples of Europe, they were of mixed colouring and type. In these early days of their great wandering, we can identify them only by their unusual practice of cremating their dead and burying them in urns.

Something made these obscure farmers restless. In tiny numbers, they began to wander over the huge expanses of Europe, putting down new settlements. Archaeologists have found their modest urnfield cemeteries nestling in the foothills of the Swiss Alps, in the gentle valleys of Champagne and on the plains of Germany. In these early days, they seem to have come peacefully, sometimes merging with existing settlements, at other times dwelling apart in isolation, but always cremating their dead and burying them in urns. And wherever they lived, they seem to have become the most important community.

The destiny of these strange folk was to be remarkable: they were to dominate much of northern Europe, to create a great culture, to be subjugated by Rome in body but never in spirit; to flee the Saxons but also to evade them, and to survive intact to the present day and once again carry their astonishing gifts of spirit and imagination all over the globe. It was at some point in the centuries before Christ that they came to the notice of the Greeks, who gave them a name: Keltoi. The Romans later took over the Greek word to describe them and it has remained unchanged to the present day: they were the Celts.

Why did they make such an impression? What was so remarkable about them? We can only say: their genius. Nothing showed that genius better than the extraordinary language they used, which was adopted wherever they settled and which became, by Julius Caesar's time, the lingua franca of all northern Europe. The Celtic language was rich; it was poetic, mystical, impassioned. With this language they created their legends, their visions and their epic tales which have passed down the centuries to present times. The Celtic language has never been destroyed and it survives intact today chiefly in the two variants of Welsh and Irish Gaelic.

It was about 1000 B.C. that a new and dramatic folk arose amongst the modest Celtic settlers. Perhaps another group joined them, or perhaps some urge already within their character was released, but suddenly there appeared on the face of history a new and seemingly unstoppable force: the Celtic warlords.

They were astonishing figures. Riding in wagons and chariots, with long moustaches flaring, their hair coated with lime so that it stood up like a headdress, wearing gorgeous collars of gold around their necks and bracelets on their arms, this new breed of warriors began to make their way west and north, to the shores of the English Channel and to the Iberian peninsula. Not only were these fiery nobles natural warriors, but they carried with them a new and terrible weapon so that when they approached the people cried out in terror:

"Here come the Celtic warlords with their long swords!"

The swords they wielded were not only long. They were made of a new metal, never before seen in northern Europe, and which had come to them from the east: it was heavy and tough, it had a fearsome cutting edge, and it could be tempered until it rang. It was iron.

Archaeologists have called this development the Hallstatt culture, naming it after an Austrian village where many remains of this warrior folk were found. With their iron swords, the Hallstatt Celts were almost invincible and became the earliest warriors of Celtic legend; few in number, they lived a life apart, rolling across the land in their wagons like gods; and when they died, these men of iron were not cremated, but buried with their chariots, wearing all their finery, as though bound for some further encounter in the after-life.

Fierce and warlike as they were however, these Celts were not destroyers. When they settled in a new land, they would build – depending on the local conditions – their modest thatched farmhouses, or, if times were troubled, well defended earthwork hillforts which were difficult to attack; if they found natives in the area, they usually left them alone, or used them as labourers. And it was in this manner that, between about 900 and 500 B.C. – the period of their greatest migration – the Celts crossed the narrow English Channel and settled in many parts of Britain.

There is no evidence to suggest that the Celts destroyed the ancient British settlements they found. They seem to have merged with them as time passed. In some parts of the island the Celts never arrived at all; and it is likely, though it cannot be proved, that there are Britons today who are almost entirely of the ancient pre-Celtic stock. But in most places where they came, the Celts settled in peace; and once again, as it had on other settlers, the island exerted its influence upon them. Separated from the rest of the world by the narrow sea, and her high chalk cliffs, the land of mists remained a magical place apart.

Then, from roughly 500 B.C. to the birth of Christ, came that great flowering of the Celts' astonishing civilisation which historians call the La Tene culture, after the great Celtic archaeological site of that name in France; it is in these centuries that the Celts of northern Europe and Britain created some of the richest and most fantastic treasures of the prehistoric world.

They made chariots, they made elaborate jewellery of gold, silver and bronze, they made pottery which they covered with swirling patterns, they made figures of animals in clay and metal which, with their extraordinary abstract quality, seem to possess an inner life of their own. They made tunics and cloaks for themselves of dazzling colours and they decked out their chariot horses with gorgeous caparisons. They made verses, endless verses, in their lyrical, mystical language, sung by bards to celebrate their ancient heroes and their gods. And they made gods. The Celtic world was full of gods: full of marvels, superstitions, magical birds and beasts. All men knew of the fierce, illogical and grimly humorous doings of the twilight world that existed, all the time, alongside the world of men; in the unlikely event that any Celt ever forgot the other world, there were always priests to remind them.

"These Celts are mad," the Romans said. "They eat like senators, they sing, they weep, and then they fight each other for pleasure."

"They are all poets: drunk with poetry," a merchant once explained.

"They are drunk with drink," came the cynical Roman reply. "And their Druid priests are disgusting."

All these statements were true. The fact was that the Romans could make nothing of the Celts. A good Roman loved systematic government, hierarchy, bureaucracy: the Celts had innumerable petty chiefs and kings, tied to each other by generations of blood vows and clientships so tangled that no logical Roman could ever make sense of them. Even their gods, like the great Dagda, the protector of the tribe, seemed to take pleasure in changing into unlikely shapes and playing tricks on mankind: not to satisfy their lusts and desires – this the Romans could have understood – but for no reason at all.

"We shall teach them to love order," the Romans said. But it was not easy.

It was Julius Caesar who first tried to tame the Celts, in Gaul. That brilliant opportunist saw the nature of the problem at once:

"We'll break up the petty kings and their clientships, replace them by magistrates," he decided. "The bigger ones we must either subdue or win over to our side by flattering them and making them rich. Then we'll educate their sons – turn them into Roman gentlemen. That always does the trick."

It was a wise policy, and to an extent it worked. But there were some who refused all blandishments. The group of tribes known as the Belgae, part Celtic, part Germanic, took to Roman culture, but refused Roman rule, and were driven across the sea. But as the years passed, the calculated Roman wooing converted many to the benefits of civilisation, both in the province of Gaul, and in the still unconquered island across the Channel. Though many Celtic tribes scorned Roman domination, their chiefs often knew the Roman merchants of Gaul who brought them the huge amphorae of wine, the gems and other luxuries they enjoyed. Ambitious rulers had heard – even if they could not quite imagine them – of the stupendous palaces of the imperial city; and they were envious. They had seen, too, the convenient written records the Roman merchants kept of their transactions, and though the Celts had no writing of their own, some of the more educated tribal chiefs could speak and even write a little Latin.

"The islanders will fight; but they'll come over to us," Claudius remarked. This was the belief of those planning the invasion. "Sooner or later these barbarians always do."

It was spring in A.D. 44, and the people of Sarum had been expecting the Romans for a month. The weather had been capricious: one day brilliant sunshine would make the chalk ridges shimmer and steam; the next, heavy grey clouds would scud over the entrance to the valley bringing an unexpected flurry of late snow or a sudden shower of hail. But today it was fine, with a warm damp wind blowing up from the south west in a clear blue sky.

They were well prepared: for the entire population had taken refuge in the dune.

In the two thousand years since the sarsens had been dragged to Stonehenge, the landscape around Sarum had not changed much. Woods of oak and ash, elm and hazel still graced the broad bowl of land where the five rivers met. To the north, the bare chalk ridges extended to the horizon and on the slopes above the valleys, fields of corn rustled in the breeze. But there were changes: sheep now grazed on the sacred precincts where the mellow grey stones of the henge, still standing in their magic circle, were seldom visited and showed many signs of disrepair. The barrows were overgrown with turf, and no new ones had been built for generations. And on the broad slopes where the farmers had sown their wheat, flax and barley for four thousand years, the land had now been more carefully divided than before, into a patchwork of small, neat rectangular fields, clearly demarcated by hedges, lynchets and earth banks. The fields were seldom bigger than two hundred feet long, and they were cross-ploughed.

Only one feature of the landscape had changed completely. The small wooded hill which stood guardian at the entrance to the valley had been completely transformed. It had been a promontory really, a natural hump jutting out from the high ground; but several centuries ago, the old promontory had been scraped bare and round the entire summit of some thirty acres, two massive banks of earth and chalk had been thrown up, with a deep ditch between them. The lightly wooded hill had been transformed into a bold, bare mound, rather unsightly, with a steep slope on every side. For the first, but not the last time in its history, Sarum hill had been turned into a regular fortress. It was a forbidding place to look at now, glaring white in the sun and dominating the landscape for miles around. The people of Sarum, using a Celtic term, called this fortress the dune.

The dune already had a chequered history. It had served as a fortress, a hill settlement, a cattle pound, a market – sometimes all at once; but in recent years it had been allowed to fall into disuse. When news came of the Roman landing, its ramparts were hastily repaired and resurfaced so that their sides, steeply packed with fresh chalk and clay, stared out bravely at the world. A new pair of gates, made of oak, were erected at the main entrance and buttressed by heavy wooden props in order to withstand any battering ram. Inside the dune, now partially restored to its former glory, a motley collection of buildings had appeared: round thatched houses, grainstores, sheep and cattle pens. Near the middle stood a well. The central focus of the dune, however, was a single pole standing near the well, twenty feet high, on the top of which was the carved head of Modron, the Celtic goddess of war, with her three ravens. Her angry face stared out blankly into space, defying all invaders. This was the community's battle standard and, according to the Druids, it made Sarum invincible.

The young man stood alone on the high wall of the dune and stared intently southwards.

"No news from Taradoc," he muttered. "But I know the Romans are near: I can feel it."

A few days ago he had sent the riverman down to the harbour with strict orders to return to Sarum and report as soon as the Romans got there. It was known that the Second Legion was moving swiftly along the south coast with instructions to destroy the hill forts of the west. They must have reached the river mouth by now, he thought, and once they did so, he was sure they would strike up river to Sarum. But Taradoc had not appeared.

"Where is the wretch?" the young man said irritably.

His eyes which scanned the country so anxiously, were blue; his figure was slight but well made, with a wispy light brown beard, a moustache, equally wispy, that he was encouraging to droop and curl up at the ends – for this was the fashion for a Celtic warrior – and a mouth that was a little too sensitive for the warrior's role he felt obliged to assume. He wore a linen tunic that reached to his knees and was gathered in at the waist by a broad leather belt from which hung a heavy iron sword. Over the tunic was a large, four cornered woollen cloak – the brat – dyed a brilliant blue and held in place at the front by a large bronze brooch. On his feet he had strong leather shoes. He had a certain air of authority, but he was young and he carried his authority somewhat anxiously; even so, if he was still uncertain of himself, something in his eyes suggested that he had a mind of his own.

The most striking part of his dress however, was not the bright cloak, nor the brooch, but a huge, heavy strip of gold he wore round his neck: it had been shaped into a ring and the free ends, which met at the front, were each fitted with a magnificent golden boss, carved in the shape of a boar's head. This was the torc, the most important ornament worn by any Celtic warrior: it was a badge of office and its huge size proclaimed that, despite his youth, this young man was the chief.

His name was Tosutigus. He was brave, but he was obstinate and he was ignorant; the fate of the dune, of Sarum, and of his family, now lay in his hands, and the plan that for many months he had carefully and secretly formed was about to cause the downfall of all three.

Tosutigus let his eyes travel along the parapet. The forces at his disposal consisted of a hundred men, six horses, an ancient chariot – for the war chariots were considered out of date nowadays – and a Druid. Since there was no question of this little garrison giving open battle to the Romans, the chariot would certainly remain unused. His men were armed with spears and arrows, both tipped with iron points, and he could rely on them to fight to the last man. But, like many of the Celts at that time, the defenders of Sarum had a still more effective weapon – which lay in the huge piles of smooth round pebbles that had been stacked every few yards along the parapet. These were the stones that the men, and some of the women, would fit into the long slings that they knew how to use so well. Swung round the head and released with the additional leverage of a fully stretched arm, the slings could hurl one of the pebbles with such force that it could drop a man stone dead at a hundred yards. In this type of fighting, the slingsmen worked so fast that their pebbles fell like a freak hailstorm, mowing their enemies down like grass.

As the people of Sarum waited to fight, and perhaps to die, they knew nothing about the plan that their young chief had pondered secretly for so long. But it was this plan which occupied all his thoughts now as he scanned the horizon for signs of the Romans, and which caused him to murmur:

"I'll make Sarum greater than it has ever been before; and my family shall be powerful kings again, as they were in ancient times."

His dynastic pride was well founded: no family on the island had an older claim to their territory. Five hundred years ago, had not his Celtic ancestor, Coolin the warrior, come riding down the great ridgeway from the north with his huge iron sword and his six faithful companions? Had they not halted at the entrance to the sacred temple of Stonehenge and there found Alana, last daughter of the house of Krona, whose noble ancestry stretched back into the mists of time? Heroic as the legend sounded, it was perfectly true; and the descendants of the union between the Celtic warlord and the last heiress of Sarum had continued to rule over a mixed population of Celtic and ancient island stock as the centuries passed. A further legend had also grown up, and had been encouraged by his family, that the first ancestors of Alana were giants who had carried the huge sarsens to the henge on their backs and built the temple in a single night. For the stones were known to be magic and the rulers of Sarum liked to remind their people that their ancestors were something more than ordinary men. Although the temple was seldom used now – for the Druid priests preferred to worship in smaller shrines or in clearings in the woods – the family still styled themselves in the ancient manner of the pre-Celtic house of Krona: lords of Sarum and guardians of the sacred henge.

But powerful they were not. Sarum had suffered many vicissitudes in the intervening centuries and by the time of Tosutigus's father it was little more than a backwater, a small settlement which the chance of history had left stranded, maintaining a precarious independence between the territories of several powerful tribes.

A century before, things had gone well. The great Belgic tribe of the Atrebates, who even had impressive sounding treaties of friendship and trade with the Roman Empire, had their stronghold to the north-east of Sarum; and the great-grandfather of Tosutigus had wisely married a princess of their royal house and secured their protection. Those had been splendid days at Sarum, when the dune was a small town, and the chief, secure in the patronage of the king of the Atrebates, held court there and hunted magnificently in the forests like his predecessors in ancient times. It was thanks to the princess of the Atrebates, also, that the ruling family at Sarum had learned to speak Latin. Even now, young Tosutigus spoke it haltingly, and was proud of his sophisticated accomplishment. But in later times, events had not turned out so well: the power of the Atrebates had waned; they were driven out of their lands; they could no longer protect Sarum, and in their place came other proud tribes, who knew nothing of the family at Sarum.

The new tribes in the east were of Belgic origin, like the Atrebates, but they were uncomfortable neighbours. As usual, the grandfather of Tosutigus, being pragmatic, had tried to secure the friendship of the nearest important tribe by offering one of their leading chiefs his only daughter in marriage. The Belgic chief had thanked him, forgotten to pay for her, and forgotten, it seemed, that Sarum existed. This at least was something to be thankful for, and for another generation the place where the five rivers met had known peace. But it was the peace of neglect and while other tribal centres grew more powerful, Sarum slowly declined.

Another generation passed, and now Tosutigus and his father were faced with another and still more dangerous problem to solve; this lay on the other side of their little stronghold, to the south west.

For in that direction lay one of the fiercest people that the Romans would ever encounter: the huge and mighty tribe of the Durotriges.

"The Durotriges in the south west will fight. They are proud and used to getting their own way," his spies warned Claudius. "They have never seen Roman arms," they explained, "and they think they cannot be defeated."

It was their hill forts that the proud Durotriges relied on: by comparison with many of these, the dune at Sarum, with its single set of walls, was puny. The great earthworks of Maiden Castle, Badbury Rings, Hod Hill and many others which are all standing to this day, covered dozens of acres; they had five, six or seven huge sets of ramparts and complex defended entrances where attackers could be trapped. The Durotriges held an enormous area in the south west of the island, including the shallow harbour, where they had fortified the hill.

The family at Sarum solved the problem in their usual way – by calculated submission.

"You must always be a loyal friend to the Durotriges," his father told him. "They hold the port, and that controls the river. If they choose, they can swallow you up like a bird swallowing a worm." And his father, following the custom of the Celtic tribes, swore an oath on his sword to fight for the king of the Durotriges whatever his cause. In so doing, he became his client, and gained some measure of protection for his petty dynasty. Sarum was left alone, to be held for the Durotrigan king as the most northerly outpost of his great chain of hill forts, and the family preserved their independence and some semblance of their dignity.

But then, a year ago, his father had died, leaving his untried young son with a proud name, but a precarious inheritance. There had been no choice, but to follow his father's policy, and only two months ago in Maiden Castle, he had knelt before the huge old man sitting on a deerskin, who was the king of the Durotriges, gazed into his fierce black eyes and sworn:

"When the Romans come, my lord, I will hold the dune at Sarum for you, to the last man."

Had the king any idea of the youth's real ambitions, he would either have laughed, or struck him dead on the spot. Instead he had turned to his council after the young man had departed and remarked cynically:

"The main Roman force will come south: they'll not trouble much with Sarum and if they take it, we can afford the loss. Let the legions come to Maiden Castle and Hod Hill – that's where we'll break their backs!"

And taking one of the bright gold coins that he had minted for himself he threw it high into the air.

"If my head is up, Sarum will stand; if down, it will fall," the huge man laughed. The coin tumbled on the grass and his counsellors gathered round to see which way it had fallen.

As Tosutigus gazed towards the south that spring morning, and considered his own plans, his thoughts were interrupted by the approach of three men whom he turned to greet politely.

The two brothers Numex and Balba were not twins, but they were close in age and so alike that it was laughable. Both were short and bow-legged, with round heads, red faces and pointed noses and though both were still in their thirties, they carried themselves with a quiet gravity that made them seem older. For numberless generations their family had always produced children with short thumbs and thick, stubby fingers who invariably became wonderful workmen. It was Numex who had made the new oak gates and carved the figure of the war goddess which stood at the centre of the dune; and it was Balba, a dyer of cloth, who had, by using a dye derived from the roots of the common buttercup, produced the brilliant blue of the young chief's cloak. Because of the dyes, which were dissolved in urine, Balba could usually be smelt even before he was seen, but his skill earned him such respect that men forgave him his pungent aroma. Both men wore tunics similar to Tosutigus's, but made of coarser cloth and they did not wear cloaks or gold ornaments. He had put these two reliable brothers in charge of the day to day running of the little camp and they had come to receive their orders.

The third figure was in stark contrast. Afleck the Druid was tall, impressive when seen at a distance, but ragged and somewhat disreputable when observed from close quarters. His brow was deeply furrowed, the lines seeming more deeply etched because they were full of dirt. Half his teeth were gone; his grey hair and long beard were filthy, as was the long brown robe that reached to his ankles. His feet were protected by open sandals with heavy leather thongs between the toes. Tosutigus had watched the Druid go down from the dune to the river at dawn that day. Taking off his sandals he had walked barefoot to a small wood where he had cut mistletoe, using a bronze knife. He had also collected herbs, moving carefully along the north side of the bushes as he did so – for the ritual of the Druids forbade the collection of herbs from any but the north side. After watching the river intently for some time, Aflek had then thrown gold dust on to the swollen waters and made his devotions to the gods before returning up the hill. The young chief eyed him cautiously.

"Well?"

"The goddess Modron has given me a sign. We shall be victorious," the old man said. "The gods protect Sarum."

Tosutigus said nothing. He knew that his ancestral lands were protected by many gods. The five rivers were protected by Sul, the healing goddess of springs; in the woods to the east there was a sacred oak tree beside which was the shrine of Cernunnos, the horned god of the forests who protected the hunting. Sometimes Cernunnos would go about in disguise, taking the form of an old man with a hood over his head: and if any man saw him then, he knew that he would have good luck all year. The fields were protected by the corn maiden, whose sacred rites were held at Samain, the great feast at the beginning of winter. And the chalk ridges were protected by Leucetius the god of lightning, who would strike dead any invader who dared to disturb the ancient tombs on the high ground. The henge, too, was protected by his own ancestors the ten giants, the greatest of whom had three heads which grew again if they were cut off. The dune was protected by Modron the war goddess with her ravens. His own family – were they not under the personal protection of great Nodens the cloudmaker, to whom they had built a shrine?

Sarum and its ruling family might have fallen from their former greatness, but they still had powerful allies amongst the gods.

Tosutigus still possessed, locked in a great oak chest, the huge iron sword of Coolin the Warrior. All Sarum knew that with this sword, centuries ago, the mighty Coolin had slain a chief from the north. Everyone knew the story of how he had then cut off his head and made the skull into a drinking cup; of how, the first time he had raised it to his lips the skull had righted itself and, in front of all his companions, had started to speak and had prophesied that as long as the family of Coolin dwelt there, Sarum would never be taken in battle.

With such protection, the people of Sarum believed, their dune was impregnable.

As Tosutigus contemplated these matters with a grim smile, he realised that the old man was still talking to him.

"You have the protection of the Druids as well," Aflek reminded him smugly. "There is nothing to fear."

The power of the Druids varied from tribe to tribe, depending upon the attitude of the ruler. The Belgae often favoured these priests because their secret network helped to stir up trouble for the Romans in Gaul. The

Durotriges also honoured the priests because they represented the Celtic gods in defiance of everything Roman. In other parts of the island, while the gods were worshipped, the Druids often had little power. Recently however, Tosutigus knew, Druid priests had travelled far and wide performing a flurry of ceremonies and sacrifices to the war gods to ensure that the Roman invasion would be beaten back. Until five years before, a community of Druids had worshipped at a sanctuary near Stonehenge, and his father had been obliged to support them. It had been costly and the Druids often complained about the meagre provisions they were given. Then they moved north west to a council of Druids that was held at the island of Anglesey, two hundred miles away, and to his family's relief they had never returned. Two months before, however, Aflek had arrived at Sarum from Maiden Castle; and the young chief had no doubt that he had been sent by the Durotriges as a spy.

Tosutigus did not reply to the Druid; for even as the old man spoke, his eye was caught by a flash of metal in the woods to the south. All four men had seen it, and all four now stared intently at the place from which it had come. Several minutes passed, and then they saw what they had awaited for so long – a column of Roman soldiers crossing a small patch of open ground two miles away.

At last. The moment had come. His plan was ready.

"Bar the gate," he said curtly to Numex: "When I give the order, everyone is to man the walls." The carpenter and his brother hurried away.

The Druid began to shout imprecations. "Modron, goddess of war, smite our enemy; Nodens the cloudmaker, protect your people!"

He seized the young chief by the arm.

"Modron will give you victory," he reassured him earnestly. "The gods will destroy these invaders."

But Tosutigus was paying him no attention.

"You Druids said they would never get across the sea," he muttered.

This was true. The year before, the Druids had sworn that the sea god would swallow up the Roman fleet before it ever reached the island's shores.

The young chief turned to face the older man.

"You must go now," he said calmly.

Aflek stared at him in astonishment.

"I will fight at your side, Tosutigus," he replied; for even if he had been sent as a spy, the elderly Druid was no coward.

But Tosutigus shook his head.

"If the Romans find you here, they will kill you," he stated. "Besides, I don't want you."

Aflek gazed at him uncomprehendingly. And then the young man revealed the plan that he had been secretly forming for so long.

"I am going to surrender the dune," he said. "I intend to join the Romans."

It had been so easy. The four Roman legions had landed in Kent in the

summer of A.D. 43, led by Aulus Plautius. They had marched rapidly
through the south east, routed the brother of the impudent chief
Caractacus and a few days later smashed the little army of Caractacus
himself. As soon as he heard that all was well, Claudius came over with
his elephants and watched the submission of the fiery Catuvellauni a few
miles north of the river Thames. Sixteen more of the island's tribes,
including the now weakened Atrebates, immediately sent messages of
surrender: some because they thought they could get advantages over
their neighbours, others because they knew the Roman legionaries would
cut them to pieces. But other tribes did not surrender; and certainly not
the proud Durotriges.

Claudius did not care. He had his military triumph, and he only stayed
on the island for sixteen days.

"Clean up the rest of this country," he told Aulus Plautius, who was
appointed the first governor of this new island province of Britannia.
Then he returned to Rome and, as he had always wanted, the senate
voted him a triumph.

"We must strike north and west," Aulus decided. "The II Legion shall
reduce the hillforts in the south west." He considered the commanders at
his disposal. "Vespasian shall lead the expedition," he added. "I can trust
him to do it well."

Vespasian was everything a Roman commander should be: already a
veteran of several campaigns he had a hard, blunt, but handsome face
that inspired respect in his men and admiration in women; he was
intelligent, cool, ambitious, and ruthless. He was also young. His
remarkable qualities were one day to bring him to the throne itself: and he
certainly did not intend to allow the islanders and their Celtic warriors to
stand in his way. The following spring the young legate led the II Legion
swiftly along the southern coast.

The first of the Durotrigan forts that he encountered was not impressive: it was a long, low hill beside a sheltered harbour, and around
the hill and its headland had been thrown a pair of walls twenty feet high
and ending with a mound at the harbour's edge. In the centre of the wall
was a large wooden gate, reinforced with heavy posts at each side, and
studded with fearsome iron spikes. Had it not been for this gate and the
walls, it was clear that nature had destined the shallow harbour to be a
quiet and peaceful place, a settlement and a port, but never a fortress. The
waters were calm and herons glided over them. But the defenders were
confident that their walls would deter the invaders. The settlement inside
the walls was similar to that at Sarum, except that there were two small
wooden jetties by the water's edge where several boats were moored, and
a collection of small barns for storing merchandise. There was also a small
round building with a hole in the roof which had a vital purpose in the life
of the harbour: for here silver coins were minted for the king of the
Durotriges which were of a sufficiently good quality to be accepted by the
merchants from Gaul.

When the hard-faced young commander saw the defences, he
shrugged with contempt. He knew what to do.

The Durotriges stood along the top of the walls. Their bright cloaks and golden ornaments made a dazzling display and as the Romans approached, they shouted challenges and shook their spears. One of the warriors waved a red flag, for red was the colour worn by the god of war; and several of the young men cried out:

"Send forward your bravest warriors, Romans, to fight us in single combat!" While others shouted: "Show us your leader that we may know him in battle."

But the Romans did not attack; they took their time. To the surprise of the natives, they calmly dug a small fortification in front of the gate. This took them two hours. Then, from the back of their column, they slowly wheeled a huge catapult and brought it to the little fortified rampart they had built, together with a cart containing several enormous rocks.

While this work proceeded, Vespasian sat on a leather stool, out of range of the walls. He took no notice of the Durotriges at all, but coolly dictated a memorandum to a scribe:

> The first fort we have encountered belonging to the Durotriges is beside the sea. There is a shallow harbour behind it, which the hill protects from the sea. The fort had two walls. As our reports suggested, the warriors of the tribe are brave but undisciplined.
>
> The gate of the fort was breached and the place taken.

"You may carry this to the governor now," he remarked to the scribe. "This place will be ours by sundown."

At a nod from the legate, the catapult was now put into action. A huge stone rocketed in a great arc and crashed against the gate, which split. A minute later, a second rock burst the entire gate wide open.

"Take it," he ordered.

Now, for the first time, the Durotriges discovered the perfect, impersonal efficiency of the fighting machine that the young commander was so coolly directing against them.

A century, eighty men in military organisation of that time, had drawn up in formation under their centurion. Now those in the inside ranks raised their shields above their heads, each shield touching the next to form a solid metal covering. Those in the first and the outside ranks held their shields in front of them or at their side so that the front and flanks were protected in a similar manner: this formation was the famous *testudo*, or tortoise and was neither more nor less than a human, armour-plated tank – a favourite formation of the Romans, and almost impregnable. At a nod from the centurion, the *testudo* moved smartly forward and went through the open gate of the fort while the spears, arrows and sling-stones of the defenders bounced uselessly off its raised shields. A second century followed at once; then a third.

Slow, mechanical, indestructible, these man-machines then set to work upon the Durotriges inside the fortress. The shield wall of the *testudo* would suddenly flash open, like a line of shutters, and the *pila* – the Romans' short, heavy, bolt-like spears – would shoot out. At close range the *pila* could drill a neat, square hole in a man's skull. Those who came within reach would receive a harsh thrust from the legionaries' short, flat-bladed swords. The Romans moved along the inside of the walls and across the open ground below the hill while the brave Durotriges dashed themselves to pieces upon their metal shell. They hacked the defenders unmercifully. By mid afternoon, as Vespasian had known they would, they had cleared the entire fortress.

The Romans took the merchandise from the barns and the boats in the harbour. The controller of the mint had just time to bury his stock of silver coins in the ground under his hut before the soldiers walked in and killed him – a little hoard which archaeologists would find nearly two thousand years later.

The massacre was watched by a single figure from a safely concealed point in the rushes on the opposite bank of the harbour. He was tall, thin and stooped, with a lean, hard face and narrow-set eyes. After he had carefully watched the gate being smashed and the Durotriges cut to pieces, and satisfied himself that the defenders had no chance of success against the Romans' fighting methods, he loped along the bank on his curious, long-toed feet, and stepped into a large canoe made of hides stretched over a wooden frame, with a broad, shallow draught. Taradoc the canny riverman made no attempt to paddle up river to warn Tosutigus and the waiting defenders of the dune at Sarum. Hugging the bank, he slipped quietly to the harbour entrance and out into the open sea.

The force which was now arriving at Sarum three days after the taking of the harbour was no more than a *vexillation* – a detachment of a single century under their centurion, with two cavalry outriders and one siege engine, similar to that used at the harbour. As Tosutigus watched the Romans approach, he noticed that there was also a single figure on horseback riding in front of the column, and he wondered who it was.

The dune was ready. Everything was prepared in order to make exactly the right impression on the Romans when they approached its gates. Only moments before, Aflek had been let down from the ramparts by rope on the northern side, out of sight of the Romans; but before he had gone, the Druid had uttered a terrible curse upon the young chief.

"May the gods turn their backs upon you, Tosutigus: for the other tribes will. Be warned – you have broken your oath to the king, and from today, all men will call you Tosutigus the Liar."

This warning proved to be correct, and it was by this name that every Celt on the island would refer to him for the rest of his life.

But Tosutigus did not care. His mind was already filled with the dreams he had for Sarum's future. It would all, he was sure, go according to plan.

The ambitious plan that he had made was in all respects a young man's plan, but there was, it must be admitted, some sense in his reasoning.

All over the island in the years A.D. 43 and 44, the tribal chiefs had been faced with a stark choice. If they resisted the Romans, they faced probable defeat followed by a military occupation. But if they went over to the empire's cause, it was well known that Rome could be generous: and in due course a number of chiefs emerged from those years as independent client kings of great wealth. The empire continued its wise policy of enriching these clients, building them sumptuous villas and educating their children as Roman gentlemen. In a generation, or at most two, the petty kings turned into provincial aristocrats, their authority was assumed by magistrates, and their kingdoms quietly slipped into the stream of provincial Roman life.

The young chief was wise enough to know that he could not hold Sarum against the might of Rome, and to guess that the Durotriges too would be defeated. So how could he survive? Only by keeping up an appearance of loyalty to the powerful Durotriges until it was safe to desert them, and then by throwing in his lot with Rome. As soon as Claudius had landed, this was his secret intention.

But Tosutigus was young, and for a long time he had nursed a plan that was more ambitious than this alone. The Durotriges hated the Romans; they would fight, he knew, hillfort by hillfort, and they would lose. The Romans would subdue them – but what then? Surely, it seemed to him, the Roman officials, as they had done in other parts of their huge empire, would look for loyal Celtic leaders, local men they could trust in the area. And that, perhaps, was where he could turn the situation to his advantage.

"After all," he reasoned, "I am a Celt who speaks Latin and who is ready to be loyal to Rome. I am not one of the Durotriges who hate the empire and whom Rome can never trust. I could be useful to the governor."

Sometimes during those months, as he had allowed his mind to dwell on the many advantages he believed himself to possess, he imagined a grateful emperor bestowing upon him a commission to rule over the fierce old king of the Durotriges himself. At the very least, he decided, I shall ask for control over the harbour, as my family used to have in ancient times. I'm sure the Romans won't want the Durotriges to have that.

Now the moment had come. In order to impress the Romans with his importance, he had ordered every man and boy on to the walls. It seemed to him that they made a formidable showing.

The Roman contingent had halted in front of the gate. The legionaries were gazing up at the high chalk walls of the dune with curiosity. The man he had noticed riding at the front had dismounted and was obviously searching the defences for weak spots.

This was the crucial moment of his plan. He strode down from the rampart and ordered:

"Open the gates."

His meeting with the Romans did not go quite as he had planned, although he had rehearsed it many times. It began with his walking alone, slowly and sedately, down the path from the dune to where the Romans waited. At the foot of the hill, he found himself facing the Roman officer whom he had seen dismount and who now stared at him with a hard, unsmiling face. He noticed the large, square chin, the jutting nose, and the intelligent brown eyes which at that moment seemed expression-less. For a second, the young Celt hesitated, then, as he had planned, he opened his arms in a friendly gesture and cried in Latin:

"Welcome! I am Tosutigus, lord of Sarum; and the ally of Rome."

Vespasian, who had led the *vexillation* himself, looked at him coldly, but said nothing. The dune had not impressed him, but if the young man did not want to fight, it would save time. He intended to rejoin the rest of the legion the next day.

"You speak Latin," he said at last.

"So did my father and his father before him," Tosutigus replied eagerly. "My grandmother," it was his great-grandmother, but this sounded better, "was a princess of the Atrebates, friends of Rome."

Vespasian nodded. He understood. This young man with his small fort wanted to ingratiate himself. It was of no importance whether he was friendly to Rome or not, but the legate would not discourage him, as long as he did not waste time.

"Tell your men to evacuate the fort," he said curtly.

Tosutigus had hoped for a more encouraging response than this, but he signalled to those on the wall to descend.

"Are there any Druids here?" the Roman next demanded.

"There was one. I sent him away," Tosutigus replied truthfully.

Vespasian looked at the landscape around him. He had no interest in Sarum, in Tosutigus or his dune. He had come inland because he had heard reports that there was a temple on the high ground which might be a cult centre of those cursed Druids. Since he intended to wipe the island priests out, he had decided to make a detour to see for himself, before continuing west to deal with the main strongholds of the Durotriges.

"Where is the stone temple?"

"To the north. A short ride," Tosutigus answered. "It is deserted," he added.

"Take me there," Vespasian ordered.

The short journey that the little party made – for Vespasian, took with him only Tosutigus and the two outriders – decided the young chief's fate. By the time they set out from the dune, the Celt had already discovered the hard-faced Roman's identity, and he was eager to impress him.

Tosutigus rode his finest horse, a chestnut. He was proud of his horses: they were not large, but sturdy animals with broad heads who did well on the wild terrain of the island. To Vespasian, who had seen the fleetest and most elegant horses that Persia or Africa could send to Rome, they seemed clumsy, heavy-boned creatures; but Tosutigus could not know this. Following the old custom of his people he had mixed the leaves of the she-yew tree with the horse's bait to make his coat shine; and mounted on this fine animal, with bridle and bit decorated in gold, he cut a splendid figure. Beside him the Roman rode on a quiet grey; the animal was stolid, and the commander wore no ornaments, but the hilt of his short sword tapped against his bronze breastplate as they went along.

A damp breeze had blown up and grey clouds were now passing over the landscape. The flocks of small brown sheep, most of which it had not been possible to bring within the dune, were grazing untended on the chalk ridges. On the slopes, the patchworks of little cornfields were empty, and the few farmsteads the riders passed, with their round thatched buildings and wattle enclosures were silent.

But deserted as the scene was, Tosutigus gazed round the rolling landscape with pride.

"It's good country," he remarked.

Vespasian nodded thoughtfully. It was, and he had already decided how he could use this rich and empty land.

"This place is yours?"

"My family has always held it," the Celt answered, indicating the whole landscape with a sweep of his hand. "The high ground is ours, and the land to the south west, towards the Durotriges. Our house is in the valley," he added.

The family's house in normal times was not the dune but a modest and comfortable place a few miles to the north: it consisted of a large enclosure similar to the farmsteads they were passing, though on a grander scale. Inside were two circular thatched houses, each thirty feet in diameter, in which the family lived, a dozen stores and outhouses, and the small shrine to the god Nodens at which the family worshipped. Since leaving the windy dune as a residence two generations before, the family had been content with their farmstead and its fine views over the valley and river below – a modest style of life typical of many of the Celtic nobles on the island at the time.

They passed numerous barrows, all overgrown with short, coarse turf and the Roman glanced at them with careless interest.

"These are the tombs of my ancestors," Tosutigus told him. He hoped that this Roman legate understood that he was a figure of some consequence in the land, but he was not sure that he did.

When they reached Stonehenge, Vespasian surveyed the huge, crumbling stone circle with curiosity. It was obvious that this temple was not in regular use.

"Do the Druids come here?"

Tosutigus shook his head.

"It was used in my father's time, but not much even then. The Druids left."

"Human sacrifice?"

The young chief hesitated. He was well aware of the Roman view of this practice, and although he was loyal to Nodens and the other Celtic gods, he had been revolted by many of the Druids' ancient customs himself. The truth was that ten years before, after a poor harvest, a party of Druids had sacrificed a child at the henge, but there had been no sacrifices since.

"There used to be," he answered.

The Roman's face registered disgust.

"The Druids are mostly further north," Tosutigus explained, "or in the lands of the Durotriges. They don't use the henges much; they use clearings in the woods." This was the truth and he hoped it would satisfy Vespasian.

"If any Druids come here, you will send them to me in chains," Vespasian ordered.

"As you wish."

Tosutigus had no particular love for the Druids and he knew that once the Romans ruled the island, they would be exterminated anyway. The Druids were irrelevant to his purposes. He glanced at the cold young legate to see if he had succeeded in making a favourable impression, but the Roman's expressionless face gave nothing away.

In fact, from the first moment when Tosutigus had come down from the dune, Vespasian had seen him for exactly what he was: a young provincial chief – hopeful, ambitious, and obviously without any real power. Vespasian understood power better than most men then living, and he could see at once that Tosutigus had nothing to bargain with except a minor fort which he had already given up. But it amused him to watch this young chief on his fine horse trying to impress him with his floundering and ungrammatical Latin and as they made their way back towards the dune, he suddenly turned to him and asked abruptly:

"And what do you want from Rome, Tosutigus?"

The young man was taken by surprise. He had not expected such a direct approach but he recovered himself quickly. Was not this exactly the chance that he had waited for so many months? It obviously was, and he had his answer ready.

"I want to be a client ruler, Vespasian, and a Roman citizen." He might have added, "and a senator too," for it was known that client kings under the empire had sometimes been given this honour and had strutted in the streets of Rome in their heavy-bordered togas and been treated as equals by the greatest men of the empire. He could think of nothing he would like more.

"You want to be a client king?" Vespasian looked at him out of the corner of his eye, and wondered: how vain and ambitious was this foolish young fellow? "What else do you want?" he asked.

Thinking that he had impressed him, Tosutigus went on eagerly:

"Let me have the harbour which the Durotriges stole from my family; I know how to run it profitably." This claim was in fact true; but it was of no particular interest to the legate, who could see that the Celt was bursting to ask for more. Without letting Tosutigus see that his questions were little more than grim teasing he asked with apparent seriousness:

"And what else?"

Tosutigus paused.

For many months he had pondered his grand design; he had even prepared his approach to the governor on the subject; and now, lured on by what he took to be the legate's interest in him – this legate who was about to destroy the powerful Durotriges and who certainly must have the ear of the governor, he threw aside his usual caution. This, he thought to himself, is my moment: it has come sooner than I expected. His hope had been to approach the governor himself with his plan, if he could only get the opportunity; but it seemed to him now that he must seek to win over this commander of the legion which was about to destroy the Durotriges, for Vespasian was probably his only way to the governor.

Slowly he drew out of his tunic a parchment scroll. It was a letter, addressed to governor Aulus Plautius, and it was the result of endless nights of secret composition. This was his plan to make Sarum great again.

The letter was not yet sealed.

"Read it," he said proudly.

Vespasian read, with grim amusement, and then astonishment. Before him, couched in a Latin and handwriting that would have made any Roman schoolboy burst out laughing, was the mind of Tosutigus – his grand plan for the reorganisation of the south-west of the island, for his personal benefit. Stripped of its fervent expressions of devotion and absurd flattery it said: Tosutigus is loyal to Rome: give him the entire land of the Durotriges to rule over and you will never repent of your choice.

"The Durotriges hate the Romans," Tosutigus explained excitedly. "They will fight to the death, but even when you have conquered them, none of their own chiefs will ever be loyal and you'll have nothing but trouble. You will either have to garrison the whole territory, which is expensive, or kill them all, and leave behind you a desert. But I am a Celt," he went on. "I understand these Durotriges and their ways, and furthermore I am loyal to Rome. I could hold their lands as your client – or some of their lands at least," he added hopefully.

So that was it. Even Vespasian was surprised by the ambition of this foolish fellow's dream: there was even a certain logic to it, he acknowledged. But it was wholly impractical – from start to finish a young man's plan. If the Durotriges were too proud to submit to Rome, there was even less chance that they would accept as their king this obscure young chief who had already betrayed his fort. The idea was absurd.

In his heart of hearts, Tosutigus knew it himself; but it was a gamble worth a try. The Roman invaders, he reasoned, knowing little of the country, might be attracted by the prospect of an easy solution to the problem of governing the area – for he did not realise the thoroughness and relentless attention to detail of the imperial administration; and besides, how else was he to revenge his family for the years of indignity under Durotrigan domination, and restore Sarum to its ancient glory?

Vespasian saw all this clearly, but his face remained impassive.

"I will convey your letter to the governor," he replied gravely.

For he had already decided how to make use of the foolish young Celt at his side, and now he craftily introduced the subject that was really on his mind.

"If you want to be a client king, you will not only need to please the governor," he said. "You must show your loyalty to the emperor himself. Claudius is impressed by action, not words."

Tosutigus waited expectantly. It seemed to him that his negotiations were going better than he had dared to hope.

Vespasian knew very well what Claudius wanted from his new

province. Before leaving the island, the lame emperor had made his wishes clear: "Gentlemen," he had remarked to Aulus Plautius and the legates in the governor's tent, "remember that I expect this conquest to be profitable to me personally." No ambitious commander would be so unwise to forget such a hint, and when Vespasian saw the rolling lands of this insignificant young chief, he also saw his opportunity.

"You must make a friend of the emperor, and impress him," he assured his companion earnestly.

Tosutigus fell into the trap at once.

"How?"

Vespasian pretended astonishment.

"Make him a present of course – land. You have plenty, but he has less of his own than you suppose."

Tosutigus frowned. This was not the way he had intended the conversation to go. He knew that in other parts of the island before the conquest began, Celtic chiefs had made gifts to the Roman emperor and in return had received both honours and lucrative contracts. But he was reluctant to part with any portion of a patrimony that had already shrunk in recent generations.

"How much would I need to give?" he asked doubtfully.

"He would not want the estates where your own home is – keep them," Vespasian replied. "But this land on the high ground, and the land you have to the south west, towards the territory of the Durotriges: give him that."

"But. . . ." Tosutigus was dismayed. "That is three fourths of all my land!"

Vespasian's look was stony.

"You have just asked him to make you a king. It's a small price to pay for what you want."

But, Tosutigus thought, I may not get what I want; and then I will have given all my land to an emperor I shall probably never see.

"And if I refuse?"

Vespasian's face was a mask.

"Perhaps you would lose it anyway," he remarked pleasantly.

The threat was obvious. If the Roman decided to take the land anyway, there was nothing he could do. The Durotriges would not make any trouble on his behalf, because he had broken his vow and given up the dune. The Belgae to the east cared nothing for him; the Atrebates had forgotten his existence. Faced with reality, and with Vespasian's naked power, he realised as a sudden cold sweat broke over his body, the incredible folly of his plan and the weakness of his position. He had no options; he was defenceless. He had even opened the gates of the fort, the only bargaining weapon that he had.

But in this assessment too, Tosutigus was wrong; Vespasian did not in the least want to conquer Sarum. For if this land were to be conquered, then it would automatically come under the control of the military, and perhaps require a small garrison in an inconvenient location. Yet here, he saw at once on the rolling high ground, were exactly the sort of valuable estates that Claudius would be glad to receive for his personal use and for his family: valuable estates, moreover, which were not claimed by any powerful tribe. The legate had no intention of losing such an opportunity to please the emperor. All that was needed, he knew, was a legal document in due form, making a personal gift of them from the present owner to Claudius: that was how such matters were done. But Tosutigus knew little of imperial administration or of Roman legal niceties. He did not understand that the transfer would benefit only Vespasian in the emperor's eyes, or that such a document would then be used by the clever military bureaucrat to persuade other chiefs to follow his example.

In fact, Vespasian would have been satisfied with half the land he had demanded, in return for which Tosutigus should have held out for at least a grant on Roman citizenship.

But Tosutigus had received a shock, and he panicked.

"It seems I have no choice," he muttered, and from that point they rode over the chalk ridges in silence.

At the dune, watched in puzzlement by Numex and his men, Vespasian quickly dictated an appropriate document to the centurion who acted as scribe. When it was done, he invited Tosutigus to sign it. It read:

> I, Tosutigus, hereditary chief and ally of Rome and on the presence of legate Vespasian, do give to Claudius Nero Germanicus, divine Emperor of Rome, all those lands previously held by me on the high ground and to the south west of the temple of stone.

It was a somewhat crude document, but for the time being it would suffice. A more detailed and formal document could be drawn up later.

Suddenly a thought struck the legate.

"We must give this place a name. What do you call this fort?"

"The dune," Tosutigus replied sullenly.

"And the stream below?"

"Afon." This was the Celtic word which meant river.

"Avon?" He shook his head. The sound did not please him. "Sorvio," he said finally. "Means a slow-moving stream. We shall call it Sorviodunum."

A.D. 60

It seemed to Porteus, as the night deepened, that the waves crashing against the rocky Welsh shore nearby made a melancholy sound. But perhaps it was his mood.

The sharp, salty wind had just found a gap between the tent flaps and it burst in, causing the oil lamp to flicker violently. But the clean-shaven young Roman who sat motionless on the camp stool inside did not allow this interruption to distract his attention. He passed a hand through his unruly mop of black curly hair – never in all his twenty-one years had he ever completely managed to control it all – and, on a new piece of parchment he wrote down, slowly and carefully, the dangerous thought that had been troubling him for the few months.

Privately, my dear father, I believe that we are administering the island badly and that there will be trouble. It's the governor's fault.

Having written this, he paused. Was it wise to express such ideas in a letter that was to travel all the way to his family's estate in south east Gaul, and which might easily be opened by spies? He was attached to the governor's staff, thanks to the influence of his prospective father-in-law. Wouldn't he be accused of treachery? He shook his head sadly, put the parchment to one side, and returned to the safer narrative of the letter he had been composing before.

Two days ago, dear parents, we exterminated the last of the Druids: and a strange business it was, I can tell you. They and their followers had gathered on a small island called Mona, off the extreme west coast of Britannia, past the territory of the Deceangli tribe we have been fighting recently.

The governor was determined to crush them, and so we prepared to cross the narrow straits with the whole of the XIV Legion and most of the XX too.

They were burning fires all along the shoreline opposite, and what with the fires, and the shrieks they made, and the surf pounding, our troops hesitated for a moment. But not for long! The infantry crossed in boats and those of us who were mounted swam across on our horses; when we got over it wasn't so bad. They fought well, but in the end they had to surrender and our own losses were not heavy.

He rested his hand. This account could safely be read out to his mother and his two sisters. The reality had been very different.

It had not been the lowering, overcast skies nor the crashing waves, nor the flickering fires along the shore that had made the legionaries hesitate; it had not been the native warriors banging their long shields with their spears to make a noise like thunder, nor the Druids in their robes shrieking the curses of their Celtic gods across the waters; it had not even been the sight of the naked sacrificial bodies the Druids threw into the hissing fires.

It had been the women.

They were a strange and terrifying sight: they were drawn up in front of their men, half naked but brightly painted and fully armed, their long hair streaming in the wind. They shook their knives and spears, they danced and gesticulated as though they were possessed; and – this was the worst of all, they uttered a high, piercing war cry, again and again, that came wailing over the water with a terrible, unearthly sound. He had never heard anything like that cry: it sent shivers down his spine.

A mutter arose amongst the men.

"It's the Furies themselves," they said. And for a moment, he had thought they would not fight, until a wise centurion shouted derisively:

"What, are you afraid of women now?"

It had the desired effect: the soldiers had pulled themselves together, and prepared to surge forward.

The battle was worse than anything he could have dreamed of. The disciplined Roman formations hacked their way through the native horde without difficulty. Men, priests and the women were butchered by the short broad Roman swords in ways that he did not care to remember. The shallows were awash with bodies; the surf was red. After the fighting he had watched as two old Druids, toothless, with their long grey robes in shreds, but still screaming their useless curses, were tied together in one of their own wooden sacrificial cages and torched in front of him.

"It's what they do to their own people," a soldier shouted. He knew this was not true: the Celtic priests meted out this cruel death to criminals only; but one did not argue with soldiers after a victory, and the two old men died horribly while the Romans laughed:

"See them fry!"

He returned to his letter, preferring to put the scenes out of his mind.

I think the governor means to return to the new town of Londinium in a few days and I shall write to you next from there, no doubt.

He was tired; it was time to close his letter.

How grateful I am, dear parents, that Graccus the senator, whom I shall soon call my father-in-law, has made it possible for me to see these things and, I hope, to distinguish myself in some way.

As for my dear Lydia, I think of her each hour, and count the days until I may see her in the imperial city, once again.

Your son,

Caius Porteus Maximus.

Porteus sighed. Lydia – when would he see her again? In a year, perhaps. He thought of her as he often did, smiling and laughing with him: it seemed like a distant ray of sunshine in this cold northern place.

It was a remarkable circumstance that he should be betrothed to her at all. She was the third daughter of Graccus, a powerful senator of ancient family; whereas he was of the provincial nobility, belonging to the second, equestrian order of Roman society – respectable, entitled to enter a civil or military career and aim for high office, but hardly a good match for the daughter of a great aristocrat. Normally they should never have met at all; but by some stroke of good fortune – a distant cousin was a magistrate in Rome and had taken Porteus to the senator's house – he had met the girl and for both of them it had been love at first sight. In such circumstances, a young man like Porteus could have expected to be thrown out of the senator's house for his presumption – politely and with no hard feelings, but firmly and permanently; and that was exactly what Graccus had tried to do. But Lydia had fallen in love: it was not a thing well bred Roman girls were supposed to do. She had complained and moped incessantly; and by the end of a month her father, who had two sons and two other daughters to think of, became bored with the whole business and gave way.

"There's nothing against young Porteus," the girl's mother reminded him.

"And nothing for him either," the heavy, grey-haired senator replied irritably. Which was perfectly true.

Young Porteus had vague aspirations towards a literary career, but these were based upon nothing more solid than some jejeune epigrams that he had circulated amongst his friends and which Lydia thought wonderful. The income from the estates in southern Gaul was enough just to maintain the family's modest social position, but no more; and although Porteus's father had encouraged him to go into law as an advocate, so far his career in Rome had not been impressive.

"The daughter of a Graccus does not marry a nonentity," the senator growled. "I suppose we shall have to make something of him."

The solution he hit upon was sensible from every point of view. He had used his influence with the newly appointed governor of Britannia, Suetonius, to have the young man attached to his personal staff for three years.

"Give young Porteus a chance either to win distinction for himself, or to get killed," he said to that crusty general. "I don't mind which."

It was an excellent opportunity. The *cohors amicorum* of a figure like Suetonius formed an informal staff around the governor: it often contained young men of aristocratic family who were being prepared for greater things, and by joining this elite group Porteus would have many chances to make important friends and to learn the inner workings of Roman administration. If the governor chose, he might appoint him to a temporary post in the new province, and at the end of his time there, the young equestrian would have fitted himself to hold important appointments in the future. Groomed for success, Graccus might be able to start him on a career worthy of a member of his family. In the meantime, he would at least be far away from Rome.

"With luck Lydia will forget him while he's away," the senator confided to his wife. "She's thirteen now, but I dare say it wouldn't be too late to find her a husband in two years' time."

"I'm sure he will do brilliantly and be a credit to us," his wife encouraged.

To Porteus the senator said severely:

"You are betrothed to Lydia. If you want to marry her, make a success of this post. If you fail, I do not want to see you again."

It was, when all was said and done, a generous bargain that the senator was making: for the governor of Britannia was a man of consequence.

Gaius Suetonius Paulinus was a pompous, red-faced and testy soldier who had distinguished himself in several campaigns, and most notably in the province of Mauretania where, as Praetorian legate, he had made a daring crossing of the mighty Atlas Mountains. War and mountains were what he understood and as soon as he had arrived in the island province he at once set out to find both.

His influence in Rome was considerable: he was a favourite of Emperor Nero.

For poor Claudius was now dead, poisoned six years before by his wife. It was his own fault: she was a young woman and the lame emperor was well into middle age: she had a young son from another marriage for whom she was ambitious and she persuaded Claudius to make the boy his successor. Once she had achieved that, she found little use for the ageing emperor. He should have realised this, and been on his guard. But Claudius had grown foolish – worse, he was even in love with his cruel young wife: she poisoned him, and young Nero succeeded.

Nero was unstable, though brilliant. Once he was emperor, he murdered the mother who had given him the throne and set out to rule in his own peculiar fashion. It soon became clear that he loved above all to appear on the stage: and with his grotesque and lewd performances he shocked the Senate far more than poor stammering Claudius had ever managed to do. Of his favourites, however, some were men of genuine merit: the philosopher Seneca was one; Suetonius the soldier was another.

Suetonius was a fine commander and he had collected about him a talented group. Amongst them was Agricola, the clear-eyed, hard-faced military tribune who had already shown early promise as a great military commander; several young bloods of the great senatorial families; and Marcus Marcellinus, the leader of this younger group. Marcus's face was almost a perfect square; his features were strong and symmetrical, with a jutting nose and handsome jet-black eyes, over which his eyebrows met. He was twenty-four, but already bore himself like a man of thirty, and had carried out several civil and military assignments with distinction; it was clear that the soldiers, and even Suetonius respected him and that he would probably follow in the distinguished path of his senior, Agricola, and perhaps Suetonius himself one day. He was tall and powerfully built and Porteus was overawed by him.

At first his life was difficult. The governor had only accepted him on sufferance; he had neither attainments nor great family to recommend him to the young bloods. It was Marcus who, after Porteus had tried for over a month to make a place for himself in the group with little success, decided that something should be done.

"It's time we welcomed young Porteus," he announced to the others. "The poor fellow's doing his best and there's nothing against him. We should give him a chance."

Thereafter life became easier. Suetonius, who had completely ignored him while they settled into their temporary quarters in the windy eastern colony at Camulodunum, now saw that the young officers were going about with him and started to give him small tasks to perform. Short as his temper was, he found nothing to complain of in the young man: he was industrious, eager to learn and not particularly stupid.

"He needs to be tested in battle," he remarked to the legates one night as they chatted over their meal, "but he could be worse." And the legates knew that, from the governor, this was as near to a compliment as anyone was likely to get.

"How did he come to be here?" one of them dared to ask him.

"I had to please his father-in-law, Graccus the Senator you know," Suetonius candidly admitted. "Foolish to refuse a favour to a man like that who can always do you some good in Rome. His daughter's going to marry young Porteus – I can't think why."

Lydia! As he stared at the shadows on the side of his tent, Porteus let his thoughts wander to his future bride. The picture that immediately arose was the same one that always did: it was a vision that was imprinted forever on his memory, that first magic time that he had seen her. The girl had been walking across the small garden in her father's house in Rome and she had not realised that anyone else was there. It was her thirteenth birthday: her long brown hair was braided and wound round her head in the fashion of that year, and she was wearing a simple white linen dress, gathered at the waist. As she passed the small fountain in the centre of the little court, the sunlight caught her so that her naked form was perfectly silhouetted through the thin material, and he saw, with a gasp of wonder, the firm lines of her body and the soft young breasts newly swollen to their first perfect fullness. It was a sight he should never have been permitted to see, for high born girls like Lydia were kept in modest seclusion until they were married, but once seen he would never forget the girl's artless grace. Porteus had fallen in love at once. At thirteen she was already of marriageable age, and he soon discovered to his delight that she was not yet betrothed. She had a perfect oval face, large brown eyes and that clear pale olive complexion that can last, almost flawlessly, for a lifetime. She was perfection. It was not long before the two young people discovered that they delighted in each other's company. Lydia was young, innocent, and self-willed. He came to look forward to her sudden flashes of childish temper, followed by laughter and brilliant smiles. And the girl thought that her eager young lover was the most brilliant young man in the world. It was flattering.

Porteus sighed. His favourite day-dream, in which he had often indulged during the lonely months in the cold northern province, was of their wedding. It was due to take place in two years and by then, he knew, Lydia would have developed into a beautiful young woman. He could see it so clearly: the torchlight procession waiting outside Graccus's house and singing the marriage hymn: "Hymen, O Hymenae, Hymen", while inside, hidden from view in the family shrine Lydia would dedicate her child's toys to the household gods, the Lares; then, following the Roman custom, she would step for the last time out of her child's clothes, and her mother's women would dress her in the long white wedding gown and the bright saffron veil in which every Roman girl of family was married. He could see it all. They would arrange her long hair in the style of the vestal virgins so that three perfect curls fell down each cheek. Ah, how he longed to run his fingers through her hair and bury his face in those long, sweet smelling tresses!

And then the torchlight procession would make its way through the streets to the bridegroom's house where the bride would place wooden fillets on the door posts and anoint the door with oil before he carried her over the threshold while the guests cried "Talassio" and his young friends made lewder calls amidst the general laughter.

They were his most precious thoughts.

Now however, his dreams were interrupted by a gust of wind from the tent flap and the head of Marcus looking in.

"Writing love letters?" The young aristocrat gave him a friendly grin.

"No. Telling my parents about our victory."

Marcus nodded.

"Not a pretty business I'm afraid; but necessary I daresay. By the way," he smiled pleasantly, "you may as well know the governor thinks you handled yourself well at the crossing. Seems to think you might make a soldier yet!"

Porteus could not help blushing with pleasure. This was praise indeed.

"I'm planning to reconnoitre the west of this island tomorrow," Marcus went on. "Thought you might like to come with me – just in case there's a little action."

"Of course." He did not think he had done anything out of the ordinary during the battle, but there was no mistaking the message that Marcus was giving him: he had been accepted.

Marcus looked down at Porteus. A nice young fellow, he thought: good material. But how in the name of all the gods had he managed to get himself betrothed to the daughter of an important man like Graccus? Perhaps there was something wrong with the girl.

"What's she like, this paragon of yours, this Lydia?" he enquired.

"I'll show you," Porteus replied, glad to have a further chance of impressing his mentor; and proudly he pulled out a miniature that he secreted amongst his papers. Silently he handed the little painting to the aristocrat.

It was no bigger than the palm of a man's hand, but the work was beautifully done and the likeness excellent. Marcus stared at it in wonder.

"She is beautiful," he marvelled.

"She is," Porteus cried enthusiastically. "We'll be married in two years when I return to Rome and then we shall visit Britannia and if you're still here, you shall meet her."

For a moment Marcus felt almost jealous at his young friend's astonishing good fortune: the girl was exquisite; it would be a brilliant marriage.

"I look forward to it," he replied thoughtfully. "Until tomorrow then," he added as he went out.

As soon as he had gone, Porteus began to add a postscript to his letter to let his parents know about the governor's good opinion of him. Then he sat silently for a period, lost in reflection.

His thoughts were not, this time, of Lydia; nor even of himself. His mind had instead returned to the political matter that had been nagging at him for so long. For young and inexperienced as he still was, Porteus was not a fool, and he had recently been learning important lessons about Roman statecraft – lessons that were affecting him more deeply than he had ever expected. After turning the matter over in his mind for some

[169]

time, he finally picked up the piece of parchment that he had formerly discarded and wrote the following.

My dear father –
This must of course be between ourselves – do not even speak of it to my mother – but I ask for your wisdom and your advice.

The problems I speak of are many, but they are all caused by the fact that while we expect the islanders to learn our Roman ways, we take no account of their own customs, and they are coming to hate us.

For example: we have built a fine new temple to the imperial cult at Camulodunum in the east and, as usual, a number of native chiefs have been honoured by being made priests. But the temple is so large, its ceremonies so magnificent – and as you know, all these costs are charged to the priests themselves – that the cost of its upkeep is too heavy for them. Instead of inspiring them with love and respect for our emperor, it is only causing them to long for their own, and less expensive Celtic gods!

Another example: we have reversed our policy towards the chiefs. The late divine Claudius, as all the world knows, favoured client kings; but our present emperor hates them and now his procurator here, Decianus Catus who you warned me was a lazy and greedy man, has been busy confiscating their property and saying it belongs to the empire. As you would expect, they are furious and they say that we Romans do not keep our word. It's true – we haven't.

Yet another, perhaps worse: many island chiefs are deep in debt to Roman creditors. They say that one of the greatest creditors of all is the philosopher Seneca. It seems amazing: I remember as a student with what admiration we studied his philosophy which told us to live a simple life, to be merciful to all men and to eschew worldly goods! Well, it seems he has millions of sesterces out on loan to native chiefs here and that he and a number of other great financiers have recently panicked and are calling in all their debts. Since the chiefs are having their property taken, they can't pay, and they'll be completely ruined!

It seems to me that if this province is ever going to be a success, we must not only win the war but also win the peace as well, and we can't do that if no one trusts us. But the governor, who is a great man, thinks only of military mountain operations to swell his reputation amongst the other generals, and the procurator is no more than a rogue. The situation is drifting from bad to worse. It is particularly serious in the east, in the lands of the Trinovantes and the Iceni.

I think perhaps others in the administration see this too, but no one says a word – if you met Suetonius, you'd see why: they're all terrified of him, and so am I!

I wish I could do something, but I don't know what. Give me your advice.

Porteus read this second missive over and grunted with satisfaction. He was pleased with its neat, epigrammatic statements; the views he expressed were both honest and perceptive. The question was, did he dare send such a dangerous letter at all when there was a risk it might be opened, or would it be wiser to burn it and say nothing?

His ambition told him it was none of his business to worry about such things; but his conscience troubled him, and this difficult question was still unresolved when he fell asleep.

He never had to make the decision. Because at dawn he was awoken by Marcus in his tent, shaking him by the shoulder.

"Wake up, Porteus: quick!"

As he struggled into consciousness he saw that the young aristocrat's face was set grimly.

"What is it?"

"It's action, my friend. The Iceni have revolted!"

There was no need for him to send the letter to his father now: it was already too late; and as he soon discovered, the revolt was worse than anything he had ever imagined.

It was the procurator's fault: King Prasutagus of the proud Iceni tribe in the east of the island had recently died leaving his widow and two daughters in the care of the emperor: but instead of protecting them, Decianus Catus had immediately confiscated most of their property and when the Iceni protested, Roman troops moved in.

It was a potentially explosive situation, created by the greed and stupidity of a worthless bureaucrat and an unsympathetic governor. Had there been a cool and more broad-minded administrator in the region to conciliate the Iceni, trouble might still have been averted.

When the troops moved in they found the Iceni in a state of justifiable rage. There were insults hurled at them and small skirmishes. Believing that their job was to teach these British natives a lesson, the officers led their men to the residence of the king's widow, Boudicca, and ordered them to confiscate her possessions. This was the final insult to the powerful tribe, and the operation turned into a fiasco. The queen's faithful servants began to attack those who, it seemed to them, had come to loot the royal house, and the Roman troops in no time were out of control. By the end of that day, Boudicca had been dragged out of her house and flogged, and her two daughters raped.

It was all that was needed. The fire of revolt against Roman oppression was lit – and the conflagration spread with a speed that astonished the conquerors.

The entire tribe of the Iceni and their powerful neighbours the Trinovantes rose at once. The arms which the Romans thought they had confiscated after Claudius's conquest suddenly reappeared and a great horde, tens of thousands strong, began to move upon the eastern colony of Camulodunum.

Camulodunum was the first of the provincial centres the Romans had founded when they arrived. Its charter called it a *colonia* – the highest rank of provincial settlement – and it contained a forum, a temple, law courts and other administrative offices; around this walled centre had already spread the farms of the retired Roman legionaries who were normally given grants of land beside these *coloniae* in the provinces where they had served. It was a typical Roman colony: rich, complacent and undefended except for a small garrison, and the great horde swept towards it like an avalanche.

"We'll burn the temples of the extortioners," they cried. "We'll destroy their gods who are devouring us and wipe out their settlements."

Caught off guard, the local garrison discovered they were powerless. Messengers requesting help raced west towards Suetonius. "Camulodunum is being engulfed," they said. But it was already too late.

Although he had come to disagree with his politics, Porteus could not help admiring the governor as he faced his staff that cold morning.

"The whole of the east's in flames," he said tersely. "This kind of fire has to be stamped out at once.

"The nearest garrison as we know is at Lindum and they've sent a messenger to say they're already on their way south. But they'll need reinforcements and plenty of them. We've no time to march on foot. I'll take the cavalry with me this morning. The XXIV and XX Legions will follow of course: forced marches. I've already sent a messenger to the garrison at Glevum, they're far closer than we are, so I've told them to march east and we'll pick them up on the road at Verulamium. Camulodunum's probably lost by now. We'll just have to try to save the port at Londinium. Be ready to start at once."

And so, with only three hundred cavalry, the fearless governor rattled down the long road that ran diagonally across the island and which later centuries would call Watling Street, towards Londinium. It was cold, damp autumn weather, and by nightfall Porteus felt the steam from his horse condensing into ice on his face. Every few hours fresh reports of the rebellion had reached them and each one was more discouraging than the last. But on Suetonius these reports seemed to have no effect at all.

"You've got to admire the old man," Porteus confided to Marcus. "The whole country's rising and he's as cool as ice."

"He enjoys it," Marcus smiled. "The worse it is, the better he likes it."

It seemed to Porteus by the end of the second day's journey that this might be true.

"Natives think we're soft," Suetonius announced as they took a much-needed night's rest by the roadside. "That's the trouble with these colonial settlements like Camulodunum. They see our retired soldiers turning into farmers on the land and think we can't fight. It's the same with every new province – natives need to be taught a lesson every generation. Now we'll do it."

Despite his brave face and his blunt speeches, however, the governor was seriously shaken by two events before he reached Londinium. The first concerned the garrison from Lindum in the north east. Their brave commander, Petilius Cerialis, had led the two thousand crack legionaries down from Lindum believing that he could quell the riot himself. He had not realised the seriousness of the revolt, and that already tens of thousands of tribesmen were up in arms; when his troops ran into them, they were completely massacred and only the commander and his cavalry managed to escape alive. This news had reached Suetonius just as he left Mona.

"Bad business," he muttered: for this was a loss – almost half a legion out of four on the island – that he could ill afford; but he gave no other sign of his fear and he pushed on down the long road with as much determination as ever.

The second event took place on the fifth day, when they reached the town of Verulamium. It was a small settlement with inadequate defences that could easily be breached. It was here that the governor expected to meet the garrison of the II Legion from Glevum before they marched together to Londinium, but when the party of cavalry clattered up, there was no sign of them.

"Where in Hades is the garrison from Glevum?" he thundered at his staff. He turned irritably to Agricola, the handsome military tribune. "Who's in charge there?"

"At present the prefect, Poenius Postumus," Agricola replied promptly. "They should have come up here by now."

"I told them to meet me here," Suetonius grumbled.

It was a quandary and for once his staff could see that the governor was hesitant.

"Well, we'd better go to Londinium to see if anything can be done and hope they catch up," he said at last. And once again the tired party pushed on, eastwards towards the port.

They came to Londinium the next morning. Although it was not an administrative centre like Camulodunum with the status of a *colonia*, it was already a large, sprawling place. Warehouses rose along the river, and the wooden houses of the traders in the muddy streets behind. There were military stores surrounded by palisades, and a makeshift forum. But unlike most Roman settlements, the majority of the buildings were still made of wood instead of stone or brick. It was a busy, informal place – a natural growth waiting to transform itself into a great city: and as Porteus looked at it, he knew that it could not be defended. There were a handful of troops at the depots; but no sign of the legionaries from the Second. The governor and his little force waited unhappily all day while ever worse reports came in. The imperial temple at Camulodunum had been razed to the ground, the colony burnt, and every Roman or pro-Roman inhabitant slain. Boudicca's horde was on its way to London now, and there were fifty, sixty, seventy thousand of them. The traders and their families anxiously crowded round the depot where the governor and his staff were waiting.

"You must save the warehouses, protect our families," they cried.

"With what?" demanded Suetonius angrily. And at nightfall he announced: "We're leaving. There's nothing we can do here. Tell these people to flee wherever they can: if they don't, they'll be cut to pieces." Then without more ado, he turned his horse and made his way out on the road back towards Verulamium.

Still there was no sign of the Second; but the following night on the south east horizon, there was a red glow, and they knew that Londinium was being burned. Before dawn reports came that the huge horde was already advancing in their direction.

"Save yourselves," Suetonius called to the people of Verulamium. "I can't." And yet again, the cavalry cortège clattered back up the road still looking for troops.

That night, once more, they saw the terrible red glow along the horizon.

"Verulamium's gone too," Porteus whispered to Marcus. And for once even Marcus's strong face showed that he was worried.

The XIV and the XX Legions arrived from Mona the next morning. They had covered the two hundred miles in a succession of forced marches and carrying heavy equipment, but the troops were battle hardened and ready for action.

"And now," Suetonius said to his staff, "we shall show them."

The battle that took place two days later was one of the most terrible and merciless examples of slaughter that has ever occurred on the island. It also proved once again that Suetonius, whatever his faults, was a great commander.

The Romans were completely outnumbered. The combined strength of the detachments of the two legions amounted to about seven thousand men: advancing upon them was a victorious horde of ten and perhaps twenty times that size, determined not only to defeat them but to exterminate every last man and destroy Roman power in the province for ever. Faced by a less able general, they might have succeeded.

Suetonius had time to choose his ground, and he chose a long, narrow, defile on a gentle slope: at the top of the slope and on each side were woods. Coolly he arranged his battle line so that the horde of the Iceni and the Trinovantes would have to advance up the slope towards its narrow point where his well-trained legionaries would be ready to receive them.

"See how well he has chosen his position," Marcus said to Porteus.

They had been sent to join the small troop of cavalry that was being held in readiness just behind the Roman line, and from this vantage point he had an excellent view of the whole battle ground.

"They'll outnumber us by ten to one, maybe more. But we have thick woods behind us and on each side: the Celts will think they have trapped us, but by choosing this position we make it impossible for them to surround us or outflank us. They'll lose most of the advantage of their numbers and they will have to come and break themselves on our wall of bronze and iron."

"And if they break through?" asked Porteus.

"They won't!" It was the growling voice of the governor himself who had come up behind him. He looked at the young man sternly, but not unkindly. "Remember this, Porteus," he added significantly, "the bigger the horde is, the more complete the confusion when things go wrong. You'll see." And such was the governor's power of command that from that moment it never occurred to Porteus to doubt the outcome of the battle.

The advance of Boudicca and her horde was the most astonishing sight that Porteus had ever beheld. They rumbled forward out of the mists early in the morning – a huge, black mass that seemed to fill up the horizon. As they drew slowly nearer, it was impossible to count their numbers: it could have been seventy thousand, it could have been two hundred thousand. Men, women and children, they surged forward – some on foot, a few in their bright old war chariots, but most of them riding in cumbersome wagons. They carried a motley collection of spears, clubs, swords and flaming torches and when they caught sight of the Roman legion, patiently standing in the sunlight with their backs to the wood there arose a huge howl of rage up and down the line. But they continued to advance slowly, inexorably, and so great was their number that half an hour passed before they had drawn themselves up at the entrance to the defile to face the Romans.

Then Porteus saw her: a gaunt white-haired figure standing proudly in a chariot drawn by two small horses. She wheeled up and down the line, in the quick darting movements that still made the Celtic chariots so formidable on open ground of their own choosing, and so useless in a confined set-piece battle of this kind. She was screaming her instructions or her encouragement at them – he could not tell which – and at each point of the line that she touched, there was a roar of approval and defiance of the hated Romans.

"Look," Marcus nudged him. "See what they're doing?"

Behind the horde, the wagons were being drawn into lines, completely sealing off the fourth side of the battle ground. It was clear that Boudicca did not intend to let any of the Romans find a way to escape.

The Celts, seeing the Romans trapped, were exultant; and Boudicca whipped up their enthusiasm further.

"We have the governor," she cried. "This place shall be the Romans' grave."

From obscure hiding places, a number of Druids had joined the horde, but everywhere the Celts carried images of their gods: the gorgon heads of Sulis and Leucetius, the horned hunting god Cernunnos, Dagda the red warrior god, Toutatis the ruler of the people, Nodens the cloudmaker, and innumerable little figures with hoods over their heads – minor gods of fertility, healing and good luck. In her own hands, Boudicca brandished a long pole, on top of which was the carved black figure of a raven.

"The raven gives victory in battle," she cried. "I am the raven!" And all along the line the battle cries echoed.

It was a fearsome sight, but Suetonius watched it calmly, and in the disciplined quiet of the Roman line, his rasping voice could be clearly heard.

"Those wagons will trap them when they want to run away."

The noise from the horde grew louder; the Romans waited in silence, and Suetonius continued to watch, a faint look of contempt on his red, weatherbeaten face. Then, while the native horde was still working itself up into a frenzy, his voice was heard once again, giving the astonishing order:

"Advance."

It was a brilliant and daring piece of generalship, and as he had calculated, it took Boudicca and her horde completely by surprise.

The long wall of Roman shields flashed as the line advanced, and the steady, rhythmic beat of the legions' march pounded the ground. The native horde, suddenly aware of what was happening, tried to collect itself into some kind of order, but the Roman advance did not give them time; men and women, children and wagons were all in a sprawling, contorted mass. Out of this huge dark body, eruptions of movement began: streams of warriors, acting individually and under no direction, hurled themselves valiantly at the Roman line, where they were methodically cut to pieces. The machine of the legions pressed on.

Porteus remained stationed with the cavalry, who were ordered to wait. He did so impatiently. At last, he thought, this was his chance to win distinction. He would perform deeds that would be reported even to Graccus in Rome.

"Let us charge," he breathed, "we can crush them with a single blow."

But the governor was in no hurry. He watched impassively as the legions did their work. It was not a valiant cavalry charge that would break the confidence of these rebels, but the steady, invincible wall of metal against which their brave warriors were breaking themselves like waves upon the shore. When their confidence wavered, then would be the time for the cavalry.

It was now as he waited that Porteus began to appreciate the crusty commander's infallible instinct: by some sixth sense he knew exactly when the heaving mass of the horde in front of him had reached the critical point of panic, and it was only then that he gave a curt nod to the military tribune beside him who promptly shouted:

"Sound the charge."

The entire Roman force, infantry and cavalry, surged forward at a run and Porteus found himself galloping over the hard ground towards Boudicca's huge army.

The rebels were already running – not from any cowardice but because their lines were in total confusion. And as the small but compact force of Roman cavalry overtook them, the cavalrymen cut them down like grass. Porteus was conscious only of the thundering horses' hoofs and the excitement of the chase: he hardly saw what he was doing as he hacked and slashed at the ragged figures streaming by; and he was surprised to see the figure of a boy of twelve, his shoulder cut wide open, fall from his own sword. Still he did not hesitate, for this was a battle to the death, but urged his horse forward into the throng of men, boys and women. To right and to left he cut, knowing that it was slaughter, and convinced it was necessary.

Finally he heard the order shouted:

"Cavalry, wheel back." He was nearly at the line of wagons: he did not want to turn back. But again he heard it: "Turn back: regroup." And reluctantly he joined the other riders, careering back to the bare ground where the governor was silently watching.

It was only when they regrouped that he saw what had happened. The cavalry charge had served its purpose well: they had driven the great horde into headlong flight, and if they had not turned back, they would have become entangled in the wagon train themselves. For everything had happened exactly as Suetonius had predicted. In turmoil, their warriors, hopelessly mixed up with defenceless women and children trying to escape from the terrible wall of metal that was rushing down upon them, had crashed into their own wall of wagons and been trapped by it. They fell over traces and wagon shafts, and were thrown to the ground by the terrified horses and oxen. The whole heaving mass became a riot of confusion; and the Roman line moved on, hacking and thrusting indiscriminately at the heap of bodies before it.

"Nothing for cavalry to do now," Marcus muttered at his side. "We'd only be in the way. By Jupiter," he added, "just look at that."

It was mass slaughter. It was no longer a battle, nor anything resembling one, as the helpless horde was pressed against its own barrier and hacked to pieces. Those Celtic warriors who valiantly tried to stand their ground, had no room to fight, and they went down like the women and children.

They now saw Agricola canter up to the governor.

"It's over, sir," he called. "Do I regroup the men and take prisoners?"

But to Porteus's surprise Suetonius's face was stony.

"No."

"There are women and children," the tribune began.

"Kill them all."

And Porteus remembered what a friend of Graccus's had told him before he left Rome:

"Suetonius – a fine general: none better. But when he is angry, then he is truly terrible."

As the massacre of women and children took place before their eyes, a silence descended on those watching, but it did not seem to affect the governor. When it was done, he turned to his staff:

"Remember, gentlemen: when the natives forget to respect Rome, they must be taught to fear her."

On the day of the battle, hardly any of the rebels escaped. Boudicca is dead for certain. The governor refused to stop to count the dead but Marcus and I think there were more than seventy thousand.

We went to Verulamium, then on to Londinium. In both places there was nothing left – just charred ground, as though the rebels had burned all the houses down and then trampled on them. I could not believe that places of such size, especially Londinium, could be so completely destroyed. All the inhabitants had been butchered – all.

As for our own people, the procurator Decianus Catus has run away to Gaul and we are to have a new procurator in his place; the most disgraceful performance of the whole business has been the behaviour of the prefect in charge of the II at Glevum. He heard about the defeat of the Ninth and so he disobeyed the governor's orders and stayed like a coward in his garrison. No wonder we couldn't find him! When he heard about our victory over Boudicca he fell on his sword.

Now the governor is taking vengeance on the whole island. *Vexillations* are being sent to every settlement in the country and any dissidents are being slaughtered. Suetonius says he will offer one choice only: absolute obedience or instant death. He means what he says.

This letter was sent by Porteus to his parents from the charred ruins of Londinium. His feelings for the governor were now mixed. He had come to admire the testy old soldier's coolness and generalship during the rebellion: for if Suetonius had made one mistake, then certainly every Roman soldier in the province could have been massacred in the general uprising that must have followed. To Suetonius therefore, he owed a soldier's loyalty. But he could not help being disgusted by the reign of terror that followed when the governor, seeing the ruins of the port of Londinium and the Roman colony of Camulodunum pounded his fist into his hand and shouted:

"Now they shall taste Roman revenge!"

Up and down the country the Romans went, killing and confiscating in a huge act of administrative anger; and as Suetonius intended, the islanders were cowed into submission. It was a correct military solution, but it left the new province poorer and more unhappy than ever, and the unease Porteus had felt before only grew stronger.

"The governor is a great soldier," he acknowledged to Marcus one day, "but he is destroying this province. The natives fear us, but they do not trust us."

"Perhaps you're right," his friend replied, "though frankly I don't think so. But no one else would agree with you. The legions are all with Suetonius and from what I hear, the emperor would put the whole province in chains if he could."

"They're wrong," Porteus insisted.

"Then all the more reason to keep quiet. Be sensible, young Porteus: forget the whole thing and let others do the worrying; just do as you're told."

This was good advice, and had he been wiser, Porteus would have taken it as his guide for the rest of his career. As it was, though he kept his thoughts to himself during the winter, he continued to ponder the matter.

In other ways, his life took a turn for the better. Suetonius, who knew nothing of his opinions, thought well enough of him after the revolt to send him on several missions, including one to the depleted garrison of the IX Legion at Lindum in the north, in the company of Agricola the tribune. And on that visit he was given further encouragement.

"Later on, we shall have some important campaigns in the north of the island," Agricola told him. "Perhaps you'd like to come on my staff?"

"Oh yes," he replied, and blushed with pleasure.

He wrote to tell his parents of what was passing; to Graccus he sent letters of respect; and to Lydia he wrote:

I think the governor is pleased with me and that by next year your father will have cause to be satisfied with my career.

Marcus continued to take a friendly interest in him. Several times he asked to see Lydia's portrait and on each occasion he told Porteus what a lucky man he was.

"I even wrote to my family to tell them what a splendid fellow you were," he said laughingly to Porteus one day. "Not good enough for that lovely girl of yours, of course!"

Late in the winter, while the snow was still on the ground, a new figure of great significance arrived on the island. He was tall, middle-aged, with a thin, kindly face and receding hair. He had two peculiarities that Porteus observed: he stooped when he spoke to people, as though concentrating intently on what they said; but when not involved in conversation his eyes often seemed to grow distant as though he were dreaming of some far-off place. He was Julius Classicianus, the new procurator and replacement for the disgraced Decianus Catus. His responsibility included all the island's finances. Under the Roman system of divided authority, he reported direct to the emperor.

"He seems a decent man, but a bit vague," Porteus commented to Marcus. "I don't think he'll make much headway here."

In this assessment he was completely wrong.

Classicianus was, like him, a member of the minor provincial aristocracy, having come originally from the town of Trier on the Moselle; but by a combination of great astuteness and honesty he had worked his way up to the highest offices in the state. Kindly he was, but he missed nothing; and within weeks of his arrival he was secretly compiling a report that was to change the province completely. Of this, naturally, Porteus had no idea.

In the early spring, a letter came from Lydia, which Porteus read with joy.

> The aunt of one of the other men on the governor's staff, Marcus Marcellinus, was here at the house recently. She told us all the high opinion that he and the governor have of you and father was pleased. Marcus has written to Rome about you. His aunt showed me a picture of him like the one I have of you. Write to tell me the news of all that you do, and tell me about Marcus also.

This was good news indeed, and Porteus was grateful for the loyalty of his friend. He wrote to Lydia at once, telling her more of his successes, and gave her a warm and friendly account of Marcus too.

It was towards the end of winter, as the snows still lingered, that the governor camped in the windy eastern colony of Camulodunum which his legionaries were busily rebuilding; and it was there one day that he sent for young Porteus and said to him gruffly:

"You are to undertake a mission."

He was delighted. Up to now, he had only accompanied the tribune or one of the *beneficarii* – the governor's personal emissaries. Now at last he was being entrusted with a mission of his own: it was clearly a chance to prove himself, and he listened eagerly as Suetonius outlined his task.

The mission was simple enough: he was to take a centurion and eighty men and make a tour of inspection of some of the minor tribal settlements in the north west of the land under Roman control, close to the territory of the Deceangli where they had been fighting recently.

"They haven't paid any taxes and they may be rebels. They're to pay at once: if they don't, kill their chief and burn down their houses," the governor ordered.

Porteus opened his mouth to protest, but then said nothing. This was his first mission, and if he started arguing with the governor he could be sure it would also be his last. He prepared to leave at once.

They reached the place ten days later: Porteus, the eighty men, and a stocky, elderly centurion, who had served under Suetonius several times before, and who hated natives.

"Hammer them. It's the only thing," he told Porteus. "Suetonius – he knows what he's about."

It was a dreary spot. Like many of the north western settlements at that time, it was poor; the tribe had been forced to abandon their earthwork, which was more a corral than a defensive fortress, and to rebuild their tribal centre at some distance from it. This was what Porteus found: an untidy clutter of huts, a small round shrine, two cattle pens each containing a small collection of thin, long-haired beasts, and a dozen small fields of barley on the hillsides. On the open ground above, however, there were many flocks of small, squat sheep who roamed over a large area. He toured the entire place carefully. The population was not large: at the centre, some five hundred people huddled together; in the foothills around, another two hundred lived in widely scattered home-steads. They were unlike those stout, thatched round houses with their wattle palisades and rich fields of corn that he had encountered all over the south: these were stone hovels, dug into the ground on windy hillsides, relics of an earlier age. The natives watched the progress of the legionaries silently. At the end of his inspection, Porteus confronted the chief – an elderly grey-haired man with a heavy woollen cloak over his shoulders. He stood in front of a gaggle of his people and stared at the Romans insolently. Porteus addressed him sharply.

"You have not paid the *annona* you were assessed last year." This was the corn levy used to feed the army. The chief did not reply but shrugged. "You have not paid the *tributum soli*, or the *tributum capitis* – your land tax or the poll tax," Porteus went on. "Why not?"

The chief regarded him dully. Finally he spoke.

"With what?"

"You have barley, cattle, sheep," Porteus replied firmly.

"We cannot pay. You can see for yourself, Roman. Your emperor is too greedy," the man replied.

"There's no statue to the divine emperor anywhere in the settlement," the centurion grumbled at his side. "And their shrine is to some native god we can't recognise."

[180]

This too was a serious matter. It was the policy of Rome to discover the characteristics of the gods the natives worshipped and to join them to whichever seemed the closest of the vast pantheon of Roman gods. In this way, the provinces passed easily into Roman forms of worship without abandoning their own ancestral gods. It was a practical compromise which usually worked; as long as they abandoned the cursed Druid sect and paid due respect to the divine emperor they were left alone. But the curious hooded figure that the centurion had found in the little shrine, who held a snake in one hand and a raven in the other, did not seem to be identifiable with any Roman deity.

"These ones are trouble," he muttered. "We'd do better to burn the whole place down."

But Porteus shook his head. It seemed pointless to destroy these miserable folk. He was also concerned to see that the taxes they had been assessed by the procurator Decius were obviously too high: for they amounted to more than half the cattle in the pens, and to two thirds of all the barley.

"I shall have their taxes reassessed," he stated. "For the moment we shall take ten cattle, and one wagon of grain."

"That's letting them off lightly," complained the centurion.

"They must pay it at once," Porteus continued. And turning to the old chief he announced: "We shall take taxes from you now, but new assessments will be made in the future – less high than these, and those you must pay promptly."

"Take the ten cattle," Porteus said to the centurion, and the Roman legionaries moved quickly into the cattle pens.

It was then that the trouble began. The natives, seeing their livestock being taken, began to jostle the soldiers and the old chief, with great foolishness, did nothing to stop them. A scuffle began as the legionaries pushed the ragged natives aside with their shields. And then suddenly, as if from nowhere, an elderly woman appeared with a spear and rushed towards them. Before anyone could stop her, she hurled the spear with ferocious accuracy at one of the soldiers. It struck him in the neck and he fell. As soon as he saw it, Porteus knew what must follow.

"Form a line," the centurion shouted. "We'll deal with them," he cried to Porteus. Before he could do anything about it, Porteus saw the battle line drawn up.

"Hold them steady," he called out to the centurion. "Don't move." But it was useless. Without taking any notice of him, the centurion and his force were already advancing with deadly efficiency towards the natives.

"These are not my orders," he shouted.

"They're the governor's orders," returned the centurion. And as he watched, the disciplined troops began to cut down the terrified people in the little settlement, while Porteus watched helplessly.

In an hour, it was all over. They had collected ten wagons of grain, fifty cattle, and the settlement was a smouldering ruin. The chief had been caught and butchered, his shrine completely destroyed.

[181]

"A good day's work," the centurion remarked with a grin. "Where to next, Caius Porteus?"

Porteus said nothing.

In the brief report of this incident that he delivered personally to the governor when they returned to Camulodunum, he said only that there had been resistance to the payment of taxes and that accordingly the settlement had been punished. He also recommended a new tax assessment for the surrounding country. Suetonius received the report casually.

"Quite right," he commented.

But as Porteus was leaving, the governor gave him a quiet, shrewd look and said:

"No centurion will risk his men in a place like that. No honour in being killed by native women. Don't hesitate next time, Caius Porteus. This province has got to be tamed."

But if the governor thought that this was the end of the matter, he was wrong. The butchering of the natives, whose only crime had been poverty, the sense that he was now actively engaged in a brutal policy which he knew would fail, preyed increasingly on Porteus's mind. All over the province, he knew, other troops were performing similar cruel and useless acts of repression, and the thought of it sickened him.

The islanders hate us more every day, he thought and it is only a matter of time before there is another rebellion, another Boudicca. Will there be another Suetonius then, too, or will the entire Roman population be cut to pieces?

He could no longer close his mind to what was being done, but what could he do about it? Should he resign his position and go back to Rome? That would probably end his career. Should he write to Graccus, or some other powerful figure to warn them of the tragic mistakes that were being made? That would be disloyal. In the end, he concluded that there was only one proper course of action, which was neither of these; but before taking it, he decided to consult Marcus, who had always taken a kindly interest in his affairs, and whose judgement he knew was excellent. He believed he could trust him.

He explained his dilemma to him at length, and Marcus listened attentively.

"I must be loyal to the governor," he concluded, "but the whole policy is a terrible mistake, and I can't stand by and say nothing." He frowned. "If he sent me out to destroy another settlement like last time . . ." he made a gesture of despair. "I couldn't."

"What do you want to do then?" Marcus asked him.

"I think I should go direct to the governor," Porteus replied, "and make my complaint to him."

Marcus nodded slowly. It was obvious that young Porteus was determined to make a fool of himself: the question was, should he try to stop him? And on this point Marcus Marcellinus now faced a difficult moral dilemma of his own: did he want his young friend to continue his successful career, or did he want him to take a foolish step which, knowing the temper of the governor, would almost certainly ruin his prospects? He was not sure. For that very morning he had received a long letter from his aunt in Rome, and as a result of what she had told him, his own motives where Porteus was concerned were now mixed. He thought carefully, not liking the choice, and being wise he temporised.

"If you do as you say, the consequences could be serious for you," he said carefully.

"Perhaps, but what else can I do?"

Marcus looked at the young man with pity. He liked young Porteus, and he could not help frankly admiring his honesty and his courage. But . . . He shrugged. After all, he knew, each man must look out for himself.

"You do what you think is right, Porteus," he said gravely. "You are a man of honour – and a brave man too," he added.

It was enough. Porteus thanked him gratefully and went back to his quarters. His mind was now at rest, and Marcus's words – a man of honour – were still ringing in his ears as he sat down to prepare what he must say to Suetonius.

It was his great misfortune that at this most critical moment of his life, he did not possess a highly important piece of information.

For the entire matter of the governor's mistreatment of the new province had already been taken up by hands which were far stronger than his. After a careful inspection of the province's affairs, the new procurator, Classicianus had been appalled by the destruction of the island's wealth.

"If we go on like this," he judged, "we shall be lucky to raise any taxes at all in a few years. This oppression must stop at once."

He had exercised his official right to send his own independent report to Rome – a document far more damning of the governor than anything Porteus had dreamed of.

Such reports were not unusual, for it was the policy of the empire to encourage the financial and military authorities to watch each other jealously: every major official was spied upon in this way, and this was how the bureaucrats in Rome could control their far-flung empire with such efficiency. When Nero received the adverse report he was furious. But there was nothing that even the emperor himself could do about it without upsetting the whole administrative machine, and unbalanced though he often was, Nero knew the value of Rome's huge system of checks and balances. Favourites or no favourites, a commission of inquiry would have to be sent from Rome to investigate Suetonius's administration of the province – that was the only correct procedure.

Private word of the adverse report reached the governor early, before it was known in the province or even leaked to his staff. And it was on the very morning when he received the news that young Porteus requested his interview.

Suetonius was in a rage – a towering rage. He had nearly refused to see Porteus, but supposing it was some minor routine matter that could be easily disposed of, he had him sent in. The young man entered smartly, his clear expression giving no hint that he was about to touch off an explosion.

[183]

"Well Porteus, be quick about it," he muttered testily.

And so Porteus stood to attention, squared his shoulders, and began.

He had worked hard to prepare his speech. It was well thought out, carefully argued, respectfully submitted; it contained exact instances of why he thought the policy of revenge was a mistake, and made practical suggestions for a new and more conciliatory policy; it was in every way an excellent speech, of which Porteus could rightfully be proud – and it contained not one word that the governor wished to hear. As Porteus went on, the general's anger turned to fury; but not a muscle in his red face moved as he listened.

Porteus had no idea of this. Even if he doesn't agree, he thought, he must be impressed with my case. And when he had finished he waited confidently for the governor's response.

Suetonius was completely silent for some time, his eyes resting impassively on this impudent young man who had just challenged him. First it had been the procurator starting a campaign against him – a shameful and outrageous campaign, but one that was at least recognised within the imperial system. And now he had discovered that there was a traitor on his own staff. For that was, unquestionably, what this young man that Graccus had wished on him had turned out to be – a disloyal troublemaker. From his long years of experience the governor knew exactly how to deal with traitors: they must be neutralised and destroyed with a single, sudden blow – and it must be a blow that they could not see coming. So his face remained a perfect mask as he considered the matter; and certain things were clear to him at once: Porteus must not be allowed to give his views to any commission of inquiry; nor must he be able to spread discord amongst the other members of the staff; nor would it do to send him back to Rome either, where he might stir up trouble with Graccus. No, something different was needed, and before long he could see clearly what it was. Without doubt he would deal with this young man. At last he spoke.

"Thank you for your valuable advice, which has been noted." He gave Porteus a polite incline of the head, and then dismissed him coolly. It was a danger signal which Porteus completely missed, and afterwards he confided to Marcus:

"I think I impressed him."

The blow fell the next day.

It was a note from the governor's office, which Marcus delivered to his quarters in the early afternoon. The note was short:

C. Porteus Maximus is transferred to the staff of the procurator.

Porteus was puzzled. What did this mean?

"Do you know about this?" he asked Marcus.

But Marcus shook his head.

"Perhaps they think you should have experience of finance; it could be a good sign," he suggested doubtfully. "There's another note too," he went on.

This was from the secretary to the procurator, in Londinium.

[184]

You are appointed as assistant to the junior procurator. Your first post will be at Sorviodunum. Proceed to this office for instructions at once.

Assistant to the junior procurator! It was a minor clerical post. And Sorviodunum! He had never been to the place but he knew it was nothing more than a staging post at a crossroads – miles from anywhere: a complete backwater.

As he gazed at the two impersonal documents, he realised with a cold horror what they meant – and knew that there was nothing he could do about it.

Suetonius's solution to the problem of Porteus was simple, and perfect. By transferring him to the procurator's office, he removed him completely from his own staff and put him in the enemy camp where he belonged. Even if his views were ever heard, it would be assumed that anything he said was because either he wished to please the procurator, or to revenge himself on the governor for dismissing him from his staff. And by sending an urgent message to Londinium, recommending that the young man would be ideally suited to a junior post in a backwater, Suetonius had ensured that the commission of inquiry was unlikely ever to see him at all. He had to go there, or be guilty of disobeying orders. There was nothing, nothing that he could do. It was a trap that had already closed. Without fully understanding all that had happened, Porteus could see that he had been neutralised.

"What can I do?" he asked Marcus; and for once his friend was at a loss. "I'm finished," the young man said sadly.

He could see the consequences quite clearly. Graccus would say that he had failed; he would lose Lydia; his parents would be disgraced. Was there some way out? He could not see it.

But why had Suetonius turned upon him so violently? He shook his head. He was still ignorant of the procurator's report.

Marcus did not know either.

"It looks as if Suetonius didn't like what you said," he muttered.

Out of consideration, Marcus sat with him for some time, though neither man spoke much.

"I have a posting too," Marcus said at last. "I am to go to Rome for a year and I'm leaving in two days. I'm sorry, young Porteus, to be leaving you like this; but perhaps something will turn up." He gave him an encouraging smile. It was easy for him, Porteus thought: he was a success.

"Let me know if I can do anything for you." Marcus said as he left.

For the rest of the day Porteus prepared to leave. Several times he wondered whether to appeal to Suetonius, but common sense told him that this was a waste of time. Instead he put his affairs in order and wrote a long letter to Lydia, asking her to wait for him while he tried to rescue his career. It was a brave letter:

I still hope to recover and to return from this province with honour. Marcus will give you news of me.

This he gave to Marcus, with a request that he would take it to the house of Graccus when he reached Rome.

"Hand this to Lydia," he begged. "Give her a good report of me, and tell her father that I have conducted myself with honour. I have no one else I can trust but you."

Marcus took the letter with a trace of embarrassment.

"I shall do what I can," he promised, "but don't hope for too much, Porteus." And with that the two men parted.

That evening Porteus made one attempt to take leave of the governor, but Suetonius would not see him, and so as dusk fell, there was nothing for him to do but to ride slowly and sadly down the long road to Londinium.

At the port of Londinium his last hopes were dashed. Perhaps, he had thought, I can at least make a good impression on the procurator and he will speak for me in Rome. But at the procurator's headquarters he found that Classicianus was absent in the north and would not return for weeks.

"You're to go to Sorviodunum at once," the secretary told him bleakly. "Governor's request. The procurator's never heard of you and you probably won't see him at all until next year."

It was only then that Porteus realised the complete effectiveness of Suetonius's action against him.

"And what am I to do in Sorviodunum?" he asked slowly.

The secretary shrugged. He was a short, bald man with many things on his mind, and he had only taken on this gloomy-looking young man, about whom he knew nothing, at the urgent request of the governor.

"There are some imperial estates there and you're to supervise them. It's a routine job," he added. "Hurry up, will you – you're expected there tomorrow." And before Porteus could argue, the bald secretary's attention was engaged elsewhere.

Sorviodunum: a place that scarcely existed. Porteus: a young Roman whom the administration had decided to forget. That night he faced the fact that his career was in ruins, and even though he did not yet understand the cause of his disgrace, there could be no mistaking its results. For the moment there was nothing he could do except go to the lonely outpost.

He wondered what he would find there.

Life had not dealt very kindly with Tosutigus since the conquest, and as he looked back, some of the memories were painful.

In the days after Vespasian left, the young chief had waited anxiously for developments. News soon arrived from the south west: every few days word came through the valleys of the fall of another of the many-walled hill forts.

"So much for the proud Durotriges," Tosutigus would mutter with grim satisfaction; and it was not long before he had convinced himself that his surrender of the dune and the signing away of his lands had been a masterstroke of diplomacy.

The fortresses continued to fall and he waited expectantly for news from Vespasian or the governor; but no message came.

By the end of the summer, Vespasian's campaign was over. The Durotrigan chiefs had fought hard, but the siege engines of the II had been too much for them; and the hard-faced tribune had cut a swathe through their entire territory from east to the far west, where he set up camp for the winter. All over the island the news travelled: "The proud Durotriges have been humbled."

But if they were humbled, they had still fought; and they had not forgotten the betrayal of the young chief at Sarum.

It was one early autumn morning that a small party of prisoners arrived from the south west at Sarum and were led into the dune by a detachment of Roman soldiers. There were twenty prisoners, men of all ages, and the Romans ordered Tosutigus's men to feed them.

"They tried to break into our camp and loot the stores," the soldier in charge explained to him. "They're bound for Londinium, to be sold as slaves."

The party rested there the night, and while the soldiers rested, Tosutigus went to inspect the prisoners. One of them, he noticed, was only a boy of ten, and as he drew close he recognised the son of one of the Durotrigan chiefs. Feeling sorry for the boy, he approached him.

"I know your father and I am sad to see you like this," he said.

But the boy only scowled at him.

"Better a slave than a traitor like you," he cried bitterly. "Tosutigus the Liar." And he spat on the ground to show his contempt.

Tosutigus turned round and walked away. So that was to be his reputation – just as the Druid Aflek had warned him. He told himself that he did not care.

"The Durotriges may hate me; but it's from the emperor that I shall get my reward," he reasoned.

The autumn passed and no word came.

The snows fell; Sarum was silent. The huge gaping circle of the dune stood frozen and empty. Each day, Tosutigus would climb its high walls and pace about on the great rim of ice, scouring the horizon for signs of the Roman messengers he hoped for. Sometimes Numex and Balba accompanied him, waddling at his side, their red faces shining in the cold air, peering with him across the snow-covered wastes – but as the months passed, he had little conviction that anything would come out of them.

Throughout the long winter, the landscape remained empty. When the snows departed, Tosutigus noticed that the chalk sides of the dune were sprouting tufts of new grass.

As the river grew to its full spate, and spring began, the people of Sarum went about their business quietly. The young chief guessed that they despised him for surrendering the dune, and compared him unfavourably with the Durotriges; already, while Vespasian's troops were busy occupying their territory, they had begun to compose songs about the feats of bravery of their chiefs who had fallen in battle. But he was not discouraged.

"You will see," he told Numex and his brother. "I have done well for Sarum."

It was a full year after Vespasian's visit that a little group of men was seen approaching across the high ground from the north east. It consisted of a tall, sallow, middle-aged man on a small horse, six slaves and six legionaries; the group came across the high ground towards the dune slowly, pausing frequently.

Eagerly, Tosutigus rode out to meet them. When he reached them, he saw that two of the slaves carried posts, on top of which rested a pair of crossed wooden bars, from the four ends of which hung small plumb lines.

"We're surveyors," the sallow man told him. "There are important roads coming through here."

When the surveyors reached the dune, they inspected it carefully, and then went down the slope to the river below.

"There's to be a road across the river," the sallow man said, "and a new settlement." He indicated a modest rectangular site by the bank.

A new settlement! The young chief's eyes lit up. So the Romans had important plans for the place.

"Just a staging post, a *mansio*," the surveyor went on. But Tosutigus was not listening. Already he had visions of an extensive town under his control.

They came to build the roads two months later: this time a whole century of eighty men with their centurion swung over the high ground, each man carrying a spade on his back in addition to his other equipment.

They began with the settlement, and they worked with astonishing speed. On the site by the river that the surveyor had marked out, they threw up a bank of earth, just as though they were building one of their walled military camps. Down the centre they laid out a single small street, with three square plots on each side of it, making a grid. And that was all. There was no forum, no space for any large official building, no temple: just a few modest plots designated for a stable block, a guardhouse, and some simple dwellings. In one corner, a rectangular area was set aside for a little orchard within the wall. The entire work was done in under two days and when it was completed, the centurion remarked:

"Well that's it. That's Sorviodunum."

But to Tosutigus, even then, the drab little enclosure seemed full of promise.

"We'll need labourers for the road," the centurion said next. "What can you give us?"

Glad to have a chance to show his usefulness, Tosutigus at once provided them with fifty men, and to these he added Numex, despite the fellow's protesting: "But I'm a carpenter!"

"Learn how the Romans build," the chief ordered him. "You'll be more useful to me then." For he knew very well that Numex would quickly learn Roman skills and bring credit to Sarum and its chief in the future.

When he saw how the Romans built their roads, Tosutigus was astounded. The first main route lay across the high ground to the north east and was to stretch in an almost straight line from the dune to the port of Londinium some eighty miles away. As the men worked he would ride out to watch them, returning home shaking his head in wonder.

First the men dug two parallel trenches, about eighty feet apart, and piled up the earth they dug into a raised causeway in the middle, roughly twenty-five feet wide. This was the famous raised *agger*. Then on top of this they packed chalk, a handspan deep and cambered down from the centre, to ensure that the road surface would be well drained. Next, they brought carts of flint from local diggings, and these the legionaries laid over the chalk, packing each flint carefully down by hand until they were three or four inches deep, and filling in with chalk to make the surface even. Finally they packed six inches of gravel on top, stamping it down until it was hard and smooth.

"Sometimes, if there are ironworks in the area, we put the slag on top," the centurion told him. "Then it rusts into a single sheet and it lasts for ever."

Tosutigus also noticed that several roads were to intersect beside the dune. "Sorviodunum will be connected to places all over the island," he thought happily. At the river Afon below, the soldiers built a stone causeway across the river bed and paved it to form an artificial ford.

"Why not build a bridge?" he asked.

"Bridges can be destroyed," the centurion replied grimly. "Fords aren't so easy to break up."

The road across the river led south west towards the land of the Durotriges; he watched with fascination as, during the next two months, the Romans laid wooden underpinnings across the low marshy ground, laid the road surface over them, and then made the road zig zag up the steep hill beyond. But it was what followed that made him gasp with wonder.

For across the rolling lands of the proud Durotriges, in a straight line that ran south west from Sarum, the Romans build a highway unlike anything the island would see again until the coming of railways nearly two thousand years later. Between its deep ditches the *agger* was almost fifty feet wide, and it rose a full six feet high. It stretched across the landscape, straight, uncompromising and magnificent for thirty miles into the Durotrigan heartland before curving south towards the coast.

This was the mighty road known as the Ackling Dyke and its message was unmistakable: Your hill forts have fallen, it stated, but hill or valley, open land or forest, all are one to Rome. We march straight across them at our will.

As Tosutigus stood on the high ground and stared at this great new highway, so utterly unlike the ancient ridgepaths of the island that he had known before, he was lost in admiration.

"They are like bands of iron over the whole land," he murmured. And for the first time he began to understand the real power of Rome.

That winter, word finally came from the governor, in the form of a dark, swarthy man from the governor's staff, with small, hard eyes. He was accompanied by a clerk from the procurator's office. He came to the point at once.

"This territory is being organised," he told the young chief. "In view of your co-operation, the governor has decided to reward you."

At last. This was what he had been waiting for.

"Which area am I to rule?" he asked eagerly.

The swarthy man frowned. Whatever was this young Celt talking about? He took no notice and continued.

"All the land of the Durotriges will remain under military occupation. Sorviodunum is excepted and will form part of the land for sixty miles to the east, which is to form a new client kingdom."

Tosutigus went pale. This was all the land that the Atrebates had occupied in their heyday; a huge and magnificent territory.

"I am to rule all that?"

The swarthy man paused.

"Rule?" He decided he must have misunderstood the young native.

Tosutigus shook his head in wonder. He had never dared to hope that his letter would have impressed the governor so much.

It had not occurred to the swarthy Roman that Tosutigus expected to rule anything and even now he failed to realise the great delusion that still filled the young chief's mind. He went on stolidly.

"The new king of all the Atrebates is the chief Cogidubnus – he's your king now. In recognition of your gift to the emperor, you are exempt during your lifetime from all taxes on your estates – both the *annona* and the poll tax."

Tosutigus stared at him, only gradually understanding what was being said. He had heard of Cogidubnus of course – a pro-Roman chief of the Atrebates with estates far away in the south east.

"He is my king?"

"Yes."

"What am I to rule them?"

"Nothing."

He turned it over in his mind.

"Is he a Roman citizen?"

"The emperor has granted him citizenship."

"Am I?"

"No."

"What am I then? What status have I?" he asked in sudden despair.

"*Peregrinus*: a native."

"So, apart from the tax exemptions, that's all I have?"

"That's all."

What Tosutigus should have realised was that the Romans were following their normal pattern in settling a new province, and that in fact they were dealing with him kindly.

The governor was wisely maintaining a military zone in the territory of the troublesome Durotriges, and rewarding the Atrebates for their longstanding friendship by, at least temporarily, restoring, their lands. This would leave the troops and administrators free to deal with the north and west of the island where most of the tribes were yet to be conquered.

At that moment, the legionaries were constructing the great road known as the Fosse Way that ran from the western part of the conquered Durotrigan lands in a north eastern diagonal across the whole of the southern half of the island. This formed the frontier from which they would advance. In time, both the client kingdom of the Atrebates and the military zone in the south west would disappear – though perhaps not for a generation. Then there would be provincial capitals, councils and native magistrates with the chance to obtain the coveted Roman citizenship. But not yet. To have excluded this obscure young chief from the military zone and to have given him generous tax exemptions was to treat him better than he had any right to hope.

But still Tosutigus dreamed.

It was the following year that he made the journey eastwards to pay his respects to Cogidubnus; and when he did so he received two more shocks.

The new client kingdom of Cogidubnus was so large that it contained two provincial capitals, the northern one of which lay on the main road from Sorviodunum to Londinium. It was called Calleva Atrebatum.

The first shock came when he saw it. He could have wept: for though only half built, Calleva was everything he had hoped Sorviodunum would be. It contained a forum, handsome buildings of wood, even a few of stone, and a generously proportioned network of streets covering many acres. But the king, he discovered, was not there. He was far away on the south coast and it was there, seven days later, that Cogidubnus and the chief from Sarum came face to face, and Tosutigus received the second blow.

Tiberius Claudius Cogidubnus – he had wisely taken the emperor's first names as his own as a mark of respect – was a large, powerfully built man, already middle-aged, with greying hair and glittering blue eyes. He had no particular interest in the young chief from the west of his territory, but greeted him courteously enough. His mind at that moment was principally occupied by the great building he had in hand. For on a splendid site near the sea the new king of the Atrebates was building a sumptuous villa.

It was everything Tosutigus had ever dreamed of, and more. With envy he followed the burly king through its rising halls and courtyards. In astonishment he looked at the mosaics that were beginning to adorn its floors: here a group of dolphins was depicted dancing around Neptune the sea god; elsewhere, a peacock strutted in a Roman garden. There were even windows with green translucent glass in them, shedding a cool light on the paved floors inside. It was a noble building, worthy, it seemed to him, of a Roman senator, and as he gazed at it he realised the vast gulf that separated his dream of power from the reality of the little *mansio* at Sorviodunum.

"This," he thought, "this is Rome."

He stayed there two days. Cogidubnus thanked him for coming and gave him a small statuette of himself. Then he returned to Sarum.

[191]

In the sixteen years that followed, Tosutigus lived quietly. When the rebel prince Caractacus fought his brave but useless rearguard action against the Romans in the south, he did not even bother to ask for help from the chief at Sarum. Cogidubnus had politely ignored him as irrelevant; the Durotriges remembered his name with contempt; but by everyone else he was almost forgotten – one of the many nameless, petty chiefs who existed in the island at this time.

The year after his visit to Cogidubnus, he had married. The girl was the third daughter of another minor chief of the Atrebates. This too, had not been without humiliation. The girl's father was poor, and Tosutigus's reputation with the Durotriges, although the two tribes had taken different sides, did not speak well for him with the Atrebatic chief: he refused to give the girl a dowry. Tosutigus took her all the same: she was a striking, red-haired girl with a tempestuous temper, who had given him a daughter and lived six more years before suddenly falling sick one winter and dying.

He had not remarried. His marriage had not been especially happy. After his wife's death he had contented himself with a woman he visited in Calleva from time to time, and his affections had centred on his daughter, Maeve, whom he adored and who looked strikingly like her mother. At forty, Tosutigus had become a quiet, middle-aged widower, somewhat withdrawn from the world, living on his estate in a provincial backwater.

The settlement was certainly nothing much to look at. Beside the dune, scarcely occupied now except for a few huts, and only used occasionally as a desultory market, the bare hard roads intersected and cut their lonely way across the empty ancient tracks and ridges. By the entrance on the eastern side there was a cluster of huts used by Balba and some of the weavers. Down in the valley below, the small settlement of Sorviodunum contained a well-run stables for the governor's messengers, a small inn where travellers could rest, and a little group of store houses. It was presided over by three soldiers who had little to do and who would gather in the porch of the largest storehouse and play at dice by the hour. The only other regular visitor was a clerk from the procurator's office who came only at intervals to supervise the imperial estate and arrange for the sale of the emperor's grain at the end of the summer.

Yet Tosutigus had some reason to be contented. Sorviodunum was at peace; though some of the western chiefs used the Boudiccan revolt as an opportunity to rebel, Tosutigus took no part in it at all. And even if Sorviodunum remained no more than a staging post, the sporadic traffic through the place was important. From the south west, by the new road through the land of the Durotriges, came the prized Kimmeridge shale – a dark, lustrous stone that the Romans mined eagerly at the coast. A new road had also been built to the west and along this came lead from the mines in the western hills, bound for the growing towns of Calleva and Londinium, from which it might be shipped to Gaul and beyond.

Moreover, the tax concessions given him had turned out to be worth more than he realised. At a time when land yielded the best return of any investment in the empire, the untaxed revenues from his estates over the years had made Tosutigus a rich man. In his farm, simple as it was, handsome firedogs of wrought iron decorated with gold stood before his hearth. His daughter Maeve wore armlets and anklets of gold, shale and amber. He ate off the finest red pottery from Arezzo and drank the best wines of Gaul. The family shrine contained ornaments of silver and gold.

Above all, he had Maeve. She was already turning into a beautiful young woman, with her mother's cascade of sumptuous red hair, flashing blue eyes and a blazing temper that, while he could still control her, caused him to laugh with delight. He had taught her what Roman ways he could but he had also spoiled her shamefully, allowing her to run wild, and swelling with pride at the easy way she had mastered every horse he had given her.

"She's both a son and a daughter to me," he often thought. And whatever the deficiencies of her education in the new Roman world, she would more than make up for by her dazzling looks and Celtic fire. He was sure of it.

"You'll marry a great chief – a prince," he told her. "Nothing less will do."

But despite all these gifts, his spirit was still discontented. When any Roman official came through, he would hurry down to the staging post wearing his toga, suddenly as eager as he had been as a young man to impress them with his Roman ways. Not a year passed without his evolving some scheme to obtain citizenship, none of which ever succeeded. A month might go by when he would stay on his farm in the valley watching his sheep and cattle, and delight in the company of his wayward daughter; but before long he would wander up to the dune, stand on its overgrown walls, and stare over the high ground as his ancestors had done before him. And for some reason, whenever he did this, his dreams of glory would return as fresh and strong as they had been when he was a foolish young man of twenty.

Despite his determination to succeed in the Roman world, the chief often spent long hours alone in the family shrine, endlessly inspecting the great sword of Coolin and turning over his grandfather's horned helmet in his hands. Then he would kneel before the little figure of Nodens, his family's protecting god and pray:

"Make me worthy of my ancestors."

Once, when she was ten, he took Maeve to the deserted henge, and pointing to the huge sarsens, he told her:

"Your ancestors built this place in a single day: they were giants, gods. Never forget that."

"Is that why I shall marry a prince?" she asked solemnly.

"The descendants of Coolin the Warrior and the ancient house of Krona deserve nothing less," he replied.

To Porteus, as his small chestnut pony clattered towards the west, the broad, hard road to Sorviodunum seemed endless. It was the middle of a cool, grey day when he left the town by Calleva and the clouds had not lifted. Now, in the early evening, he was crossing the last ridge before reaching the place that was to be his new home.

When he did so and saw the empty dune with the undistinguished little settlement below, his heart sank. On arrival, he discovered that the three legionaries in charge of the place had been warned of his arrival only the day before and it was obvious that they were not pleased to see him. They led him in silence to a two-roomed hut in one corner of the settlement which contained a couch, a camp stool, a table, a horsehair mattress and a single slave to attend to his needs.

"This is all you have?" he asked irritably.

The eldest soldier shrugged. He had never liked procurators or their staff.

"See for yourself." He indicated the little station with its mean huts, and the empty spaces around it. "There's nothing else here."

The next morning Porteus inspected the place thoroughly. He saw the sweeping ridges where the small brown sheep grazed, noted the many little farmsteads and their patchwork of fields. He saw that the imperial estate was immense and valuable, and that little care had been taken to keep its huge tracts of land in good order. At the gates of the dune he met the squat figure of Balba and could not help drawing back at the pungent smell that emanated from him.

When he had seen everything he drew his own grim conclusion.

"It's a backwater. If I stay here long I shall go mad."

When he returned to Sorviodunum, the legionaries told him he had a visitor.

"The local chief," they said.

Tosutigus had taken off the *paenula* – the hooded cloak which was the everyday costume of most Celts – and had put on a toga, which had unfortunately become splashed with mud on the journey from his farm. He had shaved his beard, but not his flowing moustaches, now turning grey; and on his feet he wore stout boots. He presented a curious, but not undignified figure.

But it was the figure beside him that Porteus was staring at: a radiant girl, dressed in a Celtic costume of green and blue, with the finest tresses of bright red hair that he had ever seen, falling almost to her waist, a pale skin that was lightly freckled, and sparkling blue eyes. She was, he guessed, about the same age as Lydia.

"I am Tosutigus, chief of Sarum," the old man greeted him solemnly. "And this is my daughter Maeve."

And to Porteus's surprise, instead of modestly lowering her gaze, as any Roman girl would do, the chief's daughter stared brilliantly, straight into his eyes.

When Tosutigus heard that a new Roman official was to be stationed at Sorviodunum, he had hurried down the valley to make a good impression; and within minutes he let the pleasant-looking young Roman understand that it was he who had given the estate to the Emperor

Claudius, and reminded him that he was exempt from taxes on the lands that he still held.

"And where have you come from? What position?" he asked.

"From the governor's staff," Porteus replied. It was true, after all, and he had no wish to explain the circumstances that had brought him to Sorviodunum. Tosutigus was impressed. Could it be, at last, that he had been given a way to get the governor's ear? Porteus, though he was aware of the effect of his words, was even more conscious of the fact that the girl, for reasons he could not guess at, was still staring fixedly into his eyes.

Maeve was fifteen; and she had indeed good reason to stare at the young Roman with his curly black hair and gentle brown eyes: for she knew something about him that no one else did.

Despite her father's desire to be a Roman, Maeve had been brought up as a Celtic child, and after her mother's death she had been allowed to run wild. The local women, the wives of Numex, Balba and others like them had taken care of her and whatever she knew about the adult world and her duties as a woman, she had learned from them. It was Maeve who carefully polished the sacred sword of Coolin and the heavy helmet in the family shrine; it was she who planted the little hedge of hawthorn near the house to ward off evil spirits. It was she who knew every story about the locality and her family: the talking head that prophesied to Coolin the Warrior, the raven that would circle the house three times when it was time for the head of the family to join the gods; and the branch of the nearby oak tree that would fall at the moment when he died – folk lore and legends that even Tosutigus often forgot. No one knew the woods and valleys better. She knew which clearings were sacred to the wood goddess Nemetona, which springs and streams were most favoured by Sulis the healing goddess; she knew that the swan flying low over the river might be the sun god in disguise, and must never be shot.

"Wound a swan, and the sun will make you bleed for hurting him," the women had told the child.

She had been well trained in her household duties. Though the daughter of a chief, she was not too proud to grind the corn herself by hand between the quernstones that the women still used, and her fingers were as deft as any on the big loom where the bright cloth was woven in the huts beside the dune.

Her father had taught her a little Latin, which she could speak; but she could not read or write. And this was the sum total of her education.

But she had recently reached an important time in her life; for she had decided it was time to find herself a husband.

Just three weeks before the arrival of Porteus, when her monthly time was ending, she had gone alone to a little clearing in the woods where there was a spring sacred to Sulis, and there she had stripped naked and carefully washed herself in the spring. The water was cold and she shivered. But as she looked at her long strands of hair and inspected the taut, white lines of her body, she was pleased.

"Good enough for any man," she said softly. And now, she sensed, it was time to look for her husband.

She had not told anyone about this little private rite, but when she came out of the woods she immediately began to count horses. For she had known ever since she was a child, that if a maiden counts horses at the start of her month, then the first man she sees after counting a hundred, will be her bridegroom.

Three weeks went by. There were not many horses in Sarum, but from time to time they passed on the road. The evening before Porteus's arrival, she had reached ninety-nine, and at the settlement she caught sight of his horse just before he walked round the corner of the stables to greet them.

So he was the one! This was Maeve's secret, and the reason why she stared at him so boldly and intently.

"He is handsome," she thought. "And young." She could see herself on his arm.

But now that the gods had given her a sign, what came next? How would the courtship take place? About this the fifteen-year-old girl was less sure.

In the months that followed, Porteus buried himself in his work. The news from Londinium was conflicting. A commission of enquiry had arrived to investigate the conduct of the governor, and it seemed to be siding with the procurator; but then it departed and nothing more was heard.

He wrote three times to Lydia and once to Marcus, but received no reply. To his father he wrote:

> Sorviodunum is a quiet place. There is no one here except a chief who speaks a little Latin, and his daughter who speaks less. The imperial estate however is large and needs organising. It should keep me busy for several months.

The estate had been neglected. The assistant to the procurator who was supposed to supervise it was busily engaged further west near the colony of Glevum, and apart from sporadic visits, had done nothing to improve the place in years. Porteus could see at once that, with a little effort, the revenue from the estate could be doubled; and he set to work to do so. If he could impress the procurator and increase the emperor's wealth, then perhaps he could win his way back into favour.

He worked hard and systematically, inspecting every field, ordering the repair of ditches, restoring cattle pens, rebuilding grain stores. He worked from first light until the ridges darkened, when he returned to Sorviodunum, ate a light meal and fell instantly asleep.

Each night, as he lay on the simple horsehair bed on the floor of the bleak little house, he dreamed of his return to Rome, restored to honour, and he dreamed of Lydia.

After the first month, he sent a brief report to Classicianus, outlining what he was doing. It was acknowledged politely by a clerk in the procurator's office. That was all.

Several times he saw the red-headed girl walking by the settlement or riding on a fine, high-stepping horse over the ridges with her loose hair flowing behind her. On several occasions the chief sent presents of game, and once a fine blanket, to his spartan quarters. But he was too preoccupied with his own plans to think much about either the girl or her father.

But on the eve of the great festival of Samain, the Celtic name for Hallowe'en, Tosutigus invited the young Roman to a feast at his house; and not wishing to offend the native chief, Porteus went.

It was already dark when he entered the wattle enclosure round Tosutigus's house, and as he did so he realised that he had been so busy and so starved of company that this was the first time he had paused to relax in several months. As he walked past the spits in the enclosure and the charcoal hearth where the women were preparing the meal, and entered the large thatched hall in the centre of which another fire was burning, he realised how much he had missed warmth and comfort in his cold, bare quarters in Sorviodunum.

To his surprise, the house was not full of local men; Tosutigus greeted him alone. Once again, he was wearing a toga and he led the young Roman to a couch near the fire.

"Let us show you that even a Celt can give you a Roman meal," he cried. "And that my daughter knows how to prepare one."

The meal that followed was better than anything Porteus had enjoyed since he left the governor's quarters, and it did indeed conform to the Roman pattern. First came the *gustatio*: oysters, brought up from the south in barrels of salted water, a salad prepared with pepper and olive oil imported from the Mediterranean, and a delicate preparation of eggs. Next came the main courses: venison, and a local dish of mutton, cooked with rosemary and thyme. There were lampreys, trout and veal. And to accompany this, the women brought in huge, square, sweet-smelling loaves of unleavened bread and the rich butter of the area. Finally, for the *mensae secundae* there were puddings made by Maeve, apples and pears. It was a magnificent meal, and accompanied not by the ale and mead that Porteus had expected, but by excellent wines from Gaul. So well did he eat and drink that he even began to enjoy Tosutigus's ponderous jokes, and to take no more notice of the endless hints that some favourable mention should be made of him to the governor.

During the meal he saw that each course was brought in by the red-haired girl and her serving women. She seemed to take no special notice of him on this occasion, but several times he found his eyes following her back and forth across the room, and he became aware of the proud carriage of her young head with its magnificent tresses shining in the firelight, and of the lilting rhythm of her walk. She wore a simple green robe that was slit up one side almost to the waist so that he caught tempting glimpses of her leg.

"A magnificent meal," he complimented the chief when they were done.

"It is my daughter you should thank," the Celt replied, and called the girl forward.

While Porteus thanked her as courtesy demanded, she stood before him with her eyes this time modestly downcast, her hair falling forward so that it covered her cheeks. Despite his love for Lydia, the young Roman felt a sudden urge to take this marvellous girl in his arms. He laughed to himself. No doubt it was the meal.

What he did not know was that with each successive course, Maeve had sprinkled his food with a mixture of herbs which she had carefully prepared that afternoon, and which the older women had promised her was a powerful love potion. Whether the herbs were aphrodisiac or whether Porteus was simply flushed with food and wine, she observed with a surreptitious glance that the handsome young Roman's eyes were glowing – she hoped with lust. She kept her eyes on the ground, but inside she felt for the first time the exhilaration of sexual triumph.

"I will have him," she thought.

Tosutigus did not know about the aphrodisiac herbs, nor that Maeve had been counting horses; but as he watched through half-closed eyelids the effect his daughter was having on Porteus, he smiled quietly to himself.

The Celtic chief was less naïve than the young Roman supposed. A month before, Tosutigus had ridden into Calleva and made discreet enquiries about him; he had met a clerk from the governor's staff and from him he had discovered the full story of Porteus's prospective marriage, his quarrel with Suetonius and his fall; and from this information he had drawn his own conclusions. He had also watched the vigorous way in which the young Roman had gone about his work on the imperial estate.

His assessment was, for once, realistic.

"He's still a good catch for my daughter," he considered.

Indeed, even in disgrace, Porteus was certainly as good a match as Maeve was likely to encounter in the backwater of Sorviodunum.

"With a different governor, or with the procurator's help, he could still go far," the Celt deduced. "And in any case, my grandchildren would be born Roman citizens. Then who knows what they might achieve!"

"I think that young Roman could be a good match for you," he had told Maeve two days before the feast, and she had smiled quietly and replied: "I think so too."

During the winter months, Porteus himself made two journeys to Calleva and one to Londinium in the hope that he might see Classicianus; but again the procurator had been absent and his hope of improving his position had to be shelved. It was on the day before he left Londinium that he had a painful experience. As he came out of a small inn, he heard the crash of horses' hoofs on the cobblestones, and looking up, he saw Suetonius and a cavalcade of twenty staff officers trotting straight towards him. He was standing alone. Neither the governor, nor the riders, many of whom he knew, could fail to see him, and a moment later he found himself staring straight into the angry eyes of the governor himself.

Suetonius did not pause, did not avert his gaze, or even scowl: he looked straight into the eyes of the young man as he passed, and gave no sign of recognition at all. His face was as blank as if Porteus had not been there. The officers following, observing the governor's behaviour, were careful not to look at him at all.

The next day, Porteus returned to Sorviodunum.

By the spring, he could already predict a modest increase in the output from the estate, and by the following year he was sure the yields would improve enormously.

"But by then, if the gods favour me, I shall no longer be here," he thought.

Several times during the long, cold months, Tosutigus took him hunting in the woods. They hunted both deer and the boar. And on each occasion their hunting brought them to a point near the chief's farm where Maeve would be waiting with a meal, accompanied by mulled ale and the heady island mead.

On these occasions, the older man would gently draw the young Roman out on the subject of his plans for the future, and from the little that Porteus let fall, it was clear to the chief that his position had not changed.

Soon after midwinter, a letter came from Marcus.

> I am afraid, my dear Porteus, that things in Rome are not going well for you at present. Graccus as you may suppose, was furious that you fell out with Suetonius. The rumour here is that after the commission of enquiry, the governor will be retired from Britannia at a convenient time, but that he will leave with honour. The emperor is in no mood to disgrace him, and will do nothing for his enemies. Frankly, you are well out of things here.

The letter gave no news of Lydia; but Porteus told himself that since Graccus was furious, she had probably been forbidden to write to him herself, and that Marcus was probably being tactful by making no mention of her.

He did not despair. He redoubled his efforts.

"By the end of summer," he vowed, "I'll return to Rome with honour."

Marcus's information was accurate. Soon after his letter arrived, news came to Sorviodunum that Suetonius had returned to Rome with honour and that he had been replaced by a new governor – Publius Petronius Turpilianus – who was reputed to be a milder man. He hoped to hear some word from the new governor, and sent him a respectful letter of welcome to remind him of his existence. But no word came.

The summer was fine and a bumper crop was expected. He felt some pride, at least, in his achievement on the estate.

Then, just before midsummer, a message came that the procurator himself was coming to inspect the place; and at this he rejoiced. At last: his opportunity had come.

Classicianus was just as he remembered seeing him – a quiet man of medium height, with a forehead over which his thinning brown hair made a tired display, and thoughtful blue eyes. He might have been a scholar rather than an administrator. Despite his high rank, he came with only three clerks and a junior procurator for escort. With the help of the legionaries Porteus had put up a large tent for him beside the little orchard, and although it was a primitive affair, Classicianus seemed quite satisfied with the arrangement. He spent an entire day touring the estate, studied every aspect of the progress in person, and inspected the accounts with his clerks. He made no comment, but Porteus could not believe that he had failed to be impressed.

It was in the evening that Tosutigus arrived at the settlement without warning. He had come to pay his respects to the procurator. On this occasion, Porteus noticed, he was perfectly dressed: his toga was a dazzling white; he wore elegant sandals; and the young Roman was astonished to see that he had even shaved off his moustache. Classicianus, appreciating at a glance the effort that must have been made by this native chief, welcomed him with every mark of respect, and invited him into the tent.

But after the initial courtesies, to Porteus's surprise, the chief gravely requested a private audience with the procurator; and Classicianus, not wishing to offend him, immediately granted it, obliging Porteus and the other officials to withdraw.

It was now, for the first time in his life, that Tosutigus conducted a successful piece of diplomacy. Standing before the procurator, the perfect picture of provincial pride, he made a short but well-calculated speech.

"I hear reports, Julius Classicianus," he began ponderously, "that you have shown respect for this island and its people, where others have not." He paused carefully, before going on. "As you will know, when the late divine Emperor Claudius came to Britannia, I made him, of my own will, a gift of the best part of my estates – those fine lands you have inspected today. They are noble estates and they have belonged to my family since a time before even Rome was great."

He paused again. "Since that time however," he went on, with a trace of anger in his voice, "I have seen my ancestral lands neglected, almost ruined by your officials, who visit them only once or twice a year. I have seen ditches fill up, fences down, farmsteads in disrepair, sheep untended. It's a loss to your emperor and a scandal to me." His voice rose in protest: "I did not give Claudius my lands to see them laid waste!" He stopped, apparently to calm down. "In this last year you have sent an official who has begun to restore them. I say begun: there are years of work to do still. But I hope, Classicianus, that this means the policy of your office will be more consistent and that you are not here to remove your official as soon as minor improvements are made, and allow my ancestral estates to fall to pieces yet again."

He bowed stiffly.

Of his plans for Maeve he had given no hint; he had not even mentioned Porteus by name. He had cleverly calculated that when the young Roman had been wished on the procurator he had probably been added to a staff that was already complete, and that Classicianus had no special position for him anyway.

The next day, Porteus brought up the subject closest to his heart. He gave Classicianus a full account of what had passed with Suetonius – which the procurator already knew. Then he burst out: "You see what I can do, Classicianus. I am transforming this backwater. Take me on to your staff. Let me help you in larger areas on the island. Take me to Londinium and give me back my honour!"

Classicianus listened kindly, but when Porteus had finished, he only shook his head.

"No, young Porteus. You are too hasty – just as, if I may say so, you were with Suetonius."

"But you yourself issued an adverse report on him!" Porteus burst out.

Classicianus frowned.

"Yes," he replied sharply. "And I am the procurator whereas you are here only on sufferance."

Porteus blushed.

"I see what you have done," Classicianus went on more gently. "Your work here is excellent. But we must not allow the natives to think that we do not take proper care of the lands entrusted to us. You must continue here for two or three years at least. Your reward will come in time."

Two or three years! To Porteus it seemed a lifetime. In two or three years would Lydia still be there? He knew very well that she would not.

Seeing his dismay, Classicianus added: "We must make a commitment to our work, young man. I myself may spend many years on this island. Perhaps I shall even die here. And I need men I can trust, not fly-by-nights. You'll get no favourable report, no honour from me if you don't stick to it here."

"I wanted to go to Rome," Porteus sighed.

"Everyone in the empire wants to go to Rome," the procurator smiled. "But with the present political situation," he added seriously, "it's a dangerous place. You're safer here, if you take my advice." And he indicated that their interview was at an end.

He left the next day, pausing as he turned on to the road to say: "While you're here, young man, build yourself a decent house." Then the little entourage cantered away into the distance.

As Porteus watched them, there were tears in his eyes.

It was two days later that Maeve arrived at Sorviodunum. She was riding a fine chestnut mare; but as she drew close, it was not only the mare that caught Porteus's attention but a second horse that the girl was leading. It was a magnificent grey stallion, heavy-set, but as good an animal as he had seen on the island. He could not take his eyes off it.

As he stared, he heard the girl laughing.

"Seen a ghost?" she cried.

"The grey," he replied. "It's splendid."

"My father bought it," she replied. "He told me to ask if you'd like to ride it today." She smiled mischievously. "If you can, that is!"

He accepted the challenge at once. But even as he swung up into the saddle, she dropped the leading rein and, turning her own horse's head, she cried: "He's not as fast as my mare!" and began to race up the path towards the high ground, her red hair streaming behind her.

Porteus laughed. Very well, if the girl wanted a race she could have one, he thought. He gave her one hundred paces start and then set after her.

To his surprise, he found that she was still pulling away from him. The big grey, strong as he was, was carrying a new rider and the track was steep; the fleet chestnut mare ahead, despite the fact that the girl was riding side saddle, was faster.

"She looks like the goddess Epona," he murmured.

Indeed, with her long, flying hair, the girl did resemble the horse goddess, beloved by both Celts and Romans, and often depicted as a wild woman riding side saddle on a prancing steed.

"She's wedded to her horse," he thought admiringly.

From ahead, above the sound of the horses' hoofs, he could hear her taunting laughter. She gained the top of the hill well ahead of him, circled the dune, and rode swiftly north west across the high ground.

On the plateau, he found that his stallion could gain on her; it was superbly strong. But they had still covered half the distance to the ruined henge before he drew level.

They slowed to a canter, then a walk. Both horses and riders were panting.

"You took your time, Roman," she cried. "But I slowed up to let you catch me."

He began to protest, then saw that the girl was laughing at him. Her eyes were sparkling. The thin linen shirt she was wearing had been half pulled off, either by accident or design; her shoulder was bare and he could see the top of one of her breasts. She was indeed a Celtic beauty.

As she stared at him, Maeve noticed the little beads of sweat running down into the soft hairs of his chest, and saw the hard excitement in his eyes. For a moment, she saw, he began instinctively to lean across to kiss her then, remembering that she was the daughter of the local chief, he corrected himself. She laughed.

"You Romans say there are four elements," she said. "Earth, water, air and fire. What are Romans? Earth?"

"Probably," he laughed in turn. "And what are you?"

"I am fire, Roman." She pushed her horse into a rapid canter. "All fire!"

They rode together over the high ground back towards the dune. He was beginning to get the feel of the grey now, to sense the animal's rhythm. When they reached Sorviodunum again, he dismounted.

"I should like to ride the grey again," he said.

"You can't," she told him gaily.

"Why not?"

"My father bought it to give to my bridegroom. I just let you ride it once."

For a second he paused.

"And who's your bridegroom to be?" he asked evenly.

"Who knows?" she replied with a laugh. "Whoever my father chooses." She turned her horse's head. "So long as he can ride," she cried. She caught the grey's leading rein and cantered away, while Porteus stared after her thoughtfully.

That night was restless. Half awake, half asleep, he lay on his hard mattress and turned over the day's events in his mind. He thought of Lydia. Which of the four elements was she? She was cool like water, it seemed to him: refreshing, sensuous. And once again he remembered her perfect olive skin. But just before he fell asleep, a vision of flaming red hair rose before him, and the sound of a voice being carried by the breeze: "I am fire, Roman. All fire."

Two days later a letter arrived from Lydia. It was very short.

My dearest Caius,
I am betrothed to Marcus and by the time this letter reaches you, we shall be married. I think this is for the best, and hope you will agree. I often think of you, and Marcus speaks of you warmly. Perhaps we shall all meet again one day.
Your loving Lydia.

It was the final blow. Yet, as he read the letter with tears in his eyes, he could not blame Lydia, and after a few minutes raging at the treachery of his friend, he had to admit that he had nothing really with which to reproach even Marcus. He had known in his heart that Graccus would never allow him to marry his daughter now, and if he could not have her, it might as well be Marcus, who was a noble fellow, as anyone else. Sadly he sat down and wrote to congratulate them both, adding a separate note to Marcus.

My dear friend,
I know Graccus would never have let me marry Lydia now – so I'm glad that the girl I love has been lucky enough to find one whom I know to be the best of fellows. Speak well of me in Rome.
Caius Porteus.

In the hope that it would drive Lydia out of his thoughts, he worked harder than ever on the estate. And to his own surprise, he began to take pleasure in the work. The land was good; often at the end of a day's work on the long summer evenings, he would ride slowly over the place, looking at all he had done and at these times it almost seemed to him that the ancient lands of Sarum were his own.

Once or twice on these rides, he had encountered Maeve, and in the evening the two of them had walked their horses quietly over the ridges. He noticed that she had become a little awkward in his presence of late, and there was no repetition of the wild ride they had taken with the grey.

At the edge of Tosutigus's valley one evening the two of them gazed over the waving fields that seemed almost crimson in the light of the evening sun, and she said softly:

"I think you like this land, Caius Porteus."

He nodded because at that moment it seemed to be true.

"It's good land," she said simply. "Worth having." And she rode quietly away.

Her message was clear; but if there had been any doubt in his mind, it was resolved shortly before the harvest when Tosutigus asked him to visit his farm one afternoon.

This time the chief was not wearing a toga, but the simple *paenulla* of the people. He had laid on no special entertainment. When Porteus arrived, the little enclosure at the farmstead was bustling with people: he passed the squat form of Balba, smelling as acrid as ever, sorting bales of newly woven cloth in the door of one of the huts. The men, helped by their women, were preparing the linings of the big circular grain pits for the approaching harvest. It was in every respect a busy Celtic farm.

Tosutigus greeted him, then motioned him to follow as he led the way to a small thatched house at the side of the enclosure and ushered him in quickly, closing the door behind him.

It was the family shrine. Inside it was dark: the only light coming from a small, high, square open window in the far wall, under the thatch eaves; but as his eyes grew accustomed, Porteus could make out the contents well enough. Opposite him, some twenty feet away, stood a small stone altar, and on it was a wooden figure whom he recognised by its attributes as Nodens the cloudmaker, a Celtic god whom the Romans had easily recognised as being one and the same as their own god Mars. Beside the image of Nodens stood a battered but carefully polished helmet with huge horns. He bowed his head respectfully, to show proper reverence for the family's gods.

"Nodens protects our family," Tosutigus stated briefly.

"Each Roman family has its *lares* and *penates*," Porteus answered. "But few families have more revered objects than these," he indicated the helmet.

"My grandfather's. He was a great soldier," the chief replied. "But there is more than this that I wish to show you, Roman."

To the side of the shrine, Porteus saw that there were two large heavy wooden chests, bound together by thick bands of iron. Tosutigus now moved to the first of these; bending down slowly, he reverently opened the lid and took from it a long, iron sword of the ancient Celtic type, pitted with rust generations ago, but obviously now carefully preserved.

"This is the great sword of my ancestor, Coolin the Warrior," the Celt said. Porteus nodded gravely. "His bride was Alana, last of the ancient house of Krona, who built the stone temple." Tosutigus closed the lid of the box heavily. He turned to face Porteus.

"We are not senators in Rome," he said slowly – and Porteus realised that he must know about Graccus – "but we are as ancient as any family on this island, and not without honour."

He moved to the other chest. Slowly he opened the lid, and to his amazement Porteus saw that it was full of coins – not bronze sesterces, but the gold *aureus* and silver *denarius*. It was full to the brim. With calm deliberation Tosutigus pushed his hand down into the chest until the coins reached his armpit. Then he drew it out again. The chest, Porteus calculated, must contain a considerable fortune – the untaxed income from the estate over twenty years. The chief closed the chest without a word.

"My daughter is a fine-looking girl," he stated, without looking at the Roman.

"She is beautiful," Porteus agreed.

"I am looking for a husband who is worthy of her," Tosutigus said, still staring at the box.

Porteus bowed his head respectfully once again.

Tosutigus said nothing more; it was obvious that the interview was over. Porteus made a few polite expressions about the chief's family and left.

In the days that followed he thought many times about his situation. He had lost his position; he had lost Lydia; he was being offered a beautiful native bride and a rich estate.

"In my present position, I'd be a fool not to take it," he acknowledged.

As he lay on his hard mattress and closed his eyes, he conjured up a picture of her, red hair flying, racing over the high ground on her chestnut mare, and he thought: I could do worse.

But then he thought of the warm skies over his family estates in southern Gaul; or of Rome with its noble basilicas, its theatres, its splendour; he compared the magnificent household of Graccus to the farmstead of this local chief, who was in truth little more than a peasant. In the middle of the night, the voice of ambition would remind him: the girl can barely speak Latin. She is beautiful: but there will be other beautiful girls in Gaul, or in Rome. You can still do better than this, Porteus.

"Perhaps," he mused, "I should return to Gaul – begin my career again."

While he was in this uncertain state of mind, he avoided Maeve and her father as much as possible, and since the harvest was coming in, Tosutigus was in any case busy on his own estate. Once he saw the girl walking near the dune, but he did not approach her.

Then came the letter from his father. It was not long.

Unfortunately, my dear son, I am unable at this difficult time in your life to give you good news to cheer you. Our steward has made some most unfortunate transactions which have resulted not only in lost revenues but a lawsuit which I fear will prove very costly. I have had to sell the vineyard, the olive grove and the two best farms and I'm sorry to say that your inheritance is much depleted.

We are not absolutely ruined, but the estate can no longer support us. Let us hope that in the coming year either you or I can find some way to improve our family's fortunes. Remember, truth, and good conduct will always triumph. Do not despair. Your loving father.

In a sense, Porteus was relieved. At least he knew now what he must do. Sarum might not be Rome, but it was all he had.

Soon after the harvest was in, he put on his finest toga, had his servant carefully groom his horse, and rode up the valley to the chief's farm.

The sense of horror, the absolute, sickening terror that seemed to arise from the pit of his stomach, the feeling of desolation, did not come to him until quite late in the wedding ceremony.

The wedding took place at Tosutigus's farm. The chief and Porteus wore togas; so did the three legionaries who were his only escort. But this was the only concession to Roman customs.

Two huge trestle tables were set up in the open enclosure and piled high with food. The men sat on benches while the women served them. It seemed to Porteus that every farmer in the region was there, dressed in their brilliantly coloured tunics and *brats*, so unlike the sober Roman dress. There were over fifty of them, including some of the more important craftsmen like Numex and Balba. The feast lasted from the early evening until late into the night, the men eating hugely the piles of venison, mutton and boar placed before them and drinking ale. The heat from the two enormous fires over which the spits were placed was so tremendous that Porteus felt his cheeks burning. The men with their heavy moustaches toasted him again and again in beer and in mead.

During the meal, Maeve did not appear; but at last, when it seemed impossible that the guests could eat or drink any more, Porteus heard the sound of bells and cymbals outside the enclosure. This sound was greeted by shouts of joy from the men; two of them ran to the gate and made a pretence of holding it closed while the party outside hammered on it, demanding entry. After they had begged to be let in three times, Tosutigus gave the order and the gates were opened.

The mummers came in to the sound of applause. There were nine of them – eight wearing blank masks painted in bright colours, with bells attached to their ankles which crashed loudly as they stamped and danced between the tables; two had reed pipes and one a pair of cymbals. The ninth mummer, a giant of a man, wore a huge wooden head carved like that of a bull with a magnificent pair of horns. They danced up and down between the seated guests, who roared their approval as the bull made clear by his lewd gesture that he represented the bridegroom. Finally, as the dancers reached a crescendo, the bull advanced towards Porteus. In his hand he was holding what seemed to be a drinking bowl, which he held out towards the young Roman while all the men shouted:

"Drink, bridegroom, drink!"

Porteus took the bowl. It contained a thick broth.

"Drink!" they shouted again, and he saw that Tosutigus was shouting with them.

He drank. It tasted salty, he thought. The men cheered.

"What is it?" he asked Tosutigus.

"An ancient recipe," the chief grinned. "I had to wash in it when I became chief, in the middle of the dune. You're really one of us now."

"But what is it made of?" Porteus asked again.

"Milk, bull's blood, herbs mainly."

Slowly Porteus looked down at the mixture, and as he did so he saw that the bowl was made of a human skull, sawn across at the brow and fitted with a golden rim. For a moment he thought that he would be sick.

Tosutigus was getting up, and the men were calling: "Fetch the bride."

It was then that Porteus experienced panic. As he looked round at the men with their big moustaches, at Numex and Balba sitting together on a bench, their solemn round faces swollen and scarlet with food and drink, at the mixture of bull's blood he had just swallowed – as he heard again the voice of Tosutigus saying "you're one of us now," – his own inner voice seemed to shout at him: Caius Porteus – is this your wedding? Are these British peasants now your people and will you never escape from this place? What have you done? Yet this was his wedding: nothing like the one he had always imagined with Lydia. And his bride was coming! I am committing myself to be part of this, he realised suddenly. My children will call these people their own. For a moment he wanted to cry out: No! Never! But Tosutigus and the mummers were already coming towards him, leading his bride. It was too late. He had committed himself for a red-haired girl, a grey horse and a single chest of gold coins. He was lost.

She was dressed in a white robe; her hair was swept back and held by a single golden clasp. She wore gold bracelets and gold anklets.

As her father led her to the place where Porteus was standing, the men all fell silent and the young man knew every one of them was gazing at his bride and thinking: if I could have her tonight . . . And in the horror of what he was doing as he stretched out his hand to take hers from her father, he comforted himself with the thought: tonight she will be mine.

Later that evening, the whole party prepared to ride down the valley to Sorviodunum; but before they did so, a servant led out the grey stallion and solemnly handed the reins to Porteus.

Then with torches blazing, they made their way down through the darkness and entered the little settlement below the empty dune just as the moon was rising. At his modest quarters, Porteus carried his bride over the threshold.

And so Porteus the Roman came to live at Sarum.

The early days of his marriage brought him several surprises. The first was Maeve. From their first night he discovered that his young wife's appetites were nearly insatiable. When they were alone together for the first time, Porteus smiled at her tenderly, anxious to reassure her; but to his astonishment the girl threw herself upon him with a happy cry; she was like a wild animal. She wound herself round him, pulled him down on to the mattress, and laughing, sat astride him while she tore at his toga with her hands. In the coming months, her behaviour did not change. She would appear suddenly when he was working and lead him back to their house; or she would ride out to where he was supervising the men in the fields and make him canter after her to some deserted spot where, without waiting for him to undress, she would again throw herself on him with a little cry of delight.

It was all so new to her – this handsome young man with his Roman ways; the excitement of her first passion. She was rich; she had not a care in the world. It seemed to Maeve that suddenly the familiar scenes at Sarum had all been recreated, in brighter colours and that each new day brought a fresh adventure. The gods had given her a husband for her pleasure; she meant to enjoy him. As to what went on in his heart, or what might lie in the future – these were areas of darkness, sealed behind doors in her mind that she never thought of opening.

Another thing Porteus discovered was that in taking Maeve as his wife, he was also marrying her father.

On the first morning after the wedding, when the sun was still hardly up, he looked out to see the chief waiting patiently outside the house. He had brought a present of sweetmeats for Maeve. Thinking that it might be a local custom, the young Roman politely ushered him in, expecting him to leave soon afterwards; but several hours passed before he did, and he promised that he would return in the evening.

He did. And the next day the same pattern was repeated. If Porteus was out, he would sit with Maeve, or go out riding with her; if Porteus were there, he would remain and engage him in desultory conversation by the hour. His presence in their small house became so much of a habit that, although at first it annoyed Porteus, he soon found that he hardly noticed the chief any more.

Tosutigus was bored and lonely at the farm without his daughter. For the first time in many years he missed the company of a woman; he was also eager to take part in his daughter's new Roman life.

"Now the young Roman is in the family," he told Balba and his brother, "we shall see some changes at Sarum." And he waited anxiously to see what they would be.

At first Porteus himself was uncertain what to do. As far as Rome was concerned, he was forgotten. His work on the imperial estate was excellent; from Classicianus he received praise, together with a handsome increase in his salary so that he was able to send money to his father in Gaul; and this act of family duty did much to relieve the pain he had felt at the failure of his career so far. But that was all. When, a year after his marriage he reminded the procurator of his hopes for a move, Classicianus said only:

"I can't spare you from Sorviodunum. Not at present." And again he warned him: "Rome is becoming more dangerous every month. Nero's court is a snake pit. Stay where you are and build up your wife's estate."

But still Porteus was impatient to leave; and to his surprise he found that Tosutigus was his ally. For when he mentioned his wish to visit the imperial city, the chief rubbed his hands enthusiastically.

"I want to see Rome before I die," he told Porteus. "Perhaps I shall meet the emperor." And almost every day after this, the Celt would cry: "Let us go to Rome together!"

It was Maeve who showed no interest.

"Rome!" she would say with a toss of her head. "What can be better than this at Rome?" And with a sweep of her hand she would indicate the rolling landscape of Sarum.

They spent their nights in passion; but although Porteus was still obsessed with his young wife's body and her tempestuous character, this lack of interest in Rome became a source of irritation between them. Each evening, when they were alone together, he would sit with her and try to improve her halting Latin. Sometimes she made a brief effort, to please him; but soon she would grow bored. "I want a husband, not a schoolmaster," she used to laugh, and pull him to her. Or, if he persisted, her voice would become toneless and indifferent, she would start to fidget and her eyes would wander, until sadly he gave up.

Hoping to interest her, he described the wonders of the great city: the seven hills with their palaces, the forum, the theatres, the brilliant debates in the lawcourts or in the senate, the magnificent libraries of the great nobles. But to all these wonders, which fired his imagination, she was indifferent.

"It's nothing to do with us, though," she once told him impatiently. And as the months went by, it was with the chief, rather than his daughter that Porteus shared these enthusiasms.

He told himself it did not matter. After all, he thought, a man doesn't have to share his thoughts with his wife. And he tried to take his passionate bride on her own terms.

Yet still it hurt him that Maeve should show no interest in matters that were so dear to him; and though he knew it was unreasonable, he was secretly angry that she made no attempt to become a Roman wife. How could she truly love him, he sometimes wondered, and despise things that were so much a part of his own character?

"If you despise Rome, it's a pity that you married a Roman," he once said bitterly.

"Are you sorry you married me?" she demanded in reply, and began to take off her robe. And as he saw her marvellous young body, and felt, as he always did, a rush of excitement, he stretched out his arms to her eagerly.

"I'm not sorry," he laughed. But he knew it was not enough.

Maeve never fully understood her husband's disappointment. Surely in choosing her, he had chosen Sarum? She loved him passionately, wildly; and in her imagination, he was a new and exciting part of the world that was her home. When he spoke of Rome, it seemed to her that he was trying to get away from her, so she tried to bind him to her all the more closely, tempting him with her body to force him to put such unwelcome thoughts out of his mind. As the months went by, if he still spoke of Rome too often, she would close her mind, refuse to think about the subject at all, and tell herself that it was a temporary obsession that would pass.

"You belong to Sarum now. Make it your home," she said as they made love together.

Sometimes however, as he lay spent afterwards, she would take a candle and hold it near his face as he dozed, anxiously looking at him to

[209]

make sure that the ugly thoughts had not returned.

Eighteen months after their marriage, Maeve announced that she was pregnant. For the time being, Rome was forgotten. And Tosutigus said to his son-in-law: "Now there's a child, it's time we made some improvements and built a house. I have the money. Build a house we can be proud of – a Roman house."

"I agree," said Porteus, "a villa."

The site he chose was half a mile up the valley to the north of the chief's farmstead and occupied by a deserted farmhouse, then only used as a place for storage. It was well situated however, on a flat shelf of ground half way up the eastern slope and overlooking the river; the views to the south west were open and to the north it was protected by a screen of trees further up the slope. Below, the ground fell away to the rich, marshy flats along the river.

Behind the site, the ground rose in a gentle, handsome sweep to the ridges above. The slope was partly open, partly wooded; some small fields had been laid out there; on the top of the ridges, sheep usually grazed.

There were two other features that recommended the place. One was shown him by Maeve.

It was a small hill, a short distance along the ridge, little more than a hump on the edge of the high ground, and he would never have paid it any attention if Maeve had not led him solemnly to inspect it. It seemed to be quite overgrown with trees, but in the centre they found a little clearing, and as he inspected the ground carefully, he saw that it formed a concave dish, about thirty-five paces across; he had seen similar shapes on the high ground.

"It's an old tomb," he remarked.

She nodded. Though neither of them knew it, this round barrow had already been there many centuries.

"This is a sacred place," she whispered. "The Druid priests used to come here and worship the forest gods."

He grimaced at the mention of the Druids, but she went on eagerly: "It is good such a place should be near to our home. I shall make a shrine here and it will bring us luck."

He looked around. It was true that the little circular clearing had a certain quietness about it that was pleasing.

"Do as you wish," he told her.

The second feature lay in the valley: for under the river Afon at the point just below the site there was a broad bank which made the stream so shallow that it could be forded. It was the best crossing for a mile in either direction, useful for men and cattle alike.

"Does it have a name?" he asked Tosutigus.

"Not really," the chief replied. "We just call it the ford."

And so, above the Afon's ford, Porteus began to build.

With the help of Numex, Balba and a small team of men, he converted the single rectangular shell of the old farm into a new home for his family. To the main room he added wings of two rooms each, to form a narrow house with a south west aspect. Then along the back of the house he added a broad corridor, in the centre of which he built out a little paved courtyard with small chambers leading off it. The walls of the house were made of clay and stone, the upper part being faced with wattle. Inside, the walls were plastered and painted white. The roof was tiled, the tiles being brought at some expense down the road from the north.

It was a crude, rectangular farmhouse, nothing in the least like the magnificent palace of King Cogudibnus which Tosutigus had so admired years before. But with its long, low façade, its plastered walls and tiled roof, it was still unmistakably Roman. Tosutigus inspected it each day, and as he saw it take shape he became excited.

"We need mosaics on the floor," he said, "and a fountain. Windows with green glass in them too." Each day he thought of a new luxury that he had either seen or heard about; and now that at last Roman civilisation had come to his estate he was anxious to achieve the most impressive results as quickly as possible. But Porteus was less ambitious.

When Maeve became pregnant, he had taken a hard decision. "For the time being," he thought, "I am going to have to stay at Sarum. So if I cannot take my wife to Rome, I'll have to bring Rome to Sarum." And to the impatient Celtic chief he said:

"A fine house can come later. We'll need more money, and skilled workmen. But first, I'm going to transform the estate."

Tosutigus was puzzled.

"The estate works very well," he said.

But Porteus only shook his head.

"It's a good Celtic estate," he said. "But it's nothing to what a Roman can do."

The changes that Porteus made at Sarum were to have long term consequences, but they were not achieved without difficulty.

He began with the land in the valley.

"Look at the fields on the lower slopes and the lands beside the river," he said to Tosutigus. "It's all rich land. But you use the lower slopes only for grazing cattle and pigs, and half the land by the river is marsh."

"The earth on the lower slopes is too heavy for our ploughs," the chief replied. "As for the marsh . . ." he made a gesture to imply that it had always been so.

"We can do better," Porteus told him. "Firstly, we could use a heavy plough – drawn by oxen, with an iron blade and a coulter that will turn a heavy soil: grow grain there and the yields would be enormous."

"And the marsh?"

"Drain it of course. Then plough."

What Porteus was suggesting was not unusual. The heavy plough had already made an appearance on the island a few generations before, and had been especially favoured by some of the Belgic tribes who had been familiar with its use in Gaul. But the farmers at Sarum and other rich chalk areas in the west had seen little need to change their ways: they had been successfully turning the easy soil on the ridges with their light ploughs for

[211]

several thousand years. The new methods were difficult and they already had plentiful crops. This argument, however, carried no weight with Porteus.

"The empire and the army have a huge need for grain," he said. "Whatever we produce, we can sell at a handsome profit."

As for the drainage, this was a Roman speciality. From this time onward, huge tracts of southern and eastern Britain were reclaimed by sea walls, causeways and ditches. Across the eastern fens, Roman engineers brought into cultivation huge tracts of land that were little better than swamps before they came. Porteus's plan was more modest.

"Those marshes," he explained to Numex, pointing at the flat expanse of land below the ridges to the north and west of Sorviodunum; "it wouldn't be so hard to drain them."

And Numex, who had helped the Roman soldiers build their roads, and learned to admire their skills, was enthusiastic. "It can be done," he agreed. But his face soon became solemn again. "The trouble is, the farmers won't work it."

"Of course they will," the Roman replied. "They'll see the sense of it."

He was wrong.

In the years that followed, Numex constructed a network of small channels that carried water off the low ground and into the river. He also built channels to convey the water draining off the slopes around the area he was reclaiming. He even introduced a series of small wooden sluices so that the flow of water could be regulated. At the same time, Porteus laid out three large fields of several acres on the rich lower slopes, and brought in two large, heavy ploughs.

"Now you'll see progress," he assured Tosutigus.

The first year, the spring river ran unusually high and the meadows were flooded. The men who had unwillingly dug the channels and ploughed the ground shook their heads; but Numex and Porteus did not despair, and the solemn craftsman patiently reconstructed his channels, and heightened the river bank. This time the experiment was more successful.

But Numex's fears were justified. Whenever Porteus ordered the farmhands to take out the heavy ploughs, they would try to find some excuse for not doing so: the traces would mysteriously have broken, or some other urgent problem would arise on another part of the estate. Complaints were made to Tosutigus; there were endless disputes about who should do the work, and by the third year of the experiment Tosutigus begged him to stop.

"They've never ploughed the low ground," he told his son-in-law. "They don't like your idea. It's not worth the trouble."

"But Romans have ploughed the low ground for centuries," Porteus protested.

"These are Celts," the chief replied simply. "They're obstinate."

"So are Romans," the younger man replied crossly. And he refused to give up.

For a generation the low ground at Sarum was cultivated; but each year the work was done under protest and done badly, and the yields were disappointing. Even Numex, having built his channels and his little sluices, was disheartened, and in later times the experiment was abandoned and the heavy iron ploughs allowed to rust. For centuries more, it was the higher ground that provided Sarum's grain.

Porteus's other improvements were more successful.

Beside the villa he built a walled enclosure, sheltered from the wind and acting as a sun trap. Along one wall he trained peaches, which he imported from Gaul, and apricots. The apricots did not do well, but as the years passed the peaches provided magnificent fruit, which had not been before at Sarum. He also questioned Maeve about the honey from which she made the heady mead: where did it come from?

"We find the beehives in the woods," she told him. "You can hear them buzzing."

Porteus only shook his head and soon afterwards Numex received orders to have six small pots made and placed in a clearing on the slope beside the walled enclosure. Stranger still, he was told to drill six holes in the side of each pot.

"What are they for?" the puzzled craftsman asked.

"Bees," Porteus told him.

At first not even Numex would believe that a swarm of bees could be induced to live in a pot. Nor did Maeve.

"You Romans!" she protested. "You want everything to be ordered, just like your empire and your roads. Well the bees won't obey you. They fly for miles until they find a place in the woods that they like. They won't live to order like you."

But Porteus quietly went on, and under his directions the next year the men trapped swarms of bees and took them to the pot hives. They were astonished when they contentedly stayed there.

Tosutigus was delighted.

"This is Roman progress," he told Maeve, who was disappointed that the bees had apparently obeyed her husband.

It surprised even Porteus that Balba the dyer volunteered as bee-keeper.

"It's the dyes I use," he explained to the Roman. "The bees won't touch me." And whether it was the pungent smell, or the chemical content of the dyes, or the fact that his skin was so hardened by the constant working with urine-based bleaches, the squat figure of the clothworker could be seen moving from hive to hive, plunging his stubby little hands into the honeycomb without ever suffering harm.

"Even the bees can't take the smell of him," Numex solemnly told Porteus.

Of Porteus's other improvements, one that especially delighted Tosutigus was his importing of pheasants. The chief inspected the handsome brown birds with their tiny heads and long trailing tail feathers, that had never been seen on the island before.

"You say we can hunt them?" he asked.

"Just let them loose in the woods. They're excellent game, and you hang them when they're dead," Porteus told him. "It gives them a tangy taste."

He imported two hundred of them, and it was not long before the woods all around Sarum were rich with their graceful, fluttering presence.

"He's even improved the hunting!" Tosutigus exclaimed with delight.

But all these changes were insignificant compared with the complex work that Porteus carried out on the high ground. It was this work that was to change the face of Sarum for fifteen hundred years.

One of the first things that Porteus had noticed after his arrival on the island was the sheep. Most of the sheep of Britain at that time were of the ancient soay type: small, agile, hardy animals with short tails, well suited to life on even the most uninviting terrain in the far north. Their fleece was not coarse, though nothing like the silky quality of the finest Roman wool, but it was coloured brown, and to Roman eyes it seemed primitive and unattractive.

"We can do much better than this," he told Tosutigus. "There are finer fleeces all over the empire." And he described the magnificent red wool that came from Asia and the region of Beatica, the pure black wool of the province of Iberia. "But the finest of all," he said, "is the wool from southern Italy: for that is pure white, and so soft it seems to melt in your hand."

"Do you want to get rid of our flocks?" Tosutigus asked in dismay.

"No. We shall cross them," Porteus explained.

Although not trained as a sheep farmer, Porteus had read the works of the great writer Varro on the subject, and had some ideas of his own. It was not long before he had made arrangements to import half a dozen of the finest sheep from Italy, and within months he received letters from the merchants to tell him that they were on their way.

The arrival of the six Italian sheep at Sarum caused a stir. They were brought to the dune one afternoon in a covered cart, and a gaggle of twenty men and women, including both Numex and Balba gathered round to watch Porteus and the chief unload them.

"Now," Porteus promised his father-in-law, "you will see something remarkable." And he drew back the flap of the cart and led the first sheep out. It came down the ramp unsteadily and stood before them.

When the crowd saw the sheep there was a roar of laughter, and Tosutigus went red from embarrassment. For the sheep was wearing a jacket which completely covered its body.

"It's bald!" they cried. "The Roman sheep is bald. It has to wear a coat!" And men and women alike hooted at the animal which stood silently blinking at them. By now Tosutigus was crimson; but Porteus was unperturbed.

"They all wear these jackets – they're called *pellitae*," he explained patiently. "It protects their wool." Calmly he undid the leather straps that held the jacket, and removed it. And now the laughter ceased.

For the sheep that was revealed was anything but bald: it had a fleece longer and more magnificent than they had ever seen before – it was so long that it trailed to the ground. It gleamed softly. And it was as white as snow.

The laughs turned to a murmur of surprise.

Some of the women moved forward to touch it, and when they did so they gasped at the delicate texture. One by one, Porteus now led the sheep out, taking off the *pellitae* and revealing the shining white fleece underneath, while the crowd, their respect now restored, watched in wonder.

But Tosutigus was puzzled.

"They're all ewes," he complained. "How will you breed without a ram?"

"We don't need a ram," the Roman answered. "The only rams we need are already here."

He was right.

In the coming years Porteus demonstrated the Roman skill in sheep-breeding by his skilful crossing with the soay stock. First he let the native rams breed with the Roman ewes. The results of this cross were mixed in colour, but their wool was coarse, and seeing these indifferent results, Tosutigus shook his head.

"I told you we needed rams," he said.

But Porteus was patient.

"It's the second cross that does the trick," he explained.

And so it proved. For when he selected the white rams from his first crossing, and crossed them again with the Roman ewes, the results were excellent: all the sheep had fine fleeces – a little coarser than the pure Roman but perfectly adapted for the climate at Sarum – and all were pure white. And when the people of Sarum saw what he had done, they treated Porteus with a new respect.

"The Roman is a fine farmer," they said.

Not only did Porteus improve the stock, but he also changed the way in which the wool was gathered.

"You pluck the sheep when their new wool grows in the spring," he told Tosutigus. "But then the sheep moult again in the autumn and much of that wool is lost. Plucking is slow and inefficient." He showed the chief some metal shears. "In future we'll use these and we can double what we collect." He also made the men comb the wool with iron combs to separate the long fibres from the short.

Before long, Porteus's flocks of white sheep were to be seen all over the high ground beside the brown soay stock. They were hardy, agile, and wore no *pellita*. But they were producing huge quantities of high grade white wool which sold well, and Tosutigus was able to say to his daughter:

"Our Roman has not only brought us his customs – he is even making us rich."

By the time that he had been married five years, Porteus could look around him with some satisfaction and feel that perhaps after all, he had made something of his life. Maeve had given him three children: two boys and a baby girl. The two boys would be given a Roman education: when they were a little older he would engage a tutor for them. The estate was flourishing. Indeed he had been so busy with his improvements that he had not even mentioned the subject of a move from Sorviodunum to the procurator's office; and though his parents had now lost almost all the estates in South Gaul as a result of the lawsuit, he had been able to send them sufficient money to keep them in modest comfort. Life, all things considered, had treated him well.

One change in his daily routine he had not forseen. This was the change in Maeve.

She had been surprised herself. When her first pregnancy had begun she had lain beside him at night while waves of nausea swept over her. She longed for the business of childbearing to be completed so that she could return to her free and easy life with her lover. But when the nausea left her and she became conscious of the warm little ball of life growing inside her, she became fascinated by it. This was a new adventure: it was taking place within herself. It was, she thought, even more exciting than the arrival of Porteus had been.

The business became even more absorbing; when the child was born, she could not take her eyes off it. She would sit for hours, staring at it in wonder; and in the months that followed her whole attention became focused on her baby to the exclusion of almost everything else. She never rode now. When she made love to her husband, it was no longer with passionate abandon, but with a warm contentment; and not many months had passed before, to her surprise, she began to look forward to having another child.

At first Porteus was pleased with this change. "My wife is growing into a woman," he thought with pride. But as two more children followed, he found that Maeve's attention had turned from him almost completely. There was always a child to attend to when he was in the house; his wife's smile for him was warm, but her eyes were focused elsewhere.

Indeed, although she never formulated the thought, it sometimes seemed to Maeve that the strange young Roman who had given her her children and who still spoke of going to Rome, was almost an intrusion into her new life. How could he fail to see the absorbing wonder of their children? Why did he sometimes turn away from her impatiently? And yet she loved him: she was sure she did: for was he not building up a fine estate for their family? Of course she loved him. She needed him.

If at times Porteus felt angry that his wife's passion for him had disappeared, he told himself that it was for the best. He had no time for it, now that he had so much he wished to do.

And when, on those occasions that she remembered to show him her affection, Maeve would come to him in the evening, stand beside him and ask: "Are you still in such a hurry to go to Rome?" it seemed to him that he was not.

The visit of Marcus and Lydia to Sorviodunum took place in the summer of 67.

As he waited by the dune with Tosutigus and Maeve, Porteus's emotions were mixed. Why had he invited them to visit him? Good manners, he told himself. How, after receiving a letter from Marcus to let him know that they were visiting the province, could he have done otherwise?

And now, after so much had happened, he was to see her again. For two days, elaborate preparations had been made for their reception at the villa. Every room was spotless; outside, even the track that curved down to the house had been freshly surfaced with gravel. Several times he had found himself snapping at Maeve or his children, unable to conceal his agitation as the time drew close; and on the morning of their arrival he had stood in front of the polished bronze mirror in his room and wondered: What will they think of me? Have I become a provincial? And more important still: Am I still in love with her? He did not know.

Maeve was apprehensive too. Although Porteus had never spoken to her of Graccus or Lydia, she had long ago learned the whole story from her father. As they waited now by the roadside, she gave a little shiver, which she hoped Porteus did not notice. She was not sure why she was afraid of Lydia. It was not of the Roman girl's beauty, for she was confident enough of her own. No, she thought, it was because the visitors were Roman, part of that other world that might make Porteus want to leave her. And she did not know what to do about it.

Only Tosutigus was completely happy. Dressed in his finest toga, he chuckled as the time approached. "The senator's daughter will stay at our villa," he announced to anyone with whom he came in contact. He was delighted to have such important Romans as his guests and secretly proud that his own son-in-law should once have been considered worthy to be betrothed to Graccus's daughter.

Although none of the party waiting knew it, their visitors had hesitated sometime before writing to Porteus. Marcus had been given an important post in Africa, a political appointment which marked him out clearly as a candidate for the highest offices. Before going there, he was fulfilling a long-standing promise to show Lydia the northern province she had heard so much about. Both of them had wondered what to do about Porteus.

"He's still stuck there in some backwater, married to a native girl. His family in Gaul lost everything I believe. He might not want to see us," Marcus had sensibly suggested.

But Lydia pointed out: "He'll be more hurt if he discovers that we were in the province and never tried to see him." And so now they were travelling to Sorviodunum; but as they came down the long road, it was Lydia who murmured: "I hope this isn't a mistake."

They travelled in a light-wheeled covered carriage with two outriders, that pulled up smartly in front of the little party by the dune; and the wheels had scarcely ceased to turn when Marcus sprang from it with a shout of welcome and seized Porteus firmly by the arm.

"Hail and well met, my dear old friend!" he cried, as though they were two commanders who had never known defeat; and to the chief, and to

Maeve, he made respectful bows that would have been appropriate for the family of Graccus himself.

He had not changed. He had grown, perhaps, a little more thickset; his broad, handsome face with its widely spaced eyes had acquired a few more lines: but they gave him a look of success and authority that Porteus had to admit suited him well. His black hair was somewhat thinner in the front and it was now easy to see exactly what he would look like in middle age – not a bad thing for a man who plans to achieve high office early. He exuded the power that belongs to a man with sponsors in high authority, and Tosutigus stared at him in admiration.

But it was to the carriage that Porteus's eyes had turned, as Lydia stepped out.

She had changed, and yet she was everything he had expected, all that he had ever imagined she would become.

The child's face and body had lost their last traces of puppy fat, and their softness had been replaced by the firm, full lines of an elegant Roman woman. As she stepped down, he was aware of her cool, strong, rounded form – the almost athletic body that he had caught a glimpse of in her father's garden by the fountain; and he was also aware that the simple grace of the girl with her classically perfect body had now acquired a subtle poise, a way of holding herself that was both alluring and yet untouchable, and which belonged only to the most elegant circles in the imperial city. Her hair was swept up lightly and piled on her head in the manner then fashionable in Rome. As she came towards him, he smelt the subtle scents with which the Roman women perfumed themselves, and realised that he had even forgotten what those scents were like. Her olive skin was flawless, and seemed to glow: obviously life with Marcus agreed with her. The senator's childish daughter who had laughed at his adolescent jokes and admired his student epigrams had turned, in the space of a few years, into a sophisticated Roman woman. It was to be expected: but it still left him speechless for a moment.

She stood in front of him, smiled gently to see that she was still attractive to him, and said softly:

"Greetings, my Porteus."

Maeve watched her with fascination. She saw at once that this girl came from another world: a world she could never enter, never even understand. So this was the Rome her husband hankered after. As they led the carriage towards the little villa, she whispered to Porteus:

"Are there many women like that in Rome?"

And Porteus, not wanting her to think he considered Lydia too highly replied:

"Yes, many."

Maeve nodded thoughtfully, and from that moment decided that they should never if she could prevent it, go there. She had also noticed the delicate and careful way in which the Roman girl held herself.

"Can she ride?"

Porteus grinned.

"I don't know. Probably not."

"I ride," Maeve said firmly, and she tossed her magnificent hair.

It was as the party came down the lane towards the villa that they hurt him. They did not mean to. He had pulled his horse over to the carriage and was bending down to pull aside the curtain so that he could speak to them, when he heard Lydia, who could not see him, exclaim softly:

"Look – oh Marcus look. That hovel: it's where he lives!"

And he heard Marcus whisper:

"We shouldn't have come. Praise everything and keep smiling."

Slowly he straightened up in the saddle. They had no idea he had heard them. As he gazed down at the little villa he had built he saw it, for the first time in years, for exactly what it was: a poor, pathetic little farmhouse in the middle of nowhere, and for a moment, all his conflicting emotions in seeing these friends from his past seemed to dissolve into embarrassment and shame.

At the house the children were brought forward to meet them, and the two boys said a few words of greeting in Latin that did them credit.

"We have two sons back in Rome," Marcus said. "But I haven't managed to teach them to speak as prettily as yours, Porteus."

Then that afternoon Porteus showed them round the place; and if he did so without enthusiasm, it was more than made up for by the voluble commentary of Tosutigus, who was anxious to show them his son-in-law's brilliant improvements even to the plaster on the walls. Marcus at once spotted the white sheep and asked him intelligent questions about how he had crossed them, as well as providing up to date information on the most recent innovations in land drainage. His enthusiasm seemed to be genuine, and Porteus was grateful for it. But he could not help noticing that when Marcus grinned, it was for just a little too long, and when he exclaimed: "Why, young Porteus, you've landed on your feet after all and got yourself a fine estate!" he could only feel that the Roman was looking for a compliment to pay.

The meal that night, prepared by Maeve and her women, would have been hard to surpass even in Rome and Porteus felt some of his pride return.

"Your Maeve . . ." Lydia had some trouble in pronouncing the name, "puts our own poor meals to shame. I can see why you chose her, my Porteus." Into this last sentence she managed to convey a trace of sadness, as if it were he who had deserted her, rather than the other way round.

She tried, also, to talk to Maeve; but after she had complimented her on the meal the conversation became strained. She spoke a little of Rome, but Maeve, while smiling politely, showed no interest; and when the talk turned to the affairs of other provinces, it became clear that the native girl had only the vaguest conception of the shape of the empire, let alone its individual parts. But Tosutigus was in his element, plying both his guests with questions about affairs of state, the doings of the Emperor Nero and the politics of Rome late into the night, until finally Porteus, with a laugh, declared to the grateful couple that it was time that his visitors were allowed to get some sleep.

[219]

"You must visit us again," Tosutigus urged them as they retired, "and we shall visit you when we come to Rome."

When Marcus and Lydia left in the morning, the whole party went together to the dune.

"Farewell, my Porteus," Lydia said with a sweet smile. "I am glad to see you so happy."

And then Marcus took his arm and said cheerfully: "Glad to see you're getting rich in your province, my dear friend. The gods be with you." But as he said it and turned away to his carriage, Porteus saw that faint but unmistakable look of embarrassment which the successful man can never perfectly hide from a friend who has fallen into another sphere.

As the little carriage bowled away down the road, Porteus suddenly realised that he had walked a dozen paces or so after them, leaving Tosutigus and Maeve behind him; and there he stood alone, staring at the little figures receding into the grey horizon. It seemed to him that the road from Sorviodunum was infinitely long. And inside him the small voice spoke and said: you have lost.

When they had disappeared, he turned slowly back to face the chief, his wife, and the dune.

In the year 68, great changes were set in motion in the empire, the province of Britannia, and in the household of Porteus at Sorviodunum.

For in the year 68, the emperor Nero was deposed and died, probably by his own hand. There then followed a period of confusion, known to history as the year of the four emperors, when several claimants, from different parts of the empire, fought for the imperial purple. During this struggle, the province of Britannia under its governor Bolanus remained on the sidelines; the three legions still stationed there all supported one of the candidates, Vitellius, and sent detachments to his army; and though the main body of each legion remained in Britannia, they remained a potential threat which each of the rivals had to take into account. Old Suetonius, now a respected senator in Rome, supported the candidacy of another claimant, Otho; but he was not punished when the Vitellian army defeated him in the battle of Bedriacum in Northern Italy. The victorious Vittellians however made one great mistake. To deter all others from opposing their candidate, they butchered every centurion in Otho's army. It had exactly the opposite effect. All over the empire, legions heard the news and felt a sense of outrage; and it was not long before other powerful commanders had collected troops and begun to move against them. One of these was the single-minded, hard-faced Vespasian, who was then in command of operations in Palestine where he was suppressing a Jewish revolt. Vitellius summoned more aid from the legions in Britannia. Governor Bolanus hesitated: and before Bolanus made up his mind, Vitellius was defeated and Vespasian took the throne. The remarkable Flavian Dynasty had begun.

It was an extraordinary series of events. Suddenly it became apparent that Rome was no longer able to impose itself on all its parts: a powerful commander of a relatively unimportant family had placed himself, without great difficulty, upon the imperial throne; and from this day, any provincial governor knew that given the right circumstances, he might do the same.

The new regime brought several changes to Brittania. On the whole, the legions in the province accepted the new emperor, and the II Augusta were delighted that their former commander had risen unexpectedly to such heights. But the loyalty of the XX Legion was less secure. Vespasian acted quickly. As legate to the XX, he sent the reliable Gnaeus Julius Agricola, who had performed so well on Suetonius's staff during the Boudiccan revolt. As governor, he replaced Bolanus with Cerialis, who had gallantly if rashly led his troops down from Lindum when Boudicca and her rebels were destroying Camulodunum. These were staunch, loyal soldiers and they were to serve both Vespasian and the province brilliantly.

They were also known personally to Porteus.

Tosutigus was delighted with these changes.

"Cerialis and Agricola – friends with whom you have served. And Vespasian – a man to whom I have spoken myself! This can only be good for us." And the next day he wrote a fulsome letter to the emperor reminding him of what he called their friendship. Porteus smiled, corrected his grammar, and let him send it. The emperor would be receiving thousands of such letters – it could do no harm.

But for once, to Porteus's amazement, the chief's boundless optimism was not ill-founded.

The first good news came when a staff officer from the new governor arrived in Sorviodunum and handed Porteus a letter.

In recognition of your loyal service and the good reports of your work for Procurator Classicianus, you are appointed as the governor's personal *beneficiarius* to oversee the building of a new baths at the place known as Aquae Sulis.

"It's an excellent appointment," the officer assured him, "and it carries a huge salary. I congratulate you."

It was a normal procedure in the Romanisation of a new province like Britannia to encourage the building of theatres, baths and other visible signs of civilisation as soon as possible; and the commencement of the great Roman baths at Aquae Sulis was to prove such a triumphant example of this process that the place which later became known as the city of Bath retained its Roman atmosphere for the rest of its two thousand year history.

Porteus knew the site well. It stood in a deep valley surrounded by a protective crescent of ridges at the southern tip of the Cotswold hills with their rich deposits of grey and honey-coloured stone, only thirty miles north-west of Sarum. There, powerful warm springs burst out of the rocks bringing up with them rich mineral solutions that were well known to have curative powers. For centuries before the Romans came it had been a place of pilgrimage, sacred to the Celtic goddess Sulis; and though the Romans knew this goddess to be one and the same as their own Minerva, it was typical of their wisdom that they chose to give the place a Celtic name so that the natives would think of the Roman spa as their own.

When the officer briefed him, the instructions were simple. He was to build a large, single bath house – handsome but simple – and situate it in such a way that more elaborate extensions could be added in the future. The budgets were generous.

"It's to be a showplace – a spa for our soldiers and a place for the natives to discover the delights of civilisation," the officer told him. "Nothing like a baths for softening these warlike Celts," he added with a grin.

One summer morning, Porteus set out to inspect the place. With him, after the little fellow had pleaded to be included, was Numex.

"I have learned how to build Roman roads," the ageless craftsman said, "let me learn more of your Roman arts. I will put them to good use for you at Sarum."

The preparations which Porteus found awaiting him were impressive. There were contractors drawn from all over the island; architects from Gaul, surveyors, masons, plumbers, and an army of workmen – it was far larger than anything he had controlled before. But so well organised were they that supervising them was comparatively light work. Already the surveyor had inspected the springs, dug trenches to examine the soil and made plans of the entire site. It was not long before a plan for the baths had been drawn up.

A massive, rectangular bath hall would be built on a north west axis beside the sacred springs, whose waters would be fed into the pool from one side. On the east side of this main hall, a smaller thermal bath would be constructed, and on the west side a suite of artificially heated rooms including the warm *tepidarium* chamber and the steaming *caldarium*, where the bathers could sit and allow the open pores of their skin to sweat profusely. The design of these first buildings would be simple, with plain, bold masonry; but this rather solemn effect would be enlivened by brightly coloured mosaics, and carvings of the Roman and Celtic gods.

It would take several years to build even the first of the baths, but Porteus set to work cheerfully. Perhaps, after all, life in the province might improve.

Numex had never been more excited. Years before, when he had helped the legionaries build the great road from Sorviodunum, he had recognised at once that the new rulers of the island, as well as being militarily powerful, were masters of building crafts and skills far beyond anything he had seen before, and when he heard about the new baths, he almost burst with curiosity. At Porteus's request, the contractors had enrolled him in the craftsmen's guild, and this meant that once he had taken the craftsmen's sacred oaths to their protectress, the goddess Minerva, he was free to join the builders and learn their secrets. From early in the morning until late at night the little craftsman waddled about the place, his round red face gleaming with pleasure, as he poked his long nose into every corner, and engaged the workers in friendly conversation. He observed how the plumbers laid their lead pipes through which water could be pumped and how they made channels with bricks to carry the excess away. He learned the painstaking work of the men who planned and laid out the mosaics, and came to admire the exact, geometric precision with which every aspect of the work was done.

But above all, he studied the intricate system for heating the baths – the hypocaust – the vast network of central heating air ducts which carried the heat from furnaces under the floors. He had never seen anything like this before, and when he thought of the primitive fires that filled the Celtic huts with smoke he laughed. "Compared with these Romans, our Celtic chiefs used to live like cattle," he said.

After two years he had mastered many of the arts of the workers he had encountered there.

The building of the Roman baths was not the only change taking place in southern Britain. Important political developments were occurring as well. Soon after Vespasian assumed the purple, he decided that the Durotriges he had conquered twenty-five years before were ready for the next stage in the process of civilisation, and a new provincial capital was laid out in the south of their territory at Durnovaria. And when King Cogidubnus of the Atrebates died a little later, his territory also was reorganised and the northern half of his kingdom formed into a new adminstrative area that stretched past Sorviodunum and on to Aquae Sulis; the capital of this being the new city called Venta Belgarum. It was in this way, at the start of the Flavian dynasty, that the ancient towns of Dorchester and Winchester were founded.

These provincial capitals were important: for each would be run by a native council – the *ordo* – drawn from the most important local men, and the chief amongst them would be elected magistrates and win the coveted Roman citizenship; so that in this way, too, the former enemies of the empire would be flattered and inveigled into its culture and government.

It was now, after having been ignored for almost thirty years, that Tosutigus at last received the recognition he had always coveted: one day, when the whole family were together at the villa, a personal emissary from the governor rode up the lane and respectfully requested an audience with the chief. When Tosutigus, flanked by Porteus and Maeve stood before him in surprise, he bowed low.

"Greetings, chief Tosutigus," he began solemnly. "The governor sends you his respects. He has received a letter from the Emperor Vespasian, who remembers you."

Porteus was astonished. Obviously the imperial secretariat was doing its job brilliantly, and was ensuring that no petty chief in the empire was left out of the huge system of flattery.

"As you know," the messenger went on," a new provincial capital is being founded at Venta Belgarum and you are one of the chiefs whose estates fall within its territory. The governor hopes that you will consent to serve on the *ordo*," he paused for effect, "and not only serve, but that you will agree to act as the first of its two magistrates. I need not tell you that this post carries with it a full grant of Roman citizenship." He was a plump, elderly man and he smiled with self-satisfaction.

So at last it had come: if not a client king, Tosutigus was to be made a citizen. Porteus was glad for him.

Then Tosutigus astonished him.

With a low bow, and a look of mock respect that confused the governor's messenger completely, he replied:

"Convey my respects to the governor, but please inform him that, flattered as I would be to receive such an honour, unfortunately I do not think my health will allow me to accept it." He coughed. "I have recently become unwell," he explained, "and so I must decline."

It was afterwards that he explained to his surprised son-in-law.

"I've heard about these councils, my dear Porteus. When you join them, you're responsible for the upkeep of the town, all its civil and religious ceremonies. It can cost you a fortune!" This was true: the honour of serving on the *ordo* had been known to ruin men in the provinces. "When I was younger I wanted to be a citizen," the chief went on, "but since you're a Roman, my grandchildren will be citizens anyway. Better keep the money – don't you think?" And although it went against all Roman notions of honour and public service, Porteus could not help laughing in agreement.

That night Tosutigus opened an amphora of his finest wine:

"To celebrate an old Celt's wisdom," he explained to his son-in-law with a wink.

It was in the third year of the work at Aquae Sulis that Porteus met the girl. She could not have been more than fifteen.

He had a small house set on the curving slopes overlooking the workers' camp, which he used whenever he was on one of his visits to the spa, and which was run by a cook and two slaves. When one of the slaves fell sick, he told Numex to find him a replacement, and the next day the squat jack-of-all-trades waddled in with a small, dark-haired girl that he had bought from a passing trader. He assured Porteus that the girl was clean and hard-working, and after a quick glance at her, the Roman thought no more about her.

Three days passed busily after this before he even addressed a word to her, but one evening as he was sitting at his table inspecting some plans for a mosaic that was to adorn the paved entrance to the baths, the girl came in to light the lamps and he glanced up at her. She seemed very small.

"What is your name?" he asked with a friendly smile.

"Anenclita," she replied softly.

This was a Greek name, meaning blameless. Slaves were often given such names which pleased or amused their owners, but he could see at a glance that she was not Greek.

"Your real name – before you were a slave," he persisted.

"Naomi."

"Where are you from?"

"From Judaea, sir."

"And why were you sold into slavery?"

"My parents were in the revolt in Palestine. The whole family was sold as slaves by Vespasian."

He nodded slowly. It was not an uncommon story. The slave trade in the empire was huge. A girl like this might find herself transported by chance – either by a trader or in the household of some official – to distant places and never see her family again. She might be lucky and spend her life with a kind family, receive manumission if her owner died, perhaps marry a freedman and have children who might in turn serve the empire and even become Roman citizens. Or she could be unlucky and be sold several times, ending up in some distant slave market like the busy one at the port of Londinium, and be worked like a drudge by a succession of masters until she died. Anything could happen. On the island, the Celts were evolving a kinder process, where a poor family might sell a son or daughter into slavery with a local owner for a fixed period only, after which the child would be returned. He preferred this method, and had already engaged several slaves on that basis at Sarum.

She was young, he noticed, with large brown eyes and a slightly frightened look; but something in her quiet, serious manner made him think she would be reliable.

"You'll find you are treated kindly here," he said, and turned his attention back to the plans.

Two days later he returned to Sarum and it was nearly a month before he was back at Aquae Sulis. He had forgotten the existence of the slave girl, but when in the evening he saw her again, he remembered their conversation.

"You are Anenclita, whose real name is Naomi," he said, and saw that she blushed a little.

The next evening when she entered he put down his work and talked to her kindly. Was she contented? Did she have enough to eat? She nodded and answered in very passable Latin that she did. She was a pretty, dark little thing, he observed, with a soft skin and a trace of childish down still on her cheeks. But in her large brown eyes there was something sad and reserved.

He learned that she had been separated from her family almost at once and had been bought by an official who was travelling to northern Gaul. The rest of the story was as he had expected. After a year, the official had returned home and sold her to a merchant who had taken her to Londinium and in turn sold her to the trader who had passed through Aquae Sulis.

"And do you hope to return to Judaea one day?" he asked idly, not thinking it likely that she would.

"Oh yes," she replied, with a new urgency. "That is the land where people worship the true God."

He stared at her in surprise, and then remembered that if she came from the province of Judaea, she must be one of the Jews, who unlike the Romans, believed in only one god.

"You do not worship Apollo, or Minerva, or any of the Roman gods?" he asked curiously.

She looked at the ground, obviously afraid that she might anger him, but still shook her head.

He shrugged.

Like all right-thinking Romans, Porteus was comfortable with the official pantheon of gods. There were gods to suit every temperament and every activity. It was a broadly-based, accommodating system. He, for instance, had experienced no difficulty in worshipping at the family shrine of Tosutigus, since it was clear that the family's god Nodens was none other than Mars in a Celtic guise, and Tosutigus had had no objection to his adding a Roman statue to stand on the little altar beside the shrine's original occupant. Similarly, at the new spa he had discovered that, as well as Sulis Minerva, the Celtic sun god was worshipped in the surrounding region, and so he had commissioned a fine gorgon's head to stand in a niche near the main bath – a bearded Celtic head surrounded by a magnificent flaming halo which the Roman workers immediately identified as Apollo. The Roman pantheon of gods seemed to him so eminently reasonable that he had never been able to understand the passion of those in the eastern provinces to limit their own gods to only one.

As the days went by, he fell into the habit of calling the young slave girl to him in the evening, and questioning her about her life and her religion. After a hard day's work, it seemed to him a pleasant way to pass the time.

As a young man and a student, he had of course been aware of some of the mystery religions of the east. There were the Jews, of course. Then there were the followers of the bull-god, Mithras, with their secret cults, and sacrifices. All over the eastern Mediterranean seaboard there were mystery cults. But for him they had only been religions that one read or spoke about, whereas the girl, it soon became plain, cared passionately about this nameless, invisible God whom, she claimed, created the world and was the source of all truth and all justice.

"The emperor is the source of all justice," he said with a laugh, "and you'd better remember it." But he noticed that when he said this, the girl looked at the ground so that he would not see the disbelief in her eyes.

He found that he enjoyed questioning her more and more – not because he understood the things she told him about her all-powerful God; but because he was fascinated to watch the passion with which she believed them.

That winter however, a new development began at Sarum which occupied all his thoughts for some time and caused him almost to forget the girl again. It was Numex who started it when he shuffled into his presence one day and suggested: "Why don't we improve the villa at Sarum – make it a proper Roman villa?" And when Porteus began to explain the problems of bringing in specialised workmen, the Celtic craftsman shook his head and said: "But I can do all those things now."

To his astonishment, Porteus discovered that it was true: the Celt had studied the Roman workman so carefully that he had, without anyone's knowledge, already designed a simple hypocaust system for the villa that would work perfectly well, and even a small bathhouse which could be supplied from a water tank fed from a stream on the slope above.

"And we can have a mosaic, with a figure of Neptune, and dolphins," the little fellow went on excitedly, "just like the one you're planning at Aquae Sulis. I know how to do that too."

Porteus laughed, but he gave the idea serious consideration; and when he discussed it with Tosutigus, the chief could not wait to begin.

"At last," he cried, "we'll have a Roman villa to rival Cogidubnus's!"

In fact, Porteus had been thinking along similar lines himself in recent months. There was no shortage of money for such an undertaking: indeed, the estate, together with his new salary was making the family so rich that they could have built a small palace if they chose. Already he had engaged an expensive tutor for his sons; and he had begun negotiations to buy a plot of land within the town of Venta Belgarum so that the family could build a house there and take part in the busy life of the new provincial capital. But more important even than the question of money was something else.

For the visit of Marcus and Lydia had had a profound effect on him and had made him change his attitude to Sarum. Seeing the two Romans had made him realise how far from them he had drifted.

Everything I have is in Sarum now, he had admitted to himself after they had gone. The estate, his wife, who would never live in Rome, his children, his position. His plan to leave this place was only a delusion. And if this was so, he thought, then it was time to improve the place. We may not be Roman, he decided, we may be half-Celtic provincials, but we can be civilised.

Now he threw himself into the new work, adding rooms, expanding the courtyard, planning every detail with Numex as carefully as if it had been the great baths at Aquae Sulis itself. To Maeve's annoyance, whole floors were ripped up, walls pulled down, and for months the villa became so uninhabitable that she and the children decamped to the old Celtic farmstead. But each time Porteus inspected the work, the round red face of Numex, his thin hair coated with chalk and grime, would emerge from some hole in the ground to announce: "We progress. Just give me time."

It was during this process of digging that Numex made a discovery. To his surprise, he found that his pick encountered stone under the main room of the house, where he had expected only to find chalk or clay. Again and again as he cut through the soil this happened, until he found that the stones formed a circle about ten feet across, which he would have to dismantle to instal the hypocaust. What he found was a dwelling house, the previous building of some long-forgotten occupant of the site before even the old farmhouse had been built. He made short work of the stone circle, but to one side he found what appeared to be a pile of rubble. And it was in this, encased in a thick envelope of clay and accompanied by three flint arrowheads, that he uncovered a small stone figure no bigger than his fist, that obviously represented a naked woman. To throw away such a thing would be sacrilege, and so he cleaned it and brought it to Porteus.

The Roman turned the little stone figure over in his hand. It was crudely carved, he thought, yet there was something very appealing about the thick, big-breasted torso it so well represented. He wondered what the figure was.

"I think it's a statue of the goddess Sulis," Numex said.

Porteus examined it again. It might be so.

"Keep it," he suggested. But Numex shook his head.

"If the statue is the goddess Sulis," he stated, "it is sacred and it must have a shrine. Let me build one beside the bathhouse."

Porteus smiled. It amused him that the Celt should think this crude little figure might be a god. "Very well," he laughed, "let the goddess Sulis Minerva have her temple by our bath."

The following day, Numex built a small shrine on the western side of the bathhouse. It was made of stone and was only four feet square; but inside it was a small altar on which he carefully placed the new goddess.

And so, after resting in the earth for nearly two thousand years, the little figure of Akun, the hunter's woman, with her thick thighs and heavy, fertile breasts was once again given a home, this time as a local goddess which, in a sense, it might be said that she was.

By the next summer, the work on the villa was completed.

When Porteus led Tosutigus to see the finished result, the chief glowed with pride. At each end of the house, new wings jutted forward. One of these contained the bathhouse. Behind, there was a large cobbled courtyard, enclosed on all four sides by an elegant colonnade. The floors of the house were now made of stone; and the principal room was paved with marble; underneath them all ran Numex's warm air ducts that conveyed heat from a furnace at the rear of the property. In the bathhouse, as the enthusiastic craftsman had wanted, there was a passable mosaic, around the borders of which Porteus had told him to depict the stately brown pheasants he had introduced on to the estate. And to Tosutigus's delight, in the principal room, there was a window fitted with thick green glass through which the sunlight dimly filtered. By the standards of Rome it was a farmhouse; by the standards of Sarum, it was a palace.

The chief clapped his son-in-law on the shoulder, and kissed old Numex on both cheeks.

"My dear friends," he beamed, "now this family has something to be truly proud of."

All these improvements were watched by Maeve without comment. She had no objection to the house; but she had no enthusiasm for it either. She was indifferent. Porteus did not mind: now that he had his sons to educate, he no longer even wished to teach her better Latin or encourage her to adopt more Roman ways. He had grown used to his wife as she was; and Maeve was content: she was still proud of her clever husband's talents and of his important position at Aquae Sulis; she was glad if the villa gave her husband and her father pleasure. But these were all part of her husband's separate interests, such as a man should have, and they need not interfere very much with his life with her.

For as their two sons grew older, their own relationship had fallen into a comfortable pattern. While she spent much of the day with her daughter, instructing her in her own Celtic ways and sometimes riding with her up to the little shrine to the forest gods that she kept in the clearing on the hill, she had more time on her hands than before. At nights, if Porteus were not too tired, she found that a flicker of her old passion for him returned; and sometimes it seemed to be answered.

But the barrier that she had put between them in recent years was not easily broken down now, and often it seemed to her that Porteus said he was tired when she suspected he was not.

She did not complain. A certain toughness, almost a coldness about the increasingly successful Roman made her, for the first time, a little shy of him.

As for Porteus, he had long ago closed off and sealed the door of his old passion for his wild Celtic bride. He no longer wished to open it again. Besides, he was busy.

The completion of the villa had occupied a good deal of his time; but when he returned for a spell to Aquae Sulis, Porteus was glad to find that the slave girl was still there, and he soon resumed his talks with her.

She told him many things he did not know, not only about her all-powerful Jewish God, but about recent events in Palestine. He listened with interest, for the girl was well informed, and it seemed to him that the whole area was in a ferment of mysticism: as she earnestly described the various sects and their quarrels, it made his head spin. There was one new sect, she told him that had been founded by a Jewish prophet who had been crucified a generation before: a Nazarene who some said was a false prophet who deserved to die, and who others claimed to be the Jewish Messiah himself. Whichever was the case, it appeared that the movement was attracting a huge following, and was spreading far beyond the confines of Judaea.

He had never heard of it. No doubt these new fanatics would give the government in Rome trouble in due course.

But always the girl came back to her idea of a single God, a God who had no physical body, no human attributes, a God wholly unlike any in his Roman pantheon; and sometimes if they had talked for some time she would gaze at him with her solemn, childish eyes and ask: "What do you think?"

To hear the girl speak in this way used to confuse him.

"You ask questions like a philosopher," he would laugh, "not like a woman."

His own education had taught him that philosophy was a subject properly reserved only for gentlemen. Such matters were to be considered quietly in the state of *otium cum dignitate* – dignified leisure – that was appropriate to men of his class.

"Never discuss philosophy with the people," his teacher had been

[229]

fond of saying: "it excites them and turns them into fanatics."

Religion, he knew very well, was not a fit subject for women: nor should it be allowed more than a passing interest by educated men. As for the spiritual passions, the commitment to unseen forces who refused to show their face, there was no place for them that he could see. The Roman virtues of balanced judgement, of sobriety, restraint, courage and manly patriotism: these were all a man needed in his path through life. It was the proper sacrifices to the gods which pleased them and which were a man's civic duty. It was a question of observance, not mystical encounter.

Yet, as he watched the dark-haired young girl reduced almost to tears in his presence at the thought of her invisible God, to whom no Roman sacrificed, he found that he was strangely moved.

It was inevitable that one evening when he had been absent from his wife for a month, he should take her in his arms. And although her religion, which was all she had to cling to, expressly forbade it, it was not so surprising either that the young slave girl yielded to what seemed to her, in her loneliness, to be his affection.

Despite the fact that the girl was only a child, the affair opened new worlds for the Roman. For now her reserve with him was gone. As they lay in each other's arms at night, Naomi would tell him stories from her holy books: stories of the prophets and their faith in Jahveh: of the ancient Jewish commanders: of Moses and his journey to the promised land. She would tell them in an ecstasy, for these stories were her most precious possessions; or she would whisper snatches from the Song of Solomon in her native tongue, her eyes taking on a faraway look as she caressed him and murmured: "Aie, Aie."

Porteus was not only moved. His imagination was fired: when she spoke, he saw in his mind's eye visions of the desert from which her stories came, and trying to apply what he heard to himself, he gave her an account of his quarrel with Suetonius in such grandiose terms that he emerged from the story almost like one of her own ancient prophets crying for justice for his people; and the girl believed in him and loved him for it.

This experience was Porteus's first and only glimpse of the religious and spiritual world; and though he only dimly understood it, he sensed its power. How different this small dark girl was from his wife; how deep her passion for her God compared with Maeve's easy pagan ways. As the months passed and the affair continued, it seemed to him that his love for the Hebrew girl was unlike anything he had known before.

He tried to be discreet about the affair, but it was foolish to think that the other servants in the little house did not know; and one morning when Numex arrived unusually early and came in to wake his master, he found the girl in his bed. Numex said nothing. He quietly went out of the room, waited outside, and made no reference to the subject afterwards, so that Porteus did not know what he thought of it, or if he told anyone what he had seen.

But whether it was Numex who had talked or the news had travelled by some other route, it was not long before his love for the slave girl was known at Sarum, as he was to discover when he returned there after a longer absence than usual during the summer.

He did not hear it from Maeve. Indeed, his wife gave no sign at all that she knew he had been unfaithful. When he arrived, she greeted him affectionately and led him gaily into the house where she had prepared a splendid meal. She fussed over him and the children and that evening, when they were alone, she made passionate love to him.

Only one thing surprised him: Tosutigus was absent from their meal. Nor did the chief appear as usual the following day, and when Porteus asked where he was, Maeve told him that her father was busy at his farm and dismissed further questions with a shrug. The next evening the same thing happened – and now there could be no mistaking the message: Tosutigus knew. But Maeve seemed unconcerned, and went happily about the house as though nothing were amiss, so that Porteus marvelled at her self-control. Two more days passed; he decided it would be wiser not to go to see Tosutigus, although by failing to do so he was indicating his own guilt; but the chief's angry absence made him feel so awkward that he finally told Maeve that he must return to Aquae Sulis for a while. Still she said nothing, and when they parted she kissed him and waved goodbye with a happy smile as though they were lovers parting for only an hour. He admired her for it.

But when he had gone, her face took on a grimmer look.

She had learned about the affair some time before, not from Numex, but from others who had seen the pair together. At first, for several days, she had felt rage and mortification; then, to her surprise, she had experienced something else – a sudden, searing passion for him, as great, perhaps greater than any she had felt when they were first married. The thought of the other girl in his arms made her tremble and grow pale; she felt an aching pain in her stomach; she wanted him. She almost forgot her children now, and spent hours inspecting her own body, looking anxiously for flaws that would make him prefer the slave girl to herself. She was even about to travel to Aquae Sulis to confront Porteus and make him give up the girl.

But first she had consulted some of the older women at Sarum whose advice she had relied upon since her childhood and they had counselled her differently.

"If you throw out the girl, he'll only find another," they told her. "There are better ways of holding a man, other remedies."

"What remedies?" she asked.

And carefully the wise old women told her what must be done.

When Porteus and Numex had arrived back at Sarum, Maeve's serving women had spent a long time with the little craftsman, at the end of which he had gone quietly to his home taking with him a small package for his wife; and when he had left with Porteus again to return to the spa, he looked even more thoughtful and serious than usual.

On the night after Porteus left, a strange event took place: Maeve, accompanied by eleven of the Sarum women, left the villa and went silently to the little clearing where Maeve had built her shrine on the hill above. As the moon rose over the trees, they sat down on the ground together in a small, tight circle, so that each woman touched the one beside her. When they were seated, two small objects were produced. One was a strip of cloth from a linen tunic that Porteus often wore, and which had been tied into a ball. The other was a little figure made of clay with a painted face, which bore a striking resemblance to the girl from Judaea.

The women began to chant softly: ancient Celtic spells that invoked Sulis, Modron and other powerful goddesses. Then one old woman solemnly reminded the goddesses that it was Maeve who was the Roman's faithful wife, and again the chants were repeated while the two objects were passed from hand to hand round the circle three times. When this was done, the piece of cloth and the little figure were placed in the centre of the circle, and each of the women in turn called out their names: "Porteus. Naomi," until the oldest woman declared: "They are named." After this, the women rose and the little circle dispersed without another word spoken.

The following afternoon, alone in the house, Maeve placed a pot over the fire and made a curious brew into which she fed roots and herbs following instructions which the older women had given her. As it boiled, it gave off a pungent, acrid smell so that she could hardly stay near it; but as she had been told to do, she tied a thread round the little clay figure of Naomi and dipped it slowly, three times into the liquid saying each time:

"Drink Naomi, and may it taste bitter."

The next night, and the following afternoon, both processes were repeated; and once again, on the third day.

It surprised Porteus to see Numex in deep conversation with the cook at the house in Aquae Sulis; and it surprised him still more when he approached the craftsman only to see him slink away without a word. But he thought no more about it.

That night, as usual, he lay with the girl and experienced an ecstasy of passion. Afterwards they had slept, while a single taper flickered in the room.

It was in the middle of the night that he woke to find he was both sweating and shaking. It seemed to him that he had been having a terrible nightmare but he could not remember what it was. He felt for the girl and found that she, too, was lying in a cold sweat, trembling violently.

"It must have been the food," he said, and the next morning, after an uncomfortable night, he spoke to the cook and warned her to take care how she prepared the meal.

The next day, he thought he saw Numex hanging about the kitchen again at dusk, but this time he could not be sure. The meal seemed to be prepared as usual. But once again, in the middle of the night, he woke and found that his body was awash in sweat, far worse than the night before; and the girl's teeth were chattering.

This time he warned the cook that the food was certainly bad and that if he had food-poisoning again, he would dismiss her.

It was on the third night that the dreams began.

At first he was aware only of a general feeling of dread, as though he were a criminal, awaiting some terrible judgement. He still recalled this sensation afterwards; but it was following this first premonition that the dream itself began. He could remember every detail.

He had found himself on the high ground at Sarum, riding on his grey stallion behind Maeve, just as he had before, all those long years ago. The whole landscape was completely silent: there was no sound even of the horses' hoofs: yet he could see her long red hair flying in the wind. She turned to look at him – but instead of smiling now, he saw with dismay that her eyes looked sad and she seemed to be urging her horse away from him, so that try as he might, the distance between them was growing greater with every pace. Again she looked back. This time her eyes were sunken and her skin was white as though she were on the point of death. It seemed to him that he must do something; he wanted to help her, to comfort her, but still she was drawing further away from him. Suddenly she vanished. He was standing alone on the empty plateau. He looked about him, wondering what had become of her. But there was no sign. And then the strange figure appeared, wearing a *paenulla*, with the hood drawn over its head; it was striding towards him rapidly across the empty ground. With relief he realised that it was Tosutigus. He called to the chief in welcome; but the figure did not answer. It drew closer. Only when it reached him did the figure remove its hood.

The chief's familiar face was white with anger. His eyes were blazing. He began to raise one arm to point in accusation, but as he did so his face was transformed into a skull, whose jaws were slowly opening and closing. As he watched in surprise, Porteus saw the skull begin to grow. Within moments it filled half the sky. Its jaws were open, moving closer. He saw that they were going to devour him. And once again he was gripped by the sense of horror he had experienced before. As the jaws closed over him, he woke shaking.

If his dream frightened him, it was as nothing to the terror he saw in the face of the girl as he started into consciousness. She was sitting up, her arms wrapped around her knees, her eyes staring straight ahead. She was trembling.

"What is it?" he demanded.

"Nothing," she replied, her voice strangely flat. "A dream."

He tried to comfort her; putting his arm around her shoulders, but still she continued to tremble.

"What did you dream?" he asked.

But she only shook her head sadly and would not tell him.

And so it continued, night after night. Porteus could find nothing wrong with the food, nothing for which he could blame the cook. But each night the terrible dreams came, and each night, it seemed to him, they grew worse. Sometimes he was attacked by snakes, at other times he was being drowned; once Tosutigus had cut off his head to use it as a drinking bowl; and on each occasion Maeve was there, with her sad eyes, moving steadily away from him.

After seven nights, Porteus found that he was almost unable to sleep; but the effect on the girl was worse. Her eyes became haggard; she would sit in a corner and moan; and by the fourth night she begged him not to lie with her. He did not know what to do.

It was the girl who finally brought the matters to a head.

"You must sell me," she said simply.

"Why?"

"The dreams. Jahveh is angry because I have broken the law: it is a great sin to lie with a man who is already married. It breaks the law of Moses. And amongst my people it is a greater sin still to lie with a married man who is not a Jew, for it brings anger upon them." And she broke down and wept bitterly.

Was it guilt that was causing his own nightmares too?

"I do not want to lose you," he told her. "The nightmares will pass. Trust me." But she shook her head and repeated: "I have sinned. Send me away or I shall not know any peace."

For three days he hesitated. He was selfish. If she stayed, he told her, in time he would manumit her and she could become a free woman again. "Perhaps," he suggested cleverly, "you will then be able to return to Judaea." But the girl was past aid; she was no longer eating, and by the third day her condition had become so mournful, her weeping both day and night so pitiable, and her pleas to him so desperate that finally, in a fit of exasperation, he shouted:

"Very well, you shall be sold a slave, it that is what your God demands! But your God is cruel."

She shook her small head sadly once more and murmured: "He is just."

The next day watched by Porteus with tears in his eyes, Numex led the girl down to the muddy forum and found a trader who was prepared to take her for a fair price; and whether it was because of the God Jahveh, or the spells of Maeve and her women, something that Numex and the cook had placed in the food, or simply the force of conscience, the affair of Porteus and the Hebrew girl was over. He did not see her again.

A few days later, Porteus returned to Sorviodunum. He was greeted warmly by his wife; he was relieved also that early that evening chief Tosutigus paid a visit to the villa to welcome his son-in-law home. The following morning, as he stood on the high wall of the dune beside the chief and gazed over the familiar rolling landscape where he had accomplished so much, Porteus realised somewhat to his own surprise that he had almost forgotten Marcus and Lydia, that he would soon forget the Hebrew girl and her demanding God, and that he was glad to be back at Sarum.

Twilight

A.D. 427

PLACIDIA SAID NOTHING. She felt tired and sad, but she knew she must not show it as she gazed at the angry scene before her. With such dangers on every side, must her little family still tear itself apart?

Her son Petrus had turned and was looking into her eyes for a sign of approval. She gave him none.

Her eyes: they at least were still beautiful: age did not change that. Fine, dark, they had been full of humour once; but now they were thoughtful, a little ironic, and resigned.

She was getting old – her husband often told her so; but still she moved with a stately grace, and the lines on her finely drawn face only added to its look of nobility. She wondered if they knew what strength was needed to keep up that graceful façade – of course not. It was the strength of a woman who knows her worth and who knows, also, that she is not appreciated by the only people she might have hoped would love her.

Yet she loved them. Petrus, her intense son, with her wonderful dark eyes but too little of her commonsense; Petrus, who thought that his quarrels with his father were for her sake, and who truly believed, in his self-centred way, that he loved her. Poor Constantius, her husband. He had already been waxing and polishing his horse's leather harness for hours, just as he did nearly every day – as if it were important. He respected her – and hated her, because he could not respect himself. And faithful Numincus. The stocky steward with his big head and short fingered hands – he loved her, admired her; he would probably have laid down his life for her. She sighed. But what was the use of that?

These three were all she had. And now they were quarrelling again . . .

It was mid-afternoon and Constantius Porteus was drunk: not very drunk, but as drunk as he usually was by that time of the day.

He was also roaring: not because he was drunk – that usually made him subside into silence – but because he was angry. And did he not have reason to be?

In his hand he still held the leather harness he had been cleaning.

Through the mists caused by alcohol and rage that obscured his vision, he could still see the group in front of him well enough: Placidia, his stately, grey-haired wife who despised him; the squat, square form of Numincus his steward, who was now standing respectfully but protectively in front of her: the fool! And lastly his twenty-year-old brat of a son, who had just finished speaking.

[235]

It was on his son that his angry eyes were trying to focus. He would teach the boy a lesson.

"You whelp!" he bellowed.

The young man was looking at him steadily: Constantius was not certain what the expression was in his son's large brown eyes – was it anger, contempt, fear? It did not matter.

"I'm master in this house," he roared. "Paterfamilias. Not you." Defiance. That was it. The short, intense young man with his dark curly hair and shining eyes was defying him. "I'll have no Germans here," he shouted. "This is a Christian house."

"Then what will you do?" the young man hurled back at him instantly: "Nothing, as usual, I suppose – except get drunk and watch my mother being killed?"

Contempt was in every word. Constantius felt his face flush with rage. The mist in front of his eyes seemed to thicken into a red fog.

He opened his mouth to shout, but his brain refused to supply the right word. Then he remembered the harness. With a huge effort, he lunged towards his son, and swung it at him with all his force . . .

There was a loud crack as the leather made contact, followed by a gasp; at the same time he stumbled, almost falling on his knees. His face broke into a foolish grin. That had taught the boy a lesson!

His eyes were clearing. He stared at them in triumph.

Then he frowned.

Something was wrong. The boy was hurling himself towards him – but not from where he should have been – and his eyes were blazing not with hurt but with anger. Numincus's round face was red, his body was shaking, and his stubby hands were clenching and unclenching with fury; and Placidia his grey-haired wife was standing quite still with a huge red mark across her face. There was blood already starting to drip from her mouth.

How had he missed?

Petrus was almost upon him, fists raised to strike. Automatically he raised his arm to shield himself. His face winced, anticipating the falling blows.

"Stop!" Her voice was firm and commanding. Despite the searing pain, she felt a little flush of pride at her self-control.

There was a second's pause. Constantius was still braced to receive the blows. He heard a cry of anguish from his son. What was happening?

Placidia's voice again cut through the silence.

"Petrus. Leave us."

"But look what he has done . . ." the young man protested furiously.

Mother and son faced each other. As Petrus looked at his mother's face, all the rage and frustration of the last few months seemed to come together in his mind. Was his drunken father going to destroy her too? He felt a wave of compassion for her; he wanted to strike his father down.

Placidia saw it all, and knew that now, more than ever, she must uphold the last shreds of Constantius's authority.

"Your father and I wish to be alone. Leave, Petrus." He did not move. "At once."

At moments of crisis her authority was still complete. Unwillingly, Petrus started to go.

"Numincus, tell my maid I need warm water. Go," she added sharply, as the steward, too, seemed to hesitate.

They were alone. The shock of seeing his wife's bleeding face had abruptly sobered Constantius. He felt his body sag with shame. He opened his mouth to speak, trying in his confused state to formulate some apology, but she cut him short.

"Your son is right," she said quietly. "You must do something. Now leave me."

He tried to make out the expression in her eyes. Did she feel nothing but contempt for him now? Was she rejecting him? He could not tell. She was staring past him, her face rigid as a statue.

Humiliated, he moved slowly away through the house.

Yes, he thought, he must do something.

Left by herself, Placidia still did not give in to the tears she longed to weep. But she wondered for how long this situation could go on.

Petrus, meanwhile, was preparing to leave the house.

The situation at Sarum was grave: there had been nothing like it in four centuries: for if the latest reports were right, the threatened invasion of barbarians might come at any time and destroy Sarum, the villa and the family. If the invaders came now there would be no Roman troops to oppose them, not even a local militia; and, worse for his conscience, Constantius had made no preparations to defend the place.

It was twenty years now since the legions had left the island. Each year he had been confident that things would get better, and that they would return. "Have faith," he told Placidia and his son. He could see them in his mind's eye – Christian legionaries marching to the aid of the Roman family at Sarum. But they never came.

Constantius Porteus was not only proud of being a Roman gentleman; he was also, like many of the landholding decurion class, a Christian too. For since the conversion of the great Emperor Constantine a hundred years before, the once despised and persecuted Christian sect had become the official religion of the empire and its army. To be sure, there were still in practice many followers of other cults, and of the old pagan deities too, but as far as Constantius was concerned, he and the emperor were Christian and that was what counted.

To be more precise, he was not simply a Christian but, like many others on the island, a follower of the British-born monk Pelagius who had in recent years made a great stir in the Roman world. The Pelagians proudly distinguished themselves from other believers by declaring that each individual Christian must earn his way to heaven not only by faith but by his actions.

"God gives each man free will," he explained it to Petrus. "And God watches our actions – for which we must answer. That's what counts."

[237]

Technically this was a heresy, but in Pelagius's native land it was a popular one, and Constantius believed in it firmly.

And so when, that day young Petrus had come out with his outrageous demand that, like some of the local towns, they should employ German heathens to defend this, a Christian villa, from attack, he had been deeply offended. Still more offensive were the taunts with which, in front of Placidia, the boy had accompanied his suggestions.

"You speak of Roman aid: but the legions have gone: the empire has deserted the island and they'll never come back." This was something Constantius could never bring himself to accept. "As for your solutions, follower of Pelagius, where is your God-given free will? Gone in drink. And what are your actions? There haven't been any." No son should speak to his father in such a way, he thought. Worst of all, in his heart of hearts, he knew the boy was right.

But now, as he made his way despondently through the quiet rooms of the house, Constantius still muttered defiantly:

"I'll save the villa. My way."

The villa of Constantius Porteus, though it was built on the same site, was a far more imposing structure than the one built by his ancestor Caius nearly four centuries before. There were eight large day rooms now, arranged around three sides of a square courtyard, with further wings to which a second storey had been added. There were extensive out-buildings behind the house which formed the home farm. Outside, the building was similarly constructed to the original – a stone base, wattled walls daubed with plaster on the upper storey, and a tiled roof; to one side the old walled garden had been kept; now it boasted beds of irises, poppies and sumptuous lilies, and – its greatest glory – a double line of rose trees down the centre. But inside, the building far surpassed the first and would have gratified every wish of old Tosutigus had he been able to see it. All traces of the original rustic farm were gone. Large, light and airy rooms led one into another. The floor of the entrance hall was made of a soft, pink marble imported from Italy two hundred years before and handsome pilasters of the same material with graceful ionic capitals framed each of the doorways leading out of it. All the main rooms had finely painted frescoes on their walls, some depicting Roman men and women in solemn, graceful attitudes, others with lively hunting scenes.

But the finest features of all were the magnificent mosaic floors, of which the family was rightly proud.

Constantius stood in the doorway of the largest room. The villa seemed very quiet. Placidia had retired with her maid to her room, and his son and the steward had disappeared. As he stood there, gazing into the room, his face softened.

On the floor, stretching for thirty feet, lay one of the villa's two greatest treasures. It was a mosaic depicting Orpheus in the happy days before his descent into the underworld to find his love Eurydice. He was picked out in brilliant reds, rich browns, and seated in a graceful, somewhat wistful attitude, with his lyre resting on his knee. Around the figure of Orpheus, arranged in concentric circles, were panels of animals, trees and birds, especially featuring the handsome pheasants with their trailing feathers for which the first Porteus had made the estate famous.

It had been made by the great mosaic workshop of Corinium which lay some twenty miles north of Aquae Sulis, and it had been installed by Constantius's great-grandfather just after the year 300. Its classical theme, with its pleasing allusions to the local flora and fauna was typical of the work which, for four centuries, had adorned provincial homes of families like the Porteuses all over the empire. "It's a Roman gentleman's villa," his father had always told him. "We've been here nearly four hundred years and I dare say we shall be here four hundred more."

As he gazed at it now, a tear ran down his cheek. The thing was so beautiful; it represented all his Roman culture; he would not let it be destroyed.

It was time for him to pray.

For nearly four centuries Britain had been Roman. Only in the far north, beyond the Emperor Hadrian's great wall, had the Picts and Scots avoided Roman rule. And for most of that time, the Porteus family at Sorviodunum had enjoyed the pleasant peace of the Roman provincial world. Ordinary freemen had become citizens. Local towns – places like Venta Belgarum in the east, Durnovaria to the south west and Calleva to the north boasted not only forums and temples, but theatres and arenas too. The baths at Aquae Sulis had been rebuilt several times, each more grandiose than the last. And the Porteus family had always assumed that the Roman Empire would go on for ever.

As the centuries passed however, great strains developed in the empire. It had grown unwieldy; and even though it had been subdivided into four parts – two in the east and two in the west – it still proved difficult to govern. Many times there were rival emperors and civil wars, and the northern island of Britain, with its normal complement of three legions, had sometimes found itself drawn into these disputes, and suffered as a result.

But something else was happening to the Roman world. It was being invaded from the east.

The great barbarian invasions of Europe were a gradual process that began in the third century. Sometimes the newcomers arrived as mercenaries, or settlers; sometimes, like Attila and his Huns they descended like a plague, only to withdraw again. They came from the distant plains of Asia, from the Baltic and Scandinavia; they had names which were to become familiar in European history – Franks, Goths, Burgundians, Lombards, Thuringians, Vandals, Saxons – and no matter how the empire managed to absorb them, there always seemed to be more.

Slowly, very slowly, the mighty Roman Empire had begun to break up.

They were dangerous times, but through the last century the island of Britannia was still prosperous and defended. The legions were there; its towns had stout walls; its shores were defended from the raids of Saxon pirates by a fleet and by fortified ports.

But for how long?

It was probably inevitable that Britain would be separated from the empire; but it is also certain, and sometimes forgotten, that the islanders took every possible action, around the year 400, to break the bond themselves by a combination of greed and bad judgement.

The first action was a manouevre by the British legions. Seeing a new emperor in Italy who was hardly more than a boy, they proclaimed one of their own commanders emperor and marched into Gaul to support him. In Italy, young Honorius was forced, for the time being, to accept this usurper as co-emperor. But the only result of this action for the island of Britannia was to leave it without its normal garrison, undefended.

Next, Burgundian and Saxon hordes crossed the Rhine and invaded Gaul, and the legions there lost control of the province. So now Britannia was isolated too.

It was exactly then that the British made their great mistake. They revolted, declared themselves independent from the empire, and threw out the imperial officials.

Constantius remembered it well. Like many of his class, he had approved of the move.

"Taxes have never been higher," he told Placidia. "The decurions like me are hit hardest of all – because we have property, they want us to pay for town repairs, roads, defence, everything. And what are we getting in return? An ever increasing army of bureaucrats to be paid, and nothing more than a skeleton force of legionaries to defend us."

And so the island had organised its own defence, paid no more taxes, and waited on events.

But nothing happened. For the moment the empire had neither time nor resources to concern itself with the island province that had revolted. There was no protest, no returning army, nothing: there was only silence.

And then, in the midst of these troubles, came news of something that for centuries had been unthinkable.

In 410, three months before Petrus was born, Alaric and his Visigoths sacked the imperial city of Rome.

The imperial city, the eternal city, the sacred symbol of Roman rule, had been humiliated by a force of landless barbarians because the city's proud senators had refused to pay them protection money. Rome had fallen. The shock waves spread instantly to the most distant frontiers of the mighty empire, and it seemed to all men when they heard it, that an age, a world – indeed, civilisation itself – had come to an end.

The empire recovered. In Ravenna, a year later, the boy emperor, Honorius, was glad to hear that his agents had murdered his usurping British co-emperor. The Visigoths meanwhile had been paid and departed. It was time to mend what was left of the western empire again.

But his plans did not include the return of the legions to Britannia. In fact, they did not include the island province at all.

"Let them fend for themselves," his harassed officials advised. "They stopped their taxes; they threw out the imperial servants. We have enough to do: let the British live beyond the sea."

The empire's resources were overstretched. The northern island was too far away. For the first time in four centuries, Rome had to turn her back on the province of Britannia.

Twenty years had passed since then: twenty years of waiting.

At first it had seemed that little had changed. There were occasional raids from Saxon or Irish pirates. A party of *bacaudae* – landless peasants – had appeared in Sarum one day and burned down one of the barns; but Numincus the steward and some of the men had driven them off. It was more what had not happened that gave Constantius concern.

There had been no new coins struck in the province. The trade with Gaul had grown slack. The ports with their warships were short of funds and so the island was poorly defended. The few remaining legionaries had not been paid and so they had turned to other occupations or left; Constantius had even heard of one selling himself into slavery. Finding that money was tight, he himself had been obliged to close the town house in Venta Belgarum which the family had maintained for generations. Others were doing the same and the town was falling into a poor state. It was as though a great wave of lassitude had covered the place, and each year matters grew worse.

Then the rumours had reached him. A large Saxon raiding party, a fleet, was preparing to attack the defenceless island. At first he did not believe it.

But the rumours grew. A merchant from London claimed he had seen the preparations on a visit to the east; and suddenly the area was in a state of panic. The city of Calleva strengthened its walls and so did Venta Belgarum. More important, Calleva negotiated through the port of Londinium to obtain a contingent of German mercenaries to supplement their own half-trained militia. Venta tried to do the same.

And that was where the quarrel with Petrus had begun.

"Let me go to Venta and hire half a dozen of these mercenaries," he had demanded. "We can quarter them at Sorviodunum. This place must be defended."

Constantius had refused. The boy had screamed at him. And now . . .

It was time to pray. God would guide them. After he had prayed, he would be reconciled with his son.

He did not know that it was already too late.

His horse's flanks were wet with lather. He had been riding hard, but now at last his destination was within sight.

He had left the villa within minutes of the angry scene with his father and he had not stopped since. He had no doubt about the urgency of his mission, and that in carrying it out he was in the right. But then Petrus Porteus always believed he was in the right: it was his only fault.

Before him, in the afternoon sun of an autumn day, lay the city of Venta Belgarum.

It was a small town, set on a hump of ground, surrounded by a thick wall. A pair of squat, heavy round turrets faced with rough hewn stone flanked the gateway which had recently been narrowed as a safety measure, and frowned towards the western approach road. Behind them he could see the town's red tiled roofs.

Petrus urged his horse forward. His eager young face with its dark eyes was pale and tense with excitement. In a quick, nervous gesture, he pushed his hand back through his curly hair.

It was this nervous intensity in all that he did which so often caused his wise and thoughtful mother to sigh, and which drove his father into his frequent spasms of rage.

"Sometimes, Petrus," Placidia would urge him, "one must compromise." After all, she could reflect, her own less than happy marriage had consisted of little else for twenty years. But Petrus always looked at her blankly when she said this.

"How?" he would ask, in perfect sincerity.

Petrus did not despise compromise: it just never occurred to him.

He urged his horse forward and minutes later was clattering through the gates.

The town was quiet. It was as though half the population had gone indoors to sleep; but the people who were to be seen looked at him curiously. He noticed that the streets were in poor repair: the cobbles were loose, weeds were growing in places, and many of the houses, like the big Porteus town house, had been left empty and abandoned by their owners because they were too expensive to keep up. The Porteus house had stood in a small, paved square. He saw as he passed that someone had built a shack in the centre of it. The cobbles made a good floor; and since the council was more concerned with defence than anything else, no one had bothered to stop it. The forum was still well kept: a clean open space with handsome porticoed buildings round it and a column in the centre celebrating an almost forgotten triumph of the Emperor Marcus Aurelius. He paused for a moment.

"Where are the Germans?"

A passer-by indicated the eastern gate.

"Outside."

A group of men were strengthening the masonry of the gate as he rode through. Immediately outside stood a small cemetery: a Christian cemetery, he noticed, since the graves were laid neatly east to west. Beside it was the German mercenaries' camp.

They were striking to look at: huge, broad-shouldered men with hard, unshaven faces, cold blue eyes and long flaxen hair which they braided in pigtails. There appeared to be about fifty of them; they lounged in front of their tents and stared at him insolently as he dismounted.

"Where's your commander?" he asked. One of them jerked his thumb casually towards a tent in front of which a slightly older soldier was sitting with a small, dark man who looked like a merchant.

They listened to him without comment as he explained what he wanted, and it was the merchant, obviously acting as their agent, who replied.

"These men are for hire, young man; but the price is high." He looked at the youth doubtfully.

Petrus allowed himself a half smile. From his belt he pulled a small leather bag of coins. Unknown to Constantius, his mother had given them to him before he left. He poured out a dozen for the merchant to see, and as he did so, the man's eyes opened wide with surprise. They were gold *solidi*, minted in the reign of Theodosius the Great, the century before. Coins like this were becoming rare on the island. The merchant's tone altered.

"For how long do you need the men?"

It was hard to say: the Saxons might attack at any time.

"Perhaps a year."

The merchant nodded thoughtfully and spoke a few words to the German in his own language. The German nodded and the merchant turned back to Petrus.

"Pick your men," he said.

Early the following morning Petrus, followed by six German warriors, rode out of the western gate of Venta Belgarum on to the road towards Sarum. There was a light mist over the ground.

They were a strange sight: a pale young man on a handsome horse riding a little ahead of six huge Germans on ponies that seemed hardly large enough to bear them, and each leading a spare pony which carried their weapons and their baggage. One of the six was older – Petrus guessed he might be thirty – and spoke a little Latin; he had placed him in charge of the others.

Just before they rode out of sight of the town, a thought occurred to Petrus, and turning his horse's head, he halted. There was, he realised, something important that he must say.

"At Sorviodunum," he addressed them, "you will remember that I am your commander. You answer to me: no one else." He paused, looking at them sternly. "I pay you," he added.

The six warriors stared at him, their faces expressionless. Finally, the oldest nodded slowly. He had understood.

Satisfied, Petrus motioned them to continue past him down the road. He thought he heard one of them laugh.

He did not follow them at once, however, but remained there, gazing back at the town reflectively. Several minutes passed, but still the young man did not move, and an observer might then have noticed that a strange look had come over his nervous young face – half dreamy, half triumphant – and would have seen that his eyes were fixed on a point above the town.

The sun was still crimson in the chilly morning sky. As it rose over Venta, it caught the tiled roofs and the grey walls, so that for a short time it seemed that the undistinguished little citadel was floating above the misty landscape. And it was now that Petrus spoke out loud words that would have astonished and horrified his father far more than the insults he had uttered in their quarrel the day before. The words came out like a prayer.

"Helios, Helios, great Sun," he murmured. "Jove – Apollo, king of all the gods: give strength to your servant."

For Petrus, son of a Christian household, was a secret pagan.

He was not alone. All over the Roman world, there were many who openly or secretly followed pagan ways despite the fact that, for a century, the upstart Christian faith had been declared the official religion of the empire; and successive emperors had never succeeded in stamping them out.

There were numerous cults: there were not only the observances of the ancient Roman gods, but also those of the Celts, the Saxons, the Goths and the many other peoples of the empire. There were the popular cults from the east with their strange rites, their mystical experiences and ecstatic states: one of these at least he knew well – the worship of the Egyptian goddess Isis – for there were several temples to her on the island. More important was the old established freemasonry of the religion of Mithras the bull god, whose themes of self-discipline and sacrifice had made it popular with the army. Since the reign of Constantine the army had officially been Christian, but Petrus knew very well that his father's faithful and long-suffering steward Numincus, himself the son of a centurion, worshipped Mithras in private, a fact which Constantius Porteus quietly overlooked. But there were other cults at Sarum that Constantius never guessed at. And these Petrus knew, because he practised them himself.

It was a similar story all over the island. Only fifty miles west of Sarum, at Lydney on the banks of the great river Severn, a large new temple to the Celtic god Nodens had been re-opened only a generation before. Constantius had been outraged, but the temple had been popular and had received many endowments.

For paganism still had many powerful friends. Had not the emperor Julian himself, that military genius, philosopher and visionary – who seventy years before, had crossed the skies of the empire in his three year reign like a meteor – had not Julian declared himself for the old Roman gods and tried unsuccessfully to restore them, in place of Christianity, to their rightful place in Rome? There were many besides Petrus to whom the gallant young pagan emperor was still a hero.

Certainly many of the old senatorial families of Rome supported the ancient religion. The Christians, they had always claimed, put loyalty to their God before loyalty to Rome: but had not the great orator Cicero centuries earlier declared that the good patriot is promised a reward in heaven? What had become of the old values – the stoicism of the philosopher emperor Marcus Aurelius, the solid virtues of the Roman gentlemen who read the classics, consulted the *haruspices* and built shrines for their ancestors? All this the Christians claimed to despise. Was it not Christian emperors who had removed the most sacred symbol of the old pagan order, the altar of victory, from the senate house? And now Rome had fallen: it was hardly surprising.

"The empire is ruled by upstart emperors, by Christians and barbarians," the conservatives said. "And look at the chaos that has resulted."

This attitude was not only the prejudice of a few diehard Roman aristocrats. Petrus remembered well the attitude of his schoolmaster in Venta Belgarum, who had been a scholarly man and a discreet pagan all his life.

"Christianity was a cult for slaves," he exclaimed. "They say that of all the gods, only theirs is the true one: what arrogance! What proof have they for such a claim?"

It was an argument which, when he brought it up at home, made his father explode; but the fact was that the blustering Constantius was never able to answer to his satisfaction.

With his schoolmaster, however, he had enjoyed many arguments. Even now, he could hear the old man's voice, demanding rhetorically: "Are we wiser than Plato and the other great philosophers of antiquity? Was Socrates, that seeker after truth, too proud to sacrifice a cock to Aesculapius before he died?"

"But the Christians teach that there is a single all-powerful God behind the universe and that man has an immortal soul," Petrus had challenged him. "Do you deny that?"

"Why should we?" the scholar replied. "No one who has read and understood Plato would deny that there is a divine idea, an unknowable God behind the universe. As for immortality: each man has a soul which apprehends, though dimly, the divine intelligence: in that sense we may say that the soul reflects the divine and is immortal."

"And how should we act? The Christians say their morals are better."

"Virtue and contemplation purify the body and the mind and direct it towards the divine soul," the old man replied calmly. "The pagan philosophers have taught this for centuries before the Christians existed."

"And the gods?" Petrus asked eagerly: "Apollo, Minerva, Mars . . ."

"They are divine agents – attributes of the divine, which is infinite and includes all creation. When we worship the gods, we worship in them the divine idea. Why should we deny them?"

"The Christians do."

"The Christians are fools," the old man retorted angrily. "First they say that their God is the only god; then they claim that he became a man; then they dispute with one another endlessly about the interpretation of God's nature – as if a man could comprehend such a mystery – and each party calls the other heretics: Arians, Catholics, Donatists, Manichees, Pelagians . . ." He shrugged contemptuously. "Argue with a Christian and you find a fanatic; read the classical philosophers and you will find reason, enlightenment . . ." He smiled wearily. "But don't say I said so or I'll lose my job."

It was an attractive philosophy: later ages would describe this abstract system as neo-Platonism. To Petrus it seemed to encompass everything: the civilisation of Greece, the virtue and grandeur of Rome; and as he thought of his Christian father's morose inaction, he decided to rebel. Courage, stern patriotism, the old Roman code of honour – it seemed to him that these were the only qualities he admired; so he became a pagan convert.

Now, as he looked back at the town where the old pagan had taught him, as he saw the roofs glinting in the sun, the top of the column erected in memory of Marcus Aurelius, the triangular pediment of the old temple, he cried out aloud:

"I will restore Sorviodunum, and then this city to the gods."

They reached Sorviodunum at midday. Petrus had intended that the Germans should camp in the settlement in the valley where half a dozen families were still living in a group of small houses protected by a small wooden palisade. His idea was that they would fortify the place properly. But when the leader of the Germans saw it, he shook his head.

"We'll camp there," he said, pointing up to the dune on the hill above. "Only place we can defend."

Petrus shrugged. "As you wish."

The dune had been almost deserted for generations. Although there was a cluster of huts just east of the entrance, the big circular space inside, with its high grassy wall, had been used by Numincus only as the estate's cattle pen for some years.

It had one occupant however, and as Petrus and his party entered, he shuffled forward from the small wooden house he occupied on the west side of the enclosure.

"This is Tarquinus the cowherd," Petrus explained.

He was very old. His back was stooped, his face wizened like a nut and his thin grey hair lay in long strands down his back. But his cunning, narrow-set eyes, which gave him away at once as belonging to the clan still known in the area as the riverfolk, were as bright and keen as a young man's. He had been widowed many years before, and as soon as his wife had died, he had abandoned his children and retired alone to the dune, where the Porteus family had decided to tolerate his presence. It was Tarquinus who, when Constantius in a fit of Christian piety had knocked down the little temple to the goddess Sulis that for centuries had stood beside the family villa, had quietly rescued the little stone figure, and built a modest shrine to house her beside his own shack in the dune. Although he was old now, the cowherd was greatly feared by many in the area, for he was skilled in the arts of magic.

He glanced at the Germans.

"You brought them."

Petrus nodded.

"They'll camp here. Keep an eye on them."

Tarquinus grinned contemptuously.

"If they give any trouble, I'll cut their throats when they're asleep."

Petrus turned his horse.

"My steward will see you're fed," he told the Germans.

Then he moved towards the entrance, the cowherd shuffling beside him. Before leaving however he glanced down and enquired quietly:

"We have an appointment tonight?"

The old man nodded. "Everything is ready."

[246]

"Good, until tonight then." And pleased with his work Petrus rode out of the dune towards the villa.

On entering the villa, he sought out his mother.

Placidia was sitting quietly with Numincus. She had grown fond of the stout little widower over the years, not only because of his loyalty to her, but because she recognised that in his quiet, modest way he was a man of talent.

It was she who had taught the steward to read. Now, he not only ran the estate from day to day, but he drew up the accounts with her himself, accounts which for years Constantius had done little more than glance at. She would still try, from time to time, to interest her husband in the details of his own estate, but he would usually wave her away with the remark: "I know you and Numincus attend to all that." Though whether it was pure lack of interest on his part, or whether there was resentment about Numincus's role, she could never be sure.

It made no difference in practice. And if she enjoyed the quiet company of the little steward, it was, she thought, one of her few pleasures in life.

He sat on a stool opposite her. He had just proposed to barter a third of the year's expected grain with another farmer for some cattle. It seemed to both of them a wise move.

"Are we right to hire these Germans?" she suddenly asked him.

He looked at her seriously.

"I think so."

"My husband does not think so."

Numincus looked awkward.

"The villa must be defended," he said slowly. "So should you be," he added, and then blushed.

She smiled. She knew that he loved her.

Then she sighed. The question was, how could she break it to Constantius without destroying his dignity?

As usual, Numincus had read her thoughts.

"Someone must take action." He said it softly, but firmly. "It's better to act than to argue."

She nodded. She was glad of his support and it was comforting.

She smiled at him. Within the limits prescribed between mistress and servant, she tried to return to the strange little fellow some of the affection he so richly deserved.

Then they both turned, as they heard Petrus coming.

Constantius Porteus was at prayer.

Since the incident the day before, too ashamed to approach his wife and son, he had spent his time alone. He had drunk nothing, so for once his mind was clear.

And he had been busy: busy making the plans that he should have made long ago for defending the villa. That Petrus had gone to Venta he had no idea. He would begin, he had decided, by arming Numincus and some of the men.

The room in which he was kneeling was remarkable. It stood at the north eastern corner of the villa and was almost bare of furniture; but it did not appear empty because it seemed to be completely filled by a huge and remarkable mosaic on the floor. It was unlike any other mosaic in the house. On a background of solid green, and presented frontally, stood a single figure in a white robe; his arms were outstretched in the attitude of prayer the Romans called *orante*; his large, pale face was round and clean shaven; under black brows, as regular and heavy as the arches of a bridge, two huge eyes stared straight ahead, apparently fixed on some landscape beyond this world. In the figure's raised hand was the Chi-Rho symbol: ℞; which signified that this staring man represented Christ. Where the Orpheus mosaic had been wistful and decorative, every line of this one was bold, striking and insistent.

Constantius prayed.

"Paternoster, qui es in coeli: Our Father, which art in heaven," he murmured. "The emperor has turned his face from us, but surely you will not desert your servants."

Besides the mosaic, there was another strange feature of the room. On the wall immediately opposite him, painted on the plaster in red, was a curious arrangement of five Latin words:

> ROTAS
> OPERA
> TENET
> AREPO
> SATOR

By themselves the words had no particular significance, except that an observant reader might notice that they formed a palindrome, for they could be read the same way back to front. But to every Christian at that date they had a well known significance, dating back to the time before the Emperor Constantine in the last century when Christians had been persecuted for their faith. For the secret of the five words was that they could be rearranged to read:

```
                    P
                    A
                    T
                    E
                    R
        P A T E R N O S T E R
                    O
                    S
                    T
                    E
                    R
```

When this arrangement was completed, two letters remained unused: a and o, which stood for Alpha and Omega, the Greek biblical description of God. It was this ancient rubric that had for several generations served as a kind of altar before which the Christian family of Porteus had prayed.

He had been at prayer some time when he was suddenly aware that he was not alone. In the doorway stood his wife, Numincus and the boy. There was a red mark across Placidia's face that made him blush. It was Petrus who spoke.

"The Germans are here. They've camped at the dune and I've hired them for a year."

Constantius felt his face grow cold and pale. He stared at them, bemused. And then he found that he was trembling.

Petrus was gazing at him steadily.

His anger rose. It was an outrage: the blinding fury of the day before was mild compared to what he felt now. But today he was sober.

He got up slowly. The disrespect, the contempt of the action cut him to the quick. He saw that they were all watching him: the boy's eyes were cold; Placidia looked concerned. With a huge effort of self-control, he stood before them and spoke evenly.

"You disobeyed my wishes." His voice shook a little, but it was very quiet.

"It was necessary, Constantius." It was Placidia who replied – gently, almost pleading. He ignored her and kept his eyes on the boy.

"You disobeyed."

"No, Constantius." Placidia again. "I told him to bring them. I urge you to reconsider."

Had she really, or was she just defending the boy?

"And how will you pay your mercenaries?" he demanded coldly.

"With gold *solidi*," the boy answered simply. "Numincus will see they are fed. We have plenty of grain."

Constantius's eyebrows rose.

"What gold *solidi*?"

"Mine." Placidia.

He started. Truly, it was like a knife stabbing him. His voice became a little husky, but still he kept his control.

"Since you and your mother wish to pay these mercenaries against my wishes," he went on, "do you also intend to let them camp on my land?"

There was no answer.

"I can send them away," he continued.

Now his son shrugged.

"You'll find them difficult to dislodge. They're armed."

The insolence of the boy! Still Constantius held on to his control.

"Numincus," he said quietly, "you will collect twenty men and bring them here. Then we will go to the dune, pay off the Germans and tell them to leave. Go now."

He paused, waiting for something to happen. But Numincus only bowed his round, balding head and stared at the floor. He did not move.

The silence continued.

Then Constantius realised that he was going to cry.

The humiliation was complete. There, in the family chapel, they had left him nothing, not even the last shred of his dignity. He looked at his wife: surely she would not do this to him? He found that he could not see properly because his own eyes were clouding over. With a desperate gesture he waved them away, and saw them turn.

Constantius waited as he heard their departing footsteps echoing in the empty rooms; he waited until they had died away into silence. Then, when he was sure he was alone, he finally sank to his knees on the floor and gave in to the sobs that shook his body. He doubled up. His head touched the cool mosaic floor, as the tears fell.

But even as he wept, a thought formed itself in his mind, a warning that he must give the family even though they had decided to despise him. It was a perceptive thought that saw clearly into Sarum's future. For if the Germans could not be dislodged by him, would Petrus and Placidia be able to control them either?

It was midnight and there was a full moon. On the hill, the silent dune was bathed in light.

Petrus had already passed the dune, however, and was walking with determined steps through the woods below. A light frost encrusted the fallen leaves that covered the ground.

He could feel his heart beating with excitement.

The clearing lay in the curve of the river, twenty yards from the water; it was a small space, less than thirty feet across, and at first glance there seemed to be nothing unusual about it.

But as Petrus reached it, a curious activity was taking place. Two men were pulling up long planks from the ground and as he watched the surface of leaves began to disappear, revealing in the centre of the clearing a circular pit. It was about eight feet across and covered with a heavy grid of wooden beams over which the planks had been laid and then concealed with leaves. At one side of the pit a wooden ladder descended into it. The pit was twelve feet deep.

As the last plank was removed, the stooped form of Tarquinus the cowherd emerged from the shadows. By his side walked demurely a young girl of sixteen. She had a pale face, narrow like the cowherd's, but not without beauty; on her feet she wore only sandals, and she was wrapped in a heavy cape made of furs. She was his niece. All three bowed to each other solemnly. The girl was to go through the important rite of initiation at the same time as Petrus.

At a nod from Tarquinus, both Petrus and the girl took off their sandals and stripped naked, the girl with a single delicate gesture slipping out of the heavy furs that had been her only covering. She did not seem in the least self-conscious; her slim, hard body seemed almost ghostly in the moonlight; but Petrus noticed that, despite herself, she shivered slightly in the cold night air as they stood side by side in front of Tarquinus. Then at a nod from him, they knelt.

Without speaking, Tarquinus now carefully unwrapped a small bundle he had been carrying and held it out towards Petrus. It was the little stone figure from the shrine, the goddess Sulis who was the guardian of the place where the five rivers met. Petrus reverently kissed it.

"Sulis, be my friend," he whispered.

For in the act which he was about to perform, it was important that the local goddess should act as a messenger and intermediary, pleading his case before the unknowable gods who ruled the heavens and who could not be approached directly by man.

The girl also did the same.

Then, at a further signal from Tarquinus, the two young people went to the ladder and began to descend into the pit, Petrus going first. When they were both down, they knelt again.

"May the gods accept their servant and make me pure." Petrus prayed aloud.

Meanwhile, Tarquinus and his two assistants had vanished. For long minutes, Petrus and the girl waited silently in the pit. And then they heard heavy footfalls above.

From the trees Tarquinus and his men had reappeared. They were leading a large, black bull.

The bull lumbered forward slowly. It was Tarquinus's magic that he could, by speaking to it softly, control the huge animal and keep it docile; but when its hoofs touched the wooden grid over the pit it halted, unwilling to go on. Still Tarquinus muttered in its ear, his skilful hands coaxed it, and finally the bull lumbered forward, its heavy tread echoing in the pit below. Petrus and the girl looked up at the huge black shadow: they could see the hairs on its long belly and feel its warm breath as it snorted impatiently.

Now came the critical moment. From his belt Tarquinus gently drew a long, narrow sword. Still whispering to calm the bull, he stepped back, and then, with a single movement, so smooth that it was hard to believe anything had happened, he drove the sword straight down to the bull's heart.

For a moment the huge animal stood transfixed, not knowing what had happened; then suddenly its hoofs slipped across the wooden grid with a clatter, and its heavy body crashed.

It was now that the stout wooden grid served its purpose. As Tarquinus moved about, hissing between his teeth, he made small slits in the animal's carcass so that the blood flowed, not too much at a time but in a steady stream through the grid and into the pit below. Gazing up at the black form outlined against the moonlit sky, Petrus and the girl shifted their position so that the warm dark stream of blood fell on their naked bodies. And all the time Petrus, lost in concentration, murmured half aloud: "May the gods make me pure."

For this was the sacred rite of the *taurobolium*, an important ceremoney of purification that was practised all over the pagan empire. Men and women who had gone through the rite in the pit knew that by doing so they had been purified and drawn closer to the gods, and they often recorded the fact on their tombstones with the word *tauroboliatus* or *lauroboliata*.

For more than an hour, Tarquinus continued his work, cleverly opening new cuts in the bull's body until he had satisfied himself that all the animal's blood had dripped into the pit. The two young people below moved about on the earthen floor, now slippery with blood, placing themselves under each new jet. Finally, when it was over, Tarquinus called quietly to them to come up; once again, while the blood dried on their bodies, they knelt before him while he recited prayers and his two assistants carefully dissected the heavy carcass on the grid and carried it away.

At last he motioned them to rise and dress again; when they had done so, all three bowed gravely, and Tarquinus led his niece away.

As she left, the girl turned back and stared at Petrus's body with a look of secret greed; but Petrus did not notice. Conscious only of the great and mystical event that had taken place, and of the wonderful fact that from this day onwards he was purified and closer to the gods, he turned away and started back towards the northern valley.

In the Orpheus room, Constantius Porteus had been drinking ever since dusk; it was now the early hours of the morning, but surprisingly he was neither tired nor drunk. He was brooding on the events of the day.

Suddenly he saw the form of his son quietly crossing the open doorway on his way to the courtyard. He started violently and rubbed his eyes. The boy was covered in blood.

For a moment even his anger was forgotten. What could have happened? Had the German mercenaries attacked him? Stumbling up, he moved with surprising speed out of the room and caught Petrus before he disappeared.

"My dear son," he cried, "are you hurt?"

Petrus turned. To his father's astonishment he wore on his face a look of calm serenity that he had never seen before. He smiled at his father. His eyes, instead of being filled with their customary hostility, were kindly. He cheerfully dropped his bombshell.

"Not hurt, father, purified."

Constantius's mouth dropped open. What could the boy mean?

"I am *tauroboliatus*, father. I am returning Sarum to the ancient gods."

Before Constantius could say a word, he was gone.

For several minutes he stood there, stupefied. His son not only disobedient but a pagan? He wondered if it was a dream, pinched himself, but knew that it was not.

A few minutes later he burst into his wife's room.

Placidia was not asleep when he came in, and as she looked up she could see by the lamplight that Constantius was very pale, though apparently sober.

He stood in the doorway; it had long been an unspoken rule that he did not enter her bedroom; though after the events of the day, she had nearly, out of simple compassion, invited him in; now, as he stood there, he looked so woebegone that she motioned him to enter.

"What is the matter, Constantius?" she asked quietly.

He made a gesture of desperation and told her briefly about Petrus.

"The *taurobolium*!" he concluded dismally. "A monstrous heathen rite." He wiped his hand across his eyes. "Did you know that our son was a secret pagan?"

She considered. "I did not know."

He stared at her.

"Did you suspect?"

"Perhaps."

He shook his head in disbelief.

"And you said nothing?"

She sat up slowly, pulled a cushion behind her and lay back, allowing her hands to fall palm upward beside her.

"I only suspected. Something about him – secretive. And he is close to Tarquinus, you know."

"I should have sent that cowherd away," Constantius moaned.

His wife's calmness about this terrible business baffled him. As he continued speaking, it was almost to himself.

"This is a Christian house. First heathen Germans, now this." He looked miserably at Placidia. "What are we to do?"

Poor man. At times, even now, she still loved him; if only he could be wise.

As for Petrus, she did not take this latest enthusiasm very seriously.

"We should do nothing. Petrus is impulsive, but he has a good heart. We must just be patient."

Perhaps, since the boy was almost all she had, she was too indulgent towards him. But she was far too sensible a woman to be blind to his faults; she knew very well that it was only her balance and good sense, and the hard work of Numincus the steward, that held the household and the estate together. Petrus with his obsessive enthusiasms was very like his father, and her secret fear was that if he failed to achieve anything and did not find a good wife to steady him, he would degenerate just as Constantius had done, despite her own unsuccessful efforts to strengthen him.

But none of these thoughts was apparent to Constantius. Although he had come to her instinctively for guidance, her calmness was beginning to irritate him.

"You seem unconcerned," he said bitterly. "Perhaps you approve."

"You know very well that I do not. I am a Christian."

In truth, she supposed that with her stern and practical attitude to life, touched, she knew, with more than a tinge of resignation, she was nearer to being a stoic than a true Christian. But she was content to be a Christian in name and had little use for heathen magic and the pagan gods.

None of this satisfied poor Constantius.

"You seem to me to condone the boy," he said angrily.

"We must be wise, Constantius. He is headstrong. There are many pagans in Sarum – you know that. Why even Numincus . . ."

At the mention of the steward's name Constantius stiffened. Only that afternoon, Numincus had disobeyed his orders; he knew very well that, because of his neglect, it was the steward who ran the estate and he was jealous of the hardworking, solemn little fellow who was always, it seemed to him, closeted with his wife.

"Numincus has nothing to do with this," he flared. "But in the morning he will acknowledge the Christian faith to me: and if he does not, I shall dismiss him."

Placidia shrugged.

"That would be foolish."

His wife despised him. It made him furious.

"No doubt it would be a blow to you," he replied with a bitter anger. "I have no doubt he is your lover."

Placidia did not reply for a moment. Then she said quietly:

"Please leave me."

Constantius, feeling once again a sense of defeat descending upon him, and too weary and angry to protest any more, walked out of the room, banging the door behind him.

Placidia closed her eyes. Before her rose the vision of Numincus: his large balding head, his red, pointed nose, his solemn eyes, and his curious, stubby little hands. She knew that the steward was devoted to her; but a lover? She could not restrain a smile.

Two events of significance took place in the next two years. The first was the coming of the Saxons.

They came in the spring: not, as had been expected, a vast horde, but a small advance party. Thirty landed in two boats on the coast of the Solent estuary, twenty miles to the south east. The main contingent travelled towards Venta, looting the farms as they passed; but they did not attack the town, whose strong walls they could not hope to breach. Despite the fact that they came near the town, the force of German mercenaries there, which could easily have sallied out of the gates and wiped them out, remained inside; for the people of Venta had decided that the mercenaries were for the protection of the town itself and refused to let them leave to save the nearby farmsteads.

A smaller contingent of ten men, meanwhile, had moved north west across the rich farmlands towards the little settlement of Sorviodunum.

Petrus had been warned of their approach the day before, and he had prepared with care.

On his orders, the families living in Sorviodunum had evacuated the place and retreated inside the dune; but he had cleverly left fires burning and the gate of the wooden palisade open, so that the Saxons would be encouraged to approach. Inside, Numincus, Tarquinus and half a dozen men were concealed by the gate. Petrus himself, dressed in the armour of Numincus's centurion father, waited with the six Germans on the little platform of land immediately in front of the entrance to the dune.

In the early afternoon, they came. The ten Saxons approached along the track beside the river; they were large men, though not as large as the German mercenaries. They were fair-haired and had long beards; and they approached Sorviodunum at a leisurely pace. They had taken several horses along the way, and two of these were pulling a farm cart which was piled high with the goods they had looted. They rode their captured horses carelessly; four of them were singing; and seeing the apparently undefended settlement, they walked their horses confidently towards the gate. Petrus grinned. At a nod from him, the Germans began to move quietly forward down the slope.

Just before the Saxons reached the gate, the men inside slammed it shut and barred it. Taken by surprise, the Saxons paused, wondering whether to fire it or break it down some other way; and it was while their attention was fixed on the gate that Petrus and the mercenaries came out of a clump of trees on the slopes above.

"The gods are with us," Petrus whispered to himself.

The victory was total. Trapped between the gate, the slope and the river, the Saxons were taken by surprise and hardly had time to defend themselves as the compact party on their sturdy ponies burst upon them, the Germans swinging their heavy axes with terrible effect. Within moments they had been driven to the ford, and several thrown into the water, while Petrus and his men dismounted to finish their work. They hacked mercilessly; and Petrus killed one of the Saxons with a thrust of his sword through the raider's throat, a blow that earned him a grunt of approval from one of the Germans. Only two of the Saxons managed to escape: the rest were killed. The cart with all its contents was left standing in front of the gate.

The mercenaries obviously enjoyed their work. Though their camp in the dune was comfortable, and they had been well fed, they had been getting bored and restless. Now however, they were smiling contentedly.

It was when the skirmish was over and the bodies of the Saxons had been stripped and tossed into a shallow pit by the river that Petrus found himself faced with a new and awkward situation, that he had not forseen. For now the leader of the mercenaries approached him.

"The cart," he pointed to the Saxons' loot, "is ours."

Petrus frowned and shook his head. Some of the contents doubtless came from local farmsteads. "It will be restored to the owners," he replied.

The German's eyes were expressionless.

"Ours."

"You have been paid."

"We killed the Saxons. The cart is ours or we go."

Petrus considered. If the Germans left, they would easily find employment with one of the other settlements; he had no doubt that the Saxons they had just encountered were nothing more than an advance party and that they would be back before long, in greater numbers. It would be foolish to let the mercenaries go.

"Very well," he said irritably.

But the German had not finished.

"We have fought. Now we need women," he stated. "A woman each."

There were a few slave girls in Sarum of course, which Numincus had already supplied, but not enough for all the Germans. Something in the fellow's manner told him that it might be dangerous to argue.

[255]

"Numincus will find you women." Perhaps some slaves could be found in Venta or Durnovaria. Angry with himself for giving in, he turned towards the gates from which Numincus was now emerging.

The day before, in one of his more lucid moments, Constantius had warned him: "Your Germans will give you more trouble than you think. Take care." It irked him to think that his father could be right.

But later that day, as he was riding slowly back towards the villa, and remembering the details of the battle and his part in it, a flush of elation came over him. Whatever his father's weakness, he had proved that he at least was a good Roman and a man.

And it was then, when he was half way to the villa, that the figure of the girl, Tarquinus's niece, stepped out onto the track in front of him.

He stopped, surprised. Since the episode of the *taurobolium* he had almost forgotten her; but as he gazed down at her now, he remembered her slim, pale body.

She was looking straight into his eyes.

"You fought today."

He nodded.

"You beat them."

He grinned. "We did."

"They say you fought as well as the Germans."

"Perhaps." He was glad to hear it.

She continued to stare up at him, saying nothing else, but now there could be no mistaking her purpose.

He thought of the words of the German, and nodded to himself. How simple it was, and how right: when a man has fought, he should have a woman.

He dismounted and followed the girl as she led the way to the place she had prepared.

The second event took place the next summer, in the year 429.

It concerned Constantius.

For some time now, the Christians of Rome and Gaul had been disturbed by the large number of followers that the Pelagian heresy had attracted in the island of Britain. It was late in the previous century that the British monk Pelagius had begun to live and teach in Rome. At first his teachings had met with only mild disapproval or even tolerance from such church leaders as Ambrose of Milan or even the great St Augustine of Hippo himself. The well-meaning monk only said that the good Christian must exercise his free will, rouse himself from his lethargy, and actively choose to serve God. Such a teaching might have been nothing more than a moral exhortation and perfectly acceptable. But unfortunately it did not stop at that, and it soon became clear that his doctrines were being developed by his followers into a full-blown heresy.

For the followers of the monk held that a man, if he was truly to serve God and win his way to Heaven, must choose God, for himself, of his own free will. And this, of course, was an obnoxious heresy.

For were it to be true that a man could really make such a choice for himself, then that man would be a separate being, an individual entity with absolute power to choose to embrace God or the Devil as he liked. How could any right thinking Christian suggest such a thing when the Church taught that man, like everything in the universe, was created by God and belonged to Him? A man could not even exercise his free will except through Providence and God's grace. "If a man could act unilaterally like that, then the nature of God is reduced to that of any pagan god, like Apollo or Minerva, that he could as well have chosen instead," they argued. The old British monk might have been harmless, but the doctrines of his followers were a dangerous heresy and they must be stamped out.

As for Britain, not only had his doctrines been popular with many on the island, but when a number of Pelagians were successfully driven out of Rome, they exiled themselves to the distant province and continued to spread their pernicious doctrines there.

It was not to be borne.

Accordingly, in 429, at the request of the outraged Church in Gaul, and with the blessing of the Pope himself, two important Churchmen, Germanus of Auxerre and Lupus, Bishop of Troyes, made a visit to the island. The Pelagians would be spoken to sternly.

A huge meeting was arranged at the city of Verulamium, where the bishops would argue their case before the leaders of the British Pelagian party. Many of these were prominent landowners, proud and powerful; and it was the thought of being present at such an august gathering that made Constantius for once pull himself together enough to make the journey.

He made careful preparations; Placidia had not seen her husband so in control of himself or so eager for many years. Neither she nor the pagan Petrus were to accompany him. He took one attendant, his two best horses, and his finest clothes, including the magnificent blue cloak that he had worn on his wedding day. He set off on a bright morning, taking the old road that led first to Londinium and then north to Verulamium.

"These bishops from Gaul may be important men," he told Placidia as he was leaving, "but they'll find we are Christians every bit as good as they are."

And though she herself had little interest in such controversies, Placidia was glad to see Constantius so roused. Perhaps this journey would be good for him, and even lessen his drinking.

It was ten days later that he returned.

Placidia was alone when he approached the villa; Petrus had gone to Durnovaria and was not expected back for three days. When the servants ran in to tell her of his arrival, she went quickly to the door of the house to welcome him. But when she saw him her face fell.

He was pale, unshaven and spattered with mud. The attendant leading the horses, one of whom was lame, looked downcast, and as Constantius stumbled into the villa without a word, Placidia could smell that he had been drinking. He disappeared to his room and was not seen again for several hours.

For two days Constantius moved about the villa quietly, drinking as usual and speaking to no one. Placidia wisely said nothing to him, and when she discreetly asked the servant who had been with him what had happened, the man could only tell her that his master had returned from the great meeting very angry and that he had been drinking ever since.

It was not until the third day that she learned the truth, when Constantius came into the room where she was sitting, sat down heavily on a couch, and blurted out:

"They say that I'm a heretic."

She said nothing, but waited.

"They say that I am damned."

She went across and sat beside him.

"Why should they say such a thing?"

"That's not all," he moaned. "They say that to be a Pelagian – a heretic as they call it – is worse even than being a pagan. Think of that! According to them I'm worse than my accursed son who stands in that pit of iniquity the *taurobolium*! Worse!"

"But why?" Even Placidia was taken aback.

He shook his head in disgust.

"Their reasoning, these men of God from Gaul: they say that the pagans have not seen the light, and so they are damned. But the heretic is worse: he, they say, has seen the light, and having seen, has turned his face from God – not damned but double damned. That's me, it seems."

"Who says this terrible thing?"

"Ah." He stood up. "Who indeed? Lupus, Bishop of Troyes said it. To my face. Told me I'd be damned as a heretic and a lot more besides."

He slumped down; and for once Placidia did not know what to say.

It had been a magnificent occasion. The visit of St. Germanus and his conversion of the Pelagians would go down in history as one of the most notable events in the story of the early British Church. A large group of the island's magnates attended, many with substantial retinues. They were splendidly dressed in the brightly coloured tunics and cloaks that were fashionable in the Roman world of that day – a far cry from the sober white toga of earlier times – and Constantius had felt his heart swell with pride to be amongst them. The grandees arranged themselves in a large circle to hear the debate between the two parties, and behind them was a large crowd of onlookers. By good luck Constantius found himself standing with a number of the important landowners at the front.

The two great churchmen had positioned themselves in the centre: and facing them were ranged a number of prominent members of the Pelagian party who were thought to be distinguished in the arts of scholarly and religious dispute.

It was an impressive debate. The Pelagians led off, making their case bravely and, it seemed to Constantius, soundly. The bishops said nothing until they had finished. Then they rose to reply. And now Constantius saw why the two men had such awesome reputations: for the islanders had never heard anything like it. With wonderful eloquence, with compelling power of argument, the two churchmen from Gaul attacked the Pelagian position, demonstrated its shortcomings, begged and persuaded the listeners to come back to the true Church. They spoke vehemently, and soon there were heads nodding in grudging admiration all around the circle. As Constantius watched, he could sense the tide beginning to turn in the visitors' favour. Several times Germanus paused, inviting the Pelagian speakers to rebut him, but they were unable to do so. Even Constantius had to confess that he had never witnessed anything better.

But the triumph of the visitors was not yet complete. Many of the landowners were unwilling to be so quickly influenced. Here and there around the circle there were murmurs. These bishops from Gaul might be eloquent and holy men, but Pelagius came from Britain and was not to be so lightly thrown over. The doctrine of submission that the visitors insisted upon did not appeal to them.

"Give what Thou commandest, O Lord," cried Lupus of Troyes, "and command what Thou wilt. We have no will but Thine. We submit."

Submit? It seemed to deny all their freedom, their claims to self-discipline, their proud island independence. In several places there was a shaking of heads.

It was now that Constantius made his great mistake. Though he had had difficulty in following the arguments, it suddenly seemed to him that he knew where he stood. Self-discipline, the exercise of the will – the things which he never achieved in his own daily life – these, he thought, were the things he most passionately believed in. Suddenly seized with courage, he stepped forward into the circle and, catching the eye of Lupus while the curious crowd fell silent, he addressed him.

Nervously fumbling for his words, not very coherently, he began to speak. He tried to say something about the Christian soldier, the man of free will who stood unaided against paganism and fought the good fight for God. Such a man, he reminded them, was not to be despised. He spoke badly, but he spoke with genuine feeling, for this was how he saw himself: was he not just such a Christian soldier fighting against his son and the heathen Germans, and the *taurobolium*? And though his words were fumbled and confused, they began to draw murmurs of sympathy and approval from others like him around the circle. Here was a man who felt as they did, and who had the courage to speak against these clever bishops from Gaul. When he finished, there was applause, and he smiled with a sense of accomplishment he had not felt in years. Constantius Porteus, decurion of Sorviodunum, has spoken, he told himself.

Lupus eyed him angrily. Here was exactly the kind of landowner, a provincial heretic steeped in pride, that he had come to defeat. Here and now, the last of these doubters must be stamped out.

"*Superbus!*" he bellowed. "Proud man, who thinks he can do anything without God." And he launched into his attack.

It was masterly. It was lacerating. Each word of it seemed to embed itself in Constantius's mind. He felt his face flush red, first with embarrassment, then with humiliation as Lupus tore his arguments apart, poured scorn on his ambitions and told him he was worse than a pagan.

Was everything he stood for wrong? Had he no friends – neither at home where his wife believed nothing and his son was a pagan, nor here where he had come to find honour amongst his fellow landowners and Christians? By the end of his speech, Lupus had converted many of the waverers, and shamed the others into submission. Constantius he had broken.

That night he returned to his lodgings alone and drank until morning. Then he had called for his horse and made his way down the long empty road.

"If I'm no better than a pagan," he confessed to Placidia, "then I've nothing left."

"You have the estate and your family," she said gently.

But she saw that he was not listening.

At the turn of the year 432 news came to Sarum that a major invasion was confidently predicted for that summer, and the evidence this time seemed definite.

Petrus faced the prospect with confidence. In the last two years he had not been idle, and nor had many other communities in the south. Settlements like Venta, if they could, had strengthened their defences still further. More mercenaries had been drafted. And in the far west, he had learned of an interesting development when a group of vigorous young men, mostly of his own age, had ridden into Sarum one day from the west and asked for him by name.

"We're forming a confederation," they told him, "local landowners like you and your family, each organising a militia on his own estate and pledged to support his fellow landowners if there's an invasion. Will you join us?"

He had agreed at once and they promised him: "Send to us for help and we will come," before riding on to the next estate.

There was a new mood of optimism in the air. There was even a rumour that the legions might return from the empire to help the former province; but no sign of them had come as yet.

As for the German mercenaries, Constantius had been proved wrong. Petrus found that by giving them some land on the slopes around the dune, and by allowing them to keep women in their camp, they were willing to stay and gave little trouble. They were paid, mostly in kind now, since the stock of gold *solidi* was beginning to run low, but it was agreed that they had the right to strip and loot any invaders they killed. He even increased their number to ten.

The families from Sorviodunum had now transferred into the dune, which was resuming its ancient aspect of a defended settlement. They lived uneasily, but peaceably, beside the Germans.

Following the visit from the young men from the west, there was a further important development. Under the organising genius of Numincus, a local militia was started. Petrus and the steward went one day to Venta where they purchased a quantity of swords and assorted armour, which they stored safely at the villa. Numincus also saw to it that every able-bodied man had a short bow and two hundred arrows – they were not impressive weapons, but useful at short range. Each morning now the stocky, grey-eyed steward would drill his twenty men as he had seen his own father do when he was a child. This militia did not look impressive beside the Germans, but they at least provided numbers of troops to man the walls of the dune if necessary.

"We'll be ready when they come," Petrus assured his mother. And to himself he promised: "We'll not only smash the Saxons; we'll restore Britannia to grandeur, given time."

Placidia watched these developments calmly; but she was worried.

Constantius had not changed. He took a nominal interest in the running of the estate and none at all in its defence – both of which in reality were in the hands of the loyal steward. For Placidia now knew only too well that Petrus, apart from his spasmodic bursts of enthusiasm, did little that was practical either. He rode his horses, supervised the work on the dune and occasionally, with obvious impatience, joined her when she went through the estate accounts with Numincus. When I am gone, she had to confess to herself sadly, he'll be little better than Constantius. His only hope was if she could find him a wife to strengthen him.

And here there was another problem. For ever since the skirmish with the Saxons, Petrus had been keeping a concubine: Sulicena, the cowherd's niece. It was a relationship which worried her.

It was not that the girl was a nuisance at the villa, since Petrus kept her in a small house two miles away; nor did Sulicena do anything she could complain about. On the few occasions when they had met the girl had been polite and respectful. It was more something that Placidia sensed, a hidden scorn and contempt behind the pale girl's deference that concerned her and she felt instinctively that she was an evil influence on her son. Worse, the girl distracted him from the more important business of finding a suitable wife. Each time Placidia raised this vital subject, Petrus brushed the matter aside, and on one occasion said to her bluntly:

"If I do take a wife, I shall still keep Sulicena as my concubine."

Placidia shrugged wearily.

"It is not necessary to tell me that, Petrus." She supposed some compromise would be reached in time, but his attitude was discouraging.

Petrus was content with things as they were. His relationship with the girl was entirely physical – her lithe, hard body and her eager sexual demands exactly satisfied his needs. Frequently he visited her and they would make love until they were spent. It made him feel a man and since he made it clear to the girl that the affair would have to end one day, it left him free.

And yet, he was conscious of a sense of dissatisfaction with his life. The worship of the pagan gods began to seem flat, when he had no one to share his belief with, except the grim old peasant Tarquinus. True, he would spend hours studying Roman history for heroes to his taste; he even read the works of the great pagan philosophers. But on the windswept ridges around Sarum, the classical world he admired seemed too far away. He felt a growing sense of emptiness. There was no outlet here for his need to dramatise himself.

Perhaps he would enter the *taurobolium* again.

"What you need," Placidia told him again, "is an intelligent woman to keep you company as a wife."

It was not until the spring of 432 that Placidia had at last persuaded him to take some positive action.

A kinswoman – recently widowed – had written to say that she had a daughter of marriageable age: that the girl would inherit a large estate to the west, near the Severn estuary: and that, though only nineteen, she ran the place with the steward as if it were her own already.

Even Petrus had to agree with his mother that it would be both foolish and insulting to a kinswoman if he did not at least visit this girl called Flavia.

"After all," Placidia said, "you don't have to do anything about her if you don't like each other."

The visit became more attractive to Petrus when he remembered something else.

"I have always meant to visit the shrine to the god Nodens across the Severn," he said. "It's supposed to be magnificent. I can see that and then visit the girl." And as he considered this he became almost keen to make the journey.

Placidia could only pray it might come to something.

From all the reports received at Sarum it seemed unlikely that the Saxons would come before midsummer that year, and so in early spring having said goodbye to his parents, given Sulicena a gold *solidus*, and taking one spare horse, he set out on the road west. His way lay through Aquae Sulis.

The roads, though overgrown with weeds in places, were still good, and he reached Aquae Sulis early the next day. It was a sad sight.

For though the town was still inhabited, it was only a ghost of its former self. The spa's problem had not been raiders, but a change in the water level in the previous century that had caused the ducts leading to the baths to silt up; and although they had been cleaned out, they soon clogged up again. As the years went by the costs of repair had grown too high. The resort had almost closed down long before Petrus was born.

As he rode through the deserted streets, gazing at the splendid but empty buildings, Petrus felt a sense of melancholy. When he inspected the shrine of Sulis Minerva, and looked at the fine gorgon's head that now gazed over the dry and empty pool, he shook his head and murmured:

"Aquae Sulis, too, must one day be restored to glory."

But how he did not know.

That afternoon, when he rode on to the town of Corinium, he found it in a better state. Its defences were strong, like the ones at Venta, and as a further precaution, the amphitheatre whose round walls stood proudly in the centre of the town had been fortified as a last place of defence. Its high, strong walls would be impossible for anyone to breach without large siege engines. He found a small inn near the town gates and spent the night there.

Soon after dawn, he rode on. As he left the town, he noticed a small building outside the walls. It was an *ecclesia*, a Christian church: a small, poor building made of wood, obviously badly attended. Some useless attempts had been made to fortify the little structure too, and Petrus could not help smiling. These poor Christians, he thought: it's the pagan gods who will save this place.

Later that day he reached the broad estuary of the Severn and took the ferryboat across to the western side. From there he rode south towards the shrine. It was a remarkable region. Ever since the conquest, coal and iron had been mined and worked in the area, and several times he passed small settlements where slag heaps rose darkly out of the thick forest on his right. On his left he could see the sparkling waters of the great river. And then, as the sun was sinking, he saw his objective ahead.

The shrine of the god Nodens the Cloudmaker was a fine sight – a cluster of temple buildings with handsome, heavy-pillared porticoes set on a promontory overlooking the broadening estuary. Smoke was rising gently from two altars in the clear spring sky. There was a pleasant scent from the surrounding woods and the wind just disturbed the sparkling surface of the river and rustled the trees below the little acropolis.

Petrus smiled. It was everything a temple should be.

Indeed, the entire place was in perfect order. By the entrance was a long wooden building that served as a lodging house, simple but comfortable, and there he found a dozen pilgrims like himself. There were eight temple priests and numerous acolytes, and they lived in handsome houses built, he learned, with money from two large bequests that had been made recently.

Since Nodens had been the traditional patron god of his family, he went at once to the two altars and left one of the dwindling stock of gold *solidi* on each.

"If I choose the girl Flavia as my bride," he promised, "she shall come here to be married by the priests and acknowledge Nodens as her god."

It was a pleasant visit. That evening he spent long hours talking with the temple priests and found them to be learned and scholarly men who reminded him of the pagan professor of his youth. In their peaceful and civilised presence, he found his faith in the pagan calling was renewed.

He was glad. He had not liked to admit even to himself his recent dissatisfaction with his chosen religion. He had gone through the *taurobolium* again the year before, this time alone, and had emerged disappointed. The mystical experience, the sense of purification, had eluded him: he had been conscious only of the sticky blood and the occasional coughing of Tarquinus above, who now seemed old and rather disreputable. In the quiet precincts of the shrine however, everything seemed different, and on the second day, as he prayed before the smoking altar, feeling the sun on his back, smelling the scented wood that the priests laid on the fire and hearing the gentle murmur of their chants, he felt a sense of peace that he had not known for many months. The shrine of Nodens was a place of healing, and he felt bathed in its benign influence.

A whole further day passed. Once again he slept at the shrine, and then the next morning, refreshed, he made his way slowly back to the ferry.

The estate of Flavia's family lay south, a day's ride away, near the old lead mines in the Mendip hills whose ore had so often passed in former centuries along the road through Sorviodunum. It was rich, rolling country; his spirits were high, and almost forgetting the cowherd's niece he told himself: perhaps, after all, I shall like her.

It was late afternoon and he was only an hour's ride away from the estate when he came upon the small port. The sun had still some way to sink, but the air was beginning to grow chilly; on a sudden impulse he decided to halt there for the night and complete his journey the next morning.

If she's a possible bride, I may as well arrive there fresh, he decided, and thought no more about it.

The little port consisted of half a dozen store houses, a small jetty and a cluster of buildings including a *mansio* for travellers to stay and change their horses. It was surrounded by a recently erected wooden stockade, the previous one having been burned down a few years earlier by a party of Irish raiders. Several small coracles of skin stretched over a wooden framework were moored by the jetty; but there was also a stout wooden vessel with a single mast, which was obviously ready to put out to sea.

He saw that his horses were stabled at the *mansio*, and the innkeeper ushered him into a long room with a fire at each end, where the evening meal was soon to be served.

His companions were half a dozen sailors and an older, weather-beaten man with a mass of reddish hair who, he learned, was master of the stout ship he had seen. It was the master who presided at the long table down the centre of the room which he now approached, and where he was quickly made welcome.

Soon they were served a huge bowl of stew, accompanied by pitchers of ale. The company chatted happily and the master mariner, at frequent intervals, made his opinions clear in a bluff way that the other sailors immediately agreed with.

After a little time, however, he began to take notice of one other traveller at the table. He sat alone at the far end, eating quietly, and seemed to be oblivious of the rest of the company. He wore a *birrhus* – the heavy cloak of brown wool for which the island had become famous – and a hood over his head. Petrus at first paid this man little attention, but in the middle of the meal, seeing his gaze shift towards him, the master mariner nudged him and said in a lower voice:

"See that fellow over there? Well, he'll be dead in a month." And he gave a decisive nod, and passed the back of his hand across his throat. "They'll slit him from ear to ear."

Petrus stared at the silent figure in surprise. Though the hood covered his head, he could see enough of the man's face to judge that the stranger was only a few years older than himself.

"How do you know?" he asked.

"He sails with us tomorrow," the mariner explained, "to Ireland. He's going to join this fellow they call Patricius and his friends. And they'll all be killed."

Petrus had never heard of Patricius and asked the mariner who these people were. The man grunted impatiently. "Missionaries," he said with scorn. "They're going to convert the heathen Irish, who are mostly cut-throats and pirates, as anyone on this coastline can tell you." It was true that in recent times, the raids of the Irish pirates on the west coast had been a constant source of trouble. "They'll be butchered." He paused before glancing at the traveller and adding: "Pity. He's a nice young fellow."

After the meal, the sailors gathered round the fire at one end of the room while the stranger quietly moved to the other fire where, drawing out a small roll of parchment, he began to read. Petrus sat with the sailors.

The evening passed pleasantly, with the sailors getting steadily but peaceably drunk while they chatted or sang an occasional chorus. As darkness fell, four of them retired to the sleeping quarters while two more dozed where they were by the fire. The stranger, who took no notice of them at all, was still reading quietly.

Petrus had drunk only a little and was still wide awake. Having nothing else to do, he found himself watching the stranger curiously. There was something in his manner that seemed modest, even retiring, yet self-possessed. After some time the other became aware of his gaze and turned towards him.

His face was indeed young, Petrus now saw: hardly older than himself; it was broad and square, with widely spaced brown eyes. His hands too, were large and strong. He might have been a pleasant young country farmer. The eyes flickered with amusement and then, to Petrus's surprise, he gave him a boyish grin.

"Not asleep yet? Seems you didn't drink enough."

As he spoke the young man pulled back his hood and Petrus saw that the whole of the top of his head was shaved, leaving a circular fringe of hair around the edge; and although at this time monasteries were still almost unknown in Britain, Petrus was aware that this tonsure meant that his companion was a monk.

It seemed that he had finished his reading, for he motioned Petrus to join him.

"My name is Martinus," he explained.

He had come, he said, from Gaul, to visit his family in Britain before making the voyage to Ireland. He asked Petrus about his own journey, and listened with interest as Petrus told him about his trip to Lydney and the visit he was planning to Flavia's family the following day.

To his surprise the young monk showed no shock that he had been to the shrine of Nodens, and when he heard about Flavia he grinned and said:

"Let's hope she's pretty, then you can marry her with a good conscience!"

When Petrus had told his own story, he felt less embarrassment at asking Martinus about himself. Was the mariner's report true? Was he going to Ireland to convert the heathen? Martinus nodded.

"Aren't you afraid?"

The young man nodded again.

"Sometimes. But it soon passes. If you're serving God, there's nothing to be afraid of really."

"But they may kill you."

Martinus gave him a gentle but unaffected smile.

"Perhaps."

Petrus was familiar with the blustering Christianity of his own father, but the young monk's quiet confidence seemed very different.

"What made you choose to serve the Christian God?" he asked.

To him it seemed a natural question, but a look of genuine puzzlement crossed Martinus's broad face.

"Oh, I didn't," he corrected. "It's God who chooses."

Petrus shrugged.

"Well, you want to go to Ireland anyway," he remarked.

Now Martinus grimaced, a little ruefully.

"Actually, I don't want to go at all."

Petrus stared at him. Was the monk playing some kind of verbal game with him, like his old professor? He did not think so.

"You don't *want* to go?"

Martinus shook his head.

"No, to tell you the truth, if I followed my own will, I'd stay on my family's farm. It's only two days' ride north of here you know. But God gave me a commandment and I joined a monastery, and now God's will is that I go to Ireland, so . . ." He made a gentle, self-deprecating movement with his big hands; and then, seeing that Petrus still looked surprised, he asked: "Do you know the story of Patricius, the man I'm going to join?"

Petrus did not, and so Martinus explained.

Patricius, or Patrick, was only a few years older, he told Petrus. His family were like the Porteus family – modest landowners of the decurion class, whose estate was in the west of Britannia. When Patricius was sixteen, Irish pirates had raided the coast where he lived; they had caught him and carried him across the western sea to Ireland, where he had been sold as a slave.

"He was used as a shepherd," Martinus said. "Cut off from everyone he loved. But he never lost his faith in God."

"Were his family Christian?" Petrus asked.

To his surprise, Martinus chuckled.

"Both his father and grandfather took Christian orders, but I wouldn't be surprised if it was to escape taxes – don't you think?"

For under the late empire it had been possible for decurions to obtain exemption from the financial burdens of holding local offices by taking priestly orders, and many local landowners had entered the priesthood for this reason. Petrus smiled: his companion's frankness was engaging.

But the story of Patricius's religious calling was another matter, and Martinus told him the story of how he used to go alone into the woods every day to pray; and how one day, after six years, he had a vision which told him where he would find a ship, several days' journey away and in a strange port he did not know, and how he found the ship which then took him home to his family.

"But that was only the start of his real life," Martinus explained. "From then on, you see, he knew that he had been chosen by God. He left his family home, went to study in Gaul, and became a monk. And then he had another vision which told him that the heathen Irish who had made him a slave should be converted to Christianity. At first the Church authorities said he couldn't go – even that he was unworthy," here Martinus's face puckered into momentary anger and disgust. "But he persisted and now he has been sent there. I'm going to join him tomorrow."

This was a new, and altogether more daring version of Christianity than Petrus had encountered before. He questioned Martinus further, and the monk told him about the vigorous monasteries of Italy and Gaul, of their great men like Martin of Tours, Germanus of Auxerre and the monk Ninian who recently founded the first monastery in the land of the wild Picts in the north of the island. He told Petrus about their bravery, the sanctity of their lives, the hair shirts and other discomforts they willingly endured to mortify the flesh. "These are true servants of God," he said. "In Ireland we shall continue their work."

Since Petrus was still curious, he gave him some account of the Church's thinkers, men like Augustine, the present Bishop of Hippo in Northern Africa. "He used to be a pagan you know, just like you," Martinus said. "He's a great scholar, and before he converted, he taught rhetoric at the finest pagan schools of Italy. It was his confessions about his early life that I was reading this evening. I copied them out when I was in the monastery in Gaul."

"Another saintly life I suppose?" Petrus asked.

Martinus roared with laughter.

"He is now. But as a young man – you should read his *Confessions*. He seems to have done nothing but fornicate, according to his account!" He grinned again. "Actually, I think Augustine boasts about it a bit." He paused, then added conspiratorially: "Even after his conversion, they say he kept his concubine for years."

Petrus was puzzled. It was obvious that Martinus was ready to lay down his life for a religion whose great men, saintly though they might be, didn't seem to him like heroes. He asked him why.

At once Martinus became serious.

"You attach too much importance to the man, too little to God," he said. "Man is sinful and imperfect. He's noble, if you like, only in so far as he turns his mind over to God directly. It's not that I or Patrick," he used the non-Roman form of the missionary's name, "can do anything in

Ireland: but God will work through us. That's exactly Augustine's point. He wants us to know that as a man, he was a pagan, a sinner, a fornicator. Whatever he's done – and believe me, in Africa he's done more than ten others could have – has only been done through God's providence and will, not his own. His own spirit, which knew only confusion before, is now at rest in the service of God."

As he spoke, the boyishness of his former manner had left him and Petrus suddenly felt himself to be in the company of a man, who although about the same age in years, was far ahead of him in maturity.

"And you – are you at peace?" he asked.

"Yes," the monk answered simply. And Petrus could see that it was true.

But to Petrus the answers the missionary gave still seemed incomplete. He might be going to heathen Ireland, but what about Britannia – and what of Rome? He thought of the deserted baths at Aquae Sulis, the cities of Venta and Corinium, fortifying themselves against the Saxons, and of the villa at Sarum under threat at this very moment.

"You may be at peace," he accused, "but our towns and villas are not. I want to restore them. I want to see Rome great again – the theatres, the temples, the baths all restored."

Martinus smiled.

"Like the shining city on its seven hills – Rome in all its glory. Civilisation, you mean?"

"Yes."

Martinus nodded understandingly.

"Even the great Jerome, a saintly Christian scholar, even he could not speak when he heard that Rome had fallen," the monk agreed. "And Augustine, too – his great work of theology is not called *De Civitate Dei* – the City of God – by chance. Many Christians love Rome and all it stands for. But there is a greater city still," he went on eagerly, "a city that no man can corrupt, no army destroy. And that is the city of the spirit – God's citadel that shines like the eternal sun. Think, my friend," he urged, with sudden passion, "if you are prepared to defend a city made by man, how much more you should be anxious to defend the faith, which is the city of the Creator of the heavens Himself."

It was a fine speech, and Petrus could not help being moved by his companion's passion. But he still shook his head doubtfully.

To his surprise, Martinus stretched out his big hand and took him gently by the arm.

"I see, my friend, that though you are a pagan, you are a seeker after truth. One day you will find it when God commands you, and then you will know peace." He gave his arm a friendly pat. "Time we slept. We both have journeys tomorrow."

Petrus considered. Had he found peace? He thought of his parents, of the girl Sulicena, of the *taurobolium*, of the tangled events and violent urges of his young life. No, whether the missionary's religion or his own were the true one, he had not found peace. As they rose, a thought occurred to him.

"When you first left your farm, you said, God commanded you. What command did God give you, Martinus?" he asked.

"The same that he gave to the apostle who bore your own name Petrus – Peter the rock," the monk replied. "He said: 'Feed my sheep'."

Petrus nodded. He knew the text.

"God does not speak to me," he admitted frankly.

Martinus gazed at him carefully.

"You have to listen, Petrus," he replied. "Sometimes He speaks very quietly."

For the rest of his life Petrus always explained that his conversion took place that night, shortly before dawn. It happened in a dream.

He was on a huge, empty downland – similar to the ridges around Sarum. "But I was not at Sarum," he would say, "I was in some other country which I took to be Ireland." The landscape was full of white sheep. But as he rode through them, he came upon a single lamb. "It was a lamb, yet bigger than the sheep; and it came towards me and stopped, dead in front of me, so that I couldn't go on. Then it spoke: 'Petrus,' it said: 'Feed my sheep'. Then it vanished."

He had not known what to make of this, but soon afterwards, though the lamb had gone, he heard its voice. And again it said: 'Feed my sheep'. And he had woken.

"Then later, that same night, I had a second dream. This time I was looking at Venta. It was definitely Venta: I saw the walls, the column to Marcus Aurelius and the gates. The sun was shining on the roofs, and it seemed to me that my old professor was still there, in the city, and that I had only just come from seeing him. As I looked back at the town, a great light from the heavens seemed to descend on the place, so that all the tops of the buildings gleamed and sparkled, as though they were made not of tiles and stone, but of silver and gold. And then I heard a voice. I could not tell where it came from, whether it came from inside my own head or from the clouds: but the voice spoke so that there could be no mistaking it, and it said: 'My city is a heavenly city, not made of bricks, but of the spirit. And my city is eternal. Turn back from worldly cares, Petrus, and walk boldly to the city of God'. Then, for the second time I awoke. The dawn was breaking. And I knew what I must do."

It was an impressive vision, and he was proud of it.

But when Petrus hurried to tell Martinus about it early that morning the monk's reaction was rather disappointing.

"If you truly wish to serve God," he said, "you must learn self-discipline. I advise you to go to one of the monasteries in Gaul. Study there for several years: it will teach your unruly spirit to submit to God. Then you may become a missionary."

Petrus thanked him politely. But he took little notice of the advice. The vision, it seemed to him, had been definitive. He had never experienced such a thing before: and now that God had spoken to him so directly, whole vistas opened up in his mind in which he could see himself in a set of new and heroic roles.

It was late afternoon the next day that Tarquinus saw Petrus riding towards him along the track that led to the big curve of the river. As he stared at the young landowner, the cowherd's cunning old eyes grew wide with astonishment.

Petrus was riding his horse at a walk, and he was followed by half a dozen estate workers. But what caused the old man to stare was his appearance.

For Petrus's head was bare, and the entire crown had been shaved completely bald.

Stranger still, as Tarquinus opened his mouth to greet him, the young man stared at him as if he were a monster, and then turned his face away. What could it mean? Confused, Tarquinus waited a little, then followed the party towards the curve in the river.

If he was surprised before, it was nothing compared to his amazement at what he saw next.

Petrus knew what he must do. And he was methodical.

When he reached the clearing where the *taurobolium* pit was concealed, he quickly ordered the men to pull back the planks and break up the wooden grid that covered it.

"Burn the wood, and fill in the pit," he ordered them. "See that it's finished tonight."

When Tarquinus, who had heard his orders, hobbled into the clearing to protest, he gave the old man a withering look and cried:

"Your iniquity is destroyed, servant of Satan!"

Then, before the cowherd could reply, he turned his horse's head briskly and rode towards the valley.

Darkness was falling when he arrived at the villa where he was eagerly awaited. A farmhand had told Numincus an hour before that Petrus had been seen, and the steward had hurried to the villa to ensure that preparations were made. A dozen welcoming torches now burned near the doorway and even Constantius had roused himself to stand with his wife and the steward to greet his son.

"Let us hope," he said, "that he has found a rich bride."

As Petrus dismounted, all three came out; to his surprise, Constantius felt his arm gripped, and found himself embraced by Petrus with an affection that he had not known in years.

It was only when the party moved inside that he, too, noticed the tonsure that had been causing the other two to stare. And as he gazed at his son's head in puzzlement, Petrus announced:

"I have news that will please you, father. I have been converted at last to the true faith of Christ." And while Constantius blinked in astonishment he went on. "Before coming here, I destroyed the *taurobolium*. There will be no more such iniquities at Sarum."

As he took this news in, Constantius felt tears come to his eyes. "My dear son," was all that he could say, "I thank God."

It was only when they were seated, and the servants had brought in a huge bowl of steaming fish, that Placidia, who had been staring at her son's tonsure thoughtfully, quietly asked:

"And what of Flavia, Petrus. Was she to your liking?"

Petrus gazed back at her serenely. A half smile crossed his face and gently he tapped his shaven head.

"Flavia? I don't know," he replied, as though it was the most natural reply in the world. "When I vowed to serve only Christ," he explained calmly, "I undertook a vow of chastity. I swore never to know woman again. So obviously there was no point in going to see Flavia. I just turned my horse's head and came back to Sarum." And while the others were still digesting this appalling news, he went on: "I've decided to join Patrick in Ireland. I shall leave in three days."

The battle of wills between Petrus Porteus and his mother lasted not three, but five days. During that time each discovered strengths in the other that surprised them.

It began that first night. While Constantius sat slumped and silent, and Numincus's sad grey eyes gazed at him in mute appeal, Placidia marshalled her forces carefully.

She had no illusions about his conversion. To her it seemed her son had simply found a new and exciting role to play. But she was careful. She argued with him gently: why did he want to do this? He told her in detail about his conversation with Martinus and his dreams. She listened carefully, then plied him with questions.

"Does God demand that you leave Sarum to be destroyed? What of us? Doesn't the Bible say 'Honour your father and mother'? Will you desert us?"

As she argued, Placidia was wise. She took care never to attack his conversion or to suggest that God had not spoken to him. She did not dispute his visions, but only the interpretation of them. "If God commands you to feed his sheep," she argued, "how can we be sure he meant the Irish. Isn't there plenty of work to be done for God in Sarum?"

But Petrus was obdurate. And when she pleaded with him that the villa might be destroyed, he answered passionately:

"It is the city of God we must defend, not the work of man. God will decide the fate of Sarum."

"And did God demand in the dream that you should be celibate?" she pressed him.

To which he only replied:

"I know my own weakness. A woman would distract me. This way is better."

They argued until dawn, and as the night wore on and she saw the quiet but unshakable determination of her son, she recognised the ruin of all her hopes. I'd rather he married the girl Sulicena and had children by her, she thought, than had none at all. Whether this was a passing enthusiasm or a genuine vocation – she was not sure which herself – it made little difference if he left for Ireland and perhaps was killed.

"You really mean to leave in three days?"

He nodded.

She wondered if she would ever see him again.

[271]

Though they argued quietly like this, hour after hour, the other two men did not join in.

Constantius had no need to. In the first place, he was delighted with his son's conversion to the true faith. In the second, he saw at once that if his son did as he suggested, then the defence of Sarum would be in his hands again. No one could argue now if he got rid of those German heathens. He would show them what he could do. After a time, during which he had quietly drunk a pitcher of wine to celebrate, he had subsided into sleep.

Numincus sat, as he usually did, only speaking when spoken to, his grey eyes blinking slowly. Some time before dawn, his eyes closed and only opened again once or twice, for a few seconds at a time.

At last, mother and son retired to their rooms.

Alone in his room, Petrus prepared his bed carefully. He did so in a strange manner.

Instead of lying down on the couch beside the wall, he began to dismantle it, removing the slats of wood on which the mattress rested and placing them on the floor. The pillow cushion he discarded. Then he stripped. Under his clothes he was wearing not linen, but a hair shirt: a coarse garment which he had managed to acquire from Martinus, and prickly discomfort of which had already brought his skin out in a rash. Dressed only in this, he lay down on the bare boards, his head on the stone floor. His feet were cold. He shivered slightly. But this, he knew, was how the great men of the Church, men like Germanus of Auxerre, mortified their flesh, and he was resolved to do likewise. And this was how Placidia found him, asleep, later that morning.

During the next day, he paid two more important visits. The first was to the dune.

He rode through the gate and walked his horse slowly past the camp of the Germans, who watched him curiously. He ignored them however, and headed for the little house at the far side of the place, that was occupied by Tarquinus. There he halted, and called to the cowherd to come out.

Tarquinus emerged suspiciously. After the incident of the day before, everyone at Sarum knew that strange changes had come over Petrus. No one could be sure what might come next.

Petrus came straight to the point.

"Bring the idol of Sulis out of the shrine," he ordered, pointing to the little hut beside Tarquinus's house.

Unwillingly Tarquinus went in and came back with the little stone figure.

"There will be no more pagan gods at Sarum," Petrus announced. "The idol must be broken up. Give it to me."

But Tarquinus clutched the little figure close to his chest.

"No."

Petrus stared at him. Was the cowherd defying him?

"I can make you," he threatened.

Tarquinus said nothing, but he did not loosen his hold. Petrus looked into his eyes and saw that they were full of hate. He had no doubt that Tarquinus was laying curses on him; but though such a thought a month ago would have terrified him, now he found that he did not even care.

"Very well," he said coldly. "You are to leave Sarum. For ever. Collect your things and go."

Without a word, Tarquinus turned and went back into his house. A few minutes later he reappeared with a few belongings. Not even looking at Petrus this time, the old man shuffled out of the dune; and once outside, he went down the path to the empty settlement of Sorviodunum and the river. Pulling a small boat from its mooring, he stepped into it and paddled down stream; only as the current caught him and swept him southwards did he turn and mutter:

"I'll be back, young Porteus. And so will she." He stroked the little stone figure. "But your Christian eyes will never see us."

From the dune above, he saw a thin column of smoke rising. Petrus was burning down his house and the little shrine.

It was a few hours later that Petrus arrived at the house of Sulicena. The girl was standing in front of the door, her large eyes watching him approach. She was dressed only in a thin robe tied with a girdle round her waist, and as he saw her slim figure he felt his familiar lust rising again.

She stepped forward, obviously expecting him to dismount, but he did not. For a second he felt his hand tremble, but he controlled it. She looked curiously at his shaved head.

"I am leaving for Ireland," he told her coldly. In a few words he explained his conversion and the vows he had taken. She stared at him in disbelief.

"You mean you'll never lie with a woman again, as long as you live?"

He nodded.

She laughed aloud, and for some reason Petrus found himself blushing. But when she found that he was serious, he saw a hint of scorn appear in her face.

Finally she moved to stand beside his horse, stretched up her arm, and before he could stop her, ran her hand down his leg. She looked directly into his eyes.

"You feel nothing?"

He felt his body tense, determined to resist.

"You don't want me any more?" she asked again.

"No."

She stepped back angrily.

"You lie," she exclaimed furiously.

He coloured, but fought it down.

"I'm leaving anyway." He suddenly felt embarrassed.

She stood quite still. Her face now showed nothing except anger and contempt.

"Enjoy yourself then, celibate," she hissed the last word scornfully, and spat on the ground in front of him. "I hope the Irish kill you."

"What will you do?" he asked. Despite his convictions, he felt guilty.

"Find a man instead of a boy," she said coldly. "Now go."

He hesitated.

"You may need money." Awkwardly he dropped a small bag of coins in front of her. She picked it up without a word. He felt a need to explain himself.

"It is only the service of God . . ." he began earnestly.

But she cut him short.

"Tell the Irish," she said flatly, and turned away, into her house.

The battle with his mother was resumed that evening.

In his desire to cleanse the villa of all pagan images, he had intended next to destroy the mosaic of Orpheus; but here Placidia succeeded in stopping him.

"When the villa is yours, you can do as you wish; but while it belongs to your father and to me, you must respect our wishes. Your father's Christianity has never been offended by the mosaic, which portrays the birds and animals of God's creation as well as Orpheus." Although he did not approve of the mosaic any more, he had to admit the force of Placidia's argument, and let the matter rest for the time being.

But this was the only argument that Placidia won that day. All that evening, as they had the night before, mother and son battled. If he must go to Ireland, it did not have to be now, she pleaded. And what of his duty to defend his own home?

His duty? His black eyes flashed with anger.

"You do not understand," he cried. "Those who love God can feel only contempt for themselves and their possessions. The duty you speak of is nothing but love of self: it is contempt for God." And as she tried to argue he added: "If God is served, it does not matter if this place is destroyed."

"But this is all I have," she said softly.

"No," he urged her. "We have God, which is more."

"And me? Do you not care what is to become of me?" she asked gently.

"Trust in God," he replied.

Placidia shook her head sadly, and, realising once again that neither her husband nor her son really loved her, turned away to hide her tears.

She did not give up. Indeed, now that she knew that she was really alone, it seemed to give her strength.

And on the third day, as he was preparing for his journey, Petrus was surprised when Numincus, accompanied by eight men, quietly appeared in his room, and before he realised what was happening, took him politely but firmly to an outhouse into which they pushed him. To his astonishment, Placidia was standing by the door, which was then barred, four of the men standing guard outside.

"I'm sorry Petrus," she explained, "but you cannot leave Sarum at present. I won't allow it."

It had never occurred to him that his mother would resort to such extreme action.

"Do you intend to keep me a prisoner then?" he demanded incredulously.

"Yes," she replied simply.

She knew that Numincus was on her side, and that the men would obey him. Later that day, Petrus ordered the steward outside to release him, but he learned his mother's strength and his own weakness when Numincus replied:

"I wish there was a better man than a Porteus to look after this place, and her. But you're all there is, so you stay."

That evening, and the next, Placidia came to reason with him. But though the outhouse was draughty and uncomfortable, he would not give in; and both mother and son secretly wondered how long this state of affairs could last.

It lasted until the fifth day after his return. Then it was resolved: not by Petrus, nor by Placidia, but by a single messenger who rode frantically down the road from Calleva with the message:

"The Saxons have come."

They had come in force this time, landing in the south east and sending several large raiding parties, each a hundred or more strong, towards the west.

As soon as the news reached the villa, Placidia knew what she must do. Stalking to the door of his prison, she opened it herself and let him out.

"You're free."

He looked at her curiously.

"Why?"

"The Saxons are coming and we are all going to the dune. I can't leave you here." Even as she spoke, he could see Numincus and some of the men loading weapons into a cart. "If you want to go to Ireland," she added, "I suggest you leave at once."

Petrus stared at his mother. The sun caught her white hair and her lined old face. His own bald head now had three days' growth of hair on the crown and he looked bedraggled. But as he looked up at her and saw her indomitable spirit, he thought that he had never felt better.

"I think I'll come with you to the dune," he replied with a grin.

By that evening, all was in readiness within the ancient fortress. A newly built oak gate lay against the earthwork wall, ready to be slid into place and buttressed against the entrance. Numincus's militia were armed and ready to mount the ramparts; and all the Sarum families, together with a quantity of livestock, were camping within the big circular space.

Petrus had also sent a horseman to the west to beg for aid from the young leaders of the militia there.

"I think we can hold the Saxons off for a short time," he told his mother. "But we were promised help, and we may need reinforcements to drive the Saxons away."

"Then I hope they come," Placidia said bleakly.

"Of course they will," he replied.

All in all, however, he was not dissatisfied with the dune's defences.

[275]

"The bowmen can protect the walls," he explained to his father; "then we can make sallies out with the German mercenaries."

The dune was also a Christian fortress.

For one point on which Petrus had insisted was that both Numincus, whose unspoken devotion to Mithras was well known, and the heathen Germans should be baptised; and in this he had had the vigorous support of Constantius. Accordingly, though the Germans had grumbled, father and son had led them down to the river below and immersed each of them in the water, making the sign of the Cross as they did so. Though neither was a priest, such a brief ceremony would have to do. In the centre of the dune he also placed a small wooden cross. It was enough.

"God will protect us," Petrus told the people as he moved amongst them, pleased with the transformation he had wrought.

But a greater transformation still was the appearance of Constantius. He was a new man. Dressed in a magnificent bronze breastplate, wearing his finest blue cloak, and carrying a long iron sword which he himself had honed to a razor sharpness, he seemed not only to have shed his customary torpor, but he was an inspiration to the defenders. Leaving the ordering of business to Numincus and Petrus, he moved cheerfully amongst the men, his grey head held erect and his black eyes no longer bloodshot, but clear and keen. Chatting to one of the bowmen on the ramparts, or sharing a joke with the women in the camp, he seemed to give them confidence, and Placidia found herself several times gazing with admiration and even affection at the man that her husband might have been.

Two days passed. Every hour Petrus looked out from the walls for some sign of the reinforcements from the west. They did not appear.

Then, on the third day, the Saxons came.

The only thing that Petrus had not forseen in his elaborate plans for Sarum's defence was that the fearsome German mercenaries would desert. But early on the third day, when the lookout on the ramparts saw a large force of Saxons approaching from the south-east and informed those below that there were at least a hundred of them, this was what happened. Nodding briskly to their women to follow them, the huge men swung on to their horses and, before anyone realised what was happening, rode out of the gate and on to the road that led north-eastwards towards Calleva. They had come to fight for pay, but not to be killed. Petrus could hardly believe his eyes; but it was obvious that there was nothing to be done.

"Close the gate," he ordered angrily.

Once again he looked towards the west. "If the reinforcements are coming," he thought, "they had better come now."

The Saxons made their way quickly and purposefully towards the dune. They took no notice of Sorviodunum in the valley below, but the whole company, some hundred strong, walked their captured horses round the north side of the old fort, inspecting its defences before they congregated again at a safe distance from the gate, to decide how they would attack. From the wall, Petrus could see each man distinctly: they were tall, blond men, most of them wearing thick leather tunics, heavy woollen leggings bound with cross straps; their leaders carrying big metal helmets, with horns let into each side. They carried swords, spears and large wooden shields with shining metal bosses. A few carried small axes.

The dune was a formidable obstacle, even for a hundred armed men, but it was obvious that they intended to take it. After a few tense minutes, he saw the body split into four equal parties which wheeled their horses away to different positions opposite the wall before dismounting. One party remained opposite the gate, the other three took up positions on the north, north west and west of the fort. Clearly there would be a simultaneous attack. Quickly Petrus split his own men into four groups: Constantius commanded by the gate, Numincus, himself and one of the estate men taking charge of each of the others.

The Saxon charge was formidable. It began with a terrible battle cry.

"Thunor!" Two of the four groups bellowed, so that it seemed to echo round the dune. Thunor, he knew, was one of their greatest gods.

"Woden!" answered the other two. And all four hammered their weapons against their shields.

"Thunor! Woden!" Again and again, the names of their gods of thunder and war rang round the fort, and the terrible hammering of the shields made some of the defenders grow pale. But Constantius's voice came clearly from the gate: "God defends us, my children." And the men seemed to take heart.

Then the Saxons charged.

The invaders found it harder than they had expected. The walls of the dune were steep and the bare slopes around them were long. Each party found a hail of well directed arrows greeted them, and while they tried to scale the walls, they were completely exposed and defenceless. The defensive capacity of the old British fort, in the absence of Roman siege engines, was shown once again.

The nearest the invaders came to success was at the gate where, by splitting into smaller groups and storming each side of the gate they managed in several cases to reach the top of the rampart. But here Constantius performed prodigies of valour, racing from one spot to another, greeting the Saxons with tremendous blows and thrusts from his sword. One Saxon he killed outright, and two others he sent single-handed rolling down the slopes, badly wounded.

Soon the Saxons were faltering. The defendants kept up a steady fire. And then Constantius made his extraordinary move.

To his astonishment, Petrus suddenly saw the main gate thrown open; and before he could even move from his position, he saw his father, mounted on his best horse, leading a party of six men on foot out of the gate at a run.

It was what he had intended the German mercenaries to do – to sally out just as the attackers faltered and cut them down as they fell back; but it had not occurred to him his father would do so instead.

What followed made him catch his breath. For while the rest of the

[277]

sortie party caught the nearest group of Saxons in the rear and cut them down with great success, Constantius had raced far ahead, entirely alone.

Galloping wildly across the open ground, he intercepted the other parties as they retreated, clipping one warrior and then another with his sword, and shouting his defiance.

"He's mad," Petrus exclaimed. "If he doesn't turn back they'll cut him off."

But Constantius, though he could not have failed to see his danger, appeared oblivious. Again and again, he spurred his horse at one group after another, his cloak flying behind him, thrusting at them with his sword before dashing off to the next group, and whipping them into a fury. Those still engaged on the wall turned and saw his act of supreme insolence, bellowed with rage, and began to hurry back. But still he taunted them and Petrus counted that already he had struck seven men down.

Gradually, inexorably, the retreating Saxons began to close in on the solitary rider. And still, instead of making off while he could, Constantius rode at one of them after another. Two more fell. Even from the wall, Petrus could feel their sullen rage. As the sun caught his father's breastplate, that flashed as he wheeled his horse about, he looked a splendid and heroic figure.

By now the attack on the dune was over and all eyes were on the insane, taunting duel that was going on below. Each time Constantius charged, the defenders cheered. Each time he engaged, there was a tense silence; and each time he miraculously managed to pull away, there was another, relieved burst of applause. Petrus did not know exactly when it was that he found Placidia at his side, staring down at the extraordinary scene as well. She, too, must have realised the inevitable outcome; but her face was rigid as stone. Only her eyes moved, from one end of the enclosing line of Saxons to the other. The circle had nearly closed.

Constantius never made any attempt to escape his fate. He seemed to be in a kind of ecstasy as he continued his single-handed battle against the entire remaining Saxon force until at last they closed in on him and dragged him from his horse. Petrus saw a knot of them close, saw their swords rise and fall. Even from there, he and all those on the wall could hear the heavy thud as the swords and axes hacked his father's body into pieces. It went on for some time. The Saxons were avenging their defeat.

"Madness," he muttered aloud. "Why did he do it?"

Placidia was staring past the Saxons, at a point somewhere over the ridges. Her face was still motionless, but there were tears in her eyes. "Poor man," he heard her murmur softly. "There was nothing else for him to do."

The Saxons did not attack again. Slowly they came back in ones and twos to drag their dead away, while the defenders watched from the walls. Petrus did not order an attack: the bowman who had defended the high walls would have been no match for the powerful Saxons on open ground.

Within sight of the wall, the Saxons made a large funeral pyre on which, for several hours, they burned their dead as was their custom. Then, without looking back, they moved away.

They took their vengeance, though. That night, from the empty farms around, the defenders saw the flames flickering in the sky as the Saxons fired them.

Petrus made everyone stay within the dune for a further day, and at night kept the walls well guarded. The next dawn, he sent out scouts who soon reported that the invaders had gone.

The villa had been thoroughly looted. But by good luck, only half of the main house had been burned down. The outhouses and barns, however, had been completely destroyed. As Petrus and his mother surveyed the damage with Numincus, the steward said thoughtfully:

"There will be much work to be done. I will try to have it completed before your return from Ireland."

Petrus paused, and realised that he had not thought of his mission in the last three days. As he stared at the charred ruins, he smiled wryly.

"My journey to Ireland is postponed for the present," he said.

And Placidia, afraid to dwell on the sensitive subject in case he changed his mind again, quickly turned the conversation to other matters.

While Sarum was busily returning to normal, a small but significant event took place. It was two days after the Saxons had left that Petrus, returning from the ridges where he had been inspecting the flocks of sheep, saw Sulicena for the last time.

She was sitting quietly in a cart. Beside her was a large, bearded man whom Petrus recognised as one of his own estate workers. They were obviously setting out on the road that led west, towards the river Severn, and the cart was full of their possessions. Though he was only a few yards away, she did not look at him. A second cart following immediately behind, contained a noisy family of children, their parents and an old woman who was no doubt the grandmother. They were, he thought, relations of Tarquinus.

Not wishing to address Sulicena, he rode over to this second cart.

"Where are you going?"

"West," they told him.

"Why?" he demanded. "Didn't we just beat off the Saxons?"

The man shrugged.

"Until next time. But they burned down our farm."

"Where will you go?"

"To the Severn. Maybe further."

He nodded slowly. He could not blame them, though whether they would be any safer in the west than at Sarum, it was hard to know. He did not try to stop them. It they had decided to go, they would find a way to leave anyway.

"Good luck, then," he said, and rode off.

Yet despite this discouraging sign, as he stood with his mother in front of the villa a few nights later, he felt a new sense of hope.

The Germans had deserted. The promised aid from the eager young men in the west had never come. Many farms had been burned. But they had survived, and he was sure they could do so again.

Opposite, the sun was sinking over the western ridge, but he could still make out, on the river below, the pale forms of the swans as they moved sedately about and on the slopes behind, he could see the tiny white patches of sheep in the dusk. Gently he took his mother's hand.

"I'll stay," he promised her quietly. "And God will give Sarum a new dawn."

Placidia said nothing. An instinct, which she did not share with him, told her that this was not a dawn, but a twilight, and she wondered bleakly what lay in the darkness beyond.

In the terrible times that followed, the young militiamen from the west never came to the aid of Petrus Porteus.

Others, like Sulicena, left him; it was the start of a long process by which, in the coming generations, many families would migrate south-westwards into the peninsula of Britain that would become western Cornwall, or across the Severn river into the hills of Wales – areas which the Saxons were never to penetrate effectively and which contain the ancient Celtic and pre-Celtic stock of Britain to this day.

As the coming of the Saxons and of their neighbour tribes of Angles and Jutes increased until they became a steady migration, the historical record almost ceases.

But the impetus of Romano–British people like Petrus Porteus and the young bloods who tried to start a militia did not die out without leaving an echo – an echo that gave rise to a legend which has grown greater with the passing of centuries.

For it was in the west, probably in the rich, rolling lands that lie between Wessex and the Welsh and Cornish hills, that about two generations after Petrus Porteus, a new and vigorous force arose. They were Romano–Britons and they seem to have been well organised. They were probably Christian; they won a great battle against the Saxons at a place, still not identified, called Mons Badonicus; and it is quite likely that they had a general named Artorius.

From references to these events in historical records, medieval historians and romancers began, some eight hundred years later, to construct a Christian and chivalric order of knights led by a king called Arthur.

Behind the legend of Arthur and the knights of the Round Table lie several elements of historical reality, however. The world of Arthur, though it is chivalric and romanticised in a way that belongs to a later era, is nonetheless a Celtic, Christian world, with ties not only to Wales and the west country but also across the English Channel to Britanny, to which, in the century that followed the end of Roman Britain, a number of British families emigrated.

The history of Sarum, too, enters an era of twilight at this point. It may be called the age of Arthur. It was the twilight, not of the feudal knight, who did not yet exist, but of the Roman world.

The Two Rivers

THE YEAR OF Our Lord 877.

In King Alfred's kingdom of Wessex, it seemed that winter that there would be peace.

The small, half walled town of Wilton, a noted royal centre, lay at the joining of two of the five rivers: the Nadder and the Wylye. To the east, just three miles away, stood the ancient hill fort of Sarum, which acted as a defensive outpost for the town. To the west, the broad valley stretched under the edge of the chalk ridges until both encountered, some fifteen miles away, the great forest of Selwood that blocked, like a wall, the sweeping open lands of central Wessex from the maze of small hills, woods and marshes that were the hinterland of the west country.

And in Wilton, resting between its streams, it seemed that the terrible darkness which had lain over the land had receded, like a threatening bank of clouds and that, this winter at least, there would be a period of sunshine.

Since the Anglo-Saxon settlement of the island some four centuries earlier, there had been many changes and disturbances. One kingdom after another – first Northumbria, then midland Mercia, now southern Wessex had become more powerful than its rivals. Independent tribes in Kent, Sussex and East Anglia had gradually lost their separate status. The Jutes of Kent and the Isle of Wight now acknowledged the west Saxon king; the old British Celtic tribes in Devon to the south west had become part of Wessex too; even distant Cornwall looked up to Wessex as a greater kingdom. Only Wales and northern Scotland had held aloof from Saxon settlement, and they would keep their isolated independence for centuries more.

But despite the rise and fall of these kingdoms, which seldom took place without some bloodshed, the Anglo-Saxon world, now converted to Christianity, had flourished for the most part in peace.

The conversion of the Anglo-Saxons had taken time.

In 597 the monk known as St Augustine, sent by the great Pope Gregory, had landed in Kent, whose pagan king and Christian queen had allowed him to make converts amongst their people. From there, the Roman Church had made steady progress in converting the Saxons, moving up the island and encountering the remains of the older Celtic Christian Church as they did so. And although the Celtic monks of Britain, many of them trained in Ireland, had drawn apart from the Roman Church of Europe, they too were finally brought into a cohesive whole, acknowledging the supremacy of the pope, at the great meeting of churchmen in 664, since called the Synod of Whitby.

Primitive as the island was compared with its Roman past, the centuries when Northumbria and Mercia triumphed were great days. The splendid courts of the kings promoted the still more significant splendour of the great religious houses such as those in Northumbria that in the eighth century produced the great historian of the Anglo-Saxons, the monk Bede. Their arts flourished. The old Latin culture, though seen through the eyes of monks, grew once again. New bishoprics were founded and the archbishop received his *pallium* from Rome. The Anglo-Saxon island seemed blessed indeed.

Until the coming of the Norsemen.

They came from the great peninsula of Jutland, at the foot of the Baltic Sea. For some time, their raids had been held in check by the powerful and holy empire of the mighty Charlemagne, king of the Franks; but after his death early in the century, their activities had increased; and when a dynastic dispute in the Danish kingdom broke it up, a new and terrible age for Europe began: the age of the Vikings.

The term meant pirate – and despite the attempts of some modern historians to rehabilitate their reputation, the facts are still beyond dispute. The heathen Vikings were cruel, destructive raiders, whose main object was plunder. In a series of raids, stretching over two generations, they descended on the island like a plague. By the time that Alfred came to the throne of Wessex, England was in effect divided into two parts. Over the so-called Danelaw in the north – most of the land above the river Thames – the Vikings had supremacy, moving freely about and levying huge tributes from the native farmers and merchants to save themselves from destruction. When they had taken all they could get, they moved camp. But Wessex had held out. Though the Vikings had made several huge raids into the southern territory, they never mastered it. And in recent years this had been thanks to Alfred.

During the last three years, the growing Viking forces, having taken all they could from the unlucky people of Northumbria and Mercia, had split into several sections. One party took over the territory in the north that came to be called Yorkshire; another annexed East Anglia. A third party, following their natural impulse, set off to raid Ireland, and a fourth, but still powerful force, moved once again upon Wessex. They swept down almost to the southern sea, but here at last they were hemmed in by the Saxon forces and a peace was arranged. In return for a payment, the Vikings swore their most solemn oath – on their holy armlet – that they would leave Wessex and trouble her no more.

They broke their solemn oath at once, and slipped west to the settlement of Exeter, where they waited for reinforcements.

But now it seemed that God had come to the aid of the people of Wessex. In sight of the shore, the Viking fleet of reinforcements was destroyed by a great storm and soon afterwards in the autumn of 877 the invaders moved back to the borders of Mercia to set up their camp for the winter.

Wessex had triumphed, and for the winter at least, it seemed there would be peace.

The eyes of the crowd turned upon the thin, grey-haired man who was standing, rather self-consciously but erect in the centre of the circle.

For a moment, however, he seemed to have forgotten them. Although everything depended on the outcome of the trial, Port could not believe that he would not win; and once it was over, he would have to make a decision about a matter that had been troubling him for the last two weeks. He shook his head in perplexity. Which course of action would bring most honour to his family? Should he please himself or his sister? Would either course bring him to the notice of the king? No decision in his life had caused him so much trouble and he knew that he must decide today.

A cough from somewhere in the crowd recalled him to the proceedings.

"Let Port make his charge," the reeve's gruff voice rang out.

Slowly and methodically he now unwrapped the bandage that bound his right arm, then held it up.

"Sigewulf smote me," he accused.

The crowd stared critically: for where Port's right hand should have been, there was only a jagged stump.

It was a frosty morning at the start of the two month midwinter period known as Yule; but despite the cold, the hundred court, faithful to its particular custom, was meeting in the open air of Wilton's market place.

The crowd of about sixty were mostly freemen farmers and their families – the men dressed in bright woollen tunics that stretched to the knee and were belted at the waist, and thick woollen leggings, the women wearing longer, but similar clothing. Opposite Port stood three older men, who would officially witness the judgement. Presiding over the conduct of the proceedings was Earldorman Wulfhere: a large, grey bearded man whose deeply pitted face had long been flushed with too much good living and whose broad, bulbous nose gave him a look of brutality. His small, restless eyes flitted continuously from face to face, as though conscious of the fact that he was one of the least liked of the powerful nobles at King Alfred's court. Since the business of the day might involve fines due to the king's reeve, his presence in that capacity was important.

Now that Port had made his accusation, the court could move on to the trial.

In doing so, it would follow the traditional Anglo-Saxon procedure, hallowed by the centuries: there would be no advocates, no jury, and no examination of any evidence. Despite these apparent drawbacks, the system worked.

For the time being, all that mattered was that the extent of the injury should be known – a hand had been lost, but not a whole forearm; and this was important.

At a nod from the earldorman, Port lowered his arm and began to bind it up again.

"Have you any other injury?"

Port shook his head.

"But he struck me four times," he added.

"The number of blows makes no difference," Wulfhere reminded him.

"Four times," Port repeated obstinately, and many in the crowd smiled; for his meticulous precision was so well known that there was a local saying: when grain is ground, Port counts each grain.

The injury had taken place two weeks before, in that very market place. Sigewulf, a local farmer, had left his horse straying in the street while he was drinking in one of the booths by the market. When he had reeled out in the dusk, he had seen Port, who was leading his horse to a post to tether it, and in his befuddled state he had decided that the fellow was trying to steal the animal. Furious, he had lurched towards him; there had been a scuffle; he had drawn his sword, waved it wildly, and as Port had raised his arm, the accident had occurred. He did not remember striking four times; but Port was adamant that he had.

Now it was Sigewulf's turn to tell his story. He was a short, thickset man whose sullen manner, even when he was sober, did not inspire confidence.

"Port attacked me," he said. "I struck him once, not four times; it was self-defence. He tried to steal my horse."

He finished. He knew the crowd was against him, but it did not matter; nor did it matter that his version of the events was improbable. For the Anglo-Saxon court took no account of evidence.

The trial had now reached its crucial stage. It was time to hear the oath helpers. At a sign from Port, three men stepped forward into the circle and announced their names and ranks. All were churls: small, free farmers.

"Upon the blood of Christ," each repeated, "I swear that Port's accusation is true."

Immediately, three churls stepped forward and swore similarly on behalf of Sigewulf.

This was the ancient oath swearing upon which Saxon justice turned. No evidence was examined, no jury asked to decide on the merits of the case: but the number of oath swearers each side could produce, together with the rank of the swearer, decided the outcome. The oath of a slave counted for nothing; the word of a churl, as a free peasant, had weight. The word of a thane, a noble, outweighed that of any number of churls; an earldorman outweighed a thane; the word of the king, of course, could not be questioned.

The apparent stalemate between the parties was broken however, as a splendid figure now stepped into the circle.

He was a tall, well-built man in his forties. He had been standing quietly at one side of the circle with a group of young men and a girl whose strikingly blond good looks marked them out as his children. He carried himself with an air of easy authority; his blue eyes seemed amused, and as he came forward, Sigewulf's face looked more depressed than ever.

"Aelfwald the thane," he announced calmly. "I swear that Port's words are true."

There was a murmur from the crowd, followed by silence. No thane stepped forward for Sigewulf. The case was over.

Wulfhere looked at the three elderly men before announcing the verdict.

"The decision is for Port," the three men agreed, without hesitation.

"So be it," Wulfhere announced. "The wergild will be paid for his hand. His lord will be compensated accordingly."

No system of law was more important than the ancient code of the wergild. Under the wergild system, every Anglo-Saxon, in common with other Germanic and Scandinavian peoples, knew the exact value of his life, and that depended on his rank. The life of a churl was worth two hundred shillings; that of a thane, like Aelfwald, six times as much, and the price to be paid for an injury, like the loss of a hand or a leg, was calculated in proportion. It was for this reason that it had been necessary for Port to show his injury to the court: the loss of a hand was one thing; but if he had lost his whole forearm, Sigewulf would have had to pay more. The wergild payments, codified in writing the century before by the great King Ine of Wessex, were essential to the ordering of society. Without them, any injury done to an individual would, under the strict code of honour of all the Germanic tribes, have meant that his family must begin a blood feud. But by paying a fixed compensation instead, most of these costly feuds could be avoided. It was a sensible system for settling disputes, which King Alfred encouraged.

The trial by open court was a primitive affair, but it had its benefits too. Since every man above the rank of slave had his individual wergild, no one, not even an earldorman, could attack him with impunity. The trial moreover, was a communal business, conducted by free men. The judgement was not simply handed down by Earldorman Wulfhere, but agreed and witnessed for the community by the three old farmers, learned in the law. It was in these quaint courts, deriving from ancient Germanic folk practice, that the common law of the English speaking people had its roots.

Under the judgement just given, Port and his family would be compensated by the family of Sigewulf, and since he was Port's lord, Aelfwald would also receive a payment because his man had been harmed.

Sigewulf could only count himself lucky that the king had been absent from Wilton on the day of the incident, as otherwise he might have been judged to have broken the king's peace and have had to pay a fine to the reeve as well.

Sigewulf shook his head sadly nonetheless. He had known the case would probably go against him, but the price he would have to pay was considerable. This was for two reasons: firstly because wergild payments were deliberately set high to encourage peaceful behaviour; and secondly, because Port belonged to a rare class in Anglo-Saxon society. He was what some folk called half a thane, and his wergild, though only half that of Aelfwald, was therefore three times that of an ordinary churl. For Port's ancestors had been noble Britons.

The ancient Roman name of Porteus had been long forgotten at Sarum, and so had most of the remains of the Roman world. Many of the metalled roads were overgrown, and some had disappeared entirely; there were new pathways in the valleys and on long journeys, travellers might easily take the old, prehistoric tracks up on the high ridges. The towns, the temples and baths built of stone, had nearly all gone, except in the great port of London where the shells of some of the old buildings lingered on. In King Alfred's new capital of Winchester, the old Venta, parts of the stout Roman wall remained; but the settlement of Sorviodunum was marshy grazing land and where the old Porteus villa had been, with its mosaics and its hypocaust, there now stood a fine timber barn with a steep gabled roof, and just below it, the sprawling farmstead and splendid oak-beamed hall of the family of Thane Aelfwald.

Not that the memory of Roman and Celtic times had died. The river Avon had kept its Celtic name; so had the river Wylye to the west. The memory of a Roman spring – fontana – was alive a few miles up the Wylye at the estate of Fonthill. And besides, though the old Roman Empire had departed from the west of Europe, everyone in its many kingdoms knew that Rome was civilisation. Was not the Bible, were not all the works of philosophy, literature and learning to be found in the churches and monasteries of Europe, written in Latin? Had not Charlemagne, the greatest emperor Europe had seen in centuries, taken care to be crowned in Rome? Had not King Alfred himself made three journeys there when still a boy? The imperial troops had long gone, but their legacy would never die.

If the Porteus family name had become obscure, this was only a matter of convention: the Saxons rarely used surnames in the Roman or the modern manner: neither Earldorman Wulfhere nor thane Aelfwald had more than a single personal name. And the stubborn Porteus family, who reminded each new generation that they had been famous Romans once, had themselves forgotten how to pronounce their own name. Over the centuries they had called themselves by names such as Port, Porta or Porter, which were recognisable to Saxon ears as terms meaning doorman or gatekeeper.

"Never forget," Port told his two young sons, as he pointed to the dune at Sarum, "when this place was taken, we were the lords of it and we fought bravely."

This was true. The Anglo-Saxon Chronicle recorded for the year 552: "Cynric fought the Britons at a place called Searobyrg and put them to flight." This was the dune, whose new Saxon name meant the place of battle. There the descendants of Petrus Porteus had fought bravely and lost; and the only survivor of the family, whose valour the Saxons admired, was honoured by them after the final surrender. It was because of this incident three centuries before that Port kept the last remnants of his nobility in the wergild which marked him out as, if not a thane, at least something more than an ordinary churl.

The old Porteus wealth was gone. The villa and most of its lands, were taken from them and given to the family of Aelfwald the thane. But not all. While the Saxons took the rich land on the lower slopes, the Porteus family was allowed to keep the bare land on the high ground; and here, in a small farmstead, sowing a little corn and pasturing the white sheep their ancestor had brought to the place, the descendants of Sarum's ancient lords had lived for three hundred years.

But today, all this could change; and this was Port's terrible dilemma. For today's events had given him a chance to raise his family to a position it had not known in centuries.

"With the money from the wergild added to what I am holding," he thought, "by sunset tomorrow I can be a thane." And not for the first time that morning he shook his head in discouragement. Yes, it could certainly be done, but to do it, he must break his word: and the promise he had made to his sister Edith was a solemn one. Worse, now that the trial was over, he was about to have to confront her. If only there were some way out.

"Well, are you coming?"

The tall figure of Aelfwald was beside him. He was smiling broadly. The two men, so strangely contrasted, liked each other, and though Port's secret ambition was to become a thane himself, he had no complaint to make about his lord.

Accompanying Aelfwald was a small retinue consisting of two of his sons, his daughter, a boy dressed in the habit of a novice monk, and a young man with a pinched, ageless face, whom Port recognised as the slave called Tostig.

Port nodded to them. It was clear from the grins on the faces of Aelfwald's children that they regarded him as something of a joke, but he did not mind. The sons: Aelfric and Aelfstan – the repetition of the first syllable in a family's name was a typically Saxon custom – were close in age. Aelfric, the eldest, was twenty-six; and the girl, Aelfgifu, was only eighteen. He bowed to her gravely. He did not dislike the cheerful, rather childish high spirits of the young men, but Aelfgifu's wild, tomboy antics shocked his sense of propriety. It was of course this which gave the thane's children such delight in teasing him.

Aelfwald looked at this little retinue contentedly. He was typical of the Saxon folk who had made the island their own: an easy-going, even-tempered man, with a mind that moved slowly, but steadily. He was not much given to argument or speculation, but once he had seized an idea that he believed in, he could be massively obstinate in defending it. The fiery Celtic peoples who had held out in Wales, despised what they saw as the slow-witted Saxon settlers who had taken their lands; but their contempt was not necessarily returned, and the two communities had long since lived on the island with only sporadic outbreaks of violence over the border.

Aelfwald had good reason to take a comfortable view of life. The thane possessed estates in several parts of Wessex, including a fine area of woodland down at the coast. His eldest son was married and he had already been able to give him handsome farms. He hoped soon to find a husband for Aelfgifu.

"Though who'll want to marry such a tomboy, the Lord knows," he complained laughingly to his wife.

Now the trial was over, he was going personally to conduct his man back to his farm where Port's wife and two sons were waiting; and that night he had invited Port and all his other dependants to a feast in his spacious hall in the valley.

But first they must pay the visit that was causing Port so much secret anguish.

Together the party moved along the mainstreet of Wilton.

It was a small, sheltered town, pleasantly situated in the angle where the rivers Wylye and Nadder ran together. The stout wooden wall around its west side, despite the fact that a Danish force had briefly overrun the place seven years before, was still only half finished, and the palisades and banks that completed the circuit had been left in some disrepair for the winter. The little river Nadder wandered along the southern edge of the town; trees flanked the river, and magnificent oaks and beeches stood on the slopes that led quietly up towards the great chalk plateau on the northern side. The two central features of the place were the small market square, surrounded by modest wooden buildings, and a large building in stone that lay just east of it. This was the Kingsbury, the royal palace; for although King Alfred was now lavishing more attention on the larger town of Winchester, Wilton was still the second most important royal town in his kingdom.

Today the palace was empty: the king was hunting in the west; but the party's destination was a third entity, that lay just beside it: a small group of buildings within their own walled enclosure, through the gate of which they now entered quietly. For this was the abbey: and it was here, in the small but distinguished group of twelve nuns, that Port's sister led her life.

There were several buildings – the nun's house, a wooden church, a refectory; but it was to a small, stone chapel with two side aisles and a steep wooden roof that they were now led by one of the nuns. It was a single structure with small windows and triangular pointed arches, but it was not without a certain quiet elegance. The nuns' greatest pride were the beautifully carved pillars on each side of the west door, whose sides were covered with a wonderful pattern of interlocking knots and whose square capitals depicted a similarly intricate design of interwoven dragons – Saxon workmanship at its best. There was a delicate smell of incense in the church, and everywhere there was evidence of its rich endowments in the gold and silver ornaments, the splendid hangings, and the finely woven altar cloth.

Aelfwald the thane often visited the abbey; he liked to pay his respects to the abbess, who was a distant kinswoman of the king himself, and to admire the stone church, which was by far the finest building in the area. And Port had come to see his sister. The abbess entered almost immediately, accompanied by Edith. The two nuns exchanged polite greetings with their guests; then Port and Edith drew to one side.

She was not an attractive woman. Thin like her brother, though ten years younger, she had a face over which the pale skin was drawn tightly, so that her appearance was skeletal, an impression made worse by yellowish eyes and pale lips which often turned blue in the winter months. She was lucky to have been accepted in the abbey, for most of the nuns were high born, and their families had given endowments far beyond the means of Port. Indeed, it was only thanks to the support of Aelfwald that she had been accepted. But she had come to the abbey with high ambitions. Several of the nuns there, including the abbess, had been trained in the great double minster of Wimborne, twenty miles to the south west, where two large, though carefully segregated communities, one of monks, the other of nuns, were ruled over by a single abbess. In previous centuries, great missionaries like Boniface, who had set out from the newly converted Anglo-Saxon island to convert the heathen tribes of north east Europe, had drawn many of their best assistants from the great Wimborne community, and Edith had hoped that from Wilton, she too might be selected for such work. But the wise abbess had soon seen that Edith was not the stuff that missionaries were made of; no invitation to go to Wimborne had come; and it was clear that she would live out the rest of her life in the little community with the other nuns.

Now she had only one ambition – and since she had time to brood, it was never out of her mind. For she alone of all the nuns had made no contribution to the abbey, and though she was never reminded of it, she felt the disgrace keenly. It was because of this, three years before, that she had given her small inheritance to her brother to keep for her, and won from him, in a weak moment, a promise that he would add to it when he could, so that the family could buy a fine gold cross to be given to the abbey. Night and day she dreamed of it: to be sure, it would not rival some of the fine jewelled ornaments given by the king; but it would stand there, simple but dignified on the altar in the abbey church, and the nuns would know that the family of Edith had given it.

Then had come the news of Port's accident and the trial that must follow. She had said nothing to anyone, but alone in her room, she had calculated, with rising excitement, the sum that she knew he must receive in wergild; and added to what she had given him, she knew that it would be enough. As the days passed, she had gone about her duties in a state of suppressed excitement; there was a new fervour in her prayers; her singing of the psalms was almost tuneful. For no reason that any of the other nuns knew, it was clear that she had some new and secret joy.

This was Port's dilemma.

It was a clearly understood rule, under the Anglo-Saxon legal system, that when a churl possessed five hides of land – a hide, depending on the quality of the land being usually between forty and over a hundred and twenty acres – he automatically had the right to the status of thane. A man like Aelfwald had many scores of hides; Port had four.

The money from the wergild, added to what he had saved, together with some of the money that his sister had entrusted to him, would be enough to buy the last hide.

For two weeks, he too had been making secret calculations; and he too had been living in a state of suppressed excitement: for there was nothing in the world that he wanted more passionately than this all-important status for himself and his family.

But he had given Edith his word: the money ought to go to her golden cross. Surely, he told himself, the money for the cross could be found later; but if that were true, then so could the money for the land – and in his heart of hearts, he did not believe that it ever would be. If he broke his promise to Edith, would anyone ever know? No. It was, and would certainly remain, their secret. Would she not rather he became a thane? He shook his head despondently. He knew what she wanted. And as he entered the abbey, thought of her pale, expectant face and of his hide of land, he did not know what to do.

Now Edith was beside him.

She took his bandaged arm in her thin hands and looked up at him tenderly.

"I am sorry you were injured," she said gently.

"It was nothing." His voice was cold. He had not meant it to be.

For a moment neither spoke. Then, like a drop of water that one has been watching form, the inevitable question softly fell.

"Did you win your case?"

He nodded miserably.

"Sigewulf paid the wegild?"

Again he nodded. She gazed up at him; then, unable to contain herself, she broke into a smile. Her smile disclosed a row of surprisingly good teeth and, for a moment, she almost looked beautiful.

"You have the wergild?" He nodded once more. "Have we enough?" she asked eagerly.

Still he could not bring himself to admit it.

"Perhaps. I do not know," he lied.

Her face fell. "Surely . . ." she checked herself. She knew she must not question her brother. "I had hoped . . ." she began. He could see the happy excitement draining out of her.

"There may be. I will see," he said quickly, unable to bear the spectacle any longer. He could not look into her eyes.

She nodded slowly. He felt wretched, almost as though he had committed violence against her frail body.

"You will tell me when it is possible," she murmured sadly. Her submissiveness gently quenched the little flame of hope she had allowed to exalt her.

He nodded. "Of course."

A few moments later, they rejoined the others.

The abbess was showing Aelfwald the latest treasure that had come to the abbey. It was a book of the Gospels – a huge, leather-bound volume, its cover studded with magnificent jewels in the shape of a cross and its pages splendidly illuminated.

Over the centuries, the art of book illumination had been brought to its wonderful flowering in the Saxon north of England and the monasteries of Celtic Ireland, culminating in such masterpieces as the great Book of Kells, completely only a few generations before, and the Gospels from Lindisfarne, the holy monastic island off the coast of Northumbria; the brilliant scholarship and craftsmanship of Mercia was well known; and in southern Britain, too, there was a fine school of illumination at Canterbury, now being emulated at Alfred's Winchester. But the invasions of the heathen Danes had destroyed most of the schools in the northern half of the country, and this magnificent volume had only recently been rescued from a monastery in Mercia: it made a splendid addition to the treasures of Wilton.

The abbess was pointing to the finely written text. Most of the uncial scripts used in England derived either from the Celtic Irish or the continental Frankish school known as Carolingian.

"See," she remarked, "the Mercian monk has adapted the Carolingian script – good, square lettering."

Aelfwald said nothing. All scripts were as one to him, for like most Saxon nobles, he could neither read nor write – a shortcoming for which King Alfred, who was painfully learning these arts himself, had several times taken him to task.

But Aelfwald's eye had been caught by something else. And it was causing him to smile.

Osric was twelve years old. A short, serious little boy, his two most noticeable features were his large grey eyes and his small hands with stubby thumbs, both of which he had inherited from his father, who was a carpenter working on Aelfwald's estate. Some years previously when, rather to Aelfwald's surprise, his second son Aelfwine had decided that he wished to become a monk, the thane had set up a small monastic cell for six monks on his estate near Twyneham, down on the coast, and installed Aelfwine there, hoping that in time he would change his mind. So far, the young man had not. And when the carpenter confided to his lord that his young son Osric had a similar ambition, the thane in his cheerful way had sent the boy down there too. "At least Aelfwine can keep an eye on him and let us know as soon as he's had enough," he remarked to the carpenter. That had been almost a year ago.

But when, three days ago, Osric had come to visit his parents, the thane had noticed that the boy did not seem to be happy. The reports of him from Aelfwine had been good, and neither the carpenter nor the thane had been able to discover what was the matter. Perhaps, Aelfwald guessed, the boy regretted his decision, but was too proud, or too frightened to say so.

He had kept young Osric with him for several days, and though he had repeatedly asked him: "Are you certain you wish to be a monk?" the boy had always assured him that he did. It still seemed to Aelfwald that the boy was unhappy, but whatever his secret, it was obvious that no one was going to find out.

But now, suddenly, Osric's face was shining. As he studied the illuminated book, followed the careful penwork, the exquisite choice of reds and blues, the gold leaf applied around the elaborate capitals, it was clear that the boy was lost to the world. It was not surprising that Osric, descendant of countless generations of craftsmen, should have been moved by such workmanship; but as soon as he saw it, Aelfwald smiled. The boy's obvious fascination had given the thane a new idea – a solution that might make young Osric happy, add lustre to his own reputation, and even please the king as well.

Resting his hand on Osric's shoulder he asked:

"Do you think you could do that?"

The boy considered slowly.

"I think so, my lord."

"And would you like to?" Aelfwald went on.

The boy's eyes sparkled. "Oh yes."

"Good. Then that's what you will do. I will speak with the king. This summer you'll be sent either to Winchester or Canterbury to learn your craft. You'd like that?"

Osric's face gave him all the answer he needed.

"Splendid. We have a new craftsman," he announced to the abbess. He smiled. Whatever was wrong with the boy, this seemed to have settled it; and Aelfwald liked to settle things.

While this conversation was taking place, a very different one was going on between the thane's youngest son Aelfstan, his daughter Aelfgifu, and poor Edith. Aelfstan was indulging in his favourite occupation of teasing.

"Yes," Aelfstan assured the nun, with a sad shake of his head, "my father says that if Aelfgifu cannot find a husband in the next two months, she's to come here as a nun." He sighed. "So far, Edith, no bridegroom has appeared."

The effect of this invented news exceeded his greatest hopes.

As she gazed up at the handsome, strapping and obviously disruptive eighteen-year-old girl, who was known throughout the area to be wilder than any young man, the nun's face registered horror. She looked from one to the other. Both brother and sister were shaking their heads despondently.

"A nun?" The idea was too awful to contemplate. "But surely . . ." she began. "Such haste . . . A year or two at least?"

"No." Aelfstan was adamant. "My father never changes his mind."

Edith's jaw had now dropped open; she tried to swallow.

"Well," Aelfstan continued briskly. "I'm sure she'll be happy here, won't you, Aelfgifu?"

"Oh yes," the girl replied gaily. And then as an afterthought: "Will I still be allowed to ride and hunt?"

"Hunt?" Edith's eyes opened wide as she tried to take in this idea.

"Occasionally?" Aelfgifu suggested. She was a fine horsewoman, and had gone out hawking with the king himself.

"No, no," the nun murmured. This terrible news had, for a moment, driven even the thought of the golden cross from her mind. "Our chief occupation is our needlework," she added seriously. For the nuns were rightly proud of the magnificent embroidery they produced, working together, silently, patiently, hour after hour.

Aelfgifu let out a guffaw of laughter that rang round the chapel, and held up her large strong hands. "I can hardly hold a needle," she cried.

"Life is very different here," Edith said anxiously, wondering what she could possibly do to avert this disaster.

"I should miss not being able to wrestle with my brothers," the girl remarked in her open, easy way. But Edith was now past speech. Her face had lost even the little colour it had.

Aelfstan now brought the teasing to an end with a warning cough. The rest of the group was beginning to stare at them curiously, and he had no wish to explain the conversation to his father. Hurriedly, and a little guiltily, brother and sister excused themselves politely and moved away, leaving Edith with her anxious thoughts. It was not until that evening that the abbess was able to explain to the by-now-distracted nun that the young people had been mistaken about the thane's intentions for his daughter; and it was only after poor Edith had left that the abbess allowed herself to lean back in her seat and shake with laughter.

As the sun sank over the valley that evening, the feast began.

The great hall of Aelfwald the thane stood at the centre of a busy community. Around the hall itself, with its massive oak beams and its raised floor were grouped the stout timber and thatched buildings of the farm. Fifty yards away, straddling the lane that wound along the valley floor, was the small village of Avonsford, consisting of a dozen cottages; and around the village lay the most striking feature of the Saxon countryside: the open fields.

This was the great change that the Saxons had wrought. Whereas before, the higher slopes had been laid bare, and the farmsteads and villas had nestled in modest clearings on the valley slopes, gradually, century after century, the Saxons had carved great swathes out of the lowland forests, smashing down woods, and scrub, as they made the rich land submit to their will. At Avonsford there were now two huge open fields, extending for hundreds of yards over the sweep of the low ground, divided by ridges into long strips, so that it looked as if some huge comb had been passed over the bare landscape. The villagers had given the two fields names – the eastern field was called Paradise, the western, Purgatory. Heavy ploughs pulled by teams of six or eight oxen had clawed up the heavy soil, just as Caius Porteus had dreamed of doing eight hundred years before. The long ridges were carefully divided – some belonging to the lord, some to the individual churls or their own lesser tenants, the freedmen or former slaves. The village worked the fields; and the lord took his share. The land on each side of the river, which Aelfwald's grandfather had drained with modest success, was now a huge meadow, where livestock was pastured.

This was the community, the basic village of England, which had now formed on the remains of the estate that had been the Porteus villa. Half a mile away, the woods began again; and these were used for pasturing swine. On the chalk slopes above, the ancient farmlands of earlier times were still used by Port and others like him to drive their flocks of sheep.

There was one other notable feature of the place: in a small field, reserved for pasture, that lay between Aelfwald's hall and the village, stood a single wooden cross. This served as the open air church for the people, winter and summer. Here the elders of the village met when there were matters of importance in the village to discuss; and here the priest from Wilton would hold a service on Sundays and on the great feast days of the church.

As the setting sun caught the edge of the furrows in the open fields, creating a striking pattern of red and black, light and shadow across the land, the entire community was making their way towards Thane Aelfwald's hall.

For tonight there was to be a great feast; and tonight, it was rumoured, the thane was to make an important announcement.

The hall accommodated a hundred people with ease. Trestle tables were arranged in two lines down the sides of the hall with a single table across the head, where the thane sat with his wife Hild, a tall, handsome woman in her fifties whose only sign of age seemed to be a light streaking of grey in her long, fair hair and a few lines in her forehead. The thane's sons and Aelfgifu were dispersed around the tables amongst his retainers.

The feast was splendid. Beef and venison were complemented by huge plates of fish that Tostig the slave had provided from the river. A few of the men drank wine, but most drank the thickly scented ale of the region, and beside each man and woman was a cup into which the servants poured the most important drink of all, the sweet and heady mead that still, as in the most ancient times, was made from honey gathered in the woods.

At the head table, the splendid enamel dishes gleamed in the light from the tapers and from the roaring fire at the end of the hall.

"The hall of Aelfwald could be that of a king," it was often said, and the thane lived up to his reputation.

In the place of honour, directly in front of him, rested the magnificent drinking horn that was one of his proudest possessions. It was the horn of that rarest and most stupendous of all beasts, the almost forgotten auroch, and it had been given by King Egbert of Wessex himself to the thane's grandfather – a long, curving and fearsome object, polished so that its whiteness gleamed, bound with six bands of gold, and so big that hollowed out it could hold eight quarts of ale.

To his great pleasure, Port found that he had been placed in an honoured position at the corner of the high table, and there with his wife – a small, mousy woman who gave him her unquestioning devotion – he sat contentedly.

The whole company seemed to be in high good humour, and if some of the hoots of laughter from the far table came from the fact that Aelfstan was giving a perfect imitation of Edith the nun's consternation that morning, both the thane and Port were fortunately unaware of it.

More than once at that gathering however, the eyes of the men had turned away from the high table where the thane sat, towards his daughter, as she and her mother, performing their proper duties as the wife and daughter of a hospitable lord, moved about the hall, offering delicacies and mead to their guests and speaking a few kind words to each. For the tomboy Aelfgifu this evening had been transformed. She was dressed in a long, red, embroidered gown with billowing cuffs of silk. On her feet were slim, elegant shoes of soft red leather. Around her neck on a golden chain hung a pendant of gold and garnets, and from her girdle hung the long silver hooks in the shape of keys that were the Saxon symbols of womanhood. Her magnificent golden hair was worn loose and spread in waves down her back, and her athletic figure stood out proudly. Suddenly the flashing eyes and laughing good humour that had made her a tomboy companion for her brothers now made her seem an even more splendid young woman.

"She's worth a thane's *morgengifu*," the men murmured. This was the gift the bridegroom had to pay his new bride on the morning after the marriage was consummated.

"For a night with her," one churl replied, "I'd pay any price."

"If you weren't already dead with exhaustion," his companions told him laughingly.

When the company had eaten, it was time for the entertainments, and for these, a stout young man with a clean shaven face stepped into the space between the tables, accompanied by a youth who carried a small harp.

For a few minutes, they sang some bawdy songs that set the listeners laughing; and these were quickly followed by riddles, most of which were familiar to the guests, but to which the stout young man had added two or three of his own. He sang them tunefully but slowly, with a formal measure, enticing the audience's concentration.

Silent my dress   when I step on the shore
Stay in my lodge,   or stir the stream.
Or my trailing gown   and the wild wind
Lift me high,   over the living:
There with the clouds,   I can sweep and soar
Over the land-bound.   Then my white wings
Echo so loudly,   ring and moan,
Sing to your ear;   when I'm not sleeping
On the soil,   or sailing on the still water:
Like a ship,   like a wandering spirit.
I am.   What am I?

"A swan," the audience cried, and the young man bowed. For all were familiar with the stately swans that moved above on the five rivers of Sarum.

The riddles were followed by songs about the old Germanic gods: Thunor the thunderer, Tiw, the god of death, great Woden, the battle god, and the mythical ancestor of the royal house of Wessex. At the end of each song, the men hammered on the table with their goblets and applauded.

Although for many generations the Anglo-Saxons of England had been Christian, the memory of the pagan past was alive, an accepted part of everyday life which no church could attempt to stifle. Were not the gods still celebrated in the days of the week, like Wodensday? Did not the code of honour that made a man loyal to his lord, the law of blood feud and wergild, and the songs and poetry they loved all come from pagan times? Aelfwald the thane did not try to cudgel his brains over the fact that the Saxon culture he loved and the Christian religion he believed in were logically incompatible. He was an Anglo-Saxon Christian: and he was content.

Now, at a nod from his companion, the youth strummed three times on the harp and the reciter announced:

"Beorwulf."

And now the hall became silent. For no poem was better known or more highly prized than *Beorwulf*; and though it had been written down, the reciter still carried it all in his head. He would not sing it, but declaim it in a slow, stately chant, letting the words, with their heavy, stressed alliteration weave their own spell round the hall. Nor would he recite it all that night, for *Beorwulf* was very long; but he would give his eager audience the parts they knew and loved best. He would tell them how the hero journeyed across the sea to help the Danish King Hrothgar; how at night Beorwulf with his bare hands, in just such a hall as this one, fought the gruesome monster Grendel and tore his whole arm from its socket; how he slew the monster's mother at the bottom of the lake; and how in his last fight, Beorwulf died slaying a dragon that lived in an ancient barrow tomb.

He began slowly, describing Beorwulf's voyage: his slow, rhythmic chant fell on the audience like waves on the sea; and around the hall, unconscious of what they were doing, men and women alike rocked to and fro on the benches, strangely moved. Port, too, was enthralled. It seemed to him that he could see the ship, sense the motion on the waters under the empty sky, feel its keel scrape when it finally beached upon the Danish sands. Like the rest of the audience, his eyes grew misty. He, with them, was transported to the echoing, half mournful, half heroic, timeless world that is the world of the sagas of all the northern peoples.

Then came Beorwulf's great oaths of loyalty to King Hrothgar, and the fights in which he redeemed them. This was the Anglo-Saxon warrior as he ought to be – loyal to his chosen lord, trusting in fate, believing in the Christian God to aid him, but pagan in every other respect.

As the reciter came to the battle scenes, his pace quickened. The words poured out, thick, gutteral, hissing, making a sound like that of the fight itself.

From Grendel's shoulder,   the gash ripped wide open,
Out sprang the sinews,   the bone-casings burst;

[296]

Beorwulf was given   glory in battle:
Broken and bleeding   Grendel was beaten:
Fled to the fens,   to his dark lair.

Like the Saxons, Port's eyes were shining; his fists were clenched and he
felt the pumping of the blood. How the hero fought!

But at last, Beorwulf fought his last battle; and after he was burned on
his funeral pyre, he was buried in a barrow, in sight of the sea; with his
brooches and his golden rings, as every warrior should be:

Kindest of Kings,   of men the mildest
Just to his people,   thirsty for fame."

The voice of the reciter died to a murmur. It was over; and for a long,
richly savoured moment all those in the hall were silent.

Then the reciter bowed and the audience, after thunderous applause,
toasted him for his excellent performance.

It was after this, when all the thanks were done, that Aelfwald the
thane rose ceremoniously from his chair and called for silence.

"It is time for a ring-giving," he announced.

No ceremony was more important than the ancient custom of ring-
giving. When the king gave his earldorman or his loyal thane a ring, it was
a symbolic bond between them which could never, with honour, be
broken. Often such rings would be engraved with a message or charm in
the ancient runic script which the northern peoples still preserved from
the pagan past and which gave the ring its particular magic value.

Aelfwald the thane, rich with many lands, liked to give rings to his
men, for it enhanced his own dignity.

Now, as the voices in the hall died away to a murmur, he pointed to
Port.

"Today," he announced, "Port received the wergild for the loss of his
right hand." There was a friendly banging on the tables and some
laughter. "And so today, my loyal friends, I give him a ring to wear on the
hand he still has." There was a roar of cheerful approval. Port inclined
his head gravely. "Keep this ring for me, Port," the thane cried, "and," he
winked at the audience, "try not to lose it!"

The hall rocked with applause and laughter. Port's face went crimson
with pleasure.

While Aelfwald held the ring high for all to see, his wife moved along
the table and ceremoniously offered Port the drinking cup. As soon as he
had drunk, Aelfwald himself followed his wife and handed Port the ring.
It was a thick band of gold with a runic inscription.

Port fitted the ring on the little finger of his left hand. Then he, too,
rapped on the table for silence. As he did so, the merriment ceased; for
although the stiff and solemn sheep farmer was regarded as something of
a joke, the pledge he must now make in reply to the ring-gift was a serious
matter which must be heard with respect.

"Thane Aelfwald is my lord," he replied solemnly. "I have drunk his mead; I have received his ring. If any man attacks him, I will defend him with my life."

There were nods of approval. The Saxon code of honour demanded that such oaths should be sworn, and Port, Celtic though his ancestors were, would be as good as his word.

Then Aelfwald raised the huge auroch's horn to his lips and cried: "Port, we drink to you." And the company drank the toast.

Several toasts followed. More rings were given and elaborate oaths sworn. Port sat flushed and happy, his wife smiling proudly beside him.

But as he looked around the great hall, the disquieting thought of that morning returned more strongly than ever.

Truly, he thought, it is a fine thing to be called a thane. And he remembered his four hides of land. For the hundredth time he made his calculations. Perhaps I could buy the hide and give Edith a silver cross, he reckoned. That would do. But he knew it would not. The image of his sister rose before his eyes, first angrily, then piteously. He tried to put her out of his mind, but without success, and he frowned with vexation.

His thoughts were interrupted by Aelfwald, who had risen once more to his feet. This time he gave the table three loud bangs, to signal absolute silence, and the hall waited expectantly. This must be the expected announcement and they wondered what it would be.

The thane's face was now serious, and he looked slowly about him to convey this change of mood to his people. Even young Aelfstan managed to look grave for once. When he judged that the company was ready, he spoke.

"Friends," he began, "we have eaten and we have drunk mead together. We have taken rings and given oaths. But there is something more important that we have not done yet." He paused. "I am speaking of our duty to God."

There was a respectful silence. It was right that a great thane should speak of such things. Did not King Alfred always spur his men on before a fight by reminding them of God's ever watching eye; had not the king's own brother won universal admiration for refusing to begin battle, when under attack, until he had finished the mass in his tent?

"This year," Aelfwald reminded them, "our lord Alfred at last forced the Viking heathens, those wasters and destroyers, to leave our land. Not only that: their fleet was smashed and sunk off our coast. And for these events we must now thank God." All around the table, those seated bowed their heads, while Aelfwald repeated the little prayer of which he was especially fond:

Greater than Thunor,
Greater than Woden,
Who for our sins
Hung bleeding and died:
To you we give thanks,
Lord Christ on the rood.

And suddenly moved himself, the thane went on:

"Our life on earth is short." He glanced up at the rest of the great hall. High in the beams were several birds' nests, and at each end through a small square ventilation hole, the birds were accustomed to go in and out. "It is like a sparrow that flies through the hall. It comes from outside, and flies away again, no one knows where. And so, friends, we travel, from darkness to darkness. For the few years of our life we live in the great hall." He paused, unable to find more words to express the transitory nature of life. "But there is a greater hall," he went on, "where life is eternal."

Port nodded slowly at the thane's words. They expressed exactly his own feelings, though he could never have spoken them himself.

"Today I have an important announcement," the thane continued. "For when my mother died, I swore an oath to her, that I would give generously to God's Church." He looked about the room. "Four years ago I established the religious house on my estate at Twyneham, where my son Aelfwine is a monk." There was a murmur of approval. "Today, I decided that Osric the carpenter's son shall go at my expense to the school at Canterbury to learn the art of illumination." At this there was applause. "But this is not enough," the thane cried. "And so, to redeem the oath I swore to my mother, I am making a new endowment." Port wondered what this could be. A gift to the nunnery perhaps? "In the field beside this place, where the cross now stands," Aelfwald proclaimed, "I will build a church. It will be made not of wood, like this hall, but of stone. And I will give land to support a priest who will minister there."

There was an awed silence. Such churches, the first of the parish churches of England, were still a rarity; and a church of stone still more so. There had only been one other in the area, just south of the place where the five rivers met, at the little hamlet of Britford, where a former king had endowed a small structure on his estate there, using stones from the ruins of Roman Sorviodunum; but no one else in the area had done such an ambitious thing in a generation. The cost of such a building, even a modest structure, would be formidable and represented a major sacrifice even to a wealthy man like Aelfwald.

Port stared down at the table. His mind was in a whirl. As he thought of his own unwillingness to redeem his own vow to his sister he felt his face go scarlet with shame.

"I am unworthy to be a thane," he moaned softly to himself.

And then, as Aelfwald sat down and the toasts were drunk again, he knew what he must do.

His face still flushed, his head spinning slightly, he rose a little unsteadily to his feet. As the hubbub around him died down, and the faces of the feasters turned towards him in surprise, he cried out, so that his thin voice echoed round the hall:

"I, Port, to redeem the pledge I gave my sister Edith, give to the nunnery of Wilton a fine gold cross, for the glory of God."

He sank down. It was done. The people applauded. His honour was satisfied. And the money was gone.

He would never be a thane now.

He sat by his wife, hardly knowing what to think. He trembled with pride: yet, though he tried to disregard it, in the pit of his stomach, he felt a terrible coldness at the great opportunity he had lost. His face now burning, he stared down into his lap, and when from the head of the table Aelfwald gave him a warm smile of encouragement, he did not see it.

In the darkness outside the hall, a light snow had begun to fall over Sarum: a token, it seemed that this winter at least, there would be peace.

It was an hour after dawn. In the little wooden chapel where the six monks performed their simple devotions, Osric rose stiffly from his knees. There was a cold, hard January frost on the ground.

It was time to begin the day, and like all his days at the monastic cell, the boy was dreading it. For nearly half an hour he had been praying alone; but his prayers had brought him no comfort. One thought, and only one kept him going: "Six months more," he whispered, "and then I'll be sent to Canterbury." If he could just work out how to get through them.

At the place where the two rivers, the Avon and the Stour, ran into the sheltered harbour by the sea, there was now a modest settlement of some two dozen houses protected by a palisade, which had acquired the name Twyneham. It meant the place by two rivers, and like Wilton, it was set in the angle between them. Opposite lay the long spit of land with its low hill that protected the shallow harbour from the turbulence of the English Channel; and along the northern side of the harbour, to the east of Twyneham, lay the broad, flat marshland that gradually turned into woods as one went further inland. It was here that Aelfwald owned a large hunting estate, and it was on the edge of the wood that he had carved a spacious, dry clearing on which the modest buildings of the little monastery stood.

The thane's endowment of a monastic cell was a rarity. In the last generation there had been fewer monks in Wessex, despite the fine old monasteries it possessed. Those that continued had often degenerated into communities where the rules were lax or almost non-existent. And though the king was constantly urging his nobles to improve the situation, few of the young men of his kingdom had been volunteering to enter monastic orders. In this respect, Aelfwine was unusual, and Alfred had warmly congratulated the thane on his modest initiative. Though the cell consisted of only a dormitory, a refectory with its kitchen, and a Chapel, in effect three enlarged huts, it did boast a fine psalter and a pair of magnificent jewelled candlesticks given by the thane's wife.

There, under the vague and somewhat informal leadership of Aelfwine, the six monks led an approximate version of the life prescribed under the great and wise Rule of St Benedict.

Osric turned to leave the chapel. At dawn the six monks had sung the first of the day's seven offices in the chapel. Before the next, Prime, he must sweep the little courtyard outside the chapel clean; and before the third service, Tierce, he must work in the kitchens, preparing the modest meal, *prandium*, that would be eaten at noon. But between Tierce and noon, when the little bell would be rung for the midday meal, he had some two hours of free time. As always, that time he would spend out in the marshes, away from the monks. And this was for a very good reason.

Now as he left the chapel, he spoke aloud a final prayer:

"Please God, do not let Aelfwine touch me again."

Why had the thane's son chosen to be a monk? It was believed by some at Sarum that it was because he had not been able to live up to the strength and prowess of his brothers.

"Even Aelfgifu could break him with her little finger," it was said; and indeed, it was well known that when she was a girl of twelve, she had humiliated him in a wrestling match before a crowd of children, and that he had never got over it. It was not that Aelfwine was weak: in any other family he would have been normal: but by the standards of his brothers and sister, he was inadequate.

Whatever his reasons were, at the age of fifteen Aelfwine had told his family that he wanted to become a monk, and since then he had never altered his mind. He was twenty-five now – a fair, sparely built young man, usually rather reserved in his manner, but whose pale blue eyes seemed to shine sometimes with an intensity that was not quite natural. To Osric it seemed that he smiled too much.

At first it was nothing: the young man had been kind to the boy his father had sent: each week he had given him religious instruction, and he had sent back good reports of him to Avonsford from time to time. The other monks, too, were kind, instructing him in his daily tasks, which were certainly not onerous. Indeed, on the land which his family leased from the thane, the work was much harder. Occasionally, during their lessons, Aelfwine used to walk about the room, and once or twice paused and rested his hand on the boy's head – a gesture which Osric had hardly even noticed at the time.

Nor had young Osric thought much about it when one day Aelfwine sat next to him, and at one point had allowed his hand to rest lightly on his leg. It had not seemed so remarkable. Osric looked up to the thane's son, even if instinctively he liked him less than Aelfgifu or his brothers. If Aelfwine showed him a small sign of affection, he felt honoured.

Often, when he was working at his tasks, Aelfwine came and spoke a few friendly words to him, or chatted with him easily about his life. When he rang the little bell attached to the side of the wooden chapel as the monks went in to their devotions, the young man usually gave him a pleasant smile. All these were small attentions which Osric was grateful for. And if Aelfwine sometimes let him walk with him and the other monks across the flat open ground to the river, or by the harbour shore, he would return more cheerful than before. But once, when Aelfwine had walked with him alone and put his arm round him, the boy for some reason felt uncomfortable. He felt his body freeze, uncertain what to do; and he had been glad when after a time, Aelfwine disengaged his arm, to point at a heron, scudding over the harbour water.

It was one evening in the late autumn that the awful thing happened.

He was alone in the kitchen, preparing the monks' food. In the corner was a roaring fire, and because of the noise of the wood crackling in the grate, he did not hear Aelfwine come into the room. When he turned, he found the young man close beside him. They had spoken a few words, he could hardly remember what, and then suddenly Aelfwine had come much closer. His face was flushed – he supposed it was because of the fire; on his forehead he noticed little beads of sweat. And the young man's eyes were shining, staring down at him meaningfully, but conveying a message he did not understand. Then, before the boy knew what had happened, Aelfwine's arms were round him, pressing him closely; and as he turned up his face, his mouth open, his large eyes wide with shock, the thane's son had kissed him.

He did not know what was happening; he was terrified. He struggled, but against the strength of Aelfwine, it was useless.

At last, the thane's son let him go.

"Remember, Osric, I am your friend."

And moments later, scarlet and panting, the boy found he was alone again.

What did it mean? Were such things done? He did not know what to think, but he felt as if he had been defiled.

From that evening, his life had been miserable. It seemed to him that wherever he went, Aelfwine was watching him, looking for a chance to come close to him. In the chapel, about his work, in the kitchen, or even in his lonely walks, he would suddenly and unexpectedly find him there, always smiling, putting his arm round him, stroking his arm or running his hand through his brown hair. His life became a series of calculations on how he could avoid him. And although Aelfwine had not tried to kiss him again, Osric knew that he was powerless to stop him if he did.

He had been afraid to say anything; and there was no one whose advice he could ask. The other monks, he knew, were a little afraid of Aelfwine and unlikely to say anything to offend him. Aelfwine was in charge of the monastery, the son of a great thane. What could he do – he was only a poor carpenter's son? And on his visit to Avonsford, when the thane and his father questioned him, he had been reluctant to speak: with the thane he had felt embarrassment, and with his father, a sense of shame.

Then the unbelievable had happened: Aelfwald had said he would send him to Canterbury. Which was why, each morning now, he whispered to himself: "Six months. Only six more months."

There was a mist that morning. It lay in wreaths over the marsh and hid the settlement of Twyneham from sight. But Osric knew the ground so well that in the mid-morning interval, he did not hesitate to move swiftly away from the clearing and make his way across the marsh towards the harbour. Every patch of shrub, every clump of rushes was a friend to him now as he walked over the ground – half stiff with frost and half boggy underfoot. The mist swirled around him.

At least he won't try and follow me today, the boy thought, and for a while he felt his spirits lift. But half way across the marsh he stopped. It seemed to him that he could hear something. Was it breathing? Was it some other sound? And was it behind or in front of him? He listened, then shook his head and went forward. A few moments later he paused again. Had he heard footsteps? Carefully, still listening, he proceeded to the water's edge. He thought he heard a heron's call.

And then he saw it.

The ship was forty yards in front of him; it was moving towards Twyneham slowly and furtively through the mist. Its eighteen pairs of oars were stroking the surface gently, its high prow slipped through the water, silent as a swan. The round, black and yellow shields that hung on the longboat's sides told him what it must be.

"Vikings," he breathed.

He turned and ran. The mist now seemed like a cloud, enveloping him. The rustle of his feet on the ground seemed like a pounding drum; he ran across the empty marsh, almost blind with fear. And in the middle of the marsh, with a gasp of terror, he ran into a tall figure, who held him in his arms. They fell to the ground together.

It was Aelfwine.

The thane's son smiled as he held Osric tightly. The mist was damp on the woollen habit he wore, and on his thick yellow hair.

"No one can see us," he breathed.

"Vikings." Osric struggled to get free but made no headway. "In the harbour. Let me go."

Still it had no effect. Aelfwine grinned and shook his head. His face came closer.

There was only one thing to do. Osric let his body go limp. He let Aelfwine kiss him; and after a moment he felt the grip on him loosen.

Aelfwine drew back, smiling.

"That's better," he murmured, gazing at the boy affectionately.

Then Osric kicked, as hard as he could, and as Aelfwine doubled up in agony, he scrambled up and ran towards the monastery. Almost at once, he could hear Aelfwine following, cursing behind him. But Osric knew the tracks better; he sped through the frozen marshes. And in his mind there was a single thought: he must warn the people in the settlement.

Almost out of breath, he raced into the little courtyard, only to find it empty. In a state of near panic, he looked about. How could he warn those people across the river at Twyneham? He saw the bell.

A minute later all six monks were standing in the little courtyard gazing with astonishment as the boy Osric frantically rang the chapel bell: not with its normal, steady toll, but with a desperate clanging that echoed through the mist. And while this was going on, Aelfwine, white with anger, hobbled towards him.

"Vikings!" Osric was shouting. "Vikings!"

The monks looked at one another. What was the boy talking about? Everyone knew that the Vikings never appeared in the winter months. But when one of them tried to restrain him Osric shook him off furiously.

It was Aelfwine who first realised the truth. With a few quick steps he

[303]

came to Osric's side and seized his arms.

"Don't touch me!" the boy screamed.

But Aelfwine, with a single wrench tore Osric away from the rope and clapped his hands over his mouth.

"Silence," he ordered. He stared at Osric and the boy saw that his eyes had lost the shining look of lust that they had had minutes before and that now they were grave. "You saw Vikings? A boat?" Osric nodded. "Then you should not have rung the bell." He let him go.

Now, as he looked about him, Osric understood what the thane's son meant. For the mist was growing thicker. In their clearing at the edge of the wood, the monastery's buildings were now invisible, not only from the river but even from twenty yards. And as he saw the terrified faces of the monks, he realised with a terrible sense of shame what he had done: he had told the Vikings where they were.

They were all silent, listening intently. There was no sound. Then Aelfwine spoke, and his voice had a quiet command.

"It will be safer if we go into the woods."

This was clearly right. They could keep moving inland; and if the Vikings found the little monastery empty, they might set fire to it, but they were not likely to bother to search for a few monks. Very quietly, the six men and the boy moved together past the chapel and out towards the cover of the trees.

Then they heard it: a deep cough, followed by a low call, some distance away on the left towards the river. The Vikings were already searching for the bell.

Quickly the little party moved forward. The edge of the woods was only twenty yards away.

There was a whistle. This time it came from in front of them. Aelfwine cursed. The Vikings were obviously in the woods as well. The first call was directly ahead of them; but seconds later there was another, this time to the right. How was it possible, Osric wondered, that they could have moved so fast? It was a question that neither the Saxons nor any of the other people who encountered them had ever been able to answer; but it was known that the Vikings moved more swiftly than ordinary men. The monks looked at Aelfwine, uncertain what to do. If the invaders had formed a line to sweep the woods, they would have to turn back.

"I know the marsh," Osric whispered. "We could hide there."

Aelfwine looked at him. His face was calm and thoughtful – it was as if the incident between them there had never taken place. He nodded. "It's a chance."

The little body of monks silently retraced their steps, past the cluster of wooden buildings and towards the harbour. But a hundred yards further they had to stop once more. For ahead of them from the direction of the water, they heard shouts in the mist; and this time Aelfwine shook his head. "No good," he said. "Follow me."

The little group, huddled together, and scarcely able to look at each other, let him lead them back to the chapel, into which he ushered them, closing the door.

"Pray," he ordered.

He was right. There was no further use in trying to dodge the raiding party who seemed to be all over the open ground. The best remaining hope was that they might either miss the little group of buildings in the mist, or become bored with searching for them. With what sounded like a single sigh, the six monks sank to their knees.

Inside the chapel now there was no sound. Osric was kneeling to one side of the rest, but he was so conscious of his heart pounding that it seemed to him the Vikings must hear it. Minutes passed and the silence continued. Osric tried to pray, closing his eyes, fighting for concentration; but though his lips silently formed the words, his ears were listening, intently, for every sound.

It seemed to him that a long time passed, and even his breathing began to steady. Perhaps, after all, their prayers had been answered.

"Let us be invisible, Lord," he prayed. "Hide us in this mist." As the silence continued, and he came to think that they were safe after all, a warm glow of hope, then of indescribable joy seemed to flow through his body. He glanced at Aelfwine, who knelt with his head bowed before the altar. "I forgive him," he whispered.

When the door of the chapel opened, it did so briskly. The Vikings who strode in wore huge metal helmets and light chain mail; they carried shields and the fearsome iron axes that had made them dreaded all over northern Europe. They did not hesitate.

What Osric saw next seemed to happen in a way that was so simple, so matter of fact, that to his own amazement, he was not even afraid.

As the helpless monks turned and rose to their feet, the Vikings – he counted eight of them – cut them down with a few quick blows. He saw the head of one young man bump, several feet from where his body was standing, on the wooden floor. As they fell, one after the other, for some reason he could not explain, it seemed the most natural thing in the world.

But Aelfwine did not fall. Not for nothing was he the son of Aelfwald the thane. As the massacre began, he ran to the altar and seized the heavy wooden cross that stood upon it. Then, rushing at the intruders, he dealt them tremendous blows, hacking right and left, and catching one of the Vikings in the eye so that he howled with pain. There was a roar of rage as they turned on him, striking at the heavy cross until it shattered and driving him back upon the altar.

It was then that one of them shouted something Osric did not understand, but he noticed that the others, with a laugh, allowed him to step forward.

The Viking did not strike at once. He seemed to be measuring the young man before him carefully. Then he grinned. Aelfwine, pinned with his back against the altar table, and with only the stump of his wooden cross left in his hand, faced him calmly. Then the Viking swung his axe.

The blow was an unusual one; but it was perfectly calculated. It smashed against the breast-bone, bursting Aelfwine's chest open as

[305]

though it was splitting a sack, and tossing his body on to its back on the floor. The Viking stepped forward. Wrenching his embedded axe to right and to left, he shoved aside the rib cages and reached into Aelfwine's chest with his hand. While the body was still shaking in its death throes, he raised it on to its knees, pulled out first one lung, and then the other, and deftly dragged them over each shoulder, where they rested like two folded wings. Then he stepped back to admire his handiwork while the others applauded. The body of Aelfwine, his mouth wide open and full of blood, his chest a ghastly palpitating mess, framed by the jagged ends of his opened rib cages, jerked and pitched forward.

This was the famous blood-eagle – an arrangement of death that the Vikings thought amusing.

Osric was numb. He did not even feel the horror. Then they noticed him.

He walked slowly towards them. They did not move. It occurred to him that since he was a child, perhaps they would not hurt him. As he reached the centre of the little nave, he saw that on his left, the door was open and that, through the clearing mist, the sun was shining. He stepped towards it.

Almost lazily, one of the Vikings swung his axe.

The news of the death of Aelfwine and Osric did not reach the thane for some time.

For on the same day, an event of much greater significance was taking place at Sarum – an event that nearly changed the history of the island for ever.

The sudden attack of the Danes upon the kingdom of Wessex in January 878 took the Saxons completely by surprise. Never before had the marauders broken their camp at midwinter. But in 878, a few weeks after Christmas, part of the Mercian force led by the Danish King Guthrum, suddenly left their encampment in Mercian Gloucester and moved with lightning speed into Wessex, taking the fortified settlement of Chippenham at once. From there, huge raiding parties swept southward over the ridges and down the valley of the river Avon. There was no army to oppose them.

Wessex, after all, was still minting new silver coins for its king: the Vikings had not done with it yet.

At the thane's farmstead at Avonsford, the evacuation was completed with speed. The messenger had arrived at the gallop from Earldorman Wulfhere with orders for the thane and his men to meet him at the dune at Searobyrg at once.

Immediately Aelfwald sent his men scurrying about loading stores and valuables into wagons making sure that everything they could not carry had been well concealed. He despatched his two sons to supervise the evacuation of the village.

"And Port, has he been warned?" he demanded.

"He has already been told," the messenger shouted. "Hurry your men." And he turned his horse back towards the dune.

Within an hour, the entire settlement was on the move, riding or walking beside the four wagons from the farm and the village, which had been piled high. Two more carts followed, filled with armour and weaponry.

Earldorman Wulfhere was waiting with a group of horsemen at the dune. His big, blotched face surveyed the approaching carts with disgust, and he greeted Aelfwald with a curt nod.

"I didn't say bring your whole village with you," he said grumpily.

"Should I have left them to the Vikings?" the thane asked, to which Wulfhere only shrugged in reply. Other trails of carts were approaching from nearby hamlets.

Both men stared at the old earthwork fortress that was meant to defend the place.

"We can't fight here," the earldorman stated flatly. "No gate and the fortifications need repair."

"We could improvise a gate," Aelfwald suggested, but Wulfhere shook his head.

"The king's ordered a general withdrawal anyway," he said. "Back to the homelands west of Selwood."

Even now, though the kingdom of Wessex stretched as far as London, it was the hinterland to the west of the huge barrier of Selwood forest, the original power base of the early west Saxon tribal group, which was still sometimes thought of as the homeland. There, west of the sweeping open ridges and broad valleys of Sarum, lay the remote fastnesses of marsh and woodland which the Vikings did not often try to penetrate.

Aelfwald was appalled.

"We're deserting the whole south? Wilton too?"

Wulfhere looked at him a little strangely, then shrugged.

"The Vikings will be here at any time. We aren't ready for them. Look at this."

The straggling wagons full of villagers who had not even had time properly to arm themselves, and the empty unfinished fort certainly did not promise an organised defence. "They'll pause at Wilton and loot it," the earldorman said calmly. "Meanwhile these people;" he looked at them with contempt, "can get away."

It seemed to Aelfwald that Wulfhere showed no great eagerness to fight, but he had to admit the truth of what he said. The earldorman was in no mood to argue anyway.

"Move your people along," he ordered gruffly, and turned away.

As he looked at the untidy procession of carts, loaded with possessions, making their disorderly way along the muddy lane that led along the valley to Wilton, Aelfwald felt discouraged. Wulfhere had not attempted to organise them; soon, as others joined them, the little cavalcade would become unwieldy. A broken wheel here, an overturned cart there – he could just see them, a few miles down the road, strung out helplessly while the Vikings swooped down upon them.

If they could manage with fewer carts, he thought. And then he had an idea.

On the west side of the bowl of land below Searobyrg there lay two tiny hamlets with Saxon names. One, beside a marsh, was occupied by the family who traditionally played the trumpets or *bemer* at festivals, and which had therefore acquired the name Bemerton; the other, on the river, he owned himself; and this was inhabited by the extended family of Tostig the slave, which had since time out of mind, supplied the best fishermen at Sarum – for which reason the place had long been popularly known as Fisherton. There, on the banks by the little cluster of thatched huts, lay six fine long boats.

"Tell Tostig to bring all his boats to Wilton," the thane ordered. "Perhaps we can load them instead of using more carts."

When he reached Wilton, the wisdom of this decision was immediately clear.

The little town was in utter confusion. The evacuation was taking place without any direction and the main street was already blocked by carts. Worst of all, no one had thought of removing the valuables from the royal palace or the nunnery. Wulfhere had not arrived. Quickly therefore, the thane took charge and soon established order, and when Tostig arrived with his six boats at the jetty south of the nunnery, the thane had no doubt how he should use them. Directing his men to the palace and the church, he saw to it that all the gold and ornaments from both buildings were carried to the water's edge and stowed in the boats until all six were full.

"Upstream," the thane commanded, "as far as you can." And he told his eldest son Aelfric to accompany them. Slowly Tostig and his helpers edged the six boats out into the stream and paddled away through the cold waters.

While the procession of carts was being organised, Aelfwald detailed his younger son to arm twenty men who would ride as an escort for the convoy. Then, satisfied that he had done all he could in the time, he started them up.

The armed escort had one addition that he had not foreseen.

As soon as Aelfgifu had seen what was happening, she had slipped away to where the men were arming. In moments she had found all that she needed and vanished into one of the empty houses by the market place. Carefully winding her long hair tightly round her head, and stripping to her shirt, she had prepared herself. Soon afterwards a tall, handsome figure in a coat of chain mail stepped into the open. On her head she wore a Saxon helmet crowned with the customary figure of a crouching boar on whose front was blazoned a silver cross. From her belt hung a short single-edged sword, and in her hand was a spear. With her splendid bearing, she looked every inch a Saxon warrior, and none of the men hurrying to their rendezvous on the western side of the town paid her any particular attention.

Only Aelfstan spotted her as she took her place at the rear of the escort, and he grinned. He had never known Aelfgifu allow herself to be left out of anything her brothers did, and this latest prank came as no surprise. He quietly moved to a position beside her.

"Better not let father catch you," he whispered, then pulled his horse away; and moments later when the thane looked about and asked where the girl was he could answer with perfect truth:

"She's here, father. I saw her a moment ago."

Despite the confusion, the town was evacuated; and as they went along the valley, Aelfwald was relieved to see Wulfhere and his men moving slowly along the ridge above them, keeping watch over the high ground on their northern flank.

It was when the procession was over a mile away from Wilton that the first mishap occurred, when the abbess suddenly noticed that Edith had disappeared, and learned that a little while before the nun had been seen hurrying towards the back of the line, although for what reason, no one knew. After a search, she was nowhere to be found and so the abbess came to report the matter to Aelfwald.

The thane turned in his saddle irritably. This was the kind of time-wasting he had hoped to avoid; but since it was a nun, he called for someone in the escort to ride back to check the town; and it was then, needing no second bidding, that one of the escorts wheeled about and cantered back along the muddy road.

The town of Wilton was empty and silent; there was no sign of the Vikings yet as Aelfgifu clattered down the main street and she was almost at the palace when she saw Edith.

The nun was staggering along the street. In her eyes there was a wild stare of determination and triumph, and in her arms was clasped tightly the huge leather bound volume of Gospels. In the confusion they had somehow been left behind, and as soon as she realised it, forgetting everything else, she had run back alone to the empty nunnery. She was almost collapsing under its weight. She stared uncertainly at the rider, whom she did not recognise, bearing down on her.

With a single, easy movement, Aelfgifu reached down and scooped Edith up, sitting her in front of her astride the horse, which she kicked into a smart canter. Edith was so taken by surprise, that she let go of the heavy book which crashed with a thud in the middle of the street behind them. She gave a high pitched scream.

"The Gospels! The Gospels!"

Aelfgifu took no notice.

"Stop. Stop your horse, foolish man." She struggled wildly, her face a picture of woe. But it was nothing to the look of horror and astonishment which crossed her face when she heard the familiar voice of the thane's daughter laughing in her ear.

"Can't stop, Edith. It's only a book."

The Gospels were not found again.

In the meantime, a far more serious discovery had been made: Port's wife and children had never joined the party at all.

It was the messenger's fault. Before he left Wilton, he had encountered the sheep farmer, who had come there on business that morning and shouted to him that he was riding to warn the thane. Naturally Port had assumed that Aelfwald would bring his wife and children too; and the thane would have done so if the messenger had not told him that Port had already been warned. It was only now, as he came back along the line of carts to greet the thane, that the astonished Port found his family was missing.

"I must go back," he cried, almost beside himself.

Aelfwald looked grimly up at the sun. It was well past noon. If the Vikings had not already reached the farmstead at Sarum, they might be very close. Even so, there was a chance that they would not bother to search for the isolated sheep farm on the high ground, when the rich farmstead and the village of Avonsford lay so invitingly in the valley below. He knew he should not do anything to weaken the protection of the wagons, but after one look at the distracted sheep farmer, he did not hesitate.

"Aelfstan," he called his youngest son. "Take six men and four spare horses to Port's farm. Go now!"

But as the men began to peel away from the cortège, he laid a restraining arm on Port.

"I forbid you," he said. The sheep farmer with his single hand was not even armed. He would be of little use if the rescue party met any of the marauders.

Port looked at him beseechingly, but the thane shook his head. The riders were already vanishing down the road.

Aelfgifu had just reached the tail end of the line when she saw her brother and his men streaming by, and though she did not know the reason, she wasted no time in hauling Edith from the horse and unceremoniously dumping her in the road; then she turned her horse's head.

She caught up with them just as they climbed the steep path that led to the dune of Searobyrg. She saw Aelfstan waving at her angrily, heard him shouting at her to go back. But since she took no notice, there was nothing that he could do. "I'm coming anyway," she cried, as her horse drew level with his; and so, serious this time, he told her their quest, as together they rode on swiftly over the ridges.

As they went, they kept their eyes peeled for signs of rising smoke that might signal the Vikings' presence but there was none; and as they drew level with the thane's farmstead below, Aelfgifu allowed herself to breathe a sigh of relief. It seemed that they were in time.

They were not.

The party of Vikings had made their way at a leisurely pace up the path from the farmstead where the main force had briefly paused on its way towards Wilton. Finding no opposition, they had not troubled to set fire to the place, and had sent scouting parties to the ridge above to see if there was anything there to plunder.

It was one of these which, just as they reached the crest, saw the Saxons coming towards them.

Aelfstan's reactions were instant. Turning to his sister he cried:

"Ride to Port's with the spare horses," and he motioned two of the men to go with her. As Aelfgifu wheeled away across the open ground, he rode down upon the Vikings to cut them off.

There were ten of them, dark, swarthy men; three carried swords, the rest axes, and they rode small, sturdy ponies. By his quick action Aelfstan had caught them before they could give chase to the rescue party, and as they were still mounting the crest, he had them at a disadvantage.

The skirmish was brief. At the first rush the Saxons knocked half of them off their horses, and sweeping down on them again, with loud whoops, they stampeded the riderless ponies and cut down three of the Vikings where they stood. The third charge brought them to stern, hand to hand fighting, but although still outnumbered, Aelfstan and his men still had the advantage of the higher ground. They killed two Vikings and wounded three more before the rest of the invaders, thinking this was an unprofitable battle, turned their ponies and made their way down the track. With a shout of triumph, the Saxons wheeled about and went to look for Aelfgifu.

Port's little farmstead lay in a long, narrow dip in the ground. The house itself was a modest five room structure with outhouses, facing south east along the dip, with a sheep pen on each side of it and a small hut for the shepherd. In front of it the dip extended two hundred yards, broadening a little towards the south east end where it rose to a lip of land. This natural declivity formed a sheltered spot within which the farm was invisible from the sweeping turf ridges above, and its inhabitants, looking out only on the bare edges of land above, lived in secluded silence, unaware of what was passing in the busier world of the valleys below.

Since Port had left early that morning the day had been uneventful. The shepherd and his son had gone up on to the ridges, and though once or twice around noon he had noticed that some of the distant sheep by the edge of the valley were stirring uneasily, he had assumed that it was only a passing fox that had made them do so. A little later, he returned to the house.

It was in the afternoon that a group of thirty Vikings passed swiftly and silently across the grazing grounds, while their smaller scouting party was having its encounter with Aelfstan. Although the sheep farm was invisible in its declivity, a thin column of smoke from the fire told them where it must be. They swooped down upon it.

Aelfgifu and her party arrived at the other end of the hollow just as the Vikings were approaching the little farmstead.

Ahead of her, by the house, Aelfgifu could see Port's wife and two children standing helplessly. Some of the Vikings already lay in her path, between her and the farm, and her two companions hesitated.

Quickly she measured the ground with her eye: it was a tiny chance, no more, but if she could just outflank the Vikings, if she could just, for a moment, get the horses to the farm, perhaps they might get Port's family away.

Hardly bothering to see if her companions were with her, she seized the reins of two of the spare horses and dashed forward. Startled into action, the other two Saxons raced after her.

It was a daring move, and it almost worked; but before she could reach her goal, the Vikings moved swiftly to cut her off.

Frantically she tried to break through them.

In the fight that followed, futile though it was, the marauders were taken by surprise at the ferocity of the Saxons. Never had they seen a warrior fight more bravely or deal more telling blows than the splendid young Saxon who led the party. Dodging the fearsome battle-axes with amazing skill, cutting and thrusting powerfully with the short, single edged sword, this handsome mounted warrior killed four men without receiving a scratch while the other two Saxons, fighting hard, were holding their own. Admiring, but furious, a group of six Vikings, made a concerted rush at them.

It was a glancing blow that knocked her helmet off, sent her hair tumbling down over her breasts, and caused the six Vikings to stare in astonishment.

"A woman!" one of them cried. A proud young Saxon woman had killed four of their number! They could hardly believe it. With a roar of fury and lust they rushed at her.

It was then that Aelfgifu experienced red anger: oblivious to all sense of danger, she struck right and left as if her rage alone could break through them and rescue the little family beyond.

So angry was she that she was hardly aware of the sudden arrival of her brother and the rest of the party. She was conscious that the Vikings were momentarily falling back; dimly she heard her brother's voice crying – "Get her away." But as she tried to strike at the Vikings again, she realised that someone was turning her horse's head, and, it seemed only a second later, she found herself galloping away across the high ground, safely surrounded by the Saxons.

She turned, to find Aelfstan, riding close by her side, smiling at her.

"Port's family," she cried. "We must get them."

But her brother only shook his head.

"It's too late. We tried."

And now, as they hurried her back towards the dune, she found that she was trembling uncontrollably.

It was fortunate that, in the heat of the little battle, she had not seen one thing; but Aelfstan had seen it, as he rode to her defence. By the farmhouse, three of the Vikings had already seized Port's wife. While two held her, the third, with a lascivious grin, was untying his belt. He was a large man, with a pock-marked face, which Aelfstan had committed to memory.

When the Saxons had been driven off, the Vikings turned their attention to the little group at the farmstead. After two more men had raped Port's wife, they decided it was not very good sport, and killed her.

The shepherd and his son were butchered too. There remained the slaves and the children.

The slaves ran to and fro, trying to escape: for three minutes the Vikings allowed them to do so in a scene that resembled a gruesome game of tag. Then they killed them. Now only Port's two children were left. The elder was seven. Two of the Vikings stepped forward with their axes.

But they stopped at a shout from the ridge above.

The man who now appeared was huge; he was older than the other warriors and although on foot, he tramped down the slope with an air of authority. He had been scouting the area alone, but finding nothing he had come across to where he had heard the sound of fighting. Now his gruff voice echoed round the area.

"Bairn-ni-kel!"

The warriors paused and looked up. His order puzzled them: do not kill the bairns: yet it was not unusual to kill children on a raiding party.

"Bairn-ni-kel." His voice was a deep roar so that the words sounded more like: Bar . . . Barn-ni-kel.

The heavy-set Viking marched across to where the children were standing. He stared around at the carnage with a look of disgust. Then he allowed his large hand to fall on the head of Port's elder son. It was clear that he was determined that the children should be spared. He gestured the two axemen away impatiently. They hesitated, but since he was known as a fearsome warrior, they reluctantly obeyed.

From the far end of the hollow, several voices began to laugh. It was not the first time that the gruff-voiced warrior had stopped such killing of children.

"Look," one of the men joked, "it's old Barn-ni-kel." For similar incidents had already given him this nickname which his descendants would carry for many generations.

Now, under his watchful eye, they looted what they could, but the children were spared.

A few minutes later, when the marauders had left, Port's two children stared at the bodies around them; then, not knowing what else to do, they climbed into the sheep pens to seek comfort where the familiar woollen bodies of the sheep kept them warm.

The journey of the people of Wilton lasted for five days. As they passed near other settlements, like the hill town of Shaftesbury, they were joined by others anxious to escape the Vikings. But as the days passed and no attack was made upon them, some of the farmers began to leave the cortège and seek shelter in the woods and valleys, reasoning that they were as safe there as in an armed camp which the Vikings might decide to attack. Aelfwald tried to dissuade them but Earldorman Wulfhere admonished him:

"Let them go. Fewer mouths to feed."

The thane's own people from Sarum however, stayed together.

The little party passed the southern tip of the great forest of Selwood and gradually the landscape began to change. There were more marshes and soon, Aelfwald knew, they would encounter the rich, red earth of England's south west. It was on the fifth day that they passed by the site of the ancient abbey of Glastonbury – where, it was said by the monks, there was a tomb of the legendary warrior Arthur, who had fought in pre-Saxon times. Soon after they passed this Wulfhere sent out scouts.

"My information is that the king is somewhere near," he told the thane.

The next morning they found him.

The camp of King Alfred at the place called Athelney was a modest and hastily erected collection of tents, huts and reed shelters set on a parcel of land protected on one side by a hill and the other by a marsh. Though it was unlikely to be attacked, the site was cold and damp. Each day, small parties of men had been arriving as word filtered through the south that the king was there; they were still too few to accomplish much, but each of them was devoted to the cause of the beleaguered Wessex king.

The arrival of Wulfhere, Aelfwald and the other thanes was an important addition to their strength, and they were taken immediately to the king's tent.

Alfred of Wessex was unremarkable to look at. He was of medium height and delicate health. In his youth he had suffered from piles and for most of his adult life he was subject to a nervous sense of his own poor health that came close to hypochondria. But whatever his psychological problems, it was his intense spirit and determination that carried him through and made him a remarkable monarch by the standards of any time.

When the earldorman and thanes came into his presence he embraced each one of them, and it seemed to Aelfwald, as the king gazed at him with his earnest pale blue eyes, that Alfred took his hand with a special fervour.

"You came. Faithful friends." The thane was shocked to see that his blue eyes were sad, almost beseeching. "Most of my thanes probably think I'm dead," he explained. "There has been no defence anywhere, you know: none at all."

The Viking attack had been a bitter blow to the ambitious monarch. For the seven troubled years of his reign Alfred had tried to give the rich lands of Wessex the security needed to undertake the great projects for which his heart and spirit yearned: the building of churches, the restoration of monasteries and schools, the revival in Wessex of the great Latin culture that had in past generations made the northern Anglo-Saxon kingdoms of Northumbria and Mercia amongst the noblest in Europe.

"We have our examples," he would urge men like Aelfwald, "both in the Anglo-Saxon kingdoms of the past and at the Frankish court across the sea." Two generations before the great Frankish Emperor Charlemagne's court had been the most sophisticated centre of culture since the collapse of the western Roman Empire and Alfred was anxious to emulate it. But the invasions of the Vikings in the north, and a lack of ambition in the south had left the whole island in a state of cultural decline and the task he had set himself was huge.

None of his plans could be accomplished – his new kingdom would be stillborn – if he could not protect Wessex from the heathen marauders.

"There is so much to do. Our towns need to be fortified. We need ships to patrol the coast," he would remind his thanes. "As for the army . . ."

The Anglo-Saxon fyrd, the armed levy of the thanes and their men from every shire and hundred, was an unwieldy and inefficient force. Each lord was only under obligation to perform a certain number of days fighting each year; it was hard to persuade the farmer warriors to fight outside their own shires, and often even loyal churls would suddenly leave to see to their harvests. In trying to make this a cohesive force against the freebooting Viking horde, Alfred was up against formidable obstacles. As for the fixed defences, the fortified towns known as burghs were the first consistent defensive systems since Roman times, and they were only just beginning to be prepared. Eventually, when it was complete, every settlement in Wessex would be within twenty miles of a burgh.

"We need four men for every pole of defended wall," he had said. "That's about a man every five feet. And if you reckon a hide of land supports one man, then we must assign land to support each burgh, according to the length of its walls."

This was the beginning of the English system of Burghal Hideage which designated land for the support of each defended Saxon town. Wilton, whose walls would be over a mile around, was allotted 1400 hides.

He had tried also to plan a naval system to protect the coast and designed a sixty oar ship to act as a model for his new fleet.

But all these preparations were incomplete and the surprise attack in midwinter had found him powerless. His ambitious plans now seemed close to ruin.

"So here I am, hiding like a criminal in the marshes," he said ruefully to the party from Sarum as they gathered round.

The news that came in during the following days was not encouraging. As further parties arrived with news, it became clear that the Vikings had free run of the whole kingdom.

"They could partition Wessex as they already have Mercia," Earldorman Wulfhere confided grimly to the thane. "Then the whole island will be Danelaw."

Although Aelfwald did not greatly care for Wulfhere or want to admit such a thing, he knew that unless they could mount an astounding offensive from the marshes, the Anglo-Saxon kingdom would be finished for ever.

But Alfred was firm. "In the spring," he promised them, "when we can rally our people, we will hit back."

Two days after his arrival Aelfwald received news that Aelfwine had been killed at Twyneham, and that young Osric was dead as well. The thane sought out the carpenter and his family and gave them comfort. Of the trouble between the young monk and the boy neither he, nor the carpenter, ever had any idea.

To his remaining sons he said:

"Now we have your brother to avenge. Nor shall we forget Osric or Port's family. They are our people too."

Three weeks passed. The force in the marshes slowly grew; but outside, nothing changed. The weather was relentlessly cold. And yet, in that ramshackle and informal camp, where the few thanes wandered in and out of the king's tent as if it were their own, Aelfwald did not lose hope.

The king was extraordinary. It never ceased to amaze Aelfwald how, in the middle of his difficulties, Alfred's active, urgent mind could switch to the higher matters that he considered so important.

"Look at these," he would say to the thane, pointing to the pile of books that always lay on the table at the centre of his quarters. "I have once again been hearing my teachers read me the history of our people written by that great man Bede, more than a century ago." He would sigh. "Why has our own century produced no such man?"

And more than once when he had confessed to Aelfwald – "I had hoped for so much. But now . . ." – and his head had dropped in despair, he would suddenly recover his spirits and exclaim eagerly: "This my friends, is the answer to despair." And he would tap a huge book. "Boethius gives us consolation. One day I will translate it from Latin into our own Anglo-Saxon tongue." Then he would poke Aelfwald in the ribs and grin: "So I shall expect you to learn to read by then, my friend."

For Boethius's *Consolation of Philosophy*, written by the last great pagan philosopher of the Roman world as he awaited execution four centuries before, was so noble a book that few Christians had any difficulty in accepting its prescriptions – that peace of mind can only be reached by the contemplation of eternal truths – and together with the works of St Augustine it had become one of the best loved books of the Middle Ages.

"Boethius, Augustine, the laws of King Ine: these are the things every educated man should know," Alfred often told the thane. "Through study, Aelfwald, we rise above our difficulties."

By mid-February, another problem had arisen: the camp was short of food. Each day scouts were sent out to forage, but each day they came back with less, and it almost seemed that the little Saxon force might have to break up for lack of supplies.

It was then that Aelfwald formed a daring plan.

When the thane sent Tostig and the boats up river from Wilton, he had not held out great hopes that they would escape capture. But, under the supervision of his son Aelfric, the fisherman had done surprisingly well, bringing the six boats across a network of rivers, occasionally crossing small strips of land, and arriving at the marsh of Athelney only three days after the rest of the party, with all the goods from Wilton still intact.

Recent reports from the scouts suggested that while there were Viking camps along the Wylye valley near Wilton, the thane's farmstead at Sarum had, so far, been left untouched.

One morning Aelfwald summoned the slave and told him what he had in mind.

He was a strange, disreputable looking fellow, the thane thought, with his lank, dark hair, his narrow-set eyes and long thin hands and toes. He reminded him of one of the long flies that lay on the surface of the stream. As Tostig listened to what was proposed, he stood in his customary attitude, his head staring at his feet, maintaining a sullen silence that might have been insolence, or might not. Whatever the slave's true thoughts, Tostig had always done his work well when he was made to, and the thane's table had always been liberally supplied with fish netted in the five rivers.

"Well, can you do it?" he asked peremptorily when he had finished.

Tostig did not look up.

"Maybe."

"You may take any men you want. Aelfstan or Aelfric can accompany you."

The slave shook his head.

"They'd only be in the way."

"As you like." This was, he knew, as much enthusiasm as he would ever elicit. "Good luck then."

That evening he watched Tostig and his family push the six empty boats into the stream and paddle away. He wondered if he would ever see them again.

Ten days later, Tostig returned.

He had done brilliantly. Using his intimate knowledge of the waterways, he had brought the boats past every Viking camp, usually at night, without being noticed. He had slipped by Wilton and gone up the Avon to the thane's farmstead without difficulty. There, as Aelfwald had hoped, he had found all the hidden stores intact. Having loaded the boats he returned, cleverly and silently, just as he had gone.

"Bring all the provisions you can find," Aelfwald had told him. "You know what we need."

The results, when Aelfwald led the king down to the banks where Tostig was unloading, brought a smile to Alfred's face.

There were ten vats of honey, two hundred cheeses, forty sacks of flour, flagons of ale, both dark and clear, two hundred pounds weight of fodder and the carcasses of twenty sheep, which Tostig had managed to preserve in the cold.

With a proud smile the thane explained: "This is the feorm I owe you for my land."

At this Alfred first roared with laughter, then clapped the loyal thane on the back; but a moment later, it seemed to Aelfwald that he was close to tears. For the feorm, the tax in kind owed by a thane to the king or his superior lord, was a reminder of how far Wessex was from its normal state of order.

"Soon Thane Aelfwald," the king said quietly, "I hope we shall return to a time when the king collects his feorm as before." Then turning to Tostig the slave he announced: "You are a freedman from this hour: I shall pay your lord Aelfwald the price of your freedom." At which, true to his character, the surly slave bowed his head respectfully, but did not smile.

[317]

But what gave the thane more pleasure even than the king's praise was the cargo Tostig brought in the last boat: two small children whom they had assumed must be dead. When he saw these, tears came to the thane's eyes too and he shouted:

"Tell Port we have livestock for him."

Later that day the two children told the sheep farmer and the thane how they had lived alone for weeks at the sheep farm, and then at the empty farmstead in the valley; and how during the massacre they had been saved by a grey-bearded Viking about whom they could tell the listeners nothing except that he was called Bar-ni-kel.

The battle of Edington which took place in the spring of 878, though it involved only modest numbers of men, ranks with those other small but vital conflicts – Hastings, the Armada, the Battle of Britain – as one of the turning points in the island's history.

As the winter drew to an end, Aelfwald was aware of a sense of anticipation growing within the community at Athelney. The king was active now: scouts were being sent out in all directions to monitor the Vikings' changing dispositions; others were sent to rally support.

It was in late March that the spirits of all at the camp were raised by a piece of unexpected news. A detachment that the king had sent into the rich lands of the south west had succeeded in collecting a sizeable force together there, and this new group had met and defeated a Viking raiding party which had crossed, in no less than twenty-three ships, from Wales. Over a thousand of the raiders were reported dead: it was the first hint of success for many months.

The thane's sons were eager to attack in force.

"We should raid Guthrum himself at Chippenham," Aelfstan urged. "Teach him a lesson."

But King Alfred waited. For too long the war with the Vikings had followed this pattern of inconclusive battles followed by a payment of danegeld and a temporary withdrawal.

"This time," he told Aelfwald, "we must force them out for good. Nothing less will do." And each day, messengers came with news of more thanes willing to meet him when he marched.

Easter came and the whole camp gathered in a nearby field where a tall wooden cross had been set up. The nuns of Wilton, and the few monks whom the king had in his entourage celebrated a mass and it was after this that Aelfwald saw King Alfred advance to the cross and turn to address them.

"The time has nearly come," he cried. "And if it is God's will, we'll drive the Vikings out of Wessex for ever. If not," he added grimly, "we'll die in the attempt."

As the thane waited eagerly for the day of departure, one problem arose that he had not anticipated. It concerned his daughter.

After her escapade with the Vikings at Sarum, he had been furious as well as relieved on her return, and for the rest of the journey he had ordered her to ride in one of the waggons with her mother so that she could not get up to any further mischief. At the camp, she had been duly submissive, confining herself to domestic tasks and helping the other women prepare food and look after the soldiers.

"My daughter is a little wild," he had confessed to Alfred, "but I can control her."

He was astonished therefore when, the evening after the mass, Aelfgifu had appeared before him and calmly announced:

"I'm coming with you to fight."

"Impossible. You're a woman," he told her.

"But I'm coming anyway," she repeated obstinately.

How dare she defy him? The whole idea was absurd.

"You'll stay at the camp," he thundered. "Let me hear no more of this."

"I fight as well as any man," she insisted.

He glowered at her. He knew that what she said was true and, secretly, he was proud of his extraordinary daughter's prowess. But it was not seemly for a young woman to behave like this and he knew that some of the other thanes smiled at him behind his back because of her.

"It's impossible," he repeated, and expected that to be the end of the matter.

It was not. The very next morning, to his fury, his two sons appeared before him to plead the foolish girl's cause.

"I've seen her fight," young Aelfstan said, "and I'd sooner have her with me than most men."

"And would you like to see her killed beside you as well?" he demanded irritably.

"No," Aelfstan confessed, "but if she's so determined to do it, then I'd rather she took the risk. And I'd rather we both died fighting together, if we lose, than leave her to her fate with the Vikings."

To the thane's surprise, his elder son Aelfric agreed.

"He has to," Aelfstan laughed, "she's threatened to break his arm if he doesn't!"

He had heard enough. It was time to assert his authority.

"I'll hear no more of this," he ordered. "Bring her here at once. If necessary I'll put her under guard."

But now the two young men were looking at each other awkwardly.

"The fact is," Aelfric confessed, "she's already left the camp. She says she'll follow us anyway, if you refuse," he explained. "If you change your mind and agree, though, then we're to let her know by leaving a sign in the woods up there," and he gestured towards the hill nearby.

Aelfwald gazed at his son in stupefaction.

"And you didn't stop her?"

Aelfstan grinned.

"How, father? She was already armed and we weren't."

The thane was lost for words. He was not sure whether he wanted to explode with fury or burst out laughing. Finally he sighed.

"I shall be the laughing stock of the whole army," he acknowledged. "Tell her she rides."

A few days later, they started.

[319]

The camp at Athelney was left with a light guard. As well as leaving Aelfgifu, it had also been Aelfwald's intention to leave Port at the camp, but when the sheep farmer pleaded with him – "Let me fight at your side my lord, as I swore an oath to do; and let me avenge my wife" – he could hardly refuse. His own wife and the abbess were placed in charge of the women, and they too were armed. Even Edith proudly showed the thane a spear that she had been given, and brandished it with such ferocity that he had to turn away so as not to let her see him smile.

The valuables were loaded into Tostig's boat so that they could be transported either back to Sarum, or if necessary, to another hiding place, and the thane ordered the former slave and his family to guard them with their lives.

As he left the camp, the last thing that Aelfwald saw was the fisherman crouched over the boat by the swollen stream, his bare feet with their long, prehensile toes gripping the bank, and his dark, narrow face concentrated on his task, oblivious to the Saxon warriors passing by. He would never know, he thought, what was passing in that curious fellow's brain.

At first it caused some amusement to the soldiers that Thane Aelfwald was accompanied not by two, but three fine warriors, and that one of them was a woman.

"She's there to protect them," they cried. But some of the others, who had ridden with her and Aelfstan at Sarum assured them: "You may laugh, but the Vikings won't." And though the stern-faced thane remained aloof from all these conversations, he felt a secret flush of pride in his brave daughter as the little force made their way from Athelney.

The place where Alfred had told his thanes to gather lay two days away, at the edge of Selwood Forest. As the little force from Athelney drew nearer, Aelfwald wondered how many they would find there. Would the thanes of Wessex prove as good as their word?

It was almost with a shout of delight that, as they finally drew close, he saw a noble army gathered to greet them. They had rallied to their king, who was also their last chance to keep their independence. Together the Anglo-Saxon fyrd moved north to confront the Viking invaders.

It was the next day, fifteen miles south of Chippenham, that they saw the long lines of helmets glittering in the sun. Guthrum was waiting for them.

As the Saxons drew up into battle line, Aelfwald stood a little to the right of the centre. He was flanked by his children: Aelfric on his right, Aelfstan and Aelfgifu on his left. Immediately behind him was Port. To all of them he said:

"This is to be the last battle. We win or die."

It was a well-chosen site – a broad piece of open ground, and fairly dry. As he looked to the right, Aelfwald noticed that there was a huge, untended field, over whose brown furrows the crows were sweeping, unconcerned by the lives of the warriors nearby; and in his heart he knew, at that moment, that they would win. The Anglo-Saxon fyrd was going to defend its fields.

It was a long battle. The Vikings fought furiously; but the Saxons were fighting for their existence. As each Saxon advance was checked by the terrible battle axes, it fell back like a retreating tide, reformed and crashed forward again.

"They're like the waves of the sea," Aelfwald thought. And indeed it seemed that no matter how many blows the Vikings dealt, the waves of Saxon warriors continued to pound upon them endlessly. Inspired by the slight figure of their king who fought with such determination amongst them, the Saxons were unstoppable.

Aelfstan and his sister fought together, side by side, and they made such a fearsome combination that few who came up against them escaped.

All the time, however, Aelfstan had a particular object in the back of his mind, and it was at one crucial point, when the Saxons broke through the Viking line, that he saw what he had been searching for. He motioned to his sister and they began to make their way towards it. For fifteen yards away, he had caught sight of a tall figure with a pock-marked face. It was the man who had raped Port's wife. His face was imprinted on Aelfstan's memory.

Fighting their way through the mêlée, it took them some time to draw close, but as they did so, some of the Viking's companions in turn recognised them, and a cry went up: "It's the Saxon woman!" From all sides, it seemed, warriors were suddenly turning on them, for the pleasure of striking the impudent woman down.

Before they knew what had happened though, they had been transformed into a little rallying point. Saxons were rushing to their defence. A cry went up in the middle of their part of the battle: "Aelfgifu!" and seconds later they saw another group, led by Aelfric, surging towards them.

For several minutes, they became the focal point of the line; the fighting was desperate; but all the time, Aelfstan was conscious that they were drawing gradually closer to their chosen object, and now, only five yards away, he guessed that the tall, pock-marked Viking had sensed that he was their quarry. Pressing forward, at the front of the fighting, they came up with him at last.

He stared at them with scorn; swivelling round, he raised his axe to smash the young woman who was glaring at him so defiantly; but not quickly enough. Before he could strike, Aelfstan made an upward swing with his sword, so quick that the Viking never saw it, and which split him open from stem to stern.

The rape at the sheep farm had been avenged.

Meanwhile, none had fought more bravely than Port. He had prepared himself for battle by strapping a small round shield of the Viking type to his right arm while in his good left hand he wielded a short, light sword with which he showed a surprising dexterity.

"You fight better with your left hand than you did with your right," the thane called to him. Certainly he was glad of Port's presence. Each time Aelfwald turned in the thick of the fray, the solemn sheep farmer was always there, either just behind him, guarding his back, or on his left side, acting like a second shield.

But it was at the turning point of the battle, when the Vikings, after seeming the first time to waver, were launching a furious counter attack, that Port performed his most noble service.

Aelfwald and the sheep farmer had found themselves unguarded for a moment, just as two huge Vikings had borne down upon them, one from each side. As ill luck would have it, the ground on which they were standing was muddy and slippery, so that when the thane despatched one with a magnificent thrust from his sword, he slipped and fell, while at his side, Port was knocked to the ground by the other with a mighty blow that completely shattered his shield. As he struggled to get up, he saw the Viking's axe raised above Aelfwald.

He knew what he must do. With a calm gesture, he raised his good arm to take the blow that was meant for his lord. While the heavy blade, deflected, bit past the bone, Aelfwald had just time to recover, raise himself on one knee and plunge his sword into the surprised Viking's heart. Then he seized his loyal retainer and dragged him from the fight.

Port lived; but his remaining hand, and most of the forearm, was gone.

Soon afterwards, the Viking retreat began; within the hour, Alfred was master of the field, and as night fell, Guthrum and the tattered remains of his horde limped into Chippenham. The Saxons camped outside.

Aelfwald himself dressed Port's terrible wound and his sons made a rough stretcher with their spears, on which they carried him. It was not long before the report of his gesture was common knowledge throughout the fyrd.

"Port swore to fight for me in my hall," the thane announced. "Never was any Saxon's vow better kept."

And the other thanes agreed:

"The sheep farmer fought like a noble today."

Port, weak though he was, felt a glow of pride. But at the back of his mind he could not help wondering: "With both my hands gone, what shall I do?"

As the Saxon force hurried after the retreating Vikings, one figure remained behind. The thane's youngest son did not leave the field of battle.

For Aelfstan still had one more duty to perform.

Alone, as the sun sank, he searched among the fallen bodies for the pock-marked Viking. It did not take him long and when he found him, he knelt on the ground. Silently and skilfully he worked with his knife for half an hour, cutting and peeling, until he had carefully separated the man's skin from his body. Then, rolling the dripping skin up, he slung it over his back and mounted his horse to ride after the others.

At dawn the next morning he found a small wooden chapel just under the walls of Chippenham, and there he nailed the flayed skin on to the door.

It was a pagan custom, but one of which, in the circumstances, none of the Saxons could disapprove.

Guthrum held out at the small settlement of Chippenham for two weeks. Alfred and the fyrd awaited him. Finally, the Viking offered his surrender, together with a promise to leave Wessex for ever. Three weeks later, Guthrum and thirty of his nobles submitted to baptism at the Saxon camp of Athelney, in the presence of Alfred and his thanes.

Among them was a new thane who had no hands.

For a few days after the surrender at Chippenham, there was an open air ceremony at which the king gave his loyal followers their rewards.

When he came to the men from Sarum, Aelfwald was pleased to see a twinkle in the king's blue eyes.

"Where is Port?" he asked.

The sheep farmer was brought forward and Alfred looked at his arms before declaring:

"This Welshman," this was the term often applied to men of Celtic descent, "fights like a true Saxon noble." He turned to Aelfwald with a look of enquiry and the thane nodded quickly: for the day before he had spent the morning with the king urging him to bestow this honour upon his loyal man. "Therefore," Alfred continued: "from today, Port, you are to be a thane." And then, followed by Aelfwald and his family, he solemnly embraced the astonished sheep farmer.

But this was not all. If Port was to be a thane, he must have land.

At a nod from the king, two monks now stepped forward. They held in their hands heavy sheets of parchment: for the granting of lands was carefully recorded in writing. There were two kinds of land that the king could grant: the ordinary land of the people on which the owner would owe him the feorm tax; or the still more valuable bookland, which was exempt from all taxes except military service and contributions to fortifications and bridges.

"Thane Port," Alfred announced, "I will give you bookland."

The sheep farmer flushed with pleasure; his eyes opened wide as the monk, holding up the charter, read it out in Latin, which he translated into Saxon as he went along.

The wording of the charter, like all such documents at that time, was resounding.

In the name of the High Thunderer, the Creator of the World, be it declared to all present, absent and to come, by the contents of this charter that I, Alfred, by the grace of God King of the Anglo-Saxons, give and concede to Port an estate in my ownership into his perpetual possession by hereditary right.

His own charter: his own land. Now he was truly a thane. As he listened carefully the monk continued.

And on account of his pleasing obedience I confirm the extent of the estate: that is, twenty hides near the river Avon, immediately north of Aelfwald's land.

Twenty hides! He was a rich man. With the income from that he could give his sister Edith not only her gold cross but put jewels on it too. He knew the land in question. It was a fine estate. He listened intently as the monk came to the definition of its boundaries, which was written not in Latin but in Anglo-Saxon, so that there could be no doubt about what was meant.

> First along the river, then at the bend, east over the meadow to the great tree; then north along the boundary furrow to the linch, and west along the dyke . . .

He knew every inch. Even as the monk recited, his precise mind was carefully calculating its income.

> Which lands include the place called Odda's farm, and the right to pasture in the meadow six oxen . . .

"Stop."

At this unexpected interuption from the sheep farmer, the monk looked up, astonished.

"There are eight oxen there, not six," Port objected.

Alfred stared at him, then seeing what kind of man he had to deal with, smiled.

"Are you sure?"

Port nodded.

At a sign from the king, the monk crossly altered the charter, before continuing.

> And to receive from the dairy farm there twenty weys of cheese, fifteen lambs, fifteen fleeces . . .

But Port was shaking his head.

"They produce twenty-five weys of cheese," he told the king.

Now Alfred and all those around burst out laughing, and even the monk could not suppress a smile. Again the charter was altered.

> That he may have and possess and present the aforesaid land to whomsoever he shall choose in all things with free will, except the fortification of fortresses, construction of bridges and military service.

He had land, and he had it for ever. The Charter ended with the usual flourish.

> If anyone shall insolently attempt to infringe this generous munificence, let him know that, on the great Day of Judgement when the deepest caves of Hell shall open and the whole world tremble, he will perish in the infernal fire with Judas and all traitors and suffer agonies for all eternity, if he shall not have previously made amends, with compensation.

It was done. Aelfwald and the others witnessed the charter. Port had lost his hands, but regained a portion of his ancient ancestral territory.

When it came to Aelfwald's turn, Alfred had a special gift: an inscribed ring and a small jewelled casket. To accompany these personal mementoes, he added a fine new farm.

The farm of Shockerlee lay just to the north west of Wilton, on the wooded slopes of the small ridge that rose between the two broad valleys of the Wylye and the Nadder rivers, and which was known as Grovely Wood.

Like many new farms, it had been carved out of the edge of the woodland, as its name – meaning the sheaves of corn, *shocker*, in the wood, *lee* – implied. It was excellent, well drained land.

When the king had passed on to the next thane, Aelfwald turned to Aelfstan and Aelfgifu and told them:

"You both fought bravely together. In my will, when Aelfric inherits the lands at Avonsford, you shall jointly own Shockerlee."

At the end of the granting of lands, Alfred addressed those present:

"Remember," he said with a smile, as his pale blue eyes searched them out one by one, "when you look at your estates in times to come, that they were won when we saved the kingdom of Wessex, at Edington."

There was one other memorial to that day however, which the king did not plan.

Two days later, Aelfstan and a group of young men were riding over the high ground near the battlefield and the young Saxon's thoughts returned to the extraordinary events of those recent months, and to the battles, side by side with his sister. In later times, he thought, who would believe the part that Aelfgifu had played.

"She should have a memorial," he cried aloud.

As he gazed up at the bare turf on the hillside above him, he saw what he should do; and calling to his friends he told them what he planned.

All that day, and for two more afterwards, the party of young men worked busily; and when they had finished, carved in the chalk hillside where they had cut back the turf and staring proudly over the valley below, there was a fine white horse, forty feet across.

Aelfstan looked at it with pride.

"That's for Aelfgifu, and our victory," he told them; and feeling that he had done a fine thing, he returned to the camp more contented than he had been for many months.

The chalk had been well dug. The white horse on the hillside remained.

Only one other surprise awaited the thane when he returned to Athelney.

Tostig had disappeared.

He had gone one night, taking one of the boats loaded with valuables with him. He had departed without warning and left even his family behind. At first the thane supposed he had gone for some legitimate reason; but he had not.

He was never seen again.

The kingdom of Wessex was by no means free of its troubles. There were still many battles to be fought and accommodations to be made with the Vikings on the island. There were also personal disappointments for the king, as when Earldorman Wulfhere, a little after Edington, suddenly and unexpectedly defected to the Vikings in the Danelaw.

But never again would the kingdom of Wessex be in danger of extinction. The burghs were fortified, new monasteries and schools were built, the nunnery where Edith remained at Wilton was re-established even more splendidly than before; and despite his many campaigns, Alfred found time, as he had always hoped, to translate his chosen classics into the Anglo-Saxon tongue.

During the rest of his reign and those of his successors, the influence and rule of Wessex was gradually extended over the Danelaw; the Scandinavian raiders mostly settled and were even converted to Christianity; and the process by which the Anglo-Saxon and Danish people gradually became fused into a single island kingdom continued steadily.

Although, for a short period before the Norman Conquest, the island came to be ruled as part of a larger Scandinavian confederacy by the great King Canute, it was no longer in doubt that the kingdom of England was a single whole, and its people English.

That this was so was thanks to the efforts of King Alfred and his thanes in the heart of Wessex, in the winter and spring of the year of Our Lord, 878.

The Castle

THE TWO FIGURES stood side by side on the wall of the castle of Sarisberie. It was a week after Easter and the weather had turned pleasantly warm.

The taller man wore a fine black cloak of wool, faced with silk and held by a golden chain across his chest; his brown hair, greying at the temples, was dressed in a curious style: it was long, and parted on both sides while the locks in the centre were brushed forward into a fringe; his beard was curled. His face was long, with an aquiline nose and two deep lines that folded from almost under his eyes to the corners of his long, thin mouth which occasionally turned down with an expression of sardonic amusement. This was Richard de Godefroi, minor Norman knight.

As he glanced down now at the stout figure of Nicholas who stood in his leather jerkin beside him, the impassive lines of his face did not mask the fact that his eyes were troubled. For the stoneworker had just asked in his native English a question that the French-speaking knight understood perfectly, but did not wish to answer:

"Why is the bishop filling the castle with weapons?"

Across the fields below lay the undefended town of Wilton where, in times of peace, the sheriff held the county court; to the north, up the valley which three generations of the Norman's family had come to love, lay the knight's English estate of Avonsford, which he held of the great Wiltshire landlord, William of Sarisberie. As he gazed out now, he could see every detail of the landscape: the day had that sparkling clarity that presages rain – like the serene face of a man, Richard thought grimly, who is about to commit treachery.

"Perhaps he means to hold the castle against the king," the stoneworker suggested.

Which was exactly what Richard dreaded.

The castle towered over the place where the five rivers met. It was far higher, and more terrible, than any building that Sarum had seen before.

On top of the huge chalk ring of the original dune on its windswept promontory, there now rose a high, nearly completed curtain wall of flint. Outside and below it lay an untidy mass of houses and allotments. Inside, in the centre of the dune, a second, inner hill had been raised by the Norman conquerors – an enormous mound, an acre across at its summit; and this was surrounded by another frowning wall. Within this central enclosure, they had built yet again – a great, grey tower. And so, like an inverted telescope, the castle soared up: from promontory to wall, from wall to inner mound, to second wall and on, up to the final massive tower with its battlements in the sky.

This was the typical Norman stronghold of mound and enclosure – motte and bailey. When William the Bastard of Normandy and his following of Norman, Breton and other assorted adventurers had conquered the Anglo-Saxon kingdom of England in 1066, he had speedily erected castles all over the land. Unlike the modestly fortified Saxon burghs, the Norman castles were tall, compact and almost unassailable. First built of wood they had gradually been converted, in the reigns of his two sons, and now his grandson Stephen, to bastions of stone. The castle of Sarisberie was not one of the largest, but it was a significant place nonetheless. It was here, when he received the great Domesday inventory of his island kingdom, that William the Conqueror had summoned his nobles to perform their oath of fealty to him – a memorable ceremony that Godefroi's grandfather had attended. Within the broad sweep of the curtain wall it even included the massive, towered cathedral that was the bishop's seat. The stone pinnacles and thatched roofs of the castle's many houses clustered tightly around the central mound with its soaring *dongeon* which hung over the landscape, heavy, dark and menacing.

The castle belonged to the king: it was held for him by the sheriff. So it had always been in the reigns of the Conqueror, and his sons Rufus and Henry, when the king was in firm control and the castle was a symbol of military rule and order. But four years ago Henry's nephew Stephen had ascended the English throne, and though his claim had been supported by most of the magnates and been sanctioned by the pope, there were already murmurs of discontent as it became clear that he was not as strong as those who had gone before. And now the castle was in the bishop's hands, instead; and the bishop was filling it with arms.

The feudal system, under which most of Europe now lay, had enormous weaknesses. In the centuries following the break-up of the empires of Rome and later of Charlemagne in the west, first tribes and then individual families had seized power over huge tracts of land which had yet to coalesce into the countries of modern Europe; and although a powerful king might assert his sovereignty over many lesser magnates, the individual feudal lords were in a state of almost perpetual dispute amongst themselves. No people claimed a single country as their nation state: Europe was a huge patchwork of estates to be bought, sold, fought for or obtained by marriage. Even a minor knight like Godefroi had estates on both sides of the English Channel. True, there were laws to govern feudal relationships and possession; true, the Church had proclaimed a Christian peace and ordered days of truce to be observed in every territory. The result, however, was only to add endless legal disputes and appeals to the long and complex process of intermittent violence that was the feudal world.

It was this system of formalised chaos that the counts and dukes of Normandy had tried to reduce to order first in Normandy and then, with more success in the conquered island of England. For at the conquest, the Kingdom of Harold had fallen, at least in theory, entirely into the hands of Duke William; and though he had granted to his chief supporters the vast estates of the leading Anglo-Saxons, they were to hold them only as his tenants in return for military service. Though trusted lords were sometimes given wider powers where the king's primitive bureaucracy was not large enough to cope, justice too – and most of the profits of justice in the form of fines – was generally the king's. Such a centralised system, such order, was unique in Europe.

It worked well, as long as the king was strong.

But Stephen was not, and already his right to rule had been challenged by the late king's daughter, and widow of the German ruler, the Empress Matilda. It was just the excuse that ambitious English nobles were looking for: where two sides might bid for their support, there must be chances for profit. In the spring of 1139 there was treachery in the air.

And no man was more treacherous than the bishop.

"I think he is a devil," Nicholas remarked, and though Godefroi gave him a stern look to discourage such impertinence, he would privately have agreed. The bishop was usually absent, but when he appeared, his great, heavy jowl and angry, watchful eyes made even the knight afraid.

Roger of Caen, a low-born adventurer, had first ingratiated himself with King Henry, it was said, because as a young chaplain he could complete the mass before the King went out hunting in less time than anyone else. He had risen rapidly to be Chancellor of England, running the whole machinery of government for Henry with a ruthless efficiency matched only by his own greed and ambition. He was a priest, but he kept mistresses and had a son who came to succeed him as chancellor. As a reward for the family's services the king had made him Bishop of Sarisberie and his two nephews Bishops of Lincoln and Ely, so that, within a single generation, his family had raised itself to a wealth and power equalled by only a few of the greatest nobles in the land.

Furthermore the ailing King Henry and weak Stephen had allowed Roger to hold castles as well: in the spring of 1139 the family controlled not only Sarisberie, but the other southern castles of Malmesbury, Sherborne and Devizes. And now they were being filled with arms. As Godefroi had warned his wife that morning: "One false move by the king and there will be anarchy."

It was all the worse for the knight of Avonsford, for he had secret plans of his own – plans which a civil war would ruin. As he looked down now at the little workman by his side he pursed his long lips and remarked in Nicholas's own language:

"You'd better pray, then."

The relationship between the two men was an easy one. When the descendants of Aelfwald the thane fought and lost at Hastings, they were deprived of most of their estates. The estate at Avonsford had been granted, along with dozens of others, to the great family of which William of Sarisberie was the present head, and they in turn had given it to the Godefroi knights as hereditary tenants. Though the thanes and minor landowners had lost their estates, the humbler folk – the semi-free villeins like the family of Nicholas – had suffered no particular harm. They now had a new lord of the manor to whom they owed services or rents and who held a summary court of justice over the estate; but this was little different from their status in the old days under Canute, Edward the Confessor or Harold. The family of Godefroi, though stern military men, had not been oppressive lords. Though they spoke Norman French, they had soon learned to make themselves understood in the local English dialect, and had treated the family of craftsmen with respect. It was Nicholas's father who had helped to build the Norman's house, and when Nicholas's skill with his hands had shown itself, Richard had let him go to work on the castle buildings in return for a modest rent to cover the manual service he owed the manor, which was easily covered by the wages he received in the castle.

One thing that the family had acquired since the conquest was a nickname. It was because of their skill in building. For often, when the Godefroi knights could not be bothered to remember the individual names of Nicholas or his father before him, they would shout: "Here, do this, Masoun," using their own Norman word meaning 'stoneworker' – and though the villagers in Avonsford still called him Nicholas, they too, half in mockery at the Norman's arrogant call, and half out of respect for his skill, would sometimes call after him: "Here, Nicholas – Masoun."

Now he looked at the knight's saturnine face thoughtfully. Although he had known Godefroi all his life, he still did not find it easy to gauge his mood; and it was important that he choose his moment carefully.

For the stoneworker had an important matter of his own on his mind, a subject that he wished to broach only at the right time. He glanced down at his short, stubby fingers while he considered whether to speak.

"You have a villein on your estate," he said finally. "Godric Body."

Godefroi knew the young fellow well – a meagre, insignificant little serf of seventeen. The boy's mother, he knew, had been Nicholas's sister; his father a fisherman. Both were dead and he had no relations, so far as the knight knew, except Nicholas and a cousin of the boy's father, who was something of a troublemaker.

"Well? What do you want?" His voice was sharp and cold; he had learnt that it was best to be severe when people asked for favours, as it was clear the fellow was about to do.

Nicholas cleared his throat.

But as he did so, the air was pierced with a scream.

Godric Body could not believe his luck.

In the first place, he had eaten meat the evening before. It was not a thing he often did, except when he snared a rabbit or received his modest share of the meat from the cullings of livestock that took place at midsummer and the start of winter. But his uncle Nicholas and his family, though humble villeins like himself with little land, were far better off. Thanks to his skill, the stoneworker often received twice the normal labourer's wage of a silver penny a day and his family not only ate meat, but on occasion shared it with their poor relation.

"My wife looks like a pear," Nicholas remarked with satisfaction as the cheerful little woman with her huge posterior bustled about the room; "and my children are like apples." As Godric looked at their rosy cheeks and round faces he had to agree that the description was exact.

If he closed his eyes, he could still taste the salted pork, smell its aroma: it brought a smile to his usually dispirited face.

Godric Body was small and thin. The narrow face which he inherited from his fisherman father always seemed to be pale and pinched; shocks of reddish hair grew unevenly, like tufts of grass, on his head, giving him an untidy look. His hands were thin and delicate and looked unsuited to the rough work which was his lot. And worst of all, he had been born with a hunchback – not a pronounced and grotesque hump, but an un-mistakable curvature that thrust his head savagely forward and caused the other children to call him Godric the rat. His parents had hoped he would not live, his mother because she feared he would be unable to work, his father because he loathed to see what he called a runt.

He lived, and he worked – painfully but with a remarkable persever-ance; and as he grew older even the villagers would grudgingly admit that the ungainly boy with the surprisingly soft and dreamy eyes could carve figures in wood with a dexterity that far surpassed anyone else at Avonsford. His parents had died when he was thirteen and since then he had lived a lonely life, completing his work on the estate painfully, uncertain of how to express himself, and nursing a single passion and ambition as to how to better his lot.

His second piece of luck was that his uncle Nicholas had agreed to speak to the lord of the manor on his behalf that very day. He knew that Godefroi, whom he dared not address himself, respected the stone-worker and he was full of hope.

Now here was a third piece of luck. For before his eyes in the small market place that lay within the castle precincts, an extraordinary scene was developing that promised to provide a rich and unforseen entertain-ment. With surprising determination, his bent little figure nudged and ducked its way to the front of the crowd to get a better view; and what he saw made his face break into a broad grin.

The two women were facing each other in the centre of the square.

The larger of the two seemed about to burst. She was a massively built figure, and the scarlet woollen robe she wore seemed to accentuate the rage that radiated from her. Despite the rolls of fat about her person, it was clear that she was powerful and dangerous. Her heavy cheeks which were, even when she was calm, as red as her dress, had now puckered up so that her eyes were no more than slits. Godric stared at her with a mixture of loathing and admiration: he knew her well: she was Herleva, wife of his own cousin William atte Brigge.

"Harlot! Thief!" the huge woman shouted; and then, her whole face contorted with venom, she hissed: "Bondwoman."

The object of these insults was a blond, handsome young woman in her mid-twenties whose slight plumpness only added to the attractiveness of which she was comfortably aware. The simple shift she wore with a girdle at the waist was light blue, and set off her hair as she tossed her head in contempt at the older woman. Godric knew her too. She was the wife of a Saxon farmer, John of Shockley.

It was true that she had been a bondwoman, a lowly villein owned, like himself, by a Norman lord until she had married the freeman of Shockley. But at the intended insult she only smiled and then cried mockingly:

"A year and a day."

The crowd laughed. It was well known that William atte Brigge had run away from the Avonsford estate when he was a boy and lived for a year and a day at the little town of Twyneham on the coast; a villein who escaped to a town for this period was allowed his freedom if his lord failed to claim him. He had become a tanner – an unpopular trade on account of the pungent smells the tannery always produced – and moved to Wilton, where he was disliked for his bad temper as much as his trade, and where he acquired the added name of atte Brigge because his house lay by a small wooden bridge over a backwater of the river.

"But your husband's a freedman," the younger woman added loudly, "because no Godefroi ever wanted to get him back."

The crowd roared its approval. It was always said that the estate had been glad to be rid of a troublemaker.

For Herleva, this was too much. With a shout of rage she hurled herself towards the young woman, and in a moment had ripped her shift off one shoulder with her huge hands and knocked her to the ground, before crashing down on top of her. It was this that caused the scream which the Norman and the mason had heard on the ramparts.

Against the weight of Herleva, the younger woman had little chance. Her hair was pulled; slaps rained upon her face. But she fought back gamely, using her greater agility to kick the older woman savagely and to open scratches on her heavy jowled face that began to bleed profusely. The crowd did nothing to intervene. No better entertainment had been seen in years. Godric, who had no love for Herleva, saw the scratches open on her face and rubbed his thin hands together for joy.

The quarrel between the two women had its roots several generations before. When the descendants of Aelfwald the thane lost their estates at the Conquest, the farm at Shockley in the Wylye valley was given to the Abbess of Wilton. She took pity on them however, and allowed them to stay on the farm as tenants. There they remained, still claiming their ancient thanely status, but living as modest farmers – free men under the law but little better off in reality than the more prosperous of the villeins. Soon after this, a dispute arose when the daughter of the family, who had married a burgess of Wilton, claimed that the tenancy had been promised to her rather than to her brother. The abbess in her court ruled against her and confirmed her brother in his tenancy; but the matter did not rest there. The burgess and his wife tried, without success, to take the matter to a higher court, and when the commissioners of the great Domesday land survey inspected the area, the clerks noted that the tenancy was in dispute. The years passed, but the burgess and his wife never lost their furious resentment: nor did their daughter, Herleva. And when she married William atte Brigge, that obstinate and greedy man had made the cause his own and sworn to the family of John of Shockley more than once:

"I'll go to the king himself. You'll be turned out before I die, I promise you."

Such lawsuits were common; they could also last for generations: the threat lay like a cloud over the farmer's life, and whenever William or Herleva saw one of the Shockley family, they never missed their chance to make matters worse by insulting them.

The screaming matches between the two women were not unusual either, but never before had one developed into a physical fight, and to Godric's delight, the fight was reaching epic proportions.

Herleva's weight had triumphed. She rolled the younger woman over and tore the clothes from her back. And as her victim screamed, Herleva, ignoring her own wounds and in an access of fury, was casting about for some object with which to belabour her.

But now the circle of spectators suddenly parted and fell silent, as Richard de Godefroi strode towards the two women. He was closely followed by their husbands – both looking frightened – who had been hastily summoned from other parts of the castle. At the sight of the Norman knight, even Herleva forgot her fury and got to her feet awkwardly. Shockley's wife pulled her torn clothes hastily over her breasts.

In the silence Godefroi's voice was icy.

"You are breaking the peace. Do you want the ducking stool or to be put in the stocks?"

The knight's words would certainly be enough in the hundred or borough court to ensure such a punishment for them; and besides the indignity, the ducking stool, in particular, could be a hazardous affair if the victim was held under the water for too long. Shockley's wife shivered.

"Take your women away," the knight ordered the two men curtly. "If they break the peace again, I'll see they answer for it in court." He waved at the crowd peremptorily. "Disperse," he cried. Then he turned on his heel and stalked away.

John of Shockley led his wife quickly from the scene. But William stood gazing at Herleva's face. His black brows contracted furiously.

He was a striking figure. In many respects he was typical of the ancient river folk who were still to be found in Fisherton and other hamlets along the five rivers. He had their long fingers and toes; and his narrow face with its close-set eyes was an almost exact replica of the face of Godric Body. But there all resemblance between the tanner and his cousin ended. William atte Brigge was tall, spare and strong: his hair was dark; and his eyes were jet-black, hard and cruel.

And he was in a rage – not because his wife had attacked the Shockley woman, but because she had made a fool of him. As Herleva drew herself up, a little shaken by what she had done, he gave her a vicious look that made even that large woman blench. Then he looked around the square.

Godric had been so engrossed by the drama taking place in front of him that he had not noticed he was the only person left after the crowd had broken up. Suddenly he realised that the tanner was striding towards him.

William atte Brigge glowered at him. The sight of his crippled kinsman, whom he loathed because he was deformed, always angered him, and now he was sure the youth was laughing at him. His mouth contracted into a snarl. As he strode across the little square, he glanced quickly about him to make sure that there was no one watching; then, seeing they were alone, he kicked the boy as hard as he could, so that he rolled helplessly on the ground. Without a word, he kicked the boy three more times before walking away. He had relieved some of his temper.

In silence Godric watched him go. The kicks had hurt. But crippled as he was, it took more than his rich cousin William to break his spirit, and as he slowly got up, he managed a grin.

"You'll pay for those kicks," he muttered. The thought gave him comfort.

It was as he left the castle for his home up the valley that he noticed John of Shockley and his wife. They were standing together in the shadow of the gateway and he could see that they were arguing furiously. He instinctively liked the farmer, and he was glad that his handsome wife had scratched Herleva. Yes, he decided, he would make William pay for his villainy.

He would have been disappointed if he could have heard what John was saying to his wife.

"You must make peace with Herleva," he urged.

"She started it. She called me a harlot," she protested.

"You must turn the other cheek; walk away."

"Never. I scratched hers," his fiery wife replied with satisfaction.

But still John only shook his head.

"We must make peace with them, not provoke them," he pleaded.

It seemed to the girl that sometimes her husband was weak. It was not lack of courage, she was sure of that; but his honest blue eyes always grew troubled at any suggestion of a quarrel. He would run his hand over his fair, close-cropped beard nervously, and search endlessly for a compromise where some other men would rather fight.

The threat from William cast a shadow over his life which nothing she could say would dispel. Each night he prayed that William would drop his suit and be reconciled, for the memory of his grandfather's loss of the family estates was like an open wound in his mind.

"Do not anger William," he used to caution his wife. "We could lose the last thing that we have."

But she would toss her head with impatience and retort: "If you're a thane, why are you so timid?"

Yet she had seen him face a bull that had broken loose, and which no other man would go near, with perfect coolness: so he could not be a coward. She did not understand it.

Nor could John of Shockley explain his feelings himself. He only knew that he loved his farm, and that to him, peace seemed more important than it did to other men.

"Will you go to Herleva?" he asked hopelessly.

She shook her head.

"Not until William comes to you."

Godefroi entered the church alone.

It was a large, three-aisled structure with heavy, rounded arches which the Normans had built in the outer ring of the castle. Like most Norman churches, it was designed in the form of a simple cross, and to this Bishop Roger was adding splendid embellishments.

He was glad to enter its quiet, solemn spaces and leave behind the noise and the brawling that had so irritated him a few moments before.

For Richard de Godefroi had important matters to consider.

The stately arches and the cool light pleased him. Forty years before when the church had first been completed, it was nearly destroyed by fire. It was then that Roger had started to rebuild this new and heavier structure on the shell of the original, and the work of rebuilding that kept Nicholas and many others so busy had been going on ever since. A few of the tombs and the pillars had been painted, but while the work on the roof continued, much of the decoration of the interior had been held over. The bare stone, so solemn and simple, suited his mood. He felt his irritation fall away and breathed more easily.

The object of his quest was a modest stone tomb that lay on the north side of the bishop's new presbytery. It was here that the knight liked to pray, and as he sank to his knees he touched the bare slab affectionately. Beneath it lay the remains of the former bishop, the saintly Osmund who had built the first church. Richard could just remember him, a quiet, white-haired man whom children used to follow in the street. It was Osmund who had brought such an air of sanctity to the cathedral on its bleak castle hill; it was he who had collected the canons and other priests who had turned the grim castle into a place of learning; and it was Osmund who had begun to set out the rules for the ordering of the cathedral and its services which later, under the name of the Sarum missal, would be used all over England and beyond. He had been, and to Godefroi he still was, the guiding spirit of the place. That the previous king had given the bishopric of this holy man to the evil Roger was a crime which even the loyal knight had found it hard to forgive.

Alone now, Godefroi raised his long, aquiline face and spoke aloud to the bishop's tomb.

"What shall I do, to save my soul?"

It was not an unusual question. Like every man from the king downwards, Godefroi knew very well that the whole world was in a state of perpetual war – not just between order and chaos, but between God and the Devil, the spirit and the flesh. This was the universal conflict, which would not be resolved until the Day of Judgement, which gave all life its dazzling colour and its terrible poignancy. Whatever his position,

[335]

feudal lord or knight, burgess or villein – even Bishop Roger himself – each man knew that he must make his peace with God, or after death suffer perpetual hellfire.

Yet for a Norman knight to save his soul, the Church had devised some attractive choices. He could, like other men, do penances; he could endow the church with lands, or better yet, he could travel.

In his grandfather's day it had been easy. When Pope Urban II, in the year of Our Lord 1095, had announced the First Crusade, the previous Richard de Godefroi had gladly gone. What more could any knight ask for than the chance to purge his soul in the warfare he knew best and most enjoyed? He thought with envy of those days and of his grandfather's tales of the privations they had endured and the brave campaigns in those distant lands under the parching sun. These had been the stories that fired his imagination when he was a child.

It was not only the thought of winning honour in arms that attracted him. Deep within him he felt a restlessness, a wanderlust that, despite his contented life on his manor, seemed to grow stronger and more urgent with the passing of the years. He could not explain it. Yet the explanation was simple. For the Norman conquerors of England were mainly Norsemen, cousins of the Danish Vikings, who had only settled in northern France a century and a half before. It was not only to England either that this tribe of adventurers had gone: they were inveterate wanderers. Norman knights had already made names for themselves as mercenaries in Italy, where they had first seized tracts of land and then become the most powerful allies of the pope. They had made themselves lords of Sicily. Kinsmen of his own, he knew, had sailed their long ships all over the Mediterranean and in those warmer climes carved for themselves splendid fiefs which made his modest manor look humble indeed. They journeyed south and served the church just as in earlier centuries, his pagan Viking forbears had roamed the northern world and when they had died, been buried or burned with their ships, so that their spirits could make the still greater journey over the soul-bridge to join their ancestors and the northern gods. The spirit of the roaming Norse adventurer – though now he spoke French and lived off the land – was still in his blood.

The crusade had been so easy: a warrior could travel, fight for God, and have all his sins forgiven him. He could have asked for nothing more. But alas, in his own generation there had been no crusade. Which left the next alternative – a pilgrimage, preferably to the Holy Land.

And this was the problem facing Richard de Godefroi. For years he had been working to provide for his wife and three children; both his estates were now in perfect order. For years, not a day had gone by when he did not dream of setting out on his life's great adventure. He yearned to go, and it was time to begin.

"I'm almost fifty," he murmured. "If I don't go soon, it will be too late."

But now, just when he was ready, a foolish king and a group of unscrupulous and powerful lords were threatening to tear the country apart in a feudal war. If it broke out, he knew he could not leave his family; and in the current uncertainty, his own feudal overlord, William of Sarisberie, would probably not give him permission to go as far as one of the shrines in Italy, let alone to the Holy Land.

He remained at the tomb of Osmund for half an hour, supposing that he was praying, but in fact weighing up the likely dispositions of the great feudal magnates; and realising with a sigh that he was reaching no conclusion, he rose at last, and made his way slowly out of the church.

It came as no surprise to him that Nicholas was waiting for him respectfully just outside the door. He gave a thin smile, and, remembering their interrupted conversation, cut the villein short before he could make a tiresome speech.

"Your nephew, Godric Body," he said abruptly. "What was it you wanted?"

As he looked out over the sunlit fields the following morning, it seemed to Godric Body that his life was not without hope. His uncle was working on his behalf with the lord of the manor, and the bruises from William atte Brigge's attack were not as bad as he had thought.

He stretched his hand down and ruffled the smooth hairs on the neck of the young dog that stood expectantly by his side. Named Harold, it was an animal of uncertain parentage, though he called it a strakur – the lowest kind of hunting dog, which roughly resembled a lurcher – and it had a black and tan coat and a bright and watchful pair of eyes. Godric looked down at his companion with a mischievous grin.

"We'll get even with William," he assured him; though exactly how he did not yet know.

He would be careful: only the week before, the reeve had grumpily warned him:

"I think you're a troublemaker, Godric Body. Take care: the frankpledge is watching you."

The frankpledge system, by which twelve men from each village were pledged to answer to the king's sheriff for the good behaviour of all those in their community, was an informal police force, but highly effective – for in the event of their allowing a criminal to escape its members were liable to a fine themselves. Godric knew that the reeve had only picked on him because he was small and weak; his crimes were confined to the petty theft of occasionally short-changing Godefroi on some of his corn or livestock; so he did not take the threat too seriously; and he continued to think of his revenge.

The life of Godric Body was bleak. He owned almost nothing. The reeve, the most senior man in the village, held a whole hide scattered, as were all the individual landholdings, amongst the strips of the two huge open fields of Paradise and Purgatory beside the village of Avonsford. Nicholas and his family held a virgate, or quarter hide – some thirty acres in all from which they could derive a modest surplus. His uncle also had forty sheep, which he pastured on the common land on the slopes above. But the lowly Godric, at the bottom of the feudal social scale, held only two acres of strip land. When his father died a few years earlier, Godefroi

[337]

took the best of the three poor cows the family pastured in the common meadow. This was not an imposition but the customary heriot payment to which the lord of the manor was entitled when a villein died. Godric also owed Godefroi four days work a week on the lord's land – hard work, from harvesting to carrying dung and weeding; and while this duty was normally shared out amongst the family of a villein, poor Godric, all alone, had to complete it by himself. This was not all he owed. At Easter he would give the local priest the customary present of Easter eggs from the dozen hens he kept beside the hut, and at harvest, a tenth of the small amount of corn from his strips went as payment of tithe to the priest as well. Alone, as long as he was fit, he could just support himself; but he needed a wife to help him. And though his mother, looking at his wretched physique, had always assured him that no one would ever marry him, the spirited little fellow had not given up hope.

He even had a candidate in mind. For the youngest daughter of the village smith had suffered a skin ailment as a child which had left her pock-marked and undeniably plain. She was a small creature with eyes that squinted so that they gave her a look of suspicion, and there was often an air of bitterness about her that was not attractive. Her family were almost as poor as his and she always looked hungry. And yet in other ways she was not, he considered, so ill-looking and he had let her see that he was interested. If the smith had had any better hope for her he would have driven Godric away; but as things were, he tolerated him; and as for Mary, she had once or twice, without great enthusiasm, allowed him to hold her hand. Despite her suspicious look, he found that he was excited by the two small breasts that had begun to jut out sharply from her thirteen-year-old chest, and he had made himself a promise that by the harvest, he would take them in his hands.

And perhaps, the smith had acknowledged to his wife and daughter at Easter, there were a few things to be said for young Godric. Whether he had inherited the skill from his mother's family, or whether it had been given him as a special gift by God to make up for his deformity, there was no question that he could carve wood with astonishing genius. His speciality was the carving of shepherd's crooks. The badgers, the sheep, the elegant swans that adorned the curving handles seemed to come to life in the hand. Godefroi had also given him a few pieces of work in the manor house, and from these he had been able to add a few pence to his subsistence wages. But he was still painfully poor.

"And he's not strong," the smith's wife complained. "The work in the fields is hard for him. If only he were a shepherd."

If only. For this was exactly what Godric wanted to be. At every spare moment from his other work, he would roam the high ground where the sheep were grazing, talking to the shepherds who guarded them, and helping gladly in the washing and shearing, without needing to be asked. There was little about the care of sheep that he did not already know; and certainly he was physically far better suited to this work than to the heavy drudgery in the fields. A shepherd, too, was entitled to a bowl of whey all through the summer, ewes' milk on Sunday, one of the lord's lambs at weaning time and a fleece at shearing. This had been the subject of his uncle's plea to Godefroi the day before.

"Make the boy one of your shepherds," he begged, "and I'll vouch for him that you won't be disappointed. He's not cut out for the fields."

Godefroi had not committed himself. He disliked being manoeuvred.

"But he didn't say no," Nicholas told his nephew.

Since it was the day after Hokeday, the second Tuesday after Easter, there was much to do. On Hokeday, the community's sheep were folded on the lord of the manor's lands where they would remain until Martinmas in November, so that the lord would have the benefit of their richest manure during the summer months for his fields. All through the morning Godric helped the other villeins to erect the stout wattle sheepfolds on the slopes above the valley. Then at noon he was summoned to help one of the teams of oxen which were harnessed two by two to pull the heavy plough. It was to turn the huge field which was to lie fallow that season. By mid-afternoon, the reeve had no further work for him, and he was told he could go.

This was an unexpected piece of good luck since there were still many hours of daylight left, and he was hardly even tired. It did not take him long to return to the village, collect his dog, and set out down the valley.

It was quite by chance that he found his opportunity to take his revenge on William that day.

He had walked down the valley with no particular object except to stay clear of the village in case the reeve changed his mind; but as it was a fine day and the dog Harold was eager to go forward, he soon found himself skirting the castle walls and turning east across the lightly wooded bowl of land below.

He had gone another mile before he stopped abruptly; for it was only then that he realised suddenly that he had carelessly entered a forbidden area.

Without thinking, he had entered the royal forest of Clarendon.

The Norman royal forests covered a huge area, almost a fifth of the kingdom, and Sarum lay at the centre of some of the greatest. To the west, between the rivers Wylye and Nadder lay the ancient woods of Grovely, and past that, running north to south just as it had in King Alfred's day, the broad band of Selwood. To the south west, where the grass-covered *agger* of the old Roman road to Dorchester could still be seen, was another hunting area, the wild and desolate region of Cranborne Chase. But it was immediately to the east of the place where the five rivers met that the largest forest in the south of the island began. Here, stretching roughly north to south, from the north eastern edge of Salisbury plain, down past Sarum and on in a huge broadening sweep that did not end until it reached the Solent, lay forty-seven miles of continuous woodland and wasteland. Through the Middle Ages the names given to its various parts would become well known in the island's history: from Savernake in the north, Clarendon just past the village of Britford below Sarum, to the so-called New Forest that stretched to the coast. Within its bounds lay not only woodland but open lawns – grasslands where livestock could graze –

and areas of wilderness. And almost the whole of it, every deer, every boar and every tree belonged to the king and was reserved for his hunting.

It was protected by strict forest laws. A man might, with a licence, pick up dead wood for his fire; but if he touched a living tree he would be fined. No farmer could turn his pigs or cattle loose to graze anywhere in this vast area unless he paid a fee to the agisters who regulated all the forest pasturing; and though a man might kill one of the unreserved warren animals or fowl – the hares, foxes, squirrels, the partridges, pheasants or woodcock – woe betide him if he touched a deer. That offence was punishable by maiming or death.

Godric knew that he had already committed a crime. For Harold had not been lawed.

It was a sensible precaution which the foresters enforced strictly: any but the smallest dogs were forbidden to enter the forest unless three claws from their forepaw had been cut off: a painless operation, but one that left the animal too lame to chase the deer. Lawbreakers were fined and their dogs might be lawed on the spot. Godric rarely entered the forest, and, having already trained Harold to help with driving the sheep, at which the young dog had shown a remarkable talent, he had no wish to have him lawed. He called the dog to him quickly and began to retrace his steps.

Before he had gone a hundred yards, he froze.

He had seen an agister.

Fortunately, the agister had not yet seen him. He was walking slowly through the wood and was not at that moment concerned with poachers. His mind was taken up with a discrepancy he had discovered in the accounts which were to be presented to the warden of the forest. Edward Le Portier was a precise man: most people thought him fussy. But he was a figure of some authority. At the Norman invasion his grandfather, who bore the family name of Port, had (to the disgust of the other thanes) decided that, since the Norman William was fighting under the pope's banner of approval, he should support him. It was a decision that the people in the area had never forgiven, but it had won the family the grant of prosperous estates, some of which lay within the bounds of the forest. The name of Port, whose Roman origin they had now long since forgotten, but to which they still tenaciously clung, had become altered to the French Le Portier, and both Edward and his father had been elected as agisters.

He was thin and dark, with a clean-shaven moonlike face; his eyes had a strange, intense stare that was completely without humour. His voice was rasping and high-pitched. And he was now only twenty yards from the youth and his unlawed dog.

By good luck, there was an oak tree a few feet away which shielded them from view. Godric went down on one knee, placed his hand gently over Harold's muzzle and held his breath. He heard Le Portier pause for a moment. But the agister had only stopped to think, and a second later he moved on.

For several minutes more, however, Godric did not move. Harold waited patiently at his side. It was only when he was sure the coast was clear that the boy stood up and left his cover. It was time to go home.

Then he saw the pig.

The pig was black. It was not large, but it was plump and moving at a leisurely pace in a straight line across the ground with its snout down. No doubt it was searching for any remaining acorns that might be embedded in the forest floor. There was nothing remarkable in this sight, except for one thing: a small brand mark on the pig's hindquarter which told Godric that it belonged to William atte Brigge.

He knew that the tanner had half a dozen swine and that he paid a fee for pasturing them loose in the forest; as he watched the animal go past, his face broke into a smile. The risks were great, but now he saw how to take his revenge. Resting his hand on Harold's back he pointed at the pig and whispered:

"Follow."

It was dusk, three days later when Godric Body called at the smith's and asked Mary to walk out with him. After some hesitation, and giving him as usual the suspicious, sideways look that should have discouraged him, she consented. But Godric was in high spirits and, without being asked, took her hand as they walked along the lower end of the huge furrowed fields. Harold bounded beside them. The first shoots of the summer crops were already showing; there was a faint chill still in the damp air so that, after a few minutes he put his arm around her. At first she shook her shoulders crossly; but when he persisted she made no further protest. At the end of the field he turned round and asked her casually:

"Can you keep a secret?"

"Depends," she replied flatly.

For a few minutes he said nothing. They started back.

"What?" she enquired at last.

He paused once again, before answering.

"I'll show you."

Slowly he led her back towards the village where his mean hut was the last of the straggling line of dwellings. She noticed that there was a thin column of blue smoke rising from it. As they reached the entrance she hesitated and he felt her shoulders hunch defensively. He grinned.

"It's inside." He led the way.

The hut was a simple affair. Under a thatch roof, the outer, larger compartment was a storeroom containing two chickens in a cage, his farming tools, several sections of wattle and half a dozen wooden stakes together with the other debris of his poor life. The floor was of earth. The inner compartment was smaller, about twelve feet square, its floor covered with dried rushes and in the middle, a small open fire in a grate under a hole in the roof. In the far wall there was a little square opening to let in some light, and this, in the manner of modest cottages, was covered with a thin sheet of lambskin, stretched and oiled so that it was translucent.

[341]

But what she noticed at once when she gingerly entered, was that on a spit over the fire was a small piece of salted port. Despite herself, her eyes brightened as she sniffed the aroma. It was a month since she had last eaten meat.

"Want some?" he asked quietly.

She stood quite still. He knew the temptation she felt.

"Where d'you get it?" Her voice was low, a little frightened.

"Doesn't matter. Want some?"

Still she hesitated. He took out his knife and began to cut a piece. Without looking at her, he could feel her weakening.

There was a chair with a rush seat in front of the fire. Slowly she came forward and sat in it.

They ate it all.

When they had done, he turned to her and looked at her seriously.

"You won't tell?"

She stared at the floor. They both knew the seriousness of what they had done. At best a thief would be fined; he might be hanged.

She shook her head.

"If they ask you ever, you had no meat," he reminded her.

She nodded.

Then she got up and he escorted her out. "There's more," he whispered as they emerged into the night.

"Where?"

He smiled.

"Nowhere they'll ever find it."

She was impressed by his caution.

Slowly he took her home; at the door of her father's cottage he kissed her on the cheek and she did not protest.

Then Godric and his dog walked home, and the young man smiled to himself once more. He had taken the first step with Mary. Now there was a bond between them.

Midsummer's Eve was to be a busy day at the manor of Avonsford, and it began with a brief but important meeting between Richard de Godefroi and John of Shockley.

On several occasions in recent months the farmer had approached the knight for advice on the continual threats from William to reopen the lawsuit against him, and although Godefroi thought the Saxon worried more than he should, he had listened patiently each time and given John sensible advice about how to proceed.

"Above all, give no sign that you're afraid of him. And in the name of God keep your wife out of trouble," he counselled.

But now he had sent for the farmer to ask a favour in return.

It concerned his own wife.

By midsummer, the political situation in England had become alarming. Only the previous week, in the little fortified port of Twyneham, a merchant from France had assured him that the Empress

[342]

Matilda was planning to cross the Channel to England later that year, and that she could count on the support of Robert, Earl of Gloucester – one of the many bastard sons of the last king – and his allies who held the great western towns of Bristol and Gloucester on the river Severn, both of which were impregnable. Despite the fact that Matilda, with her high-handed ways, had made herself unpopular in many quarters, despite the fact that both the pope and King Louis of France were staunchly for Stephen, the rebel party was convinced that it could topple him.

In Godefroi's opinion, they could be right. The good natured king had shown too many signs of weakness. Matilda's second husband, the vicious Geoffrey of Anjou, was still seeking by every means to wrest Normandy from Stephen's ally and brother Theobald. The king's support south of the Channel could crumble at any time. Apart from the glorious Battle of the Standard the previous year, when he had trounced an invading army of Scots in Yorkshire, he had few decisive actions to his credit. Now the air was thick with rumour.

As he considered the major landowners at Sarum, it seemed to Godefroi that the prospects were bleaker than ever. To the south, the huge estate at Downton, which stretched almost as close as Britford was in the hands of another of the king's brothers, the Bishop of Winchester, still furious that Stephen had not made him Archbishop of Canterbury, and dissatisfied with his position as papal legate.

"A born traitor," Godefroi had told his wife. Of the other landowners, the abbesses of Wilton and Shaftesbury, who owned much of the land to the west, would probably be neutral; as to the local families like the Giffards, Marshalls and Dunstanvilles, he was not sure. But he was certain that William of Sarisberie would turn on Stephen if it suited him, and as for the bishop with his four castles, they were already prepared for war. It was said that recently the king, usually good-natured to a fault, had become morose and suspicious. He had cause.

But what should he do himself?

When he considered his feudal position, he could only shake his head irritably. It was complex. William of Sarisberie as a tenant-in-chief of the king, owed Stephen the service of a number of knights. In theory he in turn provided them by settling the required number of lesser nobles as his own sub-tenants, each on a parcel of land sufficiently large to represent a knight's fee. But in practice, his land was instead split into many much smaller estates whose tenants might be due for only a quarter, a tenth, even a fortieth of a knight's fee – which they usually paid to him in cash. Godefroi himself was such a tenant; but he was also a trained military knight and therefore one of those on whom William would certainly call for actual service – for which he would also be paid. So although his feudal duty was to serve his lord, he was in truth no more than a part-time mercenary. But what if he were asked to fight against the king? Where then did his duty lie? And what would be the safest course? He had turned the matter over countless times in his mind, and still he did not know the answer.

One thing he had decided, however.

He looked thoughtfully at the blue-eyed Saxon farmer.

"You have a kinsman in London, I think?"

"I have. He is a burgess." John said it with pride. The free burgesses of London were already a force to be reckoned with.

The knight nodded.

"Good. I wish you to go with my wife and children to London and place them under his care. Will you do it?"

John blushed. It was an honour.

"Of course."

"I am grateful to you," Godefroi inclined his head gracefully.

John of Shockley guessed what this must mean. He wondered what news Godefroi might have.

"Will they," he hesitated, "be there for long?"

"Perhaps." It was clear the Norman did not wish to discuss it. "You'll leave tomorrow."

After John withdrew, Godefroi gazed thoughtfully about the room. His manor house was not large, but typical of the time. On the ground floor level, it consisted of a broad, vaulted undercroft, like a barn, with thick stone walls and pillars down the centre, which was used mainly for storage. Above this however, reached by an outside wooden staircase, were the living quarters. These consisted of a large, handsome hall that took up two thirds of the space, and divided from this by a heavy leather curtain was the *solar*, where the family's sleeping quarters were partitioned by screens. There was a huge stone fireplace set in the wall of Godefroi's hall, and on the north east corner of the building was a small garderobe tower where he kept his valuables. The windows of the upper rooms were large and fitted with panes of soft, potash glass – less durable than the soda glass of Roman times, but which shed a pleasant greenish light in the interior. The windows of the undercroft however were no more than narrow slits, in case the manor should ever need to be defended.

He was sitting at a large oak table. On the wall above him hung a wooden shield: on its red background was depicted an elegant white swan. The art of heraldry, just beginning, was still an informal affair, but when the fashion for a knight to have his own insignia had begun, Godefroi chose for his symbol one of the swans which, if he looked out of the window of his hall, he could see gliding silently by on the Avon below. Near the fire, darkened by the smoke, stood a wooden screen, to the ends of which had recently been fixed wood carvings of two more swans, whose graceful lines had delighted him. They were the work of the boy Godric, whom he had recently made a shepherd, and the young fellow had given them to him, unasked, to thank him for the new position. He would have young Godric do other work, he thought.

But not at present. The following day Nicholas the stoneworker was to take the glass out of the upper windows and reduce them to narrow slits, like those below: the manor was being fortified.

"Just as a precaution," he sighed.

A few minutes later when his wife, a pleasant, quiet woman, daughter of a Breton knight, came to him with their three children, he gave them their instructions.

"John of Shockley will take you to London tomorrow. I am sending money with you – half of all I have. His kinsman is a burgess who will find lodgings for you and see that you are safe."

It was a wise move. For centuries, even since the time of Alfred, London had been a world apart. It was the greatest port in the kingdom; its walls were formidable. And despite the great tower that the Conqueror had built beside it to overawe its citizens, the independent burgesses of the city would make their own terms with any king who tried to seize the crown. Not only would his wife be safe there, but if by chance he finished on the losing side in the conflict, she would be in a position in the independent city and with ample funds, to plead his case and arrange whatever financial settlement might be needed to win him back to favour. Though quiet, she was a capable woman, and he knew he could trust her.

"What do you think will happen?" she asked.

"I think the rebels will hold the west. This area will then be a battle ground. We must expect the worst."

Left alone once more, Godefroi returned to his work.

On the table lay two books and an abacus, a recent importation from the Mediterranean that Godefroi had been quick to master. Since dawn that day he had been reckoning up his accounts.

The account of the manor of Avonsford in William the Conqueror's great Domesday survey of England had been brief and simple.

> Richard de Godefroi holds Avonsford from Edward of Sarisberie. In the reign of King Edward it paid geld for 6 hides. There is land for thirty ploughs. In demesne are 10 ploughs and 20 slaves; 30 villeins and 15 bordars have 20 ploughs. There is a meadow for 4 ploughs and pasture for the beasts of the village. There is a church.

It was a typical feudal manor, consisting of the lord's own land, his demesne, farmed separately and the common land he shared with the villagers. The estate was profitable and yielded him over twenty pounds a year. The estate in Normandy, which he seldom visited but which one of his wife's family kept an eye on, yielded him another ten pounds.

In addition to this, he had some years previously bought a wardship in Devon. This was the practice by which an overlord could grant the estate of one of his tenants, which was in the hands of a widow or a minor, as payment to another landowner, who would then manage the estate and take most of its profits until the widow remarried or the minor came of age. Originally designed to protect the estate of those who were unable to manage them, the system in practice often led to terrible abuse, with the assets being systematically sold off by profiteers who finally returned only the shell of the estate to the rightful inheritors. Godefroi was a conscientious manager, but the Devon estate still brought him a useful twenty pounds a year.

Now he was considering the assets of his own estate. That spring he had decided to turn everything he could into ready cash, and midsummer was a crucial period. He had ordered the reeve to select a larger number of beasts than usual – both cattle and sheep – to be fattened for slaughter. They were in prime condition, and would be driven to market within the next few days – most to Wilton market, and a few to the new, smaller market which the burgesses now ran in the castle town of Sarisberie. On the ridges above, the sheep shearing had also begun. Half of the expected wool had already been pre-sold to a merchant from the great cloth centre of Flanders across the Channel; the rest would go to local markets. So would all the excess cheese and corn that the estate produced. He calculated that in two weeks' time, he could forward a further ten pounds to his wife in London.

At last he finished, and pushed the abacus away from him. He had done all that he could.

Before getting up, he stretched his hand out to one of the two leatherbound books that lay on the table beside the abacus. Godefroi was one of a minority of knights who was literate. Not that education was hard to find. The schools were no longer confined to the monasteries as they had been in previous centuries. And not only were there now schools of law, philosophy and literature at the great centres of Laon, Chartres, Paris and Bologna – schools that produced such scholars as the great Abelard, the lover of Heloise – but in the town of Oxford a small learned community now existed, and cathedrals like Sarisberie attracted scholars too. But few men of Godefroi's class bothered to read and write, and he was proud of this ability. As a boy he had received tuition from the canons at Sarisberie, along with other young men of Sarum, some of whom, like the great cleric John of Sarisberie, were to go to make a name for themselves as scholars as far afield as Rome. His own attainments were more humble. He read Latin well enough to work his way through a charter, or to decipher the new histories of the island, such as that of William of Malmesbury. He read English with greater ease, and one of the most treasured of the eight books he possessed was the translation of Boethius into English made two hundred and fifty years before by Alfred of Wessex. In times of stress, its stoic philosophy often calmed him. But his greatest love was the songs and tales of courtly love of the troubadour poets which he could read in his native French. This was the knightly world as it ought to be – chivalrous, civilised, where the nobles of the castle served an idealised lady as faithfully as if she were the Virgin Mary herself. It was a delicate, sunlit world, a fantasy far removed from the grim realities of the castle of Sarisberie; but it invoked an ideal of chivalry which the hard-headed knight nevertheless respected and took seriously.

A week ago he had been sent a new book, however: a small volume hurriedly and badly transcribed from Latin into French by a scribe whose handwriting was abominable. And yet the little volume – it was no bigger than his two hands held together – had given him more delight than anything he had seen in several years. With a smile on his severe face, he pulled the book to him and slipped it into a large leather pouch that hung from his belt, before striding out of the house.

An hour later he had completed his inspection of the fields and of the shearing, had seen the reeve inspect the carcasses of two sheep to make sure no murrain was affecting the flock, and satisfied himself that the quality of the wool being sheared was up to that stipulated in the contract with the Flemish merchant. Only then did he make his way to his favourite spot.

The little clearing on the hill at the edge of the high ground had always been a place of special solace to him. As it lay only half a mile up the valley from the manor, it had been the first place he could remember walking to as a child, and even now he always took the same path; up the steep track through the little beech wood that covered the slope from the valley floor, across the strip of land where the trees were thinned with scrub. Then, suddenly cresting the lip of the ridge where the trees abruptly ended, he would encounter the breathtaking sweep of the bare chalk ridges extending north and east, it seemed, for ever. And there, in a circle of trees on a little hump of ground was the clearing with its dish-like surface some ninety feet across and concave towards its centre.

It was his father who had first taken notice of this place and made it his own. That the circular mound was a barrow, or that any Celtic predecessors had worshipped here more than a thousand years before, he had no idea; but something about the place besides its fine view appealed to him, and shortly before Richard was born, he had planted a double circle of yew trees round the spot. They were tall and thick now, obscuring the view; but they also protected the place from the wind, and Richard had placed two benches there, on top of the barrow, where he liked to sit alone.

He knew of no more silent a place: it was quieter even than inside the cathedral on the castle hill. And it was open to the sky. On the bare slopes around, where the scars of the ancient Celtic cross ploughing still left traces, as though the land had been lightly etched, only the sheep now occasionally grazed on the short turf. Nobody came there.

This was the place that Godefroi called the arbour, and it was here that he finally sat down to forget his troubles for an hour and read his little book.

It was a remarkable work. It purported to be a history of the English kings, by a clerk called Geoffrey of Monmouth – a Breton by birth who had been brought up on the borders of South Wales and who had neatly calculated how to please not only his patron the dangerous Earl of Gloucester, but a wide audience all over northern Europe. The book had been completed only four years before, but already translations like those in Godefroi's hands were circulating all over the island.

One story in particular had caught the knight's attention, as it had so many others. It was the story of King Arthur. For from scraps and hints in earlier chronicles, the clever writer had concocted an extraordinary tale of a western English king in a courtly setting that echoed the world of the troubadours, and who had fought for chivalry and Christianity against the forces of darkness. It was a magnificent invention, a romantic saga like the famous *Chanson de Roland*, and a worthy tale for crusaders. With the reality of the almost forgotten general Artorius who had tried to defend the civilisation of later Rome against the heathen Saxons it had almost nothing to do, beyond the name. And Geoffrey's story still lacked many of the Arthurian world's finest features: the knights Lancelot and Percival, the tale of Tristran and Iseult, the legendary Round Table and the Holy Grail were all to be added by romantic writers a century later. But bald as it still was, the story moved Godefroi considerably. In his present mood it seemed to him better than the songs of the troubadours, better even than Boethius's sober *Consolations of Philosophy*. For here had been a Christian monarch, the proper ideal of a feudal king – a man of the stature of such Christian heroes as the mighty Charlemagne, or Saxon Alfred, or the last true monarch of the island kingdom before the conquest, the saintly Edward the Confessor, whose very touch was known to cure the disease of scrofula. Yes, there really had been great and Christian kings like Arthur.

"But not in my lifetime though," he said bitterly.

He closed the book. Perhaps, when the present troubles were over, he could throw off the cares of his life at Sarum, turn his back in disgust on incompetent Stephen, on the evil Bishop Roger and, if there was no Christian war to fight, begin his pilgrimage to the Holy Land.

"More and more," he thought, "I grow sick of this world." He longed to save his soul. "But will God grant me time?" he wondered.

It was midsummer. In the royal forest, it was the fence month when the deer were in fawn and the foresters ensured that no unwelcome intruders disturbed them. On the slopes around Sarum, it was the time for sheep shearing.

It seemed to Godric Body that the world was a brighter place than it had been before.

All morning he had helped at the sheep-washing, which was carried out in a small pool that the men had created with a wattle dam just below a bend in the little stream that ran across the edge of the high ground.

It was two months since Godefroi had let him work with the shepherds. From morning till night he had been busy on the slopes, his life now regulated by the calendar of the shepherd's year. At Helenmas at the start of May, the fat lambs had been rounded up and sold; in two days' time, at the midsummer feast of St John, while the workers in the open fields began to weed the corn, on the slopes above the old ewes would be taken away to market. Today, all the spare villeins were up to help with the washing and shearing. There were almost a thousand sheep to be got through. Expertly the men held the sheep between their knees as they worked with the iron shears to cut away the thick fleeces that the new summer growth underneath was lifting up.

He liked to see the shorn sheep scuttle away as soon as they were freed, with their close-cropped coats gleaming in the sun.

Harold usually accompanied him to his work. The dog was growing more skilled every day, and despite his youth, was learning patience, his bright eyes watching the sheep by the hour, and helping Godric to herd them from ridge to ridge. To celebrate his new life, Godric had made himself a fine shepherd's crook, and on its curling handle he had carved a figure that captured the dog's sleek, eager form and character exactly. With the crook in his hand and the dog at his side he experienced a contentment he had never known before.

Nor was this all. He had reason to believe that he was making headway with Mary.

In recent weeks, even the smith and his family had welcomed him.

"If the lord keeps him as a shepherd," Mary's mother told her, "you could do worse."

He had pressed his suit with her, gently but firmly; and he had not been slow to discover how to win her.

He wooed her with food.

The pig he had cleverly salted had lasted some time. He ate it slowly, sometimes alone so that Mary would not take his invitation for granted, and sometimes with her.

His revenge on William atte Brigge was complete. When the tanner had discovered his loss, he had been beside himself with rage and attempted to raise the hue and cry: but since the pig had never been found, he was helpless. It preyed on his mind. In Wilton and in Sarisberie he would suddenly seize a passer by and cross question them about it until, to all but himself, the matter had become a joke. And when he realised that people were laughing at him, it made his fury even worse.

"Have you seen a pig?" men in the market place would call out as soon as they saw him coming. And someone else, to anger him further, would be sure to reply:

"Yes, at Shockley farm."

Once he cross-questioned Mary; but her look of squinting suspicion easily put him off and he gave it up.

Godric had tempted the girl with a remarkable variety of foods that he had been able to trap without risk. On the common land he could take a hare, a pheasant or partridge. And there was another tasty and prolific animal he loved, a newcomer to the island – for it was only after the Norman conquest that the first rabbits appeared in the area. The natives called them coneys, and Godric was especially skilled both at snaring them, and at the delicate business of roasting the small animal's rich, dark meat.

Twice, even three times a week, he would bring Mary to his little hut to share some new delicacy, and each time he would slyly watch the eager look in her eyes as she saw the meal he had prepared for her.

Gradually her manner softened towards him. Her face seemed to have become less pinched, its lines a little fuller. Once or twice she had even smiled, and now she allowed him to kiss her; he even thought he detected the beginnings of enthusiasm. But he did not try to take matters too fast, and continued his calculated routine until soon their meetings had become, for her, a habit there was no reason to break. By the end of May it was generally known that the two were walking out together. Even Godefroi was aware of the fact, and once or twice gave the couple a friendly nod as he passed.

At their last few meetings Godric was aware of a new mood in the girl: a certain shyness and hesitancy, as though a struggle was taking place within her. The look of defensive suspicion in her eyes had changed to a softer uncertainty and fear. He had understood, and pressed on.

It was early evening that shearing day when Mary came up from the valley. She was walking alone.

In the fields, the wheat and the barley were already showing green; the hay in the meadow below was turning to gold. She left the fields behind her.

All day she had been working in the dairy beside the manor house where the great vats of milk were brought and the cheeses of cow's and goat's milk were made. She carried a small goat's cheese with her now and half a loaf of bread.

As she looked at the ridge in front of her, Mary knew that once she was over it there could be no turning back. She did not hesitate.

She had considered her future carefully. She was still very young, but then her life might well be short, nor was there any reason why it should be particularly pleasant. After that – Heaven or Hell she supposed. Who knew? Meanwhile, there were only two things she needed to know: she must eat and, if possible, she must find a man.

She had just passed puberty; soon these questions would become urgent; and her prospects were not good.

She had, for the moment, one tiny advantage. Her body was still almost that of a child, yet it had a certain awkward freshness about it that the young shepherd with his bent back, at any rate, had found appealing; and in her wisdom she had realised: I shall never look any better than I do now: probably worse.

Sometimes, in moments of weakness, she had allowed her mind to wander and consider which men she had seen that she found attractive. The knight of Avonsford was one. Handsome, greying, remote, so far from the clumsy peasant folk of the little village; so tall, so straight: she tried to imagine what might go on in his mind. He was a figure from another world, however, only to dream of. But when she thought of the men she knew in Avonsford, there were none that attracted her; and of those she had seen on her occasional visits to Sarisberie or Wilton, none that had ever spoken to her.

But Godric had spoken to her, which was why she had been so suspicious. After all, she knew she must not hope for much from life: it was her only way of protecting herself from humiliation. If he spoke to her, therefore, it was only because he could find nobody better. But he spoke to her all the same, and if that was because he thought he would not find anyone better, then at least, she conceded with a shrug, he was being practical.

For since she had always known she would have a struggle to survive, she had no use for anything that was not practical. And indeed, as time went on, it was the young man's competence that did attract her. She admired the way he carved; she liked the way he fed her; several times in the previous weeks, if she had not been so cautious she would have smiled.

Her father now spoke well of him: that was a point in his favour.

And strangely, his bodily affliction gradually became an attraction to her as well. Not because she felt sorry for him – she did not think she could afford the luxury of feeling sorry for anyone. But as she considered her own unattractive features, she was comforted by the thought: at least he can never despise me.

So it was, at the ripe season of the year, that she had struck her bargain with fate in deciding to make the little fellow with his bent back a present of her life.

As she passed, the men on the slopes turned to watch her. It was as though, by some ancient instinct, they knew what her journey meant.

The shadows were just starting to lengthen when she reached the place where the men were shearing. Over a wide area, the ground was white with wisps of wool and the dust in the air shimmered over the place like a haze. And here too, as she walked by, the men glanced up from their busy work to stare at her.

The shearing had been going on ever since early morning, and though it would probably be two more days until it was completed, the pace had slackened. Here and there men were standing together by the piles of sacks containing the fresh wool, quietly chatting. The place had the air of an untidy camp. The sharp-sweet smell of sheep-droppings was every-where.

Godric was busy helping the men collect the wool, and though Harold rose and ambled over to greet her, he did not notice her at first. When he did, he smiled and came towards her.

"Finished at the dairy?"

She nodded.

He noticed the little package she was carrying.

"What's this?"

She held out the little cheese, her face impassive.

"It's for you."

He looked at her carefully, then took it solemnly from her. She had never given him a present before and he knew what it meant: she had made her decision. The men standing nearby were grinning.

"We'll be some time," he began . . . but from thirty yards away he heard the voice of the reeve.

"Godric Body: you've finished for today."

There was laughter all around. Godric blushed, and glanced towards the reeve, who was smiling broadly. It was not often that the reeve gave him a friendly look. "Go!" he shouted.

Godric looked down at the girl. For the first time since he had started to court her, he now felt awkward.

"Shall we walk?"

She nodded. "That way." She pointed across the high ground, away from the valley.

As they moved away, and he felt the sun on his back, she slipped her arm through his. Ahead of them Harold happily bounded, chasing his own shadow across the turf.

[351]

They walked for nearly half an hour, neither saying much. Here and there was a clump of trees, but almost all the ground was bare. The grasses were just beginning to become parched. The chalk ridges were mostly deserted as the sheep had been driven to the shearing.

At the outer edge of the land where the Avonsford flocks were grazed, there was a dip in the ground, at one end of which lay a long stone building. Centuries before it had been a farmhouse; now it was used only for sheep; and on the open land a little way off there was a large, round depression in the ground, some five feet deep at its centre, which even now, at the dry height of summer, contained more than a foot of water.

Here they sat down and ate the bread and cheese she had brought.

Mary squinted at the pond curiously. There seemed to be no stream to feed it, and Godric, following her gaze explained:

"This is a dew pond. It was made up here for the sheep." And he outlined how, once in a generation, the men would go and line the bottom of the pond with clay and straw, packing them so tight that no water was lost. "And then," he went on, "when the dew falls on the ground around, it drains into the pool so that the sheep can drink here right through the summer."

And as he enthusiastically explained about it, Mary decided that she was glad he was a shepherd, and that she was even proud of him.

It was a pleasant spot, but she was not ready to stop yet; the sheep house was still too near the place where the men were shearing; so after a little time she made him get up and they walked on.

They walked together for another half an hour, with nothing, now, except the blue butterflies for company.

It was evening, but still warm when they reached the henge.

Only a third of the huge sarsens were still standing, and less than a third of the smaller bluestones within the ancient circle. The earth wall and ditch was only a little bigger than one of the earth banks dividing the strips of furrows in the open fields. The ceremonial avenue had almost disappeared and only one of the two gateway pillars remained. As the midsummer sun bathed the worn grey stones in its red-gold light, the ancient henge seemed a quiet, harmless place.

"They say giants built it," he remarked. "It's magic."

She took his hand.

"Come," she said softly.

As the sun sank over the henge, he was not aware of the fact that at dawn its first rays would run to the centre of the sacred circle up the faint path of the great avenue, nor that the moon that day rose opposite the place where the sun had set; nor in the exultation that took both of them by surprise, did he know that the place was reserved for the shedding of blood.

He knew that when she was pregnant they would marry, and he was content.

On St John's Day, 24th June 1139, the crisis that had so long been threatening Stephen's reign at last broke, and the period of English history known as the Anarchy was begun.

The trouble was not unexpected. The chances that the weak rule of Stephen would be challenged from within, or more likely, by his sterner-minded cousin the Empress Matilda, had been growing stronger every year. "There's more of the spirit of the Conqueror and his sons in the Empress than in Stephen," Godefroi himself had had to admit. And the rumours of her expected arrival were constantly growing.

But the beginning of the drama did not involve the Empress, but the Bishop of Sarisberie.

The first act took place at Oxford, where Stephen had summoned his magnates for a council meeting; and the spark that lit the fire was nothing more than a brawl at an inn between some of Bishop Roger's men and a group of retainers in the service of the other magnates, that had arisen over an argument about their lodgings. Some said that it had been planned by the king. It was possible. Several men were wounded and one knight killed.

Whether he planned it or not, it was the excuse that Stephen had been looking for: Bishop Roger's men had broken the king's peace: he was responsible. Immediately he summoned not only Roger but his son the chancellor and his two nephews, the Bishops of Ely and Lincoln into his presence. They must make reparation for the brawl, he told them; and for the time being, they must surrender the keys of their castles to him as guarantees that they could be trusted.

It was one of his shrewder moves. The bishops were undefended, away from their strongholds: they were taken by surprise; but if they were loyal, they would deliver the keys at once.

They hesitated.

The king knew what he must do. He let them return to their lodgings. Then he sent his men to arrest them.

But as usual, Stephen failed to close the trap properly: Bishop Roger, his son, and the Bishop of Lincoln were captured; but Nigel, Bishop of Ely escaped.

"And he has gone to Devizes," the excited messenger told Godefroi. "He's holding the castle and the king's on his way there now."

This was it. The picture was only too clear. The towns that lay in a great ring around the high ground of Sarum: Marlborough, twenty-five miles to the north, then Devizes, Trowbridge, Malmesbury to the north west, Sherborne to the south west, and finally Sarisberie at the centre – market towns each with their own stout castles – would become the scene of operations. Thank the Lord he had sent his family to London. Anything could happen; but as for his own position, he was going to get as close to the centre as possible, to see which way the wind was blowing. He would have to act quickly.

Within an hour he was speaking to Nicholas.

"Fortify the manor, Masoun," he told him. "I am going to Devizes."

The king's camp outside Devizes was, like so many of Stephen's operations, a hastily constructed and rather disorganised affair. It did not take Godefroi long to find the two tents occupied by William of Sarisberie and his brother Patrick, and before he went in, one of the young squires brought him up to date with news.

"Bishop Roger's in detention," he waved towards a tent where two men were standing guard. "He hasn't eaten since we left Oxford. And his son the Chancellor's in chains."

Godefroi whistled softly. This was an extraordinary reversal for the powerful upstart family.

"And in there?" He indicated the stout castle keep inside the town walls.

"The Bishop of Ely's in there. And he's got Matilda of Ramsbury there too."

This was the striking dark mistress of Bishop Roger and mother of the Chancellor.

The knight laughed. "Quite a family affair. The king really means to break them then?"

The young man gave him a curious look.

"If he can. You'd better go in."

The two brothers were standing together in the tent, deep in conversation. Several other knights crowded the place as well. When William saw Godefroi come in he looked surprised, then shot the knight a careful look of suspicion; but obviously deciding it was unlikely that the knight from Avonsford was intriguing with other parties, he came towards him with an outstretched hand. Like his brother he was a tall, spare figure with a long, fine face only marred by a brutal and slightly crooked nose.

"We didn't send for you, Richard, but we're glad you came," he said easily. "You've heard the news?"

Godefroi nodded. William turned confidentially to one side.

"It looks as if the king may win this skirmish, if he sticks it out," he murmured.

"Will he?"

William grimaced.

"God knows. He's like the wind: always moving but constantly changing direction. He starts things well but never finishes them, you know. He's just as likely to get bored and break the whole siege off."

"If he does, what then?"

The magnate looked at Godefroi carefully.

"We'll tell you what to do," he said, and turned away.

Several times that day Godefroi saw the king. Stephen went about the camp bare-headed usually, accompanied by a group of magnates. Godefroi noticed that his curly hair was thinning. He seemed cheerful though. His general, William of Ypres, had stationed his men in front of the castle gates, and was prepared to settle down to a regular siege. But on the afternoon that Godefroi arrived, a messenger suddenly ran out of the king's tent and galloped towards the town.

Even William of Sarisberie was surprised by the king's message.

"He's told them that unless they surrender, he'll hang the Chancellor in front of the gates," he explained to Richard. "As for Bishop Roger, the king says since he's started to fast, he may as well continue it indefinitely.

He's getting nothing – not even water."

But if King Stephen thought this would bring matters to a head, he under-estimated the Bishop of Ely.

"He says the king can hang and starve who he likes," the squire at William's tent told Godefroi excitedly, and William soon confirmed it.

"He's called the king's bluff," he remarked coolly. "Now we shall see."

The next morning they brought the stout, balding Chancellor out of his tent. His hands were bound and there was a noose round his neck. They put him on a horse and led him up to the castle walls before taking him back to the camp. But still there was no response from within.

In the afternoon they tried another tactic: they sent out Bishop Roger to talk to the rebels.

Godefroi watched him as six men-at-arms led him past: even under guard and after several days of starving, he was a frightening sight; his fast had done nothing to reduce his massive paunch; his heavy jowl shook as he walked. He stomped along looking neither to right nor left, and out of sheer force of habit, Godefroi shivered. The aura of power and menace he remembered had not left him.

But the conference that took place in front of the town between Bishop Roger and his nephew was a failure. Roger, with his practical eye, had seen at once that it would be better to surrender the castle and win back the easy-going king's favour; the resistance was only making his cause weaker and might cost his son's life. But Nigel of Ely was indifferent to his cousin's death, or his uncle starving, and after a short while Roger returned to the castle.

The next day the test of wills went on. William of Sarisberie grew impatient.

"If the king's going to hang the chancellor, then why doesn't he do it?" he asked irritably.

It was his lack of ruthlessness that made Stephen such a poor leader; if the king would not carry out his threat then even a humble knight like Godefroi could see that there would never be order in the kingdom.

Another day passed.

And then, unexpectedly, Stephen won everything he wanted. A messenger came out of the town and offered surrender if Bishop Roger and his son were set free. Within minutes, terms were agreed and the king walked through the camp beaming.

But the magnates were less impressed.

"It wasn't the Bishop of Ely who sent the messenger," William told Godefroi. "It was Matilda of Ramsbury: she couldn't bear to see her son hanged." He grimaced with disgust. "The king's been lucky. But if the empress invades, he won't be able to frighten her so easily."

For the time being however, Stephen was satisfied. He had the castles of Devizes, Malmesbury, Sherborne and Sarisberie: not only that, he had all the treasure and arms that Bishop Roger had amassed in them. The immediate crisis appeared to be over.

That night there was a feast, to which Godefroi was summoned by William, and the next morning the men began to break camp.

But there was one more surprise in store for the knight from Avonsford. Just as he was saddling his horse, an unexpected arrival made his way through the tents and packhorses. It was William atte Brigge.

His face was sullen but determined. He loped through the camp, only stopping to ask the way to the king. For the cantankerous tanner, hearing the king was so near, had come to seek royal justice in the case concerning the Shockley farm.

Such quests were not uncommon: the king's court existed at whatever place the king was, and any free man had a right to royal justice. Before now litigants had followed the Norman monarchs all over the island, and even across the sea to Normandy to try to get their case heard.

As soon as Godefroi saw the tanner's dark face he guessed why he was there; since he had just sent the farmer of Shockley to London with his wife, he could not help feeling responsible for him. With an oath, he hurried after him.

He need not have worried. When William atte Brigge reached the place where the king and a group of his nobles were standing, he blurted out his demands to the squire who was sent to ask him his business. He was a wronged man, dispossessed of his farm; he had come to the king for justice. His angry words tumbled out all together. He seemed to expect the king to hear the matter at once.

Stephen stared towards him in surprise, then smiled.

"Where do you come from?"

"From Wilton," the tanner replied.

Stephen turned to a group beside him.

"We have a castle near there," he cried.

There was a shout of laughter. William atte Brigge glowered in confusion.

"I'll hear your case, tanner," the king called out. "In my castle of Sarisberie." And he waved him away.

It was enough for the tanner. The nobles might be laughing at him, but the king had promised to hear his case. Satisfied, he turned to go, and Godefroi, shaking his head not only at the fellow's audacity but at the trouble it could cause his friend from Shockley, mounted his horse and headed back to Sarum.

His mind was not at rest on any count. Whatever the king's temporary success might have been, as he rode over the high ground the voice of the magnate echoed in his head:

"We'll tell you what to do."

There was something else that was wrong; and as he waited on events during the coming months at Sarum, Richard de Godefroi became increasingly filled with a sense of desolation.

It was not only the threatening political anarchy of a war between Stephen and the empress, not only the treachery in the air over Sarum, nor even the fear that in the uncertain times he might lose his lands that troubled his spirit.

It was something more profound – a sense that not only England, but all Christendom was sick – and it had been brought home to him by the sight of the bishops at Devizes and their conduct. For though he was a level-headed realist, the knight of Avonsford still believed that the Church should be sacred. And how could it be so with three such bishops as these?

"I believe in Our Lord's true Church," he confessed to John of Shockley a few days later: "Yet I no longer know where to find it."

In other times, he believed, it had been easier. No man could doubt the saintliness of Bishop Osmund. Few even questioned the authority of such great Church servants as the great Archbishop Lanfranc or the scholarly Anselm in previous reigns. Had not a former abbess of Wilton and member of the old Saxon royal house, Edith, already been made a saint? When Pope Leo announced the First Crusade, did anyone doubt that they were doing God's will in going to fight the Saracen? This was the true Church: the Church that governed the spiritual life of all Europe just as, in times past, Rome had governed the temporal world with her armies; the Church that was the undisputed voice of moral authority; the Church that ordered monarchs themselves to observe days of peace; the Church that, even if it had faults, constantly renewed itself.

Bishops should be men of God – named by the king, certainly; holding their vast lands with his permission too; but they should be drawn from the monasteries or put forward by their congregations, as they once had been. That was the knight's view. He was prepared to modify it in one respect. It had long been the practice of kings to reward their greatest servants with rich bishoprics which were, of course, only held for the servant's lifetime, and which, being church lands, cost the king nothing to bestow. This was a compromise; but he saw no great harm in it if the king's servants were worthy men. What he had seen now, however, was nothing more than three rascals from an upstart family, making a mockery of a sacred office. And even the king seemed to accept it. He felt nothing but a sense of disgust.

Church and state were both necessary; but they should be opposite sides of the same Christian coin, in harmony with each other.

But it was no longer so. In recent generations a new conflict had been born, a conflict between State power and religious authority, *regnum et sacerdotum*, that was to echo through the Middle Ages and far beyond. Who was superior on earth, the pope or a monarch? Who invested bishops with their spiritual authority and their estates – the Vicar of Rome or the king? Who chose abbots and bishops? If a priest committed a criminal act, should he be tried by the king's court or the bishop's? At its best, this quarrel was between the king and the universal Church which was determined to maintain its spiritual independence. At its worst, it was an excuse for cynical power politics between the monarch and the Church with its huge estates. It was exactly the struggle for power that was to have a bloody outcome when Thomas à Becket, Archbishop of Canterbury, was murdered in the next reign.

And now, in the months following the scene at Devizes, the dispute was to be seen at its most cynical. By his Charter of Liberties, Stephen had confirmed that the church would be free of all secular interference. Now therefore, Bishop Roger and his rascally nephews, on the grounds that they were ordained priests, claimed that the king had no right to lay hands on them. The other bishops, supported by that master of duplicity, Stephen's brother Henry, the Bishop of Winchester, supported them. By the end of August, a council of bishops had met at Winchester and tried to summon the king to them to explain his conduct.

Fortunately, by the start of September, Stephen had won his case when the Archbishop of Rouen arrived from Normandy to remind the council at Winchester that bishops had no business to be holding fortified castles anyway. The leading bishops went to the king on their knees; and after that Roger returned to skulk at Sarisberie, where he was not much seen.

But the whole affair left Godefroi depressed.

If God's kingdom on earth is like a great castle, he considered, then these councils were only putting plaster over the cracks. The foundations themselves were rotten.

It was at the end of September that the great blow at last fell. The Empress Matilda landed at Arundel, in the south east.

And it was then, to the stupefaction of Godefroi and almost every knight in England, that Stephen made perhaps the most foolish move of his reign. On the advice of the double-dealing Bishop of Winchester, the king cheerfully allowed the empress a safe conduct across his own kingdom to join her supporters who were gathering in the western stronghold of Bristol.

Whatever his motives for this extraordinary action, it ensured that, before the month was out, civil war had begun.

It was exactly as Godefroi had feared: would the troubles reach Sarum? He waited.

Godric Body and his dog moved quietly across the bowl of land below the castle walls. The afternoon sun warmed his hunched back. He kept Harold close by his side and walked with care; for he did not want to be observed as he crossed the ground where the autumn leaves were falling.

It was a few days past Michaelmas. The last of the harvest was all gathered, and in the big open fields they were sowing the new seed. On the slopes above, the last signs of the ruddle on the rams' chests, painted on so that they would leave a mark on each ewe when she had been serviced, were wearing off. Each morning now he was having to keep the sheep in their pens a little longer until the sun had dried the mildew off the turf that would give the sheep disease if they grazed on it. The warm, damp autumn season was a dangerous time in the shepherd's calendar.

Two days before, the last of the old ewes had been slaughtered and salted and at Hallowmas, the day after Hallowe'en, there would be a great feast on the slaughtered beasts in the village.

But it was not the sheep that Godric was thinking about that afternoon. It was William atte Brigge's vanished pig.

He had supposed by the end of summer that the tanner would have forgotten it; but he had not, and his interview with the king had left William so elated, that at Michaelmas he had decided to offer a reward of three marks for information about the animal. This was more than the value of the pig, but William was as obstinate as he was bad-tempered, and he was already disappointed that the reward had so far yielded no result.

Godric had been careful. It was four months since he had been near the spot in the forest where the animal's carcass was buried, and it was so well hidden that he was sure it could never be found. All the same, a mixture of prudence and curiosity made him make one more visit to the spot just to make sure it had not been disturbed.

He left the river behind and made his way slowly and cautiously into the forest.

It was a good month for hunting: hind and doe were in season and since Holy Rood in mid-September the boar was in grease and could be hunted also. He knew the foresters would be about and kept a wary eye for them.

It took him half an hour to reach the place: a sheltered dip in the ground with a thick screen of brambles in front. He inspected it carefully. The remains of the pig were three feet under ground, completely safe behind the cover. Leaves had fallen on the ground too: there was not even a hint of the animal's presence. Satisfied, he walked further on. Perhaps he might catch a coney.

He did not; and after a further hour scouting the woods in a wide arc he began to head towards home.

Dusk was almost falling when he saw the deer.

It was in a clump of saplings in a dip in the ground, and the little doe had obviously gone down there to feed; then, clearly, something had happened and he could guess at once what it was. He moved close.

She had been snared – by a cunning cats-cradle of twine woven between the saplings in such a way that it would catch the antlers of a stag as it lowered its head to eat, or enmesh the feet of smaller deer. It had done its work: the doe's fore-legs had become hopelessly entangled and one of them had broken as she struggled desperately to jump out. Now the little animal was standing there trembling pitifully.

He disliked snares: they were a cruel way to catch an animal, but he knew better than to touch one of the king's deer; on the other hand, though he could alert one of the foresters' men, he was unwilling to encounter them since Harold was with him, and the dog had never been lawed. The safest thing to do was to get away from the illegal snare as quickly as possible.

But he did not. A mixture of curiosity and concern for the doe made him instead take cover fifty yards away and wait.

The dusk began to close in. No one came. Still something – was it only curiosity? – held him there.

And then the animal began to cry.

It was not a loud noise; at times it was no more than a snuffle, followed by a little moan; but then it would rise to a whimper and conclude with an eerie, weeping cry that echoed softly across the forest floor. It was the desolate cry of an animal that has been deserted.

Darkness fell, and a light wind began to blow through the trees, making a soft rustle. It was suddenly cold. It seemed to Godric that the whole forest was still: nothing was stirring in the tall trees, silent except for the rustle as they were brushed by the wind.

Once, far away, he thought he heard a cry from a wolf. There were few wolves about at Sarum now, but occasionally they still appeared at the forest's edge and killed sheep who were not properly protected. The deer heard the sound too, and for a time fell silent.

But then, after a period of quiet, the little doe, alone and now invisible, began crying again in the darkness. She seemed to be calling him.

No one came.

At last he could bear it no longer.

He knew that a deer with a broken leg would have to be killed by the foresters; there was no question of that.

"I hid the pig well enough," he thought. "Why not a deer?"

Softly he moved out of his hiding place.

"Mary will eat venison tomorrow," he said to himself.

When he reached the deer he put his arm round her neck to calm her. She shuddered. Then, reaching cleverly for his knife, he put her out of her misery.

A moment later the doe sank to the ground, and he knelt over her.

The sudden start that Harold gave came too late for him even to rise before he felt the hand on his shoulder and heard the voice of Le Portier, the agister, who, from another vantage point, had been watching him for over an hour.

Richard de Godefroi was alone in the yew arbour, enjoying the last of the warm autumn sun and, for the tenth time, reading Geoffrey of Monmouth's story of King Arthur when he looked up angrily to see the squat figure of Nicholas advancing towards him: how dare the fellow trespass into his most private retreat?

But the stoneworker, red-faced and sweating, was not daunted by even the knight's deep frown, and his sharp question: "What now, Masoun?"

"My nephew Godric, my lord," he burst out. "They say he has taken a deer. Help us."

At which the knight rose, closed his book, and came without a word.

The situation could hardly have been worse, as Godefroi discovered when he spoke to the agister at his house in the forest.

There were several ways in which a man guilty of a crime against the Norman forest laws could be apprehended: but the most damning of all was guilt by bloody-hand – red-handed men sometimes called it; and Godric not only had blood on his hands – he had been taken in the act itself.

"And his dog had not been lawed," Le Portier told the knight: he dragged Harold out from the little kennel where he was keeping him and insisted on demonstrating that he was too big to fit through the leather hoop which had to be passed fully over any forest dog if it were to escape the operation.

"What about the boy's story?" The knight had spent an hour with Godric that morning at the house of the forester where he was being held, and had listened to his account; though it was hard to believe, he had finally decided that he was probably telling the truth.

But Le Portier only stared at him blankly. "It makes no difference," he said. "He had blood on his hands and the law says. . . ."

"We know what the law says," the knight interrupted impatiently. In a court of law the boy's explanation would be useless. "But are you sure it should go to the court? What if the boy made a mistake?"

It would be up to the meeting of the forest officers, the swanimote, to consider the matter at their own informal court of attachment before deciding whether to refer it to a formal prosecution before the king's justices, and the agister's statement would be crucial.

"Are you sure he should be accused?" Godefroi demanded.

But if the agister had any imagination, it seemed that he was determined not to use it.

"The terms of the law are clear," he said and once again gave him the same blank stare and fixed smile.

That evening the knight told Nicholas regretfully:

"I don't hold out much hope, Masoun." But he did not give up.

The month that followed was a bleak period.

Poor Godric could scarcely have chosen a worse time to fall foul of the forest laws. The swanimote was due to take place at Martinmas, the eleventh day of November, and it had been decided to hold the court of attachment immediately after it. There was less than a month to go. After that, unless it could be prevented, he would go before the justices. The court of the Forest Eyre visited Wilton usually only once in three years: but as ill luck would have it, it was due to sit there at the end of that November and, as Godefroi soon discovered, the forest officers were on the lookout for offenders.

"They expect a few you know, otherwise they say we're getting slack," one of the knights who inspected the forest told him.

Nonetheless, Godefroi did what he could, not only because he believed the young man was probably innocent, but because he was a useful worker and nephew of the stoneworker for whom he had a warm regard. He spoke at length to Waleran the warden, who oversaw the forest all the way down to the coast, and who would run the court of attachment. He spoke to the foresters and the knights of the court, and at his request, several of them had interviewed the boy. By the end of October there was considerable sympathy for his case. But as Waleran warned him:

"I'd take a lenient view; but if the agister insists that he took him bloody-handed, there's very little option: he'll have to go to the Forest Eyre."

"And then?"

Waleran waved the question away. They both knew what would happen then.

Twice he saw Le Portier; but the agister would not budge.

The news from beyond Sarum was bad as well. It was obvious that the country was drifting further into anarchy every day. Despite Stephen's success with the bishops the rebel forces were increasing their hold on the west. They took Malmesbury. Wallingford near Oxford was staunchly held for them. Soon other strongholds, including nearby Trowbridge were in their hands. As usual, Stephen raced from one trouble spot to another, always active, but accomplishing nothing. As November began, rumours reached the knight that the important Midland towns of Worcester and Hereford were about to fall to them too.

"Before Christmas," he remarked to John of Shockley, "the whole west side of England will be theirs."

He thanked God that his wife and children were safely in London.

For the farmer had done his work well, installing them safely there and, though he had both his farm and his troubles with the tanner to think of, refusing to leave for a month until he had satisfied himself that they were being well cared for by his relations. Godefroi was grateful; but when he asked the Saxon what he could do for him in return, John only laughed cheerfully and replied:

"You could slay William atte Brigge for me, my lord."

It could not be long, he thought, before the warfare reached Sarisberie; but so far everything there was quiet. A small group of the king's men held the garrison; and if William of Sarisberie, or the Giffards, or the other magnates were plotting treason, they had not yet shown their hand. As for Bishop Roger, he had hardly been seen since his return, and there were rumours that he was sick with a quartan fever. It seemed to Godefroi that the whole area lay under a cloud.

His own gloom was made deeper when, in early November, he saw the girl Mary. She was standing in the street at Avonsford as he was riding through one evening, and though her head was lowered in respect, he was aware of her squinting up at him as he passed. He paused to say a word to her, but after he told her that perhaps the young man might escape with his life, she only shook her head morosely and pointed to her stomach.

He stared at her.

"Pregnant?"

She nodded.

"We'll do what we can for him."

She looked up. Her face seemed to wear a kind of scorn, though it was hard to tell.

"He's killed a deer, hasn't he? So he'll be hung." Her voice was flat, but bitter.

He could not remember what he had replied before he had ridden on, but he knew that she was probably right.

Nor as the day approached did there seem to be any more hope. News came that the rebels now had taken not only Worcester and Hereford, but two more castles in the south west as well.

"Perhaps the forest justices will not come," he suggested to the warden; but Waleran shook his head:

"The king holds all the country except the west. They'll come."

It was only on the night before the swanimote that Nicholas came to him with a last proposal. He arrived at the manor at dusk; his round face seemed thinner than usual, drawn with worry; his short, thick fingers were clasped round a small leather pouch which he handed solemnly to the knight and asked him to open it. Godefroi counted the contents out on the table. The bag contained nine marks: six pounds: a sum that it must have taken him years to collect. Nicholas stood awkwardly, afraid to look at Godefroi, but obviously determined.

"What's this, Masoun?" the knight asked.

"For the agister," Nicholas replied solemnly.

"Nine marks."

"It's all I have my lord."

Godefroi frowned.

"You mean you wish me to bribe him?" He thought of the stiff, humourless agister, always so precise with every detail of his accounts.

Nicholas reddened, but nodded.

The knight of Avonsford was half angry and half amused.

"You really think he'd take it?"

"Men say he does," the stoneworker mumbled.

Godefroi was astounded. He had known Nicholas all his life and he knew he would not lie. Obviously there were underhand dealings at Sarum that he did not know about.

"And you dare to ask me to do this?" he thundered.

Nicholas looked at the floor. His stubby hands trembled, but he did not move.

"I am only a poor villein, my lord. The agister would not speak to me."

But he'd take the fellow's money, Godefroi thought.

"Get out!" he roared.

Nicholas left hastily. But the nine marks remained on the table.

The following morning, moved by curiosity as much as anything else, Godefroi went early to the agister's house. Without a word, he tossed him the little bag; and was astonished by the response. With exactly the same blank stare and fixed smile with which he did everything else, Le Portier carefully counted the money.

"You want the boy to get off?" he asked.

"Obviously," the knight replied drily.

The agister's expression was serene.

"Nine marks is not enough."

"It's all there is."

Le Portier shook his head. Scarcely able to believe his ears, Godefroi demanded:

"How much then?"

"For Godric Body? Twelve marks."

With a gesture of contempt the knight gave him three more marks. The agister bowed politely.

"How will you get him off?"

Le Portier considered carefully before speaking.

[363]

"The deer was a raskell, you know," he said thoughtfully. This meant that it was not fit enough for the king's hunting. "The crime would still be serious, but the court would be less interested. Fewer questions asked." He paused. "Then," he pursed his thin lips, "I saw an identical snare set the other day, and a man running away from it. Godric Body was locked up by then, so it probably wasn't him that set the original snare at all."

Godefroi listened carefully.

"As for his slitting the deer's throat," Le Portier went on, "I shall say I told him to, seeing her leg was broken. I assumed he had set the snare you see, so in that sense he was caught bloody-handed. Of course, if he didn't, he wasn't." He appeared satisfied. "Of course, the dog will have to be lawed. He'll pay a fine for that."

Godefroi could not help admiring the fellow's cleverness.

"You should have been a priest," he muttered darkly, and strode away. It was well known that the forest officers often made a profitable business out of their offices, usually by making illegal charges – a mild if reprehensible form of extortion. But the agister's calm game with the boy's life apalled him.

"I hope I see you hang one day," he called back to him; at which Le Portier only stared and gave his tight-lipped smile.

A strange fellow, the knight concluded. He knew nothing of Le Portier's distant ancestry, and the idea that the agister's Porteus ancestors had fought with the real King Arthur would have astonished him indeed. And so it was with a flash of insight that he murmured:

"As stiff and exact as an ancient Roman: but his only point of honour is the precision with which he takes money – anyone's."

As he rode to the castle of Sarisberie, his anger gradually subsided.

At least, he thought, he had saved the boy.

The meeting of the swanimote took most of the morning, but at last the court was convened.

It was held in a hall in the castle: Waleran presided. All the forest officers were present: the inspecting knights, the verderers, foresters, woodwards and agisters. Each wore on their tunic the badge of their office – a bow for the warden, a horn for the foresters. A jury of twelve was selected from those present and then the court was in session. Though it was strictly a private court, the doors were left open and a small crowd pushed their way inside. Godefroi stood at the front; Nicholas a few paces from him. Out of the corner of his eye, the knight saw both the girl Mary and William atte Brigge working their way through the throng as the proceedings began.

The warden lost no time. As Godric was brought in, he turned sharply to the agister.

"Make your statement, Le Portier," he ordered.

Godefroi watched intently as the agister rose. His face was calm and, the knight thought he allowed the hint of a smile to cross his face as he glanced in his direction.

"The accusation is not quite as previously stated," he began smoothly.

But he got no further.

For the court was interrupted by a shout.

On the morning before the trial, Mary knew very well that Godric Body was about to be hung; and as she considered her new situation, the future was bleak.

She was poor; she was ill-favoured, and soon she would have a child. If she had not secured Godric, perhaps she might have found another man, though it had always been doubtful; but who would marry her now? She knew the answer very well. And she was only fourteen.

Once again, she had to ask herself the questions she had pondered the midsummer before. Would her life be long? She thought she could see it. She might work in the manor dairy for another forty years if she was lucky; or she might work in the fields and probably die sooner. Meanwhile, there would be the child to support.

"I wish it would die," she thought.

But she was sure the child within her was healthy.

Her situation was made all the plainer for her by the behaviour of the people in the village. Nicholas was too preoccupied with his own plans to have given the girl much more than a passing thought; most of the other villeins and their families, though they sympathised, instinctively avoided her, and even her parents were cool, fearing that she might be a liability to them.

"We can't afford to keep you and the child," her mother told her bluntly. "You'll have to keep yourselves."

She had been allowed to see Godric two days before. He asked her to bring him some pieces of wood from his cottage so that he could fashion another shepherd's crook to pass the time. But when she had brought them to him, he had been withdrawn: not because he had wished to hurt her, but from a feeling of helplessness.

"Is there a chance for you?" she had asked.

He had shaken his head; and soon afterwards she had gone.

On the morning of the trial, knowing nothing of Le Portier's bribe, she went into Sarisberie; and as she had expected, William atte Brigge was in the little market place with the other men. When she asked if he were still offering the reward for information about the pig she had learned that he was. And so she told him all she knew, because, after all, she reasoned perfectly, it must be done soon so that Godric could testify to the truth of it and tell them where the pig was buried. William atte Brigge roared with exultation, and better still, he gave her the money on the spot, took her by the arm and dragged her towards the court, just as the crowd was going in.

It had seemed the sensible thing to do.

While the buzz of excitement and surprise continued, the warden considered the interruption carefully.

"You accuse Godric Body of killing a second animal in the forest?"

"I do." There was triumph in the tanner's eye.

"If the slaying occurred within the forest bounds," the warden said, "then it falls within the consideration of this court." He glanced around and down at Godric. He was conscious that time was passing. "Very well. We'll hear both charges together. You have witnesses?"

The tanner grinned. And when he pointed at Mary, the face of Godric Body fell in disbelief.

While the tanner took his place before the warden, and all eyes were upon the squinting girl, Le Portier moved quietly to where Godefroi was standing. Unobserved, he removed the small bag of coins from his belt and dropped it into the knight's hand. Shaking his head he murmured:
"No hope."

The trial of Godric Body before the justices of the Forest Eyre did not take long.

On the first day of December, as a light rain was falling, he was led out to the gallows erected the day before in the market place in the castle. Godefroi and Nicholas were in the crowd who were watching; so was Mary. But as he stood on the platform under the gallows and the rope was slipped over his head, it was not at her, but at his dog Harold, now duly lawed and brought there at his special request by his uncle, that he sadly gazed.

There was no sound from the crowd – neither the cry of triumph which it reserved for a villain, nor the moan it gave for a popular man – as the gallowsman gave him the shove that sent him off the platform to drop and dangle in the air. His small, hunched body jerked helplessly as the noose did its work; and as his pale, pinched face grew purple, his desperate eyes, even as they started from their sockets, never once left the dog.

It was soon over.

Just after he had gone, Harold suddenly slipped his collar and lurched across the cobbles to where his master's body hung, so that Nicholas had to drag him away.

In the month of December 1139, several events of significance took place in the castle of Sarisberie.

On 10th December, as he was visiting the market, Godefroi heard terrible cries coming from the bishop's house, as though a madman were raging through the place. After a few moments, a servant ran out and the knight asked him what was amiss.

"The bishop, sir. The quartan fever has grown worse. I think it is a crisis. Four men are trying to hold him down and he's quite delirious."

It was now a month since Roger had been seen outside his house, and the whole town knew that the sickness had taken control of his massive frame.

"What is he shouting about?"

The servant grimaced.

"His castles and his treasure, sir. It's the loss of them that caused the fever I think."

Godefroi stared up at the house sadly. Its thick stone walls, decorated so beautifully in the zig-zag patterns Roger particularly favoured, were a tribute to his taste and wealth.

"Does the thought of God and his Church give his mind no relief?"

"No, sir."

There was a crash from within.

"Dear God I think he's broken loose again," the man exclaimed, and hurried away.

On 11th December, Bishop Roger died.

The next event, which followed soon afterwards, was the visit of the king. A truce had been arranged for the holy season and in his customary easy-going way, Stephen treated it as though it were a lasting peace.

He rode into the castle in high good humour, inspected its solid walls, the bishop's fine house and the stout tower. The treasure he found there astonished him.

"I think the bishop was richer than I!" he cried. And he took it all.

Nor was this all. The canons of the cathedral had decided to buy an exemption from the ancient geld tax levied on their lands, and offered him the princely sum of two thousand pounds for this privilege. This was another windfall which pleased the monarch still more, and as a token of his gratitude he donated forty marks towards the completion of the cathedral roof.

"I like your Sarisberie," he remarked to Godefroi when the knight came to pay his respects. "Before he rebelled its bishop served me well; and now the diocese has made me rich."

He admired the cathedral enormously, and told the canons:

"Whatever we say about Roger now he is dead, he certainly knew how to build."

It was a few days before Christmas, when he was holding an open court in the castle hall in the presence of a group of magnates and knights which included Godefroi, that the king was surprised to see a curious party approaching. It consisted of William atte Brigge, John of Shockley, their wives, both walking demurely behind them and a little gaggle of witnesses. William, still flushed with his triumph in the matter of Godric Body and the pig, looked hard and confident; the farmer on the other hand was very pale and his mild blue eyes wore a startled, pained expression.

When they were asked what their business was, it was William who cried out:

"The king promised me justice here, when he camped before Devizes."

As Stephen stared at the tanner, he dimly remembered, and he grinned.

"The fellow's right. I did." And turning to the knights he cried. "Let's hear what he wants."

As William explained his complaint, the king listened carefully. It was long and involved and after a time, he cut him short.

"You say this matter dates from the time of your wife's grandfather?" William agreed. "That's fifty years ago?" It was.

Stephen gazed around the hall. For all his faults, he was a clever man.

He had already sized up the respective characters not only of William, but of the stolid, blue-eyed farmer who stood looking silent and woebegone throughout the tanner's litany of complaint.

"We'll grant you your wish," he said finally. "Your case shall be tried." He paused. "But not by jury."

William's face fell. Although the system was not yet in regular use, he had assumed quite reasonably that if he requested it, the king – who was well known to dislike violence – would grant him a trial by jury. For months the cunning farmer had been carefully preparing his evidence and, more important, coaching his chosen witnesses.

The king gazed at him imperturbably.

"This is an ancient quarrel, William atte Brigge. It shall be settled by the ancient and time-honoured means that applied in our predecessor's reigns for all property disputes. I order a trial by battle."

He leaned back in order to watch the reaction. The tanner's brow had clouded. He was thinking furiously.

But a still more extraordinary change had come over John of Shockley. It was as though a huge weight had been lifted from his mind. For years he had dreaded the complex process of swearing and evidence, the intricate business of courts where, though he was by no means a fool, he felt trapped and helpless against the clever tanner. But now his brow cleared; his blue eyes lost their troubled look and suddenly gazed out with a clear, bold stare. The descendant of the family of Aelfwald the thane and Aelfgifu had no fear of fighting for his lands, if God was on his side. And he believed that He was.

The king, glancing from one to the other, smiled.

But William had not come so far for nothing.

"I have the right to choose a champion," he stated.

Stephen frowned. The surly fellow was right, unfortunately. And no doubt he had the money to hire a thug who would kill this honest farmer. He wished he could deny it.

"Do you also wish to choose a champion to fight for you?" he asked John of Shockley hopefully.

But John of Shockley, if he was aware of his danger, seemed content to fight for himself.

There was an awkward pause.

And then Godefroi saw what he should do. Coolly, to the astonishment of the two parties, and the delighted grin of the king, he stepped forward.

"I am John of Shockley's champion," he announced.

He had found a way to repay the farmer for his kindness.

William was silent. No champion that he could ever hope to purchase would last for a minute before the trained skill of a knight like Godefroi, even if he dared to fight him at all. The swift blade of the Norman would slice any bold rustic or even a man-at-arms to pieces before he could get close. He looked from side to side, baffled.

"Well," said the king with a show of impatience, "do you wish to proceed or not?"

The tanner scowled and hung his head.

"No, your Majesty," he finally muttered.

"Case dismissed," the king cried, with a wink to Godefroi; and to William's fury, the entire court burst out laughing.

He was defeated – all his work for nothing, and mocked into the bargain. But as the tanner left, he turned to his wife and swore:

"One day, our family will have revenge."

Christmas came, and in the castle of Sarisberie, King Stephen in the ancient and symbolic manner of the Norman king, summoned the local magnates to him and ceremonially wore his crown. But despite the king's presence, the knight of Avonsford still did not summon his family from London.

"Let's wait and see," he said to John of Shockley.

As Christmas passed and the period of truce drew towards an end, he was conscious more than ever of a sense of desolation hanging over the dark castle on its high chalk hill.

It was in the spring of the year of the Lord 1140 that Richard de Godefroi, a Norman knight of modest attainments who had begun to grow weary of the world, discovered a satisfactory way to save his soul.

It came to him on 5th January, when he had gone to the cathedral on the castle hill to pray and, as usual, he had knelt quietly by the tomb of Bishop Osmund. The day was bitterly cold. As he knelt and whispered his Ave Marias, his breath made little clouds of mist in front of him. Yet it seemed to Godefroi that, despite the cold, there was that day a special warmth – a sensation he thought he had noticed once or twice before – coming from the stone under which the saintly bishop lay; and while he remained beside it, he experienced a sense of peace. He remained at his prayers for longer than usual that day and, as usual, ended them with the request:

"In these godless times, show me, Osmund, what I must do."

It was a few minutes later, as he left the church, that he noticed Nicholas. The fellow was squatting near the doorway, his large head bent over a piece of parchment, and he was so engrossed in studying it that he did not even notice the knight approach.

"What's this, Masoun?" Godefroi asked him.

He looked up.

"This, my lord? It's a great mystery. See," and he lifted the parchment.

It was an elaborate design: a circle divided into four segments through which there twisted a single strip, like a serpent winding back and forth in great coils until it ended in a small circle at the centre. Godefroi frowned.

"A design?"

Nicholas nodded.

"It's a miz-maze. Look." His short, stubby finger pointed to the entrance to the pattern and then traced the winding path round the serpent, back and forth, coiling back upon itself before advancing to the next segment until finally it ended in the centre. The knight admired the little maze for its perfect, teasing symmetry.

"What's it for?"

"Several have been laid out on the floors of churches," Nicholas told

[369]

him. "And some cut in the turf out of doors as well. There's even one in Rome." He looked at the design admiringly. "It's a fine decoration of course, but they call them the Ways to Jerusalem, too." He smiled. "They say that men do penance for their souls by going round them on their knees, if they can't travel to Jerusalem."

Godefroi smiled as well.

"It's as good a penance as any, I suppose," he remarked, and put the matter out of his thoughts.

It was only two days later, as he walked up through the beech wood to his favourite retreat, that the beauty of the little maze suddenly returned to his mind. And as he inspected the quiet arbour in its circle of yew trees under the open sky, he could not help thinking what a perfect spot it would be for such a construction. Could it be that Bishop Osmund had been answering his prayer?

He decided to speak to Nicholas and look at the little design again.

In February 1140, while the kingdom of England enjoyed a brief period of peace, and while the ewes were lambing in the darkened sheep-houses on the slopes below, Nicholas, called Masoun, directed a small team of men in a curious labour.

On the surface of the ancient disk barrow in its circle of yew trees, they cut a strange design: dividing the circle into four segments they laid out a winding path that led from its outer edge, through each segment in turn, until at last, exactly as on the parchment's design, it arrived at the centre. It was an infuriating path. First it seemed to be going straight to the centre, then it would turn away, advancing and retreating, looping back on itself again and again, and finally flinging back to the outer edge before curving round, entering the next segment, and repeating the process again. Only on the last of the four journeys, when it seemed the path was about to fly off to the outer edge once more, did it suddenly and unexpectedly lead straight to the centre. It was, Godefroi shrewdly realised, a perfect allegory for the spiritual life: a subtle and perfect substitute for a pilgrimage.

"The men who designed this was a wise fellow," he remarked to Nicholas, but though the craftsman nodded, he was only aware of its geometric symmetry.

The making of the miz-maze was simple. The path was two feet wide, and was marked out by cutting a furrow into the packed chalk soil on each side so that the effect was of a green grass pattern laid over a white chalk base. Its measurements had an almost mystic symmetry which especially delighted the knight: it was thirty-six paces in diameter; and the journey through the maze was 660 paces from the entrance to the opening of the inner circle and 666 paces to the exact centre.

The men worked carefully and steadily.

Three days before the end of the month, the work was completed.

In the years that followed, the miz-maze of Godefroi, lord of Avonsford was greatly admired. But it was the cool, determined piety of the knight which was admired still more, and made him throughout Sarum, an object of awe.

For it soon became known that he had set himself a secret regime – secret because he practised it at dawn, and never spoke of it. For the rest of the day he managed his estate, performed his duties at the castle or in attending on his overlord as required; but during all the years the Anarchy raged and his family remained at London, he used to go silently up to the miz-maze at dawn each day, winter and summer, regardless of the weather, and alone on his knees he would make his way slowly round it to the centre. It used to take him an hour.

Why did he do it? It was not fanaticism certainly: he was a level-headed man. It was rather a grim, self-disciplined disgust with the world that led to his penance which, though it never gave him peace of mind, brought him a certain satisfaction.

By this means, it was calculated, he travelled over a hundred miles a year and, there could be no doubt, earned himself remission from many years of hell-fire.

And who should not try to save his soul at such a time? For at the castle of Sarisberie that stared so grimly over the five rivers below and the sweeping chalk ridges above, there could be no doubt that the times were very evil.

On 1st March 1140, three days after Godefroi's miz-maze was completed, there was a total eclipse of the sun and it surprised no one that, soon afterwards, the Anarchy broke out again.

NEW SARUM

The Founding

1244

AND NOW, AT the place where the five rivers met there was a new presence in the valley: in the gentle curve of the river a mile below the castle hill, a large area had been cleared and there, where before had been only broad meadows dotted with trees, a huge building site, several hundred acres in extent, was slowly rising.

It was larger than anything the people of Sarum had ever seen before. It seemed at times like a vast, strange plant, slowly unfolding through the coating of dust which covered it like pollen – or a huge creature emerging from its chrysalis; yet already its streets with their houses of wood and plaster, and its open ground with its enormous, half-built cathedral of grey stone, were teeming with activity, and already it could be seen that its outlines were to be stately and majestic. For this was the spacious city of New Salisbury.

It was not a fortified hill, like the old Norman founding town, nor a semi-fortified burgh, like the older Saxon foundations. It lay in a broad valley; it contained large, open spaces; it had no defensive wall, no castle keep; it was built for comfort and for trade.

To understand how it came to be there, it is necessary to go back a little.

Since the troubled reign of King Stephen, England had been, for the most part, at peace. It was a peace that had been laid by Stephen's nephew and successor, the son of the Empress Matilda, Henry II. From his parents, Henry received a huge Angevin inheritance across the Channel so that during his long reign he ruled not only England, but Normandy and huge tracts of France as well. His wars were fought abroad, while to the island he had given peace and a strong administration, law codes and the King's Justice founded on trial by jury. It was a legacy to England that neither his heroic but absentee son Richard Coeur de Lion, nor his younger and unlucky son John, who had lost most of the Angevin and Norman Empire, had managed to destroy. The order and peace of England was broken briefly at the end of John's reign by the revolt of the barons that culminated in the king's capitulation and sealing of the contract known as Magna Carta, and a short invasion of the eastern part of the island by the French king. When John died soon afterwards, it was the magnates themselves who wisely expelled the French, restored peace, and gave their support to John's son, the pious boy king, Henry III.

With the peace at home had come prosperity: a spectacular new prosperity – the richness of medieval England – that provided magnificent new cathedrals, and stately towns.

It was founded upon two things: rising agricultural prices, from a rising population – and sheep.

The wool of England was some of the best in Europe, it was plentiful, and the merchants of Flanders and Italy with their huge cloth business, could not get enough of it. Vast quantities of wool were exported and, for most of the time, the taxes and excise duties on it were low. In the early thirteenth century in feudal England, there was a huge capital expansion.

They were good times for most holders of land.

Above all, they were good times for the magnates.

The magnates were powerful. They allowed the monarch to rule – but only just. When a king like John found himself in the impossible position of having too little income from his feudal dues to pay for extraordinary expenses – usually wars – they resisted his efforts to raise money at every opportunity. The crisis of Magna Carta was as much the result of this natural tension as any tactlessness or wrongdoing on the part of King John. Indeed, the monarch was even short of funds with which to run his administration.

Partly for this last reason, and partly to appease the feudal vanity of these men, successive monarchs had allowed the magnates to govern huge tracts of land for them. In these great feudal domains, variously called honours, baronies or liberties, it was the magnate, acting as the representative of the king, whose courts tried all but grave offences; it was the magnates' servants who collected the taxes and fines; indeed, in some of these areas, even the king's own sheriff was not allowed to set foot unless the king had evidence of some major abuse of privilege on the magnate's part. For this kingdom within a kingdom, the magnate paid the king either by knight service or fixed rents.

True, as time went on and the king's courts grew more developed, the scope of these feudal authorities became less; but they were still sought after, not only because such feudal authority carried prestige, but also because the revenues, even from the trial of minor cases, were still extremely valuable.

By the time of King John, a third of the hundreds of Wiltshire, each with their own courts and administration, were in private hands; a century later, two thirds of them were. Great houses like that of the Longspées who had succeeded by marriage to the estates of the earldom of Salisbury, other notables like the families of Peverel, Pavely, and Giffard, all held these private feudal domains.

And amongst the greatest of all the magnates was the Church. The abbeys of Glastonbury, Malmesbury and Wilton, the priories of St Swithuns in Winchester and nearby Amesbury, and of course the Bishop of Salisbury all held private hundreds in the shire.

They paid the king a rent for these privileges, but the profits were theirs.

And one of the most profitable possessions a magnate could have on his domain in the changing world, was a town.

There were the rents from the buildings, the proceeds of the courts, the tolls and duties on incoming goods: the value of the franchise of a town was considerable.

In the new prosperity and peace of England, the opportunities for new towns seemed to grow every day. In the latter part of the previous century, the Bishop of Winchester had founded a number, nearly all of which were yielding a handsome profit for his diocese. It was natural therefore that the Bishop of Salisbury should want to follow suit.

He had a perfect excuse – or rather a catalogue of excuses. The site of the old cathedral was unsatisfactory. The cramped hillfort with its straggling suburbs was windy and poorly watered; the glaring chalk hurt the eyes; the cathedral priests were supposed to share this confined space with the king's military garrison, who, it was claimed, even interrupted the celebration of the divine services. But to the south of the hill, in the bowl of land where the five rivers met, lay the broad meadows known as Myrifields. There was only the little parish of St Martins down there. And this large, well-watered stretch of ground already belonged to the diocese.

In the year of Our Lord 1218, Bishop Poore – the second of two rich and powerful brothers to be Sarum's bishop – obtained permission from the pope and from the pious English boy king Henry III, to move the cathedral to a new and more pleasant site in the meadows below. He also, of course, got an agreement that he might found a new town beside it.

The new city was typical of the larger foundations of its day. All over England, for nearly a century, new market towns had been laid out with sophisticated geometric plans. Some were wedge-shaped, some semi-circular; but the largest like New Salisbury were usually laid out on a rectangular grid. Such civilized urban planning had not been seen on the island since Roman times, a thousand years before.

The bishop's new city lay in the gentle curve of the river Avon which came from the north and swept round its western and southern sides like an embracing arm. It consisted of two cells. One was the cathedral precincts – the close – a broad expanse of open ground in which the new cathedral would stand and around the edge of which the houses of the priests were being built. The other was the market town beside it, with its rectangular grid of streets and a huge market place at its centre.

The two cells each had their different functions: one spiritual, the other commercial. And both together, church and priests, market and traders belonged to the bishop, lock, stock and barrel. For the city was a feudal liberty and by the charter granted in 1227, the Bishop of Salisbury was its undisputed feudal lord.

It was a hot July day. The little gang of labourers were not enjoying their work.

Nor, in particular, was a small, stocky thirteen-year-old boy with a head too big for his body, tiny stubby hands, and solemn grey eyes, who though he was working under the watch of the stern cathedral canon, could not help glancing anxiously up the street.

For in the valley north of the city, unknown to the canon, a small group

[377]

of men including Godefroi and Shockley were meeting, and soon, if their meeting was successful, they had told him they would come and give him the chance to escape from this drudgery.

Several times he looked hopefully away from his work. It was back-breaking labour and he hated it. How he longed to change his life.

Canon Stephen Portehors stared at him coldly.

Of all the people in Sarum, no one was more insignificant, more utterly unimportant, than young Osmund the Mason. Osmund knew it too, for Canon Stephen had told him so himself.

"In the eye of God, you are as small, Osmund, as a grain of dust," the priest had explained. "But remember," he added ominously, "he sees everything that you do – for not even a grain of dust can hide from the Father. Your sins will all be known."

Now the canon was beckoning. And Osmund knew why: he had sinned.

It seemed to Osmund that, wherever he looked, there was dust.

There was dust like a shimmering haze around the huge grey pile of the rising cathedral looming a few hundred yards to the south. There was dust on the broad open space of the cathedral close – the two-hundred-acre precinct around the cathedral, which stretched from the eastern boundary ditch to the river. There was dust on the piles of grey Chilmark stone around the construction site, dust on the carts, planks, scaffolding, on the coils of rope and the heaps of rubble to fill the walls; dust all over the spacious plots where the fine stone houses of the priests were being built with gardens backing on to the sweeping curve of the Avon river; dust on the river itself; dust on the long dark riverweeds that waved slowly in the stream. The swans who drifted at their secret, measured pace past the green banks were half grey with it. There was dust on the flat marshy meadows that stretched past Fisherton and Bemerton villages to Wilton beyond. All over the half-completed chequerboard of the new town beside the cathedral precincts there was dust from the lathe and plaster houses.

There was dust, he could even see it, like a pale grey mantle over the dark, half-deserted castle on its hill. And on the slopes above, on the bare high ground, whenever the wind came from the south, the sheep gave off a puff of grey chalk if you handled them. The pale blue butterflies, too, seemed to carry a subtle coating of it as they shimmered up in their summer clouds from the hard warm ground. Even that great curious circle of fallen stones to which he had once walked, eight miles away, had seemed to have collected the dust from the new city. It looked like a strange, outlying satellite of the building site itself, as if it might be arising once again, instead of falling silently into decay.

He was covered with dust himself. The dour canon too, had collected a rim of dust on his shoulders.

It choked Osmund, and irritated him.

Yet he knew he should be grateful.

"Our city is built on a rock," the canon had told him. "Our foundations are sure."

Indeed, this was literally true, for although much of the surrounding terrain was marshy, the ground the wise bishop had chosen in Myrifield was firm.

"See," Canon Stephen had pointed out to young Osmund the day before, "though this site is low, if you dig down a little you come to a thick layer of gravel." And as Osmund had looked into the trench beside which they were standing, he could see that this was so. "The gravel is strong – it will support even the greatest cathedral we could build," the priest assured him. "Be grateful that you were born at such a time, when you can see such great works undertaken, to the glory of God."

But now the priest was angry. His hair was grey and thin but his eyebrows were bushy and still mainly black, curling up at the outer corners like a tawny owl. The eyes themselves were dark brown and piercing. As he spoke, it seemed to Osmund that his voice was as hard and cutting as flint.

"Name the seven deadly sins, Osmund."

The sins committed deliberately and with knowledge, the sins that ensured that the sinner would go to hell: the priest at Avonsford had made sure he knew those from his earliest childhood.

"Anger, gluttony, envy, sloth, avarice, lust, and pride," he recited glumly.

Portehors nodded.

"And of which are you guilty today?"

How much did the canon know? Osmund considered carefully.

The work on which he had been engaged all summer, this splendid and unusual feature of the new city was, everyone knew, Canon Stephen Portehors's particular pride and joy. The water courses of New Salisbury, though still unfinished, were already much admired. Tapping off the Avon just above the city, they formed a network of stone channels that ran down the centre of the most significant streets; they varied from two to six or seven feet wide and were crossed by tiny foot bridges every few yards.

"They bring the river into the very town itself," Portehors would announce proudly. "What could be more pleasant – or more healthy?"

Indeed, they were more important to him than the streets themselves: and when a few months before he had noticed that the ground along one of the main north-south streets being laid out was not quite level, he had altered the course of the street itself, and hence the whole of one side of the new town, in order to keep his precious watercourse on even ground.

"Precision," he insisted. "The water will only run if the levels are exact."

Exact. When the labourers had heard that word they shrugged gloomily; for it was well known in Sarum that the priest and his brother in the town had their family's mania for exactness, and as soon as a word like precision was spoken, it was useless to argue. They had had to lay out the whole street and dig a new channel again.

And how the boy hated it!

Osmund the Mason. His name was a mockery to him. Though like his father and grandfather, both occasional stoneworkers at Avonsford, he too bore the nickname of 'Masoun' or Mason, it meant nothing. He was only a humble serf, a labourer who was occasionally allowed to trim the stones for these cursed water channels, if he was lucky.

For the masons were the craftsmen who worked on the great cathedral. And that was another world. True, it was a world he sometimes dreamed of. When his day's work was done, he would often walk into the magical quiet of the close and watch the craftsmen about their business in the huge building. He would see the solemn master masons, who ran the masons' guild, the elect, who came from all over the country and even from across the Channel. But they, and the ordinary masons, had all been engaged long ago. Even their apprentices were usually from their own families. Why should they take notice of a young serf from Avonsford whose father had once worked in stone?

Yet the spirit of the carver was in his blood. One day, he vowed, he would find a way – he would work in the cathedral itself, amongst those masons in their heavy aprons who strutted so proudly to their work each day.

It was over a century since Godric Body had swung on the gallows on the castle hill; a few months afterwards his son had been born; and since the baby's mother died in childbirth, it had seemed only natural to his uncle Nicholas to take the baby in and bring the boy up as his own. As a result, the children and grandchildren of Godric Body had usually been nicknamed Mason, like the rest of their adopted family, and when, eighty years after Godric's death, one of his descendants had married his short, stocky cousin, the squat body, short thumbs and large head of the Mason clan had been passed on to their son. Though typical of the busy Mason clan in his looks, however, the boy Osmund had a secret wildness of imagination, a feeling for natural forms, that derived directly from the unlucky young shepherd carver who had been hanged. It was a genius that the stolid-looking young serf, though he loved to carve, still only vaguely sensed.

At the moment, all that was offered him was drudgery, and he had to admit, he did not always work as hard as he should.

So as he gazed at the thin, greying priest he answered sadly:

"The sin of sloth."

Canon Stephen nodded.

"Yes. You are slothful because you do not like the work. But God did not make you to be happy: he made you to serve, and only by serving him will you earn any heavenly reward."

Osmund hung his large head. Though a part of him still rebelled, he knew that the canon, though harsh, was just. He turned to go.

"Stop." The voice of the canon was relentless. "That is not all. You are hiding another sin, my son."

How could he know? The youth felt the canon's eyes on his back, and did not want to turn round.

"Well?"

Osmund still did not speak.

"Then I will tell you," the cutting voice went on. "The sin is avarice." He hissed the word.

So he knew.

He was paid a penny a day; he was poor.

"Men who should know better are tempting you to work for them, when you are needed here," the canon accused. "Ungodly men."

It was true, every word. And yet it had not seemed such a crime.

For this was what he had been waiting for so anxiously all morning. The men returning from their meeting had promised to offer him a penny and a half to work for them: an excellent wage, that might last a year until the work was completed. He knew them well. They had not seemed so ungodly. He turned round slowly, wondering how the canon had found out.

"You would desert your work here for money, Osmund. You are young. But the love of money is avarice, and that is a sin." He paused, fixing the youth with his terrible gaze, then asked more kindly: "You cut stone well. They tell me you also carve wood"

Osmund nodded. He had carved a fine door for Godefroi at the manor of Avonsford and he knew the priest had seen it. But the canon's next words astonished him.

"Should you like to work at the cathedral?"

Osmund stared at Portehors, hardly daring to believe the question. To work in the cathedral with the masons – his dream? The priest regarded him shrewdly.

"They are paid a penny and a quarter a day," he said quietly, "but not more." He waited a moment before continuing. "You could start at Michaelmas, if you work well on the watercourses. Do you want to?"

"Oh yes," his voice was almost pleading. He could not help it.

"Good." The priest paused a moment. "Of course, if you work for Shockley and his friends, you will never work for the cathedral. Ever."

Osmund paled, but did not speak.

Stephen Portehors watched him calmly; he was not a canon of the cathedral for nothing.

He had seen young Osmund's work at Avonsford. He suspected the young fellow had talent.

It was at this moment that the Shockleys and Godefroi came riding down the street and the canon turned to face them.

The hair of the ferret-faced man who stood by the bridge, though it might once have been destined to shoot straight up from his head like a tuft of black grass, had – since it was rarely washed or brushed – relapsed instead into a dozen or so matted strands that stood in dispirited clumps like a small bush that had been charred. And in this tangled mess on his head, as it did on all things, the dust of New Salisbury had settled too.

William atte Brigge was about to experience the worst day of his life.

He was angry already. As he looked at the scene before him his small, close-set eyes were glittering with rage.

He had come with his small cart from Wilton that morning. He had crossed the Avon at Fisherton bridge and gone straight to the market place in the middle of the bishop's new town. There he had left it with another trader from Wilton who had a stall, and made his way past the rising cathedral building to the southern tip of the new settlement, where the river curved round before turning south on its slow way to the coast.

To a casual observer, his behaviour now might have seemed strange.

In front of him was a new stone bridge. It crossed the river in two short leaps, between which lay a little island. On his left stood the cluster of buildings that was the hospital of St Nicholas; on the island stood the little chapel of St John, both of them built there by Bishop Bingham for travellers. It was a pleasant spot, the water murmuring soothingly as it passed on either side of the island.

William crossed to the centre of the bridge. First he glanced down the road on the other side that led to the south and west; then he looked back at the rising city; next he stared glumly at the little grey building on the island. And then, suddenly seized by some inner rage, he jumped up and down, flapping his thin arms, before turning and spitting viciously at the hospital. He spat once again, this time on the dusty road in front of him. Then he cried out: "Damn that bishop and all his works," before turning and loping gloomily back towards the city.

William atte Brigge was a naturally resentful man – but today he had cause to be bitter: for the revered Bishop Bingham of Salisbury was about to ruin him.

Since the time of King Alfred and before, the town of Wilton had been the capital of the shire. Not only did the sheriff hold his court there, not only had there been a mint in the town since Saxon times, but above all it had been a thriving market, well situated at the junction of two busy rivers. True, there had been the little market in the old castle on Sarum hill. But because of the place's exposed position and its lesser status it had never seriously damaged the business of the old Saxon town in the western valley. But a quarter of a century ago when Bishop Poore had started to build his new market town in the valley, the burgesses and traders of Wilton had begun to be anxious. Soon the bishop was granted the right to hold both an annual fair, and a market day each week; its charter also gave its freemen important trading concessions and tax exemptions similar to those granted to other great cities like Winchester, or Bristol. Worse, the royal hunting lodge in the forest of Clarendon was only two miles east of the bishop's new town, and King Henry, who liked to hunt there, had a well known passion for new church building.

"The new town will soak up all the money," the Wilton burgesses grumbled. "The king's not interested in us."

They were right. But at first there had been one compensating factor. For as the trade of the area grew and the traffic on its roads increased, many traders were coming to the new settlement from the south and west, and in order to cross the river system and enter the city, they had to use the bridge at Wilton. The Wilton traders therefore benefited from the traffic. For twenty years it had seemed that the old burgh in the west might even flourish beside its new neighbour. But now, in 1244, the inevitable had happened: Bishop Bingham had built his own bridge south of the cathedral. By crossing at Ayleswade, and paying a small toll, visiting merchants could get over this part of the river system without going near Wilton at all, and the older town was suddenly cut off from the mainstream of trade.

Nor was that all. Since time immemorial, the old burgh of Wilton had held two market days a week in its little square. The bishop had only been granted one. But the merchants in the broad expanse of New Salisbury's market were trading without a licence almost every day of the week, and no one was stopping them. Despite the frequent protests to the king from the burgesses of Wilton, the new foundation was sucking its life blood away.

William's family had made little progress since their aborted lawsuit a century before. Though he bore the same name as his great-grandfather who had so uselessly challenged the farmers from Shockley, William was not a tanner but a minor wool merchant, making a precarious living by advancing money to the smaller peasant farmers on the security of their wool, which he then sold in the open market. Since wool prices were firm and the trade booming, he managed to make small gains in this developing futures market. His wife and her sister had also inherited the tenancy of a cottage on one of the Godefroi estates; as a result of this, he owned thirty sheep which he grazed above the river Avon. To supplement the family's modest income further, his sister-in-law wove a poor quality cloth on a single loom which he then sold for his own profit in the local markets at cut prices. In these ways he made a living; but he was poorer than his great-grandfather the tanner.

The family had never forgiven the prosperous farmers at Shockley.

"Those Shockley folk are thieves," he told his children. It was an article of faith. And now the Shockleys had taken a house in the new town as well, the new town that was going to ruin Wilton.

"Curse them, and curse that bridge," he muttered.

But if he was angry when he contemplated the bishop's bridge, it was nothing compared to the fury he experienced when he reached the market place.

There were a dozen people standing by his cart; some were curious, a few openly grinning. The Wilton man in whose care he had left it was looking glum; and in the centre of the group, calm but severe, stood a figure he dreaded: Alan Le Portier, the aulnager. His daughter Alicia stood just behind him.

The aulnager was pointing at the cart. "Your cloth?"

The assize of aulnage had been instituted by King Richard half a century before. It was a simple tax on cloth, together with a set of standard measures that must be observed. Alan Le Portier had chosen a different variant of the family name, but like his brother Canon Portehors, he was a thin, exacting man: and when the great William Longspée had recommended him for the post of aulnager, that grand noble had assured the royal officials with a laugh:

"You needn't worry, he's just like all his family: he'll count every fibre in the cloth if he has to."

As he approached, William looked from the aulnager's face to his daughter's. Alan was a little greyer than his brother. His thin face was refined but stern and the eyes were dark. The daughter Alicia, a pleasant looking girl of sixteen with hazel eyes was watching him curiously. She often went round the market with her father whom she admired, and she knew all its ways.

The aulnager repeated the question.

"Your cloth?"

He nodded.

"A quarter inch too narrow."

Who could have guessed that he would notice? By short-changing his customers this tiny fraction on the width, he could make a modest profit even at his discounted prices. He should never have left the cart where the piercing eyes of Le Portier might find it.

"You'll be fined of course," the aulnager told him matter-of-factly. "Better take it all back to Wilton. You can't sell it here."

William hung his head. It could have been worse: the aulnager could have impounded the merchandise; but it would still be hard to dispose of the cloth now. And it was two months' work. Without a word he took the long handles of the cart and began dragging it away. As he went, he heard Le Portier remark to his daughter:

"You have to watch that family."

He cursed them all, under his breath.

The meeting that so interested young Osmund took place by the side of the river Avon that morning, half a mile south of the village of Avonsford.

Two splendid horses and a cart had been left beside the track above the river. Twenty feet away, a little group consisting of two men and a boy were conversing in low tones; below them on the edge of the river bank, a single figure in a long black cloak with a hood was pacing up and down, deep in thought. The other three glanced at him from time to time, anxiously.

Jocelin de Godefroi, Edward Shockley and his eighteen-year-old son Peter, were awaiting the decision of the hooded man below.

"If he will agree this morning to what we ask," Edward had told his son, "it will be the most important thing I have ever done. It'll make our fortune."

Now they were waiting for the hooded man, and Shockley could hardly contain himself.

The family had prospered modestly. They had kept the farm of Shockley, which had now become their family name, but as a young man, Edward had taken the house in the new city as well, and there he had opened a small but profitable business by installing three large looms at which he employed weavers for making cloth. The times were busy; the family was trusted and well liked. Big, bluff Edward Shockley had become a member of the merchant guild of the new town; by 1240 he was a burgess of some standing and the Shockley farm was managed on a day to day basis by a villein who acted as steward.

Jocelin de Godefroi was calmer.

Since the terrible reign of Stephen, the times had favoured his family. Though Edward of Salisbury and his brother had declared for the empress against the king in the Anarchy, they had kept their influence when Stephen finally prevailed, and no harm had come to their minor follower, Godefroi. Indeed, under Henry II and Richard, the family had not only prospered but won honour for itself when the great Ranulf de Godefroi had fought with Richard Coeur de Lion in the third crusade to the Holy Land. In the little church at Avonsford, a splendid tomb bore a statue of Ranulf, lying with his sword at his side, a broad cross on his chest and one leg crossed over the other, in the traditional posture of the deceased crusader knight. The little pewter badge which had been sold to him by monks in the Holy Land as a memento of his pilgrimage, had been set into the outer rim of the church bell. For these and other deeds, the family was honoured locally. They had obtained a second estate at Sarum too, this one held directly of the king, and now that the king was choosing some of the lesser nobles for the position, there was even a rumour that a notable gentleman such as Jocelin de Godefroi might be asked to serve as sheriff.

But in one important respect, Jocelin was very different from his ancestors: for though he had two estates, he had only one home: and that was England.

This state of affairs was new. For the first hundred and fifty years after the Conquest, many a Norman and Breton had held estates both in England and across the Channel; asked to state which was home, many would have had difficulty in replying; but when King John in his disastrous wars lost Normandy to the French king, those with estates in both regions were told they must choose – either they must give up their English estates and do homage to the French king, or vice versa. The Godefroi family of Avonsford had chosen England. The loss had not been serious. Both monarchs, as feudal men themselves to whom the idea of the family was still far more important than any vague concept such as a nation, gave their vassals time to rearrange their affairs and the Godefroi estates in Normandy were satisfactorily disposed of by sale in due course. But as a result of this, Jocelin was the first of the family who had never known a second country as home and who, if asked his identity would have answered not Norman, but English.

He was a fine figure, of medium height. Unlike his ancestors in Stephen's reign, he was clean-shaven, and his hair, instead of being parted, was cut in a fringe across his forehead and curled carefully, with heated tongs, under the ears, giving his fine-boned, aquiline face an intellectual look. He wore the long cotte robe of linen that fell to his ankles and over it a surcoat lined with fox fur. His soft leather shoes, buttoned round the ankle, were embroidered with silver thread on their long points, and in his hand he held a three-cornered felt cap. On a golden chain round his neck hung two little amulets which commemorated his own two pilgrimages: one from St James of Compostella in Spain, and the other from the shrine of St Thomas à Becket, killed after his quarrel with Henry II at Canterbury, only seventy years ago. From his horse's bridle hung two tiny enamel shields an inch across, bearing his coat of arms – a white swan on a red ground.

For no family in Sarum was more devoted to the cause of chivalry than that of Godefroi. At the end of the last century, when that irresponsible paragon of chivalry Richard I had started the jousting tournaments in the broad fields between the old castle of Sarisberie and the town of Wilton, no knight had supported them more vigorously than old Ranulf de Godefroi. His son, and now his grandson, were amongst the most prominent patrons and organizers of these festivals.

For all that however, Jocelin had a good head for business, and the meeting today was about a highly important venture, so that he, too, carefully watched the hooded figure who was now, at last, coming up the slope towards them.

Now he reached them. What would the verdict be?

He was a large, well-built figure, somewhat inclined to stoutness, and he stepped heavily on the turf as he walked. As he reached them, he pulled back his hood, to reveal a dome-like, balding head, with hair greying at the temples, and a face with a fine aquiline nose, a firm, pleasant mouth and broadset blue eyes that were full of humour and intelligence. He was thirty, but already an experienced man of affairs.

"The current is strong; the ground's firm." He smiled. "You have your loan."

He spoke in French, since it was Godefroi that he was addressing; and both this fact, the rich cloak he wore and the splendid horse which obviously belonged to him suggested that he was a member of the Norman ruling class. Yet there was one strange feature of his dress: on his chest was sewn a double rectangle of white cloth about two inches across and three in length: a badge, known as the tabula, that represented the two tablets of stone which bore the Ten Commandments. For Aaron of Wilton was a Jew.

The Jews of England belonged to the king. They had mostly come from northern France and both the Conqueror and his sons Rufus and Henry had encouraged them to settle in their new kingdom where, although they were forbidden to own land or engage in ordinary trade, they enjoyed a privileged and protected status in the Norman feudal system as financiers and moneylenders. The Jews were not the only group to perform this necessary function. Both the Italian merchants and the most Christian order of Knights Templar, whose international network was large, lent money too; but in England the Jews were the most significant raisers of finance at a time when the need for ready money for the king for his crusades, foreign wars and mercenaries, was increasing and when the expanding economy of the island had no other corporate body within its feudal system for raising liquid capital. French-speaking, often cultured, and necessary to the court and greater magnates, their leaders – though outside the feudal caste as such – were closer to being aristocrats than any other group apart from the bishops and greater churchmen. And for about a century, their relationship with the Church itself – whose bishops frequently required funds to raise their great cathedrals and whose monasteries soon found themselves tempted into borrowing on the security of their huge output of wool – were usually friendly.

The community had thrived, despite a few local demonstrations against them, through the long reign of Henry II in the twelfth century as well; they became treasury agents for the king, raising finance for him on the security of the revenues that the sheriffs received from the shires, and thus anticipating the sophisticated government borrowing of later centuries. They were even allowed to hold land as tenants-in-chief of the king as well. Technically the king still owned them. The estate of every Jew escheated to the king upon his death, but this was a privilege the king rarely exercised in practice, since it hardly made sense to destroy his own bankers when they could be of such use. And useful they certainly were. By the latter part of the twelfth century, the king began to raise money from the Jewish community by the system of arbitrary taxes, the tallages, which he could impose at will. And although Henry II was moderate in his demands, by the last part of his long reign, about one seventh of his entire yearly revenue came from the Jewish community.

"We may be useful," Aaron's father had warned him. "But do not ever think we can be secure."

He had good reason for his caution. The crusaders had whipped up a general prejudice against all who could be accused of being infidels, and in England the preparations for King Richard's crusade had seen a new series of anti-Jewish riots in some cities, culminating in the terrible affair at York, when a hundred and fifty Jews trapped in the castle where they had gone for protection, killed themselves rather than face a worse fate from the armed mob. But this trouble was quickly stopped by Richard himself and, once again, the Jewish community was given relative security under the king's protection.

But the tallages increased. When Richard was captured and held to ransom on his return from the Holy Land, the little Jewish community were taxed five thousand marks – three times what was given by the burghers of the mighty trading city of London. And under his successor John, always short of money, the taxes reached ever higher levels.

Indeed, the position of the king in this became curious. For while the Church, despite the activities of its own agents, increasingly condemned the practice of lending money at interest, which it termed usury, and while the king paid lip service to this doctrine, it was the King of England, by his increasing tallages, who reaped most of the profits of the Jewish financial system he retained under his protection; and it was therefore a fact that the greatest usurer in the realm was the king himself.

Whatever the faults of the system, it was certainly well organized. There was a separate court and exchequer for the community; and there were a number of towns where the official records of all moneylending transactions were kept in the *archae*, the great chests for holding these chirograph documents. Wilton, which had long possessed a prominent Jewish community, was one of them and Aaron was one of its most senior members.

It was a century since his family had arrived there and he knew both Godefroi and Shockley well. His own grandfather had, in happier times, enjoyed long and friendly arguments with the great Ranulf de Godefroi; his father had made a small loan to Edward Shockley when he had first set up his business in New Salisbury. It was natural that both families should now have approached him to help them with this new and much more substantial venture.

Aaron turned to Shockley next.

"One question," he said seriously: "You already have a farm and your weavers in the town. Who is to oversee this new business, day to day?"

Edward pointed to Peter.

"My son."

Aaron's blue eyes took in Peter Shockley carefully. He liked the young man, had known him since he was a boy; he was steady enough, but he sensed an impulsiveness in him, that gave him a slight concern.

"Very well. But he's young," he said. "You must keep an eye on him." He began to move towards his horse.

Was it possible that he had forgotten the most important condition? Godefroi and Shockley looked at each other.

"Aaron." Edward Shockley stopped him. "You haven't said," he paused nervously, "the rate of interest."

The Jew smiled.

"Did I forget? How careless. Shall we say the usual?"

The two men sighed audibly with relief. It was better than they had dared to hope for.

In the growing economy of the thirteenth century, when liquid capital was so hugely in demand and the supply was still so limited even ordinary rates of interest were high. The normal rate was between one and two pennies in the pound per week – an annual rate of twenty-one to forty-three per cent: but when the king imposed heavy tallages on the lending community it often forced rates up and, although the king officially disallowed them, rates of sixty or eighty per cent were not unknown. Nor was this high cost of money confined to Jewish creditors. The Christian Cahorsin merchants would often make out a bond for half as much again as the amount of a loan, to be paid at the end of the current year – thus in fact charging a fifty per cent interest over what might be a period of only a few months. But business was booming and both landowners and merchants were prepared to pay the staggering rates. Aaron however had dealt with both Shockley and Godefroi families for years: the usual rate to which he referred was a comparatively modest twenty-five per cent.

The party mounted, Aaron and Godefroi on their horses, Shockley and his son in their cart; since they all had business to attend to in the new city, they rode together at a leisurely walk down the green Avon valley.

As they did so, Edward Shockley turned to his son and whispered softly:

"We'll start to build at once." And then he added, not for the first time. "This mill will make our fortune."

Peter nodded. It was a splendid venture. He would run it, and then – then, to be sure he would marry Alicia. He smiled with anticipation at the thought. Le Portier could hardly refuse a young man with a mill.

The mill in which Godefroi and the Shockleys were investing had nothing to do with grinding corn. It was for making cloth, and it was a symbol of the era.

The process of clothmaking had altered very little from the most ancient times. First the sheep were sheared and the wool gathered; then the wool was combed, or carded with a thistle to straighten the fibres and open them out; then it was washed and dried to remove surplus grease. Next, the raw wool was spun – pulled and twisted into twine with a spindle – and this slow process was accomplished by hand, for the spinning wheel was not yet invented. Only then could the business of weaving begin.

The looms on which the cloth was woven had, for the previous two thousand years, been very simple: a high cross bar over which the long strands of yarn – the warp – was hung and weighted: then the shorter strands – the weft – were threaded through them and pushed tight with a crossbar. A thousand times this simple business, threading the weft in accordance with a carefully designed pattern, was repeated by hand and slowly, inch by inch, the rough cloth appeared on the loom. This continued until the end of the long warp was reached, which was the end of that piece of cloth.

This was the vertical loom. But more recently, a far better machine had come into use. In this, the warp was held in place horizontally on a frame and wound round a revolving beam, so that a roll of cloth of unlimited length could be woven. Moreover, the cloth could easily be made in broad strips by seating two men opposite each other on each side of the loom who could pass the waft between them. This was the double horizontal loom which revolutionised the medieval textile business, and it was these that Shockley possessed.

But the newly made cloth from the loom was, as yet, unusable. The fibres were still comparatively loose, the wool full of dirt and impurities; the next and important stage was the fulling: treading the raw cloth in vats of water to which a detergent, usually stale urine, had been added. As the fullers walked the cloth in the vats which gave off their pungent smell of ammonia, the cloth shrunk and tightened, and all the remaining dirt in the wool was loosened and fell out. Then, when the fulling was completed, the acrid smelling cloth was thoroughly rinsed. Afterwards, while it was still damp, the nap was raised with a teasle of thistle heads and then the nap was trimmed with straight ended shears. Lastly, it was spread on tenter frames to be dried.

The fulling process was laborious and long – it often lasted twenty hours at high temperatures – and it was heavy work: the heavier the cloth, the more thorough the fulling had to be; so that with a thick felt for instance, the cloth was so shrunk and beaten that it became impossible even to see the original weave at all.

It was at this period of the island's history that two more important changes were beginning to take place in the wool trade. The first was a gradual increase in clothmaking. As decade followed decade, though most cloth was still imported from Flanders and Italy, English-made cloth was beginning to make headway as well. The second development was mechanical: the introduction of the mechanical fulling mill.

And it was the potential of this huge new machine that had so excited Edward Shockley.

"You see," he explained to Godefroi, "it operates just like a corn mill: the river turns the wheel, but instead of millstones, you have two huge wooden hammers on a ratchet that pound the cloth continuously. It can do the work of ten fullers: and the heavier the cloth, the more effective it is."

The fulling mill was making its appearance in many places, especially in the west of the island. Though often resisted by the local fullers, who feared it might compete with their own traditional methods, it was a far more effective way of working on the heavier cloths. It looked exactly like a corn mill, the only difference as one drew closer being the rhythmic thump of the two heavy wooden hammers, and the pungent smell from the ammonia. Already, the Bishop of Winchester had set up such a mill on his nearby estate at Downton.

"There's more cloth being made every year," Shockley argued. "If we have a mill already operating, we can profit from this growth."

All that he needed in order to do this was a parcel of land by the river at a spot where a mill race could easily be constructed, and a backer with sufficient capital resources to build the mill, or give security for the money that would be needed to do so. Naturally he had gone to Godefroi.

Under their agreement, Godefroi was borrowing the money for the mill from Aaron and would build it on the new estate he held as a tenant-in-chief and where he was free to do as he pleased without needing the permission of any superior landlord. Shockley, as the entrepreneur, in turn agreed to pay him half the receipts of the mill from all those who brought cloth to it from outside Godefroi's estates, and all the receipts from Godefroi's tenants and villeins – who would be compelled by the knight, as their feudal overlord, to use his mill. So Godefroi, using his ample lands as security for the loan, would add a valuable asset to his estate; and his feudal tenants would be compelled, indirectly, to increase his income. It was a combination of capitalism and feudalism that was typical of the times.

The building was not complicated, but solid stonework and carpentry would be required.

"Who will do the masonry?" Aaron enquired of Godefroi as they rode along.

"We've got a young fellow from my estate," the knight replied, "who's working in the town at the moment. He seems to be competent. His name's Osmund."

Aaron smiled.

"Cheaper than hiring a master mason you can't trust," he remarked.

"Exactly," Godefroi agreed.

When, half an hour later, William atte Brigge saw the little cavalcade of Godefroi, Aaron of Wilton and the hated Shockleys coming down the street, he knew instinctively that he did not like it; and when the party paused, while Godefroi turned aside to speak with a merchant, he loped across the street and sidled up to Aaron. Neither man liked the other, but as they were neighbours at Wilton, both observed a guarded politeness.

"What's up?" William asked. "Godefroi and Shockleys after money?" Aaron said nothing. "They in trouble?" he suggested hopefully.

"Not at all. A very good investment I think." Briefly he outlined the plan for the fulling mill. "I've already helped finance two others in the west," he added calmly.

But William's face clouded. His mind was making connections rapidly. His wife's loom, his sheep, the source of his miserable cloth, lay on Godefroi's estate. That could mean only one thing. His suspicions were confirmed a moment later when he became aware of the knight's horse with its enamel decorations looming over him and Godefroi staring down at him with undisguised contempt.

"Doesn't your wife's family weave cloth on my land?" he demanded curtly.

William nodded.

"Good. They'll be fulling it at my mill shortly." He nudged his horse forward and the cart bearing the Shockleys rumbled after him. William heard someone laugh; he did not know who. Nor did he look up to see.

So the cloth which he had fulled cheaply before in Wilton, the cloth from his own sheep, would now have to go to a mill run by the cursed Shockleys. He would have to pay them and Godefroi to ruin him. And there was nothing, absolutely nothing in the world that he could do about it.

Furiously he grabbed his cart and began to haul it away; but as he did so the accumulated insults of the day swelled in his mind until he could bear it no longer. Suddenly he stopped.

"Damn the bishop and his bridge! Damn that aulnager! Damn that Jew and the Shockleys!" he screamed. Taking the bales of defective cloth he hurled them onto the dusty road, and turned to make his way under the sweltering sun, back towards Wilton.

Since Aaron had halted briefly in the market place, it was Godefroi and the two Shockleys who first confronted Canon Portehors. And since he knew nothing of what had taken place between Portehors and Osmund that morning, it was without any sense of danger that the knight reined his horse and beckoned to the boy to approach him.

But before Osmund could get up from the ditch where he was kneeling, he found himself pushed peremptorily back by the priest who now strode angrily towards the knight.

"What do you want with this young man?"

Godefroi eyed the priest calmly from his horse.

"I wish to speak to him. He is my villein."

"He is busy."

Godefroi inclined his head courteously. "I shall only detain him a moment, Canon Portehors."

But Portehors did not shift his ground.

"If it is your intention to entice him from his work here, I forbid it."

Godefroi stiffened. The priest had no jurisdiction over the young fellow whereas he, as the boy's feudal lord, had.

"I'll thank you not to interfere," he said sharply.

Portehors did not move. The knight therefore ignored him and spoke to Osmund.

"We shall need you tomorrow to begin work on the mill," he said pleasantly. "Report to the reeve at daybreak."

Godefroi was about to turn away.

He had no wish to confront Portehors and it seemed to him that the incident was closed.

But to the canon it was not.

"He is engaged in the Church's work," he declared.

It had not occurred, of course, to either the canon or the knight to refer any part of this matter to the boy himself, although in theory Osmund was free to engage himself as he wished on those days when he did not owe his feudal lord labour services. To Portehors, at least, the matter was too important even to consider Osmund's wishes any longer, for now there was a point of principle at stake.

At the canon's last statement however, Godefroi frowned in surprise.

"But he is building ditches in your street." He pointed to the half finished watercourse.

Portehors hesitated for only a second.

"Tomorrow he begins work on the cathedral." In order to suit his argument, Osmund's destiny had just been altered.

Godefroi paused. Although he had a perfect right to the lad's services, he would not normally have chosen to remove a worker from the cathedral itself. But he sensed that Portehors was altering the facts, and it irked him to be put upon.

"He will work for me," he stated flatly.

But Portehors, having aroused himself, was now stubborn. His eyebrows contracted; he bristled.

"Do not insult the Church of God," he cried, "or I shall speak to the bishop; and he may speak to the king."

"That is absurd," the knight very reasonably replied. But his eyes were suddenly cautious. Portehors saw it and stood his ground.

And despite the absurdity of the argument, Godefroi was wise to be careful: for Canon Portehors and his Church could be dangerous.

There were several reasons: one was King Henry III. Ever since he had come to the throne as a boy twenty years before, the pious Henry had consciously modelled himself on the last king of the old Saxon house, the saintly Edward the Confessor. With his passion for ceremonial and for church building, he made frequent trips from his hunting lodge in the nearby forest of Clarendon to see the progress of the new cathedral and was liable to fly into a rage at anyone who got in the way of his project.

But there was more to it than the king's religiosity. The political struggle for supremacy between Church and State had already been a long one. It had begun when William Rufus had quarrelled with the saintly Archbishop Anselm, and it had reached a crisis in the quarrel between Henry II and the impossible Thomas à Becket that had ended in the murder of the archbishop in Canterbury Cathedral. It had broken out once more, in some ways more seriously, a generation later when King John had refused to accept the pope's choice of archbishop, Stephen Langton, and Pope Innocent III had then laid the whole kingdom under an Interdict. For six long years all church services, even Christian burial were forbidden, a situation that God-fearing men like Godefroi had found intolerable.

John had retaliated by confiscating Church property and retaining the income for himself; Innocent in reply excommunicated him and thereby released all his feudal vassals from their vows of loyalty to him. He had even threatened to depose the king. For Innocent was not a man to be trifled with. Finally, when he was threatened by an invasion by the French king with the pope's blessing, John capitulated, resigned his kingdom to the pope and received it back from him as a vassal. The Church had triumphed: the new archbishop was installed; and the Church's superior power, even over kings, had seemed to be established. It was a tremendous power, not to be lightly challenged, and Godefroi had good reason to be afraid of it.

The political victory was theoretical. Much more important to every man in England was the fact that Church and State could not live without one another: the king needed the Church's moral authority; the Church with its huge holdings of land, needed the king's and the laity's protection. In England after the Interdict, a new spirit of co-operation developed, which brought great blessings to the State. When the disasters of John's reign finally led to the rebellion of many of his barons and the contract of Magna Carta, it was Stephen Langton, the archbishop he had opposed, who counselled the barons to moderation and who finally drew up a charter with such wise and statesmanlike provisions, even protecting humble folk, that both kings and magnates referred to it for guidance for generations afterwards. Now it was the Church which supported England's kings and people alike against feudal power-seekers and whose high moral authority helped to prevent any return to the chaos of Stephen's reign.

This could not have happened either if the bishops themselves had not been men of stature, or if they had been out of sympathy with the state itself. Sometimes they were candidates proposed by the English Church, or by the pope; sometimes they were servants of the king; but in the island

[393]

now a period of practical compromise had set in. Church leaders usually emerged through mutual agreement; the disputes between the Church and the lay authorities were normally settled in court. Unlike the terrible days when Bishop Roger had built his castles, the bishops of Salisbury in recent generations had been worthy and distinguished men, and the respect of a man like Godefroi for the present Bishop Bingham, was high. The new city, with its stately cathedral and busy market town side by side expressed the cooperative spirit of the new era.

And so, both through caution and genuine sympathy, when the canon invoked the authority of the Church, the knight had good reason to pause.

But he was still unwilling to give way.

A little crowd had now gathered.

From his place by the ditch, Osmund looked up at the two men and hardly knew himself which one he wanted to win.

But as he watched, he noticed a slight twitch in the canon's eyebrow – it was a sign he had come to know well. And it meant a fresh and very different attack was coming. He stared, spellbound.

For Portehors was not just a stern disciplinarian. He represented a new and powerful force.

In recent years, a new movement had appeared in the English Church, led by the exacting and scholarly Grosseteste, Bishop of Lincoln. The duty of the Church, they reminded their colleagues, was the cure of souls, and nothing should interfere with that. Bishops and archdeacons had a duty to inspect the moral and spiritual condition not only of every priest in the diocese, but of the laity as well.

"It's not that I object to Grosseteste in principle," Godefroi had confided to the grey-haired Bingham. "It's just that he encourages the most narrow-minded of the Churchmen to become a damn nuisance."

It was certainly true that this puritan wing of the old Roman Church could become a source of irritation to well-meaning laymen like the knight. But Bingham had only smiled sympathetically. He was too wordly wise to take sides on any issue of reform.

Of all the narrow-minded and dogmatic priests however, both men would have ranked Portehors amongst the first.

For if Christ came with a sword, to the canon religion was to be used like a knife.

As he surveyed the knight before him now, he sensed a possible victory and it exhilarated him. He had read the constitutions of Grosseteste to the letter and he knew what he must do. Pointing his finger at first Godefroi and then the two Shockleys he suddenly cried:

"The sin of pride, Jocelin de Godefroi. I see it in you. And you, Edward Shockley: avarice is in your soul." He paused. Then his gaze rested upon Peter Shockley. "Lust," he shouted in triumph. "I see the sin of lust."

"There's lust in every eighteen-year-old boy." Godefroi muttered irritably.

But now Portehors had worked himself into a state of righteous authority:

[394]

"Do penance for your sins," he ordered peremptorily. "And do not presume to disturb God's work with your schemes."

There was an awkward pause. The crowd was growing. Godefroi hesitated. The Shockleys watched anxiously and Osmund held his breath.

It was then, quite unaware of the drama taking place, that Aaron rode round the corner. He ambled to Godefroi's side, bowed courteously to Portehors, gazed at Osmund and remarked pleasantly to the knight:

"Is this the young fellow who's going to build our mill?"

And now Canon Stephen Portehors, disciplinarian and enquirer into morals, saw it all; the depravity of what he saw acted upon him as though he had been stung.

"Usurer!" he shouted at Aaron. No crime was worse in his eyes. "Miserable sinners." He shook his long finger in fury at them all.

Aaron gazed at him coolly. The implied insult did not worry him, but there was a flicker of irritation in his eyes which he could not quite conceal and which the sharp-eyed priest did not miss. Portehors felt free to insult him further. He turned to the crowd.

"See how the ungodly Jews try to steal our labour and destroy God's work!"

Aaron of Wilton had a fault and it was one that his father had warned him against. "Never argue with a fool, Aaron," he had cautioned: "you will win." For though he was a kind and gentle man with his family, and scrupulously honest in his dealings with men like Godefroi and Shockley, he had an intellectual arrogance that sometimes made him seem harsh when he was confronted with a fool.

Because he perfectly understood the island's need for capital investment, and because he could see equally perfectly into the narrow walls of the canon's inflexible mind, he could not resist exposing Portehors's stupidity.

"Yet the Jewish community at York – before they were massacred," he remarked drily, "did God's work. They financed the building of nine Cistercian monasteries."

This was true. The great sheep-farming monasteries in the north had done a huge and successful business with the Jews in financing their magnificent buildings. But this had mostly been two generations ago, when relations were better.

Portehors looked at him furiously.

"The Church has no need of your money now," he retorted.

"Although the fourth Lateran council in Rome," Aaron went on coolly, "asked us to pay tithes to the Church."

"Which you refused to do," Portehors spat back.

Aaron smiled grimly at his inconsistency.

"True, we had contributed enough already," he replied softly. Having made his point, he was about to leave, but Portehors, blind to the fact that he was being worsted, was now aroused.

"Your only interest is to steal the land of Christians as security," he accused.

[395]

Aaron stopped. How easy it was to make a fool of Portehors.

"Land? Not at all," he answered blandly. "The Bishop of Ely, you may remember, offered the relics of the saints themselves as security for a loan."

This, too, was a fact. The evil Bishop Roger's nephew had done exactly that the previous century. It had scandalised many in the Church and caused some wry amusement in the Jewish community.

The canon flushed with anger. He knew that Godefroi and the Shockleys, watching in silence, were enjoying his discomfort.

"The king will deal with you before long."

It was not altogether an idle threat. Henry had demonstrated mixed feelings about the Jews. He had allowed a ceremonial burning of the Talmud to take place four years before and had often given the Jewish exchequer into the hands of unscrupulous foreign favourites whom he had allowed to rob the community with impunity. But his extravagant building and complex foreign affairs had left him perpetually short of money, and he still needed this source of funds.

"The king received our gold at Westminster last year with his own hands." The ceremony in which he had indeed taken the gold personally had caused some surprise, but Henry had seemed to be delighted.

"I am not concerned with that," Portehors tried another tack. "I am concerned with building a house of God."

Aaron nodded.

"And so, Canon Portehors, are we. For at this very moment the king is seeking a substantial loan from the Jewish community to rebuild his church of Westminster Abbey."

Portehors's jaw dropped. He had not known this. But the refounding of Edward the Confessor's great church was indeed financed in part by a Jewish loan in 1245. Defeated, he stared at Aaron with loathing, and then at last, having no other insult to hand, he spoke the most bitter words he knew.

"What would you know, when the Jews are crucifiers of children?"

Of all the accusations made against Jews, heretics and other supposed enemies of the Church, one of the most monstrous but most widely believed was the accusation of ritual murder. It had started a century before when the body of a child, with what were claimed to be marks of crucifixion, was found at Norwich. Immediately a group of fanatical Churchmen had accused the local Jews of indulging in necromancy and ritual child murder. The absurd claim had surfaced several times since, when those embarrassed by debts hoped to find a way of attacking the creditors they blamed for their condition.

Against this outrageous insult there was no sensible reply to make. With a look of disgust on his face, Aaron turned his horse's head and moved away. As he watched him go, a gleam of triumph appeared in Portehors's eye. He might have lost the argument, but he had sent the Jew packing. With his sense of victory restored, his demeanour became calm and grave again, and he turned his attention back to Godefroi and Edward Shockley.

"If you take this young man from God's work," he threatened quietly, "to traffic with those who crucified Our Lord, you will be candidates for excommunication."

It was a threat he probably could not carry out. There were no legal grounds for it. But as he saw that the canon was determined to make an issue of the matter, and as he had no desire for a quarrel with the Church authorities, Godefroi decided to give up. There were plenty of other masons.

"As you like," he shrugged, and with a curt nod to the Shockleys, he moved away.

And so it was, in the year of Our Lord 1244, that Osmund the Mason was saved by Canon Portehors from the two deadly sins of avarice and sloth and transferred, at the wage of a penny farthing a day, to work on the new cathedral of our Blessed Lady Mary at New Salisbury.

That afternoon Peter Shockley walked with Alicia Le Portier through the town and told her the good news about the mill.

He pushed his fair hair back from his forehead and his blue eyes shone as he explained to her with pride: "We've got the mill and my father says I'm to be in charge of it."

He was ambitious. She knew it. Ever since they were children, this simple, enthusiastic ambition had attracted her. Their conversation followed a familiar but delightful route as he walked beside her.

"I hope you're up to it." She could not resist deflating him a little: she liked to see him bounce back again.

He flushed.

"Of course I am. And that's only the beginning."

She looked at the ground, not wanting him to see that she was smiling with pleasure.

"Maybe you'll manage," she suggested in pretended doubt.

"Manage!" He outlined every detail of the fulling mill to her, explained how the heavy timber was being brought down from Godefroi's estate to make the huge hammers, the turning mechanism with its cogs and ratchets and the huge water wheel. "It'll be like the mill at Downton," he proclaimed, "but I'll run it even better."

She turned her eyes on him for a moment.

"I shouldn't think much of you if you didn't," she challenged him.

He had known her all his life; how was it that a few words from her could still send such a thrill of excitement through him? He would prove himself and then, in a year or two, as soon as he had made a success of the mill, he would marry her. The prospect had been one of the secret but fixed points in his imagination almost as long as he could remember, and as he saw it coming nearer he felt a glow of warmth and anticipation. "In a year, I'll ask her father," he promised himself.

She was a neat little figure with freckles and reddish brown hair which she wore cut short at the neck like a boy's. She was light on her feet: when he was a boy, he had been able to outrun her, but she was never far behind, and when the children of the area had gone swimming in the broad pools near Wilton, she was like a fish in the water so that not even the boys could catch her. Her only brother, Walter, was many years older and so she had come to take his place like a second son to her father, whose calm authority she admired. "I'm not a boy," she had told Peter when she was seven, "but I'm as good as any boy."

How long ago that seemed. Walter was now a successful royal official at Winchester, where his father's influence had obtained him the post of aulnager, and in the last two years Peter had watched Alicia grow up and ripen so that now it was no longer his childhood sweetheart who walked beside him but a new, only half familiar young woman, about whom there was a sense of mystery and excitement which sometimes made him tremble when he thought of her.

It was her eyes above all that he loved. They were not like any others he knew. At one moment they seemed to be hazel, though flecked with green and blue around the irises; a moment later, with a change of light, or perhaps a change in her mood, they were an astonishing violet. It was an inheritance from her mother.

"Let's go to the market," she suggested.

The big, irregular area was filled with sound and activity.

On the west side stood the squat new church of St Thomas à Becket, which served as parish church for the trading area; though the town was expanding so fast that soon another church might be needed. Near the church was a cheese market. At the opposite, east end, were pens for livestock. Near the centre, a reminder of the bishop's authority over criminals, stood the stocks. And along the south side, in several rows, were the stalls.

There were the wheelwrights' stalls and next to them Bottle Row, where not only bottles, but crockery and pewter were busily traded. There was Fish Row, Ironmonger Row, Cooks' Row, and Cordwainers' Row – this last being where a motley collection of shoemakers and cobblers stitched and tapped behind their tables. There were butchers, bakers, cloth-sellers, tailors, silversmiths, carpenters, leatherworkers, bellows-makers, glovers, hatters, yarnmakers, rabbitsellers, spicers, greengrocers, garlic sellers, and poultry merchants. There were coopers, with their barrels piled in tiers, coalsellers, salt merchants, oatmeal-sellers, dealers in hogs; and by a cross at the south east corner, the all-important wool merchants held their own market. The place was alive with all the colourful profusion of specialist trades that made up the medieval world – and which, at this time, gave family names such as carter, cooper, butcher, or tailor, to so many of its people.

They spent an hour wandering amongst the brightly coloured stalls. The crowds jostled comfortably, regardless of whether they were merchants or villeins, traders from Wilton or farmers from the outlying villages, rich priests, poor friars, or stonemasons from the cathedral. Grave canons might be seen, while their servants picked out cheeses with care; nuns from Wilton and quiet shepherds with their crooks, majestic as bishops, stood side by side at the spicers' stalls while urchins ran in the street behind them. And each corner of the market had its own, rich smells, from the soft aroma of the cheese stalls to the sharp, dusty tang of the coalsellers' quarter.

It was during their walk that Peter discreetly slipped away to purchase something that caught his eye, while Alicia pretended not to notice.

At last they moved northwards, and up the street past Blue Boar Row.

The bishop had laid out his town in roughly rectangular blocks, or chequers, each of which was divided into standard tenements. The tenements were plots of land three perches – about fifteen yards – fronting the street and seven perches deep for which each tenant paid a shilling a year ground rent and upon which he might build as he pleased. Most built houses with stores or workshops on the street level; a few – the rich – constructed purely private homes. South of the market lay New Street chequer; to the north, Blue Boar chequer and several others, still being laid out on as the town expanded.

Past Blue Boar chequer, on the street that led north towards the old castle, but before the city gate, lay the home of Le Portier the aulnager – a tall three storey timber and plaster house, with a single, steep-gabled roof hung with tiles.

When Peter and Alicia entered, the aulnager was not there, but Alicia's mother was. As she watched the two go past, Peter noticed that she gave them a curious, thoughtful look. Perhaps, he supposed, she was wondering how long it would be before he was her son-in-law.

It pleased him to see Alicia's mother. As well as her unusual violet eyes, she was one of those fortunate women whose looks, though not beautiful, were somehow so compact that she did not seem to grow old. It was another of the reasons why he had chosen the girl. I want a woman who'll last, he had always thought. Her mother had only one fault that marred her appearance: a slight stoop that made an unattractive curve at her shoulders. But her father's as straight as a rod, he had argued to himself; I think she'll grow straight.

She had. As he looked at her now, he was sure that his choice of bride was perfect.

They moved into the area behind the house.

Unlike most of the spaces at the back of each tenement, the aulnager's was not used for workshops or storehouses, but contained instead a little garden with a yew hedge, two honeysuckle and half a dozen small rose trees. In the middle of the little garden was a wooden bench.

Only when she sat down did he produce the present he had bought in the market. It was a tiny silver locket that he had seen on a silversmith's stall. It hung on a thin silver chain and had been made down at the coast at the mouth of the river, where there were small open silver mines. He produced it with a show of casualness, while she watched him cautiously. They both knew that this was an important moment.

"It's for you." He handed it to her, suddenly feeling awkward.

As she took it, her eyes were on the ground.

"And what's that supposed to mean?" With a great effort she kept her voice cool, unconcerned.

"That you're to wear it because you belong to me." He said the words with a little too much bluster.

"Do I?" She was pleased, but she did not want to sound so: she wanted him to say something more.

"Of course you do."

"Isn't that a bit of an assumption?"

But young Peter was both awkward and pleased with himself. He only shrugged.

"Perhaps I may not want to belong to you." There was a quietness in her voice that was a warning, but he chose to ignore it. Indeed, the half flush on her cheek, which told him she was unhappy, gave him a sense of power. Half man, half boy, he wanted her to give way.

"I offered you a locket," he said coolly.

She had started to put it round her neck. Now she paused.

"Is that all you have to say?" Why didn't he say he loved her?

He knew what she wanted, but now, suddenly the knowledge made him shy.

"There are plenty of others who'll wear it if you don't," he announced proudly, and stared at her in triumph.

To her it was like a blow in the stomach. She felt her face go pale. For a moment she could not speak. She summed up her strength and held back the tears she could feel welling up.

"Take it then!" She could not prevent a sob breaking out. "I don't want it, or you."

He had gone too far. He wondered how to retract; but he was not clever.

"I'm not a bad catch for you," he bluffed. "I'm a rich man."

The silence that followed seemed to him very long; but her eyes had never been more violet as she controlled her tears and finally gave him a cold and contemptuous stare.

"You're not a man, I assure you, you're a boy. And I don't want you. Please go away now." She handed him the locket calmly. "I don't want to see you any more."

There was a sickening feeling in his stomach as Peter took it silently. Then, not knowing what to do, he turned on his heel.

She would come round.

But it was that same evening that her mother took Alicia upstairs and began to change her dress, telling the surprised girl with a smile:

"You must look your best tonight, Alicia." When she asked why, her mother in turn had asked her, with a thoughtful look: "Who do you expect to marry?" And to that she had replied, not as she would normally have done: "Peter Shockley I suppose," but instead, since she was still angry: "Who knows?"

Her mother nodded.

"Shockley's a nice boy," she went on quickly, "and I like him. But he's very young. And he's only a merchant. He'll never be anything more." She pulled Alicia's hair gently back from her face, pinning it behind.

[400]

"You're a woman now, and you need an older man, not a boy."

Alicia blushed. The words suited her mood. But she wondered what was coming. Evidently something quite unusual, for she had never seen her mother's face so concentrated.

Now to her surprise, her mother slipped off the simple child's *bliaut* tunic and linen cotte that Alicia was wearing, and produced a white silk slip which she whisked over her head. Alicia had never worn such a thing before and her eyes opened with delighted surprise as it fell in soft folds over her body.

"You've nice breasts," her mother told her frankly. "We'll show them a little." And from the huge chest by her bed she pulled out a magnificently embroidered blue and gold dress which, after being gently gathered by a golden cord above the waist, fell in long folds to her feet. At the front, where the dress laced across, she left its plunging line as open as possible, so that the form of her young breasts thrust forward tantalisingly under the silk shift, making Alicia blush again. Next her mother folded a fine linen wimple in a band over the top of her head and fitted the linen cap, like a crown, over it.

Alicia stood in front of the polished bronze mirror in one corner of the room and surveyed herself. She had no idea that she could look like this, and the sight of the new person that her mother had just created made her heart race with excitement.

"And now, my child, you're a woman," she declared.

"Who is all this in honour of?" she asked.

"Your father has an important friend at Winchester," her mother explained. "Your brother is bringing him here tonight. His name is Geoffrey de Whiteheath." Alicia had heard her father speak of him before, in terms of respect. "It would be a great match for you," her mother went on. "He's a knight with a fine estate. He lost his wife and son in a fire last year. Now he wants an heir."

"Will father make me marry him?"

Her mother hesitated.

"No. But he hopes you will. He and your brother have been to a lot of trouble to arrange it."

Alicia admired both the men in her family. She was not sure what to think. She supposed she would like their choice.

"Is he very old then?" she asked anxiously.

Her mother laughed.

"No. A little grey at the temples – but that can improve a man you know." She smiled. "He'll be here very shortly."

Alicia went down the stairs first. The long dress felt very grown up: too grown up, she thought, for Peter Shockley.

Perhaps this knight would know how to appreciate her.

The third of the seven deadly sins which afflicted Osmund the Mason crept up upon him very slowly before it took him by surprise.

His life as a cathedral mason delighted him. For in entering the quiet close, he discovered another world.

On the canon's instructions, he had been taken on as an apprentice , a step above the little army of some two hundred labourers who moved the stones and carted the rubble about, but an insignificant and almost unnoticed figure on the fringe of the fifty masons, of whom the master masons formed a small and dignified elite. Above the master masons were the revered master of masters, Nicholas of Ely and his deputy Robert, whom he often saw directing the work but to whom he had never dared to speak; and most godlike of all, more honoured by the builders than even the bishop himself, Elias de Dereham, the designer of the cathedral. He had designed other buildings, including the hallowed shrine of St Thomas à Becket at Canterbury; but Salisbury was known to be his masterpiece. Elias was an old man now, and was at present away from the city; Osmund was not even sure what he looked like.

The masons had admitted him as an apprentice, but since no one knew anything about him, his existence was almost ignored, even by the other apprentices. It might have been discouraging. But one thing he knew for certain the first day that he began: this was where he wanted to be.

For the time being he was used as a spare pair of hands and given only the lowliest tasks – sawing the blocks of grey stone and helping to dress them. But he was content. In the long, hot, dusty days under the cathedral's slowly rising shadow, he was glad to watch the builders go quietly about their work in perfect order, closed off from the rest of the world in their spacious precincts. Several nights a week now he would stay in the mason's quarters, a long line of sturdy wooden huts along the north and east perimeter of the close, and he was glad to sit deferentially outside the circle of masons and listen to their talk. As for his ambitions, he kept them to himself: the masons' guild was a tight and secretive fraternity; even a new apprentice the masons knew was expected to attend to his duties patiently and wait to be spoken to.

There was one object in particular on the building site which fascinated him. In the eastern end of the cathedral, where the first chapel, lower than the main body of the church, was already roofed over, Elias de Dereham had placed a large wooden model on a table. It showed the cathedral in its finished form; any mason or labourer was free to wander in and inspect it, and Osmund used to visit this place each day.

The cathedral that he saw consisted of a long, narrow building whose simple rectangular line was broken only by the huge transepts at its centre, which gave it the form of a simple cross, and two smaller transepts near the east end. At the central crossing, the long roof line was divided into two equal parts by a low, square tower that rose some twenty feet above it and was topped with a flat roof. This was the standard design for many large churches all over Europe at that period and its plain, long, horizontal lines were the essence of simplicity.

But how elegant it was! Where the old Norman churches, like the cathedral on the castle hill, had been stout, heavy bastions with rounded arches and narrow windows set in fortress-like walls, this new building was a light and airy shell. Its windows, with their plain, gothic points, rose in two tiers – huge areas of glass that perfectly balanced the high, sheer surfaces of the building's grey Chilmark stone. Nothing, it seemed to him, could be more pure, and natural.

It was one day when he was standing beside the model, wholly absorbed in it, that he heard a voice at his side.

"You like the building?"

An elderly man with a broad, receding forehead and a hooked nose was standing there, gazing down at him curiously. Osmund wondered who he was.

"It's so," he hesitated: "so simple," he said honestly.

To his surprise, the old man smiled.

"The best things always are. You see those windows: note how there is an absence of any but the simplest tracery. Across the channel you will find the most elaborate patterns of masonry appearing in windows, and in the vaults," he added. "But I dislike all that. It's not Sarum," he smiled, "not Sarum at all."

"I think it must be the greatest cathedral in the world," Osmund said.

The designer laughed.

"Oh no. The cathedral of Amiens in France," he went on cheerfully, "is twice the volume of our church. But if you stand inside both, you will never be able to tell. And why? Because the proportions are perfect. See," he became enthusiastic, "these piers of Purbeck marble that support the vaults: the marble is so hard that we can make them thin. And where the transepts cross at the centre, the four great columns at the corners of the crossing – there we have built huge pillars whose columns will fly straight up, with no intervening capitals from floor to vaulting in a single unbroken line. Simple nests of columns. Pure line. They soar."

It was obvious to Osmund now who the old man must be. He was astonished that such a great man should speak to him.

Canon Elias de Dereham gave him a friendly look. "And are you a mason, young man?"

"No sir," he answered modestly. "But I hope to be."

"Can you carve?"

He knew that he could carve in wood. He was sure he would in stone.

"Yes," he replied unhesitatingly.

The old man nodded, and then moved on.

It was two days later that one of the masons came up to him when he was working and began to question him.

"You wish to be a mason?"

He nodded.

"If you wish to join our guild and learn the mysteries of the mason's craft, you must serve our apprentice until we decide you are worthy."

The mason's guild was still a fairly informal organisation, but he knew that usually a boy apprentice might have to serve as long as seven years before being admitted as a journeyman mason. He bowed his head.

"Very well," the man said briskly. "See Bartholomew. He'll be your mentor." And he walked away.

And from that moment Osmund knew that his life as a proper mason had begun.

Bartholomew was an apprentice only two years older than himself: a pale, surly young fellow with a shock of dark hair, already thinning, that fell over his face, and a large, running boil on the right side of his neck. He greeted Osmund without enthusiasm, but told him he might work beside him in future and learn the beginnings of his craft.

The next day Robert the master mason came to him too, asked him a few questions about himself, and then gave him a curt nod.

"Learn from Bartholomew," he ordered.

There was so much to learn. His surly mentor showed him how to turn his chisel, and explained to him the properties of the different kinds of stone.

He also showed him the many activities that went into the building, each of them with their own particular workshop.

It was a world full of wonder. He saw the great drawing board of the head mason, where, with compasses and set squares, he drew the designs for each part of the building on a linen sheet. He was surprised to see that the pencil he used was not made of lead, but of silver.

"Silver leaves a black line on linen," Bartholomew informed him curtly. He had not known.

He learned to understand the work of the joiners and carpenters who not only fashioned the supports for the roofs, but who organised the scaffolding as well. He saw the huge saw pit and the waiting piles of timber from the nearby forest of Clarendon.

On the north-east side of the close, by the gate to the bishop's palace grounds, he visited the glaziers, who were already preparing the huge quantities of stained glass that would be required – first painting and then firing the glass in their kilns. He smiled in delight to see the delicate designs of saints and biblical scenes that would gleam softly down from every wall.

There were the storehouses, the painters' workshops, the refectories, kitchens, outhouses – two decades of work had already formed a little world within a world for the builders of the great cathedral.

But most important of all, stretching along the whole south side of the church's long nave, was a wooden lean-to that formed the masons' lodge.

There were all kinds of masons – hewers, carvers, men who laid the stones, others who set the tracery; there were turners who used their lathes to polish the marble; bench masons at their tables, who fashioned the hundreds of capitals and bosses that would be needed to seal and decorate the masonry of the mighty structure. There was the place on the floor where the complex arrangements of pillars could be drawn full size. There were stacks of wooden templates that were cut to give the mason his exact cross-sections when he carved the stone.

All these things a stonemason should thoroughly understand if he were ever to be master of his craft.

He was fascinated.

The stone used for Salisbury Cathedral came from two sources. The grey limestone used for most of the building came from the quarries of Chilmark, twelve miles west of the city along the valley past Wilton. It was a wonderful, cool greenish grey, soft to the touch and easy to work.

But for the pillars that must carry the heavy roof, a very different stone was used. This was the solid Purbeck marble, quarried on the south coast near the castle of Corfe. Much of it, he knew, was the gift of a single woman, Alice Brewer, who had given the new church as much marble as they could get from her Purbeck quarries in twelve years – one of the greatest of all the sumptuous gifts the cathedral received.

Osmund loved the grey Chilmark stone. Often he would take a small piece home with him when he walked up the valley to Avonsford, turning it over and over in his hands, feeling its texture, and studying its composition.

"Each stone," Bartholomew had told him, "has a grain, exactly like wood. If you want to cut it, you must know that. And also, when you place stone in a wall, it will weather better depending on how the wind and rain strikes the grain."

Sometimes Osmund could also detect a faint second colour in the stone: the subtlest hint of blue, or rusty red; and this too he loved.

Part of his apprenticeship, he knew, would be spent at the great quarry at Chilmark where the stone was rough hewn before being transported to Salisbury.

It was in August that he was sent there for the first time, and it was in a state of excitement that he set out at dawn one day to walk along the road past Wilton.

Only the deep cart tracks scored in the road told him that anything unusual came along the western valley; and only when the tracks veered suddenly off into a wood did he guess that he must have arrived at Chilmark. In fact, there was little sign of the quarry at all until he arrived at the camp itself. He saw the miners' quarters and those of the masons who did the rough hewing. He saw the big lean-to where the stones were being cut, and the bay beside it where the carts were loaded. But where was the mine? He looked about eagerly.

As soon as he had explained his business, a friendly young miner pointed to a small cave entrance in the trees.

"That's it."

It seemed tiny. But when the young man took a torch and led him into the cave, he soon gasped with wonder.

He did not know quite what he had expected, but certainly not this.

At first, as one gently descended, the entrance opened out into a large gallery. But then, further into the rock began a huge sequence of halls, tunnels and cavernous spaces, leading in every direction – to right and left, above and far below – a labyrinth. It was only after he had been there two or three minutes, getting accustomed to the faint light from other distant torches in the shadows, that the little mason suddenly realised that the great network of halls and galleries had been so thoroughly worked that it was not so much a labyrinth, as a huge single space, subdivided by pillars of rock.

"Why," he cried, "it's like the cathedral, but underground."

It was. The galleries disappeared into the distance like aisles. In places, the vaulted ceilings were as high as those in the great building. The quarry at Chilmark, with its soft echoing spaces, was truly like a great church.

"It's the cathedral's womb," the young man at his side remarked. "And we've still enough stone down here to build a second church too."

For two hours Osmund wandered, torch in hand, through the endless caves. It gave him a pleasure he could not explain to know that the great cathedral whose vaults would soar over him had been pulled by pick and human hand, out of the bowels of the earth.

He spent two weeks at the quarry that first time, and on his return, the carters going back to Salisbury let him ride with them. There were six carts of stone to be transported that day, but to his surprise he saw that a further six carts, full of rubble and debris from the mine shafts and workshop had been added to the little procession.

"What is that for?" he asked.

"You'll see," the carter told him. And sure enough, when they had travelled five miles, the carters began, one after another, to shovel the contents of these carts on to the road. "We surface the road as we go," his companion explained. "After all, not only stone comes out of a mine, and you've to put the rubbish somewhere."

A month later, Osmund made a second, and more ambitious expedition for himself, this time down the river to the harbour. The little town by the coast now boasted both a tiny stone castle on a mound by the river, and a fine Norman priory church whose name, Christchurch, was generally applied to the town itself in preference to the old Saxon name of Twyneham. Here, looking across to the empty headland with its low protecting hill and its deserted earthwork walls, he saw the huge wooden barges enter the still harbour waters, bearing their precious load of marble from the western quarries along the coast, and begin to make their slow way up the river Avon to Sarum.

Always there was so much to learn. As the cathedral's walls slowly rose, the labourers hauled up huge barrels of chalk lime and flint which were poured into the gap between the inner and outer stone.

"It's not only quicker than making the walls of solid stone," Bartholomew explained, "but the lime rubble binds with the stone. It's as solid as can be."

And the mason marvelled as he realised that the rising cathedral was not only made of stone, but contained, locked within its walls, great cliffs of lime and chalk.

Another discovery he made one day, soon after his journey down the river, concerned the cathedral's windows. Why he should have begun, during one of his daily inspections of the model, to count them he could not say, unless it was that there was no other feature of the model he did not know by heart. But count them he did; and so it was that, to his surprise, he discovered that there were three hundred and sixty-five.

"One for each day of the year!" he cried aloud with delight. And thinking he must have made a mistake, he counted again, keeping tally on a slate. It was exact: 365.

Was it by Elias's design, or by accident? He did not dare to ask him. But one thing he was certain of: "It's a sign from God," he murmured, "that's for sure." And he crossed himself.

Osmund was a humble soul, and the more he learned, the more conscious he became of his own ignorance and of the greatness of those who had designed and organized the great cathedral. Often at the end of the day he would go to the little chapel and pray beside the model, whispering: "Blessed Mary, make me worthy to be a mason."

And it was here, one evening a few months later that he had his second and last encounter with the great Elias. The canon had just walked over from the Leadenhall, the fine house with its leaded roof that he had built for himself beside the river; and he had entered the chapel quietly. But he stopped with surprise at the sight of the young mason who, not knowing he was being watched, had just fallen to his knees and crossed himself as he gazed up at the model of the great building. When he asked kindly "What is it my son?" the intense young fellow with his oversized head and his solemn grey eyes looked up at him, and, echoing the words that Canon Portehors had spoken to him before, announced: "Oh father, I am unworthy; I am dust."

To which the architect had replied with a smile: "You forget the words of Our Lord, my son: God the Father sees even the sparrows – and the sparrows, my young friend, have eyes themselves." He tapped him on the shoulder. "Not dust, young mason: a sparrow – who uses his eyes." And Elias de Dereham passed on.

Then for a moment Osmund knew an ecstasy of happiness he had never known before. And he had almost forgotten the deadly sins.

It was nearly the middle of the night.

In the market place, the brightly-coloured awnings on the stalls were folded tight; the sheep and cattle pens were empty; the streets were silent.

Or almost so. For along the edge of the cheesemarket, where the trestle tables were stacked in piles, neatly chained beside the walls of the squat parish church of St Thomas, a single figure, dressed in a grey cloak with the long capuchon hood pulled over his head, was moving unsteadily through the shadows. There was only starlight to see by that night, but the stars were very bright. The figure moved along the western edge of the market, detached itself from the shadows, and moved up the centre of the street that led north past Blue Boar Row.

Peter Shockley was drunk.

Slowly he made his way up Castle Street.

Only when he reached the tall, severe, house of Le Portier the aulnager did he stop, look for a stone in the road and finally begin to cast it up at the topmost window of the house's pale, blank front.

Alicia was in there. It was her last night in her father's house.

At the third attempt, he succeeded in hitting her window and a few moments later it opened and her face appeared, staring down into the starlit street.

He pulled back his hood. Her hair was a little longer than before. He could make it out, falling to her shoulders, and see her white nightshirt beneath. It seemed to him that, even from that distance, he could sense the warmth and even the scent of her body beneath.

"Alicia."

She sighed. It was the third visit that week.

"Go home Peter, I can't see you."

He did not move.

"Come down," he whispered urgently.

"No."

Three times he had begged her to run away with him. "And then what would you do?" she demanded.

"Something," he replied defiantly.

It was absurd. She was beginning to find him ridiculous. And yet – because she was almost tempted, because she was angry with herself for giving way to her father, because she knew that it was useless and because she was trying to make herself believe that she was going to be happy with the pleasant, middle-aged knight from Winchester who was such a fine catch for her – she treated Peter with scorn.

"Go away and forget about me," she hissed into the darkness.

"Will you forget me?" he cried aloud.

"I already have. I'm in love with Geoffrey de Whiteheath." She withdrew her head and he saw the window close.

He did not leave. He threw the stone up again, and again, but she did not appear. He threw it harder; and then a little too hard. He heard a pane of glass break. But still he did not move away.

A moment later the door of the house opened and the tall thin form of Alan Le Portier strode out of his house. He was carrying a stick.

"Go home at once, young man," he ordered angrily. "You'll pay for my window tomorrow." He glared at him contemptuously as though he was a child. Peter felt his resentment rising.

"You've sold her," he shouted, "you've sold her to a knight!" As his words echoed down the street, several heads appeared at other windows.

Le Portier stiffened. The charge was quite untrue, but it infuriated him to have such insults thrown at him.

"You brat."

In the darkness and his fuddled state, Peter did not see him swing the stick; it caught him sharply on the arm.

"Be off," the aulnager shouted.

Peter felt a surge of anger. He staggered towards Le Portier, and would have aimed a blow at him, except that at that moment, he saw behind him the figure of Alicia. She was standing in the doorway with a candle in her hand; and her face which suddenly looked older, was gazing at him with scorn.

He stood quite still.

"Go away, you child," she said coldly, and then turned back into the house.

He stared at her, then her father. And then with a shrug he moved away down the street, watched by faces at every window.

It was his great misfortune that there was an unexpected witness to the whole business standing in the shadows fifty feet away.

William atte Brigge had lingered at a merchant's lodgings near the northern gate until late that night and he had just begun to make his way through the town when he saw the young man loitering in the street. After pausing to observe him, he had seen with interest that it was young Shockley; and within minutes, his interest had turned to a malicious grin of pleasure. The boy had already broken a window and tried to assault the aulnager. Wondering what else he might do, he followed him.

At the market place he saw the youth kick the trestle tables by the cheesemarket moodily. He watched him pick up a stone and hurl it across the empty market place. He heard him cry out in rage.

The chance was too good to miss. Casting about, William found a large piece of wood that had been used to prop up one of the stalls. A moment later he had moved swiftly through the shadows, hurled the lump of wood through one of the windows of St Thomas's church, and run quickly through the shadows towards the house of the bishop's bailiff.

His satisfaction was complete when, a few minutes later, the bailiff strode into the market place and arrested the young man who was still mooning about near the stalls.

"I saw him throw a stone through Le Portier's window," he assured the official, "and then he came down here and broke the window of the church as well. Ask in Castle Street if you want witnesses."

"I will," the bailiff promised.

Ten days later Peter Shockley, brought before the Lord Bishop's Court, was accused and promptly found guilty of causing a nuisance in the bishop's market place and breaking a church window; he was sentenced to a morning in the stocks.

As the bailiff said to Edward Shockley afterwards: "I'm sorry about your boy, Shockley, but I can't make exceptions."

The Wilton merchant's revenge was satisfactory; but it was not yet complete.

Punishment in the stocks was an unpredictable affair. A man could stand there all day and leave without a mark, or if he were unpopular, he might find all manner of objects thrown at him. With his hands and head locked in the heavy wooden yoke, he could not defend himself so he would probably emerge badly cut and bruised. Above all however, it was an undignified business, and when Edward Shockley heard the sentence he was filled with rage.

"You've disgraced the family," he thundered. "After this, you'll work at the fulling mill, but by God you'll not be in charge."

The following morning, when Peter Shockley was led out by two of the bailiff's men and placed in the stocks, it seemed to him that his life, which two months before had appeared so full of promise, was now in ruins. I've lost the mill, he thought bleakly, and I've lost Alicia. As he stared across the market place and thought of Alicia in the arms of the knight from Winchester, his eyes filled with tears; a street urchin, not out of malice but for amusement, threw an apple at him which struck him in the mouth and made his lip bleed. He had never felt so without friends.

Yet his morning in the stocks did bring him one unexpected friend.

It was mid-morning when he became aware of a figure standing quietly by his side; and though the yoke over his neck prevented him from turning his head to look, he could see a pair of feet in rough sandals and the edge of a grey robe that was none too clean. This told him that his companion must be a Franciscan.

There were two orders of friars who had become a familiar sight at Sarum during his lifetime: the Dominicans – the black-robed order of preachers and intellectuals, who had set up their first house near Wilton – and the grey friars, followers of one of the church's newest saints, Francis of Assisi. Unlike most of the priesthood or the monks, the grey friars were dedicated to a life of simplicity. They usually lived and worked amongst the poor, and they had already earned the respect of the people of Salisbury by their devotion to such humble tasks. When the first group from Italy had arrived at Sarum fifteen years before, the bishop had given them a modest house in St Ann Street just outside the close and the king, too, was known to favour them.

Though he knew their reputation, Peter had never spoken with one of the friars before and he stared with curiosity as the grey figure now moved round the stocks and came to face him.

He was a young man – little older than himself – with dark hair and a clean-shaven, sallow face.

"What brings you to the stocks?" He spoke with a strong Italian accent.

"My sins," Peter replied dismally. "And a girl," he added. "What about you?"

The sallow young man smiled. He had very white, even teeth.

"The same two things," he laughed. "I am Brother Giovanni." And without being asked, he sat comfortably on the ground in front of the stocks. "What's your story?" he demanded.

As the enquiry was friendly, and as he had nothing else to do, Peter told the friar his whole story, about the mill, his losing Alicia, and the night when he broke the window. "The funny thing is," he confessed, "I may have been drunk, but I don't remember throwing anything at the church window at all."

The friar made no comment, but his cheerful presence was a comfort to Peter and soon they were talking easily. Giovanni told him about his own life in Italy, which was that of a merchant family very like his own, and though Peter did not realise it, over an hour passed without incident in this way.

"The worst of it is," Peter told him, "my father won't forgive me either now. He says I've disgraced the family."

"He will," the friar assured him. "Give him time."

"What can I do to please him?" Peter asked.

"Work like hell, I should think," Giovanni answered with a pleasant grin.

Eventually one of the other friars called his friend away, and Peter once again resumed his lonely stand.

The sun continued to rise slowly. Little beads of sweat formed on his forehead; but the market place was occupied with other matters and although there were people standing near the stocks, no one seemed to take any notice of him.

It was nearly midday when he saw William atte Brigge lope into the open.

The trader looked about him surreptitiously as he made his way slowly towards the stocks. Peter saw that he was carrying a basket of rotting vegetables and in his hands, a turnip, and that he was grinning quietly to himself. Two little boys, guessing his intentions, joined him.

Nothing had been thrown at him since the boy's apple had hit him in the mouth; the presence of the friar had deterred the urchins from their usual sport of tossing whatever refuse they could find lying about at any victim in the stocks. But obviously William, with his hatred of the Shockleys, was determined to see that there was a little sport at his expense before the stocks were opened at noon.

When he was comfortably in range, William set his basket down and motioned the two children to take their pick of the contents; a moment later a large cabbage hit Peter in the face and the two boys hooted with triumph.

The rotting vegetables would do him little harm; but it was the turnip that William held that Peter's eyes were fixed upon. There was something about it which looked odd, and suddenly he made out what it was: cunningly embedded in it there was a large lump of flint. Its edges were razor sharp.

His eyes grew wide with horror. He opened his mouth to shout for help; but before the cry was half out, he saw the trader from Wilton coil his body like a spring and hurl the terrible missile at him with all his might.

He felt the back of his head crack against the top of the stocks as he instinctively tried to dodge; his face winced and his eyes closed tightly. He heard a thump and a cry. But he felt nothing. Could William have missed?

As he opened his eyes, he saw with astonishment that the young friar was lying three feet in front of him, struggling to get up; blood was streaming from a huge gash in his forehead. In the background, William had picked up his basket and was scurrying hastily away.

How the friar had seen what was happening and managed to throw himself in the stone's path he never knew.

"Why did you do that?" he asked in wonder.

Young Giovanni looked up at him ruefully.

"Didn't they tell you, Franciscans are all a bit simple-minded?" Then he fainted.

A number of the men in the market had seen what had happened and they stared after the departing trader with disgust. Two men hurried from their stalls to help the friar to his feet and a third went in search of the bishop's bailiff. Within minutes Peter found himself free.

The next day he and his father went to visit the friars' house. Giovanni was already up and about, but he had a large, jagged wound on his forehead that he would carry as a scar for the rest of his life. He was cheerful.

"Made it up with your father yet?" he asked.

Peter Shockley was never a religious man, but for the rest of his life he was known to make regular donations to the Franciscan friars of New Salisbury.

Although Peter Shockley had regained his father's good graces, he nearly lost his mill the following spring.

The new disaster that nearly destroyed the Shockleys' plans when the building of the mill had hardly begun was the one contingency which neither Godefroi nor Edward Shockley had even considered.

It was the fault of King Henry III, and resulted from events which had nothing to do with Sarum.

The problem lay in France. Nearly all the disasters that embarrassed Henry so many times during his fifty-six-year reign originated in his passion for intrigues across the English Channel – an interest which almost none of his subjects shared. Yet it was understandable enough. He could not forget the great empire in western France that his grandfather Henry II had ruled and his father John had lost. He would not accept that Normandy was gone. And when a few years before the new French king Louis had overrun the province of Poitou on the Atlantic coast, of which he was still at least the nominal overlord, it added insult to injury. He was determined to get his mighty inheritance back.

In order to understand the true state of affairs it must be remembered that the high politics of Europe were still entirely a feudal business. Though the English wool merchants, the Flemish and Italian clothmakers during the peace might raise their countries' wealth to new heights, the kingdom and provinces of Europe in which the merchants operated remained related to each other by family ties. The ties were endless. They crossed the continent like huge and intricate spiders' webs; and the shifting family ambitions and alliances of the rulers frequently overrode all considerations of peace, prosperity, or even common sense.

Of no one was this situation more true than King Henry III of England. His second wife was the daughter of the lord of Provence, that sunny southern region of France where the troubadour poets and minstrels had their origin. His mother Isabella, after the death of King John, had returned to France, thrown out her own daughter who was engaged to the head of the great Poitou house of Lusignan, with whose father she had once been in love, and married him herself. Henry was also cousin to the King of Aragon, who had claims on southern France, and brother-in-law to the German emperor, who was anxious to weaken the French and seize northern Italy.

To all these, and many others, Henry was a dupe.

In the year 1242 he had undertaken what was, even by his own remarkable standards of incompetence, one of the most botched and pointless expeditions of his long reign. It had begun, as always, in an elaborate intrigue – so elaborate that none of the parties probably even understood it. In this, the lords of the Midi, aided by the King of Aragon, the Lusignans and even the German emperor were to push the King of France out of the south western regions, part of which would then be returned to Henry. The enterprise was so absurd that some of the participants had even made treaties with Louis of France before it had started. The magnates of England, who already had a shrewd idea of Henry's talents for diplomacy, refused to accompany him; consequently he took a scutage payment from them in lieu of service, tallaged the Jews, and set out. His allies in the south, who had a similarly just idea of his talents as a military commander, were delighted to take his money instead. And that was the last he saw of it. The campaign fizzled out almost as soon as it began. Henry returned to England. In the space of a few months, for no return whatever, he had just lost the then incredible sum of forty thousand pounds. As usual, he was bankrupt.

In 1244 a second and apparently quite unrelated event took place in London. The body of a child was found in the churchyard of St Benet's; and some of those concerned made the preposterous claim that a Hebrew inscription had been cut into the child's flesh. Absurd though the whole business was, the canons of St Paul's Cathedral chose to believe it and the little corpse was buried by the high altar.

It was exactly what the king needed. The Jews must be guilty. He fined them – a sum three times greater than the largest levy ever taken before, twelve times the usual annual rate – sixty thousand marks. Which was, coincidentally, since the mark was two thirds of the pound, just forty thousand pounds.

Late that year, Aaron came to Godefroi and Edward Shockley and told them:

"I do not know if I can promise the loan any more. I am almost ruined."

For a week they heard no further news. It was well known that all over the island the Jewish communities were struggling to find ways to make the preposterous payment.

After a week, the other participants decided to hold a meeting.

The conference between Godefroi and the two Shockleys was one that Peter remembered for the rest of his life. For it was there that he heard views expressed by the knight that amazed him, and began the process of his political education.

One thing that was certain was that neither family could finance the mill without the loan.

"I'd have to sell Shockley," his father explained.

"And I'd gladly advance the money in cash," Godefroi declared, "but at present. . ." He made an empty gesture with his hands.

It was well known that, like many of his class, the knight of Avonsford lived up to, and sometimes even beyond his considerable means. Not that he was foolish in the management of his estates. In the booming times he took full advantage of his situation. As the population of England grew, not only the wool growers but all agriculturalists were reaping the benefits. The open fields at Avonsford were now sowed three times a year instead of twice, and the sale at New Salisbury market of his winter wheat, spring oats and barley brought him a handsome income. Not only had his flocks of sheep increased, but he had even experimented, like other landlords in the region, with new strains such as the fine-wooled Lincoln sheep, so that part of his flocks now produced the crisp Lindsey wool that fetched the highest price of all in the market. In these ways Jocelin had made sure that his ten-year-old son Hugh would one day come into a splendid inheritance.

But ready cash was another matter. A gentleman must live in the manner proper to his class. Everyone who knew the songs of the French troubadours, or read the ever more elaborate tales of King Arthur and his knights knew that. His entertainments, his passion for jousting, the handsome new wing with its fine pointed windows that he had added to the stout old Norman hall – all had taken their toll.

"There's plenty of wealth," he told his son, "but no money." And in this he was typical of many of the nobility.

The two men reviewed every option, even that of approaching the Cahorsin merchants. "But they'll rob us blind," Shockley complained. And it was only after some time that Godefroi suddenly gave way to the outburst that so surprised young Peter.

"This is all the doing of the king," he raged. "The king with his damned foreign schemes and his damned foreign family. He'll ruin us all."

In his innocence, Peter had always assumed that the knight was a loyal follower of the king. But Godefroi's next words, though they were spoken in anger, made his mouth fall open.

"I tell you Shockley, the man's a child; the only good government we've had was when he was a child, and there were regents to govern in his name. We're English. We don't need his foreigners; we don't need his extravagance and frankly, except as a figurehead, I sometimes think we don't need him."

Astonished as Peter was by such sacrilege against the pious monarch, Godefroi's view was widely shared amongst the gentry, and among the magnates too. The king might not have forgotten his lost lands, but most of his feudal subjects had. The magnates disliked the foreign favourites who were given key positions at court; the knights disliked the scutages that the king levied on the magnates and which the magnates in turn passed on to them. Several times when the king had made demands for money which his barons thought unreasonable, they had reminded him of his father's Magna Carta which limited his powers; and though he did not tell Shockley, Godefroi had heard a rumour that several of the magnates were planning to try to force a council of four on the king which would effectively administer the realm in his name.

These were heady ideas for a provincial merchant's son; he did not know what to think. But one thing he did know: the king had spent too much money and had damaged his family's business; and at some point, he was sure, something must be done. It was the most important political lesson he ever learned.

Two months dragged by. The oak already felled to make the mill machinery lay on the ground. By the empty site, two cartloads of stones lay in undisturbed heaps. And then at last Aaron of Wilton called for a meeting at the manor house.

"Gentlemen," he told them. "I have raised the money." He paused and Edward Shockley noticed the new lines of pain and worry that had collected around his eyes. "But I tell you this," he went on, "if the king tallages us like that again, it will be the last loan I shall be able to make."

"And the interest rate?" Godefroi knew very well that the Jews would be forced to increase their rates to stay in business.

"I agreed a rate," Aaron replied with aloofness. "It remains the same."

It was then that Jocelin de Godefroi disappeared for a few moments into the garderobe chamber where he kept his most valuable possessions and returned with a little leather-bound book which he placed in Aaron's hands. It was Geoffrey of Monmouth's little history, translated into French, that had belonged to his great-grandfather.

"To remember this day," he said solemnly, and he was glad to see that, for once, the Jew flushed with pleasure.

Two days later a messenger arrived at the manor and was ushered into the knight's presence. With a low bow he declared that he came from Aaron of Wilton and handed Godefroi a small package.

In the package was another small book.

It was a little set of stories called *The Fox Fables*, written by a Jew of Oxford called, in French, Benedict le Pointur, and known to the Jews as Berechiah ha Nakdan. Godefroi had heard of it, for the fables were one of the classics of the great renaissance of Jewish writing that had taken place in England the previous century, before the sporadic persecutions had begun. It, too, was translated into French and charmingly illustrated. The knight smiled. "The fellow's too proud to take a gift without giving one in return," he muttered. But he was pleased with the book, and put it in the garderobe.

"And now," he said cheerfully to Edward Shockley the next day. "Let work on our mill begin."

1248

When exactly it was that his mentor Batholomew turned against him Osmund the mason could never say with certainty. But he thought it was probably the day, about a year after he began his apprenticeship, that he brought a carving of a swan that he was making for Jocelin de Godefroi into the mason's lodgings.

It was a small piece, carved of oak, which was to fit into a niche set in the big, studded door of the manor house at Avonsford; he had worked on it for several days and he was proud of it, and by the guttering candlelight, while the masons chatted, he put the finishing touches to it.

The masons liked young Osmund. He was quiet, and modest, and never pushed himself forward unless first spoken to. When one of the men noticed what he was doing, inspected the work, and then called his friends over to see what the young fellow had done, they were delighted to find that he had such a talent.

"He can carve," they agreed. "The young fellow has the touch. We'll teach you," they promised him, "how to carve in stone."

It was a moment of acceptance. From that evening, his life changed. The older masons began to speak to him freely. Robert himself, the deputy to the great Nicholas of Ely, came by where he was working to look him over again and say a few words; and often one of the older men would call him over to where one of the more intricate pieces of work was being done and show him the techniques, the mysteries, of the mason's art.

He was discovering the broad friendship and companionship that linked, right across the whole country, the network of medieval masons.

It was not surprising that Bartholomew became cold. He was a competent, hardworking fellow, with little talent, and just enough imagination to see that the new apprentice was his superior.

He found fault with the new apprentice where he could; but it was not easy. Once or twice, when he had complained to the older masons about some supposed incompetence of the little fellow with the big round head, he had seen a look in their eyes which told him that it was their respect for him, not for Osmund that was dwindling. Soon he stopped complaining. But he did as little as possible to help his protégé, and it was all the more galling to realise that the quiet little fellow was rapidly ceasing to need his guidance anyway.

Within another three months, he scarcely addressed Osmund at all; and by the next Michaelmas, he had even begun surreptitiously placing obstacles in the young man's way – leaving a pile of dust mixed with lime beside the place where he was working so that it would blow into his face and irritate his eyes, or discreetly removing pieces of stone which Osmund was about to work.

At first Osmund was hardly aware of these small attacks. But gradually he began to sense a certain method in them; he also noticed that every time some mishap had occurred to him, Bartholomew would appear soon afterwards, apparently casually and by chance, to see how he was getting on. Several times he was aware of the young man staring at him with unconcealed malice, although he had done nothing to offend him.

Sometimes the young mason would be so frustrated by Osmund's progress that he would unconsciously scratch the sore on his neck until it bled, and Osmund would see him going by, his long pale face working with vexation and his neck scarlet with the scratching he had given it.

But Osmund paid little attention. For with the years of his apprenticeship he had entered a period of timelessness. He had watched the passing of the seasons, of course. He had been conscious that he was growing older, stronger and filling out. But he no longer measured time in such ways as he had always done before. Now he measured time by his proficiency in his craft. That was the year I truly mastered stonecutting, he would remember; or, that was the year I learned to turn stones upon the lathe.

He loved the long, peaceful days, especially in the summer when the masons would rise at dawn and work till sunset, only stopping for their breakfast and dinner, and once more in the quiet of the evening for a drink, when the first bell sounded, summoning the priests to vespers.

He still spent time at Avonsford; but he lived for his work in the cathedral and scarcely took notice of what was passing in the world outside.

It was in September of his fourth year that one of the master masons came to Osmund with astonishing news:

"We're going to make an exception and admit you to the mason's guild later this year." This was an extraordinary honour and one that Osmund had never dreamt of. There were still three years to go to make up the seven years he had expected to serve. Even Bartholomew was not due to be admitted until the following year.

"But first," the mason told him, "you must prepare a piece of work to present to the guild, to show that you are worthy."

He knew at once what he would choose.

There were many decorative features of the great gothic cathedral that he admired. There were the perfectly turned bases of the pillars, the elegant capitals with their designs of animals and foliage, the mask-like faces that peeped out from nooks and corners, the magnificent low reliefs of the former bishops on the tombs which were being moved down from the old cathedral on the castle hill. But the most intricate of all, the apogee of the sculptor's art, were the great round bosses that were fitted, like enormous studs, into the vaulting.

They depicted all kind of objects, but the most splendid and elaborate were those which took a pattern of plants as their design. The long leaves, stems and flowers wove together, crossing and recrossing each other in a lavish, magnificent display of the carver's cunning art. To accomplish one of these, the mason had not only to shape the delicate leaves with his chisel, but to work his way under them, carving the stone into layer upon layer of tracery, like a huge open knot.

"I will make a roof boss," he said, suddenly confident in his ambition.

The design he chose was splendid. In the centre of the boss was a double rose, like those he had seen near the door of Godefroi's manor. Around the edge was a ring of beech leaves; and inside this was a riot of vegetation that curled around the central flower: oak leaves, acorns, rushes, ivy, a tangled profusion that perfectly expressed the rich foliage of the lush Avon valley he knew so well. It was only twelve inches across, but it contained everything. He worked on it at dawn each day, and again by candlelight in the evening. And as the time approached for him to present it he knew that, at his first attempt, he had accomplished a triumph of the mason's art.

As Christmas approached, there was to be a meeting of the guild at which he was to present himself with his work. Two days before, it was finally completed, and placed in the box under his little bed in the mason's quarters where he kept his tools.

The next day, when he came in from his work and opened the box to put his tools away, it was gone.

It was then that Osmund the Mason suffered the third of the deadly sins. The sin of anger which now afflicted him was unlike any emotion he had known before. His little body began to shake; for a moment he could not see, as a red mist came up before his eyes, and his little hands clasped the mallet and chisel so tightly that his knuckles became white. He wanted to strike the empty box in front of him, but he was so angry that he could not even move. He knew, with absolute certainty, who had done it.

"It must be Bartholomew," he muttered.

But what could be done? In thirty-six hours he was to present his work to the guild. And now he had nothing. The rules of the guild could not be altered on this point – he must present his work or be denied admission until the following year.

Bartholomew appeared at dusk and sat down on his own bed as though nothing had happened. Osmund said nothing. A confrontation with him now was useless since he would deny all knowledge of the matter, and there was no proof.

He watched the young man stretch out on his bed. His sore seemed better than usual. His face in the candlelight had a look of calm satisfaction on it.

All that night Osmund lay awake. He knew that he must do something about the meeting the day after, but he could only think of Bartholomew. His anger was hard now, and unyielding.

A little before dawn he decided to kill him.

He felt for his chisel. He knew what to do: a single blow with the chisel – tapped with his mallet, just as if he were attacking a block of stone – on his windpipe. And after that? He considered. He could run, perhaps. But where would he go? He shook his head in perplexity and rage.

Then he had his idea; it was a long shot, but there might still just be time. As the first light appeared, leaving Bartholomew unharmed, he rose from his bed and crept out of the hut. The cold, clear air was refreshing; the cathedral was silent. Picking up a small piece of Chilmark stone, he walked out of the close and headed towards Avonsford. It seemed to him that his anger had given him inspiration.

The evening of the next day, in the large upper room of the inn, the master mason stared at young Osmund thoughtfully. The boy looked pale. It was not surprising, since it was now two days since he had slept. The master mason was also aware that he had gone missing from his work the day before, and Bartholomew had put it about that he was unable to face the guild. But here he was and so he must receive the consideration as a candidate for masonry that he had been promised. The other masons who sat at the long tables round three sides of the room looked at young Osmund expectantly.

"You have work to show us?" the master mason asked.

Osmund nodded. He held it in a small bag.

"A fine roof boss I believe?"

"No sir."

The master mason frowned.

"That is what we were promised."

"It disappeared, sir. But I have something else."

This did not augur well. Perhaps they had, after all, allowed the young man to proceed too fast.

"Show us your work," he commanded.

Osmund drew a small object from his bag. It was a little torso, about twelve inches high, like those that stared out from some of the cathedral's capitals. He stood it on the table and stepped back without a word.

And when the master mason inspected it, his eyes opened wide in surprise.

It was a figure of Bartholomew. It was Bartholomew to the life, from the mean but stupid look in his long face, to the persistent running sore on his neck. He was in the act of running away from something, but his head was thrust forward in an attitude of triumph, as though he were winning a race. His lips were parted in a malicious grin. And in his two outstretched hands he held a large round boss in the centre of which was depicted a tiny rose.

Silently the sculpture was passed around the tables. No word was said about the subject of the carving: the message was clear.

"How long did you take to do this work?" the master mason asked him.

"A day sir. And a night," he added truthfully.

The master glanced round the table at his colleagues. Several of them were now grinning broadly. As his look fell on each one, he nodded approvingly.

"Welcome to our company, Osmund the Mason," the chairman intoned.

And with those words, as suddenly as it had come, the deadly sin of anger left Osmund the Mason. It did not attack him with such terrible force again.

That night Osmund looked up at the huge unfinished cathedral and murmured:

"I think I shall work in the cathedral all my life."

1264

If anyone had told Peter Shockley that parliamentary democracy was to be born that year he could have had no idea what was meant by those terms; and if they had been explained to him, he would have laughed out loud. The idea was preposterous.

Few men in Sarum were more respected for their solid judgement than Peter. The mill which he and his father had founded had been a great success, and the rhythmic pounding of its huge oak hammers had brought them considerable wealth. It was not the only such mill in the area. There was the mill at the busy town of Marlborough, twenty-five miles to the north, and the one at Downton, six miles to the south. But at Sarum itself only the bishop's mill outside the town and the new Shockley mill were at that moment in operation, and the business was brisk.

He was a member of the merchant guild; he grew powerful in the town; he even grew a little stout. His blue eyes missed nothing concerning the mill or the weaving business and it was clear that the fortunes of the family were in good hands. There was only one problem: he did not marry.

"It isn't as if he didn't like women," old Edward complained sadly. On more than one occasion he had been obliged discreetly to pacify the fathers of girls in the town with whom his son had had relations; and with one it had been necessary to make a considerable payment to an outraged husband.

But whenever he broached the question with his son, Peter just laughed and told him: "I'll get married, father, when I'm ready. I'm not so old yet."

Indeed, it seemed that Peter might continue indefinitely in his single life in the thriving new city.

But in 1264, everything was changed.

The stage for the extraordinary events of that year was set some time before, and again, it was King Henry's foreign entanglements that led to the trouble. On this occasion it was the pope who lured him into an extravagant disaster.

The prize this time was the rich southern kingdom of Sicily which the pope, in one of the many shifting alliances of the time, had offered Henry for his son Edmund if he would lead a holy war there. Sicily was far away and the Hohenstaufen dynasty whom the pope was trying to oust by this means, was well entrenched. Henry's own brother Richard of Cornwall, who was a far wiser statesman than the king, warned that the scheme was preposterous. But Henry, as usual, was dazzled, and when soon afterwards Richard of Cornwall himself was offered the throne of Germany, Henry began to dream of a magnificent new alliance between himself, the equally pious King Louis of France and the new German monarch his brother – a Christian confederacy unlike anything that Europe had seen in centuries. With the same enthusiasm with which he might have planned a splendid new court ceremony, he plunged into a fantastic series of diplomatic manoeuvres. He made a peace with Louis by which he finally renounced all the claims he had been making for so many years in France; he even, for good measure, married the daughter of the crusading King of Castile; and he made extravagant promises to the pope to help in the Sicilian affair – promises involving sums of money he could never hope to pay.

It was typical of his schemes. It was everything that any sensible English magnate or gentleman most dreaded – a foreign entanglement with an almost unlimited budget, and absolutely no prospect of success.

"Another lunatic venture," Godefroi stormed to his family. "The Welsh are making trouble; the kingdom's badly administered, the king's already head over heels in debt – God knows there's enough for him to do here."

The situation soon got worse. For Henry had now made such tremendous promises to the pope to conduct this holy war, that if he did not keep his word, the pope had threatened to excommunicate him and place the whole country under an interdict again.

It had long been clear to the magnates that poor Henry was unfit to reign. Lesser men like Godefroi would not have disagreed. But this last venture was the last straw. The king's hopeless position also gave them their opportunity; and so in 1258 they produced the Provisions of Oxford – a new charter of liberties which was a huge extension of the Magna Carta of the reign before. And they told Henry that if he wanted their support in the Sicilian venture, in which he was now ensnared as in a net, he must agree to its terms. The terms were humiliating. There was to be a standing council which must include English magnates as well as his own close friends, most of whom were the suspected foreigners from his mother's Lusignan connections. This council would appoint the chief officers of state – in effect, it would govern the realm in his name. And Henry was now in such a financial mess that he had to give way.

The leader of this movement was one of the strangest and most controversial figures in English history: Simon de Montfort.

The founder of the Mother of Parliaments was not English at all: he was French, from one of the most notable families in the Isle de France. Nor had he the slightest interest in democratic government. He was a magnate. Twenty years before he had caused a scandal by marrying Henry's newly widowed sister when she had already been promised to a convent – according to the king, he had seduced her. And he was more concerned with the endless lawsuit to secure her dowry – which Henry had still not paid – than he ever was with the Parliament of England.

He did not even like the English: he openly despised them and agreed with the stern Grosseteste that the nation's morals needed reforming, by compulsion if necessary. He was a strict military disciplinarian who despised Henry's footling campaigns and told him so in pointed language which made the King of England wince. He was intellectual, tactless and high-handed: a European grand seigneur who saw that Henry did not know how to govern his kingdom and could not resist doing it for him.

But Montfort had energy; he had ability and charisma, and unlike poor Henry, he knew what he wanted. He crossed the sky of England's history like a meteor.

During a few months in 1258 he overhauled the entire system of government. In the king's name parliaments of barons and knights were to be called three times a year; the king's sheriffs were to be local men who would be kept in check by serving only a year a time; a massive programme of local reforms were begun. And all this, not because he was devoted to any principle, but because he saw that for the independent-minded folk in their northern island, this was the system which would work best.

In October 1258 a proclamation was read in Latin, French and English, in every shire court, and in the name of the king and the community of the realm, not only each baron and knight, but every free man in the kingdom had to swear an oath of loyalty to the new government.

On this occasion Peter Shockley was with Godefroi and his son and took the oath immediately after them.

"Now we'll get some good government for our money," Godefroi's son told him with an encouraging grin.

"And Montfort? What's he like?" the merchant asked. The elder Godefroi smiled.

"An arrogant bastard," he murmured confidentially. "But he gets things done."

The irony of the situation only appeared a little while afterwards when the pope changed his mind and decided to give Sicily to someone else. Perhaps no one in England, except Henry himself, was surprised. He had given his kingdom to Simon de Montfort and his council for nothing at all.

But the oath had been taken.

"The king must live by the Provisions now," Godefroi declared. "It's too late to go back. The issue's settled."

He was wrong. Greater forces, the currents that bore along and finally tore apart the elaborate society of the middle ages, were deep at work.

The events that followed in the next four years, like a complex ritual dance, were conducted according to the best traditions of a feudal society.

First it seemed that Henry's son, aided by Simon de Montfort, would rebel and seize the throne. Then father and son were reconciled, and Henry appealed to the pope to declare that the hateful Provisions which bound him were invalid. The pope obliged and Montfort, disgusted, went into exile. Henry immediately reverted to his previous ways, filled his court with foreigners and ignored the magnates. Predictably the barons summoned Montfort again and rebelled. The situation changed almost monthly, the king's party in the ascendant one month, the rebels humiliating him the next; it was near to civil war: but still no blood was shed.

Important though these great events were in the national context, they did not greatly disturb the peace of Sarum. The local magnates, men like Basset and the Longspées were either moderates or for the king. And when the sheriff in 1261 seemed likely to veer towards the Montfort party he was speedily replaced by Ralph Russell, the king's man, who was also given the castle to garrison. For the first time for many years, the people of Sarum were conscious again of the old castle's frowning presence above them. The new town was anxious, but subdued.

Godefroi echoed the sentiments of most men when he said firmly: "No one wants war with the king. But we must find a settlement." The problem was how to find one.

It was in 1263 that a method was agreed upon. Both sides would go to arbitration.

The man they chose to arbitrate was the saintly King Louis IX of France.

No choice, it appeared, could have been more perfect: a pious crusader king, the perfect image of everything a feudal monarch should be; a lover of peace who was now bound by treaties of friendship to England; and, since Henry did homage to him, technically, for the last French province left him – the rich wine producing region of Gascony in the south west – he was in one respect the English king's feudal overlord.

And so at Christmas 1263, King Louis of France prepared to hear the case between the King of England and a large party of his subjects.

For Peter Shockley, the crisis of 1264 that changed his own life completely and nearly broke up the family of his friends the Godefrois, began at the mill, on the last day of January.

The spring had begun very early in Sarum that year and the river swept past the mill race in full spate.

It was in the middle of the morning that young Hugh de Godefroi had come to the mill to discuss the sale of the coming year's wool with Peter, and the two men were standing outside in the cold damp air, deep in conversation when Jocelin rode by.

The knight of Avonsford was growing old, but he was still a fine, even a daunting figure who sat on his horse as proud and erect as though he was about to enter the lists. His hawklike face was now surrounded by iron grey hair, its long, sardonic lines deeply incised; but as he looked down at his son and Peter Shockley, it softened into a smile. Jocelin was proud of his son.

Hugh was nearly thirty now, a tall, handsome fellow with jet-black hair and his father's aquiline face. He had married the daughter of a Devonshire knight who had given him a baby son before being carried off by a fever. It was assumed that soon he would marry again. From the age of eighteen he had delighted Jocelin by distinguishing himself in numerous tournaments and won praise from that great enthusiast for the joust, Prince Edward himself, the king's heir. The Godefroi shield with the white swan on the red ground was now greeted with a murmur of anticipation by the crowds in the stands, and with apprehension by the other competitors. The previous summer Jocelin, now himself a widower, had handed over the running of the estates to Hugh and these days he contented himself with his books and a daily ride around his considerable domains. That morning he had just come from the old miz-maze on the hill, which he had been restoring, and he was in good humour.

The three men made a pleasant contrast: the two Godefrois with their stately ways were so obviously of the knightly caste – even their greeting to one another was spoken in courtly French – and their friend and business associate Shockley, with his broad face and solid appearance was every inch a merchant.

"And when are you both getting married?" It was a question Jocelin had taken to asking each whenever he saw them. It was asked in jest, but they knew that he was in earnest, both to see his own son settled again and to see a grandchild for his old friend Edward Shockley, who had long since given up asking his son about the prospect himself.

But before either man could even make an excuse the party was interrupted by an unexpected sight, as a cart came careering along the track towards them. In it was old Edward Shockley himself, frail and bent, but with a look of grim determination on his face; he was whipping the horse along frantically and the old cart, never designed for speed, was bumping towards them crazily. His hood had fallen down onto his back and wisps of snowy hair stood up from his balding head like an aureole. As he crashed to a halt, he cried:

"The King of France – he's declared for Henry. Montfort and the Provisions are finished."

In fact, Louis had not even hesitated. The case he heard at Amiens, where the King of England had attended in person, was quite clear to him. He had not even considered a compromise which might have saved the situation. The pope, he declared, had rightly rejected the rebellious barons and no man should ignore such spiritual authority. Henry should be given power to do whatever he wished in his kingdom, and to choose whatever friends and ministers he liked, whether it pleased his barons or not. Those, he reminded them, were the customary rights of all kings. The judgement was comprehensive, conservative and feudally correct; but it was worse than anything the English rebels had feared.

The four men looked at each other. No one had any doubt about the graveness of the crisis. This was the final arbitration – the last peaceful solution left.

It was Jocelin, finally, who broke the silence.

"They must submit."

The two Shockleys looked at him in surprise; but it was Hugh, speaking in English who protested:

"To Henry? But father, you've said yourself that he's incompetent to rule."

Jocelin shook his head.

"They must submit," he explained. "because it's King Louis's judgement – and the pope's."

"You spoke up for Montfort once," his son reminded him.

"Yes. But not now. Things have gone too far."

This, they all knew, was the heart of the matter. For over a year now the knight, as he saw the results of Montfort's work, had felt a growing sense of unease; and there were many like him who were troubled by the way that Simon and some of his party were humiliating the king. It offended his sense of propriety. True, Henry was incompetent; but the monarchy itself, whatever a king's faults, was still a sacred institution. The feudal proprieties must be observed. Whatever the cost, Louis's judgement and the authority of the pope must now be respected.

"To reform the king and the Church is one matter," Jocelin had argued to his son the year before; "but we cannot *deny* the king and the Church. There must be authority." For these sacred institutions were the only guarantees that his world knew of morality and order. "Take them away," he warned, "and you take away the cornerstone of the building; then it will collapse."

But now Hugh shook his head.

"No, father. I will not submit."

"Not to King Louis? Or to the pope?" Jocelin's voice was dangerous.

"No. They're both foreigners. And the pope's too far away. They don't understand us."

This was an argument the older man found meaningless.

"That's nothing to do with it," he thundered. "It's a matter of principle."

Still Hugh shook his head.

The aliens in England – both the friends of the king at court and the numerous appointments by the popes of Italians to rich English benefices – had irritated many Englishmen. But the dissatisfaction that Hugh was expressing lay deeper. For the judgement of the pope and King Louis, however technically correct, was an affront to the islanders' sense of natural justice.

Jocelin glared at him.

"You must obey the law," he stated flatly. "And the law proceeds from the king, sanctioned by the Church. You cannot deny that."

But Hugh only made a dismissive gesture with his arm.

"No, father. The king himself is subject to a higher law, a natural law if you like: the community of the realm: the body politic. You want royal rule – reformed, of course, but royal. Montfort has shown us something better: a political rule, to which the king himself is subject. That's the only way for the future."

And when old Jocelin heard this, he went white, not with anger but with shock.

Constitutionally Hugh's statement was revolutionary; yet it was nothing new. All through the century, such ideas had been widely discussed in the universities of Europe, and even been endorsed by such a great churchman and philosopher as St Thomas Aquinas. Indeed, from the time of Magna Carta onwards, the magnates of England had in practice forced a political, cooperative rule on her kings, but had always claimed that in doing so they were only ensuring good feudal government, in which the king would be properly 'advised'. In this way the ancient sense of monarchy as a sacred institution, and of the right of the king to govern as he wished, had always been preserved.

But despite the fact that he knew all this, when he was faced with Hugh's bald statement and his rejection of the authority of centuries, Jocelin – much as he despised the king – could only draw back in horror.

"But the pope. . ." he cried.

"Even the bishops are split," Hugh protested. "Half of them are for Montfort." It was true. Many of the bishops, with good consciences, believed that Montfort was in the right and that the king should be bound by the oath and the Provisions.

"Do you agree with this?" Jocelin suddenly turned to old Edward.

Shockley considered. The philosophical points, though he understood them, interested him very little.

"I'll tell you one thing," he replied. "The merchants of London will go for Simon de Montfort if it comes to a fight."

Jocelin shrugged scornfully. London was a formidable, perhaps decisive power; but he was a knight, not a mere merchant, and he was concerned with defending a principle which, now that it had been challenged, he knew was all important.

"You are fighting divine authority," he stated, and staring with eyes full of both sorrow and anger, he addressed Hugh in French. "I order you to submit, or you will no longer be my son." Then he rode away.

It was while he witnessed this quarrel between Jocelin and his only son, that Peter Shockley, whose opinion had not been asked, understood finally where he stood. For although he missed many of the philosophical points, his pragmatic mind, moving instinctively, had grasped the essential issue that lay beneath the high-flown argument. "It makes no difference to us whether the king rules or his council," he remarked to his father afterwards. "We need peace and low taxes for the fulling mill. And," he added ominously, "we must see that we get them."

Within a week, there was no one in Sarum who did not know about the quarrel between Jocelin de Godefroi and his heir. They no longer lived under the same roof. Though his baby son remained at the manor house in the care of his father's women, Hugh moved into a house in the new city where he lived quietly, but in open defiance of his father's wishes.

Hugh was not alone. There were many voices of discontent raised in Sarum now and in February a new and larger contingent of the king's troops arrived in the castle. The message was clear: the town remained relatively quiet and even Hugh found it necessary to conduct himself carefully. Nonetheless, in the coming weeks he disappeared twice on visits to destinations that could only be guessed at.

The months of February and March also brought fresh rumours. London was in an uproar and had declared for Simon. Montfort himself had broken his leg in an accident at the start of the year – there were rumours that he was dying, others that he was already on the move. Prince Edward was sweeping across the country with his friends from the border castles of Wales: early in April he and his father took the castle at Northampton. And now news came that Simon de Montfort was definitely in the field.

Despite these political events, the business at the fulling mill continued to thrive and at the end of March Peter began to consider enlarging the mill with a new extension. Accordingly, at Jocelin's request, Osmund the Mason paid several visits to the mill to advise on the construction.

It was one morning in mid-April, as Peter and Osmund came out of the mill after one of these discussions, that they saw Hugh de Godefroi approaching. He was riding the magnificent black charger which had borne him so many times to triumph in the lists. Behind him he led two other horses, one of which was a second charger, the other a packhorse carrying his equipment: the great suit of chain mail, that stretched from his neck to his feet, his shield with the swan on its red ground, his sword and lances, and the great helm – the solid metal head cover fashionable at the time that resembled an upturned saucepan with two slits for the eyes.

Over his leather tunic, Hugh was wearing a red cloak bearing the white cross of the crusader.

"Where's my father?" he asked.

In the two months since Hugh had left, the old knight had resumed control of the estate and, to distract his thoughts from the quarrel with his son, he had thrown himself wholeheartedly into the business. He had visited the mill every two days and Peter, though the older man never asked him, had always mentioned the fact if he had seen Hugh in the city and given Jocelin a report of him, as though he did not know of the quarrel between them. Few people at Sarum would have dared to do such a thing, but Peter suspected that the knight's regular visits to the mill were not unconnected.

"Should be by shortly," he answered.

The three men waited in silence. All knew what this visit meant. And it was not long before Jocelin came into sight.

He was erect as ever. From a distance he might have been a young man. He seemed for a moment to hesitate, but then walked his horse straight towards them; as he came up, his eyes seemed very bright and very hard. Father and son faced each other. Jocelin's eyes fixed on his son's cloak.

"Do you have the right to wear that cross, monsieur?"

Hugh inclined his head.

"Oui, monsieur. The Bishop of Worcester, and three other bishops have given us the right." That several bishops should recently have decided that his rebellion ranked as a holy war was a great coup for Simon de Montfort. "I have come to ask for your blessing," Hugh continued.

The older man nodded curtly. He need not refuse what a bishop had already granted. He dismounted and Hugh did the same.

Without a word, Hugh knelt on the ground in front of the mill. Gently Jocelin removed from his own neck the little chain on which the badge from the shrine of Thomas à Becket at Canterbury hung. Silently he placed it over the head of his son.

"I do not agree with your quarrel, but go with my blessing all the same," he said gruffly.

Hugh got up. It was curious to see the two men, Peter thought, the one so perfect a replica of the other. The reconciliation made, both men looked relieved. Hugh looked down at the little badge and touched it affectionately.

"I understand, monsieur, that your journey takes you towards the shrine of this saint," his father said wryly. "Perhaps you could kindly bring me another badge." It was a courtly jest, that Hugh smiled at: for it was well known that the forces of Montfort were gathering in Kent, on the Canterbury road.

"Certainly, monsieur," he replied gracefully. "We hope to be only briefly detained on the way."

No one spoke as he rode away; and as soon as he was out of sight, Jocelin too, having forgotten his business at the mill, mounted his horse and rode up towards the high ground. From up there, Peter suspected, the knight might catch another glimpse of Hugh as he took the road towards the east.

But neither the Godefrois, Shockley or the mason realised that there had been two other witnesses to the scene. William atte Brigge and his son John, a dark, sharp-eyed boy of seventeen, had come from behind the mill, unnoticed, just as the two Godefrois had dismounted. Hanging back by the corner of the building where they would not be seen, they had watched carefully as Hugh received his blessing. William had looked thoughtful: one never knew the value of information, but he sensed that what he had witnessed was important.

"Remember that," he said quietly to his son. "It might come in useful one day."

The battle of Lewes took place on May 14, 1264.

The town of Lewes lay near the coast, some sixty miles west of the Dover Straits and immediately below the high chalk ridge of the South Downs. It was a small place – about the size of Wilton – and it boasted a small castle and an ancient priory belonging to the monks of Cluny.

The forces of King Henry and his son Edward were camped beside the town when, after dawn, they saw the army of Simon de Montfort in battle line upon the chalk ridge above, with the Londoners on the left wing. The night before, Simon's army had been given absolution by the Bishop of Worcester. They wore crusader crosses on their breasts.

The battle was brief. Prince Edward attacked up the hill, cut the Londoners off from the rest of Simon's force, and managed to drive them into some nearby marshes through which he then pursued them for several hours. When he returned to the battleground, however, he found that his own victory had been a side issue and that in the meantime Montfort had completely routed the rest of the army. The king and his brother were prisoners, and the battle was all over.

There were very few knights killed in the engagement. One, who had valiantly ridden to the aid of the Londoners as he saw them being driven back, was trapped in their flight, toppled accidentally from his horse by men at arms who did not stop to help him, and butchered a few moments later by a group of Prince Edward's foot soldiers. He was identified afterwards by the white swan on his shield.

On the king's side, although they lost, the main battle was so brief and decisive that the casualties were not large. Amongst them however was an elderly knight, who should not have been fighting at all, named Geoffrey de Whiteheath.

It was in June that Alicia quietly returned to the house in Castle Street. It astonished her to realise that she had not been to Sarum for twenty years.

Outwardly she had changed very little: only the little lines around her eyes, which were not unattractive, suggested her age. Her hair still had no streaks of grey. As for her inner feelings – she was not sure herself.

She had not been unhappy. She had given Geoffrey de Whiteheath a child a year after their marriage, but it had been a girl, and for some reason, though she had tried, there had been no son to follow. Geoffrey had slipped into old age without the son he had married her for and she had watched his broad, handsome face gradually sink in upon itself and gather lines of age and a sadness he could not conceal. Their daughter had been married the year before and after this he had been left alone with a wife who had failed him and a fine estate which no longer brought him joy.

When – though he had difficulty clambering into his chain mail – he insisted on going to join King Henry, she knew what was in his mind and did not try to stop him. And when he bade her a loving and courteous goodbye, she had been glad to see the eager look on his old face as he rode off to his final battle, from which, she was well aware, he had no intention of returning.

The estate had passed to his brother; she was left with comfortable means, and she had left Winchester without regrets.

But what next?

"I'm neither young or old," she thought as she approached the growing city of her childhood.

She found it fuller than it had been before. The half empty chequers in the northern part of the new town were now almost all built over. People had been drawn to the thriving market town from all over the southern half of the island – from Bristol, London, Norwich, and even further afield: it was teeming.

And above its roofs now rose the long grey line of the nearly completed cathedral.

Her father had died five years before and her brother Walter had succeeded him. She spent three pleasant days in her brother's house. She inspected the cathedral and marvelled at its long, clean lines. She paid a visit of respect to her uncle Portehors, who was now very frail, but who insisted on stiffly walking beside her to show her the completed watercourses in the streets; but she saw few other faces that she knew.

It was on the third evening of her visit, when they were alone together, that her brother broached the subject that was on his mind. He was like her father, she thought, except he had developed a fulsome, pompous manner, where Alan Le Portier had always been caustic and dry.

"Have you considered the prospect of making a new alliance?" he asked.

She smiled.

"Marriage you mean? I suppose so?"

He smiled with self-satisfaction. "I've a candidate. A fine catch." He blew out his cheeks complacently.

"Really? Already?" She could not help laughing. "Who?"

"A knight with a splendid estate." He paused for effect. "Jocelin de Godefroi. He is most interested."

For Jocelin de Godefroi, at the age of fifty-seven, had emerged from his grief at the loss of his son to the realisation that he must begin his life again – not for himself, but for his little grandson.

"The boy's three," he considered as he looked at the child his son had

[429]

left behind. "If I can live seventeen years, he'll be twenty. Just about able to fend for himself." But could he do it? In seventeen years he would be seventy-four, and few men reached such an age at that time. He still had his health though: he must try. But as he gazed at the child, he knew something else was missing. "The child needs a mother and this place needs a woman," he decided. "I must find a wife."

And so he allowed the fact to be known and waited to see what happened. It was not long before Le Portier approached him.

The idea of the Le Portier girl attracted him – not a noble family admittedly, but respectable enough; besides, she'd been the wife of Geoffrey de Whiteheath for twenty years and she knew about managing an estate. And she was only thirty-six. As he thought about it, for the first time in many weeks his face broke into a smile.

Perhaps he could give her a child! He certainly felt capable of it.

"I've two estates after all," he considered. "I could leave one to my grandson Roger and the other to the child, if it's a boy." And so he sent for Walter and told him: "Bring her here to take a look at me." And he made preparations.

Alicia was standing at the corner of the market place, by Blue Boar Row, when Peter Shockley saw her. He stood quite still, staring at her, hardly able to believe that it was she. He had been out at the Shockley farm where his father now liked to spend the summer and had not been in the city for several days. He had known nothing about either the death of her husband or her own return. In a few long strides, he was in front of her.

"You have not changed." He smiled down at her.

Alicia started. She had almost forgotten him. No one had been further from her mind at that moment – she was sure of it. But there he was, a little stouter, but a remarkably good-looking man, she could not help admitting.

It only took a few moments for him to learn her story; and also the fact that she was going to see Godefroi that very day.

"He's looking for a wife," he said thoughtfully.

She smiled. "I know." And then, rather to her own surprise she heard herself say, as she gazed straight into his blue eyes:

"But perhaps he won't find one."

The courtship of Peter Shockley took one week.

He had told himself that he had not been waiting for her twenty years: it was surprising to him now how comfortably that lie fell away. He found a sense of joy and excitement that he had long forgotten suddenly awaken now in her presence; and when on the third day he took her hand and drew her to him in a kiss, it seemed the most natural thing in the world.

"It's as though we'd always been together," he said simply.

"I know," she replied.

But it was not the truth. For her, their meeting had not been – as it was for Peter – an act of fate. And the idea of marrying Shockley had not really occurred to her until later that day, when she had been eagerly ushered by her brother into the great hall at Avonsford and seen the perfectly preserved knight, his grey hair carefully curled with heated tongs, advancing towards her. He was old. In his eye, she saw at once, was a sadness. She had known both before.

"My answer is no," she told Walter afterwards, to his great distress.

It was nothing to his distress a week later when she announced that she would marry Shockley.

"But you've become a lady. A fit wife for a knight!" he protested. It had pleased him to be brother-in-law to Geoffrey de Whiteheath; to be allied to Godefroi would be an even greater advantage. "Shockley's nothing but a merchant."

"I have money," she reminded him. "I can do as I like."

And to the delight of old Edward Shockley, they were married the following month.

On the day of their marriage, Peter gave her, for the second time, a little locket on a silver chain.

For Peter, his marriage was like being reborn, and when on the night of their wedding he led Alicia to the room in the old Shockley farm which Edward and his wife had occupied before them and took her in his arms, it seemed that all his years fell away and he was, once again, the eighteen-year-old boy united at last with his bride. All this Alicia knew; and if she could not feel the same, she concealed the fact, glad to feel his happiness. So it was with surprise that in the middle of the night, she woke and pulled him to her once more, but this time with a little gasp of unexpected passion.

When Jocelin de Godefroi heard about the marriage of Alicia and Peter Shockley he became white with anger.

"This merchant goes too far," he muttered, "if he supposes he can take the bride of a Godefroi." It was not only his family pride that was hurt; the business was an affront to him personally.

For several days he brooded about it.

Peter was in such a state of happiness in the first days of his marriage that he hardly noticed the fact that Godefroi had not visited the mill on his customary rounds of the estate; and so when, two weeks after his wedding, he saw Jocelin approaching he came out to greet him quite unsuspecting. His face fell in utter confusion as the knight, sitting bolt upright in the saddle and with a distant look in his eyes, told him:

"I'm afraid I shall be wanting another tenant for this mill, Shockley. You're to leave at the end of the month."

The mortgage to Aaron had been paid off many years ago; the mill lay on Godefroi's land; Shockley might fight dispossession in the courts, but even if he won, Godefroi could make his life a misery. As the knight rode away, he gazed after him in horrified disbelief.

He did not know what to do. He had become so used, over the years, to keeping matters to himself, that for two more days he went moodily about his business, unable to decide on any course of action and unable to speak about the matter even to his wife. On the third day, however,

Alicia, who had waited patiently for his mood to pass, demanded firmly that he tell her what was on his mind; and after she had heard, she told him:

"You must ask your father to speak to him."

But Peter refused. Edward was old and frail, and besides, the Shockley affairs were in his hands now.

"I'll find a solution," he told her moodily.

Alicia said nothing. But the next morning when Peter had gone, she retired to her room for half an hour. When she had finished, she smiled to herself at the result; and at noon that day the servants of Avonsford manor were surprised to see a woman dressed not in the plain, simple cotte and pelisse of a merchant's wife, but in the richly embroidered robes of a lady, with wimple and cap, ride calmly into the courtyard and call peremptorily to one of the grooms to help her dismount.

In the twenty years as the mistress of Geoffrey de Whiteheath's household, she had learnt all the elegant ways of a lady, and when a few moments later she swept into Jocelin's hall, even he, despite her new position, automatically rose and bowed respectfully.

She wasted no time, and she addressed him in French.

"I know, seigneur, that you propose to eject my new husband from his mill."

He inclined his head stiffly, but under the steady gaze of her violet eyes he could not help himself blushing. She pursued her advantage calmly and masterfully.

"I came to see you without his knowledge since – you will forgive my conceit – I feared I might be the cause. But perhaps I am wrong and my choice of husband was of no interest to you."

The knight smiled at the neat way that she almost forced him to pay her a compliment.

"Madame," he replied, with frank admiration, and using the same terms of formal courtesy, "I should have been proud had you expressed an interest in my poor manor of Avonsford."

"Then I wish you to know, seigneur, that your manor and its occupant were of great interest to me," she replied graciously. "But after twenty years with a man whom I loved, but who was from the start my senior by a generation, I decided to try to bring happiness to the merchant whom I had deserted for him when I was young. It seems that instead I have brought Shockley only a great misfortune, and I am sorry that it should come from a man whom, if circumstances had been different, I might have loved." And with a graceful curtsey, she swept out of the room.

That evening, after visiting his little grandson, Jocelin de Godefroi went to the garderobe where he kept his books and took down from the wall the sheet of burnished steel that he liked to use as a mirror.

"You're too old for her," he told himself frankly. "But what a woman."

The next day, to his surprise, Peter Shockley received a message from Avonsford manor that Godefroi had changed his mind and that the mill should remain in his hands. He never discovered why.

Through that summer, although great events were taking place in the island, many at Sarum chose to ignore them: Peter Shockley because he was concerned with his mill and his marriage, Godefroi for sound reasons of politics.

"The business between the king and Montfort could still go either way in the end," he judged. "If I'm to preserve the estates for my grandson, we must stay out of trouble." Sarum with its garrison remained quiet, and although Montfort's party knew that he had been opposed to them, his only son had died in their cause and they did not disturb him.

The events of 1264 were fraught with both danger and opportunity. Montfort was in control again; the king and his son Edward, in whose name he was governing once more, were safely in his hands. But he was threatened on every side; the supporters of Henry gathered across the Channel and threatened to invade with Louis of France; the friends of Prince Edward, the great lords from the border with Wales were preparing to attack again, and across the Channel, another powerful voice, the legate of the pope, still refused to accept the new arrangements in England. In October he excommunicated Simon and all those who supported the Provisions.

Despite the uncertainty, however, most of the island was still with Montfort: the freemen of England had a government bound by Magna Carta and the Provisions. They had no wish to turn the clock back.

It was at the end of the year that the great event took place which made Godefroi shake his head with surprise and Peter Shockley clap his hands together and exclaim to Alicia: "At last! Now we shall see the king get some good advice."

For it was in December that Simon de Montfort summoned his most famous parliament to meet in London at the end of January.

This famous assembly was by no means a parliament of the nation. Barons loyal to Simon were summoned by writs at once while others, who were loyal to the king, were summoned late. As before, knights were called from the shires. And as well as the Bishop, the Dean of Salisbury was summoned. But it was a single, tentative innovation that gave the gathering its fame and caused Shockley such excitement. For from London and a small selection of boroughs, chiefly in the north, Montfort summoned burgesses.

"It's time they heard some of the men who run this country's trade," Peter cried.

Alicia watched her husband fondly. She had lived with men like Geoffrey de Whiteheath and Godefroi for too many years to suppose that they would listen to a mere merchant.

"The merchants will be present to reassure the towns which might be trouble spots," she said calmly. "They'll stand about and be flattered to be there, that's all."

Peter nodded.

"That may be so," he replied shrewdly, "but the point is that once they've been summoned, they'll have to be asked to future parliaments as

[433]

well. Next time, other boroughs will demand to send burgesses. And in time, those burgesses will speak."

"Perhaps," she said doubtfully. "But I wouldn't count on it."

For all that, as the days of January passed, he became excited. Wiltshire was sending knights. Had the old man wished to take part, his friend Jocelin de Godefroi might have been one of them. But there were other local Wiltshire knights like Scudamore, Hussey, or Richard of Zeals, to whom Peter knew he could speak freely. The prospect of these men being joined by burgesses like himself in their national councils enthralled him, and at the end of January he announced: "I'm going to London to see this parliament."

Alicia raised her eyebrows.

"You can't take part."

"I know." His eyes were shining. "Not this time. But I can watch."

Alicia got up and kissed him. "Go and watch then." And then, after a brief pause she added: "but mind you get back by summer, because – " she gave him a happy smile "– I'm pregnant."

At which Peter gave a great shout of joy.

For Peter Shockley, the visit in February 1265 to Simon de Montfort's great parliament in London was a disappointment.

It was not what he had expected. He had supposed that he would see a great assembly – the king surrounded by his council taking important decisions. He had hoped to witness them hearing complaints against royal officials, appointing new sheriffs and even designing a new peace with the pope and King Louis of France. It would, he supposed, be a grand affair. But when he arrived in the great port, he could see no sign of such an assembly at all. True, a large stone building with a wooden roof was pointed out to him by a friendly merchant as the hall where the assembly would meet; but each time he went by, the place seemed half deserted.

Even so, he was soon aware of activity. Little groups of men bustled about between lodgings or greeted each other in the streets – knights from the shires lounged together in the inns chatting idly but, he soon gathered, with serious purpose. It was clear that what was taking place was not a single assembly, but a huge network of informal groups and committees which would in due course come together in some common purpose. But apart from the dean, who only gave him a cursory nod, he never seemed to see anyone he knew, and after two days of fruitlessly walking about and engaging people in desultory conversations, he began to feel rather lonely.

He had hoped, also, to hear several important subjects discussed. One of these was the wool trade with Flanders, which the recent disturbances had disrupted.

"If the wool trade goes, there's no money for the king's wars or Montfort's peace," he had stated accurately to Alicia.

Another personal concern was the plight of the Jews.

He had good reason to be concerned. In numerous recent ventures,

[434]

including the extension to the mill, he had wanted to borrow money. He disliked borrowing from Cahorsin merchants and his dealings with Aaron of Wilton had been perfectly satisfactory in the past.

"The business often needs money," he told Alicia. "Why should I be put to inconvenience to get it?"

But this was exactly what had happened. For the needless persecution of the Jewish community had gone from bad to worse. There had been more ritual murder accusations, more trials; and there had been constant levies, including a second stupendous assessment of sixty thousand marks. These repeated persecutions and tallages had reduced the community to a pitiable state: to his certain knowledge, the group at Wilton was almost completely ruined.

A week before he left, he had encountered Aaron in the city. It was a shocking sight; the Jew, always so robust and only twelve years his senior seemed an old man. He walked slowly and stiffly; his once fine robe was frayed at the edges where it touched the ground. That the financier should have been reduced to such a state offended Shockley.

"I am going to the parliament," he told Aaron proudly. "And when I get there I shall say something about the treatment the Jews are receiving."

But to his surprise Aaron had taken him by the arm and begged:

"Don't do so. It can only harm you, and it won't help me." And when Peter protested the Jew reminded him: "Look what happened to the Franciscans."

It was sadly true that when, ten years before, the Franciscan order had protested against the inhumanity – and plain mendacity – of the Jewish persecutions and blood-accusations, the prejudice against the Jews had been so strong that they themselves had been universally execrated. Peter had continued his donations to the brotherhood in New Salisbury, but he knew of many others who had not.

"But Montfort's a reformer," he countered.

Aaron smiled ruefully.

"My friend, Simon de Montfort is almost as extravagant as the king. He's in debt to Jewish moneylenders up to his ears. He hates us more than anyone."

Peter had parted from him despondently. And at London, whenever he had been able to strike up a conversation with those who were taking part in the proceedings, he found that even the burghers from York and Lincoln, had little interest in these and other practical affairs which concerned him.

"There are high politics to be dealt with first, friend," one of them told him seriously. "Until we settle which party holds which castles, and whether Prince Edward will come to terms with the council as well as his father, nothing else can be done I assure you."

These were matters about which the merchant had no opinions. After four days he decided to go. But he was not discouraged – indeed, what he had seen made him more determined than ever to take part in the future.

"This is not my parliament," he thought. "But the next one will be. Or the next."

In fact, the parliament of 1265, which lasted into March, accomplished a great deal. The feudal questions of the king and prince's castles were settled, leaving Montfort secure but the royal party appeased. New officers of state were appointed, cases heard, and the wool trade with Flanders was reopened. Even Montfort's dislike of the Jews was modified later that year when he realised that he must either lift some of the burdens upon them or destroy them as a source of government funds completely.

But across the Channel, the papal legate waited – for whatever the parliament might agree, his position remained unchanged: Montfort, the defier of the pope, must be rooted out of England. And on the Welsh borders, the friends of Prince Edward, though they had sworn oaths of loyalty to Simon and the new government, were waiting too.

Back in the relative calm of Sarum however, Peter Shockley watched these great events unfolding with detachment. When, that summer, Prince Edward escaped to his friends in the west, and led them against Montfort, he hoped that Montfort would prevail. But when, on August 4, the great man was trapped and killed at the battle of Evesham, he was not downhearted.

"These are quarrels between the magnates now," he said to Alicia. "The burgesses have been allowed into the king's council: that is all that matters." And although his wife smiled at his naïvety, the merchant felt sure that events one day would prove him right.

For the next two years, a great and majestic series of feudal events took place. The friends of Montfort great and small were formally deprived of their lands. Fortunately however, since his own loyalty was well known, old Godefroi was forgiven his son's rebellion, and left in peace; Simon's son fought on but had to flee the island and his last followers, after holding out in the eastern Isle of Ely, finally surrendered. The papal legate Ottobuono with all the pomp of his position came to England and, as great churchmen had done before, arranged in his Dictum of Kenilworth a lasting settlement which would allow the rebels, on payment of stiff penalties, to regain their lands; and in the great Statute of Marlborough he not only reconfirmed the liberties in Magna Carta but added most of the Provisions of Simon de Montfort as well. The net result of all these high feudal politics was accurately summed up by the provincial merchant.

"Montfort's gone," Peter said to Alicia "but they haven't destroyed his work."

He had more cause for satisfaction than just the political settlement. For in June 1265 Alicia bore him their first child: a chubby, healthy girl with blonde hair and the most beautiful violet blue eyes. They called her Mary.

"She shall have the farm," Peter promised his wife, adding cheerfully: "All we need now is a son who shall have the house and the mill."

Alicia smiled.

But all these great events, it seemed to Osmund the Mason, passed away and dwindled into insignificance in the quiet presence of the huge building of grey stone on the valley floor.

For in the year of Our Lord 1265, the main central body of the new cathedral was almost completed.

The church, with its simple cruciform design, its long nave, and its light and airy transepts, stood peacefully in the silence of the close – eighty-seven feet tall, nearly five hundred in length, its long lead roof only broken by the single low square tower that rose a few feet above it at the intersection of the transepts – serenely unaffected by all such temporal events. As though by an afterthought, a free-standing tower containing the massive bells to summon the church's faithful to prayer, had been constructed near the north walk of the close, about forty yards from the main church, and in order that the tolling bells should be heard all over the valley, this stout stone belfry had been made two hundred feet high.

In the year of Our Lord 1265 Osmund the Mason was to begin his greatest work, and it was to be the year, also, when he fell under the spell of the deadly sin that almost destroyed him.

It was on a cold, dry day in March that he led his little family proudly into the cathedral close to see the work that he had done. This visit had become a yearly ritual ever since, ten years before, his son Edward had been born; he liked to feel that the boy, who was surely destined to be a mason too, was growing up consciously with the great church his father was building and on which he would one day work himself.

Accordingly he had escorted them down the valley from Avonsford, past the old castle hill and through the busy streets to the close. The party consisted of his wife Ann, his two daughters and the boy.

They were a strange little group. The mason, squat, short-legged, with his big solemn head and a face which his veins made rather red, walked with a certain sense of his own dignity. He was, after all, a master mason now. In the city, he was a man of importance as he moved about in his heavy leather apron, and a figure of awe to the junior masons with whom he was fair, but stern. In the village of Avonsford however, he was best known as the kindly though respected figure who would often of an evening, surrounded by his family in their cottage, carve a wooden model in his wonderful craftsman's hands for some village child while the child waited. The three women of the family all closely resembled each other: Ann was a thin, sallow woman, neither good-looking nor ugly, but about whom there always hung a faint sense of unspoken resentment. She liked to remain at her house at Avonsford with its four modest rooms and thatched roof: she had little interest in the town except when, occasionally, her two daughters took her to the market and made her buy some brightly coloured cloth or trinket after which she could be induced to smile unwillingly. She was a little taller than the mason.

Last of all came the little boy of ten, walking contentedly behind the women, with his chubby body and large head, unconsciously so closely imitating his father's stolid walk that people grinned as the family passed.

It was to him, while the three women admired the great building, that Osmund addressed his remarks.

He showed him the splendid west front, the last part of the main building to be completed, that rose like an enormous stage set with tiers of empty niches flanking the door and a huge window in its centre.

"See, there are statues in some of the niches already," he explained. "And we are making more. One day every niche will have its statue."

"Statues of whom?" Edward asked.

"Kings, bishops, saints," Osmund replied. For in the cathedral at least, if not in the world outside, the perfect medieval marriage of the spiritual and the temporal worlds was celebrated at every opportunity.

This was the one wall of the cathedral that rose, sheer, to its apex at the top of the roof, nearly a hundred feet above. Edward gazed at the wall, across at the high belfry tower in admiration, and then started back instinctively as a veil of cloud passed overhead and made the great wall seem to move towards him.

Osmund laughed.

"When the clouds pass over," he said, "it always looks as if the west front is going to topple. Come inside."

If the outside of the building was impressive, the inside was astonishing. It was not only the huge, spacious nave and side aisles which seemed, like huge tunnels, to disappear into the distance, not only the airy transepts, flooding the centre of the church with light: it was the fact that the whole of the inside was painted. For the gothic cathedral of the medieval world was a riot of colour. The vaults, the pillars, the carvings and the tombs that lay in the chantry chapels were all painted in brilliant blues, reds and greens. The effect was as bright and vivid as the market place; its carved and painted foliage seemed as lush as the Avon valley from which they had come. As the little boy gazed enraptured down the lines of graceful pillars he cried: "It's like a forest." And so it was.

"Now I will show you the carvings," his father said.

There were many to see. There were the carvings on the great stone screen that separated the nave from the long choir beyond, where the services were sung: set in the choirscreen in a line across the church stood the solemn figures of the kings of England splendidly painted in red, blue and gold, from Saxon Egbert to the present King Henry III.

"There is the great King Alfred, ancestor of them all, who ruled first Wessex and then all England," Osmund showed him. "And Edward the Confessor, the pious; then William of Normandy; and there, Richard Coeur de Lion, the crusader. Our greatest kings." For the centuries had done their work, and to Osmund it was an article of faith that all these figures, though the blood line that linked them was only a very tenuous one in reality, formed a single family of island kings. In the cathedral, the world became God's world, as it ought to be.

He pointed up to the brightly painted bosses in the roof of the choir, and led the boy to the east end of the nave where, on a high scaffolding the painters were busy on the final section of the ceiling.

Then he showed him the great stout pillars, one tiered above the other that supported the three rows of arches that led to the vaults. He led him to the central crossing of the transepts where the eye travelled up the huge pillars that stretched, not in three tiers but in a single, sheer, unbroken line right up to the crossing of the vaults.

"Feel the stone," he ordered his son, and Edward felt the smooth, hard stone of the massive nest of pillars.

"That's solid Purbeck marble," he explained. "It came all the way from Corfe, round by the sea and up the river. It's stronger than any other stone so it takes the central tower. And we never paint it."

Edward could see why. The stone's polished, blue-grey surface was a delight to the eye.

He took him up to the upper level next, and showed him the cathedral's construction.

"See how the vaults are made," he explained. "When they used to build them before, a vault was just a half circle across from side to side – like cutting a barrel in half from top to bottom. But that way, you had to support every stone of the roof while you were building it – great wooden boards on scaffolding, thousands of them. But now – look from here." From the clerestory level he pointed across the nave, and now Edward saw clearly that the pointed Gothic vaults he had seen from below were achieved by crossing pairs of arches diagonally across the nave instead of from one side straight to the other.

"They cross north east to south west, south east to north west, over the nave that runs from west to east," Osmund summarised. "They divide each section into four quarters."

"Why do you do it?" the boy asked.

"Simple," the mason replied proudly. "First, once we have got the basic cross arches up – these we call the ribs – we have the bones of our building. It's flesh, the vaulting between, we call the cells." Now he took his son up into the space above the vaults. "We fill the cells with these," he explained, and the boy saw a collection of differently shaped stones, all wedge-shaped, but some much broader than others. "They're *voutains*," Osmund told him. "Being wedges, we drop them in from above, like a peg into a hole – so once the ribs are up we can fill in the rest of the vaults from up here."

"And the different sizes?"

"Simple again. As you go higher, the vault opens out wider, so we use bigger stones." And he showed him an adjustable wooden mould that was used by the stone cutters.

"Now come down again," he ordered, and led the boy back to the floor of the church. "The most important thing," he pointed up at the soaring arches, "is that instead of all the weight of the roof falling evenly on the walls, now it's the ribs that hold it all up, and they rest on the pillars. So the walls don't have to be so thick any more and we can build these fine big windows."

When Edward remembered the heavy old Norman cathedral he had seen, still standing but nearly unused, on the castle hill and compared it with this airy new building, he understood what Osmund meant.

But it was another feature, less important perhaps, and less easy to see, which was for the mason the church's best feature. This was the series of carved heads in which he himself had specialised ever since the day he made the figure of Bartholomew twenty years before. They were everywhere, brightly and naturally coloured, peeping from the screen, from the aisles and the clerestory arches; but the finest of all were the highest up, at the end of the shafts where the broad vaulting ribs spread out to form the ceiling, so high that one had to peer carefully to see them at all.

"Yet they are the best," the mason told him enthusiastically. "There are fifty-seven of them up there in the vaults," he explained. "We've been adding them ever since the building first started."

"And how many did you make," the boy said.

"Eight," Osmund said proudly. "No one has made more."

Set just in the cleft of the V that begins the vaulting the heads were arranged in perfect symmetry: king opposite king, bishop matched with bishop, staring at each other or down into the softly echoing spaces below. They were of many kinds, by many hands: a few in Purbeck marble, most in the softer Chilmark stone.

It had taken him many years of study to perfect his technique. He had even travelled to Winchester where, the century before, King Stephen's brother the bishop had collected pagan statues from Rome. But the stylised classical heads, and the wooden staring faces produced by many of his fellow masons had never caught his imagination. He searched always, as he had from the first, for a more natural, lively form, as though he was carving in wood; and in several of his heads he had achieved this wonderfully.

"See up there," he pointed to Edward: and far above the boy suddenly saw the face of Canon Portehors, his deeply lined, frowning and disembodied face staring bleakly at them from its great height.

Afterwards he took the boy to where he had been working in the masons' lodge. Masons like Osmund were known as bench-masons, so called because unlike the lesser stone cutters and labourers, they did their work at a bench. Here the mason showed him another head he had been working on, this time of a former bishop, and on the underneath, where it could never be seen unless the head was one day dislodged from its place, he showed Edward the small mark he had chiselled in the surface. It consisted of a capital M, in the centre of which was incised the letter O.

"Osmund Mason," he explained. "My mark goes on each piece I do." This was not only a signature, but it also ensured that he would be correctly paid for each work he contributed to the cathedral. "And one day, you too will have a mason's mark," he told him. "Like this," and with a piece of chalk he drew his own mark again, but his time added an E below it for the boy's name. "It's our family mark," he said with satisfaction, before taking his son back to rejoin the others.

"But will I work here?" the boy asked anxiously. "The church is nearly finished."

Osmund smiled.

"There's more to come," he assured him. And he took him through a side door to where, running along the south of the nave, on the other side of the masons' lodge, a spacious cloister had been laid out. Leading off this, the walls of a new octagonal building were almost complete.

"This will be the chapter house," Osmund said, "where the canons and the deacons will hold their meetings. They say it will be a fine building, with many carvings. And after that we may extend the tower as well." He beamed with the thought of it. "There'll be colleges, more houses for the canons, hospitals. . ." He spread his little hands expansively: "There's work for generations of masons in Salisbury."

And indeed, as the boy walked around the close afterwards, it was plain that what his father said was true. Along the west walk that backed on to the river, fine new houses were still rising: not perhaps quite as splendid as the sumptuous hall with its leaded roof that old Elias de Dereham had built for himself – and whose colossal mortgage, twenty years after his death, was still being paid off – but handsome buildings all the same. Near the river, just before the little hospital, the new college of St Nicholas de Valle had just been built for scholars who were now coming to the new centre from Oxford. At St Ann's Gate, near the little house of the Franciscans, a new grammar school had been founded; and on the south side of the cathedral, separated from the rest of the close in its own gracious grounds, the bishop's impressive palace was constantly being enlarged.

"There's no better place for a mason to be in England," Osmund declared.

He could have added, for a priest to be, or a scholar. For under the patronage of the distinguished local scholar Walter de la Wyle, its present bishop, the new school by the river was already becoming a small but distinguished centre of learning, where not only theology but civil law, mathematics, classical literature and the elaborately precise logic of Aristotle were studied. This interest in science and the humanities, which had been stimulated by the crusaders' discovery of the Arab scholars in the Middle East, was to be found in many scholarly communities; and the transfer of scholars from Oxford, which had been unsettled recently by several disputes with the townspeople and the papal legate, was not unusual either: a similar emigration a little before had already caused the setting up of another small college in the little East Anglian town of Cambridge.

In fact, only one thing at Sarum was lacking.

"If only the pope in Rome would make our Bishop Osmund a saint," the mason cried.

For a long time the diocese of Salisbury had tried to have its saintly bishop canonised: partly, to be sure, on account of his undoubted piety but also, it could not be denied, the existence of a shrine to the saint in the new city would bring with it, in those times when pilgrimage was so popular, a huge influx of visitors from whom the diocese and its new market town would profit enormously. So far they had not prevailed at Rome. But the campaign went on.

[441]

"One day," declared the mason, who had himself been piously named after the great man, "we'll have our shrine, and you," he told Edward, "shall build it if I don't."

It was as he was returning to his workbench that afternoon that Osmund saw the girl.

At first, she did not particularly attract his notice. He was aware of a small blonde girl of about fourteen moving quietly through the nave towards the cloisters, but he thought nothing more about it until, half an hour later he saw her returning, and on enquiring who she was, a mason told him: "That's Bartholomew's daughter. She and her mother just moved into the town from Bemerton."

It explained why he had not seen her before; but he was surprised to learn that this blonde child belonged to Bartholomew, who was tall and dark. His old adversary and he were on terms of distant politeness: his former mentor had never attempted to become a carver of figures, but his painstaking if unoriginal work had earned him some respect in the guild and he was now in charge of the masons who were building the cloisters. After a moment's surprise however, Osmund put the matter out of his thoughts.

It was a week later when he saw her again. This time she was loitering by the west door, presumably waiting for her father and after a little while, out of idle curiosity, Osmund strolled over – ostensibly to look at a statue that was about to be installed in its niche in the west front – and inspected her.

She was indeed an unlikely child for Bartholomew; although, as he surreptitiously inspected her, he remembered being told that the tall mason with the weeping sore had been lucky in finding a pretty wife. Obviously the girl took after her mother. Although he did not want to pay her too much attention, his sculptor's eye noted that under her cotte there was a slim but well-formed body. The torso he judged, was a little longer than the legs and there was a hint of fullness about the waist that was not unpleasing. Her eyes were light blue; her skin was pale but, unlike in Bartholomew's, he could detect no flaws. Her blonde hair was pulled back in a braid on each side of her face and then hung loose to halfway down her back. As the sunlight caught it he noticed that her hair had a tinge of red.

It was a habit with Osmund to look at any face that interested him to ask himself how he would sculpt it and he observed her expression carefully. Was her character, despite her different appearance, perhaps like her father's? Superficially it was a simple, oval face with a sweet and innocent expression; yet he thought he detected something in the set of her eyes and the play of her lips that was – he tried to place it – feline perhaps, or even lecherous. He grinned to himself at his own imagination; it was probably playing tricks with him; and a few moments later returned to his work and forgot about her.

The months of April and May were busy. Two years ago the last bishop, Giles de Bridport had died and Osmund had designed a tomb for the respected prelate that had particularly pleased him. Above the simple raised slab with its effigy, he had decided to erect a little monument with two arches on each side. It was a borrowed design, an exact copy of one of the little wooden shrines that were used to hold the relics of saints, and it had allowed him, in the elaborately carved detail depicting scenes from the bishop's life, to show once again how stone could be carved like wood. As he now put the finishing touches to this little masterpiece, he was often in the main body of the church, and several times he saw the girl passing through on her way to see her father. Sometimes she would glance at him shyly as she passed, but usually he pretended to take no notice. Once or twice however, when she did not know he was looking, he found himself staring at her for long moments before resuming his work.

It was in the month of June, when the intricate labour on the tomb was completed, that he was introduced to the great new project that was to be his life's greatest masterpiece.

It began with a summons to the quarters of Robert the chief mason.

There he found two other master masons, one who had come from London, the other from France, both men whose work he respected deeply. Robert himself, who had succeeded the great Nicholas of Ely many years ago, was now a grey-haired man. He welcomed them politely.

"You're the three best masons," he said without flattery. "And I have a big project for you."

And without more ado he spread several large plans on parchment on the table before them.

"It's the chapter house," he began.

The chapter house, one of the greatest glories of the cathedral, was closely modelled upon the chapter at Henry III's new church of Westminster Abbey. It was magnificent. Like Westminster, it consisted of a single high chamber with eight sides. It was fifty-six feet across and at its centre a single slender pillar rose elegantly some thirty feet before it spread out like a palm tree, or a flower to form the ribs of the simple vaulting. In character with the rest of the cathedral, it was a pure, almost understated building. Years ago when Osmund had first inspected the design, it was the plans for each wall that amazed him.

"Why, they are all window!" he cried.

He was right. Each window, divided into four lights and supporting in its arch a tracery pattern in the form of a simple rose, took up the entire face of each wall from the height of about ten feet to the vaulting. The only masonry in the upper wall was therefore the solid cluster of pillars at each of the eight corners. Now it was nearing completion.

"It will be," Osmund searched for a description, "just a container for light: an eight-sided barrel of light."

Robert smiled.

"It will. That's it exactly. But it's the entrance and the lower part of the wall I want you to look at now."

From the cloisters one entered a broad, almost square vestibule, and from there a handsome arch led directly into the octagon itself. Around the lower wall of the octagon was a running stone seat and behind it an arcade of little arches, five to each wall, each arch marking the place at which one of the church dignitaries would sit.

"Now there, in the big arch at the entrance, and there," Robert indicated the lower walls of the octagon, "we have important plans." And while the three men bent attentively over the plans he went through every detail.

The design that the dean and chapter had approved was elaborate. Within the broad arch at the entrance there were to be seven niches on each side, set and angled one on top of the other along the curved line of the arch and meeting at its point. In each of these narrow niches was to be a pair of almost free standing statues – a woman in free-flowing robes, who would represent one of the fourteen virtues, and at her feet, sinking submissively, the corresponding vice. Thus Justice would subdue Injustice, Patience Anger, Humility banish Pride. It was a fine conception, and a daunting technical challenge.

But it was the design for the inside of the chapter house that captured Osmund's imagination still more.

For above the stone seats, in the spandrels between the little arches there were to be a series of delicate reliefs depicting biblical scenes, from the creation of the world to the delivery of the Ten Commandments.

"There are to be sixty scenes," Robert told them. "They're broken down into groups as follows: The Creation, the expulsion from Eden, Cain and Abel, Noah, Tower of Babel, Abraham, Sodom and Gomorrah, the Sacrifice of Isaac, Jacob, Joseph, Moses." He looked at the three men. "I want you to submit designs. Divide the work up as you like. Then we can discuss the matter again."

As they left, Osmund said a silent prayer, and it was answered soon afterwards when both his companions told him that they were more interested in the fully sculptured figures in the arch than the low reliefs in the chapter house. Reliefs, it seemed to them, were work for lesser hands. Osmund bowed submissively.

"Then I will design the reliefs," he said with a serious face, but a heart full of joy.

And he was still more excited when, at his discussion with Robert a few days later, the chief mason gave him further guidance.

"The effect that the dean and chapter want is something like this," he explained. And he produced two beautifully illustrated manuscripts, one a psalter, the other a romance, which contained flowing and expressive drawings neatly set into the irregular spaces around the text. "Could you manage something like that?"

As Osmund gazed at them he trembled. For what he was being asked to do was not to produce the usual, static figures and heads that he had already perfected, but fluid, flowing pictures in stone, full of movement and life. It was beyond anything he had ever attempted before and he knew that, more than anything else in the world, he wanted to try.

"Give me a few weeks," he said, "and I can do it."

All that summer, Osmund worked at the design; he made sketches of each scene; he practised, day after day, to achieve the lively, flowing lines that he wanted; he even made trial runs of half a dozen scenes, carving them on soft blocks of chalk that he could show the canons.

But while his two colleagues were progressing rapidly with their work on the statues of the virtues and vices, he could not seem to produce anything that quite satisfied him. Each time Robert asked him for his designs, he put him off until at the end of July the master mason had to warn him:

"The canons are growing impatient, Osmund. If you cannot produce the designs, I must give the work to someone else."

"One more month," the perfectionist mason pleaded.

And he returned to the task feverishly.

For days on end, he would think of nothing else, hardly noticing the other masons, or even his wife and children as he went to and from his work in a sort of daze. Sometimes he thought he could see them – all sixty scenes – laid out in perfect order before him; but as he tried to sketch what he saw, or tried to carve even one of the scenes with chisel on a slab of chalk, the vision would mysteriously vanish. Such a thing had never happened to him before and he could not account for it. When this had occurred, he would walk disconsolately home, or make his way quietly to the cool chapel at the east end of the choir where he would fall to his knees and pray: "Blessed Mary, Mother of God, give me strength to do this great work."

How difficult it was. Sometimes, as he whispered his prayers it seemed to him that his low, pleading voice was lost in the deep shadows of the church and returned to him, unanswered, from its high walls. At other times, though no clear vision appeared, he would feel a sense of calmness and return to his workbench to try once again to make the carvings come alive. And even though the work was slow to take shape, he knew he must have faith and comforted himself by remembering the words from the gospel that he had heard the preachers utter so many times before: "If the son asks the father for bread, shall his father give him a stone?" Surely God would not now deny him the ability to do His work, he reasoned. Surely not, but then again, the work would obstinately refuse to take shape and he would cry out in despair:

"Why, why will this stone not take shape for me?"

He was in this unhappy frame of mind one hot August morning as he walked from Avonsford into the new city. He had chosen a different route that day, taking the little path along the river bank instead of the road above, hoping that perhaps the cool river waters and the stately swans might calm his unsettled mind, and he was walking meditatively when a little ahead of him he heard the sound of children's voices laughing and shouting. There was, he knew, a large pond by a bend in the river just ahead where the children from the nearby village liked to swim and play, and thinking nothing of it, he continued towards them. A few moments later he came to a clump of reeds beside the path and as he glanced through them he saw the children in the river beyond. There were half a dozen of them, splashing gaily in the water, and as he looked at them, he stopped in his tracks and stared. But it was not the children that his eyes were fixed upon.

In the middle of the group was Bartholomew's daughter, and now, just as he caught sight of her, she rose and slipped out of the water on to the bank.

Like the children, she was naked.

Her body was just as he had imagined: the small breasts and gently rounded hips were as perfectly formed as one of the Greek statues he had seen at Winchester. Her legs were a little shorter than her body. The water dripped from her pale, flawless skin onto the river bank and her hair, now a dark reddish gold, hung in glistening wet tresses down her back. For a moment, she turned and, staring directly at the clump of reeds in front of him, she seemed to smile. Could she see him? He did not think so, but even if she had been able to, he could not at that moment have moved as he stared back between the reeds at her firm young body and the tips of her breasts. He was transfixed.

She turned in the sunlight and, laughing at something – he did not know what – ran over to where her clothes were lying.

Suddenly, blushing in furious confusion at what he had seen and at the thought that she might have caught sight of him – the dignified master mason – peeping at her through the reeds like a boy, he stumbled back up the path the way that he had come, and cut across to the road above.

By the time he reached the city, he had put the incident from his mind. Or so he thought.

But the damage was done. Try as he might to suppress it, the tantalising vision of the girl would not leave his mind: all that day she rose up constantly before his eyes, haunting in her loveliness, tempting him, even in the middle of his work, to sudden thoughts of lust And the image returned, several times, in the following days.

Not only the thought of her body, but the idea that she might have noticed him preyed on his mind; when, a week later, he saw her once again standing quietly by the west door, something compelled him to go over and speak to her.

He walked towards her slowly, trying to look dignified and un-concerned, pausing as though by a casual impulse and looking at her coolly.

"You are Bartholomew's daughter?"

He had expected her to look down modestly as she replied; but instead she stared at him curiously.

"Yes."

"And what is your name?"

"Cristina."

For a moment he wondered what to say.

"Does your father know you are here?" he asked, as though he meant to send one of the junior masons to fetch him.

"Yes."

Still she was staring at him. Was there a flicker of amusement in her eyes? Had she seen him after all, and was she sharing the secret with him? There seemed to be a hint of complicity in her look.

He felt himself beginning to blush before the girl's steady gaze. He gave her a curt nod and turned away quickly to hide his confusion. As he walked away, he felt sure she was watching him, but when he got back to the place where he had been working and turned, he saw that she had vanished.

And it was from then, for no reason he could understand, that instead of slowly disappearing, the little mason's obsession with the girl began to grow. Day after day, he seemed to see her wherever he went. Every time he caught sight of a fair-haired girl, it made him start. He would look up from his work and think he saw her in the nave or by the cloisters. His eyes would search for her in the close. Her presence seemed to fill the air wherever he was, at his work, in the town, even in the valley or at home; now, instead of being absorbed in the chapter house carvings, he could hardly concentrate on his work.

It grew worse. He knew that Bartholomew's lodgings lay in the chequer just north east of the market place, taking up half a house in a row where tuckers fulled and sheared cloth in a series of small workshops and hung it out on tenting racks to dry in the allotments behind their houses. He started to walk home by this circuitous route each evening now, often pausing on some excuse to speak to one of the clothworkers who lived there, in the hope of catching a glimpse of the girl. He knew it was absurd, but he could not help himself.

Occasionally she did pass by. But then, he would give her a curt nod accompanied by a frown of disapproval with which he hoped to mask his true feelings, before burying his head in his work.

The obsession followed him home. Several times he snapped at his wife for no apparent reason; some evenings he could hardly eat, but toyed with his food irritably. His wife was not concerned. They had lived together peacefully for so many years – with neither affection nor dislike – that she had grown skilled at reading his moods almost before they appeared. To each mood she had learned to ascribe a cause – not by instinct or insight but by simple trial and error – and so now she quieted the children and told them in her cool and placid way, "Your father's angry because his work is not going well." And so Osmund kept his torment secret.

Sometimes when he was alone with his wife at night, his mind was so full of the girl that he would turn from her irritably, shroud himself in silence and ignore her. Then Cristina would dance before him in his imagination. At other times, he would find himself so aroused by his thoughts of the girl that he would suddenly transfer his accumulated lust on to his wife and she would find herself driven before it and savagely used until she was gasping and sweating as he made love to her with an unexpected eagerness and power.

Somehow he managed to continue his work and at the start of September he showed his plans for the chapter house to Robert. He was still not satisfied with them himself, but after a few alterations the canons accepted them and told him to begin work. Some of the scenes he had designed did please him – the voyage of Noah's ark which he had cleverly depicted with eight tiny arched windows out of which animal heads were looking, the building of the great tower of Babel, and the fall of Sodom and Gomorrah, a riot of castle walls and towers tumbling down on top of each other in a crazy pattern that made him smile. But many of the other scenes disappointed him; the human figures lacked the life and movement that he wanted, and although the canons were satisfied, he would shake his head irritably as he stared at the wooden stiffness of his designs and mutter in exasperation: "It's that girl. She is a curse to me. If only I could put her out of my mind." Then he would rage against himself for his weakness and cry: "But the fault is mine, miserable sinner that I am."

Yet the more he railed against himself in this way, the worse his infatuation became.

As the end of September approached he knew that he must somehow break the spell. He stopped his walks by Bartholomew's house, and whenever the girl came into his mind, he forced himself to concentrate on something else. For a few days it would work, and Osmund would go about his business proudly; but then, just when he was not expecting it, she would appear again in the cathedral, or in the street as he made his way out of the town, and despite his new self-discipline, the feelings would return, even more sharply than before, and he would go once more to the chapel, fall on his knees and, in desperation pray: "God preserve my soul from sin."

For this, he knew very well, was the deadly sin of lust.

But if only his sin had been his greatest woe! For now Osmund discovered an even more uncomfortable affliction, as a new fear began to torment him: he started to live in terror of being found out.

For his lust was so strong, he could not believe that others did not see it. He began to look nervously at his fellow masons, searching in their eyes for signs that they were laughing at him. If someone laughed, he turned abruptly. At times he even thought he heard their voices calling: "Osmund lusts after Bartholomew's daughter – lusts after her day and night!" At home, he wondered that his wife did not accuse him, and he was surprised that the village children still clustered happily round him in the street and asked him to carve their models. One day, when he found himself face to face with Bartholomew, he discovered to his horror that he could hardly look at him for embarrassment.

Worse was to come. In the first week of October, just after Michaelmas, he was standing by the trancept where the great pillars of Purbeck marble reached up into the tower, when he saw the girl come into the nave. Thinking he was alone, he moved back so that he could watch her without being seen. As she made her way quietly up the nave, he could hear her humming to herself and as she crossed towards the entrance to the cloisters he watched the muted shafts of sunlight catch her hair. In doing so, she passed only ten yards from where he was standing, and he thought, but it must have been his imagination, that he could smell the delicate scent of her young body. As she went into the cloisters, a wild, irrational thought filled his mind and he almost shouted aloud: "I must have her; I must have this girl if I die."

With this idea taking over his very soul, he moved away from his hiding place into the empty nave.

But it was not empty.

In the opposite trancept he suddenly saw a single, dark figure, motionless as a statue, staring at him.

He halted.

Canon Stephen Portehors, very thin, leaning on a stick, his hair white but his dark eyes still piercing and terrible, continued to stare at him fixedly, seeing all.

No word was spoken, but the trembling mason was sure: he knew.

The next morning he noticed that a new figure had just been completed in the archway to the chapter house. It was the cool, flowing figure of Lady Purity, subduing Lust at her feet; and when he saw this he hung his head in shame.

From that day, he evolved a new discipline; he began to walk like a monk, with his head bowed. By keeping his eyes always fixed on the ground or on his work and never looking up or from side to side, for the next three months until Christmas, the mason kept the deadly sin of lust at bay.

Putting the distraction behind him, Osmund found a renewed pleasure in his work. Each scene of the relief, which would finally form a continuous frieze around the chapter house wall, consisted of a broad, curving V between the arches opening out into a rectangle above, and this allowed the artist many opportunities for expressive arrangements. The first scene, which began on the left of the entrance, showed the figure of God parting the clouds as He emerged to create light; the second scene showed the bearded figure of God in flowing robes, raising His right hand to create the firmament, and the subsequent scenes, showing the other days of Creation, were all completed to Osmund's satisfaction. Until he came to the sixth. This however was far more complex, for he had to depict both the Creation of the beasts, and of Adam and Eve, which required a difficult interweaving of forms that for the moment defeated him.

After several attempts he put it aside and completed the next scene, a far simpler one, in which God, depicted in a lozenge, rested on the seventh day.

But now he ran into another technical difficulty. For the design called for another five scenes on the story of Adam and Eve; and here, no matter what he tried, he could not get the figures right: his Adam was wooden, and Eve seemed to elude him completely.

The problem was an important one.

"How can I depict him – who must be every man? And how can I capture her?" he puzzled. "She must be a pure maiden, and yet the mother of all men; she is first innocent, yet she is the temptress who led Adam to his original sin: pure woman, lascivious whore, wife and mother." The contradictions, which were so necessary to express the first man and woman, seemed beyond his art. Certainly, as he looked at the work of his colleagues on the Virtues and Vices, with their standardized grace and their almost comic depictions of evil, these reliefs called for a subtlety far beyond any of the other sculptures in the great church.

So finally, with a sigh, he put these carvings aside also and went on to the three more straightforward scenes representing Cain and Abel.

It was in this way that, oblivious to all distractions, even forgetting the girl Cristina, he laboured at the carving until Christmas.

On Christmas Eve he saw her again. It was his own fault. On leaving the church on the evening before the great festival he had relaxed and allowed his gaze to leave the floor. And as he walked happily down the nave, the first thing he saw was the girl. She was kneeling before a little side altar where the candles were burning; her hair fell loosely down her back and her face was turned up towards the candles. It looked like the face of an angel.

He stared at her. Once more, as strongly as ever before, his lust rose like a wave. He was seized with an overpowering urge to take the girl's face in his hands and kiss her.

"Temptress," he muttered angrily, "disguised as an angel." And he rushed out of the cathedral and made his way back to Avonsford, vowing he would never look up from his work again.

In the new year, Osmund began the story of Noah. He was pleased with the little ark he carved, bobbing on the waves, and with the next scene of the drunkenness of Noah. By the month of March he had completed fine scenes of the Tower of Babel, which he made to look like the old castle on the hill at Sarum, two scenes from the life of Abraham, and the splendid carving, of the destruction of Sodom and Gomorrah. He showed them to Robert and the canons and received their delighted approval. Daily he was growing more confident of his techniques.

"Soon," he hoped, "I shall be able to do those scenes from the Garden of Eden."

On March 25, 1266, a wonderful event took place in Sarum.

For on that day, after twenty-six years of labour and a total expenditure of the stupendous sum of forty-two thousand marks, the main body of the new cathedral was finally completed. It was, without doubt, one of the most perfect examples of early gothic architecture in Europe.

Some eight years before, at a splendid ceremony, the king himself had ridden over from his hunting lodge at Clarendon to see the consecration of the great building. But still there were years of work to do before the interior was finally completed. Now however, every last piece of decorative masonry was finished and painted, the huge leaded windows were all installed, and there was nothing to be added to the long, gracious vista within.

In the late afternoon, a solemn high mass was held at which all the masons with their families and half the town attended. Afterwards, in the market place, there was to be a huge feast.

The sun was already sinking over the river when Osmund led his family to their place in the crowded nave. The church was full. Some two thousand people were gathered in the nave alone. His son was at his side, and the boy's eyes were wide, for he had never seen such a great concourse of people before.

As the hour approached, the congregation fell silent; the setting sun was now flashing through the great window at the west end, sending huge shafts of light, dappled with the colours of the glass, up the long aisle to the choir screen and the inner sanctum of the choir beyond.

Slowly the light faded. In the half shadow, the huge arches of grey stone loomed silently over the people, and the boy reached up for his father's hand as he gazed, awestruck, into the cavernous spaces that led towards the distant high altar.

Now junior priests rustled about, lighting candles with their long tapers. There were huge banks of candles, by the pillars in the nave, in the transepts, in the arcaded galleries and clerestory high above, along the line of the choir screen and in the choir beyond. For fully ten minutes they went about their work, and as they did so, and the light outside faded, the interior of the great cathedral was gradually transformed. The thousands of candles first glimmered, then glowed, and now set the whole fabric shining with light. And when Osmund looked up and saw the full effect of what the masons' work had accomplished his face broke into a smile of joy. For the soaring pillars and the tiers of arches gleamed with light. Red, gold, green and blue – the dazzling colours rose from the floor to the decorated vaults above and the windows shone with the reflection of the candlelight. High in the air, the faces he had carved and others had painted peeped down cheerfully at the folk below.

Little Edward tugged at his hand.

"Is this the feast?" he whispered.

And indeed, the mason thought, the church was, when fully lit, like a vast banqueting hall.

But now the west doors were thrown open and a great procession began to enter the cathedral and move slowly up the aisle. It was led by the choirboys who carried long candles and chanted as they went. Behind them came the priests, several dozen of them, their long white robes hissing on the polished stone floor, their deep voices intoning the raw, majestic harmonies of the plainsong chant. Canons and deacons swept by, and last, accompanied by two boys who held his train and by the priests who carried the sacraments, came the tall, stately figure of the bishop. He walked slowly. Over his robes he wore a magnificent cope, embroidered with gold and silver and encrusted with precious stones that glowed dully in the light. His fine ascetic face looked neither to right nor left, and his height was further accentuated by the tall mitre with its silver cross that he wore on his head. In his hand he carried the long ceremonial crook of his office, its curved head looping elegantly like the neck and head of a swan.

Solemnly he strode by, up the church's great arcade of stone. The people knelt as he passed. Finally he went through the choir screen into the inner sanctum.

It was just as he reached this point and the voices of the choir echoed from the distant altar, that Osmund saw Cristina. She was a little in front of him, on the other side of the aisle, standing beside her father. At the moment when the bishop entered the sanctum, the great west doors were closed, and as she looked round to watch this, her eyes rested on Osmund. He thought she smiled before she turned away.

Once again, his fever rose.

Soon the mass was in progress. Its soothing murmur and its distant chant spread their timeless comfort over the congregation. But to Osmund, it was a torture.

"Agnus dei. . ." the chant echoed. Lamb of God, who takes away the sins of the world. He tried to think of the Lamb, led to the slaughter, the great sacrifice of the Christian rite.

"Agnus dei. . ."

But another figure insistently presented itself before his eyes. He tried to concentrate.

The moment of the transubstantiation came. The bell rang as the priest presented the body and blood of Christ to His people.

And it must, Osmund knew, be the Devil himself who at that moment sent him a different vision, a vision that refused to be dispelled, of the girl's body, naked, arched and trembling on the high altar.

At the feast that night in the market place, where the oxen turned on huge spits and the crowd sat at the long trestle tables that stretched for fifty yards, the mason sat with his family in silence. His children chattered; even his wife's face was, for once, wreathed in contented smiles. But Osmund did not join in. Instead he sat slumped, conscious only of the terrible lust, so urgent that it made him want to cry out, which afflicted him. In an agony of despair and rage, he sullenly gorged himself with food and drink in the hope that another sin, the sin of gluttony, might drive this greater demon out. He continued until, bloated and fuddled, he slipped off the bench into oblivion.

The crisis came in June.

Since the completion of the cathedral, Osmund had finished the scenes of Lot turning into a pillar of salt and Abraham's sacrifice of Isaac. He was pleased with these because the fluidity and natural expressiveness of the figures that he strove for was at last beginning to come. It was with a sense of optimism that he now began work on the story of Isaac and Jacob.

The spring that year was particularly fine and warm. As he made his way through the lush Avon valley Osmund felt a sense of excitement, a tingling anticipation that he had not known for many years; and just as he had when he carved the roof boss as a young man, he felt that something of the rich and fertile spirit of the place where the five rivers met was showing through in his work. Sinner that I am, he considered, God has let me see some light in the darkness. And he went to his work more contented.

It was a warm morning in June; the valley was lush; a cuckoo was singing. He had walked about a mile from Avonsford when the encounter took place.

On the right of the road at this point there was a wood, and through it a winding path led down to the path by the river. It was just as he drew level with the opening to the path that he stopped abruptly and stared.

For what he saw was clearly a vision. There seemed no other explanation for it. And he knew it must have been sent by the Devil.

Quickly he crossed himself. The vision laughed.

The apparition that the Devil had sent had taken the form of the girl Cristina. She was leaning against a tree and she wore only a light shift tied at the waist and open at the front, so that it barely covered her breasts. Her hair was loose, and she was staring at him with a look of amusement. He crossed himself again, and then pinched himself to make sure he was not asleep.

"What's the matter with you?" she enquired as she watched his nervous gestures.

He stared at her. What new punishment had the Devil prepared for him?

"Who are you?" he asked hoarsely.

"You know me, Osmund Mason," she replied with a smile. "I'm Cristina."

Unable to help himself he walked over to her and gazed at her. She seemed real enough, but if so, then what was she doing here?

"What do you want?"

She shrugged.

"Maybe I came to see you. I knew you'd come by."

He knew he should go at once, whatever this encounter meant; whether he had fallen prey to a vision or the girl was real it made no difference. But he did not.

His breath was coming short as he stared at her. It was she who broke the silence.

"I've seen you watching me."

"I don't know what you mean." He felt himself blushing furiously, but he could not move.

"Yes you do," she taunted gently. "Been watching me ever since last summer. Every time I go through the church. Seen you go by my house too. Quite a few times."

Now the poor mason flushed scarlet. He opened his mouth to protest but the girl broke into a soft laugh.

"I don't mind." And she smiled: not the smile of a child, he noted, but that of an experienced woman; her eyes ran up and down his stocky frame. She shifted her position, pushing her legs out so that she was leaning back even further against the tree, and her blue eyes looked straight into his.

Then, to his astonishment, she said calmly and quietly: "You can kiss me if you want."

He stared at her. She was no older than his own daughter – he knew;

yet now it was he, the master mason, who felt like a foolish boy. What game was she playing, he asked himself, what witchcraft? He must leave her at once.

But still he could not.

She did not move; she gazed up at him. Her face seemed so soft, and her eyes had a look of hurt, almost reproach in them.

"Not if you don't want to," she murmured.

He stood very still. The wood seemed unnaturally silent. Then, hardly knowing what he was doing, whether he was awake or whether, after all, this was some dream sent by the Devil, the mason forgot all caution, stepped forward, lowered his large head to kiss her lips, and was astonished as the child threw her soft arms around his neck and pulled him to her.

How sweet her lips tasted. Her young body pressed urgently against him and the little mason trembled.

In an ecstasy of excitement, he felt himself falling to the ground with her.

Moments later, he did not even protest as, still murmuring softly, she began to tug at his clothes. Osmund the Mason forgot his fear and caution. With a cry he rose, tore his clothes off, and flushing this time with pride, stood before her naked. Now, he knew, now he would have her at last. His hands reached out.

But suddenly, with a little peal of laughter, she slipped from his grasp and darted away from him. He stared at her in astonishment.

Ten feet away, she turned, and he saw that she was smiling.

"Catch me, then," she cried. And before he could protest, she was running lightly away down the path between the trees.

His stocky, hirsute body with its small paunch bounded along the path behind her. For fifty yards he followed, conscious only of the twists in the path, the flickering light through the trees and the fact that her form, in its single white shift, was only a few tantalising yards ahead of him. The leaves and branches flicked into his face; his feet stumbled over the hard roots that lay across the path; but he hardly noticed them as he panted forward, his round face and his grey eyes shining.

They were getting near the river. But before reaching it the path passed through an open glade of grass about thirty yards long. That, he thought was where he would catch her, and as they reached it, he hurled himself forward.

She was ahead of him, almost at the far end of the glade. She had stopped. She was turning. His face lit up in a smile of triumph.

It was when he was half way along the glade that he heard the childrens' voices. They were laughing. And they came from both sides of the glade.

Before he reached her he stopped and turned to look at them.

There were more than twenty children. He recognised most of them, for they were the children of Avonsford. They were standing all round the little glade beside the trees and he knew at once that they had been concealed there deliberately, waiting for him. They were laughing and several of them were pointing at his nakedness.

He looked at Cristina. She was gazing back at him, and he saw that she, too, was shaking with laughter. Then, turning quickly, she vanished into the trees, leaving him alone to stand there, in his absurd nakedness, in the middle of the circle of children.

There was nothing to do but go back the way he came.

As he made his way back along the path, the laughter of the children was ringing in his ears. He wondered how long the girl had planned this cruel practical joke, so perfectly designed to humiliate him. Was it her own idea? Had, possibly, her father's jealous mind had some part in it? He would never know. But as the full implication of what had just taken place unfolded in a terrible vision before his eyes, he broke out in a cold sweat and his little hands clenched and unclenched in impotent fury. He saw exactly what it would mean: within an hour, all Avonsford would know; by the end of the morning, the whole of Sarum. The respected master mason in his leather apron would be transformed, probably for the rest of his life, into a figure of fun. People in the street would point at him and laugh as he passed; children – the children for whom he had so often carved little presents – would giggle when his name was spoken. As for his family. . .

He came to the place where he had stripped off his clothes. They were gone.

He was naked; now he would have to stay that way as he walked back to the village. It was the final humiliation. They had made sure that all his dignity was gone. As he considered the thought, the deliberate planning which must have gone into the morning's episode, and the way that the children had been so carefully taken into the wood to witness it, he almost broke down. Keeping close to the edge of the trees, he began his slow walk home.

In the days that followed, the consequences were everything that he had forseen. But there were some surprises. He had guessed that his two daughters would turn angrily against him; he had forseen their looks of disgust and their angry silences if he entered the house, but he had not forseen the shocked, only half-comprehending face of his little son, who knew only that his father had committed a terrible crime that he did not understand, and who now – encouraged by his elder sisters – stared at him with large, frightened eyes and refused to come near him.

Unexpectedly, his wife was kinder.

Ignoring completely the rage of her daughters or the expressive silences that greeted her in the village, she looked at the squat little mason, stripped of all his hard-won dignity, and she felt sorry for him. She knew that her pale, thin form held little excitement for him; their long marriage had held little hope of passion on either side, she would almost have been glad if, for a moment, one of them had found it. She did not reproach him but when she moved to his side to comfort him, she found that, after the long, blank, untroubled years of their life together, she did not know how. Her hand rested on his arm, and she knew that he felt it; it was all that either of them could do.

But it was when he returned to work the next day that Osmund suffered worse.

As he made his way through the city gates, he heard the titters as he passed; when he arrived in the cathedral close, he noticed that the priests gave him contemptuous looks. Once in the cathedral itself, though he tried not to look into their faces, he knew that the masons were smirking, and as he reached his workbench, he saw the tall figure of Bartholomew standing nearby, grinning broadly. He pretended not to notice; but he felt himself blushing, and more than once during the morning he thought – or did he imagine it? – that he heard voices near him whispering the name Cristina.

The hours passed and mercifully he was left alone, but although he tried to concentrate, it was impossible not to think about his misery, and by the end of the morning he was in a black depression.

"Truly," he thought, "I am being punished for my sins."

The same thing happened the next day and the next. After four days he realised with disgust that he had achieved almost nothing at his work.

It was five days after the incident that by chance Osmund saw the girl again. This time, their encounter was not planned; she did not even know that he had seen her.

It happened just outside the city, when the mason was returning home at the end of the day. As he passed the old castle, he suddenly caught sight of her on the little lane that led down to the valley bottom. To his surprise he saw that she was not alone, but walking demurely hand in hand with a boy. Involuntarily he stopped and stared down at them. He knew the boy; he was young John, the son of the merchant William atte Brigge. Neither of the young people realised they were being watched. Half way down the lane they paused, and kissed.

He watched, transfixed.

But then, to his own surprise, Osmund the Mason found that he did not care. He felt no anger, no jealousy, hardly even lust. He shrugged. She's out of my life now, he told himself.

But she was not. Despite the fact that he had come to hate Cristina, despite his misery, the haunting vision of a naked girl with cascading golden hair would still suddenly rise before him in his degradation, sending an unwanted spasm of lust through his body that left him shaking and despising himself more than ever. When, a week later, he reached his workbench and looked at the pitiful results of the previous days' work, he fell on his knees and cried in despair: "Lord have mercy on me: you have cast me down and I am sunk in sin."

He remembered the words of the priest, spoken to him so many years before and he moaned: "Truly, Lord, I am less, far less, even than the dust." Was there to be no respite from this terrible malady? As he considered the matter and it seemed to him that there was not, he felt the hot tears spring to his eyes. "Lord, I am unworthy to serve you," he murmured. "Let me die."

It was now, at this final crisis of his humiliation, that his eyes happened to turn to the unfinished scene of the creation of Adam and Eve. And hardly thinking about what he was doing, without any hope that he would be able to make anything of the task he had given up so many times before, he began sadly to carve the little figure of Adam. As he did so, he gradually became aware that he was giving it his own squat body, with its large head and short legs. Not only that, the manly little fellow he was depicting, half solemn and half eager before his God, was an all too accurate representation of his own character, stripped so naked that for a moment he paused in embarrassment. But then he shrugged. He had already been as humiliated as it was possible to be; he had no further dignity to lose, and to his own surprise, he found the almost comic little figure rather engaging. There was something, he realised, rather touching in the little man's naked pretension as he stared solemnly past God to where the future of mankind, in the form of Eve, was rising before him. As his chisel worked faster and more easily, the mason began to smile, and half an hour later, satisfied with the main outline of the first man, he turned to Eve.

Now at last he saw exactly what to do. Deftly, suddenly gifted with a knowledge he had not possessed before, he drew the outlines of Eve's body, and by the end of that day, rising from the rib cage of the first man, came in perfect detail, the form of the girl Cristina. Her body was perfect – for did not every line of it haunt his imagination? Her long hair was swept back, just as it had been when she came out of the river, and in her face – though he himself could not say how he had done it – was to be found the look of innocence and knowledge, purity and lasciviousness, the necessary but impossible combination that had defeated him for so many months.

It took him six weeks to complete the carvings of the Garden of Eden. The scene where Adam takes the apple from the tree of knowledge was the perfect representation of the master mason's proud self-importance before his humiliation; the expulsion from Eden showed Adam with head bowed, just as his own had been when he made his way shamefacedly to his work after his own fall.

If Sarum was still laughing at him, Osmund was hardly aware of it. He worked from dawn until dusk, half abstracted, in a contented passion, realising as each day passed that God, having first humiliated him, was now creating a little masterpiece through his hands.

And in this manner, he completed the spandrel carvings of the chapter house.

1289

Even before the year of Our Lord 1289, the new tower had begun to dominate the city. It seemed to be rising out of a table set in the sky.

This impression was quite correct. At the crossing of the nave and trancepts, where the marble pillars soared into the roof like four legs of a table, the masons had now in effect begun a second building – a massive square grey tower rising nearly a hundred feet over the roof. It rose in two huge tiers, its walls elegantly broken by tall lancet arches. From all five rivers it could be seen, a stately presence in the sky and when the tower was completed, yet another tall structure – a slender spire – was to be set upon it, so that Osmund the mason had remarked to his son:

"They'll build the cathedral into the clouds."

It was a noble conception, and no one approaching the new city now could help looking up in admiration at the stones above.

But on a warm September morning in 1289, it was not the tower that a little party entering the city over Fisherton Bridge stopped and stared at. Their eyes instead were fixed downwards, at a crumpled figure lying by the roadside.

It was the stout old burgess Peter Shockley who got slowly from his cart, went forward and made the identification.

"Is he alive?" Jocelin de Godefroi looked down sadly from his horse. Shockley nodded. "Just."

A light wind by the river stirred the dust that had gathered in the fallen man's clothes.

The bridge was a busy, pleasant spot. Below its narrow arches, the river with its long green weeds flowed smoothly and strongly. Just above, on the city side, the bishop's three mills ground corn for the new city's bread; a little below, the stream was briefly split by a narrow bar of land before it curved round the edge of the close, and here the poorer pilgrims on their journey east and local vagabonds, both wanting to escape the modest tolls on the bridge, would often try to ford it. The current was a little stronger than it looked and it was a favourite pastime for the city children to gather on the bridge, where they were tolerated, to watch the pilgrims downstream lose half their possessions in the water. Ducks and moorhens favoured the ford. The swans liked to nest a little below it. To the west of the bridge, a few dozen cottages straggled beside the road towards Wilton.

The figure huddled by the roadside was dressed in black. His feet were dirty and bare; his hood, which Peter Shockley had just lifted, had been pulled down over his face so that only the end of his stained and matted grey beard was visible; on his chest, the *tabula* sign that proclaimed him to be a Jew was, at the king's orders, coloured bright yellow and considerably larger than it had been in earlier decades. Flies buzzed unchecked about his head and he was only semi-conscious.

The ruin of Aaron of Wilton had taken forty years to accomplish, but the process was now complete and represented a triumph of the God-fearing over the infidel. In a long series of edicts that otherwise enlightened monarch Edward I had followed the sporadic persecutions of his pious father Henry to their logical conclusion. The Jewish community had been taxed, forbidden to practise money-lending, forbidden to trade except on impossible terms, taxed yet again; and when a few years previously almost every active Jewish trader had been thrown into jail until he had paid another, stupendous fine, Aaron of Wilton had at last been successfully ruined.

He was too old to seek his fortune elsewhere. He had no family left.

Together with the few others remaining in the little Wilton community, he had sometimes been able to scrape a miserable existence out of tiny trades in wool; more recently he had been reduced to begging. He had walked from Wilton at dawn that morning and collapsed by the bridge from sheer fatigue, and for several hours no one had cared to touch him.

The little party that stared down at him represented three generations. Frail, but still upright in the saddle, Jocelin de Godefroi had survived, carefully preserving the two estates in the valley for his grandson, for longer than he had dared to hope. And Roger de Godefroi was everything his grandfather might have hoped for: at twenty-seven he was a splendid representative of the knightly class, like his father before him, and the darling of the lists. That summer, when Jocelin had noticed that the tips of his fingers were turning blue, the knowledge that his grandson would soon inherit had only caused him to smile. The estates were in excellent condition, and not even the dry summer of the year before, when many of the sheep had contracted scab, nor the poor grain harvest of that summer could make more than a small dent in the prosperity that he had built up. He had even improved the manor house in a modest way, adding a small wing to the hall and enclosing the place with a courtyard wall. The old generation had done their work well.

Between these two in age was Peter Shockley; his large, stout, grizzled figure exuded authority; only the pressure of his constantly expanding business had prevented him from representing the borough as a burgess in the several parliaments of Edward's reign. Since his marriage to Alicia, the merchant had known contentment. Though his wife was grey, her freckled skin had stayed almost miraculously young, and only small lines of contentment filled the corners of her face.

"I'm sixty, but she makes me feel half my age," he would proudly announce.

Beside him in his cart sat two fair young people: his son Christopher and his daughter Mary.

All five gazed at the Jew, but they did so with very different feelings. Jocelin remembered the courtly aristocrat with whom he and old Edward Shockley had done business in their youth. Peter remembered a middle-aged moneylender whom he had wanted to defend at the Parliament of Montfort. Young Roger de Godefroi saw an infidel whom his knightly class was supposed to despise, and the two Shockley children saw only an old tramp, whom they had never known, but whose misfortune they knew must be his own fault, for obstinately denying the true God.

And so the Shockley children gasped with horror when they heard Jocelin de Godefroi's next words to his grandson.

"Pick him up and put him in the cart. We'll take him to Avonsford."

Roger frowned and hesitated. Must he touch this repulsive old figure? But a look from his grandfather was enough; he bowed his head respectfully and went forward. Peter Shockley helped him.

Slowly they raised him, still unconscious, and laid him in the back of the cart. The two Shockley children edged forward, so that he should not touch them.

As they completed the task, Roger allowed himself one questioning look at old Jocelin.

"Is this wise?" His grandfather was a respected knight of the shire, who had acted as a local coroner and as one of the crown escheators, and whose duty was to support the king in all things; and since it was well known that the king's policy was now to harass the Jewish community as much as possible, surely they should leave the old man where he was. But the knight only shook his head.

"To Avonsford," he ordered curtly. "He can recover or die there." And the reluctant little procession moved on.

As it did so, no one noticed that, when they had lifted the old man into the cart, the seal with which he signed his documents had slipped out from the folds of his clothes and tumbled onto the dusty road.

It was John, son of William atte Brigge, who noticed it half an hour later. He stooped and picked it up, then put it carefully into the pouch that hung from his belt.

He did not yet know what, but he would find a use for it, he was sure.

While the cart bumped along from Salisbury into the courtyard of Avonsford manor, and while Aaron was carried into the house, Mary Shockley said nothing. But as soon as they were clear of Avonsford and rattling down the valley towards the city, she burst out: "Why does the knight pick up that old Jew? And why should we carry him?"

"Aaron helped my father start the mill," Peter reminded her calmly.

"Then we should be ashamed," she replied hotly. "He's a usurer."

Peter shrugged.

"I'd have thrown the old Jew in the river," she added defiantly; at which her brother Christopher grinned. For Mary's outbursts were well known.

She was a splendid figure – a twenty-year-old girl as big as her brother and probably stronger. With her fine, athletic body and her long flaxen hair she was a perfect throwback to her Saxon forbears, except in one respect. For from her mother she had taken two features: a band of light freckles across her forehead, and her extraordinary violet eyes. Unlike her mother, Mary's eyes never varied: they were always violet and they were dazzling. As a child, she had been a tomboy, outrunning and out-wrestling all the other children; and now, though she was a striking, blonde young woman, her father had to confess: "She's a beauty, but she's still like a man – and as obstinate as a donkey." Even Alicia, with all her determination, had long since given up trying to make her daughter dress and behave in the demure manner proper to a young woman.

"If we ever find her a husband, he'll have to take her as she is," she admitted ruefully.

And when old Jocelin, chiding his handsome grandson for not yet having taken a wife, laughingly remarked that the merchant's daughter, though hardly noble, was still a fine-looking girl, Roger, the hero of the joust, protested: "Why grandfather, she'd break me over her knee."

At least her character made the settling of the Shockley properties very simple. "She'll have the farm, of course," Peter had said. "And Christopher will run the business." Both children were content with this: for Christopher was already showing a quick grasp of the expanding Shockley affairs, whereas Mary was only happy when she was over-seeing – or more likely working beside – the labourers on the farm.

But despite her tomboy appearance, Mary had one unexpected enthusiasm: she had an unshakeable belief in all things religious. Often she would be seen driving her cart from the farm to Wilton Abbey with gifts of provisions that should have been sold at the market. And though the abbey was one of the greatest landowners at Sarum, and so well known for its extravagant and lax ways that only two years before the Dean of Salisbury had been forced to threaten some of its senior members with excommunication if they did not pay some of their debts, Mary always obstinately – and to the huge amusement of her father – referred to the inmates as 'the poor nuns'.

To Mary, the wishes of the nuns and the word of the priests were law. When the nuns sighed over the debts into which the wicked money-lenders had trapped them, or the vicar of the little church near the farm spoke harshly against the evil of the Jews and their usury, she knew that they must be right.

As the cart trundled down the valley, she banged on its side and swore to her father.

"No Jew shall ride with me again. Not if the king himself asks."

In the cathedral close that morning, a painful scene was taking place. Indeed, as Osmund the Mason faced his son, he could only gasp in disbelief at the insult.

"You are telling me I may not work in the cathedral any more?"

Edward Mason looked embarrassed, but nodded.

"It's what the guild of masons have decided," he confessed.

It was hard to take it in. For a moment Osmund could not speak.

"But why?" he cried at last.

Since the completion of the chapter house and cloisters, Osmund the Mason had known peace. His wonderful carving there had earned him respect.

Each time the masons came to the great round table in the chapter house where their wages were paid, they would glance up at the wonderful carvings on the walls, and acknowledge no one had ever done anything better. Even the incident with Cristina, who had long since married William atte Brigge's boy, had gradually been forgotten. And when the work on the tower had begun, he had been glad to have a new project.

The building of the tower involved the creation of a new world. First the carpenters constructed an enormous wooden platform over the great central crossing of the nave and transepts. Like a wooden table top, resting on the four central pillars, this platform sealed off the base of the tower from the empty spaces below. Once this was done, the old roof above was removed, leaving the square platform open to the sky, and it was here, in their new and separate world a hundred feet above the ground, that the masons began to raise the four walls of the tower. The walls were solid – though not as thick as the main walls of the church below – and like them they were filled with a mixture of lime, mortar and rubble. At each corner of the great tower there was a spiral staircase.

Osmund liked working in the tower, and as its walls slowly rose, he would often stand in the shadows they cast, staring up in admiration at their solemn mass, and at the square of sky even higher above. There were fewer masons now, but there was work for his clever hands to do, and around the huge stone lancet windows, he supervised a fine decoration of ballflowers.

One thing concerned him, however. The tower had no buttresses, no outside supports to hold its stone and rubble walls together.

"As they get higher, they will spring apart," he complained to the canons. His fears were justified; careful plans were made, and he was only satisfied when an engineer showed him what they would do.

"We shall wrap the whole tower in bands of iron, all the way round, pinned in place with big bolts, right through the wall," the man explained.

"But the bands will have to be thick," the mason objected. "The strain could be enormous."

"They will be," the engineer promised. "They'll last five hundred years."

This was exactly what they did; as the walls of the huge tower slowly rose, the grey Chilmark stone was bound in with huge bands of iron.

He loved the separate world of the tower in the sky, almost silent except for the tapping of the masons, the occasional squeaking of winches raising the stones, and the rustle of the wind over the high walls above. And he was contented. Both his daughters were married. He was respected in his work. The only cause of annoyance in recent years had been his only son's joining King Edward in his wars in Wales. When that mountainous country, for the first time since Roman days, had been subdued and the English had acquired from the Welsh not only a fine new principality, but also a new skill in the use of the great longbow, Edward Mason, with his short strong fingers, had discovered that he was well-suited to master the archer's art and he had returned from the wars with honour and with a pouch stuffed with the king's silver coin. His son's skill as a longbowman had not pleased Osmund at all.

"You're a mason," he reminded him.

And though Edward often practised his archery in his spare time at the butts outside the city, Osmund never came to watch him. When at last the time came to admit his son into the company of the master masons, he did so grudgingly.

He was fifty-nine; both he and his wife had kept their health; he had still all but three of his teeth. True, it annoyed him that sometimes, when he was carving, he could not see the detail of his work clearly from close up, but he had grown so used over the years to feeling his carving with his hand that this small disability did not trouble him, and he found that his eyes picked out objects at a distance better than ever.

But lately a change had come over him.

At first he blamed his wife. Although her thin body was growing old, he had still been used to paying her mechanical attentions for which she was, at least sometimes, grateful. But recently he had found that his body did not respond as it had before. At first he had told himself that it was because his wife no longer attracted him, but as the months passed, he had to admit that this explanation was not enough. He began to stare at young girls, sometimes with lust, but at other times, challenging his own body to respond. And his body, he realised, was slowly failing him. He began to grow testy. He would snap at his wife for no particular reason, or he would deliberately stare at young women when he was with her, to suggest that they might arouse him if she did not.

At work, he had now taken to wandering unasked amongst the other masons, inspecting their work, and gruffly correcting them. And though every mason admitted that no one was a finer carver than old Osmund, these criticisms were soon resented. Often he would pick on his own son, rebuking him publicly for some piece of imagined sloppiness or poor finish, and Edward bore this patiently. But frequently he would berate others too, even his fellow master masons, telling them curtly: "The line is weak," or silently shaking his head as he gazed at their efforts. Several times Edward had privately warned him that this behaviour was giving offence, but his father had taken no notice.

At last, when these inspections had become a habit, the mason's guild acted. The work on the tower could only use a few workers and Osmund's testy comments had become too much of a nuisance.

"There are younger men who can carve," they told Edward. "It is time for your father to leave the work in the cathedral to others." It was a harsh decision, but Edward knew that if the guild had decided, it was useless to argue.

"Let me tell him," he requested.

Now Edward had delivered their message. He knew they were right. But as he watched his father's thickset body first bristle with indignation and then suddenly sag, he wished he had protested against it.

There was a long pause before Osmund spoke again.

"What shall I do?" It was terrible, after so many years, to hear the note of despair in his father's voice.

"There is plenty of work in the close."

It was true: houses for the clergy were still being built; there were still constant alterations being made to the bishop's palace even though Bishop de la Corner, a royal official, was seldom at Sarum. But none of this mattered to Osmund. Only the day before he had completed a series of carvings of little dogs' heads which were to be installed half way up the tower. He had been pleased with them. He shook his head in confusion. There were so many other carvings he had wished to do.

"But I have always worked in the cathedral," he protested. It was his home, his life.

There was another awkward pause before Edward replied.

"The guild has decided. I'm sorry." There was nothing else he could say. And after a little time, during which neither of them spoke, he turned away and started to walk towards the cathedral.

Osmund watched him go.

Was it really possible that he, the master mason, had been rejected? He could not believe it. But as he stood there, the realisation grew. It seemed to fall on him like a crushing weight.

It was worse than his humiliation by Cristina: at least he had brought that upon himself. But the recent sense of his failing powers, and now this sudden rejection by the masons' guild were terrible blows he had done nothing to deserve. He felt suddenly weak and helpless.

Edward was passing round the corner of the building; he did not look back.

The mason's shoulders hunched forward. He hung his head. "Then my life is over," he murmured. Suddenly, he was an old man.

But then, as he stared at the cathedral he had loved, and that Edward was now entering, his round face suddenly contorted into a look of furious hatred and rage.

He loathed them all: his wife, the masons, even his own son.

"Do what you like then," he muttered bitterly. "You can't carve, but you're still young." And with a curse he turned his back on the cathedral.

For in all his life, this was the first time that Osmund had truly discovered the deadly sin of envy.

Shortly after the feast of Edward the Confessor, in the month of October 1289, King Edward I of England left Westminster and rode with his attendants to Sarum.

The party was in excellent spirits, for all knew that important plans, which might change the course of the island's history, were ready to take shape. The king himself was in high good humour.

Indeed in 1289, King Edward had good reason to be optimistic.

His kingdom was at peace, and prospering mightily; its population was increasing, agriculture booming. Its huge exports of wool, except for a few years of dispute with Flanders the decade before, had grown continuously to the busy cities of France, Germany, Italy and the Low Countries. Five years before, he had also extended his territory when he had subdued the unruly Celtic chiefs of Wales, and garrisoned their mountainous country with the series of great castles like Caernarvon that he understood how to build so well. His son had been accepted by the warring Welsh as the first English Prince of Wales and their principality, for the first time since Roman days, had become united again with England.

Since then, Edward had spent three busy years in the last of his continental possessions, the rich province of Gascony whose Bordeaux wines the English loved, and whose affairs he had thoroughly organised, as was his habit.

Now he had turned his attention back to England once again.

There were two great affairs of state to be dealt with. The first was a complete and overdue reform of the royal and feudal administration. There was petty corruption everywhere. And already, within two months of his return, the vigorous king set his chosen officials, fresh from their work in Gascony, on an investigation into abuses that had half the sheriffs and justices of England trembling.

The second affair of state was still more important: for it was nothing less than the joining of England and her warlike neighbour Scotland into a single kingdom.

The opportunity had come about by chance when King Alexander of Scotland had been killed in a fall from his horse at the age of only forty-four, leaving as heiress to his kingdom the child of his daughter and the King of Norway – a little girl, Margaret. She was known as the Maid of Norway and the regents governing Scotland had at once decided that she should return from Norway to her future kingdom; they also began to look for a husband for her.

It was a heaven-sent opportunity, and Edward seized it at once. If the Maid should be married to his own son, then at last the two kingdoms could merge – a spectacular piece of diplomacy to crown the other triumphs of his reign. He had already been negotiating from Gascony with the Scots. The negotiations had gone well: now, even as he rode towards the cathedral city, four Scots commissioners were on their way to Salisbury to meet his officials there.

He was a splendid figure: tall, broad-shouldered, with a long reach that made him formidable in the joust, but at the same time, he possessed the mind of a lawyer – an unusual combination that made him one of the most remarkable monarchs of his age. Though he sometimes showed his father's dreamy and religious qualities – for he loved pageantry and had already promised the pope to go on crusade – this ruthless administrator and soldier had also learned many lessons from Montfort, not least of which was how to make use of the new parliaments to tame the magnates and to raise taxes.

His magnificent mane of hair and his beard were all white now – but the effect was still handsome. His eyes missed nothing, though, from his father, he had inherited one drooping eyelid that sometimes gave the wholly erroneous impression that he was half asleep.

His spirits were high as he rode towards Sarum. While his officials negotiated he would hunt in the forest of Clarendon, and visit the cathedral.

Soon, Osmund knew, King Edward and his retinue would walk through the great west door.

Outside, it was a bright October morning, but inside the cathedral the candles were lit and the brightly painted interior shimmered with gold and silver ornaments and magnificent hangings of embroidered silk. At the end of the nave, next to the choir, a party of knights and officials, including old Jocelin de Godefroi, resplendent in a long blue cloak, and his grandson waited to greet the monarch; below this group stood the mayor and burgesses. Osmund could see the bluff figure of Peter Shockley among them. The rest of the nave was filled with humbler folk like himself. All eyes were on the west door where very shortly the king, accompanied by the sheriff of Wiltshire and the dean of the cathedral, would appear. There was an excited murmur of anticipation.

Osmund stood a little apart from the crowd. In the last month he had become a changed man. Instead of the stocky, upright figure with a big, round head and ruddy face, there was now only a shadow of the master masons. His heavy head hung forward sadly; his shoulders were stooped; his cheeks had become hollow and pallid; the effect was made worse by his refusal to shave so that now a thin, uneven straggle of grey hairs, halfway between stubble and a beard, sprouted from his chin. His proud waddle had given way to a shuffle. In less than a month he had succeeded in turning himself into an old man. Since he had been turned out of the cathedral, he had withdrawn not only from the world of the masons, whom he carefully avoided, but even from his wife. Only in Edward's presence did he come to life: for if his son approached, his shoulders would suddenly hunch forward like a threatening animal, and his face would twist into an angry grimace.

"Here is a master builder," he would snarl, "a builder of towers who can't carve."

He had been offered other work, but he had refused it. "I'm too old. Can't see," he would explain bitterly, and when one of the canons had protested, he had shuffled away.

He had been seen in the city though, walking along the riverbank opposite the close, apparently staring blankly at the swans; but if an observer watched carefully, he would have seen that the mason's eyes shifted constantly and sadly to the soaring grey mass of the cathedral opposite.

He had only come to the cathedral today because a messenger had come from the dean with an order for him to do so.

"The king has admired the carvings in the chapter house and he wishes to see the mason who did them. You will attend the service." And so, grumbling at the order, but secretly gratified, he had come. Even so, he had insisted on standing apart, several yards from his son and his wife, in his own determined isolation.

He looked around the cathedral. It was a splendid spectacle; even now, he could not restrain a small smile of satisfaction when he saw it, and if the king were to take notice of him above the lesser masons who had dared to cast him out, so much the better. Imperceptibly, his back began to straighten.

In the crowd, heads were turning eagerly. At any moment the king would come.

And then suddenly the mason's face contracted to a frown. He glanced from side to side to see if anyone else had noticed it, but it seemed they had not. Puzzled, he shook his head.

Why was it that he had the impression that something was wrong?

He stared around the cathedral, trying to analyse what it was that had caught his attention, peering into the shadowy spaces. Everything looked normal. But still his frown remained.

Then he heard it: a faint, an almost imperceptible murmur that seemed to be coming from the ground. It was somewhere in front of him but he could not say how far. He listened carefully; was it just a whisper in the crowd; could it be the tramp of feet of the king's retinue outside, or the clergy in their heavy vestments moving about in the choir? He did not think so.

By the choir screen he could see a thin haze of incense rising: he could smell its sweet scent.

Forgetting his old age, all his senses seemed to come to life. Under his feet he was sure he could detect a subtle, insidious trembling in the flagstones, unnoticed by the crowd whose attention was elsewhere, but there all the same.

He listened again. It was more than a murmur; it was a faint creaking, and it was definitely coming from the stones of the cathedral itself.

Something was wrong.

He stared at the shapes of the great arches ahead. Was it his imagination or was there something about them that was slightly different?

A minute passed. The sound came again, but this time it was distinct – a creaking, grinding sound, followed by a faint crack from somewhere far above. And now several heads turned.

Then he saw. It was almost imperceptible, but there was no mistaking it. The central pillars of the cathedral, the four slender marble legs on which the huge tower rested, were bending.

He gazed in horror. It was as though some enormous force was trying to bend them like bows, and the fibre of the stone was trying with all its strength to resist. There was another faint, grinding crack. He opened his mouth to cry out.

But now there was another shout, from just outside the building, and before he could do anything the chant of the choir drowned out all other noise as King Edward and his retinue, their jewelled cloaks flashing in the sun, swept in at the west door.

All eyes turned upon him, except those of Osmund, who remained staring up in terror as the huge fabric of the cathedral, undetected by the folk below, quivered.

"Mother of God," he whispered. "Do not let it come down now."

The movement that Osmund had detected was part of a complex problem whose origins lay deep in the structure of the great cathedral.

Even without the tower, the outward pressure from the vaulting of the great roof had placed enormous stresses on the supporting pillars of the thin, Gothic structure. Already some of the arches in the eastern choir had settled askew, pushed towards the altar like a huge stone concertina, and at the great central intersection, the tops of the central pillars had been pressed inwards – an effect that was barely visible, but implied a massive strain on the stone fabric. Such problems were not unknown in other cathedrals, and if the settling of the structure seemed to be becoming dangerous, fresh supports – buttresses or bracing arches – were often needed. Indeed, some small, though not very effective buttresses had already been added to the main building. But no one had properly worked out the extra stress when thousands of tons of masonry were added as the great pile of the new tower rose over the central intersection. "The Purbeck marble will hold it," the masons confidently assumed.

If they were right, then they were about to see the marble stretched to its utmost limit as the tall columns, already pressed inward began to bend at the centre as well with the tremendous new load.

If they were wrong – Osmund held his breath as the king strode up the aisle.

The service was over, and while the group of priests and local notables stood in a respectful circle at the east end of the nave, several masons were summoned forward to receive a gracious nod from the king. The last of these was Osmund. A small bag of coins was placed in his hand, and he heard Edward himself announce: "Your carvings in the chapter house – very fine, Osmund Mason." He bowed low. But when he heard the king remark: "Soon there'll be no finer cathedral in England," he shook his old head so violently that the whole circle turned to stare at him.

It was then that he pointed at the tall pillars and cried: "The tower: it's too heavy. See the shafts, how they're bending." And as all eyes turned up to where he was pointing he added:"It nearly came down today."

There was silence as the group stared at the now unmistakable curve in the shafts. Then he heard the voice of one of the canons. It was polite but contemptuous.

"The mason is old, sire, and not allowed to work in the church any more. The marble will support the tower."

Moments later he was dismissed and so he could not hear all that was said after that; but there was some laughter.

He was surprised therefore when shortly afterwards, as he was making his way out of the cathedral, one of the king's courtiers came up to him.

"You're to go to Clarendon," the man ordered, "first thing tomorrow morning. The king wants wooden carvings for his apartments there."

And as he opened his mouth to make his customary refusal the courtier cut him short.

"The king's orders. Be there at first light, before he goes hunting." And then the man smiled. "The king values your carving, Mason, even if you have annoyed the cathedral canons."

There was nothing he could do except obey.

On the morning after the service, two other people made their way on foot the two miles along the road from the eastern gate of the city to the royal palace of Clarendon. No one had summoned them.

John, called Will's son, did not much resemble his father William atte Brigge in his outward appearance, for although, taken individually, he had inherited all William's features, he had contrived collectively to make something different out of them. Where William had stooped, he stood straight; he walked with a calculated sedateness that completely masked the loping gait of his ancestors. His narrow face seemed brisk and lively instead of cruel, and his eyes intelligent where Wiliam's had only been cunning. His thin lips never drew back over his teeth in a snarl, but were trained to form a winning smile. He had continued his family's modest cloth business in Wilton and even before old William died, he had somehow gained a name for honesty. Despite these differences, it was still as William's son that he was known – for men usually referred to him as John Will's son, or Wilson.

John Wilson had no enemies: there were even several men in the town who, for reasons of business, called him their friend.

But his greatest asset was his wife.

Cristina at thirty-seven was astonishing. It was as if, at twenty-five, time had ceased to move, and even women in Sarum who had claims to good looks would admit that Cristina Wilson was in a class of her own. She had given her husband five children, but she was slim as a girl. The normal lines of age had confined themselves to pleasant lines of satisfaction about the eyes. Her hair was as fair as it had been when she was a child, and she moved with a frank but modest admission of her beauty. She had done wonders for her husband's business.

It was not that she spoke much. It was not that she flirted with the merchants who dealt with him – for in a small community that could be dangerous – but her presence, her smile of encouragement to them if the prices they offered were acceptable, made them positively anxious to please. Indeed, John Wilson had often been tempted to strike outrageous bargains when a client fell under the temporary spell of her beauty, but she had always shrewdly discouraged him.

"They'll be angry with us afterwards and hate me," she warned him. "We need friends, John: we're only small people."

Sarum had long ago forgotten how she had made a fool of the mason; her mischievous mind and her rich sexuality were known only to her husband, who was careful to keep this knowledge to himself.

Today, John Wilson's face was both anxious and eager: it would be the most important day of his life.

The sun was still barely over the trees when they reached the palace of Clarendon. It was a hunting lodge really – a sprawling, spacious collection of two-storey buildings that had grown over the reigns of several kings and with no very defined plan, extra chambers for guests or kennels for hounds being added as the need arose. Most of the buildings were constructed of wood; the principal sections were tiled, the rest had wooden shingle roofs, which required constant repair.

When they arrived at the entrance to the palace enclosure and asked for the king's apartments, the guard looked at them doubtfully; but then, supposing that they were either workmen, like the little mason he had admitted earlier, or that they belonged to one of the companies of minstrels who flocked whenever the royal party was in residence, he

[469]

gestured them curtly towards a group of buildings near the centre, and a few moments later, they found themselves standing in front of the little courtyard around which the royal apartments were set.

The royal apartments were similar to the others, except that their walls were hung with dozens of antlers, from previous hunting expeditions which gleamed white in the morning sunlight. There were a dozen huntsmen waiting there and several couple of splendid hounds, whose eager, panting breath rose like steam. The huntsmen were laughing amongst themselves, obviously anticipating the king's good humour, and they took no notice of the new arrivals.

The door of the royal apartment was open and through it Wilson could see a brightly decorated room. On the floor were the coloured tiles that the local monks of Wiltshire had made their speciality. On the opposite wall he could see cheerful paintings of previous kings, set in a green border that ran round the room. And in the centre of the room, he could also see the edge of a fine carpet – a new piece of decoration that Edward's adored queen had brought to his court from her native Spain. He had never seen such luxury before, and suddenly aware of the imminent presence of the king he looked at his wife nervously for support. She smiled calmly.

"You are ready?"

He nodded, but his hand was trembling.

"Everything is at stake, John," she reminded him.

And before he had time to consider any further the monstrous thing that he was about to do, the white-haired figure of King Edward appeared, followed by a group of courtiers.

He was in an excellent temper that morning; otherwise he would not have paused when a courtier pointed the Wilton merchant and his handsome wife out to him, and told him they had a petition.

Since Edward had started the great inquiry into his administration, the court had been swamped by complaints and petitions which his efficient secretariat promptly sent to the investigating justices or the shire courts. But like that other lawmaker, his great-grandfather Henry II, it was his practice often to hear cases himself; so now, while the huntsmen waited, he gave Wilson a curt nod and standing squarely with his long legs apart and his arms folded, he prepared to listen.

"Be brief," Edward told him.

John Wilson had a pleasing manner, an air of simple straightforward-ness that years of practice had perfected. He stated his case shortly and with such obvious sincerity that Edward, though he was an excellent judge of men, was inclined to believe him.

"It's my farm," he explained. Fifteen years ago, he went on smoothly, before the recent laws had forbidden the Jews to make such transactions, Aaron of Wilton had once again lent the Shockleys money on the security of the Shockley farm. "They didn't pay, and the Jew took the farm, but he couldn't hold it," he continued; for Jews were not usually allowed to hold land and so had to sell such pledges on immediately. "The land was sold to me," Wilson stated, "and Aaron took the money. But then he let

Shockley stay on it and I've never been able to get possession. So I'm out of the money and no farm." He shrugged, as if such chicanery was something an honest man had to expect. "What's more," he continued, "since all these transactions with the Jews have been forbidden in recent years, I can't get anyone to take an interest. But that money was all I had, and I earned it honestly." It was a plausible story, and not one word of it was true.

The king nodded. He disliked the Jews, and a decade before he had not only forbidden most of their activities but he had closed the chirograph chests in which their records were kept. In the confusion surrounding the liquidation of the Jews' affairs, he knew that an administrative slip-up of this kind could well have occurred, depriving the honest man and his striking blonde wife of a tenancy they had bought in good faith.

"But this matter should have been brought to the justices of the Jewish exchequers or the shire court," he said, and Wilson noted that the king, as he had always heard, spoke with a lisp.

"Can't get justice there," he replied firmly.

Edward looked at him sharply.

"Why not?" These abuses of justice were exactly what he was determined to stamp out.

And now John Wilson, who all his life had known that the Shockleys had cheated his family out of the farm, and that Shockleys and Godefrois were his natural enemies, began his next great lie.

"Godefroi," he said simply. "He hates me and he's in business with Shockley and the Jew. He's got power in the courts so he'll see I never get justice."

For the first time Edward looked at him in disbelief. He knew old Godefroi; as coroner, he would often have to decide matters relating to dead men's estates; as an escheator, it was his duty to look after the king's interests when his tenants died. Both positions gave him influence in the local courts and scope for malpractice, but of all those who might be accused of corruption in the current investigations, the knight of Avonsford was the last the king would have expected. He stared at Wilson coldly.

"Jocelin de Godefroi is our loyal servant," he rasped.

But Wilson did not flinch.

"He and Shockley run the fulling mill together," he stated flatly, "and Godefroi is keeping the Jew in Avonsford manor now – he's been there a month."

Edward's face darkened. If the harbouring of a Jew was not a legal offence, it was certainly against the spirit of the law, which was to isolate Jews from Christians in every way possible. He turned to the group about him.

"Is this true?"

One of the courtiers nodded. "I have heard it said, sire. The Jew is very old."

The scowl remained on Edward's face.

"The man's always been loyal," he repeated testily.

[471]

It was the moment for which John Wilson had prepared himself so carefully.

"Not so loyal, sire," he interrupted. "He was with Your Majesty's enemies at the time of Montfort."

This time the king positively glared at him.

"The son was with Montfort, and he was killed. Not the father."

But, unabashed, the merchant shook his head again.

"Jocelin gave his son his blessing when he left to fight at Lewes," he said. "And Shockley was with him. It was at their fulling mill. I saw them both."

This was the piece of information he had waited twenty-five years to use against them, ever since he had stood by the mill at his father's side.

There was a terrible silence.

Although his instincts now told Edward that this man was not to be trusted, long experience warned him that his last, damning statement might be true. Perhaps, after all, the Godefrois should have been punished like the other rebels; inwardly he cursed this vicious merchant from Wilton who was ruining his day.

It was now that old Osmund, who had been standing quietly behind the group of courtiers after receiving the instructions for his work, by a single and splendid act of courage incurred the enmity of the Wilsons for his family for generations.

John Wilson had not seen the old mason come out of the royal apartments. And in his hatred for the Godefrois and Shockleys, he had even forgotten that Osmund had ever been present at the meeting at the mill, twenty-five years before. Even if he had remembered, since this was one of the few parts of his story with any basis in truth, he would never have expected what followed.

Osmund pushed his way through the circle of courtiers, stepped forward boldly and turning to the king announced:

"But I was there too, Your Majesty, when Hugh de Godefroi went away to fight, and his father cursed him at the mill and forbade him to go."

It was a lie. But sixty years of loyalty to the knight of Avonsford made him say the words with ease.

John Wilson gazed at him in stupefaction.

"You lie," he cried.

But on Edward's face there was a smile of relief. Of the two, he was more inclined to believe the old mason. Besides, he wanted to.

"Say no more about Godefroi," he snapped. "What's your proof about this farm?"

For a moment John Wilson was shaking so hard with rage that he could not speak. It was Cristina now who touched his arm and looked pleadingly at the king. Slowly recovering himself, Wilson then drew out a sealed document and handed it to the king for his inspection. Having done this, and glared at the mason, his face relaxed and he waited confidently. This would settle it.

He was hopelessly wrong.

For the document which supported his massive fabrication of fraud and revenge, the evidence which he thought was his masterpiece, was his one terrible mistake. Indeed, it was a pathetic miscalculation that no learned man would ever have made. But John Wilson, though he was persuasive and cunning, was also illiterate.

Edward read it slowly and as he did so, his brow began to clear. Seeing this, John and Cristina looked at each other with satisfaction; obviously the king was impressed. But when he began to chuckle, their look changed to uncertainty, and when a moment later he laughed out loud, they became confused. Finally, the king without a word handed it to one of his courtiers, and in a moment the man had doubled up with mirth.

For the forgery which John Wilson had paid a poor priest – one of the band of semi-employed vicars choral who roamed about Sarum – to inscribe, was so lamentable that it was ridiculous. The deed purporting to convey the Shockley farm to Aaron and then assign it to Wilson was couched in a grotesque mixture of French, dog Latin and English that no literate cleric, or even merchant would ever have perpetrated. The forms of transfer were wrong, it was not properly stamped or witnessed – it could not conceivably have passed through the hands of the highly educated Jew, even as an illicit transfer. Only one thing was genuine, and this was the seal of the Jew which Wilson had picked up out of the dust on Fisherton Bridge the month before.

Now Edward stopped laughing, and turning on Wilson he roared: "Your document is a fraud, you rogue. You're a forger. You shall go to jail!"

"But it has the Jew's seal," Wilson cried in alarm. "It must be real."

"Fool! Don't you know, a seal proves nothing?"

Wilson's face fell. It was the seal that had given him the idea. He had put his faith in it, for he had always heard that a sealed document was absolute proof in any dispute. The fact that only a few years before, the king's court, in considering a case of forgery like this, had very properly ruled that a seal, which could easily be mislaid or stolen should no longer constitute proof of authenticity was something of which neither he nor the miserable priest he had employed had been aware. He was trapped. He turned to Cristina in dismay and she immediately gave the king her most winning and appealing smile. Edward took no notice whatever.

"How dare you waste the king's time and make accusations against the king's loyal servants!" he thundered. "You shall be punished for this. Call the guard."

In a moment John Wilson found himself surrounded by men at arms.

"Hold him under lock and key until I return," the king ordered. And when they pointed to Cristina he added: "And her too."

It took several hours spent in hunting before his temper improved: not only because of the way his time had been wasted, but because, despite Osmund's defences, he could not throw off the nagging suspicion that a part of Wilson's accusations might be true. Should he investigate the matter to find out the whole truth? What for – to discover a long forgotten betrayal? He decided to put it out of his mind: the matter was in the past. He had no wish to know.

"Godefroi is my friend," he muttered. But the seed of distrust had been sown.

The fate of John Wilson and his wife was decided by circumstances that had nothing to do with the Shockley farm.

It was a thoughtful young courtier who had been involved in the Scottish negotiations who decided the issue. He had studied the pair carefully that morning; while King Edward was sitting at his meal in the evening he came to the king's side and quietly made the ingenious suggestion as a result of which, a little later, John and Cristina found themselves led into the room.

They had spent an anxious and unpleasant day. The bare hut in which they had been kept had a leaking roof. It had been used as a kennels some time before and it smelt musty. By evening the place had become cold, and by nightfall their teeth were chattering. They had been given no food. Now, suddenly, they were blinking in the bright light of the king's sumptuous apartments, faced by Edward and his hunting companions, and listening in surprise to the remarkable proposition that the young courtier was putting to them so coolly.

His logic was impeccable. The Scottish negotiations had been progressing well, but in the last week the final completion had dragged unnecessarily over some minor details, and the cause, he had discovered, was the secretary to one of the commissioners, who was against the business and had influence with his master.

"The only way to keep him happy is to amuse him," the young man explained to the king. "Then he lets things go along, even if he doesn't really approve. If he isn't amused, he just invents trivial obstacles all the time."

"How do you amuse him?"

"Women, Your Majesty. His appetite's insatiable. We've given him three local wenches already, but he got bored with them." He grinned. "But did you notice the merchant's wife this morning? She's extraordinary."

Edward gazed at the young fellow with a mixture of admiration for his cunning, and contempt for his methods. His devotion to his own Spanish wife was well known. He even used to take the queen with him on campaign.

"You want to send her to the Scot – as a price for their release?" He shook his head in disgust. "I won't do it."

"No sire, there's no need," the courtier responded. "They'll both do it of their free will." And briefly he outlined his simple plan. "Have I your permission?"

Edward grimaced.

"I suppose so."

When John Wilson heard the smiling young man make his proposal, he recapitulated it carefully:

"You're going to set me free with no trial?"

The courtier nodded:

"The king is considering it, despite your impertinent fraud."

"And when I'm free, you'll grant me a farm?"

"Precisely. Your own farm."

"But my wife has to lie for a week with the Scot?"

"If you want the farm, yes. You will be doing the king a useful service," he added with a smile.

John Wilson paused, without looking at his wife.

"If the Scot wants her for longer," he said thoughtfully, "do I get more?"

Even the courtier's bland smile faltered for an instant at the coolness of the question; but he recovered quickly.

"Perhaps."

Only then did John turn to Cristina. Neither spoke, but between them there passed a look of perfect complicity.

"She'll do it," he said cheerfully.

The young courtier smiled; the king, with his drooping eyelid watched unblinking. And an hour later a small charter granting John Wilson and his heirs tenancy of a farmstead consisting of one virgate of land with a messuage thereon was dropped contemptuously into his hands. The messuage in question was a small cottage; the land was mediocre. But it was enough to satisfy his modest aspirations. It lay next door to the Shockley farm.

The agreement between the Scots and English commissioners for the government of Scotland during the minority of its child queen, and the recommendation that the king's son should be married in due course to the Maid of Norway, was presented to King Edward at Salisbury on November 6, 1289.

After this, the king hunted in the New Forest, travelling as far south as Christchurch and the shallow harbour by the sea. He stayed in the region for a month before returning to London for Christmas, after which he held a parliament there until the end of February. During Lent, Edward was in the upper Thames valley and at Easter he stayed at his park at Woodstock. He then returned to the Sarum area when he visited the convent at Amesbury, that lay two miles from the old henge and where his mother was now a nun, for a family conference. After this, the busy monarch returned once again to London for one of the most important parliaments of his reign.

The summer Parliament of 1290 was remarkable in England's history for many reasons. The reforming legalist king had never been more active: creating order out of the creaking feudal administration, looking for ways to raise revenue from his increasingly wealthy kingdom; the settlement with Scotland was discussed, and substantial subsidies were granted by the church from its vast possessions.

He also issued some of his most famous laws. One of these was the great statute Quo Warranto by which he attempted to regulate, even if he could not completely cut back, the undisciplined power of some of the feudal magnates. The statute challenged any magnate who claimed a jurisdiction, or liberty, over an area to show by what charter he held this right. If no clear right could be demonstrated, then the jurisdiction should revert to the king. These actions were not always successful, however. One of the liberties he challenged was of the Abbey of Wilton over the nearby hundred of Chalke. But even Edward was defeated by the nuns.

And another milestone in history was passed during these proceedings when, on July 18, 1290, the King decided one further matter of great importance.

For on that day, Edward I of England in his Council at Westminster, expelled the Jews from his kingdom.

As it happened, this day was also the Fast of the Ninth of Ab in the Jewish calendar: the anniversary of the destruction of Jerusalem and many disasters thereafter.

The entire community was given until the feast of All Saints, the day after Hallowe'en, to be gone. They were to be allowed to leave under the king's protection, unmolested.

It was not a complete surprise: their position had long been untenable, and as they had been ruined, they were no longer a source of profit to the crown. It was generally believed that his mother had urged the king to expel them when he visited Amesbury. The church subsidy that immediately followed was, in part, a thanks offering to Edward for this pious act.

Two days before Hallowe'en, Aaron of Wilton was placed once again in the Shockley cart. He had decided, rather than travel to London, to embark with half a dozen others from the remnants of the Wilton community on a small ship that would leave from the port of Christchurch and cross to France. It was Peter Shockley who had insisted that his cart should be used to convey his old friend, and since he and Christopher were detained on business, he had abruptly ordered Mary, despite her protests, to accompany Aaron and see to it that he was safely put aboard his ship.

There were three carts to carry the little party and their few remaining possessions slowly down the rutted lane that paralleled the lazy Avon river south through the villages of Fordingbridge, Ringwood, and along the western edge of the New Forest to Christchurch. Though the journey was only twenty-five miles, it took two days, and it was the night of Hallowe'en when they rattled on to the cobblestones of the little town of Christchurch with its fine Norman priory and its dark little castle on a hump of turf beside the harbour.

Aaron was remarkably serene. The rest at Avonsford had restored him to something approaching his former self. Besides insisting that he accept a small pouch of silver coins, old Jocelin had seen to it that his clothes were new and his grey beard was shaved to a crisp, chiselled end; his blue eyes were bright and clear again, and he sat up, calm but alert, watching the countryside as they went along. Although he was being banished from the country that had always been his home, as he told the knight of Avonsford, he was too old to be anything but philosophical about it.

"It seems God wishes me to see more of the world before I die," he said wryly, and took his leave of the Godefrois and the Shockleys with surprising cheerfulness.

It was during this final journey from Sarum to the coast that Mary Shockley tried to convert him.

All day before the journey, Mary had pondered. Since her father had ordered her to take Aaron in the cart, she supposed that she must, and since she was taking him to banishment, it seemed to her that she was doing God's work. But she was not happy with the task. She was a bluff, good-hearted girl, perfectly formed to farm and fight like her Saxon ancestors before her. She knew that the Jews would suffer hellfire if they did not convert, and the question of how to deal with them had always seemed simple to her. "Why doesn't the king just order them to convert and kill them if they don't?" she had once asked as a child. It was how Roman had converted Saxon and Saxon Dane, in better, simpler times. But now she was to be forced to sit for two days in the cart with an old infidel close to death; and the more she considered it, the more she realized that it must be her duty to convert him if she could. So as soon as they rattled over the Ayleswade bridge and set off on the road south, she told Aaron that this was her intention.

To his amusement, the elderly, sophisticated Jew sat in the creaking cart beside the almost illiterate and forthright young woman who had earnestly told him to repent even before they reached Britford or the cathedral tower was out of sight. She pleaded with him all the way to Fordingbridge, explaining the folly of Judaism and the greater authority of her church.

He did not argue much, but she could see that she was making little headway. She was not discouraged, though.

"Don't worry old Jew; we'll save your soul yet," she told him cheerfully.

After they had crossed the river at Fordingbridge, she warned him of the danger of hellfire; she told him he must do penance for the crime of the Jews in sending Christ to the cross; she explained to him that those who, like him, saw the Saviour but closed their eyes would not be forgiven on the Day of Judgement. The old man answered her patiently, more amused than irritated by her persistence, as he explained that he had no wish to desert the God who had made His covenant with his ancestors.

They stopped at Ringwood for the night.

The second day, sensing that she had been defeated on the main issue, Mary changed her line of attack.

"Why do you practise usury," she demanded, "when the Bible and the Church says usury is a sin?"

"I do not practise usury," he replied.

She frowned.

"You lend money at interest."

"Yes, but what the Bible calls usury is excessive interest, which is different," he responded calmly. "All money must carry some interest,

[477]

otherwise no one has any reason to lend."

She shook her head. How ignorant the old man was.

"You're not supposed to charge any interest," she corrected. "The priests say so."

Aaron sighed. The profound ignorance of simple finance that this invented doctrine showed was something he could only grieve over.

"Do you deny it?" she insisted.

He gazed at her and thought what a splendid creature she was, with her frank, violet eyes, her mass of long, yellow hair and her athletic figure. He bore her no ill will and wished now that she would stop arguing with him since he was tired. But his passion for accuracy made him reply:

"I do deny that it is wrong, whatever the priests say. Excessive interest is a crime, and a destructive one, but there must be some interest."

She could see he was sincere, and her face puckered in puzzlement as the old man, tired of the argument though he was, tried for the last time to set right the fundamental prejudice that dogged all financial transactions through the Middle Ages.

"When your grandfather invested in the mill, Mary, he could only do so if his investment yielded a return. It's just the same if a man gets a farm and works it. You have to show a return or you give it up. When you sell your goods at the market, you exchange them for money. What if, now, you wish to finance someone else to build a mill or buy a farm with your money? Don't you look for some return, just as you would if it was the mill or farm you were working yourself? The return on that money is your interest rate, that's all."

She considered. It sounded logical, but she did not like it. She was silent for several minutes as they rumbled along the lane. Then her face cleared.

"But I work on the land, and it raises crops; and my brother works in the mill to full cloth. That's how we get money."

"Of course," he smiled. "But there's no difference really. When you work, the money in the farm is working, and earning its return."

Now she knew he was wrong!

"Money doesn't work, Jew!" she cried, thumping the side of the cart with her fist. "I work!"

The simple abstract principle behind almost all economic activity and human civilisation offended her practical mind to its core. "You should have been made to work with your hands," she said sternly.

For this was a solution to the Jewish problem that had been suggested many times before, not only by well-meaning landowners but even by such otherwise subtle intellects as the churchman Grosseteste and the great philosopher and theologian Thomas Aquinas.

The prejudice of otherwise intelligent people against the rules of finance upon which their lives depended was too deep, Aaron reminded himself, to be argued with. But perhaps, he considered, as he felt the winter sun on his head, they will be wiser in another generation.

"Truly," Mary thought to herself at the same time, "the old Jew is so steeped in sin that he cannot even see the difference between honest work and theft.''

And so, tolerating each other on their final journey together, they went on in silence towards the port.

On the morning of Hallowe'en, that most magical of days, when all men knew that the dead rose from their graves, a small, squat wooden ship, broad in the beam, with a single square-rigged sail, lurched away with a creak from Christchurch quay. In the hull of the boat, just able to see over its side, stood Aaron, three adults and four children from Wilton, for each of whom the captain had been paid a shilling in advance of the crossing.

The captain of this modest vessel was a stooped, narrow-faced man, one of the countless generations of river folk who had fished and traded along the rivers and the coast since long before the Romans came; he shoved his passengers roughly into a space near the mast where they would be no trouble to him. His crew consisted only of his two sons.

From the stout little boat, Aaron could see Mary Shockley as she waved a curt goodbye before turning her cart and clattering up past Christchurch Priory on to the Sarum road; and as the crew pushed off and made their way slowly into the calm, shallow harbour, he held on to the mast and strained to see all he could during his last hour in England. Hungrily, his eyes took in the long reeds that grew along the bank, and the flat, marshy area on the northern side of the harbour, where the swans nested and wild horses still roamed; to his right lay the remains of the two earthwork walls and the long, low headland that silently protected the harbour from the sea. The boat carried them past the sand bar that enclosed the harbour and through the narrow channel that led into the open sea. A few fishermen were standing on the sand bar with their boats and they silently watched the little vessel go by. Bobbing on the light swell, it pushed its blunt nose out, away from the headland, towards the Solent and the high chalk cliffs of the Isle of Wight.

Twenty minutes passed. The sail was up but they made slow progress. He turned and looked back.

There, across the brown waters, under a grey sky, lay the headland.

"The isle in the sea," he sighed. For centuries this was the name that the Jews of Europe had given to the island of Britain, hidden by its narrow Channel and shrouded in its soft, northern mists. The low, matter-of-fact headland lying quietly behind him on this cold, dull day, was so infinitely touching to him, such a sudden and poignant reminder that he was never to see England again, that, still holding on to the thick mast, he suddenly broke into tears.

The tide was very low, and the captain, chatting to his sons, seemed to be taking little notice of where they were going. It was thanks to his carelessness that suddenly, when it was a mile out from the headland, the little boat crunched aground on a sandbank in the bay. The passengers groaned and the captain cursed his own folly loudly.

There was nothing to do but for passengers and crew alike to clamber out in order to lighten the boat, and stand on the sandbank with the cold salt water coming up to their knees while the captain and his sons heaved and cursed as they rocked the boat to shift it. The process took several minutes, but finally they managed to get the little vessel free, and in order not to make the same mistake again, the captain and his sons waded several yards out to keep the boat off the sands while ordering the passengers to stay where they were. Only when it was well clear did the crew clamber on, while the captain tried to hold the bow.

Then the captain swung himself up into the boat, turning to face his passengers, still obediently waiting on the sandbank.

"How do we board?" one of the men cried.

The captain grinned.

"You don't."

The passengers looked at each other, bemused. Was this a strange joke of some kind?

"You don't board, Jew," the captain cried. "You stay on the sandbank."

"But we paid our fares."

"And this is where they get you," he chuckled.

And now, suddenly his two sons pushed off with their oars, sending the boat skidding out into the deep water.

"Tide's coming up," the captain shouted. He looked at Aaron. "Remember Moses, old man, and you can part the waters!" He roared with laughter at this excellent joke. His sons swung the boat round, caught the wind, and as the sail filled out with a snap, the boat began to tack away towards the harbour.

Only now did the little group understand that the manoeuvre with the sandbank had been a trick. They gazed at the departing boat in astonishment, scarcely able to believe what was happening.

There was a shocked silence.

"What shall we do?" The younger of the two men turned to Aaron.

"Can you swim?"

"No."

There were two men and a woman, none of them in condition to attempt any feats of physical endurance, even if they could swim. The three children were thin and silent, in a state of shock. Aaron looked around him. It was a mile to the headland and perhaps a mile and a half to the main line of the shore. The water was already over his knees.

"We'll have to try to swim," he said finally. He knew it was useless, but if they stayed there, it was obvious they would drown. No one responded.

"Perhaps someone will see us," one of the men suggested.

The coastline was bare. By the sand bar at the end of the headland, he could see the fishermen were still there. But would they rescue them? Christchurch itself was far away, hidden from view by the headland.

"Perhaps the sailors will change their minds."

Aaron did not reply.

"Better try to swim," he suggested. Still nobody moved.

The woman began to cry for help.

It was only then that he saw the storm.

The black clouds that came over the bay had seemed insignificant when they appeared on the horizon, no bigger than a man's hand. But then they had arisen suddenly and within minutes had spread out, blackening the west and rushing forward over the waters with terrible swiftness, like ominous birds of prey. The storm came in a fury. Its winds whipped the sea into a wild spray, hurling it against the headland and sending the grey black waves buffeting and thumping their weight onto the shingle shore with a crash and rattle. As the boat rounded the headland and reached the safety of the harbour, the group of fishermen who had watched the pathetic little party stranded on their sandbank and heard the faint cries across the water, had gone at last to their boat with the idea of rescuing them. But when they saw how fast the black clouds were coming, they realised that it was wiser not.

As the clouds streamed across the bay, they retired to a little hut they had built in the lee of a sand dune, and waited out the rage of the storm.

An hour later, as the winter skies began to clear, they ventured out of their shelter again.

There was no sign of Aaron and his party.

Sometimes, in later years, the fishermen at the harbour would point out from the headland to the spot where the sandbank lay, and tell their children:

"That's where they stood. That's where the Jews were drowned."

And it was said, for a generation or more:

"When a storm's about to blow, if you listen carefully, you can hear their voices, crying in the waves."

The expulsion of the Jews from England took place swiftly and quietly. Apart from a few isolated incidents, for which the culprits were mostly punished by the authorities, they were not molested.

The Church, it was agreed by everyone, had triumphed.

To mark this triumph in Sarum, the dean and chapter declared that a fine statue should be erected – a figure representing the True Church with an infidel blindfold beneath.

Osmund the Mason was briefly considered for this work; but after his outburst about the tower, it was decided to give it to another.

Mary Shockley did not hear about the death of Aaron until several days later, and when she did, she only shrugged.

"He's lost his soul anyway," she stated flatly. "I tried to save him," she explained, "so I know."

Only one matter continued to puzzle her. A week after her journey to Christchurch, the Shockley family went to the Saturday market in Salisbury, and after she had refused to buy some brightly coloured silk slippers that Alicia had pointed out, on the grounds that there was nothing wrong with her boots, she noticed a figure standing by the sheep market that she had never seen before. He was dressed in a long black robe edged with fur; his head was bald and he was more wonderfully stout than any man she had ever seen before. His flowing robe stretched

[481]

out over his huge stomach and reached to the ground in such ample curves that he resembled nothing so much as one of the mighty cathedral bells. His clean-shaven face appeared to be built up in layers of polished fat out of which his small black eyes shone and his full lips were formed into an expression of perfect serenity.

She strode across to him.

"What are you, fat man?" she enquired pleasantly.

"A merchant, lady," he replied. His voice was a rich, melodious tenor, heavily accented.

"You're from Italy," she guessed.

He inclined his head. "From Lombardy."

"What do you sell?"

"Money, my lady, only money. It's what everybody wants." His eyes had already taken her in at a glance and now flicked back and forth across the market place.

She frowned.

"Does the Church allow you to sell money?"

"Of course," he answered serenely. "I am an agent, lady, for a great Lombardy money house. The pope blesses us every day, for his Church is our greatest customer. We make many loans," he added dreamily, "many loans. Do you wish a loan?"

She stood in front of him with her arms akimbo, looking at him severely.

"Tell me your terms, fat man."

"They are easy, lady." His eyes rested on her for only a moment. "If you borrow twelve marks, I will advance you ten now. In a year, you will repay me the twelve."

She glared at him.

"And the other two?"

"My fee."

"It's interest."

For a second his smile departed and he looked pained.

"We call it a fee."

"Call it what you like. Same thing. It's usury."

He shook his head, then recovered his beatific smile.

"Money must work, lady. Money always works."

She remembered where she had heard that expression before.

"Then what's the difference between you and a Jew?" she demanded.

And now, just for an instant, the man from Lombardy allowed himself to chuckle.

"The difference," he smiled sweetly, "is that I am here."

Mary turned away, with a sense that she was being made a fool of; but for years afterwards, her face darkened if either the Jews or money-lending were mentioned: for it was the one area where her simple and unquestioning faith had been undermined.

There was at this time a man in Sarum who was generally agreed to be a nuisance.

He was an old Franciscan friar – a harmless eccentric who some claimed to be a hundred – who irritated the priests in the close considerably. A lifetime of hard labour and ascetic living had certainly taken their toll on him physically: his back was bent, his teeth gone, and his eyes were deeply sunken. The fellow was often to be seen sitting near the entrance of the close and would not have excited any attention if he had not, several times a day, risen up and began to preach.

When he did so, the effect upon him was remarkable. His back would straighten, his voice, high-pitched though it was, would carry across the close, and his eyes would gleam with a piercing brightness that was disturbing.

His sermon was always the same.

"Beware you burgesses – and you priests. This city is swollen with pride," he would cry. "But I tell you, your pride will be cast down unless you return to humility and repent." Each time he preached, his voice would grow in strength and passion. "You build a great tower into the sky, like the Tower of Babel," he would shout. "You build a church of stone, but you forget God." And then he would point with outstretched arm at the great tower above the city. "Pride and vanity are building that tower," he would proclaim. "Pride and your tower will fall."

It was not a message the canons wished to hear. Although its mighty pillars were bending, the huge tower was still to be surmounted by a slender spire which, all knew, was for the glory of God, and though they did not like to move the preacher on, they took as little notice of him as possible. Unfortunately there were a few poor souls in the city, not to speak of the urchins in the streets, who took his preachings too literally and who would sometimes follow one of the canons up the street crying "Pride, pride."

It was irritating.

Despite his deranged preaching, people often gave him alms, though he never asked for any; but even so, most passers by preferred not to get too close. Only Peter Shockley, for some reason, used to stop and converse with him; but when he once remarked that the friar was hardly older than he was, people smiled and supposed the old fellow had told him some fantastic story. The friar had a long scar running down his forehead.

It was the following spring that Osmund the mason made his last contribution to the great cathedral. It was a contribution that gave him a strange satisfaction, partly because no one ever knew about it.

The castle of Old Sarum on its bare chalk promontory had become a place apart. It was not deserted, for the garrison remained there, so did a gaol. The little town still held its small market and sent burgesses to parliament whenever burgesses were summoned. But few people from outside went to the windy promontory on the edge of the high ground for choice. The clergy were glad to be out of the place, and although small services were still held in the old Norman cathedral building of Bishop Roger, they often referred to the old town as the castle of Caesar in the mistaken belief that the dune, rather than the vanished Sorviodunum below, had been a Roman settlement.

But Osmund liked to visit the place. He had finished the carvings at Clarendon – a pleasing set of animal heads around a door. But since then, no one had offered him any work. The bleak emptiness of the castle suited his mood. He would trudge up the steep hill from the river and stare out over the new city from its battlements. It was here one day, passing a small stone building near the gates that had recently been demolished, that his sculptor's eye picked out a little grey object in a heap of rubble. Walking over to the spot he reached down and pulled out a piece of carved stone, no bigger than his fist, over whose curves he ran his stubby fingers and which caused his solemn face to break into a smile.

It was a strange little figure, of a naked woman with big breasts and strong, muscular hips; it fitted neatly into the palm of his hand and the feel of it gave him a strange sense of pleasure.

It was eight hundred years since the little figure of Akun, the hunter's woman, had last been seen; yet her presence there was not so strange. She had travelled up river with Tarquinus the heathen, and then been discreetly returned by him one day and secreted in a hidden niche in a wall in Sorviodunum where she belonged. Sorviodunum had been deserted; its buildings had tumbled down, and over the centuries its stones had been dispersed until no visible trace of them remained. Some of them had been carried up the hill, and later Norman builders had unwittingly moved the little figure, in a heap of other assorted rubble to be used as in-fill, and dropped her into a cavity in the walls of a house on the castle hill. In her eight-thousand-five-hundred-year journey, she had therefore never travelled far from the little northern valley, and now, delighted with her shape, the old mason carried her back to Avonsford.

For several days he wondered what to do with the little figure; and then a thought occurred to him that made him smile.

The tower of the great cathedral had not collapsed: he had been wrong. Though the cathedral continued to settle, it seemed that, after all, it would hold up. And though he continued to criticise the building, he secretly rejoiced that the noble structure and its many carvings were safe after all. It was thinking about the tower that gave him the idea.

It was a few evenings later that Osmund walked slowly into the cathedral close just as dusk was falling. The masons in the tower had already left for the day and the place was almost deserted so that no one saw him as he quietly entered the cathedral and moved to the staircase which led to the upper storey. It was a long climb: first to the top of the main arches, then to the clerestory above them, until finally he reached the level of the vaulting. Below him in the cavernous spaces of the nave, half lit by a dim glow from the great windows, he could not hear anyone moving about. As he had hoped, the door to one of the four staircases to the tower was open. He climbed the narrow spiral: twenty feet, forty feet, up to the first landing with its parapet and sweeping views over the city. The first stars were beginning to glimmer but set in the wall above, despite the dim light, he noticed one of the dog's heads he had carved.

"They don't want me in the tower, but they're glad enough to use my carvings," he muttered.

He climbed again, breathing heavily, and this time he came out at the top of the tower. The work on the spire had not yet begun and there was nothing above him but the open sky. He was two hundred and twenty feet above the ground.

Everywhere the stars were appearing; they seemed brighter and more plentiful than the little lights of the city below. The great stone tower thrust so high above the other buildings, belonged more to the world of the stars than the world of man.

Osmund moved around the parapet, inspecting it. There were dozens of small niches in the masonry, some containing figures, some empty, and finally he found one on the outer edge of the parapet into which a tiny head would neatly fit. From his pouch he drew a little chisel and hammer and, disregarding the height, he leaned out over the edge of the parapet and hollowed a deeper recess in the niche; when this was done, he dropped the little figure of Akun into the hollow so that just her head appeared, looking out of the lip, while her squat body was concealed. Glancing about, he saw some mortar and a bucket of water, left by the masons at the end of the day, and a few moments later the little figure was permanently fixed in place.

He grinned. The head was so small that it would probably never be noticed; but there it was, gazing northwards towards the high ground, a last contribution from the master mason, despite the wishes of the guild, to the cathedral that had been his life. He gave the tiny head a pat.

"If this tower stands up, you'll stay here now," he said.

And so it was that Akun found a new resting place in the tower of stone, high above the bowl of land where the five rivers met.

1310

And now at last the great work was almost completed.

The final addition to the new cathedral was its most dramatic feature – the crowning glory that transformed it from a splendid church into a wonder: there was nothing else like it on the island, hardly, indeed, in all Europe.

For the tapering octagonal spire, that ineffable narrow grey cone that rested on top of the tower, soared a further, astounding hundred and eighty feet. It almost doubled the height of the cathedral to over four hundred feet. Year after year it had gently risen over the stately mass of the tower, aweing even the masons who were building it.

None had been more fascinated than old Osmund. Time had taken away some of the pain of the events of 1289, and although for some years he was not a popular figure with the other masons, they tolerated his presence when, once or twice a year Edward had taken him up the tower to show him the progress on the spire. In the early years of the building, Edward had always explained: "He's getting old. This may be the last time he sees the spire before he dies." But as the years passed, this excuse became a sort of joke with the little band still working in the spire's upper reaches.

For Osmund, having passed through the grand climacteric of his life, seemed to have settled quietly into an indestructible old age. Thin and bent, his shuffle a little slower, he seemed always to be in motion, and even as he neared his eightieth year, he still walked the few miles from Avonsford to the new city at least once a week if he could not get a ride in a cart. "We'll be building another cathedral before that old man dies," the masons began to joke, as he gamely pulled himself up the tall staircases that led to the spire.

Year by year it slowly rose, and year by year Osmund climbed up to inspect it, gazing carefully at the bending pillars. The buttresses that had been added seemed to be taking the strain of the arcades; the soaring purbeck shafts, miraculously, seemed to be holding in place.

The construction of the spire fascinated him, for there were several new technical problems to surmount. The first was how to fit an octagonal spire on to a square tower – a problem which fell into two parts: how to support its eight corners' vertical thrusts, and how to counteract the eight horizontal thrusts that accompanied them. To support them, arches had to be constructed across the four corners of the tower, subdividing the area into eight bases. But now the weight of the spire was pushing upon not only the tower's corners but the middle of the walls as well, where the new arches met, forcing them outwards and threatening to split the tower apart.

Once again, the builders decided to bind the tower with bands of iron, this time just below the parapet. Thin iron bands were therefore placed around the inside and outside, fastened securely together through the masonry, and again the work was so well done that it would not be reinforced for four centuries. Next, turrets were built at the corners to act as extra buttresses against the outward thrust at the bottom of the spire's sloping walls. But it was something else that truly astonished Osmund. For on his fourth visit, when the cone had grown some twenty-five feet, he noticed that the last five feet of its walls were much thinner than the first twenty; and when he clambered up the scaffolding to inspect it, he was amazed to discover that it was only a little thicker than the span of his own small hand.

"Are you building the walls so thin right to the top?" he called down. Edward nodded. "Why then, it will be as thin as an eggshell," he cried.

"And as light," Edward remarked.

This was the key. The stone spire of Salisbury cathedral was built of masonry less than nine inches thick – an incredible thinness for a structure nearly two hundred feet high. Of the total weight of the tower and spire together, some six thousand five hundred tons, the spire represented only eight hundred.

When he descended to the cathedral floor that day and stared up at the bending pillars in the transept, Osmund, for the first time in years, allowed a hint of cautious approval for the daring building to pass his lips.

"If you brace those pillars and add more buttresses," he remarked, "it might stand up."

The work was intricate, and because of the difficulty of access, another unusual procedure was necessary: the scaffolding had to be constructed inside the spire instead of outside, the stones being drawn up using a huge, twelve-foot windlass that the labourers pulled round by hand. Nor could the stones in the sloping walls simply be laid one on top of another, as they were in the main body of the church: instead each was clamped to the next with an iron staple, sealed with molten lead, each octagonal layer being completed before proceeding to the next, so that the masons built it up in the same way as a potter lays on rings of clay.

The spire had reached a height of sixty feet when, one cold February, his wife caught pneumonia and died. He accepted it philosophically and soon afterwards moved in with Edward and his family.

By the turn of the century the old mason had outlived all his contemporaries.

Jocelin de Godefroi died in 1292; and in September 1295, Peter Shockley died, two days after Alicia. He was sixty-nine. Alicia had been taken ill that spring and during the summer he had watched her quietly fade. Shortly before the end, she had become delirious, and while he kept watch by her side, she chattered, to his great surprise, in French. He never made out what she said, nor to whom she was talking.

The day that they buried her in the little churchyard beside St Thomas's church, he complained of feeling tired. They found him dead in his chair that evening.

But Osmund went on. And when his grandchildren asked the old man, "How long will you live, grandfather?" he used to answer: "Until the spire is built."

The disasters that had struck both the Godefroi and the Wilson families by the early years of the new century were caused, indirectly, by the king.

For Edward I, the years after 1289 were times of gathering darkness. His plans for Scotland had collapsed in ruins when, in the late summer of 1290, the Maid of Norway died, and though he remained nominal overlord of Scotland, his hopes of uniting the north and south of the island peacefully under his dynasty were destroyed. Worse, his own life had been shattered in November of that year when his beloved queen, Eleanor of Castile, had unexpectedly died too. The grief-stricken king accompanied her bier from Lincoln to London, and at each place where the mournful party rested for the night, he had a fine stone cross erected. The last was the Charing Cross, at London.

On every side, it seemed things were going wrong. By the mid-nineties, England had drifted into war with France over Gascony, and both the Welsh and Scotland, which after the Maid of Norway's death now had rival claimants to its throne, had risen in rebellion against him. The peace he had won, all the work he had done, was threatened and from now on he was almost constantly at war.

And the trouble, as usual, was the cost. For while the kingdom of

[487]

England with its growing towns and thriving wool trade grew richer, King Edward himself did not. His finances still relied upon his feudal dues, his own estates, the profits from the courts, and whatever taxes he could raise by special assessments on his feudal tenants and the Church. In times of war, he knew, these were not enough. Worse, strong as he was, Edward could not enforce his will. The greatest landowner was the Church and since each generation saw more lands given to the Church by a pious nobility – land which then passed forever out of the king's control – the Church's wealth could only increase at his expense. This was another situation which he had tried to correct by insisting, in his Statute of Mortmain, that only the king should license these land grants in future; but even so, the wealth of his kingdom that was controlled by the bishops and abbots was huge. And if this was not bad enough, in 1296, in the great Bull *Clericis Laicos*, the pope had now declared that no subsidies should be paid to the king without his permission. Not only the Church gave him trouble. The very next year, when Edward held a parliament of his magnates at Salisbury, they had even refused to go to Gascony unless the king went too. "By God, earl," he was said to have cried in exasperation to the marshal, "you will either go or hang." To which the magnate replied: "By God, king, I will neither go nor hang." And so, once again, England's king found himself confronted with exactly the same problem that had forced King John to agree to the Magna Carta and Henry III to give way to Montfort. The feudal king had neither the money nor power to govern in troubled times.

The answer was wool. Roughly half the value of the kingdom now lay in its wool, and Edward made every effort to increase the wool exports from his own estates and to tax the trade of the merchants. Why, after all, should the king not profit from the greatest source of wealth in his kingdom?

It was Edward who first established the customs and excise. And in 1294 he began the tax on wool exports called the maltote.

In doing so he ruined John Wilson completely. It was Wilson's fault.

The grant of the farm, small as it was, had given the merchant a new confidence. A subtle change came over him and his wife. He trimmed his cotte with fur around the collar; Cristina, who had persuaded the Scottish secretary to part with a gold chain, wore it proudly round her neck. When they went to hear the mass on Sundays, they almost strutted down the street.

And in 1291, John Wilson began to speculate in wool.

It had seemed safe enough. Under the system known as arra, a merchant would advance money to a farmer at a discounted price on the security of his next crop of wool. There was nothing new in this, and since the wool business was booming, the risks to the merchant were slight. In his first year, by driving a hard bargain with some of the smaller wool growers, many of them villeins from nearby estates, Wilson did well.

He grew more ambitious. The following year, he not only advanced small amounts of money of his own; he borrowed sums from larger merchants so that he could advance more, using the security of the farm.

For two years he made handsome profits. He gambled more.

The effect of the maltote tax was simple. The wholesale wool exporters unable to pass on all the tax as a price increase to their customers, made up for it by paying less for their wool. And so although at the end of the thirteenth century the wool market was booming, the prices paid to suppliers actually fell. John Wilson, now the owner of large quantities of wool he had bought two years ahead and paid for with borrowed money, was left with a huge shortfall. To meet it he had to sell the house and business in Wilton, all his livestock, and the tenancy of the farm. By the spring of 1296 the Wilson family, after only half a decade of prosperity, was completely ruined.

Though he was only a boy of five at the time, John's son Walter remembered what happened next all his life.

On a cold spring day, when the little family were disconsolately huddled by the cottage, it was Mary Shockley who came striding down the path from the Shockley farmhouse towards them.

What a strange figure she had seemed: a big, bluff woman with her hair cut short and dressed like a man, as she came stomping through the mud in her heavy boots. When she reached the cottage she stood in front of them with her hands on her hips and to the boy she seemed very tall. Her violet eyes took them all in, and she came straight to the point.

"Well, ferret-face," she addressed John Wilson. It was said cheerfully and without malice. "I hear you've got to give up the farm."

John gave her a sidelong glance, but said nothing.

"Where will you live?"

John had shrugged. "Dunno."

She had grunted thoughtfully.

"I need some help on my land. If I buy this farm, you can stay on it and work for me. I need four days a week. How's that?"

To little Walter this seemed wonderful news: they would not have to leave. He could not understand the look of white anger that passed over his father's face.

"If I do that," John said slowly at last, "then I'd be a villein. I'm a free man now."

Mary did not seem interested.

"Can't help that. It's work anyway."

It was not uncommon for a free man without money to be forced to take a position giving work-rent to a landlord which made him technically a villein, and it was possible for a villein to become rich again and buy his freedom back. But after all his efforts, to be the serf of one of the hated Shockleys! He tasted his greatest bitterness.

"At least you stay on your farm," Mary said, not unkindly.

Walter remembered so well his father's sad nod. Even at his age, he knew it was a gesture of surrender, and, though he did not understand the reasons, he felt sorry for his father, and angry with the big woman who seemed to be bullying him.

"All right."

[489]

Mary smiled.

"That's settled then." She was turning to go, when she paused. She had noticed something on Cristina.

"Want to sell that gold chain?"

Mary thought she was doing the family a favour, but Walter remembered only how his mother's hand had reached up and grasped the chain, as though someone was trying to tear it from her. He did not know where it had come from.

"Maybe," Cristina had replied, dismally.

"Good," Mary said. "I like that chain."

It was the only ornament she ever bought in her life.

But what stuck in Walter's mind even more was what followed after Mary Shockley had gone. Never, during the long sad years that his father worked the Shockley land, never while he saw Cristina slowly turn into an old woman with arthritic hands, and never afterwards did the vision leave him. For it was to him, Walter, that his father had turned when Mary had gone; it was he who saw, to his astonishment, his father's calm and pleasant face suddenly contort into a look of savage hatred, and it was into his eyes that his father's, full of an age-old urgency and rage, had looked as he took him by the shoulders and exclaimed:

"We'll take this land back one day, and Shockley farm, and the mill, you understand? We'll kick him out. If I don't, you will. Don't ever forget."

He never did.

The trouble with Roger de Godefroi on the other hand, was that he overspent. The two fine estates old Jocelin had preserved for him were there to be enjoyed; nothing had given his grandfather greater joy than to see his heir cut such a fine figure at the joust: he had pleased him by being everything a young noble should be. It was natural that after Jocelin was gone, he should live in a manner befitting so fine a gentleman; he knew it was expected of him.

As a youth he had attended the king on his expeditions to Wales: the revenues from the estates allowed him to do so in style. He jousted. He could afford it. He entertained sumptuously at Avonsford; the estates almost supported this and could have recovered. He married: a lady from Cornwall. She had wonderful Celtic looks – rich brown hair and dazzling blue eyes, which were greatly admired – and a tiny dowry. He had chosen her because she was the most beautiful woman watching a tournament at which he had triumphed. He provided her with magnificent dresses from London and the knight of Avonsford and his lady were pronounced the most handsome couple in the region. The estates groaned. He built a fine walled garden and planted it with mulberry trees, nut trees, roses, vines and willows; it was only luck that he never found time to build the fine new hall he was always planning. And lastly, he made splendid benefactions to hospitals and religious orders: and this the estates could in no way support.

By these means, not suddenly but steadily over the years he extended his credit on every side.

And it was while he did so that the king's maltote tax came and the price he was paid for his wool dropped. It was from this cut in his income that he never recovered. He did nothing about it except, once, curse his steward.

By 1300, the situation was serious.

By 1305, it had become desperate.

He knew it. He was not a fool. But still he went on, for besides being a perfect model of chivalry, he was also spoilt, and inside him the small, insistent voice that sooner or later, as the centuries pass beggars almost every aristocrat, said: "If you do not keep up your state, people will scorn you."

For a man like Roger de Godefroi, there was only one way out of his difficulty.

He had two daughters now, and a baby son. The daughters would have to be married off, the son provided for, and as he admitted to himself: "I've my sword and nothing else to make my fortune."

There had been opportunities. The king had been forced to make several campaigns in Scotland against the rebels Wallace and Bruce; he should have gone, but there had always seemed to be too much to be done at Avonsford. Now he could delay no longer.

"I have to bring myself to the attention of the magnates, and the king," he told his wife. "It's now or never."

An opportunity came in 1305; for that year there was a great tournament at Sarum, in the lists between the old castle and the town of Wilton.

Retinues came from all over the country; the whole area was buzzing with armed men. The cathedral chapter with the Church's suspicion of tournaments, and already harassed by an unruly mayor and council who were trying to avoid paying the bishop their taxes, issued a furious order, with the king's authority, threatening excommunication on any of those attending who disturbed the peace of the city. It was a useless threat: the whole of Sarum was in a genial uproar. And Godefroi swore:

"This is my chance."

Of all the retinues attending the joust, none was more splendid than that of the knight of Avonsford. His grey charger was magnificent. He was attended by a squire and two pages. On his shield, his surcoat and all his accoutrements shone the noble device of the white swan on the red ground.

"If I show my skill," he explained to his wife, "the king will hear of it. On the next campaign it could mean a command – and that could be valuable."

He had planned for the joust meticulously. His weapons were splendid; he had obtained the latest armour – a light chain mail, with extra protection provided by solid plates of steel on the outer arm, legs and feet. It was the most sophisticated equipment available and he had paid dearly for it – with borrowed money. But it was a calculated gamble, for he knew that few knights were better prepared for war.

And what a magnificent affair it had been. Roger's spirits always rose when he saw the dazzling array of tents, flags and the brightly dressed crowds that made these pageants such a cheerful spectacle; and as he walked his horse along the edge of the lists, and looked at the other knightly competitors, he experienced that strange but familiar sense of timelessness that these festivals always seemed to have. "Surely," he thought, "there is nothing better in this world than to be a knight."

But that day, for the first time, he also experienced another sensation: it was quite new to him, and it was uncomfortable.

Before the proper tournament began, there was often a burlesque of some kind; on this occasion it was two women tumblers, dressed as knights, who entered the lists on horses and cavorted around grotesquely, swearing oaths in a mixture of broken French and English of the most ribald kind. The crowd applauded wildly. Even the priests of whom many, despite the bishop's strictures, were to be seen in the crowd, rocked with laughter. Pieces of the women's armour fell off; one of them wore a cooking pot on her head at which the children threw things as she whirled past, and both shook their weapons with indecent gestures while the people roared their approval. To complete this good-natured farce, the heralds solemnly sounded their trumpets and the two women with exaggerated pomp took their positions at each end of the lists. Bets were placed. Several women threw their gloves to be worn as gages, and then the women charged. Once, twice, three times they rode at each other down the lists, waving their lances in a ludicrous parody of the knightly contests until one of them was finally knocked off her horse, while the crowd, from magnate to churl, hooted with delight and derision.

Godefroi watched in silence. To his surprise, the spectacle no longer amused him. His brow darkened. Suddenly, without wanting to, he remembered his terrible debts. For all the brave show he was making, nothing could take them away. And then, as he sat on his magnificent grey charger, with weapons and armour he could not pay for, about to fight to keep his estates, he was afflicted with a terrible sense of emptiness. A wave of desolation seemed to cover him. He shook his head in surprise at the awful thought that had just thrust itself so unpleasantly upon him. Was even his own jousting perhaps, like the vulgar display of these two women, nothing more than an elaborate, a fantastic charade? His armour, his shield with the white swan gleaming upon it; was all this really, as the church's preachers often warned, mere vanity? He did not know. He tried to put the ugly thought from him. But it would not go away.

Roger triumphed at the joust that day. He was noticed and admired and as he had hoped, several magnates approached him and urged:

"Come to the next great meeting, Godefroi, when the king is there. It will be to your advantage."

The chance had come the very next year. For in May 1306, King Edward I summoned his nobles to witness the knighting of his dissolute son at

Westminster. It was an event of huge significance and one of the last acts of his reign. The king was sick and old and, for better or worse, his son Edward would soon succeed him. It was an occasion full of pomp and feudal ceremony. The prince performed his vigil in Westminster Abbey and was knighted the next day. Then he in turn knighted some three hundred young noblemen at the high altar, and after this there was a huge feast.

The Feast of Swans – King Edward's last great ceremony – was remembered for long afterwards. Every symbol of Arthurian chivalry was worked into the proceedings. Men said it was as if the Round Table had been reborn. This was no idle show. Edward, with deliberate calculation, was determined to spare no effort to impress upon his nobles the feudal duties they owed his son, by appealing to their chivalry. His calculation was, as always, sound and Godefroi, as he watched the magnificent feast from one of the lower tables, felt his heart expand with joy and loyal emotion.

By an astounding chance the king had chosen as the theme for the feast, the image of two swans: no doubt Godefroi assumed, to symbolise himself and his son. There were splendid hangings representing swans around the walls: and at the end of each table was a chair with a high back carved in the same shape. For King Edward knew very well that though his nobles might swear loyalty to a man upon one day, it would be the symbol that they remembered in later times and which might keep them steadfast.

But the high point came when two swans were brought in and placed upon the table before the king. Old Edward, though he had been brought to Westminster on a litter, rose to his feet, squared his broad shoulders as he had used to do when he was young, and swore before God and the swans that he would go to Scotland yet again to crush the rebels, and after that, turn on the infidels in the Holy Land. It was a rousing speech, a heroic vow worthy of the chivalrous king, and the whole hall rang with applause.

Soon after this Godefroi's moment arrived. Two magnates, walking together up the table to pay their respects to the king, beckoned to him to join them. His heart beating excitedly, he walked beside them. Surely it must bring good luck that the king had chosen the device on his own coat of arms as the theme for such a feast. He was wearing it now, as a badge upon his tunic. He pushed his chest out, so that the king could not fail to see it.

Even as an old man, Edward I was impressive. Though his large form was slumped in his chair, Roger noticed at once the great mane of snow white hair, and the famous drooping eyelid. But his handsome, leonine face was terribly sunken and it was obvious that he was ravaged with pain. Nonetheless, he gave a slow, but courteous nod to the two magnates.

"This is Roger de Godefroi, Your Majesty," one of them said pleasantly. "He distinguished himself at the Sarum tournament last year."

While he spoke, Roger saw that the king's eyes were fixed on his badge; but it was impossible to tell what he was thinking.

For a moment Edward was silent. Then, in little more than a whisper he said:

"So I heard."

His eyes had not left the badge.

"His own coat of arms is a swan, sire. A coincidence," the other said hopefully.

Edward did not reply; nor did his eyes move.

"He is the grandson of Jocelin de Godefroi, whom Your Majesty will remember," the first continued, "and he is anxious to serve you in Scotland."

There was silence. In the back of his mind, Edward remembered a scene. It had been at the time of the negotiations with the Scottish commissioners, before the confounded Maid of Norway died and caused him all this trouble. The details came back to him now. There had been doubt about the family's loyalty: a hint of duplicity. Perhaps it had all been untrue, but he had no time to take chances.

For a second the great eyes flashed into Godefroi's face. They were not unkind, but they were tired.

"You come rather late, monsieur," he said calmly. "I have all the men I need."

Roger bowed. The king's eyes moved on, to rest elsewhere. The interview was over. As were Godefroi's hopes.

A year later, Edward I was dead, and the ignominious reign of his son began. The times had been depressing. Edward II was as unfit to rule as his father had been outstanding. He infuriated the magnates by ignoring them in favour of his favourites. He was thought to be a homosexual.

By 1309, the king's favourite, Piers Gaveston had been banished the kingdom, the Bishop of Salisbury being one of those who had insisted upon his departure. In that year, also, at Sarum, the river Avon had flooded its banks, run across the close, and burst through the cathedral's great west doors, eddying around the stone tombs in the nave.

But all these national and local disasters meant nothing to Roger.

For by the end of the year he had sold the second estate.

He was not completely ruined. He managed to retain the fulling mill, and the original estate at Avonsford with its modest manor house was still intact. But the fact remained, half his inheritance was gone and the days of splendid living were over.

There was nothing he could do. He managed the Avonsford estate as best he could, but his heart was never in it. Steady application was needed; he did not know how to apply himself steadily. In a fit of enthusiasm, he restored the old miz-maze above the valley and would spend long hours up there alone. But he was neither praying nor reading, and he himself would have had difficulty in saying how he had passed the time.

To his son Gilbert, as the boy grew up, he gave only one piece of advice:

"Go to the wars if you can. If you do well, perhaps you can get back the estate I lost."

He hoped the boy would forgive him. But he was not sure that he would. And Gilbert would gaze at his father, and draw his own conclusions.

High on the pinnacle, like a series of eagle's nests, the little scaffolding had hung round the top of the spire.

For the last fifty feet of the slender spire, as it tapered to its final, miraculous point, it had been necessary to reverse the previous method and construct the scaffolding around the outside of the cone. It was held there by horizontal supports which passed through the shell of the masonry.

And now the work was done, the scaffolding dismantled, retreating from the dizzying height where the cone was so thin that it was hard to imagine it sustaining even a man and a bucket. As it was withdrawn, the holes through which the supports had passed were filled with stone plugs with iron handles so that they could be opened and used again for future repairs.

Crowning the spire was the capstone – a series of stones in fact, laid in four courses and welded together with cramps of iron. And over the capstone was set the great iron cross.

The cross of Salisbury Cathedral was not only a necessary ornament. A rod from its centre passed directly through the capstone, like a root, and down to the wooden framework inside the spire, to which it was connected with a tightening mechanism. By this means the ingenious masons ensured that the interior stress of the cone could be adjusted.

One other item had been needed: and though it was not a structural feature, there was no question that it was as important to the safety of the building as anything the clever builders conceived. Inside the capstone they had reverently placed a small circular casket lined with lead which contained a little piece of cloth. It was a fragment of the Blessed Virgin's robe.

When this was done, the capstone sealed, and the great cross tightened to the framework, almost a century after it had been begun the cathedral church of Our Lady, the Blessed Virgin Mary at Sarum was at last complete.

It was soon after this completion, on a darkening afternoon in late December, that Edward Mason found himself in the nave of the great cathedral – and staring at the old man in disbelief.

"Impossible."

But Osmund was obdurate, and nothing Edward could say would make him listen to reason.

For on the eve of Holy Innocents Day, also called Childermas – that is, on December 27 – in the year of Our Lord 1310, Osmund the Mason in the eightieth year of his life, had fallen into the last and greatest of all the seven deadly sins.

Worse. He seemed to have decided to destroy himself.

[495]

Childermas eve was an important day in the year: for on that day, in Sarum, a curious and delightful event took place: the festival of the boy bishop.

The nave of the great church was crowded. The ceremony was about to begin. They had come from all over Sarum to witness it. The merchant Shockleys had come; Mary Shockley, now grey-haired, had stomped in from the farm to join them. From Avonsford, Roger de Godefroi had brought his son Gilbert, and although neither John nor Cristina had chosen to come, young Walter Wilson had even deserted his eel traps in the river to slouch across the fields that afternoon to see the fun.

It was an extraordinary, and good-humoured business, begun some time in the century before. On this day, in the best tradition of topsy-turveydom, the boy choristers were allowed to take over the cathedral and the priests take second place. Not only this: the boys had elected their own boy bishop who would rule the cathedral for the festival.

Despite the completion of its lovely spire, the cathedral and its priests had not always been popular with the people of Sarum of late. There had been, first, a spirited dispute between the mayor and the bishop over the bishop's feudal right to tax the town. The bishop had won. Then there were always the vicars' choral – a mass of junior and penniless fellows ranging from former choirboys who rang the bells to ordained young men without benefices – who were generally a rowdy nuisance and whom the townspeople complained about. And then there had been, despite Bishop Simon of Ghent's best efforts, a general decline in standards in the close. It was partly caused by the number of its canons who were absentee Italians, granted these rich benefices by the pope; but whatever the reason the once scholarly precincts, despite the extraordinary cathedral in their centre, were regarded with less respect than they had been before.

Today however, it seemed that all these grudges were forgotten as the people came to witness the charming ceremony.

"Perhaps," Edward thought as the congregation hushed, "the old man will forget this madness." He could only hope so.

They had been allowed a good place by the crowd, out of reverence for Osmund – for it was generally believed, and could have been true, that he was the oldest man in Sarum.

The ceremony began with the choristers solemnly dressed in copes and holding lighted tapers, leading the boy bishop to the altar of the Blessed Trinity and All Saints. There the lesson for Innocents Day, from the Book of Revelation was recited, before the choirboys sang the verses:

Sedentem in supernae

The music echoed softly through the great church.

As Osmund listened, he smiled contentedly. He was so very old. His big, round head was completely bald, except for the few fine wisps of white hair just behind his ears. The limbs of his once squat body were now so thin they seemed almost reduced to the bone. Yet he was still sprightly and he had all his faculties; and when he took Edward's arm to walk, he did so because it pleased him and not because he really needed to.

He had come to the cathedral with his family that afternoon to admire the newly completed spire and make his annual tour of the building before the boy bishop's service. He enjoyed doing this: pointing out a statue here, a capital there, even a distant boss in the vaulting, describing each in intricate detail to his patient son and grandchildren, and telling them the name of some long dead mason who had carved it. For only he could remember their names now, and after him, these anonymous artists would be forgotten. This, he knew, was as it should be.

"A mason does not need a name," he used to say. "He lives on in the stone."

The boy bishop was fuming the altar – swinging the heavy silver censer to and fro vigorously and sending up clouds of white smoke. The rich scent of the incense wafted towards Osmund and he sniffed it with pleasure. The last light of the December afternoon was fading from the coloured windows.

It had only been after a particularly thorough inspection of the nave and choir an hour before that the indefatigable old man had led his family into the cloisters. From there they had entered the chapter house.

And it was in the chapter house that he had committed his sin.

Now the choristers were making their procession through the church. The boy bishop, a fair-haired lad with a mischievous face, was striding boldly up to the great bishop's throne. In his hand he held the bishop's staff with its elaborate, curling handle. It was twice his height, which added to the comic aspect of the ceremony. He turned and, in plain chant, blessed the people. Despite his mischievous face, Osmund noticed he had a sweet voice. Then he sat on the throne and the choir began to chant the lovely evening service, the compline.

Sometimes on these days, the boy bishop would preach a sermon, usually admonishing the choirboys, singly and by name, for their sins while the congregation tried not to laugh. And then, when the service was over, he and all his fellow choristers would be given a prodigious feast by the canons. For this one day in the year, they too would be allowed to gorge themselves on veal, mutton, duck, sausage, woodcocks, plovers – all the rich and varied foods with which the five valleys and the high ground supplied the fortunate canons of Sarum.

The boys were looking forward to their feast: the congregation was in good humour. But Osmund's thoughts had returned to the chapter house.

He had not entered the place for several months. The dull afternoon light had been falling softly from the eight huge windows on to the walls. Silently he had stood, just apart from the others, and slowly turning he had let his eyes travel round the spaces between the arches of the canon's tall seats.

There they were: the sixty low reliefs – from the Creation to Moses receiving the Law: his sculptures. And as he gazed at them, he knew they were perfect.

Whatever his faults, he had been a humble man. He had known satisfaction in his work; he had known delight when he caught the spirit

[497]

of some animal or man he had wanted to depict; he had known pleasure when his work was praised, and a modest sense of self-respect when he was certain that a piece was well-executed.

But now the great cathedral was completed. He knew its wonders, every stone.

And as he stared at his work, done so long ago, he experienced for the first time in his life the fierce, overwhelming exultation that, had old Canon Portehors still been alive, the priest would have told him at once, with a terrible admonition, was the greatest of all the seven deadly sins.

For suddenly, overcome with emotion, the old man had grabbed his son by the arm, and cried:

"I did those. I carved them all. And there's nothing better in the cathedral. Nothing better in all England."

"They are excellent," Edward agreed quietly.

"Excellent?" He laughed, so loudly that it echoed round the stillness of the cloisters outside. "Excellent? There's no mason living," he shouted, "there's been none at Sarum since the cathedral was started who could do what I have done." He walked over to the little scene of Adam and Eve, stood on the canon's seat beside it and ran his hand over the carving. Then, turning to his family in triumph he reminded them:

"I made this. I made it all."

And so at last, in his eightieth year, Osmund the Mason fell easily into the most deadly sin of pride.

As they returned through the cloisters, the old man seemed flushed with exultation. He seemed to forget his age as he almost skipped along. And when they entered the shadowy nave again, his keen eyes could still pick out in the half light a dozen reminders of his craftsmanship. The tomb of Bishop Gyles, a boss here, a capital there, even the stern face of Canon Portehors peeping down from the vaulting far above. The whole cathedral suddenly seemed to belong to him. What fools those masons had been, he remembered savagely, who had sent him ignominiously down from the tower. What were they? Fools and knaves, he almost shouted aloud: knaves like the worthless Bartholomew.

And in this mood of elation, just before the choir entered, he had turned to his horrified son and announced:

"Tomorrow morning we shall visit the tower," and then added: "And I shall climb the spire."

It was an unusual morning for December – both warm and clear.

The two men stood at the parapet: the old man eager and excited, the younger somewhat anxious and ill at ease.

It had been useless to argue with Osmund.

"If I prevent him going to the tower today," Edward had told his wife, "he'll only find some way of sneaking off another day. It's better if I go and keep an eye on him."

"He'll never get up the stairs anyway," she had remarked.

Edward was less sanguine. And now he had been astonished by the way his ancient father had mounted them: slowly, to be sure, but

[498]

steadily, stopping only at the clerestory level and once again at the first of the two landings in the great tower.

"The old man's like an ant," he muttered. "He just won't be beaten." And tiresome as the business was, he could not help admiring the old fellow's incredible persistence.

As for Osmund, as he went up the familiar spiral staircase in the tower, he never remembered feeling better in his long life. Perhaps it was because he felt like a part of the building itself that the climb seemed easy; perhaps because his mind was fixed on the objective ahead. When at last he came out into the open air at the top of the tower his head was singing and he had to steady himself for a moment; but soon his face relaxed and he began to walk slowly round the parapet, beneath the huge sloping walls of the octagonal base of the spire.

He seemed to have forgotten his insane idea of the day before. Indeed, to Edward's relief, he scarcely glanced at the spire. He seemed to have forgotten Edward too as he paced about, staring out at the view, examining the masonry and muttering to himself. He went round several times. Twice, on the northern side, he leaned out and inspected a tiny stone figure, buried in a niche, with a curious, primitive little woman's face that stared out over the town. It seemed to give him a special satisfaction, though Edward could not imagine why.

After a time, since Osmund appeared to be circulating the place indefinitely, Edward sat on the parapet to let him go about his business. The morning sun was surprisingly warm.

And it was only after several minutes on one of Osmund's slow circuits that Edward realised he had disappeared. Assuming the old man must have started to descend, he inspected the four staircases, but found his father on none of them. Only then did he run round the base of the great octagonal spire and look up.

The iron rings were set a little further apart than Osmund would have liked. They stretched in a straight, but dizzying line from the base to the cross nearly two hundred feet above. But by treating each ring as a small individual obstacle, he was able to mount slowly, resting his feet on one ring and pulling his body up to the next with both his small hands together clutching one of the rings above. Gently, calmly, he mounted the steep, sheer face of the cone, pausing frequently. Twenty feet, thirty feet: he was already thirty feet up when Edward saw him.

Edward gazed up at his father. What should he do? His first thought was to hurry up the daunting spire after him; but then he considered – if the old man were to slip, could he really hope to catch him?

Then he shrugged. If his father was determined, in his eightieth year, to break his neck in this spectacular way, why should he stop him? With a rueful grin he watched the determined little figure make his solitary way towards his objective. His instinct told him that, despite his age, the mason would not fall. He hoped his instinct was right.

"He'll go up and come down again just like he said," he said aloud, to reassure himself. And if the old man succeeded, it would be something to tell his grandchildren about. Behind him, the great bells in the belfry sounded the hour. It was ten o'clock.

How silent the air was. The soaring octagon of the spire rose majestically, straight at the blue sky, in its separate region above the world to which it was obviously so serenely indifferent: indifferent to the Shockleys and their mill, to Godefroi in his manor, to the sheep on the high ground that had paid for its very stones; it was indifferent to the market, the close, to even the bishop himself; to drought and flood below, seed time and harvest; the spire was above these things.

Osmund took his time. He rested when he wanted. And at last, a little before the bells sounded the half hour, he came to the dizzy point where he could stretch his little arms right round the spire, as he touched the silent capstone in the sky. He was aware that, far below, people in the close were staring up. There was now a faint, just discernible breeze in his face coming from the west.

He had done it. The cathedral, and all that was in it, was his.

His long-sighted eyes were an advantage. Below, he could see every detail of the houses in the close. He could see the market place. Behind the city, on the ancient hill, he could make out individual figures moving about on the castle walls. On the rolling ridges, everywhere, he could see the tiny white dots of the sheep. Eight miles away, directly in line with the old castle hill, he could even make out the broken circle of grey sarsens at Stonehenge. And beyond that, ridge after ridge, extending northwards like a sea.

And as he gazed over Sarum, so high in the sky, even the old mason's newfound sin of pride dissolved in the air, lost at the wonder of the place.

After a little time, he came down.

The Death

1348

ON A WARM August morning, a little after dawn, the small ship had passed the low headland and come slowly through the sheltered harbour waters to tie up beside the quay at Christchurch. The ship contained a cargo of wine, from the English province of Gascony in south west France. The sailors, eight bluff, healthy fellows came briskly down the gangplank and were welcomed by the men on the waterfront. Soon afterwards, they began to unload.

They did not know about their passenger and his small companion.

He arrived alone – except for his companion. His coat was black. He had come in a crate, into which, at the French dock, he had accidentally strayed; now, as soon as it had been deposited on the quay, he left it immediately. For he did not care for the company of men. A small, solitary figure, he moved unnoticed along the edge of the waterfront looking for a convenient place to hide; seeing none, he made his way, pausing from time to time, up the little lane that led past the edge of the priory churchyard and soon afterwards he came to a row of small gabled houses, huddled together. He could tell that they were already occupied, and since strangers in his experience were seldom welcome, he and his small companion moved on, keeping discreetly to the side of the lane so as not to excite attention. Soon he came to a cobbled street.

He could not decide whether he was hungry or not, after the long voyage. There were not many people about, but a cart rumbled by on its way towards the quay and splashed him with mud, which he did not mind. Fifty yards further he saw that there was a stream on his right; and immediately beside it was a hump of ground on which rose the thick, dark walls of the little castle of Twyneham with its stout tower that faced the priory. Amongst its stones, he guessed, there would be passages, litter, scraps of food and sewers leading down to the stream. He could smell the faint tang that always arose from such an area, welcome to a scavenger like himself. Gratefully he made towards it, for he was getting tired.

It was as he reached the castle wall that he discovered his mistake. Three grey-coated guardians of the place, all male, stood facing him, each standing just behind the shoulder of the next. He made a tentative signal that he had come in peace; but first the front one, then the other two, bared their teeth at him. They began to advance, menacingly. He did not hesitate, but scuttled away to the edge of the stream, taking his companion with him. There he turned, saw them still watching him, and despondently went back to the street.

He felt unwell. He had experienced a brief shivering fit just before he had left the boat; now he found that his head was pounding. He made his way along the lane out of the little town, crossing a stone bridge. Through a hole in the side, he could see the river Avon moving below at a steady pace, its long green river weeds swaying from side to side and for some reason this made him giddy.

On the other side of the bridge, fifty yards along the bank, was a small mill; but this was not what he wanted, for he did not care for the company of humans. He cast about for something else, somewhere to rest. He had travelled nearly five hundred yards from the boat and he felt very tired. Then, close by, he saw a pile of rubbish by the water's edge. He entered it.

An hour later his breath was coming in gasps. When he tried to rise, he had difficulty, but in his confused state he felt the need to do so and forgetting that the rubbish heap was, at least, a shelter, he staggered out onto the river bank. No one noticed him. His companion came with him.

Slowly now, and with pain, he started to drag himself forward, hardly knowing what he was about, but determined: I must find a quiet place, a shelter where I can be alone, he thought. It took him fifteen minutes of spasmodic movement to reach the wooden walls of the flour mill, and although it was bound to be occupied, he did not care: finding a hole, he crawled into a store room. He halted beside a sack of flour.

And now something terrible began to happen to him. As he shook with fever, he was vaguely conscious that he was starting to bleed. He could feel the blood in his mouth: it seemed to be coming from his gums. Strange and terrible sensations came from his body too: his breath came in gurgles. There was fluid of some kind in his lungs; could this, too, be blood?

Half an hour later, he was dead. His companion stayed with him for a little while.

When the house rat came past the corpse of the strange black sewer rat, which had no business to be there, he saw that it was surrounded by a pool of blood. He sniffed the corpse cautiously, uncertain what to make of it: and it was at this point that the flea, the companion which had been living on the body of the black rat for a week, left the corpse and transferred itself to the house rat. Soon afterwards the house rat and the flea moved on to another part of the building.

It was the following morning that the flea made an unusual move. It did so because it was ravenously hungry. For some reason, when it fed on the house rat, its hunger was not satisfied. And so, when a cart containing a man and a ten-year-old boy stopped at the mill and the boy wandered by some sacks of flour where the house rat was scavenging, the flea which normally did not feed on humans, left the rat to try the boy. It was no good. A few minutes later the flea hopped back to the rat.

The reason for this failure on the part of the flea was that the blood of the black rat which it had been secreting in its stomach had developed a new and hideous life of its own, breeding bacteria that had already sealed off the entrance to the flea's stomach so that it could not draw in any fresh blood. When the flea tried to ingest blood from the boy, it was unable to do so, and it spat the blood, together with bacteria from the entrance to its stomach, back into the boy's skin before leaving him.

The boy's name was Peter Wilson.

It is a tiny life-form, a small collection of cells. Under a powerful microscope, the little bacterium has a shape that resembles nothing so much as a safety pin.

It is asexual: like other bacteria, it replicates itself by splitting in two.

The bacteria form colonies, residing in the bloodstreams of small rodents, from which fact medicine has allotted them the name *yersinia pestis*, and these live for the most part quietly and in peace. They have done so – and still do today – for who knows how many centuries, in obscure regions in places round the globe from the Crimea, to India, and the United States of America.

Normally the *yersinia pestis* bacteria are contained by antibodies and do not overwhelm the other cells in the blood of their hosts and this stable condition, which may last indefinitely, is called the chronic condition of the disease.

Why is it then that at isolated periods, something extraordinary occurs? Why, after remaining in this peaceable state for perhaps a hundred years, should the little cells suddenly spring into hyperactivity, replicating themselves with an urgency that develops into a kind of seething rage, a rage that turns into an explosion? What is the alteration in the environment, the unexpected catalyst that begins the process? Various explanations are offered by science, but no definite answer is known.

Whatever its first cause, once the sudden expansion begins, it is almost unstoppable. Nothing but a barrier of the highest mountains, a polar ice-cap, or an impassable sea, seems to bring it to a halt.

Or almost nothing. Modern science has found preventative treatments which were effectively applied when the disease began to break out in the United States of America in the 1970s so that only a few lives were lost. But the third pandemic of the plague, which killed some ten million in India at the turn of the century, is still continuing, although contained, to this day.

In the 1340s, such an explosion occurred.

It began in central Asia. From there it spread outwards – eastwards to China, southwards to India, and southwest along the old trading routes to Asia Minor and Turkey. By December 1347, probably carried by ship, it simultaneously appeared in Constantinople and the borders of Greece, Genoa in north west Italy and Marseilles in southern France. Then it swept, like a madness, through the whole of western Europe. No one had seen such a thing before.

The Black Death is a single form of bacterium which is transmitted mainly in two ways, called the bubonic and the pneumonic plagues.

The bubonic plague is usually carried from host to host by fleas. No less than seventy-two possible host animals have been identified, from rabbits, hares and squirrels, dogs and cats, to – the best known – rats. The different forms of infected animal population are then grouped into two, so that we speak of two varieties of the disease: the sylvatic form to be found amongst non-domestic rodents like squirrels, less likely to have intimate contact with humans – this is the form found in the United States today – and the murine form, usually transmitted through rats, and therefore likely to reach the human population.

With the pneumonic plague, the same bacteria are transmitted from one infected human to another, by tiny droplets in the breath.

The Black Death travelled round Europe in a huge clockwise curve, from Italy round the west and ending in Scandinavia and the Baltic.

That it struck so particularly virulently and spread so completely may have been due to several causes. The population of Europe in the previous century had greatly increased, to a level it was not to reach again until the eighteenth century. A series of bad harvests may have created famines during the first half of the fourteenth century and lowered the resistance of some of the population. It is also thought that the rat population, especially the black household rat, had increased substantially in the thirteenth century – indeed there may have been few if any rats on the island of Britain before that time. All these circumstances, however, are only suggestions – proof is lacking. Indeed, only one definitive statement about the circumstances favouring the reception of the plague emerges from history. It came from the Medical Faculty of the University of Paris, in the year 1348.

In the year of Our Lord 1345, on March 20, there was a conjunction of the planets Saturn, Jupiter and Mars in the House of Aquarius.

The conjunction of Saturn and Jupiter portends death and disaster.

The conjunction of Mars and Jupiter portends pestilence in the air.

For Jupiter is warm and humid and draws up evil vapours from earth and water; and Mars is hot and dry, and kindles the evil into an infective fire.

We must therefore expect a terrible calamity.

In the first months of 1348 the plague struck Venice and Pisa. By March it had reached the crowded city of Florence where the people, labelled thirty years earlier by their exiled poet Dante as wolves, died more like flies. Southern France was already in its grip. By June it had reached west to central Spain and taken in almost all France to north of Paris. Some time afterwards it reached the shores of England.

When the flea bit Peter Wilson, and the bacteria entered his blood they travelled with him up the river Avon. Though they had travelled over seven thousand miles, they were still teeming with fury.

Walter Wilson and his youngest son Peter arrived back at Sarum that night, and went straight to the Shockley farm.

It was several years since Mary Shockley had died and the farm had passed to her nephew William, who spent most of his time in the city. Of the five children of John Wilson, only Walter remained on the farm; though he had been well treated, both he and his family continued to hate the Shockleys because they were their masters.

Peter Wilson was glad to get home. Neither he nor his family thought about the plague during the next forty-eight hours.

Nobody at Sarum did.

The one exception was Gilbert de Godefroi.

The strange behaviour of Gilbert de Godefroi, which for several days made people say that the knight had turned eccentric was caused by a letter he received on the day of Peter Wilson's return. It came from a cloth merchant, newly arrived in London from the continent.

Before this, Godefroi had heard vague rumours of a plague in the south of France; but he had given them no particular thought. The letter was more explicit:

> This terrible plague is raging in Paris already. Even as I travelled north, it seemed to me that it was following hard upon my heels. No one knows what to do. They say that it is spread in the air and through the breath of those who carry it. Some believe they can save themselves by holding herbs before their noses. In the south, those who can have been fleeing from the pestilential cities where the disease seems to breed. Soon, I promise you, it must cross to England. Get herbs, avoid the city; clean your house and do not leave it. And set your affairs in order.

It was an ominous ending.

The merchant was a man he respected. As soon as he received this letter, therefore, Godefroi had a long discussion with his wife; then he swung into action. The courtyard of the manor house was cleaned out and washed down; fresh rushes were laid on the floor of the old hall; a manure heap that was situated near the buildings was completely removed in carts to a point half a mile away. Quantities of supplies were brought into the cool store rooms, and baskets of fresh herbs taken to the big stone kitchen or placed in the hall and solar. If the plague came, the manor house could virtually seal itself off from the outside world.

"It's the foul air from the city and the breath of the townspeople which carries this plague," Gilbert announced to his puzzled servants. He also inspected the village and ordered his tenants and villeins to take similar precautions, even burning down one small house which had been used as a piggery and from which he decided evil vapours might be arising. Then he ordered the vicar to say extra masses to ask for God's deliverance for the villagers. The people of Avonsford did as they were told, but they were baffled. What was this plague the lord of the manor spoke about? No one else was making such preparations. But Godefroi was resolute. He had no idea whether these precautions would be effective, but he could think of no others. It was not only his duty as lord of the manor to take care of his people. He was determined that if possible, nothing of his estate should be lost.

"At all costs," he said to his wife, "I'll preserve what we still have at Avonsford."

It was a phrase she knew well. Since his father's careless loss of the family's second estate when he was a boy, Gilbert had been obsessed with preserving what was left. The memory of Roger's spendthrift ways remained with him like a nightmare and made him excessively cautious in everything that he did. Once as a youth, with Roger's encouragement, he had left Avonsford to seek his fortune: that had been in 1314 when he had gone as a squire on the king's disastrous campaign in the north. It had been a fiasco: the campaign had ended in the crushing defeat of the English by the Scots of Bannockburn – a defeat that effectively ended hopes of a unified kingdom of England and Scotland for centuries; and he had returned discouraged and much the poorer. As a young man, he had little stomach for public affairs, for the court of Edward II disgusted him. His disgust was justified. First there had been the bisexual king's favourites Gaveston and Despenser, and their years of misrule. Then, even more shocking, the queen had left and become the open lover of the great Lord Mortimer. It was a disastrous reign and when Parliament had finally deposed the king, Godefroi had felt a sense of relief. Soon afterwards his enemies had murdered Edward horribly in Berkeley Tower; he had been shocked, but not surprised.

Since then, times had been better. The new king, Edward III, soon showed himself to be a wise and competent governor. Indeed, when the king gave his trusted friend Montagu the vacant earldom of Salisbury ten years before, Godefroi had a chance of advancement: for the new earl, who now became Gilbert's feudal overlord, kept a large retinue and a court of his own. But once again, Gilbert was cautious; instead of coming forward, he remained quietly and safely at Avonsford. "One's always either in or out of favour at a court," he told his wife. "Why take the risk?"

He had not gone to the French wars either. And this had probably been a mistake.

The old disputes with the French had smouldered on since Edward's grandfather's time and had been complicated because now, through his mother, the English king had acquired a claim to the French throne. At first young Edward had made the same mistake as his ancestor Henry III and tried to build up a great European alliance; as usual it had been unsuccessful, ruinously expensive and almost started a new barons' revolt. But young Edward, unlike his great-grandfather, was flexible. Soon, he hit on a better way: small armies from England, without expensive and untrustworthy allies and comfortably paid for by English wool, had made straight for France. Their strength lay in the Welsh and English archers with their longbows, and also in the fact that the well-trained knights who accompanied them were not too proud, when it was needed, to dismount and fight side by side with ordinary men. In a series of short, daring campaigns they humiliated the proud but disorganised feudal cavalry of France. At Crécy, only two years before, Edward and his gallant son the Black Prince had routed the French king. The next year, the port of Calais had been taken. And when the Scots had played their usual trick and raided the north of England when they thought the English were busy with France, they were beaten and their King David captured. For the first time in many generations, war was popular in England. It was profitable, there was plunder, and there were French knights to ransom.

Gilbert regretted that he had not fought at Crécy. The profits could have been used at Avonsford. For his mind seldom left the manor now.

He made some modest improvements: he installed a bathroom with a large wooden tub which the maidservant filled with hot water once a week; he rebuilt the kitchen with a stone vaulted ceiling and two huge fires set in the walls. But though some of the richer landowners were building fine stone halls on the ground level of their houses, he stuck conservatively to the old Norman hall on the upper floor with its narrow windows. "It did for my grandfather," he stated with finality.

The estate, too, was cautiously run. On the demesne land that he cultivated for himself, he had sharply reduced his activities from those of his father's day; in order to ensure the maximum yield from the minimum investment, he now raised crops only on the best land.

Indeed, when he compared the estate accounts of today with those of two decades before he was surprised at the change himself. They were as follows:

Acres of lord's demesne

	Wheat	Bere	Barley	Peas	Vetch	Drage	Oats	Total
1328	66	31	64	10	15	10	50	246
1348	48		53		10	10	33	154

The flocks of sheep were smaller, too, than in his father's and grandfather's time and he withdrew them from the poorer pastures on the high ground. But their wool was of a higher grade. Not only the acreage under cultivation had been reduced: he now needed fewer labourers and so more of his villeins paid him money commutations instead of service, increasing his modest profits further. Other men with larger operations might make a killing in good years, but careful Gilbert was never in trouble.

If sometimes his wife admitted to herself that her husband was a little too cautious, if sometimes she secretly wished that by bolder action he had built more of a reputation, she quickly reminded herself that his unadventurous life had all been for her and the boy; and she was contented. So was Godefroi.

By the afternoon of the second day as he sat down in his hall for the main meal, Gilbert was satisfied that he had done all he could for the manor and the village. But the most important decision of all had still not been taken, and so it was now, when the great salt cellar and the *nef* containing the spices were set upon the table, that he turned to his wife and asked:

"What about our son? What should we do?"

She looked at her cautious husband fondly.

Although Rose, daughter of the Winchester knight Tancred de Whiteheath had been chosen for Gilbert by his father, and had brought only a modest dowry, their marriage had been an unqualified success. "The only good bargain my father ever made," Gilbert would say contentedly. With her long pale face and her tall, willowy figure she was known at Sarum simply as the lady of Avonsford. But her most striking feature was her hair. When they married, it had been dark, but when she was thirty, it suddenly turned, not grey but snowy white, and the effect was, surprisingly, to make her look even more beautiful: "The lady of Avonsford is lovely; she is white like a swan," the villagers used to say.

The knight of Avonsford and his wife had been in love for twenty years. Of their three children, two had died in infancy, one of them a girl; Rose wished she had been able to give her husband more. "I should like a daughter. She would be like you," he had often told her, and she had loved him for this simple compliment. But one child had survived, Thomas, and he was their greatest joy.

Indeed this was the problem. Like many Englishmen of his class, Godefroi had sent his son to receive part of his education at the castle of another lord. The boy was fifteen now, a page; in due course he would become a squire and then, perhaps a knight. To teach him his knightly duties and the manners of a gentleman, Gilbert had chosen his own brother-in-law, Ranulf de Whiteheath – a sensible choice, not only because he was the boy's uncle, but also because the Whiteheath establishment was considerably larger and more splendid than Avonsford. He had even heard that Ranulf used silver forks – a most unusual sophistication when most men even of his class were content with knives alone.

"You'll see how things should be done," he told Thomas; "and one day at Avonsford, if we find you a rich wife, you'll be able to live as a noble really should."

With this new threat of the plague, though, he was not sure what to do. Should he summon the boy home, or leave him at Whiteheath? He hated not to have Thomas at his side at such a time, but which was the safer place?

This was the difficult question he and Rose debated during their meal.

It was the normal custom at Avonsford for a musician to play while the lord of the manor supped, and then for the vicar of the little church, who in the absence of any other priest acted as a private chaplain to Godefroi as well, to read to the lord afterwards. Today however, Gilbert had dispensed with the musician, a peasant from the village who played the bagpipes atrociously.

At the end of the meal, they were still uncertain what to do. Perhaps, after all, this plague the merchant spoke of would not come.

It was now that Godefroi saw the priest enter and, not wishing to disappoint him, nodded curtly for him to begin. Perhaps his recital would help him to decide.

He was a balding young man in his twenties with gap teeth and a high-pitched voice; but he read clearly. Now he stood respectfully before the table and pulling out a little book that Godefroi had lent him announced: "The tale of Sir Orfeo."

There was no poem that Gilbert loved more than this popular ballad. In this recent courtly version, the legendary Orpheus had become an Arthurian knight, Dame Euridice his lady, and the underworld to which he journeyed to find her had become the faery kingdom. It would have pleased Godefroi to know that, several feet under the ground of the manor house there lay a broken Roman mosaic celebrating its hero; but he would scarcely have recognised the Romano–British Orpheus depicted there.

It was a haunting tale.

> Orfeo was a king
> In England, a high lording.
> Orfeo most of anything
> Loved the delight of harping.

As he recited the gentle cadences of the bitter-sweet poem, the vicar's high voice became almost tuneful; and Gilbert, who knew it so well, nodded encouragement from time to time.

It was the sense of sorrow in the early lines that moved the knight, as the poem told how Euridice sleeps with her ladies under an orchard tree and awakens half mad after a dream in which the faery king has told her that he will steal her away the very next day.

> Where'ere thou be thou wilt be fetched
> And torn apart your limbs be all
> None can help you, no one shall:
> Tomorrow lady, we shall call.

And Gilbert smiled and shook his head as the tale related how poor Sir Orfeo took all his useless precautions, standing guard over his queen with a thousand armed knights.

> They formed in ranks on every side
> And said with her they would abide
> And die there for her, every one
> Before the queen be from them gone
>   And yet from the midst of that array
>   By magic she vanished away.

Gilbert closed his eyes with a smile of contentment as the story related how Sir Orfeo became a ragged minstrel and beggar, wandering the world in search of his wife. For all his cautious management of his own estate, he identified with the pilgrim knight who gave up everything completely. He listened intently, familiar as the tale was, as Sir Orfeo at last saw the faery king, hunting in the forest with his lords and ladies. And then came, for him, the most touching moment of all, when the ragged Sir Orfeo sees that one of the ladies is his own lost wife, and approaches her.

> Then he beheld her, and she him too
> And neither to other a word did speak;
> She for pity, to see him so,
> Who had been a king, now so weak.
> And then a tear fell from her eye:
> And the other women the tear did spy
> And made her swiftly ride away.

What was it about that meeting and parting, as though the hero's wife were separated from him by a pane of glass, that always made the tears start from Godefroi's eyes? Was it the sense of loss? He was not sure exactly.

But soon his eyes were glowing with delight again as Sir Orfeo followed the riders back to the faery castle and played his harp before the faery king. And when he was offered a reward for his playing, Gilbert's face relaxed in pleasure as Sir Orfeo replied:

> 'Sir', he said, 'I beseech thee
> That thou wouldest give to me
> That fair lady that I see
> That sleeps under the orchard tree.'

And at last, having won his queen, the king, still disguised as a minstrel, returns to his astonished court and faithful servants:

> To Winchester at last came he
> That was his own city.

And then Gilbert reached out and took Rose's hand and whispered:

"I'd have wandered a hundred years to find you." And his wife, turning her head and smiling, squeezed his hand in return and said:

"I want us all to be together. Send for Thomas tomorrow."

Before the young vicar left, Gilbert asked him if he had heard any news of the plague. He replied confidently that he had not.

"But I pray every hour for my little flock at Avonsford," he replied stoutly, "and I'm sure we shall be spared."

Gilbert himself was less certain; and the next morning, after he had sent his groom on horseback to Winchester to collect his son, prepared himself to ride into the city to see if there was any news.

It was just as he was leaving that he was stopped at the courtyard gates by a small but extraordinary delegation.

The Mason family now consisted of six people: Edward's two grandsons, John and Nicholas; their widowed stepmother and her three young children. Since the death of their father Richard, three years before, John and Nicholas, both in their late twenties, had worked hard to support the second family Peter had left behind, and the house the whole family occupied in Avonsford, though crowded, had an air of cleanness and prosperity about it that pleased the knight. Though both men had followed the family calling as masons, John was also a bowman, and had recently returned from Crécy with a modest fortune in booty that was now the family's reserve against times of trouble.

But it was their stepmother Agnes who ruled them all. Godefroi gazed at her with a mixture of dislike and admiration. She was a small, square-jawed woman whose precise age he could never guess, with sandy red hair and little grey eyes that were honest, but seemed to dart about constantly. With her busy, jerky movements, she often reminded him of a red squirrel; she defended her little family with a fiery determination that did not make her popular in the village, and the aggressiveness in her nature that he sensed behind the respect she had to show him always made the knight feel uncomfortable in her presence. All the same, he had to admire her spirit.

It was this little red-haired woman who now stood in front of him, while John and Nicholas, their large heads respectfully bared, kept silent, and holding her arms akimbo bluntly announced:

"Sir, we want to rent the old sheep house. What's the price?"

He looked down at her in surprise. The old sheep house was still standing – a long, stone building that lay in a dip some distance away on the high ground. But since he had reduced his flocks, the ridges around it had not been grazed, and the place was now deserted and tumbling down. What could she want it for? Not wishing to waste time he shrugged.

"Sixpence a year." It was a nominal figure.

Agnes nodded.

"Can we take it right away?"

"Take it when you like," he answered. And without paying her any more attention he rode away.

As soon as he was gone she turned to the two men.

"Hurry," she told them. "We must be gone at once."

As soon as he entered the city, Godefroi went straight to the house of William Shockley. It was a natural choice, for few men were better informed. His house stood in the High Street, and though his primary business was in the export of wool and cloth, he had turned the whole floor on the street level into a store. Here one could find oysters from Poole, wine and fruit, woad, soap and oil imported through the lesser ports like Christchurch and Lymington or the great and growing port of Southampton on the south coast; there were herrings and salt fish brought over from Ireland through the trading city of Bristol in the west, and from more distant markets, pepper, dates, ginger, and fine silk clothes shipped through Southampton or the huge emporium of London. Not only was it a delight to inspect these wonders, but the carriers who brought them also brought news, and this was what made the merchant doubly valuable. He was the soul of the place, a big, bluff figure with a ruddy face, inclined to stoutness, and who loved to wear the brightest and most splendid clothes that he could find. His loose flowing surcoat, buttoned at the front, that fell like a dress to his knees, was of the most gorgeous brocade, worked with gold, that he had brought from London. His capuchon was wound into a huge turban on his head and he usually strutted amiably about the store, dispensing information.

But today, as soon as he saw the knight, he drew him to one side and whispered to him gravely.

"You have heard of this plague? It has come to Southampton."

"When?"

"Yesterday. Word reached me this morning. Two dead already."

"Is the city prepared?" Godefroi asked.

Shockley grimaced.

"I warned the mayor and the aldermen. It's all I can do; but no one believes me and anyway, in the city, what precautions are possible? Personally," he admitted, "I'm taking the family to the farm today."

Godefroi nodded grimly. The merchant had six children and he could hardly blame him for wanting them out of the teeming streets of Salisbury.

When he left a few minutes later, he found that the merchant's assistants had strapped two small panniers onto his horse. "Malmsey wine, just in from Christchurch," William explained. "It's a good protection against disease."

The arrival of the Black Death at Sarum was discovered that afternoon.

The two carts containing William Shockley, his plump wife, their six children, and two servants, had trundled slowly out of the city on the Wilton road in the early afternoon; an hour later they had reached the small collection of timbered buildings beside Grovely Wood that was the Shockley farm. William and his wife were both relieved to be there; the children anxious to run into the spacious freedom of the surrounding woods.

He had sent word ahead and was glad to see that the Wilsons had opened the house to air it and already lit the fire in the main room where the food would be cooked. The house however, though prepared, was silent and deserted.

"Damn that Wilson," he remarked. The fellow should have waited to help them unload; it was not the first time he had been guilty of slackness; and irritably he had stomped down the path that led to Wilson's cottage, accompanied by two of his children.

The surly villein was standing at the door. As usual, he made no move to welcome the merchant as he came up and when Shockley told him pleasantly enough to go up to the farm to help, he started off without a word. Meanwhile, as they always did, the two Shockley children dived into Wilson's cottage to satisfy their curiosity, and it was his fair-haired daughter of twelve who now came out with a puzzled expression and called to her father:

"Come and look at Peter."

The fire in the dark little room had gone out and Wilson's wife was sitting silently, as she usually did, in one corner. In the other, young Peter Wilson lay on a bed of straw. As he entered, Shockley was not conscious of anything especially wrong, beyond the general air of silent hatred he always sensed when he went into Wilson's little dwelling, but as he came near him, he had a sudden sensation that the boy was very hot. He bent down to look. And as he did so, Peter Wilson sat up bolt upright, and with a terrible retching sound, coughed into his face.

"Out of here. Out!" he roared at his astonished children. A moment later all three had tumbled out of the cottage and were running up the path again. "We leave the farm at once," he cried.

As they passed Walter Wilson, Shockley was almost certain that the cottager had grinned.

Rose de Godefroi's cook, Margery Dubber had her own ideas about how to deal with all kinds of illness. She was a large, stolid middle-aged woman with greenish eyes that stared in different directions; when the two women unpacked the Malmsey wine from Christchurch and Rose gave her the recipe for its use, neither eye looked convinced.

"You must boil the wine until a third of it's gone," Rose told her. "Then add peppers, ginger and nutmeg and let it simmer for an hour more; then I want you to add this Treacle Venice." She produced a thick syrup made from honey. "And aqua vitae," she added. Rose suspected that the spirits were the best part of the cure. "Boil them all up again and we'll keep the plague at bay." And so, morning and evening, the Godefrois and their entire household now began to drink this fortifying brew.

But as soon as she was by herself the cook muttered:

"If the plague comes here, it'll be Margery Dubber's cures they need."

When they had taken the bottles of Malmsey wine from their straw packing, neither the cook nor Rose had noticed the flea which had fallen out of the basket and leaped at once into the deep folds of the lady's cloak.

News that the plague had reached the Shockley farm came to them the next day; but at Avonsford there was still no sign of it.

The only thing disturbing the Godefrois' calm was the failure of their son Thomas to arrive.

If anything was needed to confirm the view in the village of Avonsford that Agnes Mason was not only wilful, but a little strange in the head, it was her behaviour two days after the lord of the manor began his mysterious preparations for the invisible plague.

The knight's actions seemed odd; but then the workings of a noble's mind were often beyond their ken, and could not be questioned. For a villager to behave as Agnes did, however, was inexplicable and outrageous. Why did the two Mason men stand for it?

Within an hour of receiving the knight's permission, she led her little family out of the village and up onto the ridges. She and her two stepsons each pulled behind them a small handcart piled high with provisions – grain, household possessions, clothes, and certain other items, the need for which her family could not understand.

When they reached the sheep house, she sent the two brothers back to the woods, telling them: "Find all the firewood you can and bring it here." Meanwhile, she inspected their new accommodation. The holes in the roof and the crumbling wall had not interested her; but the earth floor and the ground around the wall did. For half an hour she looked into every cranny on her hands and knees before finally pronouncing: "No rats. Not even a spider."

Her next action was stranger still.

Pointing to the crumbling wall she told her two puzzled stepsons:

"Take stones from there and place them round the house."

And she went to a point fifty yards from the building and paced out a circle round the sheep house, pausing every five paces to make a mark in the ground where she wanted them to put a stone.

"But why?" they asked.

"I will show you," she promised; and since they were used to obeying her, they did as she had said.

By late afternoon there was a circle of sixty-three stones around the house.

The building itself was adequate: one end was in a good state; the roof was easily repaired; their quarters were spacious and airy. But there was one problem.

"There's no water here," they complained.

And now for the first time Agnes smiled in triumph.

"Yes there is." And taking a wooden pail with her she led them out of the hollow and strode a quarter of a mile across the open high ground. "There," she said.

It was a dew pond. No sheep had used it for years now, and it was a generation since the bottom had last been re-sealed; but there was still a layer of water, about a foot deep in the centre; and it was clean.

"That is our water," she declared.

When they returned, she pointed to the ring of stones.

"The stones will protect us," she explained, "because they are our barrier: nothing – no stranger and no living animal – is to come inside the circle." And now she told them why she had insisted that they bring with them not only John's longbow, but also the little bows and slings he had made for the children, with which they often hunted birds.

"If anything comes near we'll drive it away with stones from the slings; if that doesn't work, we'll kill it with the arrows," she announced.

"How will we know if anything's coming?"

"We'll keep watch," she answered simply. "Night and day."

John looked at her curiously.

"And what if people come?"

"They must not enter the circle," she replied, "or I'll shoot them."

As the family stared at her in astonishment, they knew that she meant it.

"It is necessary," she stated, with a fiery determination, and they knew better than to argue.

The truth was that Agnes Mason hardly knew what she was doing herself.

When the knight had spoken of the plague's approach at Avonsford, and while the villagers had scoffed, she had thought long and hard about the matter. For unlike them, she not only believed the knight, but she saw why the plague was coming, too. And it was this terrible knowledge, which she kept to herself, that made her consider all the more carefully, searching in her mind for clues as to what she should do. The mind of Agnes Mason, though she could not read and write, was stored with a remarkable stock of information. There was the knowledge her mother had carefully handed on to her – not only about the care of her little household but a huge store of folklore and herbal cures; there were the strange if garbled accounts her father had given her about his journeys with old King Edward to Wales and Gascony. All these she remembered perfectly: for ever since childhood, she had had an extraordinary ability to memorise. Her brothers and sisters used to say: "Ask Agnes. She never forgets anything." But above all, it was her vivid imagination that had been filled almost entirely from a single source: the Bible, as related to her by the vicars of Avonsford in their perfunctory sermons or, more important, the public preachings of the friars when they drew their audiences to them in the market place or by the roadside. The images they evoked coloured all her thoughts. The words they spoke, some terrible, others comforting – these were the mighty truths that echoed in her mind.

She had thought hard.

And certain things she knew. She knew this plague was sent by God, as a punishment for men's sins; when she was still a child, the vicar had told her of the fall of Babylon, the great flood, the destruction of Sodom and Gomorrah. She had seen them in the windows and carvings in the churches. These things were to be feared – and expected. She remembered the words of Moses from the Book of Deuteronomy, as they had been translated to his audience by the terrifying old Franciscan friar who had preached in Sarum when she was a little girl.

"But if thou wilt not hearken unto the voice of the Lord – cursed shalt thou be in the city and in the field. The Lord shall send upon thee cursing because of the wickedness of thy doings. The Lord shall smite thee with a consumption and a fever, and an inflammation and an extreme burning, and with mildew, and madness and blindness, and with a sore botch that cannot be healed . . ."

The list of terrors had been endless, and the piercing eyes of the old man had seemed to hypnotise her. And now the divine punishment had come. This must be the plague the knight spoke of.

Was there no hope? She knew that the villagers of Avonsford, though not especially wicked, were unlikely to escape God's wrath. But surely her own sins, and certainly those of her three little children, were not so great? Good men in the past, men like Noah, had been shown how to escape these terrible visitations: she cudgelled her brains for some information that might save her children.

At last she thought she had it.

"It's the animals that spread the plague," she announced.

There were few, if any, at Sarum who would have agreed with her. From the knight down to the humblest cottager, they believed that sicknesses passed either by contact with humans who were infected, or by inhaling evil vapours which were carried by the wind and rain. But

Agnes alone had decided otherwise. For she remembered another sermon she had heard, twenty years before, from a thin, pale Dominican friar with a cold, hard voice who had preached on the Wilton road. He had warned them:

"Evil is all around you. The world is unclean." And quoting from the book of Leviticus he had declared: "The coney and the hare, because they chew the cud but divide not the hoof, they are both unclean. Of their flesh shall ye not eat and their carcase shall ye not touch. And the owl and the cuckoo and the bat; also the creeping things that creep upon the earth: the ferret and the lizard, the weasel and the mouse, all these shall be abominations unto you. Touch these," he cried, "and you shall be defiled."

Few people took much notice, but Agnes remembered. The more she thought about it, the more she believed this might be the means by which God would spread His righteous rage.

And gradually her plan had begun to form.

"We must go away from the village," she urged. "Away from contact with unclean animals, like the preacher said. We must live apart until this plague has passed."

"How?" the two brothers had demanded.

And then her inspiration had come, and she had declared:

"I know a place."

For the rolling, high ground, bare and uninviting, was in some places empty of man and beasts. It's as bare as the sea, she thought. The more she considered the great chalky wastes, open only to the sky, the more she grew certain that this was the region that God had prepared for them.

"We'll go up to the high ground to escape the plague," she said. "We'll be safe up there."

At first they had not wanted to go. But she had been persistent. "Think of our children," she cried – for she always called them 'our' children, in the same way that her stepsons referred to her as 'our' mother. "Will you leave them to the plague?" And at last, as they always did, John and Nicholas gave in to her determined will.

But now that she had led them on the journey to the high ground, she realised that her problems had only just begun. For having got them to go, how would she keep them there?

She did not know. For years, Agnes had taught herself to be strong. The brothers relied on her and she encouraged this, for if she could not keep her two quiet stepsons at home, how would her children be fed? With her own plain, strong looks and her three young children, she was unlikely to find another husband to look after them. Some day the two brothers would marry and she would lose her hold on them, but secretly she prayed that day would be delayed as long as possible. And so she had made herself strong, to dominate the brothers and feed her children. So far it had worked.

She had taught herself to be patient; it had not been easy. How they secretly irritated her, these two men who were so necessary to her, with their quiet grey eyes and their slow and quiet ways. Their father, a skilful man who physically resembled them, had had a quick temper and a wicked sense of humour to match her own fiery mind. But his two sons were like slow-moving streams, never even in flood, on which she knew the little boat of her family must sail. How she longed for the company of different men, and how carefully she concealed her frustration, for she sensed that if she ever allowed her temper to flare up, she would lose their loyalty. But she had been patient. She had even come to love them over the years.

And now her authority was to be tested. For if her plan was to work, she must never allow her authority to slip, even for a moment: there must be no sign of weakness.

The first test came that evening.

It was about an hour before dusk, when the family had finished the light meal of wheatcakes she had made, that John quietly rose and began to walk out of the little compound.

An instinct made her follow him.

"Where are you going?"

He grinned cheerfully.

"To the miz-maze. Catch some coneys."

The miz-maze of the Godefroi knights, only two miles away to the west, had been allowed to fall into disrepair. Although the pattern of the maze could be clearly seen in the turf, it had not been re-cut for years; for Gilbert, probably because it had been such a favourite haunt of his father's, had never cared for the place and seldom went there. In the circle of yew trees around it, where the soil was soft, a thriving colony of rabbits had now sprung up – a warren which could have been a modest but valuable asset to Gilbert if he had shown any interest in it. It was the one corner of the estate where discreet poaching was never noticed.

But now Agnes shook her head.

"You must not go there. Coneys are unclean." She reminded him of the warning in Leviticus.

"They sell well enough in the market," he protested, gazing at her stubbornly.

"They carry plague," she said.

His grey eyes were unconvinced, and as she faced him, she sensed that this was a crisis. If he went to catch coneys now, her authority would be undermined and she would never hold the little family together in the difficult days ahead.

"The plague is about to strike," she said with certainty. "It may be in Avonsford already. Think of the children."

He hesitated.

"We must stay together here," she pressed on quickly, "and never leave until it has passed. You'll see what happens to the others."

John said nothing, but to her relief, he turned back.

Just before he went back with her into the sheep house she put her hand on his arm.

"Promise me, until the plague has passed, that you will obey me," she asked.

Again, he gazed at her unwillingly, and though she stared back at him with steadfast eyes she was inwardly praying: "Let him obey Your will, dear God."

Slowly, grudgingly, he nodded and walked inside. It was enough for the moment.

But by the next morning, she had failed.

Of the two brothers, Nicholas was the one she feared less. He was fairer than John and even milder in temper; he was employed as a cathedral mason in the constant repair of the fabric that the great building required, and when John had gone to the French Wars, it was Nicholas who had stayed at Sarum to look after Agnes and the children.

Yet it was Nicholas, just before dawn, who slipped out of the sheep house unnoticed and set off towards the city.

And when she saw what had happened, Agnes pursed her lips and said nothing, but she knew what she must do.

He was glad to get away from Agnes. Sometimes she frightened him. For if she supposed that she concealed her fiery temper from her stepsons, she was mistaken. She might have swallowed her impatience, but the waves of it emanated from within her like heat from a forge, and they disturbed him.

As for her faith in isolation from the plague, Nicholas did not believe in it.

The sun was up as he walked off the high ground into the city below, and the dew was glistening on the cathedral roof.

As he passed the city bar, his mind was already occupied with the work he intended to do in the cathedral that day and it was only when he reached the market place that he noticed that something was strange. Usually by now the place would be bustling, but today for some reason only half a dozen stalls seemed to be opening. He thought nothing of it and followed his usual tour round the eastern end of the market and down the High Street. Shockley's store, he noticed, was still shut up for the night. No one in the High Street seemed to be stirring except for the black rats who were swimming after a little pile of rubbish that was drifting down the water channel in the middle of the street.

He turned along New Street; here too there were few people about, and concluding that for some reason the city was rising late that day, he turned left into Minster Street and through the fine new stone gate that led into the cathedral close.

Nicholas loved the close. A decade before when the king had given permission for the bishop to dismantle the old cathedral on the castle hill above, he had watched while they carried the stones of the old building down into the valley and he had helped when they used them to replace the old ditch with a splendid new wall around the close. It had interested him to find the old masons' marks on many of the stones he was using. The wall, with its stout stone gateways on the north east and southern sides had added greatly to the secluded dignity of the place, sealing it off with a resounding finality from the rest of the world like a vast cloister in the centre of which the stately grey cathedral with its gracious spire was set.

But why was the place so quiet? As he entered, the porter at the gate gave him a strange look, and as he gazed across the tranquil lawns there did not seem to be a priest in sight.

He went into the cathedral. That, too, was silent. He walked up the nave.

How he loved the soaring pillars with their gentle bend under the tower! Across the little transept in the choir, his father had built the strainer arches – shaped like the Gothic arches, one inverted above the other – that had helped to buttress the choir against the eastward drift it had suffered since the tower was built. One day, Nicholas believed, the canons would decide to put arches like that across the bending pillars at the great central crossing of the church. But no one wanted to spoil the unbroken line of the soaring pillars, and so far they had not bent any more since the spire was completed.

"The spire holds up by our faith," the priests liked to joke.

For an hour he went quietly about his work, a small repair in one corner of the cloisters; then, wondering why there was still no one about, he went out into the close again.

It was the porter at the gate who told him.

"You haven't heard? The plague came to Sarum yesterday. They say it's in the city now."

"Who has it. How many?"

The man shrugged. "No one knows. Half the people are staying indoors."

As Nicholas walked through the streets, he found it was true. The only crowd was outside Shockley's store, and they were hammering on the door and on the shutters over the windows. When he asked one of the women why, she cried:

"He's got herbs in there. Cures to prevent the plague. But he won't open his doors to anyone. Coward," she yelled. "Viper." But the Shockley house remained silent.

He wandered all over the town, trying to get definite news. There was plague in the outlying farms, he heard, but no one knew which. A man had fallen into one of the water channels with it, a trader in the market told him; but no one else had heard of the incident. People were coming out of their houses now, asking each other what was happening, but no one seemed to have definite infomation. Some people said that Shockley the merchant knew more, but his house was still closed.

At the end of the morning, he decided to return to Avonsford. The place had changed completely. In the main street, a group of villagers, no longer scoffing, were anxiously looking at the sky for signs of the dark clouds they expected to bring the plague. They glanced at him cautiously, but he passed on.

Was it possible, he wondered, that Agnes might be right after all in choosing the isolated sheep house? The threat of the plague seemed to be all around him here.

He went to the family's cottage, collected an extra jerkin and two blankets and began to make his way out of the village again.

It was just before he left that he saw the first real sign of the panic that was about to grip the area.

The priest's house was little more than a cottage, for his stipend was modest, and it was only more dignified than the other village houses because it stood just apart from the line of the main street and had a small paddock beside it.

To his surprise, as he went past, the priest ran out from it into the lane and seized him by the arm.

"My sheep, Nicholas," the gap-toothed vicar cried. "Come quickly and look at my sheep."

And when he followed him, Nicholas saw three sheep lying in the paddock. They were all dead. At the vicar's urging he looked at them.

"Well, what killed them?" the priest asked him anxiously. He kept running his hands through his thin hair.

Nicholas shrugged. "A murrain I suppose."

"You don't know?" the vicar demanded plaintively. Nicholas gazed at the dead sheep again but did not answer. "It's the plague," the priest suddenly cried in despair. "The plague. We're all lost." And to Nicholas's amazement, he burst into sobs.

He had not heard that sheep could catch the plague. He wondered if it were true. The vicar was still weeping as he turned up the lane.

It was mid-afternoon when he reached the sheep house. He smiled to himself as he saw the curious circle of stones around it. For all her faults, he thought, Agnes was a remarkable woman. And as he considered the place in its isolated setting he could not help admitting that it was undeniably safer than the city or the village. She is right after all, he admitted to himself. She'll bring us through if anyone can.

He smiled, too when he saw his youngest half brother, a dark-haired boy of four solemnly standing guard by the door with his little bow and arrow. He heard the boy cry out happily as he advanced towards him.

The morning had seemed to pass slowly for Agnes. John had not given her any trouble, but it had been difficult to contain the children within the circle of stones, though somehow she had done so.

The place was astonishingly quiet. Far from the trees, even the birds scarcely seemed to visit it, and most of the time they had only the drifting clouds for company. No animals had come near except once, soon after dawn, when a fox, scenting their occupation, had cautiously approached. As soon as it saw her, it began to lope away, but not before she had skilfully loosed a stone from a sling that struck it hard in the hindquarters and caused it to scamper off, to the delighted cries of the children.

Noon passed. The children dozed while she sat quietly by the entrance. There was no wind; the only sound was the gentle scraping of John's knife as he fashioned a new arrow for one of the children's bows. An hour later she let the little boy take her place while she slept.

Now his cry had awoken her.

For a second the sun hurt her eyes as she ran out, shook off her sleep and stared anxiously into the hard yellow light of the afternoon.

He was only a hundred yards away; her little boy was about to run towards him.

And now she was fully awake: for this was the test.

"Back into the house and stay there," she ordered. And then, seizing the child's bow, she went out to the line of stones.

He was surprised when Agnes called to him to stop.

She was standing there with the child's bow in her hand, her square chin thrust forward in the look of determination he knew so well. He saw his brother John, emerging from the sheep house behind her. He smiled.

"Where have you been?" Her voice was hard.

"To the city. And to Avonsford." He started forward again, but she raised her hand.

"Has the plague begun?"

He shrugged.

"Maybe. They said a man died in the city, but I never saw him. The vicar," he jerked his thumb towards the village, "says his sheep are dead of it." He grinned as he remembered the man's sobs. "Looked like the murrain to me."

Again he moved forward. John was still approaching behind her.

And then, to his amazement, she calmly fitted a little arrow to the bow and drew it.

"No further."

Her body was square and rigid, as an archer's should be. She held the bow steadily. And the little arrow was pointing straight at his heart.

"Go back," she told him. "You must not come in here again."

She saw the look of bewilderment on his face. It hurt her as though he had been her own son. But she knew she must not flinch.

Determined, she forced herself to stare straight into his eyes so that he could see she would shoot if she had to, and though for a second her hand trembled, she thought of her three children and it became firm again.

Nicholas hesitated.

If he took another step, she must do it. But could she? And if he forced her to shoot, what next? She had no idea.

They faced each other in silence. Neither moved.

Now John was at her elbow. She could hear him breathing.

"Let him in, mother," he said softly. From the tone of his voice she knew at once that he thought she had gone mad.

"You promised to obey me," she reminded him. Why did he not understand?

"Let him in." This time it was an order.

She did not move. And she did not take her eyes off Nicholas. If she gave in now, everything would be destroyed.

John started to reach out, to take the bow from her.

"Touch me and I'll shoot him." She heard her own voice, hard and authoritative. It surprised her, but she was glad it was so convincing.

She did not see, but she sensed his hand draw back.

"If the plague's in the city, he may be carrying it," she said calmly. "The risk is too great. If he carries it, we may all die."

John said nothing. She knew he did not believe her.

Then, to her astonishment, it was Nicholas who spoke.

"She is right. I will go." He turned to go, and then, with an afterthought he called: "I'll come each day and tell you when the plague has passed." He strode away. Slowly she lowered the bow.

John was gazing at her. His mild round face was contorted with rage; his voice was edged with contempt.

"What have you done?"

The anger and reproach in his voice cut her to the quick. But she did not show it.

"Saved us," she replied bluntly.

Rose de Godefroi displayed the first signs the next day. At first no one noticed.

She had been proud of her simple precautions. She felt sure that at Avonsford, she had created a safe haven for her husband and her son.

But as dusk fell and the household had just drunk the potion of Malmsey wine she had prepared, she suddenly felt faint. She steadied herself quickly; Gilbert had not noticed. A few minutes later the faintness passed and she dismissed the tiresome sensation from her mind. Half an hour later, she suddenly began to shiver. The candles were lit; in the half light neither Gilbert nor the serving woman realised. Quietly she retired to the solar.

Soon afterwards, she vomited.

She knew what it was. She had no shadow of a doubt.

Gilbert had probably nodded off in his chair in the hall. She was glad to have a little time to herself to consider what to do.

There was only one thought in her mind: how to save the others in the household. There was little use, she guessed, in trying to send them away. However the plague had reached her, it had probably infected its chosen victims in the manor already.

But then she thought of her son. It had been so many months since she had seen his cheerful face and tousled head. How she had longed for his visit. If she were to die, she must prepare herself to do so without seeing him – he must not come to Avonsford now; that was certain.

No word had come from the Whiteheath manor – perhaps this very moment Thomas was on his way. She trembled, now, even to think of it. In a moment she must get up and warn her husband to send messages to stop him coming. If only she did not feel so weak. She closed her eyes.

It was the sound of clattering hoofs on the cobblestones that awoke her with a start. A glance at the shortened candle beside her couch told her that an hour had passed. And now she was not only wide awake but seized with panic. A horseman arriving at the manor after dark – it could only be Thomas.

She struggled to her feet, and, stumbling, crossed to the window before peering out into the courtyard below. A servant had opened the door. By the light of the torch he carried, she could make out a figure dismounting from his horse. She rattled the window desperately. He must not come into the house. The figures below took no notice. She reached out for something with which to break the glass, but then again the dizzy faintness overtook her and she fell back.

It was a few minutes later that Gilbert de Godefroi stood at the open doorway staring at the form of his wife. She was lying on the floor, her white hair covering her face like a shroud.

The messenger from Ranulf de Whiteheath who was waiting in the yard below, had brought him a simple message:

"My master was away when your groom arrived. Your son is well but we have heard that the plague has reached Sarum. Do you still wish your son to return?"

And it was only when he had revived her and brought her to her bed again that she looked at him calmly but sadly and said:

"You must keep the boy away."

That night she lay alone in the solar while, at her insistence, Gilbert slept in his chair in the hall. Both only slept fitfully, and several times he went to look at her. "You will feel well soon," he promised her, and at first light he made her drink some Malmsey wine. Soon afterwards she was sick again.

The buboes began the following evening: three little red rashes, under each armpit and in the groin. Before dark, they had already swollen into boils that made her cry out in pain, and as night fell the word spread through the village:

"The lady of Avonsford has the plague."

She tried to keep her husband calm, but she did not succeed. He sent for the vicar, but word came back that the gap-toothed priest, terrified by the sight of his own dead sheep, had fled. As he gazed at his lovely wife, with her snow-white hair spread round her head on the pillow like an aureole, and saw with horror the way her body was being torn by the wracking pains, he remembered the haunting words of the poem they had heard two nights before, and they came back to him with a terrible new force:

And torn apart your limbs be all
No one can help you, no one shall;
Tomorrow, lady, we shall call.

He could not bear to think that she could be taken from him.

"God save us all," he cried, helplessly.

He did what he could. He filled the room with herbs. He prayed himself, night and day; he sent for other priests and at last two were persuaded, for a handsome fee, to come out from Salisbury. But the hideous buboes grew: the one in her armpit was soon the size of an apple, white and hot, as the disease took its inevitable course. By the third day of her illness, he was desperate for any remedy.

It was when he had reached this point of despair, that Margery Dubber asked to apply her cures. She had been brooding for two days in the kitchen, waiting for someone to summon her. Everyone in the village knew that her cures for all ailments were the best, and more than once she had dropped a broad hint to that effect to the knight. He had taken no notice. Now however, seeing his wretched state, she went up and suggested herself boldly.

Godefroi was ready to agree, but Rose would not. Her eyes were sunken now, black with pain, but she found strength to raise her head, stare at the cook and order: "No."

But the next day she was too weak even for this; and so early in the afternoon, Margery, her two skewed eyes gleaming with satisfaction, was allowed to march into the sick room.

Her cure was simple. She had used it on swellings before, so why should it not work for the plague as well?

"You take a live frog," she explained to Godefroi. "Press its belly against the boil. That will take the venom away."

"And then?"

"Hold it there until the frog bursts," she said. "Then take another."

Rose was hardly aware of what was happening at first, and when she realised, she only cast her eyes up to heaven and said nothing.

It was not a success. Though she pressed them hard against the growing buboes, the frogs died without bursting, and after a few hours Margery Dubber shook her head.

"She'll not be cured," she announced as she left for the village.

That night, alone in the hall, the knight slowly read the tale of Sir Orfeo to himself, and waited.

Nicholas Mason spent one day at Avonsford. During this time, two men fainted in the fields and were carried home.

The next morning he went up to the sheep house; remaining outside the circle of stones, he told them how the plague had come to Avonsford and then, supposing the risk of catching it must be about the same in one place as another, he walked into the city.

The change there was extraordinary. There were people in the streets now, but they hurried about anxiously with handkerchiefs over their faces. Already, several people had died – no one knew how many – but even as he walked through the market place, he saw a cart carrying two bodies lumber out towards the city gates. There was no organisation; the mayor and aldermen were locked up in their houses like everyone else.

When he passed the Shockley house, he found no crowd by the door. People walked past on the other side of the street, and though no one knew exactly what was going on inside, terrible retching sounds could be heard from time to time from within.

"They've all got it," a neighbour told him, "in the lungs. They say the Wilson boy gave it to them at the farm and William Shockley's vowed to turn them out for it." He shrugged. "He'll not live to do it though." And as if to confirm this, a fit of coughing started within and both men hurried away.

A number of people were leaving the city. He saw a small train of covered wagons at the corner of New Street, containing several families including that of Le Portier, the aulnager. He asked the wizened driver of the first cart where he was taking them.

"North," the fellow grimaced. "They tell me to drive north. Who knows where they'll end up?" His hard narrow face broke into a grin. "They pay me. I'll take them all the way to hell if they pay me."

The close was silent. There was not a soul to be seen. Even the vicars choral, those rowdy junior priests who, only the week before, he had seen exercising their dogs in the cloisters and drinking merrily on the green, seemed to be staying indoors in their lodging houses.

It was as he walked across the empty close towards the cathedral that he was surprised to be hailed by a loud voice.

"Mason!" He knew the voice at once.

Of all the undisciplined young clerics, the vicar choral Adam was the most hopeless case: he was considered a nuisance even by their own lax standards. This was not due to any evildoing on his part – indeed, there was not an ounce of malice in his nature – but because he was such a madcap. He was constantly involved in practical jokes or idiotic fights; never was a young man so obviously unfitted to be a priest. Yet when he was asked why he did not follow some other occupation, he gave the same answer that many another young fellow would have given at that time.

"How else is a poor man to eat and hope for advancement?" For outside the church, there was little scope for a youth who had no money and connection, and who wanted to be anything more than a humble apprentice.

Adam could be recognised half a mile away, not only because of his loud voice, but because instead of a modest habit he wore a tight-fitting tunic, a cotte hardie, and a broad belt embroidered with gold, just as if he were a young man of fashion. Irrepressibly foolish as Adam was, the quiet mason could not help liking this cheerfully outrageous extrovert, with his childlike honesty.

"See Mason," he shouted, so that his voice echoed round the precincts, "the world has changed today. Only you and I about and not a priest to be seen."

It was remarkable. At a time when one in fifty of the population was in some form of holy orders, the cathedral city was teeming with priests. That morning however, it was as if they had melted into the moss on the walls of the buildings. "The silence is wonderful," Adam called, and his raucous guffaw of laughter seemed to shake the shutters.

"Aren't you afraid of the plague," Nicholas asked.

"Me? No. I've the cure." He pointed to two pouches that hung from his magnificent belt. "Six garlic in one. Six onion in the other. The plague won't come near me."

Nicholas wondered if this was a joke, though it was no stranger than the other remedies people were trying.

"It's true," Adam assured him, and his big, open face broke into a happy smile. "Watch me, Mason, and you'll see." And he strode away towards the town.

Nicholas spent the day working in the cathedral. In the evening he returned to Avonsford where he learned that the buboes had appeared on

Rose de Godefroi. Two more people in the village, both women this time, had been afflicted, one with the terrible buboes, the other in the lungs.

The next morning he went up to the high ground again. This time he stopped well outside the circle of stones.

"Stay where you are. Do not come down," he told them. "The plague is everywhere and it is spreading."

Yet never in his worst nightmares had Nicholas imagined what, in the next ten days, was to follow. The start of the plague had given little hint of it.

At times, he wondered if everyone at Sarum would die. The contagion seemed to swirl and eddy round the city like the waters when the river flooded.

Some were consumed by the plague at once, and died within hours; in others it took the pneumonic form and its victims died coughing blood and mucus; the stronger went down more slowly with the buboes that, in their final stage, spread across the body in a terrible, pestilential swelling that left the body of the dead victim a loathsome and infectious mass of suppurating sores. Of those who caught the plague in its pneumonic form, none lived. Of those who suffered the buboes, about sixty per cent died.

Each day he watched the carts roll through the city picking up the dead. By the end of the first week they were being buried indiscriminately in trenches outside the city gates. One morning he saw the door of the Shockley house open and three pairs of arms unceremoniously drop the bulky form of William Shockley on the ground outside, before slamming the door again. He lay there for two hours before a passing cart decided to pick him up; the next day his wife followed. The day after, two of their children and a servant. But these events were hardly remarked in the general horror. Nor was the news that Rose de Godefroi had died at Avonsford.

The close fared no better than the rest of the town. For two days the gate was closed, in a useless attempt to seal its sacred precincts off from the contagion in the town, but then the porter at the gate succumbed, and it was left open.

Some of the priests emerged to do their duties in ministering to the dying. The friars never hesitated, moving quietly from door to door, apparently undisturbed in their holy work.

But over the whole city a strange fear and lethargy had fallen. The evil spirit of the plague had seeped like a noxious vapour into every nook and cranny of the city. And when the suppurating corpses of the victims were brought into the streets, there was indeed a sickly, terrible stench that turned the stomach. It seemed to Nicholas that men's souls were filled with terror, and the sense of that, too, was almost palpable.

Only one figure seemed untouched, and this was Adam. Each day he was in the city, Nicholas would see the strange fellow ambling about, in his tight tunic and his broad belt with the pouches of onions and garlics swinging from it. Astoundingly, he still seemed cheerful. People said he was mad.

Nicholas himself remained calm. He reasoned, fatalistically, that if he were a chosen victim, then there was little he could do about it. He was careful all the same. Like most people, he held a cloth over his mouth and nostrils when he walked the streets. He kept himself to himself, ate alone, and avoided any contact with those who were infected. Taking these precautions, he went into the city most days, working quietly in the cathedral and returning periodically to the sheep house on the high ground to give his reports.

The event that caused him to panic took place a week after Shockley's death. He was carefully crossing a street in the city when, as he stepped over the water channel that ran down its centre, a corpse he had not seen tumbled sideways off a cart in front of him and fell heavily into the stream, splashing him from head to foot. The sudden soaking shocked him. It was as though he had been attacked, and afterwards he felt defiled. The next day, when the family in the cottage next to his at Avonsford came down with the plague, he decided to take further precautions.

"I shall be coming only every two days now," he told Agnes and the family. "Because I shan't be at Avonsford any more. I'm going to a safe place until the plague has passed."

"Where?" John asked him.

And now Nicholas smiled.

"No folk or animals where I'm going," he replied. "I'll go to Salisbury tower."

The cathedral was quiet as dusk fell, and there was nobody to see as he climbed the steps that led to the tower. No one had questioned him when, saying it was for maintenance work, he asked for the keys of the tower doors the day before. Probably it was already forgotten that he had them.

He was carrying a bucket containing bread, two flagons of ale, cheese, salted meat and a quantity of fruit: enough to last several days. Carefully he made sure that the stairs in all four corners of the tower were locked before he made his way up to the parapet. Now nobody could disturb him.

Soon it was dark. The great cathedral below him was silent. It was so warm that he decided to spend the night on the parapet under the stars. He looked up at the soaring spire above him. He knew that, nearly forty years before, his great-grandfather Osmund had climbed to the top the year before he died. Perhaps he would do so too, to celebrate, when the plague had passed.

How pure the air was, far above the stench of the city streets. With only the grey stones for company, and the open sky, he lay there comfortably, feeling safer than he had done for a week, and fell asleep.

He stayed in the tower all the next day. It was strange how much of the life of the city he could see from up there. He noticed that in the city, the dead were being brought out and carried away soon after dawn; three corpses were brought out of houses in the close that morning. He watched a dispute between the carriers and a junior clergyman about how much they should be paid. He could not hear their words, but it was clear what was being said. The carriers offered to leave the canon's body where it was. Then they were paid. He could see everyone who came in and out of the close; he saw the carts rolling on their dismal journey to the city gates. Several times he watched Adam in his broad belt, walking jauntily back and forth into the town, and laughed aloud with pleasure at the sight. That night, once again, he slept comfortably under the stars.

But the next morning he received an unpleasant shock. He had decided to pay another visit to the sheep house, and so that he could get safely clear of the city before the contagious corpses were brought out, he had started to descend from the tower a little before dawn.

He fumbled his way down the endless spiral tunnel of the stairs, locking the door carefully behind him. As he emerged into the cathedral however, he saw a faint light flickering in the shadows, and out of curiosity, he went towards it. He soon wished he had not.

The little family must have sneaked into the cathedral during the night. They were standing now, five of them, with long candles in their hands by the tomb of Bishop Osmund. Obviously they had carried their father in with them; for now they had laid him, stripped entirely naked, on the tomb.

There had been many claims of miraculous cures from people touching or standing near the revered bishop's tomb. The priests, still hoping that one day the pope would be persuaded to canonise Osmund, did nothing to discourage these claims. Now silently, hopefully, a middle-aged woman and her two sons and two daughters gazed at the wretched figure before them.

It was an eerie and terrible sight. He was in the last stages of the disease. The buboes had spread all over his chest, and the poor fellow, hardly knowing what was happening, was shaking uncontrollably on the cool, hard slab.

Nicholas turned quickly and hurried away. He continued to shiver until he was well out of the city.

At the sheep house, the family appeared calm. He offered to bring them more food, but they refused.

"We have enough grain," Agnes told him. "That and water – it's all we need."

But the strain of their strange isolation was obviously taking its toll.

John seemed sullen, though after his description of what was taking place below, he showed no inclination to move from their sanctuary. The children were silent and withdrawn. Agnes too looked tired.

After standing for several minutes and giving them what words of encouragement he could from outside the circle of stones, he left them.

He was installed in the tower again early that evening with a fresh supply of food when the extraordinary movements in the cathedral's structure began.

At first he thought he must have been mistaken – the whole thing just a trick of the eye.

There was a light, refreshing breeze that was sending small white

[528]

clouds drifting across the evening sky. It was just as he lay back and watched them pass overhead, that it suddenly seemed to him that the top of the spire had moved.

It must have been the motion of the clouds. He waited until the sky was clear again and looked up once more. There was the cross, high above.

And again it moved.

Not very much, to be sure. He sat up. But as he did so, he felt the building below him shift, so that he fell back against the edge of the parapet. Then he sat very still. A feeling of sickness and panic came over him. Was the cathedral settling on its foundations yet again? Could it be that, after all, the bending pillars below were at last going to break and the whole mighty structure come tumbling down in colossal ruin? He stared up at the spire again, in dread.

He started to get to his feet. And now he could feel the whole structure shifting – so much that he had to steady himself. A bead of perspiration broke out on his brow, which suddenly felt very hot. Glancing up he saw with horror that the spire was swaying wildly; the stone floor under his feet was tilting. Dear God, the cathedral was coming down! The floor tilted violently as he fell face down upon it.

Several minutes later, he came to. Strangely, the spire, the parapet, the masonry were all in place. In the west, the sky was glowing a deep magenta red and in the sky above, the first stars were starting to appear.

He put his hand to his forehead. It was burning. A momentary giddiness and nausea enveloped him.

Now he realised. The cathedral had not moved at all.

He was shaken by several spasms of trembling that night. In the bright starlight, he found that his eyes were swimming. Several times not only the spire but the constellations: Orion, the Plough, the Bear, joined in a wild dance around the sky after which, each time, he was sick.

In the morning, he felt the boils in his armpits.

At dawn he prayed:

"Mother of God, save your servant."

He had served the cathedral all his life. They said that people could survive the buboes. Surely the Blessed Virgin would protect him.

He did not try to move from where he was; even if he had wanted to, he did not think he could have made it down the deep spiral stairs. He tried to drink only a little ale at a time, realising that he might need to conserve his supply of liquid.

By the afternoon the agonising pains had spread to his groin as well. He wanted to weep, but his body refused him even that relief.

He spent another night alone, while the plague continued remorselessly to take over his body.

By the following dawn, he knew he would not survive. He remembered the wretched man he had seen in his last extremities, stretched on the tomb below, and the grotesque, rotting corpses he had seen carried through the streets. He had no wish to be reduced to that final, loathsome state.

Painfully he dragged himself to the edge of the parapet. The city was gradually stirring below.

He gazed out, over the sweeping ridges to the north, and as he did so, he was vaguely aware of a tiny stone face, in a niche in the masonry a few feet to his right, gazing in the same direction.

For an hour he remained there. Three times he was forced by the pain to cry out.

Then he saw the figure of Adam in his broad belt walking jauntily through the close. He watched him until he had gone out, past the belfry and on through the gate into the town beyond.

Only when he could see the strange fellow no longer did he drag himself to the parapet and launch himself, with a huge effort, as far out into the air as he could go.

Gilbert de Godefroi forgot entirely about the Mason family and the sheep house. Half of Avonsford had died.

He himself sat, day after day, in the hall of the old manor. Often he would pick up the poem of Sir Orfeo and read it to himself while his eyes filled with tears as he thought of his own vanished wife.

Each day he waited, too, for news of his son.

For two weeks, none came.

Agnes Mason and the family remained on the high ground for a total of six weeks.

For Agnes, the week after Nicholas's last visit was the worst.

On the second day when he did not appear, all the family knew what it must mean. John said nothing, but she knew what he was thinking – she had been thinking the same thought herself. For each time he appeared, still healthy, after she first turned him away she had known with greater certainty: he was not contagious when I refused to let him in – if he catches the plague now, it will be my fault. Now, day after day, she prayed that he would come again, and each day, John's sullen silence was worse than a hundred accusations.

There was another problem too. She had chosen the deserted spot so well that no one ever came there, and as the weeks passed it was impossible to know whether it was safe to leave or not.

A month passed. Their food ran low; worse, the weather was so dry that the dew pond became almost empty, with only a small chalky puddle at the centre.

"One more day and we shall have to leave." John stated, and she could not deny it.

But that night it rained, and the next morning the whole family walked over to the dew pond and found a fresh supply of clear, clean water.

They held out for two more weeks, living off grain and water. A kind of lethargy descended upon them. They walked slowly, like people in a dream. Each day the bare ground around the circle of stones was empty and there was nothing to do but watch the clouds.

It was a morning in mid-September when, at last, Agnes turned to John and stated:

"I can't go on any more."

It was her first and only sign of weakness. When she said it, she wanted to break down and cry. But she could not.

An hour later, taking an almost empty cart with them, the bedraggled little party slowly made their way across to the edge of the valley.

And when they came down into Avonsford, they discovered that in their absence, the world had changed.

1382

When Edward Wilson looked back, he could not deny that it was old Walter who had changed the family's destiny.

How fortune's wheel had turned: what a tale of triumph it was. And of vengeance.

What a pair they had been.

But it was Walter who had seen his family's moment in history. Like a sailor sensing the turning of the tide, he had known exactly when and how to move; he had seized his opportunity and driven them forward.

For the Wilson family, the critical moment was the Black Death.

He was fifteen when the plague arrived. When young Peter suddenly fell sick he and his other brothers and sisters were ordered out of the house. They stayed in Grovely Wood, sleeping out, but returning periodically to the cottage to collect scraps of food. Then the rest of the family went down, one by one: his mother, his brothers and sisters – some with the disease in the lungs, others with the buboes, until only he and his father and his brother Elias – a half wit but with the strength of an ox – were left. Elias stayed at the cottage then, while he remained in the wood. And finally, even Walter succumbed. He saw the swellings under his father's arms; then he fled.

Three weeks he stayed in Grovely Wood, and lived well enough, for the Forest Laws were temporarily forgotten. He set snares for a variety of small animals; he even killed a young deer. And no one came by to trouble him. Several times, he wandered towards one of the nearby villages, watching cautiously from a vantage point; but as he saw the people there carrying out their dead for burial, he retreated back into the safety of the wood. Often he considered returning to Shockley farm but the terrible memory of his family dying there made him tremble and he avoided the place.

And then he saw his father.

It was early one morning. Walter was moving slowly, limping up the slope from the direction of Shockley, one foot dragging in the newly fallen leaves so that he made an uneven rustling sound as he moved that was strangely frightening. His face was distorted with pain and, even from fifty yards off, Edward could see that the buboes had spread to his neck. Obviously he must be dying, but what had made him go into the woods to do so the boy could not guess. He did not wait to find out, but fled. As he did so, he heard his father cursing behind him.

He did not go back to the spot but spent the day roaming the edge of the high ground before returning to another part of the wood to sleep.

Darkness had fallen and he was just dozing when he felt the long thin hand close over his throat. He tried to scream, but the steely grip prevented him. He knew it was his father.

"Fool," Walter's voice hissed, close by his ear. He smelt his father's breath. For some reason it smelt of fish.

He let his body relax. Perhaps if he could get his father off guard, he could suddenly slip out of his grip. But the steely hand only tightened.

"Want to slip away? Think I'm going to give you the plague?"

Of course he did. He heard Walter laugh softly.

"Still afraid of me?" Walter seemed pleased at the thought. All his family had been afraid of him.

Then Edward felt his other hand being taken and, though he fought with all his strength, it was pulled slowly but inexorably towards his father's face. Now Walter was pressing it against something – a small, hard bump.

"That's my neck," he hissed. Edward groaned as his hand was shifted again, and jammed against something hairy this time where there was another hard bump. "Armpit," Walter whispered. "I had the plague. Didn't kill me though. Gone now; you won't catch it." He released Edward's throat, but kept a hold on his arm. "You come with me," he muttered. "Work to do."

Edward smiled now, at the thought of the days that followed. They were a revelation.

Elias never even caught the plague. "Too stupid to catch anything," his father commented sourly. The rest of the family were neatly buried in a small trench above the cottage. "Half Sarum's dead," Walter informed him the next morning. "Go to your cousins. Bring anyone here who's alive. Get back by evening."

"Why?" he asked. But when Walter made to strike him he ran quickly off and did as he was told.

The little group – the remnants of Walter's brothers' and sisters' families was not impressive. There were two widows, a boy and a girl, both under twelve who looked thin and frightened, and the husband of one of his sisters, who was thin and sickly looking. One other brother, whose family had escaped the plague, had refused to come. But to Edward's surprise Walter seemed pleased with this little company.

"Put them in the cottage," he ordered. And then, with a sudden and uncharacteristic grin directed only at him he murmured: "And keep them there."

The next morning there were more surprises.

"Shockley's dead," Walter announced. "So's his family. Good riddance. One boy's left though: Stephen." He nodded to Edward. "You come with me: we're going to see him."

When they arrived at the house in the High Street, they found it in a state of chaos. He felt sorry for the boy, who was about his own age. Stephen had been through worse, Edward realised, than he had, since he had remained in the house in Salisbury throughout the plague and seen every one of his family die while being spared, by some miracle, himself.

If his father had sworn to destroy the Wilsons, poor Stephen Shockley had neither the desire nor the energy to persecute anybody. He was exhausted and he looked at them dully. Walter came straight to the point.

"You hold the tenancy to the farm from the Abbess. What are you going to do about it?"

Stephen looked blank. He did not know.

"My family's all dead, except this one." He jerked his thumb at Edward. "You've got no one to work the land."

Still Stephen stared at him hopelessly.

"If you don't work the land, you'll have to give it up."

Now the boy reacted. It was as if he had been slapped in the face.

"We've always had the farm," he protested.

Walter shrugged.

"Are you going to work it yourself?"

Stephen fell silent. They all knew he could not. The Shockley business in the town, and the fulling mill in the Avon valley were worth more than the farm. Whatever skill and energy Stephen had must be applied to these businesses first. But if he could not work the farm and pay the abbess her rent, she would repossess it.

"I'll get more labourers," he suggested hopefully.

Walter shook his head. "You won't find them," he stated. "Most of them are dead around Shockley." This was perfectly true and Stephen knew it. There was a pause. Then Walter said, in a voice that sounded more like a sad admission than a threat:

"Fact is, I've had other offers."

Was his father bluffing? Edward did not know. And certainly Stephen Shockley didn't. Walter's face was expressionless.

The young merchant was in a quandary, and in this he was not alone. The problem he faced was repeated all over the country. For the Black Death – the Pestilence or General Mortality as contemporaries rightly called it – had carried off something like one third of the population of England. It may have been more. Not since events described, seven centuries before by the Saxon historian Bede, the chroniclers noted, had there been such a mortality. Estimates are that in the whole of Europe in the years 1347 to 1350, about twenty-five million were lost. Its effects had varied from area to area, town to town, even from one estate to another – some were hardly affected, others saw an entire village completely destroyed.

Already, as he wandered about Sarum, Edward had heard widely different stories. But one thing was certain. Many fields would be untilled that year, and every landlord in the region was anxiously looking for labourers. Within a week of the first sign that the plague was passing on, farmers were out offering astonishing wages to anyone who would come and work for them.

"You owe me two days' work," Stephen reminded him. This was the condition of villeinage that Walter had inherited. But instead of acknowledging the fact, Walter now only shrugged.

"That was before the plague."

The young merchant looked at him thoughtfully. He was not a fool and he was well aware that in the general chaos in the countryside, villeins were already deserting their own cottages, breaking their feudal obligations, in return for high wages. Technically they were breaking the law, but in practice, when half the landowners were conniving with them, it would be futile to protest about it. If Walter deserted him, the farm would be empty and he would probably lose it. The villein had outmanoeuvred him and he knew it.

"So what do you want?" he asked.

That had been the beginning. And how clever his father had been.

"Go to the abbess," Walter told the young merchant. "Tell her you can't pay as much for the land."

"And then?"

"I'll pay you a fixed rent for it and make what I can. I'll try and find labourers, but if I can't, the boy here and I will have to do our best. That way we all survive and you keep your farm for no trouble."

There was sense in this. The abbess of Wilton from whom the Shockleys held the farm had many properties already vacant because of the plague. She would be glad enough to keep a good tenant even at a reduced rent for the time being. As for Stephen, he certainly hadn't the time to oversee the farm and try to find workers, who would in any case cost him more. The fact that he himself already had a workforce concealed in his cottage was something Walter carefully did not mention.

It worked. Two days later both Wilton Abbey and Stephen Shockley were receiving a sharply reduced, fixed rent for the farm. And Walter Wilson, now a subtenant instead of a villein, had the use of all the Shockley land for four pence an acre – less than half its value the year before.

But when Edward grinned at his father and said happily: "So we're Shockley's tenants now, not his villeins any more!" Walter turned on him viciously.

"Fool. We only need Shockley this year. Next year, we kick him out."

And when he looked puzzled, Walter only grunted.

"You'll see."

His father's extraordinary foresight was shown again when they discussed how to farm the land that first year. He had assumed that they would look for stock, including sheep, so that at worst they could get some return from selling wool. But Walter shook his head.

"This year, corn," he announced. "Sow every acre we can. Especially wheat."

"But half the people are dead," Edward suggested. "There'll be fewer mouths to feed – no market for corn."

But Walter only gave him a look of contempt.

"They'll be crying out for corn," he answered curtly.

And by the next summer they were. For in the confusion following the plague, many fields still lay uncultivated, and furthermore, there was a tendency amongst lawlords to put all their efforts into making sure their own demesne land was sown and harvested and then to keep back most of their corn and store it in case of further trouble. As Walter had forseen, there was a shortage and the price of wheat had soared.

In the autumn of 1349 the Wilsons, while they paid Stephen Shockley a pittance, made a huge profit.

It was not their only source of wealth. For the commodity even more in demand than corn was the labour to produce it. And Walter possessed that too.

For the little group – the old man, Elias, the two women and the children – were all, undeniably, his. Each, individually, had nowhere to go. And so he housed them, he clothed them, he fed them. And he terrorised them. He did it by sheer cunning and force of character.

They worked the Shockley land: he made them plough until they almost dropped. At harvest time, when extra help should have been called in, he kept them in the fields from before dawn until night fell. As the harvest time drew near its close, and the work was not finished, he even lit torches in the fields so that they could work on after dark.

At other times, when the work was lighter, he hired them out, singly or as a group, insisting that their day's wages should be paid directly to him. If they complained he would snarl: "Look after you, don't I?" And his menacing character was so strong that they were too frightened even to run away.

Once Edward told him: "I think the women will die if you work them so hard."

But Walter was not concerned. "They'll last a few years," he said gruffly. "That's all we need them for."

Between his own children he made a strict differentiation. Elias was a work horse. He was half as big again as his father, and though he had the same long hands and close-set eyes, it was as if some supernatural force had first flattened and then twisted his body: his face was broad and usually wore a look of blank stupidity; his shoulders were hunched; his walk was ungainly. "His mother must 'a looked at the moon before he was born," Walter remarked cheerfully. But he was strong, and he was anxious to please. "The idiot loves me," Walter explained. "He'll make my fortune." And indeed, though he would curse and even whip the young man as he went about his work, he could often find local farmers prepared to give him the incredible sum of two pence a day for Elias's services because he was so willing and so strong.

But Edward was let off lightly. He worked, as Walter did, but reasonable, regular hours. And often his father would take him with him on his busy trips around Sarum.

"Don't talk. Just listen," he was always told curtly. And that is what he did.

It was a year after he had first rented the farm from Stephen that Walter came home one evening with a broad grin on his face. He nodded to his son:

"Young Shockley's in trouble."

It was hardly surprising. Though nature had made him slight, where his father had always tended towards corpulence, he resembled William Shockley in many ways, not least in having a shrewd business brain. But though he was a capable, intelligent boy, and the abrupt death of his family had made him mature for his seventeen years, the sheer weight of the Shockley businesses had swamped him. When Walter had paid him a visit, he had found the boy showing every sign of being harassed, constantly pushing his thin flaxen hair back over his head in a nervous gesture, his pale blue eyes unable to conceal the fact that he was worried.

Fundamentally, there was nothing wrong with his affairs. The store and the fulling mill were both excellent businesses. But he was still learning how to manage them at a time of crisis which would have tested even an experienced merchant. And he had run out of cash.

The next day they went to visit him; and once again his father astonished him. For Walter was courteous, even generous.

"You're already running two businesses," he remarked pleasantly; "no man can do more than that. I want to make you an offer." He paused. "Let me take over the tenancy from the Abbey and I'll give you three years' rent for it. Fifteen pounds."

As he watched, Edward could not tell which one of them was more surprised – himself or young Shockley. It was more than a fair offer, and a substantial sum of money. Though he could not read or write, he could reckon with lightning speed, and he knew that, with the whole profit from their sales, together with the money saved from hiring out the family, Walter could not have produced such an amount. He must have stolen it, he thought to himself.

"You have that?" Stephen queried.

"An inheritance," Walter said coolly.

The youth considered. He was loath to give up the farm which had been in the family so long, but such a sum, in his hands now, would tide over the Shockley business where he knew his own future lay.

He nodded.

"Yes. I'll take it."

And with those words, the farm which King Alfred had given his Saxon forbears nearly five centuries before, and which had given him his name, passed forever out of the family's hands.

The next day, the former villein and new tenant of Shockley had a brief interview with the steward at Wilton Abbey. Edward was not asked to come. He never discovered how his father had done it, but the rent on the farm was lowered again.

"Now we've kicked those damn Shockleys out," his father told him. "And this is only the start."

"What's next?" Edward asked. But Walter did not say.

The next year, 1350, was a bad harvest; but they managed to salvage some of their corn and sold it at a handsome profit.

During this time, a subtle change began to take place in their relationship. For although his father would still occasionally strike him and frequently scowled at his foolish mistakes, he noticed that sometimes Walter would turn to him, apparently for advice, when they were doing business, and would even send him to attend to small matters by himself.

For he had shrewdly observed that people liked his son better than they did him. It did not worry him in the least; but he saw at once how it could be used as a weapon.

"You just smile. Soften them up," he would instruct Edward, and it was not long before the two of them had evolved a system of negotiating in this way that was devastating.

In the summer of 1350 Walter was ready for his next big step.

Edward still laughed when he remembered that day, when they had called for the first time upon Gilbert de Godefroi, and he had followed, so perfectly, his father's instructions.

The Black Death had taken a terrible toll upon the knight of Avonsford. He had one consolation, perhaps the greatest: he and his son had been spared. But both his wife and almost the entire village of Avonsford had been lost. The Masons, Margery Dubber and half a dozen more remained. The rest all lay in a trench beside the little churchyard. And now the knight was in deep difficulties.

The first year after the plague, this had not been so. For although the villeins and free tenants who should have worked his land had gone, he still had the right to the heriot tax payable when a peasant died. From the possessions of the dead he had collected some twenty pounds, which had at least kept the estate's accounts in balance. During the previous year he had paid high wages to cultivate at least part of his own demesne lands, but this had brought him no actual profit. And he had also been hard hit, like many others, by a murrain which had carried off most of his sheep. The Avonsford estate needed badly to be restocked and to find fresh tenants.

Thus it was that Walter Wilson and his son presented themselves respectfully at the manor house one morning, to enquire what land might be available.

They had walked all over the estate with the knight and his son. The land, Edward could see, was good, though untended; but it was the knight's son Thomas, a young man of his own age, who fascinated him most of all. He had never spent any time close to such a person. It was not only his pale, fine face and dark hair that made him so strikingly handsome, not only his splendid, athletic body; it was his bearing, the way he walked, the way he addressed others. How elegantly the fellow carries himself, he thought, and he was not ashamed frankly to admire him.

He did not forget their purpose, though. At each place they came to, Walter would survey the land silently. Occasionally he would mutter, or even sigh, but he seemed, out of deference to the knight, to hold back from speaking. But the more he saw, the more depressed he looked.

At last he shook his head.

"Land's tired."

It was true that in recent years Gilbert had used dung and marl fairly intensively to improve the yield from the land – a fact of which Walter was well aware – but to say the land was exhausted was an exaggeration.

"Don't think I can do anything with it," Walter said. "Sorry." He turned to go.

As he did so, Edward watched the knight. He saw Gilbert's face fall. It was his turn now.

"Let me put sheep on it father," he suggested. "Graze them above and then fold them here, let them dung it. I could work some of this land."

Walter glared at him.

"Land's no good, you fool," he snapped. "Can't make any money."

"We could do something."

"Better land elsewhere."

He looked sad, as if having to acknowledge that this was true.

"You said I could take on a piece of land. . ." he began, then looked at the knight and his son, as though pleading with them for support.

Walter paused.

"And what do you think it would cost?"

Edward looked confused.

"Maybe . . . a penny an acre." That was only half what Godefroi had wanted, but Walter made a sound of disgust.

"You'll ruin us."

This carefully calculated discord between them was kept up throughout the rest of the negotiations. It was clear that Godefroi wanted tenants, and that at present he had not enough takers. Half an hour later they had left with an agreement which was so advantageous to them that, once out of sight, Edward and his father had to lean against a tree they were laughing so hard.

For a pitiful rent they were to get almost a third of his best fields while, apparently as a favour, paying a small rent for a huge tract on the high ground above that the knight had not expected to rent at all.

"We could graze a thousand sheep up there – if we had them," Edward cried.

"And we can fold them on those fields. They'll yield plenty," Walter reminded him.

"That knight's a fool," Edward declared. "He doesn't know what he is doing."

This was not quite correct. Gilbert did know what he was doing, even though the choice he had made was still wrong.

The options open to the lord of Avonsford were simple. He could invest in his own land – restock it and, if necessary, pay higher wages. Or he could find good tenants and lease it out, withdrawing from the everyday business of agriculture almost entirely. Other men in his position were following either course. But now, at this critical point in history, the knight's cautious nature had done him a great disservice: or to be more cruel, he had lost his nerve. He was not prepared to risk the investment; he was not prepared to wait, as he should have, for the right tenant. He had simply played safe by accepting a rent that was too low rather than risk getting none. Indeed, he was pleased to have got anything for the marginal land on the high ground on which poor but extensive terrain Wilson could now graze his few sheep, forgetting that in the process, he was getting far too little for the good land.

As they turned to home, for the first time in his life, Edward felt his father's bony hand clap him on the back.

The thing which had surprised him most of all, however, had been the behaviour of young Thomas. For while the negotiation went on, the knight's son watched with a mixture of bafflement and scorn. He had taken no part in the discussion and it was obvious that, while too polite to say so, he felt nothing but disgust for the whole business.

"That Thomas," he said to his father in wonder. "He doesn't even care."

Walter nodded.

"He'll fight, but he'll never work," he replied.

For the years at Whiteheath had turned young Thomas into a most perfect squire. He carved to perfection; he sang, he could even, a little haltingly, read and write. And though English was his native tongue, he could speak a few phrases in Norman French – enough at least to exchange compliments with any French noble he might be lucky enough to capture in war. For war – and only war – was what he was made for. He had been as thoroughly trained in all its aspects as any of his ancestors. If another campaign came, he might grow rich; if not, it was clear that he would never take more than a cursory interest in his estate.

In the next four years, Edward scarcely set eyes on young Thomas, since the young squire was often away. But he came to know every corner of the Avonsford estate, and there was hardly an inch on his part of it from which he did not wring a profit.

For those with initiative, the 1350s were good years at Sarum. Despite the shock of the Black Death, the area soon picked itself up again, and in this respect the south and west of Wiltshire was more fortunate than many parts of the country.

For not only was the wool trade recovering there, but a new and formidable business was starting to grow: the manufacture of cloth.

In former times, England had exported her wool and imported cloth from the continent. The home manufacture had been mainly confined to the cheap burel cloth made at towns like Marlborough, to the north of Salisbury Plain, and a limited quantity of the heavier broadcloths which had especially benefited from the vigorous pounding in Shockley's fulling mill. But now a lively market for broadcloth began to develop not only in London and other major settlements, but on the continent as well. All over the area, there was more work for weavers, fullers and dyers. New mills were being built and merchants like Shockley were prospering. Nor were the great landlords left out. They supplied the wool. The Bishop of Winchester, the abbeys, and new feudal families who had gained royal favour, like the Hungerfords, were building up huge flocks of sheep on the rolling chalk ridges, on estates that stretched above Sarum for dozens of miles right across the northern sweep of Wessex.

It was a good time for those with initiative: and no men had more than Walter Wilson and his son. Walter got the better of every deal he made; and he continued to drive his little labour force unmercifully.

Only one person ever defeated him.

Agnes Mason and her little family had remained at Avonsford; but certain things had changed.

For although the family still held together, their life could never be the same after the experience on the high ground.

John had taken over his brother's work at the cathedral, and though Nicholas's death was seldom mentioned, Agnes was aware that her stepson treated her with a reserve, a distance, that was new. She was not surprised, nor was she dismayed when, six months later, he married and moved to another house in the village.

He still came, each day, to make sure that the family was not in need, but Agnes found that even without his help now, she was able to manage. Godefroi had not raised the rent on their cottage, and while she and the knight came to a new agreement that she would give the Avonsford estate three days work each week, he paid her well for these days and she had her older children to help her besides. Indeed, she soon found that she was better off than ever, since labour was scarce and she was able to sell the rest of her days either to Godefroi or to local farmers for handsome wages. Each week the square-jawed widow would visit the local landholders with her children, selling their free days to the highest bidder and though they could never achieve the rates that Elias Wilson got, they did well all the same, for they were known to be steady and reliable.

It was not surprising therefore that when Walter Wilson concluded his deal with Godefroi, that shrewd opportunist insisted as part of it that the Mason's three days paid labour should be given to him. To her annoyance, Godefroi had weakly given way.

"You work under my orders now," he curtly informed Agnes at once, and to Edward he remarked: "We'll work those cursed people till they drop."

For although Agnes was scarcely aware of the fact, Walter had not forgotten that it was old Osmund the mason who had spoken against his father to King Edward on the day of John Wilson's accusation at Clarendon, and when Edward had looked surprised at his father's vehemence he was reminded sharply: "We've a score to settle with those Masons too."

But he had reckoned without Agnes.

Their relationship had been calm for a month; Agnes had worked her usual three days and, although he had grumbled, Walter had paid her the same wages she had received before. But then he started to apply pressure. First he demanded an extra hour a day; she quietly refused. Then he demanded that not only she, but two of her children as well, should work all three days; this she simply ignored. When he tried in his usual way to terrorise her, she did not even complain, but her jaw set in the firm line her family knew so well and all his threats were useless.

Edward watched his father's mounting fury, but decided to stay out of the quarrel himself.

"There's no profit in that family," Walter would storm. "I'll get rid of them." But for the time being, as Agnes knew very well, there were no cheaper workers to be found, and so he had to put up with the infuriating situation.

It was not until a year later, in 1351, that he thought he saw his chance to get the better of her.

His weapon was given to him by Parliament.

For the free market in labour that had allowed Walter Wilson to make some of his most rapid gains had also, very naturally, produced a sharp reaction. It was not that the problem was new: wages in England had been rising steadily since the start of the century. But the sudden, acute labour shortages that occurred all over the country as a result of the Black Death had produced examples of wage increases that were spectacular. Nor had landlords liked losing their peasants, whatever their feudal obligations, when neighbours tempted them away with higher wages.

"It's outrageous, what labourers are being paid," Walter stormed.

"But that's how we made so much money," Edward protested.

"Not any more, fool," his father reminded him curtly. "We're the ones who pay, now."

All over the country, not only feudal landlords like Godefroi, but those acquiring lands at cheap prices – merchants, freemen, or former serfs – were in the same position, and they naturally came to the same simple conclusion: those working on the land were asking too much. There were protests about labour costs by 1349. By 1351 the Statute of Labourers was passed in Parliament, regulating wages through the courts.

It was armed with this new weapon that Walter, accompanied by his son, faced Agnes and her children at their cottage and told her curtly:

"I'm cutting your wages."

To his surprise she only shrugged.

"Then I'll work for someone else."

"I can take you to the shire court for that," he warned her. The Statute forbade desertion for higher wages. But Agnes was not impressed.

"And what does Elias get paid?" she demanded.

"None of your business," he snarled. His own little workforce was of course being paid the highest wages in the area.

"You'll pay me the same, and from now on you'll pay the two elder children full wages too," she retorted calmly. "Take me to court if you like." With a brisk nod she closed the door and left him standing there.

Although it was against the Wilson interest, Edward could not help admiring the stubborn woman who stood up to his father so firmly; and he knew very well that Agnes was right. For the Statute of Labourers, in practice, could only be enforced where local landlords wanted it to be; if farmers were anxious to employ labourers on any terms they would simply disregard it. Walter was in no position to take Agnes to court, but before he left Avonsford that day he swore to his son:

"Damn that woman. I'll get even with her. You'll see."

It was in any case only a minor irritation. In the next few years Walter not only sold his grain, but drove an ever-increasing flock of sheep up on the high ground, and here again he took advantage of Gilbert de Godefroi's conservatism and drove them on to pastures, out to the old sheep house beyond, that the knight had not used for years.

One other measure from Parliament was directly useful to them at this point. For years, the king had given a monopoly of wool exports to the merchants of the Staple – the oligarchy of rich traders who operated only through a single mart or Staple, usually across the Channel. This made it easy for the king to levy customs duties and also put at his disposal a small group of monopolists who would make him large loans. But this system angered the smaller wool traders who managed in 1353 to obtain a new Ordinance of the Staple which allowed local trading.

"Now we can sell our wool through Winchester or Bristol," Walter exulted, and by expert trading, and occasionally misrepresenting the quality of his wool, he soon increased his profits still further.

But then, in 1355, came his greatest chance of all. For in 1355, Thomas de Godefroi went to war.

Few campaigns in history have been more glorious than that of the Black Prince in 1355. Even Edward Wilson was moved to admiration by the splendour of it. As for Thomas de Godefroi, it seemed to the young knight that his hour had finally come.

"Thinks he's one of King Arthur's knights," Walter remarked scornfully.

It was true. But it was not surprising. For the whole proceedings were bathed in the golden light of chivalry. Some ten years before, Edward III had vowed to establish a round table at Windsor, and both the huge table itself and a building to house it had been begun. Of still more significance, on St George's Day 1348, that noblest and most self-conscious of chivalric institutions, the Order of the Garter was inaugurated with the Black Prince and the Earl of Salisbury amongst its founder members. To a young man like Godefroi, they seemed glorious days. A great and chivalrous king was surrounded by his sons – Edward the Black Prince, John of Gaunt, Lionel of Clarence – great men in their own right, all of them, yet steadfastly loyal to their father. This was kingship as it was meant to be.

Though Thomas certainly did not know it, the chivalrous notions that he had learnt in the splendid hall at Whiteheath, and which were now reaching their greatest flowering, came from several sources. The courtly troubadours of southern France had supplied the idea of courtly manners, and that every knight must serve a lady. The Church, with its cult of the Blessed Virgin, had reminded the knight that it was the lady of religion he must serve. The stoic philosophers of ancient times, through the writings of Boethius a thousand years before, who was so well-loved that the Saxon King Alfred had chosen to translate him, had told the nobleman that he was above the triumphs and misfortunes of this world, which he must suffer bravely and gracefully. This was the final amalgam, with its philosophical, religious and sexual appeal, that was now so wonderfully mixed together in the tales of King Arthur and his chivalrous knights; and there was no finer exponent of the knight's calling than Edward, Prince of Wales, the Black Prince.

"He's only a year or two older than me," Thomas would remind himself as he strove to emulate his hero.

For if the plague had left the country a dark and desolate wasteland, it seemed to Thomas that the glittering triumphs of English arms and chivalry were shining through the darkness.

The enthusiasm for the campaign amongst most of those taking part went far beyond chivalry. Never had the prospects of profit been better: for the highest and the lowest. A Welsh foot soldier was paid two pence a day; a mounted archer six pence – and this when the yearly wage of a ploughman was supposed to be about twelve shillings a year, so that even the foot soldier would earn the labourer's yearly wage in just seventy-two days. It was not only wages that attracted, in any case: it was plunder. Every foot soldier stood a good chance of finding loot in the rich provinces of France; as for a knight, he would hope to capture a nobleman.

"There's your path to fortune," Gilbert reminded his son. "We must have a knight to ransom. That'll save the estate."

The ransoms were huge. A French knight could often be sold back to his family for over a thousand pounds. Indeed, so valuable were captured nobles that a thriving commodity market in them had developed. Captives were sold between knights, or even to syndicates of merchants for cash against an anticipated ransom, so that a French nobleman might after a little time find that he was owned by a confusing collection of men spread all over the country, each of whom had a percentage interest in his life.

But if the remedy was clear, there was one problem: the cost of entry.

It was not only the armour with its burnished plates for the forearm and the front of the leg. It was not only a squire and a servant to accompany the knight. It was also the warhorse. For the high-bred charger, the destrier, was a necessity. With names as high-sounding as their noble owners, these splendid equine aristocrats were often imported from as far away as Spain and Sicily. Wonderful to look upon, magnificent in action, one of these beasts could cost an astounding hundred pounds.

And as usual, the estate was short of cash.

In his six years of trading since the plague, Walter Wilson had done spectacularly well. Exactly how he had managed to save a hundred pounds even Edward could never quite work out. But it was the possession of this remarkable sum that now allowed him to make the most brilliant transaction of his career.

For late in 1354 he lent this entire sum to Gilbert de Godefroi to equip his son Thomas for the war. He even lent the money without interest or fee of any kind – his conditions were cleverer than that. It was a loan which, in the circumstances, Godefroi was glad to accept.

"The terms are these," he explained to Edward. "If he takes a knight, he repays the loan, plus one twentieth of the ransom; if not, then he either repays the loan without interest, or he loses his security."

"And what's his security for the loan?" Edward asked.

Walter grinned.

"Some of his best fields – and the fulling mill."

How cleverly his father had baited the trap! Edward chuckled as he thought of it. If young Godefroi captured a knight, there was a good chance of profit; but if not, then they both knew very well that the Godefroi estate would be more short of cash than ever.

"You see," Walter muttered. "We'll get that Shockley mill."

Although Edward had no liking for young Thomas de Godefroi, he watched the preparations for the war with admiration, and he could see why the young noble, who had viewed his own estate with so little interest, should be so full of enthusiasm now. Many parties of men came through. There were the Welsh foot soldiers, dressed in green and white. There were men at arms, knights and squires. One of the most splendid sights was the mounted archers. They rode proudly, their six foot bows of yew, maple or oak slung behind them; they even rode about the battlefield, only dismounting to shoot their deadly hail of arrows – up to twelve in a minute with a range of almost four hundred yards and a force that could penetrate armour. And Thomas himself looked handsome, Edward had to admit, as he rode out of Sarum, with the white swan on his surcoat, on his way to seek his fortune.

The campaign of the Black Prince against King John the Good of France was a triumph beyond even Thomas's hopes. In 1355 they had campaigned around Bordeaux. The next year they had pushed further still. And on September 16, 1356, against a much larger French force, the twenty-five-year-old Prince had led his army to the great victory of Poitiers.

It was the stuff of legend.

Before the battle, Thomas had heard the stirring address the Black Prince made to his troops; and with the prince he had knelt to ask God's blessing; he had joined in the triumph when the King of France himself was captured, and he had been standing just outside the legendary feast when the prince, in his most famous gesture of chivalry, treated the fallen king like an honoured guest. What knights had been captured – the flower of French chivalry. And what ransoms agreed. The King of France was to pay three million crowns – five times King Edward's yearly income. Huge territories had been gained as well. How proud he was to have acquitted himself with honour in these noble proceedings: why, even the prince himself had smiled upon him.

There was only one problem: he had fought so valiantly, pressing on into every fray, that he had forgotten to capture a knight. He was returning almost empty-handed.

He was one of the few that did so. Almost every man at arms found plunder. Many even stayed on in the distracted kingdom for several years, forming themselves into mercenary companies whose profiteering would be remembered in France for generations. But when he had been invited by a friendly knight to join one of these, he had refused.

"A Godefroi fights for honour," he had stated coldly, "not for money."

And so honour was all that he brought back.

It was not enough.

Gilbert and his son behaved with quiet dignity, as befitted them, when they transferred some of their best fields and the profitable fulling mill into Walter Wilson's hands. By this transaction Walter became a direct tenant-in-chief of the king. But more important, he was Shockley's landlord.

Edward had never seen him so exultant.

"We've half ruined those Godefrois," he cried in triumph. "Now we'll kick out that cursed Shockley too."

But it was this plan that caused Edward, for the first time, to contradict his father.

In their many negotiations, which were always carefully orchestrated, he always played the soft role to his father's hard one; and no one valued more than Edward his father's blunt manner and vicious calculation. It had served them well. But he had also noticed in the last year a look in men's eyes which told him that they resented Walter, and several times recently he had been convinced that his softer approach could actually have brought them more. Moreover, young Shockley had done well in Salisbury. He was getting influence.

"Stephen Shockley's a member of the city guild now," he pointed out. "Why quarrel with him? We need friends, not enemies."

Walter stared at him, amazed. "Shockley? A friend?"

Edward shrugged. "Why not? If he's useful."

The older man was silent. His life had been led for revenge, and he had been successful. He longed to humiliate a Shockley. But his clear-sighted mind told him his son was right. He scowled.

Edward went on. It was something, he realised, that he had wanted to say for some time.

"Make him a friend. Soon we'll be richer than Shockley. That's what I want."

The two generations faced each other and then, to Edward's surprise, the older man gave way.

"Do what you like, damn you." And he turned away.

The next day Edward Wilson went into the city of New Sarum and after a satisfactory interview with Bishop Wyvil's steward, transferred the mill at a handsome profit to the bishop, who he knew had always wanted to get it.

"Now the bishop's our friend as well." He smiled.

Sometimes in the years that followed, he had to admit that old Walter might, after all, have been right; for the profits they could have reaped from the fulling mill were handsome. The cloth industry, in particular the production of broadcloth, was booming. But then so was every other aspect of their business. Though other parts of the country were still suffering from the shock of the plague, Wiltshire, and the city of Salisbury in particular, were thriving. And the Wilsons still continued to thrive more than most.

It is often supposed – quite erroneously – that the Black Death of 1348 was an isolated event which was not repeated until the great plague of 1665.

In fact, throughout the intervening centuries, there were numerous outbreaks of the plague; and probably the most severe of all, almost as terrible as the original, was the second visitation of 1361. It raged in London with a particular fury.

The plague had been in London for a week when Agnes Mason once again gathered her family together and prepared to lead them to the high ground.

"We'll go to the sheep house," she told them. She knew it had not been used that year.

The group that set out from the village this time was rather different. Agnes's children were grown: her elder girl had a husband now. But they had quietly loaded the carts under her directions, just as they had twelve years before. Only John was missing. Agnes had invited her stepson and his family to join them, but when he had refused she was not surprised and had not pressed the matter.

She herself had changed though. Her reddish hair was grey; twelve years had seen her body grow thin, and a nagging arthritis made her walk with a slight limp. It was not only her body that had started to fail her with the passing of the years: there was a weariness of spirit about her this time as she led them up the path past the manor.

It was as she had just reached the crest of the ridge overlooking the valley that they met Walter Wilson.

Edward always remembered the encounter.

His father had stood in the middle of the path, scowling at them and barring their way. The party stopped, eyeing him nervously. But it was only Walter and Agnes who spoke.

"Where are you going?"

"To the sheep house."

Walter shook his head.

"I'm using it." It lay on land where he had grazed his sheep from time to time, even though it had been deserted that year.

"You're not," she replied firmly.

"Going to tomorrow," he retorted sourly. "Not yours anyway. Stay out."

"The lord of the manor let me use it before," she told him.

"He won't now. I rent this land."

Neither of them moved, but Agnes guessed that what he said might be true. She shrugged.

"I'll go elsewhere then."

But Walter had no intention of letting her pass.

"You owe me three days' work," he reminded her.

"The plague's coming."

"Damn the plague. You work."

"I'm leaving the village," she said with quiet obstinacy.

But Walter only shook his head again.

"Anywhere you go on the high ground," he said, "I'll set the dogs on you." Then he grinned. "Send you dead rats too," he added.

She stared at him, and for the first time Edward saw her falter; for she knew Walter would be as good as his word. He had not forgotten how she had humiliated him over her wages and now he was getting his revenge.

"Want to take me to the shire court?" he snarled.

There was a long pause.

"God will strike you down," she said quietly.

Walter laughed.

"After he's sent you the plague," he chuckled.

Without another word, she turned round and the party went back down the path into the village.

"Suppose you think I should have made friends," Walter remarked to Edward. But Edward had only shrugged. He knew the Masons were not important.

"We live in dark days."

How many times, Edward Wilson sometimes wondered, had he heard Stephen Shockley's favourite phrase? Many times, certainly, for since he had moved with his family into the city of Salisbury after Walter's death, he had assiduously cultivated the merchant's friendship.

Shockley's verdict was one that most people would have agreed with.

There had been the repeated plagues – not only the plague of 1361, which had carried off Agnes Mason – but another in 1374. The triumphs of the middle of the century had faded. The Black Prince had died; his son Richard who had now ascended the throne, showed few of his father's noble and warlike qualities; and the splendid possessions in France, except for a small area around Bordeaux and the Channel port of Calais, in little more than a decade had all been lost. Indeed, there had even been fears of invasion so that a rampart around the new open city had been started and partially built. Not only the state was troubled: the Church itself was now divided. For over half a century the popes had found it necessary for their safety to live in Avignon, in southern France. But at least their rule had continued from there. In 1378 however, the great schism had begun. Like rival emperors in the Roman Empire, there were now rival popes: the French supporting one, the English and Netherlands another.

"There's nothing you can trust any more," Stephen Shockley used to complain to his family.

But through all these dark days, Edward Wilson kept his own counsel, and passed on to his children a very different view of the world, with equally good reason.

"Most men are fools," he told them. "When things are bad, the world is full of opportunities."

The life of Walter Wilson had proved it. When he had died in 1370, he had left behind him, besides a quantity of cash that his son never divulged, the following property, duly itemised in the newly fashionable documents known as Wills:

> A messuage, a carucate of land and seven acres at Winterbourne, which are held of the Earl of Salisbury; at Shockley, two virgates, held of the Abbess of Wilton. At Avonsford, two hundred acres held of the king; from the Bishop of Salisbury, near Avonsford, a messuage, a dovecote, a carucate of arable and ten acres of meadow.

The family, besides their substantial cloth interests, now ran over a thousand sheep on the high ground.

And each year the family became richer – as did many others. Not only former villeins like Wilson, or merchants like the Shockleys profited. Great men like John of Gaunt's retainers, the Hungerford family, had ever larger sheep interests on the chalk downs; all over the south western part of the country, weavers and fullers and cloth dyers were setting themselves up as the new cloth business boomed. The production of English broadcloth multiplied nine times in the half century after the Black Death. When Richard II came to the throne in 1377, Salisbury was the sixth greatest city in the kingdom.

Though his methods were different from his father's, Edward Wilson never failed to take advantage of every opportunity. One of these was a joint venture with the Shockleys for making cloth.

"This will feed you and your children," he told his young family as he proudly showed them the new cloth. "It's better even than broadcloth. They called it ray."

The new cloth was a speciality of Salisbury, and it was, as he predicted, to prove hugely popular. Salisbury ray was heavy, with a single background colour, like the broadcloth, but woven across it were patterns of coloured stripes giving an effect like a bright tweed.

Unlike the broadcloth, the different coloured threads had to be dyed before they were woven.

"See, it's dyed in the wool," Edward explained.

It was a sturdy cloth, often delivered rough to the customer who then gave it its final shearing, and it was not long before the Shockleys and Wilsons were turning it out in huge quantities.

Above all, as he looked at the changing world about him, the far-sighted Edward was able to tell his children:

"Stick to trade, and even the king will have to do what we want."

This was true. For now at last the power that Peter Shockley had only dreamed of when he witnessed Montfort's parliament the century before was starting to become a reality. All through the century the lesser men – the knights and burgesses – had been making their presence felt at the parliaments King Edward III had had to call. They had successfully imposed their wishes on the king back in 1353 over the Staple. In the 1360s, the hated maltote tax on wool had been almost abolished. But most dramatic of all had been the so-called Good Parliament of 1376, the year before King Edward died. The magnates and bishops had met in the

White Chamber of the king's palace; but the gentry and burgesses – the Commons – had held their own meeting in the octagonal chapter house of Westminster Abbey, that had been the model for Salisbury's own.

Now for the first time they had come to the bar of the magnates' house and made their demands – and those demands had been remarkable: namely that they would not vote taxes until the king had dismissed several of his ministers, who had embezzled the funds they had been voted before, and that the king should also send away his mistress who was in league with them. Demands like this had been made before by unruly feudal barons, but never with such bluntness by mere burgesses and minor gentlemen. Not only this: the Commons got their way.

Underlying this political progress was also a financial need. For all his successes in the French wars – whose ransoms alone had brought huge sums into the king's coffers, Edward III had a growing financial embarrassment. By the 1340s he had, some said unscrupulously, bankrupted the Italian Peruzzi and Bardi bankers by refusing to pay his debts to them, and when the monopolist wool merchants of the Staple lent him money after that, a combination of his spending and the Black Death bankrupted many of them too. Edward was forced to look to wider sources of income: the city merchants of London, the church, the customs duties; as for Parliament, the principle of no taxation without represent-ation was becoming established anyway, but now it was not just a case of the merchants – as Peter Shockley once had done – hoping that the king would hear their advice. "He'll listen to the Commons' demands," Wilson stated flatly.

The Commons generally favoured local magistrates, chosen by men like themselves, to sit in local courts and maintain the peace – and so the system of amateur local justices slowly began. The Commons disliked the foreigners appointed to English benefices. "Those popes at Avignon send men to Sarum you never see and who can't speak English if they do turn up," men like Wilson and Shockley agreed. But this time they not only agreed, their burgesses in the Commons forced the king to do something about it and appoint more Englishmen instead. One other event, seldom remarked in histories, but significant nonetheless had taken place in 1362. For in that year, the antiquated use of Norman French in the law courts was abolished. Gilbert de Godefroi had still understood it and mourned its passing. Few others did. Within a generation, Langland's *Piers the Ploughman* and the *Canterbury Tales* of Geoffrey Chaucer with its huge, courtly Anglo-French vocabulary had been written in something very close to modern English.

"England is ours now," Edward Wilson told his children. It was a confident boast, but not an idle one. Few men understood the world better than Edward Wilson.

But if he thought he understood the world so well that he could no longer be surprised, he was wrong.

The events of 1381 amazed him. And when he thought about the unlikely person who had set the drama in motion and the strange part which he personally had played, he used to grin with amusement.

It was Stephen Shockley's son Martin who caused the uproar.

It had been a point of special pride with the burgess that his son, though not a priest, should be a scholar. This was not unusual: for though the landed gentry and the magnates usually did not trouble much with education, there were many sons of merchants, or even poor men if they could find a patron, to be found in the colleges of England. Stephen had been so determined to do the thing well that, seeing how the colleges in Salisbury had fallen into decline he had sent his son to the University of Oxford itself.

"But damn it Wilson," he moaned afterwards, "I wish I hadn't."

For at Oxford, Martin Shockley heard the lectures of John Wyclif.

The great forerunner of the Protestant Reformation was not a heroic figure. He was a timid, ill-tempered academic who, as a priest, himself derived income from several benefices which he seldom visited. But when challenged, he became obstinate, and this was his strength.

From the philosophical notion that a man may know God directly, rather than blindly follow the logic-chopping dogma of the Church, he was soon preaching doctrines that were utterly subversive.

He developed what he called his theory of lordship – that only the good, not the wicked should govern, or even own the land. The authorities protested. He promptly went further and announced that if the pope showed himself to be too worldly, he should be deposed. By 1379 he had denied publicly that the bread and wine in the mass were transubstantiated into the body and blood of Christ and, even worse, said that the Bible should be translated into English so that ordinary men could receive the word of God direct.

It was this denial by his followers, known as Lollards, of the power of the priest to make God, that was so particularly objectionable, and their reading of translations of the Bible that proved them to be subversive.

Yet, even in high places, they were not without friends.

There were magnates and ordinary gentlemen who would be glad to weaken the power of the Church. There were taxes being paid to Rome which both the king and his parliament would rather have seen go to the exchequer. This Wyclif with his denial of the pope's power could be a useful weapon. It was for this reason that the great John of Gaunt, brother to the Black Prince and uncle of the new King Richard II supported and protected the obstreperous academic.

Meanwhile in Oxford, the debate raged. And to an idealistic young man like Martin Shockley, Wyclif's lectures were not just heady stuff, but the beginning of a new world.

On an unusually chill day in May, the entire Shockley family went to the cathedral to celebrate the return of their son Martin from Oxford.

It was a pleasant domestic scene – Stephen, a well-to-do merchant in sprightly middle age, his pleasant, comfortable looking wife Cecilia, and

[550]

their five children of whom Martin, at twenty, was the eldest. Stephen was proud, glad that his son was home at last.

"It's time he took a hand in the business," he said to his wife.

The family sat quietly in the nave, wrapped in heavy cloaks as the priests came by to say their morning mass. Because of the cold, the canons were dressed in their heavy almuces – the capes lined with fur which the more important clergy favoured at the time – and their breath rose like steam as they chanted. There were not many others in the congregation – about thirty sat in the nave.

It had been some time since the family had seen Martin, and his brothers and sisters could not resist stealing furtive glances at him. He was a handsome young man, with his mother's rich brown hair and his father's slim build and brilliant blue eyes.

He had arrived late the previous evening, and apart from a little light conversation, none of the family had talked much before retiring for the night. There was a slight tension and intensity in his manner that Cecilia noticed and it worried her; but as he got happily into bed beside her, Stephen made light of it.

"They tell me the Oxford scholars all look thin and nervous," he told her. "Too much reading and thinking. He'll be all right once he's settled in the business here at Sarum."

The mass was over. The priests were coming back through the cathedral. The Shockley family respectfully bowed.

And then they stared. For something extraordinary was happening.

Martin was stepping out into the aisle, and he was shouting. What was he saying?

"Whores and thieves!" the young man cried at the astonished priests. "Your mass is an insult to God."

For a moment the little procession stopped, staring first in disbelief, then in fury, at Martin and his father.

"Criminals," Martin shouted again. But now, with a cry of fear from his wife, Stephen launched himself towards his son and dragged him out of the church.

Within minutes, standing beside the belfry tower, Stephen had learned the truth; and half an hour later, when he had locked his son safely in the Shockley house, he explained to Cecilia and the other children.

"He's become a follower of Wyclif."

He knew about Wyclif of course: how his preachings and writings had caused a storm at Oxford, how John of Gaunt had taken him to Parliament to make trouble for the Church, and how he had been inconclusively tried by an ecclesiastical court where, thanks to his friends at court, he had only been reprimanded, so far.

"But the man's a troublemaker and our son's a fool to listen to such stuff," he announced.

"Perhaps he's a little feverish," his mother suggested.

But Stephen shook his head. "Give him a potion if you like," he said, "but if he's not careful he'll end up in the bishop's prison – and so will we," he added gloomily.

His fears seemed to be justified when the next day a sallow young priest named Portehors arrived from the dean.

"Not only the dean, but Bishop Erghum himself is anxious to know about this young man," he gave Stephen a piercing look, "who has abused the priests in the cathedral."

And since there was nothing else to do, Stephen replied sadly:

"Then you'd better see for yourself."

The interview which followed, in which he took part himself, left him more depressed than ever. Portehors was two inches taller than Martin, two years older and, if it was possible, two shades paler. His grandfather Le Portier had fled the city at the time of the Black Death but when he became a priest, he had reverted to the name Portehors to stress the connection with the canon of the same family name in the previous century. Like all his family, he was painfully precise, and he questioned the young man carefully.

"You are familiar, I understand, with the preachings of the heretic Wyclif?"

"I am," Martin answered proudly.

"And you find yourself in agreement with what he says?"

"Yes. Mostly."

"For example?"

"You priests – the canons especially. You have rich benefices. You let your lands around Sarum for huge profits. You live like noblemen."

"Is that wrong?"

"Yes. Christ taught that his disciples should give up their worldly goods."

"The Church does not say so."

"The Church is wrong."

Young Portehors winced as though he had suffered pain.

"You think Christ's followers should give up their worldly goods?"

Martin nodded. "Of course."

Portehors smirked.

"You are wrong. Since you read the Holy Scriptures," this, too, Martin knew was a presumption in a layman that was almost a crime, "you will remember that in the garden of Gethsemane, when the soldiers came to arrest Our Lord, the apostle Peter tried to attack them."

"Of course."

"And do you remember what Our Lord said to him?" He paused only for effect. "I will translate: he said – 'Put up thy sword!' "

Martin nodded.

"You note the words: *thy* sword. From this it is clear," Portehors recited the explanation as if by rote, "that the Apostles had personal possessions of their own. Our Lord did not, you notice, rebuke Peter for *possession* of a sword, but only for the *use* of it at that time and place." He smiled. "So you see, the scriptures do not condemn personal property, even in the hands of St Peter himself."

It was exactly the kind of preposterous logic through which the lesser scholastics delighted to exercise their ingenuity. Martin was familiar with the method and said nothing.

Seeing that he had not impressed him, Portehors asked crossly: "What else?"

"I'm against the endowment of chantries and the singing of obits by which your priests are paid to pray for a man's soul, because he thinks that by feeding your mouths he can get time off his punishment in hell. I'm even more against the sale of indulgences where you give him time off without even troubling to pray for him. I'm similarly against the foolish practice of burning lights."

"There's nothing wrong with lights," Stephen burst out. He himself had long belonged to a small confraternity of friendly merchants who had burned lights to a chosen patron saint. "It's an act of respect."

"And you pay the church when you do it," Martin remarked. "The Bible enjoins a simple life, poverty, good works, and prayer. It says nothing about Caesarian prelates like our lord bishop at Sarum."

This last phrase was a favourite of Wyclif's: it perfectly described the worldly servants whom the king made bishops as a reward for their services. Though the system saved the king, and hence his subjects a great deal of money, since clever and powerful men could take their rewards from the huge Church revenues instead of fleecing the treasury, it was anathema to the followers of Wyclif. Both the previous bishop, Wyville, and the present Bishop Erghum were men of this stamp.

Portehors was silent after this appalling impertinence.

"Anything else?" he asked dangerously.

"I'm against foreigners being given appointments in the cathedral by the pope when they never turn up."

"They are not. The bishop has stopped it."

For once Martin had slipped up. For two years before, partly in response to the growing agitation caused by Wyclif's sympathisers, this practice at Salisbury had been stopped.

"Perhaps, like Wyclif, you would like to depose the pope," Portehors suggested sarcastically.

But here his self-confidence made him careless.

"The pope. Which one?" Martin asked pleasantly.

And at this Portehors could only scowl.

"Do you deny that the body and blood of Christ are present in the mass?" he asked suddenly. This was the dreadful notion of these heretics who denied the power of the priest to make God.

Martin looked at him coolly. He decided not to give the young priest such an easy heresy to accuse him of. "I'd like my priests to be men of God," he replied contemptuously.

Appalled as he was by his son's folly, Stephen could not help admiring his sturdy spirit; and when soon afterwards Portehors left, he went quietly to the store where he and Wilson kept their cloth and spent several hours there alone, scarcely able to decide whether he privately agreed with his son or not.

Two days later, he received a definite, but quiet warning to keep Martin under control; that was all.

For although young Portehors would gladly have seen the arrogant young merchant put to the rack, the Church authorities – perhaps because they were easy-going and frequently corrupt – took a generous view of the reformers. There was no Inquisition in England; and Archbishop Sudbury of Canterbury himself had only moved slowly and reluctantly against Wyclif even when the Oxford scholar was at his most tempestuous.

"And who are the best Christians?" Stephen asked his son a few days later.

"The poorest friars, and the mystics," Martin answered at once.

The merchant could not, in his heart, disagree. It was a conclusion that many men, in that century shot through with the darkness of the Black Death, had come to. At this very time, great mystic writers like Thomas à Kempis and Julian of Norwich were writing books on the spiritual life that would be classics for centuries to come. When all the world's riches could so visibly turn to dust, how could a thoughtful man fail to turn from the world?

But whatever his occasional thoughts might be, Stephen Shockley was a practical man.

"You've made your protest," he told his son simply. "But you must consider your family now. You must either leave my house, and Sarum, or you must hold your beliefs in private."

At first it seemed that Martin world refuse even this; but finally, after his mother had pleaded with him, he unwillingly agreed to say no more for the time being.

"Though at Oxford, or in London," he assured his father, "it will be different."

And Stephen was forced to confess to his wife: "I don't think he'll stay here for long."

The uneasy peace between Martin Shockley and the cathedral canons was shattered by the events of June 1381.

The Peasants' Revolt did not come to Sarum. It was from Kent and Essex that the great horde came, enraged by the king's new poll taxes which fell most heavily upon the poor. At London, they had elected Wat Tyler as their leader and then terrorised the city for days.

Fortunately it was soon over. The brave young King Richard had gone out to face them and promised to grant their demands; then his followers had killed Tyler, and soon afterwards, all the king's promises forgotten, the rebel leaders had been horribly punished. Sensible men like Stephen Shockley had breathed a sigh of relief.

But more worrying to those in authority was the sense of general unease in the countryside. The rebels in the east had been roused by the hedgerow preacher John Ball whose followers chanted the rhyme:

When Adam delve and Eve span
Who was then the gentleman?

It was an ugly, seditious thought, and not to be tolerated. There must be masters and servants or the whole fabric of society would collapse. As for their demands that serfdom be ended and the Statute of Labourers abolished, that could not be either. True, the old feudal obligations had been gradually lessening for a century and a half, and the Statute of Labourers had frequently failed to hold wages down. But to demand that ancient obligations should be forgotten was another matter. That was a question of principle.

It was not surprising that many, especially in the Church, blamed Wyclif for these disturbances – though in fact anything that threatened the revenues from his small estates would have irritated that absentee landlord considerably.

"He sets his face against authority, and he encourages foolish and ignorant men to think they can take the law into their own hands," Portehors told Stephen Shockley sententiously, soon after news of the troubles had reached Sarum. "I hope your son will soon learn his lesson."

But even Portehors would never have imagined the wickedness and folly of what Martin did next.

For during the riots, Sudbury, the Archbishop of Canterbury was killed by the mob.

And it was on the morning that news of this terrible event was circulating in the market place that Martin Shockley let out a great cry and shouted: "Good! There's one damned worldly prelate less!"

There was no doubt about it. There were fifty witnesses.

And now the bishop struck.

Bishop Erghum of Salisbury was not a man to be trifled with.

He also had a most unusual passion – for mechanical clocks.

These were still a great rarity. When the bellringers in the tall belfry tolled the hours, they were regulated not by any mechanical device, but by long candles, with marks on their side, whose accuracy was occasionally checked with a great hour glass. Erghum intended to change that.

It was while he was studying the design for the new clock – a large, cumbersome mechanism driven by weights hung from ropes and regulated not, as yet, by a pendulum but by a less accurate set of drums and wheels – that he was interrupted by an excited and scandalised Portehors with the news of Martin Shockley's conduct in the market place.

To Portehors's disappointment he did not rise from his chair in a towering rage; he only stared down at the picture of ropes, flywheels and gears and waved the young priest away. But if Portehors had looked more closely, he would have seen that the bishop's face had set like a mask.

The next week they brought Stephen Shockley the news.

The bishop was going to excommunicate the Shockley family; and he was going to repossess the mill.

It was a terrible punishment, but the death of the archbishop and the fear of the revolt was causing a reign of harsh repression all over the country. The so-called Lollards who followed Wyclif's teachings were heretics and their possessions could be forfeited.

"The bishop is my landlord," Stephen reminded his son. "Now we'll lose the mill through your folly."

Yet even under this threat, Martin was unrepentant.

"John of Gaunt supports Wyclif," he reminded his father. "So does the Earl of Salisbury himself, and other magnates, too."

"The bishop can't reach as high as Gaunt," Shockley replied, "but he can crush us."

His fears were well-founded: Erghum proved himself to be so strong that he even forced the great Earl of Salisbury to appear at Sarum and do penance for his Lollard sympathies in the cathedral. The Shockley family could be dealt with summarily and easily.

In the late summer of 1381, Stephen Shockley was about to lose his most valuable possession.

Edward Wilson used to laugh out loud when he remembered the events of the next few days. It was a story he loved to tell his children.

Stephen Shockley had been distraught.

"And then," Edward would relate with a grin, "he came to me for advice." He used to chuckle before he went on. "I told him not to worry."

His business with Stephen Shockley had gone well; he had no wish to see his partner ruined, or to strengthen the hand of the bishop who as the feudal overlord of the town, interfered in its affairs too much. He also had one piece of information which Shockley did not possess.

This was that young Portehors was not, as he seemed, a paragon of virtue. For over a year in fact, he had been having an affair with the wife of an ironmonger in the town. She was a large woman, far from good-looking, and it had always amused Edward Wilson to think of the pale, thin priest in her company. The young priest had been discreet, but not cautious enough, and several people in the city knew about his visits to her.

It was this weakness that gave Edward Wilson his idea. He said nothing more to Shockley.

Three evenings later, a remarkable set of circumstances took place, all by chance.

By chance Stephen Shockley was detained by a merchant until late in the evening on the other side of the town; by chance also, the Shockley children were out of the house, and by chance, therefore, Cecilia Shockley found herself alone in the house in the High Street.

It was an hour after dark, and she had already retired to bed when she heard the noise. Thinking it must be one of her family, she called out. There was no reply.

Puzzled, she turned to one side, where she knew there was a candle, but before she could even find it, the door of the chamber swung open, and a tall, thin figure entered the room.

Cecilia Shockley was a plump, good-looking woman with a soft, gentle face; her normal expression was one of happy submissiveness to her husband. But she was not a nervous woman, nor physically weak.

And so she fought long and hard, and screamed loudly as the thin young man, whose face was covered by a hood, threw himself upon her and tore away the nightshirt she was wearing. She could not get the hood off his face, but she managed to kick him soundly, disregarding the oaths he muttered as he seized her by her long hair. He was strong, and determined, and as she felt his long arms close around her, she knew she was going to be raped. But she kept fighting.

It was the shouts in the street outside that saved her. For suddenly, when she herself was near the end of her resistance, he heard them, panicked and fled, leaving her shaking and hardly able to move.

It was by chance that Edward Wilson should have been passing the house at that time with two of his apprentices, who heard her screams.

Just as it was also chance, no doubt, that young Portehors should have received a mysterious and urgent message from his lover to meet her at the corner of the market place after dusk that evening so that, when she failed to arrive for the appointment, he should have been seen loitering there, not far from the scene of the crime. It was bad luck for him that Wilson and his apprentices should have chased the thin figure down the street and then lost him, only to see Portehors a few moments later.

But it was no chance that Edward Wilson should have requested a private interview with Bishop Erghum himself the next morning.

As always, he was deferential.

"You've heard that someone tried to rape Shockley's wife last night, Your Grace."

Erghum nodded. The family was disgraced, but he had no sympathy for crimes of this kind. "Bad business," he said bleakly.

"Your Grace, I saw the man who did it."

Erghum looked surprised.

"Then tell my bailiff at once, man. He'll lock him up."

Wilson looked at the floor carefully while he paused.

"I should prefer not."

Erghum scowled at him. What was the fellow up to?

"Why?"

"It might be unwise, Your Grace. In these troubled times." He paused again. "It was Portehors, Your Grace: your chaplain."

Erghum glowered at him.

"Nonsense. He has an irreproachable character."

Wilson shook his head.

"Not quite." And he outlined, in meticulous detail, what was known of Portehors's affair with the ironmonger's wife. "Of course, he's a young man . . ." he suggested indulgently.

The bishop eyed him warily. His instinct told him that part of the story might be true.

"And you identified him running out of Shockley's house?"

"I fear so," Edward bowed respectfully.

"Anyone else see his face?"

"My two apprentices. But I have told them to say nothing. After all, we surprised him before the worst . . ."

"Yes. Yes."

Erghum now saw what he was driving at, but he waited for Wilson to make the next move.

"The city is very disturbed at present," Wilson went on calmly. "No harm was actually done. But if after Your Grace's known anger with the Shockleys an affair of this kind were to come to court, I thought . . . the townspeople . . ." he trailed off and waited in an attitude of apparent obedience for the bishop's instructions.

Though Bishop Erghum knew that he could never be sure exactly what Wilson had done, he thought he could guess most of it; and he admired the rogue's cunning. It was also true that there had been troubles between some of the rowdier elements in the town and his bailiff recently; with the tense situation in the whole country at present, it was madness to tempt them to fury over a crime by his chaplain real or supposed.

He's caught me nicely, he thought, and aloud he said: "So you want me to leave the Shockleys alone?"

Wilson said nothing.

"Control their boy," Erghum growled. "I'll have no Lollards here. You understand?"

Wilson bowed deeply, and the bishop waved him away.

Stephen Shockley was delighted when Wilson suggested that Martin go to Calais to conduct some business for him that autumn. It took the young man several months. And during this time, the bishop seemed to have forgotten about the mill. Cecilia Shockley's assailant was never found.

And in later years, when Edward Wilson looked back on his long life, he never had reason to alter his favourite opinion, but could only laugh when he remarked:

"Most men are fools."

The Rose

1456

THERE WAS AN air of excitement in the town. Already, many of the narrow gabled houses were sporting decorations of flowers or richly dyed cloths from their overhanging eaves. In the streets, groups of brightly dressed men and women were moving cheerfully about, some to inns, others to the halls of the craftsmen's guilds from which the sounds of celebration could be heard. It was early evening, but it would still be light for many hours.

For tomorrow was a great day.

It was by coincidence that the four intriguers each left their houses in the different wards of the city exactly as the former Bishop Erghum's clock in the great belfry in the cathedral close struck six o'clock.

Each of the four men had a particular task to accomplish that evening. Their names were Eustace Godfrey, Michael Shockley, Benedict Mason, and John Wilson.

The excitement in the city of Salisbury had nothing to do with events in the outside world to which, for over half a century, its citizens had consistently paid as little attention as possible.

Yet there had been no lack of drama in England's recent past. The valiant son of John of Gaunt whose huge Lancastrian estates lay over tracts of Wessex near Sarum, had seized the throne from his unhappy cousin Richard II, and so begun the rule of Lancaster. Next, the usurper's son Henry V had won most of the kingdom of France at his famous battle of Agincourt; though since then, inspired by that strange sixteen-year-old girl Joan of Arc, the French had been gradually winning their country back again. They were stirring times.

In Sarum however, these great events abroad were only noted because of a brawl between a party of soldiers on their way to France and some of the town youths on Fisherton Bridge. Apart from this, the town paid its modest subsidies and took no further notice.

"There's no profit in these foreign wars any more," Shockley told his son. "It's trade we want."

Now yet another drama was unfolding. For only the year before the battle of St Albans had begun that high feudal drama, that sequence of battles between the rival branches of the royal family, Lancaster and York, that would later be known as the Wars of the Roses – a misleading title, as it happens, since though the white rose was the emblem of the house of York, the red rose was only adopted by the royal house in later, Tudor times.

Lancaster, in theory, meant the king. In practice, however, it meant his council, which had for thirty years been dominated by powerful magnates: first, until his death, by the French king's great uncle Beaufort, Bishop of Winchester, and now by his strong-willed wife, Margaret of Anjou.

For Henry VI of England was another of those unfortunate weakling kings, like Henry III two centuries before, who were such a feature of medieval history. Like his ancestor, he had a passion for building; but he also had a more serious disability. For unfortunately, when his father after Agincourt had married the daughter of the mad King of France, he had probably introduced the French king's mental instability into the house of Lancaster. Only two years before, poor Henry VI had remained for months at nearby Clarendon during one of his fits of insanity.

The citizens of Salisbury cared nothing for these royal quarrels either. If royal visitors came, its aldermen donned their robes to receive them. They supplied minstrels to Clarendon. But the battles between the factions of Lancaster and York were fought by retainers or hired mercenaries and the people of the town went steadily about their business, wiser in their humble trading than the noble lords in their dynastic folly.

And what of the great event so eagerly anticipated at the cathedral? For in 1456, after centuries of application, the most recent negotiation, which itself had been started almost fifty years ago, seemed close to success. At last Sarum was to see its great Bishop Osmund canonised. Salisbury would have its own saint. The business might be concluded in months. Even now, the representatives of the dean and chapter were working for the great cause in Rome. No one doubted the value of the would-be saint, and his miracles – meagre though they were – were believed.

But the stately cathedral was sealed off in its private world behind the walls of the close, and the citizens of the town paid little attention to that either. For although the great schism had been settled in the early years of the century and the popes ruled over a united Catholic Church from Rome once more, that rule was passive. No terrible Interdicts fell upon the king or his people; Italy was far away and there were few foreign priests on the island now. The townspeople had their craft guilds and religious fraternities, with their own chapels and chantries – not in the huge and solemn cathedral but in the smaller parish churches of St Thomas, St Martin and St Edmund in the town itself. Religion too was a local affair, from which the outside world of bishops and popes could be excluded.

As far as the cathedral was concerned, the citizens of Salisbury cared about only one thing: the fact that the Bishop of Salisbury was still the city's feudal overlord: and this they hated, not because his rule was oppressive, but because they resented any interference.

This resentment was nothing new. Even a century and a half before, the mayor and aldermen had tried unsuccessfully to throw off this feudal yoke and get a town charter of their own; but in recent years the friction between the bishop and the town he owned had become greater. The last bishop, Ayscough, had been especially unpopular and when Jack Cade led a brief and confused revolt in Kent six years before, a party of Sarum men, inspired by the rebellion, actually killed the bishop on Salisbury Plain. The ringleaders were hanged and the king sent a quarter of Jack Cade's dismembered body to be strung up in the market place to encourage the people to good behaviour in future. But the quarrel still went on. Successive mayors had done all they could to ignore the new bishop, and only two years ago, mayor Hall had tried once again to get a new town charter from the king.

"The truth is, we don't want the bishop – and we don't need him," Shockley remarked. It was a parochial self-confidence which most of the merchants in Salisbury shared.

For no place in fifteenth century England was more fortunate than Sarum.

Two things mattered: first, it was so perfectly situated.

To the north lay the sweeping chalk ridges where huge flocks of sheep grazed, and beyond them one entered the rich cheese and dairy country of north Wiltshire.

"Chalk and cheese," the men of Wiltshire would say to describe their country. And Salisbury was the central market for all.

While wars and trading disputes in Europe had weakened many of England's ports, Salisbury lay at the centre of a network of the three most successful: to the east was London, to the west Bristol, and to the south, closest of all, lay Southampton.

Second, the region produced cloth. And cloth was the key to everything. When Shockley and Wilson had started to engage in cloth exporting the previous century, they had joined a growing business. Now it had surpassed all others. While the trade in exporting raw wool had gradually declined, hitting many great cities like Winchester, Lincoln and Oxford, the areas that were strong in cloth had boomed. Salisbury lay at the very heart of the business. Not only did the city itself manufacture its rays and other textiles, but all over the western part of ancient Wessex, from Wiltshire to Somerset, the huge broadcloth business was at its greatest. Fortunes were being made by great merchants and landowners, like the soldier adventurer Fastolf. Every village now seemed to have its weavers and dyers, every stream – and swift flowing streams were abundant – its fulling mill. The place where the five rivers met was a focal point for trade, drawing in wealth all over the rich heartland of Wessex.

The town was organised for business: from the lowliest apprentice serving his seven long years' apprenticeship in his craft, to the great men of the council of forty-eight and the inner group of twenty-four merchants who directed its affairs.

But today, in the thirty-fourth year of the reign of King Henry VI, the place was organised for a great festivity.

For tomorrow was the eve of the feast of St John.

There were several feasts of St John. There was the feast of St John of

Patmos in May; of St John's Day in Harvest in August, to remember the beheading of John the Baptist; but by far the greatest celebration was the one about to take place: the feast of the Nativity of John the Baptist. And the importance of this great feast was not surprising: for the Nativity of St John fell on Midsummer's Day.

On Midsummer's Eve 1456, well aware of the town's good fortune, the citizens of Salisbury had reason to celebrate.

At six o'clock, Eustace Godfrey left his house in the Meadow ward at the south east corner of the city.

His handsome face was determined but cheerful as he made his way towards New Street. He wore a long, red robe lined with fox fur – his best – and on his head was a small circlet of gold. For the plan in his head this evening would, he was sure, put his family on the road back to their former glory; and as always when he began a new project, he was optimistic.

For tonight he was going to marry off both his children.

His confidence seemed well-founded.

"After all, anyone in this city would be proud to marry a Godefroi," he reminded his wife.

It was his grandfather who had finally sold the Avonsford estate. Like nearly every landlord in England, even great magnates like John of Gaunt and the Bishop of Winchester, the Godefroi family had found it was more economic to let all their land to tenants; for rising wages and a general agricultural depression had gradually made their estates too costly to run themselves. But whereas the large landholders still had handsome rents to live on, the Godefrois had not, and they failed to keep their expenditure down. By 1420 the lords of Avonsford had sold their manor and the remaining land to the Earl of Salisbury and, no longer lords of anything, they had gone to live in Salisbury.

By the time of Eustace's father, the family themselves had adopted the anglicised name of Godfrey by which they were known in the town; though it still annoyed Eustace to discover a lowly merchant or craftsman who bore the same name and to think that other men might not make the distinction.

For he was still a nobleman. When the reeves collected the rent for his house he always made sure that their records correctly entered: Eustace Godfrey, Gentleman. He was pleased that the tall, four-storeyed house with its courtyard was in the ward furthest removed from the bustle of the town and nearest to the precincts of the close and the handsome old hall of the Grey Friars. From the top floor windows he could see the roof of the bishop's palace: and when recently some houses in the close, formerly reserved for the clergy, had been rented to laymen, he had nearly moved to one of them. He liked to feel that he lived close to the bishop.

His most treasured possession was the heavy parchment scroll that bore the splendid Godefroi family tree. Nothing gave him more joy than to know that his wife, the daughter of a brewer from Wilton and to whom he had been devotedly married for twenty years, still looked at this document with awe.

Almost equally treasured were his children: Oliver, a good-looking, intelligent young man of nineteen studying for the law, and Isabella, sixteen, slim and dark, of whom he could only shake his head and murmur: "She is a jewel."

Now it was time that the boy should make an alliance and the jewel should be bestowed.

He had considered the opportunities carefully, and also the advantages his children had. About the former he was optimistic but a little hazy; about the latter, certain.

"You have a noble name," he told Oliver. "And equally important – you have connections."

And connections there were, of a kind.

There was the bishop, for instance.

Godfrey did not share the townsmen's scorn of the cathedral – indeed, during the last half century the diocese had been blessed with several distinguished and scholarly bishops, great men like Chandler and the noted preacher Hallam. The ancient Use of Sarum had even been adopted as the best order of church services in St Paul's Cathedral in London now. The present incumbent, Bishop Beauchamp of Salisbury, was a figure of great importance, close to the royal house where other members of his noble family held high office. He was also chaplain to the noble Order of the Garter, and often at Windsor, which lay in his own diocese. Godfrey had taken care to draw himself to Beauchamp's attention; only months before, he had made a modest donation towards the expenses of the negotiations for Osmund's canonisation in Rome. When the bishop passed, he bowed politely and always, he noted carefully, the bishop had returned the bow with a smile. They had spoken on several occasions, which gave Eustace the opportunity to explain carefully to the bishop exactly who he was. The fact that Beauchamp, now that he knew, did not greatly care, had never occurred to him.

Once, he had met an even greater figure: for the old connection of his family with the knights of Whiteheath had not been completely forgotten, and on one of his visits to their estate, he was taken into Winchester and introduced to the great Beaufort himself. From this single meeting, when the mighty Bishop of Winchester conversed with him freely, although Beaufort himself had now been dead nearly ten years, he liked to think that he was in touch with the royal Council itself.

That was not all.

"These are dangerous times," he told Oliver. "We need a foot in both camps."

The great royal house of York, cousins to the king, had not only raged against the dominance of the Bishop of Winchester and the Lancastrian Council. When the king had gone mad two years before, the Duke of York had been made protector of the kingdom; the king had recovered but since then there had been a constant struggle for power between the two factions, until in May 1455 the dispute broke into an armed conflict at the battle of St Albans. Since the start of the year, the country had been quiet. The energetic queen was once again in control with her Council; York had returned as the King's Lieutenant to Ireland. But there was still only a weak and half mad king with a single baby son. Who could tell what might happen next?

Of all the magnates on the Yorkist side none were greater than the members of the powerful family of Neville. Their estates were vast and they had acquired them by marriage, intrigue, and by fraud. By marriage with the Montagues they had obtained the earldom of Salisbury and successfully claimed the ancient right to the third penny – a third of all the royal revenues arising in the county. The earl, though seldom seen in Wiltshire, still held huge estates there; his possessions even included the little castle by the harbour at Christchurch, and if the Yorkist party were to take power he would surely become stronger than ever. Even now, though the Lancastrians ruled the Council, the earl and his mighty son Warwick held the fortified town of Calais just across the Channel, which they refused to give up.

"We're known to the earl," Eustace told Oliver seriously. His secret hope was always that one day the magnate, who now owned Avonsford, would return his broken estate to him with enough money to put it back in order. He had made several journeys to London during which he had contrived to get himself into the earl's company and remind him of their common interest in the place. He did not know that the earl's steward had several times recommended disposing of the unprofitable manor if they could find a buyer, and that this very week it was being offered to the bishop for a sharply reduced price.

While the town did its best to ignore the feudal goings-on, Godefroi longed to take part. Often he would calculate the relative local merits of the nearby Lancastrian estates of the Bishop of Winchester or the Yorkist ones of the earl; or he would consider the value of the friendship of the Bishop of Salisbury with the huge estates of the diocese, who managed to remain on good terms with both parties in the dispute.

So he wove his web of hopes and dreams.

"The family's well placed," he claimed cheerfully. All that was needed now to succeed was money.

He had tried to provide it.

First he invested in wool, buying quantities through an agent from local farmers for the export market. He invested heavily. But as a Flemish merchant complained to him:

"The trouble with English wool is that by the time you've paid the king's tax on it, your raw wool costs almost the same as finished cloth." This was indeed the effect of the fact that the king levied customs on raw wool but not on finished cloth: while the cloth trade boomed, the wool trade was now only profitable for the huge merchants of the Staple and after a few years of steady losses, Godfrey gave it up.

Then he tried to import wine from Gascony. This was a failure too. For after the successes of Joan of Arc had inspired the French to fight, and since the parochial English Parliament had kept the king short of funds for the war, year by year England's share of France had been whittled away until finally, to Godfrey's despair, the possessions in Gascony which had always been England's stronghold had been lost as well. For a few months in 1453, he was full of hope when the great commander Talbot led an expedition to take Gascony back again. Salisbury even contributed fifty marks towards the cost. But Talbot was killed and the vineyards of Bordeaux were never to be in English hands again.

His trade with Gascony was at an end.

"I'll never be a merchant," he admitted, half with pride, half ruefully. And though he was only forty-two, it was to his son that he turned and said: "It's up to you to save the family now."

If he laid the task upon his son rather than himself, however, at least he knew what the boy must do.

"The law and Parliament," he said. "That's your way forward."

In principle this idea was sound. More than ever before the sons of the gentry and the merchant classes were attending the schools where an excellent education for laymen, as well as priests, was available. Oliver had been sent to the school in Winchester established by the great chancellor Bishop Wykeham the century before; he had also spent two years at the recently founded King's College in Cambridge. He was an intelligent boy with the capacity to be a good lawyer; his only fault was that he was lazy. But if he worked, Eustace told him, there were certain to be opportunities for him in the service of the king or of one of the magnates who kept their own courts of retainers and placemen.

As for Parliament, there was the place really to further the family fortunes. The character of that body was changing. There were re-strictions on the electors in each shire now – only those freeholders who could show an income of forty shillings a year, might vote. It had become an arena for complex power-broking. The representatives of the boroughs and shires might not always be burgesses and local knights: more and more were outsiders, professional men in the pay of a magnate.

"God knows, John of Gaunt used to pack Parliament," Eustace remarked. "But young men like you are making a career out of being placemen there now."

A good example of the cynical processes at work lay right beside the city. For the half-deserted castle on Old Sarum hill had still retained its former right to send two members to the Parliament.

"Why in the Parliament of fifty-three," Godfrey pointed out to his son, "the two members for Old Sarum were a pair of London merchants – total strangers." And so the ancient hillfort had begun its long career as a convenient token constituency for the use of ambitious parliamentary men.

Sometimes, when he thought of his ancestors, these manoeuvrings depressed Godfrey.

"In the old days," he said sadly to his wife, "we fought."

But those days were long past. Warfare, too had changed. Even before Agincourt, his own grandfather had complained of the new cannon that were changing the old spirit of gentlemanly warfare. And besides, the new plate amour that was worn by any man of rank was far beyond Eustace's purse even if his son had shown an aptitude for soldiering.

But Eustace was optimistic. No doubt the boy would do well. As for his lovely daughter, who could resist her?

All that was needed was money – for his own resources were dwindling. And that meant marriage. Indeed in the last year the need had become urgent, but now Eustace Godfrey thought he had found the right candidates – merchants, to be sure, but rich.

Confident that he was going about the matter in a sensible way, as he set out on his mission that evening, Eustace was smiling.

He was also comforted by another thought.

For once his children were settled, he would be relieved of his chief responsibility. There would be nothing further that he had to do in his life. It was a pleasant prospect. He knew in his heart – perhaps he had always known – that he was doomed to be a failure in the busy world of Salisbury. His real vocation, he felt sure, was as a religious man and a scholar. He was always to be seen in the cathedral when a mass was being celebrated. Sometimes he would even attend all seven of the canonical hours. There was nothing he enjoyed more than to waylay the learned priests in the close and discuss with them the writings of the great mystics of the time like Thomas à Kempis or that remarkable woman hermit from East Anglia, Julian of Norwich; or to dispute with them the merits of the popular theory, which he stoutly maintained, that the people of England descended from none other than the displaced inhabitants of ancient Troy. He had even given a small volume on this preposterous subject to the new library that the dean and chapter had recently built overlooking the cathedral cloisters.

Yes, when the children were settled, he would be able to devote his time to these more agreeable pursuits; and it was with this happy prospect in mind that he went on his way.

His first call would be on John Wilson.

Michael Shockley was confident too, but he had good reason to be.

The house he left that evening was appropriate to his status in the city: it was a big, double-fronted, ponderous building with heavy oak beams forming the frame, thin wood coated with plaster between, and upper storeys which jutted out, overhanging the street. It lay in the northern Market ward of the city, in the Three Swans chequer, and it fronted on to the northern section of the old High Street which, since it seemed so long, had been given the new and delightful name of Endless Street. The house was solid and sensible, like Shockley himself.

He wore a short tunic, gathered tightly at the waist to exaggerate his broad chest and a tightly fitting hose that displayed to advantage his muscular calves. His object that evening was simple and straightforward: he was going to make certain that he was elected to the forty-eight.

There were, to be precise, seventy-two notable citizens who ruled the town of Salisbury: the twenty-four seniors, headed by the mayor and containing the aldermen of the town's four wards, and below them the body of forty-eight who took some of the more junior posts and who elected the seniors. The previous month, one of the forty-eight had died and his place was to be filled the next day.

"It's time I was chosen," he told his wife, "and I've got the support."

He was thirty-nine and he had many friends, partly because he was a good-hearted, easygoing fellow, but also because he had earned them.

The Shockleys had prospered, never dramatically, but steadily. The fulling mill was kept busy, especially with the heavy undyed broadcloth that sold so well, but Michael had also set up a small business producing the lighter worsted cloth that could still be fulled by manpower rather than by machine. It was a tactful move, for as well as producing a modest extra profit, this activity made him popular with the small craftsmen who were the backbone of the town. The expanding Shockley enterprises employed a number of fullers, dyers, and weavers and Michael never failed to make contributions to their trade guilds and social fraternities. His own son Reginald had also been enrolled in the powerful Tailors' Guild as well. A rich merchant he might be, but he always reminded his son: "If you want the Shockley business to prosper, you must always show the craftsmen you are one of them."

He had had his share of trading misfortunes. The merchants who traded with the Netherlands, known as merchant adventurers and often funded by the great merchants of the wool staple, had been hit by the wars with Burgundy. And the huge eastern trade across the North Sea and into the Baltic, a trade which reached far into eastern Europe and even into Russia, had already been disrupted by disputes with the German traders of the Hanseatic towns. Shockley had imported pitch and fur from Russia and sent cloth to the Netherlands, and both these parts of his business had suffered. But these reverses had been more than balanced by his successes. Only two months before he had imported a load of twenty-five tons of woad for making dye through the port of Southampton on which he had made a handsome profit.

As he turned out of Endless Street, a group of tailors standing by the corner smiled at him and when one of them shouted: "You'll soon be one of the forty-eight, Shockley," he replied with a grin.

Minutes later he reached his destination: the little church at the west side of the market place. The man he was to meet was already waiting for him.

As they came together at the church door the great man gave him a friendly nod:

"So you want to join the forty-eight?"

"Of course."

"Are you ready to contribute?"

"How much?"

The great man looked at him thoughtfully, assessing his wealth.

"An extra arch on this church," he said with a smile.

There were several great merchants in Sarum, but none were better known than John Halle and William Swayne. Some believed that John Halle was the greater. It was said that he owned half the wool that came off Salisbury Plain; he had already represented the borough in Parliament and petitioned the king to get a new charter for the town. He was rich, arrogant and loud-mouthed. But powerful as Halle was, he was not a richer nor a greater man than his rival William Swayne, who had already served as mayor and whose voice in the council carried authority.

It was William Swayne now who walked with Michael Shockley into the little church of St Thomas the Martyr.

No project was dearer to the great man's heart than the rebuilding of the church. Nearly ten years ago, when part of the chancel near the altar had fallen down, it had been the merchants Swayne, Halle and Webb, together with members of the gentry like the Hungerford, Ludlow and Godmanstone families, who had decided not only to rebuild it but to extend the whole church as well. Though many helped, the prime mover was Swayne and he intended the result to redound to his glory. He was even building, at his own expense, an entire aisle as a chapel for the powerful Tailors' Guild, of which he had become the patron. And here there would be two chantries, where priests would say masses for the souls of the living and the dead – one for the tailors, and one for himself and his family. The chapel was no small size: the renewed church would be splendid indeed.

"So if you want to join the forty-eight," he told Shockley frankly, "I shall expect to see you contribute to the building."

It suited Shockley very well to do so.

"I'm already a good friend to the Tailors' Guild," he reminded Swayne. "I'll be glad to contribute to their church."

A few minutes later they parted. He had Swayne's support. He walked across to the corner of the market in a state of happy excitement.

It was as he went by the poultry cross that the look of contentment on his face suddenly froze to one of rage.

There were very few things that disturbed the good temper of the merchant, but this was one of them. His blue eyes glittered in an angry stare. For he had just seen Eustace Godfrey.

It had been such a small, such a foolish event – truly nothing more than a chance and thoughtless remark made in a moment of irritation that had ended, ten years before, the centuries of good feeling between the two families. To this day, Godefrey still regretted it, but since there was nothing that he could do to remedy the fault, he too had allowed the bad feeling to settle and harden until it was like a carapace.

In those days he had been richer and more arrogant, and when his pretty little daughter Isabella, playing in the cathedral close with young Reginald Shockley one morning, ran up to him with the boy and announced: "Reginald will be my husband, papa, when I'm grown up," he replied coldly but almost without thinking: "A Godfrey does not marry a mere merchant," and sent the boy away. He was sorry for his words almost as soon as he said them, but they could not be unsaid. And when his tearful and humiliated little son told Michael Shockley about it, the merchant swore an oath.

"You'll not marry the daughter of that damned lord-of-nothing either," he exploded. And the two men had never spoken since.

Now, coming face to face at the poultry cross, the two men gazed straight through each other as they passed. But after Godfrey had gone the merchant grunted:

"You'll never sit on the forty-eight. I'll see to that."

But at the corner of Cross Keys chequer a few moments later, Benedict Mason was delighted to see Godfrey. He had been looking for him.

The modest house of the Mason family lay in Culver Street where they occupied half a tenement in Swayne's chequer. The street had also been the quarters of the town prostitutes until a few years before when Mason and other citizens of St Martin's ward had persuaded the council to drive them out. Now it was a quiet street like any other. Though he only occupied part of the house, Benedict rented most of the workshop area behind, and here, with the help of two journeymen, he carried on his business as a bellfounder. Bells from Salisbury were installed all over southern England; but the work was sporadic and his own business was small; on a day to day basis, he was a brazier, turning out copper pans in his workshops, which regular trade allowed him to live comfortably and support his family of six children.

He was a short, stout man, with a round face punctuated by a long, pointed nose, the end of which glowed red in all weathers. When he and his equally short, squat wife waddled down Culver Street followed by their children they resembled nothing so much as a family of ducks.

Benedict Mason was a member of the Smiths' Guild, which included goldsmiths and blacksmiths as well as braziers, and he was also one of a small fraternity who paid contributions to ensure that a mass was said for its members at St Edmund's church at least once a year and that the great bell was rung – at the considerable cost of twelve pence – when any of its members departed the world.

But his pride and joy was in making bells. Near his furnace was the pit with its centre post in which the clay mould for a new bell would be made; every day when he went to work, he would look lovingly at the carefully shaped wooden boards which would be rotated round the centre post to shape and smooth the clay. When each bell was finished, it bore his name, carved in the metal: BEN. MASON ME MADE.

And of all the bells he had ever made, the one he wanted to make now would be the greatest.

For after two centuries of disappointment, it really seemed at last that Salisbury was to get its own saint. The envoys from the chapter had been in Rome for many long months now; hundreds of pounds had been spent and although nothing definite was known, he knew it was widely rumoured that this time the long quest might be successful and old Bishop Osmund finally receive the recognition due to him.

"And then they'll be needing a bell," he announced. He could see it clearly: a magnificent bell, four, perhaps five feet across, with a deep mellow tone. It would be placed in the belfry in the close, above the clock, and its splendid chime would summon the priests to mass.

The problem was – how to convince the cathedral canons? And how to secure the commission for himself?

Benedict Mason might be modest, but he was also persistent. For weeks he had tried to get the attention of the priests for his idea. He had even approached William Swayne himself. But Swayne was only interested in St Thomas's and none of the priests had taken much notice of the humble bellmaker: he needed a more important figure to plead his cause.

Then he had thought of Godfrey. Godfrey, after all was a gentleman: it was said he was even close to the bishop. He had prepared his case carefully and was on his way to his house at the very moment when he saw him walking away from the poultry cross.

His approach was masterful – which is to say that he bowed as low as if Godfrey were the bishop himself and humbly asked if he might speak a word.

"It's the townspeople, sir," he began. "Even Swayne. They won't do anything for Saint Osmund." And then he unfolded his tale. The great bishop might be canonised at any time, he explained, and surely it was fitting that the people of the city should contribute something to honour him. "But they won't, sir. They only think about St Thomas's," he complained.

Godfrey listened carefully. What the bellmaker said was all too true. Though he himself took an active interest in the cathedral – from the library in the cloisters to the new strainer arches that were at last being built to reinforce the bending pillars under the tower – it always appalled him that there were so few in the town who shared his enthusiasm. There was an air of laxness in the close too – the spire needed repair, someone had even opened a shop on the ground floor of the belfry – and he deplored it.

"So what do you suggest?"

"A bell, sir. St Osmund's bell, a present from the city, to call the priests to prayer."

Godfrey considered the idea.

"And why are you telling me?"

Now Benedict Mason was ready with his master stroke.

"The town needs someone to give a lead, sir," he said earnestly. "A gentleman with the ear of the bishop: someone the people would listen to with respect." He watched Eustace's reaction carefully. "As for the cost," he added, as though as an afterthought, "for St Osmund, I'd make the finest bell for . . ." he spread his hands.

Godfrey could picture it. Indeed, as the implications of it dawned on him, he felt his pulse quicken with excitement. Although he had taken little interest in the doings of the town or its parish churches, it had annoyed him that when the landed families like the Godmanstones had been asked to contribute to the rebuilding of St Thomas's, Swayne and his followers had not even bothered to approach him. He had nothing to contribute, but it irked him to be ignored. This new idea was better though. He could take the lead himself, raise contributions. If Swayne could have his chapel, Eustace Godfrey, could for a much smaller expenditure, have his bell, and it would be a pleasant thing to be able to approach the bishop as a benefactor of the cathedral. The more he considered it, the more it pleased him.

"You're right," he told the bell founder. "Come to my house tomorrow and we'll see what we can do."

After all, by tomorrow, the family's financial position should be much improved.

There were several reasons why John Wilson was known as the spider.

One was that, when other men wore brightly coloured clothes he was invariably dressed in black; another was his curious way of walking, which he seemed to do by fits and starts, hovering silently at a corner of the market place, then suddenly moving forward towards some object, so that it was hard to keep track of his movements. Yet another was that for half a century, no one in Sarum had ever been certain of the true size of the Wilson fortune, nor the extent of the family's network of operations. All that was known was that since the time of Walter and his son Edward, it had been growing. John's father had made one massive gain that the world knew about when he had traded huge quantities of inferior embroidered silk to other cities for a short time, before the cities in question protested. And more recently, a merchant vessel of John Wilson's had captured a French ship – an act of piracy that was not discouraged in the wars with France – which had yielded him yet another fortune.

He might be nearly as rich as the great Halle and Swayne: he might not. But since his operations were invisible, and since people could never be sure when they were going to be caught up in them, he was likened to a spider and his business to a spider's web.

The spider was a pure merchant, having little to do with the craftsmen's guilds, and he was not popular. His son Robert who acted as his agent in the port of Southampton, was seldom seen in Sarum, but was said to be like his father.

At six o'clock, John Wilson left his splendid house in the New Street chequer; no one noticed him leave. He had two important visits to make, and as usual, he knew exactly what he was doing. The first was to the house of the great John Halle.

At seven o'clock, as Lizzie Curtis walked along the edge of Vanners Chequer opposite St Edmund's Church, she had a sense that she was being watched. Twice she glanced into alleys as she passed by, but she could not see anything.

She was sure that she had heard something though: a scuffle of feet and a rustling noise behind her.

It was light; there were people in the houses. Whoever was following her, she did not care. She tossed her head to show it, and this time she was sure she heard a laugh.

There were two things about Lizzie Curtis that mattered, as she knew very well: she was pretty and she was rich. Her father was one of the greatest butchers in the town, and he had no other child. And so, although she was intelligent, and friendly, she knew that there was no need for her to be either. She was seventeen.

She wore a bright blue surcoat over a trim yellow cotte, so fine it was almost like a petticoat. On her feet were yellow felt shoes that she slipped into pretty little wooden clogs, painted red, so that she made a dainty sound as she clip-clopped down the street. It was warm and the street was dusty, so she scooped up one corner of the outer garment in her hand, showing her petticoat and a tantalising glimpse of her ankles as she went by. The white wimple on her head did not hide the soft brown hair that peeped out in ringlets around her ears.

Was she being followed? There was an air of bravado about her as she tripped along, pretending not to care.

Lizzie Curtis cared what people thought of her. Every time she said something or made a gesture, she thought about it afterwards, remembering in detail people's reactions. When she was alone, she practised expressions in front of the silver mirror her father had given her. And whenever she saw a fine lady in the town, she would study her every move, committing it to memory. She collected all the clothes she could – but the brightly coloured articles she saw in the market place never seemed to satisfy her imagination. She had a little coterie of friends, girls of her own age or a little younger, and they remained her friends as long as they admired her. Since she was often funny and usually courageous, the other girls followed her most of the time without complaint.

One matter she often thought about – how would she make men admire her too? She was not certain yet, and as she was unsure, she generally played hard to get: flirting just enough to lead them on, then tossing her head and treating them with scorn. So far she had only tried this technique on the youths she met in the town, and it had seemed to work satisfactorily. Once she had been careless and let a young apprentice kiss her, but then, terrified that he would boast about it, she had pretended to be angry and flounced away.

Lizzie Curtis knew what she wanted. She wanted to be a fine lady – one of those gorgeous figures occasionally to be seen in the town wearing magnificent cloaks trimmed with ermine, and tall, fantastic headdresses made of tissues or brocades and studded with jewels, that rose over their heads in the spectacular if uncomfortable fashion of the time. Could her rich father find her a husband who could give her such things? He would have to be a gentleman, for the wives of merchants, however rich, were not permitted to wear the dress of the nobility and so she supposed that this ambition would not be satisfied.

She was thinking about this very subject as she tripped along.

They attacked her at the corner of Parson's chequer.

It was done so suddenly that she did not even have time to scream before they held her; there were six of them. Hustling her across the street they pulled her to a doorway; she felt one of them holding her hands, then she felt the rope. Moments later she was bound securely.

And then she knew what was happening and with a sigh of relief she smiled. She gazed round their faces.

"How much?" she asked.

There were many ways of raising money for the parish church or for charity. The most usual were the scotale evenings when beer was sold at rowdy parties by the church, but more amusing was the practice of roping, when groups of youths carrying a rope held women and girls to ransom in the street and threatened to tie them up if they did not pay a fine. This practice was reserved for Hocktide, however, soon after Easter, which was why, as an afterthought, Lizzie cried:

"Tisn't Hocktide anyway. I'll pay you nothing."

She knew them all now: Reginald Shockley was the eldest, a pleasant-faced boy of her own age; the youngest was little Tom Mason, the bellfounder's son, who was staring at her with enormous admiring eyes.

"A penny," they cried.

"Nothing," she protested.

"A ha'penny then or stay there," Shockley suggested.

She shook her head, laughing.

"You'll get nothing, I tell you."

They considered.

"A kiss then," one of them cried, and there was applause.

"Never," she tossed her head.

"Why not?"

"I'll kiss the man I marry," she assured them. This was a tactical mistake.

"I'll marry you," each of them offered.

"You're none of you good enough," she answered.

"Tell us who you'll marry then," one of them suggested, "and we'll untie you." To which she agreed.

So they untied her and she told them:

"I want a knight with a castle – who'll do as I say."

And though the words were spoken in jest, there was enough truth in them to make Reginald Shockley look sad, which she noticed with interest.

She liked him; although they had never been particular friends. But as the roping party moved away, she called him back, and to his astonishment gave him a kiss before running away, leaving him blushing happily in the middle of the street.

Apart from the welcome interruption by Benedict Mason, Godfrey had passed an irritating two hours. When he first arrived at Wilson's house, they told him that the merchant had just gone out. Three times he went back, each time without any luck and the confidence he had felt when he began the evening was beginning to ebb away.

The streets were nearly empty now. Many of the craft guilds had feasts – some of them repeated for several nights – before the great day, so that most of the folk seemed to be indoors.

It had been annoying, too, seeing Michael Shockley: doubly so because

[573]

the merchant he had insulted ten years ago was now certainly richer than he was.

The clock in the belfry was striking eight when he returned for the fourth time to be told that Wilson was now at home.

He wished, as he entered, that he could recover the confidence he had felt when he began.

John Wilson's house occupied a corner tenement so that it was, in effect, two houses. The entrance was through a handsome stone arch over which there was a solar chamber. It led into a walled courtyard and beyond that, there was a pleasant garden. The buildings formed an L-shape round the courtyard and were partly wooden and partly stone. Everything about the place confirmed the impression that, whatever the real extent of Wilson's fortune might be, he was certainly rich.

Moments later, he was ushered into the main hall.

John Wilson sat at a large oak table. He did not get up when Eustace entered, but motioned him to a chair opposite him. To his surprise, he saw that the merchant was not alone: for standing in the corner, he recognised the silent figure of his son Robert.

Although Wilson's hall was not large, it was comfortable. It had a high, hammer beam roof with little figures carved on the ends of the rafters; the windows were of rhenish glass, from Germany, prettily decorated with roses and lilies in the powdered style in which the continental glass-makers specialised. In front of him was a plate of salted tongues which he was eating with a silver spoon, and a bowl of raisins. As an act of courtesy, he pushed the bowl of raisins towards Eustace, but neither he nor his son spoke.

"It is a personal matter," Eustace remarked, glancing at Robert.

Wilson did not look up from his place, but nodded curtly.

"It concerns your son," Godfrey persisted. But if he expected the merchant to take the hint and send the young man away, it did not work.

"Concerns you," Wilson called over his shoulder. "You'd better stay."

Eustace felt less confident of his mission every second. In the silent moments that followed, Wilson ate a salted tongue.

"I have a daughter, Isabella," he began at last.

He did not dwell on her beauty, although, since neither father nor son spoke a word, it was hard to know whether they fully appreciated it or not. But he did explain, firmly and at some length, her ancestry. He also explained the position of the Godfrey family now, as he saw it, and here, several times, Wilson interrupted him.

"You were in the Gascon trade?"

"Yes. I still hope to resume it."

Wilson shook his head.

"No good."

"Talbot's expedition to Bordeaux failed, but many of the Gascons like English rule." This was true. "We may yet live to see a king of England crowned king of France again."

Here Wilson halted with the salted tongue only half way to his lips.

"Hope not. With France as well it makes the king too powerful." This was a view many men in Parliament had formed in the early years of the present king's reign: the English squires and merchants had no wish for a powerful half-foreign king that they could not control. "Gascony's finished anyway," Wilson remarked, to close the subject.

But when Godfrey outlined his own connections to the bishops, to the royal house, and his intention that his son should stand for parliament, Wilson finally stopped eating, and leaned back in his chair, his hard, narrow-set eyes staring at him in curiosity and wonder, that Eustace mistook for admiration.

"You need money for such fine connections," he said at last.

Godfrey inclined his head in acknowledgement.

"I've got money," Wilson remarked pleasantly. "No connections."

The irony of this remark was lost on Eustace. Wilson's trading connections would have made him gasp if he had been capable of understanding them. There were the part shares in the two-masted ships that set out from the western port of Bristol for the trading emporiums of Spain and Portugal. There were his extensive connections in London. Above all, there was the huge business of import and export which Robert oversaw at Southampton. While the old wool business of Winchester had declined, the sophisticated cloth business of Salisbury had burgeoned through the ever-growing southern port. The great convoys of Italian galleys that visited Flanders and London never failed to call there and take up huge quantities of the Salisbury rays he still dealt in. And from these and other traders Robert bought silks and satin velvets, pepper, cinnamon, ginger, even oranges from the warm Mediterranean and sent them to his father at Sarum. There was almost nothing Wilson did not have a hand in that was profitable. It was these southern markets, especially the Italian connection through Southampton that had allowed Salisbury to outstrip most other cities in England. But of the details of these crucial businesses, poor Godfrey was largely ignorant.

Thinking that he had impressed Wilson he came straight to his concluding point.

"With help, my son can raise the family to new heights. And I can assure you that I shall secure him a good marriage. I propose that your son Robert should make an alliance with Isabella that could be useful to both our families."

He had brought himself to say the last words in a tone that suggested he was prepared to regard the lowly Wilson family on a par with his own; he was proud of this piece of diplomacy.

Now he looked at them both expectantly.

The small, hard man in the chair appeared to be thinking, but he did not speak. What of Robert himself though, Godfrey wondered – what did the young man for whom he had proposed this fine alliance make of it all?

Like his father, Robert was thin and sallow, but his face was a little broader and more oval-shaped. He wore his hair in the fashionable manner, covering only the top of his head and cut in a circular fringe above the ears, below which his head and face were immaculately clean shaven. He did not move from the corner but, in the half shadow, his face seemed to be expressionless.

Robert Wilson seldom spoke. Though he was twenty-one, he might have been twice that age; there was no hint of youth about him. Even as a boy, he had always held himself severely and, some suspected scornfully, apart from the other children. No one had ever seen him indulge in any amusement. Indeed, Eustace suddenly realised, he knew very little about the young man except that he was reputed to be a highly respected businessman already and that, as John Wilson's heir, he must have a large fortune. If he spoke little, his dark brown eyes took in everything, and if his face never gave any hint of what he was thinking, John Wilson was obviously impressed with his ability, for he now trusted him with the Southampton business entirely.

For a moment, in the rather disconcerting silence, Godfrey wondered whether he had done the right thing. But he put the thought from him. The boy could not be so bad. Times were changing. His lovely Isabella must have a rich husband and there was an end to it.

Since no one spoke, and the fact he could not see Robert properly was beginning to irritate him, Godfrey suddenly called out:

"Well Master Robert, what do you think?" It was an attempt at heartiness that sounded, he realised, rather forced.

In reply, Robert moved forward into the light so that Eustace could see his face. But instead of speaking, he only looked at his father inquiringly.

And now at last John Wilson was ready to give his opinion. He laid down his fork carefully on the table and pushed the plate away from him, resting his arms in the space it had occupied. When he spoke his voice was very quiet so that Godfrey had to lean forward slightly to hear it, but his soft words seemed to cut into the space between them like a knife.

"When the city of Salisbury lent the king money on the security of the customs dues of Southampton, the Bishop of Winchester tried to embezzle the dues and leave us out of pocket. Why should I have wanted his friendship?"

There had been some accusations of this kind in the past, Godfrey knew, but it seemed to him beside the point.

"He was on the king's council," he reminded the merchant. But Wilson seemed not to hear him.

"You talk of Parliament." He spat a raisin seed from his mouth. "Parliament is useless. It only exists to vote taxes for the king, who should live off the revenues of his own estates. I've no interest in the king, his Council, or his Parliament." At these words Godfrey was speechless. Still Wilson went on, in little more than a whisper now. "As for the Bishop of Sarum," he remarked contemptuously, "all I know is that his servants start riots in the town and kill chickens." Two years before, it was true, one of the bishop's rent collectors had apparently had a fit of insanity and run through the townspeople's gardens killing some poultry with a sword. It was an isolated incident, but Wilson went on with scorn: "The bishop's servants are vipers and the bishop himself is a nuisance. I wish he'd get out. We don't want him."

It was the longest speech the merchant had taken the trouble to make for years. It exactly expressed the attitude of John Halle and many other merchants in the city, but it shocked Eustace Godfrey profoundly to hear the words so savagely spoken to his face.

Still Wilson had not finished. More than Godfrey realised, he himself represented long memories of feudal power and oppression that the Wilsons had resented for centuries and now, finding Eustace in his own power, the merchant could give vent to feelings he had brooded over all his life.

"I am a merchant; my grandfather was born a villein. I have no interest in your bishop, your magnate or your king. I hope they all kill each other in their wars – like they did last year at St Albans. Let them fight some more and die many more. As for your daughter, she's got no money and we don't want her."

Having finished, he grabbed the plate with both hands, pulled it back towards him and without looking up again, continued to eat the remainder of the salted tongues. Robert did not move or speak, but looked at Godfrey with what might have been mild curiosity.

Shaking with fury, but utterly impotent, Eustace slowly rose and walked out of the room. He hoped his exit was dignified, but he was not sure.

It was a tribute to his remarkable persistence that after only half an hour, he was ready to try again.

His call this time was on Curtis the butcher. For Lizzie would certainly make an excellent bride for Oliver.

"She's an heiress and she's good-looking," he had explained to Oliver, "and she isn't spoken for yet."

He arrived at nine o'clock at the butcher's house and this time, chastened by the last meeting, stated his case more simply, though dwelling generously on his son's attainments and prospects.

To his relief, he received a polite welcome. Indeed, the heavy-set butcher was attracted by the thought of marrying his daughter to a gentleman who, if fallen in the world, could still boast noble blood.

"He's very little money," Godfrey stated frankly.

"Wouldn't matter. I've plenty," Curtis replied. "The trouble is," he confessed sadly, "you've come two hours too late. I promised her to Wilson's boy this evening."

Godfrey's face fell. While he had been walking round the town waiting for him, the merchant dressed in black had been quietly stealing all his hopes away.

"I'd change my mind, even though he's rich," Curtis went on. "But," he grimaced, "I daren't annoy the spider."

And so Eustace Godfrey returned to his house near the close, still empty-handed.

After Godfrey had left them, John Wilson and his son had not shifted their respective positions for some minutes.

The merchant had quietly finished his meal, his son silently watching him.

Only then did John Wilson speak.

"That man's a fool."

Something in Robert's impassive face suggested that he agreed.

John Wilson took a raisin and chewed it thoughtfully.

"That girl, Lizzie Curtis, I got for you. She's not stupid." He glanced up. "Might be a bit of a handful though."

And now Robert spoke.

"I'll know how to handle her." The words were said very quietly.

John Wilson looked at his son curiously.

"Think so?"

"Oh yes." And for the first time that evening, his lips formed into a thin smile.

Wilson shrugged.

"Do what you like," he remarked, and got up from the table.

The procession of keeping the Midsummer Watch, on St John's Eve, was a magnificent affair. The houses were decorated, some with dozens of lamps hanging over their doorways, others with bundles of birch, or wreaths of lilies and St John's wort.

At the head of the procession, riding on splendid horses, came the mayor and the council members magnificently dressed in long gowns of scarlet-coloured Salisbury ray. With them came the symbols of their Fraternity, a figure of St George followed by his dragon. It was only two centuries since St George had become a popular saint, but since then numerous societies had adopted him and he had even become the patron saint of England itself. There were cheers as the men carrying the figure shook it until the armour in which he was dressed clanked loudly.

Behind them came the members of the guilds: the butchers, saddlers, smiths, carpenters, barber surgeons, fullers, weavers, shoemakers: there were nearly forty guilds in all, each with their sign and their particular livery. At the head of the smiths two archers with their longbows proudly marched: Benedict Mason was one of them.

But the greatest sight of all was the rich and powerful Tailors' Guild: for with them they brought the finest figure in the carnival: the Giant and his companion Hob-Nob.

The giant was huge – over twelve feet high and dressed in the magnificent robes of a proud merchant. His headgear was the height of fashion – a huge turban over a wide circular brim, with the free end of the cloth draped around his neck and hanging down his back. Below it, his big broad face gazed benevolently over the crowd. This handsome figure – pagan as he certainly was – represented the Tailors' Patron, St Christopher. In front of him, bobbing wildly from one side of the street to the other, went the hobby horse, Hob-Nob. In the form of a small horse and carried by a single man, this comic figure not only cleared a path for the giant but made frequent attacks upon the crowd, snapping at any one within his reach, to the delight of the children. The giant was a treasure of the town: in storage he was carefully preserved from the attention of rats by bags of arsenic and, in perfect condition, he was brought out in all his towering splendour on the great feast days of the year.

As he saw the procession go round the town, Godfrey's heart was heavy. His wife, his children too, were happy in the city, but he was not. He belonged to no guild; he would never be asked to join the seventy-two, nor did he wish to. It seemed to him he had no place in Sarum's busy life he could call his own. Slowly he started to walk along the street while the procession stamped past. The minstrels, the pie-sellers, the boister-ous apprentices and solemn seniors of the guild, all dressed – as the laws insisted – to suit their station: he walked silently past the rich pageant of the city that could not include him. At the corner of Blue Boar chequer he saw Michael Shockley and his family. The merchant was dressed in a tunic of dazzling green and red, his chest puffed out like a turkey cock. He had even donned a pair of magnificent shoes with toes so long that they had to be curved up and fastened to garters round his knees with golden chains. The following day, no doubt, he would be chosen to join the forty-eight; next year he would ride with the Council in a scarlet cloak. Godfrey avoided him.

It was just after he had passed the George Inn that the figure of the bellfounder came puffing up beside him. His whole face was now as red as his pointed nose usually was, and the nose itself had taken on a deep magenta hue.

"Will you be seeing the bishop soon, sir, about the bell?" he panted.

He had forgotten the bell; even that failed to raise his spirits now.

"Soon, soon," he promised, and continued on his way.

It was more in order to escape that he walked disconsolately through the gate into the quiet of the close. Even there, the sounds of the festivities of the summer solstice followed after him.

It was just before nine o'clock the next morning, as the members of the

Tailors' Guild, carrying their lighted tapers, were solemnly passing into St Thomas's Church that William Swayne met Michael Shockley at the edge of the churchyard. The great merchant's face was dark with anger.

"We've been cheated," he exploded, "that cursed John Halle."

Shockley stared at him in confusion.

"You mean the forty-eight?"

"I mean John Halle has another candidate no one knew about and he's already got enough of his henchmen to support him. I can't get you into the forty-eight."

Shockley was silent for a moment.

"Who?" he asked finally.

"John Wilson – the one they call the spider." Swayne grimaced in disgust. "God knows what he paid Halle for that."

For as usual, Wilson had moved quietly, but effectively.

There was a great feast in the guildhall after the service. There were baked duck, roasted pheasants, hedgehog, peacock, hogs – all the delicacies of the splendid medieval cuisine. There were minstrels with harps, gitterns and trumpets. There was ale and mead.

And in the midst of these festivities, John Wilson, still dressed in black, led his son to the place where Curtis the butcher sat, and Lizzie looked up at the young man who was to be her husband. It was their first meeting in some years.

He smiled politely, but his eyes were cold.

Something told her that she might not be happy.

In the year of Our Lord 1457, the canonisation of St Osmund of Salisbury was made absolute. It had cost the dean and chapter the astounding sum of seven hundred and thirty-one pounds – as much as the yearly revenue of some bishoprics.

There is no record that any bell was made in his honour, although the guilds made his day, 15th July, an occasion for another yearly procession through the town.

In 1465 a great dispute began between the citizens of Salisbury and Bishop Beauchamp. It was sparked off by a dispute between the two great rival merchants John Halle and William Swayne over who had the right to use a plot of land in the churchyard of St Thomas the Martyr. The bishop as feudal overlord had granted Swayne the right to build a house for a chantry priest there, but Halle declared that the plot belonged to the town corporation. Swayne began to build. Halle and his men tore part of the building down. But the origin of this dispute was soon forgotten, for the real quarrel lay between the citizens, led by Halle, and their overlord the bishop. They were determined to end his feudal rule and Halle was summoned to appear before the king himself and his council, where he spoke so intemperately that even Edward IV decided to put him in goal, where he remained for some time. The dispute dragged on for nine years before the King's Council finally decided for the bishop.

"The charter is clear," Godfrey told his family. "The city belongs to the bishop and there's nothing the merchants can do about it." The final triumph of the bishop was one of his few consolations, as his own fortune continued gradually but inevitably to decline. He paid Bishop Beauchamp a personal visit to congratulate him, and was delighted that he was received.

It was strange that when even those citizens who were Halle's enemies, like Shockley, supported him in his fight against the bishop, John and Robert Wilson, to whom Halle had acted as a patron, remained completely silent during this time. No word of either condemnation or agreement came from the handsome house in the New Street chequer.

But then John Wilson already had other plans.

A Journey from Sarum

1480

YOUNG WILLIAM WILSON did not move. He watched.

The damp, cold April morning mist had formed a fine coat over him; tiny droplets of which he was not even aware hung from the hairs of his thin eyebrows and his nose.

He had not eaten the day before.

But though he was cold, damp and hungry, he forgot those facts, and on his narrow sixteen-year-old face, there appeared a smile.

He could not see the river, though he knew it was there, a hundred yards in front of him; nor could he see the top of the ridges which were also enveloped in the mist. But he was beginning to see the outlines of the ground: a tree here and there, a hint of the track leading up to the high ground, for the sun was rising over the ridges now and starting to warm the hamlet and the manor of Avonsford.

He watched in the silence as slowly the yellow morning sun appeared and the mists began to dissolve. It was a moment he knew well and that he loved: for then the mists would slowly part, the upper layer drawing softly back like a veil up the valley slope before dissolving in the morning sunlight, leaving only the lower layer resting over the ground.

As he watched, two things happened.

Suddenly, from within the mist that covered the river water, he heard a beating of wings and then, out of its wreaths, came six swans. Their powerful wings whirred and moaned as they rose from the silent, invisible stream and swept down the valley.

At the same moment, the veil lifted off the foot of the slope behind the river and revealed the house.

How beautiful it was. Its long grey, uneven line with its gabled ends seemed to hover over the mist below, floating like a boat. Despite himself, he smiled.

He stayed quite still for whole minutes, wrapt in the beauty of it, almost forgetting that it was this house and its occupant who had destroyed everything he had. For this morning he had come to take his final leave.

"I will go," he murmured sadly, "as soon as the swans return."

The new manor house at Avonsford was certainly a fine affair – finer even than young Will could know, since he had never been inside.

It occupied the same site as the old building that had belonged to the Godefrois. But their crumbling house had been so neglected for fifty years that only bits of it had been incorporated into the new structure. Built of the same grey stone it was now a splendid residence.

"Fit for a gentleman to live in," the owner had remarked with truth.

The owner of this gentleman's house was Robert Forest.

It was ten years since John Wilson and his son Robert, merchants of Salisbury, had moved out of the city; and to mark this change in their social status from merchant to gentleman, they had taken a new surname, Forest, which seemed to them to suggest an ancient connection with the land.

For some years after that, John Wilson had continued his spider-like existence in the house in New Street chequer, seldom seen outside, but still becoming secretly richer each year, while Robert and his family had lived at Avonsford Manor. The manor was leased from its new overlord the Bishop of Salisbury for a term of three lives, but it was a lease which could be extended by future generations and the Forests had immediately set to work to make improvements that would make the house worthy of their newfound gentility.

It consisted of a spacious central hall, on each side of which was a large chamber with a handsome bay window. One of these, the larger, was a fine solar not unlike the original hall of the Godefroi knights. It had a high arched ceiling displaying dark oak beams and a bay window at one end with glass almost to the floor, which flooded the room with light. But it was the smaller room on the other side of the hall that was Robert Forest's particular pride: for this was called the winter parlour. It had a fine window too, though smaller, and a huge fireplace in front of which he and his family could sit; but its glory was the splendid wooden panelling round its walls, so perfect that once inside, the visitor felt as though he had entered an intricate wooden box, and every panel of this was carved in the new and elegant linenfold design.

When old John had seen it and queried the choice, Robert told him: "It's the latest thing. All the gentry are doing it – those that can afford to." And the old man had offered no further comment.

It was in the winter parlour, in a heavy oak display cupboard that he also kept the small collection of books that belonged in a gentleman's house. There were several books on heraldry and gentility; there was an illustrated manuscript of Chaucer's *Canterbury Tales* and also a new prose version of the tales of King Arthur. It was compiled by an obscure knight who had served at least one term in goal for theft, called Thomas Malory, but since Robert Forest had heard a nobleman recommend it, he had purchased the book at once.

There was one other item of which he was proud.

"I saw it in London," he told his father. "A man named Caxton, who was governor of the mercer's guild, has started to make these things with a machine." And he showed old John a handsomely bound book – a collection of philosophical sayings – that was of interest not because of its contents but because the letters had been made by a printing machine rather than by hand.

"With this printing machine he can turn out books by the yard," Robert explained, and old John agreed that the new invention was remarkable. But he frowned nonetheless as he inspected the page.

"Why, these words are written in different dialects," he complained. It was true. Caxton had, as most men did, his own views about how English words were to be pronounced and had chosen to spell them accordingly. The result on the newly printed page was a curious mixture of dialects from several different parts of the island.

"See – he writes 'plough' like a northerner," the merchant-turned-gentleman complained: for as written, the word would have sounded more like 'pluff', or 'rough'. "This won't do."

Robert said nothing. He was not interested. But his father was right, and the confused and illogical spelling chosen by Caxton's whim was to be the hallmark of written English from then on.

Upstairs, above the parlour, were bedrooms with scented rushes on the floors, and behind the house was a courtyard with kitchens and storerooms grouped around.

Indeed, it was a remarkable fact, of which the present occupants could have no idea, that the newly laid out manor house fitted almost exactly over another, deeply buried floorplan – that of a Roman villa, that a family named Porteus had built on that site, with roughly the same degree of sophistication, more than a thousand years before.

Beside the house was a small family chapel with a little turret into which Benedict Mason had been commissioned to install a new bell. On the other side of the house was a squat stone tower, twenty feet high, and on top of that was a wooden structure pierced with numerous small entrance holes. This was the dovecote, around which several dozen doves made their peaceful cooing and fluttering. Just past the dovecote, Robert had built a walled garden in which neat rows of hedges formed a framework for arbours and beds of roses. The whole place was a little heaven.

Sometimes, it was true, there were screams and cries of pain from the house, but if they heard them the villagers only shrugged.

Robert Forest was a rich and increasingly powerful man. If the quiet, dark-eyed squire of Avonsford chose to beat his wife or his children for some offence, it was his right.

"There's good order at the manor," it was said, sometimes with a nervous laugh.

It was bad luck for young Will that Robert Forest had turned him out. There were several reasons.

He was the only one of a family of five children to survive. His mother had died when he was ten, and after struggling on for six more years in the little cottage in Avonsford, his father had died that January. This was the problem: for the family's lease was a copyhold, expiring at the death of the tenant. The yearly rent had not been high, but rents were rising now, and not only would the new rent be higher, but the squire as lord of the manor had the right to the old heriot death duty and also to a new entry fine before he would renew the lease at all. And Will had no money.

The village was small: the few other tenants were poor: no one had offered to help him. They could not. Nor had Forest.

"If you can't pay, you're out," the steward told him. "The master says so."

Which was not surprising, for two reasons.

The first was that Robert Forest had other uses for the cottage.

Since the Black Death the century before, the village of Avonsford had never recovered. Its population had remained meagre and, by chance rather than any design, the families in the place had formed into two groups at opposite ends of the straggling village, while the houses between gradually decayed and were pulled down. The larger group lay at the south end; the smaller, where Will lived, at the north. The northern cluster was reduced to only four cottages now, but around them were outhouses and a plot of common land where they had the ancient right to graze livestock: a fact which made Robert Forest angry.

"It's a waste of good land," he remarked drily each time he passed it. "Five acres I could use."

The new lord of the manor had come to his decision that winter. He would rehouse the northern families in the southern group where there was already one vacant cottage and where he now built two more. The death of old Wilson in January made matters easier. Will, having no money, would not have to be rehoused at all but could be turned out. It was obviously a sensible decision.

The second reason was more subtle, but equally powerful.

Young Will Wilson was his cousin.

A distant cousin to be sure. When old Walter's brother had refused to join the rest of the motley family collection that formed a labour gang for that cunning survivor of the Black Death, he had probably saved his own little family from ruthless exploitation. But while Walter's descendants had risen to these new heights of affluence, his brother's family had remained poor peasants ever since. Over a century had passed: four, five generations. But Robert Forest had silently suspected, and secretly verified the connection as soon as he had taken over the estate. It was not a connection he wished to remember.

All through his childhood, Will had often noticed how sourly Forest looked at him if he chanced to pass the cottage, but since Robert Forest never smiled, he had not attached great significant to it.

And if ever he asked his father about the Forest family, his father had looked at the ground and told him only:

"They were rich merchants; now they're gentlemen. Nothing like us."

For although he too had been aware of the connection, Will's father, guessing Forest's likely feelings, was wise enough never to mention it.

"Why does he glare at our cottage?" the boy asked. "I've seen him."

"Just his way," his father had answered. "Show him respect, Will, and it'll be enough."

It had not been.

To Will however, the Forests were distant figures. Robert's wife and two children, a boy and a girl a little older than Will, were seldom seen away from the manor house. On Sundays, they usually worshipped at their little private chapel rather than the small and half derelict church in Avonsford. But occasionally he would see them and would always wonder at how quiet and reserved the two children looked as they walked behind their grey-haired mother, still handsome but so severe that she frightened him.

"She wasn't always like that," his father did once admit to him. "I remember when she was a merry young girl called Lizzie Curtis." He grimaced. "He at the manor, Robert Forest, changed that."

Will had not fully understood what this meant until one day, when he had to help his father mend the entrance to the dovecote, he saw her walking alone in the walled garden and noticed that when her husband entered the place and came up to her unexpectedly, she instinctively flinched back from him in fear. He kept his distance from the lord of the manor as much as he could after that.

It was the previous month that Forest had turned him out. The way it happened had filled him with amazement.

Though his neighbours had left, he had been staying in the little cottage because he had nowhere else to go. The steward knew he was there, of course, but if he saw him about the place, ignored him as completely as if he had been a dead man. Will guessed that matters would soon come to a head.

The men came one morning: a gang of ten – four from the estate and six hired from the town. In a single day they knocked down the four cottages. They took no notice of him at all as he stood quietly with his few possessions, watching them at work. At the end of the day, his little cottage was rubble. He slept in a hayloft in the southern part of the village that night. His neighbours there had not been quick to offer him food: he did not blame them – they had their own families to look after. Eventually however he had been given some wheatcakes. The next day he watched as the men came once more, this time with carts, and carried away any stones or other materials that could be re-used. Again he stayed in the hayloft. The third morning, the men brought heavy ploughs from all over the estate and four teams of oxen. All day they ploughed up the ground where the cottages had been, and the common land around it. In the evening, when they had done, it was hard for him to believe that the place which had been his home had so completely vanished under the naked, raw brown earth. The day after that, they began to plant the hawthorn hedge that would surround Forest's new five acre field.

This was the process known as enclosure. It took many forms: sometimes open fields with their time-honoured strips, ridges and banks which were so economically wasteful, were converted to single ploughed fields; or the peasants' corn fields might be converted to cattle and sheep pasture; sometimes these enclosures were made by mutual agreement, sometimes by compulsion, or often, as in the case of Avonsford, by a mixture of the two.

Although the process was already well known in many parts of England, because it was mainly open sheep country, the practice of enclosure was never such a striking feature of life at Sarum as it was in other areas. But enclosures there were, and it was Forest's enclosure that forced young Will Wilson off the land.

Since it was obvious that Forest did not want him there, the villagers did not encourage him to stay with them. For several weeks he tried to find shelter and scrape a living. Local farmers gave him a day's work here and there, and shelter for the night, but no home. In the city, the closed community of the craft guilds showed little interest in the penniless and friendless young labourer when he tried to find a place as an apprentice. One of the inns told him he could clean out the stables, but after the innkeeper hit him for obeying an order too slowly, he decided to leave.

What was he to do?

"There's nothing for me at Sarum," he sadly decided. "Plenty for others, but not for me." He missed his poor cottage in the valley at Avonsford. "If even that's gone," he finally decided, "I may as well try my luck elsewhere."

And so it was on an April morning that he had come to the Avon valley to see the sunrise for the last time before he took his leave.

The mists were clearing now; he could see the river water and the long green weeds. People were stirring at the manor house. As the last trails of mist drifted downstream on the river the swans returned and, arching their powerful wings, made their comfortable landing on the water.

He turned to go.

He had said his farewell to Avonsford; now there was one last visit to make – to the great cathedral in the valley, whose graceful, soaring spire had been the dominating landmark of his short life. He would take one more look, pray there, and then be on his way.

It was difficult to wrench himself away from Sarum.

There was, however, one problem with his plan. When he left the city, where should he go?

He had no idea. He supposed one place was as good as another. It was a question he had been asking himself for over a week, without coming to any conclusion; and now the time had come.

"I shall go to the cathedral and ask St Osmond," he murmured. It seemed the sensible thing to do.

It was as he came towards the little wooden bridge below the village that he saw her.

The lady of the manor.

She was standing in the middle of the bridge, apparently staring down the river, but she turned to watch him approach.

She was wearing a long, black cloak and her head was bare, so that the grey hair fell half way down her back.

He hesitated for a moment, for he was a little afraid of her; then he corrected himself.

"What's she or the lord of Avonsford to me now?" he muttered and pressed forward.

She continued to watch him, impassively.

He wondered what this fine lady was doing down by the river so early; but who knew what was in the minds of the gentry? As he came close, he could not help thinking:

She's old now, but she must have been beautiful once.

In fact, Lizzie was forty, though she knew she looked more. She had walked alone down to the river because just after dawn her husband, waking in a bad temper and after a few angry words when she foolishly contradicted him, had seemed about to strike her. Now that she was visibly growing old, she had supposed that his violence towards her might grow less, but it had not. Rather than begin the day with pain, she had quickly left the house and walked down to the bridge.

She too was watching the mist lift over the lovely manor house.

How strange to think that this place – everything that high-spirited girl Lizzie Curtis, had ever dreamed of – was now nothing more than a prison. On bad days, she thought grimly, she had known it to be more like a torture chamber.

She had to think hard to remember herself as she was – those light-hearted days seemed so far away. But when she remembered, she smiled sadly at the irony of her life. Oh yes, she had got what she wanted – wealth, fine clothes, a manor house – all of them: at the price of long cold years that made her wince as she looked back on them.

Lizzie had been gazing downstream. How many times she had done the same thing from the house, always with the same thought. In an hour or two, the water passing her would be flowing gently round the big curve in the river by the edge of the city; some of it would be diverted into the water-channels that flowed through the streets; some of that water would even flow past her childhood home. If only she could dive into the stream and travel southwards with it.

She would have left, countless times. Except that she knew very well that Robert would have kept their children, would probably have kidnapped them if she had tried to spirit them away. She could not bear to think of them left alone with him.

Which was why a new development in recent years had been all the more terrible.

For the children, despite her husband's cold and sometimes cruel treatment of them, were starting to side with him against her.

It was nothing sudden, nothing obvious. It was a quiet, unspoken business.

When they were young and their father came into the room, looking around with his cold, menacing eyes, they would watch him nervously, keeping as close to her as they could. They were both pale, thin little creatures and it had seemed to her that they needed protecting. When Robert began one of his rages, both the little boy and the girl would cling to her, or try to hide behind her if they could. How often had she borne the brunt of his cruelty to protect them.

But now they were almost full-grown. Robert seldom directed his anger towards them any more, but chiefly at her. And when he did, cursing her horribly in their presence, she was first astonished, then hurt to find that they did nothing to defend her. They hardly even looked shocked. Instead she would see their two small, narrow faces turned towards her, their eyes calmly watching, measuring, as carefully and dispassionately as a cat watches a wounded bird.

They no longer needed her. They were her husband's children.

Lizzie watched the young fellow coming towards the little bridge. She recognised him and tried to remember his name. Of course. He was the Wilson boy her husband had thrown out of his cottage. She gazed at him curiously, then smiled to herself.

The boy's features were familiar in more ways than one. They reminded her of Robert's father, old John Wilson, the spider. Years ago, when she had first seen the boy and his father, and noticed this similarity, she had wondered if they might be the same stock; but she had never mentioned the subject to her husband for fear of how he might react. After all, he was a Forest these days.

Now the boy was on the bridge.

"You're Will Wilson, aren't you?"

He nodded, looking up at her cautiously.

"What are you doing here?"

"Leaving, lady."

"Leaving? You mean for good?"

He nodded again.

"Leaving Sarum. Nothing for me here."

"So where will you go?"

"Dunno."

And then, to his absolute astonishment, the lady of the manor said, as though she really meant it:

"How I envy you."

The statement was so senseless that he could only stare at her in disbelief. Then it occurred to him that she might have gone mad. That would account for her wandering by the bridge at this early hour. Perhaps she was going to drown herself. Well, it was no concern of his.

Seeing his face, she laughed.

Yes, she was obviously mad. He wondered if she would try to stop him passing.

"Leaving your family at Avonsford?"

He had no idea of the hidden meaning in her words.

"All dead, lady."

She did not pursue the point. The thought of leading this boy back to the manor and introducing him to Robert as his cousin gave her a moment's amusement.

She put her hand inside her cloak and felt the little purse at her belt. As she thought, there was a gold coin in it. She pulled it out.

"Here," she said with a smile. "Take it. Good luck on your journey."

He took the gold piece in astonishment. This was a major windfall. He took it quickly before the madwoman changed her mind. Then he hurried past.

A few minutes later, still watched by Lizzie, he rounded the corner of the lane and turned south towards the city.

He wandered about in the huge church for some time before approaching his objective. How magnificent it was, with its soaring arches and the

[589]

richly painted chapels and chantries below. There were many of these splendid memorials to the great nobles like Lord Hungerford, where the priests said masses every day. Old Bishop Beauchamp was near to death now, it was said; no doubt there would soon be a new and splendid chantry built for him too. But though these sumptuous little chapels and impressive tombs reminded him of his own insignificance, there was only one monument in that great church that he approached with real religious awe.

The shrine of St Osmund was outwardly magnificent. It was not only painted and gilded: it was even studded with gems so that it glowed and glittered as the red and blue light from the high windows fell upon it. It was right, of course, that the saint should be honoured with all the ornaments that money could buy.

But to Will the little gleaming shrine was a magical place apart.

"God himself touches the spot," the priest at Avonsford had told him, and he knew it was true. For in the cathedral, the holy body of the saint himself was present. The bodies of saints did not suffer corruption, like those of other men. He knew that too. They remained perfect and sometimes gave off a sweet odour. Some said there was even a warmth that came from their tombs. The very light that touched the jewelled shrine was holy, a direct shaft from the saint's body to God.

"Touch the shrine," the priest had assured him, "and you are touched by the saint himself." Many had been healed of sickness by doing so.

Will knew about relics – they were holy objects you could touch. Once when he was ten, he met a pilgrim on the road outside Fisherton and the man showed him, in a little casket, a rusty sliver of metal. "It's part of a nail from the true cross," he confided, and Will looked at the nail with reverence and with awe. "You can touch it," the pilgrim offered, but the boy had not dared, for he was suddenly overcome with the fear that if he touched a relic that had touched the body of Christ himself, he would probably be struck dead on the spot for his sins. He dreamed about the nail for years afterwards.

Almost every church had its relics, kept in little boxes and venerated by the people: shards of wood from the cross, a lock of hair belonging to one of the saints, a sliver of bone. But these were nothing compared with the holy shrine of St Osmund.

And so it was that now Will knelt before the gleaming shrine of Salisbury's saint and prayed fervently:

"Which way shall I go? Guide me, Osmund. Send me a sign."

He stayed there some time. The shrine glittered in the half light; and in the end, though no sign had yet come, he felt comforted. "I will watch for the sign," he thought. "Osmund will send it." And he made his way out.

It was while he was walking along the edge of the market place that his attention was distracted from his journey for a time by a curious sight.

It was a little procession: a priest, two acolytes carrying lighted tapers and six choirboys were solemnly leading a stiff old man round St Thomas's churchyard. Behind the old man walked a little group of people who appeared to be family and friends, amongst whom he recognised the burly form of Benedict Mason the bellmaker. The choirboys sung a psalm while the old man, dressed in a coarse wool habit, like that of a friar, and with simple sandals on his feet, followed silently, his bald head bowed.

"What is it?" he asked a bystander.

"An enclosure," the man told him, and seeing the boy's look of puzzlement he explained: "He's going to be a hermit. They're taking him to his cell."

Will had never seen such a thing before.

"Who is it?" he asked.

"Eustace Godfrey."

Will had never heard of him.

The ceremony of enclosure, as opposed to the agricultural practice of that name, was a grim and stately affair. First the priest had recited a mass for the dead in the church, at which Eustace had made his vows and put on the coarse woollen habit he was henceforward to wear. Now he was making the slow procession to his cell. Will watched, fascinated.

At the north door of the church, the little group stopped. In the recent rebuilding, a large porch had been added to this side of the church and over it was a large chamber that was reached by a staircase. This was to be Eustace's cell, inside which he would remain in prayer and meditation until the day he died. Now, while Eustace waited below, the priest and his acolytes went up the stairs to bless the cell.

Will was not able to see the part of the ceremony which followed, since it took place inside. Its symbolism was gruesome.

First Eustace was summoned up the stairs. Inside the chamber he was ordered to lie down on the hard wooden board he was to sleep on in future and then, while he folded his hands as though he were dead, the priest said over him the funeral rites. One of the two acolytes swung a censer, the other held out a bag of earth from which the priest scooped up handfuls and scattered them over Eustace's body. Then he sprinkled holy water over him.

"Eustace Godfrey," he announced when it was done. "You are dead to the world. Eustace Godfrey," he continued, "you are alive only unto God."

Then he turned and all three came down the stairs, closing the door and ceremonially locking it behind them.

"Eustace Godfrey has entered his tomb," he cried to the crowd of watchers. "Pray for his soul."

In fact, his enclosure was not as complete as the ceremony suggested. Before being licensed to become a hermit, Eustace had had to satisfy the archdeacon at the cathedral not only that his desire and vocation for the spiritual life was genuine, but also that he could support himself in a decent state in the place chosen for him. Entombed though he was, a servant would bring him food and clean his chamber every day; his son and daughter could visit him. The retirement into a life of solitary prayer was not, at least in England, uncomfortable. On the other hand, he must stay where he was, perhaps for many years, until he died.

With this arrangement Eustace was quite content. Indeed, the step he was taking that day was not illogical. His attempts to come to terms with the busy city, attempts that he had made as conscientiously and valiantly as any of his ancestors had gone to war or ridden in the lists, had all ended in failure. His lovely daughter had finally, at the age of twenty-eight, married an elderly farmer from Downton. There were no children. His son had not gone to the Inns of Court or made his way in London: he had settled in a modest house in the Blue Boar chequer where he traded unsuccessfully in wool, and drank more than he should. Eustace had continued to invest his dwindling resources, sinking nearly half of what he had in a venture with a Scandinavian merchant while England was in dispute with the merchants of the German Hanseatic League. In 1474 a peace had been signed with the Hansa: the Germans had regained their trade, and Godfrey and his Scandinavian partner had been almost ruined.

It was the combination of these disasters working upon his own natural inclinations that had turned his mind finally to the mystical world. Year by year, he had gone to hear more masses each day; his readings had for a long time been confined to the works of the mystics: Thomas à Kempis, *The Cloud of Unknowing* and his favourite Julian of Norwich.

By the turn of the year he had no more desire to live in the house near St Ann's Gate.

"I have done with the world," he told his children. And it was true.

Nor was it unusual. There were hermits in most dioceses: it was a natural path for a man like Eustace to choose. If he could no longer be a courtly knight at Avonsford, if the busy, noisy merchants of Salisbury would not help him regain his fortune, God at least would accept him, in understanding silence, as a Christian gentleman. When the priest had left, he got up slowly and smiled. For the first time in many years he was happy.

One other figure who had watched the ceremony with particular approval was Benedict Mason.

The bellmaker, in his last years, had become successful, and also amazingly stout. Because he considered Godfrey to be a pillar of the church, Benedict had always felt there was a bond between them and he had bustled across the market that morning to make sure that he was present to witness such an important event. To do so, he had put on his brightest blue hose and red jerkin the combination of which gave him the appearance of a well fattened turkey cock. He crossed himself repeatedly during the mass and glowered at any of the others in the crowd who were not doing so too.

When the service was over and Godfrey was safely in his cell, he did not immediately depart, but lingered a few moments by the door. Then he went back into the church: there was something he wanted to look at, just once more.

Will followed him in.

The new church of St Thomas the Martyr was the showpiece of the town, and the town had much to be proud about. For never had the citizens of Salisbury been so wealthy.

York and Lancaster were still disputing for the throne; but while the great nobles like Warwick the Kingmaker might cynically change sides, the mayor and corporation of Salisbury had calmly sent money and troops to both sides at once. One by one the mighty feudal figures fell. The king's brother, the Duke of Clarence, with his great park at Wardour just fifteen miles to the west, had been killed only recently – drowned in a butt of Malmsey wine it was rumoured. Another brother, the deformed Richard of Gloucester, who now held many of the old Earldom of Salisbury's estates, was lurking in the wings. And Salisbury still cared not one jot for any of them.

The present king, Edward IV, was of the house of York. All that mattered to the citizens of Salisbury was that he was rich – both with land from magnates who had fallen in the feudal war, and with a huge payment from the French king, after he had threatened to invade France. Consequently he had no need to summon parliaments and demand taxes. Which was just what the citizens of Salisbury liked.

And Sarum, left in peace, grew rich. True, in the ten-year battle between Halle and the bishop, the townsmen had been forced in the end to give in. The bishop remained their feudal overlord. But no one else had bothered them.

The church of St Thomas the Martyr contained everything the townsmen could wish. There was the splendid chapel of the fraternity of St George; there were the chantries of Swayne and other leading families, and the chantry of the Tailors' Guild. The other parish churches in the city too, had similar memorials to their burgesses' pride and wealth, but none were more lavish than those of the new church of St Thomas. Its staff of clergy was huge: over twenty priests, sixteen deacons, ten subdeacons, ten chantry priests – nearly sixty men in all, to serve a parish of two or three thousand souls. It seemed to Will, whenever he went past, that there was always a mass or obit being said – sometimes several at once, and when the offices were not being said, then candles were being lit.

The style of the new building was the so-called perpendicular – with thin spreading arches and broad windows. The roof did not have the sophisticated fan vaulting to be found in the greater churches like the new King's College chapel at Cambridge or its sister church at Eton; instead it had a handsome wooden-beamed roof, from every joint of which there seemed to be staring a broad-cheeked angel; the walls were decorated with bright floral motifs. Everywhere there were little painted shields, some bearing the escutcheon of a local family, others the red cross of St George, and still more with the arms of one of the guilds on them. It was here that the mayor and corporation had their seats reserved, and here that the ceremony of making a new mayor was religiously performed.

But its greatest and most striking glory had only just been completed: this was the huge painting that spread from one side of the nave to the other above the chancel arch.

It ws the painting of Doom.

Will was afraid of the Doom painting – with good reason. He could not read or write. He knew little even of religion except for what he had

[593]

picked up from the occasional mumbled sermons of the priest at Avonsford or the knockabout religious mystery plays that the mummers sometimes performed in the city after Christmas. These plays, where one of the actors took the part of the devil, and another of his victim, were not unlike a Punch and Judy show; they reminded him that he would be soundly punished for his sins; but they were hardly frightening.

What he saw before him now was very frightening: for he had no doubt that it was an accurate picture of the terrible Day of Judgement. On the big wall over the arch that led to the choirstalls, towering over him and staring down into the nave, was the figure of Christ himself, seated on a rainbow, his hands raised and outstretched. Behind him were the splendid towers of the heavenly city. On his right hand, the naked dead were being raised by angels from their graves; some were escorted to the heavenly city: but many more were passing to the space on Christ's left hand, the infernal regions where a great beast with a savage, gaping mouth was devouring them. It reminded Will of the ceremony he had seen one Whitsun at St Edmunds, where a huge painting, vividly depicting a skeleton in a grotesque, macabre dance, had been carried round the church to remind the people that they were soon to die. He would die soon – he knew that, and when he did, he would be shoved down the beast's gaping mouth to the fires of hell; he was sure of it.

At one side of the Doom painting there was a full length, life-sized portrait of St Osmund. Assuming that this was exactly what Salisbury's saint must have looked like, he gazed at it with awe.

The painting disturbed him too much; it was overpowering, and a few minutes later he was outside, on his way out of the town.

But the painting did not disturb Benedict Mason the bell-founder at all. As far as he was concerned, the more colour and ornament in the church the better.

It was one feature in particular that he had gone inside to look at: a small window on the south side – or to be exact, the lower portion of the right hand light of one window. For here, only a week before, he had installed at his own expense about a yard of stained glass. Will had not even noticed it when he went in, but Benedict stared at it with pride. It depicted in orange, red and blue, the figure of St Christopher who was blessing two small standing figures below him which, though they were crudely formed, could be recognised as the stout bell-founder and his wife. Underneath them in a clumsy gothic script were the words:

Gloria Dei. Benedict Mason et uxor suis Margery.

It was a modest memorial, nothing like the fine chantries of the nobles or the richer merchants, just as year after year his gifts of candles, wool and cheese for the church had been modest. But together with the obits which would be said for his soul by the priests when he died and the bells in Wiltshire churches which bore his name, the little stained-glass window would ensure his immortality, and the thickset craftsman was satisfied.

Of his ancestor Osmund the Mason who had carved such wonders in the cathedral he knew nothing at all. And so it was with genuine pride that he told his wife:

"I'm the first of our family to leave his mark in this city."

He did not notice young Will at all.

The dark thunderclouds that had appeared from the west, had already gathered overhead as Will passed the deserted castle hill of Old Sarum.

They did not bother him.

But still he had not solved his problem: which way should he go? He had been watching carefully but there had been no sign.

The sun, shining through the thickening veils of brownish cloud, was filling the huge landscape with a threatening orange glow. The atmosphere was growing close and heavy, building up the trembling, almost tangible tension that presages the great electric release of a thunderstorm.

In front of him, as far as the eye could see, lay the bare rolling ridges of Salisbury Plain. The scene was varied: from where he stood, into the middle distance, cleared ground was interspersed with fields of growing corn. Further away, however, there was no corn, only a bare grey-green expanse like a sea, on which he could see the myriad tiny white dots of the distant sheep.

The sky itself seemed to be growing closer to the land, as though it was about to envelop it, take the whole rolling plateau in vast unseen hands and shake it to and fro.

He stood in front of the ancient dune, a pathetic, diminutive figure, homeless, orphaned, friendless, with two shillings and the gold coin to his name in the whole world. His long thin fingers grasped a stick he had broken from a tree on the way up to the high ground; his thin face with its small, narrow-set eyes, stared over the huge, threatening landscape ahead. He might indeed have been a wandering figure from an earlier age, when men still hunted for their food; and still he had no idea where to go.

And then he grinned.

The storm that was about to break did not bother him. The weather was not too cold. If he got wet, his clothes would dry on him. Empty and uninviting though the landscape looked, he knew that, if one searched carefully, there were always ways to survive. There were shelters built for sheep; there were farms, villages, hamlets where a boy could usually scrounge a meal. Better yet, there were religious houses – monasteries, priories, small granges – where the monks, for all the jokes people made about their easy life, never refused food and shelter to a stranger.

He had asked St Osmund for guidance. It had yet to come. But even so, though he could not say why, some ancient instinct deep inside him knew, with an infallible certainty, that he was a survivor.

In the absence of any sign, he must make a choice: there were several alternatives. He could head towards the north western settlements of Bradford or Trowbridge – both thriving cloth towns. Beyond, a few days' journey further, lay the Severn river and the mighty port of Bristol. Or he

[595]

could turn south east instead and make for Winchester or the port of Southampton. Further still, to the east, lay London itself. That was too far he thought, though its unknown possibilities tempted him. Wherever he went, whatever he did, he had turned his back on Sarum.

"I'll try Bristol," he finally decided; and began to walk.

The roadway, like most of England's roads, was in reality no more than a recognised route over which people travelled. It had no surface, it was not marked out in any way: it was simply a broad path stretching across the high ground, trodden down by foot and scored with the marks of hoof prints and cartwheels which had passed that way over the centuries. In some places, where the ground was soft and travellers had fanned out to find a firmer surface, the trackways might spread hundreds of yards across; in others, a hard ridge between escarpments might narrow the road naturally to only a few. Ancient, as primitive as it had been in prehistoric times, this was the road.

He had gone a mile and was beside the last of the cornfields before the storm broke; when it did, it was not what he expected.

Will knew two kinds of storm at Sarum. The first, the more usual, was when the sky cracked and split open – with thunder and lightning, sheet or forked that might seem like crashes and flashes of fury but which carried with them also a sense of relief. "The ground's waiting for it," he would say, to express the feeling that between sky and earth there was a complicity, as if the bare high ground willingly bore the powerful fury of the storm, its flashes of lightning and torrents of rain for a space, before it moved, with a departing rumble, to some other quarter of the distant ridges, or to the wooded valley in the south. He liked these storms. He enjoyed the noise and the thrill of the lightning, sensing the relief in the sky as the whole atmosphere concentrated itself to release its pent up tension. He would grin with pleasure as, accompanied by the faraway muttering and distant flashing of the storm, the swollen rivulets and streams poured off the chalk ridges into the valley below.

But there was another, mercifully rarer kind of storm. And today, when he was a mile from cover of any kind, it was one of these that broke.

He thought, for nearly an hour, that he would die. It did not seem possible that any rage in the heavens could be so great. It seemed that the sky, the whole lowering dome of the universe about the high ground had come together not to release, but to destroy. The lightning did not crack nor the thunder roar: they came together with a single huge bang as though the world were staring up into the mouth of a cannon. And, scarcely pausing, this terrible assault of sky upon earth crashed again and again. Worse: the storm did not move, it stayed where it was, an electric maelstrom, directly above him, pouring its rage down upon him while the whole plateau trembled.

"God help me," he cried. St Osmund's comforting shrine seemed suddenly far away, ineffectual. "Mother of God," he begged, "save me."

But the great stanchions of forked lightning struck at the ground all around him, time and again until he could only believe that the storm was searching him out, personally, for destruction. He was utterly alone. Half a mile away, he knew, was a flock of sheep. Were they as frightened as he was? Might not the storm in its appalling rage choose some of them instead of him? The rain drove down so hard, so relentlessly that he could not see even half way to the sheep.

At one point for a few moments he thought the storm had begun to move; but then it returned to him, even more furious than before, with all the force of nightmare. Survivor though he was, he fell to the ground, huddled into a ball like a baby and lay, feeling utterly naked on the ground as the storm beat upon him.

It was then that the supernatural event, the terrible wonder occurred.

It was a single shaft of lightning. The bang was so loud, so absolutely sudden – the gigantic force of it seemed to cleave the ground apart so directly under him – that, for an instant, he thought he had been struck. He very nearly had.

But even his terror was forgotten as he stared in front of him.

For the lightning, having struck the ground some twenty feet from where he lay, had not vanished, but raced eastward along the surface of the earth, carving a swathe of fire in a dead straight line for a hundred yards through the field of growing corn. There before him, to his astonishment, where a second earlier had been a drenched field, lay a black and smouldering path like a giant pointer.

As he gazed at it, he suddenly became aware that the storm, having apparently caused this terrifying phenomenon, had begun to move away.

He got up slowly. The rain was already slackening off. Cautiously he went forward and inspected the spot where the lightning had struck. Except that it was now blackened, it seemed like any other spot on the ground.

But why should it leave this huge scorched trail, so absolutely straight, across a field of corn? He had never seen such a thing before.

And how indeed could Will – who had never heard of the Romans, or their legions, who knew nothing of the lost settlement of Sorviodunum or the villa of Porteus – how could he know that buried underneath the cornfield, for a thousand years, a small, metalled Roman road had lain hidden, along which, since it was a perfect conductor, the huge bolt of lightning had earthed itself?

For long minutes Will stood there, oblivious even to the storm rolling away over the ridges to the north. The charred path – the pointer – lay before him.

"Mother of God and St Osmund," he murmured at last. "It must be the sign."

The sign did not point northwest to Bristol. It pointed east. Nothing could be more clear.

"I will go to London then," he decided.

New World

1553

A GLORIOUS NEW world was being born, and it was a dangerous place for people of conscience.

As Edward Shockley stood that April morning amongst the small crowd in St Thomas's church who were watching Abigail Mason and her husband Peter set about their self-appointed task, he had a sudden premonition that they would soon be in danger. It was Abigail he feared for.

And yet, what they were doing would certainly meet with the approval of Bishop Capon, the justices of the peace, the king himself.

They were breaking one of the church windows.

Peter Mason was on his knees; Abigail stood over him. The pieces of stained glass already lay on the stone floor and Peter was pounding them carefully with a hammer. He glanced up frequently, his gentle, round face smiling, silently asking for approval which Abigail, very calm in her simple brown smock, quietly gave him.

"'Tis the Lord's work thou dost, Peter," she told him.

Yet it seemed to Shockley that her eyes were fixed on something beyond her husband while she encouraged him, as if this necessary but minor act of destruction almost bored her.

But then Abigail was a rare spirit – one of the few in Sarum with a fixed purpose in life. She had vision, and strength.

How he admired her for it.

"Abigail Mason knows what she believes," he reminded himself sternly. "She does not lie." And he shook his head sadly at his own weakness.

The little window which, three generations before, Benedict Mason had so proudly installed as a memorial to himself and his wife had lasted surprisingly long. The king's commissioners had thought it too insignificant to bother with; and since Benedict had seven descendants living in Sarum now, Peter Mason, for fear of offending his cousins, had hesitated to deface the tiny memorial himself. But Abigail had been firm. She had spoken to him, lovingly but firmly again and again, and now at last it was done. No one had dared to object. It was the Lord's work.

She did not even glance at the little crowd who were watching. Though she was short, her pale face was set so firmly and her deep brown eyes were so calm that she seemed a being apart. Stern as she was, there was something about her, besides her courage, that Edward Shockley found strangely attractive – he could not formulate it into a thought, however, and whatever it was, the feeling was probably sinful. He turned away from the dutiful couple and looked about the church instead.

St Thomas's Church had changed completely since he was a child. Even its name had been altered, for King Henry VIII, in the plenitude of his almost totalitarian power, had roundly declared that Thomas à Becket, the martyred archbishop who had defied the king, was no martyr but a rebellious subject. Accordingly the church beside the market place was no longer called St Thomas the Martyr but dedicated to another St Thomas, the Apostle, instead. It was the commissioners of the present boy king Edward VI though, who had really altered the look of it. The old statue of St George had been torn down and smashed; most of the carvings had been broken up too. The chantries of Swayne and the Tailors' Guild had been destroyed and their endowments confiscated. Two hundredweight of brass – thirty-six shillings' worth – had been carted out of St Thomas's alone, as well as most of the stained glass. The pride of the merchants and the guilds, their shrines, chantries and memorials, had all been humbled in the name of the true God. Why, even the great Doom painting had been white-washed over.

"There'll be no more popish idols," one of the workmen accomplishing the destruction had told him proudly. "We'll soon have the place cleaned up."

It was the same everywhere. St Edmund's church was bare: the fraternity of the Jesus Mass was dissolved. As for the cathedral itself, the destruction had been remarkable. Not only the services at the chantries of Bishop Beauchamp and Lord Hungerford had been ended, but two thousand pounds-worth of gold and silver plate – the treasure of centuries – had been removed. The jewel-encrusted shrine of St Osmund, the city's pride, had been stripped and broken up. Altars had been taken down to be replaced by plain tables, the ancient latin liturgy changed to simple English; even the men who tended the candles had been dismissed. So far the cathedral's windows had not been touched, but no doubt that would come too.

This was the will of the protestant boy king Edward VI.

The Reformation had come to Sarum

As Shockley left the little drama at St Thomas's and made his way slowly across the town, his mind turned to another scene that had taken place an hour before in his own house. As he remembered it, he winced.

His five-year-old daughter, Celia, staring at him with wide, frightened eyes. His wife Katherine, her look of hurt and reproach before she burst into tears.

It was his fault, of course.

If it had not been for the Reformation, he would not have needed to lie.

But then who in Sarum could have ever have expected that a Tudor king would start a Protestant Reformation in England?

Ever since 1485, when their victory over the unpopular Yorkist Richard III at Bosworth had put the upstart Welsh dynasty on the throne, the

Tudors had done everything to make their rule unquestioned, and, above all, orthodox. Since their own claim to the throne, through a lucky marriage into the house of Lancaster, was rather obscure, Henry VII had married a Yorkist princess. The great feudal nobles were tired and weakened by the Wars of the Roses: the Tudors with their strong central government and their courts, like the mighty Star Chamber, soon awed them into submission. And where Henry VII consolidated his position, his son Henry VIII shone.

He was everything a northern Renaissance prince should be. Scholar, musician, poet, athlete. Under Henry, had England not defeated the invading Scots at Flodden, and trounced the French at the Battle of the Spurs? He was extravagant, certainly, but when he went to meet the French king at the sumptuous pageant known as the Field of the Cloth of Gold, he showed himself to be magnificent.

Above all, in matters of religion, he was orthodox. For his writings in support of Rome, the pope had given young Henry VIII his glorious extra title: Defender of the Faith. Was his wife not the daughter of the most Catholic King of Spain, and aunt of the Holy Roman Emperor Charles? When Luther's Protestant movement had begun in Germany, and when milder reformers like Erasmus had questioned the malpractices of the Roman Church, the northern island of England with its faithful king had remained conservative and sternly apart.

Certainly, nothing could have been more Catholic than Sarum and its bishop.

For Henry's great servant Wolsey had given the bishopric of Salisbury with its great estates to no less a person than the legate to England, Cardinal Campeggio.

Of course, the great Italian Cardinal was seldom present. The running of the diocese was lax. The cathedral choristers had dwindled to under a dozen. But what did that matter as long as England and Sarum were orthodox? When seditious printed books such as a series of Lutheran tracts, or Tyndale's translation of the New Testament into English appeared in England, King Henry VIII and Wolsey very properly burned them and Campeggio wrote, from Rome, to assure them: 'no holocaust could be more pleasing to God.'

Sarum would never have known the Reformation but for that cruel accident of nature. It was not that Queen Katherine failed to give the king a son – for she had given him no less than four sons and three daughters in their almost twenty years of marriage; but except for one daughter, Mary, all her children died in infancy. True, the king had one son, born out of wedlock, whom he had made Duke of Richmond. But it was a legitimate heir that was needed.

And Sarum would never have become Protestant, it might perhaps be argued, if it had not been for the bishop. For Campeggio's role in the king's great matter was extraordinary. First, he had suggested that the illegitimate Duke of Richmond should marry his own half-sister Mary and inherit the crown – an idea, it seemed to many, more worthy of the Italian bishop's contemporary Machiavelli. Then when Henry asked the pope to annul his marriage, and the embarrassed pope craftily turned the case over to Wolsey and Campeggio for trial it was Campeggio's conduct that decided the outcome. It was a difficult situation. For at that moment, France and the Hapsburg emperor Charles, the queen's nephew, were fighting for control of northern Italy. Charles was powerful: his dominions extended from Spain to the Netherlands. He had even held the pope captive for a time. If the pope granted the annulment he would be a laughing stock in Italy and anger Charles as well.

The subtle Bishop of Salisbury had known what to do. While Wolsey fretted and Henry grew more furious, he had prevaricated while he watched the situation in Italy. The Emperor Charles had won, the case was withdrawn to Rome and no annulment came. Henry's patience had run out; Wolsey had fallen and the next year the King of England had started to withdraw his kingdom from the Church of Rome.

And if the Bishop of Salisbury had not prevaricated? Had he agreed to annul the marriage? Who can tell? Perhaps Sarum would be Roman Catholic still.

Shockley still trembled when he remembered the old king. When England left the Church of Rome, the constitution was, at least in theory, a more absolute rule than modern history has witnessed until the rise of the twentieth century totalitarian state. For by making himself – and all English monarchs since – the spiritual head of the English Church, Henry VIII became, in his own kingdom, both king and pope in one, a claim that no medieval monarch would ever have dreamed of. When brave men like his chancellor Thomas More protested, they were executed. His terrible and unpredictable power seemed to fall across England like a shadow. Anne Boleyn gave him a daughter, and was beheaded. Jane Seymour gave him a son at last, then died. Anne of Cleves was repudiated; Catherine Howard executed. Henry's queens crossed the stage of history like victims going to a sacrifice.

But at Sarum, frightening as Henry was, life had not changed so much. For although the king had broken with Rome, he still showed himself to be a conservative Catholic at heart.

True, he had promoted men with Protestant leanings: the gentle and scholarly Archbishop Cranmer, who had given him his needed dispensation to marry Anne Boleyn; at Sarum, Boleyn's former chaplain, Shaxton was made bishop when Cardinal Campeggio was sent packing. But in nearby Winchester, Bishop Gardiner remained, sternly Catholic.

True, for a time, he had let the reformers make some changes. At Sarum, Shaxton good humouredly threw away a quantity of hairs, gobbets of wood, bullocks' horns and other objects venerated as relics, and discouraged the people from kneeling to images of the saints and lighting candles. But later, seeing the Protestants becoming too strong, the king issued his famous Six Articles, whose orthodoxy was accompanied by such heavy penalties that Shaxton of Salisbury was forced to resign; and when he decided that priests should not be married, he even made poor Cranmer send his wife abroad.

For the church of Henry was Catholic in almost everything except acknowledging the authority of the pope. Indeed, on the great central question of Transubstantiation, Henry threatened anyone who denied it with burning – after all, had he not done so, then his new English Church and her priests would have been inferior to the Church of Rome.

Yet all the same, Sarum had changed – in two important respects.

The first was the Dissolution of the Monasteries. The minor houses had gone soonest. Edward Shockley remembered, as a boy, watching the men carrying two small crosses and items of furniture out of the Grey Friars' old house near St Ann's Gate. There had only been a handful of Franciscans there anyway, and half the place had been let to a tenant for years. Even so, he had been conscious that a world was passing away. But then, a few years later, the greater houses, Amesbury to the north and next-door Wilton had gone. And that had been another matter.

For the king, the closing of these often decrepit religious houses was chiefly a means of rising money and rewarding his friends. Amesbury went to the family of Jane Seymour; Wilton, with its huge and ancient estates, to a man rapidly rising in the royal service, Sir William Herbert.

But the effect on an area could be considerable. It was at Sarum. For centuries, when men looked west, they had seen the rich tracts around Wilton and known – those are the abbey lands. Passive, sleepy since Saxon times, one could be certain that, whatever else was happening, the old abbey estates would not change much. But look west now, and one saw the seat of a new and vigorous family power; for come what may, Sir William intended that the family of Herbert should be a mighty power in the land.

The second change was less obvious, but would have profounder consequences. This was the order, in Bishop Shaxton's time, that every church in the diocese must buy one of the newly printed English bibles, translated by Coverdale and Tyndale. Henry had come to doubt the wisdom of this piece of Protestantism too. Late in the reign he decreed that only nobles and the gentry might read them aloud in their own homes – and that ordinary women and the lower orders were not to read a translated Bible at all.

But it was too late. The damage was done. Even Henry VIII could not close his subjects' minds, once they had been opened.

Edward Shockley had read his Bible.

He had lied. That was the trouble.

When he was in love.

It did not seem such a lie at the time. And anyway, he and Katherine Moody were meant for each other. Even her parents said so.

He and Katherine made a good-looking couple. Seen side by side, they seemed to fit together like two halves of a single entity, so that, once they were betrothed, old John Shockley his father had laughed, remarking that it was hard to imagine how they had ever been apart. They complemented each other in every way – her thick, light brown hair to his thin, yellow locks; her eyes were pale azure, his startling, deep blue. And his easy belief in himself, as the sole heir to the Shockley mill, was perfectly matched by her almost submissive desire to please.

It was two years before old King Harry died and he was doing business in the western city of Exeter when he first saw her. Both of them felt an instant attraction that had fortunately never left them since; and it was not long before he discovered that her father was a clothier, that she and her brother would each inherit a modest fortune, that she was unsure of herself, and that, in every way, she suited him admirably. He had fallen in love. He was twenty-one and she was seventeen.

There was only one problem: the Moodys were Catholic.

He was not surprised. He knew very well that in Wessex, the further one travelled into the hinterland, the more people clung to the old ways. If the Moodys, far to the west in their village near Exeter, longed for their Church to return to Rome, it was only to be expected.

It did not seem so important. His own parents, though they grudgingly accepted the king's break with Rome, were certainly no Protestants. His father John had once called the reforming Bishop Shaxton a heretic to his face; and there were still Roman missals to be found in many a Wiltshire church. He supposed his parents and Katherine's would find little to disagree about.

And what of his own views? He supposed that as long as he went to whatever Church the king ordered, no one should find fault with him. It was true that in private, he personally found much to support the Protestants in his Bible readings; if he liked to hear the service in English and thought that men like Cranmer and Shaxton had been right to attack the old popish superstitions – was there any need to bring the subject up and risk a refusal from his prospective father-in-law who lived so far away? He did not think so.

He remembered the interview with old William Moody all too well.

"We are a Catholic family," Moody reminded him, "and my daughter will only marry into a family of the same mind."

"My parents are Catholic and regret the break with Rome," Edward replied truthfully, hoping this would be sufficient. He looked down modestly.

But an instinct cautioned the older man. As Edward looked up again, Moody's piercing grey eyes seemed to probe into his soul.

"There were reforms at Sarum," he observed quietly.

"Under Shaxton," Edward agreed, "but the king replaced him with Bishop Capon, who enforces the Six Articles."

Indeed, everyone knew that Bishop Capon, a former monk, had got his preferment because he was most anxious to do the king's will, whatever it might be.

But Moody was not satisfied.

"And you, young Edward Shockley, are you sure you care nothing for the doctrines of the Protestants?" His balding head had jutted forward, almost accusing. "Let there be no mistake," he went on, "if you cannot in conscience swear to that, my daughter will never find happiness."

He had thought of the submissive girl's sweet smile, of her fresh young body and of his own desire.

He had not faltered. He had looked William Moody in the eye and sworn:

"I am a Catholic, in a Catholic family."

Katherine loved him, he was certain of it; that was all that mattered. If in the future there were any disagreements, he felt sure that with her submissive nature, she would not give him any trouble.

Three months later, having promised also to be a good friend to her ten-year-old brother, he was married.

He had lied.

His married life proved to be delightful. He and Katherine had taken lodgings near the Shockley house and there they enjoyed a first year of happiness.

Each evening, they would sit together at supper and often, before they had finished the light meal, they were both trembling with anticipation. His days were filled with work for his father, his nights with wild passion. And though she sometimes looked at him timidly for a sign of approval for the changes she had made about the house or the food she served, it was not long before she had gained a happy confidence and even a passionate aggressiveness in their lovemaking.

During that year, the subject of religion scarcely arose.

They went to mass together in the town or the cathedral but otherwise they seldom discussed religious matters. Since they both agreed, as she thought, there was no need.

Occasionally he had read the English Bible and she had looked concerned. But he had reminded her that the king permitted it and she had not thought proper to argue with her husband.

He was kind to her, and firm. And she loved him.

In 1547, several events took place to change their lives. The first was the death of his father, leaving him in sole charge of the business. Since his mother was ailing, they had moved into the Shockley house and he had installed his mother in the smaller house next door with a nurse to look after her.

Now he was a man of responsibility. He was ready for it, but it kept him busy and he saw slightly less of his wife. But Katherine was content. Her pale eyes were shining, her timidity was in abeyance. She was pregnant.

But it was a third event which made a much greater difference to their home, and which cast a cloud over their lives.

For in 1547, King Henry VIII of England died, to be succeeded by his only son, the pious boy king Edward VI.

He had not realised what it would mean.

Edward VI was only a boy. He ruled under the guidance of protectors, first his Seymour uncle, then the powerful and scheming Duke of Northumberland. He had favourites whom he trusted – like Sir William Herbert of Wilton, whom he made Earl of Pembroke. Some said he was under Cranmer's influence too. But whatever his advisers may have urged, there was no doubt that the precocious young king had a mind of his own – and that he was Protestant.

And now the Reformation had really come to Sarum.

To his astonishment, Bishop Capon, that strict upholder of King Henry's orthodoxy, turned just as sternly Protestant, it seemed within the day. His regime was soon all the boy king could desire.

Everything had changed: the chantries with their priests and their masses for the souls of the dead; the altars, statues, gold plate; the seven services and high masses: all were gone in five years. Now there were two plain services a day and a communion once a month; the ancient Use of Sarum, which in Henry's day had been the form of service in most of the Canterbury archdiocese, was now replaced by Cranmer's English Prayer Book – fine in its way, but to some ears at least, empty of the mystery of the old Latin liturgy. Bishop Gardiner at nearby Winchester had been deposed. The clergy were told that priests might marry and their children be considered legitimate.

Edward Shockley was too busy with his work to worry about these changes much, but when he thought about it, he viewed them with mixed feelings. He was sorry to see some of the old chantries go, but when he heard the fine sermons of some of the reformers and as he grew better acquainted with the beautiful, melodic periods of Cranmer's Prayer Book, he came to the conclusion that the honest Protestantism of the new regime was in many ways an improvement on the harsh authoritarian orthodoxy of the previous reign. The fact was, he had been half in sympathy with Cranmer before and as new Protestant tracts came into the country from Europe, he read them to himself privately and became increasingly converted to their views.

But on Katherine the effect of the change was devastating. He had understood, of course, that she was a devoted Catholic; but he had not expected her, as the first reforms of the new king began, to go into a state of shock. Yet this was what happened.

She refused to go near the Protestant Communion table. She wept to see the images of the saints smashed and the chantries in nearby St Thomas's desecrated. Often, when he had come into the house now, he would find her tearfully at her rosary; and often at their meals together she would ask him anxiously: "What shall we do?"

She wrote long letters to her father and received the stern reply that she should maintain the true faith with strictness in private and wait upon events. Above all, he had reminded her, she should obey her husband who as a good Catholic would guide her best.

He remembered her father's warning. He understood it better now. But what could he do? At first he did nothing. He told her to be discreet. He told her to be patient. Seeing her fret, he even tried, once or twice, to make light of the matter. But this upset her so much that he even feared she might miscarry with the child.

He soon found himself protesting his own Catholicism in an effort to comfort her while urging her, for the sake of the child, to show discretion.

How submissive she was. Sometimes it moved him to see her pathetically and hopefully looking to him for the reassurance and comfort he knew in his heart of hearts he could not give. At other times it would irritate him when she turned to him and cried:

"If only we had a priest!"

There was only one answer: he was firm with her. Her father had told her, and she knew it was her duty to obey him. For the sake of the business and the child, he knew he could demand her cooperation.

It was a strange situation. Outwardly, Edward Shockley conformed to the new Protestant regime, which in his heart he believed in. At home, he maintained that he was a good Catholic in secret, to pacify his wife.

Celia was born and he supposed that for the time being, his wife might be contented.

Was it her submissiveness that made him sometimes bully her? Did he still enjoy her company? Certainly, her young body, now in its first, perfect fullness, still drove him to heights of excitement which he assumed were passion. And at such times, secure in her belief in him, the passion was returned.

The rift that gradually opened between them did not appear until Celia was about a year old. It was his fault. Perhaps, if she had not been so anxious to please, he could have held out for longer; but occasionally he began to tease her. Sometimes it would be no more than a light-hearted remark; at other times there would be an unstated criticism of her in his words. These comments were usually about the dogma of the Catholic priests, or perhaps the absurdity of some sacred relic that had been done away with. Poor Katherine could sense that such remarks were intended as a challenge, but she was not sure whether they were a criticism of herself or of her church. Was he no longer a good Catholic? Or did he mean that he no longer loved her?

He was young. Sometimes he enjoyed making her unhappy. Sometimes it even excited him. But as the months passed, a certain coldness began to develop between them. Several times he had found her looking at him suspiciously, and once she had turned to him and frankly demanded:

"Are you not a Catholic?"

He had told her that he was, but this time he realised that she feared he might be lying.

When he lay beside her at night, though she did not turn away from him, he could feel her resentment coming from her like a wave; and as the months went by he found that he returned it, if only in some sort of self-defence.

She was still submissive, still dutiful; but because he sensed she might not love him, it no longer gave him pleasure to get his way. Sometimes he would lie again to please her, swear to his Catholic faith, and for a time it would seem that their relationship had returned to where it had been before. But always he suspected she secretly doubted him.

He guessed correctly, however, that she had made no mention of her doubts to her family, for to do so would have been to admit that her husband was a traitor.

During the last few years though, their marriage had been peaceful enough. The old attraction had for periods returned. She had become pregnant again, but miscarried.

Celia was being brought up as a Catholic, in the secrecy of the home. But once or twice already the child had been heard to utter remarks which might have given him trouble in the city.

"Let the child be taught the Catholic faith when she is older," he ordered Katherine. "But not until she has reached an age when she can understand how to keep silent. After all," he added to comfort her, "Cranmer's Prayer Book is but a translation taken mostly from our old Use of Sarum." This was true, but it failed to console her.

And then there had been the scene that morning. He went out early but had returned to the house briefly before going on to St Thomas's church.

She had not heard him coming in. It was as he came up the stairs to the big room that overlooked the street that he heard her gentle voice saying to the child:

"And then the priest performs a miracle and the bread and wine become in very truth the body and blood of Our Lord."

He felt himself grow cold. What if the child should say such things in public? For this was the doctrine of Transubstantiation. Every Catholic must believe in the power of the priest, when he raises the Host to perform the great miracle that transforms bread and wine into the body and blood of Christ. Every Lollard in the past and every Protestant now denied it. The orthodox Henry VIII in his Six Articles had insisted upon it. But to his son Edward VI, to Cranmer, and to Bishop Capon it was anathema.

He stormed into the room.

"No! I will have her taught no popish doctrines." He pointed his finger furiously at his wife. "I forbid it, Katherine, and you will obey me."

He saw her look of anguish but he did not care.

"You call it popish?"

"I do."

"Then," he would never forget the pain he saw in her eyes, "do you not believe?"

And at last in his anger he cried:

"No, foolish woman. I do not."

So now she knew, beyond all shadow of doubt, that all these years he had despised her and that he had lied.

It was a relief to turn his thoughts back to business.

For today could be a turning point in his life. If the meeting he and Thomas Forest were about to have with the Dutchman were successful, the Shockley family might succeed in its long ambition of scaling the heights of Sarum's merchant society.

"I could even be mayor one day," he thought with a thrill of excitement.

Once again it was the old fulling mill which was central to the family's success.

In recent decades the cloth business of England had been changing. The lighter cloths, the rays or kerseys that Salisbury had made so successfully were no longer in such demand; the city with its medieval craft guilds, proud of their skills and set in their ways, tried to continue as before. But the old Italian trade through Southampton had almost gone; even in England rays were less in fashion.

But for the Shockleys with their fulling mill, there was a new opportunity. "Forget the Italian trade," John Shockley urged his son. "Get to Antwerp if you can."

It was the heavy cloth that was in demand – the simple undyed broadcloth, twenty-five ounces to the yard, as heavy as a modern overcoat – thick, felt-like material that the mighty hammers of the fulling mill could pound day and night. This was the cloth that the merchants from the Netherlands and Germany were clamouring for, and their great market at Blackwell Hall in London was the focus of the trade that then flowed to Antwerp, the Baltic and beyond.

But it was the men of west Wiltshire, not the craftsmen of Salisbury who flourished: for the conditions of the new trade were different. The western cloth-makers had suffered before from a disadvantage: for although they had swift-flowing streams to drive their fulling mills, the water in those streams from the chalk and lime ridges of the west was so hard that it would not take the dyes properly and it was hard to obtain an even colour. But for the growing trade in undyed broadcloth these conditions were perfect.

There were other changes too. Though the cloth was still woven in the same way on a two-man loom, enterprising merchants in the west had brought them together near to their fulling mills in what were sometimes almost factory conditions. Indeed, when the monasteries were dissolved, one western clothier had bought up the ancient Abbey of Malmesbury and turned the place into a huge cloth-works.

This was the way in which fortunes were being made, but few at Sarum, with its rich old market, its medieval guilds and their long established practices, were doing so. Some were, however.

"Look at the Webbe brothers," he would cry admiringly. "They've not only gone into broadcloth but they actually export it to Antwerp themselves."

This powerful pair of merchants had done exactly that, cutting out the middlemen on the way and making themselves a fine name in the town.

The trouble was, as he ruefully acknowledged, that he had not the resources to invest in such a large scale enterprise.

But now Thomas Forest had offered to supply his young friend Edward Shockley with exactly that. His plan was well-calculated to suit both men.

Thomas Forest was a gentleman. Of that there was no doubt. At the manor of Avonsford, which he had largely rebuilt, his father had added to the family's social status in several ways. He had acquired an imposing coat of arms – a splendid if garish creation featuring a lion rampant on a field of gold, which was proudly displayed over the fireplace in the hall and also on his tomb in the little village church. As well as this proof of gentility, he had commissioned, shortly before he died, another addition for the manor: a fine portrait of himself. It was not, admittedly, by the great Holbein who had painted the king and the leading figures in the land; but it was by a competent follower, a young man from Germany who had given his narrow, cunning face an austere dignity which it certainly never possessed. This painting of portraits was a new fashion in England, at least amongst the gentry: but Forest had shrewdly realised its value in stamping the family's importance on the minds of anyone who visited the house, and though he groaned at the price, he paid it.

"Get yourself painted, Thomas," he instructed his son. "We're a new family now, but one day . . ." He could see the long line of family likenesses that would one day hang on the walls of the gallery.

Thomas Forest continued his good work of raising the family's status with, if possible, even more urgency than his father. He married the daughter of a rich clothier from Somerset, who had, through her mother, some claims to noble ancestry that had yet to be defined. She brought an impressive dowry. The estates were mostly let to tenants: the last remnants of the old village he therefore knocked down and built some fresh cottages a mile away. This allowed him to make a handsome new three hundred acre enclosure around the house in which he kept deer. Cottages, fields and hedges were all swept away and replaced by an open space planted with clumps of trees: the resulting deer park stretching towards the river was a much more agreeable prospect than the straggling houses of the peasants. At the dissolution the Forests had not obtained any of the great estates, but they had bought at cheap prices a number of farms that had belonged to the lesser friaries and it was on one of these, where there were some under-employed tenants, that Forest now proposed to set up a weaving business. He also supplemented his income by acting as steward for several small estates which the crown or the church were too lazy to manage properly themselves. By paying a low rent for them and then managing them through his own steward with ruthless efficiency he was adding handsomely to his revenues every year. Soon he hoped to join the ranks of the Justices of the Peace: for that was the first step on the ladder of full acceptance into the gentry and could lead to parliament, the king's court, and who knew what titles and riches.

Shrewd though he was, however, Thomas Forest as a rising gentleman had no wish to soil his hands with any personal involvement with trade – at least, not visibly. And so young Edward Shockley with his fulling mill was exactly what he needed.

"I can provide the money to set up as many looms as we want: we'll put them on one of my farms and we'll make enough broadcloth to keep your mill going full time – build another mill if we need to. And I want you to run the whole thing, Edward, because I can trust you."

Thomas Forest had a memorable face – sallow and narrow-set, but dignified with jet black hair and eyes and a long, thin moustache that drooped almost to the line of his jaw, so that when he was displeased he could look as grim as an executioner; when he chose to be pleasant however, he had a warm smile which he would accompany with a disarming and courtly inclination of his head. To Edward Shockley he was always particularly courteous.

He offered the young merchant generous terms, and at one of their meetings Shockley suggested:

"What we should do is try to export our cloth ourselves – cut out the middlemen, like the Webbes do."

To his delight Forest nodded.

"I agree. And I want you to go to Antwerp to find us an agent."

Shockley made the journey that February with high hopes. But before he went, Forest gave him careful advice.

"We want a man who can trim his sails to the wind – a privateer."

Edward knew what he meant. The situation on the continent, with the recent wars in Italy and the constant unrest between Protestants and their Catholic rulers in Germany and the Netherlands, was always uncertain. Only the year before the English had finally thrown the powerful German Hansa merchants out of London and English exporters could therefore expect harassment from them in return. The merchants who did best in these stormy times were the bold adventurers and opportunists.

"We must also find a man we can control from a distance – someone who needs us more than we need him." He gazed at the young merchant thoughtfully. "Find a man with a weakness."

Shockley had pondered this advice carefully on his journey to Antwerp. He stayed ten days in the busy port on the tidal river Schelde, with its Gothic cathedral, famous for possessing six aisles, and whose towering western spire reached seventy feet higher than even Salisbury's. He visited its great guildhalls, markets and printing works, astonished by the scale of every building he saw. There were a thousand foreign merchant houses: English and French, Spanish, Italians, and Portugese from the south, from the north, Germans and Danes. And on the sixth day, in a street of tall brick-gabled buildings, he found his man.

He was a huge, blond Fleming aged about thirty-five; he was clever and knew the markets well; he had a large family; he was looking for business. And he was in debt.

"If he can't pay soon, they'll take his house away," Shockley told Forest.

"He sounds like our man," the landowner agreed.

He was taking the Fleming to meet Forest at Avonsford that day. If Forest approved, then the deal between the three of them would be struck and the business would be ready to begin.

There had been a brief shower of rain just before Edward collected the Fleming from the George Inn that afternoon, and as they rode up the Avon valley glistening in the sunlight, he was glad that the place was looking its best.

For although he and Forest were intending to make use of the big foreigner, he was uncomfortably aware that the merchant, used to the huge metropolis of Antwerp and the mighty castles and palaces of Germany and France, might be a little contemptuous of the market town and modest manor houses of Sarum. The evening before when they had dined together at the inn, his companion had expressed the general view of the continentals when he leaned back comfortably and remarked:

"You English live poorly: but I grant that you eat well."

He need not have worried, however. For as they passed through the stone gateway and rode down the newly planted avenue that led through the deer park, the Fleming nodded in warm approval.

It was when they came in sight of the manor house however, that his companion reined his horse and stared in open-mouthed amazement.

"It is beautiful," he said in frank admiration. "I have never seen such a thing better done."

For when the Forests had rebuilt Avonsford Manor fifteen years before, they had incorporated into it a remarkable feature. And as a result, with the sun glancing off the still wet walls, it presented a most extraordinary sight.

"It's like a chequerboard," the Fleming cried in delight.

No description could have been more apt. The house now consisted of two large, gable-fronted wings between which stretched a two storey central section long enough to contain a row of five fine windows; in the middle of this now perfectly symmetrical arrangement was a broad, low-arched doorway. But the striking feature of all this, and what had excited the merchant's admiration, was the stonework of the walls. For here the Tudor masons had demonstrated one of the triumphs of their local craft. The entire façade was divided into perfect squares, about a foot across, and these had been alternated between local grey stone of a light shade and carefully knapped flint which was darker. When the sunlight caught it after a shower, this flint gleamed almost like glass.

It was a design that had been used in this and other regions where grey stone and flint had been found since Roman times, but nowhere was it more elegantly and precisely done than in the five valleys around Sarum.

As the two drew closer to the gleaming grey building however, it was another feature that caught the visitor's eye. Edward saw to his amusement, as they approached the entrance, that the Fleming's gaze was so fixed upon this last ornamentation, that he did not even notice Thomas Forest had come out of the door to greet them.

He was staring at the chimneys.

"My God," he shouted this time, so that his voice echoed around the whole house, "what do you call those?"

"Chimneys," Forest answered quietly.

In the reign of Henry VIII, a brief but never-to-be-forgotten fashion appeared in the architecture of England, and one which was not found anywhere else in Europe. For the English took it into their heads to create chimney stacks unlike any that the world had seen before. They were always made of red brick, and placed on top of great and medium sized houses, wholly irrespective of whatever material, plaster, brick or stone, the rest of the building was made of. They were huge. Their stacks rose in ornate columns, often heavy spirals, and were crowned with still more bulky capitals of brick or tile, carved into elaborate shapes. The capitals of the brick chimney stacks at Avonsford were particularly splendid and cumbersome, being octagonal in shape with overhanging scalloped edges. They proclaimed, if such a proclamation were needed, that the owner of the house aspired to the highest social status, that in time the house itself would grow to be as elaborate as its chimneys: they were its greatest and most preposterous glory.

The meeting went well, and after less than an hour, Forest concluded the deal. Its terms were simple. The Fleming was to act as exclusive agent for the new venture; Forest would finance any other dealings he wished to undertake. He would also pay off the merchant's debts, taking his house in Antwerp as security. In effect, by the end of the afternoon, Forest owned him.

"And the secret of him is," young Shockley had confided to Forest beforehand, "he likes to live well and he spends his money as fast as he makes it: he'll never pay off his debt to you."

When the matter was satisfactorily clinched, the three men fell to talking of general matters.

Sitting comfortably in the big panelled hall the merchant grinned knowingly at them both and asked:

"So – you English are Protestant this year, like us. Soon you will change your minds again, ya?"

Shockley opened his mouth to protest, but to his surprise Forest made only a sign of caution.

"In Antwerp there is a rumour that your boy king is sick. He will die soon. What then?"

"Nonsense," Shockley protested. Only the previous year the fifteen-year-old king had passed through Sarum and he had seen him with his own eyes: the boy had looked pale, but he had smiled and acknowledged the loyal cheers of the crowd with every sign of healthy enjoyment. It was true that there had been news of a temporary sickness that February, but a London merchant had told him the young king was better now.

To his surprise, once again, Forest did not deny the charge.

"The country will follow the religion of the monarch," he told the Fleming quietly.

"Whatever it is?" Shockley asked sharply.

"I think so."

The Fleming laughed.

"It's true what they say then – you English believe in nothing." And he slapped his knee in amusement.

Hearing these words, Shockley's face clouded. He remembered Abigail and Peter Mason that morning. He thought of his own, foolish admission of his Protestantism to Katherine a little earlier. Could it really be, now, that the country would change religion again?

As he left, he asked Forest anxiously:

"So you really think the king is so ill?"

Forest took his arm confidentially:

"Concentrate on the new business, Shockley. Don't worry about politics or religion. Just follow Bishop Capon." He gave him a warning look. "If trouble comes, keep your head down, that's all."

The Fleming was in a boisterous mood as they rode back to the city. He understood perfectly the hold Forest now had over him, but he was relieved at the same time to be free of his debts. As they passed the old castle hill and approached the city gates he blew out his cheeks and demanded:

"So where are the girls in Sarum?"

Abigail Mason's face was always perfectly still. Edward had noticed that for a long time.

Her broad, pale brow was always placid; her brown hair pulled tightly back; her face, which receded to a firmly chiselled angle at the chin, was never allowed to give way to any animation.

It was as though a Tudor painter had depicted her face and body in severe, chaste lines on a wooden panel before she had been allowed to step into the world and assume a life in the flesh. Her mouth was carefully held in a modest line. Was there a hint of bitterness there he sometimes wondered? If so it was perfectly controlled. Her eyes were deep brown but gave nothing away. There were often dark rings under them. A generation earlier, instead of being a Protestant, she might have been a nun.

Abigail Mason wanted a child. She was twenty-eight.

Once, when she was twenty-five, she had thought that she was pregnant, but it had turned out to be a false hope. She did not know why she had failed. True, her husband had not been able to arouse her to any great passion, but she was sure that this was not important.

Was it her fault they had no child? She knew most people supposed it must be. The Mason family was plentiful; her husband's cousin Robert who lived at Fisherton nearby, had six healthy children. And yet some instinct told her that she could have one still. She did not know how she knew, but she was sure it was so.

How she longed for it. When she saw a baby carried in the street, she was irrepressibly drawn to it; when she saw Robert's wife suckle her child, she could not help an almost greedy expression coming over her placid face as she ached to do the same. Was it a sin to long for a child of her own? She prayed for it every night. And still it had not come.

She was firm with herself. Her father, a dour London bookbinder who had taken up the Lutheran persuasion, had taught all his children that they must suffer: it was to be expected. She suffered.

Peter Mason was of medium height and, unusually for his family, thin. But on his rather delicate body there rested, cheerfully, a large, round, balding head. He was a gentle, simple man and it was a tribute to Abigail's calm sense of duty that his broad face lit up with an innocent smile of pleasure whenever he saw her.

They occupied the same house where old Benedict had had his bell foundry; but they only rented half the space. The bell foundry had been discontinued thirty years ago and Peter made cutlery now. He, too, hoped for a child; apart from this he was contented.

She wished, sometimes, that he had more ambition. She wondered if, without her, he would even have served God as he should. It had taken her much persuasion to bring him to destroy the idolatrous window in St Thomas's church. But if Peter Mason was not all she might have hoped for, "I must be grateful for what I have," she would remind herself. And life in their house was quiet and pleasant enough.

Except for one thing: about that, she knew, something must be done; it was as important as the church window; and as she walked back with Peter that morning she reminded him:

"You must act now, husband. You promised me."

It was a confrontation he dreaded. He wondered if he could put it off until tomorrow.

When Nellie Godfrey left the George Inn with the merchant from Antwerp that evening, she had a feeling that he might give trouble. He was a large man and though he had taken a quantity of wine, she was not sure whether it had made him drunk or not. She glanced up at him shrewdly. She thought she could handle him: she could most men. Carefully but firmly she steered him towards her lodgings, and when the Fleming swung his great arm to pull her to him in the street she laughed and disentangled herself.

"Wait."

Nellie Godfrey had a remarkable combination of gifts which made her attractive to men. She knew about them, but they came naturally: a gay, lively, outgoing nature combined with a body of such heavy sensuousness that the air around her seemed almost palpable with the aura of it.

She was below medium height, so that her head with its short, dark brown hair hardly came up to the Fleming's chest. She wore a bright red half-open bodice laced across the front with ribbons and with high red and blue pads on the shoulders. Under this was a chemisette of thin white linen. She wore a full-bodied skirt to the ankles, dainty leather shoes and a jaunty little linen cap. Her best features were accentuated by her short stature: a pair of dazzling blue eyes with a flicker of hazel around the irises, that were always staring up beguilingly, a brilliant smile that revealed two rows of small, perfectly white teeth, and a pair of magnificent heavy breasts. It was when she came close however, that men became aware of a rich, thick sense of warmth that seemed to rise from below her breasts, carrying with it the heady sensuous scent of musk with which she perfumed herself whenever she could afford it.

"That woman," Thomas Forest remarked to Shockley, "was made to be loved by many men."

She liked her sensuousness: she was excited by it herself.

But she had a greater gift still. All her lovers felt they had received – as well as the rich warmth of her magnificent body, the triumph of holding her through her titanic orgasms – a share of her genuine affection, and a sense of an inner softness, a vulnerability in her nature that was touching.

Nellie often considered it, and she was satisfied that she liked most of her lovers. True, she sometimes had to sell herself to men she did not care for; but most of the time she had made her living by being the mistress of a few chosen men in the city. They paid her of course, she had to eat; but it was their presents, which she did not ask for, that were important to her. She would take them out when she was alone, sit up in bed with them and survey them, murmuring: "He loves me a little, I think," or even: "He loves me more than his wife." And when, satisfied, she put her presents away again, she would sometimes cry a little; but this was something nobody ever saw.

It was over seventy years since old Eustace Godfrey had become a hermit, sixty-five since he had died. Three generations had passed since then, and none of them had done well. By her grandfather's day, the last of the Godfrey money had all gone. Her father had been a drunkard and she and her only brother Piers had been orphaned when she was thirteen. Piers was a carpenter: a worthy, quiet fellow who often did small jobs for Shockley, who had befriended him. He had supported Nellie when she was a girl and he still loved her; but he was ashamed of her now. She could not help that.

"Our family was noble once," he reminded her; it was two centuries, seven generations since any Godefroi had lived at Avonsford though and her brother's foolish idea meant little to Nellie.

"Won't buy me anything, will it," she would retort fiercely.

Indeed, the fact that they bore the same name as the brother and sister was now an embarrassment to the worthy merchant Godfrey family of Salisbury whom Eustace had once despised. They had reached the apex of the town society, had even supplied a mayor of the city.

"Nellie Godfrey's no kin of ours," they were quick to say if her name was mentioned.

At the age of twenty-two, Nellie made a modest living. She owned several small pieces of jewellery, though they were worth less than she thought; she had a few fine dresses a rich merchant had given her. But though she was not unhappy with this achievement, the future was beginning to look uncertain. And when her brother pleaded with her: "What will you do next Nellie?" she could only cry impatiently: "Something," and refuse angrily to discuss the matter any further.

She had never wanted to sit at a spinning wheel or marry a poor artisan like her brother: the boredom of the prospect appalled her lively mind; but what were the alternatives?

"You won't even get any husband," Piers warned. "Your reputation's gone."

She knew it was true. She would not admit it but she was frightened. Yet some force inside drove her onward.

"I'll think of something," she would repeat defiantly, as her bright blue eyes looked out at what she could see of the world in Sarum, and watched for an opportunity.

She reached her lodgings in Culver Street. The Fleming had been ambling contentedly beside her, swaying a little and humming to himself; now he looked at the modest tenement and cried:

"Today I see a fine house like a chequerboard. Now I see a house I like even better – because it has a woman in it!" And his laugh echoed down the street.

"You must keep quiet," she whispered, and hustled him through the doorway of the little courtyard and up the stairs.

Nellie Godfrey had never been in trouble with the authorities. This was partly owing to a certain tolerance among the town authorities and the bishop's bailiff, partly to her own friendly relations with some of the leading merchants, and not least because she was discreet. The innkeepers of the larger inns were glad to have her available for their more prosperous clients and she was careful never to offend the more straight-laced part of the city population by flaunting herself in public. Once or twice there had been murmurings, but each time powerful men in the town had either quashed them or warned Nellie to go away for a while.

The big Fleming knew nothing about this; nor did he care. He had just saved his wife and family; the arrangement with Forest and Shockley had given him a new lease of life. He was not drunk with wine, but he was maudlin with happiness and once upstairs in Nellie's two chambers he would not be quiet. Moving heavily about on the creaking floors he continued humming to himself; then he began to sing, and though Nellie took his arm and tried to kiss him in order to quieten him down, it had no effect.

Quickly she began to unlace the heavy front of her dress, peeling it down over her wonderful breasts.

"Come," she begged.

It seemed to work. His broad face lit up into a happy smile; stepping across the room he took her breasts in his big warm hands, lifting them slowly with an almost childish wonder.

She might have guessed, but she had not realised the big Fleming was so strong; only now did she discover that she was completely in his power.

He meant no harm. He was only happy. But as he sat his huge frame on the bed, she was astonished that he could lift her on to his lap like a child. Holding her still with one arm, he undressed her, gently but firmly, inspecting every inch of her pale skin with the same placid concentration she had seen earlier, when he had inspected the Wiltshire cheeses at the inn. He was humming to himself as he did so: strangely, she felt like a child again and the big man's power was curiously comforting. For no particular reason, she laughed.

"At least he's quiet," she thought as this methodical performance went on.

But when he had finally completed his work and she was entirely naked, he calmly picked her up and placed her on the heavy oak bed – "Just like a piece of meat he's going to baste," she smiled to herself – as he peeled off his heavy stockings and tunic. Then placidly picking her up again, he began to make love to her.

At first he was gentle, still humming to himself as though in a dream and she found his slow caresses – his huge hands surprisingly sensitive – were not unpleasant. His breath smelt a little of wine, more of cheese; she was used to that. But soon the Fleming began to pant. His tongue and hands seemed to want to explore and possess every part of her: they roved, felt, squeezed. "He's kneading me like a lump of dough," she remarked to herself, and wondered how to respond. The big merchant did not require any response. His face was growing red, his eyes bulging: their stare of lust seemed hardly to see her at all.

And now, as his excitement mounted, he grew wilder. He picked her up, whirled her round the room, his voice rising to a shout of joy and lust. She was helpless to do anything about it. She tried to put her hand up to his mouth to restrain him, but it was the last gesture she could make before he crashed with her on to the bed and thrust hungrily into her.

For a moment her eyes opened wide. He was huge; she could only hold on to him as best she might while he thrust wildly, again and again until she wondered if even the stout oak frame would give way. She thought the climax must soon come; but she was mistaken.

It lasted over an hour. Sometimes he carried her in triumph round the room; then he would hurl himself with her upon the bed. Several times they fell together on the floor with a crash that shook the whole house. Her attempts to quieten him broke like futile waves upon the shore. He broke into song; he roared his triumph; he handled her as easily as if she had been a child's doll, while every board in the room seemed to creak in protest as he cavorted about. He fairly bellowed in the exultation of his power, his happiness, and his relief from his debts.

"He's not a man, he's a bull," she thought. It was half exciting, half comic. After a time, realising that the huge Fleming was and would remain, completely out of control, she could do nothing but give in, and, as he crashed with her once more upon the bed, come again and again.

It was dawn when the big merchant rolled contentedly out of her lodgings.

And it was soon after dawn, when Nellie was still asleep, that the group of her neighbours, commandeered by Abigail Mason and led, shamefacedly and unwillingly by Peter, met to discuss what must be done.

At eight o'clock that morning, Peter Mason and his wife made their way to the house of the alderman of the ward and there Peter reluctantly demanded that the shameless harlot whose night revels had shaken the whole tenement and alarmed its neighbours, should be brought before the bishop's bailiff and the justices.

"You know what this will mean?" the alderman said. Peter looked at the ground.

"Yes," Abigail replied fearlessly. "She'll be whipped."

It had taken her three years to persuade her husband to do his duty; she could have taken the matter into her own hands, but there would have been less satisfaction in that. She wanted Peter to act as a God-fearing man should, not for herself to have to do it for him. And at last, the day before, he had promised after destroying the idolatrous window, to take action at last. If he had had any second thoughts, the incredible racket that the Fleming had made, that had echoed all over the tenement and out into the street had surely sealed the matter.

"It's God's law that the harlot be punished," she reminded him. "And it's your duty to your wife to have the painted woman put out of our house." Peter nodded sadly. He supposed that it was.

By noon, the alderman was speaking to the bailiff.

It was at noon also that Piers Godfrey came to the house of his friend Edward Shockley to ask: "Can you save Nellie?"

Edward Shockley had known Piers all his life; the carpenter had often done small jobs in the Shockley house and made the family a fine oak table.

"I'll do what I can," he promised. But he was not optimistic.

The penalties for most kinds of misbehaviour were severe. The justices of the peace, that body of local gentlemen who were now taking over more and more of the routine local law and administration that had been done by sheriff and shire knight in the past, had the right to return vagrants to their parishes, put disturbers of the peace in the stocks, even to stop the common people playing unauthorised games. Vagrants, the parents of bastard children and harlots were all liable to a fiercer punishment: they were tied to a post in the market place and publicly whipped until they bled. If Abigail persisted in her complaint the authorities would have no choice but to carry out this sentence.

As he walked quickly to the Masons' house in Culver Street, Edward wondered what kind of reception he would get. What would it be like to cross swords with the redoubtable woman he admired?

She ushered him in politely. He noticed that Peter was standing by the door, looking awkward, wishing no doubt that none of this business was happening.

He stated his case briefly: Nellie was not a bad girl; the family was poor; in his foolish enthusiasm he even promised to be responsible for her future good behaviour. He could see out of the corner of his eye that Peter Mason was looking hopeful, and emboldened by this, he begged Abigail to withdraw her complaint.

She stared at him as though he were a child.

"Dost thou not know, Edward Shockley, that it is the sin that we punish, not the sinner?"

Yes, he knew it, but in his mind's eye, he could not help seeing poor Nellie's magnificent back bared and cut to ribbons at the cruel whipping post.

He met her calm, dispassionate eyes and flushed.

"Perhaps she will reform," he suggested; but under her steady gaze, the suggestion seemed absurd. He searched in his mind for something else.

He remembered the story of the fallen woman in the New Testament. "Which of us shall cast the first stone?" he was about to say; but as he considered Abigail's own perfect morality, that, too, seemed a hopeless argument.

"Let the Justices decide the punishment," she said quietly; and then more gently and even with a smile she added: "Thou art a merciful man Edward Shockley. After her punishment, then will be the time for thou and I to show mercy to the sinner."

How certain she was. He could not be so stern himself; but he was not so pure as Abigail. He left her sadly, knowing the young woman must suffer.

Nellie Godfrey had other plans. Surreptitiously, Peter Mason had warned her. A little before noon she had made her way to her brother's house, where he found her when he returned from Edward Shockley. She was carrying a single bag over her shoulder which contained most of her moveable possessions.

"I'm leaving," she told him flatly.

He began to protest, but she cut him short. "My life's over here, brother. They're going to whip me in the market place."

He nodded dismally.

"But if you run . . ."

"I'll be a vagrant. I'll take my chances."

"Where will you go?" he asked unhappily.

"West." The big port of Bristol was a place where she could take lodgings without too many questions being asked. She could earn a living there.

He sighed. He supposed she would be a harlot there too; the port could be a violent place. He did not like to think about her likely final fate.

Silently he went to the little chest where he kept his valuables. From it he carefully counted out fifteen pounds: it was almost all he had. He handed it to her.

But Nellie only smiled, kissed him, and put the coins back in the box. "I have money," she said, and turned to the door.

"Will I see you again?" Piers asked.

She turned; her brilliant blue eyes took in her gentle brother with complete, resigned understanding, just as they had already taken in the world.

"Shouldn't think so," she said, and was gone.

It was just as she was walking briskly towards Fisherton Bridge that Edward Shockley came up with her.

"I couldn't stop them," he told her.

"Don't worry. I'm going."

The sun was warm. As Nellie walked along the road towards Wilton, she was not uneasy in her mind. She guessed that the bailiff, once her absence was discovered, would make no great effort to go after her. Indeed, she even felt a sense of relief that, because of the sudden crisis, she was being forced to take her life in a different direction.

"Whatever happens," she vowed, "this time I won't go under."

Less than a mile out from Fisherton Bridge, as she passed the village of Bemerton, she saw a carter who offered to take her to Barford, the other side of Wilton.

Just as she was climbing into his cart she was surprised to see Edward Shockley on an old chestnut horse come riding up. Before she could even say anything, the young man had dropped a small pouch into her hand, muttered, "God be with you," and, blushing scarlet, wheeled the old horse round and cantered slowly away. The bag contained ten pounds.

Nellie Godfrey stayed that night at the old western hill town of Shaftesbury, eighteen miles away, and the following morning continued, northwards this time, upon her way.

On July 6, 1553, Edward VI of England, the pious Protestant boy king breathed his last.

The news had been expected for a month, but now, all England waited with trepidation to see who would succeed.

The answer, when it came, proved to be one of the oddest episodes in English history.

For in July in the year of Our Lord 1553, the throne of England was given to Lady Jane Grey.

It was an extraordinary situation. The two daughters of Henry VIII had been passed over; their brother Edward, perhaps to secure the crown for a known protestant, had left it in his will to a cousin in the female royal line whose claim to the throne was, at best, distant. This was the so-called 'devise' of King Edward.

In fact it was a plot, and it had little to do with either Edward or Lady Jane Grey. Cranmer and the Protestant party wanted to keep out Edward's Catholic sister Mary, daughter of Henry VIII's Spanish queen. But the prime mover was a far more cynical figure: for the Duke of Northumberland, Protector of the Realm while King Edward was a boy, had no wish to give up his power. Young Lady Jane, still only a girl, would be his puppet; and he made sure of it by hastily marrying her to his son. He was supported by an unlikely and even craftier figure: King Henry of France. Henry had no interest in either Protestantism, Northumberland or Lady Jane Grey; but his own son was married to the young Mary Queen of Scots, another cousin of the English Tudor house, and the more Edward's surviving sisters could be weakened, the better the chances that one day the Queen of Scots might inherit the English throne as well and make his family monarchs of France, Scotland and England.

The attempt to make Lady Jane queen was a gamble, but for a short time the gamblers seemed in control.

On 15th July, at the Tower of London, the Privy Council sent a stirring message to the burgesses of Salisbury. They must know, it said, if Catholic Mary succeeded,

> whereof was like to have followed the bondage of this realm, the old servitude of the antichrist of Rome, the subversion of the new teaching of God's word . . .

The Privy Council's message was signed by Cranmer, other bishops and magnates – including Lord Pembroke of Wilton.

For one other detail of the conspiracy emerged that day. Not only had the Protector's son married Queen Jane, but Pembroke had just married his own son to Lady Jane's sister Catherine. There could be no doubt of the new Earl's ambition.

The gamble to crown Lady Jane failed miserably. Mary Tudor was not the daughter of Henry VIII and a Spanish princess for nothing. She rallied a huge party to her. She promised religious toleration. She seemed – it was a trick she had from her father – to be almost jovial. And above all, whatever Cranmer's annulment of her mother's marriage might make her in the eyes of her enemies, she was, and all England knew it, the true heir to the crown.

She advanced on London. The mood of the people swung towards her. The Privy Council sent the Duke of Northumberland out to confront her – and as soon as he was gone, changed sides behind his back.

None more quickly than Lord Pembroke of Wilton who now swore loudly that he would defend her to the death with his sword.

So ended the reign of the uncrowned Queen Jane. The unhappy girl was put in prison, Northumberland executed, and Pembroke's son wisely never consummated his marriage to her sister.

Edward Shockley stood before his wife. He was about to submit.

It had taken three months and he could not help admiring her for it. They had been painful months for him, for it was not easy to endure her mistrust.

After the scene in April, there were three days during which she was very quiet, but during which he could see that she had been weeping frequently. He avoided her partly out of shame at what he had done, partly because he was angry with her for making him feel guilty.

He wondered once or twice if she might return to her father's house; but she had not, and he was thankful for that at least.

The question had remained – what was to happen? She made no further attempt to teach the child any popish doctrines: he felt sure he could trust her not to disobey him.

But she was hurt and that could not be undone.

Nor, it seemed, could he win over the child. Little Celia now looked at him with fear. It was only natural. She did not understand exactly how, but she could see that her father had hurt her mother; and she also had the clear impression, though nothing was ever explained, that her father had committed some terrible crime. If he went towards her now, her pale eyes, just like her mother's, opened wide and she shrank from him. When she did so, he cursed under his breath, and that made her more frightened still.

For a month Katherine had been distant at nights until, in a fit of rage one evening he demanded his conjugal rights. She submitted: it was her duty. But her look of meek suffering, almost martyrdom, irritated him so much that he gave it up with an oath.

And every few days, she would meekly beg him:

"Soften your heart, Edward. As a child at least, you must have been a Catholic once. Are you sure, now you are a man, it is not pride in your own mind that makes you turn from the authority of the Catholic Church?"

Authority. He understood what she wanted very well: it was the ancient demand of the Roman Church: admit that you are nothing, submit.

He would not.

Besides, after lying to her for those years, it was a relief to tell her the truth at last.

After six weeks had passed however, a slight change occurred. She went about her daily business quietly. She even welcomed him to her bed. She tried in all things to please him. And only once a week, on a Sunday, did she gently and lovingly sit beside him and beg him to reconsider.

"Not to please me," she explained seriously, "but to save your soul."

Inwardly he groaned.

How kind she was. How wronged. But whether she was weeping or, as now, coaxing, it was hard, week after week, to endure her sad mistrust.

And now he was about to give way.

It was Thomas Forest who persuaded him.

They had discussed the whole question the day before.

The new queen had only been on the throne a week and she had promised religious toleration. He had wanted to believe it, but the landowner assured him:

"Queen Mary will make England Catholic – by force if necessary."

Already there were hints for the observant in Sarum, of what might be to come.

"I've spoken to Bishop Capon," Forest explained, "he's the best weathervane."

"He's a vigorous Protestant."

Forest shook his head.

"That was last week. He's changing. You must think of your safety and our business, Edward, and be ready to do the same."

Which had made Edward Shockley think of his wife.

He looked at the situation calmly. He suspected Forest was right and the talk of tolerance was only a pretence.

Unless he wanted to risk his life therefore, he would have to profess Catholicism again.

But what of Katherine? If he did so to comply with the new regime would she ever believe he was sincere? Surely not. He had already lied to her before.

Which led to a simple conclusion. Unless he was to endure years of her disbelief and distrust, he must convert now, apparently of his own free will.

He stood before her now in the guise of a penitent.

"Katherine, I ask your forgiveness. I spoke with fear in my heart, and with anger. I believe in the Catholic faith in which I was raised and I wish to return to it."

"Are you sincere, Edward?" Her pale blue eyes were doubtful, yet he saw the hope in them.

"I swear."

"Will you confess to a priest?"

"With all my heart." He smiled.

There were tears in her eyes.

"I have prayed for this, Edward, three long months."

"And I thank you for your prayers."

How easy it was. He kissed her, though not without a secret sense of shame.

Forest was right.

Not only did Capon change sides again, but Bishop Gardiner was soon back at nearby Winchester. Within months, Parliament had granted Mary everything she demanded except the return of the English Church to Rome. All talk of toleration was forgotten. The Protestant bishops Latimer and Ridley were thrown into prison. Poor Archbishop Cranmer was arrested.

Worse, the thirty-seven-year-old queen longed for a Catholic husband and a child. Within a month she had chosen Philip of Spain. In order to make sure of support in the council Philip's father the Holy Roman Emperor sent a gift of two thousand crowns to several key men. Lord Pembroke was one of them. And when Parliament protested at this intrusion of Spain into England's affairs, Mary told them to mind their own business.

The news that came to Sarum left no doubt of the new queen's strength.

In January a rebellion led by Wyatt, son of the minor poet, collected a large body of men and marched from Kent to London. At London they were crushed by Lord Pembroke and on the convenient suspicion that they were implicated, Lady Jane Grey and her husband were now beheaded. Mary's half sister Elizabeth, it seemed, was also under suspicion, but since nothing could be proven, she was allowed to remain under supervision at the country palace of Woodstock.

Meanwhile, Bishop Capon deprived of their livings fifty-four clergymen of the diocese, who had been obeying his previous, Protestant instructions.

But the event which made Edward Shockley most nervous of all came in June 1554, when the Marquis de las Novas, personal emissary of King Philip of Spain, landed ahead of his royal master at Plymouth and was conducted thence by Lord Pembroke to Wilton House where he was greeted by a magnificent company led by Pembroke's son, and including the sheriff of the county and two hundred gentlemen. Of these, none was better horsed or more splendidly dressed than the sallow squire of Avonsford, Thomas Forest.

Two weeks later the King of Spain and his fleet arrived at Southampton. They proceeded at once to the ancient city of Winchester, where they were married with all ceremony by the newly reinstated Bishop Gardiner, after which Lord Pembroke ceremonially carried the great sword of state in front of the Spanish king.

And though Forest assured him Philip alone could not inherit the English throne and that the Spanish connection would benefit English trade with Spain's possessions in the New World and the Netherlands, he voiced the feelings of most Englishmen when he grumbled bitterly:

"I have no wish to be even half ruled by a Spanish king."

Abigail Mason had grown very quiet of late. But the reason, Edward Shockley discovered, was greatly to her credit.

In August 1553 she had seen, with absolute clarity, what was to come.

"The true religion will be outlawed. Soon there'll be nothing left but the Latin mass in every church," she explained with disgust to her bemused husband. "We must leave."

"Where shall we go?" he had asked.

And to his astonishment she had replied:

"Geneva, of course."

He had stared at her open-mouthed, first in amazement, then in dismay.

"But how shall we find the money?"

"If it is the Lord's will, then we shall find a way."

His question was not unreasonable. Of the several hundred Protestant families who fled the regime of Mary Tudor, nearly all were gentlefolk, rich merchants or scholars. The number of humble artisans who could afford the luxury of escape to the continent probably numbered only a few dozen. Peter knew of no one else at Sarum who would even attempt such a bold venture.

But if they were to go, then her choice of Geneva was, at least for her, a natural one. For the Swiss city of Geneva was the home, the holy city, of the man she admired most: John Calvin.

"'Tis the City of God," she reminded her husband.

In Geneva, the severe moral disciplinarian Calvin ruled with a Protestant regime as all-embracing and as fiercely doctrinaire as any opposing Catholic regime that Mary Tudor could have dreamed of imposing upon England.

Of all the Protestant leaders – Luther and his followers, who were still at root only reformist Catholics, or the more advanced teachers like Zwingli who emphasised that the communion was nothing more than an act of remembrance – it was the severe and logical Frenchman, Calvin, in his Swiss retreat, who appealed most to her own stern sense of duty. It was Calvin who insisted, by a process of simple deduction from the Bible, on one of the most terrifying if logical doctrines to emerge from the Protestant Reformation: the doctrine of predestination.

Predestination, though it could be deduced from St Augustine himself, was in the eyes of the Catholic church a heresy: for it denied that a man could exercise free will to follow the path of righteousness and, by God's grace, reach heaven.

Even Shockley, when he used to admit his Protestantism, felt uncomfortable with this doctrine.

"If all is predestined, then there's no point in prayer, good works, anything," he complained, "since nothing we do can alter our fate."

But to Abigail this was not the point: the logic of her case was unassailable. "Some are chosen, some are not," she told Peter. And when he asked anxiously: "Are we chosen?" she would only reply: "Perhaps."

"We must obey God's law and trust in Him," she declared. "God's law is denied in England now. We'll go to Geneva."

And so, during the month of August, the couple collected all the money they could and made their preparations.

They never left.

For at the end of August 1553, the wife of Peter's cousin Robert Mason suddenly and unexpectedly died in childbirth, and the distracted Robert was left in the cottage at Fisherton with no help, a surviving baby and a brood of young children. Peter and Abigail were with them when it happened.

It took Abigail one day to decide what must be done; the choice she made was selfless.

"We must stay," she told Peter, with tears, for once, in her eyes. "It cannot be God's will that we should leave our cousin alone like this."

"We shall not go to Geneva then?"

She shook her head sorrowfully.

"Not yet. We must stay," she replied sadly, "and suffer."

"Then I had better unpack my tools," the cutler replied, with secret relief.

From that day, Abigail had two families to care for.

Shockley had many matters, other than religion, to consider at this time.

For three years the harvests had been poor; there was a sense of discomfort and unease in the countryside and it was hard not to be affected by it. More serious, from his point of view, was that the booming cloth market had led to overproduction.

"Our Fleming may be a good trader," he told Forest, "but every month the merchant adventurers are complaining there's too much cloth coming into Antwerp. Prices are falling. Are you sure we are wise to be setting up for more production now?"

But to his surprise Forest only smiled.

"What will happen when the glut gets worse?" he asked his young partner.

"Merchants will be ruined," Shockley replied.

Forest nodded.

"Exactly. In a year or two there'll be a crisis. But it will pass. The underlying market is strong. And when the crisis comes, we shall be trading, and we'll buy up spare cloth at cheap prices from those who can't afford to keep it any longer." He smiled. "I've got enough money to ride out a dozen storms, Shockley. Let's get to work."

The two men would often ride over to Forest's secondary estates, which lay the other side of Wilton to where the workshops were being set up, and whenever they passed the gates of Lord Pembroke's great house there Forest would remark:

"That's the man to watch, Edward. He's even importing cloth workers from overseas."

It was on one of these occasions that they saw a strange sight.

Just as they came to Pembroke's gates, a coach with outriders came

[625]

rumbling by from the west at such speed that they had to pull violently to one side to let it past. As it did so, the outriders flung stones at the gates, and from inside the coach Shockley heard a string of curses, apparently directed at the house. With a tremendous racket and much splashing of mud, the extraordinary cortège rumbled out of sight.

"What was that?" Shockley asked in amazement.

Forest grinned.

"That was Lord Stourton," he replied.

Shockley knew him by name of course. Though their contact with Sarum had been sporadic over the centuries, everyone had heard of the ancient lords of Stourton who had ruled over parts of west Wiltshire for centuries. But he had never caught sight of him before.

"What's he doing here?"

"He's taken a hatred to Lord Pembroke," Forest told him.

"Why?"

"Who knows? Perhaps because the Herberts came here recently; perhaps because they're so powerful." He shook his head. "Only a fool makes an enemy of Pembroke. But Stourton's always making enemies. Some say he's mad."

Once they encountered Pembroke himself. He was riding quietly along the lane with two gentlemen, and to Forest's profuse salute he gave a courteous but brief nod in reply. Shockley studied him as he passed and noted his long, aquiline face and hard, thoughtful eyes. Forest turned to him afterwards:

"Well?"

"Not a man I'd cross," Edward confessed.

It was during this time that one minor but significant change took place in the Forest–Shockley affairs.

There were so many sides to the new business that Forest suggested to Shockley one day:

"We need a new pair of hands – someone to watch over the weavers, day to day."

To this Shockley readily agreed and both men decided to look out for such a man.

Shockley was surprised however when, two weeks after he had mentioned it to her, Katherine said to him with a smile:

"I think I have your man for you."

"Who is that?"

"My brother John." And she explained.

The proposition she put to him had considerable merit. The boy was only nineteen, but he had spent all his life close to his father's business and there was little about making cloth he did not know. He was eager to work for Shockley, it seemed, because there had been some friction between him and his father recently.

He was a pleasant, open-faced young man with slightly reddish hair. His pale eyes at first seemed a little ingenuous, but it was soon clear that in the workshop where he oversaw every detail of the spinning and weaving process, quietly but ruthlessly, he missed nothing. He spoke little, even when he was with his sister.

Forest approved of him.

Since he chose to lodge separately from his sister and brother-in-law, and as there was no available place for him on Forest's estate, he took the lodgings in the tenement in Culver Street that had been vacated by Nellie Godfrey.

He was quiet, but he was a Catholic. Abigail – who Shockley often saw when he dropped by to see the young man – tolerated his presence in silence, but she was prepared to admit:

"At least there are no more harlots here."

Abigail was often at the house at Fisherton. She had found a young woman to suckle the baby, but all the other duties of keeping the little cottage and feeding Robert Mason's family fell to her. Often Peter would walk the mile from Culver Street to Fisherton and eat with them before returning contentedly to his workshop in Culver Street, and Shockley guessed that the simple fellow was glad enough not to be on his way to Geneva. He often looked in upon the cutler in his workshop and never heard a word of complaint about his lot except once when he secretly confided:

"I miss Nellie, though."

For Abigail Mason, the two years that followed Queen Mary's accession were an increasingly difficult time. She had no doubt that she had done right in staying: that at least was some comfort. But the Catholic conditions were hard to bear. She avoided attending mass. This might have brought her into trouble with the authorities; but since it was known that she was looking after two households, and since no one was ever sure whether she was at Fisherton or in Salisbury, her absence could be conveniently overlooked.

And besides, she was quiet.

"I would speak out," she told Shockley one day at Culver Street. "But there are our cousin Peter's children to look after as well as our-selves . . ." and she quietly spread her hands. "I pray each day for deliverance," she added.

She was ceaselessly at work. The dark rings under her eyes seemed to grow darker so that sometimes she looked gaunt and hollow-eyed. "She's like a deathshead," Shockley sometimes thought. But she went about her business, silent and indefatigable, and when once John Moody offered to let Peter join his own meal at Culver Street one day, she quietly but firmly refused.

"You would not eat with Catholics?" she asked Peter, and her husband, after pausing for a moment agreed that no, he supposed he would not.

In the spring of 1554, Abigail Mason herself observed a subtle change in her own behaviour for which she reproved herself. The trouble was Peter.

It was not easy to bear his indifference to her suffering: not that he meant any harm – far from it. Indeed, he was so eager, always, to please her. He would bring little gifts for Robert's children; he would greet her

[627]

sometimes with little posies of flowers when she returned tired in the evenings. Yet always, in his broad, affectionate, rather foolish smile, she could see clearly that he was untroubled by their predicament.

"Dost thou not grieve that we are unable to go to God's city of Geneva?" she several times asked him and Peter, wanting to please her but plainly confused, would look troubled before replying hopefully:

"Are we not doing God's work here?"

And she knew that he was relieved because he was not being asked to move from his little workshop.

Most of the time Abigail was silent. But sometimes alone with her husband and hearing of the raising of a new altar in some Wiltshire church, or the celebration of a dirge in the city, she would cry out:

"How can you smile, Peter Mason, when such things are done? How long are we to suffer the Roman Antichrist – or will you just stand weakly by?"

At such times, Peter would hang his head, confused and ashamed more on account of the scorn he sensed in her voice than any clear perception that he had sinned. On three occasions he led Shockley to one side and asked his advice.

"She will speak out in public one day," he told the merchant. "I fear it and I fear for her, Master Shockley."

Hearing it, Edward Shockley too was troubled – for he, too, feared that Abigail's resolute nature might bring her into direct conflict with Bishop Capon, and he dreaded the consequences.

It was on the third occasion that Peter had said quietly:

"My wife is not like me: she is brave and strong." And Edward, though he agreed, had been sorry to see the cutler look so ashamed.

Strangely, though he even went to mass upon occasion, Abigail felt less friction with Robert at Fisherton. Unusually for the family, he had a thick shock of dark hair; he had a powerful, burly figure, and firm convictions.

"This rule is a great iniquity," he told her. "But I'll not oppose it until these children are grown," and he gestured towards his six children.

"Does thy conscience trouble thee?" she asked.

"Yes," he told her frankly, "every day. But this is a time to suffer in silence. That's my judgement."

And though she was not sure if he was right, she understood his decision, and bowed her head in respect.

"May we pray to God in the proper manner in private?" she asked.

To this Robert Mason did agree; with Robert leading their prayer, Peter, Abigail, the six children and several of their neighbours would meet discreetly in Fisherton and conduct their Protestant services each week with a good conscience.

There was no question about one thing at least: Robert's children needed her. It was a comfort in her adversity to have them about her. The baby in particular she cherished; indeed, it was hard sometimes to draw herself away from it, and often when she arrived back in Culver Street she would stand silently at the door of her husband's little workshop and gaze at him wondering:

"Will God perhaps, after all, grant us a child?"

If she could not quite respect her husband over the all-important matter of religion, she could not fault his conduct. Not only did Peter try to help her, but he never complained. Often she was at Fisherton longer than she had intended, but when she came to him at last and apologised for her long absence he would smile sweetly and answer: "I am well enough here," so that at times she wondered if perhaps her absence was a relief to him.

Was it that thought, she asked herself, that several times made her burst out at him in renewed anger at his indifference to the terrible events of Mary's reign?

Edward Shockley watched all these developments in the Mason household with mixed feelings. Sometimes, when he looked at simple Peter and his intense, passionate wife, he could not help feeling a tinge of contempt for the cutler; but no sooner had he felt it than he rounded upon himself:

"And you Edward Shockley, who understand these things more plainly than Peter Mason. Aren't you going to mass with the rest like the coward you are?" he would demand of himself.

For certainly there were no more perfect Catholics in Sarum now than Edward Shockley and his wife Katherine.

Each week, with her brother John, they went to mass and Edward solemnly raised his eyes at the elevation of the Host.

Katherine was happy; and he had to admit, that as far as his home life went, so was he. She was pregnant again.

And yet, despite this happiness, like a man who is unfaithful to his wife when he is happy with her, Edward Shockley was tempted to lead a double life.

He knew about the Mason family's illicit prayer meetings because Peter Mason had told him; and it was one day in the late spring that he had astonished the cutler by suggesting that he join them one day.

"Only, you must not speak of it," he made him promise.

Peter was delighted, and if Abigail was not, she pursed her lips and said nothing.

He liked the prayer meetings for several reasons, not least of which was that it made him feel proud of himself.

He might lie in public when he raised his eyes at the elevation of the Host; he might lie in private to his wife. But at least here, with these good people at their secret prayers, he felt he was being honest.

The meetings were illicit and dangerous. The thought that he might be discovered frightened him. But he felt sure he could trust the Masons.

"Of course," he remarked to Abigail one day, "though I pray in private, with my wife and family to consider, I cannot speak out." He watched her, hoping for the sign of approval.

Abigail said nothing at first, but she turned to look up at him with her deep brown eyes; he noticed how pale her face was, how dark the shadows were under her eyes; and she gazed at him now for fully half a minute. It was a look of perfect understanding, of resigned contempt, and of gentle condemnation that he would never forget.

"Ask God and thy conscience, Edward Shockley," she said at last. "Do not ask me."

He blushed deeply and did not raise the subject again.

It was after one of those meetings that he experienced an anxious moment. For as they came together out of the little house in Fisherton, Edward Shockley suddenly caught sight of John Moody. He was standing in the lane, about a hundred yards away, and since he was in the act of turning, it was impossible to be sure whether the young man had seen him or not.

He hurried away, and put the incident out of his mind.

In the year of Our Lord 1554, at the end of November, after Parliament formally submitted to him as papal legate, the kingdom of England was received back into the Church of Rome.

That this had been achieved, despite the earlier wishes of Parliament to remain free of Rome, was due to the determination of three people: Mary, her husband Philip of Spain, and the legate himself, Cardinal Pole.

The last was a remarkable figure. He was of English royal blood. His only ambition, to be pope, and his mission, to return England to the fold.

He was frankly disgusted by what he found.

The English Parliament would only vote for a return to Rome on condition that none of the Church lands taken by King Henry and now in their hands were to be restored – a greedy pragmatism that appalled him. As for the Church of England, the Protestant success, he roundly told the English Catholic clergy, was chiefly their own fault. If they had not so utterly neglected their duty, the people would have held the Roman Church in more respect. "You've only yourselves to blame." Now however, action was called for: and the first task was to place worthy priests in every parish.

"There's only one problem," Forest remarked caustically to Shockley: "no worthy priests."

The shortage of priests was chronic: even the august Cardinal Pole could not immediately change that. The Catholic reform of Queen Mary was, in religious terms, an undistinguished affair.

But certain things the queen and cardinal could do. If they could not supply sound Catholics, they could root out and destroy heretics, and from the end of 1554 they set out on that course.

They were dark years for the queen as well as her subjects. Tortured by the misery of a false pregnancy when all she wanted in the world now was a child; made still more desperate by the coldness of her husband Philip, who soon returned for long periods to the continent; the reign of Bloody Mary was steeped in misery.

While the Protestant preacher John Knox thundered from outside the realm that good Englishmen should overthrow their tyrants, the tyrants in question set about their terrible work.

In 1555, the burnings began.

When news came that two of England's greatest Protestant bishops,

Latimer and Ridley, were publicly burned, Shockley could only shake his head in despair.

"We shall this day light such a candle, by God's grace, in England as shall never be put out," Latimer had cried out. It seemed to Shockley that by killing such men Pole and the queen were offending ordinary Englishmen more deeply than they realised.

"Cardinal Pole's giving orders to dig up dead heretics too and burn their bodies," Forest told him one day with grim amusement. "You can't say the man isn't thorough."

But it was in the spring of the following year that another event, much less heroic, stirred the hearts of many Englishmen still more.

For poor Archbishop Cranmer, the author of the English Prayer Book had honest doubts. Had it been right to deny the Holy Father in Rome and put in his place as head of the Church the terrible figure of Henry VIII? Had it been right to annul the marriage of the blameless Katherine of Spain, whose daughter was now queen? Was it right to deny the doctrine of purgatory, Transubstantiation and the rest, about which there were so many divisions even amongst the reforming parties? Cranmer had held the new English Church together and risen to great heights – but had he, after all, perhaps been wrong?

It was not just his death they wanted. It was a confession. They kept him waiting for a month; they worked upon his doubts; they argued with him, wearied, probed, assaulted his mind. They carefully flayed the raw nerve of his doubting conscience. And they broke him. They broke him twice.

Edward Shockley was standing on Fisherton Bridge, talking to Peter and Abigail Mason when a passer-by gave them the news.

"Cranmer has recanted. Signed the document with his own hand – says he was wrong all along!"

For a second all three looked at each other in amazement. Edward spoke first.

"They'll burn him now. They've got what they wanted." He felt bitter.

But Abigail, looking at the two men, only said bleakly:

"He had not strength. We'll not speak of him again." Then, without a word, she walked away from them and the two men knew that they, too, were included in her quiet contempt.

Almost harder to bear at this time was the attitude of his own wife. For when little Celia heard of the burnings and asked what they were for, it was Katherine who, with her sweet, trusting face, told her: "Your father will explain."

Then, when he found he could not, she assured the little girl: "It's to save their souls from worse hellfire, is it not, Edward?" And he was forced to agree. How strange he found it, knowing his wife's gentle nature, to realise that this was truly what she believed.

In Edward Shockley's memory, the month of March 1556 was a time of blood.

The first execution was of the irascible Lord Stourton, who had thrown such curses at Pembroke's gates. For ordering his servants to kill a Wiltshire man named Hartgill, he was hanged with a silken rope in Salisbury market place. The servants were hanged with plain hemp. The crowd found it an amusing affair.

Not so the second execution.

Bishop Capon had been active. Though the persecutions were most active in the Protestant strongholds of London and the eastern counties, the bishop did not intend to allow his own diocese to fail in its duty to the queen. It was not long before he was in luck.

Three obstinate men in the parish of Keevil – a tailor, a freemason and a farmworker – who all knew Tyndale's English Bible well and could quote parts of it by heart, were foolish enough to tell their priest that purgatory was a sham.

"They called it Pope's Pinfold," Peter Mason told Edward excitedly. This was a term implying that purgatory was a source of cash for the Holy Father, since as long as Catholics believed in it they would buy indulgences. It was an impertinence that clearly needed more investigation.

Capon questioned them at once. Their answers to his questions left no further room for doubt. In his presence they called the pope an Antichrist; they denied Transubstantiation and called the mass idolatry, and one, questioned about the wooden statues of the Holy Family and the saints, boldly replied:

"They're good, I should think, to roast a shoulder of mutton on."

"'Tis they who will roast," Peter Mason judged. "They say Bishop Capon's determined to burn them."

He was indeed.

A few days later, soon after news came that Cranmer himself had been burned, in the field outside Fisherton, the three Wiltshiremen, undressed to their shirts, were brought forth. They were allowed, all three, to kneel and pray together, and then one, John Maundrel, was offered the queen's pardon if he would repent: whereat he cried out loudly: "Not for all Salisbury." John Spencer the freemason declared: "The most joyful day I ever saw." Then they were burned.

William Coberley, the tailor, burned slowly; after a long time, however, the fire drew his left arm from him. Then, it was recorded:

he softly knocked on his breast with his right hand, the blood and matter rising out of his mouth.

Edward Shockley had gone alone to witness the grim business. Katherine had prefered to pray for the three men at home.

Yet as he watched, he found that his eyes kept returning to one sight which struck him with surprise.

It was not the three victims that Edward Shockley gazed at with wonder on that savage spring day. It was Peter Mason.

For he was standing beside his wife, his mouth half open, staring straight in front of him, with a strange look of excitement on his simple face, as though he had just received some secret vision. As the minutes

[632]

passed, and the three unfortunates before them were consumed, Shockley looked from the rising smoke back to Peter several times, and on each occasion, it seemed to him, the cutler was separated from the crowd around him in his curious ecstasy.

He wondered what it meant.

Captain Jack Wilson was a good-looking forty and he had been sailing thirty years.

Conventionally handsome, no. He had lost three teeth, though only one of the gaps could be seen. His long, black matted hair was streaked with grey. But in his careless way, he was magnetically good-looking; and when at the inn he lay back in his chair and stretched his long, strong form, there was a sense of cat-like power about him that told women that the years meant nothing to him.

Even at a distance, he was unmistakable. Other sailors in the port of Bristol would be seen coming from their ships with the slow rolling gait of sailing men; but Jack Wilson, no matter how long he had been at sea, still came on shore with the same loping walk. Some men, though with no ill feeling, called him the wolf.

"He's a good friend to any man unless it's the captain of a ship at sea with a cargo he wants," a sailor told Nellie. "Then he's a wolf all right."

Many privateers like this were half way to being pirates, though they usually took care only to attack the ships of countries with whom England was on bad terms.

"And with women?" she asked.

The fellow laughed. "A wolf again."

Nellie Godfrey decided to marry Captain Jack Wilson the day she first saw him.

She had done well in Bristol: better than she had dared to hope. Thanks to her savings, and Shockley's present, she had been able to make her way in the busy port with care, scouting for some time before finding a protector. When she did, he was perfect: a rich widowed merchant who had, for the time being, no need for a wife, but a sufficient need for a mistress to set her up comfortably in lodgings.

He was a bluff, burly middle-aged man with a red face and a deep purse. She gave him comfort and, keeping a thoughtful eye on the swollen red veins in his face, excitement. The merchant was generous too, as long as she never asked for anything; if she suggested a present, though, he shut up like a clam. It did not take long to learn his ways.

She had made a few friends, all women. Apart from this, she kept herself to herself and saved her money.

"It's a start," she considered. "I've had luck."

She had – but not enough, a small voice told her, to send word to her brother. She could tell him she was safe, of course; she could tell him a merchant was keeping her. But at this thought she only shrugged. She wanted more than that: for it was hardly progress.

"One day," she told herself, "I'll send him word I'm married."

There was no question, of course, of the merchant marrying her. A rich burgher of the city would never do that. And indeed, she had no wish to marry him.

"Three nights a week with the merchant is well enough," she admitted cheerfully; "but to spend my days with him as well . . ."

And yet. She had never entered his own house, where his children lived, but she could see it – for he had proudly described it for her often enough. Yes, she could see it very clearly: its solid oak table, the gleaming pewter and silver in the hall and in the kitchen, the handsome, embroidered counterpanes upon the beds. Perhaps I could even bear the merchant for a house, she thought. And for long hours she would lie, alone in her room, dreaming of that other house she would one day call her own: she could see its broad fires, its sparkling cleanliness; she could smell the great saddles of mutton, the roasts, the spiced dishes and baskets of fruit she would heap proudly upon the table, and see the faces of her children . . . Her children. The merchant's mistress thought of them each day: the vision was her secret comfort; it was almost an obsession.

But there was the rub. What kind of man would marry her? And what kind of man, come to that, could she put up with patiently herself? "Any good man," she would murmur sometimes; then laugh at herself. No, not any man.

Captain Wilson had been taken to sea, despite his mother's protests, by his father when he was ten. His father had told the owner of the ship that the boy would make himself useful or be thrown overboard. He had made himself useful.

His grandfather had come from Sarum, he knew. He had been the first to go to sea, and had become, in the fullness of time, master of a small ship. He could remember old Will Wilson very well – a small but sturdy man, equal to any crisis.

"Found my first ship in London," he always used to say. "God sent me a sign in the thunderstorm – a bolt of fire, right through a field. Lucky I followed it."

His family used to laugh in secret at his tale, obviously invented. But then they, too, knew nothing of Roman roads either.

Captain Jack Wilson was already a successful man when Nellie saw him at the inn.

He had never married, though he had numerous children in London, Bristol and Southampton. He gave their mothers handsome presents of money when they were born, then never troubled about them. The life of the port was easy going. He had a child in Spain that he did not even know about.

"And that," she thought as she watched him at the inn, "is my man."

He was staying there a week, then going on business to London, she discovered. She must act fast.

Within the hour she was talking to him. She made no advances at all; but she learned his business and surprised him by how much she understood of the trading affairs of the port. The merchant had been useful to her there.

She soon discovered that he was planning to sail his little ship to the Baltic. There was a newly formed Muscovy company, he started to explain.

"I know," she cut in, and gave him not only details of the company but an accurate account of the recent attempt by Willoughby and Chancellor to find a route through to the fabled Cathay by the North East Passage. This, too, she had learned from the merchant.

He looked at her with interest.

"Do you trade south, to the Barbary coast?" she asked.

Yes, he told her, he had been to the Mediterranean, but the Barbary pirates were a match even for him.

"I don't mind a fight," he said easily, "but not if there's no profit."

After a time she left him, and she noted, as she surreptitiously glanced back, that his eyes followed her with interest.

The next day she repeated the process. And the next. When he tried to find out more about her circumstances and invited her to sup at the table with him, she politely refused.

The fourth day, she did not go to the inn until the evening. When she did, she slipped past the main room unseen, and with a small bribe to one of the serving girls, she had herself let into his chamber. Most of those staying at the inn shared rooms, sleeping on boards or mattresses. But Captain Jack Wilson was a fellow of means. He had his own room with – for it was the best at the inn – a stout oak bed. She undressed, got in, and waited.

It was towards midnight that Captain Jack Wilson made his way easily up the stairs. He had been sorry not to see the handsome woman that day. He had a girl with him.

They entered the chamber together.

And as they both stared at her in surprise she announced coolly:

"You won't be needing her tonight."

She had burned her boats. For the merchant had been expecting to see her that night. But she was confident she could succeed; and on the third night with Wilson, she put it to him squarely:

"Time you had a wife. You won't find better than me." She looked him straight in the eye. "And I'm descended from the nobility."

Wilson gazed at her. He thought of his roving life, his forty years, the many women he had known. Were they so important to him, any of them?

This woman, who had calmly walked into his bed and thrown a rival out, this woman had a fire, an inner strength and determination he had not met before.

"By God," he suddenly thought, "I've money enough of my own; I could do worse."

Two months later Nellie Godfrey got her house. It was at Christchurch.

But why, Shockley wondered, why had Peter Mason performed this act of madness?

Each time he thought of it, he remembered the day only a few months before, when he had seen the cutler staring so strangely into the middle distance at the execution of the three heretics.

Was it then that he had decided to do it? Was it before even that, some day when he heard Abigail's scornful words for the men who, like himself, had not the courage to speak out? It was impossible to know: for one thing was certain – Peter Mason was not saying.

The cutler had chosen his time well. Shockley was there.

He would never forget how that morning, at the moment of the elevation of the Host, the quiet form of Peter Mason had suddenly walked into the aisle and approached the altar table. For a second no one noticed him: then they assumed that he must have some private purpose – an unexpected call of nature perhaps – for moving from his place. He reached the front and then turned to face them. The priest and his assistants glanced back at him, irritated. Then, looking rather drawn and pale, Peter Mason said something. His voice was so soft, no one heard. He gazed at them, clearly expecting something to happen. Again he opened his mouth and Shockley strained to hear. This time there was a little gasp from the front rows.

That was all. He stood there, very still, with that curious, half puzzled smile on his face, waiting. After a little time, the priest ordered two of the men to lead him out.

Peter Mason had denied the Transubstantiation.

Few men were more eager than Bishop Capon and his chancellor to prosecute heretics; yet even they, it seemed, hesitated. Indeed, for an entire week, nothing happened, and the rumour in Salisbury was that Peter Mason had become a little weak in the head.

Edward Shockley was uneasy. He was concerned for Peter Mason, but also for himself.

He had been to the prayer meetings less of late. He told himself he was too busy; but he knew very well that it was also the sense of Abigail's secret scorn that kept him absent.

He had no wish, however, for attention to be drawn to the existence of the little group. He thought of John Moody. Had he seen him after all, that day when he came out of the prayer meeting? Had he guessed, spoken of it to anyone – even perhaps to Katherine? He spoke slightingly of the foolish Protestant heretics to her and watched her reaction. There was none he could detect. But his mind was still not easy. No doubt there were others, too who might have seen him in the Masons' company on those occasions. When he saw Abigail in the street the next day, he avoided her.

He did pay one visit to Peter though, at his workshop, and urged him not to repeat the offence: to which Peter had replied only with that same, distant half smile that made it impossible to know whether he had understood or not.

But the next Sunday, when Peter stood in the churchyard of St Edmunds, and afterwards went into the cathedral itself and made his declaration in front of the bishop, there could be no question. It was an open challenge. Before the end of the day, he had been taken by the bailiff.

The priests questioned him. They gravely asked him if he denied Transubstantiation: he did. Would he accept the supremacy and authority of the pope? He quietly shook his head. Did he deny purgatory, the power of holy relics; did he refuse to raise his eyes at the elevation of the host? Did he deny all the tenets of Holy Church? He did.

The priests were fair with him. Would he not recant? He would not.

One of the canons, a tall, elderly man who had watched him intently, then intervened.

"But why do you refuse all these, Peter Mason?" he asked, not unkindly. "Give us your reasons." And for a moment Peter's brow furrowed, as if he could not remember; but then it cleared. "These superstitions go against the true revealed religion; they are popish practices," he recited; and contentedly awaited their verdict.

There could only be one verdict; but it was qualified by the canon who had interrupted as follows:

"We think thou art a simpleton, Peter Mason. Consider well that thou mayst yet escape death by a timely repentance."

As he was led away, his cheerful round face showed no sign of fear.

Not so Edward Shockley.

Each of the next two days he waited in dread for others of the little Protestant prayer group to be brought for questioning. Would Peter be asked for accomplices and would he name them?

What if they took Robert or Abigail – or what if they took him himself?

How would he answer if they asked him whether he denied Transubstantiation? He trembled at the thought. And then a worse one occurred to him. What if he denied his secret Protestantism but Abigail and the others insisted to the priests that he was one of them?

Several times during the day he would break out into a sweat; and once or twice in the big workshop he thought he had caught his young brother-in-law gazing at him with a cynical smile: John Moody whose pale blue eyes missed nothing – certainly he knew.

Was it possible that one of his own family might denounce him to the bishop? He had been kind to John, and to Katherine of late. Surely they would not.

It was three days after Peter's arrest that Edward Shockley stood in the market place and saw John Moody walking towards him with a strange look on his face. He felt himself grow pale.

The young fellow came beside him.

"There is something I must say."

"Well?"

"Peter Mason. I know how well you know him."

Now he was ashen.

"I scarcely know the man."

John Moody frowned.

"But I thought . . ."

"The Masons are nothing to me."

What did that expression on his brother-in-law's face mean? He dreaded to know, yet he must find out. He paused anxiously.

"I had thought you could speak with him," John Moody said. "Something must be done."

"He's said what he believes. What can anyone do?" he replied guardedly.

To his surprise now, John took a different tack to what he had expected.

"I've seen him at his house – every day. 'Tis not what he believes." He grimaced, "'Tis what his wife believes. Yet it will kill him."

"And you wish me. . . ?"

"To urge him to recant."

Edward stared at him. Then, after all, the young man did not suspect him.

"Yet we are good Catholics," he challenged him, watching the young man's face carefully for any hint of cynicism about the claim. "Do we say that a heretic is not to be punished?"

"I think," Moody answered him gravely, "that there are other ways to save a man's soul than through the fire. You should help him."

He considered the idea for several hours. If he went to see Peter, might not people suspect complicity? What if Peter let fall a careless word? And again, if he urged Peter to recant, Abigail might be furious and even denounce him. On the other hand, what would young Moody think if he refused such a Christian act? Could that be seen as suspicious? He turned it all over in his mind for several hours.

He liked Peter Mason. Perhaps he was too fearful. If they were going to arrest him, they would have done so already. Finally, he went to see the prisoner that evening, at a time when he was alone. He only meant to stay a few minutes.

The room at Fisherton gaol in which he was being kept contained only two other prisoners, a man and a woman. It was furnished with two small benches and a wooden table. He and Peter Mason sat opposite each other. There were no priests about.

They had not seen each other for a week, but he saw no great physical change in the prisoner except that he was a little thinner. His manner however, was altered completely. Instead of the cheerful, eager, simple-minded fellow he had known, he found a stranger, mild-mannered, but withdrawn – as if he had already entered some other private world that gave him a comfort he could not share. He was almost serene.

The two men conversed in low tones for half an hour.

"Many of us, your friends, wish you would not take this matter to the bitter end," Edward told him. But Peter only smiled gently.

"A man may outwardly conform yet keep his heart pure, praying in secret," he also suggested hopefully. But it was as if Peter had not heard.

Suddenly however, he began to talk of his little workshop, of things that he had made, of Nellie Godfrey who used to come past his door before she was driven away. "I wonder what is become of her now," he murmured. And sensing that these thoughts of happier times were a comfort to him, Edward encouraged him and added his own memories. He forgot the time.

They were still talking of these things when Abigail arrived with Robert. He looked at her nervously, but she seemed to take little interest in him beyond acknowledging him calmly.

She was pale – paler than ever. The rings under her eyes were so deep and black that they seemed to have been branded permanently onto her face. She was very quiet, as though her sense of duty had taken her into a region of the mind that lay beyond mere sadness.

Though he knew it would be wiser to depart, some instinct – perhaps just curiosity – kept him still in the room.

As the three of them spoke in low tones, Abigail and Robert giving quiet words of comfort – she with placid composure, he with occasional nods of his head and short, nervous gestures – while Peter sat on the bench and listened with his head bowed. It seemed to Edward that there was something agitated about him, yet he could not say what.

After a time, he looked up, his eyes a little softer, more uncertain, nearer to the simple Peter that Shockley had known before.

"Tomorrow, they mean to burn me," he said.

Robert Mason shifted his feet awkwardly. Abigail looked at him steadily.

"'Tis God's work thou didst," she said quietly, as if this was enough.

"It was right to speak?" There it was: the almost puppy-like face of the friend that he knew so well, looking hopefully to his wife for approval.

"God's work is hard," she replied.

Then Peter, with a dignity Edward had not seen before, stood up and gravely turned to his cousin Robert.

"I commend my wife to your care," he said gravely; and Robert bowed his head.

Edward could bear it no more.

"Yet will you not recant?" he cried, breaking into their solemn meeting unashamedly. "They will accept a recantation even now. Believe in your heart what you will, until better times come, Peter Mason, but conform in body only, not in spirit."

Why such anguish in his voice, when there should only have been sweet reason? Was it that he himself, faced with Peter's sacrifice, now felt guilty?

He glanced at Robert, whose eyes fell; at Abigail: how steady she was, how certain.

"Each man must follow his conscience," she said quietly.

He looked at Peter again.

And then, for less than a second, yet unmistakable, terrible, never-to-be forgotten, he saw in Peter Mason's eyes a look that he had not seen before: a look of perfect comprehension. It was a look that told him the foolish fellow understood, perhaps, more than he about the world, a look that was accompanied by a pain and anguish that even Abigail and Robert did not see as he said, very gently:

"How can I?"

Chance caused Nellie Wilson to bring her husband to Sarum that day.

She had meant to send word to her brother Piers, then had a better idea. Instead of finding a poor priest to write a letter for her, she would arrive in person. It would be a small but happy triumph. As the two Wilsons came into the city in a small cart on a fine autumn morning, she was in a festive mood. She wondered why the people were all walking towards Fisherton.

Moments later, all her happiness had gone and she was racing towards the place herself.

He had already been brought to the stake when she arrived, and the fire was just being lit.

Two things she saw at once. The first was that the sheriff's men had decided to be merciful: for they had prepared a quick fire.

"Thank God for that at least," she murmured.

The slow fire burned the more fiercely, for the dry wood was left uncovered so that the victim was licked by the naked flames to die an agonising death. The quick fire was kinder, for here the fire was packed with damp leaves so that the sentenced man soon asphyxiated before his body was roasted.

The second thing she noticed was that one of the canons, a tall elderly man, was standing beside him, talking to him calmly but seriously, obviously urging him to recant; and then she saw where poor Peter's eyes were looking – at Abigail and Robert, standing at the inner edge of the circle of spectators.

They did not at first see her.

Nor, to begin with, did Edward Shockley, who was standing with his wife and John Moody not far from the Mason group.

When the fire was lit, Edward looked at his wife and wondered:

"Do the flames truly purify his soul?"

But his wife did not trouble to look at him. She and her brother instead sank to their knees.

And once again, Edward felt a sense of shame, as he stood between the two sets – Mason and Moody – of true believers.

Did the fire purify? He stared, not at flames, but billowing smoke. The sheriff's men, thank God, had done their job with the leaves efficiently. He could not see Peter.

By looking down at the kneeling figures, he had missed one small act in the drama. Just before the smoke engulfed him, Peter had for some reason turned his gaze away from Abigail, and seen Nellie. For a second he had stared in astonishment, and then he smiled, as he used to do, his simple-hearted, affectionate smile.

As the crowd began to disperse, Edward Shockley did not move; and thanks to this he witnessed a further small encounter. For long after Peter had gone, and the naked flames were consuming the thin remains of his body, Abigail Mason looked across and caught sight of Nellie, through the thinning crowd. She was staring at the stake. There were tears running down her cheeks.

For a moment Abigail did not move. Then her face set. She came towards Nellie slowly, Robert walking just behind her.

Her voice was quiet, but carrying as she reached Nellie, turned to where the Sheriff's men were still standing with the town bailiff by the fire and announced:

"Arrest this woman. She is a harlot."

Nellie looked at her, and pursed her lips thoughtfully.

It was Captain Wilson's voice which rang out for all to hear.

"No more she ain't. She's my wife." He stared, first at Robert, who now looked embarrassed, then at the sheriff's man. "Would any care to dispute with me?"

No one seemed inclined to move.

"And who's this pasty-faced scold?" he asked the crowd that had now turned to watch this new spectacle. "Who's this tittle-tattle, this cold-eyed witch?"

There was an audible laugh in the crowd.

Then Nellie Godfrey's voice rang out as she made her own, lightning deductions from what she saw of the family group before her.

"Why," she shouted – and it seemed to Edward Shockley that there was not a man or woman that side of Fisherton Bridge who would not hear. "'Tis Abigail Mason who's just burned her husband so she can get another."

Edward stared. Was it possible that Abigail had grown paler? She visibly buckled, as if she had been hit and winded. And she said not a word.

He looked from one to another. He saw Abigail's eyes smouldering with rage and hate – the hate not of someone who has been found out, but who has been told a truth about themselves they did not realise.

As he stared first at the terrible fire, then at the pale figure who stood before it, it seemed to Edward Shockley, tortured for so long by his own conscience, as if the scales had fallen from his eyes.

The agony of England and Mary Tudor was nearly over.

In Sarum, in 1557, Bishop Capon died, Queen Mary appointed three vigorous Catholic preachers to uphold the faith at Sarum, but the bishop himself was not immediately replaced.

In 1557 also, Philip of Spain made one of his rare visits to his unloved queen. He came only for troops, to be used in his quarrel against the French. The English unwillingly supplied them, and Pembroke led seven thousand men to rout the French. It was a brief triumph. In January 1558, after Pembroke himself had returned, the French struck back and attacked Calais. Philip, more anxious to make gains for Spain in Italy, let them take it. So fell the last territory England was ever to hold in France. The loss was a saving to the British exchequer, for Calais had been expensive to keep, but a blow to England's prestige.

It broke Mary's heart.

But neither her husband nor her people cared for the Catholic queen any more. Cardinal Pole, her great ally, had been recalled from England by a new pope, who hated the proud aristocratic legate. In November 1558, isolated and sick, Mary Tudor died.

During her reign, some two hundred and eighty were burned: a small number, as the dismal records of religious persecution go, but enough to tell the islanders that they wanted no more. The last victims due to stand at the stake in Sarum were never executed. The under-sheriff, given the writ for their execution, tore it up. Before it was renewed, the queen had died.

Mary's burnings were over, and it was time for England to find a compromise in this new world between the dangerous extremes that had destroyed so many people of conscience.

It was fortunate for the people of the island that, at this point in their history, two people with the necessary political and spiritual talents should have appeared upon the national stage: Elizabeth I of England, and Bishop John Jewel of Salisbury.

1580

It was mid-afternoon and few people were about. Edward Shockley had been to the village of Downton to the south and had made his way up, past the edge of old Clarendon Forest, returning to Salisbury a little earlier than expected.

At the corner of the street he paused, in mild surprise.

A stranger was coming out of his house. He appeared to be an artisan of some kind. He would have hailed him, but a moment later the stranger had turned right towards the market place and Edward was too tired to follow him. Odd though. He wondered who it was.

He went slowly down the street. It was good to be home.

There were few more contented men in Sarum than Edward Shockley. At last he had found peace.

For years he had lived in fear; worse, he had lied to his wife and despised himself. Now, as he looked back, it seemed to Edward Shockley that there were several causes. One, to be sure, was his own weakness. He did not deny it. But there had been another cause, too. He had not known what he believed himself. He had had a conscience, of a kind, but no cause.

Now he had one. It was the cause espoused by the queen. It might not seem noble to his wife, or to Abigail: but to him, and to many Englishmen, it was a cause with wisdom, and one, this time, that he was prepared to stand up for.

The cause was peace – and compromise.

The years of Queen Elizabeth's reign, thanks to her clever diplomacy, had given her island kingdom mostly peace, so far at least.

As for the religious settlement, to Shockley it seemed a masterpiece. It was a compromise. Copying her father, Elizabeth was Supreme Governor of the Church. The Prayer Book of Cranmer, with small changes, was restored. All people must attend church. Office holders must swear the

Oath of Supremacy. The communion was taken in two kinds: bread and wine; the services were said in English. All this was Protestant, but moderate.

And many Catholics liked the English services, which were so arranged that there was little there to offend them anyway.

For the rest, there must be no disorder; the enforcing of the oaths could be as lax as they pleased. As for what men believed in their hearts . . . Unlike her half sister, Elizabeth had little religious feeling. She only knew the fear of persecution. She would, she said, make no window into men's souls; let them believe what they liked: so long as they went to her church, or paid a small fine.

And up and down the country, while strict Catholics or extreme Puritans denounced the changes, men like Edward Shockley heaved a sigh of relief.

It was imperfect, hypocritical, cynical – and absolutely sensible.

Around her, the new queen had gathered a number of sound advisers including Pembroke, who for the fourth reign in succession, kept himself in high favour, and that sage councillor William Cecil. They understood the value of her cautious approach, and they helped her to make wise appointments. One of these was the gentle scholar and friend of Cranmer, Matthew Parker, who was made Archbishop of Canterbury; another was the new Bishop of Salisbury, John Jewel.

It was Jewel who transformed the Sarum diocese by his endless hard work and preaching. It was Jewel, also, who wrote one of the most important documents in the history of the Anglican Church: his *Apology*.

The *Apology* won Edward Shockley's mind and heart.

"It is so simple you cannot argue against it," he told his family with delight. "Our English Church is no new invention, no denial of authority: 'tis an exact return to the Church as it was set forth in the Scriptures – in the early centuries, before Rome added its own doctrines and practices to muddy the clear waters. We celebrate Our Lord with bread and wine – as He ordained we should. We have bishops, as did the early Church; but there is nothing in the early Church concerning a pope at Rome, nor many of the Roman pomp and vanities; we have purified England of copes and altar cloths, relics, indulgences and superstition: that is all."

And it was Jewel who finally taught Edward Shockley to come to terms with himself. Shockley always remembered the interview.

The bishop was such a small, slight fellow, with a sweet, thin, irregular face and gentle but hugely intelligent brown eyes. Study had made him prematurely old: his hair was thinning. But he was so wise.

He had imbibed advanced Protestant doctrines while he was in exile on the Continent in Mary's reign, but at Sarum he was cautious.

"The spire was struck by lightning just before I came," he joked to Edward, "so I took it as a warning to be careful. Here in Sarum," he explained, "there are still many false shows from the old popish days: fine chalices, the robes of the priests, the altar cloths," he ticked off the items that were to be found in churches all over the diocese. "In Basle or Geneva, we should have laughed at them. But now I have returned to

England, I see that I must be patient, Master Shockley. Patience is my guide. I shall change these things gradually. And you, too, must learn to be patient – even with yourself. God will judge you soon enough."

Now that he felt he had nothing to fear, his sense of shame disappeared. He was frank with Katherine about his admiration for Jewel, but as he pointed out, as long as the family outwardly conformed, that was enough. She might teach their son and daughter what she liked on that condition.

On this basis their marriage had continued without undue friction, ever since. Their children were married now. The girl was a secret Catholic; his son was not.

He saw Abigail Mason marry Robert and have two children. She was still as pale as ever; but he noticed that she and her family quietly attended Elizabeth's church services rather than pay the fine. He often thought of poor Peter with affection, and wondered whether Abigail did.

Once or twice during these years he also saw Nellie Wilson, who had now grown into a respectable married woman at Christchurch. She became a little stout, and her husband grew so rich by his voyages that he was on a nodding acquaintance with the gentry. He never alluded to her past; indeed, there were few at Sarum besides Abigail Mason who could even remember her. As for Piers Godfrey, he died and left a little family of artisans to whom Edward sometimes gave a little work.

There was only one storm cloud on the horizon threatening the peace he loved so much – Catholic Spain. For Philip of Spain was arming for an invasion; and already he had supported a rising in Ireland.

The Spanish king had a Catholic rival to Elizabeth, her cousin Mary Queen of Scots – thrown out of Scotland by the dour Protestant followers of John Knox, safely confined in England, but a rallying point for every Catholic rebel.

Philip had papal support too. Since Elizabeth had failed to return her kingdom to Rome, he had excommunicated her and, worse, he had even secretly offered plenary indulgences – remission of all their sins – to certain gentlemen who had offered to assassinate her. Subtle and determined Jesuits like Edmund Campion were even now touring the country in secret, telling good Catholics they must not attend Elizabeth's church and stirring up all manner of trouble.

It was all leading up to a Spanish invasion.

And this was the important subject which nowadays occupied his mind more than any other. He had been pondering it all the way from Downton and it was about this that he planned to address Salisbury council the following month.

Katherine was surprised to see him back so soon.

He asked her who the stranger was.

"I hardly know," she told him. "A goldsmith I think, who knows John. He only came to pay his respects." She smiled. "There is something I think would interest you more though – Thomas Forest came here two hours ago. He wants you to visit him at Avonsford."

And at this news Edward Shockley immediately forgot all the other matters that had been on his mind.

What in the world, after so many years, could Forest want with him now?

The rift between Edward Shockley and Thomas Forest had opened gradually. But for years he had supposed it was complete.

It had begun because, for once, Forest had been wrong in a business assessment.

Their joint cloth venture had not been a great success.

For their main market, the Netherlands, had been sadly disrupted. The cause was Spain, which tried to impose its Catholicism and the cruel rule of the Inquisition on an unwilling population. The brutal troops of the Duke of Álva had been valiantly opposed by the Dutch forces of William of Orange. And the effect, for years, had been chaos. The great Antwerp cloth trade had suffered, and so had the cloth merchants of England.

Shockley's trade was hit. He fought back, finding markets for his best broadcloth, and set up business in striped kersey and lace as well.

"But though it provides enough to keep us," he told his family, "the profit is not nearly enough to satisfy Forest."

And so, a little before Bishop Jewel died, he had bought Forest out, for a modest figure. It was an arrangement that worked well. His son and John Moody ran the business now.

He had made one other change too. Since the Antwerp business had gone, he had let the Fleming pay off the debt on easy terms, so that his family should be provided for, then he had ended their arrangement.

While the younger men ran the day to day business, his own concern turned increasingly to the affairs of the city. Which included the poor.

It was this that caused the rift with Forest.

The Poor Laws of Elizabeth were not generous; but they admitted, for the first time, that the charity of individuals and the Church might not be enough to help the army of poor. Not that one should be lenient. Able-bodied vagrants were still to be whipped and a hole bored through the gristle of their right ear. Persistent vagrants could even be executed.

There were plenty of poor in Sarum. Not only was the Sarum cloth trade in a recession, but on the land, things were worse. Spain's decades of importing gold from the New World had brought about a huge increase in bullion that had spread inflation to every part of Europe. Corn prices rose, and the tenants on their farms had to pay more for their necessities. The fines paid on entering a tenancy went up and the peasantry were hit hard. Forest was an active landlord.

"He's found better seed; and he folds more sheep on his fields than ever," Shockley conceded. "It's his poor tenants that suffer."

And the problem of the poor increased.

Elizabeth's solution was simple and practical. She decreed that a poor rate was to be levied compulsorily to pay for the helpless; and she set up apprenticeships and workhouses for poor children and families. The whole business was managed by the Justices of the Peace.

Forest was now a Justice of the Peace.

"If a man's got even one leg, Forest will say he's fit to work," Edward complained. There was a new workhouse in the city now, the Bridewell. "He treats the poor in there as if they were animals."

Edward Shockley was constantly trying to help the poor. Moody helped him. Forest once angrily complained that half their apprentices were taken from the poor house, and both Shockley and Moody had laughingly to admit that this was true.

There was another source of good workmen though, besides the poor house. For Lord Pembroke had encouraged a number of Flemish weavers fleeing the religious persecution to settle at Wilton. Although he was a Catholic himself and they were Protestants, Moody seemed to have a natural understanding with these skilful men and employed several of them for Shockley.

"So with our Flemings and our vagabonds," Edward used to claim cheerfully, "we do very well."

It did not make him popular with Forest.

Time and again, when Forest tried to deny the poor their aid, Shockley and his helpers raised the issue again. At first Forest had attempted to ignore them, but Shockley had grown too powerful for him. He was elected to the inner council of twenty-four – he was a man of consideration in the city.

The result of this, by 1570, was that Forest completely avoided him. When they met, it was in strictly formal settings; and though Edward himself was affable, Forest was cold and distant.

His favourite moment came in 1574.

For that was the year of the visit of the queen.

She came first to Wilton. There was a new earl now, not such a dour figure as his father, and a favourite with Elizabeth. On Friday 30th September he entertained her magnificently at his great house; on Saturday, he had prepared an elaborate banqueting house made of leaves in Clarendon Forest, but then the rains came and Elizabeth dined in the lodge. Even so, the deer were coursed with swift greyhounds, and the queen was said to be pleased.

And then, on Monday, after the afternoon dinner, the queen and her court came to the town.

They were magnificently dressed, the men in their tight-fitting under and over-robes, white ruffs at the collar and wrists, and short cloaks; the women with their stately, big-shouldered gowns that fanned down from a narrow waist to the ground, and huge ruffs that hugged their cheeks, rising to above the ears. But in both men and women, it was the material that made the cloth merchant gasp. Splendid silks, dazzling, heavy brocades of every colour.

"Why," he murmured, "they'd stand up by themselves."

His family were watching from a respectful distance as he stood with the other council men, dressed in their scarlet gowns, while the lesser merchants stood behind them, robed in black gowns lined with taffeta or silk, and watched the mayor solemnly present the usual offerings to a visiting monarch – a solid gold cup filled with coins to the value of twenty pounds in gold.

She came to him.

"No man has done more for the poor in Salisbury than Master Shockley," the mayor kindly declared.

She stared at him, and, for a moment, he was aware of her pale, plain face with its high cheekbones, pock-marked skin, and eyes that measured everything.

"Good, Master Shockley." He blushed.

She was about to move on when she paused.

"Who are the Justices who look after the poor?" she demanded.

"Thomas Forest" she was told, "is one."

"Well, where is he?"

Forest came forward and made a graceful bow.

She turned to Shockley – half terrifying, half mischievous.

"Does he perform this duty well?"

All eyes were upon him. There was an awkward silence. He looked at Forest, who had gone a little pale.

Then he spoke the truth.

"No, my lady," he answered.

"Ha!"

To his astonishment, she broke out into a loud, raucous laugh.

Forest had scarcely spoken to him at all after that.

It was a brief moment of glory. But he had met her. His family and the town had seen it.

"The only trouble was," he chuckled afterwards, "she almost ruined us."

It was not just the present to the monarch, which was usually returned as charitable gifts. It was the fees charged by her staff.

"They're like a plague of locusts," he protested.

There were bakers, littermen, footmen, musicians, porters, yeomen, the serjeant-at-arms, who took a full forty shillings; the king of heralds, who took fifty; and the trumpeters who provided the fanfares when the queen entered the city and who demanded three pounds in gold.

"Never again, we pray!" he cried. It was not only the aristocrats in their houses who dreaded the honour of a royal visit; it was the burghers of every town in the country too.

So what in the world, he wondered, could Forest want with him now?

The Forests began their wooing of Edward Shockley in September 1580 with an invitation to Avonsford Manor.

He did not hesitate about going.

"Forest's sure to be up to something," he thought cheerfully. "I wonder what."

When he arrived, he found two surprises awaiting him.

The first was that the Wilsons of Christchurch were staying there: not only old Jack, and his wife Nellie, but their three fine seafaring sons as

[647]

well. It made him smile both with pleasure and amusement to see them: for one was the image of the father, another the male likeness of Nellie, and the third a tall, big-chested amalgam of the two.

Nellie had not grown fat, but she had grown stout and it suited her. Her hair was grey, but her eyes still sparkled; she still favoured a doublet that laced across the front; she wore a modest ruff, and she set the whole off with a jaunty little conical brimmed hat in which she stuck a feather. Her three hearty sons, all in their twenties, obeyed her even faster than they obeyed Captain Jack.

For a second, as they came face to face, he saw her hesitate. He understood. He bowed low.

"Mistress Wilson."

If the Forests were not even aware of who she was, the secret past of Nellie Godfrey would never pass his lips. She saw it in his eyes and gave him a grateful smile.

He had no doubt they were all there for a reason, but Forest was obviously in no hurry to enlighten them.

He was more concerned that they meet his son.

Giles Forest was a pleasant-looking young man of the same age as the eldest Wilson boy. But there the resemblance ended. Slim, dark, with fine, delicate features and tapering fingers, his thin legs encased in a silken hose, his hair teased into curls, he was the perfect model of the courtier. He had spent the last few years at Oxford, and so to Shockley the young man was almost a stranger. But it was clear at once that he was determined to make himself agreeable to the merchant.

The other surprise was a change which many people might not have noticed. But Shockley did, the moment he entered the hall.

It was the Forest coat of arms.

He remembered it well from his youth: a proud lion in a field. Or so it had been.

But now, resplendent in the place of honour, painted on a wooden board, rested a far more impressive and complex affair for every visitor to see. He stared at it in wonder.

For though the proud lion, which had now for decades proclaimed the Forest's gentility, was still to be seen, it had been shifted into the second of the four quarters into which the shield had now been divided. In the first quarter now resided another and older emblem: a white swan on a red ground: the ancient arms of Godefroi. To this had been added a little badge, a difference, to show that the family came from one of several branches of the Godefroi line.

It was young Giles Forest who explained the change to him.

"Those are the Godefroi arms," he said, "for the family of Forest descends from them, a famous ancient line from whom we had these lands by marriage. And those," he pointed to another quarter, "are the arms of the lords de Whiteheath, another Norman family from whom we derive and there," he concluded proudly, pointing at the fourth quarter, "are the ancient arms of Longspée, the ancient earls of Salisbury."

Shockley was impressed. He had an idea that the Forests had come out of Salisbury a few generations before but he could not remember the details.

"I had not known the family was so noble," he remarked respectfully; and the pleasant young man beside him bowed.

"I will show you our pedigree," he promised.

For, like many other rising families at the time, the Forests had been to the College of Arms where, just then, resided some of the greatest rascals in the history of genealogy. There, one of the Kings of Arms had performed one of the favourite miracles of his trade. Putting the new arms the family had recently obtained into second place, he in no time discovered a far more ancient and noble origin for them in the ancient family of Godefroi, and since there seemed to be no claimants to their arms about, he kindly gave them, 'differenced' to make it seem more plausible, to the Forests. There was no question of a possible connection. It was a fabrication, pure and simple.

But once the Godefroi ancestry was admitted, why then, to be sure, all manner of splendid connections could be found in the perfectly genuine pedigree of the ancient knights of Avonsford. As he went back in time however, as an added bonus to the family who were paying him so well, the herald allowed his imagination to run riot, and added to the pedigree he drew up not only knights, but even magnates, like Longspée, to whom the Godefrois had never been more than tenants. It was a magnificent affair, and by this means, yet another rising Tudor family rooted itself in a fictitious Norman past.

That Nellie might have some connection with the ancient swan on its red ground never occurred to anyone; she was not even fully aware of it herself. But stout Nellie Wilson of Christchurch even if she guessed what had been done, had no intention of digging up the memory of Nellie Godfrey of Culver Street. And as for the children of her brother Piers, they knew her only as the rich aunt who sent them presents and their father as a carpenter. The Forests were secure.

There were other new treasures in the house: a fine portrait of Forest, a delicate miniature, the size of a man's hand, of his son; a fine arras. The party admired them all.

They dined well. Forest provided a succulent swan. And as a special course he added a curious vegetable Shockley had never seen before. It was pale in colour and had a pasty texture, and it tasted sweet.

"What is it?" he asked.

"'Tis from across the ocean, from the Spanish New World," Wilson explained. "A rare taste."

It was. Forest had obtained the first of the sweet potatoes from South America, that were soon to be followed by their cousins, the ordinary potato, back to the old world.

It was after dinner that Forest took the men aside and opened the discussions.

"Captain Wilson has plans for new voyages that could bring enormous profits," he explained to Edward. "He wants to find people in Sarum to supply the money, and so I thought you should come to hear him." Then he motioned Wilson to commence.

It was an extraordinary story.

"First," Wilson explained, "consider Russia."

Shockley had known something of this trade. For twenty years English merchants had been trying, by crossing Russia, to get to the ancient and lucrative Persian trade routes. They had met with small success. But with Russia itself, trade was booming, encouraged by a new Czar, Ivan, who would later be called 'the terrible'.

"Russia has oil, tallow, tar, hides – hundreds of thousands of them, timber for masts," Wilson enumerated. "With Spain threatening us more each day, all the ship-building materials from Russia will have a ready market here. Similarly, consider Poland and the territories about her. They too have shipping materials – and they want your broadcloth, Master Shockley. Only last year the Eastland Company was formed for this trade. It will weaken those damned Hanse merchants and strengthen us."

Forest nodded in agreement.

"Then there's Cathay. Frobisher is trying to reach it by going north west. Even the queen has invested. And now there's to be another attempt to get there by travelling the other way, over the top of Russia. Mercator and Hackluyt are advising them. Whichever gets there, we could take part in the new trade in the future.

"There's a new company being formed to trade with the Levant too. Luxury trade."

He looked from one man to the other. Then, a huge grin spread over his face.

"Of course, there's another kind of trade too." He paused. "And here I have news for you. Drake's back."

Everyone knew that Francis Drake, the adventurer from Plymouth had set off three years before to circumnavigate the globe. Those traditionalists who still refused to believe the earth was round claimed he would fall off the edge. Others who accepted the idea of the globe, still did not expect to see him again. Even the queen, who had invested money with the gallant half explorer half pirate had done so with misgivings.

"Well, he arrived yesterday," Wilson announced coolly. "He's raided Spanish lands and Spanish galleons on the way and," he paused again for effect, "his cargo includes one and a half million pound sterling's worth of gold bullion!"

Both men were silent. It was a stupefying sum.

Wilson now moved swiftly to his demands.

"I have three fine sons. I want joint stock companies for three fine ships. I want investors from Sarum, Master Shockley; and we can all make a fortune."

In a way, Shockley agreed with the suggestion. It was also true that, since the great days in the last century of men like Halle and William Swayne, the merchants of Salisbury had not been as adventurous as they should. These new opportunities were dazzling.

One thing puzzled him.

"Are you suggesting piracy as well as trade when you speak of Drake?" he asked.

"Yes," Wilson told him frankly. "And the queen herself would be glad to hear of it, so long as we raid the Spanish."

This was true. Long ago the pope had granted all the New World trade to faithful Catholic Spain. "Though what right he has to do it I do not know," Wilson maintained. The English merchants and their queen certainly wanted a share of it. Then there was the deeper political question. The Spanish king had long ago given up hope of bringing England back to the Catholic fold by persuading her wily virgin queen. He had made peace with England over the Netherlands and the renewed trade with Antwerp had been good for English merchants, but he had not forgiven the obstinate Protestant islanders. Sooner or later, he would invade, and anything English adventurers could do to weaken Spain's shipping or deprive her of bullion was to be encouraged.

"I shall do what I can," Shockley agreed.

But still he suspected that this was not all he was there for.

It was just before he left that Forest confirmed this suspicion, when he drew him apart and asked him:

"Would you yourself like to invest in this venture?"

"Yes. But . . ." Shockley grinned, "it could only be a modest sum . . ."

Forest looked at him carefully.

"A token from you would be enough. But if you would give your support, then I shall see to it that a part of the profits are yours." He paused to see Shockley's reaction.

Edward kept calm. His face gave away nothing.

"A twentieth," Forest said softly.

A twentieth! It could be a huge amount. Shockley's eyebrows rose; but still he made no comment. Forest was certainly making the offer for a reason. He waited to hear it.

"I ask in return one thing," Forest went on.

Shockley nodded. "Ask it."

"My son. Let him accompany you about your business in Salisbury. Let him converse with the merchants there." He smiled. "He knows Oxford – perhaps too well. But of trade he knows nothing."

Shockley had no objection to this at all. Forest went on.

"There is more." He grimaced wryly. "Unlike his father, he cares for the poor. Let him know what should be done for them." He bowed, as though this admission had cost him something. "Whatever our differences in the past, Edward Shockley, I value your counsel highly."

Shockley looked across at where the elegant young man was standing, with some surprise. A Forest concerned with the poor?

However, he readily agreed to do as Forest asked.

Why was it though, as he left, that he felt so certain that this was not all that Forest wanted?

He was a pleasant young man; indeed, it sometimes seemed to Edward that the dark, good-looking Giles Forest had been designed chiefly to please. He expressed great interest in the poor and investigated the workhouse minutely. He smiled charmingly at the inmates and talked to them so that, by the time he left, there was not one of them who did not believe that if young Giles Forest were only able to do so, he would certainly improve their lot.

Shockley took him round the market, the fulling mill and introduced him to Moody and the weavers. And every one of those he met, even old Moody, believed he was their friend.

He stood at the street corner. It was exactly the place where he had stood before, on that day he had returned early from Downton.

Indeed, until that moment he had forgotten the previous incident entirely.

It was dusk.

But there could be no mistaking the fact that a figure had just slipped unobtrusively out of his house. Was it the similarity of the incident, or was it also the figure himself that had brought that earlier occasion back to his mind so sharply? He could not be sure, but this time he thought it was another man – perhaps it was the darkness, but it seemed a taller, thinner figure who had furtively come out: a figure, he could not help the thought, similar to Thomas Forest.

He hurried forward, but the mysterious figure slipped away, and although this time he followed quickly, his quarry somehow eluded him in the alleys near St Thomas's Church.

He went back to the house, puzzled.

It was quiet inside. Perhaps his wife and her maidservant had gone out for some reason. Could the strange figure have been a thief?

Slowly he mounted the stairs.

Katherine had not heard him. She was standing in one corner of the big front chamber where there was a chest in which she kept her valuables. The chest was open. He saw her carefully count back a handful of gold coins into a small pouch – a pouch he recognised and in which he knew she normally kept the considerable sum of ten pounds. Even from where he stood, he could see the pouch was almost empty.

She closed the lid and turned the key in the lock. Then she stood, gazing meditatively through the shutters.

When he stepped into the room, she started violently.

"Who was here?"

"Here? Nobody?"

He frowned.

"I saw someone leave."

"Not this house."

He paused, trying to make sense of it. Had she been younger, he would have supposed such a stranger might have been a lover. Was it possible? Could it be Forest?

"Where are the servants?"

"They went to the cathedral."

He remembered now that he had heard there was a special service that evening; even so, it was strange that his wife should have been left alone in the house.

He looked at her suspiciously, surprised that she seemed so self-possessed. Then he decided to say no more, and went heavily down the stairs again.

He would unravel the mystery in due course, but one thought in particular occupied his mind: whatever was going on – and he could hardly believe she was unfaithful – in all their years of married life, it had never occurred to him that she could lie.

There were other important matters to occupy his mind though. For the long-awaited council meeting was held two days later.

It was a source of frustration to him, which sometimes almost bordered upon rage, that although in certain matters he could usually command support among the seniors, on this, which was closest to his heart, he could get none.

He pleaded. He thundered. The message was as simple as it was obvious:

"We must prepare for war with Spain. We must set aside funds and vote supplies." And most recently he had sometimes added menacingly: "It will look ill if we do not support the queen and her Church."

Each month the situation became more serious. There was an air of unrest in several parts of the country.

For once, under the threat of Spanish-inspired insurgency, Elizabeth had been forced to take stern religious measures, subjecting Catholics who refused to conform outwardly to enormous fines; and the secret agents of her servant Walsingham were everywhere.

And in Sarum, no one would listen.

He made a powerful speech that day. He saw nods of approval, and believed that, for once, he had got through.

Until a stout burgess rose.

"Wars are expensive, Edward Shockley. Let us hear no more about them here."

"But if the Spanish come . . ." he protested.

"There is an arms store."

A collection of pikes and antiquated swords.

He had failed again.

But in another sense, his words had struck home more than he knew, and in unexpected ways. For it was only three days later that a small deputation from Wilton came to see him. They greeted him respectfully, then came straight to their point.

"Edward Shockley, we are the neighbours of John Moody. You must tell him to leave your business. We no longer want him and his family amongst us."

"Why?"

"They are Catholics."

"But they conform," he protested.

[653]

It had been a struggle. Though the Moodys were deeply concerned by the messages the Jesuits brought – that the comfortable assumption that Catholics might attend the Church of England services was false – he had after many hours persuaded John Moody to sacrifice his conscience, at least for the time being.

"Catholics are traitors. They think treacherous thoughts."

He glared at them. Treachery was one thing: religious faith another. This was the whole point of the Elizabethan settlement.

"Moody will work for me as long as he pleases," he stormed. The next day he told Moody about it, so that he should be on his guard. "But they'll have to prove treason against you," he assured him, "before I cease to be your friend."

It was with an unquiet mind that he faced the winter.

There was one unexpected interlude of pure pleasure however, that took place shortly afterwards.

For as part of his plan – whatever it was – young Giles Forest invited him to accompany him, one fine day, to the great house at Wilton.

It was a large party, gathered to watch one of the companies of actors who came frequently to Lord Pembroke's splendid estate, and though he knew there must be an ulterior motive, Edward was delighted to go.

He had never been inside Wilton House before.

It proved to be a noble building.

"Though it is smaller, it has features like the queen's great palace of Nonesuch," Giles told him. "They say that Holbein himself designed it for Lord Pembroke," he added.

It had a long, grey façade with a splendid square tower at its centre, an elaborate formal garden at one side and a peaceful view over the river Nadder that flowed softly just a few hundred yards from its door. It was, Shockley thought appreciatively, a place to linger.

Shockley had met Lord Pembroke before a few times in the town, but never on terms of any intimacy, and he was curious to see him in his own home.

"He's not at all like his father," Giles said. "He's a scholar."

It was widely believed that the first earl, though he was one of the shrewdest men in the kingdom, could neither read nor write. Not so his son.

"As for his new wife . . ." Giles had murmured, "the poets write for her to read."

For after wisely failing to consummate his marriage to the politically dangerous sister of Lady Jane Grey, he married first one of the mighty Talbot family, and then, after she died, the extraordinary Mary Sidney.

"He was over forty and she was only sixteen, but it's a brilliant marriage," Giles remarked. "They live like princes."

They did indeed. It was believed Lord Pembroke kept over two hundred personal retainers who wore his livery. His wife, though not rich, was a niece of the queen's favourite Dudley, Earl of Leicester. Her brother was the brilliant courtier, soldier and author, Sir Philip Sidney.

And, as young Forest remarked, half the playwrights and poets of the kingdom came to Wilton as to a great renaissance court.

It was a day to remember. There were many ladies and gentlemen there, names like Thynne of Longleat, Hungerford, or Gorges, who was building a grand new house called Longford Castle by Clarendon Forest – gentry whom he seldom met. There was pleasant talk, too: of the poet Spenser who had dedicated his delightful *Shepherd's Calendar* to Philip Sidney, and of Philip Sidney himself.

"He was in temporary disgrace with the queen," a courtly gentleman explained to him. "He was here all this summer composing a poem for his sister. 'Tis called *Arcadia* and they say it will be a wonder when it is completed."

Though he had no courtly ways himself, Shockley had been well enough schooled to take pleasure in the elegant and literary company he found there. He also came to understand young Forest better.

For there had been times, in the last month, when he had wondered if, despite his charm, Giles Forest was perfectly sound in the head.

It was not what he said, but the truly extraordinary manner he sometimes had of speaking.

"In my concern for the poor, Master Shockley," he had announced, "I would neither be mistaken of purpose, neither misconstrued of munificence; I mean to work for the poor – for I am not mean; but in order that the poor may work – for I am not foolish."

Hearing this elaborate word play Shockley had sometimes had to beg Giles to speak more plainly. Yet now, at Wilton he observed that many of the younger men who had been to Oxford had this same affectation. Almost every subject they discussed, however trivial, was treated as though it were an elaborate dispute in some court of law, with the pro and con of a sweetmeat, the weather, a fine horse discussed with equal gravity; yet at the same time, the most intricate and serious matter of politics was reduced to exactly the same intricate word games.

This Elizabethan fashion amongst the young exquisites of the universities and court had reached its height with the publication of a book by the writer Lyly the year before.

"'Tis called *Euphues*, Master Shockley," a fantastically dressed youth assured him. "'Tis our bible," he added with a laugh.

Though he could only watch these artificial manners with wonder, Shockley found the young men pleasant. They wrote sonnets after the manner of Petrarch; they practised archery – not very seriously but, they explained to him, because it developed the body: "Beauty of body, beauty of mind," they claimed. Once he had got used to them, he thought better of young Forest.

The play was a short historical piece, and mediocre. But Shockley did not mind.

For it was just afterwards that he came face to face with Pembroke himself.

He was middle-aged and looked a little tired; but he was still a handsome man with a fine, sensitive face.

Shockley bowed respectfully. The second earl might not be as great a national figure as his father, but he was still a formidable figure. As Lord Lieutenant of the county he was the queen's own representative. He was in charge of the military, he headed all the local Justices; his vast estates stretched over such a wide area he had even a few years before had his own survey made, like William I and his great Domesday Book, to discover just what he had.

And so Edward blushed with pleasure when the great man smiled warmly at him and said:

"Master Shockley, I have heard of you: the one man in Salisbury who is ready to defend it when war comes."

One of the guests had told Edward that the earl was a student of heraldry. But when, thinking to please him, Edward mentioned that he admired the fine new coat of arms of his friends the Forests, he was puzzled when Pembroke burst out into laughter. He did not discover why.

But the day had been a delightful interlude.

Or was that all it was?

It seemed to Edward Shockley, as he and Giles Forest rode back to Salisbury together that the young man was going more slowly than necessary. He appeared reluctant to let Shockley go. Dusk was falling.

And suddenly it occured to him that there was another possible reason for young Forest's invitation to him that day: it kept him away from his own house.

He looked at the young man thoughtfully. Could he really be intriguing with his father in such a way – while Thomas Forest spent time with his wife? With a Forest, he decided, anything was possible. Bidding Giles an abrupt farewell, he cantered away towards the town, before the surprised young man could stop him.

It was dark when he reached the street. He paused at the corner. The street was empty. And then, as he walked, the door of his house opened, and a single figure – he was sure it was the same he had seen before – slipped out of the shadows and entered.

He dismounted and stole forward. The house seemed quiet. Softly he moved through the little archway beside it that led to a courtyard behind. There was a back staircase. He mounted carefully and a few moments later he was on the upper floor of his house. Whatever his wife and Forest were doing, he would soon know.

There was a light in the bed chamber. He moved to the door.

But to his surprise it was empty. He thought now that he would hear muffled voices in the hall below, and was about to descend the stairs when he noticed that in the chamber his wife's chest was open. Curious, he crept across the room and looked in it.

It was half empty. The bags of money she kept there had all gone. But as he gazed down in surprise, something else caught his eye. It was a letter, left carelessly in the empty space where the money had been.

At first he could not believe it; yet as he looked at the small scrap of paper there could be no possible doubt.

He did not know what it was that he thought it might be; but certainly not this.

At first, as he gazed at it, he felt horror. Then, naturally, rage. For a moment he felt fear as well. What if some other hand than his had found the letter?

Rest assured, your gifts are well received. And when she, the heretic, who now sits on the throne is removed, and the true faith restored, the good faith, lady, of you and your brother shall have its reward, just as now you are storing up treasures in heaven.

As to the royal Jezebel, we may hope ere long to hear good news concerning her.

Now he understood. Treason. The Jesuits have got at her, he thought. At his wife and his brother.

He felt himself grow cold. His wife had betrayed him. Worse even than that, she was clearly aiding with money the Catholic supporters of Spain – the very people who would wreck everything he believed in.

He thought of her quiet, submissive ways, of the years they had spent, he supposed, contentedly together. He remembered his own, long, deception of her. Now it was she who had lied.

He had almost forgotten the visitor. Quietly now, still holding the letter, he moved back to the head of the stairs.

They were standing by the door now: a tall, elderly man, of similar build but otherwise not in the least like Forest. He was wrapping himself round in a long cloak. He saw his wife kiss his ring.

A moment later he saw the door open and made out quite distinctly, the face of John Moody, who evidently had come to collect the priest.

He stepped back into the bedchamber.

And now Edward Shockley had to make the most important decision of his life.

For several long seconds he stood there. There was so much to consider.

However minor his wife's part in this matter, it was treason. He knew very well where his own loyalties lay – with Queen Elizabeth. That being so, what could he do except tell Walsingham's men about them. His wife might go to prison; John would be put to the rack – they would want to know his accomplices.

Moreover, if he did not inform on them then he was an accomplice, and liable to terrible punishments himself.

How long, he wondered, had she lied to him?

It was as he thought of their years of marriage that he took his decision. It was brave. He did not know if it was right.

Very carefully, he replaced the letter exactly where he had found it. Then he stole out of the house.

He would keep an eye on his wife to make sure that she neither did, nor came to, any further harm.

The times were dangerous, for people of conscience.

What he did discover, a few days later, was Forests' real game.

It was so simple, he was amazed he had not seen it before.

It was all a question of politics, and, of course, the Forests' social ambition.

The mark that a man had entered the gentry was that he became a Justice of the Peace. Whether he had any desire to either help the community, or sit in judgement on his fellow man had nothing to do with it, at least in Forest's case and many like him. This he had already achieved. But the next, and grander step, was to sit as a Member of Parliament. There were two ways to do so. The first was to be chosen as one of the two knights of the shire. But this was still out of reach of the Forests. Under the general guidance of Pembroke, this honour passed, usually, in rotation amongst the greatest county families; Penruddock, Thynne of Longleat, Hungerford, Mompesson, Danvers, and a dozen more. But after this, there were still the two citizens returned by Salisbury, and the two burgesses from fifteen boroughs. Indeed, so rich was the county of Wiltshire in parliamentary seats, having thirty-four in all, that already ambitious men from far afield came there to find seats, and since the townspeople were often unwilling to pay the heavy expenses of their own burgesses attending Parliament, they were often glad to have a rich gentleman who could pay for himself. Many of the boroughs were also under the control of the local magnate. The few electors of Wilton almost always did as Pembroke told them; in the north, the Seymour family controlled the towns of Marlborough and Great Bedwyn; the Bishop of Winchester controlled several boroughs. Why, there was even the deserted hillfort of Old Sarum, which had been bought by a gentleman named Baynton, but which still, though long since empty, had a handful of electors in the village below who duly sent their two burgesses to Parliament.

Forest was looking for a borough for his son.

So far he had failed to find one. Pembroke had politely refused him: he had good men of his own; so had a dozen others.

It was November when Forest broached the subject to him.

"My son wishes to stand for Salisbury," he told Edward. "I hope you will support him: your word carries weight."

Of course! This was the reason for the bribe, for the introduction to Wilton, and, no doubt, for Giles's unexpected interest in the poor. In all the boroughs in Wiltshire, the citizens of Salisbury were the most independent: even Pembroke himself, ten years before, had only been able to foist a candidate upon them once.

"Truly I must be his last port," he considered. And, the thought could not help occurring to him, that Forest would be prepared to pay handsomely for the service.

He waited a day. The struggle with his conscience was short.

"I've no objection to your son," he told his one-time partner. "But the burgesses will choose their own members. Giles will have to speak to them himself."

Forest's face was a mask.

"Will you vote for him?"

"No."

It was so easy to say. It was only the truth.

He never heard a word about his share in Wilson's profitable voyages again.

In the year of Our Lord 1585, the city of Salisbury was required by Her Majesty's Privy Council to make contributions towards the expenses of the anticipated invasion by King Philip II of Spain.

> We understand it be your honour's pleasure and commandment, that there should forthwith be provided, in readiness for the service of Her Majesty, a last of powder and five hundredweight of matches, to be kept here as a store.
>
> Whereupon we have had consideration, and so find that the charge of this provision will require a great sum of money to be presently levied and disbursed . . . our humble suit is . . . it would please you to respect the poor estate of this City, subject to many charges to maintain a great number of very poor people . . . and to mitigate as much as may be thought convenient. . . .

It took Queen Elizabeth's Privy Council three applications before the burghers of Salisbury finally, and most unwillingly, raised a loan to pay for the modest precautions against the invading force that was to become known as the Spanish Armada.

In 1586 John Moody and his family left Sarum. The sour mood of the time had made them feel unwelcome. Edward Shockley did not try to stop them. They did not have to go very far. Fifteen miles to the west, in the villages around Shaftesbury, they found a region where, under the aegis of the great Catholic family of Arundel, a community of recusant Catholics survived. Here they found friends, and a chance to worship as they wished, although in secret. As far as Edward Shockley knew, no more Jesuits had come to his house in Salisbury.

Events then moved swiftly. In 1587, after she had become involved in a plot of high treason against Elizabeth, that was probably set up as a trap by the subtle Walsingham, Mary Queen of Scots was executed. Her son James in Scotland protested: but not very loud, for he never liked her, and it was clear that he himself, as long as he remained on good terms with the English, was the most likely person to succeed the childless Elizabeth when she died.

Not so Philip of Spain. That most Catholic of monarchs could no longer hold back after such an outrage. In 1587, a chain of beacons were lit on hills all over the south of England to announce that the great fleet of galleons called the Spanish Armada had been seen off Plymouth.

It was a stupendous force. The mighty galleons that rolled down the channel very nearly succeeded in their conquest.

"The fact is," one of the seafaring Wilson boys confided to Edward Shockley afterwards, "even Drake couldn't have stopped them. All we did was follow them."

But thanks to a series of fortunate winds, and one brief, but successful engagement, Philip's huge fleet was blown first up the Channel, then northwards to the rocky coasts of Scotland where many were wrecked.

"We were saved by luck," Shockley declared, "not by preparation."

But, fantastic luck though the wreck of the Armada was, England was saved, and the island returned once more to years of peace; even Edward Shockley, as he entered his old age and the last decade of the reign of Elizabeth, was, in his modest way, optimistic for the future.

In particular, he loved to go to Wilton House, to which, about once a year, he was invited to see the players. Many troops of actors passed through the great mansion in those sunlit years. Once at least, they included an actor named William Shakespeare.

The Unrest

1642: August

THE FUNERAL GUESTS were leaving. Inside, the family waited tensely as, one by one, the visitors filed past the big oak staircase, out of the panelled hall and through the low doorway of the big farmhouse into the afternoon sunlight outside.

As soon as they had gone, the family conference must begin – the conference that might break the Shockleys for ever.

If only it were not necessary. If only the coming civil war, which had all Sarum in an uproar, need not intrude into the sanctuary of the family home, which should always be inviolate. For months they had all known that it could come to this. Now, with their father gone . . .

Sir Henry Forest went first. Before leaving the hall he turned, his cautious black eyes taking in all the remaining family, and bowed stiffly. Sir Henry Forest, Baronet, their senior neighbour – their friend, if he was any man's friend. Which side would he take in the coming conflict? Who knew? When he had gone, others followed suit: friends, neighbours, old Thomas Moody with his son Charles, from Shaftesbury; after them, tradesmen like the Mason family and others of Salisbury; lastly the farmworkers led by Jacob Godfrey. For three generations now, since Piers Godfrey the carpenter had worked for the Shockleys in Salisbury, the Godfrey family had remained close to the Shockleys. Many had tears in their eyes: for all felt a real regret and affection for the memory of the widower William Shockley whose sudden death had taken Sarum by surprise.

Now the family was alone, but the hall was quiet – each of them knowing that, once this last silence was broken, they might never be at one again. The four Shockleys stood, as motionless as the banisters on the broad oak stairs that gleamed darkly behind them, waiting. From outside, where the footsteps had departed, they could hear the distant, sullen tolling of the church bell. Four of them: three brothers and their sister.

Margaret Shockley: twenty years old, magnificent, with her proud, strong body, her golden hair and blue eyes that could flash with such splendid anger that people in Sarum used laughingly to say: "She's the best looking of all the boys." Tall Margaret waited silently.

One thought filled her mind: The baby.

He was hers to take care of – hers and no one else's – and they were not going to stop her, any of them. The baby, resting in an upper room. He needed her.

He was still so small and defenceless. He had been hers ever since her poor step-mother, during that terrible, endless labour two years before had turned to her and whispered: "If the child lives, Margaret, he'll be yours." Her three brothers had all been there too, she reminded herself, just three days ago when William Shockley mustered his breath to say:

"Margaret: whatever your brothers do, you must live here and look after Samuel." Then he had paused before adding: "And my water meadows."

Little Samuel – that tiny, fair-haired bundle of joy. Jacob Godfrey's wife had had him to nurse at her breast – and how Margaret would have loved to be able to do that too. But it was she who had done everything else, rocked the baby in her arms, taken him with her into her bed and, week after week, lain happily, feeling his tiny warmth beside her.

Her father's water meadows – those wonderful man-made irrigation systems running down beside the River Avon below the farm that he had bought when he was young. He had built them before she was born and they had made his farm the finest in the area; she would look after those too.

She looked at her brothers. Edmund, at thirty the eldest, the head of the family now: always serious, dutiful, sober, his brown hair cut straight, just above the shoulder; he had their mother's hazel eyes, their father's broad, rather heavy-set figure. Obadiah, the Presbyterian minister, hater of priests and bishops; though he was only twenty-seven, the black hair that was plastered close around his pale oval face before curling up at the shoulders was already greying at the temples. His eyes were slate-blue, striking, even from a distance, such as when he was in the pulpit. Obadiah, with his arrogant, lisping speech; as a child he had been vain; he was full of spiritual indignation now he was a man: a born Puritan preacher, she thought. People did not love Obadiah. He knew it, and could not forgive them.

And Nathaniel: fair like herself, gallant, only twenty-three. Even now, how nonchalant he looked, his golden hair falling past his shoulders, his elegant lace cuffs a contrast to the solemn plain cloth of both brothers; in his hand was the long clay pipe he loved to point casually at Obadiah whenever he swore one of his favourite blasphemous oaths, just to make sure the preacher did not miss it. Her own Nathaniel, her kindred spirit whom she loved even though he was often irresponsible.

She knew her brothers so well.

In the coming crisis she might have to protect Nathaniel. And she knew she must protect the child.

When she thought of the causes of this great storm that was about to engulf them, to Margaret at least it seemed that the whole matter was the fault of the king – the king and his terrible doctrine of divine right. That was why Sarum and half the country was up in arms; that was why her family was about to be torn apart; and in her heart, she cursed him.

When old Queen Elizabeth died childless at the turn of the century, the logical and proper choice as her successor had been her cousin James Stuart of Scotland, the sober-minded son of the beheaded Mary Queen of Scots.

At first it had seemed the new regime would bring happy times. England and Scotland, though each remained a separate kingdom with its own Parliament and Church, at last shared a single monarch. The king and both his peoples were mainly Protestant. There had been peace, at last, with Spain. And had not the start of the Stuart dynasty seen such glories as Shakespeare's greatest plays performed in London, the opening up of the trade with the newly found continent of America, and the preparing of the noblest book in the English language – King James's Authorised Bible? Why had it all turned sour?

Because James and his son Charles understood neither of the countries that they ruled.

They hated the Protestant Presbyters of Scotland who would have none of their bishops; they despised the proud Parliament of England.

Worse: the self-styled scholar James believed that kings ruled by divine right and that no one, even parliaments, should interfere with their actions.

Worse still: his son Charles I, governing through his hated favourites Buckingham and Strafford, had vigorously put his father's ideas into practice.

It was Edmund, at last, who broke the uneasy silence, motioning his sister and brothers to sit at the old oak table. He himself sat in the chair at the head.

He looked unhappy. It was obvious that he had been steeling himself for this job for many hours. The other three waited silently as he opened the proceedings.

"The king's commission of array is issued and he has raised his standard at Nottingham. Parliament has voted Lord Essex ten thousand men to oppose him." He paused, looking from one to the other. He looked at young Nathaniel sternly. He knew where Obadiah stood.

"This family will fight," he declared, "for the Parliament." It was an order. If it was obeyed, the family might still come through together.

There was a long pause. Then young Nathaniel, very quietly:

"Brother Edmund, I cannot."

A sound of disgust from Obadiah. Edmund winced. He had expected as much, yet hoped not to hear it.

He put a restraining hand on Obadiah, who was about to leave the table.

"Stay," he commanded gently. "Let us not part like this. One last time, we shall discuss."

Up and down the country, during those days, families were faced with the same terrible decisions. Great issues were at stake, fundamental to the constitution of State and Church, that would cause not only the kingdom to be riven, but brother to fight brother, to kill or die.

The final debate within the Shockley family was conducted in a calm and solemn manner. The arguments were familiar to them all, but now came the irrevocable taking of positions. The questions which must decide the issue came almost like a catechism.

EDMUND: Do you say that the king may rule without Parliament?
NATHANIEL: He has the right to do so.
EDMUND: But it is not the custom. Can the king tax illegally? What of ship-money?

No issue had been more furiously fought than the tax, owed only by ports, that Charles had tried to impose on inland towns as well. In Parliament, brave men like Hampden and Pym opposed him. At Sarum, the Sheriff in successive years was unable to collect even half of it.

NATHANIEL: If the king needs money for war, his loyal subjects should support him.
EDMUND: To any amount? Is that right?
NATHANIEL: The Parliament just called granted him nothing. Is that right?
EDMUND: May the king summon men before his prerogative courts and ignore ancient common law?
NATHANIEL: He has the right.
EDMUND: Do you approve?
NATHANIEL: No. But this is not cause to take up arms against him.
EDMUND: So – you believe then, that the king is not subject to the laws and customs of this realm but may do as he pleases?

Here was the heart of the matter. The privileges of Parliament, the ancient common laws, the liberties of Magna Carta, the custom, won centuries before, that the king cannot tax without the consent of Parliament: these were the rights that the parliamentary lawyers claimed that the king must observe. If a king is free to alter ancient privileges and customs, then, they claimed, the liberties of the people are left at the whim of tyrants.

NATHANIEL: The law derives from the king.
EDMUND: Not in England.

Indeed, part of the trouble between king and Parliament was that the constitution of England was not the Stuarts' model. In Spain and France, Catholic rulers were building absolute, centralised monarchies beyond anything Charles I tried, that were to last another hundred and fifty years. But then they had not the combination of Puritan merchants and an ancient Parliament trained in dispute and conscious of its privileges to oppose them.

OBADIAH: Do you refuse the rights of Puritans to worship as they please?
NATHANIEL: I support the English Church – as does the king.
OBADIAH: So he says. Do you support Laud and his bishops then?

Nathaniel laughed. He had hardly ever met a man that did, certainly not in Sarum.

The High Church Laud, whose authoritarian ways had driven numbers of Puritans across the dangerous ocean to America, was scarcely popular even with Charles's supporters, and least of all his attempts to summon laymen to answer charges before his ecclesiastical courts. In Sarum, such ideas were especially unpopular.

For early that century, after over three centuries of dispute, the townspeople of Salisbury had at last persuaded the king to grant them a charter of their own. The town was no longer subject to the bishop's court: now the bishop only ruled the close. The interfering churchmen were being driven back.

NATHANIEL: Laud has improved the discipline and church services. I support the rule of bishops.

OBADIAH: And papists? Do you want England papist? With a foreign papist army in the hands of the king, to impose his will upon us?

NATHANIEL: I trust the papists will not rule the king.

OBADIAH: They already do. We may expect an army of Irish papists here any day.

And now Nathaniel blushed. For the subject of Charles's sympathies for the papists was one that made many of his fervent supporters uncomfortable. His queen, Henrietta Maria of France, was Catholic. Her priests were at court. The increasingly Puritan people of England had not forgotten Mary Tudor – Bloody Mary – and her terrible burnings; nor the wily Jesuits who urged treason and supported Spain in the reign of good Queen Bess. They had not forgotten the plots, real or supposed, of that other Frenchified Catholic, Mary Queen of Scots, nor, most terrible of all, the plot of Guy Fawkes and other Catholic extremists to blow up the houses of Parliament – King, Lords, Commons and all – one fifth of November, early in James's reign.

As for the threat of an avenging army of Irish papists being brought over, that had been terrifying Englishmen for the last two years.

EDMUND: It seems to me, Nathaniel, that you disapprove what the king does, yet you defend his rule. What have we seen recently that makes you think the king will change his ways?

Indeed, the series of events that started the Civil War, the spark that lit the conflagration, had shown Charles I at his worst – and most foolish.

First, he had insulted the Scots. For in 1638, Laud contemptuously told the formidable Presbyterians of Scotland, whose church effectively controlled the northern land, that they must abandon their Puritan ways, submit to rule by his bishops and follow the Anglican rites of the English Prayer Book – which did not, after all, vary so greatly from the original Roman Use of Sarum from which Cranmer had derived it. Scotland had risen, signed the Covenant to preserve its own Presbyterian rule and marched into England.

Charles was helpless. Like the medieval kings before him, each time he overreached himself, he found he had no money.

He tried every means to raise it, and failed. The troops he called for did not materialise. In Wiltshire, when they found they were not to be paid, they rioted and it was all Lord Pembroke could do to quieten them.

Since he needed money, Charles had to call a Parliament.

He was in a trap. Parliament voted him no funds; its Presbyterian members sympathised with the Scots anyway; the Scots, cannily, stayed camped in the north.

Then the great Parliament of 1640, known in British history as the Long Parliament, struck. It demanded the impeachment of the king's most trusted councillors. Soon Strafford had been executed at the Tower of London in front of a cheering crowd and Archbishop Laud was in prison. It was humiliation for the king. The Irish rose in revolt. Still Parliament voted no money but passed the Grand Remonstrance – a massive indictment of his rule.

The proud Stuart king then made the mistake that ended medieval monarchy in England for ever.

He came to the House of Commons in person, to arrest Pym, Hampden and three other members. It was the final provocation. To cries of "Privilege and Parliament", London went into revolt, Charles was forced to flee: and the country was ready for civil war.

Was there still hope of reconciliation now? Some said there was. The eminent lawyer Hyde had been writing brilliant pamphlets for his royal master, showing that a settlement was possible. In return, Parliament had set conditions that would put the king entirely under their control. They no longer trusted him.

MARGARET: So why, Nathaniel, do you support the king? Is not Parliament a better ruler than a tyrant king with a papist army under his control?

How could he explain? For many, the ties to the king were simple – the personal ties of a great nobleman whose family had been advanced by the Stuarts, or the natural conservatism of a country peasant who supported the old ways.

And a young man with no great noble connections, from Sarum?

Nathaniel's feelings for the monarchy ran deep. Of course, there was the style of the king's court. He had caught some of the flavour of it when, two years before, he had spent six months at the Inns of Court while he was trying, without much application, to make himself a lawyer. Charles I, great collector of art, patron of men like Inigo Jones the architect and great painters like Van Dyck; Charles, with his cosmopolitan court; Charles, whose wife was half a Medici; Charles who had already erected small but brilliant classical buildings in London. How could an imaginative, light-hearted young student from Sarum not be dazzled by the outward trappings of these sophisticated European wonders?

But more important, the monarchy had always been there. Whether or not the notion of divine right was a Stuart invention, kingship was certainly sacred: it was part of the natural order, the divine hierarchy. It went back into the mists of time. Why, was not the English king

descended from the old Anglo-Saxon royal house that produced Edward
the Confessor? Did not, even nowadays, the king touch men and cure
them of the King's Evil – scrofula?

The king was a brilliant man. A good man – he was even faithful to his
wife.

It must be wrong therefore, for Parliament men, mere factions, to set
themselves up against the ancient and lawful authority of kings. Destroy
the sanctity of kingly rule and you are on the road to chaos.

He could not express all these feelings. They would hardly have
impressed dour Obadiah anyway. But he must try.

NATHANIEL: But can you not see – once you destroy kingship, you
destroy the natural order. Even if the king be wrong, he is
the anointed monarch: our ancient privileges are bound
up with his. Take away the king, and who governs?

OBADIAH: Men of God.

NATHANIEL: Presbyters. Why, their tyranny would be worse than the
king's. I have heard it said: new Presbyter is but old
priest writ large.

EDMUND: The king may rule, but only by consent of Parliament.

NATHANIEL: Then Parliament usurps the king – steals his ancient
rights. Tell me this, by whose authority do they then rule
instead? Who calls them to govern? I say, if the old order
is gone, then there's no authority in England. The
Parliament might as well be summoned by the people
themselves.

EDMUND: That is a foolish charge.

NATHANIEL: It is not. If you destroy the authority of the king, Brother
Edmund, then it will one day be the mob, the people
themselves who will rule. And that would be chaos and
tyranny combined.

EDMUND: I see we shall never agree.

The debate of the Shockley family was over. There was nothing more to
say.

Nathaniel looked at his eldest brother with affection. Though only a
few years separated them from the two older brothers, he and Margaret
had grown up like a second family of old William. The stern side of their
father's nature was reserved for his two older sons and the youngest boy
and girl, though they were not spoiled, led a more free and easy
existence, creating their own little world apart. In a way, it seemed to
Nathaniel, they had been children longer. He was sometimes sorry for
Edmund who, he knew, always laboured hard under the burden of being
the next head of the family. He remembered the times, as a child, when
his serious older brother used to come and play with him gazing almost
wistfully at his childish pranks. Edmund was a good scholar. He had
studied the law with stern application. One day he might even have gone
into Parliament.

But all that must be set aside now. They were children no longer.

"You mean to fight for the king?" Edmund asked gloomily.

"I do."

It was a serious business, yet, having made his decision, he felt almost cheerful.

There was a long pause, while Edmund looked grave.

"A house divided against itself cannot stand," he said with sadness. "You must leave this house."

Nathaniel smiled. How like his eldest brother: the melancholy voice of authority. He could see that it was said almost against Edmund's own will.

"I have no wish to do so," he replied blandly.

"I am sorry for it. But I am head of the family now."

Obadiah nodded in support.

Poor Obadiah. Their father never liked him, and though William had tried to disguise the fact, Obadiah certainly always knew it.

He had not been kind to Obadiah himself: in fact, he had teased him ever since he could talk. He had always hurt his brother's morbid vanity by refusing to take him seriously. Once, when he was ten, he had taunted him into such a frenzy that the thin, dark adolescent, who then was suffering from painful face acne, had rushed at him in an uncontrollable rage and bitten him on the hand. He had never forgotten it. Obadiah would not be sorry to see him go.

He gazed at his brothers mildly.

"I run the farm." It was Margaret. They had almost forgotten her. Now the three brothers turned.

She had taken little part in their arguments. She had no wish to. Besides, an instinct for self-preservation had told her that she must keep clear of the conflict. She had the child to think of. But now she knew she must be firm.

"Our father left me in charge of it: you heard him. And I shall never close the doors to any of my brothers, whichever side they take."

The will of William Shockley was very clear. Each of the three brothers was left a sum of money: Margaret, because she alone of his children properly understood them, was left half the water meadows together with the tenancy of the whole farm until her marriage or death, when they were to pass to young Samuel. "Though naturally," William had added, "if you do not marry, I shall expect you to leave the water meadows back to Samuel, who is less provided for than his brothers."

It was not said as a challenge to Edmund, just as a statement, and she shrewdly noticed that Edmund looked almost relieved.

"It is true that the farm is in your care," he conceded.

Obadiah scowled.

"And which side do you take, sister?" Nathaniel enquired, with a glint of amusement in his eye.

"I am neuter." This was the term the neutrals used.

"And Samuel?" Again, that faintly mocking tone. "Is he not a good Royalist?"

"I thank God he is too young to understand this folly," she answered hotly.

Samuel. At the mention of the baby's name, Edmund and Obadiah had looked at each other. Why did Nathaniel have to remind them of the child? Now the moment she had dreaded had come.

"Samuel." Edmund looked thoughtful. "We must decide what is to be done with him."

She knew there had been words spoken behind her back, but she was ready.

"He stays here with me." She spoke with finality. "You heard our father tell me to care for him, too."

Nathaniel said nothing. Edmund seemed to be turning the idea over in his mind. But Obadiah was looking at her coldly. She knew he suspected that she was not a true Puritan at heart.

It irked Obadiah that he had never gained any influence in the family while his father was alive. He meant to correct that now.

"Our sister is young." He smiled at her. His smile, she thought, was always ominous. "It is not right that she should be left to care for the child alone, without some wiser hand to guide her."

He gave his elder brother a meaningful look, which she understood at once to mean: "We must keep the child away from Nathaniel."

She must be careful.

"I have you to guide me, Obadiah," she said submissively, "and Edmund."

"We may not be here," Obadiah answered coldly.

"Where else could he go?" Edmund asked him.

"I know a preacher in London whose family will give him a godly home until these troubles are over."

While this was going on, Nathaniel had calmly lit his pipe. Now he removed it from his mouth and observed quietly.

"The child is but two years old, brother Edmund. It has no need to be preached at yet. Besides," he added, "if the king advances upon London there might be fighting there."

Edmund weighed all the arguments. Then he gave his verdict.

"It was our father's will the child stay here. He shall do so for the present. If the war comes to Sarum, then our sister can move him to a place of safety."

It was a temporary reprieve but she was glad of it. Obadiah seemed about to protest, but Edmund, having now asserted himself once more, gave him a look that quelled further argument.

"We shall speak of this again," Obadiah promised.

The family arguments were resolved, for the time being at least. Despite the outcome, she sensed in the brothers a feeling of relief that it was over.

And then – strangest of all, it seemed to her – the brothers calmly sat and discussed the coming war they meant to fight against each other.

"London, and the east are for Parliament of course," Edmund remarked. These were the great Puritan and merchant strongholds.

"Don't forget, you'll have all the ports as well," Nathaniel reminded him. The trading sailors of England had no love of the Stuarts whose friendship with the Catholic powers who were their trading rivals infuriated them; even now, they had not forgotten how James I had cynically executed the sailor adventurer Sir Walter Raleigh to please the Spanish ambassador. "The sailors will never forgive the Stuarts for Raleigh," he laughed.

"The north and west will stay Royalist, I think," Edmund said. The old feudal landlords and tenants in the countryside still believed in the sacredness of the king, whatever crimes he committed.

"And Sarum?" Margaret asked.

Like many parts of England, the situation in Sarum was complex. The town, like other cloth towns, was naturally for Parliament. Most of the local gentry were for Parliament too. Even the Seymours in the north of the county had havered before royal appointments and titles had secured them for the king. Other old names – Hungerford, Baynton, Evelyn, Long, Ludlow, fine old families – were for Parliament. These local men, solid Justices, with their English Bibles, their independent customs and increasingly Puritan outlook, had no use for this king with his European ways and Catholic sympathies, who despised the Parliament in which they and other gentlemen sat and expected to be listened to.

"Some of the gentry in Wiltshire country will go with the king," Edmund said. "The Catholics like Lord Arundel of course; Penruddock; Thynne of Longleat I think; the Hydes." The large Hyde family, more recently settled near Salisbury, were cousins of the king's great lawyer, and respected supporters of the king.

But Nathaniel shook his head sadly.

"Arundel's old; Thynne's crippled by a lawsuit; Penruddock's a politician, not a soldier. Whereas, brother, you have Lord Pembroke. Though he's no commander, the Pembroke influence still weighs in the balance." For the earl, after seeming to hesitate, had accepted Parliament's offer of the lord lieutenancy that spring and so effectively declared himself against the king. He had hated both Buckingham and Strafford and his example would be followed.

"Yet," Nathaniel said with a laugh, "I still have the bishop with me."

Although many of his clergy – half those even in Salisbury town, were Puritans, Bishop Duppa, a good High Churchman like his predecessors, had been made tutor to the royal princes.

"Much good it will do you," Obadiah replied grimly.

"And Sir Henry Forest?" Nathaniel enquired. "Which way will he jump, brother?"

To which, for once, serious Edmund allowed himself a smile.

"Why, with the winning side, my dear Nathaniel, to be sure."

Sir Henry Forest, Baronet, had decided to walk home. It was not far.

He had respected William Shockley and he had not been sorry when, twenty years before, the cloth merchant had bought the fine old farm that lay next to his estate at Avonsford, enlarged the house so that it was almost a small manor, and settled in the Avon valley.

He had a shrewd idea of the arguments in the Shockley family now, and guessed correctly that the brothers would be split apart.

Sir Henry Forest smiled. They did not realise it, but their falling out might be to his advantage.

As for which side he would take in the war with the king – he had not decided.

The time of the Stuarts had been good for the Forest family. After making several lucrative investments in the new tobacco trade with America, Forest's father had done better still with the recently formed East India Company whose trade in the Far East was bringing all manner of new luxuries to the busy trading island.

It had not only been good for them financially: for it was the Stuarts, as one of their expedients to raise money, who had invented the new title of baronet. By acquiring this dignity a man would be called Sir Henry, like a knight, but unlike a mere knight, pass the title on to his male heirs in perpetuity, like a lord. It was a brilliant idea, perfectly aimed at rising families like the Forests, and Henry had gladly paid the considerable sum into the king's coffers to see his family ennobled at last. Once on the ladder of nobility, there were higher titles to be had – baron, viscount, earl. Why, to secure his allegiance, Seymour had even been made a marquis, only one rank below a duke! Forest had every reason to support the Stuarts.

But was it wise to join the king when so many in Wiltshire were against him?

"I have no desire to be at odds with the country," he had told his wife that morning.

By the word 'country' he meant not England, but only the county of Wiltshire. But the usage of the day conveyed very accurately the independence of each shire, with its magnates and gentry who administered justice, raised the levies when needed, and usually nowadays – still more than in the previous century – sat for the boroughs in Parliament instead of the burgesses.

"I'll follow Pembroke," he decided. "Besides, let them fight a battle first, so I can see which way the wind blows."

It was as he walked along the path above the river that Sir Henry Forest, turning to look towards the water, forgot the Civil War again.

For there they lay: William Shockley's proudest achievement – the water meadows: a little masterpiece of scientific irrigation, stretching across the valley bottom – acres of green, rich grazing, man-made, worth a fortune now. They lay next to his estate; but he had no water meadows of his own.

He stared at them thoughtfully, his eyes narrowing.

If those Shockleys fell out with each other, he might have those water meadows yet.

1643: August

The first event that Samuel Shockley could remember to the end of his long life, took place when he was three.

To him it seemed the happiest of days.

He was riding on Nathaniel's shoulders and they were entering the cathedral.

The sunlight was catching Nathaniel's long, fair hair; his uncle's strong hands held his feet and he leaned over to play with the long silky strands of his pointed beard.

He did not understand what they were doing, but he knew it was important. Everything his uncle Nathaniel did was important: he was winning the war.

The sun was warm. Little Samuel always remembered the sunshine that day.

For Margaret, it was a day first of bright sunshine, but then of gloom.

How pleasant it was, to ride into the city in the little cart with Nathaniel. Her Nathaniel, in his brightly coloured doublet, his breeches tucked into his boots with their folded tops and lace edgings. Nathaniel gaily wearing his broad-brimmed Cavalier's hat, and smoking his long clay pipe.

"The best pipes in England are made by Gauntlet of Wiltshire," he declared, as they drove along, and showed little Samuel the tiny stamp of a gauntlet under the bowl of the pipe that was the mark of the famous maker.

Nathaniel that long summer. Her Nathaniel. As they walked gaily through the close with the child, she could see that people mistook them for husband and wife. "And with Samuel, my brother and the farm to look after," she thought with a smile, "what would I do with a husband now if I had one?"

The war had gone well for Nathaniel – badly for Edmund and Obadiah. The forces for Parliament were poorly organised and badly led. At Edgehill in the north, the king's dashing young cousin Prince Rupert had trained the Cavalier squires in the new Swedish tactics of lightning charges and swept all before him. Lord Pembroke had gone to London and the gentlemen supposed to lead the Parliamentary forces in Wiltshire – Hungerford and Baynton – had quarrelled. Everywhere the king's cavalry and Cornish infantry were winning; one after another, the towns of Wiltshire fell; and in May 1643, Seymour, whom the king had made Marquis of Hertford, swept down to Sarum from Oxford, captured the city, and imprisoned the mayor for three weeks.

Obadiah had gone to London. Edmund was with the Parliamentary forces – Margaret did not know where.

But with the Royalists came Nathaniel.

"And as well for our property that I am here and Edmund is not," he cried happily, as he first strode into the hall. For with the Royalists in the ascendant at Sarum, the known supporters of Parliament were being fined and plundered.

Thank God for the farm. To the Shockleys, it had always been a place of refuge. By sheer good luck William Shockley had sold up the old fulling mill and the cloth business and moved his young family to the farm just a few years before one of the worst attacks of the plague in centuries had come to Sarum. The plague had missed Avonsford this time and the

Shockleys had not only been safe, but had been able to send generous supplies into Salisbury to help the heroic mayor John Ivie in his fight to save the townspeople. And later, being wealthy, he had sent money when Ivie tried to run a brewery for the benefit of the town's poor – a venture the other brewers soon scotched.

Now, with the Civil War, the town seemed scarcely in a better state. The population was down, the cloth industry sunk in depression, and many merchants had been fined by both the opposing sides. Some of the cathedral plate had also been taken.

But the farm was rich, and as safe from the war as it had been from the plague.

Even such a well-known Parliamentarian as John Ivie himself cheerfully came to call, as he had done in years gone by. For, Royalist or not, it was impossible to dislike Nathaniel.

At first glance the cathedral seemed quiet as they walked up the nave.

It was only when they reached the transept where the great bending pillars soared that one became aware of a small group of men busily engaged.

When they arrived, the four men were briefly resting and drinking beer; but already there was a pile of wooden casing on the ground beside them, and loaded on a small cart, half a dozen long pipes, each with a number chalked upon it.

They were dismantling the cathedral's great double organ.

"I spoke to the dean the other week," Nathaniel explained. "I warned him it should be done and I am glad he has taken my advice." Then he took little Samuel and showed him the great pipes, explaining to him where the air entered and left them to produce the sound.

"What are they doing?" Samuel asked.

Nathaniel laughed. "They're hiding the organ from your uncle Obadiah," he said. "Obadiah does not like music."

The dour dislike of the Puritans for anything conducive to human happiness had taken many forms. A Puritan like the famous Prynne could even find it necessary to write a tract denouncing the evil of long hair. And now this dislike had extended to music with the threat of an Act of Parliament to order the demolition of all church organs in the land.

The dismantling of the great organ of Salisbury Cathedral was a wise act of foresight on the part of the dean and chapter. When the Act was passed the next year, Salisbury's organ was already safely hidden away.

To Samuel this seemed a fine adventure. When they had inspected the organ, Nathaniel carried him back through the close and into the market place, pointing out St Thomas's Church as they went.

It was here, to his delight, that Nathaniel had discovered that the curate, John King, was a secret Royalist.

"If the news of the Royalist forces is good, he orders a psalm of rejoicing – if Parliament's won a battle, he calls for a psalm of penitence." He roared with laughter. "Why I go to church more than ever I did before," he cried, "just to see what psalm he'll light on next."

And though Samuel did not really understand all this, he laughed happily at his uncle's infectious good humour.

Just as they were leaving the city, they met their cousin young Charles Moody.

Perhaps because old Edward Shockley fifty years ago had warned his grandson William to be wary of them – though he would never be specific as to his reasons – the Shockleys seldom saw their Catholic Moody cousins. But recently Nathaniel's support of the king had opened communications between the two families. Occasionally now, one of them would ride over from Shaftesbury to discuss the military situation with him; and the most frequent visitor was young Charles Moody. He was a dark, intense boy of twenty who followed both Margaret and Nathaniel about so closely that, as Nathaniel joked, it was hard to tell if he hero-worshipped him, was in love with her, or both. "He wants to fight in the next campaign," he explained. "I've promised he shall ride at my side."

The party rode back to Avonsford together. Samuel liked his cousin Charles and frequently amused them by his demands to ride with him. "Another Cavalier!" they cried. And though he was very young, he always afterwards remembered the journey as well as the visit to the cathedral. It had been a perfect day.

Yet his sister only remembered the ending of that day with gloom. For it was only after Moody had left them, and Mary Godfrey had taken Samuel upstairs, that Nathaniel walked up the slope with Margaret on the edge of the high ground and there confided to her:

"I think our cause is lost."

"But the king is winning everywhere. Soon he will march on London, and Parliament is near to surrender. Or is it the Scots you fear?"

For there had been so many demands for a settlement with, or rather a surrender to the king that the leader of the opposition had even begun a new negotiation with the Scots, who were now demanding that their own Presbyterian rule should be made compulsory in England – to Obadiah Shockley's delight.

But Nathaniel shook his head.

"No. Parliament will court the Scots but never agree with them." He grinned. "Poor Obadiah. Our Parliament has grown used to ruling the church. In Scotland, it's the Presbyterian church which rules. The English Parliament can pretend what it pleases, but it will never submit to that. No," he explained, "the king and Parliament will not agree, nor will Parliament submit and see her leaders hanged. But as time passes, only Parliament can win."

"Why?"

"Firstly, our strategy is flawed. The king means to advance from the north and west upon London. But always in his rear he will have the ports and the cloth towns – Hull in the north, Plymouth and Gloucester in the west. He cannot advance safely, nor will London easily submit."

"But his army is better trained."

"So far, yes. But the Eastern Association is growing, and there is a new commander there, a cousin of Hampden's, a squire like ourselves called Cromwell. 'Ironsides' they call him. He is training a new force that will make Lord Essex's cohorts look like rabble. Fairfax in the north, too, is a skilful commander. Wait until these men take the field."

It was true that, up to date, the Parliamentary forces had, like the Royalists, been led almost entirely by aristocrats and gentlemen, some of them dedicated, some cynical, but very few trained in warfare. So far this had given the king an advantage.

"Perhaps the king will find larger forces to oppose them."

"He can't. No money." Nathaniel sighed. "A long war is always won by wealth, sister – and the trouble is, Parliament has the purse strings." He kicked a stone irritably. "Do you not know, every time the king's men buy provisions, even arms for their men, they pay duties on them. And the duties go to London where they are held by Parliament. All our taxes go to Parliament. We Royalists actually pay our own opponents, who besides, being merchants, have always more ready money than we have. 'Tis a phantasm, a ghostly thing, this victory of the king. Whatever appears today, will vanish tomorrow."

It was a dark insight. She looked at him thoughtfully.

He was silent for a little time. He seemed to be brooding about something else.

Finally he said:

"I had a dream." He paused. "About Edmund."

"You fought?"

He frowned.

"We met. Somewhere. Perhaps in battle, I cannot tell."

"What happened?"

"I cannot remember. I know only that we met. I suppose it must have been in battle. And then . . . I woke, unhappy."

She said nothing for a few moments.

"If you met in battle, what would you do?" She asked slowly.

He stopped and stared at the ground.

"I do not know." He sighed. "Each day I have prayed it may not happen."

"But you fear it will?"

He nodded. "I feel we shall meet."

They walked a little further. How melancholy he looked.

"But you still believe, don't you, in your cause?"

He stared at the ground moodily.

"Oh yes. Of course."

Then he kicked another stone.

1644: October

All that year in England, the balance of advantage swung from side to side.

At Sarum, the Royalists seemed to have triumphed. Local Parliamentary commanders – Hungerford, Baynton, Evelyn, either deserted, intrigued with the king, or were disgraced. Fifteen miles to the west, the gallant young Edmund Ludlow had finally had to give up the Arundel's Catholic stronghold of Wardour Castle and yield it back to the Royalists. The strongholds were nearly all held for Charles.

But away in the north of England, where the Royalists had been so strong, the fearsome new army of Cromwell and Fairfax, using Prince Rupert's cavalry methods but with their own iron discipline, together with the Presbyterian Scots had utterly crushed the Royalists at Marston Moor.

"We ran like rabbits in the end," Nathaniel ruefully told his sister afterwards. "Parliament has the north now, and it bodes ill for the king."

But in the south west, the Royalists were still strong. For although in June, Lord Essex and his Parliamentary army hurried through Sarum swearing boldly that they would crush the Royalists of the south west, only last month word came that Essex had capitulated in Cornwall.

There was constant movement.

To and fro across Wiltshire the various armies had gone: Parliamentary Ludlow and Waller, Royalist Goring.

Two days before, the king himself had clattered through the city's streets, leaving a strong force of artillery at the great house beside Clarendon Forest on the east side of Salisbury, and a large garrison at Wilton on the west. Margaret had heard he was coming, and curiously, made her way down to the city, taking little Samuel with her.

"See," she told him as the long cortège of horses went by, "right or wrong, there is the king." And although he was only four, Samuel always remembered the tired-looking man with the fine, oval face and long nose who rode thoughtfully down the high street.

Nathaniel was at Wilton.

But it was not Nathaniel she found at the farm on her return.

It was Edmund.

She had not seen him for nearly two years. He had changed so much that for a moment, she scarcely recognised him. His hair which, like most of the gentlemen, including Cromwell, in the Parliamentary forces, he wore long before, had now been cut to the short fringe that gave the Roundheads their name. It was not the haircut that struck her most though, but the fact that so much of his hair was gone. His face was haggard, his clothes worn almost threadbare.

But there was something else about him – a look in his eyes that she could not explain, but which troubled her.

"I need rest and food," he told her, then looked nervous. "Or are you Royalist now?"

"I am your sister," she replied, "But you must not be seen. Royalist troops are everywhere." And turning to little Samuel beside her, who was staring curiously at the stranger she told him: "Say nothing to anyone about your uncle. It's a secret." Then she put him in her own room upstairs and locked the door. He slept for fifteen hours.

"Lord Essex gave up," he told her bitterly, as they sat together in her room the next day. "We want no more aristocrats leading us now: we need Cromwell and his men."

How haggard he was. He seemed to be almost mumbling to himself, and again, she was conscious of some deeper alteration in him: it was as if, where her dear Nathaniel might secretly doubt the success of his cause, her older brother had begun to doubt himself.

Apparently reading her thoughts, he looked up sadly.

"I have changed," he said.

And then, in a voice sometimes weak from fatigue, sometimes strangely urgent, he told her something of what he had seen: of the rich nobles who fought only for profit, hoping to gain confiscated Royalist estates if they won; of the Presbyterians, like Obadiah, who wanted to substitute their own religious tyranny for that of the king.

"But I have seen better men than these – simple, godly men, who fight for a noble cause," he went on. "Better men, Margaret, than Obadiah: better men than I. True religious men who fight for freedom to worship as they please. These are the men who fight for Cromwell. And so shall I." He spoke with a new humility, born of mental suffering; she liked him better for it.

"You mean the Sectaries?"

"Call them what you will."

There were many such men in the army, she knew, and their voice was getting stronger: political and more often, religious radicals: men who believed they were fighting to establish a new order in England, led by tough, professionally-minded officers – Cromwell's 'plain men' – who might not be gentlemen but who knew their business, which most of the gentlemen in the Parliamentary Army had shown they did not. Their exact political aims were not yet clear; but they were increasingly powerful.

Margaret looked at him thoughtfully, wondering where this would lead.

"How long will you stay?" she asked.

"Until tomorrow."

The morning passed quietly. Only Mary Godfrey and a servant girl were in the house, and neither was aware of Edmund's presence.

During the afternoon he slept again.

It was in the late afternoon that the soldiers came. They were led by Nathaniel.

"We are searching the area for Roundheads," he told her cheerfully, as he stood in the hall. "Some were seen yesterday."

Margaret looked at him steadily.

"What will they do with them when they catch them?"

"Hang them, probably. But we haven't found any yet."

"I have seen none," she said. "But your men should search the barn and outhouses."

They did, thoroughly, for a quarter of an hour, and found nothing, while Nathaniel and his sister chatted quietly in the hall.

It was just as Nathaniel was turning to leave that little Samuel, coming down the stairs from his afternoon's sleep, and seeing Nathaniel's friendly face, ran forward with a happy cry and whispered as Nathaniel swept him up into his arms:

"Shall I tell you a secret?"

The two men stood opposite to each other in her bedchamber. Little Samuel, smiling with innocent pleasure, stood at Nathaniel's side.

She had been forced to unlock the door since Nathaniel had calmly offered to break it down if she did not.

A strange contrast they made: the younger brother in his handsome tunic edged with lace; the elder, who had hurriedly dressed, hoping to escape, seeming shrunken from his former state, in his plain brown jacket and the ugly Dutch breeches, like long shorts cut off abruptly at the knee, which many Puritans favoured. His grey woollen stockings, she noticed, were full of holes.

They looked at each other in silence. Then Nathaniel spoke.

"Well brother Edmund, they have cut thy hair in an abominable fashion."

Edmund tried to smile. His eyes looked hunted. Nathaniel turned to his sister.

"I remember, sister, that you told me, when some wished me to leave, that no brother of yours should be refused a place in this house."

"I did," she replied, "nor shall they."

"Very well."

And then, with that charming smile she knew so well, he turned back to Edmund.

"Forgive me if I do not stay to greet you, brother Edmund, but my men await me outside." His eyes twinkled. "We are looking for Parliament men."

He strode from the room.

Nathaniel. She loved him.

1645: January

But it was that winter little Samuel remembered best of all.

For that was when his sister Margaret, while both her fighting brothers were far away, put on armour, took up her sword and went into battle herself.

First, though, came his own dramatic part in the battle of the belfry.

The new city in the valley, unlike its predecessor on the hill, was never designed to be defended. Now, for the only time in its history, the military had actually made the city into a temporary fortress. Or rather, since there was no other area with an existing wall around it, the Royalists had tried to fortify the cathedral close. It had not worked. In a small skirmish near Christmas, a contingent of Ludlow's Roundheads had easily fired the gates and taken the tiny garrison prisoner. Now they held it, using the high belfry as a watch tower.

It was generally expected that the Royalists would return, but no one knew when.

It was foolish of Margaret to go into the city that day; but without Nathaniel for company, she had grown tired of the farmhouse and decided to seek a change of air.

It was a crisp, cold day and she and Samuel had taken the cart into Salisbury. She had made a few purchases and stopped to talk to one or two acquaintances in the market place, while the little boy watched her with increasing boredom. There was an air of lassitude about the town that day. Finally, thinking to amuse him, she led him down the High Street towards the cathedral close. The gate of the close was open. By the belfry, she knew, there would be half a dozen soldiers lounging about, and the sight of armed men never failed to interest him.

It was as she expected. Three soldiers were leaning against the wall of the belfry near the door and they gave Samuel a friendly nod as he came by. They were big men, with leather doublets and one of them wore huge leather riding boots; none had their armour on and only the booted soldier was carrying a sword.

Margaret and Samuel made a slow tour of the choristers' green. As it was now early evening, and the cold damp was beginning to make them shiver, they turned back towards the gate to go home.

It was just as they did so that suddenly, ahead of them, pandemonium broke loose.

To shouts from the gateway, a large figure on a horse burst into the close and rode to the belfry before reining, staring at its upper storeys and bellowing:

"Fools! Did I not tell you to keep watch?"

His voice echoed round the close and Margaret identified him immediately as the gallant young commander, Edmund Ludlow.

Seeing Margaret and the child approaching the gate, he now impatiently waved them back.

"Away from the gate," he cried, "the Cavaliers are coming. They're coming into the market place."

They were indeed. A large party had moved down unannounced from Amesbury that day and already the advance guard had approached down Castle Street. The men in the belfry whose job it was to keep watch, had failed to do so.

Now all was activity. Men were running in and out of the belfry pulling on steel breastplates and helmets. Figures suddenly appeared high on the upper storeys of the tower where they should have been before, while all around people came out of their houses and, taking little notice of Ludlow's irritated commands, formed a little crowd near the gate staring up the High Street.

So far there was nothing to be seen.

Margaret wondered what she should do. Alone, she might have been tempted to leave the close quickly by St Ann's Gate and see if she could work her way out of the city. But glancing down at the five-year-old child at her side, she dismissed the idea – she could not risk his getting caught in crossfire in Salisbury's streets.

But she could not stand outside in the cold either. They must take shelter for a while, preferably in a house as far away from the belfry as possible. She glanced about at the people in the street to see if there was a face she knew.

Ludlow had quickly gathered a small force of ten men whom he sent hurrying up the High Street. Now he was collecting more. It looked to Margaret like only a couple of dozen men, but they were preparing at any moment to march out of the close behind him. She heard someone say that here were reinforcements on Harnham Hill nearby.

Meanwhile, the little knot of people by the gate had grown larger. Many of them were good-humouredly laughing as they waited to see the soldiers leave. From the town there was still neither sight nor sound of the Cavaliers. Evidently the people of the close refused to take Ludlow and his little force very seriously.

It was just then that Margaret saw what she was looking for in the crowd – an elderly woman she knew slightly who had a small house on the east side of the close, between St Ann's Gate and the bishop's palace. That would be as safe as anywhere, she judged and taking Samuel by the hand, she moved quickly towards her.

Fortunately, the woman was glad to see her. She not only agreed but seemed pleased at the prospect of company. She was even garrulous.

Margaret was relieved: so far so good.

When he was five there was no more exciting sight in the world for Samuel Shockley than a group of fully armed soldiers. He was so delighted by this new turn of events that he even forgot the cold. Ludlow's troop had gathered itself into some kind of order, and since Margaret had now solved the problem of their immediate safety, she good-naturedly let go his hand and let him move a few feet to where he could get a better view of the proceedings.

Even so, he found that he could only see the commander himself and his horse because of the thickening crowd in front of him.

The people were kindly however, and happily it was not long before several hands helped him through to the front. How magnificent the soldiers were – every item of their dress seemed full of mystery. The huge boots that reached halfway up the thigh, the great heavy gloves with their wrist guards, the long swords, the breastplates glowing dully in the fading light, the steel helmets with their face guards. As he looked up at these huge forms they seemed to the boy like so many trees. What power they all had. Surely, when such mighty figures marched, nothing could withstand them.

They began to move. His heart thrilled with excitement. He watched them with fascination and with longing.

It was as the troops passed under the gateway into the High Street that two ten-year-old boys beside him moved out and began to follow them.

No one tried to stop them; after all, the street ahead was empty. Nor, when the excited little boy a second later began to dog their footsteps, did anyone take particular notice: they assumed the little fellow must belong to them. So it was that quite unknown to Margaret, as the dusk fell Samuel left the close with Ludlow and his men.

Fifty yards up the High Street the two boys turned into a house. Samuel, well contented that he was marching with the soldiers, continued on his way.

To right and left people were pulling the shutters tight and barring their doors. No one had time to concern themselves with the curious little figure in his solitary march up the echoing street.

The High Street was not long; at the top of it the soldiers turned right towards the Poultry Cross and the entrance to the market place.

Soon Samuel too was nearly at the Poultry Cross.

The plan of Edmund Ludlow was daring. Although he did not know the numbers of Royalist troops advancing, he guessed that they must be considerable. His own total contingent in the city numbered only sixty. His only hope therefore of halting the Royalist advance was by a brilliant bluff. Leading a handful of men, he intended to make a spirited charge into the market place against the enemy's vanguard, while a trumpeter stationed by the Poultry Cross would by his bugle calls give the wholly erroneous impression that a much larger body of Roundhead troops were following close behind.

Shots were being fired ahead. There were almost three hundred Cavaliers forming a line in the market place. But with his thirty men gathered in the alley by the Poultry Cross, Ludlow gave the order and they charged. By the Poultry Cross, the bugler sounded wildly.

Nobody thought of looking behind them, where they might have seen a little figure lurking in the shadows.

Samuel stared. They had left him behind. Not understanding what was happening, the little boy followed after them.

How big the market place seemed. He could see the men running ahead of him and his legs struggled to catch up with them. He waved his arms excitedly. The line of Cavaliers in front of him held no terror.

Then the two groups clashed, and he stopped in astonishment. It was not what he had expected.

For a short time, Edmund Ludlow's plan worked. The Royalists saw the eager troops issuing from the broad alleyway in front of the Poultry Cross, led by young Ludlow himself on his splendid horse. It never occurred to them that he only had thirty men. Taken by surprise, they scattered and were driven across the open space. In the gathering darkness and confusion, nobody noticed the small figure standing hesitantly in the middle of the market place.

Men were running everywhere. Ludlow himself had taken out his sword and was locked in hand to hand combat with a Royalist officer. Their two horses wheeled and clattered not fifty yards from where the child was standing. On his left, Samuel saw a group of three foot soldiers engaged in what seemed like a crazy dance. They were shouting. He heard the crash of steel, then saw one of them fall. There was a huge red gash in his side from which blood was pumping. The two Roundheads who had struck him turned and ran past him to their next quarry.

The excitement he had felt vanished. Suddenly the huge heavy figures seemed very threatening, and they seemed to be on every side.

So this was fighting. He did not like it at all.

Suddenly, he thought of Margaret. Where was she? He wished she were here to protect him. Although men were fighting behind him now, he turned to run back past them.

It was just as he was turning that the Royalist colonel whom Edmund Ludlow was fighting tried to make a dash for it across the market place to Castle Street. Ludlow did not mean to let him go. Wheeling about, he kept at his side, heading him off towards the centre. Locked together, the two riders raced over the ground.

They were bearing down upon him. Both men's faces were set, concentrating only on each other. Neither saw, in the failing light, that there was a small figure standing helplessly directly in their path.

How huge the horses seemed. They were almost upon him, but he was so petrified he could not move. He closed his eyes.

It was the Cavalier who saw him. Frantically he jerked the reins, swerved and almost turned his horse completely into Ludlow's. There was a confused crash of hooves as the two horses collided. They were so close to the child that he was conscious of their smell and one of the horse's tails whisked across his face.

The manoeuvre was so sudden that Ludlow was caught completely by surprise. As the Cavalier wheeled away, his own horse slipped and fell and he was thrown to the ground.

Ludlow never saw the child. Half-dazed himself, and intent on his prey, he seized his horse's bridle almost as soon as it had struggled up and swung himself into the saddle, wheeling the animal about. He had picked up his sword in his right hand. As he turned, he swept it low in a great arc, and did not know there was a child in its path. Indeed, so intent was he on his pursuit that he never noticed the end of the blade had encountered human flesh or that the little fair-haired figure below him had crumpled on the ground. A few minutes later, in Endless Street, he succeeded in taking the Cavalier colonel captive.

In the close Edmund Ludlow was in a hurry. The prisoners, including Colonel Middleton whom he had just taken in single combat, were being pushed into the belfry. It could not be long before the Royalists regrouped and advanced again.

Twelve more of his men had arrived from Harnham Hill. He could only hope that, in the darkness, he could now make them look like fifty.

It was tiresome about the woman and child. A fine, handsome woman too. She had been frantic, pestering the men even as they rushed their prisoners through the gate.

"No, ma'am," he cried, "I have seen no child."

But his prisoner had.

"In the market place," Colonel Middleton had called, "A fair-haired child." He had grimaced. "I fear he was struck down," he said.

Now the woman wanted to go out and look for it. He had to forbid that. The Cavaliers would be there at any moment.

It was silent in the market place.

Samuel Shockley lay near the centre. There was a shallow wound on the top of his head where Ludlow's sword had grazed it and he could feel something warm and sticky dripping from the place. Fifty feet away, two large bodies lay very still.

He was too shocked to cry.

He got up slowly. From Castle Street he could hear sounds, but the market place was deserted. Where had everybody gone?

The sounds were coming closer. He must get away. The alley that led to the Poultry Cross was dark, but he feared the shadows less than the approaching sounds. He stumbled towards it.

Inside him, for the first time in his life, a small voice warned: there is no one to save you.

He reached the Poultry Cross just as the Royalists re-entered the market place from Castle Street. Suddenly he noticed that he was shivering violently.

The Poultry Cross was a small six-sided structure, each side consisting of an open gothic arch. It was roofed over and had a low wall around it. It seemed a good place to hide. Yet as he saw the troops massing in the market place, and guessed they might approach his way, he realised that he was still exposed. Gingerly, he began to move.

There was a faint light upon the Poultry Cross from a nearby upper window and by it, a trooper in the market place could see that a figure was moving there. No doubt it was the Roundheads again. Calling to those nearest him, he went down on one knee and a moment later, four muskets were pointing at the place. Peeping over the wall, Samuel found himself looking straight at them.

He understood now. They meant to kill him. In a few moments, he realised, they would come closer. He stood up to run.

In doing so, he saved his life. For only as he stood could the trooper see in the pale light that it was a child. The trooper shouted, only one of the four muskets was discharged and that was aimed high.

Samuel heard the shot as he ran and wondered if he were dead.

It was Margaret who saw him when he was two thirds of the way down the High Street. He was moving slowly, a picture of dejection and terror. For some reason he had moved from the shadows at the side of the street into the middle, beside the water channel. His little round face was staring hopelessly towards the gate.

At the other end of the street behind him, the advance guard of the Royalist force had just appeared.

She called to him.

Across the gate in front of her a line of Roundhead troopers was

[683]

forming, nearly blocking her view. Samuel did not seem to have heard her.

"Let me through."

The troopers with their back to her maintained a solid wall. She looked for an officer. Ludlow was at the belfry.

"Let me pass."

She began to manhandle them. They cursed her. She could see the Royalists preparing to charge.

"Samuel!"

This time he heard her. He stared at the gate, but hesitated, looking from Royalists to Roundheads and back again. It was as though, in his shock, the child had become suddenly listless.

The muskets were pointing down the street in his direction. It seemed clear to Samuel that all the soldiers meant to kill him, and he could no longer tell the difference between them.

Miserably he gazed from one to the other. The water channel was just below him.

"Jump into the water!" she cried.

He heard her and understood. He glanced again at the troops advancing down the street; they were breaking into a run. The freezing water below looked uninviting. He did not move. He was going to die, he thought.

She screamed at him. Why did he still hesitate?

And still nothing happened. The musketeers were taking aim at the Royalists.

How she broke through them she would never know. She heard curses, was vaguely aware that a musket had clattered to the ground and that she had trodden on a man's back. Then she was running, frantically, nearly falling, and at last, just as the first shots rang out, throwing herself at the child and falling with him into the icy water.

Samuel Shockley remembered little of the rest of that night.

He did not remember that as soon as the troops had passed, Margaret had clambered out of the water channel and then struck him once, with the palm of her big hand, not in anger but because, at that instant, she could find no other way to give expression to her relief. He vaguely remembered being carried round to St Ann's Gate, but he slept through the battle of the belfry.

Apart from some early and spirited charges by Edmund Ludlow, the battle was really a siege, while the several hundred Royalists surrounded the high belfry tower and waited. Since the light would show the enemy how pitifully few his forces really were, Ludlow quietly withdrew through the southern gate of the close just before dawn, and then went up Harnham Hill to watch events.

An hour after dawn, Samuel did awake. And so it was that through the upstairs window of the little house where they were sheltering, he saw the Royalists commandeer the cart of a passing collier and use his load of charcoal to burn down the belfry's studded door.

The battle of the belfry was over.

But it was later that morning, when the little cart containing Samuel and his sister arrived back at the farmhouse that Margaret Shockley's battle began. For she was met by a long-faced Jacob and Mary Godfrey at the door.

"I did what I could," Jacob explained, "but there were two dozen of them."

The house was in a shambles. The Royalist troops on their way down the valley from Amesbury, had passed several farms; in each, they had swept through like a plague of locusts. Food stores, clothes, blankets, silver, even the pewter plates in the kitchen; they had cleaned out everything, cheerfully but firmly holding Godfrey and his wife at sword-point while they did so. Samuel followed Margaret round while Godfrey dejectedly led her from room to room. She had heard stories of looting before, especially of the troops under Royalist Goring, but as she saw the extent of the damage, she began to shake with rage. And when she had seen all, she stood in the hall, and smashed her hand down on the oak table.

"Never again," she cried. Looking sternly at Godfrey, she commanded, "Bring all the farm hands at the front door at dawn tomorrow. Tell them to bring whatever weapons they have. We are going to fight."

Godfrey looked uncertain.

"We?"

"Yes. We are going to fight against the war. I shall lead them."

The events of the previous day had decided her. Up to now, to hold the family together, she had been neutral, trying not even to consider which cause was the more just.

Now she no longer cared. They had nearly destroyed her child. They had attacked the farm.

"I am at war," she announced, "with all soldiers."

Rather to her own surprise, by the end of the next day, she had collected men from two other local farms to add to her little band, swelling her numbers to ten. Three more men appeared from the Forest estate. Forest himself was in the west, though whether he had joined the Royalist or Parliamentary side no one seemed to know. "Which is just what he wants," Margaret remarked. But his deserted estate workers were glad to find a leader. And by the next morning a force of fifteen appeared.

They were not impressively armed; but soon she had organised each man with either a musket, a sword or a pike. Margaret herself, wearing a breastplate that had belonged to her father and wielding a large, heavy sword, her hair scooped up and stuffed into a tall steel helmet looked the most impressive of them all.

She drilled the little group, made them stand, charge, and push their pikes together; then she told them:

"I care not which army they be, no soldiers shall enter our farms."

Samuel was allowed to watch. How splendid his tall sister was: and just how effective the little group was was proved two days later when a dozen soldiers, more than a little drunk, came to the gates of the property and found their way barred. When they tried to push their way in, the farm hands suddenly drew weapons and charged them. To their astonishment the soldiers found themselves in hand to hand fighting – and losing.

The leader of the farm hands was a handsome young fellow in an old-fashioned helmet, who gave such sword blows that two of them were driven back.

It was only when a chance blow knocked her helmet off, and Margaret's cascade of golden hair fell down that one of the soldiers cried:

"God's blood, 'tis a woman."

"Whose side are you on, Amazon?" another cried with a laugh.

"We are against plundering soldiers," she answered.

And not caring to fight a woman, the surprised soldiers withdrew.

Samuel saw it all, looking over the fields from the top of the house.

The news of Margaret Shockley's fight was all over the valley in hours. By the next day, it was the talk of the five rivers, and soon she heard of others who were following her example.

"If a woman can do it," the farmers in the five valleys said, "so can we."

In fact, Margaret soon discovered her little skirmish in the Avon valley had been part of a much wider movement that was growing independently all over central Wessex.

"The people of Sarum don't like being disturbed," she remarked to Godfrey. "Other defence bands will spring up like mushrooms."

They did. Later in the year, led by a Wessex gentleman, Sir Anthony Ashley Cooper, they formed an association several hundred strong at Sarum alone. The Clubmen of Wiltshire, as they called themselves, were in action for about a year. They were formidable. They wore white ribands in their hats and took as their motto 'truth and peace'.

"By which we mean – don't touch our property," Margaret stated flatly.

She marched with them on every occasion.

1645: June

How determined their battle looked.

It was drawn up in the traditional manner – foot in the centre, horse on the wings. In the centre were the regiments of Waller, Pickering, Pride and other noted commanders; further across, Ireton's wing and past them a party of dragoons; opposite, the most powerful force of all, the massed regiments of iron cavalry, seven great bodies of horse, under Lieutenant-General Cromwell. And last, in front of the whole, in the centre, the brave body of advance troops jokingly called the forlorn hope. This was the new model army commanded by Fairfax.

Between them, Broadmoor Farm, surrounded by hedges and ditches. Behind the Roundheads, two more farms and a way off to the south west, the little town of Naseby. The summer morning was growing warm.

For months the king had led the Roundheads a pretty dance, darting from Royalist Oxford to the north west and back again while they relentlessly followed him. Now, in the very centre of midland England, the combined armies had come up with each other in full battle array.

Nathaniel rode with the northern horse that day, on the left flank. The whole army had moved forward from its chosen position because the impetuous Prince Rupert when reconnoitring had caught sight of the Roundhead cavalry and, refusing to believe they would stand and fight, had urged the whole Royalist army forward. Their position was less favourable now; the enemy had not budged; but the Roundheads were still outnumbered.

He glanced to his left. Beside him, on a piebald, was young Charles Moody. He had kept the boy beside him, as he had promised.

His dark eyes were shining; he was eager for battle, convinced that the king's cause was sacred, and just, and that the rightful Roman Church would still be brought back to England. A brave boy, unskilled in battle.

"Stay close to me," he said calmly.

He wondered if Edmund was in the army opposite.

How splendid the Royalists looked as they advanced. Despite himself, Edmund Shockley could not help admiring them: the serried ranks of foot in the centre with Prince Rupert's Bluecoats behind them; the splendid cavalry of the northern horse on one wing and Rupert's Life Guards on the other. Noble regiments all. Now they were in position. Because of the ground he could not see most of the infantry now, but he could make out the lines of cavalry and, on a hillock in the background, he could just see the royal standard fluttering where the king himself was watching.

Oh, but the men around him – they were men of God. And the officers too. Since the all-important Self Denying Ordinance had passed through Parliament, the new model army had been rid of the time-servers, the lords and rich gentlemen who had led so badly; most officers were still gentlemen, to be sure: but dedicated to the cause and not too proud to welcome others, like the redoutable Colonel Pride, who was the son of a lowly drayman. There were independents, too, men who had refused to take the Presbyterian Covenant but who worshipped in their own sturdily independent ways and who despised the cynical men in Parliament who paid – or promised to pay – the army.

They were disciplined. They fought for a cause. And each day he felt more privileged to be with them.

It was ten o'clock. And now there was a movement, from the enemy's right. Prince Rupert was thundering forward.

He whispered the army's battle cry to himself: "God our strength". Outnumbered, they would need God's help that day.

The battle of Naseby was closely fought. Although the Royalist army, because of Prince Rupert's original advance, was not properly supported by cannon, his dashing attack on the enemy's flank seemed about to carry the whole day. If the other Royalist wing could have matched it . . . But opposite them lay Cromwell.

[687]

For while Rupert pursued the broken left, Cromwell's mighty right moved forward, and though part of their advance was slowed by the treacherous ground of a rabbit warren, they were unstoppable. The Royalists fought well, but by the time Rupert turned from his work, he found the army of Fairfax still holding firmly and the army of Charles in disarray. He raced back to regroup. But the king was leaving the field.

It was in Cromwell's first charge that Nathaniel found himself driven off towards the centre. Ten minutes later both he and young Moody found themselves unhorsed and faced with a line of approaching infantry. The battle continued around them furiously.

"God our strength." It seemed to Edmund that there was dust everywhere. Dust covered the men, the horses; dust on every helmet so that they did not flash in the sun but glowed in an orange haze; dust on the colours they proudly carried; dust on his sword. Dust and blood. The smell of powder. The crash of steel and muskets behind him. No one fired a musket here, at close quarters. You seized the barrel and swung it like a club.

Half a dozen Royalists were in front of him in a whirling mêlée. He went towards them.

The nearest had his back turned: a Roundhead, one of God's soldiers, had fallen in front of him. With a rush Edmund came up to the Royalist, his sword and his arm pointed in a dead straight line at the kidney; the perfect attack from the rear: he thrust, deep, felt the blade burst through the leather and pass through, all the way through. The man sank. Quickly, his boot was on the man's side, dragging the long strong blade out again as the flesh gripped upon it.

Nathaniel, the colour draining from him, looked up at his brother, and recognised him.

Edmund saw nothing but his face. He did not see the Royalists close by; he did not see them falling back; was not aware of his own companions driving them before their pikes.

He did not pause to see him die, nor to speak a word, nor even look at him. "God our strength," someone was shouting. He strode away, his sword useless in his hand, and in a daze made his way, he did not know where or how, through the battle.

1646: June

She was glad to have Edmund home. After the death of Nathaniel at Naseby, she had felt a terrible emptiness and in part he filled it.

It was a relief, too, to have his quiet presence there when her strident brother Obadiah came on one of his occasional visits from London. At such times he protected her, and she almost felt that he and she made a team as she and Nathaniel had done before.

Edmund had changed. There was a new gentleness about him. Every day, hand in hand, he would walk out with young Samuel; sometimes he would spend hours quietly playing with the boy on the grassy bank beside the house.

Edmund's presence seemed also to underline that a new era had begun.

For the war had been effectively won at Naseby. It was not only a military victory over the king: in his hurried departure Charles had left not only baggage but caskets of correspondence, which proved beyond a doubt that even then, he was secretly negotiating to bring a Catholic army from overseas to subdue the island. It was just what Parliament needed. The letters were published at once. And thanks to this Charles Stuart lost the equally important battle for his subjects' minds. For if there had been waverers there could be no doubt in any Protestant Englishman's mind now: treacherous, papist Charles Stuart and his rule must be crushed.

In the months that followed Naseby, Parliamentary troops had taken siege train and cannon from one Royalist stronghold to another in a long mopping-up operation that destroyed many a fine Royalist house. The royal garrison near Clarendon had fallen the previous October, when Cromwell himself had come through Salisbury. In April that year, Lord Pembroke kept the king's daughter, Princess Henrietta, at Wilton while Fairfax prepared to take Charles's last stronghold at Oxford. Now Oxford had fallen and the king fled.

Everywhere the triumphant party was taking authority. In Salisbury a good Parliament man, Dove, friend of Ivie, sat as Member instead of Robert Hyde. Ludlow the commander now sat as a Member for the shire. Even Sir Henry Forest firmly declared himself for Parliament: "So 'tis certain we have won," Edmund Shockley remarked to his sister wryly.

Sarum had been quiet. Though a huge force of ten thousand clubmen had met the Roundhead army near Shaftesbury the previous year, Cromwell's troops had been well-disciplined and there was no looting. Now Margaret hoped she could look forward to better times.

Strangely, despite the victory of his cause, Edmund was pessimistic. It seemed the war had brought him nothing but sadness, and though he was always so pleasant with her and the child, if she came upon him suddenly when he was alone she would often see a haunted look in his eye, as though some deep anguish troubled him.

Sometimes, after he had been sitting for hours alone, lost to the world, she would hear him mutter:

"For what have we fought?"

Occasionally he had nightmares too. Once in the middle of the night she heard him cry out in his sleep: "Nathaniel!"

But she did not understand the depth of his agony: for she knew nothing of the terrible secret of Naseby.

From time to time Obadiah would come down from London. He seemed less uneasy with himself than he had ever been before. The Presbyterians were stronger every day: their stern Puritan church, with its councils and elders, was a mighty force in the land now. Not only was Obadiah's party in the ascendant, but away from his family he had made a name for himself and won respect. Whatever his faults, Edmund occasionally reminded his sister, Obadiah was a good scholar.

It was on a visit of Obadiah's early in 1646 that Margaret caught a glimpse of the doubt troubling Edmund's mind, when the two brothers had discussed the political situation.

There was much to discuss. For now that the king was almost defeated, what should be done next? Was Parliament to rule without him, or was the king to be returned under strict conditions? And in either case, what sort of rule should England now have?

Obadiah had no doubt.

"Parliament will rule now, with or without the king. And England will be Presbyterian."

Obadiah had been in London for most of the war, preaching and acting as tutor to the children of a number of prominent Parliament men. Edmund knew very well that the uncompromising attitude he expressed exactly reflected the views of many Members of the Parliament now in power.

"But not all those against the king's tyranny are Presbyterian," he reminded his brother. There were Anglicans, Baptists, many Sectaries.

"They must be crushed, like the Catholics," Obadiah replied. "There shall be one religion in England and Scotland now."

Had not the troubles of the past been due to the failure of England to achieve a single unified religion? So Obadiah thought.

"Your rule will be strict."

"Yes."

"And the army?" He thought of the men he had fought with: not Presbyters but lovers of religious freedom.

"The army will be disbanded as soon as its work is done."

"And paid? Some of our cavalry have not been paid by your parliament for forty weeks," he reminded Obadiah.

"They will be paid as far as is possible," Obadiah replied.

"Then," the question he had so often asked himself recently, "what have we fought for?"

"For the rule of a Presbyterian parliament, the abolition of all bishops, the destruction of the Anglican Church, and the extirpation of the papists."

"That is freedom?"

"Yes."

"And who shall elect this Presbyterian parliament?"

"Those who do so now."

Edmund pursed his lips.

"Those who fought," he reminded Obadiah, "want more than that."

The Model Army had provided more than an efficient fighting force; with its new cadre of junior officers and independent-minded men, it had become the focus for radical thought. The stout yeomen and artisans Edmund had come to know and respect were speaking of new freedoms: not only freedom to worship, but for free men to elect their representatives to Parliament.

"They say that every man who owns a household should vote,"

Edmund stated. "There are a few who even say all men should vote."

"Servants too?" Obadiah's face clouded. He knew all about these radicals – Levellers they called themselves. They had stated their obnoxious views for decades, but no one took any notice of them. If the army was breeding such ideas, the sooner it was disbanded the better.

"And you, Edmund, do you condone these Levellers?"

Edmund considered.

"To give the vote to every man," he said, "cannot be right. But if a man has an interest in his country – in the land or in a corporation – then I cannot see the harm in it. Indeed," he concluded, "I think it should be a natural right."

Was it possible that Edmund, head of the Shockley household, was expressing such views?

"This will lead to nothing but an heretical democracy, a monster, chaos," Obadiah cried. "If that were the result of our battle, why then I'd sooner have fought for the king," he exploded.

"And there are those in Parliament who would still prefer the king to the rule of free men," Edmund replied with shrewdness.

"You have changed," Obadiah said bitterly.

"It is true," Edmund admitted. "But it seems to me that we have fought a war against the tyranny of the king, only to replace it with another of Presbyters."

Obadiah came to Sarum less after that.

It was not until he was a man that anyone explained to Samuel what had really happened on that warm June day a week after Obadiah had left.

He remembered only seeing a mud-spattered figure ride up to the house and that he had run outside and across the field to where Edmund was speaking to Jacob Godfrey. He remembered eagerly leading Edmund by the hand to see who the visitor was. And he remembered their entering the hall.

Charles Moody had ridden straight from Oxford. Ever since Naseby he had faithfully followed the king, but now the cause was lost, he was returning home.

"I could not go to my own house without first coming here," he explained.

He had come to pay his respects to Nathaniel's family. And he had brought Nathaniel's sword.

He had been carrying it reverently for a year, and now at last, he laid it on the table in front of her, together with a lock of Nathaniel's hair.

Having done this important duty, he stepped back.

"Forgive me," he went on, "but after Naseby, I could not write." And he seemed to swallow.

Margaret smiled. She understood. He looked so tired, so pale. There were lines of hurt around his eyes. It was sad to see how the war had marked its young men.

It was strange; she had almost forgotten Nathaniel that day. It was a deliberate act of forgetting, to lessen her pain, but now, seeing young

Charles who had ridden away with him the year before, it was as if Nathaniel were back in the room with her. She smelled his pipe, heard his laugh.

What was young Moody speaking of? His condolences, of course. She nodded absently and thanked him.

"I was with him, you know," he said softly.

With him. At the moment. Suddenly that moment seemed so near, so vivid.

"Was it . . . did he suffer?" She felt she should not ask, but suddenly had to know.

"It was quick, thank God." He paused, then resting his hand on her arm: "But that it should have been Edmund who . . ."

What was he saying? She stared at him, trying to make sense of his words. It was Edmund who. . . ?

"Edmund?"

My God. She did not know. Why had he assumed. . . ? Had Edmund never. . . ?

Thirty seconds later, as Samuel happily led Edmund into the room he stared in astonishment at his sister, white as he had never seen her before, and at the young man in his filthy leather doublet who turned, eyes blazing with scorn and shouted at Edmund, "Murderer!" before storming out of the house.

She was still shaking an hour later as she strode along the edge of the river above the valley.

Several times she had stopped, staring blankly across the ridges that lay on her right, empty and baked in the June sun. The blue summer sky seemed harsh. The ground was hard and dry.

No, she could not go back. She did not know what to do. Each time she walked on.

It was half an hour more before she finally halted. On her left there was the beech wood that belonged to Sir Henry Forest. Ahead of her was a small mound: a curious place, once a rabbit warren, with a circle of old yew trees around its top. Suddenly feeling the need to be surrounded by something, she pushed her way through the circle of trees.

It was a quiet spot: no one came there nowadays. Inside the circle of yews was an open space, overgrown with weeds and a few small shrubs. She inspected it. There seemed to be a faint pattern on the ground, incised in the chalky soil, as though someone had made little furrows in the turf, but it was hard to be sure. The circle of trees made a green shade. She sat on the ground with her head in her hands.

Nathaniel.

She stayed there some time, turning the events of the last few years over in her mind, and it was not for a long time, until her grief and anger had run a full course, that she understood at last that there was a greater pain even than hers, and saw what she must do.

Edmund was sitting alone outside on a small stone bench near the house when she returned. He was leaning forward, very still, his shoulders hunched; in his hands he was holding one of Nathaniel's long clay pipes. He was staring at the little stamped sign of the gauntlet under the bowl.

He did not move as she approached, did not look at her.

Yes. As she looked at his silent misery, she knew what she must do.

Quietly, she put her arms around his stooped shoulders.

"You poor man."

And then at last, after waiting for over a year, Edmund Shockley broke down and wept.

1653: December

It was when he was thirteen that Samuel began to understand that Obadiah was his friend – and that he was not only his friend, but that he was also wise. For unlike Margaret, Obadiah was a man of learning.

And sometimes now, though he was no less fond of her, he started to treat some of Margaret's opinions with a smile.

On the subject of Margaret, however, as on all subjects, Obadiah was firm.

"You must honour your sister Margaret as you would your mother," he declared. And Samuel never heard the preacher say a word against her in those days; despite the fact that Margaret, when he was alone with her at the farm would often cry:

"Beware of Obadiah, Samuel. He is a viper."

She could not be right. On his visits to them at the farm, who could have been more kindly than Obadiah towards him? Was it not Obadiah who had honoured him, that very January, by giving him a little leather-bound copy of the great John Milton's pamphlet on the Reformation?

"Read it carefully," Obadiah had enjoined in his serious way: "for none has explained better than Milton why the prelates and the papist superstitions needed to be done away with."

He had even heard Obadiah remark to a gentleman in the close that young Samuel had the mind of a scholar – which, considering his very modest attainments with the pen, was unhoped-for praise indeed.

As for Obadiah being a devil, no one in Sarum other than Margaret seemed to say so. For Obadiah Shockley was reckoned a great man by then; and what could anyone have to fear from him?

The world was a better place for Obadiah now. For Presbyterians ruled.

The king was dead – executed after intriguing too many times. Two Wiltshire men, including Edmund Ludlow, had signed the death warrant. Now the Protector, Cromwell, ruled over a Presbyterian Parliament instead.

It was firm rule – when young Ludlow opposed Cromwell's dictatorship he was told to stay at his post in Ireland or face arrest if he came back. As for Parliament, this was the Barebones Parliament – a small number of compliant men nominated by the Presbyterian congregations. The three Wiltshire men – Eyre, Ashley Cooper and Greene – were all sound, conservative fellows, to Obadiah's liking.

And no place seemed more utterly Presbyterian than Sarum.

For the cathedral priests had gone: the whole panoply of ecclesiastical dignitaries that had ruled the diocese of Sarum for six centuries – bishop, dean, archdeacons, canons with their accompanying vicars choral and choristers – Parliament had removed them all. It had taken most of their lands as well, and those solid Puritan townsmen, Ivie and Dove had gone to London to obtain some of these possessions for the town. The town council ruled the close now; they had opened it up.

It was the parish priests and preachers who ruled – men like Strickland of St Edmunds and his colleagues at St Thomas's and St Martin's – all staunch members of the Presbyterian Westminster Assembly. They preached from pulpits that had been moved, in the Presbyterian manner, to the centre of the church. They preached in the cathedral too.

"'Tis just what every church should be now, a parish church for preaching," Obadiah explained to Samuel and Margaret. And when Margaret objected that the great building seemed to her to be something more than a mere local church, he replied impatiently: "Only the papists in the past made the thing so monstrously large."

The building had not gained from the change in regime. That very year, the tower of St Edmund's church had collapsed; and although the belfry door had been renewed, other damage done by the soldiers in the chapter house had not. Even that was not all. When, to defend England's trading interests against constant and arrogant Dutch competition, Cromwell had been forced to fight a brief war with the Netherlands too, a party of Dutch prisoners had been casually left, this very year, in the cloisters for weeks. "And a fine havoc they have made in there as well," Margaret said with disgust. Part of the close was a rubbish dump; in another area, butchers had set up a little abattoir and were selling their meat there too. The bishop's palace was made into tenements, and partly used as an inn; coaches had been allowed through on the north east and western sides and had churned up the turf and broken gravestones in the churchyard.

But if the buildings had not gained, the local vicars had. For now, instead of their lowly lodgings in the town, the council had bought them fine houses in the close where they lived with all the dignity of the canons they had ousted.

Obadiah had a house in the close. He lived in sober state.

He did not go often to the farm, but he let Samuel know that he was always welcome at the handsome house in the close and Samuel was proud that his brother was such an important man in the city. The preacher took a genuine interest in the boy, too, because he saw that he had a quick intelligence.

Besides, as he quietly but remorselessly reminded Margaret, it was he, Obadiah, who was in practice head of the family now. It was something Margaret could not deny.

If only Edmund had been there.

But Edmund had gone.

Samuel always remembered him as a quiet, gentle figure.

After the visit of young Moody, and his strange outburst, Samuel could sense that some kind of watershed had been passed. There was a new closeness between Margaret and Edmund and a feeling of peace and family affection came over the whole household. It was Edmund who acted as his first tutor, teaching him to read and write and parse a little Latin.

Yet there was also, after a little time, a sense of withdrawal. Edmund was still head of the family, but he seemed content to leave the running of the farm to Margaret and Jacob Godfrey. He grew a little thinner each year. Samuel remembered him mostly sitting or walking alone, not unhappily, but thoughtfully, as if some great debate were occupying his mind.

Then, in the spring of 1649, just after King Charles was executed, he left.

It was over a year before Samuel saw him again. Whenever he asked his sister where Edmund was, she had answered only: "Near London;" and if he asked when he would return she would only say: "I do not know."

Edmund did not return, but one spring they visited him.

It was a long journey, almost to London; but when at last their little carriage bumped up St George's Hill, Samuel found to his surprise that their destination was an extensive farm, not unlike those he knew at Sarum. And his surprise was greater still when, staring at a group of roughly dressed labourers trudging up the slope towards the house, he saw Edmund amongst them.

"Why does he work with the labourers?" he asked in surprise.

"Because he chooses to," Margaret answered. And then she explained: "Your brother Edmund has become a Digger."

A Digger: he had not met the term before; he wondered what it was.

Of all the curious groups and sects thrown up by the ferment of the Civil War, the Diggers were amongst the most curious: but also, like many extremists, the most logical. Indeed, when Obadiah and Edmund had quarrelled about who should have the vote, the Presbyterian had been right to accuse Edmund of tendencies which would lead to what he called chaos.

For if the Levellers had demanded a vote for all free men of property, the Diggers believed that all men should be free.

"And if true freedom lies in the owning of land and goods; why then, should not – if all men are to be free – all goods be held in common?" So Edmund urged his sister and his ten-year-old brother that day as they sat at the big table in the farmhouse where the Digger community of St George's Hill lived together.

"All we have here, we hold in common," he explained. "We labour together as friends." He showed them round the place proudly.

So this was the practical result of Edmund's long agony and self-questioning.

"'Tis like a monastery and a nunnery all together," she joked.

"There is no religious rule," he assured her seriously, and she wondered how long the community could last upon such easygoing terms.

[695]

She watched him carefully. He seemed so thin. There was a new gleam in his eye: was it a gleam of inner peace, or some suppressed desperation? She did not know.

They spent a pleasant evening together. He was clearly happy to see them both. But he seemed equally happy when they left the next morning.

Samuel was puzzled.

"Does he mean we should not keep the farm?"

"He wants no part of it."

"I wonder why he does not want the farm."

"He has been unhappy."

Samuel considered. He could not make much of this.

"Is he happy now?"

"I wish I knew."

He had died after a wasting sickness eighteen months later. The reports brought to Margaret told her he died contented. The community of Diggers did not last, but remained one of the more determined of the early European essays in practical communism.

With only Margaret and Obadiah to look to, it seemed to Samuel, therefore, that in his life there were two worlds. There was the Avon valley, where Margaret ruled, and Salisbury, where Obadiah held court. Avonsford was his childhood, Salisbury the outside world. One, much loved, held him back: the other, undiscovered territory tempted him forward.

Obadiah Shockley bided his time.

By the time he was twelve, Samuel was a bright, fair-haired youth who looked even more like his sister than Nathaniel had. Quick-witted, he knew everything there was to know about the farm, the water meadows and, thanks to Jacob Godfrey, he already had a thorough understanding of the farm accounts. He had been given some schooling – pressed by Obadiah, Margaret had seen to that. She had engaged a young clergyman to come out to the Shockley farm three days a week to tutor him. He had made excellent progress.

But above all, Margaret taught him to know the local countryside.

"I may not be a scholar like Obadiah," she said defiantly, "but I understand the land."

There was seldom a day they did not walk five or ten miles.

He knew the Avon valley, every inch of it, all the way up to Amesbury in the north and past Stonehenge beyond.

Each part had its particular characteristic.

There were the slopes and meadows near Old Sarum, where the villagers still held extensive common land.

"But they are ploughing it into fields now," she explained, "where they can close-fold their flocks." Soon he was familiar with the complex set of bye-laws that regulated the villagers' intense cultivation of their jointly owned flocks and hedged fields.

Sometimes, they would follow the Avon downstream, past the

cathedral, over the bridge and south to the little village of Britford, at the edge of old Clarendon Forest. Once or twice they walked further still, southwards five miles to Downton before turning back upstream. Or they would go to the city and then walk north east, past the great sweeping slope called Bishopsdown and into the long valley of the river Bourne, on whose eastern side lay the huge forbidding ridges that led away towards Winchester – magnificent country to gaze at, but a long, hard haul to walk over. But above all it was the western side of Sarum that Samuel Shockley loved. To the south west of the cathedral close lay the open fields that led to the village of Harnham with its mill. Behind that, the huge ridge of Harnham Hill rose like a protective wall. "That's the place with the best views," he would say: for from Harnham you could see the whole city – cathedral, close, market place and chequers laid out as clearly as on one of Speed's maps.

And to the west: Herbert country he called it.

It was a good description. For there, in the broad, shallow valley that ran to Shaftesbury in the west, lay the huge, well-managed estates of Lord Pembroke, head of the Herbert family. Even if the recent earls were lesser figures than their Tudor forbears who had made Wilton House like a Renaissance court half a century before, their power and influence was formidable. He loved to walk out from the city, past the next door villages with their Saxon names, Fisherton, and Bemerton, to King Alfred's old town of Wilton itself. Sometimes he would walk past Wilton, up on to the ridge to the west and into Grovely Wood where, nine hundred years before, the small farm in the clearing long since forgotten had given his own family their name.

Herbert country. The words also had another important meaning for Margaret – one that made Obadiah scowl.

For whenever they went to Wilton, they never failed to walk through the hamlet of Bemerton and stop there to view a small, grey stone and flint rectory and, on the other side of the lane from it, a little village chapel hardly the size of a low barn, into which they would go to say a prayer.

Each time they did so, Margaret would say the same thing as they came out.

"I remember him. Your father was his friend."

For Margaret was eleven years old when the great poet George Herbert died.

"Was he of the great family at Wilton?" Samuel had once asked when he was young.

"A distant cousin," she told him.

"Did he go often to Wilton House then?"

She had smiled sadly.

"I don't think so. He was a poor cousin, you see."

"He went everywhere else in Sarum though, didn't he?"

"Everywhere."

For though he had only been at Bemerton a few short years, George Herbert had left an extraordinary memory behind him in the slow, quiet days before the Civil War.

"There was not a house in his parish he hadn't visited a dozen times," she assured him; and then added firmly: "There were good priests in the Anglican Church too, whatever Obadiah may say."

And that was the trouble. Who could deny that the author of the finest religious poetry written in the English language was a saintly man? Who could deny that when, during the few years of his perfect ministry at Bemerton, George Herbert had poured out his entire poetic work before tragically dying. "His gentle spirit," as Margaret liked to say, "was touched by God." Not even Obadiah could quite deny that.

But Herbert was an Anglican; he had delighted to go to the cathedral to hear the singing; he had even written a guide for priests on how to perform their duties.

Often, Margaret would cry, even in Obadiah's presence:

"A good Anglican priest – aye, with bishops and all – was as good as any Presbyter. Think of George Herbert."

It was a dangerous thing to say.

How different, how stern, was the world of Obadiah.

Though it often seemed a little frightening, Samuel was conscious, from the first, of the preacher's moral stature and his power.

Why, Obadiah even knew Cromwell himself; and Cromwell was Samuel's hero.

For Cromwell could do everything. He had not only defeated the wicked king. He made the Scots and Irish obey him; and generously gave scores of Irish estates to the loyal army men whom Parliament had never paid. Even Parliament bowed to Cromwell: he was strong; he was just; his all powerful hand was guided by God.

Samuel had almost forgotten Nathaniel now and his light-hearted ways. He knew what he thought of the Royalists. They were traitors. And there were a number lurking near Sarum too – gentry like the Penruddocks, the Mompessons and the numerous Hydes. When the foolish Presbyterians in Scotland had signed a covenant with the king's son (as if one could trust a Stuart's word) and proclaimed him Charles II, he remembered the excitement when the young man had then invaded England. Cromwell's loyal troops had soon crushed him at Worcester; but after that there had been those at Sarum, including the Hydes and an infernal Anglican priest named Henchman, who had helped him on his dramatic flight to the southern coast. Already a popular tale was growing about how the young man had been forced to hide up an oak tree.

One must keep watch, Obadiah warned him, when there were such traitors so close at hand.

He would serve Cromwell one day. The boy felt a warm glow when he thought of the great man's righteous cause. Like a good Puritan, he began to use Biblical phrases in his speech and he would stand in front of a mirror and practise stern looks. Margaret sometimes made light of these enthusiasms, but he disregarded her. For there had been no men like Cromwell, he knew, since the time of the Old Testament prophets.

Although as he passed his thirteenth birthday, young Samuel

modelled himself upon his hero, he sometimes caught himself in acts of enjoyment. And then he was angry and ashamed. The delights of the eye, let alone food and drink, these were the lusts of the flesh, and as sinful as dancing and the maypole. He had a weakness for beauty.

"These things belong to children," Obadiah explained. "But as you grow to be a man, you put off childish things and learn to take joy only in walking the paths of righteousness." He longed to be strong, and to be a man.

When he was thirteen, Samuel inadvertently committed a sin that proved to him he was still utterly weak.

He had been walking past the gates of Wilton House.

Ever since he was seven, the place had been specially fascinating to him, for in that year, the great Tudor mansion had burnt down, and each year afterwards, mighty building works had been continuing to replace it. Now a new house was standing there and he had often gazed at its stately outlines from the road.

Today however, as he started towards it, he saw a short familiar figure coming from the house.

Old William Smith was a plasterer. The year before he had done work for Margaret at the farm and ever since, Samuel knew, he had been busy at the great house. The dust that covered his grizzled head suggested that he had been hard at work that afternoon. He greeted the young man, and seeing the direction of his gaze he asked him.

"Want to go in?"

Samuel hesitated.

"There's only us workmen and the housekeeper there," Smith assured him. "The family's in London."

And so it was that Samuel Shockley saw inside one of the great masterpieces of English baroque architecture. He had never seen such a place before.

There had been, would be, far larger country houses; there had been, most assuredly would be, far greater parks. Was it the setting by the river that made the park so perfect? Was it the long grey lines that made the new house grow out of the ground with the same, stately simplicity of the cathedral less than three miles away?

"Old Inigo Jones himself designed the state rooms," Smith told him; and he admired the perfect single cube, leading into the magnificent double cube of the great salon with its big rectangular windows looking over the park.

These rooms, some of the noblest in all England, were certainly impressive. And yet:

"It's a friendly place," the boy remarked.

For, except in a few cases, the English version of the stately baroque movement of Europe had somehow contrived an island character of its own. In place of the European style, with its huge, high volumes, its Roman arches and great marble staircases, its domes, pediments, pilasters and sumptuous paintings whose tortured forms seem to be striving to climb out of their already splendid spaces into the empyrean itself, the English version in that century was altogether a more friendly affair. Lacking Europe's feudal princes, her Catholic Inquisition, lacking that sense of awe – and, in Wilton's case, building on a former abbey whose site and stones perhaps retained their quiet, contemplative air – the northern English usually made their country palaces feel like large manor houses: grand to be sure, but still domestic homes; this intimacy was their grace and charm.

And the new house at Wilton, with its stately proportions, its magnificent collection of Vandykes and its painted cube and double cube looking over the gentle stream of the river Nadder where moorhens and swans bobbed and glided over the lazy river weeds, was just such a place.

Samuel Shockley looked at the sumptuous furnishings, the splendid paintings and the lovely setting. And he experienced only delight. It seemed to him there could not be a finer way to live.

It was only as he returned home afterwards that he realised his weakness and his sin.

"These are the world's shows," he murmured. "They are there only to ensnare and to deceive." And trying to put the charming vision from him, he went on his way, disgusted with himself and chastened. Obadiah would never have been taken in by such a place, he considered, nor great Cromwell. They were strong, and stern.

It was in this frame of mind that he arrived at the Shockley farm to find Obadiah on a visit to Margaret. As soon as he arrived, he could sense a tension in the air.

They were standing in the parlour, in front of the fire. Margaret was gazing at her elder brother defiantly; Obadiah had a prayer book in his hand.

As Samuel entered the room, Obadiah was holding the prayer book up. His pale face was grave as he announced:

"This book is a work of iniquity."

For the Puritans had dispensed with Cranmer's melodious Book of Common Prayer. It was altogether too papist. In its place they substituted their own plain Directory. Gone were all the familiar ceremonies – not only the communion, but the time-honoured rituals that celebrated the sacred events of men's lives – the burial, even the marriage service. In place of the marriage, a brief, bleak recording of vows before a justice.

This was the Puritan rule. And Margaret hated it.

Worse, she used the Prayer Book each Sunday in the privacy of the farmhouse and she did so in Samuel's presence. It was something that Obadiah had suspected, but only last week Samuel had thoughtlessly allowed a remark to drop that made Obadiah sure. The view of the Presbyterian was clear. It must be stopped.

But Margaret was defiant.

"I prefer the Prayer Book to your dull Directory."

"And you use it in front of Samuel?"

"Yes."

Obadiah sighed. Even if his sister had insisted on her own way with the

Prayer Book, it was obviously wrong to bring the boy up on a book that was anathema to the authorities.

He glanced at Samuel who was standing beside him.

"Foolish and wicked woman," he said in exasperation.

But Margaret only laughed angrily. She snatched up the book.

"Obadiah," she cried in scorn, "Obadiah the biter!"

It was the nickname Nathaniel had given him after Obadiah had bitten his hand. He had not heard it for twenty years, had even forgotten it. But now, suddenly, the pain and humiliation of his brother's taunts came back to him vividly. For a second, he was no longer the respected preacher, but the unhappy adolescent. It was an affront to his dignity.

And she had said it in front of the boy.

Samuel was staring at Margaret in surprise. He did not see the viperish look Obadiah gave her before he recovered himself.

Had Margaret been wise she would have apologised. Instead, in her fury at his attack on her Prayer Book, she said:

"Go preach in churches. You do not deceive me. A biter by nature you were and always will be." Then, turning to Samuel, "Did you not know, Samuel, that your brother Obadiah bites. He'll nip off your hand in a moment, if you do not take care."

Samuel looked from one to the other in astonishment. How could Margaret address the preacher in this way? Did she not owe him respect?

Much as he loved her, she must be mistaken.

Remembering his own sin that morning when he had taken such pleasure in the house at Wilton, he solemnly went to Margaret and took the book quietly from her hands. Then he threw it in the fire.

"We should not look at the book any more, sister Margaret," he said gravely, and left the room. He hoped he had expiated his sin.

Margaret gasped in astonishment.

But if Samuel had seen Obadiah's smile, he would have been even more surprised. For the expression on the face of the brother whom no one had loved, was a twisted smile of revenge.

It was soon after this incident that he saw Obadiah again at an exciting event.

This was the trial of Ann Bodenham, for witchcraft.

The trial was a sensational affair and, because he pleaded with her, Margaret, who refused to go herself, finally agreed to let him do so in a party which included Obadiah and Sir Henry Forest and his two children.

The court was packed. The list of her crimes was truly terrible: not only had she been addicted to popery in her youth, but she had spoken of evil and unlucky days. It was fortunate for Sarum, he discovered, that the great Matthew Hopkins, the witchfinder general, should happen to have been passing through Sarum at that time or she might never have been discovered. But once he investigated her, the terrible truth soon came out. Years before, the court learned, she had been a servant to the notorious Doctor Lambe, who had been torn to pieces by a London mob in 1640 when they had discovered he was a sorcerer. Obadiah shook his head sadly at this revelation.

"Lambe was a friend of the king's favourite Buckingham," he told Samuel. "Beware of papists and other wicked men, Samuel; they transmit their evil like the plague."

Hopkins himself was present during the trial, and Forest pointed him out to the boy: a sad-faced but otherwise unremarkable man.

"But a great servant of God," Obadiah assured him, and Samuel looked at him curiously.

Even the revelations about Lambe were nothing to what followed. For next the court learnt that when the servant of a gentleman in the close had called at her door, five spirits had appeared at the old woman's call, disguised as ragged boys, and then, before his eyes, that she had transformed herself into a cat!

"I spoke to the servant myself," Obadiah murmured. "'Tis true."

"Margaret says this trial is great nonsense," Samuel said.

"She is wrong," Obadiah replied. "Evil must be rooted out."

And Sir Henry Forest, with a grim smile added:

"Nonsense or not, as a magistrate I'll tell you, she's about to be found guilty."

She was. And Samuel was furious that Margaret would not allow him to go to see the execution at Fisherton the next day.

But more important to Samuel Shockley than the trial was the conversation he had with Obadiah afterwards. For the preacher took him to one side and said:

"I believe, Samuel, you are eager to do God's work. Have you considered a profession?"

He had not.

"If you have the will, I perceive you could be a fair scholar. That opens many doors. Should you like that?"

He blushed with pleasure that Obadiah had such a good opinion of him.

"Then you must come to live with me in Salisbury for a time," the preacher said. "For your schooling has been neglected."

Now brother and sister faced each other once again. They had not met since the incident with the Prayer Book.

For a few minutes he had tried to smile, thinking it would make his task easier; but before long he had given it up.

"The boy has intelligence. He could be a fine scholar."

"I have taught him all he needs to know."

In a way, she was right. After a few more years of his desultory lessons with the young clergyman, Samuel would be as educated as most farmers. But was it enough?

"You have taught him nothing." He did not even try to humour her.

She looked at him bitterly. In her heart, she knew that what Obadiah said was true, but she would not concede it.

She knew only one thing: she did not want to give the boy up.

She had tried not to notice the years passing. She was a woman of over thirty now, long past the age when she should have married. She had lost her father and two brothers; she had brought the child up during those terrible years as though he had been her own.

"If I lose him now," she thought, "then what is left for me?" The farm? Obadiah?

She was aware that sometimes people laughed at her. The exploits of the young woman in her early twenties, the dashing defence of her farm against the soldiers – these had been long ago. Her forthright ways were only thought eccentric now. She had a favourite cat; she fed birds each morning at the door and gave them names; she talked to the cows in the field above the house. She was becoming an old maid.

Obadiah was aware of it of course. He never said anything, maintained his customary cold reserve, except when she taunted him. But often in his eyes she could see a faint look of scorn which was painful to her.

But she still had Samuel.

Obadiah had appeared at Michaelmas, and come straight to the point.

"It is time Samuel was put to school in Salisbury," he told her. "He shall live with me."

She understood. It was not only schooling Samuel would receive, but a strict Presbyterian upbringing, away from her Anglican influence and the Prayer Book. If the suggestion had been made by anyone but Obadiah she might have agreed.

"I refuse."

His face was motionless. His hair was all iron grey now. He looked so severe in his plain grey Puritan clothes. His lisp nowadays sounded harsh, adding an extra edge to his words. He had not come to temporise.

"I can compel thee. I am head of this family now."

"Try," she blazed back. "Will you kidnap the child?"

He paused, gazing at her thoughtfully.

"We shall speak of this again."

She was not so foolish as to think that she had won.

He was back a week later.

"Do you still refuse?"

In fact, she had considered carefully. She was aware, also, that the boy was excited by the idea. If she tried to hold him back, sooner or later she would lose.

But the more she considered the business, the more certain she became that she must keep the boy from Obadiah.

It was not only jealousy, not only her loathing of his dour Puritan ways. It was something else she knew about him, and that she had known ever since she was a child.

Perhaps Obadiah hardly knew it himself.

He was cold.

True, he could sometimes show a passionate anger when he was scorned or crossed. But that was all the emotion he possessed.

He thinks only of himself, she considered. If he takes the boy, he will train him to be his servant, but nothing more. He will impress him with his learning, but Samuel will live in a tomb. She would not have him take away the boy's heart.

And so, when he appeared again, she cried:

"No. He shall never be thine, Obadiah. Not in a thousand years."

"I can claim him," he warned.

"You cannot, nor shall you see him any more. If you come near the farm again, I will have the men set the dogs on you."

He was ashen with anger.

"You will regret this folly."

"I shall not."

"Why are you so wilful, ignorant woman?"

"Because I know you," she told him frankly, "and I know your heart is evil."

She looked into his eyes, and knew that she was right. For they were not hurt, nor angry, but completely cold.

From that day began a strange period in Samuel's life.

He was forbidden to call on Obadiah. If he went to Salisbury, she accompanied him. He knew that the farmworkers had orders to report at once if the preacher was seen approaching the house. It was like a state of siege.

The Godfreys or Margaret always seemed to be within sight, wherever he was; and it was clear that Margaret feared that Obadiah might try to kidnap him. When he asked her:

"But is not Obadiah my friend?" she shook her head and replied:

"He is no man's friend. You will see when you are older."

Samuel himself was not sure what to do. He had no wish to leave her. Yet surely this strange situation could not continue.

It was not destined to. For unknown to Samuel and unknown to Obadiah, Margaret Shockley had already made other plans.

There were in any case, several other events taking place in the days after Michaelmas which took Samuel's mind off the quarrel with Obadiah.

The first concerned the water meadows. For they had to be repaired.

Samuel Shockley loved his water meadows. He understood their complex workings. For they were not only the glory of the Shockley farm but also brought to its final perfection the system of corn and sheep farming that had been the mainstay of the Sarum area for more than two thousand years.

The principle of growing corn was simple – one sowed fields, and fertilised them by folding the sheep upon them to manure them. The more sheep, the more corn could be grown, and for many centuries the only limiting factor had been the amount of feeding for the sheep on the Downland. If only more grazing could be found!

It was there all the time, potentially, in the rich valley bottoms, where for centuries there had been only bog or half-drained meadows. The trouble was, no one, at least since Roman times, had known how to drain them.

"But now we have the floated meadows," Samuel would say proudly.

It was a magnificent system.

At the top of the meadows, water was drawn off the river Avon into a channel. This was the main carriage that ran like a raised spine down the centre; off this flowed the carriers – smaller channels that ran along the tops of the meadows' big furrows and over the sides of which, called the panes, the carefully regulated water supply spilled before being collected in drains that carried the excess water away. At its widest point, the Shockley water meadows were over two hundred yards across; the main carriage was half a mile long, and the whole system was regulated by an elaborate series of hatches – little wooden sluice gates raised and lowered with iron ratchets. That was the main carriage system. But there were dozens of little carriers, each of which could be individually controlled by stops of turf inserted or removed by the controller of the meadows.

For this was a new and most important figure on the farm, who watched over the operation of the floated meadows as carefully as a shepherd over his flock: indeed, he was second only to the shepherd in the hierarchy of the farm. This was the drowner – a position proudly occupied on the Shockley farm by Jacob Godfrey's second son William.

"You see," William the drowner used to explain to Samuel, "all through the winter and early spring, by controlling each raised channel, I can keep the whole surface of the meadows covered with a thin layer of water, and the water is always moving through the system so it drops its rich mud on to the earth and enriches it. It keeps the earth warm too," he explained, "like a blanket, so that all the time, underneath the surface, the richest grass is growing. Then when the sheep have taken the best grass from the ridges, we let the water run off and bring them down here – the best grazing in Sarum." It was indeed – and all over the area others like Lord Pembroke in his meadows at Harnham, were building similar systems.

Above all, Samuel loved to come and watch the meadows when they were flooded; for then, as William Godfrey would murmur lovingly:

"See how the water moves over the meadows, never still. You can feel the grasses growing underneath."

It had been that year, in late summer, that William the drowner announced that extensive repair work on the channels was needed.

The meadows at that time of year were high with hay. Margaret had stomped around them thoughtfully.

"We could extend them too," she pointed out.

But where were the hands to do it? The Shockley farm had not enough labour.

It was just before Michaelmas when she and Samuel had been visiting the city that Margaret had suddenly clapped her hands with delight.

"I'll have some of those Dutchmen out of the cloisters," she said. "Holland is all ditch and dyke – they'll know how to do the work." It was an eccentric solution, but sensible.

In later years Samuel always smiled to remember how she had applied to the city authorities to let her take half a dozen of the men, and how, when they had told her it was impossible since they might escape, she had come back the next day with a sword and pistol in her belt and told them firmly: "You are speaking to a Wiltshire Clubman."

The Dutchmen had come. By winter the Shockley's floated meadows would be better and more extensive than ever.

And Sir Henry Forest watched with envy.

The second event was very small and took place on the same day as the hiring of the Dutchmen. Though in a way, as he grew older, it seemed to Samuel Shockley more memorable than many greater happenings.

For just before visiting the cloisters, as he and Margaret were standing quietly near the huge north transept, they discovered something which only a few people, and certainly not Obadiah, knew at that time.

They discovered the secret of Salisbury Cathedral.

He appeared as if from nowhere, from behind a pillar, it seemed, in the north aisle of the choir. He had not seen them.

He shuffled, almost silently towards the chapel at the east end, and started when Margaret caught up with him: he was old, perhaps seventy, with a large round head on his small, stooped body, and his grey eyes stared at her defensively. He was carrying a little bag of tools.

"You work here?" she asked.

"Perhaps, lady. Perhaps not."

"What is your name?"

"Zachary Mason."

She noticed lime and mortar on his hands.

"Why, you've been repairing somewhere here. I'm sure of it."

He did not reply.

"Do you know who I am?"

"Yes, lady. You're the sister of Obadiah Shockley." There was a hint of bitterness in his voice.

"True. And my brother's a fool," she said impatiently. "I thought this place was neglected. Praise the Lord if it's not."

He looked at her cautiously.

"Are you the only one?" she asked.

"Perhaps not."

A thought struck her.

"Who pays you?"

"We are paid."

She reached into her purse and drew out a coin. The old man shook his head.

"We are paid," he said quietly, and shuffled away.

"I believe," she told Samuel a week later, "that it's the Hydes who pay them."

Certain it was that, throughout the period of Cromwell's Commonwealth, workmen slipped quietly into the great cathedral and repaired it, almost unseen, thanks to the generosity of a noble local family.

A third event appeared to have no significance at all.

It was one day when the Dutchmen were working in the water meadows, guarded by Margaret and Samuel, that a little open carriage came along the lane above and stopped. When the single occupant stepped out however, the Dutchmen became excited and one of them begged Margaret to let them have words with the visitor.

"Who is he?" she demanded suspiciously.

"His name is Aaron," the men told her.

"What is he?"

"A merchant from our country," the man explained. "A Jew," he added.

Samuel gasped. One of the Biblical people of Israel. He stared at the single figure, fascinated.

For like most of the population of England, Samuel had never seen a Jew.

Surprisingly, it was Oliver Cromwell who let them in again, after their almost total absence for three hundred and sixty years. Indeed, it was one of the few complaints Obadiah had against the great leader that, being an army man, he was too tolerant of religious sectaries. Of late there seemed to have been more than ever – Baptists, Anabaptists, Brownists who insisted that each individual congregation received its own divine inspiration without requiring the guidance of any central body; there were the new folk, the followers of the preacher Fox, whom men called Quakers and who claimed an individual divine right. A lucid but infernal preacher called Penn had even had the audacity to preach their nonsense in Wiltshire. "He should have been whipped and bored through the tongue," Obadiah had explained sadly to Samuel. As for letting in the Jews – that was insufferable.

They came, often, from Holland, whence they had fled from persecution in Spain. They were not allowed to be English subjects, but were given leave to move about their trading business quietly.

Aaron had landed recently. It seemed he was known to half of the prisoners already. He brought messages from their families, money, and of course, the ability to perform any business transactions the prisoners might require.

He stayed for half an hour, an elderly, bald-headed man, who seemed to regard all around him with a wary amusement.

Samuel inspected him thoroughly but was rather disappointed. He had not expected a Jew to look like an ordinary man.

Afterwards, Aaron had returned to his lodgings at Wilton.

It was a week after her final defiance of Obadiah, that Margaret paid her secret call upon Sir Henry Forest.

She told no one about it.

As Forest heard what she had to say, he was astonished, but he listened carefully. Finally he summed up:

"So you want me to take the boy – in effect as my ward?"

She nodded.

"And you wish him to be educated with my children?"

"That is the key. They are similar age. I have heard they have a good tutor. He must receive the best education."

[707]

"My tutor is excellent. A good university man." He paused. "You think I can keep the boy from Obadiah?"

"Certainly. He would not dare attack you. And he could hardly complain if his brother were receiving the same education as the children of Sir Henry Forest."

For this was the conclusion that Margaret Shockley had reached. She did not suppose any longer that she could hold the boy. She was not even sure that she could deny Obadiah. With Forest, however, Samuel would still be at Avonsford, but quite out of Obadiah's clutches.

She could not help smiling to herself at how she was out-witting the dour Presbyterian.

Forest nodded thoughtfully. His dark, narrow-set eyes were calculating.

"Obadiah Shockley would not give me much trouble," he agreed.

"Will you do it?"

"I like your boy. He has talent too. It's right he should be educated," he told her frankly. Then he smiled. "You have guessed the price of my agreeing?"

She nodded. Of course. It was worth it.

The terms were simple. For taking over the complete education of Samuel Shockley, including his time at Oxford and, if he wished, the Inns of Court, Margaret's water meadows were to pass into his family's ownership, with the stipulation that Margaret should enjoy the life tenancy of the water meadow for a nominal rent. It was an excellent bargain for both sides.

Until the deeds were drawn up and sealed, however, they would remain secret.

Aaron the Jew liked to travel early in the day. This was partly because he normally slept poorly and woke by dawn. It was also that he had found, all his life, a special uplifting of the spirit in the dawn chorus. Even now, despite the fact he was middle-aged, it gave him a thrill about the heart.

He drove his little carriage himself up the Avon valley, just as the first light was coming over the ridges above. By the time he reached Avonsford, the sky was lightening quickly, but as yet there was no one about.

It was just past the manor house that he stopped and stared in surprise.

On the slope above there was a small wooden sheep house. It undoubtedly belonged to the manor.

Why therefore should a figure he clearly recognised as Obadiah Shockley the preacher be coming surreptitiously out of it?

Shockley was not aware of him. Quickly he strode up towards the footpath on the ridge above.

That afternoon, while Samuel and Jacob Godfrey were up on the high ground an unexpected visitor came to call upon Margaret. His name was Daniel Johnson.

He was a quiet, serious man with a polite manner. He had come, he explained, from Obadiah.

"And since my horse went lame halfway here, I had a long walk," he added a little ruefully.

Margaret was a little sorry for him; and since she was feeling somewhat elated after her meeting with Forest, she saw no harm in hearing him out.

He pleaded the case for Samuel's education well. He said that Obadiah was hurt she should deny him his natural role in helping to bring up the child. She judged that, having listened to her brother, the man was possibly quite sincere. What could she say to him?

He was agreeable at any rate. He had a pleasing way of listening to her so that she was encouraged to go on. She gave him her rough and ready views on many subjects. He was interested to learn about how she had fought for the Clubmen, dressed in men's armour. He asked if he might see round the farm, and she showed him her cows, speaking to them gently as they nudged shyly away from the stranger. Proudly she took him to the floated meadows. On their return she even, at his request, showed him the nearly tame birds that she called by name. He seemed well pleased with everything he saw. At one point, while she had to attend to one of the farmworkers he even spoke in a friendly way to the serving girl and gave her a shilling.

As far as Mr. Johnson's mission was concerned, she returned his politeness, but was non-committal. Soon she would have the documents signed by Forest and that would be the end of the matter.

They parted amicably, having reached no conclusions.

She was surprised a few minutes later to see that Samuel who had just come in, was white as a sheet. And why should he look at her so strangely when he asked who her visitor had been?

"Mr. Johnson," she told him, "from Obadiah. He was pleasing enough."

"Johnson? He called himself that?"

"Why not?"

For a second he paused, as though suddenly he was not sure whether to speak.

"'Twas Matthew Hopkins," he blurted out, "the witchfinder general. What does he here?"

The birds she called by name. The cows she spoke to. The serving girl he gave a shilling to. She felt the colour drain from her face.

Obadiah.

Worse. With his influence as a preacher and with Matthew Hopkins on his side . . . the evil cunning of the man. She had fallen into a terrible trap.

Late that afternoon, one of Sir Henry Forest's sheep died.

The agreement between Sir Henry Forest and Margaret Shockley was signed and sealed the next day. It was agreed that Samuel would begin his life at Avonsford Manor the following month, when Lady Forest and her children came back from a visit to her family.

Margaret returned home thoughtfully afterwards. If he knew the boy was safely with Forest, would Obadiah still attack her? Or would he attack all the more, to try to annul the agreement? Were agreements by people found guilty of witchcraft still valid? She did not know.

She had no illusions though. Whatever his plan, if Obadiah and Matthew Hopkins attacked, she would have little chance of surviving.

When she got back she summoned Samuel and told him:

"You're to live with the Forests. It's a great opportunity." And she explained to him both about Forest's fine tutor and about the water meadows. "You will have companions of your own age as well," she added.

That evening, the second of Forest's sheep died. When the shepherd and steward opened the dead animal up to look for signs of murrain, they could find none. They could not tell what either sheep had died of.

The two men chose their spot well – by a small clump of trees on the path that led to the water meadow. As they expected, the boy came by in the early afternoon, and Obadiah hailed him softly.

"Samuel. We must speak with thee."

They were grave, the two men. Hopkins, as always, quiet and pleasant; Obadiah sorely troubled.

"It is hard, Samuel, to think such a thing of our sister," he said sadly. "Still I pray God it may turn out to be false."

"But you must be observant," the witchfinder said. "Anything you see may be significant."

Was it really possible that Margaret, his Margaret, was practising witchcraft? Ever since the day before he had been worrying about the significance of Hopkins. Yet despite the respect he had for the two grave men, he could not bring himself to think that it was so.

As though reading his thoughts, Obadiah reminded him:

"The devil is subtle, Samuel. He may choose to possess even those we love."

When they asked him what she had done in the last day, he could only tell them about her transaction with Forest.

Obadiah was taken aback by this news. But he quickly recovered to take advantage of it.

"That land was meant to come to you, Samuel," he said. "She has sold your patrimony to pay Forest. Yet had I not offered the same education to you myself for nothing?" He shook his head. "Hers is a disordered mind. I fear the worst. We shall try, if we can, to get your land back."

And as he considered this, whether or not he thought she might be a witch, Samuel Shockley felt a touch of anger towards his sister.

The accusation was made the very next day. He would demonstrate, Hopkins promised, that by her unnatural behaviour in dressing up as a man, by her speech with animals and by other signs, Margaret Shockley had shown herself to be steeped in the arts of necromancy. For good measure, it was subjoined that she had bewitched her neighbour's sheep, and the death of two of Forest's was adduced as evidence.

It was a damning charge and all Sarum was buzzing with it. The matter would be laid before the Justice of the Peace – Sir Henry Forest – the very next week, but there seemed little doubt that he would send the matter forward to the Assizes for trial. The fact that the bewitched sheep belonged to him was not held to prejudice the matter in any way.

The next day, however, Sir Henry Forest received a most unexpected call.

It was from Aaron the Jew.

After hearing about the accusation, it had taken courage for Aaron to go to Forest. As a Jew, his position in England was tenuous. Did not his people know to their cost, for centuries of persecution, the terrible risks of calling attention to themselves? Had he any need to make enemies of powerful men like Obadiah? Margaret Shockley was nothing to him, nor Sarum, where he might only stay a month before passing on.

But it was written in the law: Thou shalt not bear false witness. It was written in the law, and if he did nothing, his conscience would not let him rest. He had seen what he had seen.

Briefly, without suggesting what it might mean, he told Sir Henry how he had seen Obadiah.

Forest listened, and as he did so, he grew thoughtful. When the Jew had finished, he thanked him, then, choosing his words with care:

"This is a delicate matter," he warned, "and I advise you to say nothing about it. I shall investigate it diligently though. Be assured of that."

Then he dismissed the man.

For some time after Aaron had gone, he considered the business in every aspect. Then drew out the agreement he had made with Margaret only days before. Even in the event of her condemnation and death, he judged that it might still be valid. Without her life tenancy at a low rent, the value of his acquisition would be raised many times.

Forest considered carefully, then decided to remain silent and wait upon events.

Margaret Shockley foresaw the next move against her.

That same day, she packed Samuel's possessions into three large boxes and placed them in the cart. Then she drove the boy round to Avonsford Manor.

"It's best he remains with you," she told the baronet, and reminding him of their agreement she pointed out: "'Twill be easier for you to keep your part of the bargain if he is already safely in your hands. Not so easy if Obadiah's already got him."

Forest took him in without a word.

Two hours later, Obadiah and six men arrived at the farm. They had come for Samuel. She noticed that neither Jacob Godfrey nor any of the farm hands made any attempt to stop him.

"You come too late," she told Obadiah. "He is safe with Sir Henry Forest, where even you can't touch him."

"I am the head of the family, impudent woman," he said with icy coldness. "Forest will yield him to me."

"I think not. He's an interest in keeping the boy. He's also a magistrate before whom you are to bring me," she added shrewdly.

Obadiah scowled, but let the subject drop.

Before he left however, when the two of them were alone together for a moment, she asked:

"If you can't have the boy, Obadiah, why bother to persecute me?"

To which, with all the hatred of the past in his dark eyes he softly replied:

"So that you burn."

She nodded.

"And then you'll truly be head of the family," she answered.

But it was no word spoken by Obadiah that day that hurt her, nor the fact that the Godfreys and the farmworkers were suddenly silent and awkward if she came close to them. It was the fact that, as they got into the cart to go to Avonsford, young Samuel sat as far away as possible and that at the manor, he had gazed at her once, with fear and doubt in his eyes, before leaving her without a word of farewell. And in that, she had to confess, Obadiah had won, since he had taken away from her the love of her only child.

Aaron was not satisfied. He had spent a lifetime in business with all kinds of men and, although he had no idea of the reason, he knew that Forest was going to conceal what he had told him.

And now he was in a quandary. For even if he had the courage to raise the matter himself, what would the word of a Jew count against a powerful Presbyterian? He would do nothing but invite persecution for himself or any other Jews who passed that way.

Then he saw the boy in Wilton. He was sitting in Sir Henry Forest's carriage, but the merchant he had been speaking to pointed Samuel out and told him, "That's the Shockley boy." He remembered him vaguely from the day in the water meadows.

There could be no doubt. It was a sign from God.

It did not take Aaron long to tell Samuel what he had seen. He did not say that he had told Forest, but he explained:

"I cannot testify. It will do you no good. Yet, for the love of God," he urged, "do something. Watch the sheep house."

But his heart sank when he looked into the boy's eyes, and saw they were disbelieving.

There were four days before Margaret was due to appear before the magistrate.

That night, another sheep was found dead.

Yet Samuel Shockley was not unmoved. He was confused. Was he to believe that the men of the party of his hero Cromwell, the stern Presbyters of Sarum, were frauds? Or was he to believe, as he already half did, that his sister was a witch?

He no longer even knew what he wanted to think.

Alone in the big manor house with Sir Henry Forest, of whom he was rather afraid, he plucked up courage to ask him what would happen to Margaret and the baronet had told him:

"She must come before me and I hear the charges. If I think there's a case to answer, then I send her to gaol until she can be properly tried by judge and jury at the Assizes."

"And will you send her for trial?"

"Probably," Forest told him frankly. "Unless she can refute the charges." He thought of the Jew.

"How can she refute them, sir?"

"Evidence. Reliable witnesses who will stand up in court and prove she did not do what she is accused of."

A Jew would be useless.

He wondered whether to tell Forest about the sheep house but decided against it. What if he wanted to get up before dawn to watch it and the dark, severe man opposite him forbade it? What would the magistrate think of the word of a Jew anyway? No, he must make sure for himself. He would have to act alone.

"And if there is no evidence to save her?"

Forest did not answer. The boy had seen the trial of Ann Bodenham.

Samuel noticed that there was an increasing awkwardness about the baronet's answers; he supposed it was because of the likely outcome.

He slept badly that night. The Jew's story came back to him again and again.

Just before dawn he got up and slipped out of the house. But though he wandered about near the sheep pens until the sun was well up, he saw nothing.

The next two nights the same thing occurred.

No doubt the Jew had lied. Probably he hated God's ministers.

But the last night before the session, when he thought of Margaret, and all that she meant to him through his childhood, he was overcome with grief.

"I will save her somehow," he vowed. Then he cried himself to sleep.

It was almost dawn when he woke. The big stone manor house was silent. Quickly he slipped on his clothes and hurried out.

In the valley, it was cold and silent. He waited.

The first hint of light was coming over the ridges. He looked hopefully up and down. Nothing.

Until he saw a figure below in the shadows.

It was tall, wrapped in a black cloak, and it was moving towards him.

Obadiah Shockley moved silently along the river's edge. This would be his last journey. One final sheep would die, on the day she left the farm, then no more. Such proof had already impressed Hopkins and would be devastating at the trial.

By the water's edge, a single swan pushed out into the river, so as not to encounter him.

The sheep house lay some way up the slope and he drew level with it. Obadiah left the valley bottom and made his way swiftly towards it. How tall he seemed in the faint light.

It was while Obadiah was coming up the slope that Samuel realised what he must do. Running quickly down from his vantage point, and keeping the sheep house between them, he reached the door a hundred yards ahead of Obadiah. A slight dip in the path gave him a second when

[713]

the preacher could not see the door of the sheep house and he used it to slip inside.

His heart beat wildly as he looked for a place to hide. The sheep stirred uneasily. There were three pens there and a space in the far corner where a handcart stood beside two bales of hay. In a moment he was behind them.

When Obadiah entered he was swift. Hardly bothering even to glance round, he walked straight to the nearest pen and selected a sheep at random. Then reaching to his belt, he pulled out a little pouch and poured out some small pellets into his hand. He fed them to the sheep. Whatever they were, he had prepared them well; the sheep ate pacifically from his hand. As soon as the sheep had eaten most of the pellets, he stepped back, took a last, cold look at it, and was gone.

Samuel waited as long as he could, until he reckoned Obadiah must be twenty yards away, then raced across to the sheep. He prised open its mouth. It was still half full. Reaching in, he pulled out all he could until he had half a handful. Then he waited, several minutes, until he was sure that Obadiah would be gone.

He had decided what to do.

It was an informal court, for in recent years the operations of the justices had been less well organised than in former times. To suit himself, Sir Henry Forest had convened it in the great hall of his own manor house.

But a court it was, a petty session, with its proceedings properly recorded and forwarded to the next quarter sessions. The magistrate sat on a high-backed chair, behind an oak table, raised on a low platform, and he looked impressive.

There was a crowd of fifty standing pressed against the back wall of the hall. For there were few in Avonsford who were not curious to see the Shockley woman brought before the magistrate by her own brother.

As Margaret and her accusers came forward, Sir Henry Forest's stern face gave nothing of his own feelings away.

In fact, his feelings were very mixed. Like many justices, who were mostly of the gentry, he did not believe in witchcraft. Still less did he believe in most of the evidence presented at witchcraft trials. On the whole by this time, local justices and the judges in the Assize courts were trying to discourage these prosecutions. But the state of popular opinion was still some way behind them. Secretly, Forest despised the proceedings from beginning to end. But wisdom taught him to give the people at least some of what they want. If they wanted to burn Margaret Shockley as a witch and her brother and Matthew Hopkins were set on it, then he supposed she would have to burn. In any case, he did not have to try the case, only send it to a higher court.

The private revelation of the Jew however made him uneasy. He looked at the parties before him warily.

Margaret's face was pale. It's expression registered nothing except contempt. Since it was clear to her that every hand was now against her, she looked at no one, not even Samuel.

But the evidence, briefly recited by Hopkins, was devastating. Her dressing up in men's clothes, and fighting with a strength which, he suggested, could not be natural; her conversation with animals; her command over birds, which she knew by name. Catholics had come to her house in the war – he had discovered Charles Moody. She had threatened to set her dogs on a Presbyterian preacher. And now, no less than four sheep had died on her neighbour's estate. Clearly all these argued malignant powers.

Forest had to admire the thoroughness of the case. He looked about for anyone to contradict the charges. He did not expect anything.

But now, Samuel stepped forward and to everyone's astonishment announced that he had testimony. Forest frowned.

"Are you sure?" What could he know?

He was sure.

His face was very pale, his back straight. Samuel Shockley stood in the middle of the great hall and told them what he knew. He told them how a passer by had seen Obadiah in the sheep house. Obadiah shrugged, as though it meant nothing. The crowd murmured. He told them how for three mornings he had waited and watched. Obadiah said nothing but began to look uneasy.

Then he described, moment by moment, all that he had seen that morning, up to the point when Obadiah left the sheep house. And the crowd in the court fell silent.

As he went on, Obadiah's face grew ashen. He began to tremble, not with fear but with rage. Was yet another of his family, a new generation, to ridicule him – to destroy his hard-won reputation? He began to shake with rage. He would destroy this boy.

His anger made him incautious.

"'Tis a lie," he cried. "All a lie to save his sister who is sunk in sin."

It was too much. Now Samuel feared neither Obadiah, nor Forest, nor the witch hunter any longer. And as he exploded, he used the Old Testament gestures and phrases which were all he knew.

Reaching into the little bag at his side, he marched to the table and poured the contents out upon it.

"Then what is this?" he shouted. "Poison! This is what I pulled, from the sheep's mouth, after you left." He turned to Forest. "Feed it to a sheep and see how it does. Search him and his house and you may find more."

Obadiah's mouth had fallen open. He almost staggered back.

"Viper!" the boy cried, raising his arm and pointing his finger at the preacher: "False witness." His blue eyes flashed with rage. "See him grow pale, who tried to murder his sister. Abomination of desolation," he cried, carried away with the grand Biblical words that suddenly welled up within him, "sitting in the temple where it ought not." And then, overcome with rage at what had been done to Margaret, at how he himself had been made to doubt her he added the words of contempt that only he, Margaret and Obadiah understood: "Biter."

Without waiting to be told what to do, he walked to the back of the court.

Long before the boy had finished, Forest had seen what to do. After this, the Jew, too, might speak. He could see trouble ahead – it must all be stopped.

He beckoned Obadiah and Hopkins to approach him.

"Withdraw this matter." He looked at Hopkins. "This case will not work in Sarum."

Hopkins nodded. He had no wish to spoil his cause. There were plenty of witches elsewhere. Obadiah said nothing and was ignored.

"The complaint is withdrawn," Forest calmly announced to the crowd, and moved swiftly on to other business.

There was a happy reunion at the farm between Samuel Shockley and Margaret that afternoon.

But to Samuel's surprise, a week later, it was Margaret who insisted he return to the Forests.

"Come and see me here, Samuel," she told him. "But it is time, now, that you learned to be a scholar."

Aaron the Jew left Wilton for Southampton soon afterwards. As he took the road from Wilton, he met Sir Henry Forest, who looked at him cautiously.

Aaron was wise. He looked down and did not meet Sir Henry's eye.

1688: December

Doctor Samuel Shockley stepped over the watercourse in New Street, which still stank despite the cold weather, and made his way swiftly towards the close.

Today was a great day; today England was having a revolution and in a few hours he would meet the man who would soon be the new king.

"Then, thank God, we shall have seen the last of these accursed Stuarts who bring us nothing but trouble," he told his wife and family. "Better times are coming." He was always an optimist.

Doctor Samuel Shockley looked his most magnificent today. On his head a huge, full-bottomed wig that reached below his shoulders. It was a rich brown colour and, his wife assured him, went well with his blue eyes; it gave him the dignified aspect proper to a respected physician. Under a cloak that hung open over the shoulders, he wore an elegant, grey-pink coat with handsome gold buttons round the cuff and at the side pockets, a shirt with fine lace ruffs made at nearby Downton, silk stockings, grey buckskin shoes with raised heels and tied over the instep with pink ribbon. In his hand he carried a cane with a silver head. Though he walked quickly, he was careful to keep his shoes clean from the horse droppings and variegated refuse that filled the street.

Before the prince arrived, he had two duties to perform: one to see the bishop; and the second . . . he frowned. He was going to have to be very firm with the Forest boy.

He entered the close – a pleasant place now. On his left, close by the gate, was the long brick building of the College of Matrons, founded by the bishop five years before for the widows of clergymen. He liked the solid, quiet house with its little cupola in the centre and its gardens behind and had several elderly patients there. He came by the choristers' green. Just here, he remembered with a smile, in August 1665, he had been presented to King Charles II, who had stayed two months in Salisbury with his court while the Great Plague was raging in London.

Of Salisbury, with its river and water courses down the streets that witty and cynical monarch had afterwards remarked:

"'Tis a good place for breeding ducks and drowning children." But he had done the clothiers of Salisbury a good turn after his visit by often wearing their medley cloth, and for this royal patronage they were duly grateful.

When Samuel Shockley looked back he had much to be grateful for. There was the farm, the home from home, where his dear sister Margaret had lived alone but contented until just three years before. He had visited her every week except while he was away at Oxford. Sir Henry Forest had honoured his bargain and given him an excellent education. He had been happily married ever since the year of the Great Fire of London and he had three children he adored.

He was not without malice. At the Restoration of Charles II he had been frankly delighted when Obadiah along with two thousand other Presbyterians, had lost his living; and he had not pretended to be sorry when the preacher had been killed a year afterwards in an Edinburgh street brawl.

He looked round the close with satisfaction. Thank God that ever since the days of Obadiah, it had returned to normal: bishop, dean, canons and choristers, were all back with their benefices restored; the cathedral cared for; the Book of Common Prayer and the ceremonies he loved – the morning and evening service, the marriage service – all in use again: Anglican normality. It meant the communion service, even if it was only three times a year in the smaller parishes – a sacred rite. It meant, once a year, the perambulation, led by the vicar with the village boys of the parish boundaries. He and Margaret had always joined that.

It had also meant, in Sarum, some fine men as bishops: Henchman, who had helped Charles escape after Worcester, Hyde, of the numerous Wiltshire family; and now his own dear Seth Ward, getting old, but always a delight. How many hours had he spent with the great man, cheerfully discussing Hobbes's philosophy, Donne's poetry, or Mr Newton's new telescope?

Only one thing annoyed him as his eye travelled round the close. This was the house of Doctor Tuberville.

Tuberville. It never ceased to anger him that, while his own sound medicine was respected, that cunning quack Tuberville, with his random blood-lettings, his potions – why he had even told a short-sighted man to smoke – Tuberville, that necromancer, had made a fortune.

But he soon smiled again when he glanced up at the cathedral spire – another reason why he loved the bishop. For it was Bishop Ward who had called in his friend Christopher Wren to survey the cathedral and repair the spire. He had liked Wren. His father had been rector at the Wiltshire village of East Knoyle. He was a good common-sense Wiltshireman like himself. And the great architect of St Paul's had done his work superbly.

"I found the old iron bands up there still in good working order," he told Shockley. "Those ancient masons knew what they were about. I only hope we do our work so well."

There were two reasons for his visit to the bishop that morning. One was usual: the other concerned young Forest. He entered the bishop's palace.

"Ah, Samuel, dear friend." Seth Ward – his big broad face, heavy-lidded, clever eyes, big hooked nose. He was sunk in a chair; he was in one of his moods. "I fear I am unwell."

Fellow of The Royal Society, friend of Wren, Pepys, Newton, fine administrator, brilliant mind, when not worried into fits by the dean, scholar, who had built up at Salisbury one of the finest medical and scientific libraries in the country – and raging hypochondriac.

"There is only one thing worse than your imagined illnesses," Shockley told him cheerfully, "and that is your invented cures." For Ward would even invent potions when he had been through all those the doctors could dream up. "I suppose you've been consulting that rogue Tuberville again."

He did not linger long over Ward's health, but came straight to the point.

"I need your help with young Forest." And he outlined the disgraceful case, and his own plan for solving it. Ward laughed.

"I feel better. I will support you."

"Thank you. Then I must be gone."

As he left, Ward held him back for a moment.

"Prince William will be here shortly. You think this revolution is for the best?"

"Undoubtedly." He smiled. "But then you know, unlike you, I am a Whig."

In his opinion, the Stuarts had finally destroyed themselves.

For when, after Cromwell had died, the English Parliament had finally invited Charles II to return to his kingdom, it was with a clear understanding.

The English had killed a king: tried a Commonwealth, and not liked it. Now the gentry in Parliament had decided to return to normal.

Which meant their rule – gentry in the shire, gentry as justices, lords lieutenant; local men, in charge of local militia, not paid armies; gentry administering old English common law, gentry supporting the Church of England; and gentry in Parliament in control of taxes. It was conservative; it was not what the Presbyterians and Radicals had fought a civil war for; but it was at least familiar and certainly no military tyranny. It was safe. The Clarendon Code and the Test Act that the gentry passed through Parliament barred all except Church of England men from public office: that kept out dangerous Radicals and, above all, papists. There was also to be no foreign interference. That was the understanding. Shockley, for one, liked it.

But for twenty-five years the obstinate Stuarts had done everything they could to thwart it.

Charles II secretly plotted with his cousin Louis XIV of France to invade, and declared himself a papist on his death-bed.

His brother James was even worse: he did not even trouble to hide his intentions.

"He'll turn us Catholic and use French or Irish armies to do it," Shockley told Seth Ward. "That's why I'm a Whig."

For the programme of the new party who had been given this curious name, was to exclude Catholic James from the succession. The king and his court Tories had fought back.

They had removed from office most of those who opposed them. Good men – Hungerford, Thynne of Longleat, Mompesson, and many more – Deputy Lieutenants and Justices had all been removed. All seven Wiltshire boroughs, including Salisbury, had lost their charters. Charles bribed, bullied and packed every borough and shire to get a parliament to support his brother.

Charles had manipulated and won. James had succeeded peacefully. But not for long.

"And by God, sir," Shockley now remarked to Ward, "he has given us Whigs our ammunition."

Sarum might have liked the new king for he was married first to the daughter of the great lawyer Hyde, made Earl of Clarendon – a good local man whose cousin was bishop, and a loyal Anglican too. That marriage produced two Protestant daughters, Mary and Anne. But now the king had married again, a Catholic princess, and the people of Sarum did not like that at all. They had soon seen enough of the new rule.

Parliament had been dismissed. Arundel of Wardour, as great a Catholic as any in the land, was in high office; the king was clamouring for the Test Act to be repealed, and even his two Hyde brothers-in-law were dismissed for not supporting these moves towards Rome. The brief rebellion of Monmouth against these changes had taken place south west of Sarum; but the terrible trials of Judge Jeffreys that followed its collapse with their massive executions (and the Bloody Judge tried five hundred men a day) had filled even the king's local supporters with disgust, just as the news of Louis XIV's recent persecution of Protestants filled them with fear. At Salisbury, the mayor and five councillors were dismissed by the king.

"He has made sure that he offends every class in England. Even Tories are turning Whig. And now he has a son . . ."

This had been the final straw. Until then, James's heirs had been his Protestant daughters. But with the birth of a Prince of Wales to his new Catholic wife, there seemed no hope for the Protestant island.

The succession had to change, and who more natural than Mary and her husband, that upstanding Protestant Dutchman, declared foe of the Catholic King of France, William, Prince of Orange?

The revolution was quick and easy. Doctor Shockley liked to say he had even played a small part in it himself. For when James and his forces camped in Salisbury the month before, and the townspeople had subserviently welcomed them, Samuel Shockley had not.

When James was afflicted with a nosebleed and the messenger came running to the doctor's house, Shockley refused to attend him.

"Send Tuberville to His Majesty," he suggested, and muttered, "Perhaps the quack will cut his head off."

"This will be remembered," the flunkey warned him.

"Good."

James had soon gone. Now William was about to enter the city. Clarendon himself, so recently a minister of James, had arrived in the town with other Wiltshire Hydes to greet him.

It was as he walked away from the bishop's palace that Samuel Shockley noticed a curious sight. Two white birds had risen from the lawns beside Ward's home and circled the roof before flying silently away towards the river.

He knew the local tale, which spoke of white birds appearing when a bishop is about to die, and for a second felt a pang about the heart. Then he put the thought from him: he was a scientist, a man of reason.

This was a day of celebration.

But first, young Forest. He had summoned him to his house. The young man was waiting there: dark-haired, quiet, polite. He had the same superficial charm as his father, the same coldness beneath, which was no doubt why, although they had been educated and gone to Oxford together, Shockley and his father had never become real friends.

Young George Forest was twenty.

Shockley did not waste time.

"You know why I have sent for you."

"No, Doctor Shockley." He was lying of course.

"I have a patient – Susan Mason. Does that help you?"

George Forest said nothing. He waited.

How tedious duplicity was. Shockley sighed.

"She is with child, young Forest."

Still he said nothing.

"You are surely not going to deny that you are the father, sir?"

It was the usual story. The young man had seen her at the inn, visited her as a light diversion, no doubt charmed her. It had taken him three weeks to persuade her even to confide in him who her lover had been. She was a pleasant, simple girl, with large grey eyes – attractive in a way – and only sixteen.

"Do you intend to marry her?"

George Forest stared at him in amazement. The heir to a baronetcy, a Forest, marry an inn-keeper's daughter?

"I see. Are you aware that her father has discovered her condition sir, and turned her out? She is quite defenceless."

It was a miserable business. Mason the innkeeper, a short, choleric man, with a large red and angry face, had simply thrown her out of the house.

[720]

"I don't care who the father is," he stormed. "You were not forced. You admit it. I have three other children to look after. You dishonour me. Leave my house."

Shockley had been to see him twice; but Mason was adamant. There was no help from that quarter.

The boy blanched. That at least was something. But still he said nothing. His cautious eyes gave nothing away. Why was it, Shockley wondered, that a vicious boy was even more unpleasant than a vicious man?

George Forest had not known. He had not known because he had studiously avoided her. When she had tried to speak to him once in the street, he had quickly turned away.

"Who knows what lovers she may have had," he finally suggested.

Shockley exploded.

"Nonsense, sir, and you know it." The boy was even worse than he thought. "I've seen the girl. I've been a doctor nearly thirty years. I know. It's yours."

At least Forest had the sense not to try to answer him back. He paused, surveying him coldly.

"You may be grateful I have not spoken to your father. You shall do that for yourself. But you will make the girl an allowance."

George Forest looked doubtful.

"Perhaps," he said thoughtfully, "thirty pounds would take care of the child."

Shockley snorted.

"Fifty a year."

It was a handsome sum, but he meant to get it for the girl.

George Forest looked at him straight in the eye.

"My father would never agree to such a thing."

That, Shockley knew, was perfectly true.

Which was why, that morning, he had taken a certain precaution.

"If you do not, then you will be brought before the bishop's court," he said calmly. "He has the power to fine and excommunicate you. I do not think your father would like that."

It was one of the benefits of the Restoration, Shockley thought, that, at least in theory, the Anglican bishops had gained these rights to try moral offences of various kinds, including, as it happened, bastardy. He smiled at young Forest blandly. The disgrace would be tremendous.

The boy was white as a sheet. But he was thinking.

After a pause he replied carefully:

"I do not think the bishop would wish to attack the Forest family."

It was a shrewd reply. For although these trials could take place, in practice it was rare for a bishop to prosecute a member of the gentry. At worst, a gentleman might be discreetly fined.

But Shockley only shook his head.

"You are wrong. I have been with Bishop Ward this very morning. He is ready to prosecute. I have his word on it."

There was dismay in the young man's eyes, then astonishment, and

[721]

then, Shockley saw it quite clearly, though it only lasted a moment, respect – for a clever trick and a worthy adversary.

"I will speak to my father."

"You have until this evening."

He had won. They both knew it.

There was a commotion in the street outside. The Prince of Orange was coming. Their business was done and they moved to the door.

"Clarendon's here," George remarked pleasantly. Now that the bargaining was over, he was already his normal self again. "Do you think there will be fighting?"

"No. I think James's men will desert."

Young Forest nodded thoughtfully.

"And where does your father stand in this matter?" Shockley enquired, equally pleasantly. He had not seen the baronet for a week.

George now gave him a charming smile.

"With Pembroke, I believe."

"But Lord Pembroke is still in London. He has not declared himself yet."

"I know."

The Forests did not change.

The young man looked at him curiously.

"What about you, Doctor, are you pleased with this glorious revolution?"

And now Shockley smiled. "It is not a revolution, George," he replied. "It is a compromise."

He looked forward to a better world.

The Calm

1720

THE SHOCKLEYS WERE ruined. Completely. It was his fault.

"Madness, sir." Immediately after breakfast, for the remaining five years of his life, he would repeat this same sentence. "To gamble – no other word for it – the future of the family: gamble all, lose all. I'm no better than a criminal."

For in 1720 the then eighty-five-year-old Doctor Samuel Shockley, scientist, rationalist, incurable optimist and one of the most respected inhabitants of Sarum, invested his entire fortune in the greatest orgy of unsupported speculation that England has ever seen – the South Sea Bubble. And when, within a year, it had burst, taking half the investment of the kingdom with it, Doctor Samuel Shockley was utterly ruined; as was his family.

He lived five years more, making small but useless attempts to regain some of what was lost. He reproached himself every day. It was said that only his will to overcome his guilt and shame kept him alive. When, by 1725, he knew it was useless, he was soon gone.

The madness which seized Shockley seized half England, and it was very understandable. For in the year 1720, it had really seemed that nothing – not even a gamble – could possibly go wrong. England at last was rich and at peace.

The country had a new dynasty. The protestant William and Mary had been succeeded first by Queen Anne; then when she died without heirs, the crown was offered not to the closest in hereditary line, but to her unobjectionable and quite definitely Protestant German cousin: George, Elector of Hanover.

True, he spoke not a word of English; true – this was a pity – he preferred Hanover to England; true, he did not try to understand his new country and was often absent from it in his beloved Hanover; true, he had divorced his wife and detested his son the Prince of Wales. He was short, fat and looked stupid, though he was an able commander. But he was not a Catholic; he would not, like the Stuarts, threaten the English Church with papist intrigue. The English were indifferent to him, but he was safe. His descendants ruled England ever since.

The country had military peace. It had been won for Queen Anne in that series of brilliant campaigns against the threatening megalomaniac King Louis XIV of France – who had tried to overawe all Europe – by the great John Churchill, first Duke of Marlborough. Blenheim, Oudenarde, Malplaquet: his heroic victories were on the lips of every schoolboy: they ensured that, for two decades, England would be safely at peace.

The island was united too. The joining of the kingdom of Scotland with England and Wales had taken place in the sense that the Stuarts were kings of both independent kingdoms; but by the Act of Union in 1707, the kingdoms were joined by Parliament; and the Hanoverian kings, though they were still greater strangers north of the Scottish border than south of it, were undoubted kings of a united island.

Almost. There remained the last male claimants of the old Stuart royal house – James Francis Edward, son of James II by his Italian wife and himself married to the granddaughter of the Polish king – known, sometimes facetiously, as the Old Pretender. The English mostly did not want him because he was Catholic. The Scots called him their own, but chiefly because he was a Stuart. The French, anxious to weaken Protestant England, supported him, but half-heartedly. In 1715 he tried to invade the kingdom – and was at once and humiliatingly driven out. Some did support him. The die-hard Tories led by Bolingbroke who did so, destroyed their own political careers with the Hanoverian kings for a generation. The Pretender and his son remained in France, always a vague threat, but often forgotten. The island had better things to do than worry about the passing of the Catholic Stuarts.

It was time to forget civil war and religious conflict: it was time to get rich: and that, in 1720, was what thousands of investors tried to do.

The story of the South Sea Bubble began with Marlborough's wars against the French. They cost many millions, and rather than raise all the money in taxes, Parliament wisely decided to go into debt. The government debt, around forty million pounds, seemed huge; the largest creditors were the Bank of England – a stronghold of the Whigs – and the East India Company; the proposal was that in order to lighten the burden on the government, a new company, the South Sea Company, would take over the debt and pay the interest in return for trading concessions in the south seas. If the trade went well, then the company might make a handsome profit. And on that basis it sold shares to the general public. There were many reasons for the scheme. The Tories who started it disliked the strength of the Whigs at the Bank and wanted another large financial group of their own to rival it; the Government wanted to be free of the interest it owed. A similar scheme had been set up in France by the financier John Law: surely it would work in England. Indeed, before it began, the scheme was already so popular that soon the company had taken over most of the debt – some thirty millions.

It was a gamble. It was the spirit of the age.

"The possibilities, sir, are endless, I assure you," Doctor Shockley told the dean, the canons, and his son.

In the imagination, they were. And so were the number of satellite companies that grew up overnight around the great South Sea Company. The trading in shares between these became so complex that it was as impossible to unravel as it was nonsensical. In the main company the £100 shares rose in the first six months of 1720 to £1,100. And still there was no enterprise underneath it all, no profit: nothing but a great mountain of paper trading powered by . . .

"Wind, sir. It was all wind. A hot gas, blowing up a huge bubble . . . all my dreams." This was Shockley's lament: he was precisely right.

When the crash came he was fortunate in having a little, a very little, in the original shares which had been exchanged for actual government debt. When that greatest of eighteenth century politicians, Robert Walpole, was brought in to clear up the mess, he arranged that these shares should be redeemed by the government, though at roughly half their original worth. But for those who had invested in the rocketing stocks that rose with the Bubble – stocks invented to satisfy investors who had long lost all sense of reason – for them there was nothing.

"There is nothing Walpole can do for this family. Nothing. I own shares in a company for trading in human hair, another for mining gold in Wales, and another for buying a peat bog in Ireland," the old man declared, shaking his head in disbelief. "And as for this," he produced a huge prospectus. "What was its purpose, sir? I cannot tell you."

In the aftermath of the Bubble, an enterprising publisher produced a pack of playing cards, each card depicting one of the fraudulent investment schemes that had collapsed with the crash, accompanied by a satirical verse. Doctor Shockley would play with these morosely by the hour.

In 1725 he died. A year later his son Nathaniel also died, of a sudden heart attack. The modest house on the north side of the close passed to his young grandson Jonathan, and it was in his hands that the meagre family fortune now lay. A few years later Jonathan married the daughter of one of the cathedral canons: a pleasant girl with carrotty hair and protruding teeth, with whom he was happy. She brought enough money to renew the lease of the Shockley house, and she was respectable. Through her father's influence Jonathan found employment with Sir George Forest as general manager of his estates. In this position, he was treated, as a matter of courtesy, as a gentleman; but with a faint, unspoken condescension that reminded him, each day, that he was nonetheless really only a dependant, a sort of superior steward. He was a tall, fair man who carried himself well, and cultivated an occasional terseness of manner to mask the slight awkwardness he felt inside.

In 1735 his only son Adam was born.

1745

The ten-year-old boy was almost bursting with suppressed excitement.

Each day, as more news came in, he looked at the sedate, unruffled calm of Salisbury close, waiting for the horsemen to appear. Each day, he watched his father eagerly. Soon, his father would take down the family sword, and then he would ride. It was young Adam Shockley's secret plan to ride with him.

For Bonnie Prince Charlie was marching from the north. And the

Shockleys would surely ride to join him.

No object in the Shockley household was more venerated than the sword of Nathaniel Shockley, which Charles Moody had brought back from Naseby. It hung high on the wall over the stairs, gleaming dully – a daily reminder to the boy of the family's romantic Cavalier past.

It was a past that Jonathan liked to refer to.

"Some Shockleys were for Parliament in those days," he conceded to Adam, "but the best of us were for the king."

It gave the boy the feeling that his family, too, had been one of the loyal band of true gentlemen like the Penruddocks and Hydes who had been loyal to a sacred cause.

And did not his father sometimes after dinner pass his hand over his wine glass, with a dour flourish, in the Jacobite sign to toast the true Stuart king over the water? The family fortune might be lost, there might be a German king on the throne and Whig politicians who tolerated religious free-thinkers, but Jonathan Shockley, a solid Tory if ever there was one, at least enjoyed this show of loyalty to a past when, by supposition, the family was more noble and the times better.

Now the time had come. The Pretender's son, the dashing Charles Edward was on his way south. From the border to Derby, not a hand had been raised against him by a people who were still indifferent to Hanoverian rule.

Each day, when Adam Shockley went to ride his pony, he whispered to it:

"We'll go too."

How strange it was, therefore, that even now, Sarum close could still be so quiet.

Sarum close. It was a good place to be born a gentleman. It was even fashionable.

The choristers' school young Adam attended, run by its famous headmaster Richard Hele, provided not only the choirboys for the cathedral, but an excellent preparation for the sons of the local gentry and merchants before they went on to the great schools of Winchester and Eton. Had not the Lord Chancellor, one of the Wiltshire family of Wyndham, been one of its notable old boys? And the great Mr. Addison, essayist and editor of the *Spectator*, had he not been at school in Salisbury too? As for the world of fashion, that was run by the redoubtable, the indefatigable, Mr. James Harris who lived at the fine house by St Ann's Gate, not a hundred yards from their own. On the south side of his house he had set an elegant sundial which bore the legend: 'Life is but a walking shadow'. Mr. Harris's grandfather, on his mother's side, was no less a person than the Earl of Shaftesbury. Mr. Harris organised the subscription concerts in the cathedral and the Assembly Rooms; there were balls, especially after the races held above Lord Pembroke's estate near the edge of Cranborne Chase; there were literary societies, clubs, and a theatre. The great composer Handel himself had performed next door to Mr. Harris's house.

On any day one might expect to meet members of the local gentry – Eyres, Penruddocks, Wyndhams, even perhaps one of the Herberts from the great house at Wilton. Why, even prominent citizens of the town bore historic names – like the deputy recorder Edward Poore, descended from the very family that had founded the cathedral five centuries before; or his wife Rachel, whose kinsman Bishop Bingham had ruled the diocese soon afterwards.

Sarum close. One did not even have to know the inhabitants to understand the place. One glance at the buildings told you that it had entered the age of elegance.

The square Georgian façades were to be seen all round the close: at Mr. Harris's house in the north east corner, in several fine houses backing on to the river on the western side, like Myles Place and the nearly rebuilt Walton Canonry, in the smaller terraced façades appearing on the eastern side near the gates to the bishop's palace. Some were stone, some brick, some stucco. But the finest, the noblest of all was the north side, facing the choristers' green: Mompesson House. It was always said that Sir Christopher Wren himself had made the first designs; since then the Mompesson family and after them their relations the Longuevilles had remodelled the interior with a splendid new staircase and elegant plasterwork; quiet, solid, modest in size yet stately in proportion with its two storeys, its row of seven large rectangular windows with three dormers in the roof above, its light grey stone blending perfectly with the mellow red brick of the similar houses on each side of it, Mompesson stared from behind its iron railings unabashed – as though conscious of its own domestic perfection – towards the grass of the churchyard by the cathedral's stately western façade. At each end of the railings that enclosed the few feet of lawn in front of the house stood a stone pillar with a heavy square lamp on top of it. The home of the Mompessons was everything a gentleman's county town house should be.

Not that the close was perfect. In the graveyard round the cathedral, the broad acres of lawn were thoroughly unkempt. After a heavy rain the place looked as though a herd of cows had marched through it; the ditches round the old belfry stank; it was perhaps to be regretted that Mr. Brown the sexton used to sell beer in the belfry, and when Mr. Henry Fielding the author had recently occupied the small house near Mr. Harris's young Adam Shockley could remember with delight the echoes of the rowdy parties that had emanated at all hours from that little house and which so amused his father and shocked his mother and the other ladies of the close.

But this did not matter. The elegance of the eighteenth century was robust and common sense.

There was plenty in Salisbury, from the suspected adultery of one of the canons, to the rich, pungent and variegated smells in the streets to remind Adam that life had its seamy side as well.

Sarum was unchanging. The great cathedral with its dominating spire spoke more eloquently than any words for the security of the Church of England. The Settlement that had brought the Hanoverians to England guaranteed its easy ascendancy. The Test Act ensured that any man wanting public office must swear the oath of loyalty to the English Church – and if Protestant dissenters were released from this obligation each year by a special indemnity, the principle remained and the troublesome Catholics were denied any office.

True, there were other religious voices at Sarum: a community of Quakers at Wilton, Wesleyans, who had heard the great John Wesley himself preach on Salisbury Plain, Deists, who believed that God would reward a good man's life regardless of his church, and even the occasional Jew. It did not greatly matter. Whatever men's private opinions might be, whatever sects might be tolerated, the placid Church of England ruled and was unmoved.

Sarum was independent. The government of England might be in the hands of the great Whig oligarchs close to the king – men like Walpole and after him the Duke of Newcastle and his brother – but still half the House of Commons consisted of the solid country members who mostly called themselves Tories, and who cared not a rap what the king or his ministers thought of them. These were the men that Sarum sent. For the county, as before, the local gentry stood – the Goddard or Long families usually in the north, Wyndham or Penruddock in the south. There was Wilton, for the Herbert interest. And in Salisbury, the burgesses sent independent gentlemen of their own choice. Recently, they had taken to sending as one of their members one of the family of a rich turkey merchant named Bouverie who had bought the great estate south of the town beside the ancient forest of Clarendon. But they did so because he gave generously to the town. Even a Herbert could not interfere with the Salisbury election.

Then there was Old Sarum: still deserted: an empty, windswept, grassy mound overlooking the little village of Stratford-sub-Castle in the Avon valley below. The ancient pocket borough still had, nominally, eight electors with the right to send members to Parliament and the custom was for them to meet by a tree below the old hillfort to make their choice. In practice, it was the landlord of the place who decided.

And Old Sarum belonged to the Pitts. For around the turn of the century both the ruin and much of the village below had been bought by one Thomas Pitt whose discovery of a huge diamond had given him the nickname Diamond Pitt. Owning the borough was more profitable than ever. Would-be members of Parliament were paying well for a seat; one could even pawn the borough to another landowner. And for the whole of the eighteenth century, with one break when they pawned it to the Prince of Wales, the family which produced two of England's greatest Prime Ministers owned Old Sarum.

This was the world that young Adam Shockley knew. One would have to say that, in the great calm of eighteenth century England, it was typical.

Prince Charlie's advance was rapid. His Highland army took Preston. Then, the large if disorganised force moved on to Derby. George II was abroad; England was short of troops, but the king's son, the Duke of

Cumberland, was collecting a force to oppose him. The French, who had promised to support the Stuart heir, did not.

Bonnie Prince Charlie had made his call.

And nothing happened.

Adam could not understand it. Day after day, while he was white with excitement, his father went gruffly about his business at the Forest estate, as usual. The friends who had often sat with him after dinner showed no sign of arming either.

In the first week of December, he could bear it no longer. One morning, he confronted his father.

"When are we going to ride," he demanded, "to fight for the Prince?"

Jonathan Shockley looked at him in surprise. What was the foolish boy talking about? It was a fault of his character that, while he enjoyed a quick and rather caustic turn of mind, he did not always bother to explain himself to his slower-witted son. He would read the vicious diatribes of the Tory poet Alexander Pope to his friends, or sit by himself of an evening and laugh till he wept at the dry satire of the author of Gulliver's Travels, that other fine Tory, Dean Swift. But when it came to such mundane matters as his child, he did not always trouble to while away the hours in his company.

"You may be," he said with a snort. "I haven't time." And he left the house.

It was a betrayal. Mortified and confused, Adam went up to his room and wept.

The truth of the matter was that, in England at least, the Jacobite cause had been dead for a generation. Of course, when things went wrong, a country gentleman would curse those damned Hanoverians and men with a certain turn of mind like Jonathan Shockley, might speak of the king over the water. But what was the good of a cause to a gentleman after dinner, if it was not already lost? Besides, the Stuarts were still tainted with Catholicism. No sane man in England wanted that trouble again.

The next morning, soon after dawn, Adam Shockley went quietly to the place where Nathaniel's sword hung. Carefully, he took it down. He had never held it before. It was heavy. But as he looked along the great steel blade he felt a thrill of excitement and awe. Once again, the ancient sword would do its work in the service of the true-born king.

Five minutes later he was in the stables with his pony, and soon afterwards, the gate keeper of the close, who had only just opened the gate at dawn, was astonished to see the small figure on his pony canter by, in possession of a sword that seemed almost as big as he was.

There were few people stirring as he left the town and took the road towards Wilton. At Wilton he took the northern road that led up the Wylie valley towards Bath. He had a guinea in his purse.

It was not until he was almost past Grovely Wood that Jonathan Shockley, cantering on his big grey mare, came up with him.

The gatekeeper had come to the house soon after dawn, to enquire if he knew his son had left. When he had heard the man's story and seen the sword gone from the wall he was at first completely baffled. But then he remembered the boy's foolish question of the day before.

"By God," he thundered to his horrified wife, "the young fool's gone to Derby."

It was reasonable to guess, therefore, that he would have taken the main north western road.

"I'll horsewhip him," he swore.

But as he came up to him now, and saw his small face set with determination and the ludicrous sword bumping at his side, Jonathan Shockley suddenly felt a wave of affection for his son. As he took the pony's bridle he said kindly:

"Come Adam, you'll fight in a better cause, another day."

And so it was that from that day, though he wept with rage the next spring when news came of the final defeat of the prince at Culloden, Adam Shockley lived with a new hope and determination in his heart.

The Stuart cause might be lost, but he would still be a soldier.

After the Forty-five, as the rising came to be known, Jonathan Shockley no longer passed his hand over the glass. But at dinner, if he chanced to see his son, he would call to the company:

"Take care, gentlemen. Here comes a damned dangerous Jacobite."

1753

He stood before his parents and smiled.

"You are sure you want to be a soldier?"

He nodded. He was certain.

His father was sitting on a tall-backed chair; his mother standing beside it with her hand resting on her husband's shoulder. They were a good-looking couple, both greying now, his father the more robust of the two. He thought he saw a little twitch at the corner of his mother's mouth and he noticed that, once or twice, she had blinked her eyes rather rapidly. There was a frown of concern on Jonathan's broad face.

He was sorry to disappoint them but he could not help it.

He knew very well what his mother would have liked. Elizabeth Shockley had always hoped her son would be a clergyman. True, many church benefices were poorly paid and some parish curates nearly starved. But her family still had some influence that might have got him preferment. Many a rector or prebendary lived like a gentleman and at Sarum at least, the dean lived like a lord.

All the great men of her own youth had been clergymen. Sarum had been full of distinguished figures – Izaac Walton, the writer's son, who had improved the cathedral library; Dean Clarke, the great mathematician; Bishop Sherlock, friend of the queen and denouncer of the Deists. She had always dreamed of seeing her only son a great man like one of these.

But there had always been one problem as his headmaster Mr. Hele had explained:

"The boy is a credit to you, madam, but he will never be a scholar. I think you must forget the church."

Adam had not been sent to Winchester or Eton after the choristers' school, but to a modest local establishment run by one of Jonathan's friends.

He was not stupid, but like an animal whose body is not yet co-ordinated, his brain often seemed to move clumsily and at times, to his shame, a kind of fog seemed to descend upon its operations. The year before, when in order to bring the English calendar in line with that of continental Europe, the date had been moved by eleven days, he could not shake off the feeling, shared by many of the illiterate folk that the eleven days had been lost. And when he heard his father laughing at a little group of labourers in the street who were crying, "Give us back our eleven days," he began to defend them.

"They were on the calendar but they've been taken away."

"Of course," his father replied, "but that doesn't make the sun rise and set any less does it?"

"No but . . ." Blushing, he felt the fog descending upon him before breaking off, embarrassed by the look of wonder on his father's face. It had taken him another two days to sort the business out clearly in his mind, to his own satisfaction.

He was slow, and did not pick up received ideas as well as the cleverer boys, but the conclusions he slowly and clumsily reached were at least his own.

As for Jonathan, he had simply hoped that his son might do something to mend the family fortunes.

But he wanted to be a soldier. One day he would be a great commander like his hero Marlborough. For years, ever since the rising of '45, he had dreamed of going to fight, of wearing a fine uniform with its bright red coat and broad lapels like those of the officers that he saw riding through the town from time to time.

There were so many places to fight.

And there was one great enemy: France.

Admittedly, England's foreign policy in recent decades had not always been clear. There had been distractions, like the small war with Spain, who cast covetous eyes on Gibraltar. And the king had sometimes made alliances to protect his native Hanover, which were not even in England's interest. But however the complex web of alliance, treachery, and diplomacy between the many states of Europe might change, one thing now seemed certain: the French meant to avenge their defeats by Marlborough and they would attack English possessions wherever they could.

If England intervened in the War of the Austrian Succession where Frederick the Great of Prussia was locked in combat with half Europe, it was only to weaken the French. If ships were sent to the West Indies, it was to protect her trade against the French; soldiers in America and in India were there to save her possessions and trade rights – always from the French. This was the single-minded strategy of that great man, loathed by the king but loved by the English people, William Pitt.

It was generally understood in 1753 that the French were about to attack English interests overseas again and that, whether he liked it or not, the king would have to call upon Pitt to direct the war.

This was the prospect that made young Adam Shockley's eyes shine and his heart beat with excitement. Recently, the great Thomas Arne had composed two stirring anthems, *Rule Britannia* and *God Save the King*. He hummed them to himself continually.

And now he had begged his father:

"Get me a commission in a regiment that is going to India."

"Which means I shall lose him," Adam's mother murmured sadly.

She had thought she might lose her only child the year before, when there was a brief outbreak of the dreaded smallpox in the town. On Jonathan's suggestion, the whole family had taken the new vaccine of Dr. Jenner, despite the warnings of all their friends. "Better to have the disease in the natural way," Forest had told him. This departure from his normal conservatism had been successful: none of them had caught the disease. But there was no vaccine against the unhealthy climate of India; few of the young men who ventured out there in that century to earn their livings, let alone who went to fight, were ever seen by their families again.

Jonathan was looking at his son thoughtfully. It was so obvious that the fair, broad-faced young fellow had set his heart on the matter. He also realised that he had no idea what a difficult thing he had asked. Should he explain? Should he disappoint the boy? What else, in any case, would young Adam do?

"If you must go to India," he suggested, "let me try to get you into John Company, where you might make your fortune. Forest has connections there and would help you." The East India Company, affectionately known as John Company, concerned itself nowadays with administering the British trading colony in India; but it held out many opportunities for shrewd young men who wanted to make their fortune.

But Adam could think only of his uniform.

"Please father," he begged again, "buy me a commission."

"You know the expense of a commission is considerable," Jonathan reminded him.

He saw the boy's face fall. At the same time, he felt his wife's hand squeeze his shoulder. He glanced up at her. Their eyes met.

"Very well," he sighed. "We shall see what can be done."

It was the next day that Adam was taken by his father to Avonsford Manor.

He had often visited the place in his childhood. He loved the handsome house, its pleasant park, and above all, the little church in the hamlet below, where he used to go to admire the stout, square, box pews that contained the worshippers like so many loose boxes. As a child he could hardly see over the edge unless he stood on the wooden bench inside. Then there were the hatchments – the big diamond-shaped wooden boards with the coats of arms of the departed members of the Forest family and their wives painted on them – that hung in cumbersome splendour from the tiny pillars. But best of all he liked to inspect the open fireplace in front of Sir George's splendid pew, and the big brass poker he rattled when he thought the curate was preaching too long. Sir George was often away, but when he encountered the dark saturnine landowner, he was usually given a quiet nod which seemed to be approving.

His father did not tell him the object of his visit, but he realised it must have to do with his career and accordingly he was on his best behaviour.

The interview he was granted was brief.

While Jonathan explained his son's desire to fight in India, he felt the baronet's cold eyes resting upon him. But looking into Forest's long, thin face, it was impossible to tell what he was thinking.

After a few questions, he was curtly dismissed, while his father remained with Forest for some time. When Jonathan reappeared, Adam thought that his father was looking tired.

"It's arranged," he said. "Forest has given me an introduction to a regiment, so I daresay we shall get you in."

"He is kind," Adam cried delightedly. And was so pleased that he hardly noticed that his father had pursed his lips.

In the early autumn of 1753, Jonathan Shockley and his son took a stage coach at the Black Horse Inn, the famous 'flying machine' that raced them up the turnpike roads to London in a single day. The adventure had begun.

Mr. Adam Shockley, Ensign of the 39th Regiment of Foot. At last.

The uniform was the most handsome thing he had ever seen: a long scarlet coat, faced with green, ornamented with white lace; scarlet waistcoat and breeches, white gaiters, white cravat, buff belt.

He never forgot that first moment of joy, that pure thrill of excitement, when he saw himself in the glass of the London tailor where his father had proudly taken him.

He was a man. A dozen gold buttons gleamed down his chest. His hair was 'clubbed' – plaited, turned up and tied with ribbon.

His father watched him and then, unnoticed, turned away; he had just remembered that he would probably never see the boy again.

The days had fled by: from a tearful parting with his mother, to the journey up the broad new turnpike roads, the wondrous entry into the collection of scattered villages and elegant parks that made up all but the very centre of London, the finding of an inn and the series of meetings between his father and numerous gentlemen in crowded coffee houses. Joining a regiment, it seemed, involved long whispered conversations, negotiations he did not understand, as well as the delivery of the letters of introduction from Sir George Forest. It also required money.

For one did not become an officer without paying for the privilege: naturally.

To be an ensign in one of His Majesty's Foot regiments cost £400. This was the humblest officer rank. To purchase a lieutenant's commission cost £550; a full captain £1,500. For £3,500 a gentleman of means could buy a lieutenant colonelcy; and a young man of great family and fortune who was known to the king, might find himself a general in his twenties.

"Everything is paid for, in this world," Jonathan said ruefully.

The £400 was paid to the Commander-in-Chief at the Horse Guards.

For two days he and his father walked about London. He saw the noble old Abbey of Westminster, the hall where Parliament met, the royal palace of St James, and the bustling maze of city streets around the splendid dome of Wren's St Pauls.

But his mind was already far from the great city on the river Thames. The 39th was due to sail from its camp in Ireland to faraway Madras within weeks, and he was going to join them.

There was only one thing that his father had not told him.

1758

Adam Shockley sat in the little hut. Outside, on the square of the cantonment, the sun was no longer beating down so relentlessly.

Very soon he had an engagement that he was looking forward to. He was dining with Fiennes Wilson – and that was always a spendid business.

He half closed his eyes and allowed his mind to wander over the events of the last few years.

What an extraordinary time it had been. What a triumph for English arms and the bold foreign policy of Pitt.

First the six month voyage to Madras; then the encounter with the massive, steaming Indian subcontinent: its exotic, dark-skinned people in their colourful dress, its dust, heat, monsoons – wild fluctuations of climate he had never imagined; in Sarum his eye had been used, day to day, to seeing the lush greens of the countryside, or the red brick and grey stone of the town. Here, life itself had a different hue – saffron, ochre, cinnamon met the eye, and as for the smells, they had assaulted him, rich and heady, as soon as he walked off the ship. How could he describe them: urine, jasmine, cowdung, he could pick out these strange and pungent aromas from the land, but they were mixed with so many others, the bitter-sweet scents of cooking that rose from every house, of spices, perfumes: no, he could not describe them. But he knew that he had a thrilling, tingling sense that he was more sharply alive than he had ever been before.

His life at first was pleasant. The little regimental canton was a modest collection of buildings, but there was so much to see, especially when one sauntered out into the warm evening after the relentless furnace of an Indian afternoon. There were amusements, like pig-sticking, or watching the native women in their subtle and exquisite dances. And he knew soon, there would be action.

For several years the French government forces and the East India Company – independent but backed by British arms – had been manoeuvring for control of the huge Indian trade in tea, coffee, silks and spices. Up to 1756, their action had mostly been confined to alliances between different Indian princes and to occasional skirmishes.

But now the incipient war was coming out into the open. Pitt demanded action. At the time he arrived in Madras, the regiment knew it could not be long before there was action.

First however, there was a brief wait.

It was during this period that Adam first met Fiennes Wilson.

Sir George Forest had supplied the letter of introduction. His father had handed it to him just as he was leaving, together with twenty pounds in gold; but he had not fully understood the value of the letter until one of the lieutenants who was well versed in India told him:

"Fiennes Wilson? He's a friend of Warren Hastings, and the other young bloods of the East India Company here."

He understood that Wilson, of the wealthy Christchurch family, was attached to the East India Company in some way, but he knew little of Hastings or other names the lieutenant mentioned.

"Those are the men in John Company that are going to build India," his lieutenant told him. "And make fortunes for themselves," he added.

The vast accumulations of capital the India merchants could make were well known. Men of moderate means when they left England might return years later, if they survived the climate, with tens of thousands of pounds – nabobs they were called – who bought estates and even titles for themselves back in England.

"An introduction to Fiennes Wilson and Warren Hastings is a valuable asset," the lieutenant went on, "make good use of it, young fellow. I envy you."

Fiennes Wilson was a tall young man of twenty-five. His face was so finely drawn and perfectly proportioned that he seemed to have stepped out of the classical world. His black hair was thinning, giving his forehead a look of greater height than it actually had.

To Adam, within minutes of their first meeting, he seemed like a Greek god and a hero.

It was not surprising. Fiennes Wilson had all the charm and easy manners of a young aristocrat; his eyes were sympathetic; he laughed easily; and he had a great deal of money.

He took in the young fellow at a glance and welcomed him like an old friend of the family.

"This is Mr. Adam Shockley," he told his other guests at their first dinner, "a friend of Sir George Forest's. You're an old Sarum family, I believe, Mr. Shockley."

Adam soon found that the other rich young men in Wilson's circle knew people in Sarum with whom he was on nodding acquaintance – Wyndhams, Penruddocks and the like – and after the first evening he imagined himself very much at home.

It was a pleasant thing, he decided, to be a gentleman from Sarum.

Wilson was in Madras only briefly. He had taken the house of an East India Company man who had returned to England for some months, and he lived in splendid style. The men he entertained there were fine fellows. And some rather fine native women came to the place too, it was rumoured. These Adam had yet to see, but he lived in hope.

[735]

He had already made inroads on the twenty pounds from his father, but he did not allow this to worry him. Life was such an adventure.

The climax of his stay in Madras had been when young Wilson had sent him a note inviting him to come hunting.

He had never seen anything like it – a full-blown affair with native noblemen and young English bloods riding elephants, and using cheetahs to chase the quarry – a far cry from the humble pig-sticking that was the usual sport of other ensigns. It lasted three days, and they killed a quantity of game including numerous bison and three tigers.

By the time this was over, although he was no spendthrift, the twenty pounds was down to five, and Adam might have been seriously concerned, if another event had not put all other thoughts out of his mind.

For now news came of the Black Hole of Calcutta.

It was a strange business – the former minister of an Indian prince who was supported by the French, had taken refuge with the British in Calcutta. The prince, Suraj-ud-Dowlah, then attacked Calcutta and after the women and children had escaped, the one hundred and forty-six Englishmen left there were put in a single prison room: they were left there in the murderous August heat and only twenty-three survived.

This was the signal: the Black Hole must be avenged.

And then there followed an extraordinary negotiation.

For the commanding officer of the 39th regiment, Colonel Adlercorn, refused to lead it. This was because Governor Pigot in Madras would not guarantee him a great enough share of the spoils if the expedition were victorious; nor would the Colonel engage to return if summoned.

It was because of this squabble that a brilliant, but bored young official of the East India Company, Robert Clive, was given command instead. In 1756, Clive, with a portion of the 39th, sailed north to Calcutta.

The ensuing campaign was short and brilliant, and culminated the following June when Clive's 1100 whites, 2100 natives and ten field pieces faced the huge army of Suraj-ud-Dowlah – 18,000 horse, 50,000 foot and 53 pieces of heavy ordnance served by French gunners.

What a glorious day that had been. He had watched the council of officers; seen Clive hesitate and seemingly take counsel with himself under some mango trees. Then, despite the odds, they had charged. At first, Adam had assumed he was going to die. Instead, they had won an astonishing victory. He felt like a hero.

Following the custom of the time and country, the treasury of the Indian prince was open to the victors. For himself Clive took the fabulous sum of £160,000, though the Indians thought this modest. Another half million was distributed to the army and navy. Young Ensign Shockley, recently arrived, had taken part in the battle and received £500. The British were now the controlling power in India, and he was in funds.

It was good not to feel poor. He guarded the money carefully, but all the same, he felt free to spend a little on himself. There were other campaigns still to be fought. If he could see more action, there might be a chance of obtaining further windfalls.

For the time being, however, he was back in Madras, enjoying a little leisure.

The company was a large one that evening, some twenty young men sat down to dine. Some he had met before, but there was a contingent of hard-faced young fellows that were new to him, but whom Wilson seemed to know well. The talk was partly of the campaigning, which he could join in, and of East India Company affairs, about which he was a listener rather than a participant. There was the usual personal badinage, and often references would be made to great names or estates, which he recognised but seldom personally knew.

It pleased him though, to be accepted as a junior member of such a company, and he ate and drank in a state of great contentment.

There were undercurrents in the conversation tonight, however, that he detected but did not fully understand. All the company seemed aware that something was going to happen. There were occasional nods and winks, some directed, he thought, at him. There was also, as the evening wore on, a constant barrage of conversation from the group he did not know about racing, wagers and gambling matters. He knew Salisbury races well enough and he prided himself that he could play a fair game of whist; he could take a hand at cribbage, and everyone was familiar with vingt-et-un and quinze. But these men spoke of other games that he had never even heard of.

Once or twice he tried to smile knowingly when some remark was made to him that he did not understand; but he felt a little uncomfortable. He drank more wine than usual.

Was it his imagination, or had Fiennes Wilson changed? At the smaller dinners he had been to, and when he had gone hunting, Wilson had always been kindly towards him and paid him special attention. Perhaps it was just the larger company, but now his friend's face seemed rather distant. There was a new hardness in his eyes too, that almost matched those of his gambling friends. As Adam gazed along the table at him, he felt a faint sense of disappointment. He drank some more, and talked earnestly to the man on his right – though afterwards he could remember nothing of what he had been saying.

It was well into the evening that the girls came in. There were ten of them. "Enough to go round us all," someone cried.

"I'll share with Shockley," the fellow opposite him remarked loudly. "He looks too damned drunk to need his share." It was a joke. But the tone of the man's voice was unfriendly.

There was laughter at this and he glanced at Wilson. But his friend's eyes only returned a hard glazed stare, which said – fend for yourself.

There was music. The girls danced. He had seen dancing before, but never anything so good. Sinuous, fluid, erotic, they entertained them for half an hour and Adam, who had only lost his virginity with a girl in the town the month before, felt a strong desire for them. Though he had to admit, the gibe about his being too drunk was probably correct. For the time being, however, the girls retired and the young men continued drinking.

[737]

It was a little later, when he had leaned back in his chair and closed his eyes for a moment that he heard the conversation two places to his left. It was between one of the men he didn't know and another, who had been on the hunt with him, and who he had thought was his friend.

"Who's the young fellow?"

"Shockley."

"Never heard of him. What is he?"

"Nothing much. A dependant of Wilson's of some kind."

"Oh."

They had gone on to discuss other matters.

He kept his eyes closed. A wave of coldness passed over him, then he blushed. He opened his eyes a little. No one was looking at him.

A dependant. It had not occurred to him they did not accept him as one of themselves. He was younger of course; but he thought he was a gentleman.

Suddenly the realisation came over him, and as he thought of his father's modest house and the frown on his face when he had originally to pay for the commission, he saw exactly how he must appear to the young blood on his left. A dependant – was that all he was?

One or two of the girls reappeared, not to dance, but to sit with the men. He saw that Wilson had one on his knee.

There was talk of further entertainment. Would they have more dancing, music, cards? Someone suggested that they needed a song.

It was then that Wilson looked up. His eyes were heavy-lidded now. His handsome, Grecian face looked slightly debauched; but his eyes as they moved round the table seemed to miss nothing. They came to rest upon Adam.

"Shockley," he said, "will give us a song."

Adam blushed furiously. His mind went blank.

"Quite right," someone cried. "Sing, Shockley." And again – was it his imagination? – he thought he detected contempt in the voice.

He could think of nothing. There was a look of arrogance on Wilson's face now.

"You must sing for your supper," he announced, flatly, and when he still hesitated: "Sing, damn you."

"He can't sing," the man opposite called, "let's play cards."

There was a general chorus of agreement. Wilson ceased to look at him and turned his attention to the girl.

The table broke up in a desultory fashion. Several men disappeared, presumably with the girls. A few gathered in little groups at each end of the table where they contrived to drink together. The rest moved to where card tables were being set up.

He was left alone.

It was a blow to find that Wilson despised him for being poor. He supposed he could not blame him.

But yet something inside him rebelled. He was a gentleman from Sarum, whatever these strangers might think of him. A descendant of

Cavaliers. He had a little money too, after Plassey. He would be nobody's dependant.

Wilson was sitting at one of the table ends. Adam ignored him. He went to the card tables instead, and quietly watched. After a while, when someone left a game and he was asked if he cared for whist, he nodded. He knew how to play. And when one of the men looked doubtful and asked him if he was sure he cared to lose, he gave him a calm look and remarked casually:

"I haven't spent my Plassey money yet."

The man shrugged and said no more.

The next morning, when Adam Shockley did his reckoning in the cold light of day, he found that he had lost just four hundred and twenty pounds. With the thirty he had spent since Plassey, he had forty pounds left.

He was resigned. A gentleman must pay his gambling debts.

"But I need a new campaign," he muttered.

It was unfortunate then, that shortly afterwards, the 39th were ordered back to Ireland.

They took a tiger with them as a mascot, and saw the great comet predicted by Halley on the way.

1767

Lieutenant Shockley looked at Madame Leroux, and then he stared thoughtfully out to sea at the dot on the horizon he knew must be the English packet. If the news the ship brought was good, he would marry her, no matter what the opposition in the regiment.

She did not know it. He had allowed her to prepare to leave.

In the year 1767, Lieutenant Adam Shockley, no longer of the 39th, but of the 62nd Foot, was a good-looking, broad-chested man of thirty-two whose fair hair was thinning. His face was bronzed and weatherbeaten. He was respected as a sound, even-tempered officer to whom many of the younger fellows came for advice.

For four years now, he had been on the sultry island of Dominica in that part of the West Indies then called the Charibees.

And for almost a year, he had enjoyed the company of Madame Leroux.

She was a strange woman; her husband, who had been killed at sea by a privateer, was a French merchant and, insofar as she was anything, she was French herself. Her age, Shockley supposed must be between twenty-five and thirty. Still more indeterminate was her race. Her skin was pale, her hair almost white and formed naturally into short, frizzy curls. The rumour was that she had negro blood. There was a languid, sensuous quality about her: she was a being apart. Though the French had lost the island to the British, she had not troubled to speak more than rudimentary English and she generally treated the new occupants with silent disdain.

"It's not my business where you go, Shockley," the major had said to him one day, "but Madame Leroux is not popular with us, you know."

Adam did not care. During the warm nights he had known a sexual passion richer than anything he had experienced before, and by day even with his own mediocre French, he had come to love her gentle, mocking humour.

And what else was there for him now, in any case? He would not be the first poor English officer in a warm outpost to take a foreign or unsuitable wife.

The years after Plassey had seen a series of English victories. Wolfe had taken Quebec and secured Canada for the English. The last battles of the Seven Years War in Europe had been fought and won. At Minden, the death of a superior officer had given him the chance to be promoted lieutenant on the battlefield. But after that, there had been few opportunities either for battle promotion or for profit. What commissions came up – captain lieutenant or full captain – were usually snapped up by rich young men from the Guards. Soon after the accession of the new king, George III, he had transferred to the 62nd in the hope of action and reward in the West Indies, but had seen little of either and was almost as poor as before.

One sad event had taken place just after his arrival there: his mother had died.

His father wrote to him gloomily about it and warned him that, although there would in time be something due to him from certain interests she had with her family, the funds would take time to come through and would in any case be small.

He was surprised, within the year, to hear from Jonathan that he had married again and that his new wife was already pregnant. There had been no more word in his father's letters about the funds coming to him; and he had not cared to ask.

So he had settled down, on the lush and sultry island of Dominica, to several years of garrison duty where the only military activity was to train men in parade ground tactics that he suspected would be useless for anything but a set-piece battle, and the only casualties from such tropical sicknesses as malaria.

In this enforced and enervating idleness, until he struck up his friendship with Madame Leroux, Adam Shockley had two principal sources of pleasure. The first was his correspondence with his father.

Jonathan Shockley wrote well. His caustic wit, which had sometimes been daunting and confusing to Adam as a boy, came through far better in his letters to his son now that Adam was a man. He kept Adam abreast of Sarum affairs – of the weakened cloth trade, the doings of Mr. Harris, and the scandal of young Lord Pembroke temporarily deserting his young wife – so that Adam could almost feel he was back in the close and hearing his father's voice. He often gave him useful information, too, about more general political affairs.

Above all, he served as a conduit for his son's other new-found pleasure. For Adam now developed a taste for books.

"I have made a late start upon my education," he confessed to one of the other lieutenants, "but the truth is I have never enjoyed any kind of learning until now."

Very soon, half of what he could save from his pay was going on purchases of books, which Jonathan willingly sent out to him, often with his own pungent comments upon them. Father and son wrote to each other on the merits of Dr. Samuel Johnson's great dictionary. Numerous lighter works – Defoe's *Robinson Crusoe*, and Swift's *Gulliver's Travels* arrived; then heavier matter: Clarendon's great volumes of history, Milton's *Paradise Lost*, and the more recent philosophical works of Hume and Bishop Berkeley. He even read Voltaire, and admired that great man's mockery of the confusion and humbug of the day's organised religion.

"With great minds for company, a man is never lonely," Adam concluded.

Jonathan's comments on political events too were thought provoking. One letter which came soon after the American colony had protested about the English Parliament's levying of a stamp duty tax on them, always remained in Adam's mind.

I was vastly amused to hear that the colonists' ambassador – I know not how else to describe the man – Mr. Benjamin Franklin, being in London at the time the said Stamp Act was first brought in, made haste to procure for three of his friends positions as stamp masters, which I am assured would have given them little exertion but a handsome income each of £300 a year!

And now, my dear Adam, I shall give you my view of the American colony which, I am proud to say, is shared by none.

For 'tis clear to me that the most foolish thing we ever did was to beat the French so handsomely. The gentlemen of the colony, having no great threat made against them any more will soon be grown indifferent to England for whose army, and the expense thereof, they will think themselves no longer in need. There's the rub. Excuses will be found, but they'll not pay taxes across the ocean.

And then – the government will try to compell them. 'Tis there that you will next fight.

But today it was a far more important letter he was awaiting.

She had been his mistress for nearly a year. It was a situation that suited them both. But, as she had said to him quite frankly, it was time that she married again. And since, she pointed out, there appeared to be no prospect of her doing so on Dominica, it was time for her to move on.

"I shall go to a French island," she told him, looking into his eyes a little sadly.

The message could not be clearer. If he wished to marry her, he must say so. But on a lieutenant's pay and her tiny income, it was impossible.

On a captain's pay, it might be done. Furthermore, a captaincy was becoming available shortly. The price was seven hundred pounds. He had two hundred saved.

That was why he had written with urgency to his father to enquire what sums might be due to him from his mother's family.

The mail the packet was bringing would be in his hands by morning.

My dear Son,

You naturally ask whether there is some money due to you from your mother.

It was a matter I had long meant to acquaint you with yet which, I must confess, had escaped my memory these last few years – namely, that when you determined upon gaining a commission before you went to India, it was necessary to purchase the same at a cost of £400.

What neither I nor your mother told you at that time was that such a sum was not readily available; and accordingly it was agreed that it should be borrowed from Sir George Forest, which loan, thanks to the high opinion he had of you, was made at no interest, but upon condition that, upon the decease of either one of us, the loan should be repaid forthwith.

Your mother had from her family a portion of £500. I have accordingly repaid Sir George Forest's loan of £400, and the remaining £100, my dear boy, is at your service. Pray let me know how and where you wish to receive it.

Yr affectionate father J.S.

They had not told him.

Madame Leroux left two weeks later.

It was three months after that, that several of the troops began to go down with malaria.

1777: October 6

It was the eve of battle. Below them on the left flowed the Hudson River; on their right was the battered little group of buildings called Freeman's Farm. On the opposite high ground, three thousand yards away, lay Gates and the American rebels. Eight miles behind them, Saratoga. The place before them was called Stillwater.

It was the eve of battle, and Captain Adam Shockley felt uneasy.

The essence of the plan, a good and sound plan which, faced with the dithering incompetence of Lord North and his ministers, had been drawn up by George III himself, was that General Howe and his large force should come from the south while General Burgoyne came down from Canada. The two should then meet and trap the American rebels against the east coast. Howe had delayed in Philadelphia.

"Some say he cares more for the rebel cause than our own," complained one of his fellow officers to Shockley.

Whatever Howe's reason, the plan was already half ruined and the forces at Stillwater were now waiting, with increasing desperation, for General Clinton to come up through Albany with urgently needed supplies.

But for ill-luck, Captain Adam Shockley would not have been there at all.

By 1769, when the regiment – or rather the handful of officers and seventy-five troops remaining after their sickness in the tropics – had returned to build up its strength again in Ireland, Adam Shockley was suffering from malaria. The voyage home and a rest at the barracks restored him, but at thirty-five he felt himself to be middle-aged. Nonetheless, he set about the business of recruiting, and at the same time tried to build up his own strength. He walked, rode, and drank little, and although he suffered a few minor relapses, pronounced himself fit enough to carry on. Since the regiment was so short of men, no one suggested he should give up his duties.

The recruiting was slow. In the years that followed, out of four hundred and sixty-four recruits, one hundred and five deserted; but still the numbers were steadily growing, and it was enough.

"It's the old hands like me who hold things together," he declared with perfect truth. The army was full of men like him – middle-aged lieutenants who could not afford higher commissions but who knew the regiment and had seen service. "I daresay I shall die a poor lieutenant," he said with resignation.

His opportunity came out of the blue – a letter from Fiennes Wilson, now a powerful man in the East India Company, working with Warren Hastings who had become the greatest man in India. It offered him a post in the company:

> We are looking for a man of sense and judgement and Sir George Forest recommended your name to us.
>
> I remember your visit here in the glorious days of Plassey, as does Mr Hastings.
>
> The position would not make you a nabob, but would certainly be rewarding.

He could not go; the doctor he consulted was adamant.

"You've spent your time in a hot climate, Mr. Shockley, and you've already paid the price. If you go to India now, I can't answer for you. You mustn't think of it. Only a cold climate for you, sir, now. The colder the better."

He had remained in Ireland and it was from there that he had watched the situation in America grow worse, just as his father had predicted. When the dumping of excess tea into the America market to aid the finances of the East India Company had sparked off the Boston Tea Party, he was not surpised. As the skirmishes of Lexington and Concord gave way to the fighting at Bunker Hill and Boston, he rejoiced. It must mean action – his one chance of promotion. If there must be fighting, he hoped it would be a compaign of interest, and he was full of curiosity when he learned that Generals Gates and Lee, both former British officers, were leading rebel forces and were being joined by a new and powerful figure, Washington, the landowner from Virginia.

The regiment was ready. After what seemed to Shockley an endless delay, in April 1776 they left the west of Ireland for Quebec.

Not, of course, that there was any question of the rebels succeeding. Why, more than half the colony was loyal to the British crown. New York alone was supplying fifteen thousand regular and eight thousand five hundred militia to the British army, when Washington had about twelve thousand under his own command.

"Besides," the major assured Shockley, "I know something of this Washington. The only reason he's against us is that our ministers denied him, and others like him, the right to conquer tracts of their own in Ohio. The man's a gentleman. His brother married into a family with six million acres – think of it, Shockley."

"Yet he leads the rebels," Adam pointed out.

"Rabble. And I dare say Washington knows it." He smiled knowingly. "I'll tell you a thing. I know a merchant in England that corresponded with him once, this Washington. Sent me a copy of some of the fellow's words: look at this." And he produced a small piece of paper on which a single sentence was written:

Mankind when left to themselves, are unfit for their own government.

"There, sir. Now don't tell me that when Washington has tried to wring a few concessions from our ministers, he won't abandon these cursed radicals to their fate."

Shockley had heard that part of the reason why the southern states had started to fight was in the hope of repudiating their debts to English merchants. The men of the north, he supposed, wanted to escape taxes. But the air of blustering confidence amongst some of his fellow officers worried him. He had a feeling the American rebels would turn out to be more tenacious than that.

In June 1776, under the command of Brigadier General Fraser, the 62nd helped to hold off and then scatter two thousand of the rebels who had advanced upon the town of Sorel on the St Lawrence river. Two hundred rebel prisoners were taken. After this victory, known as the Battle of Three Rivers, part of the British force, under General Burgoyne, moved down to Fort St John.

It was a successful action. The 62nd had distinguished itself, and to his great delight, Adam Shockley at last found himself promoted to captain.

"We've driven the rebels out of Canada," Burgoyne told his new captain. "Now we'll crush them above New York."

One other event had occurred meanwhile, that seemed to give the lie to this confident boast. For a month after Three Rivers, thirteen provinces in North America took the flag of the stars and stripes and made their Declaration of Independence.

The Declaration called forth one of Jonathan Shockley's most characteristic letters from Sarum:

As to this Declaration of Independence, I confess myself utterly astonished. That all men are born free and equal is an assertion against the history and constitution of every civilised country.

There's not a word of such a thing in Magna Carta to be sure.

Then the assertion that all men have the right to the pursuit of happiness; I cannot imagine why it should be thought so. Certainly there's no word about happiness in the Bible, nor in any of the canons of the Christian religion. Indeed, I scarcely think our Puritans in England would have tolerated such a notion for a moment; for your Calvinist makes a virtue of being miserable upon every opportunity.

No, my dear Adam, these are the vapourings of enthusiasts and demagogues, and soon will pass.

Yet it was the very day after the successful battle of Three Rivers that Adam Shockley decided the English cause was lost.

He was a small fellow, barely sixteen years old, and he was sitting very quietly with the other prisoners. When he had been taken the day before it had amused the men that the musket they took from him was so much larger than he was.

He was not only small, he was narrow – there was no other word for it. It was not only his thin face, and close-set eyes, not only his thin, spidery hands; his whole body seemed not more than a foot across at the shoulder.

Yet – Shockley noticed it about nearly all the prisoners – the boy had a sort of inner calm about him, not at all like the boisterous good nature of his own men. His dark eyes stared at his captors without fear or anger; it was almost as if he pitied them.

His name was John Hillier.

Feeling sorry for the boy, Shockley strode over to him.

"You have a Wiltshire name, Mr. Hillier," he said with a smile. "Plenty of Hilliers around Sarum where I come from."

The boy nodded calmly.

"My grandfather left Wiltshire," he replied, gazing at Adam without either respect or insolence.

"Oh. Why was that?"

"His wife's family turned Quakers, captain. They were more welcome in Pennsylvania than England." He spoke with the quiet assurance that it was England who had lost by their move. "Then my grandfather went to join them after."

Shockley thought of the little community of Quakers he remembered at Wilton. They had been tolerated – just. He couldn't say he blamed the Hilliers and their Quaker relations for leaving.

"But you and your family, you are not Quakers?"

"No," he said simply. "Quakers don't fight. I do."

"And what do you hope to gain from this fighting, Mr. Hillier?" he asked pleasantly.

The boy looked at him in surprise.

"Freedom," he said simply.

Shockley would have liked to sit down beside him to talk, but thought that, as an officer, he should not; and so their conversation was

[745]

conducted in this strange fashion, with the young captive sitting on the ground and the bluff British officer standing in front of him. Despite this, they spoke easily enough.

"Tell me then, Mr. Hillier, what is the freedom you seek?"

"That no man should be taxed without representation, sir. That all men should be free and entitled to vote. These are both English common law, I believe, and written in Magna Carta. These liberties were denied us by the king."

Shockley almost burst out laughing; but checked himself in time.

Neither common law – that collection of ancient uses which protected a man's property and gave even a serf a right to be tried before he was hung, nor the great charter that Archbishop Langton had drawn up between King John and his barons had a word to say about representation and tax, let alone voting. The very idea was absurd. But he could see that the boy believed it and so for the time being he said nothing.

He tried another tack.

"You say you accept the English laws, Mr. Hillier, yet you deny the authority of the king. How can you be an Englishman then?"

"How is the king one," the boy retorted bitterly, "when he sends German mercenaries against us?"

But Adam countered swiftly.

"And 'tis well known you seek an alliance with England's greatest enemy, France."

Now Hillier did not reply, but Shockley was not trying to confound him. He returned therefore to the general argument.

"What if, Mr. Hillier, those rights you speak of were not to be found in common law and the charter?" he asked gently. "What would be your argument then?"

The boy thought, but only for a moment.

"There are natural laws, above those made by man; God gave us reason, and reason tells us these things are just."

Adam stared at him. It was astounding. He knew from his schooldays, and from his subsequent reading that such arguments could be made. Aristotle, two thousand years before had spoken of universal law; the great Churchman Aquinas had named it too – though strictly subservient to Divine Law, as revealed in the Bible, that in turn came from God's Eternal Law, which no man could know. It was one thing for philosophers to speculate about such matters, or for clergymen turned sceptics to ridicule the rule of bishops behind closed doors; but here was this young fellow unblushingly using such grand philosophical language in the belief that it gave him the right to deny the authority of Parliament and the king. It sounded like anarchy. Yet the young fellow spoke so quietly.

It was now that young Hillier drew from his pocket a small pamphlet. Its title was *Common Sense* by the radical writer Tom Paine.

"There's much in here that explains our cause," he stated. "Read it, if you wish."

Adam had heard of the pamphlet. It had been written the previous year and copies had spread all over the colony. It was plain sedition, he had heard. He shook his head. He wanted to hear from the boy himself.

"What authority do you accept, then?"

"My conscience," he said simply.

There Adam saw the whole matter with absolute clarity. The fact that John Hillier's constitutional arguments were incorrect – it was this that had infuriated the English Parliament about the rebels more than anything else; the fact that he was using ideas of freedom and justice over which philosophers could argue; the fact that he knew nothing of the centuries of subtle adjustment between the authority and rights of Church, State and individual, of the arguments of the Reformation, the Civil War, and the Glorious Revolution: none of these mattered. The struggles of the old world, though they had produced a measure of freedom, would be forgotten in the new.

He looked down with fascination at the boy. He seemed sensible enough.

"But if we do as you say, then, the people themselves would rule," he said. "Are you not afraid of that?"

And now it was John Hillier who stared at him in astonishment.

"Why should I be?"

The conversation haunted him.

As they prepared for the offensive down the Hudson river to New York, and as his fellow officers predicted sweeping victories, his own sense of foreboding would not leave him. True, they were a well-trained force. When the order for the infantry to advance was given: "Spring up": no regiment in the line did so with more energy than the gallant 62nd. Already the jaunty little regiment was known as the Springers. He had even done what he could to train them in the more flexible fighting methods that were needed in that rough terrain. Only General Howe had done so before, when he had taken seven companies for some combat training on Salisbury Plain three years before. But so much was missing. It was not just the parade ground tactics: nor the interrupted supply lines and poorly coordinated higher command. It was in the hearts of the men.

"We pay our men poorly, and then we deduct their uniforms, their utensils, everything imaginable from their pay. They know no one cares for their welfare. And no chaplains care for their souls," he complained to his colonel. "Only the Wesleyans we so despise seem to take an interest in the poor soldier."

"The rebels are worse supplied. Even the Americans begrudge them food, because they pay for it with their own worthless paper money," the colonel countered.

But in his heart Adam was thinking:

"They can lose a dozen campaigns; but if they don't want us here, then one day they'll win the war."

He wrote to his father:

We have left Fort St George in splendid order, in a force under Burgoyne of about 8,000 men: Major Harnage has brought his wife and the general is encumbered with no less than six members of

Parliament. The men march well; and each company is allowed three women.

We have, so far been successful against the enemy in every encounter; though we lost 200 men in the swamps around Ticonderoga, which we took, most of them falling to the sharpshooters who take a constant toll of our staunch parade ground fellows. There seems little we can do about it.

Our supplies are beginning to run somewhat low.

And now it was October. Tomorrow they would fight again at Stillwater.

It was two and a half weeks since their first battle at Stillwater and they had remained in the camp at Freeman's Farm ever since. It had been a victory for the British, of course. They took the farm in a hard day's fighting, attacking the place in three columns and in classic style. There was only one problem: the 62nd in the centre column had been almost destroyed.

Four times they had charged the Americans, with bayonets fixed, and forced them to retreat into the woods; and four times they had run into the sharpshooters who lurked there, not only concealed on the ground, but up in the trees as well. It was a dastardly way of fighting: and highly effective. Major Harnage was carried from the field badly wounded; the adjutant, a lieutenant and four ensigns were killed. By sunset, only sixty men of the 62nd were fit for further duty.

The red coats had won, but at a cost they could not afford.

And still the supplies had not come.

On the night of October 6, 1777, Captain Shockley slept badly. Where was General Howe with his great force? Where was Clinton with his much needed supplies and reinforcements? Nowhere, it seemed. He got up in the morning feeling despondent.

For much of the battle known as Saratoga, Adam Shockley was a spectator; for the 62nd, being so reduced in numbers, was left to guard the camp when, at about noon on 7 October, General Burgoyne ordered the advance.

At first it seemed the British might prevail. Until, that was, the American second in command, Arnold, having been confined to camp by General Gates after a quarrel, disobeyed orders, leaped on his horse, placed himself at the head of three regiments he knew well and, without so much as a by-your-leave, smashed clean through the British centre and stormed the British redoubt.

From the camp above, Shockley watched in horror.

Darkness gave them the chance to abandon the camp for a piece of high ground by the river. The next day the Americans covered their right flank and they withdrew to Saratoga, leaving their wounded to the rebels. The day after that, the Americans came round behind them. It poured with rain. There were sharpshooters everywhere.

It was on this day, 9 October, that Captain Adam Shockley, while inspecting a barricade that a party of his men were erecting, felt a sudden blow in the shoulder followed, a moment later, by a searing, red hot pain and looked up in astonishment to find himself lying on the ground and his uniform covered with blood, before he fainted.

A sharpshooter had got him.

Five days later, when Saratoga capitulated, Captain Adam Shockley, fortunate to be only wounded in the shoulder, was one of the handful of men who remained of the five hundred and forty-one who had constituted the 62nd regiment.

Of the few who did remain, some in the next two years were sent to Virginia, others escaped to New York. The regimental band defected to the rebels and served in a Boston regiment. In 1782, the Springers regiment was reconstituted and by chance, when regiments of the line were given county titles that year, were called The Wiltshire Regiment.

The defeat at Saratoga was a turning point. From that time on, though the fighting continued, until Cornwallis's surrender at Yorktown in 1781, the British Government looked not for victory, but for the least damaging peace they could negotiate. America was going to be lost.

He only received one letter from his father at this time. It was very brief, and informed Adam that his second wife had died, leaving him alone with his two children.

His own captivity lasted a little over a year. He was not badly treated; indeed his captors and he had many discussions and he left them finally with a sense of friendship that surprised him.

But at last, in the spring of 1779, with the wound in his shoulder nearly healed, Captain Adam Shockley returned, for the first time in over twenty years, to his family home in Sarum.

He wondered what he would find there.

1779

A damp March wind from the west, small grey clouds chasing across a clear, pale blue sky. Sweeping ridges of brown earth and short grass, neatly arranged into large fields marked off by walls of loose grey stone.

The stagecoach: four fine horses, well-matched, two chestnut and two greys, driver and a man in the coachman's box both in tall hats, almost conical; up front three chilled passengers, one a woman, their faces reddened by the wind; one man behind gazing down at the huge open basket where the luggage was stowed. Inside, four men paying full fare, sitting in comfort on leather upholstery, windows pulled up, very warm. The huge wheels gliding smoothly.

The Bristol to Bath stagecoach was indeed a fine, rapid and fashionable conveyance as it rolled easily along the turnpike road.

Turnpikes: Bristol to Bath; Bath via Warminster down to Wilton; Wilton to Sarum. Put another way: medieval port, to Roman spa, to Saxon capital, to the bishop's new city, already five centuries old.

Turnpikes: there had been nothing like these broad roads in England since Roman times, fourteen hundred years before. They were installed now on all the main routes between major towns, as hard and smooth as a gravel drive. They supplanted the old cartways and tracks that had been used – except during the more civilised Roman period – as the principle roads since prehistoric times.

They were privately run: each set up with its charter of authority from Parliament, each with its shareholders; and its toll gates. Some of the turnpike trusts owned the right to toll large stretches of highway, some only two or three miles; but they were profitable and efficient. The Forest family was a major shareholder in several of them.

To Adam Shockley, returning after so many years, England was a surprise.

"Why the whole country," he remarked, "it's all fashioned by man!"

For the landscape of England and the landscape of America had nothing in common at all. The latter was virgin forest or open land in which man made his modest habitation. But in England, even on the sweeping empty ridges, the hand of man had cut down, shaped, and rearranged wood, ploughed field and pasture for thousands of years. If there were woods, it was because landowners chose to keep them there for shooting or for timber. If there were wastes, it was because, like as not, human hands had once cut down the forests that covered them and the ancient soil had eroded away. True, there were still prehistoric heaths and ancient forest where the hand of man had left little or no impression – but few if any lay along the route of the Bristol to Bath express. England was a country fashioned by men: he had forgotten.

It was early afternoon when Adam arrived at Bath. He had decided to remain there the night.

And Bath, too, was a revelation.

For thirteen centuries nothing much had been done about the spa town of Aquae Sulis. At the start of the century, in the reign of Queen Anne, the place had been little more than a run-down provincial town with a small trade surrounding its mineral springs. The huge complex of Roman buildings with their magnificent halls and baths had all but disappeared under centuries of mud.

And then that inveterate – and successful – gambler, Richard Nash arrived.

It was the Bath created by Beau Nash that Adam Shockley now entered with wonder.

There were elegant streets, squares and crescents, all built in the classical Georgian style with pediments, urns, pilasters, like so many Greek or Roman temples and all done in the mellow, creamy-grey stone of the region; there were the assembly rooms where, like the great Mr. Harris at Sarum, Beau Nash had presided over the exquisite social gatherings he had so carefully fashioned himself, and where the fashionable could gamble when they were not taking the cure. There was the hot bath, the king's bath, the great pump room where both sexes, discreetly segregated when necessary, immersed themselves in the curative saline springs or drank the mineral waters. There were obelisks to commemorate royal visits. There was even the Royal Mineral Water Hospital where the poor could obtain treatment. And, crowning glory, a quarter of a century ago, a little before the great Beau Nash had died, parts of the old Roman baths themselves had come to light.

Adam walked the streets in a daze. He forgot that his scarlet uniform was unquestionably shabby; that his grey bob wig looked as though the moths, having tasted it once, had left it alone, that his neckcloth was no longer gleaming white and that his shoes had old-fashioned buckles. As he saw the fashionable world pass him by, men carried in sedan chairs, women wearing fantastic piles of hair, with their footman and flunkeys everywhere in attendance, as he stared at the broad classical vistas of the town, so strange after the long years overseas, he murmured:

"I might be in Rome."

He might indeed. And it was only because he was now returning home almost as a stranger, that he saw it so clearly.

Not for nothing was the century of elegance known as the Augustan age. For did not Britain like the Rome of that great emperor, have an empire of which she was the civilised centre? Even if America was almost lost, there was still Canada, India, the West Indian islands, Gibraltar. Were not her Georgian buildings severely classical in design, her country houses modelled on those of the Italian Palladio – and therefore Roman? What did her children study if not Latin and Greek? Young men of means visited Italy on their Grand Tour. And when men of education debated in Parliament, did they not drop Latin tags in their speeches like so many senators, even if they had long since forgotten how to construe? A gentleman not only collected classical busts in his house, like as not he had one made of himself. In literature, the late poet Alexander Pope was as great a master of metre and wit as any Latin poet of the silver age. Had not the elegant periods of Addison's prose been as well-judged as Cicero's in the greatest days of Rome?

It seemed to Adam Shockley that they probably had. It was not the Renaissance in England but the eighteenth century that was the true classical age, and poets, architects, painters, and ordinary gentlemen were out to prove it. Why, even the religious tolerance, the easy scepticism of the English Church towards other sects, exactly paralleled the amused tolerance of civilised pagan Rome to the cults of the people they conquered. 'Rome has seen it all'. So it seemed had England. Rational, sceptical, civilised and fairly tolerant – it seemed to Adam Shockley that he had returned from a new to an ancient world.

He spent one night in the Roman city of Bath, and drank one glass of mineral water in the morning, before taking the coach to Sarum.

How familiar it was, the rolling ridges, the empty spaces filled only with the white dots of sheep. He watched eagerly for the first sight of the spire peeping over the horizon.

When he was still five miles from Sarum he noticed one change in the surroundings: it was the sheep. For contrary to anything he would have expected, they seemed bigger.

Could it really be so? The sheep on the Wiltshire ridges had not changed in centuries – stout, sturdy animals with clumsy heads, moderately fine wool and, both rams and ewes, strong curling horns.

The horns were the same, but the sheep seemed to stand taller and to be more powerfully built in their forequarters. The wool seemed to have disappeared from their bellies. They were better looking than the sheep he remembered, but he was surprised at the change.

Sarum at last. It was late afternoon when he arrived. There was the spire, soaring over the city: the streets with their water channels down the middle seemed the same as ever. How calm it was.

The wars in Europe twenty years before, the present struggle in faraway America: these things had hardly touched the city: why should they? The stately cathedral, its quiet close, the medieval market town beside it – these things did not change with the centuries.

In Sarum, for a century, it had been a period of calm.

He made his way eagerly to the house in the close. He had sent a letter from Bristol before leaving, so that his father should be expecting him. As he came through the stout old gateway into the close he suddenly laughed. It was as though he were a child again.

The door was opened by a pleasant young maid in a modest green and white striped dress, a white apron on which she had spilt some flour, and a mob cap tied round with a kerchief over her hair, from which a roll of brown hair was peeping. She gave him a look of fearful wonder, as though he were General Washington himself, and fled down the hall crying: "'Tis the captain."

A moment later his father appeared, hastily putting on his wig before holding out his hands.

"The hero returns."

He was thinner, a little gaunt, and before the wig was on, Adam could see that there were only a few wisps of his own grey hair remaining: but otherwise Jonathan at sixty-seven was astonishingly unchanged. He wore the same long blue frock coat, somewhat frayed, that he remembered, the same white silk stockings and knee breeches of a gentleman.

"Your brother and sister return to the house shortly," he said. "They are eager to meet you."

How good it was to be back in the house. Little had changed. The wainscot in the parlour seemed to be stained a little darker; in his bedroom there was a fine new four poster bed and on the walls there was one of the bright new wallpapers that had only just been coming into fashion when he was a boy. He could detect many small changes made by his father's wife – for Jonathan would certainly never have made any – but as he sat down opposite his father in the comfortable old leather-covered elbow chair, he felt very much at home.

His half brother and sister were a delight. If he had felt any secret jealousy of them before he came, it vanished the moment he saw them.

They both had dark hair, from their mother, but in other respects he saw all the Shockley looks in them – strong, broad faces, light skins, blue eyes. The girl, Frances, was fifteen; her brother Ralph was ten. They looked at him with shining eyes and before he could even rise, Frances ran across the room and kissed him.

He fell in love with her at once.

For the next hour he did nothing but answer their questions: about the war in America, the West Indies, about his whole life it seemed. But the first question of all came from Ralph who, as soon as he heard he had come from Bristol, gazed up at him with large solemn eyes and asked hopefully:

"Did you see the highwayman?"

"It's all the boy thinks of," Jonathan explained. "It seemed that in recent months a highwayman had been making a point of robbing travellers on the roads around Bath; indeed, he had made such a nuisance of himself that the Forest family, who had shares in so many turnpikes, had even offered the astounding sum of £500 for his capture.

"He stole ten pounds from a coach with a lady in it the other day," Jonathan told him with a laugh, "and he doffed his hat so politely to the lady that a gentleman riding by at the time supposed him to be her personal acquaintance."

"I didn't," Adam had to confess, "but I'll look out for him next time I go there."

"Don't come here again without seeing him," Frances cried, "or however you fought in America, Ralph will think nothing of you at all." And she laughed gaily at her brother.

"But tell us about Washington," Jonathan continued.

There was so much to tell, and much to hear. Mr. Harris was still alive, but very old. Yes, there were still theatricals in the close with the Misses Harris, Miss Poore, and the other young ladies of the close in which Frances Shockley also took part. There had been a great visit from the king and queen last year, and King George had reviewed the local militia on the high ground near the town. Why, to be sure, Frances supposed it was very much the same in the close as it was when he was a boy. When she told him about the school for young ladies she attended, Adam could only smile as he thought of his own easy and genteel days at school there.

His father, too, had news: Sir George Forest had died recently but his son Sir Joshua was as shrewd a man as his father. Jonathan himself had only given up his employment as their steward two years before, despite his advancing years.

"I might have continued longer," he explained, "but Forest has left Avonsford, and his new estates are too widely scattered for an old man like me."

The manor house at Avonsford, with its chequerboard stone, flint walls and its modest park, no longer suited young Sir Joshua Forest. It had done so while the family was content to figure as gentry, but Sir Joshua wanted something more.

"You remember the Bouverie family who took over the estates by Clarendon," his father said. "They've become earls of Radnor now: nearly as great as Pembroke himself." He smiled. "And young Joshua Forest means to do the same thing. He's kept some of the estates around Sarum, but he's purchased many more in the north of the county and he's building himself a great nobleman's house there. All too much for me to care for."

"Does he still appear in Salisbury?"

"Oh yes. He has a fine house in the close now for when he comes to visit. You'll see it, for I'm particularly instructed to inform him when you arrive. 'Tis not every day that Sarum sees a heroic captain back from America, my dear boy. You're quite a figure you know."

And so it proved. Despite the fact that he had not yet seen a tailor and cut a sorry figure, his sister Frances proudly conducted him round the close the very next morning. Before they had reached the choristers' green he found he had four invitations to dine, and the most anxious entreaties from three sets of elderly spinsters to call upon them as soon as possible.

"Why all the old ladies of the close will gobble you up in a week," Frances cried in delight.

The cathedral itself was shut that year for repairs, and he saw with sadness that the old belfry had had its tower and most of its bells removed.

"They say it was unsafe," Frances explained, "but then it took them twenty years to do anything about it. We move slowly here, brother Adam, but we get there in time," and she happily took his arm.

His reception was no less warm in the town. For when, later that day, he entered the coffee house in Blue Boar Row where the gentlemen of the town liked to meet, he had a similar experience.

But the greatest accolade, he thought, took place that evening when young Ralph, came alone to his room and asked with great solemnity if he could, please, see his wound.

The month of March was a time of continuous delight. He had forgotten it was possible to feel so happy. He bought new clothes; he even acquired some of the newly fashionable shoes with a diamond ornament instead of a buckle. "More fit for a woman than a man I'd have thought," he protested laughingly when Frances insisted he buy them. She did not let up. Before he knew what had happened, she had taken him to buy a new wig as well, with splendid short side curls, worn with a tight plait behind, turned up and tied with a ribbon at the nape of his neck. She fitted it on his head and arranged it herself.

"It's the latest fashion for a military man to wear his hair," she assured him. "They call it the Ramillies style."

He submitted to all this cheerfully. It was seldom enough, he thought, that he had had a woman to tie his hair.

"I look like a fop," he remarked with a grin, when all these improvements were completed; but she only laughed and kissed him.

It did not take him till the end of the month to love his sister and brother. They were both so artless and high-spirited. He went to watch Ralph at his studies at school; he sat through and admired the theatricals in which Frances took part.

"My children keep me young, now their mother's gone," Jonathan remarked cheerfully.

But there were serious matters to be discussed too.

"I've been able to provide for the children," Jonathan told him after he had been there a week, "not handsomely, but enough to keep them from penury. And their mother has a brother at Winchester who has engaged to look after them if anything should happen to me. But I'm afraid that doesn't leave anything for you. What do you intend to do?"

It was a question he had several times asked himself, and at present he did not know the answer. For the time being he was on half pay. He must either resume active military service, or sell his commission. The commission would give him a useful sum, but not nearly enough to live on.

"Is there anything for me to do here?" he asked.

"Not much," Jonathan had replied. And he had carefully outlined the local economy.

They had talked for an hour. He had forgotten, once one made allowances for his Tory prejudices and his carping wit, what a sound, clear mind his father had. Despite his age and retirement, there seemed to be very little going on in Sarum that he did not know about.

"Our landowners are doing well. They don't like the land tax of course, but some of them are passing it on to their tenants. Corn prices are rising, so the landowners' incomes are good. But the tenants are being hit – not only by taxes either. With rising prices many landlords, I'm afraid, are being tempted to grant only short leases so they can raise rents. We were doing it on the Forest estates, though I didn't enjoy having to go round the tenants and tell them, as you can imagine. So if you've a mind to farm, I'd advise against it – you haven't the money."

He asked his father about the sheep he had seen on the high ground. Were they not different to the sheep he had known as a child?

Jonathan sighed.

"I told Forest not to try it but he did," he answered, "as did many others." The Wiltshire farmers had experimented with an improved strain of the ancient breed – a heavier animal with larger legs and its belly free of wool.

"It's a handsome animal, but it doesn't thrive on our downland pasture and it's liable to goggles – half of them are sick already. It's true that the old breeds could be improved, but the only region in South England that has really made strides is on the Sussex downs, where they're a breed of sheep with much finer wool. It should be introduced in Wiltshire, but our people have been too slow about it so far, so we suffer."

There were parts of the cloth industry that were growing it seemed: cottons, flannels, serges and fancy-cloths. Salisbury bone lace was excellent. But most of these were businesses run by tradesmen and craftsmen. "Hardly of much interest to you," Jonathan said.

Then there was the carpet business at Wilton. Adam remembered this being started when he was a boy, and how Lord Pembroke had patronised the venture to produce carpets as good as the French.

"The workshops burned down ten years ago," Jonathan told him. "They've been rebuilt again, but they're making similar carpets at Southampton now; and it's said the ones from Kidderminster in Worcestershire are even better."

"In short," he concluded, "Sarum is getting by, but it's not expanding, and it's a difficult place for a gentleman without much money."

"I don't know what I shall do," Adam confessed.

"Get yourself a rich widow in Bath," his father advised him frankly. "Plenty of them I dare say. That's my advice."

It was perfectly reasonable advice; but Adam was not sure he wanted to take it.

Just before the end of March Adam Shockley had a strange encounter.

He was sitting one morning in the coffee house in Blue Boar Row, reading the newspaper when he was interrupted by a voice.

"There is a chair opposite you, sir. May I take it?"

"Of course."

He glanced over his paper – and saw nothing.

"I'm obliged, sir," the voice announced. Adam glanced under his paper and made the acquaintance of Eli Mason.

He was just over four foot high. He might have been forty; or thirty. His head was large, red and round. His nose was pointed: his ears stuck out so absolutely at right angles that one could only think they had been stuck there as an afterthought; his body seemed puny, yet, as he positively bounced up on to the seat, it was clear that he was extremely agile, and he projected an aura of cheerfulness that amounted to bonhomie.

He smiled at Adam.

"How d'ye do, sir."

"How do you do."

"You like your newspaper?"

"I think so."

"Well printed."

"Well enough."

"I printed it," he said with cheerful satisfaction. He held up a pair of small hands with fingers and thumbs that looked almost like stumps, and Adam saw that they were stained black with ink.

"Eli Mason, sir," he said. "And you, I am informed, are Captain Shockley, back from the wars."

"I am, sir," Adam replied, and put his paper down.

It was a sound little paper, not as large as the *Salisbury Journal*, which had been started earlier that century, but it contained some well-written articles and a good supply of advertising.

"We print a thousand copies," Eli explained. "Not as many as the *Journal* – that has a four thousand circulation – but it's good work for our presses all the same."

Everything worthwhile in Sarum, it soon turned out, was printed by Eli and his family, and Adam was delighted with his pride in his work. Soon the talkative little fellow was giving him all the gossip of the town, and Adam listened, fascinated.

For though he had been a month in Sarum, it was the first time he had had a conversation with a tradesman.

It was not so surprising. There were families in the close whose fathers

[756]

might have been aldermen, but they were gentlefolk now. Jonathan Shockley might be poor, but it would certainly never have occurred to him to invite one of the prosperous traders of the town to dine at his table, any more than he would have expected to meet them at the house of one of the canons in the close or a local gentleman in his manor house. The children of gentlefolk and tradespeople might meet at school, but afterwards, unless luck or talent raised the tradesman's child into a different class, their paths would diverge and scarcely cross again.

But Adam, when he was in America recovering from his wound, had come to know another kind of men: independent farmers and merchants who did business together and who married and lived their lives without the sense that they were somehow less fine than a layer of gentry above them. Though he was their prisoner, he had begun to appreciate them, and often related their views on life to the self-possessed Hillier boy he had encountered back on the St Lawrence river. As he chatted to Eli Mason, he almost thought himself back amongst them.

He was soon talking to Eli on easy terms, discussing the relative merits of his printing presses as against others and asking him about his business as cheerfully as any tradesmen.

"And what will you do now, Captain?" Eli asked.

"I wish I knew," Adam confessed without embarrassment. "There's not much in Sarum for a captain on half pay."

Eli considered.

"Sell your commission?"

"Not enough to live on."

Eli considered again.

"Man like you should be married," he said.

"Can't afford it," Adam smiled.

"Rich widow?"

"That's what my father said."

"You don't want one?"

"Don't think so."

"What work would you do, Captain?"

"Anything, I dare say," Adam laughed.

"Anything? Fine gentleman like you?"

Adam grinned.

"You mean, a gentleman shouldn't work, Mr. Mason?"

Eli looked down at the table thoughtfully.

"It's not often," he said slowly, "that a fine gentleman like you, Captain, stops to talk for half an hour with a tradesman like me."

Adam glanced at his paper and said nothing.

He would have been surprised indeed to know what was in the little fellow's mind at that moment. For in Eli's brain, a single thought had formed: this one at last, this is the man.

After a short pause he said:

"My family live nearby, Captain. They'd be glad to meet an officer home from America. Would you shake my brother's hand?" And as he saw Adam hesitate he added anxiously: "We're not gentry, Captain. Oh no. Not gentry. We're only small people."

Supposing by this that they must be a family of dwarfs like Eli, and not wishing to offend, Adam Shockley agreed to come.

Ten minutes later, when Eli led Captain Adam Shockley into the modest parlour of a house in Antelope Chequer, he was surprised to see before him not a family of dwarfs, but Benjamin Mason, ironmonger and printer, his wife Eliza, their two children, and Benjamin's sister Mary, none of them below average height.

Eli announced enthusiastically, "Here's Captain Shockley. Fine gentleman. Needs a wife," and all the people in the room burst out laughing.

Adam Shockley did more than shake the hand of Benjamin Mason. He spoke to him for some time. He learned that he was, in a modest way, a substantial tradesman in the town; that he had built up his father's business of making scissors into an altogether grander affair; that he owned a hardware store and a printing works; that he and his wife looked after his brother Eli, who had for some reason never grown to full height, and his young sister Mary – a quiet, good-humoured young woman of, Adam guessed, between twenty-five and thirty. Benjamin Mason was somewhat like a full-grown version of Eli, except that his ears did not stick out, and he carried himself with a certain gravity. He wore no wig; his unpowdered hair was neatly drawn back and tied; he wore a plain, dark brown coat and grey woollen stockings. His children kept staring at the splendid captain, who smiled at them, and tugged at their father's sleeve, but he quietly rested his hand on them and told them not to interrupt. Surprised as he was by Adam's sudden arrival in his house, he was delighted to get the opportunity to question him about America, and particularly about the state of religion there.

"We are Methodists, Captain," he explained to Adam. "By that I mean that, with John Wesley, we desire no break with the established Church of England, but only to reform it and increase its dedication to preaching and acting upon God's word. I trust that does not offend you?"

"Not at all," Shockley assured him.

Indeed, though his father, as a point of Tory principle, still denounced the Wesleyans, it was hard to see how any sensible Church of England man could complain of many of their ideas. They disapproved of the practice of clergy holding benefices they never visited but from which they drew income and they urged the clergy to preach.

"The Reformation was intended to cure just such abuses in the Roman Church," Benjamin Mason observed calmly; "yet now we find them in our own."

But the talk was not all of religion, and it soon became clear that Benjamin's children were as anxious to inspect the captain's wig as their father was to learn about America's religion. Adam was glad to oblige them by taking it off, and explaining to the family how his sister had forced him to buy it.

"'Tis her attempt to make a plain man fashionable," he said with a laugh, "but I fear the imposture will soon be discovered."

All this time, he noticed, Eli Mason perched contentedly on a plain wooden chair near the door, taking no part in the conversation but apparently well pleased with what was going on. And the girl Mary sat composedly beside her sister-in-law, watching him with a quiet smile, but leaving her brother Benjamin to do the talking.

She seemed very quiet. Her dress was grey and plain; her face, a little pock-marked, but not unattractive, sometimes lit up in a smile, but mostly gave nothing away; her hands, folded in her lap, were still. Her eyes, rather beautiful he thought, were grey and for the most part looked downwards; her light brown hair, rather wiry and frizzed, obviously declined to be subdued, but seemed to be discreetly tolerated by the head and body to which it was attached.

"And what does your sister do?" he asked Benjamin, with a polite bow towards the lady in question.

"Oh, she manages everything you see in this house or in my business Captain Shockley," the merchant replied with a laugh. "She is the practical one of the family, are you not Mary?"

To which Mary only smiled.

Two days later, the highwayman struck again, north west of Wilton on the turnpike of the Fisherton Trust in which Sir Joshua Forest had a considerable stake.

Young Ralph Shockley was beside himself with excitement.

"Take me with you," he begged Adam. "We'll ride out and catch him." And it was all Adam could do to get out of the house after dinner that evening to go to the Catch Club for a game of whist.

In the next month, Adam saw Eli Mason several times in the coffee house; once, at his special request, he visited the printing shop to see the little fellow eagerly at work amongst the great fonts of type which he reached by standing on a stool.

"You see," he told Adam proudly, "I am small, Captain, but my family are glad of me: I work."

Several times also, Adam called upon Benjamin Mason to spend an hour in conversation with him. He found the Wesleyan trader well informed upon many topics and each time they discussed the news from America eagerly. The French fleet had joined the American rebels the previous autumn and still neither the forces on land or at sea seemed to be making any headway against the rebels; though an English force had taken some of the French islands in the West Indies, news came that Dominica had fallen to the French.

"They're welcome to the place," Shockley told Mason with a rueful smile. "All I ever had out of it was an attack of malaria."

But much as he enjoyed his talks with Benjamin, he admitted to himself that he also came to see Mary Mason.

She only came into the room occasionally; but when she did, Benjamin often turned to her to ask her opinion on the matter under discussion, and

[759]

though she always gave her answers in a quiet voice, he noticed that they were well-judged and even revealed a sly wit.

"Can we win the war with America, Miss Mason?" Adam asked her.

"No, Captain Shockley," she replied. "Even Pitt would have ended this war; as it is, I think the war will end Lord North instead."

He laughed. The great William Pitt, made Lord Chatham, had died the year before; and poor, dithering Lord North, the present prime minister, was hopelessly unequal to his wartime task.

"That," he concluded to himself, "is a very sensible woman."

One day when he was talking to Benjamin and his sister, the merchant was called away, and for half an hour he remained in his chair, chatting easily to her, answering her questions about his life.

She had none of the artificial manners of the women he saw in the fashionable world; she would have probably laughed outright at the notion of being coy, and if anyone had ever told her it was out of fashion to have a mind of her own, she would have politely ignored them.

By chance, he met her walking once on the footpath that led across the fields from Salisbury to the little village of Harnham. They walked together to the village, admired the peaceful mill and the mill race, and then strolled back to the city together. He found that he liked the walk and took it almost every day after that. Three or four more times he met her there or up on Harnham Hill, and it was on these walks that the thought gradually formed in his mind:

"If I had the money, I'm not sure I wouldn't marry her."

He did not allow the thought to take definite shape.

"You're too poor and too old," he reminded himself.

For as the weeks passed, he had still failed completely to solve the question of how to earn his living. And though he was happy to be in the family house with his father and new brother and sister he was coming to love, he could not help feeling uneasy.

Then, on 30 May 1779, Sir Joshua Forest came to Sarum.

Joshua Forest was in his early thirties: of medium height; very dark, very thin, with a long acquiline nose, and thin, tapering hands. He was friendly to all, with studied civility.

"And his eyes see every fly on the wall," Jonathan remarked when he described him.

Sir Joshua had been in London; then he had been at his new house in the north of the county; now he had come to spend a month at Sarum.

"He has just sent a man round," Jonathan told Adam as he came in from a talk with Eli in the coffee house that morning. "You're invited to dinner this very day." He looked at his son thoughtfully. "Keep your wits about you and you may hear something to your advantage," he added. But when Adam asked him what he meant, the older man would not tell him.

It was four o'clock in the afternoon when Captain Adam Shockley presented himself at the house of Sir Joshua Forest, Baronet. The hour of dining was usually about three, but Sir Joshua, it was known, liked to dine late.

The house of Sir Joshua Forest lay the other end of the close from the Shockleys. It was a big, rectangular brick building, partly faced with grey stone. In front of it lay a gravel drive and a lawn. At one side, behind a low wall, was a path leading to the coach house and stables behind. The main floor was raised; before the front door was a set of handsome curving steps.

There were several splendid coaches on the gravel when he arrived, on the door of the largest he noticed the elaborate arms of the Forest family.

The door was opened by a powdered footman, and a moment later Adam was walking across the polished black and white marble floor of the hall. On the walls above the handsome staircase that rose up three sides of the hall were portraits of the Forest family. On a pedestal in one corner stood a marble bust of Sir George. Over the doors that led off the hall there were classical pediments with plaster mouldings above them. From the ceiling high above, on a twenty foot rope, hung a splendid chandelier with crystal glass that Sir George had acquired in France.

On his left, a second footman opened the tall white panelled door of the drawing-room, and he was ushered in.

They were all men in the room. Two or three of the local landowners; a clergyman he did not know, but clearly a wealthy one; two strangers, presumably from London; and of course, his host.

"Welcome Captain Shockley. We are honoured you are come to join us."

He fitted very well the description his father had given him. But there was one thing about Sir Joshua, as he advanced in his exquisite coat of crimson silk and lace, that Jonathan Shockley had not troubled to convey.

He was perfect.

He had learned the art in Italy and France during a grand tour that had lasted four years. He had learned it thoroughly.

There were many things that a man might study on the Grand Tour. He might read a little history. He might get a smattering of French, German and Italian. He might, if he had the introductions, meet the rulers and important men in half a dozen countries who could later be useful to him in a public career. He might, as the present Lord Pembroke had done, make a detailed study of horse breeding and riding at those incredible continental schools of equitation where the horses performed with all the precision of a modern ballet dancer, and bring back horses, illustrations and a handbook he had himself composed, to Wilton.

Or – this was rare, but it was what Sir Joshua Forest had done – he might study manners.

For in Italy and France, Forest had acquired that most elusive of eighteenth century aristocratic arts – the perfect manner. His manner was so artificial, so polished, that it actually put you at ease. He was as perfect as a china figure that can be turned admiringly this way and that. Even when he moved across the room, his body was held in such perfect posture that one hardly thought he had moved at all. His face, though it smiled amiably, or sometimes frowned, returned quickly and easily to perfect serenity. The physical body, beautifully dressed, infinitely polite even to the lower orders of humanity on the rare occasions when they were noticed, had become almost a marionette. This was the perfect manner of those who dwelt apart in the aristocratic world. If a man like Captain Shockley met them, they could – if they chose – be most agreeable. No man can quarrel with a work of art.

Sir Joshua Forest was a minor work of art.

He introduced Adam to his fellow guests: the men from London were both Members of Parliament. The clergyman – a large, powerfully built man who, he soon understood, held half a dozen rich livings – said several kind words about his valour in the American campaign; and the company in general did him the honour to speak to him as though they might have known him all their lives. In short, they practised the art, known then as condescension – which meant not at all what is meant by the word today, but rather the art of letting a man know, through perfect politeness, that you do not seek to patronise him.

"We shall plague you with questions, Captain," his host said easily.

It was not long before they moved from the drawing-room with its elegantly designed plaster ceiling to a somewhat smaller room.

"Since we are a small company of friends, gentlemen," Forest announced to them, "we shall dine in the green room."

It was a small room looking over the gardens at the back of the house. The walls were covered with green damask. A narrow table had been set in down the middle, under a beautiful plaster carving in the ceiling representing a swan, one of the family crests. On the long wall was a fine picture representing the death of Wolfe at Quebec, and on the shorter wall, over a Chippendale table hung another similar heroic picture of Clive of Plassey. It was a handsome, pleasant, masculine room.

On the table was laid a magnificent dinner service which, being a man of fashion, Forest had ordered from China, every piece proudly bearing his coat of arms. Splendid, plain silver and crystal glasses completed the picture.

As soon as the gentlemen sat, the talk began. It was Forest's pride that at his dinners the talk should be good, and he gently guided the conversation with an invisible hand.

The dinner was stately.

First came the fish: a huge pike, fried sole, and trout. It was accompanied by a white German wine.

The talk was easy: of Sarum and county matters. Forest asked him how the place had changed in his absence, which was not much; both the gentlemen from London seemed to know Mr. Harris and his son. Lord Pembroke was now in London and Lord Herbert his son now en route from Munich to Vienna on his Grand Tour. It was clear at once that all the men present knew these noble figures personally, but they put him so much at his ease that he felt almost as if he did too.

The clergyman, Adam discovered, had the living of Avonsford amongst his benefices: but he had only once visited the place.

"It's a small place," he explained pleasantly, "I have a young curate who does what work there is there, I dare say, very well."

They spoke of local Members of Parliament, of how effectively in past years Sir Samuel Fludyer had promoted the otherwise lacklustre cloth trade of Chippenham.

"The borough told him he should stand for them in Parliament so long as he promoted their cloth, and by God he ran round like a draper for years," laughed one of the country gentlemen.

"From what I hear," Adam observed, "Salisbury needs a Member to do very much the same. They need a man prepared to appear at court in the best Salisbury cloth and ready to say where he got it."

He was pleased that this was well received.

"It's just what I have said," Sir Joshua concurred. "Our merchants here still have good cloth to sell, but they fail to press their case strongly."

Next came a forequarter of lamb, and good claret.

The talk turned to the Government and the war.

"The folly of poor North is," one of the London men remarked, "that half our cavalry – and God knows he's reduced the regulars to a pitiful state – are stationed with Ward at Bury, miles from anywhere. If the rumour's true that the French fleet is coming, they can land where they please, unopposed."

"And our navy's so much under strength," a country gentleman remarked, "that a privateer from America, like this cursed John Paul Jones, can act the pirate off the coast of Ireland, like he did last year, quite unopposed."

"Our greatest security," the clergymen announced, "is that the French do not know how unprepared we are – and could never believe the folly of our ministers."

The company then all wanted to hear his views on America. He told them frankly, relating all he knew about the kind of men who opposed them. He told them about the Hillier boy, his belief in Tom Paine's pamphlet and in his natural rights. They were spellbound. When he had done one of the country gentlemen said bleakly:

"I do not like one word of what you have told us, Captain Shockley. I oppose utterly the political notions you say these people have. But I'm vastly obliged to you because for the first time in five years I think I understand what this matter of America is truly about." There were murmurs of assent. "I think now that our cause is lost," he concluded.

"And yet," Forest said, "here's the trouble. And it's what the king fears. If we grant such rights of self-government to America, and such radical notions are seen to hold sway there, why Ireland will want to follow her, and the West Indies. We can't have that."

Now the boiled chicken arrived. Also a pig's face, tongue and veal roasted with truffles. There were peas and beans for vegetables, and more wine. The conversation passed naturally to political arguments at home. They discussed Burke the statesman and philosopher, who sympathised with the Americans but defended the English Constitution just as it was.

"Burke's right," Forest remarked, "that our strength comes not from a set of rights we claim overnight, but from the deep pattern of our history and institutions. That's what makes a nation great."

"Very good, Joshua," cried the younger of the MPs, "it's even given us Lord North!" And the whole company laughed.

It was generally agreed however, that the ancient system of British laws and government could hardly be bettered.

"Consider our laws," the clergyman said. "Who here has read Blackstone's *Commentaries*?"

These huge volumes had appeared ten years before. They showed, beyond a doubt, that the common laws and privileges of the English came from ancient Saxon times – also that they could hardly be improved upon.

Two MPs both made faces which suggested that they might be familiar with the great work, but preferred not to be questioned too closely, but since, as it happened, Adam had perused it during his long and tedious garrison duty before the American war he answered calmly:

"I have. Though I'd have preferred it if Blackstone had allowed for some improvements to be made."

"There," Forest said in delight. "Captain Shockley has you." And giving Adam a smile with a new warmth in it he announced, "Captain Shockley is a man of learning."

They discussed other matters. Wilkes, that persistent trouble-maker in the Commons, had suggested a bill to reform the parliamentary representation and abolish some of the pocket boroughs like Old Sarum with their handful of electors in order to give more votes to the developing cities and the middle classes.

The company denounced it as infamous, but when Forest asked Shockley what he thought, Adam paused before replying.

Personally, he thought it reasonable, but he had no wish to offend his fellow guests; so he contented himself with saying:

"A little reform early may be wiser than none until it is too late."

This seemed to satisfy the party, and the conversation moved on.

But for the first time he became aware that in some indefinable way he was being tested, and he remembered his father's word of caution to him before he came. He wondered what was coming next.

Not another question, it turned out, but the next course: pigeons and asparagus, teal, woodcock, a pair of whistling plovers, and more red wine.

The conversation turned to lighter subjects: to Mr. Gibbon's new book on the fall of the Roman Empire, Mr. Sheridan's new play, a fine painting by Gainsborough; and although Shockley realised that Forest's hand was gently guiding them for some, no doubt carefully calculated purpose of his own, he could not help admiring the art with which it was done.

Though he had not stepped into the fashionable world, Adam was glad to find that on most matters he could hold his own. But even in this genial banter, his instinct told him that Forest was noting carefully everything he said.

Obviously Sir Joshua was satisfied, for suddenly he declared:

"I think Captain Shockley would be interested in a curiosity that was recently discovered," and he left the table for a few minutes to return with a small piece of parchment which he passed round. "This was found in a box at Avonsford Manor just before we left the place," he explained. "Who can tell me what it is?"

It was a single drawing. It was hard to guess the date, but it could hardly have been less than two centuries old.

It depicted a circular maze – not one in which a man would get lost, but one in which he would follow a winding path symmetrically arranged in four sectors that would lead him tediously back and forth until he finally reached the centre. Under it was the legend:

MAZE AT AVONSFORD

"And I found the place," Forest said. "I'm sure of it: in a circle of yew trees on a hill above the manor. I could even see faint traces of marks upon the ground which seemed to correspond with this plan. What is it Captain Shockley?"

Adam had to confess he had no idea.

"I believe 'tis one of those formal arrangements they cared for so much in the time of Queen Elizabeth," one of the party suggested. "Usually they were made with hedges."

"'Tis what I supposed," Forest agreed.

But it was the clergyman, glancing carelessly at the parchment, who shook his head.

"No sir. I know something of antiquities and I can tell you it is far older than that. This is a pagan design sir, from before Christian or even Roman times. It's as Celtic as Stonehenge." And he spoke with such finality that no one could doubt this was the history of the miz-maze. That a medieval knight had made his lonely pilgrimage upon it, none of that distinguished company ever knew.

Now came a lobster. A further choice of wine.

The wine was very good. Adam was not in the least fuddled, but he felt warm and relaxed. Each course, he realised, had brought a new topic of conversation, yet Forest had turned the subject so neatly one never noticed the change. He gazed at the lobster before him. How was it they were now discussing agriculture? He could not remember.

"The time for the small farmer is nearly over I'm afraid," Forest was saying. "All my tenants are on short leases now and I've had Acts of Parliament to enclose three thousand acres in the north of the county. But I'm not sure I shall do it even so. Some say I shouldn't."

Shockley knew that in the cheese and dairy country to the north there had been a deal of enclosing of land. A landlord had to apply for an Act of Parliament to take over common land in this way, but this permission was easily got. Some protested that poor farmers were being driven off the land, yet could not deny that the newly enclosed areas were usually more efficient.

"What is your opinion, Captain Shockley?" Forest asked.

It was a trap. Adam had drunk a quantity of wine, but he saw it clearly enough.

"I think the change is inevitable," he replied. And remembering a long and informative conversation he had had recently about the subject with

[765]

Benjamin Mason he added: "There's another consideration you did not mention. Many small farmers earn the extra money they need to survive by encouraging their wives and daughters to spin. But there is a new invention coming into use – the mechanical spinning jenny. It's appearing in this county already. Once that's in general use, there'll be no need for the spinsters and I think that will tip the balance in these parts. When the small farmers can't survive, then they won't require the common land at all and the objections to enclosure won't exist. I regret it," he admitted, "because I'll be heartily sorry to see the passing of a way of life I knew as a child. But it will happen." He paused for a moment before adding: "As to your question – enclose now or not – then I say every man must answer to his conscience. If you hurt a man by doing so, compensate him fairly."

He stopped. Why was he so dissatisfied with his answer, every word of which he believed and knew to be true? He frowned.

But the effect upon the table was dramatic. Every eye was turned upon him in admiration. Finally Forest spoke.

"That's the most damned sensible speech, sir, I ever heard in my life."

And then Adam knew why he despised himself for what he had said, true as it was. It was because it was a politician's speech. He had told them exactly what they wanted to hear. If Forest chose to rack rent or dispossess, he could do so, armed with such advice, secure in the knowledge that he had only his conscience to answer to.

It seemed to him that a sort of relief descended on the table. If he was being tested, then the examination was over.

He raised the question of sheep as well, and recommended the introduction of the Sussex breed to replace the failed new Wiltshire animals. This, too, seemed to meet with approval.

Now came apricot tarts, gooseberry tarts; custards; also a trifle and, for those with a more savoury tooth, stewed mushrooms. And more wine.

"Do you care to hunt, Captain?" the clergyman asked.

"Not at present," Adam confessed.

"Hunting the fox is the best sport in the world," the clergyman said pleasantly. "Lord Arundel has a fine pack of hounds – we call it the South and West Wiltshire – not twenty miles from here. Perhaps you'd care to join us in the new season."

The tarts were followed by dessert – a melon, oranges, almonds and raisins.

Decanters of port appeared on the table.

A mood of satisfaction descended upon the company, contentedly aware that they had done the duty of every gentleman in England and eaten all that it was physically possible to consume with dignity.

At the second glass of port it became clear that Forest and the clergyman had the clearest heads, but Adam was keeping pace with them.

"I recently had a long conversation with a Wesleyan," he remarked to the clergyman. "What do you think of them?"

"They are enthusiasts," the younger MP interrupted, "like all reformers. The line between an enthusiast and a fanatic is too thin to see."

But to Adam's surprise, the hunting clergyman with many benefices was tolerant.

"To tell the truth, Captain Shockley," he replied candidly, "I think better of them than they do of me. They say we live too easy in the Church and preach too little. 'Tis often true. They say we have no fire. I don't deny it." He sipped his port thoughtfully. "Wesley, you know, is an honest man: a fine one. If he can reform the existing church – if he adds salt to our meat – let him do so. I care less for his followers, though." A brief expression of distaste flitted across his large, fleshy face. "They complain that the Church of England is become a social institution. So it is. And 'tis very well. They want to break with us – Wesley doesn't – and there I oppose them. For I believe in the institutions of society. They are conducive to morality and to order, and," he smiled mischievously, "with such comfortable fellows as we presiding, are greatly inclined to tolerance – which few reformers are."

Shockley grinned. It was hard not to like the man.

"Forest," called the comfortable clergyman, "Captain Shockley and I lack port."

At the third glass of port there came over him that sudden sense of unreality which tells a wise man not to drink a fourth.

It was with the third glass that the talk turned to philosophy.

"No hard, dry Aristotle for me," the clergyman remarked in a comfortable, mellow tone. "Give me men of large ideas. Give me Plato." He surveyed the table to see how many of the party were still alert. "I am for Bishop Berkeley," he announced. "That everything is only in the mind."

"Expound," Forest demanded. The clergyman obliged.

"You can only tell me anything about the world, Forest, by what you see and feel. Take any object – tell me its shape, its colour, its taste – they are all qualities which are represented in your own mind. Its existence therefore is only in your own mind. To be, is to be seen. Without you to see it, therefore, I claim that the object has no existence." He leaned back in his chair and stared round the company with amusement. "Is there a man here sober enough to dispute with me?"

Ah, but in the long years of his exile, Adam Shockley had had time to read; and he knew the answer to Berkeley.

"Certainly," he said, and kicked the table sharply so that one of the country gentlemen started up from his sleep. "I kicked the table and it informed me that it did exist. Perhaps you'd care to do the same."

"The evening goes to Captain Shockley," Forest announced, "by a length and a half at least."

As he crossed the close that evening, Adam knew that he had done well. Whatever reason Forest had for inspecting him, he had been satisfied, for as he paused at the door, Sir Joshua had asked him to come to see him at ten o'clock the following morning.

How pleasant it was to be back in the civilisation of England: how thin and poor the colonies seemed after such an evening as this. He walked, fairly steadily, back home as the evening sun was sinking and the lamplighters made their quiet progress round the close.

Yet something was wrong. Was it the wine, or the company; was it something said at dinner? He shook his head slowly. No. It was something else.

He continued his walk. Far ahead, over the close wall, a long bank of pale cloud was catching the orange glow of the setting sun. On his right, the cathedral soared, so quiet and stately. The whole world seemed at peace.

But still, something was wrong. He paused, this time, to consider. It was something deep in his mind, important, increasingly urgent. He frowned. Was it just that he had had too much to drink?

The whole dinner and the conversation swelled up before him in his mind. There had been fish and gossip; boiled chicken and the constitution; game, pigeon, asparagus, and the strange picture of the mizmaze; lobster and enclosures; fruit tarts and religion; and finally port and the clergyman's philosophy. The images, tastes and rich scents of the meal, accompanied by the echoes of their conversation, of deep and laughing voices, went through his mind. He frowned. Which course, which of the subjects had so disturbed him?

No, it was none of these.

With a sad smile of recognition, he realised what it was that was troubling him. And then he murmured:

"My God, then, what shall I do? I'm too old to make another journey."

The realisation had only grown more definite in his mind the next morning when he called upon Forest.

He was led, this time, straight to a small library upstairs. It was a gem of a room, done up in the pseudo-gothic fashion some architects favoured, with heavy plaster bosses in the ceiling and gothic arches also done in plaster, which formed handsome recesses for the shelves of leatherbound books. On the table were several recent issues of the *Gentleman's Magazine*.

Sir Joshua rose and gravely motioned him to a leather chair.

"Would you care, Captain Shockley, to act as my agent? You would be in charge, of course, of all my estates."

He had guessed such an offer might come. His father, when pressed, had admitted it to him that morning. His own successor, it seemed, had been a failure and he had himself written to Sir Joshua to suggest he consider his son.

"I dare say they tested you pretty well last night," Jonathan laughed. "You can be sure he'd already made every enquiry about your military record."

It was a staggering opportunity: an excellent salary and the opportunity to manage estates that spread over three counties.

"You could live at Sarum if you pleased," Jonathan said. "You'd be set up for life."

He asked for a short time to consider it and Forest, though a little surprised, readily agreed.

"I have to depart for London on business in a few days, Captain Shockley. Let me know upon my return."

He promised he would.

But what he could hardly admit to himself, and certainly not to his father, was that he did not want it.

There was no one to discuss the problem with. Forest had offered him the chance he needed. Why with this new position and the money from his commission, he could even afford to marry. If he turned it down, was there any man in Sarum who would not think him a fool?

So it was perhaps natural that the only person he did discuss it with should be a woman, the very next day, when he happened to meet Mary Mason on the footpath to Harnham Mill.

"The devil of it is," he confessed to her as she walked silently by his side, "I'm not at home in Sarum any more."

"Tell me why, Captain Shockley," she asked.

How could he explain? How could he tell her about the long miserable years in the tropics when he had so longed to be back at home; of the years in Ireland when he had thought that a house back in the close was all that a man could desire; of the year spent in captivity in America, of his long conversations with the men who had captured him; of the Hillier boy and the impression he had made upon him? How could he explain how he had come back, with wonder and joy to his home and suddenly found that in some strange way, while he had been absent, the civilised world had grown old? The dinner at Forest's was the culmination of a process that had been in gestation for two months.

"It's me that's changed," he concluded, after trying to put a few of these thoughts into words. "I suppose I've seen freer men in a new land, and when I come back I find our old society, civilised though it is, too full of restrictions, too fond of order. It's as though I couldn't breathe." He paused, puzzled by his own thought. "It's not that I want to reform England, Miss Mason. I'm not a political fellow. But I want," he searched for words, "a wider horizon, larger freedoms."

"And how would you like to live?"

"Oh," yes, he knew the answer to that well enough, "if I were young, if I had my life again – do not say this to others, I pray – but I'd go and live in the new colonies, in America."

It had taken longer than he himself realised, but the captive Hillier boy had finally converted him.

Mary Mason looked very thoughtful, but made no comment, letting him talk, and pour his heart out. Only at the end of the path as they came into Salisbury did she turn to him and say quietly:

"I cannot advise you, Captain Shockley, except to tell you that you must follow your heart."

Then she left him.

His heart. He smiled ruefully as he watched her go. "Why then, Miss Mason," he thought to himself, "I think perhaps I'd take Forest's cursed offer and marry you."

For the first time in his life, he could not make up his mind.

In June 1779, French and Spanish ships, over sixty in number, appeared off Plymouth, where, unknown to the enemy, the ammunition did not even fit the defenders' guns.

Sir Joshua Forest was detained in London.

And Captain Adam Shockley, thinking that the local militia might be called out, let it be known that he was ready for service if needed.

But in Sarum, a still more exciting event now took place.

Its author was Eli Mason.

It was in the second week of June that Eli, having received certain confidences from members of his family, and having perused items in the newspaper concerning the most recent exploits of a certain gentleman, hit upon his extraordinary plan. He told no one in the family what he meant to do, but he needed one accomplice.

Accordingly, he called upon Captain Shockley. When Adam heard what he wanted, he burst out laughing and declared:

"If you want my help, you shall have it. Are you prepared to take the risk?"

He was indeed.

"I have all my savings," Eli declared. "They'll be at your service."

One fine morning a week later the Salisbury-to-Bath stagecoach rolled out of the city.

Adam Shockley had been as good as his word to Eli, and although it had been known for several days that he was going to Bristol to make an important transaction, no one had any inkling of what it was he intended to buy. He had only one companion from Salisbury, an elderly lady. His luggage included a large and heavy portmanteau that was stowed in the basket behind.

The portmanteau, well padlocked, contained Eli Mason's savings, and as Adam sat quietly in the coach with his fellow passenger, he could not help thinking of the trust Eli had placed in him and hoping for the game little fellow's sake that the business would not miscarry.

The journey was delightful – along the Fisherton turnpike to Wilton; a brief pause there, then along the line of the Wylie river before turning up on to the high ground.

Soon they were up there, rolling over the broad ridges; there was a glimpse of the top of the spire, then it vanished. What a noble country it was, nothing but sheep, the great sweep of the high ground, and the open sky that seemed to touch it: that familiar, bare and timeless landscape. Wherever he was in the world, he knew his thoughts would always return to the high ground above Sarum.

For an hour the coach made its solitary way across the great windswept tract.

It was several miles outside the town of Warminster that the disaster occurred. It took even Adam Shockley completely by surprise.

He had waited behind a tiny clump of trees, and stepped out, a single figure on horseback, so quietly and quickly that neither the coachman, his guard, who carried a blunderbuss which, in his confusion he fired the wrong way, nor the passengers had any time to react. He was well-dressed, rode a fine bay horse, and wore a mask over his face. One of his two double-barrelled pistols was levelled calmly and precisely between Adam Shockley's eyes as he threw open the door and politely said:

"Your valuables, please."

The elderly lady produced two rings and gold to the value of ten pounds. The highwayman seemed satisfied with this. Shockley had almost nothing to give him except a gold watch and some small coins. He parted from the watch reluctantly, wondering if this would satisfy the rogue.

It did not.

"Luggage," he called peremptorily to the coachman.

The portmanteau.

If only he had had a gun, it seemed to Adam that, though the highwayman was still covering him with his pistol, he might still have had a chance. But, like a perfect fool, he had come unarmed. Why had the idiot of a guard panicked?

The coachman and the guard, both shaking a little, were manhandling the large portmanteau out of the basket. They placed it on the ground.

Eli's savings.

"Yours?" the highwayman asked.

Adam nodded.

"Key."

If he could just distract him.

He shook his head.

"The key's at my brother's house in Bristol."

The highwayman looked at him. "He must guess it's a lie," thought Adam, "but perhaps he will search me, and then . . ."

The highwayman wasted no time. In two strides he was by the portmanteau. With one shot from his pistol he blew off the padlock and raised the lid.

Even he gasped, as he saw that it was full of gold coins.

"No!" Shockley bellowed and started out of the coach. The highwayman swung both pistols towards him, there was a crash of spilling coins.

Caught completely off guard, the highwayman looked down in astonishment to see, squatting in the portmanteau from which he had pushed off the shallow tray of coins, the diminutive figure of Eli Mason, cheerfully holding two small pistols, both of which pointed straight at his midriff.

"Your guns, please," said Shockley calmly.

And as the highwayman reluctantly threw them down, Adam grinned at his little friend.

"You were right Mr. Mason, it worked."

The reward of five hundred pounds was handed over promptly to Shockley and Eli Mason by Sir Joshua Forest on his return two weeks later.

"Best five hundred pounds I ever spent," he assured them. "Not only have you caught my highwayman, but you've given me a story to dine out on for years."

Shockley did not keep his share.

"Your plan, your risk. I only gave the word," he said, and finally only accepted fifty pounds to keep the little fellow happy.

As for his business with Forest, it was agreed he would call upon him two days later. "Though why you still haven't made up your mind," Jonathan said crossly, "I cannot imagine."

The highwayman turned out to be a young man named Stephen Field, who came from Warminster. No one at Sarum knew anything about him; he was held at Fisherton goal. That his grandfather, who had worked at an inn at Bath, had been born the son of Susan Mason and George Forest he did not even know himself. It made little difference since he was due to hang.

When Eli Mason returned home with his reward, he carried out the rest of his plans, and this part he had not confided to Adam.

He went straight to his sister's room, dumped the bag of gold in front of her, and stated proudly:

"That's your dowry for when you marry, from your brother Eli." And before she could protest, he added firmly: "Better marry Captain Shockley, sister, if I was you."

The next day, in the early evening, when Mr. Jonathan Shockley was out at the house of Mr. Harris for his regular game of whist, and the two young Shockleys were away at Wilton, Adam Shockley alone in the house was surprised to receive a caller.

Miss Mary Mason requested to see him on private business.

Wondering what she could want, he ushered her into the little parlour on the first floor.

She came straight to the point.

"I wish to know about land in America, Captain Shockley. I understand that it is at a much lower price than land here."

"Certainly," he informed her.

"One could buy a tolerable farm for five hundred pounds? In a state like Massachusetts or Pennsylvania?"

"I would say yes."

"And for, say, a thousand one could stock it too?"

"I think so."

"Your commission is worth fifteen hundred pounds, I believe."

"It is."

"And do you still desire to go to America, Captain?"

He had been pondering the question all day.

"In my heart, yes," he told her frankly.

"If you went, you would probably not return."

"I know."

To go out at his age alone though, he had been thinking. Could he face it? But she was speaking.

"Then will you take me to wife?"

He blinked. What had she said?

She repeated it, calmly and seriously.

"Would you take me to wife, Captain Shockley? On condition we go to America as soon as peace is signed?"

He gazed at her in astonishment.

"An old dog like me?"

"Yes," she replied matter of factly.

"I've been wounded. And I've been sick in the tropics," he warned her.

"Pennsylvania is hardly the tropics."

A grin spread over his face.

"Then by God, Miss Mason, I will."

"Good." She looked about her calmly.

"Where is your bedchamber, Captain Shockley," she enquired.

He frowned, puzzled.

"In the next room," he gasped. "Why?"

Quietly and methodically she now began to take off her gown. His eyes opened wide in astonishment.

"Shouldn't this wait until we are married?" he asked.

She shook her head.

"Best not."

At the Assizes that autumn, Stephen Field, notorious rogue and highwayman, aged twenty-six, a slim, handsome fellow with ringlets of black hair that made him look more like a cavalier than a common thief, was sentenced to death.

A week later, the deputy sheriff of the county recommended to the secretary at the War Office that the said Stephen Field, having received sentence of death for highway robbery, should be reprieved on condition of entering into the service. As a result, Stephen Field, along with many other able-bodied criminals, entered His Majesty's army instead of being hanged. He was fortunate: this method of recruiting was discontinued the following May.

The last letter that Adam Shockley ever received from his father was characteristic. It came in 1790, when he and Mary had been in Pennsylvania for seven years.

My dear Adam,

I thank you for your letter, received last year. Sarum is quiet as usual, but perhaps you will be interested to learn that great changes are being made in our cathedral by Mr. Wyatt the architect. The old belfry is gone – dismantled – grassed over and I do not mourn its passing. The view of the church is much improved. So will shortly be that great area of crooked tombstones and mud we call the graveyard. 'Tis all smoothed over, the gravestones gone, and laid out as lawns.

But the church – the screens are removed, the antique coloured glass is all broken up, and, if you please, thrown in the town ditch. The Hungerford and Beauchamp chantry chapels are gone too. I cannot describe to you adequately the effect of the fellow Wyatt's labours – 'tis a most astounding work of destruction. There has been nothing like it since the Reformation. The entire church within is now like a single great barn, with plain light, plain stone, nothing to stay the eye as it strays from one naked grey surface to another.

'Tis greatly admired.

Forest is recently made a lord. He had not forgiven you for deserting him. He owns both land and cotton factories in the north, I understand; but his affairs grow too large for my poor comprehension now.

I am sorry that you never saw young Mr. Pitt come to power. He is the third son, you know, of the great Chatham, and I am bound to say has acted as boldly in peace as ever his great father did in time of war. William Pitt younger is a most economical fellow – as we need after all our wars with your America. He now taxes not only the windows of great houses but even my modest number. I was obliged to brick one of them up. And he taxes us not only for our manservants, of whom I now have none, but serving girls as well. I tell my Jenny, who is a good girl, that though Mr. Pitt may consider her a luxury, she shall nonetheless never be put out of doors by me.

The king was mad last year but is recovered. The Radicals complain he was never sane.

There has been a Revolution in France. King Louis is imprisoned, I think, and his queen too. We await to know what this portends. The enthusiasts say 'tis the dawn of a new age. I hope not.

And now I turn to a most disagreeable matter. Your sister Frances is to be married. The name of the man is Mr. Porteus, a young clergyman of very substantial income.

Your sister has become a great favourite of our Bishop Barrington who – except for his allowing the ass Wyatt to ruin the cathedral – I think highly of. I fancy by marrying your sister, Mr. Porteus seeks to please him; and since I shall leave her but a small income, and Ralph without a protector in the world, I suppose I should be glad of his offer. Frances is twenty-five now and so it is more than time she was settled.

So there the matter rests. I have had to accept him. Ralph is full of radical notions. I shall send him to talk to Porteus who, you may be sure, has none.

I grow very old. My three score years and ten were done nine years ago. But many Shockleys are cursed with long lives.

I regret that you cannot see Mr. Porteus. You would relish him.

Pray give my duties to your good wife.

Yr. affectionate father,

J.S.

Boney

1803

IT WAS THE dead of night; there was no moon. In the shallow harbour below the small but ancient town of Christchurch no sound broke the cold stillness of the October night, except the faint murmur of a light wind.

The harbour was empty.

On the island side of the harbour, the flat marshes extended for several miles before giving way to the gravel, peat and sandy soil of the huge deserted heath that led towards the vast tracts of the New Forest. There was not a light to be seen.

Had anything changed in that empty region by the sea? Very little. Medieval kings no longer hunted in the great forests that still stretched from the coast up to Clarendon and beyond. But the deer still inhabited them. Men living in their tiny thatched cottages, in deserted hamlets, still had their ancient rights to gather wood, still lived their quiet and secluded existence. Furze cutters, charcoal burners, small folk who might not see a stranger in months, still held their tiny habitations on scores of miles of heathland to east and west of the little harbour. The little town of Christchurch with its square-towered Norman church and its long since ruined little castle, still nestled at the place where the two rivers Stour and Avon ran together into the harbour, and its people still sometimes used the old Saxon name of Twyneham to describe the place.

One thing had changed. The brown and turbulent waters of the English Channel had drawn a little closer, eating steadily year by year, century by century, into the soft sandy coastline, just as, thousands of years before, it had broken down the ancient barrier of chalk. It had taken a good part of the headland now. The southern end of the old earthwork walls that had protected the Celtic camp were already sliding onto a sand and shingle beach. The low hill at the centre of the headland had been remorselessly attacked by sea and weather too. Seen from a distance from the sea, it now looked as if the hill had been cut from end to end with a knife.

But the long headland and its sand bar was still there, losing its contact with the sea by only a few inches a year, still sheltering the still harbour waters and their mud flats on the inland side, where fishing boats could safely moor, where swans nested and herons stalked the flats or skimmed over the waters.

One thing had changed: the place had acquired a new name. For an antiquarian had hit upon the notion that the old Celtic hillfort was in fact the camp of none other than the legendary Saxon chief Hengist, one of the first of his race to colonise the island. It was spurious history, but popular, and the new and evocative name of Hengistbury Head soon became so firmly attached to the place that people thought it did indeed come from the mists of antiquity.

The harbour was empty. Behind it could be heard the gentle hiss of the sea. The sea was empty too, or so people hoped.

For on the other side of the English Channel in the ports of northern France, a huge armada of transport ships was being prepared. One still night when the sea was calm – as soon as the transports could be well enough organised and defended against the British naval squadrons – they would push out into the Channel, and fall upon the English coast. The people of Christchurch trembled at the thought. As well they might.

For the army of Napoleon Bonaparte, on the French coast, was invincible; against it could only be pitted a small force of British regulars and a half-trained local militia, some of whom carried only pikes.

This was the nightmare of England, caused by the French Revolution.

Of course, there were still those – extreme Whigs and Radicals, men like the brilliant Charles James Fox – who spoke with favour of the new age of liberty, equality and fraternity they believed had begun in France. When the Revolution came, idealistic young men like the poet Wordsworth truly believed they beheld a new and happier dawn. But that was before the terror of the guillotine, the killing of the king and queen and the astonishing conquests of young Bonaparte. Few in England praised the Revolution now. Italy had fallen to the French; Egypt nearly been annexed. If he had not been stopped by Nelson destroying his fleet and supplies, the extraordinary conqueror who modelled himself on Caesar and Alexander would have marched across Asia to India itself.

Worse still, when Bonaparte took the Hapsburg province of the Netherlands the thing England always dreaded most happened – the whole opposite Channel shore fell into the hands of her enemy. The powers of Europe had fought to a standstill: there was an uneasy peace which was soon broken. And the one man who stood like a rock through all these storms, William Pitt the Younger, son of the great Chatham and perhaps the greatest minister the island had ever known, even Pitt had gone, resigning his post because King George refused to give the Irish Catholics the vote.

Now the brief peace was over. Who knew what move Bonaparte with his mighty armies would make next? England had only her navy to protect her, and she stood alone.

A sound: a faint splash, followed by the soft creak of an oar on wood: almost indistinguishable from the water lapping on the muddy shore of the harbour. A sound, but no light.

Young Peter Wilson waited patiently on the bank in front of the carts.

The luggers began to arrive.

There were seven of them: long, light vessels, with well-rigged forsail, carrying oars as well, with decks for only a few feet at stem and stern. Otherwise they were open, for quick unloading of their precious cargoes. They were manned by crews of strong men, and being so light and easy to handle, they could run ahead of almost any of the revenue cutters who tried to arrest them.

"Here comes the moonrakers' run," Peter whispered.

For Peter Wilson was a smuggler.

To pick him out and call him a smuggler would have been absurd. There was hardly a person he knew in Christchurch or the surrounding region, from gentlemen, like the rich Wilsons in the manor near the town, to the humblest peasant, who was not involved in some way in the trade. He himself came from a family of ten. All of them were. So were their cousins – a vast network of sea and rivergoing people, some descended from the many illegitimate children of Captain Jack Wilson, before he married Nellie Godfrey, others deriving from who knew what ancient sources; some, like Peter, had thin and narrow faces, but they came in all shapes and sizes, and they infested the rivers, the ports, and the heathland villages for miles around. Slippery Wilson, his father, did well. But he was only a minor figure compared to the great, the legendary Isaac Gulliver, the father figure of smuggling in the whole area south of Sarum. Gulliver had organised tonight's run, paid for it and drawn his profit. The contraband would pass that very night along roads his men guarded, rest at inns he owned, and in this way pass westwards across open heathland, up over Cranborne Chase and then down to Sarum.

Peter always took part when the luggers landed at Hengistbury Head. He knew every inch of the headland and could have driven a cart of rum and brandy safely across it with his eyes closed.

Tonight's cargo consisted of a little tobacco, but chiefly brandy, rum and Geneva spirits. As the luggers came in close, dozens of men sprang forward and began to help unload. The work was accomplished in a quarter of an hour. Then twenty carts, each with an armed man riding up front, wound slowly along the headland, past the earthwork walls, and made their way westward. They were unlikely to be troubled by the excise men, who knew better than to interfere on land; some years the smugglers travelled in broad daylight, but in times of war it was wisest to be discreet.

In fact, the smuggling business was pestilential to the government for reasons which had little to do with the contraband itself, or the charming sideline of taking eloping couples to be married in the island of Jersey. For the smugglers exported gold, of which England was running perilously short, to pay for the contraband from France: the fantastic sum of over ten thousand guineas a week was leaving the island this way. And the smuggling sailors did not hesitate to sell information to the French about England's naval and shore defences.

But Peter Wilson knew nothing of that. Tomorrow, at Sarum, he would be handsomely paid. Then he would buy a wedding ring. For the very next week, on his nineteenth birthday, Peter Wilson was going to be married. He smiled to himself contentedly as they began the run into the moonraker country.

No one knew when the men of Wiltshire first came to be called moonrakers; but it was smuggling that gave them the name.

[777]

A party of Wiltshire smugglers, hearing the excise men approaching one night, had pushed their load into a pond. Later, thinking the coast was clear, they had begun to try to get the barrels out again with poles and rakes. They had just started, however, when the excise men returned. It was then, when the excise men demanded to know what they were about that one of the men, pointing to the reflection of the full moon in the water explained: "See that cheese – we're trying to pull it over here," and he began slowly to rake the water. Slow and simple these Wiltshire men, the excise men had concluded as they rode away. And slow and simple, when it suited them, the Wiltshire men had always been, especially when it came to getting the better of interfering government officials.

Peter Wilson liked the run into moonraker country.

"I'll buy that ring tomorrow," he thought.

Doctor Thaddeus Barnikel paused before the door.

Could he go in?

Of course he could. He must. He had particularly been asked to come on urgent business, by the owner of the house.

He looked at the door worriedly. If only he could trust himself not to give everything away; if only he did not blush; if only at this moment he were not trembling.

He had been particularly summoned, on a matter of delicacy. Discretion was required. He was a doctor.

Still he paused.

It was pleasantly warm. The morning mist, hours ago, had given way to a mellow autumn sun. All around the close the yellowing leaves were gently falling in the faint northern breeze. They rustled along the north walk, gathered along the edge of the choristers' green, piled into the stone corner of the little lodge by the south gate that led to the old bridge.

The cloistered seclusion of Salisbury close, with its cathedral rising like a stately tree, its sweeping lawns, and its low, receding lines of gracious houses, always seemed to Doctor Thaddeus Barnikel to have a poignant melancholy all its own in the Michaelmas season when the leaves were falling. But perhaps it was just his mood. The summer birds that infested its gracious old houses – the swallows, swifts, martins and the small company of starlings in the trees, had all long since risen with their shrill, busy cries and wheeled away, leaving the precincts to its year-round inhabitants – a few sparrows and thrushes, the daws who were sombrely picking over the green by the plane trees, the rooks in the elms, gazing down like so many black-robed canons in their stalls, and lastly a pair of kestrels who nested in the cathedral tower and from time to time circled the spire in a manner plainly suggesting that they were the true owners of the ancient building.

Only half the leaves were down, and the sun found warm and subtle colours everywhere upon the precinct's crumbling surfaces. It was not only the green and moss in the crevices, not only the tawny and golden leaves, nor the grey-green Chilmark stone, the long-leaded roof of the cathedral or the delicate shades of the red brick, red tile and the stuccoed fronts of the houses; no the joy of the cathedral close was in the lichen. It was everywhere, in every nook and cranny, on great stone surfaces or the uneven churchyard wall: greens, yellows, rusty reds, ochres, creamy blues, light browns: the living lichen with its subtle colours grew everywhere.

He knew why he was summoned.

Had she not come to him privately, three months before, and begged him to speak to the young man?

He had done so.

It was a long interview. He made the position very plain. He warned, persuaded, even begged. And it had been useless. First the fellow rambled, then laughed at him, finally told him, in a friendly way, to mind his own business.

"Can you see no danger?"

"Frankly Doctor, no."

"But what of your wife, man?" he had burst out. "Do you not realise you are giving her pain, and anxiety?"

"She has been to you?" The young man looked at him shrewdly.

"It would have been through concern for you if she had," he replied.

"Doctor," there was a trace of anger in his voice now. "There is nothing about which you need concern yourself, and nothing to fear."

What more could he have done?

The house before which Doctor Barnikel stood was a handsome brick and stone fronted building on the northern side of the close.

The house belonged to Canon Porteus, who lived there with his wife Frances. He was not afraid of either of them. He was certainly not afraid of the young man. No, he hesitated because she would also be there.

He stood by the gate for a full minute.

It was while he did so that, from the tradesmen's entrance at the rear, the small figure of Peter Wilson emerged and walked away. Barnikel smiled. He had only to look at the scruffy young fellow to guess that he had been with the housekeeper delivering contraband.

"After all," he murmured, "even the clergy must have their brandy, too."

It seemed to break the spell. He went in.

It was ten years since Doctor Thaddeus Barnikel had come to Sarum from a village north of Oxford.

He was thirty-five, an excellent and respected doctor and he had soon built a solid reputation in the city. He lived in a pleasant, modest, white-fronted house in St Ann Street.

He was a kindly man. No one in Sarum had ever seen him say a cruel word, or lose his temper: indeed, the last time he had done that was twenty years ago, and even then, it had been because he saw a man in Oxford whipping his dog so viciously he thought it would be maimed. At that moment, to his own surprise, he had been suddenly transformed into a state of towering rage. A minute later, when the dog's master picked himself up off the ground, he found that his dog was no longer in his possession but being carried away in the arms of a slightly chubby, red faced but determined fifteen-year-old. And the boy's attack had been so sudden and so devastating that the fellow had not cared to argue but had slunk away.

Thaddeus kept the dog, named Spot, which had lived on for ten years.

He was now a well-built, broad-chested man, just over average height, with thinning hair and, despite the fact that he was a respected doctor, a tendency to blush sometimes in the company of women. Surprisingly he was still unmarried.

"A strange name, Barnikel," old Bishop Douglas once remarked to him. "What's its origin?"

"Danish, I believe," he replied. He had heard of the legend of the Danish warrior who cried. 'Bairn-ni-kel'; but he smiled at this as no more than a charming myth.

She was there.

She was sitting quietly beside Frances Porteus in the drawing-room, working on a piece of embroidery, and she looked up as he came in.

"I fear my husband has not yet returned, Doctor Barnikel," Frances Porteus said politely. "But we expect him presently. Pray sit with us until then."

Barnikel bowed.

He tried to keep his attention on the older woman.

There had been a time, not so long ago, when Frances Shockley had been a gay young woman. Many in Salisbury could remember it. But that was before she had married Mr. Porteus.

"You must marry, I've no doubt," her father had told her. "But you'll never change him – make no mistake about that. I only pray he may not change you too much."

By the time Barnikel arrived at Sarum she had already been married four years; and whenever he met her it had seemed to him that there was an unhappiness in her eyes, as though her natural gaiety had been trapped. Ten years later, that look, too, had completely vanished and he did not know whether to be sorry or glad. For Frances Porteus, though she had no children, was now a most staid and proper matron.

"I trust Porteus is not harsh to you," old Jonathan Shockley said, just before he died.

"Oh no," she answered. "Never. But," she had allowed herself to sigh, "he is very correct and – he is sombre."

She sat on her chair now, bolt upright, stitching.

But it was to her companion that Barnikel's eyes kept straying. He could not help it.

Agnes Bracewell was not beautiful. She was a quiet, pleasant, dark brunette with a face that was a little too broad across the brow, lightly freckled, and cheeks that dimpled just above the corners of her mouth when she smiled. Her front teeth pointed slightly inwards, but this was not unattractive. On her wrists the dark hairs grew slightly more thickly than one expected. Her father had been a major in a good line regiment;

she was his favourite and never much displeased him. She was twenty-five. She wore spectacles to do her embroidery.

Agnes had first come to Sarum three years before; and there was only, for poor Barnikel, one tragedy in this.

For Agnes had come as young Ralph Shockley's wife.

Young Ralph Shockley. He was in fact the same age as himself, and for over a decade now he had been a schoolmaster, but his manner was still so boyish, his enthusiasms and flights of fancy so sudden, that Thaddeus still thought of him as young. It was Ralph's boyish good looks and infectious humour that had first attracted Agnes. Thaddeus sometimes found them tiresome. But then, he considered ruefully, he was prejudiced.

It was because Ralph and Agnes's own little house in New Street was being redecorated that Frances and Porteus had invited them to spend a month in their house in the close until the work was completed. Perversely, it was Ralph who insisted they accept the invitation.

Knowing what he did, Barnikel had felt a sense of foreboding ever since he heard of it; and he had no doubt that was why Porteus wanted to see him.

He glanced at the two women. Did they know why he was there this time? It was impossible to tell.

He sat politely, making demure conversation.

He was conscious of the long case clock ticking softly in the hallway outside; of the shaft of afternoon sunlight in one corner of the room, of the tiny particles of dust spiralling in the sunbeams; he was conscious of the dark, solemn portrait of Canon Porteus staring bleakly down from the wall opposite. He was conscious of the needles of the two women rising and plunging with a tiny tick through the canvas of their embroidery, and of Agnes Shockley's breast quietly rising and falling.

She was nothing exceptional.

"But then," he reflected with typical modesty, "nor am I."

Why was it that, whenever he saw her he was filled with a protective urge? Why was it that, when they spoke, there fell between them that wonderful silence of perfect understanding, the silence that made him yearn to take her in his arms and kiss her?

"Ah, if only," he often thought. If only it had not been that pleasant, self-centred young fellow with his boyish good looks that she had met. "I should have known how to treat her," he thought.

He saw her often in that small, genteel community. And the passion, which he strove so hard to conceal, only grew worse.

"I am constant," he laughed at himself ruefully. "And quite without hope."

There was nothing he could do about it.

Ten slow minutes passed. Then the canon arrived.

"Ah doctor," he bowed gravely. "You are most kind to come. Let us speak in my study."

Barnikel rose.

"I do not wish to be harsh." Porteus fixed him with his black eyes. "I must show charity." The last word sounded like the tolling of a dismal bell.

Nicodemus Porteus was a pillar of the community – straight and narrow. His thin hair, grey at the temples, was cut short on top but allowed to blossom out in curls at the sides, and it was a great pity that some fifteen years earlier, gentlemen had ceased to wear wigs or even to powder their hair; for Porteus's high narrow head was made to wear a wig, and his hair such as it was, would have looked better powdered. But since the French Revolution both these fashions had passed leaving Porteus, so to speak, stranded on his own. His appearance was as bleak as a winter tree. His clerical black silk stockings and black knee-breeches hugged the thinnest legs in Salisbury close; his black frock coat was tightly buttoned up the front, and the two starched white tabs of his clerical cravat poked over the top of it.

He was a careful man. Soon after he and Frances married, the pleasant house in the close had been offered them by the dean and chapter. He spent a whole spring morning making a precise survey to determine whether, if by any chance the cathedral spire should ever topple, it would reach his house.

"Not by fifty feet," he told Frances, and took the house.

He was a diligent man. It was he who discovered – this was the word he used – that the name Porters, which his father, the northern cloth manufacturer bore, must surely be a corruption of the ancient name of Porteus; so diligent was he that he had made this discovery already by the time he was nineteen and still an obscure undergraduate at Oxford university. Accordingly, and in deference to antiquity, he changed his name at once; besides it put a further distance between the cloth mill, which was, alas, middle class 'trade', and the gentleman he was determined to become. His delight in discovering, through the records in the cathedral library, that there had once been a Canon Portehors at Salisbury, knew no bounds. "Another variant of Porteus," he claimed.

"Like the Poores," he would quietly maintain, "the Porteus family may be said to have a . . ." he would pause to give effect to the under-statement, "somewhat lengthy connection with Sarum." Indeed, after a decade of saying it, he even believed it himself.

The fact, buried deep in the past, that his claim was true, that he really was descended from the old Porteus family who had fled Salisbury to escape the Black Death, was something that Nicodemus Porteus never knew.

He was observant. When he arrived at Sarum, with money but no friends, it did not take him long to discover that Frances Shockley was a favourite with the bishop, that she had no money, that she was considered a lady all the same, and that, if he were to marry her and take care of her young brother, the bishop, though he disliked him, would still favour his cause for Frances's sake. And by taking careful thought, he even made himself so agreeable to Frances that she consented to marry him.

No man in the last, lax years of the eighteenth century, was more assiduous in his duties than Nicodemus Porteus, no man more proper towards his wife and her family, no man more worthy, as the nineteenth century began, to be made a canon of the cathedral.

The ambition of Canon Porteus was one day to be dean. For of all the offices at Sarum, this was the jewel. The days when the huge estates of the middle ages produced vast revenues for the diocese were long past. Indeed, Salisbury diocese was now comparatively poor. But by accidents of history, certain offices had remained rich while others declined, and the office of Dean of Salisbury carried with it the fantastic income of some two thousand pounds a year. Even his own substantial means only gave him a fraction of such a sum.

"On that," Porteus reminded Frances solemnly, "a man might live as a considerable gentleman."

As dean he might almost move in the circle of Lord Pembroke, Lord Radnor, or at least Lord Forest, whom he had already assiduously cultivated. The dignity of the office, together with the income would set the seal on his social ambitions. When he knelt before his bed with his wife each night and prayed aloud for the poor, those at sea, the sick and the diocese, it was always this unspoken prayer, from his innermost heart, that rose, pure and shining into the night sky over Sarum:

"Lord, let me one day be dean."

It was not surprising that Canon Porteus should be concerned about his brother-in-law, Ralph Shockley.

"I confess," he now told Barnikel, "I confess to you, doctor, that he sometimes displeases me. But this," he added regretfully, "it is my Christian duty to bear. No sir," he went on, "it is a waywardness in his thoughts, a lack of judgement that I almost think could indicate . . ." he looked very grave, "a mental imbalance. I fear for him, doctor. I fear still more for his wife and two children." He allowed his pale hand to rest on a large concordance that lay on his desk, as though the hand might absorb wisdom and patience from that weighty tome. "I have not been ungenerous towards him, and this he must know."

Barnikel bowed his head. It was certainly unthinkable that Porteus could be generous to anybody without their being acutely aware of the fact.

"Yet my wiser counsel is, I fear, ignored."

"I see."

"I should like you to dine with us today, doctor, observe him, form your own conclusions. And, since my voice does not prevail, speak with him yourself, as you think best."

Barnikel had no wish to do any of these things; but he found it hard to refuse.

"What form, exactly do these disturbing signs take?" he asked curiously.

"Ah," the canon raised his long arms in a gesture of despair, "that you will see, all too soon; I think I hear his arrival now."

At first – to someone that is who did not know the canon's sensitive nature – at first it might have seemed that all was well.

Ralph Shockley came into the house cheerfully. His tangled yellow hair fell over his brow; he was dressed as a gentleman should be in the tight-fitting pale trousers of the day, tail coat and cravat, but he had somehow acquired a small tear in his trousers at the knee, his coat was covered in chalk dust, and his cravat, if it had ever been well-tied, had long since taken on a life of its own. Of all these improprieties he was unaware. Porteus was not, but greeted Ralph as affably as he was able.

Ralph then went upstairs to see his two children, stayed there despite being summoned to dinner, for a quarter of an hour, and then, still very cheerfully, reappeared. He had not tidied himself.

As they went in to dinner Agnes came quietly to Doctor Barnikel's side and whispered:

"I pray you will keep the peace between them."

"Is it so bad?"

"It has been getting worse all month. Each day I fear there will be an explosion. 'Tis like a powder keg on a fuse." She touched his arm lightly. "Help us, doctor," she murmured, and looked appealingly into his eyes.

He would, he thought, have fought Bonaparte's armies single handed if she had asked him.

The case of Ralph Shockley was simple enough. He had been nearly twenty when the French Revolution burst upon Europe; like many young men, he was swept along by ideals which seemed to him to be the dawn of a new world. Barnikel remembered some of the young man's excited chatter even a few years later. Since then he knew that Ralph occasionally expressed reformist views – for abolition of the rotten boroughs, or religious toleration – ideas which, though they would certainly be anathema to Canon Porteus, were not so terrible.

Ralph Shockley's error however was one of judgement. Faced with the towering conservatism of his brother-in-law, he was unable to resist teasing him with reformist opinions, and would do so until the canon began to grow pale. It was childish. It was like a boy bouncing a ball against a cliff.

And it was a mistake – greater than he knew.

Now he appeared. He was pleased to see Barnikel and welcomed him warmly.

Indeed, as the company sat down to dinner, there was little outward sign of tension. As usual, Ralph began to talk at once.

As soon as he did so, Barnikel could see trouble ahead.

"I have been to see our cousin Mason," he announced.

Poor Porteus winced.

It was not that Daniel Mason, like his father Benjamin, was a Wesleyan: better that, at least, than one of the less respectable sects like Baptists or Quakers; it was that Daniel Mason was a tradesman and that his wife's brother insisted – incorrectly too – in referring to him as cousin.

"He is not, in fact related to you," he observed coldly.

"Well, my brother Adam married Mary Mason," Ralph replied. "But even if he's not my cousin, I like to think of him as one."

Porteus suffered in silence.

"Daniel Mason says the cloth trade has never been better," Ralph went on cheerfully. " 'Tis the wars of Bonaparte you know, doctor. Thanks to the disruption abroad, our clothiers here have the world markets all to themselves." The declining cloth trade of Salisbury, though a poor and meagre business compared with the mighty trade of former times, had been given a temporary boost by the disruption of her competitors' trade in Europe. "By God, doctor," he broke out with a laugh, "I ought to give up schoolmastering and become a clothier! Don't you agree, sister?'

Frances murmured something that no one heard. Porteus's silence deepened.

Ralph's attention now turned to his plate, where a trout lay.

" 'Tis a rather small fish," he said plaintively.

"It is what is provided," Porteus said coldly.

"Excellent fish," Barnikel said with warmth, and saw that Frances looked at him gratefully.

"Perhaps," said Agnes, "Dr. Barnikel has seen the latest cartoon by Mr. Gillray." How could he not have – Gillray's brilliant satirical drawings were sold all over the land. Barnikel took up the theme at once and related a cruel one he had seen mocking the Whigs.

This line of conversation worked very well and even allowed Canon Porteus to soften a little. He and Agnes promptly set to work. They discussed the poems of Walter Scott and his excellent magazine, the *Quarterly Review*, the lyrical ballads of Wordsworth and Coleridge's *Ancient Mariner*; Porteus was pleased to commend some fine prints by Ackerman of various churches, and the new and remarkable dictionary of furniture produced by the great cabinet maker Sheraton. Barnikel smiled to see how adept Agnes showed herself at keeping the conversation in these pleasant channels, and even Frances seemed to come to life.

The fire got under way slowly, and despite Ralph's irritating manners, it was not he but Porteus who started it. It was Frances who inadvertently gave him the excuse by remarking pleasantly that she had received a letter from her late brother's family in America.

Porteus inclined his head and smiled.

"I trust they do well."

Although he disapproved of their connections with the Mason family, Canon Porteus made a special distinction for the Shockleys in America. This was for two reasons. In the first place, they were his wife's own family and therefore, much as he regretted the disloyal secession of the American colonies, it was his duty to treat the Shockleys of Pennsylvania with courtesy. In the second place, they were so far away that they were never likely to trouble him. And so he always referred to them with a charitable kindness that even extended, sometimes, to remembering their names.

"Their eldest boy is away at school."

"I am pleased to hear it," Porteus said politely.

Now he had his opening.

With a meaningful glance at Barnikel he coolly observed:

"My young brother-in-law thinks the Americans are more fortunate than Englishmen here."

At once, Barnikel saw Frances and Agnes look anxious; but Ralph only smiled easily.

"I can't say I'm sure of that," he replied, "though of course, they have not suppressed the writ of Habeus Corpus." He eyed Porteus calmly. "But then they have no prime minister like William Pitt," he added with a mischievous twinkle in his eye.

Barnikel could not help smiling. It was a fair retort. For the previous decade, when the fear of sedition in England reached its height after the French Revolution, the great William Pitt the younger had suspended the ancient writ of Habeas Corpus, and a number of editors, authors and preachers had been held in prison without trial. There had been other measures too: correspondence with France was declared treason; meetings of more than fifty persons without a licence were made illegal; and in 1799, the Combination Acts forbade workers to form any union or association to bargain over their wages or conditions.

Despite the fact that it was he who had invited the response, Barnikel noticed that the canon's fingers were white where they gripped the table. Any criticism of the great patriot Pitt had this effect on him.

The doctor decided to defuse the situation.

"What you say is true. But you will agree surely that those were temporary measures, caused by fear of the French, and probably necessary."

Ralph smiled.

"I'll agree that some of them were, certainly. Though I do not say that to suspend liberties even then is right."

"Perhaps not." The doctor looked round encouragingly, "We must hope for peace at all events," he added, as if to close the matter.

Porteus had other ideas.

"I fear Ralph does not care for Mr. Pitt," he said coldly.

But still the younger man refused to disagree.

"On the contrary," he replied pleasantly, "I applaud him over many matters. 'Tis well known he favours the end of slavery as well as the emancipation of Catholics. Indeed," he added cheerfully, "if England ends slavery, she will have far surpassed America in her freedoms, I'll admit."

It was true that Pitt had resigned when the king refused to allow Catholics to vote or hold office, and Wilberforce the Evangelical who campaigned tirelessly against slavery, was the statesman's close friend and had enlisted his support. But Ralph also knew well that these were the two issues, the only two, on which Canon Porteus could never reconcile himself to his hero.

Why, Barnikel wondered, was it necessary for the younger man to tease his prickly brother-in-law in this way?

"I daresay after a month of him I should be tempted too," he considered. Then he looked at Agnes who was now glancing at her husband in mute appeal and thought: "But I should not give in to it."

An uneasy silence fell over the table. The canon had brought the doctor to witness Ralph's waywardness. So far he had only been made a fool of.

As for Ralph, Barnikel could see very well that, instead of being content with his little victory, he would soon be ready for another passage of words.

They ate a joint of roast beef. Barnikel tried to turn the conversation to other topics. He talked of local matters, of an extraordinary duel he had heard took place at Oxford, of his recent visit to the coast at Brighton where the Prince of Wales was building his outrageous pavilion.

"He is recklessly extravagant," Porteus said sadly.

"Certainly, but you should see the place he is building," Barnikel told him. "It's like an oriental palace for some Indian maharajah."

"Do you suppose, doctor," Frances asked, ignoring for once the canon's look of disapproval, "that he keeps a harem there as well?"

"Not a doubt of it, madam," he replied with a laugh.

But their attempts to steer the conversation failed. For now the canon was ready to strike again.

Looking sombrely at the doctor, then at his wife and Agnes he announced quietly:

"It will be a sad day when his father dies. King George III is our last hope."

It was said matter-of-factly, but it was obviously well calculated. Barnikel saw Ralph Shockley flush and Agnes murmured to him:

"This is how it always begins."

"Our hope for what?"

"Stability, sir."

Barnikel saw Agnes looking at him in mute appeal. Ralph's smile had gone.

"You mean lack of change?" he asked coldly.

"Precisely. I am against religious toleration, because it weakens the Church of England."

"And reform of Parliament – you are happy that Old Sarum returns two members to Parliament at the whim of its owner while large bodies of men in northern cities have no representatives at all?"

"How members of Parliament do their duty to the king is far more important than who sent them there."

"And poor half-starved labourers should still live in feudal servitude in England, and men be sold as slaves abroad?" he asked indignantly.

Porteus did not answer. He had set out only to goad Ralph, and he had succeeded, but a small muscle in his pale cheek was flexing irritably.

Ralph's face had become flushed. He shrugged his shoulders contemptuously and glanced at Barnikel. Seeing no look of support he turned to Porteus again.

"Well, I am against ancient despotism," he said angrily. "And I am for the Rights of Man and Charles James Fox. Perhaps after all," he went on evenly, "we need a revolution here."

There was a terrible silence.

Even Agnes, though she knew he did not mean it, was shocked.

"How can you say such a thing, when Bonaparte himself is across the Channel?" she protested.

[787]

"I say it because I see very plainly that England is a tyranny too," he said acidly, "where the vote is restricted to a few, where religious freedom is not allowed, where the poor have no rights. The French Revolution may have turned into a despotism; but the original idea was good: liberty, equality, fraternity; those are the principles I believe in."

Now Porteus turned to look at Barnikel. His expression said – "There, I told you so". But his hand was shaking with anger.

Agnes was gazing at him imploringly. He must try to keep the peace.

"Let me argue against you, Ralph," he began. "And see, Porteus," he cried hopefully, "if you do not find my reasoning just."

And then, for a moment, Barnikel paused. What did he think? Which man did he actually agree with?

When he spoke, it was with perfect certainty.

"The French overturned a despotic king. But in England the very rights we have – imperfect though they may be – do not need to be snatched from a tyrant for they derive from centuries of our history: from Saxon common law, from Magna Carta, from the legislations of our parliaments, from the principles of the new monarchy set up in 1688.

"Are we so wise, have we the right, to throw away our own ancestral privileges for the sake of a Utopia which, in practice, has failed? I say no. Most Englishmen say no. Our monarchy, our Church, are old and noble institutions. They form," he searched for a word; "they form an organism," he went on, "like the human body itself. This, sir, is the English nation. Throw that away in the cause of a supposed perfect liberty and you may lose all. Continuity, inherited rights and privileges, sir, are the very things that make a nation. It is breaking with them that sets up tyranny."

This was the very case made by the great Edmund Burke in his celebrated *Reflections* on the French Revolution. It was the perfect expression of what was acceptable to most thinking Englishmen. It was also, though he did not realise it, the perfect statement of the old world's view, derived from feudal village, medieval guild, local courts and councils that liberty is primarily a corporate affair, in contrast to the new world's view that it is first and foremost an individual business. It was the grand statement of English political compromise.

He blushed. He was not used to making speeches.

"Well said, doctor." Agnes's eyes were shining with admiration.

He blushed deeper still.

Even Porteus, still speechless with suppressed fury, bowed stiffly towards him to indicate that he approved of what he had said.

On Ralph it had no effect at all.

"Nonsense," he cried, "Tom Paine answered that with his *Rights of Man*. Each generation makes its own government. And if you believe in the natural rights of man and in reason, then the only true government is a democracy where every man has a vote. If your traditions don't give you that, then throw them out of the window."

Barnikel tried to interrupt him, but Ralph went on furiously.

"As for your monarchy, your inherited peerage, your rotten boroughs, your established Church, what have they to do with democracy? Sweep them away."

It was the voice of the early revolution. It was insanity. Barnikel buried his face in his hands.

"That is treason." It was Porteus who spoke, or rather, since his throat was constricted in a white hot fury, hissed the words. "You speak against the king as well as the Church."

"Your Church," Ralph retorted. "From which you derive income from – it is five or six benefices?"

Though restrictions had been placed on how far apart the parishes held by a single clergyman might be, it did not stop Porteus having three, in each of which he had a poor curate and from which he derived a modest income. This last jibe was even more insupportable to him than the rest.

"Their income was useful to you," he thundered, "when I paid for you to go to Oxford."

"And no doubt you think you have the right to own my opinions because of it," he shot back furiously.

It was the last straw. Porteus rose. His long thin body shook so violently that the silver on the table rattled.

"Viper!" he screamed. "Viper in the bosom of this family! Ingrate! Traitor! Leave this house, sir. Leave this house at once!"

Only Barnikel, at that moment, had an inkling of the danger Ralph Shockley was now in.

Late evening in the little town of Christchurch. The priory church, with its Norman arches and square tower, dark; the little ruined castle on its mound beside the priory, dark; the river Avon flowing beside both on its way to the silent, shallow harbour inside its protecting headland, also dark; the white swans, nesting on the river bank, hidden in the dark. The houses had lights, but their shutters were mostly closed and so the light of lamps or candles was little more than a bright slit or a flicker above the street. There was a lamp though, glittering in its iron bracket at the corner of the street, lighting the cobbles below.

Now there was light and sound, as the door of an inn opened and Peter Wilson, only a little the worse for drink came out and began to walk down the narrow street towards his home. The door swung closed behind his departing figure, withdrawing the intruding sound and glare of the inn from the intimacy of the quiet shadows in the street.

Peter Wilson was not quite sober but he was happy, having been well paid the day before. He had bought his ring. He felt it in his pocket. He turned the corner.

And now, suddenly, there were too many shadows. They were behind him, before him; one of the shadows had materialised into a large, dark figure, not at all shadowy, who clamped a large hand over his mouth.

Without thinking, he bit the hand. There was a muffled curse.

"Damn the little whelp."

Then something very hard, crashed against the side of his head.

He was down; the sky was very red. A huge pain throbbed at the side of his head. Two figures were tying his hands. He was not unconscious then, only knocked down. And now he knew what had happened.

"Press gang," he muttered.

"Right, young sir," a chuckle just behind his left ear. "Now keep quiet while we get some more or this cudgel will tap you again," and the said wooden club tapped, painfully, against the rising bruise where he was hit before.

"But," he said aloud, so they could all hear him, "I'm to be married next week."

A guffaw of laughter.

"Quiet you fools." A midshipman.

"You're to be married, matey, to the King's Navy." The same voice, close by his ear again.

"Shsh. Here comes another."

His hands had been securely tied.

Ralph stayed at Doctor Barnikel's house while he waited for the storm to blow over.

Agnes and the children remained with Frances Porteus.

Ralph remained cheerful.

"The old stick will get over it," he told Barnikel as they dined together.

But the doctor was not so sanguine.

"You should go and apologise to him – the sooner the better," he urged.

Ralph laughed, but refused.

"Doesn't he owe me an apology too?"

"Perhaps. But you provoked him."

Ralph went to his work at the school as usual. It did not seem to him so serious a matter.

The next day, when Agnes came to him and demanded: "I beg you, Ralph, to submit to him," he was furious, however.

"You take sides against me then?"

"No. But I am your wife and you have two children. Canon Porteus has influence here."

"And I have principles," he responded petulantly, "even if my wife has not."

"It is only another week until our own house is ready," Ralph told Barnikel. "We can manage as we are until then. After that," he added, "damn Porteus."

But two days after the quarrel, it was Agnes who approached the doctor in the street and begged him:

"Doctor, if you can, persuade my husband to apologise to Canon Porteus. I fear the consequences if he does not."

"Do you know what he intends?"

She shook her head sadly.

"No. He is very correct with me, of course. Yet . . . I fear him," she said simply.

The summons came the next day. It was to Lord Forest's house.

He had changed remarkably little since the days when Adam Shockley knew him. He was an old man now, but upright. His manners were perfect, and he missed nothing.

There was a second great house, outside Manchester now, as well as the mansion in the north of Wiltshire and the house in Salisbury. But he still spent three months a year at Sarum.

It seemed to Ralph that Lord Forest was ageless and timeless. To his dying day he would remain what he always had been: perfect courtier, careful politician and shrewd investor.

He wondered what Forest wanted with him.

He was ushered by a footman into a small room overlooking the gardens behind the house, which Forest used as a study. Lord Forest was standing in front of the fire, grey-haired, very thin and erect.

Canon Porteus was standing beside him.

Forest greeted him courteously, then asked the two men to sit while he remained where he was. He came straight to the point.

"You know of your family's long association with us," he said pleasantly. "And so you will know that my questions are not directed by any malice." He gave a shrewd glance towards Porteus as he said this. In fact Forest had never forgiven Adam Shockley for refusing his offer; but he had nothing against the young man now before him. "You know I am also," he continued, "a governor of your school."

Ralph had forgotten. It was only a small private school, one of several in Salisbury which had sprung up in recent years, while the choristers' school had somewhat declined. The fact that, technically, it had a board of governors at all was something which both the school and the governors themselves, who included Forest and the old bishop, had almost forgotten. Five years before, he could have bought the school himself if Porteus had been prepared to advance him the money; but though Frances had urged the idea, the canon had refused.

"There is still, I fear, a certain instability in his character," he explained, "that makes me feel he is not yet ready for such a responsibility."

Ralph gazed at Forest now, wondering what was coming.

"I understand you hold certain views," Lord Forest went on. "Radical views."

"Such as reform of the rotten boroughs. And I support Mr. Fox. Is that what you mean?"

Forest bowed pleasantly.

"I am proud to know Mr. Fox very well," he said suavely. Canon Porteus looked aghast. "Though I by no means always agree with him." He looked at Ralph thoughtfully. "You also hold republican views?"

"That is my affair," Ralph snapped.

"Quite so. And there I propose to leave it," Forest replied equably.

Porteus frowned. Ralph looked at them both.

"Is that all?"

"Almost." Forest gazed at the ceiling for a moment. "These are difficult times, Mr. Shockley," he went on. "The possibility of a French invasion is always with us. In such circumstances, a man, whatever his views, must be wise." He paused. "May I have your assurance that, whatever may be your private reflections on these matters, you will not seek to express them to your pupils in the school? You understand me I am sure."

He did indeed. Nor had he, as far as he could remember, ever tried to convert his pupils to his point of view. Normally he would not have hesitated to agree.

But it was the sight of Porteus, sitting smugly opposite, his own brother-in-law who had obviously taken all this trouble to humiliate him, that infuriated Ralph.

"Do you mean that, even if I am asked my opinion, I should lie?" he asked coldly.

And now Porteus burst out.

"It means, sir, that you will keep your seditious treason to yourself! That you will not attempt to infect the minds of your charges with your infamy."

"Enough, Porteus," Lord Forest said mildly but firmly.

But now Ralph was pale with rage. This was just the tyranny he despised.

"I am not obliged to give any undertakings whatever," he answered furiously.

"Ha!" It was an explosion, half of triumph, half of rage that broke from Porteus.

"Are you sure, Mr. Shockley that you would not prefer to consider this matter," Forest asked.

"There is nothing to consider."

Forest sighed.

"Very well. I must tell you Mr. Shockley that in my view it would be unwise – most unwise – for you to continue at your post for the time being. Tempers run high on these matters, you know. We must be prudent. I shall speak to the other governors, but you should consider yourself relieved of your post."

Ralph looked at him in horror. He had not realised it would come to this. Had Forest the power to do such a thing? He tried to remember who, apart from the old bishop, the governors were. But then as he considered Forest's huge estates and his connections he realised his own folly. Of course Forest could. Trust Porteus to be thorough in such a matter.

"But . . . my wife and children," he burst out.

"Ah," Porteus cried. "So you have remembered them." He turned to Forest. "I shall of course see they are provided for."

"That will be all gentlemen," Forest said. It was an order to depart.

It was Thaddeus Barnikel who managed to discover exactly what had taken place. It was far worse even than he had feared.

"Porteus has already warned several of the boys' parents; and the bishop," he told Ralph. "Even without Forest, there would have been demands to remove you that could not have been resisted. He's done his work thoroughly."

"And if I go to apologise to him. If I retract?" Ralph asked miserably.

"Too late I fear. His mind is . . ." he pressed his hands together to demonstrate: "closed like a vice." He grimaced. "I must tell you that at present, no one in Sarum will employ you."

It was late that morning that Forest sent for him again. The interview took place in the same room as before.

"I understand Canon Porteus has turned Sarum against you. I had not realised myself how far he intended to go," Lord Forest confessed.

Ralph nodded sadly.

"It will blow over," Forest told him. "You must be patient. In the meantime, I think you must consider a post outside Sarum."

"It seems I must consider anything."

"Very well. My grandchildren need a tutor and I think you will do. You will be paid the same that you had here, but your wife had best remain at Salisbury."

It was a good offer. As good as he could hope for at present.

"Are you not afraid I shall make them into revolutionaries?" Ralph asked wryly.

Forest allowed himself a thin smile.

"There is little danger of that."

"I accept. But I must make clear that I wish to return to Sarum as soon as possible."

"That is understood." Forest looked at him thoughtfully. "In the current political climate, Mr. Shockley, you must not deceive yourself. It will take some time."

Ralph hung his head.

"I fear, Lord Forest, I have been very foolish," he said frankly.

The parting of Ralph Shockley and his wife was a sad business.

Before him he saw a woman who had not shared his quarrel. But worse than that, he knew she had been right, and now by his foolishness he had wronged her. The sense of guilt made him irritable.

And Agnes saw an immature boy. Could it be, if he was prepared to bring such misery down on her and the children for the sake of a moment's pride, that he really loved her? It felt to her like a rejection.

"He is, in effect, deliberately leaving me," she thought. He could not appreciate her very much. "I can only wait then," she considered, "for him to grow a little wiser, even if he does not really love me." If he was unstable she must be firm. Aloud she said:

"We shall await you here in Sarum. I hope your return will be soon."

"You will visit me though."

She shook her head.

"No. We shall wait for you."

He saw her intention: to take a superior moral position.

"You may wait a long time," he snapped.

"I hope not." Now she looked down. His tone hurt her and, for a moment, she thought she would cry. But she knew she must not. A tearful parting, a moment of weakness shared with him, and he would shift all the blame for his troubles on to Porteus.

So now she was strong and looked at him evenly.

"We shall wait here," she repeated.

Then she turned and left.

Ralph did not speak to Porteus again, but he did go to see his sister Frances.

"I could not stop him," she explained sadly. "I tried to argue with him for a whole night."

He looked at her with a heavy heart. For a moment he thought he could see the light in his sister's eyes that he had known before her marriage. Then it was gone.

"Pray, my dear brother," she continued earnestly, "whatever your opinions in the future, for all our sakes let them remain unspoken."

There was nothing he could say.

It was after he had taken his leave of Frances and his wife that he had a last brief word with Barnikel.

"My wife will be much alone, doctor," he said. "And I may be gone two years. She will need a friend. May I place her in your care?"

Thaddeus Barnikel swallowed but gave him his hand.

"You may."

In the year 1804, great events were stirring: events that were critical for Britain.

In January Napoleon changed his plans and decided that the fleet of armed transports he had been preparing would not be strong enough, and that he would need the French navy to accompany them as a protective escort.

It was a powerful fleet, for it contained not only the French navy, but the ships of France's allies the Spanish as well: a total greater than England's fleet.

"He will have to engage our navy and smash us first," Forest explained to Porteus; "That's his object now. Then he'll ship his army across, and it will be huge."

"Our army is still small."

"It is."

"So all now rests upon a single naval engagement."

"When it comes, yes."

From February to April, King George III suffered another of his bouts of madness.

Then, in May, the feeble ministry led by the well-meaning Addington collapsed and – "by the grace of God" said Porteus – William Pitt returned to power. Ironically, on the same day, May 18, Napoleon Bonaparte in his final departure from the supposed democracy of the French Revolution, crowned himself Emperor.

In the history of England, no man, not even Churchill in the twentieth century, ever assumed for himself during a period in office the heroic status of William Pitt the younger. His thin, meagre form with its long, upward-turning nose, and its nearly impossible angularities (his almost total lack of a posterior caused cartoonists to dub him 'the bottomless Pitt') was driven by such concentrated passion, such acute nervous energy, and such a driving and selfless zeal for the cause of his country in its desperate years of crisis, that the House of Commons was not only dominated by him, but awed.

"I think the man lives on his passion and upon air," Barnikel said to Canon Porteus. He had heard that Pitt's personal life had been one of great disappointment; but whether his political passion was an outlet for his frustration, or whether it would have been there anyway, he had no means of judging. Of his greatness, and of his firmness of purpose in resisting Napoleon, there was no doubt.

"He has the strength of the prophets, sir," Porteus answered, "because he serves a noble cause. He is pure." And it was clear that the canon considered himself cast in the same mould.

The plan by which Pitt saved his country from destruction in the years 1804 to 1806 was twofold. The first object was to form an alliance with the unwilling European powers that would force Napoleon to remove his gathering army from the northern coast of France. His second was to blockade the French navy in port so that they could not get out and destroy England's own.

At first the alliance seemed harder to achieve. The Europeans had no wish to fight Napoleon again. He had already proved that on the field of battle he was their master. As long as France remained within her natural frontiers on the continent, they would do nothing.

But fortunately there was one hope: Czar Alexander of Russia wanted to expand, north into the Baltic and south to Constantinople. Here Pitt found an ally against the threatening power of France. But he needed more. Austria held back; Prussia, cynically, seemed ready to sell her services, and the right to cross her territory, to the highest bidder.

Napoleon had ninety thousand men at Boulogne, and two thousand transports. Like Emperor Claudius, eighteen hundred years before, he seemed about to sweep all before him on the northern island.

And then, as so often in his meteoric career, Napoleon overreached himself. Not only did he parcel out Germany as casually as if he were cutting up a cake, but in the spring of 1805 he had himself crowned King of Italy. It was too much. The message was clear.

"He means to gobble up all."

Mighty Austria joined Pitt's alliance and the stage was set for a massive conflict.

1805: September 15

The mission of the little frigate *Euryalus* is seldom recorded in works of general history. Yet no ship in the British navy played a more important role in saving England during the fateful autumn of 1805.

"We were Nelson's watchdog," the crew would recall proudly. "We were his extra eye and arm."

And if he had to serve in the King's Navy instead of smuggle safely at home in Christchurch, Peter Wilson counted himself lucky that it was this ship, of all the others, that the press gang had taken him to.

For the press gang system was a wholesale business. The press tenders were everywhere in the Channel waters around the Solent. One of their favourite places to lie in wait was near the western tip of the Isle of Wight, ten miles from Christchurch, where they would send gangs aboard every ship entering the port of Southampton to take some of their men. But they raided frequently along the coastal towns as well.

On the night he was pressed, Peter found himself aboard a receiving ship lying out in the bay. He had been stripped, and the ship's doctor, after a cursory inspection, pronounced him sea worthy. Then they took him down into the hold.

He knew what to expect. Over the top of the hold was a grate. Above he could see the shadowy outlines of four marines with loaded muskets standing guard. Around him in the cramped space were, he estimated, thirty other men, some of them taken the day before. The hold was now so full that all the men were pressed together. The stench was terrible. In his pocket he still had the ring he had been carrying. It would not be long before someone tried to get that. He took it out and, in the darkness, slipped it over his little finger. It stuck at the joint, but, though it made him wince, he pushed it over. "Now," he thought, "they'll have to cut my finger off to get that." What would follow next? They would probably be taken, he guessed, to rendezvous with the other tenders. There would be all manner of recruits: experienced sailors taken from merchant vessels, sometimes quasi-legally, raw recruits like himself, and 'Lord Mayor's men' – those who had joined the navy to escape from the law or other misdeeds. Then they could be distributed anywhere in the fleet. If they were lucky the pressed men might join a ship with a kindly commander. If not . . . a cruel captain could exact terrible punishments for all kinds of offences: he had heard of men being given several hundred lashes, or worse, being keel-hauled: dragged under the ship on a rope so that, if you did not drown, the barnacles on the hull ripped the flesh off your body.

It was while he contemplated these horrors, and the fact that he had lost his home and his bride, that he heard a voice above remark.

"These are all to be put ashore at Buckler's Hard. There's a new ship there."

He knew Buckler's Hard. It was a small inlet a few miles along the coast from Christchurch, where the heathland at the southern end of the New Forest ran down to the sea. There was a dockyard there where they built ships.

And it was there, praise be to God, that he joined the *Euryalus*.

The *Euryalus* was a small vessel: a thirty-six gun frigate with three masts: a trim, speedy little vessel, designed by Sir William Ruse, surveyor of the King's Navy, commissioned in 1803: her captain, the Hon Henry Blackwood. From the moment that Peter Wilson walked on board, he knew he was in luck.

Being only a frigate, the *Euryalus* had none of the impersonality of the huge hulks with seventy-four or ninety-eight guns. Being newly commissioned, she had no bad tradition of cruelty, which some of the older ships had. And her captain was a kind and dashing figure.

"You're in luck with this one," one of the seamen told him. "Lucky as if you'd got Nelson himself."

He learned his seamanship fast. It came to him naturally; and apart from the occasional blow from the bo'sun's rattan – which was more a genial reminder of his authority than a punishment, he escaped harm. He learned the menial duties of swabbing the deck and the endless, hand-tearing work on the canvas, but he loved to swarm up the rigging and out along the arms, feeling the salt breeze in his face as he waited the order to unfurl the sails.

Because his sight was excellent, and he loved to be up there, he was often sent aloft to act as lookout.

One other circumstance had made him into a kind of mascot amongst the ship's company. When he first stood in line with the other recruits and the master demanded his name, he answered:

"Wilson, sir." Then added, he did not know why, unless it was to remind himself of his home: "Of Christchurch."

There was a roar of laughter.

"Damme," cried the master, "not another one." And so he learned that the ship contained a young midshipman, Robert Wilson, son of Sir Wykeham Wilson, whose estate lay just outside Christchurch. He gazed at the boy curiously – several years his junior, but an officer of course. He had only seen Sir Wykeham once or twice and never seen his son before. He was a tall, dark, good-looking young fellow who seemed to have an easy way both with the other midshipmen and the men. However, he did not suppose that the young gentleman would ever address a word to him, unless it was an order. He was surprised to be proved wrong. That very afternoon, the boy strode over to him.

"We Wilsons of Christchurch must stick together," he said with a pleasant grin. And from that day, whenever the young midshipman was on duty and he was up aloft as the lookout, he would make a point of crying up: "What do you see, Wilson of Christchurch?" And this harmless, good-hearted joke somehow made his exile from home seem a little less bitter.

It was a happy ship. Though Captain Blackwood never addressed him personally, he was conscious of his kindly and professional rule at all times. "The men of the *Euryalus* eat well," the men said. But once, when they had been long at sea and supplies were running low, an old seaman remarked to Peter: "Mark this, young Wilson: Blackwood sees to it his officers eat no better than we do when supplies are short. Not many do that."

He was often lonely. But he did not despair. Every day when he got up, and again, when he went to sleep, he would finger the wedding ring on his little finger and murmur: "She'll be there, when I get back." It comforted him.

The frigate was kept continually busy. First they were employed off the coast of Ireland; then under Admiral Keith, watching the port of Boulogne.

"For God's sake don't fall asleep when you watch up there," Robert Wilson said to him once in a serious tone. "If ever Boney gets his army out of there, you and I will never see Christchurch under English rule again."

But it was in the summer of 1805 that events really began to move quickly.

The huge French fleet under Villeneuve was poised to strike, but first it had to try to shake off the British. Villeneuve got out to open sea; then he made a feint towards the West Indies. Nelson followed. Villeneuve doubled back. It was a game of cat and mouse. Nelson made for Gibraltar; Villeneuve went north towards the Channel but another British force, in an indecisive action, turned him back. Nelson returned to England. Where would Villeneuve go next?

The crisis was approaching. Back in England awaiting his instructions, Nelson was convinced that the French masterplan intended Villeneuve to come out into open sea, unite the French fleet, and then strike south at the Mediterranean, pinning down the allied forces in Italy while Napoleon made a mighty sweep across central Europe. He was correct. By late summer 1805 this was Napoleon's plan. But first Villeneuve had to get out. Where was the French Admiral, and what would he do next?

On August 14 Villeneuve arrived in Cadiz, where Admiral Collingwood and his force were keeping watch.

"He can't refit his ships there. There are no supplies," Robert Wilson remarked. "He'll have to come out into open sea soon. Keep your eyes peeled, Wilson of Christchurch."

But the mission of the *Euryalus* was to be a more important one than watching.

"You're to make for Portsmouth," Captain Blackwood was told. "To tell them Villeneuve's here. As fast as you can."

So it was the little frigate *Euryalus*, playing the first part of her particular role in history, that sailed, at lightning speed, to fetch the great Admiral Nelson.

They reached the Isle of Wight on September 1. By the next morning, Blackwood called upon Nelson at Merton. Then, on to the Admiralty.

It is often thought that Admiral Nelson saved England from immediate invasion in the great events of autumn 1805. This is not in fact so. For on August 9, just before the *Euryalus* had begun her dash home, another event of great significance had taken place. Austria had declared war on France.

The response of Napoleon was immediate. He would fight the alliance on land and he would win. But in order to do so, he had to withdraw the huge army threatening England from Boulogne. He did so, as was his habit, with amazing speed. On the day when the *Euryalus* passed the Isle of Wight, Boulogne was already almost empty.

But for Nelson, now given unrestricted command of the fleet, this was not the point.

If by a single blow he could now smash the French fleet once and for all, he could make it impossible for Napoleon to invade England not only this year, but any year. This was his ambition – his mission – nothing less.

On September 15, 1805, Nelson's flagship *Victory* sailed from Spithead. In its company rode Captain Blackwood's little squadron of frigates: *Euryalus*, *Phoebe*, *Naiad*, *Sirius*, the schooner *Pickle* and the cutter *Entreprenente*. They arrived off Cadiz to join the rest of the fleet on September 28, Nelson's forty-seventh birthday.

Then they waited three weeks. Meanwhile the *Euryalus* kept watch.

Night and day, while Nelson and his fleet of twenty-seven huge warships waited patiently on the horizon, the little frigate hung in sight of the harbour mouth. Behind her stretched, at intervals, the chain of her sister frigates so that her messages could be passed back to the waiting fleet.

"What do you see, Wilson of Christchurch?" The haunting question would echo in his mind all his life.

"Nothing yet, sir."

Nelson even sent several of his ships away, in the hope of tempting them out. Nothing happened.

And then one day after three weeks, young Peter Wilson saw it: a distant mast near the harbour mouth. Then another. And another.

"They're moving!" he cried in excitement, before correcting himself: "Ship ahoy." In moments, not only Robert Wilson but Captain Blackwood himself and every officer was on deck, training their telescopes on the spot.

"Are they coming, sir?" he heard Robert Wilson ask.

Then Blackwood's voice, very calm.

"Not yet, I think." And then, glancing up, breaking all normal rules, the captain himself: "Well done, Wilson of Christchurch."

Blackwood was right. For three more days, Villeneuve's fleet hung about near the harbour mouth. Each day it seemed they might break loose. Each day, tantalisingly, they held back.

Awesome though the thought of the huge battle that would follow must be, Peter Wilson found himself praying: "Please Lord, let them come soon." The suspense was almost more than he could bear.

And then, on October 20, they came: Thirty-four huge ships of the line, rolling majestically out to sea, every one of them capable, with their huge banks of cannon, of blasting the little frigate out of the water with a single broadside: he counted them, all thirty-four, as they came; and as he saw this terrifying fleet he wondered: "Can anything withstand them?"

The huge fleet made southwards towards Gibraltar, past Cape Trafalgar. And the little frigate *Euryalus* followed, as close as she dared, while Nelson and the main fleet lurked just over the horizon. And as they went, and he felt the hissing salt surf in his face, young Peter Wilson smiled grimly to himself and murmured:

"We're Nelson's watchdog all right."

They watched the fleet all day and all night. The enemy was constantly moving about. Each time Villeneuve's ships changed their tack, *Euryalus* fired a signal gun. Every hour, she burned a blue light to show the English fleet that she was watching. And every signal she made was passed back, from frigate to frigate, and along the chain of battleships to the *Victory* herself.

They did their work well. Not a motion of the French fleet was missed.

Then Nelson came out into the open, and bore down upon them.

He did what he had been planning to do for months: he divided his own force into two, one half, the weather column, he led himself, the other, the lee, was led by Collingwood in *Royal Sovereign*. Then, aiming to converge somewhat above the centre of the huge, crescent-shaped line of the French, they began their approach.

The performance of the *Euryalus* had been faultless. As he made his formation at six o'clock that morning, Nelson summoned the little frigate to *Victory*'s side and ordered Captain Blackwood aboard to congratulate him.

"We shall surprise the enemy now," he declared. "They won't know what I am about."

As the advance began, *Euryalus* rode proudly by Nelson's side.

"One eye and one arm," an old seaman told Peter, "but you see what he does with what he's got left!"

At eight o'clock Villeneuve reversed course, but he could not now avoid Nelson's battle.

The final approach began. At 11.45am, the famous signal from the flagship went out:

"England expects every man to do his duty."

"And when we have," Midshipman Robert Wilson remarked, "I dare say it'll be the end of the French." Then under his breath he said a prayer.

As for seaman Peter Wilson, he said no prayer; but he gave the wedding ring a nervous squeeze and muttered: "You see me safe out of this."

The battle began at noon.

The great sea battles of the tall-masted sailing ships were slow, ponderous, stately affairs – at least until they came in close. The final approach took an hour. There was a gentle Atlantic swell; the wind a slight breeze from west-north-west; the day was clear, and as the huge crescent of the French fleet stood before them, Peter Wilson stood with the older seamen and watched with fascination. There was Collingwood, in almost parallel course with them, leading the mighty British warships: *Mars, Bellerophon*, under John Cooke, *Achilles, Revenge*, and others. There, ahead of them, was the huge *Bucentaure*, the flagship of Villeneuve; close by it, *Neptune, Heros, San Leandro*.

"See there," one of the sailors pointed far down the French line. "Recognise her?"

"By God I do," cried another. " 'Tis one of ours." And he showed Peter, far in the distance, where the English ship *Swiftsure* that had been captured by the enemy some years before, now sailed in the French line.

"We've another to match her," he laughed.

For it was one of the curiosities of the battle of Trafalgar that in Admiral

Collingwood's column under Captain William Rutherfurd there now sailed a new British ship, once again named *Swiftsure* – so that two British ships of the same name fired upon each other from different sides.

The two collisions of the British columns with the French – first Collingwood, then Nelson – were unlike anything Peter Wilson could have imagined. As he saw the *Royal Sovereign* split through the line first, saw her, minute after minute edge with painful slowness between the enemy ships who poured broadside after broadside in to her, he could not believe that any ship could survive. Even from a distance, it seemed to him the whole sky must crack open with the roar from the mighty guns.

"And that," he would say afterwards, "was before we entered the mouth of hell ourselves."

Nelson made the most of every inch of his journey. First he headed towards the van. Then, suddenly, he swung up, straight at the centre and at Villeneuve himself. It was a daring move. And Peter Wilson, as the little frigate bobbed by *Victory*'s side, thought the world had come to an end.

For by crossing the line as he did, Nelson exposed himself to withering enemy fire, to which he could not reply, for half an hour. As crash after crash shook the ships, it seemed to Peter that he was in the midst of a huge thunderstorm; the cannon-balls that whizzed over the water, smashing their way through sides, sails, rigging sending up a shower of sparks and splinters were like thunderbolts. It seemed it would never end. Then they were through right in amongst the enemy line: *Victory* and *Temeraire*, locked in mortal combat with the *Bucentaure* and *Redoubtable*. This was the close fighting at which the English navy excelled.

The battle lasted all afternoon. It reached its height between one and two, as more and more of the English ships ploughed into the French line. At 1.45, the flagship *Bucentaure* struck its colours. Three more ships were taken soon afterwards. In Collingwood's column the battle went even better. By half past three, he had taken eleven ships, more was still falling. Amongst those taken back that day was the original *Swiftsure*.

It was in early afternoon that they knew Nelson was hit. They saw the signals from *Victory* to Collingwood in *Royal Sovereign*. But in the blistering engagement, there was so much to do that Peter Wilson had little time to think about it. For soon afterwards the *Euryalus* played another key role in the battle when she was summoned by Collingwood to his side. He was in acting command now, but except for a tottering foremast, all *Royal Sovereign*'s masts were down. So it was that *Euryalus*, hanging close by the stricken ship's side, made from her own masts the signals to the fleet for the second half of the battle of Trafalgar.

Her final honour was at the end of the battle, when Collingwood transferred his own flag to her and, though her own main and topmast rigging had been shot away, the mauled little ship towed the mighty *Royal Sovereign* from the battle.

When did Peter Wilson know that Nelson was gone? The tragic knowledge seemed, in retrospect, to colour the whole day, as though someone had placed a dark filter over the whole thundering, echoing sky.

[801]

But it was not so. It was in late afternoon, just as he had been busy on the deck running up the colours for a signal, that he saw Robert Wilson look towards *Victory*, turn, tears in his eyes, and say:

"He's gone, Wilson of Christchurch. He's gone."

The victory of Trafalgar broke the French fleet for ever. It was never again able to launch any attack more important than an occasional raid on commercial shipping. The threat of invasion was over.

But the threat from Bonaparte in Europe was not.

Two days before Trafalgar he had forced the Austrians back at Ulm. And in December at the extraordinary battle of Austerlitz, he advanced straight to the centre of the massive joint army opposing him and broke the Austrians and Russians in a single hammer-blow. The British forces in Germany had to be hastily withdrawn. Pitt's grand alliance had utterly failed. Instead of crushing the upstart tyrant, the coalition had collapsed and now Napoleon had taken whole pieces of the crumbling Austrian empire as well.

Broken by the news in January 1806, William Pitt the younger died.

Napoleon was still at large.

But none of this mattered to Peter Wilson. For in 1806, he was allowed to go home.

When his family discovered he had been at Trafalgar he was treated as a hero. He walked happily round Christchurch and his friends gave him free drinks. It was all very satisfactory.

His fiancée, not expecting to see him again, had married.

He shrugged, then grinned.

"When I go courting again," he announced, "I've already got the ring."

Three weeks later, he delivered a keg of brandy to the house of Canon Porteus.

Things were back to normal.

Though he lived in comfort at the Forests' estate in the north, and though he was never in any physical danger, of the two men exiled from home – Peter Wilson and Ralph Shockley – it was Shockley who suffered more. The experience changed him: for if the contemplation of revolutionary theories had made him truculent and argumentative, the knowledge of real suffering, as it always does, gave him a certain quietness.

Neither the conditions of his own life, nor his pupils was the problem. The Forest boys were ten and eight years old: both dark and slender with long, pale faces. They did as he asked, learned their lessons quickly and gave him no cause for complaint. Their grandfather made periodic stays in his several houses; their parents were mostly in London, but although they were left alone with their tutor in the huge northern house, the boys seemed quite contented. He soon decided that they were, more than any other children he had known, strangely self-sufficient. *They take what they need from me. They are polite. And that is all,* he thought.

There was something else. As he saw more of the Forest family on their periodic visits, and of their guests on these occasions, he began to understand it better.

They treated him well; as tutor, he was almost like one of themselves, yet though the good manners, even of the children, made them capable at times of a delicacy towards him that would never have occurred to Porteus, he sensed that, deep down they simply did not care what he thought. There was no personal animosity towards a man of the middle classes like himself in the charmed lives of these aristocrats: in a way, it made all dealings with them very easy and restful. But sometimes it seemed to him that he could see in their eyes a callousness that only comes from generations of living selfishly apart.

"They are hard, these aristocrats," he murmured.

The house, by the standards of the great houses of the time, was not enormous, but it covered several acres and had fifty bedrooms besides the servants' quarters – a maze of numberless chambers in the roof reached by back stairs into which he never penetrated. There was a fine landscaped park, and a tree-lined drive a mile long. The stone arch through which one entered the drive was so broad and high that it seemed to frame a sizeable portion of the sky.

It was not the family nor the house that troubled him: it was what he saw outside the park gates.

The first revelation came three months after his first arrival at the northern house when old Lord Forest came to spend a few weeks with them. He heard the steward remark that his lordship was going into Manchester to inspect some of his property and Ralph asked if he could accompany them. Forest had no objection. Thus, on a crisp February morning, he found himself rolling through the Lancashire countryside towards the growing city.

The countryside was beautiful: rolling ridges of oak woods dipping down to broad valleys where the farms lay in their rich fields. The new industries in the cities and the minefields had begun to bring wealth to the area, but had not yet scarred it or raised into the sky the great cloud of grime that was to darken the face of so much of northern England. It seemed to Shockley, as they went along, that the cottages and farmhouses had about them a richer air than the often dilapidated little villages he was used to seeing in the bare sheep country around Sarum.

"They do well here, by comparison," Forest remarked. "The north grows richer than the south every day."

They came to the outskirts of Manchester. These had about them the atmosphere of a military camp. Everywhere Shockley looked it appeared that new buildings were going up: a warehouse here, a factory there; on a nearby slope, two rows of neat terraced brick houses, solidly built, suggesting a new, if somewhat regimented prosperity. With so much fresh activity, such a plethora of carts, piles of materials and digging, it seemed as though the whole surface of this part of the world was being scraped by a huge rake before a new raw world was planted.

Then they reached the cotton mill.

It was a long brick building, three storeys high, with big staring, rectangular windows and large doorways every dozen yards. Even before the carriage door was opened, he could hear the hum of machinery from within.

But nothing had prepared him for what he saw next, and he never forgot it.

The cotton industry of England owed its truly remarkable rise to two machines, and to two minerals. Like the production of woollen cloth, cotton too requires two processes – spinning yarn and then weaving it. The first machine was for spinning. Since long before the Shockleys first opened their fulling mill, only two major innovations had taken place in the process of spinning yarn. The first was an elementary spinning wheel on which the yarn could be wound, the second, which had only come the previous century, was an improvement on the spinning wheel – the jenny – on which multiple spindles could be set. But now this improvement on the old spinning wheel was fast disappearing. For hardly surprisingly, the principle of the jenny had been extended. By means of a powered system to drive it, the basic spinning wheel, now become a monster machine, could drive eighty, a hundred or more spindles. The familiar whirr and click of the spinster in her cottage was passing forever from the countryside of England, leaving behind it only a name, applied for some reason to unmarried rather than married women. This was the first part of the story.

The reason for Manchester's triumph lay in a development of the jenny. At first, the yarn from the jenny, lacking the careful handling of the old spinning wheel, was not so strong. It was good enough for the cross thread, the weft, but not for the warp – the lengthwise thread which took the strain on the loom. Then came Arkwright's water frame; an improvement on an earlier machine which, by a system of rollers spinning at different speeds could stretch and then twist a yarn which was, though a little coarse, consistent and strong enough for warp and weft. In order to produce a cotton to rival the finest imported from India, one further refinement was needed: a machine to produce yarn that was both fine and strong. It had appeared in the 1780s, a combination of the jenny and Arkwright's water frame. It was invented by Samuel Compton. And, being a combination of exciting inventions, it was called the Mule.

It drove all before it.

"The Mule and the power loom will change everything," Forest told him.

It was this that Shockley was about to see.

For the second invention that had ensured the triumph of the north was the mechanical loom. For centuries the business of weaving had been done by hand. When Shockley and Moody, two and a half centuries before, had organised their weavers into a primitive factory, it had still been no more than a collection of men, sitting in pairs at the loom, tossing the shuttlecock between them that threaded the weft across the warp. But now, Edmund Cartwright had set up a steam-driven power-loom.

"So," Lord Forest remarked, "to make cotton we hardly need weavers any more."

And the two minerals that were about to transform the world? Iron and coal, which together produced machines, driven by steam.

It was all this that Ralph Shockley saw as he entered the cotton mill.

But it was not the huge machines, the seemingly endless lines of thread that turned and clicked like so many soldiers on an eternal parade ground; it was not the monotonous thumping of the great steam engine that, in another area, drove the looms: it was not the fact that, as he saw for the first time a full scale northern factory at work and understood, at that instant, what it really meant – that the old ways, the Wessex ways his ancestors had always known, would soon be gone forever: it was not even the terrible, mechanical din and inhumanity of the place that turned his stomach.

It was the fact that half the machines were manned by ragged children.

Forest glanced at him.

"Children are cheaper," he remarked calmly. "We treat them better here than in other factories. I won't allow them to be flogged."

And for once Ralph Shockley had the sense to be silent. As he looked about the huge, pulsating monster he realised also, for the first time, that he personally was completely powerless.

"As powerless," he would afterwards recall sadly, "as those children."

Doctor Thaddeus Barnikel had no illusions.

"It will be many months before Porteus allows him to return," he told Agnes. "And Porteus will decide everything."

The canon, indeed, was only reflecting the mood of the city at that time, which was both warlike and conservative. Long before his final triumph, the council had awarded Nelson the freedom of the city. In an astounding act of generosity, the city had even offered to equip six hundred volunteers for the wars. Some of the Wiltshire Volunteers had been drilling in the cathedral cloisters. They had made rather a mess of the place, and one of them had made charcoal drawings of his comrades on the walls. But nobody seemed to mind what was done in the cause of the war. A few in the close even wore the white cockades of the royalist Bourbon cause. To the canon's huge delight, a series of local petitions against Catholic emancipation had even been prepared. All his causes were in the ascendant.

"If Porteus tells them Ralph is a traitor, he'd better not show his face here," the doctor concluded.

Sarum thought of nothing but the war. Porteus, cold and self-righteous, could be inflexible.

In the months after the departure of Ralph, Barnikel often saw Agnes. She lived now at her own small house in New Street; but most afternoons, when Canon Porteus was out, she would be found with Frances, and it was there that Barnikel would call, twice a week, before escorting her back to her own door, where he left her. He gave presents to the children. Sometimes, either with Frances or alone, he would walk with her, but always in some public place, usually in the cathedral close.

Several times he also met Frances alone and would ask her whether

Porteus showed any signs of relenting.

"Not yet doctor, I fear," she would reply stiffly, and it was impossible to tell what she really felt about the matter. The nearest hint came early in 1805 when one day, without meeting his eye she remarked: "My husband is like Mr. Pitt, doctor. His passion is very great, but it is for his country."

"I think your brother is a man of passion too," he replied.

But she shook her head.

"Ralph has sudden enthusiasms, which pass. That is not passion. He knows nothing of passion."

He wondered what else her strange life with Porteus behind the closed doors of his house, and his mind, had taught Frances; he wondered if there lay in her words a message of understanding for him too.

For the passion of Thaddeus Barnikel for Agnes, like a charcoal fire, gave little outward sign, but it burned all the same with a steady, relentless heat, as fierce as any furnace.

"The truth of the matter is," he confessed to himself, "she is my whole life."

Ralph wrote frequently: usually to Agnes, once or twice to Mason.

He told Mason of his visit to the cotton factory and received a depressing letter in reply.

The terrible machines you describe still, thank God, have scarcely appeared in Wiltshire and I see no prospect of such things at Salisbury.

Our own broadcloth industry continues very weak. Two more poor weavers went out of business last month. It is sad to see the old Sarum broadcloth trade entering its final decline.

To Agnes he wrote tenderly, and told her his return could not be long delayed.

Apart from his work as tutor, he was not idle. The horror of what he had seen at the cotton mill drew him back to the city again and again. He would take a horse and ride over there on a spare day; or he would go further and visit the port beyond. He soon discovered that what Lord Forest had told him was perfectly true: there were far worse places than his mill.

But worst of all, he visited the mines, where the precious coal to fuel the great machines was dragged up, "As though," he wrote to Agnes, "from the infernal regions themselves."

To Mason he wrote:

I have seen mines, three hundred feet deep, lit by candles – and considered safe until the gases snuff the candle out. Safe that is, unless there is an explosion below, from which the other day I saw bodies brought out with no more concern than if they had been so many rats killed down their holes by terriers.

Worse even than the dead, are the living. In some mines they still use little boys to open and shut the ventilation doors below ground, and I have frequently seen little girls, harnessed like mules, dragging baskets of coal up ladders, for ten hours a day.

Yesterday, at one such infamous place, I saw what I took to be a small black dog emerging from a mine shaft. I went over to it to find that the black creature, though it went on all fours and could indeed have been taken for an animal, so utterly degraded was its filthy condition, was not a dog but a child, sent by its parents down to work. It – I say it – was four years old.

We know poverty at Sarum; but we have nothing, I thank God, like this.

These conditions, in England, were to persist for some time.

To his wife, however, Ralph, through delicacy did not think it proper to describe such terrible particulars. He wrote only in general terms.

There are things here that seem to me, more than ever, to be a crime against human freedom and dignity: I see conditions that are worse, I believe, than slavery. Porteus himself would agree with me I think, but it is useless, I suppose, for me to communicate with him at present.

And Agnes, seeing nothing of her husband, and like most well-meaning folk at Sarum, knowing nothing about the conditions to which he was referring, assumed that he spoke of conditions on the estate or his relationship with the Forest household, and shaking her head sadly, wondered if he would ever grow up to be a mature man. So that when Frances tentatively asked her: "Do you think Ralph is growing any wiser in his absence," she could only reply, "I trust so," without much conviction.

The resistance of Canon Porteus to Ralph's return took everyone by surprise. It was awesome.

"And the devil of it is," Barnikel confessed after a year had passed, "he's only to stir up trouble at the school and in the close, for his position here to be quite untenable. He must either return with Porteus's blessing, or not at all."

He thought the triumph of Trafalgar, which the town celebrated joyfully, might provoke a change of mood. But the gloom of Ulm and Austerlitz and the death of Pitt made the canon sourer still and the mood of the town more conservative than ever.

By the end of summer 1806, Ralph was reaching another conclusion. He wrote to Agnes.

Since it seems the vindictiveness of Canon Porteus has closed Sarum to me, I have asked Lord Forest if he will help me find a post elsewhere, if possible in London, where there are many schools and where I may be reunited with my wife. He has engaged, if I will tutor the two boys until next summer, to find me a good post with a generous salary by next September.

The letter arrived on the day that Thaddeus Barnikel was to escort Agnes to an open air entertainment.

The sport of single-stick combat was similar to fencing except that the weapons in question were sticks rather than pointed swords, so that the worst injury a man was likely to get was a bruise or two. Unlike the great bare-fisted prize fights that took place occasionally on the downs, single-stick combat was, in Barnikel's opinion, fit for a woman to see. The purse was handsome and they saw some excellent contests. It was afterwards, as they walked through the town, that Agnes told Thaddeus about Ralph's letter, and his plans for her to leave Sarum.

"To London?" He swallowed. For a moment could not speak.

For it was only then that he realised how much a part of his life she had become. "Though we have never even touched," he realised sadly, "it's almost as though we were married."

"I should be sorry if you left," he said at last, and they walked in silence for a little time.

They were outside the door of her house in New Street. There were no people about at that moment. She stopped.

"I fear that in London, my husband would soon cause as much trouble for himself and his family as he has caused in Sarum," she said with a gentle smile. It was the first time in two years that she had said a word to him against Ralph. He looked down. "Besides," she went on steadily, "I have no wish to leave Sarum – or my good friends."

Then, before she left him and went through her door, she reached out and gently touched his arm.

He did not move for some time. By that tiny sign of affection she had told him that, although neither of them could ever mention the subject, she loved him. This moment was the crowning glory of Thaddeus Barnikel's passion. He turned into the close and watched the soft rays of the sunset fall on the cathedral.

Ralph was surprised, a few days later, to receive a letter from Agnes saying that she did not wish to leave Sarum.

The years 1806 and 1807 brought two events that made Ralph Shockley more optimistic.

The first was that, after the tragic death of Pitt, and in an attempt to unite every shade of opinion in the country behind the government, Charles James Fox, his radical hero, was brought into the ministry. He was to die within the year, but before he did, he championed through Parliament that most noble piece of legislation, prepared by Wilberforce and other good men, the Act that prohibited British participation in the slave trade.

"England has turned her back on slavery. Perhaps soon she will stop the terrible traffic in children too," he exclaimed hopefully.

Perhaps with this change of heart in the ministry, there would be a change of spirit in the country and in Sarum too.

There was not. By 1807, Fox had gone and the mood of the country was as belligerent and reactionary as ever.

"It is Bonaparte, by threatening us, who stops all change in England," he concluded.

And still he had not solved the question – "how was he to get back to Sarum?"

In the year of Our Lord 1807, the old Bishop of Salisbury at last died. Canon Porteus was apprehensive.

"When a bishop dies," he confessed to Frances, "one is always afraid there may be change."

In July, the new bishop was enthroned. He was a pleasant-faced, intelligent, active man named John Fisher; he was destined to be one of Sarum's finest bishops, and Mrs. Porteus, Agnes and Doctor Barnikel were all given excellent seats to view the splendid ceremony in the cathedral.

It was in the Porteuses' house afterwards, thinking himself alone, and overcome with love for the woman who sat quietly on the sofa beside him, that Doctor Thaddeus Barnikel commited his indiscretion.

Porteus was in his study; Frances had left the room for a moment. He looked across at her. When she smiled, as she did now, her smile was so gentle, so easy that he could not help thinking "She is really, if the truth be told, mine." And in an access of love, he allowed himself to reach out, take her hand, and kiss it. She did not stop him: how could she, after all his years of devotion? Their backs were to the door; and so they did not see that it had opened and that Frances was silently watching them.

She closed the door again. She did not blame either of them. But suddenly she knew what she must do.

"It is time for Ralph to return," she murmured.

The next day, she went to see the new bishop. She was with him for nearly half an hour, and when she quietly emerged from the bishop's palace, it might have been noticed that she was smiling – or to be exact, she was almost grinning, as she had not done since she was a girl.

That very evening, an extraordinary interview took place in Canon Porteus's study.

There in the door, stood Frances. It seemed to Porteus that she looked different: her face was relaxed, fuller, somehow than he remembered seeing it of late. It reminded him of the rather wayward girl he had married all those years before. He frowned.

"It is time, Canon, that my brother came home."

What was this?

"I prefer, Mrs. Porteus, not to discuss the matter."

"I must insist."

He sighed. He must be reasonable. Taking off his spectacles he explained to her, quietly but with remorseless logic why, at present, such a thing was impossible. The political situation; the reputation of the family; the new bishop.

"You surely would not have me do something so . . . reckless to my reputation at the very moment when a new bishop has been installed. A bishop who," the thought appalled him, "may wish to make changes."

"Yet I must insist."

She was leaning against the doorpost. The posture, he could not help thinking, seemed unladylike. And was there a glint of amusement in her eye?

"I have seen the bishop," she said quietly.

He started violently in his chair.

"You have spoken to him, you mean, Mrs. Porteus."

She nodded.

"Without my permission? Without consulting me?"

"Yes."

He put his spectacles on again and peered at her. Was such a thing possible?

"You need not concern yourself on his account," she went on. "The bishop is quite of my opinion. He thinks Ralph should return."

"But I, Mrs. Porteus," he replied with asperity, "may think otherwise."

"I hope you will reconsider, then. For if you do not, then I shall leave this house and ask my sister-in-law to take me in at New Street."

He could not believe his ears. Yet he could see she was serious.

"But . . . my position."

"Your position, Canon, would only be improved in every way by my brother's return. I will even," she added drily, "say you are forgiving and generous. That might secure us another prebend."

He looked at her cautiously.

"I find your conduct towards me has greatly changed, Mrs. Porteus."

She understood him.

"If you show leniency towards Ralph, Canon, my conduct will always henceforward be as you would wish – as it has been until now," she said.

"I will consider the matter carefully."

"Thank you."

She closed the door quietly as she left. Suddenly she felt very tired. She wondered, idly, if Ralph was worth it.

Another small interview took place in Mr. Porteus's drawing-room a week later. It was between Agnes and Doctor Barnikel. This time it was she who took his hand.

"I am aware, doctor, that you have an attachment to me."

He did not blush. He bowed his head in silent acknowledgement.

"And before my husband returns," she went on gently, "I wish you to know that, had circumstances been otherwise," she gave him an affectionate smile, "had I not been married already, that attachment would have been returned."

"You honour me." His voice was husky.

"Thank you, doctor, for always behaving to me not only with such kindness, but with such propriety."

He was about to speak, when there was a noise at the door.

"Ah." She smiled. "And now here come the children."

1830

It was Agnes who made the bargain, and Ralph who honoured it.

"You may think what you like about reform; but I will not go through such trouble again, nor must your children. You must promise me to be patient."

On his return from exile, Ralph had promised.

"But I never thought," he said ruefully, "that there'd be no reforms in England for twenty years."

The first quarter of the nineteenth century was a strange and unhappy period. Afterwards, men liked to remember it for Wellington's great victories over the French, for the colourful extravagance of the Regency and reign of George IV; for its poets: Wordsworth, Coleridge, Keats, Shelley and strange, saturnine Byron, for its novelists: Jane Austen and Walter Scott. But these were the rays of sunlight in a world that was mainly dark.

Ralph had promised. He returned to his work at the school, and gradually, as the months passed, a stiff but polite relationship between him and his brother-in-law was established. They could even disagree.

And there was much to disagree about.

From the battle of Trafalgar, the defeat of Napoleon had taken a decade. At first it had seemed that, like another Caesar, he would rule all Europe.

"He has made a pact with the Czar of Russia," Barnikel said: "he will rule all Europe and the Czar will rule all the east, including India. Surely now you agree he is a tyrant."

"I agree that England must oppose him," Ralph said. "But it is also true that he brings civil and religious freedoms to the countries he conquers when before some of them knew only despotic kings."

He never allowed himself to say such things to Porteus however.

For years England stood alone: only her navy saved her. Then, slowly the tide began to turn as Arthur Wellesley won the title Wellington by pushing the French out of Portugal and Spain, and Napoleon made the fatal mistake of invading Russia. When he was finally defeated, the people of Sarum wore white cockades in their hats to celebrate the return of the Bourbon kings to France. And when Ralph declined to celebrate the return of the old regime to France, Porteus contented himself with rebuking him mildly.

"You have seen how the Revolution and Napoleon have turned poor Europe upside down," he reminded him. "You know it is true that the Corsican adventurer has caused the death of nearly one and a quarter million men. Can you not see that, even if the old regimes were imperfect" – this was an astonishing admission from Porteus, Ralph had to admit – "yet the legitimate monarchs of Europe at least preserved order in the world?"

"I agree that all Europe believes so," Ralph replied. "And that itself may be enough to preserve peace."

In a way, he knew it was so. For a generation and more, the cause of 'legitimacy' – invented by the subtle brain of France's great statesman

Talleyrand – was something more than a reactionary love of the old monarchic regimes. Legitimacy meant order; it meant that upstart adventurers could not overturn the world; it meant a return to peace and prosperity. In good conscience the monarchs of Europe, glad to be rid of Napoleon who had so humiliated them, and destroyed their people, formed new general alliances to preserve a permanent peace throughout Europe, and the religious-minded Czar even tried to start a Holy Alliance dedicated to Christian principles.

But as the years passed, the legitimist cause of the monarchies led to other, less attractive results: the revival of the Inquisition in Spain; the attempt by the Bourbon rulers to return all the South American trade to the old Spanish monopoly, and a general suppression of all dissidents because they might be revolutionaries. They were dark, repressive times.

At home, not even Porteus could pretend that Britain's own monarchy gave any cause for joy. While Wellington was still struggling to wear down the French in the Iberian peninsula, George III finally went mad and his extravagant son became Regent. The Regency and reign of George IV were marred not only by his wild spending but also by his separation from and quarrels with his wife Queen Caroline. When, at his coronation in front of a large and delighted crowd, she tried to force her way into Westminster Abbey but was turned away at the door, even Porteus acknowledged to Ralph:

"It is hardly surprising that the republicans are encouraged when our monarchy allows such scenes to take place."

"I'm not sure George IV isn't a little mad like his father," Barnikel confided. "His fantasies and vanities grow even stranger than the palace he's built at Brighton. You know that although he never set foot over the Channel, he has so persuaded himself he fought Bonaparte that he even told Wellington – Wellington if you please – that he led a charge at Waterloo!"

It was in the second decade of the century that a sad rift took place in the Shockley family.

"The truth is that Napoleon broke our friendship with our cousins," Ralph said generously. He could have blamed Porteus.

For during the long years of Britain's isolation, Napoleon tried to bring her to her knees by enforcing a trade blockade. Thanks to her navy, the island could block Napoleon's trade in turn; and for years the extraordinary system continued whereby both sides tried to block trade with third parties while, unofficially, enough English cloth was still getting through to the continent to clothe Napoleon's armies, whom they were fighting.

The British Navy stopped and searched all merchant shipping, including American vessels.

"They don't admit it, but they want a crack at Canada," Mason observed, "and they'll complain about our search ships just to pick a quarrel."

Whether this was fair or not, it was an added irony that the inconclusive war, in which the United States unsuccessfully attacked Canada and

British ships fired upon Washington, actually began after an agreement between the disputing parties had been reached but before news of it had crossed the Atlantic.

With the start of hostilities came a furious letter from their cousins, demanding to know what England meant by its action.

"I do not think," Canon Porteus observed, "that we should reply." And so the correspondence between Frances Shockley and her cousins ceased.

"It's up to me to write to them now," Ralph told Agnes.

But here laziness intervened. He meant to write. He almost did, a dozen times. But the months passed. Then years. The little war drifted to its close. He still meant to write.

In 1823, when England was so anxious to keep the Bourbon powers from taking over the South America trade, a friendly atmosphere was made between Great Britain and the United States which resulted in the famous doctrine of President Monroe that the United States would tolerate no European rule in its southern sphere of influence.

"Monroe's our best ally," Ralph declared; to celebrate the fact he took pen to paper and wrote to his cousins.

He received no reply.

But far more than the situation abroad, however threatening, it was the tragedy at home in England that filled Ralph's thoughts.

For it was the poor in England who suffered most terribly in those dark years, and nowhere in the countryside was the situation worse than at Sarum.

"I promised not to quarrel with Porteus," Ralph said to Agnes. "But the truth is that even if I wanted to, I don't know what can be done."

The problem was a long-standing one. Nor was it much helped by the Poor Laws or the system of relief known as Speenhamland. This last, begun by the justices of Speenhamland in Berkshire, was a system of supplementing the wages of the poorest workers from parish funds, with the result that often the farmers simply paid them even less – a simple case of good intentions and bad economics

And even in 1815, when Napoleon was exiled to St Helena, there had been little for the poor at Sarum to rejoice about; for the peace brought with it the worst agricultural conditions in generations. The war had left the government hugely in debt. For years it had also refused to honour its notes with gold, and printed more paper money. There was rampant inflation; bread prices rose sharply while wages did not. A labourer whose wages after the American War of Independence had bought fourteen loaves, could now buy only nine; yet the new income taxes rose, and the poor had to pay.

"The government has borrowed money from the rich: now the poor must pay taxes so that they receive their interest," Ralph pointed out. In fact, between a third and a half of the government's revenue went in interest.

Now, however, at the end of the war, the combination of returning soldiers and the ending of huge government war contracts produced both unemployment and a general depression. Corn prices fell. But still this didn't help the poor. For the landowners in Parliament brought in the Corn Law. Its provisions were simple: at a time when continental Europe had massive surpluses to sell, no one in England might import corn until it had reached the price of eighty shillings a quarter. The landowners would be protected.

"It's infamous," Ralph protested. "It actually ensures that the poor will starve."

"It's worse than that," Mason explained to him. "It's stupid as well. The landowners and farmers themselves can't sell grain at that price, so they're no better off either. Everyone loses. The only people profiting are the corn merchants: they're stockpiling corn to drive the price up quickly, buying cheap imports as soon as they're allowed to, then reselling for high profit."

"Then why do the Tory landowners continue to support the Corn Law?"

"Simple," the merchant told him. "Prejudice and stupidity. They want to control everything, just as they did during the war. They won't listen to merchants like us, who could explain the benefits of free trade."

Many times on his visits to Mason and his family, Shockley had been treated to lectures on the subject of free markets and the reduction of tariff barriers, for Mason was a believer in the doctrines of Adam Smith.

"He wrote his book when America declared independence," he complained, "yet our ministers still have not understood his message."

Ralph was not so sure. He felt uncomfortable with Adam Smith's doctrines which seemed to him to describe too harsh and cruel a world, however free.

"But the Corn Law," he agreed heartily, "ought to go."

It stayed. The agricultural poor were starving. Craftsmen, especially weavers, were being thrown out of work by the new machines. A terrible and cruel peace seemed to be taking over from the long years of war. And reactionary ministers, in reality as confused by the dawning industrial age as the unhappy people, clamped down on all reform. When the unemployed rioted, when the so-called Luddites tried to break up the machines they thought were destroying their livelihood, they were crushed.

True, as the 1820s wore on, there were hints of reform. A rising figure in Parliament, Robert Peel, though certainly a Tory, began a modest reform which included founding the first London police force and removing some hundred offences from the list that carried the death penalty. Trade improved too, and some of the duties that Mason hated were removed.

But in Sarum, it seemed to Ralph Shockley, nothing ever changed.

Of all the many voices in England demanding reform at this time – voices, Ralph knew, far more powerful than his – none was more powerful than that of the great journalist and describer of poverty, William Cobbett. His weekly, *The Political Register*, was Ralph's bible, and though he never allowed Porteus to know it, he would buy up extra copies of it and surreptitiously leave them sometimes where he knew some of the poorer farm workers or labourers might find them. It was an easy way for the schoolmaster in his fifties to make himself believe he was agitating for change. But sometimes his outrage at the poverty he saw overcame him and once, to Porteus himself in his own house, he cried:

"Why, Canon, beasts of burden are better treated than our farm labourers."

To which, for once, Porteus made no reply – Ralph was never sure whether he was silent from contempt or from shame.

In all these years, it was the memory of a single day and of two encounters which always remained in his mind.

It was an overcast morning in late spring and he went walking on the high ground. There were sheep everywhere: not the old long-horned sheep – they had all gone now – but the new, more economical breed from the south downs. Hornless, except for the rams, with their true fleeces – three of them could feed, it was said, where only two of the ancient stock could have fed before. Wherever there were no sheep, there were fields of recently sown corn.

He liked the sweeping, desolate landscape: he had walked for an hour without seeing a single human being.

Then he saw the boy.

He was, at first, hardly more than a speck, a tiny figure standing all alone in the middle of a huge, furrowed field.

Ralph came slowly towards him. The boy stayed where he was. Ralph noticed the birds sweeping over the surface of the furrows cautiously, wheeling and dipping around its edges.

Only when he came to the edge of the field and stopped there did the boy move towards him. He was a handsome young fellow with a mass of unruly brown hair and a long, thin, slightly hooked nose. He could not have been more than ten; his jaunty bearing reminded Ralph of his own son at that age, although as he drew close, he saw the young fellow was pitifully thin.

"All alone?" he enquired pleasantly.

The boy nodded. "You're the first person I seen all day, sir."

"What are you doing here?"

The boy waved his arm at the huge field.

"Frightening birds off."

"What time did you come here?"

"Dawn, just after."

"When do you go home?"

"Dusk, just afore."

"Have you eaten today?"

"No, sir."

"And who sent you here?"

"My father, sir."

"What does he do?"

"Works on farm."

"His farm?"

"No. Mr. Jones."

"Where's that?"

"Avonsford."

Ralph nodded. Obviously this was an outlying field.

"So," he said with a smile, "you're a human scarecrow?"

" 'Sright."

"What's your name, scarecrow?"

"Godfrey, sir. Daniel Godfrey."

"Daniel Godfrey: human scarecrow."

It was a common enough sight. He wondered how many days that spring Daniel Godfrey would stand alone in a field all day, waving his arms at the circling birds.

Thoughtfully he made his way back, passing the deserted hill fort of Old Sarum before strolling down into the valley. It was below Old Sarum near the old tree where the three remaining electors met to vote their members to Parliament that he saw the second lonely figure.

But this time he knew exactly who he had to deal with: and he went boldly towards him.

There were many things that Ralph Shockley came to like about Bishop Fisher during Fisher's eighteen-year reign at Sarum. One was the care he took of his diocese. It was Fisher who revived the old office of the rural deans to supervise and help the outlying parish clergymen, who could otherwise be sadly cut off. It was also a mark of Fisher's wisdom, Ralph thought, that he had never offered Porteus any further office. Yet another point in the bishop's favour was that he was one of a kindly and distinguished family. It was his own nephew John Fisher, who was archdeacon of Berkshire and who occupied the fine old Leadenhall in the close while his uncle lived at the bishop's palace.

And it was Archdeacon Fisher's close friend who stood before him now, a sketch pad in his hand, his eyes intent upon the deserted hill fort above them.

John Constable made many visits to Sarum; he stayed at Leadenhall many times; he corresponded with Fisher for nearly twenty years. He painted scenes of the cathedral with its stately spire from Old Sarum and from Harnham which were to become world famous. But it was on this single day that he met his most outspoken private critic.

For, with the thought of poor Daniel Godfrey fresh in his mind, Ralph Shockley now went straight over to where the great man was standing and, presuming on their slight acquaintance, interrupted his work.

The scene that Constable had just lightly sketched was a view of the old fort, surrounded by sweeping slopes of grazing sheep.

Glancing at it, Ralph came straight to the point.

"It won't do, Mr. Constable. I complain of your scenes, because they are too pastoral – you make our Sarum too beautiful, our countryside too kind."

And then he told him of the poor human scarecrow he had just seen, and reminded him about the pitiful condition of the agricultural labourers around Sarum.

"Why do your pictures not show these, too?" he demanded. Constable said nothing.

But Ralph, suddenly flushed as he used to be when he was young, had not done yet: pointing up to Old Sarum he cried:

"There, you know, lies the most rotten borough in all England – a deserted ruin that returns two members. Do you paint that iniquity, too, as a cheerful scene?" And he reminded him of the need for reform.

It was only after he had gone on in this vein for some time that Constable turned his kindly eyes upon him and Ralph noticed for the first time that the painter's face was tired and strained.

"These things concern me too, Mr. Shockley," he answered patiently, "though I am only a painter."

"But notice," Ralph would declare proudly in later years, "how over Constable's late works depicting Sarum, there is a dark and brooding air. I think perhaps I put that there," he would tell his children.

He had had no more encounters that day, but returned to the quiet of the close.

"The peace of the place!" he would say, in recalling that day. He had wandered into the cathedral. "And there I saw another wonder." For the great west window had recently been restored, using ancient stained glass salvaged from many places: it gleamed softly in the afternoon light, and remembering how indefatigable Canon Porteus had been in promoting the cause of this lovely addition to the cathedral he chuckled:

"There's something, at least, that he and I can agree about."

"And there, I thought, I saw the whole of Sarum, as it has been in my lifetime," he explained, "the good and the bad: the beauty of our cathedral, and the misery of our countryside. That's why I have always remembered that day."

In the year 1830 a terrible event took place at Sarum.

The people of the city were appalled, but it did not surprise Ralph Shockley in the least.

For in November 1830, the countryside rose.

There was nothing new in a riot. Luddites had often rioted and broken machinery in the north. There had been small riots in Sarum from time to time, when the cloth workers tried to increase their wages or fight new machines.

"They break a few heads, but they make their views known," Mason used to remark to Ralph.

But this was something different.

There had been two terrible harvests. At the same time, farmers too, like the clothiers, had been introducing new machines. The riot was not a single rising: there were dozens of small mobs, Ralph heard, burning ricks and attacking machinery all over Hampshire and Wiltshire.

"It's the start of a revolution," Canon Porteus prophesied grimly.

"It's the start of agricultural reform, more like," Ralph corrected.

It was neither.

The riot at Salisbury was one of the most serious.

On November 23, 1830, a large mob moved across the ridge on the north-east side of the city known as Bishopsdown. They found a threshing machine and broke it up.

"There are thousands of them, and they're armed," a young clergyman assured him as he hurried down the High Street towards the cathedral close. "The Yeomanry is out already. They've come to kill us."

Ralph did not believe him and, telling his son to take Agnes to the Porteuses' house, he set out across the town. Soon he crossed the market place, turned east past the Black Horse and Swayne's chequers, and came out on the patch of open ground on the eastern edge of the town known as Green Croft. Then he could see them, on the slopes above.

They were an impressive group – not thousands but several hundred and they carried bludgeons, iron bars and odds and ends of the machinery they had broken up. They were angry and desperate. He watched calmly as they swept down towards the town.

Standing by the corner he found a young weaver with whom he had shared Cobbetts Register many times.

"The people in the close think they've come to kill them."

The weaver shook his head.

"It's Fige's Iron Foundry they're after," he said. "Machines, not people."

"It's what I thought."

Now there was a cheer as that notable Salisbury gentleman, Mr. Wadham Wyndham, rode boldly out towards them at the head of a small force of special constables. The constables looked apprehensive. Wyndham did not.

Then he noticed something else. Waiting a little behind them was a large detachment of Yeomanry.

The procedure was simple, and Wyndham followed it correctly. First he addressed them and urged them to disperse. They came on. Then he ordered the Riot Act to be read. Still they did not move. They were almost all at Green Croft now.

There was no alternative. Wyndham ordered the Yeomanry to charge.

The battle did not last long. The Yeomanry were trained and armed; the labourers were not. In minutes they had been driven back to St Edmund's churchyard and beyond. Some got away; some did not. Ralph watched the débâcle sadly.

"They captured twenty-two of them," he told his family that evening. "Canon Porteus can sleep safe in his bed."

It was a similar story in other places.

On December 27, 1830, a special Assize was opened before Lord Vaughan and Justices Alderson and Parke. Three hundred and thirty-two prisoners involved in the riots were tried. Ralph Shockley attended. It was a terrible business that left him profoundly depressed. Some of the prisoners were little more than children. Most, he guessed, had been swept into the riots for little more reason than that the rioters were passing and they had nothing better to hope for. The sentences were much as he expected.

For during Ralph Shockley's lifetime, one of the most convenient discoveries ever to aid the administration of British justice was made: the continent of Australia was found.

"By placing men down there," Canon Porteus reminded him, "they are as safely isolated from humanity as Napoleon on the island of St Helena. Escape is impossible. And that being so," he added generously, "it is hardly necessary, I understand, to incarcerate them in cells."

Twenty-eight of the prisoners were transported for life; one hundred and eighty-three were either sent to prison or transported for lesser terms.

It was while Ralph Shockley watched one group of prisoners being led out that he thought he recognised a face. He frowned. Then he remembered: it was the boy, Daniel Godfrey, the human scarecrow. He was a youth now. He had just been sentenced to transportation.

And so, although neither of them had the least idea of it, a descendant of Saxon Shockleys saw the last in the male line of the noble Norman family of Godefroi leave Sarum to which they had come seven centuries before.

But now at last, it seemed to Ralph Shockley that a new age had begun.

For in 1830, not only had a new monarch, William IV the sailor king ascended the throne, but more important, having been forced by the great Irishman Daniel O'Connel at last to grant votes and full liberties to all British Catholics, the last of the reactionary prime ministers, the Duke of Wellington, fell from office and, after twenty years in the political wasteland, the reforming Whigs came in again.

"Lord Grey is prime minister," Ralph cried, "and his programme is reform."

The Great Reform Bill of 1831 was the greatest step towards democracy in England since Simon de Montfort's parliament nearly six hundred years before. It was not intended to be, any more than Montfort's was. The Whig aristocrats who fashioned it had no intention of encouraging so dangerous a notion as votes for the people. It was intended only to remove the pocket or rotten boroughs, to give representation to new communities who had none, and to allow the vote – though not a secret ballot – to substantial freeholders in the boroughs. True, the preposterous idea of allowing the vote to all householders, regardless of the value of their property, was suggested in the course of the debates. It was even voted upon. It received one vote.

"But," as Porteus truly said, "if you allow the middle classes so many votes, then the lower classes will want them next. It must be opposed, sir, tooth and nail."

It was. For a year the Bill was sent back and forth between Commons and Lords. The Government resigned and called a snap election which it resoundingly won.

"The Bill, the Bill and nothing but the Bill," was the cry. And each time he walked out of the town, Ralph Shockley would look up at the old hillfort of Old Sarum, where under an elm tree the preposterous charade of holding an election had been carried on by a handful of bought electors for so long and cry: "Old Sarum, you'll soon be gone."

"And after that," he told his wife happily, "there'll be reforms of the factories, child labour, and even education. Thank God I've lived to see these better times."

It was Agnes who first noticed the change in Canon Porteus.

At first she thought nothing of it. They were all getting old, she supposed. Even Ralph, though he still sometimes had the enthusiasm of a boy when an idea like the Reform Bill excited him, was past sixty. Frances, as the years had passed had grown more and more staid and withdrawn, and her one rebellion against her husband had not only never been repeated but, Agnes suspected, had even been forgotten. If, during the passage of the Reform Bill which signalled an attack upon everything he stood for, the canon seemed unusually silent, she supposed it was only natural.

"You have won your cause, and he is old," she said to Ralph. "Do not agitate him by referring to it now."

For the best part of a year, Ralph hardly saw Canon Porteus.

"Ever since the election," he joked, "poor old Porteus has hardly left his house."

On June 26, 1832, the bells of Salisbury rang and every light in the city was lit to celebrate the passing into law of the Great Reform Act.

Ralph Shockley led his family in triumph the very next morning to stand upon the earth walls of Old Sarum.

"Just a pleasant old ruin again," he said contentedly. "No longer an infamy."

At first, no one thought anything of it.

It was some time since he had been seen about, but if he had decided to pause to look at something, few had the courage to interrupt the stiff old canon in his reverie. Perhaps it was unusual that he was not wearing his usual black, broad-brimmed hat. No doubt he was about to go inside again.

He was standing by the corner house on the east of the choristers' green and opposite the entrance to the close. He seemed to be looking at something at the far end of the green, a little to the left of Mompesson House.

Several passers by, bowing politely to the venerable figure and receiving no acknowledgement, tried to follow his gaze to see what it was that had so engaged his attention. But feeling it impolite to linger there without his invitation, they soon passed on and went about their business. Once a cart from the town had to make a detour to get round him and the driver silently cursed the arrogance of the clergy and the gentry who did not deign to move for him.

He was standing there when Ralph Shockley and his family left the house in New Street to walk to Old Sarum. He had not moved when they got back.

Around the middle of the day some urchins came by. They had less reverence for the motionless old figure in his antiquated black silk stockings who stood there like a petrified tree. They began to play a game around him.

And it was one of these children, early in the afternoon, who noticed something strange: something which, when he pointed it out, caused them all to go into peals of laughter.

For at the motionless canon's feet there had now appeared a little puddle.

It was Doctor Barnikel who, mercifully, came by just afterwards, who understood what had happened, and who led poor Porteus home.

"I fear," he told Agnes that evening, "his mind may not recover."

The canon did not speak again.

It was, there was no doubt of it, a blessing that, on October 1 – the very day when Porteus had been brought to the old Manor House at Fisherton Anger where Mr. William Finch ran his commodious and comfortable private asylum for the insane – the canon should have had a second seizure, this time a stroke, and died.

"I am only sad," Frances confessed, "that he should have lived to see the reforms."

But the duty of Frances to her late husband was not over. She set out to protect his memory too.

She could not deny that his mind had been affected at the end – too many people knew. But in the year after his death, a minor change took place in Salisbury that gave her her opportunity: gas lights were introduced into the streets.

It was with amazement therefore that, in August 1834, Ralph Shockley heard his own sister say, with perfect seriousness:

"My poor husband, you know, was entirely well until the gas was introduced."

"But he died before that," he protested.

Frances ignored him completely.

"That gas is dangerous," she maintained. "It turned my poor husband's mind and killed him. It ought to be removed."

"Let her think it," Agnes begged him when he told her.

"The gas never hurt anyone," he grumbled, irritated at his elder sister's folly.

But, just to prove him wrong, Frances fainted by one of the lamps, the very next week, just as it was being lit.

"It's the noxious fumes," she said afterwards. "They made me faint. And when I think what they did to my poor husband . . ."

From this time on, she fainted by the gas lamps several times a year.

In 1834 Doctor Thaddeus Barnikel, beloved by all but always unmarried, suddenly died. In his will, he left the bulk of his estate to Agnes Shockley.

Ralph was not surprised.

"I always knew he loved you," he said pleasantly, "even before I had to go away."

"He was a kind friend," Agnes answered.

"That's why I asked him to look after you," Ralph added. "Just to make sure he never . . ."

Agnes looked at him in surprise.

"Wasn't that taking a risk?"

"Oh no. Not with him," he replied cheerfully. "Or you, of course," he added, just a moment too late.

Empire

1854: October

THE AFTERNOON SUN gleamed on the railway lines.

As she stood on the platform at Milford station, and looked back eastwards towards Southampton, the shining metal tracks seemed to promise a distant, brighter destiny, a larger world.

It would be hers, very soon.

Jane Shockley was going to leave Sarum. She was going to serve. She wanted it so passionately.

She was of medium height, her hair a very light auburn brown with, sometimes, a flash of red. Her blue eyes looked out with a directness that could be disconcerting. Her face was not beautiful. "My nose," she used to lament with a laugh, "is too big." But she was considered, by those at her school who knew about such things, very passable.

She picked up her small valise. The whalebone stays pinched her. "I wish our stomachs," she often complained, "were not supposed to be quite so unnaturally small." Where was the porter?

A thought suddenly struck her. Service or passion. Which had she really been seeking? She smiled at herself. Both, probably.

She moved along the train towards the engine, hissing by the station house.

She was back at Sarum – but not for long.

True, they had rejected her at the interview. She did not blame them. But they had also told her what she must do, and nothing was going to stop her now.

She looked up at the familiar scene – there they were, her childhood friends, the huge, bare chalk ridges in their great horseshoe, staring down at the city they enclosed. In the north, the mound of Old Sarum, and there, in the centre, was the spire, scraping the silent blue sky above. Sarum. She loved the place. It was and always would be part of her.

But yesterday she had seen Florence Nightingale.

Like everything to do with the remarkable expedition of Florence Nightingale, it had all happened so fast.

It was only ten days since the article by Russell in the *Times* – one of the most dramatically influential that august journal ever printed – had startled all England like a thunderclap. Wounded British soldiers, who had gone out to fight England's just and necessary war to halt the advance of the despotic Tsar Nicholas on the Crimea, were being treated worse than animals in the disgraceful hospital conditions in Scutari.

It was a challenge to the empire. Why, even her allies the French were sending out fifty Sisters of Mercy. In such circumstances, could England do less?

Jane Shockley had seen the letter in the *Times* appealing for nurses a few days later. She had hesitated. Was she worthy? Then in Wilton, by chance, she had met Mrs. Sidney Herbert.

"Go and see them at least." It was all the encouragement she needed.

The role played by the Herbert family in the expedition of Florence Nightingale was decisive. By God-given good fortune, it was a younger son of the old Lord Pembroke, Sidney Herbert, who with his wife chanced to be friends of the redoubtable Miss Nightingale with her little hospital for gentlewomen in Harley Street. He also happened to be a junior minister conducting the war.

He had acted completely on his own initiative – invited Miss Nightingale to go, though female nurses had never been used on campaign before, found funds, and provided the Herbert house in Belgrave Square as headquarters of the enterprise.

The Herberts and Florence Nightingale moved quickly. The interviews for nurses at Belgrave Square started three days after the *Times* article.

They had not taken long with Jane. She was interviewed by Miss Stanley and Mrs. Bracebridge; they were friendly but frank with her.

"Your qualifications from the Salisbury Training College are admirable for a teacher, and we see you are sincere, but you are not trained as a nurse."

"I hoped – I thought perhaps – you might have room for a few volunteers willing to learn," she suggested. And then with inspiration: "Are not trained nurses hard to find?"

The two women smiled ruefully.

"Yes. But we shall find them."

Jane sighed.

"Those that come must be very dedicated," she remarked.

And it had been then that the unexpected voice behind her had cut through the room like a knife.

"Not at all."

She had not heard her come in. There could be no doubt who she was. She walked to the table.

"They are coming for money." A strong, pleasant face, piercing eyes, a mouth that twitched with amusement. "You look shocked," she laughed. "None of them," she went on, "save perhaps one has dedication, a sense of mission," she sniffed, "yet." She gazed at Jane. "But they're trained. I have Roman Catholics, Anglicans, Tractarians, and others who may be anything. But they are trained. Are you serious in wanting to nurse?"

"Yes." She thought she was.

"Get training in a hospital. Then I can use you."

"How shall I apply?"

"Why, use the penny post girl! What a question."

She blushed.

"I shall."

"A great empire needs many dedicated servants," the great woman smiled. "Good luck."

Empire and service.

A British empire that stretched all round the globe; a British empire that, directed by strong men like Palmerston, would swiftly humble any who failed to show respect to her citizens; an empire where Englishmen grew rich, thanks to free trade and Mr. Gladstone's low taxes. Empire and free trade: this was the combination that most English towns, even sleepy Salisbury, favoured.

Service and empire: serving the mighty East India Company, and living well besides; serving as officers, administrators, missionaries: these were things the Shockleys of Sarum did. Nothing thrilled her more than to receive the letters from her brother Bernard on his plantation in India, or her Uncle Stephen the missionary, from Africa – messages from the empire, that wide and exciting world.

Her upbringing in Salisbury close had been conventional. Though her father, Ralph's elder son had died of consumption when she was only nine, old Frances Porteus had conveniently died the same year and left them the tenancy of her house in the close and a modest fortune besides.

"There's nothing to stop you marrying well," her mother always told her. And certainly Sarum was not short of pleasant society – Wyndhams, Jacobs, Husseys, Eyres – good county or near county families with educated menfolk into which a well brought up girl with a little money should be pleased to marry.

"Why must you always want something more?"

"I don't know, mama."

She had insisted on going to the training college. That was well enough. The regime was strict. Young gentlewomen were given a training that enabled them to teach, if the family circumstances were so poor that they had to work, or to manage their households with great efficiency if all went well and they married.

She had insisted upon teaching. There were twenty-five private day schools in Salisbury now. Her mother had shaken her head. The girl was getting eccentric.

And then, six months ago, her mother died.

She was twenty-three. She had a pleasant house in the close, five hundred pounds a year, a cook, a housemaid, two horses stabled in the town, pleasant neighbours, and had turned down two perfectly acceptable offers of marriage. She enjoyed her work. She should now, of course, find a companion since it was not proper for an unmarried woman to live alone. But she hesitated.

Why was it she read those letters so avidly from overseas? Why was it she scanned the newspapers for news when other young ladies quietly did their needlepoint? Why must she, as her mother used to complain, always have opinions?

"Men have opinions. Women listen."

"I suppose," she said to her mother, a month before she died, "I am looking for a cause."

"There are any number of them, my dear." There was the College of Matrons by the close gate, Eyre's almshouses, Hussey's almshouses,

Blechynden's almshouses for poor widows – the list of charities and needy folk in Salisbury, to which Mrs. Shockley never failed, like every other Sarum lady, to devote herself was endless.

"No. Something more."

"In Sarum, Jane? What could there possibly be? And why?"

There had been no answer.

After her mother's death she had thought of going to visit her brother. Or even her missionary uncle. "Madness," she had been told of the latter idea.

Now Florence Nightingale.

Beside her bed, as always, two books: Wordsworth's poems and the love sonnets of Elizabeth Barrett Browning.

> How do I love thee? Let me count the ways.
> I love thee to the depth and breadth and height
> My soul can reach . . .

She knew them all by heart. She loved the moving story of how the poet Browning had rescued Elizabeth from her father and eloped with her.

"But no Browning comes to elope with me from the close," she laughed sadly to herself.

It was morning. Outside, the sun was already well up. The leaves were falling from the trees around the choristers' green. Below, she could hear Lizzie the housemaid scurrying about.

Sarum. Life was slow. But it was pleasant.

But today was a day for decisions. She knew they must be made now, while the spirit of adventure was still strong. Was she to go to London to train? If so, how soon? Difficult decisions, uncomfortable ones. She lingered lazily for a moment in bed before beginning such a fateful day.

There was a knock on the door: Lizzie with a letter, from Bernard.

Before the girl had even closed the door, she had slit it open.

My dear Sister,

With the loss of dear Mama you are entirely alone at Sarum and this perturbs me. Harriet joins me in suggesting most warmly that you come out to spend at least half a year here. Your two nieces and nephews long to see their aunt – we have made you out to be a dragon so don't disappoint us on any account. You will find amusement here and some society, a change of air, I need hardly say. There are some young fellows here too, quite gentlemen, who perhaps . . . but I run on.

This war in the Crimea is already having a remarkable effect upon our fortunes – for the better! Here in Hoogly District, as you may know, we have a large crop of desi – jute as it's called in England. We do an excellent trade with America already, even with a firm called Bradley and Shockley – isn't that a coincidence? But more important, this war in the Crimea has cut off the supply of Russian raw flax and hemp to

Dundee, and we are quite supplanting them with our jute instead. The profits are remarkable. However, I shall tell you more when you come here, and you can see for yourself.

There was much more, but she broke off. Dear Bernard. Ten years her senior. Ten years in India now; he always wrote her letters full of his practical business, just as though she were a man, which was why she so loved to receive them. She would keep the rest until later.

She dressed quickly. Then she made straight for the cathedral.

Whenever she had to make a major decision, Jane Shockley always walked in the cloisters. They were so quiet, so peaceful. In the first year of Queen Victoria's reign, Bishop Denison had planted two cedars of Lebanon in the centre and already they were beginning to spread a small shade over the grass of the little graveyard there, making the place more delightful even than it had been before. She walked by the chapter house. Both cloisters and chapter house were being repaired that year by Mr. Clutton the architect. Just recently the restoration of the wonderful series of low reliefs in the chapter house had been begun and, since the door was open, she walked in and spent several minutes admiring the lively carvings of the Creation and the other Old Testament scenes. She liked the silent antiquity of the place. During repairs to the walls recently, the workmen had found some coins from the time of Edward I, nearly six hundred years before.

It was hard to decide. Now that the prospect of travel to the Crimea had gone, to be replaced by several years' grinding hard work at a hospital, probably in London – was she still certain she wanted to be a nurse? Why not go out to India: that was a more exciting prospect. Or even stay here in Sarum, here with her friends, amongst these quiet scenes that she loved? It was tempting.

For once, she could not make up her mind. Annoyed with herself, she walked slowly out of the cloister and into the main body of the cathedral.

And there she saw it.

It was only a tattered object, on a stick: a single flag, hanging out at an angle just out of reach on the wall. They were the colours of the Wiltshire Regiment, and the little plaque beside them stated that they had been carried in Sicily in 1806–14, the United States of America, 1814–15, been lost by the Ganges 1842 and recovered eight months later. Placed in the cathedral April 1848.

Why should that flag suddenly move her? Was it the far off places, the thought of the soldiers there and in the Crimea? Was it the reminder of empire and service? Might it be guilt at her own easy life? Perhaps.

Slowly she walked towards the door. A disused flag and a twenty-three-year-old girl. A strange combination.

"But trailing clouds of glory do we come."

The line from her favourite Wordsworth poem, the *Immortality Ode*, suddenly came to haunt her. Clouds of glory. That was it. The tattered flag hanging so modestly there seemed, that morning, to bring her a fresh vision. A vision of service, and sacrifice, a vision of distant places and of her own heroism. She knew what she must do. It was time to write those letters to the hospitals.

Joseph Porters stood, erect but with his head slightly bowed, and stared at the drains.

"Progress, sir, and empire. That is our destiny. Make no mistake."

Porters nodded absently as Ebenezer Mickelthwaite, agent to Lord Forest, expressed these trenchant views.

"And these drains, these houses?" he interposed quietly.

"Safe. Safe as the Bank of England."

"I think not. They are pestilential. We shall have cholera here again."

Mickelthwaite eyed him. The lengthy disquisition he had just made on the empire was for the purpose of making Porters change the subject and it had not worked.

"The expense of your improvements would be very great."

Porters shrugged.

"It mainly falls on the council rates."

"Not all. Anyway, we pay rates."

They were standing in the middle of the chequer, looking up the centre strip into which the assorted refuse from some forty courtyards and tiny allotments seeped to form a black, muddy morass that was something between a drain and a swamp. It produced a dank, alkaline stench – a persistent presence in winter, in summer a vicious enemy that rose to strike.

"The water is utterly foul."

"Yet I heard that when they sunk a new well hereabouts, they discovered a mineral spring."

"So it was thought, from the colour and pungency of the water, which people were drinking. In fact, Mr. Mickelthwaite, they had penetrated a cess pit."

The situation in the city had become a scandal. The centres of the old chequers, where often no new drainage had been constructed in centuries, were disease-ridden. The water channels down the streets, though they seemed at high water to be clean, were in fact polluted and constantly drawing in more poison from the area around.

"They call this city the English Venice," Mickelthwaite said defensively.

"I call it an open sewer." He was getting impatient. "In any case, Mr. Mickelthwaite, you have lost your battle, all of you, and I am recommending the complete drainage of this chequer, new sewers, drains for every house. It will all be dug up. And those workshops," he pointed with disgust to a collection of buildings that resembled two lines of wooden hovels stacked one on top of the other – "those will have to go."

"We get rent from them," Mickelthwaite growled.

"Not any more. You'll have to build again."

He started to go. Behind him he heard the agent mutter: "That damn doctor." He smiled, and turned. "This is progress, Mr. Mickelthwaite," he said softly.

[828]

The battle had been a fierce one. For many years, the water channels had been under the control of the city's directors of highways, who had done little to improve them; as for the insides of the chequers, they were under the control of individual landlords who had usually done nothing at all.

In 1849, cholera struck Salisbury. There were some fifteen hundred cases, deaths in hundreds. A certain Doctor Middleton, visiting the city and seeing its sanitation was appalled. He protested. Reluctantly the council commissioned a survey of the water sources. Deep drainage was recommended. But that would be expensive. The council clerk did not record the medical evidence and threw Middleton's letter away. And so Doctor Middleton began his campaign.

There was one problem for the council: the Public Health Act of 1848 – another of the many acts that passed through the nineteenth century parliaments and began England's modern education, sanitation and factory conditions. The council could be forced to appoint a board of health.

"And then," Mickelthwaite had explained gloomily to Lord Forest, "the whole matter will leave the highway directors' control – the health board will oversee not only the water channels but the chequers as well. And worse, if they recommend improvements, they can be levied on the general rates."

"Which I pay."

"Exactly."

For Lord Forest, who had long since given up his grandfather's house in the close, whose interests were all in the industrial north now, or in his Indian plantations, and who only twice visited Sarum in his life, still owned half of one of the city chequers.

"Do what you can," he told the agent.

The battle had raged two years. A group of councillors who owned quantities of slums, and with whom Mickelthwaite had discreetly allied himself, fought tooth and nail. They lost.

It had been early the previous year that Joseph Porters, civil engineer, had obtained a post in Salisbury and travelled down from Leicester to inspect the place.

He set to work cheerfully, filling in the old water channels and inspecting the chequers. He had been as appalled as Doctor Middleton by what he had seen.

But he enjoyed the sleepy close, with its comfortable gentry and ecclesiastics in tall black hats, the busy market town with its sudden influxes of livestock, the sheep fair at nearby Wilton, the racecourse up on the high ground.

"There are years of work here," he declared, with some satisfaction; and he looked for comfortable lodgings.

Joseph Porters was thirty-seven. He wore, always, a buttoned frock coat, grey waistcoat, white shirt, tie in a small, neat bow, side-whiskers clipped rather short, and black top hat. His hair was sandy and thinning. He was not quite without humour, but did not feel sufficiently confident of himself to take any chances with his appearance. He had worn a moustache when young, but had abandoned it later because it did not seem to go with his half-moon spectacles.

Since his arrival in Salisbury, two things had fascinated Joseph Porters. The first was in the drains. For as these were cleared, they revealed a fantastic quantity of articles, the refuse and careless droppings of six centuries – combs, shears, clay pipes, coins – a treasure trove for the antiquarian. Though he had no training in this field, he began to study them, and it was soon a regular occurrence for the workmen to stand back respectfully while Mr. Porters so far forgot his dignity, and the whiteness of his shirt, as to poke about in the mud for half an hour at a time before hurrying back to his lodgings in Castle Street to store his new found treasure and change his shirt.

"In time," he told the dean, "we shall need a small museum for all this, you know."

The second – it had taken Porters some time to dare to admit to himself the second thing that had fascinated him – was Miss Jane Shockley.

The little library in the Shockley house was upon the main upstairs floor. It was a modest, pleasant room, and less full of the Victorian clutter that had now appeared in the drawing-room where heavy draperies on the tables, two potted palms, an ornate clock, a bowl of wax flowers and four china figures had already forced their way in.

The library only contained, besides its floor to ceiling bookshelves, two leather armchairs, an uncovered walnut table, and a bureau, at which Jane was writing.

It was three in the afternoon and she had already composed four letters, when, glancing out of the window, she saw Joseph Porters in the street below.

"Oh dear."

Why had she ever spoken to him? She remembered their first meeting perfectly. It had been a year ago, not long after he had arrived: she had been in a boisterous mood with a group of other young ladies from the close when one of them had pointed to the thin, serious man standing beside his workmen and said: "That's Porters. Drains. Very glum." They burst out laughing and she, more to show off than anything, boldly marched across the street, gazed into the empty watercourse and declared: "Well Mr. Porters, I've come to inspect you and your drains."

He was so harmless, so dedicated. He had taken her quite seriously and, for half an hour, there and then, had explained every detail of the business to her, from the need to stop cholera to the medieval wonders lurking in the mud below. She had been trapped: without being rude she could not get away. For a full thirty minutes she stood there while he lectured her and her friends stood in the doorway of Surman's Boot Shop and held their sides.

"In fact," she said defensively afterwards, "he was very interesting. And indeed," she added, for she had listened to much of what he had told her, "the council behaved abominably."

It was hard, after this, not to speak to Mr. Porters politely when she saw him. In fact, though the young ladies sometimes teased her by asking after her drains, she had more respect for Porters's opinion than theirs. Almost in defiance of them, she consented to sit with him at the St Cecilia annual music festival and walked with him round the horticultural fête.

"He is also a considerable expert on the subject of dahlias," she informed her friends.

Once they had even spent a day together – as members of a group, of course, when one of the canons had taken a party to visit a sarsen cutting works at Fyfield on the far side of the plain. Mr. Porters had even given them a little talk explaining how the hard stones, now popular as curbing stones, were exactly those used thousands of years ago at Stonehenge.

He was a remarkably interesting man and she enjoyed his company.

But more than this – oh dear.

Lizzie opened the door. His card was on the little silver salver.

"Mr. Porters, Miss Jane."

Could she say she was not at home? He would take it too much to heart. It was all her own fault.

She laid down her pen.

"Please show him up." If only she could make him dislike her, it would all be so much easier.

He had not been in the library before. What a light and pleasant room it was. He peered round quickly before remembering that it was bad manners to do so. Books round the walls. On the table, a catalogue from Prince Albert's Great Exhibition of three years before; beside it, a more modest version of the Salisbury exhibition in the guildhall that had followed it.

In the largest bookshelf, and given pride of place, stood huge leather-bound folios of Hoare's mighty history of Wiltshire together with their companion, Hatcher's history of Salisbury.

No more impressive work had ever appeared in the county: a huge historical Domesday book that listed every parish in every hundred, with their monuments, country houses and the landed families who had owned them since feudal times. Every gentleman should have a set and indeed, the gentry of Wiltshire had widely subscribed to the project. The last volume, on the city, told a more modest though more detailed historical account of the doings of the townspeople over the centuries, and this had been prepared not by Hoare, a gentleman, but by Hatcher, a modest man of the middle classes like himself. When the books were issued, Hatcher's work had been praised, but the poor author himself had been completely ignored.

The sight of these huge volumes in her house momentarily depressed Porters.

Beside the catalogues on the table lay three issues of Mr. Dickens's last serial *Hard Times*, Thackeray's *Vanity Fair*, a copy of *Wuthering Heights* and a volume of Lord Byron's poems. The last, though he had only glanced at them once, he thought rather unfitting for a lady, though he had been told that it was mostly ladies who read them.

"I trust I do not intrude upon you."

"Not at all."

He glanced once more, disapprovingly, at the volume of Byron.

"I fear I do not read poetry."

"No." Her heart sank. He would not, of course. "Please sit down Mr. Porters."

He flushed. She knew how much courage it had taken him to call upon a woman who still lived alone.

"Lizzie will bring in tea directly," she told him.

Then, as usual, they talked. As long as he spoke of things he understood, he was very agreeable company. They discussed the new railway lines that must soon come to Sarum. It was a particular enthusiasm of his.

"The council has already petitioned Parliament – it is absurd that we still only have the line to Southampton. Why, they are the new turnpike roads of the age. We need a London line. And the Great Western too. This town could still be the Manchester of the south, Miss Shockley."

She smiled at his enthusiasm.

"I'm not sure the people in the close would like that, Mr. Porters."

"And would you say they were right, in this age of progress?"

"No. I think you are," she told him frankly.

He beamed.

"It will come, I promise you."

They discussed the Great Exhibition in London and the marvellous Crystal Palace of glass that had contained it, to which no less than six million had come.

"You know that Mr. Beach's cutlery was exhibited there?" She did not. He smiled. "He is very proud of the fact."

"You manage to know everything Mr. Porters." She would make a point of complimenting Mr. Beach, all the same.

"The Great Exhibition had an effect on this household," she told him laughingly. "I bought a gas cooker for the kitchen."

"A noble invention," he agreed. "And does your cook like it?" he asked quizzically.

He was not stupid.

"You unmask me at once. She tried to light it with a tinder box and took so long she nearly blew the house up. Now it sits there to mock me, Mr. Porters, quite unused."

"Reforms take time."

She saw her opening.

"I am become quite a reformer myself of late. I am quite persuaded of Chartism, Mr. Porters."

She saw his mouth open. He closed it directly.

"Chartism?"

"Indeed."

"The Chartists were quite finished, Miss Shockley, when their great demonstration failed six years ago."

"But their cause is just."

"One man, one vote?"

"Yes."

The Chartist movement with its call for secret ballots and universal suffrage for men had seemed like revolution to many and had certainly been successfully crushed. Yet when she thought about the matter, Jane had always found it hard to rebut the Chartists' arguments. She feared them, of course; after all, if all men vote, and only a few have property, then might not the majority vote to destroy property of the few? It was exactly the fear her ancestors had faced in the Civil War two hundred years before.

Did she truly believe what she said?

She did not know. But it had shocked Mr. Porters.

"These are dangerous ideas, Miss Shockley." He looked worried.

"Why Mr. Porters, surely you are not against reform? Look at the Mines and the Factory Acts of Lord Shaftesbury. Are you for repealing those reforms and putting children back in the mines as they used to be?"

"Not at all."

"Or for taking away the Health Board and having cholera back in Salisbury?"

"Naturally not."

"Then if you care for the welfare of the people you must agree with me."

He looked perplexed. Please God she had broken his attachment to her.

"I cannot agree with you."

"Well, Mr. Porters, there it is then."

They spoke of other things over tea. But as Porters gazed at her, his thoughts were not what she had intended.

"She is a little wild," he thought, "and discontented. She needs a husband to settle her, not a doubt about it. But what strength, what honesty."

It was after tea that she broke the news.

"I am leaving Sarum shortly, Mr. Porters, so we may not meet again."

His cup rattled as he held it. He cursed himself inwardly.

"Indeed?"

"I am to go and train as a nurse. In London probably. I hope to join Miss Nightingale."

For a moment he did not speak.

"I am sorry to hear it. You will be a great loss to Sarum, I'm sure."

"Sarum will do very well without me," she laughed. "Glad to lose a Chartist, I expect."

He was silent for a little time.

"How soon do you leave, Miss Shockley?"

"Any day," she smiled. "I fear we may not meet again."

She had done it. She had got rid of him, quite painlessly.

But something was wrong. As she gazed at him now, she could sense it; his fingers were trembling, there was something in the attitude of his bowed head; he was clearing his throat. Just before he spoke, she saw it coming, with horror.

"Miss Shockley," he had to clear his throat again. He glanced up at her face, saw shock, but ploughed on. "Before you leave I must say something to you."

Should she stop him now? Was it crueller to cut him off or listen? She flushed with embarrassment at the choice. He saw the flush, mis-interpreted.

"I believe – you have been kind enough to let me be your friend . . ."

"Of course." But it was only a whisper. What should she do?

"I have observed that you are very different in your attitudes to most young ladies of your station."

Was she? Or was it only a pose? Faced with the awfulness of Mr. Porters she was not sure.

"I realise of course that I . . ." he faltered. That he was not a gentleman. It was too painful. He could not say it. "That I am a modest man with a modest fortune, but I dare to hope that you are aware how greatly I admire your extraordinary qualities of mind."

It was so terrible. For indeed, in his way, he was a better man than most she had met. But . . . he did not even understand. They would not be received.

"Should you reconsider your intention to leave, Miss Shockley, it would do me the greatest honour to . . ." again he paused, suddenly uncertain of what expression to use . . . "ask for your hand."

It was over. She was completely silent. She tried in her mind to frame words of kindness, but they would not come. She sat, staring at the richly patterned carpet on the floor.

The silence seemed eternal.

At last, feeling he must say something, he spoke.

"It is a remarkable coincidence, Miss Shockley, that you and I are already connected." It had been his trump card, to be saved for use in time of social need. In the long silence, it seemed he might as well play it now. "My grandfather's cousin lived here in Sarum, only he spelt our name differently: he was Canon Porteus."

His claim to gentility, to a sort of cousinship with her. It was worse than anything she could have imagined.

"Thank you, Mr. Porters. But I am afraid my mind is quite made up."

He hung his head.

"May I hope?"

Why, why did she hesitate when she must be firm? Because she was embarrassed and could not find words? It was no excuse.

"I am truly touched, Mr. Porters, but you see, I am quite determined to nurse."

"Should you ever reconsider . . ."

"I thank you."

He got up to leave.

"A curious coincidence about the canon."

"Yes indeed."

Then he had gone.

She would have to go and nurse now.

On October 21, 1854, the *Salisbury Journal* quoted the *Times* article on Scutari. It also noted that a letter from one Lieutenant Henry Foster, of the 95th, who had visited Scutari, completely denied there was anything amiss with the conditions there. It seemed, the *Salisbury Journal* concluded, that the *Times* correspondent was acting upon mere hearsay.

"Perhaps Miss Jane," Mrs. Brown, the cook, suggested, "it's as well you didn't go after all."

On October 22, a letter came for her.

It was from Africa.

My dear Niece,
Our dear friend Crowther, the astounding negro clergyman of whom I have told you so much, has returned in the Pleiad from a triumphant expedition up the Benue, which is you may remember a tributary of the Niger. He feels that the several kings and chiefs he encountered are ready for Christianity – praise God. Crowther speaks still, and most movingly of his meetings in England three years ago with that great man Palmerston and our queen and consort of Windsor. Indeed, it must surely have been thanks to royal interest in our mission that the government sent us the Pleiad. When I tell him he is lucky he only smiles and tells me – "God provides."

Jane had long admired the extraordinary black missionary Samuel Crowther with whom her uncle worked in the Niger. It thrilled her to think of his career, from slave, to lay preacher, to fully ordained clergyman. One day, her uncle had written her, he fully expected the dedicated Nigerian to be a bishop. God's work done by a black man with a great soul. That was progress indeed. She read on.

The expedition returned without any malaria. No sickness at all.

But alas, the same cannot be said for your uncle. I fear my health is failing and I cannot continue here any longer. Indeed Crowther's descriptions of all he saw in England have made me long to see it once again. I pray that God will spare me long enough to do so.

I was sorry indeed to hear of the death of your dear mother. But God moves in mysterious ways. What a blessing now that you should be at Sarum at our old house, where I trust you will be glad to receive, if I fear somewhat briefly, your loving uncle, Stephen.

P.S. I am to take the next packet which leaves, I understand, not long after this.

She stared at the page in disbelief. Her uncle, the saintly missionary she so revered, was coming – and she was to keep house for him: there was no mistaking his meaning. Nor, any doubt, she supposed about her duty.

Later that day, as she gazed at the railway lines by Milford station, it seemed to her they came together, closing her off.

No nursing. No India. At least for the moment.
But soon, she would get free.

1861

Jane Shockley's passion began when she was thirty.

She was standing on the steps of the guildhall, a big square building given to the town, like the hospital too, by Lord Radnor. It stood at the east side of the market, a reminder not only of the continuing presence, from their seat near old Clarendon, of the Bouverie family in Sarum's affairs, but also, it always seemed to Jane, its strong lines reminded the beholder of a certain solid severity that was needed, but usually missing, in Sarum's affairs.

As if echoing such thoughts, the short, stout man at her side shook his large round head sadly, glanced up at her and announced:

"Moral, not material progress is what is needed in Sarum now, Miss Shockley."

She nodded. Of course. And if anyone was going to provide it, she had no doubt it would be Mr. Daniel Mason, Methodist and temperance enthusiast. She looked down at him fondly.

"I shall convert you to temperance yet, Miss Shockley," he declared pleasantly. "You see if I don't."

And indeed, it was not only the non-conformists – the Wesleyans, Baptists, Congregationalists and others along with the now-tolerated Catholics, abounding in Sarum – who had joined in the mighty temperance cause. Two years before, when Mr. Gough the temperance orator had come to Salisbury, no less than fifteen hundred, from every creed and class had crowded into the markethouse to hear him. "Many of the Anglican clergy in the parishes are worried by the drink problem," Mason assured her. Evangelicals like the great Shaftesbury with his reforms of factory conditions and public health: aristocrats and Roman Catholics: all, she knew, were equally anxious to take the moral high ground in this new age of progress. Why, Florence Nightingale, returned to England after the war, had read Mr. Lees's tract on prohibition to Queen Victoria herself.

"But reform is never easy," Mason continued as he gazed around the market place. "Why," he pointed, "just look at that."

She looked at the little group he had indicated, a drunken father and two pathetic children.

"It is disgusting," she agreed.

He glanced at her quickly.

"You agree temperance is needed for them?"

"It certainly appears to be."

"Come then, Miss Shockley," he said in triumph. "You shall meet them."

It was a Tuesday market day at the end of summer. Not a very lively one. It was late afternoon. An air of torpor hung over the area.

Near the middle of the market place a line of cattle stood lethargically, tethered to rail; nearby were half a dozen pens made of hurdles, containing sheep – but the best had all been sold at the big fair in July. Carts, unhitched and resting at strange angles, some covered, some with open wood frame sides, stood everywhere, and with just as much apparent randomness, small stalls sprouted here and there, untidily from the ground. Carters in smocks, men in leggings and open shirts, farmers in great coats and stovepipe hats; here and there a woman in a big hooped crinoline, her dress and bonnet apparently the vehicle for as many small ribbons as they could carry: all seemed to move with an almost dreamy slowness in the large, warm, dusty space. Around the edge of the market place, the lines of shops sported heavy awnings which occasionally flapped reluctantly in the faint breeze. The movement of air brought familiar smells – of cattle, cow pat, dust, of a stall nearby selling jumblies – the popular gingerbread cooked on a griddle. And she could smell, too, the faint aroma of the heavy consumption, all around, of strong Wiltshire beer.

It was the market as she had always known it – with one important and significant difference.

At the far western end, beyond the old cheese market by St Thomas's, stood a new building, with a big front of three Roman arches and a classical pediment in stone, that had given Mr. Porters particular joy. It was the new covered market house. And it was also a railway station.

In the last five years, Salisbury had at last become a railway town. The London and South Western to Southampton, the Andover to London line, the Wiltshire, Somerset and Weymouth's line – part of the broad-gauge Great Western network – had all been gathered together at a handsome new station at Fisherton; and the short distance from this new complex to the market place was now covered by a special track.

"At last," Porters had exclaimed, "this is not only the centre of Salisbury Plain, but we're part of the modern world."

In a sense he was right. The trains whisked in and out with a clamour and hiss of steam; the city grew as ever more people came from the outside world to see and often settle down by its ancient charm. But the old heartbeat of the five sleepy valleys, their innumerable hamlets, and the sweeping ancient spaces of the chalk ridges and their flocks of sheep – these, breathing slowly to the gentle rhythm of the Sarum market days, did not greatly change.

And a market town was now what Salisbury was. It had reverted, though few of its people knew it, to a far more ancient role in the place where the five rivers met – to a role before the great cloth trade of England arose, a role perhaps before even Wilton was built or the little staging post of Sorviodunum was founded. Like the Roman roads before them, the new metal tracks only overlaid a more ancient and unchanging pattern; once more Sarum was a market and religious centre at the great natural collecting point of the sweeping upland plain.

Poor Mr. Porters had wanted to change that. He had fought hard, with many on the city council, to obtain the big railway coach building works for the town.

"A second Manchester," he eagerly told her once again.

They had failed. The new factories had been set up in Swindon, away to the north-east of the county.

She was not sorry.

The group that now confronted her consisted of a man and two small children – a girl of about six, she guessed, a little boy a year or two younger. The girl wore only a faded green cotton print dress with a tear down the back and old stockings, one white, one grey. The brown slippers on her feet were split at the toes. She had found, somewhere, a large woollen shawl with a fringe which, draped over her shoulders, hung down to her feet. The boy was even more dishevelled: ragged shirt, patched cotton trousers, bare feet. He was eating an orange which had smeared his face. They were sitting on the tail of a cart, viewing the world with apparent indifference.

Inside the cart, propped up against a bale of straw and apparently sleeping, was a man of about forty.

"My most depressing case," Mason explained. "The mother died recently. Two children. Believe it or not, the man is a farmer." He pointed to the sleeping figure, with his half untied neck-cloth and unshaven face who now opened his eyes. "Jethro Wilson."

The sleepy eyes had opened very slowly, but focused at once.

"Waal . . . Miztur Mason." It was a slow, easy drawl. He looked calmly from the determined Methodist to the young lady at his side. "Come to reform me, I suppose." And with surprising ease, he got up.

He had been handsome, she thought. His long hair, dirty and matted, might once have been a rich brown, like his side whiskers. His tall, lean body, his long aquiline face, suggested power. Was it laziness, drink or contempt for the world that made him move so slowly and carelessly about his business? He looked at his children and, with just a small motion of his head, sent them scurrying to harness the cart.

"You've been drinking," Mason accused.

"Had a few. Slept it off."

"Your children are a disgrace, man. You know it."

Wilson looked at them thoughtfully.

"They can harness the cart."

"I beg you, Wilson, consider them, if you don't consider yourself."

"What would you do for them?"

"Much. Educate them. Teach them to know God."

"They know the country."

"Not enough. You know it."

"Mebbe."

"We shall speak again."

"Mebbe."

The cart was ready. The two children scrambled in. He lifted a broad-brimmed hat and placed it on his head; then he gave the small pony a lazy flick with his whip and they began to move slowly away. After they had gone fifteen yards, he turned and, looking straight at Jane, slowly raised his hat, still silently looking at her for a moment after he had returned the hat to his head.

"Impudent rogue," Mason muttered; and turning to Jane he remarked: "If you could help me reform him, or at least save those children Miss Shockley, I should think it the best of all our efforts."

They had often worked together, over the last few years. There were in Sarum, God knew, enough poor souls to care for.

"And Miss Shockley," he always told his family, "is most unusual."

She was indeed. She taught at a school, though she certainly had no financial need to do so. She spent weeks, during the long summer holidays, acting as a nurse in Lord Radnor's Infirmary and never went there without a copy of Miss Nightingale's *Notes on Nursing* tucked into a pocket of her dress.

"We should have lost her long ago, if it weren't for her uncle," Mason would say.

The advent of her Uncle Stephen had been one of the great disappointments of her life. He was brought to Sarum, one bright December day, by the little steam train from Southampton – a thin, gaunt figure in his fifties, with blue eyes, which seemed never quite to focus, peering out of a yellowish face. He was liberally wrapped in a shawl and a blanket and walked stiffly with a stick. He spoke very quietly, always let her know what he required, and never considered, even for a moment, that his niece might ever wish to leave him or, if she did, that it would be possible for her to do so.

It had never before crossed her mind that a lifetime of service might make a man selfish.

"But I fear, my dear, my stay will not be long," he had told her sadly when he first arrived. And so he did still, from time to time, as he moved stiffly about the town, enjoying the reverence that was his due; really, she admitted wryly to herself, predicting his departure had become almost more of a promise to her than a regret.

"Can you really find time to teach when there is so much to be done here?" he would sometimes ask, a little querulously.

"Oh yes, uncle," she would reply, and escape, if she politely could, into the close.

Porters had proposed once again, by the choristers' green.

"If it were a question of also looking after your uncle, then I should be honoured . . ."

"Quite impossible," she assured him, and begged him not to speak of it again.

He had assumed a new role in her life now, which seemed to heal his wound and which she could tolerate – that of adviser. For it was clear to Porters that young Miss Shockley was still wayward and must be in need of advice.

He had settled in the city. The new railway station and the influx of people had caused a huge building programme on the western Fisherton side of the town and on the northern side where some of the Wyndham family estates lay. Railway cottages in rows, suburban villas, even big, neo-gothic houses on handsome sites were springing up. There was plenty of work for Porters. He had bought a villa.

And so thanks to these circumstances, Jane Shockley found herself still in Sarum, often busy with community service. If she was restless, she gave herself as little time to be so as possible.

She liked Mr. Mason and his Methodists. She even admired his efforts to get a regular temperance movement going in Salisbury, which despite much agreement on the subject in principle, had only met with sporadic success.

"I really can't say I'm prepared to go the whole way and never touch another glass of beer," she declared. For she thought it one of the small delights of the era that the inhabitants of such genteel places as the close no longer disdained to drink a glass of beer in preference to wine. "I always do, at every meal," she assured Mr. Porters, who was not sure whether to be shocked or not.

But she visited the workhouse with him, when her old friends in the close usually preferred to stick to the pleasant almshouses, and there were few places in Sarum she had not seen and understood.

"It's the farm labourers on the plain that worry me the most," Mason explained. "They have the hardest lot."

But today, as Jethro Wilson and his two wretched children drove the cart away, he clarified:

"I always lament the lot of the poor farmers on the plain, Miss Shockley. But that man," he glared after Jethro, "has only himself to blame."

The great Michaelmas Fair at Salisbury that came at the end of the harvest time, was not a proper fair – for little important business was done. But it was carefully kept up all the same, for money was freely spent. There were harvest accounts to settle, clothes to buy, entertainments of every kind to spend money on and the market place was crowded with brightly coloured booths. It lasted three days and on the first two, Monday and Tuesday, it was open until eleven at night for all the peep-shows, rides and pleasures that the fairground folk who journeyed across the plain could provide.

It was on the Tuesday, at nine o'clock, that she saw Jethro.

He was standing stock still by the gothic arches of the big poultry cross. Occasionally he swayed a little from side to side. By the light from nearby windows, she could see that his face was red; he appeared to see nothing around him at all. His beard had several days' growth. His two children were sitting miserably under the cross, half-dressed and shivering, but the handful of by-standers were paying no attention to them.

She gazed at them. Nobody moved. She went over.

His lips were moving, very slowly. He seemed to be mouthing words, but she could not hear anything as she stood beside him.

Then the little boy spoke:

"He's singing, miss."

"Are you cold?"

"Yes, miss."

Singing. She drew closer. He was staring down the street towards Fisherton bridge, and was completely oblivious to her.

She put her ear close to his lips.

"Ther vly be on the turnip."

Barely a whisper: the raucous old Wiltshire song, sung at every celebration. She listened again.

"Ther vly be on the turnip."

It was just the first line: he was repeating it, under his breath, again and again.

"Will he be like this for long?"

The little boy shrugged.

"Dunno, miss."

"His brain's stopped," the girl volunteered.

"So I see." She looked at them. "You'll die of cold. You'd better come with me." Rather to her surprise, they got up obediently. She began to turn towards Brown Street, where Mr. Mason lived.

"No you don't, damn you." He had suddenly been galvanised into life. He had both children held by the neck. His eyes were blazing at her. "Temperance bitch."

"He don't mean it, miss," the girl said.

"I do," he roared. He released the children, clenched his fists, and shaking with rage, took a step towards her.

"Run, miss."

"Certainly not."

She faced him calmly.

His eyes seemed to stand out; he raised his arms as he stepped forward. Then he crashed to the ground.

"I thought he would," she murmured.

It was a surprise to her when, two days later, she visited Daniel Mason at the little temperance hotel he had set up for himself near the Greencroft on the city's east side, and was told that Jethro Wilson had undergone a change of heart.

"It may not be permanent, but it is a start," Mason remarked.

"Mr. Mason, you are a wonder. How did you do it?"

He shook his large head and smiled at her.

"As a matter of fact, Miss Shockley, you did."

"I? I did nothing, except bring them to you."

"Not according to Jethro Wilson. His children are here. They spoke of your kindness continually. And he has been told that he attacked you."

"He didn't. He lurched towards me."

Mason gave her a quick, shrewd look.

"He thinks he did, Miss Shockley, and the shock is doing him good."

She smiled.

"As you wish. Is he a perpetual drunkard?"

"No. From all I know of him, he comes into town occasionally but then drinks heavily for several days – heavily to the point at which you saw him. His wretched children then have to put him in the cart and take him home. They fend for themselves like neglected animals."

"It is terrible."

"Yes. But the best news is," Mason told her excitedly, "that he is prepared to give them up and put them in our care. See him," he urged. "He is already much changed."

He was indeed.

The figure who now respectfully rose from his chair in the little room Mason had provided, was shaven and washed. He had been provided with a clean coat; it was brown and went well with the now shining mane of russet hair that was combed straight back over his head. His black eyes, no longer swollen and reddened took her in with a strange gentle intensity she had not encountered before.

"I am sorry for the other night, miss."

He was still a little pale she noticed. He must have drunk heavily indeed.

"It is forgotten."

"Not by me. I never tried to strike a woman before."

A woman, he had said, not a lady; as though she had been one of his own kind. For some reason she did not mind.

"Are you better now?"

"I was far gone."

"You were indeed." She smiled. "How long is it since your wife died?"

"Three years," he answered quietly. "Giving birth."

"And you have no one to look after them?"

"An old woman. A farm hand and his boy. That's all there is – except for help at harvest."

"Where is your farm?"

"Winterbourne – on the edge of the plain."

"How big?"

"Fifty acres."

She sighed.

Of all the combinations, this was the worst. For in recent generations, a great change had taken place at Sarum.

Beginning with the threshing machines which the rioters had attacked back in 1830, the process of industrialisation had come to the Wessex region in many forms. Already, not only threshing machines, but the first steam ploughs had begun to appear in Wiltshire.

"Even paying the ploughman more, and adding the cost of fuel," Mason told her, "the steam plough cuts a deeper furrow for only a third of the price."

Rich men like Lord Pembroke could afford to purchase a fine Brown and May steam engine from Devizes. Enterprising men with access to capital, like Lord Pembroke's consulting agent Mr. Rawlence, could afford to build up flocks of prizewinning sheep.

She had questioned Mason about the situation many times in the course of their work together.

"The cloth trade's weak, and a thousand acre sheep farmer up on the downs can keep over twelve hundred sheep with only three men and a couple of boys. There are many more farm labourers than available work, so the labourer is to be had for cheap. Our men are the lowest paid labourers in the county, you know," Mason explained. "That's why you see them leaving for Australia – or here in the workhouse."

"So it is hard for the labourers; what about tenants like Jethro Wilson?"

"Hard for them too. Landlords are looking for tenants to improve their land and give them a better return for as little outlay as possible. That's why many of the biggest will only give a farmer a one year lease. Men like Jethro Wilson are getting thrown out."

"Yet new men are coming in all the time. From the north."

Mason grimaced.

"The fact is, most tenant farms are still a good proposition if you're forward-looking. And the trouble is, most of our poorer sort aren't. That's why when the Scots discover the low cost of our labour, they come south as fast as they can."

She had sometimes noticed strange accents in the market.

She had made other inquiries about the subject, which confirmed everything Mason had said and told her much more besides.

So now when she questioned Jethro Wilson, she had a shrewd idea of his predicament: too small to be economic, too poor to improve. And probably, certainly, too backward to take steps to save himself.

And yet, as he stood before her now, gazing at her with his surprisingly quiet, keen eyes, she wondered – might there be hope for him after all?

"Your children. Mr. Mason says you're prepared to put them in his care."

" 'Tis not the workhouse. I'd never allow that."

"No."

"He says a Methodist farmer will take them in if I pay for keep and they'll get schooling until I've put the farm to rights."

"I see."

"Me with no wife. I think it's for the best. For the time being."

"So do I."

He seemed thoughtful.

"I must reform myself, miss." He said it not with shame, but with a quiet certainty that she found far more impressive.

"It would be as well."

"Thank you, miss."

Then she said it. Partly on impulse, partly out of curiosity to learn more about the subject.

"I think I shall come and see your farm, Mr. Wilson."

She went the next week.

There were many hedgerows on the high ground above the valleys – huge, untidy hedgerows, six, seven feet high or more, sometimes loaded with great tangles of ripe blackberries, bristling with nuts, elderberries, sloes – a storehouse which even the intense occupation of mice, red squirrels and visiting birds could never completely plunder. There were hedgerows enclosing fields around old Sarum and over the high ground far beyond.

She rode out over the plain, taking the old turnpike road.

The main roads were covered with tarmacadam now. But once off these, they were still often no more than dusty lanes or mere tracks and it was not long before she was passing along these more primitive, rutted ways. Then, leaving the world of close hedgerows she came out onto the bare, empty waste, and rode on, quite alone, for nearly an hour, until, coming over a ridge she saw in a dip below her the village she was looking for.

So this was Jethro Wilson's Winterbourne. She had not been there before, but it was just as she had imagined it probably was. There were dozens of villages in Wessex with that evocative Saxon name. The stream that flows in winter, the winter bourne. Nearly always they collected an extra name, to distinguish them from their neighbours: but for Jane Shockley, this one of many such places was always to be just Winterbourne.

It lay on the very edge of the high ground, in a dip. On each side of its single little street, a line of cottages, with a mixture of brick, stone and plaster walls, and mostly thatched. There was a small stone church without a tower. Behind the houses, small fields with hedgerows extended a little way up the slope. There were two yew trees in the churchyard, a little windbreak of trees on the church's northern side. And all around, the bareness of the chalk ridges, where the sheep were grazing.

The windswept ridges and their sheep: there were half a million sheep on Salisbury Plain.

She rode slowly down the slope and into the village street.

It was very quiet. It was as if the great harsh light of the open spaces above had been carried by the wind itself so that, in the dip where the village lay, it had been softened, filtered.

The children in the street were mostly barefoot; from their doorways, their mothers watched her curiously. It was possibly years, she realised, since this deserted hamlet on the edge of the empty plain had seen a lady riding side-saddle pass along their dusty street.

The thatched cottages, she noticed, each bore the same little decoration – a thatch pheasant, set perkily near one end, staring to the south west. This was the thatcher's mark, his signature, and would appear in each of the villages he visited to do his wonderful work.

But the most important feature of the place lay on her left: the bourne.

It was empty. Dry as a bone. Strands of straw, twigs, husks from nut-filled hedgerows, stinging nettles and dockleaves were all the small trench contained. From the roadway, over this ditch, three little wooden bridges led to the path that passed along the front of the cottages on the left.

It had been dry all summer, for such is the nature of the winter bourne. But when the November rains began to fall upon the high ground, when snow and ice covered the rolling ridges and then the great thaws of spring set in, then the waters would descend, sometimes a steady stream, sometimes a deluge, cascading off the uplands, down slopes, down grassy ravine and chalky gulch: the waters would descend off the great bare spaces and flow joyously, carrying all before them, into the channels of the winter bourne. For six months of the year the quiet, deserted hamlet would quiver into renewed life beside its briskly running stream.

This was the ancient magic of the winter bournes round the edge of Salisbury Plain.

A child directed her to Jethro Wilson's farm, which lay up a small track, two hundred yards from the main street. The track was overgrown and rutted; her horse picked her way up it gingerly.

"I have come to see Mr. Wilson." Why did she suddenly feel awkward?

"He'll be back presently." There was no invitation to enter. Obviously this was the old woman who kept the place, a thin, hard-faced, sharp-eyed creature in a red and purple shawl. She gave Jane a strange, measuring look before closing the side door.

It was – it had once been – a typical farmhouse with a low fence of wooden railings, once painted white, across the front. A narrow path led thirty feet from the little gate to the front door, hardly ever used except for a wedding or a funeral. There was a room with a window each side of the door, and three smaller windows above. On the left hand side, a wing went back another thirty feet, in which a door and a motley collection of small windows seemed to have been set at random. The walls were brick and stone. Behind the wing was a once splendid addition enclosing the vegetable garden: a long chalk wall. They were one of her favourite features of the region, these chalk walls. Quarried from the sides of ridges, solid white chalk, cut into huge blocks and stacked, two feet thick, seven or eight feet high, soft to the touch, and surmounted by a coping of thatch that jutted out with an overhang of up to a foot, to protect the soft sides from the weathering of continuous rainwater.

It could have been a fine place. But it was not.

Jethro Wilson's farm was utterly desolate.

The paint was peeling from the window frames and the paths around were overgrown; the thatch, turned grey with age, was falling slowly apart; the two thatch pheasants that had once stood proudly on the roof of the house and on the top of the chalk were now nothing more than broken frames. She sighed. Nothing was sadder than a run-down farm.

Yet when he appeared a few minutes later, Jethro seemed in good spirits. His shirt was open at the neck and he had a day's growth of beard; but as he came to her side, the place seemed to take on a more hopeful aspect.

He motioned towards the farmhouse, a little ruefully.

"A lot to do, miss."

"Yes."

"Do you want to see round?"

She did.

He took her into the walled garden first. There were two damson trees and an old mulberry, whose soft fruit had been gathered in a basket. There was also a pear tree but it seemed to be dying. In the beds, she saw potatoes and carrots.

"If you don't repair the thatch on that wall, the chalk will wear away. Worse, the water will seep inside and then crack the wall when it freezes."

He nodded. "Have to mend the house too."

"Can you do it?"

He shrugged.

"I dunno, miss."

"Show me the rest," she ordered.

It was a pitiful farm, though there were many others like it. His sheep were out on the ridge above and they walked slowly up there together. She inspected them.

"All Southdowns? No Hampshires?"

"They're less trouble."

"And they give less in return too," she said briskly.

In the last few years, a great change had taken place in the vast population of sheep above Sarum, and Jane knew all about it. The hornless Southdowns which had replaced the old long-horned Wiltshire stock in the last century were now being replaced themselves with another, even more productive breed, the Hampshires.

The Hampshires produced lambs which fattened earlier: they gave a better return; but they were as Jethro said, more trouble, and certainly more expense, to feed.

"I don't like hurdle sheep," he added. "Have to feed them root crops in a field instead of just turning them loose on the downs like a grass sheep."

"Even so, all the best farmers are changing to Hampshires," she reminded him.

He did not seem to be very impressed, but strode on before turning.

"I can't afford the investment," he said quietly.

It was very likely true.

"But what about the agricultural societies?" she suggested. "Can they help? And what about your landlord?"

Many farmers had found the machinery and investment needed in the new age too much for their individual purses; but for more than a generation now, clubs had been formed of small farmers who banded together to buy machinery and make capital investments. In a similar spirit, Mr Rawlence had recently set up a loan company for improving landlords.

"Landlord's an old man. Won't spend anything," Jethro replied. "As for the societies," he gestured towards the little hamlet and the bare downs above: "we're cut off here, you see." She noticed that when he said it, there was a faint glint of satisfaction in his eye, and she understood. There were many in those quiet, desolate regions, miles away from the bustle of the city and its market, who had no longing for change.

They began to walk down the slope again.

"Have you any relations who could help?" she asked.

He laughed softly.

"Relations? I've relations all over the five rivers. Hundreds of them – down south to Christchurch, and north to Swindon, I'spect. Hundreds of us Wilsons." He gave her a slow smile. "I don't know them; they don't know me. It's that sort of family." She nodded. She thought she could see them: fishermen, small farmers, quiet people who had lived in the area since who knew when. "The ones down at Christchurch were smugglers, so they say." He chuckled. "More money in that."

"No doubt."

Away from the city, on his own ground, where he seemed to move with such ease, there was something strangely attractive about his tall, strong figure and his gentle, half-mocking humour.

It was just before they reached the farmhouse again that he remarked:

"Over there," he pointed to an overgrown area along the edge of an old ditch, "is where you can find pigs."

"Pigs?"

He grinned.

"Hedgehogs. They call them pigs up here." He moved over to the brambles and showed her the ground, which was a mass of roots and fallen leaves. "You follow along here. Then you break down the ground and you find them."

"How do you know where to look?"

"You know. Sometimes," he said simply. "They taste better'n rabbits; that's what all the folk up here say."

She had never thought of such a thing before. How strangely simple, how primitive it was: harsh nature at the edge of the chalk ridges as it had been, she supposed, for thousands of years. A world on her very doorstep that she had sometimes ridden past, but never known.

"I fear we don't know much about hedgehog hunting in the close," she said wryly.

"No."

He was observing her quietly: she was aware of it. And how strange it was, she thought, that here in this poor hamlet, on the edge of the open wilderness, this half-reformed drunkard farmer with his simple life should make her feel uncomfortably as if he knew something about her that she did not know herself. He said nothing: he remained inscrutable and distant.

"I don't drink now," he said gently.

"That is good." She smiled. "Thank you for letting me see your farm."

"Will you come in, miss?"

"Thank you, no. I must return."

He conducted her to her horse, and with an ease she found almost disconcerting, he stooped, offered his hand for her to rest her foot upon and then lifted her coolly into the saddle.

His side whiskers, she noticed as she was lifted, were a little longer and there was a hint of grey in them that, if he had not been little more than a peasant, would, she thought, have made him look distinguished.

She turned her horse, and began to move away.

It was only as she turned to look back at him, where he was still standing, that she noticed the figure of the old woman, standing by the back door, gazing after her with a kind of scorn.

She rode slowly, meditatively back over the high ground. In the distance there was a line of smoke, and a faint red glow along the ground of fire, where some farmer was burning the stubble rather late.

Jethro Wilson's children were with a good methodist farmer at the village of Barford St Martin by Grovely Wood. They gave little trouble, Mason reported, except that sometimes they were rather wild, "and absolute pagans, you know, Miss Shockley. Pagans." He would shake his large round head. But the money for their keep came regularly from Jethro and the system seemed to be working well.

In the month of November, she almost forgot him; for Uncle Stephen had one of his afflictions – namely a heavy head cold which, he assured her, might at any time develop into pneumonia. Even the doctor expressed mild concern on one occasion, so it was necessary for her to be with him continuously when she was not teaching. But by the start of December, both the doctor and her uncle could at last agree that he was recovered.

It was at the start of December that she met Daniel Mason by the entrance to the close.

"Bad news, Miss Shockley. I fear Jethro Wilson must have fallen to drinking again."

"Why so?"

"The payments for his children have ceased. They were due a week ago and there has been no word from him."

"Perhaps he is sick."

"Perhaps. I am trying to get word to him today."

"There is no need, Mr. Mason," she assured him. "I know his farm and I shall ride over there this afternoon."

She was glad to get out of the town and clear her head after the month tending Uncle Stephen. It was a bright harsh day, and as she came down into Winterbourne at last, she walked her horse carefully on the slippery street where water had flooded the edge of the little bourne and then frozen.

The farmhouse was not deserted. A thin column of smoke rose from the chimney, but she had to hammer several times upon the door before it was finally answered, not as she had expected by the old woman, but by Jethro himself.

He had not been drinking much: she was sure of that, although she thought she could smell a little gin on his lips. But he had several days' growth of beard now and his whole appearance was unkempt. His face seemed thinner, and a little wasted. The nurse in her told her he had not eaten.

"May I come in?"

He motioned her silently towards the parlour.

The fire in its huge brick hearth was low. He had pulled a small wooden chair close to it for greater warmth. The place was not much furnished. On the table in the middle of the room, there was the remains of a loaf baked several days before. There was a single easy chair, covered with a coarse cloth, which he offered her.

"Well Mr. Wilson? Mr. Mason sent me about your children."

He nodded slowly.

"My money's run out. They'll have to come back here."

"With no money?"

He stared at the fire.

"I have a cow to sell. Best price'll be at the next market. I'll pay what I owe them and take the children back." He grimaced. "Not much of a Christmas to offer them."

"Do you want to sell the cow?"

He looked discouraged. "It's a loss, miss."

"Then how will you manage?"

"We get by."

He turned to face her. It was sad to see the strong figure of a month ago so strained and almost stooped now.

"I shall have to give up the farm, move elsewhere."

"What can you do?"

"What is there to do?"

She tried to think. The cloth trade had improved a little, but it was still poor. There was the carpet factory at Wilton, which now employed over two hundred people; she had heard that the tanning works in Salisbury was starting to look for extra men. There were paper mills down the Avon at Downton; and of course there was the railway. She could not see the man at her side in any of these occupations.

"I was at a meeting once when they read out a letter from a man named Godfrey in Australia," he said. "You'd hardly believe the good life the farmers have out there. And the food! Half the men there were for taking the boat out at once."

"Many do. Would you?"

He sighed. "I don't want to, miss. There is a possibility," he went on. He could give up the farm, leave Sarum, and go to the other side of the plain. "To the one cousin who speaks to me!" he grinned. He had a family farm up in the cheese country, and he needed help. "I could go there, but I'd be working for him then," he explained. "And," he paused before concluding quietly: "I'd not like that."

She could imagine.

"This farm could still be made to work," she urged him.

He gave her a gentle look, as though she were a child.

"Not by me."

It irked her to see the man dragged down like this, through ignorance and lack of capital as much as by his own fault. And suddenly, on an impulse she cried:

"Would you accept help – financial help – to improve?"

"Where from?"

She smiled at him hopefully.

[849]

"From me."

The investment of Jane Shockley in Jethro Wilson's farm was not a huge outlay.

"Besides, when we do the accounts, I shall take a return on my investment," she told him.

But it was by far the most exciting project she had ever undertaken.

He went about the business quietly. He was neither assertive nor submissive because of their financial arrangement, and as far as the farm was concerned, he seemed to accept the improvements as necessary evils. The first thing she did was to introduce new stock: "Hampshires," she insisted. "You could grow root crops on the lower part of your land as well," she told him. She took advice from farmers and landowners she knew, who were so surprised and then amused at her enthusiastic and sometimes pointed inquisitiveness, that they often gave her their best and most expert advice.

"It may be cheaper to import manure for the two west fields," she announced one day. "I'll see about it." And though he looked surprised, he did not oppose her.

She was wise, however. With the single farm labourer, and his gawky son, and the old woman who came each day to keep house, she had nothing to do at all, maintaining her distance as if she had been a complete stranger. Indeed, with Jethro himself she claimed: "All I do is make a few suggestions and keep accounts."

But not a week passed without her riding over to Winterbourne to watch his progress.

The children remained with the Methodist farmer and his family.

"You have no wife," she reminded Jethro, "and they are receiving proper schooling there."

But if the changes came at the initiative of Jane Shockley, she soon realised that she herself was receiving a greater, and far more subtle education than any she was giving. Few people knew where she rode to across the plain; they would have been more surprised still to see her walking with the tall farmer along the edge of the high ground, listening and nodding as he pointed out every detail of the tiny, delicate life forms in those huge waste spaces.

He looked well; his colour and strength had long since returned, and each time she visited the farm, she noticed how his lean, powerful form seemed to belong in those windswept regions. "He is like an animal," she sometimes thought. On a warm day, as he moved lazily along the edge of the ridge, or sat on a stone outcrop watching the sheep, she could picture him as a lizard. On a windy day, as the clouds raced over the land and his thin narrow face with its deepset eyes faced into the weather, he seemed more like a hawk. And when he carefully, softly approached some little animal he meant to trap, she would think: "Ah, but most of all, he is like a cat."

He never went to church and she did not try to make him. "He can be reformed," she believed, but never in Mason's manner.

He still drank, but only a little. The binges in Salisbury seemed to be a thing of the past. His hair now was always sleek, his black eyes clear.

As she looked at him, she could not believe he did not have women, but she never saw them, and never asked.

How she relished her time in his presence. In a place where she saw only a lonely furze bush, in a bare landscape that in certain lights, could almost have been the tundra, he would find tiny bright flowers; a quarter of a mile away, he would somehow discern a hare or a rabbit; with a pointing finger, he would seem to bring to life from the motionless landscape a pipit, a wheatear or another of the tiny birds that inhabited the plain and would burst with sudden life over the rim of the valley. He would see, where she peered and made out nothing, a cranefly or even the elusive hoverfly. Once, when they were walking by a field, a huge cloud of light blue butterflies rose directly in front of them, without warning and in their hundreds, so that the air was suddenly full of a flickering blue haze. She was so taken by surprise, that without thinking what she was doing, she grasped his strong arm and burst out laughing at the wild pleasure of the place.

She spoke of these experiences to no one. They were her secret escape, and often she would pass most of the day with him, insisting on the same food that he and the men ate – a piece of bread, if they were lucky, a piece of cheese for lunch and then, in the farmhouse, some potatoes and a little bacon at teatime, prepared by the old woman who continued to gaze at her in surly silence.

She enjoyed these days. An instinct told her it would be better not to discuss the matter with anyone, beyond telling Daniel Mason that she had made a loan to Jethro Wilson in the hope of keeping the farm going, and providing for the children. Once a month Jethro would now come into Sarum, see Mason, and then visit his children, "Who I really believe, in time, will become members of our church," Mason delightedly and optimistically assured her. But she had no doubts about the wisdom of what she was doing herself.

Once, it was true – the only time she had spoken to her – the old woman had suddenly turned to her when the men were out of the kitchen and said:

"You're a proper fool. He's no good – not where women is concerned."

But she had put this cryptic sentence out of her mind as merely spiteful.

No, she thought, he belongs to the subtle, silent life along the edges of Salisbury Plain.

The spring, so-called Lady Day market was held in April. It was a modest affair, given over mainly to selling cloth, and now falling into disuse, but Jane insisted that he buy some blankets for the farm there and even gave him a small present of money to do so. She had been careful not to interfere in his house, though she longed secretly to do so, but she felt some basic improvements could be made.

It was in the afternoon during this fair, while her Uncle Stephen was at tea in the house of one of the canons nearby, that, on her instructions,

Jethro Wilson presented himself at the back door of the house and was ushered into the library.

He looked about him with mild curiosity, as she sat at the bureau where she had been working. Though she had never seen him trouble to write anything down, she knew he could read, and discovered, when it came to doing business, that he had a shrewd head for figures.

"I have prepared accounts," she told him, "and I want you to see them." She showed him what they had spent on livestock, and other improvements, and the anticipated returns. "We shall have sheep to sell in July, and lambs. The cattle I think we should hold until December. There's the corn too."

He picked up the sheet of paper and walked over to the window, leaning against the panelling by the window frame to study it. As the light caught his long face in repose she smiled to herself. How strange it was: Mr Porters, the man of education, had looked so awkward and uncomfortable in the library; yet Jethro Wilson, his long frame leaning so unselfconsciously by the bookshelves, Jethro Wilson the poor farmer, no longer shabby, had exactly the careless ease of a gentleman who has owned a library all his life.

He returned the paper to her with a smile. As he did so, she noticed for some reason the sound of his frock coat brushing against the leather of the chair. Why did that please her?

"I must go to Barford now, to see the children."

"Of course."

It was only minutes after he had left that she had stepped outside into the close; and she had hardly gone ten yards before she met Mr. Porters. His face was troubled. She had not seen him so agitated since he first proposed to her.

"Ah, Miss Shockley. You have had, ah, a visitor."

She gave him a pleasant smile.

"Yes indeed. How did you know, Mr. Porters."

He blushed.

"I . . . could not help observing. I happened to be passing."

"And you are here still."

She gazed into his embarrassed, anxious eyes.

"I was . . ." his voice tailed off. "Miss Shockley, the man who visited your house, is Jethro Wilson I believe."

"Yes indeed." She saw no reason to explain any further.

"If you will permit me . . . please do not think me impertinent . . . I am aware from Mr. Mason that you have been most kind, most generous concerning him and his unfortunate children."

"Mr. Mason and I believe he is somewhat reformed."

"Somewhat?"

"I think myself, Mr. Porters," she considered, without disapproval she realised, of Jethro's free and heathen spirit, "that with a man like Jethro Wilson, complete reform is out of the question."

"Ah. Quite so." He looked relieved. "His visit to your house was unusual," he ventured.

"Most."

"Quite so," he repeated. "You would not be aware, of course," he was struggling to find his way into his normal, more comfortable advisory role, "that this Wilson has . . . something of a reputation."

"Really?"

"Yes indeed." He paused. "The two children, for instance, may not be his only ones."

"Ah yes." It would not surprise her in the least. She thought of his eyes, sometimes mocking.

"One must be careful in one's dealings, I think, with such a man." And he made her a little bow, as if he were a schoolmaster giving advice to a favourite but erring pupil.

"Why thank you Mr. Porters," she said, with a brilliant smile.

And she walked towards the High Street, half amused, and feeling the warm, damp April breeze on her cheek.

The farm began to prosper that summer – modestly, tentatively, and certainly not sufficient for the money she had put into it to bring any return; but like a small flower, it was at least showing some signs of life in the wilderness. Jethro seemed contented. Once or twice when she went there, she was not invited in, and she had thought she had caught a glimpse of a female face at an upstairs window; remembering what Porters had said she paid no special attention: she supposed that was his business.

But sometimes, as they spoke together and she saw his eyes resting quietly on her she wondered: did he feel anything for her?

There were many times when, as she left the city for the glorious ride over the high ground, she would have liked to bring him presents. Occasionally, if she were to spend a few hours there, she brought some delicacy that she could eat herself and then leave at the farm. To do more than this seemed improper, but the children were a different matter and often, when she knew he was due to visit them, she would bring some small present that he could take with him. All these he accepted, sometimes with a shrewd look, but with good grace.

"He really is like a cat," she thought to herself good-humouredly. "They never refuse cream, but they never need you either."

Sometimes, as she rode back to Sarum after one of her visits, she would allow her mind to dwell upon those faces she thought she had seen at the window. What were they like, Jethro's women, she wondered? Village girls, farmers' wives perhaps? How much, even now, did she really know about the folk on the plain? She had no wish to be one of them; yet sometimes she daydreamed about what it would be like, if she lived in another world, to be loved by him. Then she would kick her horse into a canter, feel the wind in her face and laugh at herself.

"That's one thing, Miss Shockley, you will never know."

They had their quarrel in July. It was soon after the big sheep fair where they had had their first modest success. Looking over the accounts she had concluded that they should be in a healthy position by next March, when Jethro's lease came up for renewal; but she had to admit to herself: "With only fifty acres, no matter what money we spend, we can never be more than marginally profitable. We need more land." She said nothing to Jethro, but some careful enquiries with land agents soon told her what she wanted, and one day as they stood beside the chalk wall she said:

"There's another fifty acres coming up for lease next spring. It's only half a mile off. I think we should take it on. That would give us a hundred acres and increase the profits."

She had expected him to be pleased. He was not.

"Too much."

"But it would be more economical."

"I like what I have."

"But think of the extra space."

"Space!" He looked at her with contempt he did not try to hide. "Space, you call it." He gestured to the hamlet behind them and the slowly opening valley beyond; then he pointed up to the high ground and its endless ridges. "I have space enough here."

She knew what he meant; she respected it; yet intellectually she was impatient.

"If you just look at the accounts . . ." she began.

"Accounts," he spat the word out. "I know them." Indeed, she knew that he understood the figures very well indeed. "Accounts, woman." The expression conveyed a universe of contempt, not for her, but for the very underpinnings of her life, that she had never thought of before. "I live," he said savagely, and turned on his heel to walk away.

She rode home very thoughtfully that day.

She saw him a week later in Salisbury. It was evening and he was drunk: not badly so, but enough. She came up with him just as the light was fading and he was climbing slowly into his cart. He saw her but took no notice.

"How uncommonly rude the ordinary people are," she thought furiously, as she stood in her crinoline and cloak and stared at him. "Why does one waste one's time on them?"

She saw him flick his whip and, as the little pony slowly started up, he took his old, broad-brimmed hat and crammed it on his head.

"I see you are drunk." She did not shout the words, but spoke them loud enough for him to hear. Two or three passers-by turned to stare.

It was just before he reached the corner that he turned. Very slowly, just as he had the first time they met, he raised his hat in a salute, his ironic eyes gazing straight into hers as he rolled away.

She waited two weeks before she went to the farm again. She was no longer angry: indeed, she could see his point of view. He had his own life – primitive no doubt, but one that gave him his own, strange freedom. It was foolish of her to try and tie him down, turn him into something he was not.

"He's just a wild animal," she thought, as she rode across the open. And yet, she admitted to herself, there was a challenge, even an excitement in trying to reform and tame a wild animal. Perhaps one day she might even persuade him to add another fifty acres.

Neither of them mentioned the other farm, or the incident in the town. They spoke quietly, almost distantly, as they always had before. But as she stood with him on top of the ridge that day, looking back at the little farm with its chalk wall and mulberry tree, she suddenly glanced into his eyes and it was as though, for an instant, there was a complicity between them: this was their farm, their wilderness, a place apart, whose ancient ways would never change.

"Perhaps," she suggested playfully as she mounted her horse to leave, "you'll allow me to make some improvements to the house."

He came briefly to the Michaelmas Fair that year having made a number of sales a week before. As Lizzie the housemaid was leaving her, she had spent the first day of the fair, which was also a hiring fair for servants, touring the booths in the covered market and speaking to applicants. It was only on the second day of the fair that she sat down to do the accounts for Jethro's farm, and examined the latest figures.

They were surprisingly good. He had presold the corn at exceptional prices; he had obtained figures for their lambs and some of the cattle that could only have been achieved, she knew, with incredible cunning. If the December sales went as well – several times, as she looked over the figures, she laughed out so loud that it brought a message from her uncle Stephen in the drawing-room below to ask if she could be quieter.

To have got so far, in their first year: she could hardly believe it. Her respect for Jethro increased further.

It was early afternoon when she finished, and so great was her sense of triumph that she decided to go and tell him the good news at once, even though he would not have expected to see her for another week. Within an hour, she was riding out, past Old Sarum, on the familiar route.

He was coming down the slope when she arrived. He had left the boy tending the sheep on the ridges above; the mid-afternoon sun was still warm.

"Come inside," she told him in triumph, "and see what you have done."

When she had taken him through the figures he seemed pleased.

" 'Tis better than I thought," he confessed.

"It's wonderful. Indeed," she said on impulse, "I think we should have a glass of beer. Could you procure such a thing?"

It came in large pewter mugs, wonderful to handle. There was nothing she knew of more cool and refreshing than Wiltshire beer. They drank slowly.

"There is enough to mend the thatch," she ventured.

He did not seem to mind this.

"It should be done," he agreed.

"Does it leak?"

"A little."

She sipped her beer reflectively. She was curious to see the rest of his house, but was not sure if she dared to ask. One was never taken out of the parlour of a farmer's house. Then she thought of a solution.

"The children: may I see where they sleep?"

He stood quietly. " 'Tis upstairs. You have to stoop."

He led her to the narrow wooden staircase that was set opposite the front door; she followed him up.

The children's room had two small windows, one each side of the house. It contained a wooden rocking-horse, a chest of drawers made of pine, and two low beds. She walked over and gently pulled the rocking-horse by its stiff mane.

"I made that, for the first," he said quietly. It was beautifully worked.

"I didn't know you were a carpenter."

"Have to, to farm."

"I suppose so."

She turned and went out onto the little landing. The room in which he slept lay opposite; the door was open.

"My room," he said half apologetically. "Not much furnished."

She stepped in.

There was a huge oak chest at the far side, opposite it a mahogany chest of drawers. By the door, on a stand, hung a long, embroidered smock. The bed was covered by a white cotton counterpane with a pattern of blue flowers upon it: left, she imagined from the days when his wife was alive. It was somewhat bare, but pleasant. She moved to the window and stared out at the little valley below.

Then she turned.

How strange it was. They came from worlds between which the boundary was not just wide, but completely, irrevocably impassable. Neither would ever normally expect to penetrate beyond one room in the other's house; he had come to her back door and, were she not such a regular caller, she would walk to his front.

And now he was watching her, from the other side of the room. Yes, he was tall and handsome, she thought. He did not belong to any class when he was up on the high ground; yet what was he here, in this cottage? At that moment, she hardly cared.

The late afternoon light was streaming in through the window; she felt it warm on her arm. There was a faint aroma of beer in the room. She found that pleasant. Her eyes travelled around it once more, noting with pleasure the clean white and blue counterpane.

He was perfectly still. His eyes were watching her, saying nothing, giving nothing away, understanding, she sensed, everything that she might think.

How warm it was. The beer seemed to take her half a pace towards the comfortable edge of sleep.

She looked up at him again. He smiled, slightly, but did not speak.

Silence. They shared the silence, as the sun shone into the little room. She noticed the grain in the glass making a little tracery pattern on the floor and on the edge of the counterpane. She felt her own heart-beat, slow and steady as the seconds passed and still, neither of them spoke. There seemed, that afternoon, to be a special magic in the place.

And the silence. It was the silence of the bare ridges above, where the breeze hissed, that bred the numberless, tiny bright flowers and all that half-invisible wildlife, timelessly; it was the silence of the little valley, of the winter bourne waiting patiently for the November rains. It filled the village, the chalk-walled garden with its mulberry tree behind the house, the room where they were now, facing each other, to her own amazement, in the most perfect understanding.

She watched him. She looked at him with wonder. Why was it that she felt so relaxed with him, as though she had known him all her life?

She remained, basking in the flow of light, by the window.

Then, as she knew it must be, it was Jethro who moved.

He did so very slowly, never letting his eyes leave her, like a cat, she smiled to herself. No, not like a cat though, for their eyes had met, and this room, and everything in it, was shared. Very softly, reaching out one long arm, he pushed the door of the room slowly shut.

There was no need. There was no one else in the house. The wooden latch fell with a faint click.

Her heart missed a beat. Now she was aware of it, beating faster.

She stayed by the window. It was perfectly safe. He was not barring the door. He was standing, very quietly, where he had stood before and his expression was as calm as if they were meeting in the middle of Salisbury close. He would not stop her, she knew: she had only to leave. She stood in the sunlight by the window and did not move.

Was, at last, the completely impossible to happen – so inconceivable that never once had she troubled, needed, allowed herself to think about an idea she would otherwise have had to strike down at its birth? Was it possible that at the age of thirty she could even think of such a thing, when in the close . . . ?

She stared at the blue and white counterpane and found herself half smiling, as though all her life, or rather perhaps in some former life, she had been here, known that counterpane before.

She looked up at him once more, still standing by the warm window.

He must move now. She could make no appeal.

Very slowly, as gently as she herself might have approached to feed a bird, he moved towards her.

As she turned, uncertain, looked up, and felt the warm sunlight on her back, it was as if all the rivers in the valleys had begun to run. She had not known such a thing before.

He never spoke. That was as it should be. All that happened was in the great silence of the afternoon, broken only by faint sounds that to her seemed as faint and distant as the tiny cries of the birds on the ridges above.

How was it he knew her so well?

"You are somewhat late, my dear," her Uncle Stephen complained. "Your rides are too long."

"Only this afternoon, uncle," she replied.

As she sat in the hip-bath that Lizzie had prepared for her, in the familiar surroundings of the house in the close, she knew one thing with absolute certainty.

The impossible had happened. It could never happen again.

She was sure she could trust Jethro: he understood as well as she. She did not believe the boy tending the sheep above had any idea; neither the old woman or the farmhand had been there.

For naturally, if any notion of what had taken place that afternoon reached Sarum close, then she would be finished for ever. Not a door in the place would be open to her. Her Uncle Stephen as head of the family would rightly ask her to leave the area. She could never marry and the name of Shockley would be permanently dishonoured.

She wanted none of those things. They filled her with a sense of horror. It was as though she had stepped out, over a vast chasm, as in a dream, and managed to get back. But from now on, she vowed, she would be circumspect.

For three weeks she did not go back to the farm.

When she did, he seemed to understand. He was exactly his normal self, touched his hat in front of the farmhand and his boy, and he could discern nothing in their glances that suggested they had any inkling of what had passed.

Alone with him for a moment she said simply: "It must be forgotten." And he nodded calmly and said nothing more.

But when later he took her foot as usual to lift her into the saddle, she found that she was trembling.

The rest of that year went by quietly. She went to the farm only every two weeks now, and spent less time there. The thatch was not mended. But at the cattle sales in December, Jethro did well again, and with luck the lambing season would bring a goodly addition to the new Hampshires as well.

During the month of January, when there were snows, she only visited the place once, and in February, another of Stephen Shockley's solemn flirtations with death took place and kept her in the city throughout the month.

Yet all that winter, alone in her room at night, she would lie awake and think of Jethro and admit to herself frankly: I ache for him. More than once she had decided on impulse to ride out to the farm and reached the door of the house – once she had even ridden to Old Sarum and the edge of the high ground – before deciding sadly to turn back.

In the first week of March, Stephen Shockley, was, reluctantly, nearly well again, and since the lease on Jethro's farm was due for renewal at the end of the month, she had decided to make a long visit there at the end of the second week.

Before this, however, there were other things to think of. For that spring, an important and joyful event took place in England, which necessitated a considerable celebration in the town: this was the wedding of Queen Victoria's eldest son, the Prince of Wales, which was to be celebrated with feasts and a great parade on March 10.

It was on the morning of that day that Jane went for one of her customary walks around the cathedral and the cloisters. She was interested that day to find the door of the chapter house open and one of the canons ushering Bishop Hamilton himself and a group of men she did not know out of the place. After saluting the bishop as he passed, she paused, looking curiously into the chapter house.

"Do you know who that was, Miss Shockley?" the canon asked.

"No."

"The great Sir Gilbert Scott, who is undertaking the restoration in the cathedral. He was seeing what Clutton did in the chapter house. Do you want to come in?"

It was some time since she had entered the fine octagonal building with its slender central column and huge windows. She admired it. Clutton had done his work so well: as she walked around and surveyed the wall carvings, she could not help smiling at the scenes so densely crammed with action between the severe arches: even their slightly foreshortened, clumsy figures had, she thought, an archaic grace, and gave her a hint of the former, medieval Sarum that she thought was almost gone. The figure of Adam and Eve in particular caught her eye. Adam's head had been beautifully restored, and his little body and Eve's remained just as they had first been carved. She smiled, and thought of Jethro.

She was walking from the north door of the cathedral towards the choristers' green when she met Daniel Mason. He bustled up to her.

"I have a commission to you, Miss Shockley," he announced. "The money owed you by Jethro Wilson. With, I believe, some interest." He smiled with satisfaction at this last proof of the drunkard's reform. "I told him five per cent was acceptable."

She stared at him, bemused. What was he talking about?

"Have you not heard? He is gone."

She felt the blood drain from her face.

"Where?"

"He has a cousin in the north, who died this last month and left him his farm." He laughed. "Not only the meek, but reformed drinkers inherit the earth, it seems."

She was still staring at him. It seemed to her, suddenly, that all the houses in the close had begun to perform a strange and solemn dance.

"But his farm?"

"At Winterbourne? He has given it up: the lease was due, as you may know. He has returned your loan – with interest, as I say – collected his children from Barford and gone. I understand the farm is up on the edge of the cheese country – small but quite respectable." He smiled. "He has the chance to do very well now."

She hardly heard him. Jethro had gone. With not a word to her.

"Where is the farm?"

"That I do not know."

"Thank you." She began to stride towards the house.

"Your money, Miss Shockley."

"Later."

She was leaving the close in fifteen minutes, having told the new maid not to expect her until evening. Dressed in her black riding habit, she strode quickly through the gate into the High Street.

He had gone. Why should he not? Had she not avoided him? She knew the sensible answer to these and many other questions. And she knew also that it felt like being stabbed with a knife.

She plunged into the busy street. She frowned impatiently at the thick crowds, pushing her way through them. And then, at the corner of New Street, she came face to face with the giant.

She had forgotten the parade. She had forgotten, too, that the old Salisbury giant of the ancient Tailors' Guild, with his companion Hob Nob, was to have one of his periodic outings on this occasion. The giant moved steadily forward, but at a snail's pace. The varnish on his huge face, in line with the upper windows of the old medieval houses, was black with age; he still wore a big tricorn hat from the previous century and smoked a long clay pipe. But she was in no mood for him now.

"Let me through."

But the crowd would not. They seemed to bunch together more tightly than ever as she now brusquely elbowed her way through. It was like a dream, she thought, where one was straining to go forward but making no progress. Then, with a scream of pleasure, the line of children in front of her suddenly parted as the hobby-horse, Hob Nob, rushed to attack them. She saw her chance and darted through the gap, only to find, a moment later, that Hob Nob was attacking her – good-naturedly, but persistently. Every step she tried to take, he rushed in front of her, ducking, weaving, and harrying her. The crowd roared its delight at this by-play.

It was then that she lost her temper.

"Out of my way you fool," she suddenly shouted, and raising her riding crop she struck, not in play, but hard, so that she almost broke the hobby's head with her first blow and caused the fellow inside to howl with pain and rage with her second.

There was a gasp of horror from the crowd. She did not care, and strode away through them while they parted before her with looks of rage.

"If I wasn't a lady they'd lynch me," she muttered, but went on her way regardless.

Twenty minutes later, an astonished groom had saddled her horse, and she was gone.

The farmhouse was deserted. It looked emptier than ever. More of the thatch had come apart and she noticed where recent frosts had cracked the lower parts of the chalk wall. Discouraged, she started back into Winterbourne.

"Well." The voice came from behind her. "Come looking for him have you?"

It was the old woman. She was standing by a tree in the lane, eyeing her coldly.

"Yes. Where is he?"

"Gone. As well for you."

She ignored this. "Tell me where he is."

"Where Jethro Wilson is? You're not the first woman to ask that." She laughed mockingly. Jane gave the old woman a severe look. How dare she be impertinent.

"The name of his new village please," she demanded curtly.

" 'Tis over the other side of the plain, near Edington." Reluctantly she explained how to find the place. But as Jane wheeled her horse round she called out for the first time with a hint of kindness in her voice: "Kind lady – you stay away from him." Jane rode on.

The journey there and back would take her all day; but she was already well across the high ground, and she knew tracks that would take her swiftly to the right road.

As she came up over the familiar ridge and glanced back, the memories of their time together flashed back with a terrible vividness. She must find him, even if it was only for a few minutes, to see his face again.

The storm blew up in early afternoon. She had covered many miles. Before her stretched an expanse of open heathland, about five miles across, she believed: and after this the country gave way to the richer vales where Jethro's new farm lay.

The storm was brooding and heavy; she licked her finger to determine the direction of the wind. By cutting across the heathland following a diagonal path she thought she could just head it off.

Five minutes later she was soaked, and could no longer make out the lie of the land. She pressed on.

The storm was so thick the sky over the heath did not seem to be grey, but brown. Twenty minutes later she was lost.

"And the trouble is," she thought, "I may be heading back into the plain. I can't tell."

She was.

It was nearly half an hour more before she passed an ancient dewpond on a bare expanse of turf. It was filling rapidly. Another five minutes went by.

Then, through the driving rain, directly ahead of her, she saw them – a group of painted wagons, standing in the middle of nowhere.

She gave a little gasp of fear, and reined her horse sharply.

Gypsies.

The wagons seemed to be tight shut, their owners presumably inside them; but even so, she automatically looked around her anxiously in case there were figures lurking there.

She wheeled about, and urged her horse away. One could never be sure with gypsies.

Five more minutes passed. On a grassy slope, her horse slipped and almost fell, and she wondered whether to dismount and lead him. She had no idea what course she was following.

The wagons. They were in front of her again. All she had done was to approach them from another angle.

Once again she turned.

It was ten minutes later that she came upon them again.

She could have cried. She started to turn away again, then gave up. She was too tired to go on.

Slowly and gingerly she made her way towards them.

They eyed her strangely after she had rapped upon the caravan door; but they took her in, and to her relief a few moments later a gypsy woman was helping her to undress and wrap herself in a blanket. Then she sat in the crowded little space with its strange, rich smells, gazing at the heavy embroidered cushion on the bed along one wall, and at the little family in front of her, whose four children, after eyeing her with suspicion, were now staring at her with shy amusement.

The man gave her a sideways look.

"They're waitin' to see you catch cold."

"I fear I shall. Wouldn't you?"

He shook his head.

"No."

And she remembered what she had always heard: gypsies did not catch cold.

What did she know about gypsies? That they were short and dark; that they stole sheep and hid them by burying the carcasses beneath their fires. Now she was sharing their caravan.

The storm did not abate until it was dusk, and when she looked out over the darkening, empty landscape and glanced back at her sodden clothes, she knew it was useless to go on. The nearest hamlet, they had told her was some six miles away.

"Would you give me shelter for the night?"

The woman nodded.

Later that evening she saw the woman carry out several black objects which looked to her like stones but which she soon discovered were lumps of old meat that had been soaked in salt and which now the woman was quietly boiling over the fire in a pot. She ate, glad that it was hot and salty, and that night, in one corner of a caravan, with her clothes already dried, her horse attended to, and the gypsy woman lying so near to her they almost touched, she slept a deep sleep.

She paid them and left at dawn.

She had never seen the spring dawn over the plain. Great bands of saffron yellow, orange and magenta light filled the eastern horizon. How sweet the wet turf smelled. Patches of furze, and here and there, delicate wild flowers were showing the first hint of colour and blossom in that cold March spring. The horizon was shimmering; the open sky had been washed clear and blue by yesterday's rains; the red sun was filling the distant sweeps of ground with an orange glow. It grew lighter. Nearby, a lark was rising.

As she looked towards the sunrise, over that beautiful, harsh emptiness, she knew that she wanted Jethro. It was so simple, this primitive, ancient world up on the high ground.

She wanted to be with him, as she had been before, on the edge of the great chalk nakedness of the plain.

As she came slowly down into the valley, where the farmhouses were stirring, the poignancy of this desire and longing grew: she ached again.

And yet, she knew it could not be.

She was not surprised by what she found.

The farm was a pleasant, white house with a tiled roof and an air of modest prosperity about it.

She sat on her horse and looked it over carefully. Jethro had been lucky. One of the children appeared, saw her, ducked back into the house, and a few moments later a dark-haired young woman appeared.

She moved with a slow, casual insolence, taking Jane in with curiosity. She stood in front of her.

"Lookin' for Jethro?"

"Yes."

The look in the girl's eyes was not hostile, not suspicious, just curious. But also it told her, beyond the shadow of a doubt that she knew. She knew. Not, probably, that she had been told. She knew by instinct. And strange to say, it did not even make her blush.

Why should it? She had just spent a night with the gypsies and seen the dawn rising, over the plain.

"I'm Jethro's woman now." She said it quite factually, flatly. There was a pause. "He went out early. Be back in an hour. You want to wait for him?"

Jane smiled. Why, now of all times, should she feel such calmness, a lifting of the spirit? She almost laughed. Should she wait for Jethro? There seemed no point. She had seen his farm, his woman.

"No," she smiled. And with a wry irony, "I was just passing."

She turned her horse.

As she rode slowly up the slope and reached the beginning of the high ground again, she thought she caught sight of him, a solitary figure moving along the edge of the ridge. She did not turn towards him; she nudged her horse forward and became, once again, a part of the plain.

The scandal of Jane Shockley's adventure took years to die down.

By nine o'clock the previous night, the houses in the close themselves seemed to be huddling together in a speculative murmur. She had gone out in the early morning in a hurry – the groom had been questioned. She had attacked Hob Nob in the street with her riding crop – the whole town was buzzing with that. And now she had completely vanished – no one knew where.

Only one man had an inkling. Which was why in this early morning a search party was sent far out onto the plain, since Mr. Mason had told them he thought she might have gone riding there. More than this Mr. Mason, with quiet wisdom, did not choose to say.

Stephen Shockley was beside himself: so much so that from the hours of nine until eleven at night, he had stood with his stick in the hall, motionless, refusing a chair, and receiving a constant stream of folk from the close as the drama continued.

But the greatest scandal of all had been when Miss Shockley, somewhat unkempt, arrived back at noon the next day and announced as though it were the smallest thing in the world, that she had been caught in a storm and spent the night with gypsies.

After that, it was universally agreed, poor Stephen Shockley had begun the long but irrevocable process of his last, bitter decline.

It was a month after this that Mr. Porters made the Christian, not to say heroic gesture of offering, if not to restore her reputation, at least to force the shocked scandal to subside, by offering, once again, to marry her.

To his astonishment, she refused. He retired to his villa shaking his head and concluding – what else could one do – that he had probably been lucky, since Miss Shockley was, it must be supposed, a little unbalanced.

1889

To a casual visitor entering the quiet city of Salisbury on that warm Sunday morning it might have seemed impossible that anything could disturb its sedate calm.

Yet in fact the place was in a state of seething controversy in which, as in centuries past, a powerful bishop was at war with half the town.

Had the visitor entered the even greater stillness of the close itself, it would certainly have seemed that the brisk woman of sixty with her long white dress, her parasol and her elegant, buttoned kid walking boots, who was stepping into a landau in the north walk, must be the very quintessence of respectability. As respectable, say, as the severe, grey-haired man who was politely handing her in.

And indeed, in a general sense, when Miss Shockley and old Mr. Porters set out together for Cranborne Chase that August morning, they still were.

It was very quiet. There was movement in the close, of course, but it was subdued, as if the place was patiently aware that the bell for matins was about to ring.

By the choristers' green, an ancient water cart, that sprayed the road surface to keep down the dust, was making its creaking rounds, pulled by a horse which, like the battered straw hat on its head, had seen better, but not quieter days.

From Mompesson House, Miss Barbara Townsend, swathed in shawls, made her way across to the south gate, carrying her sketch pad and water colours. And now, through the gate from the High Street an ox cart lumbered slowly in, containing no less a figure than one of the cathedral's residentiary canons and his family, come to spend his obligatory three months in the close and perform his cathedral duties.

Today, however, Jane Shockley was in a state of suppressed excitement. For tomorrow she was going into battle against the bishop. And the day after that . . . She smiled inwardly. The day after that, she would cause an even bigger stir.

There had been no scandal attached to her for thirty years. Since her Uncle Stephen's death she had lived alone in the house in the close. Ten years before, her brother Bernard had returned to England, but he had gone to live on the edge of the New Forest near Christchurch. She had become, in the manner of Victorian ladies of Salisbury close, rather formidable. The night with the gypsies had not, of course, been forgotten. But the younger folk in the close no longer believed it. She was as respectable a figure as one of the Hammick, Hussey, Townsend, Eyre or Jacob families who formed the principal aristocracy of the place.

Indeed, so successful had she become over the years at projecting a forthright and rather daunting image of herself that her opinion was much sought after and she generally got her own way.

The landau began to roll out of the close.

It was just as it entered the High Street that a stout, elderly man hurried forward and hailed the coachman. As the landau stopped, he came beside it and looked in. For a moment his face fell.

Mr. Porters and Mr. Mason stared at each other with distaste: they were on opposite sides in the bishop's great controversy. Then Mason addressed himself to Jane.

"You will not forget us tomorrow, Miss Shockley? You will come and speak?"

She looked at him evenly. The old relationship from the time when she had looked after Jethro had been replaced by something tougher.

"Yes, Mr. Mason, if I can count on you in turn."

He looked uncertain.

"If not, then of course . . ."

"You can count on me," he said hurriedly. Her presence, evidently, was important to him.

She smiled.

"Drive on, Baynes," she called to the coachman.

As the carriage left the city and began to rise up the slope to Harnham Hill, she felt quietly elated. She had secured Mason for her cause. He might not do much, but every person she could get was important. Now her eyes turned back to Porters. How upright he sat, his straight back hardly touching the carriage seat. He reminded her – it was a cruel thought – of a solemn moth that had been pinned to a board. She was sure she could win him over too, to add to her little collection.

For that was the real reason why she had agreed to his suggestion that they visit Cranborne Chase together that day. It was a chance to test her arguments out on him.

They went up Harnham Hill. Looking down on the city, she marvelled at how it was spreading. The new suburbs of which Mr. Porters was so proud stretched half way to Old Sarum now. The world was changing.

But Porters was not looking at the view as he pursed his lips. He was brooding about Mason and the bishop.

The great battle that was rocking Salisbury, and that had even caused questions to be raised in Parliament, concerned the city's schools. There were not enough of them and more must be provided. The question was, what sort of schools and who was to run them? The large community of non-conformists, led by men like Mason, wanted non-denominational schools run by the state boards that the great Education Act of 1870 had provided for. The bishop would not hear of it. He and the Conservatives were determined to provide an Anglican school instead. The bishop would not give way, he declared, as long as he had a penny in his pocket. Besides, Conservatives agreed, why should the ratepayers' money be used when funds had been offered to supply an Anglican school from private sources?

Bishop Wordsworth was a brilliant and powerful man, one of the remarkable family that had produced in the last century numerous formidable minds including the great poet. Many in Sarum knew of the family dinners when Wordsworth would decide beforehand whether to converse in English, Latin or classical Greek. And no one was surprised that so far the non-conformists of Salisbury had been defeated by the bishop at every turn.

To Jane Shockley it seemed unfair.

"I fear Mason's business is a mistake. I am sorry, Miss Shockley, that out of motives of kindness you encourage him." He was jealous of course. Even now, he still wanted to monopolise her. She smiled and ignored the rebuke as the landau slowly crested the hill.

Porters supported the bishop, not because his sympathies were strongly in either direction, but because he was sure that Wordsworth's case under the Education Act was correct.

"Which is not the point," Jane had tried to explain to him.

It was certainly useful for Mason to have her on his side: after all, she was a respected lady of the close, on good terms with the bishop. Her presence there would suggest that the non-conformists might yet find unexpected friends.

The whole conservative establishment of the city was against the non-conformists – Swayne, Hammick, the *Salisbury Journal*. Someone had even tried to persuade old Lord Forest to raise the question in the House of Lords. But since he had sold off his last half chequer of property in Salisbury some years before, he had refused to take any further interest in the place. But they were all wrong. It was daring of Mason to have chosen the White Hart Hotel for his meeting too, she thought, for it was a favourite Conservative meeting place. Yes, there should be fireworks at the meeting tomorrow, and she looked forward to it.

But today they were bound on a very different mission. They were going to Cranborne Chase.

The great sweep of land that lay south west of Sarum had always been a desolate place. Across it, nearly two thousand years before, the Romans had built the road that went to the heart of the territory of the proud Durotriges. A few small settlements had sprung up there in later Saxon times and medieval kings had hunted there. But generally speaking, the place had retained its character from prehistoric times, with a combination of forest, clearing, and bare wilderness dotted with sparse hamlets. It invited few visitors.

And yet, the Chase in recent years had become one of the most extraordinary places in England.

For in the middle of the Chase lay a great estate – some twenty-five thousand acres – recently and unexpectedly inherited by a talented man, known to history as General Pitt-Rivers.

So it came about that, in the 1880s, the people of Sarum were suddenly aware that in the empty region to the south west, something very strange was happening.

First, parts of the estate were thrown open to the public and pleasure grounds set out with picnic sites, swings and a bandstand. There were fireworks displays and hired singers; and the public was encouraged to use bicycles by the great man in order to reach these pleasures. But, in a sense, these activities were only a lure. For Pitt-Rivers had two serious missions in life. One was the pursuit of archaeology; the other was the education of the people. It was the museum he built at Cranborne Chase that was the key to it all.

Jane had never been there and Porters was eager to show her everything. He showed her where the general had found and excavated a farm of Roman times; he showed her an opened barrow, from a still earlier period. But his excitement rose to its most intense when he brought her to the latest excavation: for here, as though cut through in cross section by a knife, lay, in all its perfection, the carefully constructed *agger* of the great Roman road to the south west.

"He's found a staging post," Porters explained, pointing to the area most recently laid bare. "He's found drains, coins . . . a treasure trove." His face was shining as he remembered his own more modest finds in the old water channels years before. Those had all been placed in the little museum in St Ann Street now, but the Salisbury museum was small compared to the general's.

He led her round it as proudly as if it were his own. Painting, pottery, crafts, agricultural implements: it was a huge collection already. But it was not only the size of it that impressed Porters.

"See the way he has arranged it, Miss Shockley," he explained. "All arranged by type so that you can see, over time, the *evolution* of each artifact. That is what Pitt-Rivers wants to tell the people: that Darwin was right and that species, and cultures too *evolve*. He wants to educate them so that they can improve themselves."

She smiled to see him so enthusiastic.

"You believe society can improve then, Mr. Porters?"

"I believe it is evolving all the time."

She nodded. It was exactly what she wanted him to say.

For it was only as they made their way back from the wonders of Cranborne Chase that she broached the subject in her mind.

"You believe in human progress?"

"Certainly."

"And that each generation men raise themselves a little higher, develop their gifts further?"

"I do. That is progress."

"Does this apply to women as well as men?"

"It does."

"Then when will society evolve sufficiently to give women the same rights and freedoms as men?"

He looked worried. Why was it, she wondered, that Porters was so full of ideas for progress, so happy to follow a visionary like Pitt-Rivers, and yet so cautious the moment he was faced with any idea that might challenge authority?

And Porters in turn thought: is she, once again, going to become wild and unpredictable and do herself harm? He tried to soothe her.

"I am in favour of some reform, yes. The property act for married women . . ."

"That allowed a married woman to keep what was hers instead of being robbed by her husband? What of it?"

"It is a start."

"The campaign for women's equal suffrage began over twenty years ago," she reminded him. "Yet woman have nothing. No woman has a vote. Yet ever since the Great Reform Act, the franchise for men has been extended. Why is democracy only for the male? Is this Darwin's evolution?"

The arguments were falling out as she had planned. Though he did not know it, Porters was her guinea pig. She awaited his response.

"These matters have been discussed in Parliament and refused."

"Not quite. The bills passed their second readings. They should have been made law. But the cabinet always holds them up."

"Yet in some areas in the north, the suffrage movement is declining among women," he countered.

"Only because they are discouraged by the men who do nothing."

She looked at him accusingly.

"You should take care, Miss Shockley, that you do not speak too much of this in Sarum. Dr. Pankhurst who leads the movement is a man not liked in all quarters. He is a socialist and a republican you know." For Mrs. Pankhurst was second fiddle to her husband as yet.

"Florence Nightingale supported the movement, and she is neither," Jane snapped. To her this was the final word, but to her fury he seemed unimpressed.

"I am starting a suffrage society in Sarum in two days," she proudly told him. "And if, as you say, you believe in progress, you will support me."

He shook his head.

"I cannot."

She glared at him. She had been so sure that she would win the argument.

"Then, Mr. Porters, I think you had better not call at the house again."

The meeting at the White Hart Hotel was boisterous. There were people from both sides present, including the leader of the non-conformists Mr. Pye-Smith.

But the speech of the evening, which brought the hall to a hush, came from Miss Shockley.

She spoke very simply, and only about what was in her own experience.

"It is true that at an Anglican school, we will allow those of other churches to absent themselves when Anglican matters are discussed. Yet, as one who has taught, I can tell you, these children in practice are left outside in cold corridors and sometimes bullied. More often, if the truth is told, the wishes of parents are ignored and the children are given Anglican religious instruction anyway.'

And when the objection was made that the bishop himself had offered to provide a new higher grade school to give extra places, it was she who quietly reminded them:

"Fees of nine pence a week are proposed. But many non-conformist poor, in my experience cannot afford that. The bishop," she concluded, "wants the Anglican church to control Sarum. It did so in the middle ages, but it need not do so now."

That brought thunderous applause.

It was flushed with such a sense of triumph therefore that, at the end of the evening, she reminded Mason that he had promised to announce her own meeting, the following night. It was a perfect opportunity since many in the hall were women that evening.

He blushed.

"Not now I think, Miss Shockley."

"Mr. Mason, you promised not only to announce me but to support me."

He looked embarrassed.

"With so many people . . . all sorts," he began.

Could this be the brisk temperance reformer she had known in years gone by?

"Mr. Mason," she reminded him coldly, "you promised."

"At a more intimate meeting . . ." he pleaded.

The people were already filing out of the room.

She stood up.

"There will be a meeting of the Women's Suffrage Society, in this same hotel, tomorrow night at seven," she cried.

But no one was taking any notice.

On Tuesday evening, at six o'clock, the parlour maid came in to announce that there was a new moon.

Half an hour later Jane Shockley walked through the quiet close.

Old Mr. Sturges was conveying a young lady to a party in his ancient bath chair – a magnificent wooden contraption with a leather hood whose purpose was, in theory, to ensure that young ladies' satin slippers did not get dirty by walking in the street, but which in practice was more of a solemn ritual within the close. In the High Street, an old woman carrier had gone to sleep beside her cart.

Although she had spent the day pinning up notices of her meeting and informing everyone she knew, she was not hopeful any more.

She waited at the White Hart for an hour. Nobody came.

Except a contrite Mr. Porters who claimed that upon reflection, her arguments of two days before had finally convinced him.

She knew it was not true.

She let him walk her home.

The Henge II

1915: September 21

DARK DAYS. IN far-away Gallipoli, the advance of the forces of the British Empire had ground to a halt. In France, a new offensive was about to begin. On the fifth of the month, in hard pressed Russia, the czar himself had assumed the supreme command of the armed forces.

Dark days. As it was now clear that the Balkan campaign had failed, all chances of a short end to the most terrible conflict that the world had yet known seemed to have receded over a horizon riven by lowering flashes and packed, to who knew what depth, with black thunderclouds.

In the New Theatre, Salisbury, the little crowd was half expectant, half amused. The auctioneer paused, feeling that, after all, the moment should be invested with a little drama, yet half afraid that murmurs of derision might intervene instead and adversely affect the sale.

He cleared his throat.

"Lot 15. Stonehenge."

The heir to the local Antrobus estate had already been killed in action. Now his father, Sir Edmund Antrobus, had died. The estate – a huge tract of Salisbury Plain – was for sale; and it included Stonehenge.

The old monument had nearly been sold before. A decade earlier, the American John Jacob Astor had tried to buy it from Sir Edmund for the British Museum. The staggering price of £25,000 had even been mentioned. But Sir Edmund had feared it would fall under control of a government department and after tiresome negotiations, the matter had been dropped.

Others, too, had shown an interest in the place. An organisation called The Church of Universal Bond had suggested that ownership be transferred to a public company of Druids and Antiquarians. By act of Parliament two years earlier, Stonehenge was also protected against demolition and export.

The bidding was not excited. The price rose quietly to £6,000, then seemed to stop.

It was then that a local gentleman raised his hand.

He did so, he confessed afterwards, on impulse.

Mr. Cecil H. E. Chubb, of Bemerton Lodge, Salisbury had begun his adult life with a brilliant Cambridge degree in science and law. But he had never practised his profession. Instead, he had taken control of the Fisherton House Asylum in Salisbury, which had been left to his wife by her adoptive father. He had also recently bought an estate.

It seemed to him a good idea that a local man should own the place.
He bought it for £6,600.
In 1918 he gave it to the nation.
Lloyd George made him a baronet the same year.

The Encampment

1944: May

SOON THE MIGHTY offensive of D-Day would begin. No one of course, not even the Supreme Commander could be certain of the date. But, God willing, very soon. The time for the European war's last act was drawing near.

In the month of May, 1944, had a German spotter plane been granted free access to the southern coast of England for an hour or two, it might well have directed its flight to a point a few miles west of the Isle of Wight, to the low hill and sheltered harbour at Christchurch and thence followed the little river Avon up its lazy course to the north.

Had it done so, its careful observers might have picked out several things to interest them.

They might firstly have noticed numerous small air bases. They might have made out Hurn, at Christchurch, Ibsley, just north of the small town of Ringwood, some ten miles inland, Stoney Cross, on their right hand side, in the New Forest; or others, carefully camouflaged, where a close inspection would have revealed numbers of P-38 Lightnings and P-47 Thunderbolts to astonish them and send them scuttling back across the Channel with the news.

But the spotter plane would probably first have continued on its way north, over Fordingbridge, Downton, and up the Avon to that great junction at the foot of Salisbury Plain, where like the outstretched fingers of a man's hand, five rivers met.

It would have been an obvious place to aim at: for it was a point on the map well known to anyone in the Luftwaffe. It was, after all, a perfect natural signpost. The pattern of the five rivers, even seen by starlight from thousands of feet above, was completely unmistakable. It was for Sarum that the bombers had usually made on the huge and devastating runs when, coming in from the west and taking their precise directions from the rivers as from a compass, they branched off to devastate the port of Bristol, or the unlucky midland towns of Birmingham and Coventry.

Indeed, though the citizens of Salisbury did not know it, the city had almost been a target too: for when the plans for the series of so-called Baedicker raids on English cathedrals had been drawn up, the cathedral at Salisbury, after Coventry and Canterbury, had been third on the list. The raids had been called off after only Coventry Cathedral had been destroyed, and the people of Sarum remained unaware of their lucky escape.

There were other reasons to go to Sarum. The high ground of Salisbury

Plain, for some forty years, had been a military training ground. There were several army stations there – no doubt there would have been something to see. A sharp-eyed scout might have realised that many of the country roads round the old cathedral city had been slightly widened and their ditches filled in; that around Old Sarum hill the roads were marked out in white – both suggesting the movement of tanks.

Having inspected Sarum, the plane might have turned north-east and followed the valley of the river Bourne in which direction it would have noticed other airfields.

But only if it had been able to come down, almost to touch the ground, would the plane have been able to see anything of the real secret of the area.

For as the great day approached, there was hardly a larger concentration of troops and armaments anywhere in Britain than there was at Sarum.

All over the plains, from Old Sarum north, trucks, tanks, weapons carriers, personnel carriers, jeeps, more tanks, and yet more tanks lay camouflaged, parked row upon row along the hillsides, by the edges of the trees, along the huge uncut hedgerows. English, Australian, Canadian, American troops, swarmed around the sleepy old city. In Lord Pembroke's great house at Wilton resided the headquarters of Southern Command.

Sarum, for the first time in its history, had become one of the greatest encampments in Europe.

"The place is so loaded with armaments," it was generally agreed, "it's a wonder it doesn't sink."

Lieutenant Adam Shockley, pilot, Squadron 492, of the 48th Fighter Group, had taken the bus from Ibsley to Salisbury in the middle of the morning.

It was good to have a day's rest. The squadron, with the two others at Ibsley, had been making almost daily sweeps over Northern France in their P-47s, attacking radar stations, airfields and bridges after having received intensive bomber training on their arrival at the end of March. The raids were continuing intensely. He knew the invasion could not be very far away.

Of the city of Salisbury with its grey-spired cathedral, its market place and curious round earthwork he knew nothing at all, except what he had seen from the air.

The bus moved slowly. He wished he had managed to hitch a ride in a car. It was hard to believe that this road, with just room for two cars to pass, classified as a major highway. The little town of Fordingbridge, a village really, was picturesque beside the river. They passed through Downton, and a few miles further, came to a dip. On the right he saw the wall of what he supposed must be a great estate. He grinned. He was used to seeing stone walls round some of the old estates near his home in Philadelphia, "But these English walls are really built to keep you out," he thought. On the right, a signpost to the village of Britford.

Then he saw the spire. Almost dead ahead, and a minute later he was gazing across the broad valley floor to the ancient city.

It was a peaceful-looking place. He wondered what he would find there. Nothing much, probably.

Brigadier Archibald Forest-Wilson leant back in the rear seat of the little Morris that was serving as his staff car that morning and half closing his eyes, contemplated the back of the neck of the pretty young woman who was driving him. There was so much activity on the plain that day and such pressure on vehicles that the smartly dressed young A.T.S. volunteer had reverted to a practice from the start of the war – the car was her own.

The pool of A.T.S. drivers was fairly large, but she had often driven him before, between the various camps around Salisbury Plain and he had noticed her fair hair and striking blue eyes with pleasure.

They had come across the chalk ridges from the Gunners' camp at Larkhill, and now they were dropping down the long, tunnel-like avenue to Wilton. He smiled at the prospect ahead of him.

The officers' club at Wilton was a very special place. No matter what the rationing might be, it was mysteriously always possible to get a whisky and a steak there. "And nobody but a bloody fool would ever ask how that fellow does it," he thought fondly of the local man who ran this excellent establishment.

D-Day would be coming soon. He would miss it, of course, since he had been given a staff job. He was not sure if he were sorry or not. His career had been skilfully conducted: he had usually been able to see which way the wind was blowing. A spell in the Grenadiers, several shrewdly timed transfers including a year in military intelligence in the War Office. He had always been good with high ranking officers' wives: too good some said. Too good, it was always understood, for his own well-born, rather fluffy little wife, married young, who had left him and then died. And now, would he make it to general? Probably not. Perhaps, if he stayed on after the war; but he was not sure he wanted to. He had several more interesting irons in the fire in the business world that he had been keeping warm when there was time; he might stand for Parliament as well. Why not? He could afford it. Good war record. He was sound, as they said.

Archibald Forest-Wilson was a very fortunate man, but dissatisfied. Tall, dark, with a long, saturnine face, a short moustache he confined to the centre portion of his upper lip, heavy-lidded black eyes under black eyebrows that turned upwards at the corners, his face was like a falcon's. With men he was hard; with women, extraordinarily gentle – a combination which fascinated the latter in particular. He was an excellent shot. But his greatest love was fishing. He was skilful with the dry fly; it was a joy to watch him cast, but it was with the wet fly that he really knew happiness, trailing it, subtly, seductively under the surface, tempting the fish on to the hook, feeling their play and reading their mind from the tug and pressure beneath the surface of the water. There was something very deep, even primitive in Forest-Wilson that loved, above all, this manner of fishing.

Thoughtfully he watched the golden curls on the back of his pretty driver's neck and noticed how she held her head.

Damn his father, though, he reflected. True, he had very sensibly married the second daughter, and co-heir of the last Lord Forest. The Wilsons had had to give up the house near Christchurch in the last century, when their fortunes had dipped but this marriage had made his father a rich man and he had bought an estate near Winchester. But then, when he had the chance to buy a title from Lloyd George, he had quibbled about the price. The fool, his son now thought, as he bumped into Wilton. He could probably have taken the old Forest title; as it was, there was just the estate, no more, and that was not enough. For Archibald Forest-Wilson was an ambitious man. The war would be over soon: it was time he married again, got an heir. Perhaps, even – why not? – that title.

Once again he found himself gazing at his driver: a nice girl – one of us. He had spoken to her several times. How old was she? Twenty-five maybe, twenty-six? He was forty-three. A bit old. But then, age gave him some advantages too.

The little car bumped past the gate of Wilton House and drew up by Kingsbury. He got out lazily.

"You're going off for the day now I think, aren't you, Patricia?"

"Yes, sir."

He smiled pleasantly.

"I'm sorry I can't offer you lunch, but the general's expecting me. Perhaps you'd be free some other day – assuming nothing more dramatic intervenes."

"That sounds very nice."

Her smile was proper. So it should be to a brigadier. But he had easily taken in every detail of her: good legs, good figure, nice breasts, neither large nor small, stunning eyes. The short golden hair and the buttoned A.T.S. uniform certainly suited her very well. Hadn't he asked her if she hunted once? Yes he had. She had said yes.

Hunting bored him personally, but he usually liked women who did.

"Well," he said easily, tucking his swagger stick under his arm, "I must be getting along."

Patricia Shockley. A nice girl: and interesting too, perhaps.

At half past one Patricia Shockley sat opposite the large, burly form of John Mason in the narrow little restaurant near the entrance to the close called the House of Steps. It was just that: a medieval house, with heavy beams, and an extraordinary number of small steps and staircases between its many rooms and landings. It was also one of the best places to eat lunch.

But Patricia Shockley was not enjoying it.

What could she say?

"Tell me, is it because I'm not in uniform?"

There were little beads of sweat on the front of his head, where the hair was rapidly thinning. Would he sweat so much if he did not insist on wearing, even at the start of summer, that heavy brown suit of herringbone tweed and those heavy brown shoes, always polished until you could see your face in them, and which required those thick brown socks? Did he wear a woollen vest and underpants too? She imagined he did.

He was thirty-five. He might have been fifty. More. Sometimes she could almost scream.

Now. Should she tell him it was because he was not in uniform; should she tell him the truth; should she think of some other excuse? If in doubt, she decided, the truth.

"John, I'm just not in love with you. I'm sorry."

"I thought perhaps . . ."

"Because I let you kiss me? No."

"I see. That wasn't my fault."

Of course not. Nothing was ever John Mason's fault. It was not his fault that his weak lung had prevented him getting into the army, though it preyed on his mind and made him feel guilty every day. Thank God women aren't handing out white feathers in this war, she thought. As it was, John Mason had done more for the war effort than ten other men. He had done just enough of his work as a solicitor to pay his bills. All the rest of his time was devoted to war service. In the early days, he had been one of the few to take the threat of gas seriously and help organise some first aid volunteers; the volunteer fire brigade; the A.R.P. wardens; Mrs. Roper's hospital car service for ferrying patients about; and the system of inviting officers and G.I.s into Salisbury houses for a meal: there was almost nothing he had not had a hand in. He was an excellent organiser.

And no, it was not his fault she had felt sorry for him, let him take her out several times and, one evening kissed him and let him return her kiss. She had thought it would do him good.

Would she have gone further – if he had not immediately become so serious and asked her to marry him? No. She did not think so.

"Perhaps later you may . . ."

"No." She must be absolutely firm. "Please forget me."

He looked at her hopelessly.

"I'll try."

She refused to feel guilty any more. Enough was enough.

It was absurd of him, John Mason thought dismally, to suppose this lovely, golden-haired girl in her trim uniform could possibly be interested in him. Yet behind her outgoing ways, he was sure he could see something vulnerable, childlike, that needed protecting. He would have protected her.

The coffee came. Thank heaven, she thought, that whatever the rationing, coffee was always in plentiful supply.

She was going to say: 'We'll have lunch next week." Then she thought better of it. "I think we'd better not meet for a little while, John."

"It's all right," he said.

"No it isn't." She got up. "I must go."

[877]

She fled.

John Mason sat and considered. She had said: "It isn't." Did that mean she was upset? Clearly she was. And if she was upset, then she must at least feel something for him. She cared. He sipped his coffee moodily: he would not entirely give up hope.

The people of Sarum had done their best to make the huge influx of Americans welcome. But often they were puzzled. Two years of familiarity had ironed out many difficulties for both sides now, but misunderstandings remained.

The growing mutual respect with regard to the fighting itself had been a help. In 1942, the arriving Americans had often been contemptuous of their allies who had failed to win the war. At the same time, the first batch to reach Sarum in the summer of 1942 had come straight from training in Florida and arrived to face the English summer dressed in cotton and without a greatcoat between them. Even by English standards, that summer had been exceptionally cold and wet. The new arrivals who had made their scorn rather plain now retired in droves to hospital with 'flu and even pneumonia. It had not been a good beginning.

The Africa campaign had changed all that. The contempt had gone; so had the arrogance. "Our boys were like a bunch of bananas," a cheerful G.I. informed Patricia: "some green, some yellow, some plain rotten." They had a new hero, too, that they shared with their allies: the British General Alexander.

The citizens of Salisbury also learned to know them better. For the American army, they soon concluded, organised itself in a somewhat different way; unlike the English, whose smaller numbers usually forced them to try, at least, to convert every soldier into a fighting man, simple observation soon taught the people of Sarum that in the U.S. Army there were two very distinct categories: those groups who had been selected as only good enough for support duties – clerks, paymasters and the like, and the combat troops, who, though they seemed to lean up against any free-standing object in a casual way that was surprising, had a tough, resilient quality about them that had to be admired. Soon, anyone in Sarum could tell one group from the other at a glance.

"Our best men seem like coiled springs," Patricia had once remarked to Forest-Wilson; "theirs are like rubber."

"And just as indestructible," he assured her.

Despite their respect for the fighting men, however, it was less easy for the townspeople to accept it when they heard their modest terraced houses referred to as slums; and although there was some fraternisation, it was soon clear to the girls of the town, the English nurses and the women in the services stationed nearby, that the visitors found them and their rationed clothes dowdy. When the first American nurse arrived at the hospital with the unheard-of luxury of nylon stockings, there was an outcry.

Of course, there was the problem of money. The further down the scale in rank one went, the more striking the difference. For instance, the generals or senior officers that Patricia drove around the plain were about as well off as their American counterparts. A colonel was a little poorer, but not so much as to be noticed. A major however, made only two-thirds of his American colleague, a captain, half; an American second lieutenant was two and a half times as well off as his English equivalent. But below this, in the bulk of the enlisted men, the difference was truly extraordinary. The private in the U.S. Army made, in English currency, the princely sum of three pounds, eight shillings and ninepence a week. This was almost five times the pay of an English private.

Faced with this spending power, the people of Sarum were simply flabbergasted. It was for most of them the first time that they had realised that their island, at the heart of the mighty British Empire, was poor.

The lingering misunderstanding between the locals and their visitors however, concerned two things: attitude, and food.

The problem lay partly with the G.I.s who, being homesick, endlessly told the Sarum folk how much better life was back home. Partly the fault also lay with the U.S. authorities who, to counteract this homesickness, sent their men a vast selection of foodstuffs utterly unobtainable to their hosts, and who, it seemed, had also forbidden their men to drink British milk on the grounds that it was dangerous. And partly, the everyday habit of America was to blame: for the people of Sarum had never seen waste like this before. Food was left on the side of plates, paper, string cheerfully discarded, things were used once, and thrown away, on the simple principle, completely incomprehensible to the islanders, that there would always be more.

There was blame to be apportioned on the other side too, and this was even simpler: the people of Sarum thought their country was the best. Were they not still the British Empire?

But on one thing both visitors – to whom it was a novelty – and townspeople came to a surprising and total agreement; this was the benefit of British fish and chips, eaten off British newspaper. The G.I.s' consumption of this impressed even the locals.

The most important rendezvous and general information post for the G.I.s in Sarum was the Red Cross Club in the High Street. Besides the usual canteen and recreation rooms a most important service was provided by volunteers at the information desk: the flower service. Nowhere else in Sarum was it possible for an American G.I. or officer to arrange for flowers to be sent home.

It was here that Patricia Shockley went immediately after leaving John Mason. She felt in need of reassurance, and her friend Elizabeth, a sensible young married woman, who was doing a stint at the desk that afternoon, always provided sage counsel.

"I did right, didn't I?"

"Absolutely. You couldn't do anything else."

"Thank God for that. Will he leave me alone now?"

"I shouldn't think so. He looks persistent."

"Damn."

The young American Air Force officer who now entered made his way towards them. He had a light, athletic walk: his blue eyes seemed to take everything in.

"I must be off," Patricia said. But she lingered for a moment.

"This is flowers?" he enquired of Elizabeth.

"It is. To America, I assume?"

"Right. Philadelphia."

"You will wish to send red roses, of course, with long stems?"

"That's right. How did you know?"

Elizabeth groaned pleasantly.

"Because no American we have yet encountered at this stall has ever sent anything else. Except one, who sent his mother a poinsettia for Christmas, but I expect he came to a bad end. We couldn't I suppose interest you in carnations, tulips, gladioli . . . ?"

"Roses. Red," he laughed.

"For your fiancée?"

"No such person. My mother. It's her birthday."

"Red roses, to Philadelphia, then." Elizabeth leaned forward with mock confidentiality. "Do tell us though, Lieutenant, why is it always red roses with American servicemen?"

"Because it's what they expect us to send."

"Ah." She nodded. "You wouldn't like to surprise them?"

"No."

"And the name?"

"Shockley. Adam. For Mrs Charles Shockley."

It did not take them long to find out all about him, including the fact that he had never been to Salisbury before.

Yes, his family had come from England once, but he did not know from where. Yes, the name Adam was common in his family. Patricia tried to remember. There had been an Adam Shockley, she was sure on the family tree that her father lovingly preserved in his study. He had gone to Pennsylvania, she thought.

"There's a chance we may be related," she told him. "There aren't that many Shockleys about, you know."

"And what is there to do in Salisbury now that I'm here?" he asked.

"If you've a couple of hours I'll show you round," she offered.

"Are you sure . . ."

"I'd be happy to. I'm off duty," she replied. Besides, it would be a relief to put John Mason out of her mind.

She showed him the cathedral and the close, with its sedate old houses and the shady plane trees round the choristers' green. She showed him the river with its long green river weeds and its swans. She took him past the poultry cross and into the market place. He was astonished by the age of everything he saw.

"You really mean that little gabled house," he had pointed to a little timber house with an overhanging front in New Street, "has been there just like that for six and a half centuries?"

"Yes. Funny isn't it?" She grinned. "And you realise, don't you, that this is only the new town? The old town's up there." And she waved in the direction of Old Sarum.

"It's incredible," he admitted.

They wandered through the market. It was a market day, but there were not many stalls and the place seemed rather bare. In particular he was puzzled by the odd assortment of crockery that seemed to be on sale on a number of stalls.

"Don't they have any that matches?" he asked, "any sets?"

"Not nowadays," she answered. "This is wartime. People are glad to pick up any old cup and saucer they can."

He nodded. It was foolish of him to have forgotten the terrible shortages over here.

"What do you miss most?"

"Nylon stockings," she told him at once.

They had tea at the Bay Tree, where they had one more attempt at establishing their family connection. It did not get far, but they cheerfully swapped information about their respective families. His father was a successful lawyer, she learned, living in that large, comfortable and endless suburb, the Philadelphia Main Line. She told him something of her own family: about their rambling house with its two paddocks in the New Forest, a few miles from Christchurch; her father, a retired colonel, "Who organises anything that moves within a five mile radius," she explained; her brother in the navy.

"When this is all over, you should come and see us, Cousin Adam," she laughed.

How delightful she was. She seemed to find everything so amusing. He wondered how one asked for a date in this ancient city and concluded there was only one way to find out. He asked.

"That sounds very nice. When did you have in mind?"

"I'm flying tonight. But tomorrow I'm not."

"Tomorrow then. But you must let me pick the restaurant. I know the territory."

When he asked himself, towards the end of that extraordinary and frantic period before June 1944, exactly when he had known – known with absolute certainty that they were going to have an affair – he concluded that it was at the precise moment when she had opened the door of that dark, Victorian house she shared with a dozen other A.T.S. drivers on Milford Hill.

He had been thinking about her – except for the harrowing moments just before he had released two 1,000-pound bombs at a target spitting a fury of fire at him the previous night – he had been thinking of her almost continuously. Her golden hair and her laughing eyes were before him, like a lighted beacon that makes a great halo in the cloud, through that night all the way home.

It was a time of high excitement: for those who flew the P-47s from the bases at Ibsley and Truxton, or the P-38s from Stony Cross in the New Forest. They were either relaxing and bored at the base, or caught up in the heady game of sweeping over northern France, often face to face with death, as they pounded the enemy in preparation for Operation Overlord.

Was it really possible that during this existence, when life was being lived at the edge, Patricia Shockley was also going to happen?

She would know what it must mean. A few, snatched moments – passion caught and taken when you can, in the knowledge that each time may be the last.

All day he had wondered about her, and asked himself: was she, also, thinking of him? He had made arrangements in the hope that she was.

It was when she opened the door, and gave him a shy smile, that he knew in a flash that she had been.

"I brought you a present," he said.

It was two pairs of nylon stockings.

"Oh, you lovely man."

They did not dine in the city, but just outside, across the meadows in the place used by the cognoscenti of the area: the Old Mill at Harnham.

"It really is a mill," he said delightedly, as they mounted the rickety oak staircase with its wide treads to the upper room. It had window seats, dormer windows, and a grand piano.

"It was a flour mill – and probably a fulling mill before that," she told him. And she explained the significance of the term. "You'd never think this sleepy old place had once been one of the foremost cloth towns in England, would you?"

"What else?" he grinned.

"Constable painted some of his best known pictures, of the cathedral, from here."

"It'll do then." He smiled. "Every damn thing around here has some piece of history attached to it."

"It does," she agreed.

It was an excellent dinner – the best that could be had in Sarum. He ordered a very passable bottle of red wine. And then, when it was over and they were both bathed in a warm glow, they walked together across the moonlit water meadows with the silent grey shape of the cathedral rising in front of them. At the little wooden bridge over the river, she let him kiss her.

After some time she asked:

"What are your plans now?"

He smiled.

"Funny you should ask. I'm staying over until the morning at the White Hart."

"Really?"

"Yes. I booked the best room they had, just in case my wife turned up."

"I see. Her name, of course, would be Shockley."

"I guess it would."

She put her arm through his.

"Lead me there, Shockley."

Half an hour later, looking up at the lovely figure who had suddenly rolled over and was now triumphantly astride him, Adam remarked in some surprise:

"You seem to be taking control of this situation here, Shockley."

"Not at all,' she murmured happily. "I'm just a little hungry."

It was nine o'clock when John Mason called at the house on Milford Hill to see her.

The girl who had answered the door went in to look for her. He heard voices inside, then one calling from her room:

"She went out with an American airman. Nearly two hours ago."

He felt a sensation in the pit of his stomach.

"She seems to be out," the girl said tactfully.

He turned and walked away. The night was warm. He wondered if she would be out late. Perhaps if she came back soon, he could speak to her.

John Mason paused at the bottom of the hill and waited.

At ten o'clock he decided to go: except that since she was bound to return soon, it seemed foolish not to wait a few minutes more. At ten thirty, a drunken G.I. came by. He wondered whether to do anything about him; the drunken man was waiting near the A.T.S. house. After a few minutes Mason walked back up the hill and told him to leave.

"Why?"

"I'm a lawyer and if you don't I'll call the Snowballs."

The man cursed him, but the white-hatted military police that the locals now called Snowballs could be rough, and the English lawyer was bigger than him. He went away. John Mason felt better.

At midnight, he knew in his heart that he was wasting his time.

A little after one in the morning, he walked sadly home.

The affair of Adam Shockley and Patricia Shockley was conducted in a series of meetings, usually in the afternoon, in the month of May.

They were never easy to arrange. Once they met at Fordingbridge; another time at Downton; for both lay between his base and Salisbury. But one beautiful afternoon, he rode into Salisbury on the bus and she took him in the car up to Old Sarum and the high ground.

"I'm going to show you the rest of Sarum," she told him.

"But what if we want to . . . ?"

"Don't worry," she cut in. "We'll find somewhere." And after they had viewed the ruins of Old Sarum and gazed out over the plain, with its huge cargo of camouflaged vehicles, she drove him up the little Avon valley and parked at Avonsford. "Come on," she cried, "we're going to have a picnic." While he carried the small basket she had provided and she brought a rug, she led him up a track to the top of the ridge. "There," she said in triumph as the wonderful view opened up before them. "I discovered this place last autumn; isn't it divine?"

There was a cluster of trees at the top of a little mound nearby.

"What's that?" he asked. And since she did not know, they made their way across a fallow field towards it, only to be surprised as a huge host of blue butterflies rose like a cloud all around them.

At the top they found a circle of trees, mostly yews, with a glade of grass in the centre.

"It's a strange place," he remarked.

"It's also completely deserted," she said. The grass was warm and dry, and bathed in the afternoon sunlight.

With a chuckling laugh, she spread the rug and lay down upon it, loosening her jacket as she did so.

"Picnic?" she asked.

Adam Shockley had never known greater happiness than in these brief interludes with Patricia. It was not long before his fellow pilots realised his good fortune and began to tease him about the curious messages that would sometimes be left for him by the telephone – cryptic but full of suggestion, like the one which read simply: "Downton, 2.30."

"Who is she?" they asked, and when he would not tell them she became Downton 2.30 to the whole station.

Patricia, too, went about in a glow of good health, though for her it was interspersed with periods of anxiety whenever he was away on a raid and she had not heard from him. Often she found herself sleepless at nights and lying with tears on her pillow at dawn.

Forest-Wilson asked her in a kindly, languid way to dinner one evening; but she refused. He said nothing but she suspected from the half-amused, half-compassionate look he gave her that he had guessed the reason. He did not bring up the subject again.

A few days later, Forest-Wilson noticed she was wearing nylon stockings. "He's an American then," he deduced.

They were both careful never to mention one subject – their own lives after D-Day. That was taboo. The moment for them was now, in these few brief weeks, to be enjoyed while it lasted. Once, when he began to speak of the possibility of their meeting later in the year, she cut him off quickly.

"Don't let's think about it. It's bad luck."

But to himself he thought, several times, that when this war was over, he would not mind at all if Patricia Shockley made a trip to Philadelphia – a permanent one.

Yet there were times when she puzzled him.

They talked a lot, in their brief times together. It was one of the things he liked about their relationship most. But she had such strong and unusual opinions on many subjects that at times the things she said baffled and even disturbed him.

The first time he had noticed something strange was in a shop in Fordingbridge, where the elderly woman had addressed her as miss with a deference that he suspected had nothing to do with her uniform.

"Was that the English class system at work?" he asked laughingly. But instead of making light of it, she looked angry.

"I'm afraid so. After the war it will all stop though." He noticed she was prepared to speak about after the war in a general sense.

"Does it matter so much?"

She pointed to the four initials in brass on the shoulder of her uniform. "You see those initials: F.A.N.Y.? They call us the fannies. We're the part of the A.T.S. that act as drivers for the officers."

"So?"

"How do you suppose we're chosen?"

"By driving skill, I guess."

"Wrong. By accent – the way we speak. And . . . if someone knows us. Class, in other words. It's nicer for the officers."

He shrugged. It was the kind of thing he had always heard.

She grinned. "Actually, I suppose most girls from lower class backgrounds can't drive, so I'm exaggerating. But even so, it's got to change." She was vehement. "I'm a rebel of course," she added.

He didn't mind her being a rebel. But he wondered what form her rebellion meant to take.

On the next occasion they met she said something even stranger. They had seen a G.I. buying an armload of goods in the market place and she had shaken her head disapprovingly.

"It's terrible, their having so much money," she remarked, as though it were a statement of fact.

"You mean, it makes the English people jealous."

She stared at him in complete astonishment.

"Of course I don't. I mean it's bad for them, for the G.I.s. Nothing to be jealous about."

This he had not been able to make much sense of; but he had not felt like pursuing the subject at the time.

In fact it was only after that perfect time on the hill above Avonsford, when they had made love, eaten their picnic and made love once again, and then sat on the outer edge of the little circle of trees, gazing out over the ridges that he had decided to find out a little more about her opinions. It would be hard, he thought, to find a more perfect girl to settle down with. But, he grinned to himself, it would be wise to find out a bit more about the strange processes that went on in her mind.

"You say everything's going to change after the war. What do you mean by that?"

She leaned back against a tree, staring towards the horizon.

"You really want to know that? Now?"

"Yes."

She sighed.

"Oh well, if you must." She pulled up a long blade of grass and began to wind it around her finger. "No one agrees with me, you know. I mean, if you ask any of the other girl drivers, or the people living around Sarum – what will it be like after this is over? – they will all, everyone of them tell you: 'We'll just go back to normal.' You know what normal is?"

"Just working I suppose."

"No. Leisure. Domestic servants. Cheap labour. And exploitation. It's how it's always been."

"But you think that will change?"

"Yes. With the whole class system. The war's changing that. The

[885]

ordinary people feel they've been ordered around too much in the services, but they've got used to being something other than servants in people's houses. They'll demand a change."

"Is that good or bad?"

"Neither. But the old class society will collapse, and I think that's a good thing too."

"Welcome to America," he said with a smile.

"Oh, I don't think we want anything like that," she said.

He was puzzled. "Why not?"

"Too capitalist. All greed."

He remembered the scene in the market place, and her anger at the G.I.s' wealth.

"So let me get this straight. You want the people to be free, but they mustn't get rich, is that it?"

She laughed. "You're trying to make me look stupid, but in a way, yes."

"My God, are you a socialist?"

She considered carefully. "No. I mean, not like the Russians – or the fascists for that matter, who began saying they were socialists. But capitalism . . ." she looked for words " . . . it's unfair. And it encourages greed."

"Money's bad?"

She tapped him on the arm with her blade of grass.

"What a question to ask when you're almost in sight of Salisbury cathedral. Of course it is. Money is the root of all evil."

"It's what you do with it," he suggested, but she shook her head. "Well," he went on, confident of his ground, "your Labour Party here may agree with you, but I don't think the Conservatives will, nor most of the country folk around here. They're capitalists."

But to his surprise she disagreed.

"No they're not. The real Conservative has a sort of feudal outlook: he wants everything to stay the same but he looks after his people: he feels responsible for them. And he doesn't think they should be tempted into running about after money."

"Which he has, but he can handle – is that it?"

"Something like that. I suppose you could say many people feel God arranged the classes the way they are."

"And the socialists – your Labour Party – want the state to organise everyone: but they don't want the poor to get ahead too much either. So they'll just break up the wealth of the rich and then keep everyone from succeeding."

"There are other kinds of success than money."

"Sure." A thought had just struck him. "So in fact, the right wing and the left wing in this country – the old guard Conservatives and the Labour people have exactly the same outlook – a kind of religious paternalism. And the capitalists are just the bad guys in between."

"I hadn't thought of it. Yes. I suppose that's quite true."

"Nor had I, until I talked to you," he confessed. "Frankly, I didn't come over here to fight for either the feudal aristocracy or the socialists," he added irritably. "I thought this was the home of democracy and individual liberty."

"It is. And common law. And we abolished slavery first," she added with a laugh. "But you can't just put the individual first. It isn't fair."

"Life isn't fair, lady."

"Not yet."

"But why can't you just give everyone a chance to make as much money as they like?"

She stared at him in surprise.

"Because if one man makes money, he must be taking it away from someone else."

It was a fundamental attitude of European life that Adam Shockley had not encountered before.

"But, you just create more," he said.

"You may," she conceded. "But," she waved her arm over the landscape, "in the last few thousand years, this place has been pretty well picked over."

"That's pessimistic," he countered. "Optimism wins."

She grimaced. It had not occurred to him that she would find this idea repugnant.

"If life's a game. But perhaps God put us here to suffer."

"Do you believe that?"

"I think so."

For several minutes neither of them spoke. He found what she had said disturbed him profoundly. He thought about the implications.

"One thing underlies all of what you say," he suggested finally. "It seems to me that all you believe concerns the past. Either people want to preserve it, or destroy it."

"Yes. There's such a legacy of unfairness and exploitation. It's got to be changed."

"Fine. But what then. What's the future?"

"The future? Well, not as cruel as the past I suppose. Pensions, free hospitals, free schools."

"Socialism? Labour Party?"

"Not necessarily. No. Just reform, wherever it's from."

"I don't think you're all that interested in the future."

She paused, and thought.

"I think that may be a fair criticism," she said at last. "With so much history around in a place like this, I suppose it's difficult not to put the past first."

Perhaps after all this was the real secret, Adam considered, of Sarum. He wondered if perhaps Patricia would not be happier there than in the U.S.A. But then, there was no need to think about that now. They had agreed to enjoy the moment.

Although she never told him so, Patricia Shockley owed Brigadier Forest-Wilson a debt of gratitude.

It was in the last week of May that he happened to offer the high ranking U.S. Air Force officer a lift from Southern Command H.Q. into Salisbury.

It was, so the theory went, one of the benefits of the way that F.A.N.Y. drivers were chosen that they were all, by definition, discreet and reliable. Security at Sarum was tight. As Overlord approached, if a man in a sensitive job went sick, he was liable to be whisked into an isolation. But Patricia had noticed on several occasions that things were sometimes said in the back of the car which she could hear and which, she assumed, might have been secret.

Their destination was Odstock – a bleak spot, over a low ridge just south-west of the city where a collection of low buildings and Nissen huts constituted a small British hospital with an American one beside it.

As they bowled along, she only caught snippets of the conversation. But what she heard electrified her.

"Of course, if your men could take out . . ." It was Forest-Wilson speaking. "Certainly a great help . . . effective . . . trouble is, too fortified."

"Could be done." The American.

There was more murmuring she did not catch. Then Forest-Wilson.

"Seems too much of a sacrifice. I just don't think anyone'd come out alive."

"If we did, though . . . Day after tomorrow?"

"Perfect. Who would you use?"

"Oh. Either some of the Ibsley or Thruxton people I guess. Leave it to me."

The day after tomorrow. She was on the telephone within half an hour. She kept very cool.

"Darling, could you get one day's leave – I mean a night?"

"Maybe. I'm owed a couple."

"Downton. The day after tomorrow. Could you manage it. Just to please me?"

"I'll ask."

"Ask right away."

"O.K." He sounded puzzled. "Why then?"

"It's my birthday."

"I thought it was October."

"No." Or not, she thought, as she put the receiver down, this year it isn't.

He confirmed the next day.

"Listen, I can do it, but are you sure you can get leave yourself?"

In fact she was not.

"Yes," she lied.

"Only there's a mission I'd like to volunteer for. It sounds interesting."

"I'll be there. I promise. By four o'clock."

"O.K. But if you get held up . . ." Damn him. He was more interested in his blasted mission than her. "If say, you aren't there at five, I can get a ride back to base."

"I'll be there," she promised.

She had worked it all out with such care.

Her last run was to Wilton at three in a staff car. Then another girl would take it on. She had twenty-four hours leave.

Early that morning she had parked her own little Morris safely at Wilton. That gave her, say forty minutes to get over to Downton. She had plenty of petrol. She guarded her coupons jealously. Nothing, surely, could go wrong.

She arrived at Wilton at half past four. The meeting at Larkhill had gone on late. Hurriedly she raced to the little Morris in Kingsbury Square and started the engine.

It spluttered slightly. She took no notice. Moments later she was bowling out of Kingsbury Square.

She skirted Salisbury on the Harnham side and soon was on the road that led south down the Avon. She passed Britford; Lord Radnor's estate by the ancient forest of Clarendon lay on her left.

It was just after this, as she came up a slight incline, that the car engine died.

She pulled into the side of the road. It was a quarter to five.

She tried to start the car. It was no good. Soon it was ten to five.

Desperately she looked for a car or a bus, but the road was empty: nothing seemed to be moving. She noticed some cherry blossoms on the ground that stirred slightly in the faint breeze. The minutes passed.

The car which finally appeared came along the road in the opposite direction, at a careful pace. It was driven by John Mason. She hailed him frantically.

"You've got to get me to Downton."

"I've just come from there."

"I know. Please John. Can we hurry?"

He looked at her gravely. "Is it so urgent?"

She answered by getting into his car.

He rested his hands on the wheel. Then he sighed.

"I think I can guess what this is all about. I wouldn't have thought it was so urgent."

"You can't guess. Really. Please hurry."

Reluctantly he turned the car. It seemed to him ironic that he should now be expected to ferry her to her lover. Whatever she said, that must be the reason for the journey.

They got to Downton in five minutes and with a hurried kiss, she fled into the long, thatched inn.

She was always glad, in after years, that she had been in time. They made love with a passionate urgency that night and afterwards she cried.

He wondered why; only she knew it was from relief.

As the night of June 5, 1944 ended and the dawn of June 6 broke, the people of Sarum did not sleep.

Overhead, hour after hour, passed one of the greatest airlifts the world had yet seen. The planes were lit; their throbbing engines made the whole city reverberate and tremble. The black cloud seemed to be endless as the planes, many of them trailing gliders behind them, passed along the Avon valley and over the cathedral spire.

Adam Shockley and the squadrons from Ibsley were giving convoy and beach cover.

He felt a strange sense of elation that dawn as he joined the huge, humming concourse. He smiled to himself as they sped high over the quiet river and he thought of the sleepy city and its tall grey spire a few miles behind him. He thought of Patricia. For a moment, too, he remembered their conversation, her fervent denunciation of what she saw as the world's unfairness. Then he grinned. That was her trouble – perhaps the trouble with the English in general. They all wanted to be nice guys. Maybe, after this was over, he could cure her of that.

As they passed over the still waters of Christchurch harbour with its narrow headland, and out over the Channel, Adam Shockley drew his final conclusion on Patricia and Sarum: locked in the past, but worth defending. Then he put both out of his mind, as they swept towards France.

Later that morning, Patricia Shockley picked up Brigadier Forest-Wilson at the entrance of Wilton House.

"It's Bulford camp, please."

There were still planes crossing overhead and it was impossible not to think of him: where was he now? Over France, over the Channel?

She felt numb as she drove.

When they arrived at Bulford she was able to put a call through to Ibsley. He was back. They would meet again in a day or two. She returned to her staff car, trying to look as calm as she could and she believed she had succeeded when, a few minutes later the brigadier reappeared and asked her to take him to Wilton again.

In the rear seat, Forest-Wilson watched the back of her neck thoughtfully. One shrewd glance at her as he came out had been enough though. The offensive was only a few hours old and already she was radiant. "He's an airman then," he deduced, "and he's back." Then he smiled to himself. The American air bases would be moved to France soon.

It was hard, he considered, for people in a wartime romance to know how serious it was; for how could anyone know anything under such conditions? Perhaps this one would last – but there was only one way to find out.

He would ask her out to dinner again in a month or so.

He was a good fisherman.

The staff car bumped along the road over the rolling ridges of Salisbury Plain, suddenly emptied, once more, of its unaccustomed traffic.

The Spire

1985: April 10

ALREADY THE CROWDS were gathering in the close.

It was not often that the city of Salisbury had a royal visit: and this one, besides, was probably the most important for the cathedral in seven hundred years.

On the station platform, Lady Forest-Wilson smoothed her skirt. She had sent the three other members of her little house party into the close ahead of her, and now she was waiting.

She wondered if her tweed suit was a wise choice. She was an elegant woman, but as she grew older she had developed a dread of looking frumpish. She pulled the little pocket mirror out of her bag, glanced in it quickly, and dropped it back again. She was still good-looking. Grey of course, but she liked the way her hairdresser had teased her hair forward, giving it more wave and body. Did it make her look a little square and severe? No. She reassured herself: it was just a good bone structure.

It was hard not to be a little nervous after forty years.

Her nervousness had showed that morning. Her daughter Jennifer noticed it at once. Her son-in-law hadn't. But then, she thought privately, Alan Porteus never noticed anything that wasn't a number on a balance sheet.

"I know several accountants who aren't dreary at all," she had confided to Sir Kersey Godfrey the day before. "I've never been able to understand why she had to marry that one."

Kersey had noticed of course. Dear Kersey noticed everything. He had said nothing at first, just quietly read the paper at breakfast. But when Jennifer had gone out, that handsome, grey-haired man asked, with a mischievous smile;

"Is he married?"

"Who?" But she had blushed.

"The American you have to meet today."

"His letter mentions a wife."

"Good."

He had turned back to his paper. She had watched him for a moment.

"Kersey."

"Yes?"

"Damn you."

He had been staying at the house at Avonsford for three weeks. It was an experiment. Since Archibald had died ten years ago, she had been

[891]

entirely alone there, except for Jennifer's occasional visits and she was not sure how she would take to having a man about the place again. To her relief, it had been a very agreeable experience. Jennifer, of course, had asked the inevitable question.

"Do you?"

"None of your business."

"People think you do."

"My dear, I simply couldn't care less. The village always thinks something about everyone, in any case."

As for the next question, was she going to marry him, she was quite straightforward.

"Would you mind if I did?"

"Not at all."

"Well, if he asks me, and I think he will, then I shall say yes, so long as we spend four months a year here at Avonsford."

Not that Kersey's own home at Melbourne wasn't infinitely grander. There was the property an hour's flight away and the huge house in Melbourne with its wonderful art collection. She had visited Sir Kersey Godfrey's establishment and admired it for what it was: three generations of highly successful businesmen, building patiently and with taste and culminating in Kersey, who had done so well he had earned a knight-hood. He had taken her to see the small sheep farm the family had owned in the last century, too.

"I respect his roots, and he respects mine," she explained. She had spent all her married life with Archibald Forest-Wilson at Avonsford: and her family had been Sarum people before that. She could not bear to lose all contact with the place, and she had every hope that Kersey Godfrey would agree to her request. He was retired now. He could spend his time where he liked.

She smiled to herself. Thinking about Kersey relaxed her – a good sign.

As for the American.

She felt her heart miss a beat. The train was coming in.

He came straight towards her. How sunburnt he was. To an older woman's eyes, his creased, tanned skin was even better looking than that of the unlined young pilot she had known before. His blue eyes were positively startling. But as he held his hand out, the grin was the same.

"Recognised you at once." He turned. "This is my youngest daughter Maggie."

A fair-haired, blue-eyed, girl of eighteen, the same height as she was and with a powerful handshake. She was carrying a grip.

"So," Adam Shockley remarked, "you said today would be a good day to visit."

"A very special day. Come to the car though. We must hurry to park."

They went to the small carpark near Crane Street bridge, on the west side of the river, only a short walk from the close.

Then she led him over the bridge.

She told herself she was not excited, but as they turned into the High

Street she realised that she had been sufficiently distracted to leave her bag in the car. With an effort, she forced herself to be calm. She owed that to Kersey Godfrey. Definitely.

It had been a surprise after all these years to hear that he was coming to England. They had kept in touch after the war, writing regularly for a year until she got married. They exchanged cards at Christmas since then. She knew, of course, that he had become chairman of a construction business in Pennsylvania, and that he had five children. Maggie, the youngest, his letter explained, now had to visit England.

"I do pentathlon," she told Patricia.

"She also beats the hell out of her brothers and sisters," Adam laughed. "Maggie's a total tomboy."

"Not total," Maggie corrected wryly, and Patricia gave her an encouraging smile.

It was just before they went through the old gate from the High Street into the close that Maggie suddenly turned to her.

"So I guess you must have been dad's girlfriend," she said, so loudly that the policeman standing just behind them could hear.

To her horror, Patricia blushed furiously.

Adam only chuckled ruefully.

"I apologise. Maggie's quite uncontrollable," he explained. And then, to change the subject he quickly went on.

"So tell us about the royal visit. You said it was to do with the cathedral."

"It is indeed." She gazed up at the great building affectionately. "The fact is, unless something is done soon, the spire is going to fall down."

It was true. The passing of the centuries, and in particular the twentieth century with its increased pollution, had worn down and attacked the Chilmark stone so that all over the west front and on the soaring spire, it had crumbled disastrously.

Most worrying was the state of the spire itself, where the delicate stone shell was now so worn in places that it was hardly thicker than the length of a man's finger.

Could it really be, after seven and a half centuries, that the mighty spire was in danger of collapse – that the awful fear of the medieval masons might be realised, and the whole structure keel over, wrench the tower open and bring the entire cathedral down?

Even Maggie was awed.

"You mean the whole thing could come down?"

"I'm afraid so. If we don't put it right."

"And that's what this visit's all about?"

"Absolutely. We need six and a half million pounds and we haven't got it. All the income the dean and chapter can get goes into the maintenance. The Prince of Wales is coming here to help start the appeal."

Adam considered.

"It's a lot of money, but I imagine you should raise it without much difficulty."

[893]

"We're going to raise a million in the Sarum diocese, maybe more. After that, it may be difficult."

"But it's one of the wonders of the world!"

"True. But try raising six million pounds in England."

Shockley laughed. When he thought of some of the expenditures of the big American foundations it didn't seem so large a sum.

Maggie looked dubious.

"You sure it's safe to go inside?"

"Of course. It's all under control. We aren't stupid, you know," she added rather tartly.

But it was something else she heard that caused her to frown thoughtfully. For it was just as they were entering the church that she heard Adam turn to his daughter and whisper:

"You see what I told you. This whole place is like a museum."

It was meant as a compliment to Salisbury, of course. She was well aware of that. And certainly it was true that to any outsider coming to the ancient city, and particularly the quiet close, it might seem as if they had stepped back in time.

Yet, something was wrong, profoundly wrong, with that statement. She frowned, trying to decide exactly what it was.

They were all sitting together – good seats, halfway up the nave. She knew many of the people there. In the row just in front of them was Osbert Mason.

It was so unexpected, she thought, that when the late John Mason had finally married five years after the war, the son he produced should have been so much shorter than he was. True, the quiet librarian from London he had married was a short woman, but even so. It had, in some ways been a sad business. Poor John. He had set his heart on having his only son succeed him in his solicitor's office. Yet young Osbert had shown no desire whatever to be a lawyer – indeed, it had been a problem to get him even to finish school. This was not because the boy was stupid either; it was just that he had a passion for working with his hands. So much so, that he had become a carpenter and now ran a small, but profitable business in custom-made furniture, with a little works outside Avonsford. He was thirty-five now and had already made a name for himself. All power to him, she thought, but naturally it was disappointing for his father. Surprising too. John had not been aware of any bent towards handicrafts in his family.

He turned, now, and nodded his large balding head at her solemnly.

Punctual to the minute, as the crowds gazed upwards and the television cameras followed its path, the bright scarlet and blue helicopter had descended out of the spring afternoon sky, and shortly afterwards the Prince of Wales had made his way into the stately cathedral, where he was to read the lesson. The spire appeal had begun.

The works to be undertaken were formidable. The first and most vital was to insert, within the cone of the great spire, an octagonal brace, a framework to take the weight of the spire at its weakest point while the stonework around it was rebuilt. It was a delicate task. And after this, the crumbling west front would be tackled too. The masons would use the old Chilmark stone again, just as they had seven centuries before.

The workshops were in nearly the same place as before: the office of the clerk of works was where the masons' lodge had stood; there was a glaziers' workshop, a plumbery, a carpenters'. Nor, in the essentials had the working methods changed – only the power which drove and heated the same basic machines of saw, lathe and kiln had needed to be improved.

It was a sense of continuity that pleased Patricia Forest-Wilson, as she looked around her and heard the strains of the great Willis organ.

A museum, he had said. If so, she thought with a slight irritation, then perhaps she was a museum piece. She glanced at the faces of the two men beside her – both of them more bronzed than those around them, one probably from a Caribbean sun, the other from the Australian summer from which he had recently come. Two attractive men she thought, and felt rather pleased with herself. Archibald had been a handsome man too. She liked to think she had only had the best. As for a museum piece – she was not. That was that.

Adam leaned over towards her. She saw Kersey's eyes following him.

"Seems brighter than I remember it," he whispered.

She nodded. It was.

In recent years much work had been done in the cathedral. Some, like the restoration of the library, where new cases to hold its priceless medieval books had been made from the old plane trees in the close, was invisible to the casual visitor, though still important. But one had only to look around the main body of the cathedral to notice signs of new life. Here and there, on walls and on the ancient tombs, careful restoration and cleaning had revealed fragments of the medieval paint which had once made the place a riot of colour. In every chapel, splendid embroidered cushions and hassocks, lovingly made by local hands had recently appeared; and the new Sarum Group of embroiderers had won national renown for the chasubles and copes, and the dazzling altar cloths that caught the eye with such force. Today, even the flowers in the cathedral had been arranged, she could see, by a professional artist's hands. It seemed to her that there was a new and more vigorous spirit in the place than there had been before.

But a greater wonder was at the east end, where a huge new stained glass window had been installed only five years before. The Prisoners of Conscience Window was the work of the famous French glass designers, Gabriel Loire and his son Jacques, whose workshop was outside another cathedral city, Chartres. It was good, Patricia thought, to see the old colours return to the windows too.

And then she knew why Adam Shockley was wrong.

It was not a museum after all – neither the quiet close nor the bustling town, neither the great house at Wilton nor the medieval cathedral with its soaring spire. All were as alive as on the first day they were made. For ancient forms could be re-used, medieval forms and colours recreated,

[895]

and new forms would be found at Sarum. They might come slowly, almost invisibly, but they would come because their roots were deep. England had been ruined by two devastating wars; but here, as elsewhere, the ancient culture of Europe would put forth its vigorous flowers again.

She smiled. She was pleased with the thought.

After the service, while the prince was taken to tea at the old bishop's palace, now the cathedral school, Patricia led her little party back towards the car.

Shockley and his daughter had to return to London that evening and she had promised to show them Stonehenge.

As they left the close, she moved to Kersey Godfrey's side and linked her arm through his, smiling up at him happily. She touched his hand.

"You're coming to show them Stonehenge, aren't you?" she murmured.

"If I'm not in the way."

She squeezed his arm.

"You're not."

They crossed the bridge and walked along to the little car park.

"It's only twenty minutes drive, if that," she explained. "Kersey and I will take you there."

They reached the car. Then she paused and stared.

"I don't believe it."

Young John Wilson had been lucky that day. It was his thirteenth birthday.

He had stood in the close to watch the royal helicopter arrive. Then, when the prince had been greeted and moved into the cathedral, he went away. It was twenty minutes later that he walked past the car park near Crane Bridge.

The place was deserted. Idly, he moved about amongst the cars.

The big maroon Volvo was parked in one corner.

And on the driver's seat lay an expensive woman's handbag. The door was locked. But there was a little pile of bricks beside the wall nearby.

There were no people and no police about: all in the close, no doubt, waiting to see the Prince of Wales. He moved in quickly.

There is a particularly delightful spot at Sarum – it is on a little island below Crane Street bridge – a strip of grass between two streams where the river Avon makes its gentle curve round the western side of the close.

On the opposite eastern bank, the gardens of the handsome close houses run down to the stream. On the western side, the meadows stretch, broad and placid, towards Wilton.

There are long green riverweeds in the stream; moorhens, ducks and swans make the place their habitation. There are trees along the island's bank. It is a quiet timeless, place where, by the hushed sounds of the riverbank, one can measure the even greater and more dignified silence of the cathedral close next door.

It was here that John Wilson loitered.

Having extracted the cash, he had thrown the bag and the rest of the contents into the stream where it had slowly sunk just opposite the gardens of the North Canonry.

It was a rich haul: a hundred pounds. His small narrow face broke into a grin.

Soon he would catch his bus home.

He knew nothing of museums, little about the cathedral. About Old Sarum and the high ground he knew only that, even now in spring, they were bare, cold and windy.

But if he thought about the matter at all, he supposed that here, at the place where the five rivers met, life would go on, as it had always done before.

Acknowledgements

I AM DEEPLY indebted to the following, all experts in their respective fields, who with great kindness and patience read different parts of this book and corrected errors. Any errors that remain, however, are mine alone.

Dr. J. H. Bettey, University of Bristol; Mr. Desmond Bonney, Royal Commission on the Historical Monuments of England; Miss Alison Borthwick, formerly of the Archaeological Section, Wiltshire County Council Library and Museum Service; Dr. John Chandler, Local Studies Officer, Wiltshire County Council Library and Museum Service; Miss Suzanne Eward, Librarian and Keeper of the Muniments of Salisbury Cathedral; Mr. David A. Hinton, University of Southampton; Dr. T. B. James, King Alfred's College of Higher Education, Winchester; Mr. K. H. Rogers, County Archivist and Diocesan Records Officer, Wiltshire County Council; Mr. Roy Spring, Clerk of the Works, Salisbury Cathedral;

Thanks are also due to the following, all of whom gave valuable help and advice in different ways:

The Right Reverend John Austin Baker, Bishop of Salisbury; The Very Reverend Doctor Sydney Evans, Dean Emeritus of Salisbury; Mr. David Algar; Miss S. A. Cross, formerly of The Museum of the Wiltshire Archaeological and Natural History Society; Mrs. Elizabeth Godfrey; Sir Westrow Hulse, Bt.; Mrs. Alison Campbell Jensen; Dr. P. H. Robinson, Curator, The Museum of the Wiltshire Archaeological and Natural History Society; Mr. Peter R. Saunders, Curator, Salisbury and South Wiltshire Museum; Mr. and Mrs. H. S. Taylor-Young; Mrs. Jane Walford.

I am grateful to the Director of the Wiltshire County Council Library and Museum Service for kindly allowing his library to become my second home over a period of more than three years, and to the staff of Salisbury Library for much valuable assistance.

No thanks can be enough to Mrs. Margaret Hunter and the staff of Saxon Office Services, Shaftesbury for their unfailing help and good humour in the typing and constant altering of the manuscript.

I have also been most fortunate in finding an agent, Gill Coleridge of Anthony Sheil Associates and two editors, Rosie Cheetham of Century Hutchinson and Betty Prashker of Crown Publishers who early on had faith in this project and gave me such unfailing help and encouragement.

I am deeply grateful to my wife Susan, my mother and the Hon. Diana Makgill for their respective patience, unstinting help and hospitality.

Special thanks are also due to Miss Alison Borthwick for her expert maps and illustrations.

Finally, and most important of all, I owe the greatest possible debt of gratitude to Dr. John Chandler whose book, *Endless Street* opened the doors of Salisbury's history to me and has been my constant companion. For over three years, with unfailing patience and courtesy he has guided me towards my objective, and without his kind help and expert advice this book could not have been written.